U. S. Grant

THE HISTORY

OF

JO DAVIESS COUNTY

ILLINOIS,

CONTAINING

A HISTORY OF THE COUNTY—ITS CITIES, TOWNS, ETC.

A BIOGRAPHICAL DIRECTORY OF ITS CITIZENS, WAR RECORD OF ITS VOLUNTEERS IN THE LATE REBELLION, GENERAL AND LOCAL STATISTICS,

PORTRAITS OF EARLY SETTLERS AND PROMINENT MEN,

HISTORY OF THE NORTHWEST, HISTORY OF ILLINOIS,
MAP OF JO DAVIESS COUNTY, CONSTITUTION OF THE UNITED STATES,
MISCELLANEOUS MATTERS, ETC.

ILLUSTRATED.

WILDSIDE PRESS

The reproduction of this book has been made possible through the sponsorship of the Heritage League of Northwest Illinois, Stockton, Illinois.

A Reproduction by
UNIGRAPHIC, INC.
1401 North Fares Avenue
Evansville, Indiana 47711
nineteen hundred and seventy-seven

Preface.

Nearly sixty years have come and gone since white men came to occupy and develop the rich mineral and agricultural lands of the Fever River country. These years were full of changes and of history, and had some of the vigorous minds and ready pens of the early settlers been directed to the keeping of a chronological journal or diary of events, to write a history of the country now would be a comparatively easy task. In the absence of such records, the magnitude of the undertaking is very materially increased, and rendered still more intricate and difficult by reason of the absence of nearly all the pioneer fathers and mothers who came here more than half a century ago. Of those who came here in pursuit of fortunes and homes, between 1821 and 1827, and who founded the City of Galena, only a very few are left to greet those who now come to write the history of their county—a county second to none in point of historic interest. The struggles, changes and vicissitudes that fifty years evoke are as trying to the minds as to the bodies of men. Physical and mental strength waste away together beneath accumulating years, and the memory of names, dates and important events become buried in the confusion brought by time and its restless, unceasing changes. Circumstances that were fresh in memory ten and twenty years after their occurrence, are almost, if not entirely, forgotten when fifty years have gone, and if not entirely lost from the mind, they are so nearly so that, when recalled by one seeking to preserve them, their recollection comes slowly back, more like the memory of a midnight dream than of an actual occurrence in which they were partial, if not active, participants. The footprint of time leaves its impressions and destroying agencies upon every thing, and hence it would be unreasonable to suppose that the annals, incidents and happenings of more than fifty years in a community like that whose history we have attempted to write, could be preserved intact and umbroken.

The passage of several years was recorded on the pages of time after the first settlement was made at Galena by white men, before any written records of a public nature were made. The first and only record we were able to find was a poll book of an election held in *Fever River Precinct*, *Peoria County*, *August* 7, 1826—one year previous to the organization of Jo Daviess County—and this record, with the names of 202 voters, was procured from the archives of the County Clerk's office at Peoria. With this single exception the gentlemen entrusted with the duty of writing this history were forced to depend upon the memory and intelligence of the few surviving pioneers for a very large share of facts and information herein presented, until after the organization of the County and the first session of the County Commissioners Court, in June, 1827. For reasons already indicated, it is not to be expected that this volume will be entirely accurate in all its details of names, dates, etc., or that it will be so perfect as to be above and beyond criticism, for the book is yet to be written and printed that can justly claim the meed of perfection; but it is the publishers' hope, as it is their belief, that it will be found measurably correct and generally accurate and reliable. Industrious and studied care has been exercised to make it a standard book of reference, as well as a book of interest to the general reader.

In the absence of written records, recourse was had to the minds of such of the "Old Settlers" as have been spared to see the wilds of 1821–'5 reduced from Indian hunting grounds and camping places to the abode of thrift, wealth, intelligence, refinement—schools, colleges, churches and cities. In seeking to supply such missing links by personal interviews, different individuals would render different and conflicting, although honest and sincere, accounts of the same events and circumstances. To sift these statements and arrive at the most reasonable and tangible conclusions, was a delicate task, but a task we sought to discharge with the single purpose of writing of incidents as they actually transpired. If in such a multiplicity of names, dates, etc., some errors are not detected, it will be strange, indeed. But, such as it is, our offering is completed, and it only remains for us to acknowledge our obligations to the gentlemen named below for the valuable information furnished by them, without which this history of Jo Daviess County would not be so nearly perfect as it is.

To Captain DANIEL SMITH HARRIS, Dr. E. G. NEWHALL, WILLIAM HEMPSTEAD, Esq., JOHN LORRAIN, Esq., DANIEL WANN, Esq., Capt. GEORGE W. GIRDON, H. H. HOUGHTON, Esq., J. M. HARRIS, R. S. NORRIS, Esq., Judge W. R. ROWLEY, L. A. ROWLEY, Esq., FREDERICK STAHL, Esq., GEO. FERGUSON, Esq., ALLEN TOMLIN, Esq., D. W. SCOTT, Esq., WM. H. SNYDER, Esq., W. W. HUNTINGTON, Esq., B. C. ST. CYR, Esq., A. M. HAINES, Esq., STEPHEN MARSDEN, and others of Galena; AUGUSTUS SWITZER, Esq., Mayor THOMAS MAGUIRE and C. S. BUSH, Dunleith; HARVEY MANN, of Vinegar Hill; W. O. GEAR, of Okahoma, Iowa; HIRAM B. HUNT and JAMES W. WHITE, of Hanover; Hon. H. S. TOWNSEND, of Warren; WILLIAM T. GEAR, of Guilford; Hon. E. B. WASHBURNE, Gen. A. L. CHETLAIN, Gen. JOHN C. SMITH, of Chicago, this paragraph of acknowledgement is therefore respectfully dedicated.

To the venerable Mrs. FRENTRESS, widow of ELEAZER FRENTRESS, wife and mother of the first white family to settle in what is now Dunleith Township, we are also indebted for the early history of that part of the county.

To the press of Galena—Messrs. BROWN and PERRIGO, of the *Gazette*, and Messrs. CUMINGS and SCOTT, of the *Industrial Press*—to the county, city and various township authorities, to the ministers and official representatives of the various churches, and to the Principals and Teachers of the schools of the county we are also under obligations for statistical and historical information, without which this volume would be incomplete. To the parties named above is due, in a large measure, whatever of merit may be ascribed to this undertaking.

To the people of the county in general, and the people of Galena in particular, our most grateful considerations are due for their universal kindness and courtesy to our representatives and agents, to whom was entrusted the labor of collecting and arranging the information herein preserved to that posterity that will come in the not far distant by-and-by to fill the places of the fathers and mothers, so many of whose names and honorable biographies are to be found in the pages of this book.

In conclusion, the publishers can but express the earnest desire that before another fifty years will have passed, other and abler minds will have taken up and recorded the historical events that will follow after the close of this offering to the people of Jo Daviess County, that the historical literature of the country may be fully preserved and maintained complete from county to nation.

H. F. KETT & Co., Publishers.

March, 1878.

CONTENTS.

HISTORICAL.

ILLUSTRATIONS.

LITHOGRAPHIC PORTRAITS.

CONTENTS.

JO DAVIESS COUNTY WAR RECORD.

BIOGRAPHICAL TOWNSHIP DIRECTORY.

ABSTRACT OF ILLINOIS STATE LAWS.

MISCELLANEOUS.

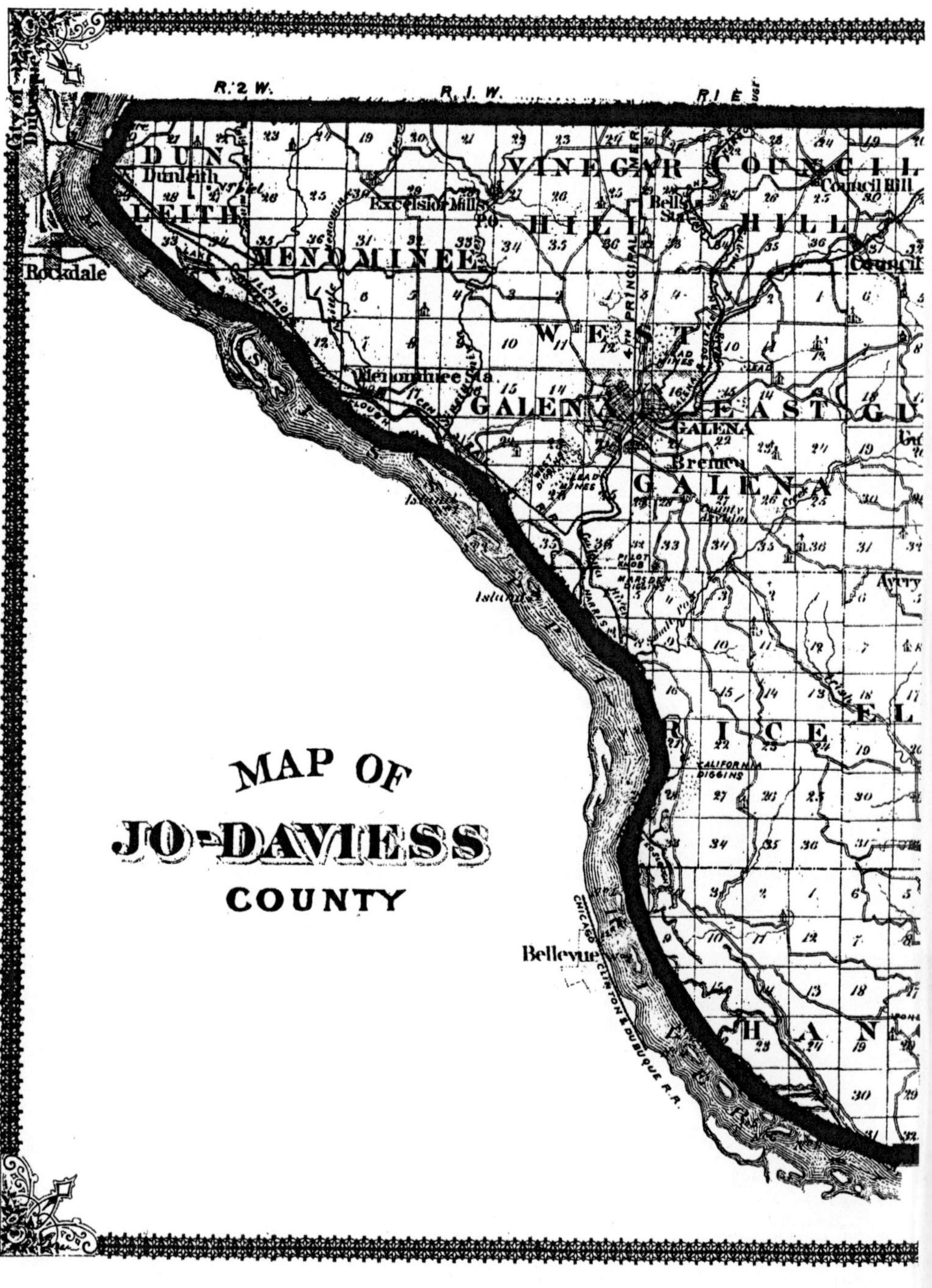

MAP OF
JO-DAVIESS
COUNTY
R. 2 W.
R. I. W.
R. I. E.
DUN LEITH
Dunleith
Rockdale
MENOMINEE
Excelsior Mills
VINEGAR HILL
COUNCIL HILL
Council Hill
WEST GALENA
EAST GALENA
GALENA
Menominee Sta.
Bremen
LEAD MINES
4TH PRINCIPAL MERIDIAN
PILOT KNOB
RICE
CALIFORNIA DIGGINS
Bellevue
CHICAGO CLINTON & DUBUQUE R.R.
HANOVER

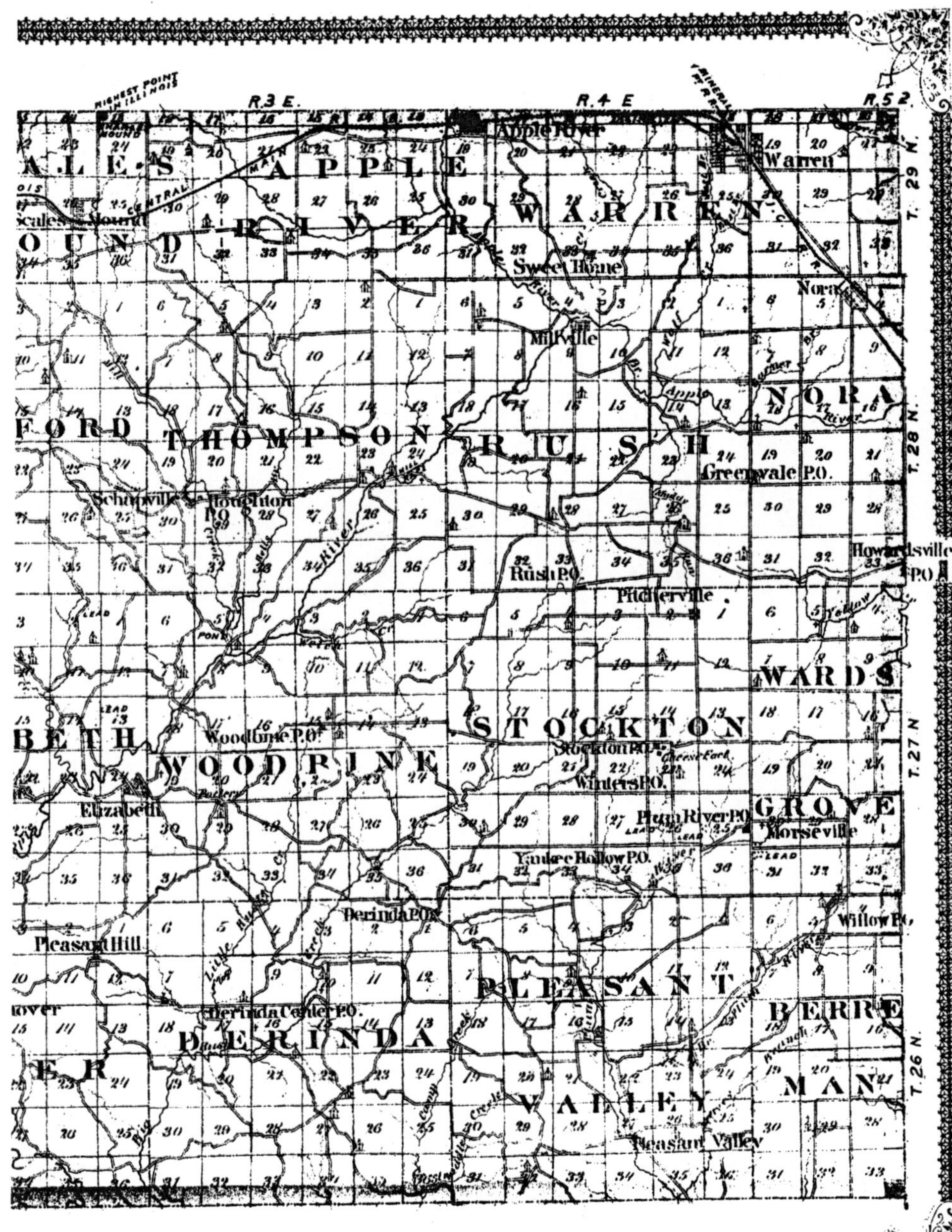

HIGHEST POINT IN ILLINOIS
R.3 E.
R.4 E.
R.5 E.
T. 29 N.
T. 28 N.
T. 27 N.
T. 26 N.
APPLE RIVER
WARREN
THOMPSON
RUSH
NORA
STOCKTON
WARDS GROVE
WOODBINE
PLEASANT VALLEY
BERREMAN
DERINDA
Apple River
Warren
Scales Mound
Sweet Home
Nora
Millville
Greenvale P.O.
Schapville
Houghton P.O.
Rush P.O.
Pitcherville
Howardsville P.O.
Woodbine P.O.
Stockton P.O.
Winters P.O.
Elizabeth
Plum River P.O.
Morseville
Yankee Hollow P.O.
Derinda P.O.
Willow P.O.
Pleasant Hill
Derinda Center P.O.
Pleasant Valley

The Northwest Territory.

GEOGRAPHICAL POSITION.

When the Northwestern Territory was ceded to the United States by Virginia in 1784, it embraced only the territory lying between the Ohio and the Mississippi Rivers, and north to the northern limits of the United States. It coincided with the area now embraced in the States of Ohio, Indiana, Michigan, Illinois, Wisconsin, and that portion of Minnesota lying on the east side of the Mississippi River. The United States itself at that period extended no farther west than the Mississippi River; but by the purchase of Louisiana in 1803, the western boundary of the United States was extended to the Rocky Mountains and the Northern Pacific Ocean. The new territory thus added to the National domain, and subsequently opened to settlement, has been called the "New Northwest," in contradistinction from the old "Northwestern Territory."

In comparison with the old Northwest this is a territory of vast magnitude. It includes an area of 1,887,850 square miles; being greater in extent than the united areas of all the Middle and Southern States, including Texas. Out of this magnificent territory have been erected eleven sovereign States and eight Territories, with an aggregate population, at the present time, of 13,000,000 inhabitants, or nearly one third of the entire population of the United States.

Its lakes are fresh-water seas, and the larger rivers of the continent flow for a thousand miles through its rich alluvial valleys and far-stretching prairies, more acres of which are arable and productive of the highest percentage of the cereals than of any other area of like extent on the globe.

For the last twenty years the increase of population in the Northwest has been about as three to one in any other portion of the United States.

EARLY EXPLORATIONS.

In the year 1541, DeSoto first saw the Great West in the New World. He, however, penetrated no farther north than the 35th parallel of latitude. The expedition resulted in his death and that of more than half his army, the remainder of whom found their way to Cuba, thence to Spain, in a famished and demoralized condition. DeSoto founded no settlements, produced no results, and left no traces, unless it were that he awakened the hostility of the red man against the white man, and disheartened such as might desire to follow up the career of discovery for better purposes. The French nation were eager and ready to seize upon any news from this extensive domain, and were the first to profit by DeSoto's defeat. Yet it was more than a century before any adventurer took advantage of these discoveries.

In 1616, four years before the pilgrims "moored their bark on the wild New England shore," Le Caron, a French Franciscan, had penetrated through the Iroquois and Wyandots (Hurons) to the streams which run into Lake Huron; and in 1634, two Jesuit missionaries founded the first mission among the lake tribes. It was just one hundred years from the discovery of the Mississippi by DeSoto (1541) until the Canadian envoys met the savage nations of the Northwest at the Falls of St. Mary, below the outlet of Lake Superior. This visit led to no permanent result; yet it was not until 1659 that any of the adventurous fur traders attempted to spend a Winter in the frozen wilds about the great lakes, nor was it until 1660 that a station was established upon their borders by Mesnard, who perished in the woods a few months after. In 1665, Claude Allouez built the earliest lasting habitation of the white man among the Indians of the Northwest. In 1668, Claude Dablon and James Marquette founded the mission of Sault Ste. Marie at the Falls of St. Mary, and two years afterward, Nicholas Perrot, as agent for M. Talon, Governor General of Canada, explored Lake Illinois (Michigan) as far south as the present City of Chicago, and invited the Indian nations to meet him at a grand council at Sault Ste. Marie the following Spring, where they were taken under the protection of the king, and formal possession was taken of the Northwest. This same year Marquette established a mission at Point St. Ignatius, where was founded the old town of Michillimackinac.

During M. Talon's explorations and Marquette's residence at St. Ignatius, they learned of a great river away to the west, and fancied —as all others did then—that upon its fertile banks whole tribes of God's children resided, to whom the sound of the Gospel had never come. Filled with a wish to go and preach to them, and in compliance with a

MOUTH OF THE MISSISSIPPI.

SOURCE OF THE MISSISSIPPI.

request of M. Talon, who earnestly desired to extend the domain of his king, and to ascertain whether the river flowed into the Gulf of Mexico or the Pacific Ocean, Marquette with Joliet, as commander of the expedition, prepared for the undertaking.

On the 13th of May, 1673, the explorers, accompanied by five assistant French Canadians, set out from Mackinaw on their daring voyage of discovery. The Indians, who gathered to witness their departure, were astonished at the boldness of the undertaking, and endeavored to dissuade them from their purpose by representing the tribes on the Mississippi as exceedingly savage and cruel, and the river itself as full of all sorts of frightful monsters ready to swallow them and their canoes together. But, nothing daunted by these terrific descriptions, Marquette told them he was willing not only to encounter all the perils of the unknown region they were about to explore, but to lay down his life in a cause in which the salvation of souls was involved; and having prayed together they separated. Coasting along the northern shore of Lake Michigan, the adventurers entered Green Bay, and passed thence up the Fox River and Lake Winnebago to a village of the Miamis and Kickapoos. Here Marquette was delighted to find a beautiful cross planted in the middle of the town ornamented with white skins, red girdles and bows and arrows, which these good people had offered to the Great Manitou, or God, to thank him for the pity he had bestowed on them during the Winter in giving them an abundant "chase." This was the farthest outpost to which Dablon and Allouez had extended their missionary labors the year previous. Here Marquette drank mineral waters and was instructed in the secret of a root which cures the bite of the venomous rattlesnake. He assembled the chiefs and old men of the village, and, pointing to Joliet, said: "My friend is an envoy of France, to discover new countries, and I am an ambassador from God to enlighten them with the truths of the Gospel." Two Miami guides were here furnished to conduct them to the Wisconsin River, and they set out from the Indian village on the 10th of June, amidst a great crowd of natives who had assembled to witness their departure into a region where no white man had ever yet ventured. The guides, having conducted them across the portage, returned. The explorers launched their canoes upon the Wisconsin, which they descended to the Mississippi and proceeded down its unknown waters. What emotions must have swelled their breasts as they struck out into the broadening current and became conscious that they were now upon the bosom of the Father of Waters. The mystery was about to be lifted from the long-sought river. The scenery in that locality is beautiful, and on that delightful seventeenth of June must have been clad in all its primeval loveliness as it had been adorned by the hand of

Nature. Drifting rapidly, it is said that the bold bluffs on either hand "reminded them of the castled shores of their own beautiful rivers of France." By-and-by, as they drifted along, great herds of buffalo appeared on the banks. On going to the heads of the valley they could see a country of the greatest beauty and fertility, apparently destitute of inhabitants yet presenting the appearance of extensive manors, under the fastidious cultivation of lordly proprietors.

THE WILD PRAIRIE.

On June 25, they went ashore and found some fresh traces of men upon the sand, and a path which led to the prairie. The men remained in the boat, and Marquette and Joliet followed the path till they discovered a village on the banks of a river, and two other villages on a hill, within a half league of the first, inhabited by Indians. They were received most hospitably by these natives, who had never before seen a white person. After remaining a few days they re-embarked and descended the river to about latitude 33°, where they found a village of the Arkansas, and being satisfied that the river flowed into the Gulf of Mexico, turned their course up the river, and ascending the stream to the mouth of the Illinois, rowed up that stream to its source, and procured guides from that point to the lakes. "Nowhere on this journey," says Marquette, "did we see such grounds, meadows, woods, stags, buffaloes, deer, wildcats, bustards, swans, ducks, parroquets, and even beavers, as on the Illinois River." The party, without loss or injury, reached Green Bay in September, and reported their discovery—one of the most important of the age, but of which no record was preserved save Marquette's, Joliet losing his by the upsetting of his canoe on his way to Quebec. Afterward Marquette returned to the Illinois Indians by their request, and ministered to them until 1675. On the 18th of May, in that year, as he was passing the mouth of a stream—going with his boatmen up Lake Michigan—he asked to land at its mouth and celebrate Mass. Leaving his men with the canoe, he retired a short distance and began his devotions. As much time passed and he did not return, his men went in search of him, and found him upon his knees, dead. He had peacefully passed away while at prayer. He was buried at this spot. Charlevoix, who visited the place fifty years after, found the waters had retreated from the grave, leaving the beloved missionary to repose in peace. The river has since been called Marquette.

While Marquette and his companions were pursuing their labors in the West, two men, differing widely from him and each other, were preparing to follow in his footsteps and perfect the discoveries so well begun by him. These were Robert de La Salle and Louis Hennepin.

After La Salle's return from the discovery of the Ohio River (see the narrative elsewhere), he established himself again among the French trading posts in Canada. Here he mused long upon the pet project of those ages—a short way to China and the East, and was busily planning an expedition up the great lakes, and so across the continent to the Pacific, when Marquette returned from the Mississippi. At once the vigorous mind of LaSalle received from his and his companions' stories the idea that by following the Great River northward, or by turning up some of the numerous western tributaries, the object could easily be gained. He applied to Frontenac, Governor General of Canada, and laid before him the plan, dim but gigantic. Frontenac entered warmly into his plans, and saw that LaSalle's idea to connect the great lakes by a chain of forts with the Gulf of Mexico would bind the country so wonderfully together, give unmeasured power to France, and glory to himself, under whose administration he earnestly hoped all would be realized.

LaSalle now repaired to France, laid his plans before the King, who warmly approved of them, and made him a Chevalier. He also received from all the noblemen the warmest wishes for his success. The Chevalier returned to Canada, and busily entered upon his work. He at once rebuilt Fort Frontenac and constructed the first ship to sail on these fresh-water seas. On the 7th of August, 1679, having been joined by Hennepin, he began his voyage in the Griffin up Lake Erie. He passed over this lake, through the straits beyond, up Lake St. Clair and into Huron. In this lake they encountered heavy storms. They were some time at Michillimackinac, where LaSalle founded a fort, and passed on to Green Bay, the "Baie des Puans" of the French, where he found a large quantity of furs collected for him. He loaded the Griffin with these, and placing her under the care of a pilot and fourteen sailors,

LA SALLE LANDING ON THE SHORE OF GREEN BAY.

started her on her return voyage. The vessel was never afterward heard of. He remained about these parts until early in the Winter, when, hearing nothing from the Griffin, he collected all his men—thirty working men and three monks—and started again upon his great undertaking.

By a short portage they passed to the Illinois or Kankakee, called by the Indians, "Theakeke," *wolf*, because of the tribes of Indians called by that name, commonly known as the Mahingans, dwelling there. The French pronounced it *Kiakiki*, which became corrupted to Kankakee. "Falling down the said river by easy journeys, the better to observe the country," about the last of December they reached a village of the Illinois Indians, containing some five hundred cabins, but at that moment no inhabitants. The Seur de LaSalle being in want of some breadstuffs, took advantage of the absence of the Indians to help himself to a sufficiency of maize, large quantities of which he found concealed in holes under the wigwams. This village was situated near the present village of Utica in LaSalle County, Illinois. The corn being securely stored, the voyagers again betook themselves to the stream, and toward evening, on the 4th day of January, 1680, they came into a lake which must have been the lake of Peoria. This was called by the Indians *Pim-i-te-wi*, that is, *a place where there are many fat beasts.* Here the natives were met with in large numbers, but they were gentle and kind, and having spent some time with them, LaSalle determined to erect another fort in that place, for he had heard rumors that some of the adjoining tribes were trying to disturb the good feeling which existed, and some of his men were disposed to complain, owing to the hardships and perils of the travel. He called this fort "*Crevecœur*" (broken-heart), a name expressive of the very natural sorrow and anxiety which the pretty certain loss of his ship, Griffin, and his consequent impoverishment, the danger of hostility on the part of the Indians, and of mutiny among his own men, might well cause him. His fears were not entirely groundless. At one time poison was placed in his food, but fortunately was discovered.

While building this fort, the Winter wore away, the prairies began to look green, and LaSalle, despairing of any reinforcements, concluded to return to Canada, raise new means and new men, and embark anew in the enterprise. For this purpose he made Hennepin the leader of a party to explore the head waters of the Mississippi, and he set out on his journey. This journey was accomplished with the aid of a few persons, and was successfully made, though over an almost unknown route, and in a bad season of the year. He safely reached Canada, and set out again for the object of his search.

Hennepin and his party left Fort Crevecœur on the last of February, 1680. When LaSalle reached this place on his return expedition, he found the fort entirely deserted, and he was obliged to return again to Canada. He embarked the third time, and succeeded. Seven days after leaving the fort, Hennepin reached the Mississippi, and paddling up the icy stream as best he could, reached no higher than the Wisconsin River by the 11th of April. Here he and his followers were taken prisoners by a band of Northern Indians, who treated them with great kindness. Hennepin's comrades were Anthony Auguel and Michael Ako. On this voyage they found several beautiful lakes, and "saw some charming prairies." Their captors were the Isaute or Sauteurs, Chippewas, a tribe of the Sioux nation, who took them up the river until about the first of May, when they reached some falls, which Hennepin christened Falls of St. Anthony in honor of his patron saint. Here they took the land, and traveling nearly two hundred miles to the northwest, brought them to their villages. Here they were kept about three months, were treated kindly by their captors, and at the end of that time, were met by a band of Frenchmen,

BUFFALO HUNT.

headed by one Seur de Luth, who, in pursuit of trade and game, had penetrated thus far by the route of Lake Superior; and with these fellow-countrymen Hennepin and his companions were allowed to return to the borders of civilized life in November, 1680, just after LaSalle had returned to the wilderness on his second trip. Hennepin soon after went to France, where he published an account of his adventures.

The Mississippi was first discovered by De Soto in April, 1541, in his vain endeavor to find gold and precious gems. In the following Spring, De Soto, weary with hope long deferred, and worn out with his wanderings, he fell a victim to disease, and on the 21st of May died. His followers, reduced by fatigue and disease to less than three hundred men, wandered about the country nearly a year, in the vain endeavor to rescue themselves by land, and finally constructed seven small vessels, called brigantines, in which they embarked, and descending the river, supposing it would lead them to the sea, in July they came to the sea (Gulf of Mexico), and by September reached the Island of Cuba.

They were the first to see the great outlet of the Mississippi; but, being so weary and discouraged, made no attempt to claim the country, and hardly had an intelligent idea of what they had passed through.

To La Salle, the intrepid explorer, belongs the honor of giving the first account of the mouths of the river. His great desire was to possess this entire country for his king, and in January, 1682, he and his band of explorers left the shores of Lake Michigan on their third attempt, crossed the portage, passed down the Illinois River, and on the 6th of February, reached the banks of the Mississippi.

On the 13th they commenced their downward course, which they pursued with but one interruption, until upon the 6th of March they discovered the three great passages by which the river discharges its waters into the gulf. La Salle thus narrates the event:

"We landed on the bank of the most western channel, about three leagues (nine miles) from its mouth. On the seventh, M. de LaSalle went to reconnoiter the shores of the neighboring sea, and M. de Tonti meanwhile examined the great middle channel. They found the main outlets beautiful, large and deep. On the 8th we reascended the river, a little above its confluence with the sea, to find a dry place beyond the reach of inundations. The elevation of the North Pole was here about twenty-seven degrees. Here we prepared a column and a cross, and to the column were affixed the arms of France with this inscription:

Louis Le Grand, Roi De France et de Navarre, regne; Le neuvieme Avril, 1682.

The whole party, under arms, chanted the *Te Deum*, and then, after a salute and cries of "*Vive le Roi*," the column was erected by M. de LaSalle, who, standing near it, proclaimed in a loud voice the authority of the King of France. LaSalle returned and laid the foundations of the Mississippi settlements in Illinois, thence he proceeded to France, where another expedition was fitted out, of which he was commander, and in two succeeding voyages failed to find the outlet of the river by sailing along the shore of the gulf. On his third voyage he was killed, through the treachery of his followers, and the object of his expeditions was not accomplished until 1699, when D'Iberville, under the authority of the crown, discovered, on the second of March, by way of the sea, the mouth of the "Hidden River." This majestic stream was called by the natives "*Malbouchia*," and by the Spaniards, "*la Palissade*," from the great

TRAPPING.

number of trees about its mouth. After traversing the several outlets, and satisfying himself as to its certainty, he erected a fort near its western outlet, and returned to France.

An avenue of trade was now opened out which was fully improved. In 1718, New Orleans was laid out and settled by some European colonists. In 1762, the colony was made over to Spain, to be regained by France under the consulate of Napoleon. In 1803, it was purchased by the United States for the sum of fifteen million dollars, and the territory of Louisiana and commerce of the Mississippi River came under the charge of the United States. Although LaSalle's labors ended in defeat and death, he had not worked and suffered in vain. He had thrown open to France and the world an immense and most valuable country; had established several ports, and laid the foundations of more than one settlement there. "Peoria, Kaskaskia and Cahokia, are to this day monuments of LaSalle's labors; for, though he had founded neither of them (unless Peoria, which was built nearly upon the site of Fort Crevecœur,) it was by those whom he led into the West that these places were peopled and civilized. He was, if not the discoverer, the first settler of the Mississippi Valley, and as such deserves to be known and honored."

The French early improved the opening made for them. Before the year 1698, the Rev. Father Gravier began a mission among the Illinois, and founded Kaskaskia. For some time this was merely a missionary station, where none but natives resided, it being one of three such villages, the other two being Cahokia and Peoria. What is known of these missions is learned from a letter written by Father Gabriel Marest, dated "Aux Cascaskias, autrement dit de l'Immaculate Conception de la Sainte Vierge, le 9 Novembre, 1712." Soon after the founding of Kaskaskia, the missionary, Pinet, gathered a flock at Cahokia, while Peoria arose near the ruins of Fort Crevecœur. This must have been about the year 1700. The post at Vincennes on the Oubache river, (pronounced Wă-bă, meaning *summer cloud moving swiftly*) was established in 1702, according to the best authorities.* It is altogether pròbable that on LaSalle's last trip he established the stations at Kaskaskia and Cahokia. In July, 1701, the foundations of Fort Ponchartrain were laid by De la Motte Cadillac on the Detroit River. These stations, with those established further north, were the earliest attempts to occupy the Northwest Territory. At the same time efforts were being made to occupy the Southwest, which finally culminated in the settlement and founding of the City of New Orleans by a colony from England in 1718. This was mainly accomplished through the efforts of the famous Mississippi Company, established by the notorious John Law, who so quickly arose into prominence in France, and who with his scheme so quickly and so ignominiously passed away.

From the time of the founding of these stations for fifty years the French nation were engrossed with the settlement of the lower Mississippi, and the war with the Chicasaws, who had, in revenge for repeated

* There is considerable dispute about this date, some asserting it was founded as late as 1742. When the new court house at Vincennes was erected, all authorities on the subject were carefully examined, and 1702 fixed upon as the correct date. It was accordingly engraved on the corner-stone of the court house.

injuries, cut off the entire colony at Natchez. Although the company did little for Louisiana, as the entire West was then called, yet it opened the trade through the Mississippi River, and started the raising of grains indigenous to that climate. Until the year 1750, but little is known of the settlements in the Northwest, as it was not until this time that the attention of the English was called to the occupation of this portion of the New World, which they then supposed they owned. Vivier, a missionary among the Illinois, writing from "Aux Illinois," six leagues from Fort Chartres, June 8, 1750, says: "We have here whites, negroes and Indians, to say nothing of cross-breeds. There are five French villages, and three villages of the natives, within a space of twenty-one leagues situated between the Mississippi and another river called the Karkadaid (Kaskaskias). In the five French villages are, perhaps, eleven hundred whites, three hundred blacks and some sixty red slaves or savages. The three Illinois towns do not contain more than eight hundred souls all told. Most of the French till the soil; they raise wheat, cattle, pigs and horses, and live like princes. Three times as much is produced as can be consumed; and great quantities of grain and flour are sent to New Orleans." This city was now the seaport town of the Northwest, and save in the extreme northern part, where only furs and copper ore were found, almost all the products of the country found their way to France by the mouth of the Father of Waters. In another letter, dated November 7, 1750, this same priest says: "For fifteen leagues above the mouth of the Mississippi one sees no dwellings, the ground being too low to be habitable. Thence to New Orleans, the lands are only partially occupied. New Orleans contains black, white and red, not more, I think, than twelve hundred persons. To this point come all lumber, bricks, salt-beef, tallow, tar, skins and bear's grease; and above all, pork and flour from the Illinois. These things create some commerce, as forty vessels and more have come hither this year. Above New Orleans, plantations are again met with; the most considerable is a colony of Germans, some ten leagues up the river. At Point Coupee, thirty-five leagues above the German settlement, is a fort. Along here, within five or six leagues, are not less than sixty habitations. Fifty leagues farther up is the Natchez post, where we have a garrison, who are kept prisoners through fear of the Chickasaws. Here and at Point Coupee, they raise excellent tobacco. Another hundred leagues brings us to the Arkansas, where we have also a fort and a garrison for the benefit of the river traders. * * * From the Arkansas to the Illinois, nearly five hundred leagues, there is not a settlement. There should be, however, a fort at the Oubache (Ohio), the only path by which the English can reach the Mississippi. In the Illinois country are numberless mines, but no one to work them as they deserve." Father Marest, writing from the post at Vincennes in 1812, makes the same observation. Vivier also says: "Some individuals dig lead near the surface and supply the Indians and Canada. Two Spaniards now here, who claim to be adepts, say that our mines are like those of Mexico, and that if we would dig deeper, we should find silver under the lead; and at any rate the lead is excellent. There is also in this country, beyond doubt, copper ore, as from time to time large pieces are found in the streams."

HUNTING.

At the close of the year 1750, the French occupied, in addition to the lower Mississippi posts and those in Illinois, one at Du Quesne, one at the Maumee in the country of the Miamis, and one at Sandusky in what may be termed the Ohio Valley. In the northern part of the Northwest they had stations at St. Joseph's on the St. Joseph's of Lake Michigan, at Fort Ponchartrain (Detroit), at Michillimackanac or Massillimacanac, Fox River of Green Bay, and at Sault Ste. Marie. The fondest dreams of LaSalle were now fully realized. The French alone were possessors of this vast realm, basing their claim on discovery and settlement. Another nation, however, was now turning its attention to this extensive country, and hearing of its wealth, began to lay plans for occupying it and for securing the great profits arising therefrom.

The French, however, had another claim to this country, namely, the

DISCOVERY OF THE OHIO.

This "Beautiful" river was discovered by Robert Cavalier de La-Salle in 1669, four years before the discovery of the Mississippi by Joliet and Marquette.

While LaSalle was at his trading post on the St. Lawrence, he found leisure to study nine Indian dialects, the chief of which was the Iroquois. He not only desired to facilitate his intercourse in trade, but he longed to travel and explore the unknown regions of the West. An incident soon occurred which decided him to fit out an exploring expedition.

While conversing with some Senecas, he learned of a river called the Ohio, which rose in their country and flowed to the sea, but at such a distance that it required eight months to reach its mouth. In this statement the Mississippi and its tributaries were considered as one stream. LaSalle believing, as most of the French at that period did, that the great rivers flowing west emptied into the Sea of California, was anxious to embark in the enterprise of discovering a route across the continent to the commerce of China and Japan.

He repaired at once to Quebec to obtain the approval of the Governor. His eloquent appeal prevailed. The Governor and the Intendant, Talon, issued letters patent authorizing the enterprise, but made no provision to defray the expenses. At this juncture the seminary of St. Sulpice decided to send out missionaries in connection with the expedition, and LaSalle offering to sell his improvements at LaChine to raise money, the offer was accepted by the Superior, and two thousand eight hundred dollars were raised, with which LaSalle purchased four canoes and the necessary supplies for the outfit.

On the 6th of July, 1669, the party, numbering twenty-four persons, embarked in seven canoes on the St. Lawrence; two additional canoes carried the Indian guides. In three days they were gliding over the bosom of Lake Ontario. Their guides conducted them directly to the Seneca village on the bank of the Genesee, in the vicinity of the present City of Rochester, New York. Here they expected to procure guides to conduct them to the Ohio, but in this they were disappointed.

The Indians seemed unfriendly to the enterprise. LaSalle suspected that the Jesuits had prejudiced their minds against his plans. After waiting a month in the hope of gaining their object, they met an Indian from the Iroquois colony at the head of Lake Ontario, who assured them that they could there find guides, and offered to conduct them thence.

On their way they passed the mouth of the Niagara River, when they heard for the first time the distant thunder of the cataract. Arriving

IROQUOIS CHIEF.

among the Iroquois, they met with a friendly reception, and learned from a Shawanee prisoner that they could reach the Ohio in six weeks. Delighted with the unexpected good fortune, they made ready to resume their journey; but just as they were about to start they heard of the arrival of two Frenchmen in a neighboring village. One of them proved to be Louis Joliet, afterwards famous as an explorer in the West. He had been sent by the Canadian Government to explore the copper mines on Lake Superior, but had failed, and was on his way back to Quebec. He gave the missionaries a map of the country he had explored in the lake region, together with an account of the condition of the Indians in that quarter. This induced the priests to determine on leaving the expedition and going to Lake Superior. LaSalle warned them that the Jesuits were probably occupying that field, and that they would meet with a cold reception. Nevertheless they persisted in their purpose, and after worship on the lake shore, parted from LaSalle. On arriving at Lake Superior, they found, as LaSalle had predicted, the Jesuit Fathers, Marquette and Dablon, occupying the field.

These zealous disciples of Loyola informed them that they wanted no assistance from St. Sulpice, nor from those who made him their patron saint; and thus repulsed, they returned to Montreal the following June without having made a single discovery or converted a single Indian.

After parting with the priests, LaSalle went to the chief Iroquois village at Onondaga, where he obtained guides, and passing thence to a tributary of the Ohio south of Lake Erie, he descended the latter as far as the falls at Louisville. Thus was the Ohio discovered by LaSalle, the persevering and successful French explorer of the West, in 1669.

The account of the latter part of his journey is found in an anonymous paper, which purports to have been taken from the lips of LaSalle himself during a subsequent visit to Paris. In a letter written to Count Frontenac in 1667, shortly after the discovery, he himself says that he discovered the Ohio and descended it to the falls. This was regarded as an indisputable fact by the French authorities, who claimed the Ohio Valley upon another ground. When Washington was sent by the colony of Virginia in 1753, to demand of Gordeur de St. Pierre why the French had built a fort on the Monongahela, the haughty commandant at Quebec replied: "We claim the country on the Ohio by virtue of the discoveries of LaSalle, and will not give it up to the English. Our orders are to make prisoners of every Englishman found trading in the Ohio Valley."

ENGLISH EXPLORATIONS AND SETTLEMENTS.

When the new year of 1750 broke in upon the Father of Waters and the Great Northwest, all was still wild save at the French posts already described. In 1749, when the English first began to think seriously about sending men into the West, the greater portion of the States of Indiana, Ohio, Illinois, Michigan, Wisconsin, and Minnesota were yet under the dominion of the red men. The English knew, however, pretty conclusively of the nature of the wealth of these wilds. As early as 1710, Governor Spotswood, of Virginia, had commenced movements to secure the country west of the Alleghenies to the English crown. In Pennsylvania, Governor Keith and James Logan, secretary of the province, from 1719 to 1731, represented to the powers of England the necessity of securing the Western lands. Nothing was done, however, by that power save to take some diplomatic steps to secure the claims of Britain to this unexplored wilderness.

England had from the outset claimed from the Atlantic to the Pacific, on the ground that the discovery of the seacoast and its possession was a discovery and possession of the country, and, as is well known, her grants to the colonies extended "from sea to sea." This was not all her claim. She had purchased from the Indian tribes large tracts of land. This latter was also a strong argument. As early as 1684, Lord Howard, Governor of Virginia, held a treaty with the six nations. These were the great Northern Confederacy, and comprised at first the Mohawks, Oneidas, Onondagas, Cayugas, and Senecas. Afterward the Tuscaroras were taken into the confederacy, and it became known as the SIX NATIONS. They came under the protection of the mother country, and again in 1701, they repeated the agreement, and in September, 1726, a formal deed was drawn up and signed by the chiefs. The validity of this claim has often been disputed, but never successfully. In 1744, a purchase was made at Lancaster, Pennsylvania, of certain lands within the "Colony of Virginia," for which the Indians received £200 in gold and a like sum in goods, with a promise that, as settlements increased, more should be paid. The Commissioners from Virginia were Colonel Thomas Lee and Colonel William Beverly. As settlements extended, the promise of more pay was called to mind, and Mr. Conrad Weiser was sent across the mountains with presents to appease the savages. Col. Lee, and some Virginians accompanied him with the intention of sounding the Indians upon their feelings regarding the English. They were not satisfied with their treatment, and plainly told the Commissioners why. The English did not desire the cultivation of the country, but the monopoly of the Indian trade. In 1748, the Ohio Company was formed, and petitioned the king for a grant of land beyond the Alleghenies. This was granted, and the government of Virginia was ordered to grant to them a half million acres, two hundred thousand of which were to be located at once. Upon the 12th of June, 1749, 800,000 acres from the line of Canada north and west was made to the Loyal Company, and on the 29th of October, 1751, 100,000 acres were given to the Greenbriar Company. All this time the French were not idle. They saw that, should the British gain a foothold in the West, especially upon the Ohio, they might not only prevent the French settling upon it, but in time would come to the lower posts and so gain possession of the whole country. Upon the 10th of May, 1774, Vaudreuil, Governor of Canada and the French possessions, well knowing the consequences that must arise from allowing the English to build trading posts in the Northwest, seized some of their frontier posts, and to further secure the claim of the French to the West, he, in 1749, sent Louis Celeron with a party of soldiers to plant along the Ohio River, in the mounds and at the mouths of its principal tributaries, plates of lead, on which were inscribed the claims of France. These were heard of in 1752, and within the memory of residents now living along the "Oyo," as the beautiful river was called by the French. One of these plates was found with the inscription partly defaced. It bears date August 16, 1749, and a copy of the inscription with particular account of the discovery of the plate, was sent by DeWitt Clinton to the American Antiquarian Society, among whose journals it may now be found.* These measures did not, however, deter the English from going on with their explorations, and though neither party resorted to arms, yet the conflict was gathering, and it was only a question of time when the storm would burst upon the frontier settlements. In 1750, Christopher Gist was sent by the Ohio Company to examine its lands. He went to a village of the Twigtwees, on the Miami, about one hundred and fifty miles above its mouth. He afterward spoke of it as very populous. From there he went down the Ohio River nearly to the falls at the present City of Louisville, and in November he commenced a survey of the Company's lands. During the Winter, General Andrew Lewis performed a similar work for the Greenbriar Company. Meanwhile the French were busy in preparing their forts for defense, and in opening roads, and also sent a small party of soldiers to keep the Ohio clear. This party, having heard of the English post on the Miami River, early in 1652, assisted by the Ottawas and Chippewas, attacked it, and, after a severe battle, in which fourteen of the natives were killed and others wounded, captured the garrison. (They were probably garrisoned in a block house). The traders were carried away to Canada, and one account says several were burned. This fort or post was called by the English Pickawillany. A memorial of the king's ministers refers to it as "Pickawillanes, in the center of the territory between the Ohio and the Wabash. The name is probably some variation of Pickaway or Picqua in 1773, written by Rev. David Jones Pickaweke."

* The following is a translation of the inscription on the plate: "In the year 1749, reign of Louis XV., King of France, we, Celeron, commandant of a detachment by Monsieur the Marquis of Gallisoniere, commander-in-chief of New France, to establish tranquility in certain Indian villages of these cantons, have buried this plate at the confluence of the Toradakoin, this twenty-ninth of July, near the river Ohio, otherwise Beautiful River, as a monument of renewal of possession which we have taken of the said river, and all its tributaries; inasmuch as the preceding Kings of France have enjoyed it, and maintained it by their arms and treaties; especially by those of Ryswick, Utrecht, and Aix La Chapelle."

This was the first blood shed between the French and English, and occurred near the present City of Piqua, Ohio, or at least at a point about forty-seven miles north of Dayton. Each nation became now more interested in the progress of events in the Northwest. The English determined to purchase from the Indians a title to the lands they wished to occupy, and Messrs. Fry (afterward Commander-in-chief over Washington at the commencement of the French War of 1775–1763), Lomax and Patton were sent in the Spring of 1752 to hold a conference with the natives at Logstown to learn what they objected to in the treaty of Lancaster already noticed, and to settle all difficulties. On the 9th of June, these Commissioners met the red men at Logstown, a little village on the north bank of the Ohio, about seventeen miles below the site of Pittsburgh. Here had been a trading point for many years, but it was abandoned by the Indians in 1750. At first the Indians declined to recognize the treaty of Lancaster, but, the Commissioners taking aside Montour, the interpreter, who was a son of the famous Catharine Montour, and a chief among the six nations, induced him to use his influence in their favor. This he did, and upon the 13th of June they all united in signing a deed, confirming the Lancaster treaty in its full extent, consenting to a settlement of the southeast of the Ohio, and guaranteeing that it should not be disturbed by them. These were the means used to obtain the first treaty with the Indians in the Ohio Valley.

Meanwhile the powers beyond the sea were trying to out-manœuvre each other, and were professing to be at peace. The English generally outwitted the Indians, and failed in many instances to fulfill their contracts. They thereby gained the ill-will of the red men, and further increased the feeling by failing to provide them with arms and ammunition. Said an old chief, at Easton, in 1758: "The Indians on the Ohio left you because of your own fault. When we heard the French were coming, we asked you for help and arms, but we did not get them. The French came, they treated us kindly, and gained our affections. The Governor of Virginia settled on our lands for his own benefit, and, when we wanted help, forsook us."

At the beginning of 1653, the English thought they had secured by title the lands in the West, but the French had quietly gathered cannon and military stores to be in readiness for the expected blow. The English made other attempts to ratify these existing treaties, but not until the Summer could the Indians be gathered together to discuss the plans of the French. They had sent messages to the French, warning them away; but they replied that they intended to complete the chain of forts already begun, and would not abandon the field.

Soon after this, no satisfaction being obtained from the Ohio regarding the positions and purposes of the French, Governor Dinwiddie of Virginia determined to send to them another messenger and learn from them, if possible, their intentions. For this purpose he selected a young man, a surveyor, who, at the early age of nineteen, had received the rank of major, and who was thoroughly posted regarding frontier life. This personage was no other than the illustrious George Washington, who then held considerable interest in Western lands. He was at this time just twenty-two years of age. Taking Gist as his guide, the two, accompanied by four servitors, set out on their perilous march. They left Will's Creek on the 10th of November, 1753, and on the 22d reached the Monongahela, about ten miles above the fork. From there they went to Logstown, where Washington had a long conference with the chiefs of the Six Nations. From them he learned the condition of the French, and also heard of their determination not to come down the river till the following Spring. The Indians were non-committal, as they were afraid to turn either way, and, as far as they could, desired to remain neutral. Washington, finding nothing could be done with them, went on to Venango, an old Indian town at the mouth of French Creek. Here the French had a fort, called Fort Machault. Through the rum and flattery of the French, he nearly lost all his Indian followers. Finding nothing of importance here, he pursued his way amid great privations, and on the 11th of December reached the fort at the head of French Creek. Here he delivered Governor Dinwiddie's letter, received his answer, took his observations, and on the 16th set out upon his return journey with no one but Gist, his guide, and a few Indians who still remained true to him, notwithstanding the endeavors of the French to retain them. Their homeward journey was one of great peril and suffering from the cold, yet they reached home in safety on the 6th of January, 1754.

From the letter of St. Pierre, commander of the French fort, sent by Washington to Governor Dinwiddie, it was learned that the French would not give up without a struggle. Active preparations were at once made in all the English colonies for the coming conflict, while the French finished the fort at Venango and strengthened their lines of fortifications, and gathered their forces to be in readiness.

The Old Dominion was all alive. Virginia was the center of great activities; volunteers were called for, and from all the neighboring colonies men rallied to the conflict, and everywhere along the Potomac men were enlisting under the Governor's proclamation—which promised two hundred thousand acres on the Ohio. Along this river they were gathering as far as Will's Creek, and far beyond this point, whither Trent had come for assistance for his little band of forty-one men, who were working away in hunger and want, to fortify that point at the fork of the Ohio, to which both parties were looking with deep interest.

"The first birds of Spring filled the air with their song; the swift river rolled by the Allegheny hillsides, swollen by the melting snows of Spring and the April showers. The leaves were appearing; a few Indian scouts were seen, but no enemy seemed near at hand; and all was so quiet, that Frazier, an old Indian scout and trader, who had been left by Trent in command, ventured to his home at the mouth of Turtle Creek, ten miles up the Monongahela. But, though all was so quiet in that wilderness, keen eyes had seen the low intrenchment rising at the fork, and swift feet had borne the news of it up the river; and upon the morning of the 17th of April, Ensign Ward, who then had charge of it, saw upon the Allegheny a sight that made his heart sink—sixty batteaux and three hundred canoes filled with men, and laden deep with cannon and stores. * * * That evening he supped with his captor, Contrecœur, and the next day he was bowed off by the Frenchman, and with his men and tools, marched up the Monongahela."

The French and Indian war had begun. The treaty of Aix la Chapelle, in 1748, had left the boundaries between the French and English possessions unsettled, and the events already narrated show the French were determined to hold the country watered by the Mississippi and its tributaries; while the English laid claims to the country by virtue of the discoveries of the Cabots, and claimed all the country from Newfoundland to Florida, extending from the Atlantic to the Pacific. The first decisive blow had now been struck, and the first attempt of the English, through the Ohio Company, to occupy these lands, had resulted disastrously to them. The French and Indians immediately completed the fortifications begun at the Fork, which they had so easily captured, and when completed gave to the fort the name of DuQuesne. Washington was at Will's Creek when the news of the capture of the fort arrived. He at once departed to recapture it. On his way he entrenched himself at a place called the "Meadows," where he erected a fort called by him Fort Necessity. From there he surprised and captured a force of French and Indians marching against him, but was soon after attacked in his fort by a much superior force, and was obliged to yield on the morning of July 4th. He was allowed to return to Virginia.

The English Government immediately planned four campaigns; one against Fort DuQuesne; one against Nova Scotia; one against Fort Niagara, and one against Crown Point. These occurred during 1755–6, and were not successful in driving the French from their possessions. The expedition against Fort DuQuesne was led by the famous General Braddock, who, refusing to listen to the advice of Washington and those acquainted with Indian warfare, suffered such an inglorious defeat. This occurred on the morning of July 9th, and is generally known as the battle of Monongahela, or "Braddock's Defeat." The war continued with various vicissitudes through the years 1756–7; when, at the commencement of 1758, in accordance with the plans of William Pitt, then Secretary of State, afterwards Lord Chatham, active preparations were made to carry on the war. Three expeditions were planned for this year: one, under General Amherst, against Louisburg; another, under Abercrombie, against Fort Ticonderoga; and a third, under General Forbes, against Fort DuQuesne. On the 26th of July, Louisburg surrendered after a desperate resistance of more than forty days, and the eastern part of the Canadian possessions fell into the hands of the British. Abercrombie captured Fort Frontenac, and when the expedition against Fort DuQuesne, of which Washington had the active command, arrived there, it was found in flames and deserted. The English at once took possession, rebuilt the fort, and in honor of their illustrious statesman, changed the name to Fort Pitt.

The great object of the campaign of 1759, was the reduction of Canada. General Wolfe was to lay siege to Quebec; Amherst was to reduce Ticonderoga and Crown Point, and General Prideaux was to capture Niagara. This latter place was taken in July, but the gallant Prideaux lost his life in the attempt. Amherst captured Ticonderoga and Crown Point without a blow; and Wolfe, after making the memorable ascent to the Plains of Abraham, on September 13th, defeated Montcalm, and on the 18th, the city capitulated. In this engagement Montcolm and Wolfe both lost their lives. De Levi, Montcalm's successor, marched to Sillery, three miles above the city, with the purpose of defeating the English, and there, on the 28th of the following April, was fought one of the bloodiest battles of the French and Indian War. It resulted in the defeat of the French, and the fall of the City of Montreal. The Governor signed a capitulation by which the whole of Canada was surrendered to the English. This practically concluded the war, but it was not until 1763 that the treaties of peace between France and England were signed. This was done on the 10th of February of that year, and under its provisions all the country east of the Mississippi and north of the Iberville River, in Louisiana, were ceded to England. At the same time Spain ceded Florida to Great Britain.

On the 13th of September, 1760, Major Robert Rogers was sent from Montreal to take charge of Detroit, the only remaining French post in the territory. He arrived there on the 19th of November, and summoned the place to surrender. At first the commander of the post, Beletre refused, but on the 29th, hearing of the continued defeat of the

French arms, surrendered. Rogers remained there until December 23d under the personal protection of the celebrated chief, Pontiac, to whom, no doubt, he owed his safety. Pontiac had come here to inquire the purposes of the English in taking possession of the country. He was assured that they came simply to trade with the natives, and did not desire their country. This answer conciliated the savages, and did much to insure the safety of Rogers and his party during their stay, and while on their journey home.

Rogers set out for Fort Pitt on December 23, and was just one month on the way. His route was from Detroit to Maumee, thence across the present State of Ohio directly to the fort. This was the common trail of the Indians in their journeys from Sandusky to the fork of the Ohio. It went from Fort Sandusky, where Sandusky City now is, crossed the Huron river, then called Bald Eagle Creek, to "Mohickon John's Town" on Mohickon Creek, the northern branch of White Woman's River, and thence crossed to Beaver's Town, a Delaware town on what is now Sandy Creek. At Beaver's Town were probably one hundred and fifty warriors, and not less than three thousand acres of cleared land. From there the track went up Sandy Creek to and across Big Beaver, and up the Ohio to Logstown, thence on to the fork.

The Northwest Territory was now entirely under the English rule. New settlements began to be rapidly made, and the promise of a large trade was speedily manifested. Had the British carried out their promises with the natives none of those savage butcheries would have been perpetrated, and the country would have been spared their recital.

The renowned chief, Pontiac, was one of the leading spirits in these atrocities. We will now pause in our narrative, and notice the leading events in his life. The earliest authentic information regarding this noted Indian chief is learned from an account of an Indian trader named Alexander Henry, who, in the Spring of 1761, penetrated his domains as far as Missillimacnac. Pontiac was then a great friend of the French, but a bitter foe of the English, whom he considered as encroaching on his hunting grounds. Henry was obliged to disguise himself as a Canadian to insure safety, but was discovered by Pontiac, who bitterly reproached him and the English for their attempted subjugation of the West. He declared that no treaty had been made with them; no presents sent them, and that he would resent any possession of the West by that nation. He was at the time about fifty years of age, tall and dignified, and was civil and military ruler of the Ottawas, Ojibwas and Pottawatamies.

The Indians, from Lake Michigan to the borders of North Carolina, were united in this feeling, and at the time of the treaty of Paris, ratified February 10, 1763, a general conspiracy was formed to fall suddenly

PONTIAC, THE OTTAWA CHIEFTAIN.

upon the frontier British posts, and with one blow strike every man dead. Pontiac was the marked leader in all this, and was the commander of the Chippewas, Ottawas, Wyandots, Miamis, Shawanese, Delawares and Mingoes, who had, for the time, laid aside their local quarrels to unite in this enterprise.

The blow came, as near as can now be ascertained, on May 7, 1763. Nine British posts fell, and the Indians drank, "scooped up in the hollow of joined hands," the blood of many a Briton.

Pontiac's immediate field of action was the garrison at Detroit. Here, however, the plans were frustrated by an Indian woman disclosing the plot the evening previous to his arrival. Everything was carried out, however, according to Pontiac's plans until the moment of action, when Major Gladwyn, the commander of the post, stepping to one of the Indian chiefs, suddenly drew aside his blanket and disclosed the concealed musket. Pontiac, though a brave man, turned pale and trembled. He saw his plan was known, and that the garrison were prepared. He endeavored to exculpate himself from any such intentions; but the guilt was evident, and he and his followers were dismissed with a severe reprimand, and warned never to again enter the walls of the post.

Pontiac at once laid siege to the fort, and until the treaty of peace between the British and the Western Indians, concluded in August, 1764, continued to harass and besiege the fortress. He organized a regular commissariat department, issued bills of credit written out on bark, which, to his credit, it may be stated, were punctually redeemed. At the conclusion of the treaty, in which it seems he took no part, he went further south, living many years among the Illinois.

He had given up all hope of saving his country and race. After a time he endeavored to unite the Illinois tribe and those about St. Louis in a war with the whites. His efforts were fruitless, and only ended in a quarrel between himself and some Kaskaskia Indians, one of whom soon afterwards killed him. His death was, however, avenged by the northern Indians, who nearly exterminated the Illinois in the wars which followed.

Had it not been for the treachery of a few of his followers, his plan for the extermination of the whites, a masterly one, would undoubtedly have been carried out.

It was in the Spring of the year following Rogers' visit that Alexander Henry went to Missillimacnac, and everywhere found the strongest feelings against the English, who had not carried out their promises, and were doing nothing to conciliate the natives. Here he met the chief, Pontiac, who, after conveying to him in a speech the idea that their French father would awake soon and utterly destroy his enemies, said: "Englishman, although you have conquered the French, you have not yet conquered us! We are not your slaves! These lakes, these woods, these mountains, were left us by our ancestors. They are our inheritance, and we will part with them to none. Your nation supposes that we, like the white people, can not live without bread and pork and beef. But you ought to know that He, the Great Spirit and Master of Life, has provided food for us upon these broad lakes and in these mountains."

He then spoke of the fact that no treaty had been made with them, no presents sent them, and that he and his people were yet for war. Such were the feelings of the Northwestern Indians immediately after the English took possession of their country. These feelings were no doubt encouraged by the Canadians and French, who hoped that yet the French arms might prevail. The treaty of Paris, however, gave to the English the right to this vast domain, and active preparations were going on to occupy it and enjoy its trade and emoluments.

In 1762, France, by a secret treaty, ceded Louisiana to Spain, to prevent it falling into the hands of the English, who were becoming masters of the entire West. The next year the treaty of Paris, signed at Fontainbleau, gave to the English the domain of the country in question. Twenty years after, by the treaty of peace between the United States and England, that part of Canada lying south and west of the Great Lakes, comprehending a large territory which is the subject of these sketches, was acknowledged to be a portion of the United States; and twenty years still later, in 1803, Louisiana was ceded by Spain back to France, and by France sold to the United States.

In the half century, from the building of the Fort of Crevecœur by LaSalle, in 1680, up to the erection of Fort Chartres, many French settlements had been made in that quarter. These have already been noticed, being those at St. Vincent (Vincennes), Kohokia or Cahokia, Kaskaskia and Prairie du Rocher, on the American Bottom, a large tract of rich alluvial soil in Illinois, on the Mississippi, opposite the site of St. Louis.

By the treaty of Paris, the regions east of the Mississippi, including all these and other towns of the Northwest, were given over to England; but they do not appear to have been taken possession of until 1765, when Captain Stirling, in the name of the Majesty of England, established himself at Fort Chartres bearing with him the proclamation of General Gage, dated December 30, 1764, which promised religious freedom to all Catholics who worshiped here, and a right to leave the country with their effects if they wished, or to remain with the privileges of Englishmen. It was shortly after the occupancy of the West by the British that the war with Pontiac opened. It is already noticed in the sketch of that chieftain. By it many a Briton lost his life, and many a frontier settlement in its infancy ceased to exist. This was not ended until the year 1764, when, failing to capture Detroit, Niagara and Fort Pitt, his confederacy became disheartened, and, receiving no aid from the French, Pontiac abandoned the enterprise and departed to the Illinois, among whom he afterward lost his life.

As soon as these difficulties were definitely settled, settlers began rapidly to survey the country and prepare for occupation. During the year 1770, a number of persons from Virginia and other British provinces explored and marked out nearly all the valuable lands on the Monongahela and along the banks of the Ohio as far as the Little Kanawha. This was followed by another exploring expedition, in which George Washington was a party. The latter, accompanied by Dr. Craik, Capt. Crawford and others, on the 20th of October, 1770, descended the Ohio from Pittsburgh to the mouth of the Kanawha; ascended that stream about fourteen miles, marked out several large tracts of land, shot several buffalo, which were then abundant in the Ohio Valley, and returned to the fort.

Pittsburgh was at this time a trading post, about which was clustered a village of some twenty houses, inhabited by Indian traders. This same year, Capt. Pittman visited Kaskaskia and its neighboring villages. He found there about sixty-five resident families, and at Cahokia only forty-five dwellings. At Fort Chartres was another small settlement, and at Detroit the garrison were quite prosperous and strong. For a year or two settlers continued to locate near some of these posts, generally Fort Pitt or Detroit, owing to the fears of the Indians, who still maintained some feelings of hatred to the English. The trade from the posts was quite good, and from those in Illinois large quantities of pork and flour found their way to the New Orleans market. At this time the policy of the British Government was strongly opposed to the extension of the colonies west. In 1763, the King of England forbade, by royal proclamation, his colonial subjects from making a settlement beyond the sources of the rivers which fall into the Atlantic Ocean. At the instance of the Board of Trade, measures were taken to prevent the settlement without the limits prescribed, and to retain the commerce within easy reach of Great Britain.

The commander-in-chief of the king's forces wrote in 1769: "In the course of a few years necessity will compel the colonists, should they extend their settlements west, to provide manufactures of some kind for themselves, and when all connection upheld by commerce with the mother country ceases, an *independency* in their government will soon follow."

In accordance with this policy, Gov. Gage issued a proclamation in 1772, commanding the inhabitants of Vincennes to abandon their settlements and join some of the Eastern English colonies. To this they strenuously objected, giving good reasons therefor, and were allowed to remain. The strong opposition to this policy of Great Britain led to its change, and to such a course as to gain the attachment of the French population. In December, 1773, influential citizens of Quebec petitioned the king for an extension of the boundary lines of that province, which was granted, and Parliament passed an act on June 2, 1774, extending the boundary so as to include the territory lying within the present States of Ohio, Indiana, Illinois and Michigan.

In consequence of the liberal policy pursued by the British Government toward the French settlers in the West, they were disposed to favor that nation in the war which soon followed with the colonies; but the early alliance between France and America soon brought them to the side of the war for independence.

In 1774, Gov. Dunmore, of Virginia, began to encourage emigration to the Western lands. He appointed magistrates at Fort Pitt under the pretense that the fort was under the government of that commonwealth. One of these justices, John Connelly, who possessed a tract of land in the Ohio Valley, gathered a force of men and garrisoned the fort, calling it Fort Dunmore. This and other parties were formed to select sites for settlements, and often came in conflict with the Indians, who yet claimed portions of the valley, and several battles followed. These ended in the famous battle of Kanawha in July, where the Indians were defeated and driven across the Ohio.

During the years 1775 and 1776, by the operations of land companies and the perseverance of individuals, several settlements were firmly established between the Alleghanies and the Ohio River, and western land speculators were busy in Illinois and on the Wabash. At a council held in Kaskaskia on July 5, 1773, an association of English traders, calling themselves the "Illinois Land Company," obtained from ten chiefs of the Kaskaskia, Cahokia and Peoria tribes two large tracts of land lying on the east side of the Mississippi River south of the Illinois. In 1775, a merchant from the Illinois Country, named Viviat, came to Post Vincennes as the agent of the association called the "Wabash Land Company." On the 8th of October he obtained from eleven Piankeshaw chiefs, a deed for 37,497,600 acres of land. This deed was signed by the grantors, attested by a number of the inhabitants of Vincennes, and afterward recorded in the office of a notary public at Kaskaskia. This and other land companies had extensive schemes for the colonization of the West; but all were frustrated by the breaking out of the Revolution. On the 20th of April, 1780, the two companies named consolidated under the name of the "United Illinois and Wabash Land Company." They afterward made strenuous efforts to have these grants sanctioned by Congress, but all signally failed.

When the War of the Revolution commenced, Kentucky was an unorganized country, though there were several settlements within her borders.

In Hutchins' Topography of Virginia, it is stated that at that time "Kaskaskia contained 80 houses, and nearly 1,000 white and black inhabitants—the whites being a little the more numerous. Cahokia contains 50 houses and 300 white inhabitants, and 80 negroes. There were east of the Mississippi River, about the year 1771"—when these observations were made—"300 white men capable of bearing arms, and 230 negroes."

From 1775 until the expedition of Clark, nothing is recorded and nothing known of these settlements, save what is contained in a report made by a committee to Congress in June, 1778. From it the following extract is made:

"Near the mouth of the River Kaskaskia, there is a village which appears to have contained nearly eighty families from the beginning of the late revolution. There are twelve families in a small village at la Prairie du Rochers, and near fifty families at the Kahokia Village. There are also four or five families at Fort Chartres and St. Philips, which is five miles further up the river."

St. Louis had been settled in February, 1764, and at this time contained, including its neighboring towns, over six hundred whites and one hundred and fifty negroes. It must be remembered that all the country west of the Mississippi was now under French rule, and remained so until ceded again to Spain, its original owner, who afterwards sold it and the country including New Orleans to the United States. At Detroit there were, according to Capt. Carver, who was in the Northwest from 1766 to 1768, more than one hundred houses, and the river was settled for more than twenty miles, although poorly cultivated—the people being engaged in the Indian trade. This old town has a history, which we will here relate.

It is the oldest town in the Northwest, having been founded by Antoine de Lamotte Cadillac, in 1701. It was laid out in the form of an oblong square, of two acres in length, and an acre and a half in width. As described by A. D. Frazer, who first visited it and became a permanent resident of the place, in 1778, it comprised within its limits that space between Mr. Palmer's store (Conant Block) and Capt. Perkins' house (near the Arsenal building), and extended back as far as the public barn, and was bordered in front by the Detroit River. It was surrounded by oak and cedar pickets, about fifteen feet long, set in the ground, and had four gates—east, west, north and south. Over the first three of these gates were block houses provided with four guns apiece, each a six-pounder. Two six-gun batteries were planted fronting the river and in a parallel direction with the block houses. There were four streets running east and west, the main street being twenty feet wide and the rest fifteen feet, while the four streets crossing these at right angles were from ten to fifteen feet in width.

At the date spoken of by Mr. Frazer, there was no fort within the enclosure, but a citadel on the ground corresponding to the present northwest corner of Jefferson Avenue and Wayne Street. The citadel was inclosed by pickets, and within it were erected barracks of wood, two stories high, sufficient to contain ten officers, and also barracks sufficient to contain four hundred men, and a provision store built of brick. The citadel also contained a hospital and guard-house. The old town of Detroit, in 1778, contained about sixty houses, most of them one story, with a few a story and a half in height. They were all of logs, some hewn and some round. There was one building of splendid appearance, called the "King's Palace," two stories high, which stood near the east gate. It was built for Governor Hamilton, the first governor commissioned by the British. There were two guard-houses, one near the west gate and the other near the Government House. Each of the guards consisted of twenty-four men and a subaltern, who mounted regularly every morning between nine and ten o'clock, Each furnished four sentinels, who were relieved every two hours. There was also an officer of the day, who performed strict duty. Each of the gates was shut regularly at sunset; even wicket gates were shut at nine o'clock, and all the keys were delivered into the hands of the commanding officer. They were opened in the morning at sunrise. No Indian or squaw was permitted to enter town with any weapon, such as a tomahawk or a knife. It was a standing order that the Indians should deliver their arms and instruments of every kind before they were permitted to pass the sentinel, and they were restored to them on their return. No more than twenty-five Indians were allowed to enter the town at any one time, and they were admitted only at the east and west gates. At sundown the drums beat, and all the Indians were required to leave town instantly. There was a council house near the water side for the purpose of holding council with the Indians. The population of the town was about sixty families, in all about two hundred males and one hundred females. This town was destroyed by fire, all except one dwelling, in 1805. After which the present "new" town was laid out.

On the breaking out of the Revolution, the British held every post of importance in the West. Kentucky was formed as a component part of Virginia, and the sturdy pioneers of the West, alive to their interests, and recognizing the great benefits of obtaining the control of the trade in this part of the New World, held steadily to their purposes, and those within the commonwealth of Kentucky proceeded to exercise their civil privileges, by electing John Todd and Richard Gallaway, burgesses to represent them in the Assembly of the parent state. Early in September of that year (1777) the first court was held in Harrodsburg, and Col. Bowman, afterwards major, who had arrived in August, was made the commander of a militia organization which had been commenced the March previous. Thus the tree of loyalty was growing. The chief spirit in this far-out colony, who had represented her the year previous east of the mountains, was now meditating a move unequaled in its boldness. He had been watching the movements of the British throughout the Northwest, and understood their whole plan. He saw it was through their possession of the posts at Detroit, Vincennes, Kaskaskia, and other places, which would give them constant and easy access to the various Indian tribes in the Northwest, that the British intended to penetrate the country from the north and south, and annihilate the frontier fortresses. This moving, energetic man was Colonel, afterwards General, George Rogers Clark. He knew the Indians were not unanimously in accord with the English, and he was convinced that, could the British be defeated and expelled from the Northwest, the natives might be easily awed into neutrality; and by spies sent for the purpose, he satisfied himself that the enterprise against the Illinois settlements might easily succeed. Having convinced himself of the certainty of the project, he repaired to the Capital of Virginia, which place he reached on November 5th. While he was on his way, fortunately, on October 17th, Burgoyne had been defeated, and the spirits of the colonists greatly encouraged thereby. Patrick Henry was Governor of Virginia, and at once entered heartily into Clark's plans. The same plan had before been agitated in the Colonial Assemblies, but there was no one until Clark came who was sufficiently acquainted with the condition of affairs at the scene of action to be able to guide them.

Clark, having satisfied the Virginia leaders of the feasibility of his plan, received, on the 2d of January, two sets of instructions—one secret, the other open — the latter authorized him to proceed to enlist seven companies to go to Kentucky, subject to his orders, and to serve three months from their arrival in the West. The secret order authorized him to arm these troops, to procure his powder and lead of General Hand at Pittsburgh, and to proceed at once to subjugate the country.

With these instructions Clark repaired to Pittsburgh, choosing rather to raise his men west of the mountains, as he well knew all were needed in the colonies in the conflict there. He sent Col. W. B. Smith to Holston for the same purpose, but neither succeeded in raising the required number of men. The settlers in these parts were afraid to leave their own firesides exposed to a vigilant foe, and but few could be induced to join the proposed expedition. With three companies and several private volunteers, Clark at length commenced his descent of the Ohio, which he navigated as far as the Falls, where he took possession of and fortified Corn Island, a small island between the present Cities of Louisville, Kentucky, and New Albany, Indiana. Remains of this fortification may yet be found. At this place he appointed Col. Bowman to meet him with such recruits as had reached Kentucky by the southern route, and as many as could be spared from the station. Here he announced to the men their real destination. Having completed his arrangements, and chosen his party, he left a small garrison upon the island, and on the 24th of June, during a total eclipse of the sun, which to them augured no good, and which fixes beyond dispute the date of starting, he with his chosen band, fell down the river. His plan was to go by water as far as Fort Massac or Massacre, and thence march direct to Kaskaskia. Here he intended to surprise the garrison, and after its capture go to Cahokia, then to Vincennes, and lastly to Detroit. Should he fail, he intended to march directly to the Mississippi River and cross it into the Spanish country. Before his start he received two good items of information: one that the alliance had been formed between France and the United States; and the other that the Indians throughout the Illinois country and the inhabitants, at the various frontier posts, had been led to believe by the British that the "Long Knives" or Virginians, were the most fierce, bloodthirsty and cruel savages that ever scalped a foe. With this impression on their minds, Clark saw that proper management would cause them to submit at once from fear, if surprised, and then from gratitude would become friendly if treated with unexpected leniency.

The march to Kaskaskia was accomplished through a hot July sun, and the town reached on the evening of July 4. He captured the fort near the village, and soon after the village itself by surprise, and without the loss of a single man or by killing any of the enemy. After sufficiently working upon the fears of the natives, Clark told them they were at perfect liberty to worship as they pleased, and to take whichever side of the great conflict they would, also he would protect them from any barbarity from British or Indian foe. This had the desired effect, and the inhabitants, so unexpectedly and so gratefully surprised by the unlooked for turn of affairs, at once swore allegiance to the American arms, and when Clark desired to go to Cahokia on the 6th of July, they accompanied him, and through their influence the inhabitants of the place surrendered, and gladly placed themselves under his protection. Thus the two important posts in Illinois passed from the hands of the English into the possession of Virginia.

In the person of the priest at Kaskaskia, M. Gibault, Clark found a powerful ally and generous friend. Clark saw that, to retain possession of the Northwest and treat successfully with the Indians within its boundaries, he must establish a government for the colonies he had taken. St. Vincent, the next important post to Detroit, remained yet to be taken before the Mississippi Valley was conquered. M. Gibault told him that he would alone, by persuasion, lead Vincennes to throw off its connection with England. Clark gladly accepted his offer, and on the 14th of July, in company with a fellow-townsman, M. Gibault started on his mission of peace, and on the 1st of August returned with the cheerful intelligence that the post on the "Oubache" had taken the oath of allegiance to the Old Dominion. During this interval, Clark established his courts, placed garrisons at Kaskaskia and Cahokia, successfully re-enlisted his men, sent word to have a fort, which proved the germ of Louisville, erected at the Falls of the Ohio, and dispatched Mr. Rocheblave, who had been commander at Kaskaskia, as a prisoner of war to Richmond. In October the County of Illinois was established by the Legislature of Virginia, John Todd appointed Lieutenant Colonel and Civil Governor, and in November General Clark and his men received the thanks of the Old Dominion through their Legislature.

In a speech a few days afterward, Clark made known fully to the natives his plans, and at its close all came forward and swore allegiance to the Long Knives. While he was doing this Governor Hamilton, having made his various arrangements, had left Detroit and moved down the Wabash to Vincennes intending to operate from that point in reducing the Illinois posts, and then proceed on down to Kentucky and drive the rebels from the West. Gen. Clark had, on the return of M. Gibault, dispatched Captain Helm, of Fauquier County, Virginia, with an attendant named Henry, across the Illinois prairies to command the fort. Hamilton knew nothing of the capitulation of the post, and was greatly surprised on his arrival to be confronted by Capt. Helm, who, standing at the entrance of the fort by a loaded cannon ready to fire upon his assailants, demanded upon what terms Hamilton demanded possession of the fort. Being granted the rights of a prisoner of war, he surrendered to the British General, who could scarcely believe his eyes when he saw the force in the garrison.

Hamilton, not realizing the character of the men with whom he was contending, gave up his intended campaign for the Winter, sent his four hundred Indian warriors to prevent troops from coming down the Ohio, and to annoy the Americans in all ways, and sat quietly down to pass the Winter. Information of all these proceedings having reached Clark, he saw that immediate and decisive action was necessary, and that unless he captured Hamilton, Hamilton would capture him. Clark received the news on the 29th of January, 1779, and on February 4th, having sufficiently garrisoned Kaskaskia and Cahokia, he sent down the Mississippi a "battoe," as Major Bowman writes it, in order to ascend the Ohio and Wabash, and operate with the land forces gathering for the fray.

On the next day, Clark, with his little force of one hundred and twenty men, set out for the post, and after incredible hard marching through much mud, the ground being thawed by the incessant spring rains, on the 22d reached the fort, and being joined by his "battoe," at once commenced the attack on the post. The aim of the American backwoodsman was unerring, and on the 24th the garrison surrendered to the intrepid boldness of Clark. The French were treated with great kindness, and gladly renewed their allegiance to Virginia. Hamilton was sent as a prisoner to Virginia, where he was kept in close confinement. During his command of the British frontier posts, he had offered prizes to the Indians for all the scalps of Americans they would bring to him, and had earned in consequence thereof the title "Hair-buyer General," by which he was ever afterward known.

Detroit was now without doubt within easy reach of the enterprising Virginian, could he but raise the necessary force. Governor Henry being apprised of this, promised him the needed reinforcement, and Clark concluded to wait until he could capture and sufficiently garrison the posts. Had Clark failed in this bold undertaking, and Hamilton succeeded in uniting the western Indians for the next Spring's campaign, the West would indeed have been swept from the Mississippi to the Allegheny Mountains, and the great blow struck, which had been contemplated from the commencement, by the British.

"But for this small army of dripping, but fearless Virginians, the union of all the tribes from Georgia to Maine against the colonies might have been effected, and the whole current of our history changed."

At this time some fears were entertained by the Colonial Governments that the Indians in the North and Northwest were inclining to the British, and under the instructions of Washington, now Commander-in-Chief of the Colonial army, and so bravely fighting for American independence, armed forces were sent against the Six Nations, and upon the Ohio frontier, Col. Bowman, acting under the same general's orders, marched against Indians within the present limits of that State. These expeditions were in the main successful, and the Indians were compelled to sue for peace.

During this same year (1779) the famous "Land Laws" of Virginia were passed. The passage of these laws was of more consequence to the pioneers of Kentucky and the Northwest than the gaining of a few Indian conflicts. These laws confirmed in main all grants made, and guaranteed to all actual settlers their rights and privileges. After providing for the settlers, the laws provided for selling the balance of the public lands at forty cents per acre. To carry the Land Laws into effect, the Legislature sent four Virginians westward to attend to the various claims, over many of which great confusion prevailed concerning their validity. These gentlemen opened their court on October 13, 1779, at St. Asaphs, and continued until April 26, 1780, when they adjourned, having decided three thousand claims. They were succeeded by the surveyor, who came in the person of Mr. George May, and assumed his duties on the 10th day of the month whose name he bore. With the opening of the next year (1780) the troubles concerning the navigation of the Mississippi commenced. The Spanish Government exacted such measures in relation to its trade as to cause the overtures made to the United States to be rejected. The American Government considered they had a right to navigate its channel. To enforce their claims, a fort was erected below the mouth of the Ohio on the Kentucky side of the river. The settlements in Kentucky were being rapidly filled by emigrants. It was during this year that the first seminary of learning was established in the West in this young and enterprising Commonwealth.

The settlers here did not look upon the building of this fort in a friendly manner, as it aroused the hostility of the Indians. Spain had been friendly to the Colonies during their struggle for independence, and though for a while this friendship appeared in danger from the refusal of the free navigation of the river, yet it was finally settled to the satisfaction of both nations.

The Winter of 1779–80 was one of the most unusually severe ones ever experienced in the West. The Indians always referred to it as the "Great Cold." Numbers of wild animals perished, and not a few pioneers lost their lives. The following Summer a party of Canadians and Indians attacked St. Louis, and attempted to take possession of it in consequence of the friendly disposition of Spain to the revolting colonies. They met with such a determined resistance on the part of the inhabitants, even the women taking part in the battle, that they were compelled to abandon the contest. They also made an attack on the settlements in Kentucky, but, becoming alarmed in some unaccountable manner, they fled the country in great haste.

About this time arose the question in the Colonial Congress concerning the western lands claimed by Virginia, New York, Massachusetts and Connecticut. The agitation concerning this subject finally led New York, on the 19th of February, 1780, to pass a law giving to the delegates of that State in Congress the power to cede her western lands for the benefit of the United States. This law was laid before Congress during the next month, but no steps were taken concerning it until September 6th, when a resolution passed that body calling upon the States claiming western lands to release their claims in favor of the whole body. This basis formed the union, and was the first after all of those legislative measures which resulted in the creation of the States of Ohio, Indiana, Illinois, Michigan, Wisconsin and Minnesota. In December of the same year, the plan of conquering Detroit again arose. The conquest might have easily been effected by Clark had the necessary aid been furnished him. Nothing decisive was done, yet the heads of the Government knew that the safety of the Northwest from British invasion lay in the capture and retention of that important post, the only unconquered one in the territory.

Before the close of the year, Kentucky was divided into the Counties of Lincoln, Fayette and Jefferson, and the act establishing the Town of Louisville was passed. This same year is also noted in the annals of American history as the year in which occurred Arnold's treason to the United States.

Virginia, in accordance with the resolution of Congress, on the 2d day of January, 1781, agreed to yield her western lands to the United States upon certain conditions, which Congress would not accede to, and the Act of Cession, on the part of the Old Dominion, failed, nor was anything farther done until 1783. During all that time the Colonies were busily engaged in the struggle with the mother country, and in consequence thereof but little heed was given to the western settlements. Upon the 16th of April, 1781, the first birth north of the Ohio River of American parentage occurred, being that of Mary Heckewelder, daughter of the widely known Moravian missionary, whose band of Christian Indians suffered in after years a horrible massacre by the hands of the frontier settlers, who had been exasperated by the murder of several of their neighbors, and in their rage committed, without regard to humanity, a deed which forever afterwards cast a shade of shame upon their lives. For this and kindred outrages on the part of the whites, the Indians committed many deeds of cruelty which darken the years of 1771 and 1772 in the history of the Northwest.

During the year 1782 a number of battles among the Indians and frontiersmen occurred, and between the Moravian Indians and the Wyandots. In these, horrible acts of cruelty were practised on the captives, many of such dark deeds transpiring under the leadership of the notorious frontier outlaw, Simon Girty, whose name, as well as those of his brothers, was a terror to women and children. These occurred chiefly in the Ohio valleys. Cotemporary with them were several engagements in Kentucky, in which the famous Daniel Boone engaged, and who, often by his skill and knowledge of Indian warfare, saved the outposts from cruel destruc-

INDIANS ATTACKING FRONTIERSMEN.

tion. By the close of the year victory had perched upon the American banner, and on the 30th of November, provisional articles of peace had been arranged between the Commissioners of England and her unconquerable colonies. Cornwallis had been defeated on the 19th of October preceding, and the liberty of America was assured. On the 19th of April following, the anniversary of the battle of Lexington, peace was proclaimed to the army of the United States, and on the 3d of the next September, the definite treaty which ended our revolutionary struggle was concluded. By the terms of that treaty, the boundaries of the West were as follows: On the north the line was to extend along the center of the Great Lakes; from the western point of Lake Superior to Long Lake; thence to the Lake of the Woods; thence to the head of the Mississippi River; down its center to the 31st parallel of latitude, then on that line east to the head of the Appalachicola River; down its center to its junction with the Flint; thence straight to the head of St. Mary's River, and thence down along its center to the Atlantic Ocean.

Following the cessation of hostilities with England, several posts were still occupied by the British in the North and West. Among these was Detroit, still in the hands of the enemy. Numerous engagements with the Indians throughout Ohio and Indiana occurred, upon whose lands adventurous whites would settle ere the title had been acquired by the proper treaty.

To remedy this latter evil, Congress appointed commissioners to treat with the natives and purchase their lands, and prohibited the settlement of the territory until this could be done. Before the close of the year another attempt was made to capture Detroit, which was, however, not pushed, and Virginia, no longer feeling the interest in the Northwest she had formerly done, withdrew her troops, having on the 20th of December preceding authorized the whole of her possessions to be deeded to the United States. This was done on the 1st of March following, and the Northwest Territory passed from the control of the Old Dominion. To Gen. Clark and his soldiers, however, she gave a tract of one hundred and fifty thousand acres of land, to be situated any where north of the Ohio wherever they chose to locate them. They selected the region opposite the falls of the Ohio, where is now the dilapidated village of Clarksville, about midway between the Cities of New Albany and Jeffersonville, Indiana.

While the frontier remained thus, and Gen. Haldimand at Detroit refused to evacuate alleging that he had no orders from his King to do so, settlers were rapidly gathering about the inland forts. In the Spring of 1784, Pittsburgh was regularly laid out, and from the journal of Arthur Lee, who passed through the town soon after on his way to the Indian council at Fort McIntosh, we suppose it was not very prepossessing in appearance. He says:

"Pittsburgh is inhabited almost entirely by Scots and Irish, who live in paltry log houses, and are as dirty as if in the north of Ireland or even Scotland. There is a great deal of trade carried on, the goods being bought at the vast expense of forty-five shillings per pound from Philadelphia and Baltimore. They take in the shops flour, wheat, skins and money. There are in the town four attorneys, two doctors, and not a priest of any persuasion, nor church nor chapel."

Kentucky at this time contained thirty thousand inhabitants, and was beginning to discuss measures for a separation from Virginia. A land office was opened at Louisville, and measures were adopted to take defensive precaution against the Indians who were yet, in some instances, incited to deeds of violence by the British. Before the close of this year, 1784, the military claimants of land began to occupy them, although no entries were recorded until 1787.

The Indian title to the Northwest was not yet extinguished. They held large tracts of lands, and in order to prevent bloodshed Congress adopted means for treaties with the original owners and provided for the surveys of the lands gained thereby, as well as for those north of the Ohio, now in its possession. On January 31, 1786, a treaty was made with the Wabash Indians. The treaty of Fort Stanwix had been made in 1784. That at Fort McIntosh in 1785, and through these much land was gained. The Wabash Indians, however, afterward refused to comply with the provisions of the treaty made with them, and in order to compel their adherence to its provisions, force was used. During the year 1786, the free navigation of the Mississippi came up in Congress, and caused various discussions, which resulted in no definite action, only serving to excite speculation in regard to the western lands. Congress had promised bounties of land to the soldiers of the Revolution, but owing to the unsettled condition of affairs along the Mississippi respecting its navigation, and the trade of the Northwest, that body had, in 1783, declared its inability to fulfill these promises until a treaty could be concluded between the two Governments. Before the close of the year 1786, however, it was able, through the treaties with the Indians, to allow some grants and the settlement thereon, and on the 14th of September Connecticut ceded to the General Government the tract of land known as the "Connecticut Reserve," and before the close of the following year a large tract of land north of the Ohio was sold to a company, who at once took measures to settle it. By the provisions of this grant, the company were to pay the United States one dollar per acre, subject to a deduction of one-third for bad lands and other contingencies. They received 750,000 acres, bounded on the south by the Ohio, on the east by the seventh range of townships, on the west by the sixteenth range, and on the north by a line so drawn as to make the grant complete without the reservations. In addition to this, Congress afterward granted 100,000 acres to actual settlers, and 214,285 acres as army bounties under the resolutions of 1789 and 1790.

While Dr. Cutler, one of the agents of the company, was pressing its claims before Congress, that body was bringing into form an ordinance for the political and social organization of this Territory. When the cession was made by Virginia, in 1784, a plan was offered, but rejected. A motion had been made to strike from the proposed plan the prohibition of slavery, which prevailed. The plan was then discussed and altered, and finally passed unanimously, with the exception of South Carolina. By this proposition, the Territory was to have been divided into states

A PRAIRIE STORM.

by parallels and meridian lines. This, it was thought, would make ten states, which were to have been named as follows — beginning at the northwest corner and going southwardly: Sylvania, Michigania, Chersonesus, Assenisipia, Metropotamia, Illenoia, Saratoga, Washington, Polypotamia and Pelisipia.

There was a more serious objection to this plan than its category of names,— the boundaries. The root of the difficulty was in the resolution of Congress passed in October, 1780, which fixed the boundaries of the ceded lands to be from one hundred to one hundred and fifty miles square. These resolutions being presented to the Legislatures of Virginia and Massachusetts, they desired a change, and in July, 1786, the subject was taken up in Congress, and changed to favor a division into not more than five states, and not less than three. This was approved by the State Legislature of Virginia. The subject of the Government was again taken up by Congress in 1786, and discussed throughout that year and until July, 1787, when the famous "Compact of 1787" was passed, and the foundation of the government of the Northwest laid. This compact is fully discussed and explained in the history of Illinois in this book, and to it the reader is referred.

The passage of this act and the grant to the New England Company was soon followed by an application to the Government by John Cleves Symmes, of New Jersey, for a grant of the land between the Miamis. This gentleman had visited these lands soon after the treaty of 1786, and, being greatly pleased with them, offered similar terms to those given to the New England Company. The petition was referred to the Treasury Board with power to act, and a contract was concluded the following year. During the Autumn the directors of the New England Company were preparing to occupy their grant the following Spring, and upon the 23d of November made arrangements for a party of forty-seven men, under the superintendency of Gen. Rufus Putnam, to set forward. Six boat-builders were to leave at once, and on the first of January the surveyors and their assistants, twenty-six in number, were to meet at Hartford and proceed on their journey westward; the remainder to follow as soon as possible. Congress, in the meantime, upon the 3d of October, had ordered seven hundred troops for defense of the western settlers, and to prevent unauthorized intrusions; and two days later appointed Arthur St. Clair Governor of the Territory of the Northwest.

AMERICAN SETTLEMENTS.

The civil organization of the Northwest Territory was now complete, and notwithstanding the uncertainty of Indian affairs, settlers from the East began to come into the country rapidly. The New England Company sent their men during the Winter of 1787–8 pressing on over the Alleghenies by the old Indian path which had been opened into Braddock's road, and which has since been made a national turnpike from Cumberland westward. Through the weary winter days they toiled on, and by April were all gathered on the Yohiogany, where boats had been built, and at once started for the Muskingum. Here they arrived on the 7th of that month, and unless the Moravian missionaries be regarded as the pioneers of Ohio, this little band can justly claim that honor.

Gen. St. Clair, the appointed Governor of the Northwest, not having yet arrived, a set of laws were passed, written out, and published by being nailed to a tree in the embryo town, and Jonathan Meigs appointed to administer them.

Washington in writing of this, the first American settlement in the Northwest, said: "No colony in America was ever settled under such favorable auspices as that which has just commenced at Muskingum. Information, property and strength will be its characteristics. I know many of its settlers personally, and there never were men better calculated to promote the welfare of such a community."

A PIONEER DWELLING.

On the 2d of July a meeting of the directors and agents was held on the banks of the Muskingum, "for the purpose of naming the new-born city and its squares." As yet the settlement was known as the "Muskingum," but that was now changed to the name Marietta, in honor of Marie Antoinette. The square upon which the block-houses stood was called "*Campus Martius;*" square number 19, "*Capitolium;*" square number 61, "*Cecilia;*" and the great road through the covert way, "*Sacra Via.*" Two days after, an oration was delivered by James M. Varnum, who with S. H. Parsons and John Armstrong had been appointed to the judicial bench of the territory on the 16th of October, 1787. On July 9, Gov. St. Clair arrived, and the colony began to assume form. The act of 1787 provided two district grades of government for the Northwest, under the first of which the whole power was invested in the hands of a governor and three district judges. This was immediately formed upon the Governor's arrival, and the first laws of the colony passed on the 25th of July. These provided for the organization of the militia, and on the next day appeared the Governor's proclamation, erecting all that country that had been ceded by the Indians east of the Scioto River into the County of Washington. From that time forward, notwithstanding the doubts yet existing as to the Indians, all Marietta prospered, and on the 2d of September the first court of the territory was held with imposing ceremonies.

The emigration westward at this time was very great. The commander at Fort Harmer, at the mouth of the Muskingum, reported four thousand five hundred persons as having passed that post between February and June, 1788—many of whom would have purchased of the "Associates," as the New England Company was called, had they been ready to receive them.

On the 26th of November, 1787, Symmes issued a pamphlet stating the terms of his contract and the plan of sale he intended to adopt. In January, 1788, Matthias Denman, of New Jersey, took an active interest in Symmes' purchase, and located among other tracts the sections upon which Cincinnati has been built. Retaining one-third of this locality, he sold the other two-thirds to Robert Patterson and John Filson, and the three, about August, commenced to lay out a town on the spot, which was designated as being opposite Licking River, to the mouth of which they proposed to have a road cut from Lexington. The naming of the town is thus narrated in the "Western Annals":—"Mr. Filson, who had been a schoolmaster, was appointed to name the town, and, in respect to its situation, and as if with a prophetic perception of the mixed race that were to inhabit it in after days, he named it Losantiville, which, being interpreted, means: *ville*, the town; *anti*, against or opposite to; *os*, the mouth; *L.* of Licking."

Meanwhile, in July, Symmes got thirty persons and eight four-horse teams under way for the West. These reached Limestone (now Maysville) in September, where were several persons from Redstone. Here Mr. Symmes tried to found a settlement, but the great freshet of 1789 caused the "Point," as it was and is yet called, to be fifteen feet under water, and the settlement to be abandoned. The little band of settlers removed to the mouth of the Miami. Before Symmes and his colony left the "Point," two settlements had been made on his purchase. The first was by Mr. Stiltes, the original projector of the whole plan, who, with a colony of Redstone people, had located at the mouth of the Miami, whither Symmes went with his Maysville colony. Here a clearing had been made by the Indians owing to the great fertility of the soil. Mr. Stiltes with his colony came to this place on the 18th of November, 1788, with twenty-six persons, and, building a block-house, prepared to remain through the Winter. They named the settlement Columbia. Here they were kindly treated by the Indians, but suffered greatly from the flood of 1789.

On the 4th of March, 1789, the Constitution of the United States went into operation, and on April 30, George Washington was inaugurated President of the American people, and during the next Summer, an Indian war was commenced by the tribes north of the Ohio. The President at first used pacific means; but these failing, he sent General Harmer against the hostile tribes. He destroyed several villages, but

BREAKING PRAIRIE.

was defeated in two battles, near the present City of Fort Wayne, Indiana. From this time till the close of 1795, the principal events were the wars with the various Indian tribes. In 1796, General St. Clair was appointed in command, and marched against the Indians; but while he was encamped on a stream, the St. Mary, a branch of the Maumee, he was attacked and defeated with the loss of six hundred men.

General Wayne was now sent against the savages. In August, 1794, he met them near the rapids of the Maumee, and gained a complete victory. This success, followed by vigorous measures, compelled the Indians to sue for peace, and on the 30th of July, the following year, the treaty of Greenville was signed by the principal chiefs, by which a large tract of country was ceded to the United States.

Before proceeding in our narrative, we will pause to notice Fort Washington, erected in the early part of this war on the site of Cincinnati. Nearly all of the great cities of the Northwest, and indeed of the whole country, have had their *nuclei* in those rude pioneer structures, known as forts or stockades. Thus Forts Dearborn, Washington, Ponchartrain, mark the original sites of the now proud Cities of Chicago, Cincinnati and Detroit. So of most of the flourishing cities east and west of the Mississippi. Fort Washington, erected by Doughty in 1790, was a rude but highly interesting structure. It was composed of a number of strongly-built hewed log cabins. Those designed for soldiers' barracks were a story and a half high, while those composing the officers quarters were more imposing and more conveniently arranged and furnished. The whole were so placed as to form a hollow square, enclosing about an acre of ground, with a block house at each of the four angles.

The logs for the construction of this fort were cut from the ground upon which it was erected. It stood between Third and Fourth Streets of the present city (Cincinnati) extending east of Eastern Row, now Broadway, which was then a narrow alley, and the eastern boundary of of the town as it was originally laid out. On the bank of the river, immediately in front of the fort, was an appendage of the fort, called the Artificer's Yard. It contained about two acres of ground, enclosed by small contiguous buildings, occupied by workshops and quarters of laborers. Within this enclosure there was a large two-story frame house, familiarly called the "Yellow House," built for the accommodation of the Quartermaster General. For many years this was the best finished and most commodious edifice in the Queen City. Fort Washington was for some time the headquarters of both the civil and military governments of the Northwestern Territory.

Following the consummation of the treaty various gigantic land speculations were entered into by different persons, who hoped to obtain from the Indians in Michigan and northern Indiana, large tracts of lands. These were generally discovered in time to prevent the outrageous schemes from being carried out, and from involving the settlers in war. On October 27, 1795, the treaty between the United States and Spain was signed, whereby the free navigation of the Mississippi was secured.

No sooner had the treaty of 1795 been ratified than settlements began to pour rapidly into the West. The great event of the year 1796 was the occupation of that part of the Northwest including Michigan, which was this year, under the provisions of the treaty, evacuated by the British forces. The United States, owing to certain conditions, did not feel justified in addressing the authorities in Canada in relation to Detroit and other frontier posts. When at last the British authorities were called to give them up, they at once complied, and General Wayne, who had done so much to preserve the frontier settlements, and who, before the year's close, sickened and died near Erie, transferred his headquarters to the neighborhood of the lakes, where a county named after him was formed, which included the northwest of Ohio, all of Michigan, and the northeast of Indiana. During this same year settlements were formed at the present City of Chillicothe, along the Miami from Middletown to Piqua, while in the more distant West, settlers and speculators began to appear in great numbers. In September, the City of Cleveland was laid out, and during the Summer and Autumn, Samuel Jackson and Jonathan Sharpless erected the first manufactory of paper—the "Redstone Paper Mill"—in the West. St. Louis contained some seventy houses, and Detroit over three hundred, and along the river, contiguous to it, were more than three thousand inhabitants, mostly French Canadians, Indians and half-breeds, scarcely any Americans venturing yet into that part of the Northwest.

The election of representatives for the territory had taken place, and on the 4th of February, 1799, they convened at Losantiville—now known as Cincinnati, having been named so by Gov. St. Clair, and considered the capital of the Territory—to nominate persons from whom the members of the Legislature were to be chosen in accordance with a previous ordinance. This nomination being made, the Assembly adjourned until the 16th of the following September. From those named the President selected as members of the council, Henry Vandenburg, of Vincennes, Robert Oliver, of Marietta, James Findlay and Jacob Burnett, of Cincinnati, and David Vance, of Vanceville. On the 16th of September the Territorial Legislature met, and on the 24th the two houses were duly organized, Henry Vandenburg being elected President of the Council.

The message of Gov. St. Clair was addressed to the Legislature September 20th, and on October 13th that body elected as a delegate to Congress Gen. Wm. Henry Harrison, who received eleven of the votes cast, being a majority of one over his opponent, Arthur St. Clair, son of Gen. St. Clair.

The whole number of acts passed at this session, and approved by the Governor, were thirty-seven—eleven others were passed, but received his veto. The most important of those passed related to the militia, to the administration, and to taxation. On the 19th of December this protracted session of the first Legislature in the West was closed, and on the 30th of December the President nominated Charles Willing Bryd to the office of Secretary of the Territory *vice* Wm. Henry Harrison, elected to Congress. The Senate confirmed his nomination the next day.

DIVISION OF THE NORTHWEST TERRITORY.

The increased emigration to the Northwest, the extent of the domain, and the inconvenient modes of travel, made it very difficult to conduct the ordinary operations of government, and rendered the efficient action of courts almost impossible. To remedy this, it was deemed advisable to divide the territory for civil purposes. Congress, in 1800, appointed a committee to examine the question and report some means for its solution. This committee, on the 3d of March, reported that:

"In the three western countries there has been but one court having cognizance of crimes, in five years, and the immunity which offenders experience attracts, as to an asylum, the most vile and abandoned criminals, and at the same time deters useful citizens from making settlements in such society. The extreme necessity of judiciary attention and assistance is experienced in civil as well as in criminal cases. * * * * To minister a remedy to these and other evils, it occurs to this committee that it is expedient that a division of said territory into two distinct and separate governments should be made; and that such division be made by a line beginning at the mouth of the Great Miami River, running directly north until it intersects the boundary between the United States and Canada."

The report was accepted by Congress, and, in accordance with its suggestions, that body passed an Act extinguishing the Northwest Territory, which Act was approved May 7. Among its provisions were these:

"That from and after July 4 next, all that part of the Territory of the United States northwest of the Ohio River, which lies to the westward of a line beginning at a point on the Ohio, opposite to the mouth of the Kentucky River, and running thence to Fort Recovery, and thence north until it shall intersect the territorial line between the United States and Canada, shall, for the purpose of temporary government, constitute a separate territory, and be called the Indiana Territory."

After providing for the exercise of the civil and criminal powers of the territories, and other provisions, the Act further provides:

"That until it shall otherwise be ordered by the Legislatures of the said Territories, respectively, Chillicothe on the Scioto River shall be the seat of government of the Territory of the United States northwest of the Ohio River; and that St. Vincennes on the Wabash River shall be the seat of government for the Indiana Territory."

Gen. Wm. Henry Harrison was appointed Governor of the Indiana Territory, and entered upon his duties about a year later. Connecticut also about this time released her claims to the reserve, and in March a law was passed accepting this cession. Settlements had been made upon thirty-five of the townships in the reserve, mills had been built, and seven hundred miles of road cut in various directions. On the 3d of November the General Assembly met at Chillicothe. Near the close of the year, the first missionary of the Connecticut Reserve came, who found no township containing more than eleven families. It was upon the first of October that the secret treaty had been made between Napoleon and the King of Spain, whereby the latter agreed to cede to France the province of Louisiana.

In January, 1802, the Assembly of the Northwestern Territory chartered the college at Athens. From the earliest dawn of the western colonies, education was promptly provided for, and as early as 1787, newspapers were issued from Pittsburgh and Kentucky, and largely read throughout the frontier settlements. Before the close of this year, the Congress of the United States granted to the citizens of the Northwestern territory the formation of a State government. One of the provisions of the "compact of 1787" provided that whenever the number of inhabitants within prescribed limits exceeded 45,000, they should be entitled to a separate government. The prescribed limits of Ohio contained, from a census taken to ascertain the legality of the act, more than that number, and on the 30th of April, 1802, Congress passed the act defining its limits, and on the 29th of November the Constitution of the new State of Ohio, so named from the beautiful river forming its southern boundary, came into existence. The exact limits of Lake Michigan were not then known, but the territory now included within the State of Michigan was wholly within the territory of Indiana.

Gen. Harrison, while residing at Vincennes, made several treaties with the Indians, thereby gaining large tracts of lands. The next year is memorable in the history of the West for the purchase of Louisiana from France by the United States for $15,000,000. Thus by a peaceful mode, the domain of the United States was extended over a large tract of country west of the Mississippi, and was for a time under the jurisdiction of the Northwest government, and, as has been mentioned in the early part of this narrative, was called the "New Northwest." The limits of this history will not allow a description of its territory. The same year large grants of land were obtained from the Indians, and the House of Representatives of the new State of Ohio signed a bill respecting the College Township in the district of Cincinnati.

Before the close of the year, Gen. Harrison obtained additional grants of lands from the various Indian nations in Indiana and the present limits of Illinois, and on the 18th of August, 1804, completed a treaty at St. Louis, whereby over 51,000,000 acres of lands were obtained from the aborigines. Measures were also taken to learn the condition of affairs in and about Detroit.

C. Jouett, the Indian agent in Michigan, still a part of Indiana Territory, reported as follows upon the condition of matters at that post:

"The Town of Detroit.—The charter, which is for fifteen miles square, was granted in the time of Louis XIV. of France, and is now, from the best information I have been able to get, at Quebec. Of those two hundred and twenty-five acres, only four are occupied by the town and Fort Lenault. The remainder is a common, except twenty-four acres, which were added twenty years ago to a farm belonging to Wm. Macomb. * * * A stockade incloses the town, fort and citadel. The pickets, as well as the public houses, are in a state of gradual decay. The streets are narrow, straight and regular, and intersect each other at right angles. The houses are, for the most part, low and inelegant."

During this year, Congress granted a township of land for the support of a college, and began to offer inducements for settlers in these wilds, and the country now comprising the State of Michigan began to fill rapidly with settlers along its southern borders. This same year, also, a law was passed organizing the Southwest Territory, dividing it into two portions, the Territory of New Orleans, which city was made the seat of government, and the District of Louisiana, which was annexed to the domain of Gen. Harrison.

On the 11th of January, 1805, the Territory of Michigan was formed, Wm. Hull was appointed governor, with headquarters at Detroit, the change to take effect on June 30. On the 11th of that month, a fire occurred at Detroit, which destroyed almost every building in the place. When the officers of the new territory reached the post, they found it in ruins, and the inhabitants scattered throughout the country. Rebuilding, however, soon commenced, and ere long the town contained more houses than before the fire, and many of them much better built.

While this was being done, Indiana had passed to the second grade of government, and through her General Assembly had obtained large tracts of land from the Indian tribes. To all this the celebrated Indian, Tecumthe or Tecumseh, vigorously protested, and it was the main cause of his attempts to unite the various Indian tribes in a conflict with the settlers. To obtain a full account of these attempts, the workings of the British, and the signal failure, culminating in the death of Tecumseh at the battle of the Thames, and the close of the war of 1812 in the Northwest, we will step aside in our story, and relate the principal events of his life, and his connection with this conflict.

TECUMSEH, THE SHAWANOE CHIEFTAIN.

TECUMSEH, AND THE WAR OF 1812.

This famous Indian chief was born about the year 1768, not far from the site of the present City of Piqua, Ohio. His father, Puckeshinwa, was a member of the Kisopok tribe of the Swanoese nation, and his mother, Methontaske, was a member of the Turtle tribe of the same people. They removed from Florida about the middle of the last century to the birthplace of Tecumseh. In 1774, his father, who had risen to be chief, was slain at the battle of Point Pleasant, and not long after Tecumseh, by his bravery, became the leader of his tribe. In 1795 he was declared chief, and then lived at Deer Creek, near the site of the present City of Urbana. He remained here about one year, when he returned to Piqua, and in 1798, he went to White River, Indiana. In 1805, he and his brother, Laulewasikan (Open Door), who had announced himself as a prophet, went to a tract of land on the Wabash River, given them by the Pottawatomies and Kickapoos. From this date the chief comes into prominence. He was now about thirty-seven years of age, was five feet and ten inches in height, was stoutly built, and possessed of enormous powers of endurance. His countenance was naturally pleasing, and he was, in general, devoid of those savage attributes possessed by most Indians. It is stated he could read and write, and had a confidential secretary and adviser, named Billy Caldwell, a half-breed, who afterward became chief of the Pottawatomies. He occupied the first house built on the site of Chicago. At this time, Tecumseh entered upon the great work of his life. He had long objected to the grants of land made by the Indians to the whites, and determined to unite all the Indian tribes into a league, in order that no treaties or grants of land could be made save by the consent of this confederation.

He traveled constantly, going from north to south; from the south to the north, everywhere urging the Indians to this step. He was a matchless orator, and his burning words had their effect.

Gen. Harrison, then Governor of Indiana, by watching the movements of the Indians, became convinced that a grand conspiracy was forming, and made preparations to defend the settlements. Tecumseh's plan was similar to Pontiac's, elsewhere described, and to the cunning artifice of that chieftain was added his own sagacity.

During the year 1809, Tecumseh and the prophet were actively preparing for the work. In that year, Gen. Harrison entered into a treaty with the Delawares, Kickapoos, Pottawatomies, Miamis, Eel River Indians and Weas, in which these tribes ceded to the whites certain lands upon the Wabash, to all of which Tecumseh entered a bitter protest, averring as one principal reason that he did not want the Indians to give up any lands north and west of the Ohio River.

Tecumseh, in August, 1810, visited the General at Vincennes and held a council relating to the grievances of the Indians. Becoming unduly angry at this conference he was dismissed from the village, and soon after departed to incite the southern Indian tribes to the conflict.

Gen. Harrison determined to move upon the chief's headquarters at Tippecanoe, and for this purpose went about sixty-five miles up the Wabash, where he built Fort Harrison. From this place he went to the prophet's town, where he informed the Indians he had no hostile intentions, provided they were true to the existing treaties. He encamped near the village early in October, and on the morning of November 7, he was attacked by a large force of the Indians, and the famous battle of Tippecanoe occurred. The Indians were routed and their town broken up. Tecumseh returning not long after, was greatly exasperated at his brother, the prophet, even threatening to kill him for rashly precipitating the war, and foiling his (Tecumseh's) plans.

Tecumseh sent word to Gen. Harrison that he was now returned from the South, and was ready to visit the President as had at one time previously been proposed. Gen. Harrison informed him he could not go as a chief, which method Tecumseh desired, and the visit was never made.

In June of the following year, he visited the Indian agent at Fort Wayne. Here he disavowed any intention to make a war against the United States, and reproached Gen. Harrison for marching against his people. The agent replied to this; Tecumseh listened with a cold indifference, and after making a few general remarks, with a haughty air drew his blanket about him, left the council house, and departed for Fort Malden, in Upper Canada, where he joined the British standard.

He remained under this Government, doing effective work for the Crown while engaged in the war of 1812 which now opened. He was, however, always humane in his treatment of the prisoners, never allowing his warriors to ruthlessly mutilate the bodies of those slain, or wantonly murder the captive.

In the Summer of 1813, Perry's victory on Lake Erie occurred, and shortly after active preparations were made to capture Malden. On the 27th of September, the American army, under Gen. Harrison, set sail for the shores of Canada, and in a few hours stood around the ruins of Malden, from which the British army, under Proctor, had retreated to Sandwich, intending to make its way to the heart of Canada by the Valley of the Thames. On the 29th Gen. Harrison was at Sandwich, and Gen. McArthur took possession of Detroit and the territory of Michigan.

On the 2d of October, the Americans began their pursuit of Proctor, whom they overtook on the 5th, and the battle of the Thames followed. Early in the engagement, Tecumseh who was at the head of the column of Indians was slain, and they, no longer hearing the voice of their chieftain, fled. The victory was decisive, and practically closed the war in the Northwest.

INDIANS ATTACKING A STOCKADE.

Just who killed the great chief has been a matter of much dispute; but the weight of opinion awards the act to Col. Richard M. Johnson, who fired at him with a pistol, the shot proving fatal.

In 1805 occurred Burr's Insurrection. He took possession of a beautiful island in the Ohio, after the killing of Hamilton, and is charged by many with attempting to set up an independent government. His plans were frustrated by the general government, his property confiscated and he was compelled to flee the country for safety.

In January, 1807, Governor Hull, of Michigan Territory, made a treaty with the Indians, whereby all that peninsula was ceded to the United States. Before the close of the year, a stockade was built about Detroit. It was also during this year that Indiana and Illinois endeavored to obtain the repeal of that section of the compact of 1787, whereby slavery was excluded from the Northwest Territory. These attempts, however, all signally failed.

In 1809 it was deemed advisable to divide the Indiana Territory. This was done, and the Territory of Illinois was formed from the western part, the seat of government being fixed at Kaskaskia. The next year, the intentions of Tecumseh manifested themselves in open hostilities, and then began the events already narrated.

While this war was in progress, emigration to the West went on with surprising rapidity. In 1811, under Mr. Roosevelt of New York, the first steamboat trip was made on the Ohio, much to the astonishment of the natives, many of whom fled in terror at the appearance of the "monster." It arrived at Louisville on the 10th day of October. At the close of the first week of January, 1812, it arrived at Natchez, after being nearly overwhelmed in the great earthquake which occurred while on its downward trip.

The battle of the Thames was fought on October 6, 1813. It effectually closed hostilities in the Northwest, although peace was not fully restored until July 22, 1814, when a treaty was formed at Greenville, under the direction of General Harrison, between the United States and the Indian tribes, in which it was stipulated that the Indians should cease hostilities against the Americans if the war were continued. Such, happily, was not the case, and on the 24th of December the treaty of Ghent was signed by the representatives of England and the United States. This treaty was followed the next year by treaties with various Indian tribes throughout the West and Northwest, and quiet was again restored in this part of the new world.

On the 18th of March, 1816, Pittsburgh was incorporated as a city. It then had a population of 8,000 people, and was already noted for its manufacturing interests. On April 19, Indiana Territory was allowed to form a state government. At that time there were thirteen counties organized, containing about sixty-three thousand inhabitants. The first election of state officers was held in August, when Jonathan Jennings was chosen Governor. The officers were sworn in on November 7, and on December 11, the State was formally admitted into the Union. For some time the seat of government was at Corydon, but a more central location being desirable, the present capital, Indianapolis (City of Indiana), was laid out January 1, 1825.

On the 28th of December the Bank of Illinois, at Shawneetown, was chartered, with a capital of $300,000. At this period all banks were under the control of the States, and were allowed to establish branches at different convenient points.

Until this time Chillicothe and Cincinnati had in turn enjoyed the privileges of being the capital of Ohio. But the rapid settlement of the northern and eastern portions of the State demanded, as in Indiana, a more central location, and before the close of the year, the site of Columbus was selected and surveyed as the future capital of the State. Banking had begun in Ohio as early as 1808, when the first bank was chartered at Marietta, but here as elsewhere it did not bring to the state the hoped-for assistance. It and other banks were subsequently unable to redeem their currency, and were obliged to suspend.

In 1818, Illinois was made a state, and all the territory north of her northern limits was erected into a separate territory and joined to Michigan for judicial purposes. By the following year, navigation of the lakes was increasing with great rapidity and affording an immense source of revenue to the dwellers in the Northwest, but it was not until 1826 that the trade was extended to Lake Michigan, or that steamships began to navigate the bosom of that inland sea.

Until the year 1832, the commencement of the Black Hawk War, but few hostilities were experienced with the Indians. Roads were opened, canals were dug, cities were built, common schools were established, universities were founded, many of which, especially the Michigan University, have achieved a world wide-reputation. The people were becoming wealthy. The domains of the United States had been extended, and had the sons of the forest been treated with honesty and justice, the record of many years would have been that of peace and continuous prosperity.

BLACK HAWK AND THE BLACK HAWK WAR.

This conflict, though confined to Illinois, is an important epoch in the Northwestern history, being the last war with the Indians in this part of the United States.

Ma-ka-tai-me-she-kia-kiah, or Black Hawk, was born in the principal Sac village, about three miles from the junction of Rock River with the Mississippi, in the year 1767. His father's name was Py-e-sa or Pahaes; his grandfather's, Na-na-ma-kee, or the Thunderer. Black Hawk early distinguished himself as a warrior, and at the age of fifteen was permitted to paint and was ranked among the braves. About the year 1783, he went on an expedition against the enemies of his nation, the Osages, one

BLACK HAWK, THE SAC CHIEFTAIN.

of whom he killed and scalped, and for this deed of Indian bravery he was permitted to join in the scalp dance. Three or four years after he, at the head of two hundred braves, went on another expedition against the Osages, to avenge the murder of some women and children belonging to his own tribe. Meeting an equal number of Osage warriors, a fierce battle ensued, in which the latter tribe lost one-half their number. The Sacs lost only about nineteen warriors. He next attacked the Cherokees for a similar cause. In a severe battle with them, near the present City of St. Louis, his father was slain, and Black Hawk, taking possession of the "Medicine Bag," at once announced himself chief of the Sac nation. He had now conquered the Cherokees, and about the year 1800, at the head of five hundred Sacs and Foxes, and a hundred Iowas, he waged war against the Osage nation and subdued it. For two years he battled successfully with other Indian tribes, all of whom he conquered.

Black Hawk does not at any time seem to have been friendly to the Americans. When on a visit to St. Louis to see his "Spanish Father," he declined to see any of the Americans, alleging, as a reason, he did not want *two* fathers.

The treaty at St. Louis was consummated in 1804. The next year the United States Government erected a fort near the head of the Des Moines Rapids, called Fort Edwards. This seemed to enrage Black Hawk, who at once determined to capture Fort Madison, standing on the west side of the Mississippi above the mouth of the Des Moines River. The fort was garrisoned by about fifty men. Here he was defeated. The difficulties with the British Government arose about this time, and the War of 1812 followed. That government, extending aid to the Western Indians, by giving them arms and ammunition, induced them to remain hostile to the Americans. In August, 1812, Black Hawk, at the head of about five hundred braves, started to join the British forces at Detroit, passing on his way the site of Chicago, where the famous Fort Dearborn Massacre had a few days before occurred. Of his connection with the British Government but little is known. In 1813 he with his little band descended the Mississippi, and attacking some United States troops at Fort Howard was defeated.

In the early part of 1815, the Indian tribes west of the Mississippi were notified that peace had been declared between the United States and England, and nearly all hostilities had ceased. Black Hawk did not sign any treaty, however, until May of the following year. He then recognized the validity of the treaty at St. Louis in 1804. From the time of signing this treaty in 1816, until the breaking out of the war in 1832, he and his band passed their time in the common pursuits of Indian life.

Ten years before the commencement of this war, the Sac and Fox

Indians were urged to join the Iowas on the west bank of the Father of Waters. All were agreed, save the band known as the British Band, of which Black Hawk was leader. He strenuously objected to the removal, and was induced to comply only after being threatened with the power of the Government. This and various actions on the part of the white settlers provoked Black Hawk and his band to attempt the capture of his native village now occupied by the whites. The war followed. He and his actions were undoubtedly misunderstood, and had his wishes been acquiesced in at the beginning of the struggle, much bloodshed would have been prevented.

Black Hawk was chief now of the Sac and Fox nations, and a noted warrior. He and his tribe inhabited a village on Rock River, nearly three miles above its confluence with the Mississippi, where the tribe had lived many generations. When that portion of Illinois was reserved to them, they remained in peaceable possession of their reservation, spending their time in the enjoyment of Indian life. The fine situation of their village and the quality of their lands incited the more lawless white settlers, who from time to time began to encroach upon the red men's domain. From one pretext to another, and from one step to another, the crafty white men gained a foothold, until through whisky and artifice they obtained deeds from many of the Indians for their possessions. The Indians were finally induced to cross over the Father of Waters and locate among the Iowas. Black Hawk was strenuously opposed to all this, but as the authorities of Illinois and the United States thought this the best move, he was forced to comply. Moreover other tribes joined the whites and urged the removal. Black Hawk would not agree to the terms of the treaty made with his nation for their lands, and as soon as the military, called to enforce his removal, had retired, he returned to the Illinois side of the river. A large force was at once raised and marched against him. On the evening of May 14, 1832, the first engagement occurred between a band from this army and Black Hawk's band, in which the former were defeated.

This attack and its result aroused the whites. A large force of men was raised, and Gen. Scott hastened from the seaboard, by way of the lakes, with United States troops and artillery to aid in the subjugation of the Indians. On the 24th of June, Black Hawk, with 200 warriors, was repulsed by Major Demont between Rock River and Galena. The American army continued to move up Rock River toward the main body of the Indians, and on the 21st of July came upon Black Hawk and his band, and defeated them near the Blue Mounds.

Before this action, Gen. Henry, in command, sent word to the main army by whom he was immediately rejoined, and the whole crossed the

Wisconsin in pursuit of Black Hawk and his band who were fleeing to the Mississippi. They were overtaken on the 2d of August, and in the battle which followed the power of the Indian chief was completely broken. He fled, but was seized by the Winnebagoes and delivered to the whites.

On the 21st of September, 1832, Gen. Scott and Gov. Reynolds concluded a treaty with the Winnebagoes, Sacs and Foxes by which they ceded to the United States a vast tract of country, and agreed to remain peaceable with the whites. For the faithful performance of the provisions of this treaty on the part of the Indians, it was stipulated that Black Hawk, his two sons, the prophet Wabokieshiek, and six other chiefs of the hostile bands should be retained as hostages during the pleasure of the President. They were confined at Fort Barracks and put in irons.

The next Spring, by order of the Secretary of War, they were taken to Washington. From there they were removed to Fortress Monroe, "there to remain until the conduct of their nation was such as to justify their being set at liberty." They were retained here until the 4th of June, when the authorities directed them to be taken to the principal cities so that they might see the folly of contending against the white people. Everywhere they were observed by thousands, the name of the old chief being extensively known. By the middle of August they reached Fort Armstrong on Rock Island, where Black Hawk was soon after released to go to his countrymen. As he passed the site of his birthplace, now the home of the white man, he was deeply moved. His village where he was born, where he had so happily lived, and where he had hoped to die, was now another's dwelling place, and he was a wanderer.

On the next day after his release, he went at once to his tribe and his lodge. His wife was yet living, and with her he passed the remainder of his days. To his credit it may be said that Black Hawk always remained true to his wife, and served her with a devotion uncommon among the Indians, living with her upward of forty years.

Black Hawk now passed his time hunting and fishing. A deep melancholy had settled over him from which he could not be freed. At all times when he visited the whites he was received with marked attention. He was an honored guest at the old settlers' reunion in Lee County, Illinois, at some of their meetings, and received many tokens of esteem. In September, 1838, while on his way to Rock Island to receive his annuity from the Government, he contracted a severe cold which resulted in a fatal attack of bilious fever which terminated his life on October 3. His faithful wife, who was devotedly attached to him, mourned deeply during his sickness. After his death he was dressed in the uniform presented to him by the President while in Washington. He was buried in a grave six feet in depth, situated upon a beautiful eminence. "The body was placed in the middle of the grave, in a sitting posture, upon a seat constructed for the purpose. On his left side, the cane, given him by Henry Clay, was placed upright, with his right hand resting upon it. Many of the old warrior's trophies were placed in the grave, and some Indian garments, together with his favorite weapons."

No sooner was the Black Hawk war concluded than settlers began rapidly to pour into the northern parts of Illinois, and into Wisconsin, now free from Indian depredations. Chicago, from a trading post, had grown to a commercial center, and was rapidly coming into prominence. In 1835, the formation of a State Government in Michigan was discussed, but did not take active form until two years later, when the State became a part of the Federal Union.

The main attraction to that portion of the Northwest lying west of Lake Michigan, now included in the State of Wisconsin, was its alluvial wealth. Copper ore was found about Lake Superior. For some time this region was attached to Michigan for judiciary purposes, but in 1836 was made a territory, then including Minnesota and Iowa. The latter State was detached two years later. In 1848, Wisconsin was admitted as a State, Madison being made the capital. We have now traced the various divisions of the Northwest Territory (save a little in Minnesota) from the time it was a unit comprising this vast territory, until circumstances compelled its present division.

OTHER INDIAN TROUBLES.

Before leaving this part of the narrative, we will narrate briefly the Indian troubles in Minnesota and elsewhere by the Sioux Indians.

In August, 1862, the Sioux Indians living on the western borders of Minnesota fell upon the unsuspecting settlers, and in a few hours massacred ten or twelve hundred persons. A distressful panic was the immediate result, fully thirty thousand persons fleeing from their homes to districts supposed to be better protected. The military authorities at once took active measures to punish the savages, and a large number were killed and captured. About a year after, Little Crow, the chief, was killed by a Mr. Lampson near Scattered Lake. Of those captured, thirty were hung at Mankato, and the remainder, through fears of mob violence, were removed to Camp McClellan, on the outskirts of the City of Davenport. It was here that Big Eagle came into prominence and secured his release by the following order:

BIG EAGLE.

"Special Order, No. 430. "WAR DEPARTMENT,

"ADJUTANT GENERAL'S OFFICE, WASHINGTON, Dec. 3, 1864.

"Big Eagle, an Indian now in confinement at Davenport, Iowa, will, upon the receipt of this order, be immediately released from confinement and set at liberty.

"By order of the President of the United States.

"Official: "E. D. TOWNSEND, *Ass't Adj't Gen.*

"CAPT. JAMES VANDERVENTER, *Com'y Sub. Vols.*

"Through Com'g Gen'l, Washington, D. C."

Another Indian who figures more prominently than Big Eagle, and who was more cowardly in his nature, with his band of Modoc Indians, is noted in the annals of the New Northwest: we refer to Captain Jack. This distinguished Indian, noted for his cowardly murder of Gen. Canby, was a chief of a Modoc tribe of Indians inhabiting the border lands between California and Oregon. This region of country comprises what is known as the "Lava Beds," a tract of land described as utterly impenetrable, save by those savages who had made it their home.

The Modocs are known as an exceedingly fierce and treacherous race. They had, according to their own traditions, resided here for many generations, and at one time were exceedingly numerous and powerful. A famine carried off nearly half their numbers, and disease, indolence and the vices of the white man have reduced them to a poor, weak and insignificant tribe.

Soon after the settlement of California and Oregon, complaints began to be heard of massacres of emigrant trains passing through the Modoc country. In 1847, an emigrant train, comprising eighteen souls, was entirely destroyed at a place since known as "Bloody Point." These occurrences caused the United States Government to appoint a peace commission, who, after repeated attempts, in 1864, made a treaty with the Modocs, Snakes and Klamaths, in which it was agreed on their part to remove to a reservation set apart for them in the southern part of Oregon.

With the exception of Captain Jack and a band of his followers, who remained at Clear Lake, about six miles from Klamath, all the Indians complied. The Modocs who went to the reservation were under chief Schonchin. Captain Jack remained at the lake without disturbance until 1869, when he was also induced to remove to the reservation. The Modocs and the Klamaths soon became involved in a quarrel, and Captain Jack and his band returned to the Lava Beds.

Several attempts were made by the Indian Commissioners to induce them to return to the reservation, and finally becoming involved in a difficulty with the commissioner and his military escort, a fight ensued, in which the chief and his band were routed. They were greatly enraged, and on their retreat, before the day closed, killed eleven inoffensive whites.

The nation was aroused and immediate action demanded. A commission was at once appointed by the Government to see what could be done. It comprised the following persons: Gen. E. R. S. Canby, Rev. Dr. E. Thomas, a leading Methodist divine of California; Mr. A. B. Meacham, Judge Rosborough, of California, and a Mr. Dyer, of Oregon. After several interviews, in which the savages were always aggressive, often appearing with scalps in their belts, Bogus Charley came to the commission on the evening of April 10, 1873, and informed them that Capt. Jack and his band would have a "talk" to-morrow at a place near Clear Lake, about three miles distant. Here the Commissioners, accompanied by Charley, Riddle, the interpreter, and Boston Charley repaired. After the usual greeting the council proceedings commenced. On behalf of the Indians there were present: Capt. Jack, Black Jim, Schnac Nasty Jim, Ellen's Man, and Hooker Jim. They had no guns, but carried pistols. After short speeches by Mr. Meacham, Gen. Canby and Dr. Thomas, Chief Schonchin arose to speak. He had scarcely proceeded when, as if by a preconcerted arrangement, Capt. Jack drew his pistol and shot Gen. Canby dead. In less than a minute a dozen shots were fired by the savages, and the massacre completed. Mr. Meacham was shot by Schonchin, and Dr. Thomas by Boston Charley. Mr. Dyer barely escaped, being fired at twice. Riddle, the interpreter, and his squaw escaped. The troops rushed to the spot where they found Gen. Canby and Dr. Thomas dead, and Mr. Meacham badly wounded. The savages had escaped to their impenetrable fastnesses and could not be pursued.

The whole country was aroused by this brutal massacre; but it was not until the following May that the murderers were brought to justice. At that time Boston Charley gave himself up, and offered to guide the troops to Capt. Jack's stronghold. This led to the capture of his entire gang, a number of whom were murdered by Oregon volunteers while on their way to trial. The remaining Indians were held as prisoners until July when their trial occurred, which led to the conviction of Capt. Jack, Schonchin, Boston Charley, Hooker Jim, Broncho, *alias* One-Eyed Jim, and Slotuck, who were sentenced to be hanged. These sentences were approved by the President, save in the case of Slotuck and Broncho whose sentences were commuted to imprisonment for life. The others were executed at Fort Klamath, October 3, 1873.

These closed the Indian troubles for a time in the Northwest, and for several years the borders of civilization remained in peace. They were again involved in a conflict with the savages about the country of the

CAPTAIN JACK, THE MODOC CHIEFTAIN.

Black Hills, in which war the gallant Gen. Custer lost his life. Just now the borders of Oregon and California are again in fear of hostilities; but as the Government has learned how to deal with the Indians, they will be of short duration. The red man is fast passing away before the march of the white man, and a few more generations will read of the Indians as one of the nations of the past.

The Northwest abounds in memorable places. We have generally noticed them in the narrative, but our space forbids their description in detail, save of the most important places. Detroit, Cincinnati, Vincennes, Kaskaskia and their kindred towns have all been described. But ere we leave the narrative we will present our readers with an account of the Kinzie house, the old landmark of Chicago, and the discovery of the source of the Mississippi River, each of which may well find a place in the annals of the Northwest.

Mr. John Kinzie, of the Kinzie house, represented in the illustration, established a trading house at Fort Dearborn in 1804. The stockade had been erected the year previous, and named Fort Dearborn in honor of the Secretary of War. It had a block house at each of the two angles, on the southern side a sallyport, a covered way on the north side, that led down to the river, for the double purpose of providing means of escape, and of procuring water in the event of a siege.

Fort Dearborn stood on the south bank of the Chicago River, about half a mile from its mouth. When Major Whistler built it, his soldiers hauled all the timber, for he had no oxen, and so economically did he work that the fort cost the Government only fifty dollars. For a while the garrison could get no grain, and Whistler and his men subsisted on acorns. Now Chicago is the greatest grain center in the world.

Mr. Kinzie bought the hut of the first settler, Jean Baptiste Point au Sable, on the site of which he erected his mansion. Within an inclosure in front he planted some Lombardy poplars, seen in the engraving, and in the rear he soon had a fine garden and growing orchard.

In 1812 the Kinzie house and its surroundings became the theater of stirring events. The garrison of Fort Dearborn consisted of fifty-four men, under the charge of Capt. Nathan Heald, assisted by Lieutenant Lenai T. Helm (son-in-law to Mrs. Kinzie), and Ensign Ronan. The surgeon was Dr. Voorhees. The only residents at the post at that time were the wives of Capt. Heald and Lieutenant Helm and a few of the soldiers, Mr. Kinzie and his family, and a few Canadian voyagers with their wives and children. The soldiers and Mr. Kinzie were on the most friendly terms with the Pottawatomies and the Winnebagoes, the principal tribes around them, but they could not win them from their attachment to the British.

After the battle of Tippecanoe it was observed that some of the leading chiefs became sullen, for some of their people had perished in that conflict with American troops.

One evening in April, 1812, Mr. Kinzie sat playing his violin and his children were dancing to the music, when Mrs. Kinzie came rushing into the house pale with terror, and exclaiming, "The Indians! the Indians!" "What? Where?" eagerly inquired Mr. Kinzie. "Up at Lee's, killing and scalping," answered the frightened mother, who, when the alarm was given, was attending Mrs. Burns, a newly-made mother, living not far off.

KINZIE HOUSE.

Mr. Kinzie and his family crossed the river in boats, and took refuge in the fort, to which place Mrs. Burns and her infant, not a day old, were conveyed in safety to the shelter of the guns of Fort Dearborn, and the rest of the white inhabitants fled. The Indians were a scalping party of Winnebagoes, who hovered around the fort some days, when they disappeared, and for several weeks the inhabitants were not disturbed by alarms.

Chicago was then so deep in the wilderness, that the news of the declaration of war against Great Britain, made on the 19th of June, 1812, did not reach the commander of the garrison at Fort Dearborn till the 7th of August. Now the fast mail train will carry a man from New York to Chicago in twenty-seven hours, and such a declaration might be sent, every word, by the telegraph in less than the same number of minutes.

VILLAGE RESIDENCE.

PRESENT CONDITION OF THE NORTHWEST.

Preceding chapters have brought us to the close of the Black Hawk war, and we now turn to the contemplation of the growth and prosperity of the Northwest under the smile of peace and the blessings of our civilization. The pioneers of this region date events back to the deep snow

A REPRESENTATIVE PIONEER.

of 1831, no one arriving here since that date taking first honors. The inciting cause of the immigration which overflowed the prairies early in the '30s was the reports of the marvelous beauty and fertility of the region distributed through the East by those who had participated in the Black Hawk campaign with Gen. Scott. Chicago and Milwaukee then had a few hundred inhabitants, and Gurdon S. Hubbard's trail from the former city to Kaskaskia led almost through a wilderness. Vegetables and clothing were largely distributed through the regions adjoining the lakes by steamers from the Ohio towns. There are men now living in Illinois who came to the state when barely an acre was in cultivation, and a man now prominent in the business circles of Chicago looked over the swampy, cheerless site of that metropolis in 1818 and went southward into civilization. Emigrants from Pennsylvania in 1830 left behind

LINCOLN MONUMENT, SPRINGFIELD, ILLINOIS.

them but one small railway in the coal regions, thirty miles in length, and made their way to the Northwest mostly with ox teams, finding in Northern Illinois petty settlements scores of miles apart, although the southern portion of the state was fairly dotted with farms. The water courses of the lakes and rivers furnished transportation to the second great army of immigrants, and about 1850 railroads were pushed to that extent that the crisis of 1837 was precipitated upon us, from the effects of which the Western country had not fully recovered at the outbreak of the war. Hostilities found the colonists of the prairies fully alive to the demands of the occasion, and the honor of recruiting

A PIONEER SCHOOL HOUSE.

the vast armies of the Union fell largely to Gov. Yates, of Illinois, and Gov. Morton, of Indiana. To recount the share of the glories of the campaign won by our Western troops is a needless task, except to mention the fact that Illinois gave to the nation the President who saved it, and sent out at the head of one of its regiments the general who led its armies to the final victory at Appomattox. The struggle, on the

FARM VIEW IN WINTER.

whole, had a marked effect for the better on the new Northwest, giving it an impetus which twenty years of peace would not have produced. In a large degree this prosperity was an inflated one, and with the rest of the Union we have since been compelled to atone therefor by four

SPRING SCENE.

PIONEERS' FIRST WINTER.

years of depression of values, of scarcity of employment, and loss of fortune. To a less degree, however, than the manufacturing or mining regions has the West suffered during the prolonged panic now so near its end. Agriculture, still the leading feature in our industries, has been quite prosperous through all these dark years, and the farmers have cleared away many incumbrances resting over them from the period of fictitious values. The population has steadily increased, the arts and sciences are gaining a stronger foothold, the trade area of the region is becoming daily more extended, and we have been largely exempt from the financial calamities which have nearly wrecked communities on the seaboard dependent wholly on foreign commerce or domestic manufacture.

At the present period there are no great schemes broached for the Northwest, no propositions for government subsidies or national works of improvement, but the capital of the world is attracted hither for the purchase of our products or the expansion of our capacity for serving the nation at large. A new era is dawning as to transportation, and we bid fair to deal almost exclusively with the increasing and expanding lines of steel rail running through every few miles of territory on the prairies. The lake marine will no doubt continue to be useful in the warmer season, and to serve as a regulator of freight rates; but experienced navigators forecast the decay of the system in moving to the seaboard the enormous crops of the West. Within the past five years it has become quite common to see direct shipments to Europe and the West Indies going through from the second-class towns along the Mississippi and Missouri.

As to popular education, the standard has of late risen very greatly, and our schools would be creditable to any section of the Union.

More and more as the events of the war pass into obscurity will the fate of the Northwest be linked with that of the Southwest, and the next Congressional apportionment will give the valley of the Mississippi absolute control of the legislation of the nation, and do much toward securing the removal of the Federal capitol to some more central location.

Our public men continue to wield the full share of influence pertaining to their rank in the national autonomy, and seem not to forget that for the past sixteen years they and their constituents have dictated the principles which should govern the country.

In a work like this, destined to lie on the shelves of the library for generations, and not doomed to daily destruction like a newspaper, one can not indulge in the same glowing predictions, the sanguine statements of actualities that fill the columns of ephemeral publications. Time may bring grief to the pet projects of a writer, and explode castles erected on a pedestal of facts. Yet there are unmistakable indications before us of

the same radical change in our great Northwest which characterizes its history for the past thirty years. Our domain has a sort of natural geographical border, save where it melts away to the southward in the cattle raising districts of the southwest.

Our prime interest will for some years doubtless be the growth of the food of the world, in which branch it has already outstripped all competitors, and our great rival in this duty will naturally be the fertile plains of Kansas, Nebraska and Colorado, to say nothing of the new empire so rapidly growing up in Texas. Over these regions there is a continued progress in agriculture and in railway building, and we must look to our laurels. Intelligent observers of events are fully aware of the strides made in the way of shipments of fresh meats to Europe, many of these ocean cargoes being actually slaughtered in the West and transported on ice to the wharves of the seaboard cities. That this new enterprise will continue there is no reason to doubt. There are in Chicago several factories for the canning of prepared meats for European consumption, and the orders for this class of goods are already immense. English capital is becoming daily more and more dissatisfied with railway loans and investments, and is gradually seeking mammoth outlays in lands and live stock. The stock yards in Chicago, Indianapolis and East St. Louis are yearly increasing their facilities, and their plant steadily grows more valuable. Importations of blooded animals from the progressive countries of Europe are destined to greatly improve the quality of our beef and mutton. Nowhere is there to be seen a more enticing display in this line than at our state and county fairs, and the interest in the matter is on the increase.

To attempt to give statistics of our grain production for 1877 would be useless, so far have we surpassed ourselves in the quantity and quality of our product. We are too liable to forget that we are giving the world its first article of necessity — its food supply. An opportunity to learn this fact so it never can be forgotten was afforded at Chicago at the outbreak of the great panic of 1873, when Canadian purchasers, fearing the prostration of business might bring about an anarchical condition of affairs, went to that city with coin in bulk and foreign drafts to secure their supplies in their own currency at first hands. It may be justly claimed by the agricultural community that their combined efforts gave the nation its first impetus toward a restoration of its crippled industries, and their labor brought the gold premium to a lower depth than the government was able to reach by its most intense efforts of legislation and compulsion. The hundreds of millions about to be disbursed for farm products have already, by the anticipation common to all commercial nations, set the wheels in motion, and will relieve us from the perils so long shadowing our efforts to return to a healthy tone.

Manufacturing has attained in the chief cities a foothold which bids fair to render the Northwest independent of the outside world. Nearly

GREAT IRON BRIDGE OF C. R. I. & P. R.R., CROSSING MISSISSIPPI RIVER AT DAVENPORT.

our whole region has a distribution of coal measures which will in time support the manufactures necessary to our comfort and prosperity. As to transportation, the chief factor in the production of all articles except food, no section is so magnificently endowed, and our facilities are yearly increasing beyond those of any other region.

The period from a central point of the war to the outbreak of the panic was marked by a tremendous growth in our railway lines, but the depression of the times caused almost a total suspension of operations. Now that prosperity is returning to our stricken country we witness its anticipation by the railroad interest in a series of projects, extensions, and leases which bid fair to largely increase our transportation facilities. The process of foreclosure and sale of incumbered lines is another matter to be considered. In the case of the Illinois Central road, which formerly transferred to other lines at Cairo the vast burden of freight destined for the Gulf region, we now see the incorporation of the tracks connecting through to New Orleans, every mile co-operating in turning toward the northwestern metropolis the weight of the inter-state commerce of a thousand miles or more of fertile plantations. Three competing routes to Texas have established in Chicago their general freight and passenger agencies. Four or five lines compete for all Pacific freights to a point as as far as the interior of Nebraska. Half a dozen or more splendid bridge structures have been thrown across the Missouri and Mississippi Rivers by the railways. The Chicago and Northwestern line has become an aggregation of over two thousand miles of rail, and the Chicago, Milwaukee and St. Paul is its close rival in extent and importance. The three lines running to Cairo *via* Vincennes form a through route for all traffic with the states to the southward. The chief projects now under discussion are the Chicago and Atlantic, which is to unite with lines now built to Charleston, and the Chicago and Canada Southern, which line will connect with all the various branches of that Canadian enterprise. Our latest new road is the Chicago and Lake Huron, formed of three lines, and entering the city from Valparaiso on the Pittsburgh, Fort Wayne and Chicago track. The trunk lines being mainly in operation, the progress made in the way of shortening tracks, making air-line branches, and running extensions does not show to the advantage it deserves, as this process is constantly adding new facilities to the established order of things. The panic reduced the price of steel to a point where the railways could hardly afford to use iron rails, and all our northwestern lines report large relays of Bessemer track. The immense crops now being moved have given a great rise to the value of railway stocks, and their transportation must result in heavy pecuniary advantages.

Few are aware of the importance of the wholesale and jobbing trade of Chicago. One leading firm has since the panic sold $24,000,000 of dry goods in one year, and they now expect most confidently to add seventy per cent. to the figures of their last year's business. In boots and shoes and in clothing, twenty or more great firms from the east have placed here their distributing agents or their factories; and in groceries

Chicago supplies the entire Northwest at rates presenting advantages over New York.

Chicago has stepped in between New York and the rural banks as a financial center, and scarcely a banking institution in the grain or cattle regions but keeps its reserve funds in the vaults of our commercial institutions. Accumulating here throughout the spring and summer months, they are summoned home at pleasure to move the products of the prairies. This process greatly strengthens the northwest in its financial operations, leaving home capital to supplement local operations on behalf of home interests.

It is impossible to forecast the destiny of this grand and growing section of the Union. Figures and predictions made at this date might seem ten years hence so ludicrously small as to excite only derision.

ILLINOIS.

Length, 380 miles, mean width about 156 miles. Area, 55,410 square miles, or 35,462,400 acres. Illinois, as regards its surface, constitutes a table-land at a varying elevation ranging between 350 and 800 feet above the sea level; composed of extensive and highly fertile prairies and plains. Much of the south division of the State, especially the river-bottoms, are thickly wooded. The prairies, too, have oasis-like clumps of trees scattered here and there at intervals. The chief rivers irrigating the State are the Mississippi—dividing it from Iowa and Missouri—the Ohio (forming its south barrier), the Illinois, Wabash, Kaskaskia, and Sangamon, with their numerous affluents. The total extent of navigable streams is calculated at 4,000 miles. Small lakes are scattered over various parts of the State. Illinois is extremely prolific in minerals, chiefly coal, iron, copper, and zinc ores, sulphur and limestone. The coal-field alone is estimated to absorb a full third of the entire coal-deposit of North America. Climate tolerably equable and healthy; the mean temperature standing at about 51° Fahrenheit As an agricultural region, Illinois takes a competitive rank with neighboring States, the cereals, fruits, and root-crops yielding plentiful returns; in fact, as a grain-growing State, Illinois may be deemed, in proportion to her size, to possess a greater area of lands suitable for its production than any other State in the Union. Stock-raising is also largely carried on, while her manufacturing interests in regard of woolen fabrics, etc., are on a very extensive and yearly expanding scale. The lines of railroad in the State are among the most extensive of the Union. Inland water-carriage is facilitated by a canal connecting the Illinois River with Lake Michigan, and thence with the St. Lawrence and Atlantic. Illinois is divided into 102 counties; the chief towns being Chicago, Springfield (capital), Alton, Quincy, Peoria, Galena, Bloomington, Rock Island, Vandalia, etc. By the new Constitution, established in 1870, the State Legislature consists of 51 Senators, elected for four years, and 153 Representatives, for two years; which numbers were to be decennially increased thereafter to the number of six per every additional half-million of inhabitants. Religious and educational institutions are largely diffused throughout, and are in a very flourishing condition. Illinois has a State Lunatic and a Deaf and Dumb Asylum at Jacksonville; a State Penitentiary at Joliet; and a Home for

Soldiers' Orphans at Normal. On November 30, 1870, the public debt of the State was returned at $4,870,937, with a balance of $1,808,833 unprovided for. At the same period the value of assessed and equalized property presented the following totals: assessed, $840,031,703; equalized $480,664,058. The name of Illinois, through nearly the whole of the eighteenth century, embraced most of the known regions north and west of Ohio. French colonists established themselves in 1673, at Cahokia and Kaskaskia, and the territory of which these settlements formed the nucleus was, in 1763, ceded to Great Britain in conjunction with Canada, and ultimately resigned to the United States in 1787. Illinois entered the Union as a State, December 3, 1818; and now sends 19 Representatives to Congress. Population, 2,539,891, in 1870.

A WESTERN DWELLING.

INDIANA.

The profile of Indiana forms a nearly exact parallelogram, occupying one of the most fertile portions of the great Mississippi Valley. The greater extent of the surface embraced within its limits consists of gentle undulations rising into hilly tracts toward the Ohio bottom. The chief rivers of the State are the Ohio and Wabash, with their numerous affluents. The soil is highly productive of the cereals and grasses—most particularly so in the valleys of the Ohio, Wabash, Whitewater, and White Rivers. The northeast and central portions are well timbered with virgin forests, and the west section is notably rich in coal, constituting an offshoot of the great Illinois carboniferous field. Iron, copper, marble, slate, gypsum, and various clays are also abundant. From an agricultural point of view, the staple products are maize and wheat, with the other cereals in lesser yields; and besides these, flax, hemp, sorghum, hops, etc., are extensively raised. Indiana is divided into 92 counties, and counts among her principal cities and towns, those of Indianapolis (the capital), Fort Wayne, Evansville, Terre Haute, Madison, Jeffersonville, Columbus, Vincennes, South Bend, etc. The public institutions of the State are many and various, and on a scale of magnitude and efficiency commensurate with her important political and industrial status. Upward of two thousand miles of railroads permeate the State in all directions, and greatly conduce to the development of her expanding manufacturing interests. Statistics for the fiscal year terminating October 31, 1870, exhibited a total of receipts, $3,896,541 as against disbursements, $3,532,406, leaving a balance, $364,135 in favor of the State Treasury. The entire public debt, January 5, 1871, $3,971,000. This State was first settled by Canadian voyageurs in 1702, who erected a fort at Vincennes; in 1763 it passed into the hands of the English, and was by the latter ceded to the United States in 1783. From 1788 till 1791, an Indian warefare prevailed. In 1800, all the region west and north of Ohio (then formed into a distinct territory) became merged in Indiana. In 1809, the present limits of the State were defined, Michigan and Illinois having previously been withdrawn. In 1811, Indiana was the theater of the Indian War of Tecumseh, ending with the decisive battle of Tippecanoe. In 1816 (December 11), Indiana became enrolled among the States of the American Union. In 1834, the State passed through a monetary crisis owing to its having become mixed up with railroad, canal, and other speculations on a gigantic scale, which ended, for the time being, in a general collapse of public credit, and consequent bankruptcy. Since that time, however, the greater number of the public works which had brought about that imbroglio — especially the great Wabash and Erie Canal — have been completed, to the great benefit of the State, whose subsequent progress has year by year been marked by rapid strides in the paths of wealth, commerce, and general social and political prosperity. The constitution now in force was adopted in 1851. Population, 1,680,637.

IOWA.

In shape, Iowa presents an almost perfect parallelogram; has a length, north to south, of about 300 miles, by a pretty even width of 208 miles, and embraces an area of 55,045 square miles, or 35,228,800 acres. The surface of the State is generally undulating, rising toward the middle into an elevated plateau which forms the "divide" of the Missouri and Mississippi basins. Rolling prairies, especially in the south section, constitute a regnant feature, and the river bottoms, belted with woodlands, present a soil of the richest alluvion. Iowa is well watered; the principal rivers being the Mississippi and Missouri, which form respectively its east and west limits, and the Cedar, Iowa, and Des Moines, affluents of the first named. Mineralogically, Iowa is important as occupying a section of the great Northwest coal field, to the extent of an area estimated at 25,000 square miles. Lead, copper, zinc, and iron, are also mined in considerable quantities. The soil is well adapted to the production of wheat, maize, and the other cereals; fruits, vegetables, and esculent roots; maize, wheat, and oats forming the chief staples. Wine, tobacco, hops, and wax, are other noticeable items of the agricultural yield. Cattle-raising, too, is a branch of rural industry largely engaged in. The climate is healthy, although liable to extremes of heat and cold. The annual gross product of the various manufactures carried on in this State approximate, in round numbers, a sum of $20,000,000. Iowa has an immense railroad system, besides over 500 miles of water-communication by means of its navigable rivers. The State is politically divided into 99 counties, with the following centers of population: Des Moines (capital), Iowa City (former capital), Dubuque, Davenport, Burlington, Council Bluffs, Keokuk, Muscatine, and Cedar Rapids. The State institutions of Iowa—religious, scholastic, and philanthropic — are on a par, as regards number and perfection of organization and operation, with those of her Northwest sister States, and education is especially well cared for; and largely diffused. Iowa formed a portion of the American territorial acquisitions from France, by the so-called Louisiana purchase in 1803, and was politically identified with Louisiana till 1812, when it merged into the Missouri Territory; in 1834 it came under the Michigan organization, and, in 1836, under that of Wisconsin. Finally, after being constituted an independent Territory, it became a State of the Union, December 28, 1846. Population in 1860, 674,913; in 1870, 1,191,792, and in 1875, 1,353,118.

MICHIGAN.

United area, 56,243 square miles, or 35,995,520 acres. Extent of the Upper and smaller Peninsula — length, 316 miles; breadth, fluctuating between 36 and 120 miles. The south division is 416 miles long, by from 50 to 300 miles wide. Aggregate lake-shore line, 1,400 miles. The Upper, or North, Peninsula consists chiefly of an elevated plateau, expanding into the Porcupine mountain-system, attaining a maximum height of some 2,000 feet. Its shores along Lake Superior are eminently bold and picturesque, and its area is rich in minerals, its product of copper constituting an important source of industry. Both divisions are heavily wooded, and the South one, in addition, boasts of a deep, rich, loamy soil, throwing up excellent crops of cereals and other agricultural produce. The climate is generally mild and humid, though the Winter colds are severe. The chief staples of farm husbandry include the cereals, grasses, maple sugar, sorghum, tobacco, fruits, and dairy-stuffs. In 1870, the acres of land in farms were: improved, 5,096,939; unimproved woodland, 4,080,146; other unimproved land, 842,057. The cash value of land was $398,240,578; of farming implements and machinery, $13,711,979. In 1869, there were shipped from the Lake Superior ports, 874,582 tons of iron ore, and 45,762 of smelted pig, along with 14,188 tons of copper (ore and ingot). Coal is another article largely mined. Inland communication is provided for by an admirably organized railroad system, and by the St. Mary's Ship Canal, connecting Lakes Huron and Superior. Michigan is politically divided into 78 counties; its chief urban centers are Detroit, Lansing (capital), Ann Arbor, Marquette, Bay City, Niles, Ypsilanti, Grand Haven, etc. The Governor of the State is elected biennially. On November 30, 1870, the aggregate bonded debt of Michigan amounted to $2,385,028, and the assessed valuation of land to $266,929,278, representing an estimated cash value of $800,000,000. Education is largely diffused and most excellently conducted and provided for. The State University at Ann Arbor, the colleges of Detroit and Kalamazoo, the Albion Female College, the State Normal School at Ypsilanti, and the State Agricultural College at Lansing, are chief among the academic institutions. Michigan (a term of Chippeway origin, and signifying "Great Lake), was discovered and first settled by French Canadians, who, in 1670, founded Detroit, the pioneer of a series of trading-posts on the Indian frontier. During the "Conspiracy of Pontiac," following the French loss of Canada, Michigan became the scene of a sanguinary struggle between the whites and aborigines. In 1796, it became annexed to the United States, which incorporated this region with the Northwest Territory, and then with Indiana Territory, till 1803, when it became territorially independent. Michigan was the theater of warlike operations during the war of 1812 with Great Britain, and in 1819 was authorized to be represented by one delegate in Congress; in 1837 she was admitted into the Union as a State, and in 1869 ratified the 15th Amendment to the Federal Constitution. Population, 1,184,059.

WISCONSIN.

It has a mean length of 260 miles, and a maximum breadth of 215. Land area, 53,924 square miles, or 34,511,360 acres. Wisconsin lies at a considerable altitude above sea-level, and consists for the most part of an upland plateau, the surface of which is undulating and very generally diversified. Numerous local eminences called mounds are interspersed over the State, and the Lake Michigan coast-line is in many parts characterized by lofty escarped cliffs, even as on the west side the banks of the Mississippi form a series of high and picturesque bluffs. A group of islands known as The Apostles lie off the extreme north point of the State in Lake Superior, and the great estuary of Green Bay, running far inland, gives formation to a long, narrow peninsula between its waters and those of Lake Michigan. The river-system of Wisconsin has three outlets — those of Lake Superior, Green Bay, and the Mississippi, which latter stream forms the entire southwest frontier, widening at one point into the large watery expanse called Lake Pepin. Lake Superior receives the St. Louis, Burnt Wood, and Montreal Rivers; Green Bay, the Menomonee, Peshtigo, Oconto, and Fox; while into the Mississippi empty the St. Croix, Chippewa, Black, Wisconsin, and Rock Rivers. The chief interior lakes are those of Winnebago, Horicon, and Court Oreilles, and smaller sheets of water stud a great part of the surface. The climate is healthful, with cold Winters and brief but very warm Summers. Mean annual rainfall 31 inches. The geological system represented by the State, embraces those rocks included between the primary and the Devonian series, the former containing extensive deposits of copper and iron ore. Besides these minerals, lead and zinc are found in great quantities, together with kaolin, plumbago, gypsum, and various clays. Mining, consequently, forms a prominent industry, and one of yearly increasing dimensions. The soil of Wisconsin is of varying quality, but fertile on the whole, and in the north parts of the State heavily timbered. The agricultural yield comprises the cereals, together with flax, hemp, tobacco, pulse, sorgum, and all kinds of vegetables, and of the hardier fruits. In 1870, the State had a total number of 102,904 farms, occupying 11,715,321 acres, of which 5,899,343 consisted of improved land, and 3,437,442 were timbered. Cash value of farms, $300,414,064; of farm implements and machinery, $14,239,364. Total estimated value of all farm products, including betterments and additions to stock, $78,027,032; of orchard and dairy stuffs, $1,045,933; of lumber, $1,327,618; of home manufactures, $338,423; of all live-stock, $45,310,882. Number of manufacturing establishments, 7,136, employing 39,055 hands, and turning out productions valued at $85,624,966. The political divisions of the State form 61 counties, and the chief places of wealth, trade, and population, are Madison (the capital), Milwaukee, Fond du Lac, Oshkosh, Prairie du Chien, Janesville, Portage City, Racine, Kenosha, and La Crosse. In 1870, the total assessed valuation reached $333,209,838, as against a true valuation of both real and personal estate aggregating $602,207,329. Treasury receipts during 1870, $886,-696; disbursements, $906,329. Value of church property, $4,749,983. Education is amply provided for. Independently of the State University at Madison, and those of Galesville and of Lawrence at Appleton, and the colleges of Beloit, Racine, and Milton, there are Normal Schools at Platteville and Whitewater. The State is divided into 4,802 common school districts, maintained at a cost, in 1870, of $2,094,160. The charitable institutions of Wisconsin include a Deaf and Dumb Asylum, an Institute for the Education of the Blind, and a Soldiers' Orphans' School. In January, 1870, the railroad system ramified throughout the State totalized 2,779 miles of track, including several lines far advanced toward completion. Immigration is successfully encouraged by the State authorities, the larger number of yearly new-comers being of Scandinavian and German origin. The territory now occupied within the limits of the State of Wisconsin was explored by French missionaries and traders in 1639, and it remained under French jurisdiction until 1703, when it became annexed to the British North American possessions. In 1796, it reverted to the United States, the government of which latter admitted it within the limits of the Northwest Territory, and in 1809, attached it to that of Illinois, and to Michigan in 1818. Wisconsin became independently territorially organized in 1836, and became a State of the Union, March 3, 1847. Population in 1870, 1,064,985, of which 2,113 were of the colored race, and 11,521 Indians, 1,206 of the latter, being out of tribal relations.

MINNESOTA.

Its length, north to south, embraces an extent of 380 miles; its breadth one of 250 miles at a maximum. Area, 84,000 square miles, or 54,760,000 acres. The surface of Minnesota, generally speaking, consists of a succession of gently undulating plains and prairies, drained by an admirable water-system, and with here and there heavily timbered bottoms and belts of virgin forest. The soil, corresponding with such a superfices, is exceptionally rich, consisting for the most part of a dark, calcareous sandy drift intermixed with loam. A distinguishing physical feature of this State is its riverine ramifications, expanding in nearly every part of it into almost innumerable lakes—the whole presenting an aggregate of water-power having hardly a rival in the Union. Besides the Mississippi — which here has its rise, and drains a basin of 800 miles of country — the principal streams are the Minnesota (334 miles long), the Red River of the North, the St. Croix, St. Louis, and many others of lesser importance; the chief lakes are those called Red, Cass, Leech, Mille Lacs, Vermillion, and Winibigosh. Quite a concatenation of sheets of water fringe the frontier line where Minnesota joins British America, culminating in the Lake of the Woods. It has been estimated, that of an area of 1,200,000 acres of surface between the St. Croix and Mississippi Rivers, not less than 73,000 acres are of lacustrine formation. In point of minerals, the resources of Minnesota have as yet been very imperfectly developed; iron, copper, coal, lead — all these are known to exist in considerable deposits; together with salt, limestone, and potter's clay. The agricultural outlook of the State is in a high degree satisfactory; wheat constitutes the leading cereal in cultivation, with Indian corn and oats in next order. Fruits and vegetables are grown in great plenty and of excellent quality. The lumber resources of Minnesota are important; the pine forests in the north region alone occupying an area of some 21,000 square miles, which in 1870 produced a return of scaled logs amounting to 313,116,416 feet. The natural industrial advantages possessed by Minnesota are largely improved upon by a railroad system. The political divisions of this State number 78 counties; of which the chief cities and towns are: St. Paul (the capital), Stillwater, Red Wing, St. Anthony, Fort Snelling, Minneapolis, and Mankato. Minnesota has already assumed an attitude of high importance as a manufacturing State; this is mainly due to the wonderful command of water-power she possesses, as before spoken of. Besides her timber-trade, the milling of flour, the distillation of whisky, and the tanning of leather, are prominent interests, which, in 1869, gave returns to the amount of $14,831,043.

Education is notably provided for on a broad and catholic scale, the entire amount expended scholastically during the year 1870 being $857,816; while on November 30 of the preceding year the permanent school fund stood at $2,476,222. Besides a University and Agricultural College, Normal and Reform Schools flourish, and with these may be mentioned such various philanthropic and religious institutions as befit the needs of an intelligent and prosperous community. The finances of the State for the fiscal year terminating December 1, 1870, exhibited a balance on the right side to the amount of $136,164, being a gain of $44,000 over the previous year's figures. The earliest exploration of Minnesota by the whites was made in 1680 by a French Franciscan, Father Hennepin, who gave the name of St. Antony to the Great Falls on the Upper Missisippi. In 1763, the Treaty of Versailles ceded this region to England. Twenty years later, Minnesota formed part of the Northwest Territory transferred to the United States, and became herself territorialized independently in 1849. Indian cessions in 1851 enlarged her boundaries, and, May 11, 1857, Minnesota became a unit of the great American federation of States. Population, 439,706.

NEBRASKA.

Maximum length, 412 miles; extreme breadth, 208 miles. Area, 75,905 square miles, or 48,636,800 acres. The surface of this State is almost entirely undulating prairie, and forms part of the west slope of the great central basin of the North American Continent. In its west division, near the base of the Rocky Mountains, is a sandy belt of country, irregularly defined. In this part, too, are the "dunes," resembling a wavy sea of sandy billows, as well as the Mauvaises Terres, a tract of singular formation, produced by eccentric disintegrations and denudations of the land. The chief rivers are the Missouri, constituting its entire east line of demarcation; the Nebraska or Platte, the Niobrara, the Republican Fork of the Kansas, the Elkhorn, and the Loup Fork of the Platte. The soil is very various, but consisting chiefly of rich, bottomy loam, admirably adapted to the raising of heavy crops of cereals. All the vegetables and fruits of the temperate zone are produced in great size and plenty. For grazing purposes Nebraska is a State exceptionally well fitted, a region of not less than 23,000,000 acres being adaptable to this branch of husbandry. It is believed that the, as yet, comparatively infertile tracts of land found in various parts of the State are susceptible of productivity by means of a properly conducted system of irrigation. Few minerals of moment have so far been found within the limits of

Nebraska, if we may except important saline deposits at the head of Salt Creek in its southeast section. The State is divided into 57 counties, independent of the Pawnee and Winnebago Indians, and of unorganized territory in the northwest part. The principal towns are Omaha, Lincoln (State capital), Nebraska City, Columbus, Grand Island, etc. In 1870, the total assessed value of property amounted to $53,000,000, being an increase of $11,000,000 over the previous year's returns. The total amount received from the school-fund during the year 1869–70 was $77,999. Education is making great onward strides, the State University and an Agricultural College being far advanced toward completion. In the matter of railroad communication, Nebraska bids fair to soon place herself on a par with her neighbors to the east. Besides being intersected by the Union Pacific line, with its off-shoot, the Fremont and Blair, other tracks are in course of rapid construction. Organized by Congressional Act into a Territory, May 30, 1854, Nebraska entered the Union as a full State, March 1, 1867. Population, 122,993.

HUNTING PRAIRIE WOLVES IN AN EARLY DAY.

EARLY HISTORY OF ILLINOIS.

The name of this beautiful Prairie State is derived from *Illini*, a Delaware word signifying Superior Men. It has a French termination, and is a symbol of how the two races—the French and the Indians—were intermixed during the early history of the country.

The appellation was no doubt well applied to the primitive inhabitants of the soil whose prowess in savage warfare long withstood the combined attacks of the fierce Iroquois on the one side, and the no less savage and relentless Sacs and Foxes on the other. The Illinois were once a powerful confederacy, occupying the most beautiful and fertile region in the great Valley of the Mississippi, which their enemies coveted and struggled long and hard to wrest from them. By the fortunes of war they were diminished in numbers, and finally destroyed. "Starved Rock," on the Illinois River, according to tradition, commemorates their last tragedy, where, it is said, the entire tribe starved rather than surrender.

EARLY DISCOVERIES.

The first European discoveries in Illinois date back over two hundred years. They are a part of that movement which, from the beginning to the middle of the seventeenth century, brought the French Canadian missionaries and fur traders into the Valley of the Mississippi, and which, at a later period, established the civil and ecclesiastical authority of France from the Gulf of St. Lawrence to the Gulf of Mexico, and from the foot-hills of the Alleghanies to the Rocky Mountains.

The great river of the West had been discovered by DeSoto, the Spanish conqueror of Florida, three quarters of a century before the French founded Quebec in 1608, but the Spanish left the country a wilderness, without further exploration or settlement within its borders, in which condition it remained until the Mississippi was discovered by the agents of the French Canadian government, Joliet and Marquette, in 1673. These renowned explorers were not the first white visitors to Illinois. In 1671—two years in advance of them—came Nicholas Perrot to Chicago. He had been sent by Talon as an agent of the Canadian government to

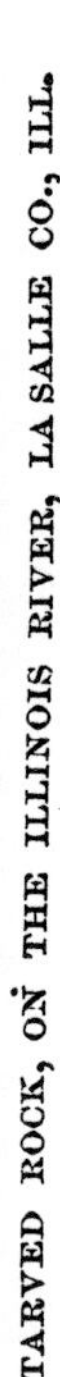

STARVED ROCK, ON THE ILLINOIS RIVER, LA SALLE CO., ILL.

call a great peace convention of Western Indians at Green Bay, preparatory to the movement for the discovery of the Mississippi. It was deemed a good stroke of policy to secure, as far as possible, the friendship and co-operation of the Indians, far and near, before venturing upon an enterprise which their hostility might render disastrous, and which their friendship and assistance would do so much to make successful; and to this end Perrot was sent to call together in council the tribes throughout the Northwest, and to promise them the commerce and protection of the French government. He accordingly arrived at Green Bay in 1671, and procuring an escort of Pottawattamies, proceeded in a bark canoe upon a visit to the Miamis, at Chicago. Perrot was therefore the first European to set foot upon the soil of Illinois.

Still there were others before Marquette. In 1672, the Jesuit missionaries, Fathers Claude Allouez and Claude Dablon, bore the standard of the Cross from their mission at Green Bay through western Wisconsin and northern Illinois, visiting the Foxes on Fox River, and the Masquotines and Kickapoos at the mouth of the Milwaukee. These missionaries penetrated on the route afterwards followed by Marquette as far as the Kickapoo village at the head of Lake Winnebago, where Marquette, in his journey, secured guides across the portage to the Wisconsin.

The oft-repeated story of Marquette and Joliet is well known. They were the agents employed by the Canadian government to discover the Mississippi. Marquette was a native of France, born in 1637, a Jesuit priest by education, and a man of simple faith and of great zeal and devotion in extending the Roman Catholic religion among the Indians. Arriving in Canada in 1666, he was sent as a missionary to the far Northwest, and, in 1668, founded a mission at Sault Ste. Marie. The following year he moved to La Pointe, in Lake Superior, where he instructed a branch of the Hurons till 1670, when he removed south, and founded the mission at St. Ignace, on the Straits of Mackinaw. Here he remained, devoting a portion of his time to the study of the Illinois language under a native teacher who had accompanied him to the mission from La Pointe, till he was joined by Joliet in the Spring of 1673. By the way of Green Bay and the Fox and Wisconsin Rivers, they entered the Mississippi, which they explored to the mouth of the Arkansas, and returned by the way of the Illinois and Chicago Rivers to Lake Michigan.

On his way up the Illinois, Marquette visited the great village of the Kaskaskias, near what is now Utica, in the county of LaSalle. The following year he returned and established among them the mission of the Immaculate Virgin Mary, which was the first Jesuit mission founded in Illinois and in the Mississippi Valley. The intervening winter he had spent in a hut which his companions erected on the Chicago River, a few leagues from its mouth. The founding of this mission was the last act of Marquette's life. He died in Michigan, on his way back to Green Bay, May 18, 1675.

FIRST FRENCH OCCUPATION.

The first French occupation of the territory now embraced in Illinois was effected by LaSalle in 1680, seven years after the time of Marquette and Joliet. LaSalle, having constructed a vessel, the "Griffin," above the falls of Niagara, which he sailed to Green Bay, and having passed thence in canoes to the mouth of the St. Joseph River, by which and the Kankakee he reached the Illinois, in January, 1680, erected Fort *Crevecœur*, at the lower end of Peoria Lake, where the city of Peoria is now situated. The place where this ancient fort stood may still be seen just below the outlet of Peoria Lake. It was destined, however, to a temporary existence. From this point, LaSalle determined to descend the Mississippi to its mouth, but did not accomplish this purpose till two years later—in 1682. Returning to Fort Frontenac for the purpose of getting materials with which to rig his vessel, he left the fort in charge of Touti, his lieutenant, who during his absence was driven off by the Iroquois Indians. These savages had made a raid upon the settlement of the Illinois, and had left nothing in their track but ruin and desolation. Mr. Davidson, in his History of Illinois, gives the following graphic account of the picture that met the eyes of LaSalle and his companions on their return:

"At the great town of the Illinois they were appalled at the scene which opened to their view. No hunter appeared to break its death-like silence with a salutatory whoop ot welcome. The plain on which the town had stood was now strewn with charred fragments of lodges, which had so recently swarmed with savage life and hilarity. To render more hideous the picture of desolation, large numbers of skulls had been placed on the upper extremities of lodge-poles which had escaped the devouring flames. In the midst of these horrors was the rude fort of the spoilers, rendered frightful by the same ghastly relics. A near approach showed that the graves had been robbed of their bodies, and swarms of buzzards were discovered glutting their loathsome stomachs on the reeking corruption. To complete the work of destruction, the growing corn of the village had been cut down and burned, while the pits containing the products of previous years, had been rifled and their contents scattered with wanton waste. It was evident the suspected blow of the Iroquois had fallen with relentless fury."

Tonti had escaped LaSalle knew not whither. Passing down the lake in search of him and his men, LaSalle discovered that the fort had been destroyed, but the vessel which he had partly constructed was still on the stocks, and but slightly injured. After further fruitless search, failing to find Tonti, he fastened to a tree a painting representing himself and party sitting in a canoe and bearing a pipe of peace, and to the painting attached a letter addressed to Tonti.

Tonti had escaped, and, after untold privations, taken shelter among the Pottawattamies near Green Bay. These were friendly to the French. One of their old chiefs used to say, "There were but three great captains in the world, himself, Tonti and LaSalle."

GENIUS OF LaSALLE.

We must now return to LaSalle, whose exploits stand out in such bold relief. He was born in Rouen, France, in 1643. His father was wealthy, but he renounced his patrimony on entering a college of the Jesuits, from which he separated and came to Canada a poor man in 1666. The priests of St. Sulpice, among whom he had a brother, were then the proprietors of Montreal, the nucleus of which was a seminary or convent founded by that order. The Superior granted to LaSalle a large tract of land at LaChine, where he established himself in the fur trade. He was a man of daring genius, and outstripped all his competitors in exploits of travel and commerce with the Indians. In 1669, he visited the headquarters of the great Iroquois Confederacy, at Onondaga, in the heart of New York, and, obtaining guides, explored the Ohio River to the falls at Louisville.

In order to understand the genius of LaSalle, it must be remembered that for many years prior to his time the missionaries and traders were obliged to make their way to the Northwest by the Ottawa River (of Canada) on account of the fierce hostility of the Iroquois along the lower lakes and Niagara River, which entirely closed this latter route to the Upper Lakes. They carried on their commerce chiefly by canoes, paddling them through the Ottawa to Lake Nipissing, carrying them across the portage to French River, and descending that to Lake Huron. This being the route by which they reached the Northwest, accounts for the fact that all the earliest Jesuit missions were established in the neighborhood of the Upper Lakes. LaSalle conceived the grand idea of opening the route by Niagara River and the Lower Lakes to Canadian commerce by sail vessels, connecting it with the navigation of the Mississippi, and thus opening a magnificent water communication from the Gulf of St. Lawrence to the Gulf of Mexico. This truly grand and comprehensive purpose seems to have animated him in all his wonderful achievements and the matchless difficulties and hardships he surmounted. As the first step in the accomplishment of this object he established himself on Lake Ontario, and built and garrisoned Fort Frontenac, the site of the present city of Kingston, Canada. Here he obtained a grant of land from the French crown and a body of troops by which he beat back the invading Iroquois and cleared the passage to Niagara Falls. Having by this masterly stroke made it safe to attempt a hitherto untried expedition, his next step, as we have seen, was to advance to the Falls with all his outfit for building a ship with which to sail the lakes. He was successful in this undertaking, though his ultimate purpose was defeated by a strange combination of untoward circumstances. The Jesuits evidently hated LaSalle and plotted against him, because he had abandoned them and co-operated with a rival order. The fur traders were also jealous of his superior success in opening new channels of commerce. At LaChine he had taken the trade of Lake Ontario, which but for his presence there would have gone to Quebec. While they were plodding with their bark canoes through the Ottawa he was constructing sailing vessels to command the trade of the lakes and the Mississippi. These great plans excited the jealousy and envy of the small traders, introduced treason and revolt into the ranks of his own companions, and finally led to the foul assassination by which his great achievements were prematurely ended.

In 1682, LaSalle, having completed his vessel at Peoria, descended the Mississippi to its confluence with the Gulf of Mexico. Erecting a standard on which he inscribed the arms of France, he took formal possession of the whole valley of the mighty river, in the name of Louis XIV., then reigning, in honor of whom he named the country LOUISIANA.

LaSalle then went to France, was appointed Governor, and returned with a fleet and immigrants, for the purpose of planting a colony in Illinois. They arrived in due time in the Gulf of Mexico, but failing to find the mouth of the Mississippi, up which LaSalle intended to sail, his supply ship, with the immigrants, was driven ashore and wrecked on Matagorda Bay. With the fragments of the vessel he constructed a stockade and rude huts on the shore for the protection of the immigrants, calling the post Fort St. Louis. He then made a trip into New Mexico, in search of silver mines, but, meeting with disappointment, returned to find his little colony reduced to forty souls. He then resolved to travel on foot to Illinois, and, starting with his companions, had reached the valley of the Colorado, near the mouth of Trinity river, when he was shot by one of his men. This occurred on the 19th of March, 1687.

Dr. J. W. Foster remarks of him: "Thus fell, not far from the banks of the Trinity, Robert Cavalier de la Salle, one of the grandest characters that ever figured in American history—a man capable of originating the vastest schemes, and endowed with a will and a judgment capable of carrying them to successful results. Had ample facilities been placed by the King of France at his disposal, the result of the colonization of this continent might have been far different from what we now behold."

EARLY SETTLEMENTS.

A temporary settlement was made at Fort St. Louis, or the old Kaskaskia village, on the Illinois River, in what is now LaSalle County, in 1682. In 1690, this was removed, with the mission connected with it, to Kaskaskia, on the river of that name, emptying into the lower Mississippi in St. Clair County. Cahokia was settled about the same time, or at least, both of these settlements began in the year 1690, though it is now pretty well settled that Cahokia is the older place, and ranks as the oldest permanent settlement in Illinois, as well as in the Mississippi Valley. The reason for the removal of the old Kaskaskia settlement and mission, was probably because the dangerous and difficult route by Lake Michigan and the Chicago portage had been almost abandoned, and travelers and traders passed down and up the Mississippi by the Fox and Wisconsin River route. They removed to the vicinity of the Mississippi in order to be in the line of travel from Canada to Louisiana, that is, the lower part of it, for it was all Louisiana then south of the lakes.

During the period of French rule in Louisiana, the population probably never exceeded ten thousand, including whites and blacks. Within that portion of it now included in Indiana, trading posts were established at the principal Miami villages which stood on the head waters of the Maumee, the Wea villages situated at Ouiatenon, on the Wabash, and the Piankeshaw villages at Post Vincennes; all of which were probably visited by French traders and missionaries before the close of the seventeenth century.

In the vast territory claimed by the French, many settlements of considerable importance had sprung up. Biloxi, on Mobile Bay, had been founded by D'Iberville, in 1699; Antoine de Lamotte Cadillac had founded Detroit in 1701; and New Orleans had been founded by Bienville, under the auspices of the Mississippi Company, in 1718. In Illinois also, considerable settlements had been made, so that in 1730 they embraced one hundred and forty French families, about six hundred "converted Indians," and many traders and voyageurs. In that portion of the country, on the east side of the Mississippi, there were five distinct settlements, with their respective villages, viz.: Cahokia, near the mouth of Cahokia Creek and about five miles below the present city of St. Louis; St. Philip, about forty-five miles below Cahokia, and four miles above Fort Chartres; Fort Chartres, twelve miles above Kaskaskia; Kaskaskia, situated on the Kaskaskia River, five miles above its confluence with the Mississippi; and Prairie du Rocher, near Fort Chartres. To these must be added St. Genevieve and St. Louis, on the west side of the Mississippi. These, with the exception of St. Louis, are among

AN EARLY SETTLEMENT.

the oldest French towns in the Mississippi Valley. Kaskaskia, in its best days, was a town of some two or three thousand inhabitants. After it passed from the crown of France its population for many years did not exceed fifteen hundred. Under British rule, in 1773, the population had decreased to four hundred and fifty. As early as 1721, the Jesuits had established a college and a monastery in Kaskaskia.

Fort Chartres was first built under the direction of the Mississippi Company, in 1718, by M. de Boisbraint, a military officer, under command of Bienville. It stood on the east bank of the Mississippi, about eighteen miles below Kaskaskia, and was for some time the headquarters of the military commandants of the district of Illinois.

In the Centennial Oration of Dr. Fowler, delivered at Philadelphia, by appointment of Gov. Beveridge, we find some interesting facts with regard to the State of Illinois, which we appropriate in this history:

In 1682 Illinois became a possession of the French crown, a dependency of Canada, and a part of Louisiana. In 1765 the English flag was run up on old Fort Chartres, and Illinois was counted among the treasures of Great Britain.

In 1779 it was taken from the English by Col. George Rogers Clark. This man was resolute in nature, wise in council, prudent in policy, bold in action, and heroic in danger. Few men who have figured in the history of America are more deserving than this colonel. Nothing short of first-class ability could have rescued Vincens and all Illinois from the English. And it is not possible to over-estimate the influence of this achievement upon the republic. In 1779 Illinois became a part of Virginia. It was soon known as Illinois County. In 1784 Virginia ceded all this territory to the general government, to be cut into States, to be republican in form, with "the same right of sovereignty, freedom, and independence as the other States."

In 1787 it was the object of the wisest and ablest legislation found in any merely human records. No man can study the secret history of

THE "COMPACT OF 1787,"

and not feel that Providence was guiding with sleepless eye these unborn States. The ordinance that on July 13, 1787, finally became the incorporating act, has a most marvelous history. Jefferson had vainly tried to secure a system of government for the northwestern territory. He was an emancipationist of that day, and favored the exclusion of slavery from the territory Virginia had ceded to the general government; but the South voted him down as often as it came up. In 1787, as late as July 10, an organizing act without the anti-slavery clause was pending. This concession to the South was expected to carry it. Congress was in session in New York City. On July 5, Rev. Dr. Manasseh Cutler, of Massachusetts, came into New York to lobby on the northwestern territory. Everything seemed to fall into his hands. Events were ripe.

The state of the public credit, the growing of Southern prejudice, the basis of his mission, his personal character, all combined to complete one of those sudden and marvelous revolutions of public sentiment that once in five or ten centuries are seen to sweep over a country like the breath of the Almighty. Cutler was a graduate of Yale—received his A.M. from Harvard, and his D.D. from Yale. He had studied and taken degrees in the three learned professions, medicine, law, and divinity. He had thus America's best indorsement. He had published a scientific examination of the plants of New England. His name stood second only to that of Franklin as a scientist in America. He was a courtly gentleman of the old style, a man of commanding presence, and of inviting face. The Southern members said they had never seen such a gentleman in the North. He came representing a company that desired to purchase a tract of land now included in Ohio, for the purpose of planting a colony. It was a speculation. Government money was worth eighteen cents on the dollar. This Massachusetts company had collected enough to purchase 1,500,000 acres of land. Other speculators in New York made Dr. Cutler their agent (lobbyist). On the 12th he represented a demand for 5,500,000 acres. This would reduce the national debt. Jefferson and Virginia were regarded as authority concerning the land Virginia had just ceded. Jefferson's policy wanted to provide for the public credit, and this was a good opportunity to do something.

Massachusetts then owned the territory of Maine, which she was crowding on the market. She was opposed to opening the northwestern region. This fired the zeal of Virginia. The South caught the inspiration, and all exalted Dr. Cutler. The English minister invited him to dine with some of the Southern gentlemen. He was the center of interest.

The entire South rallied round him. Massachusetts could not vote against him, because many of the constituents of her members were interested personally in the western speculation. Thus Cutler, making friends with the South, and, doubtless, using all the arts of the lobby, was enabled to command the situation. True to deeper convictions, he dictated one of the most compact and finished documents of wise statesmanship that has ever adorned any human law book. He borrowed from Jefferson the term "Articles of Compact," which, preceding the federal constitution, rose into the most sacred character. He then followed very closely the constitution of Massachusetts, adopted three years before. Its most marked points were:

1. The exclusion of slavery from the territory forever.
2. Provision for public schools, giving one township for a seminary,

and every section numbered 16 in each township; that is, one-thirty-sixth of all the land, for public schools.

3. A provision prohibiting the adoption of any constitution or the enactment of any law that should nullify pre-existing contracts.

Be it forever remembered that this compact declared that "Religion, morality, and knowledge being necessary to good government and the happiness of mankind, schools and the means of education shall always be encouraged."

Dr. Cutler planted himself on this platform and would not yield. Giving his unqualified declaration that it was that or nothing—that unless they could make the land desirable they did not want it—he took his horse and buggy, and started for the constitutional convention in Philadelphia. On July 13, 1787, the bill was put upon its passage, and was unanimously adopted, every Southern member voting for it, and only one man, Mr. Yates, of New York, voting against it. But as the States voted as States, Yates lost his vote, and the compact was put beyond repeal.

Thus the great States of Ohio, Indiana, Illinois, Michigan and Wisconsin—a vast empire, the heart of the great valley—were consecrated to freedom, intelligence, and honesty. Thus the great heart of the nation was prepared for a year and a day and an hour. In the light of these eighty-nine years I affirm that this act was the salvation of the republic and the destruction of slavery. Soon the South saw their great blunder, and tried to repeal the compact. In 1803 Congress referred it to a committee of which John Randolph was chairman. He reported that this ordinance was a compact, and opposed repeal. Thus it stood a rock, in the way of the on-rushing sea of slavery.

With all this timely aid it was, after all, a most desperate and protracted struggle to keep the soil of Illinois sacred to freedom. It was the natural battle-field for the irrepressible conflict. In the southern end of the State slavery preceded the compact. It existed among the old French settlers, and was hard to eradicate. The southern part of the State was settled from the slave States, and this population brought their laws, customs, and institutions with them. A stream of population from the North poured into the northern part of the State. These sections misunderstood and hated each other perfectly. The Southerners regarded the Yankees as a skinning, tricky, penurious race of peddlers, filling the country with tinware, brass clocks, and wooden nutmegs. The Northerner thought of the Southerner as a lean, lank, lazy creature, burrowing in a hut, and rioting in whisky, dirt and ignorance. These causes aided in making the struggle long and bitter. So strong was the sympathy with slavery that, in spite of the ordinance of 1787, and in spite of the deed of cession, it was determined to allow the old French settlers to retain their slaves. Planters from the slave States might bring their slaves, if they would give them a chance to choose freedom or years of service and bondage for their children till they should become thirty years of age. If they chose freedom they must leave the State in sixty days or be sold as fugitives. Servants were whipped for offenses for which white men are fined. Each lash paid forty cents of the fine. A negro ten miles from home without a pass was whipped. These famous laws were imported from the slave States just as they imported laws for the inspection of flax and wool when there was neither in the State.

These Black Laws are now wiped out. A vigorous effort was made to protect slavery in the State Constitution of 1817. It barely failed. It was renewed in 1825, when a convention was asked to make a new constitution. After a hard fight the convention was defeated. But slaves did not disappear from the census of the State until 1850. There were mobs and murders in the interest of slavery. Lovejoy was added to the list of martyrs—a sort of first-fruits of that long life of immortal heroes who saw freedom as the one supreme desire of their souls, and were so enamored of her that they preferred to die rather than survive her.

The population of 12,282 that occupied the territory in A.D. 1800, increased to 45,000 in A.D. 1818, when the State Constitution was adopted, and Illinois took her place in the Union, with a star on the flag and two votes in the Senate.

Shadrach Bond was the first Governor, and in his first message he recommended the construction of the Illinois and Michigan Canal.

The simple economy in those days is seen in the fact that the entire bill for stationery for the first Legislature was only $13.50. Yet this simple body actually enacted a very superior code.

There was no money in the territory before the war of 1812. Deer skins and coon skins were the circulating medium. In 1821, the Legislature ordained a State Bank on the credit of the State. It issued notes in the likeness of bank bills. These notes were made a legal tender for every thing, and the bank was ordered to loan to the people $100 on personal security, and more on mortgages. They actually passed a resolution requesting the Secretary of the Treasury of the United States to receive these notes for land. The old French Lieutenant Governor, Col. Menard, put the resolution as follows: "Gentlemen of the Senate: It is moved and seconded *dat de notes of dis bank* be made land-office money. All in favor of dat motion say aye; all against it say no. It is decided in de affirmative. Now, gentlemen, I bet you one hundred dollar he never be land-office money!" Hard sense, like hard money, is always above par.

This old Frenchman presents a fine figure up against the dark background of most of his nation. They made no progress. They clung to their earliest and simplest implements. They never wore hats or caps

They pulled their blankets over their heads in the winter like the Indians, with whom they freely intermingled.

Demagogism had an early development. One John Grammar (only in name), elected to the Territorial and State Legislatures of 1816 and 1836, invented the policy of opposing every new thing, saying, "If it succeeds, no one will ask who voted against it. If it proves a failure, he could quote its record." In sharp contrast with Grammar was the character of D. P. Cook, after whom the county containing Chicago was named. Such was his transparent integrity and remarkable ability that his will was almost the law of the State. In Congress, a young man, and from a poor State, he was made Chairman of the Ways and Means Committee. He was pre-eminent for standing by his committee, regardless of consequences. It was his integrity that elected John Quincy Adams to the Presidency. There were four candidates in 1824, Jackson, Clay, Crawford, and John Quincy Adams. There being no choice by the people, the election was thrown into the House. It was so balanced that it turned on his vote, and that he cast for Adams, electing him; then went home to face the wrath of the Jackson party in Illinois. It cost him all but character and greatness. It is a suggestive comment on the times, that there was no legal interest till 1830. It often reached 150 per cent., usually 50 per cent. Then it was reduced to 12, and now to 10 per cent.

PHYSICAL FEATURES OF THE PRAIRIE STATE.

In area the State has 55,410 square miles of territory. It is about 150 miles wide and 400 miles long, stretching in latitude from Maine to North Carolina. It embraces wide variety of climate. It is tempered on the north by the great inland, saltless, tideless sea, which keeps the thermometer from either extreme. Being a table land, from 600 to 1,600 feet above the level of the sea, one is prepared to find on the health maps, prepared by the general government, an almost clean and perfect record. In freedom from fever and malarial diseases and consumptions, the three deadly enemies of the American Saxon, Illinois, as a State, stands without a superior. She furnishes one of the essential conditions of a great people—sound bodies. I suspect that this fact lies back of that old Delaware word, Illini, superior men.

The great battles of history that have been determinative of dynasties and destinies have been strategical battles, chiefly the question of position. Thermopylæ has been the war-cry of freemen for twenty-four centuries. It only tells how much there may be in position. All this advantage belongs to Illinois. It is in the heart of the greatest valley in the world, the vast region between the mountains—a valley that could feed mankind for one thousand years. It is well on toward the center of the continent. It is in the great temperate belt, in which have been found nearly all the aggressive civilizations of history. It has sixty-five miles of frontage on the head of the lake. With the Mississippi forming the western and southern boundary, with the Ohio running along the southeastern line, with the Illinois River and Canal dividing the State diagonally from the lake to the Lower Mississippi, and with the Rock and Wabash Rivers furnishing altogether 2,000 miles of water-front, connecting with, and running through, in all about 12,000 miles of navigable water.

But this is not all. These waters are made most available by the fact that the lake and the State lie on the ridge running into the great valley from the east. Within cannon-shot of the lake the water runs away from the lake to the Gulf. The lake now empties at both ends, one into the Atlantic and one into the Gulf of Mexico. The lake thus seems to hang over the land. This makes the dockage most serviceable; there are no steep banks to damage it. Both lake and river are made for use.

The climate varies from Portland to Richmond; it favors every product of the continent, including the tropics, with less than half a dozen exceptions. It produces every great nutriment of the world except bananas and rice. It is hardly too much to say that it is the most productive spot known to civilization. With the soil full of bread and the earth full of minerals; with an upper surface of food and an under layer of fuel; with perfect natural drainage, and abundant springs and streams and navigable rivers; half way between the forests of the North and the fruits of the South; within a day's ride of the great deposits of iron, coal, copper, lead, and zinc; containing and controlling the great grain, cattle, pork, and lumber markets of the world, it is not strange that Illinois has the advantage of position.

This advantage has been supplemented by the character of the population. In the early days when Illinois was first admitted to the Union, her population were chiefly from Kentucky and Virginia. But, in the conflict of ideas concerning slavery, a strong tide of emigration came in from the East, and soon changed this composition. In 1870 her non-native population were from colder soils. New York furnished 133,290; Ohio gave 162,623; Pennsylvania sent on 98,352; the entire South gave us only 206,734. In all her cities, and in all her German and Scandinavian and other foreign colonies, Illinois has only about one-fifth of her people of foreign birth.

PROGRESS OF DEVELOPMENT.

One of the greatest elements in the early development of Illinois is the Illinois and Michigan Canal, connecting the Illinois and Mississippi Rivers with the lakes. It was of the utmost importance to the State. It was recommended by Gov. Bond, the first governor, in his first message. In 1821, the Legislature appropriated $10,000 for surveying the route. Two bright young engineers surveyed it, and estimated the cost at $600,000 or $700,000. It finally cost $8,000,000. In 1825, a law was passed to incorporate the Canal Company, but no stock was sold. In 1826, upon the solicitation of Cook, Congress gave 800,000 acres of land on the line of the work. In 1828, another law—commissioners appointed, and work commenced with new survey and new estimates. In 1834–35, George Farquhar made an able report on the whole matter. This was, doubtless, the ablest report ever made to a western legislature, and it became the model for subsequent reports and action. From this the work went on till it was finished in 1848. It cost the State a large amount of money; but it gave to the industries of the State an impetus that pushed it up into the first rank of greatness. It was not built as a speculation any more than a doctor is employed on a speculation. But it has paid into the Treasury of the State an average annual net sum of over $111,000.

Pending the construction of the canal, the land and town-lot fever broke out in the State, in 1834–35. It took on the malignant type in Chicago, lifting the town up into a city. The disease spread over the entire State and adjoining States. It was epidemic. It cut up men's farms without regard to locality, and cut up the purses of the purchasers without regard to consequences. It is estimated that building lots enough were sold in Indiana alone to accommodate every citizen then in the United States.

Towns and cities were exported to the Eastern market by the ship-load. There was no lack of buyers. Every up-ship came freighted with speculators and their money.

This distemper seized upon the Legislature in 1836–37, and left not one to tell the tale. They enacted a system of internal improvement without a parallel in the grandeur of its conception. They ordered the construction of 1,300 miles of railroad, crossing the State in all directions. This was surpassed by the river and canal improvements. There were a few counties not touched by either railroad or river or canal, and those were to be comforted and compensated by the free distribution of $200,000 among them. To inflate this balloon beyond credence it was ordered that work should be commenced on both ends of each of these railroads and rivers, and at each river-crossing, all at the same time. The appropriations for these vast improvements were over $12,000,000, and commissioners were appointed to borrow the money on the credit of the State. Remember that all this was in the early days of railroading, when railroads were luxuries; that the State had whole counties with scarcely a cabin; and that the population of the State was less than 400,000, and you can form some idea of the vigor with which these brave men undertook the work of making a great State. In the light of history I am compelled to say that this was only a premature throb of the power that actually slumbered in the soil of the State. It was Hercules in the cradle.

At this juncture the State Bank loaned its funds largely to Godfrey Gilman & Co., and to other leading houses, for the purpose of drawing trade from St. Louis to Alton. Soon they failed, and took down the bank with them.

In 1840, all hope seemed gone. A population of 480,000 were loaded with a debt of $14,000,000. It had only six small cities, really only towns, namely: Chicago, Alton, Springfield, Quincy, Galena, Nauvoo. This debt was to be cared for when there was not a dollar in the treasury, and when the State had borrowed itself out of all credit, and when there was not good money enough in the hands of all the people to pay the interest of the debt for a single year. Yet, in the presence of all these difficulties, the young State steadily refused to repudiate. Gov. Ford took hold of the problem and solved it, bringing the State through in triumph.

Having touched lightly upon some of the more distinctive points in the history of the development of Illinois, let us next briefly consider the

MATERIAL RESOURCES OF THE STATE.

It is a garden four hundred miles long and one hundred and fifty miles wide. Its soil is chiefly a black sandy loam, from six inches to sixty feet thick. On the American bottoms it has been cultivated for one hundred and fifty years without renewal. About the old French towns it has yielded corn for a century and a half without rest or help. It produces nearly everything green in the temperate and tropical zones. She leads all other States in the number of acres actually under plow. Her products from 25,000,000 of acres are incalculable. Her mineral wealth is scarcely second to her agricultural power. She has coal, iron, lead, copper, zinc, many varieties of building stone, fire clay, cuma clay, common brick clay, sand of all kinds, gravel, mineral paint—every thing needed for a high civilization. Left to herself, she has the elements of all greatness. The single item of coal is too vast for an appreciative handling in figures. We can handle it in general terms like algebraical signs, but long before we get up into the millions and billions the human mind drops down from comprehension to mere symbolic apprehension.

When I tell you that nearly four-fifths of the entire State is underlaid with a deposit of coal more than forty feet thick on the average (now estimated, by recent surveys, at seventy feet thick), you can get some idea of its amount, as you do of the amount of the national debt. There it is! 41,000 square miles—one vast mine into which you could put any of the States; in which you could bury scores of European and ancient empires, and have room enough all round to work without knowing that they had been sepulchered there.

Put this vast coal-bed down by the other great coal deposits of the world, and its importance becomes manifest. Great Britain has 12,000 square miles of coal; Spain, 3,000; France, 1,719; Belgium, 578; Illinois about twice as many square miles as all combined. Virginia has 20,000 square miles; Pennsylvania, 16,000; Ohio, 12,000. Illinois has 41,000 square miles. One-seventh of all the known coal on this continent is in Illinois.

Could we sell the coal in this single State for one-seventh of one cent a ton it would pay the national debt. Converted into power, even with the wastage in our common engines, it would do more work than could be done by the entire race, beginning at Adam's wedding and working ten hours a day through all the centuries till the present time, and right on into the future at the same rate for the next 600,000 years.

Great Britain uses enough mechanical power to-day to give to each man, woman, and child in the kingdom the help and service of nineteen untiring servants. No wonder she has leisure and luxuries. No wonder the home of the common artisan has in it more luxuries than could be found in the palace of good old King Arthur. Think, if you can conceive of it, of the vast army of servants that slumber in the soil of Illinois, impatiently awaiting the call of Genius to come forth to minister to our comfort.

At the present rate of consumption England's coal supply will be exhausted in 250 years. When this is gone she must transfer her dominion either to the Indies, or to British America, which I would not resist; or to some other people, which I would regret as a loss to civilization.

COAL IS KING.

At the same rate of consumption (which far exceeds our own) the deposit of coal in Illinois will last 120,000 years. And her kingdom shall be an everlasting kingdom.

Let us turn now from this reserve power to the *annual products* of the State. We shall not be humiliated in this field. Here we strike the secret of our national credit. Nature provides a market in the constant appetite of the race. Men must eat, and if we can furnish the provisions we can command the treasure. All that a man hath will he give for his life.

According to the last census Illinois produced 30,000,000 of bushels of wheat. That is more wheat than was raised by any other State in the Union. She raised In 1875, 130,000,000 of bushels of corn—twice as much as any other State, and one-sixth of all the corn raised in the United States. She harvested 2,747,000 tons of hay, nearly one-tenth of all the hay in the Republic. It is not generally appreciated, but it is true, that the hay crop of the country is worth more than the cotton crop. The hay of Illinois equals the cotton of Louisiana. Go to Charleston, S. C., and see them peddling handfuls of hay or grass, almost as a curiosity, as we regard Chinese gods or the cryolite of Greenland; drink your coffee and *condensed milk;* and walk back from the coast for many a league through the sand and burs till you get up into the better atmosphere of the mountains, without seeing a waving meadow or a grazing herd; then you will begin to appreciate the meadows of the Prairie State, where the grass often grows sixteen feet high.

The value of her farm implements is $211,000,000, and the value of her live stock is only second to the great State of New York. in 1875 she had 25,000,000 hogs, and packed 2,113,845, about one-half of all that were packed in the United States. This is no insignificant item. Pork is a growing demand of the old world. Since the laborers of Europe have gotten a taste of our bacon, and we have learned how to pack it dry in boxes, like dry goods, the world has become the market.

The hog is on the march into the future. His nose is ordained to uncover the secrets of dominion, and his feet shall be guided by the star of empire.

Illinois marketed $57,000,000 worth of slaughtered animals—more than any other State, and a seventh of all the States.

Be patient with me, and pardon my pride, and I will give you a list of some of the things in which Illinois excels all other States.

Depth and richness of soil; per cent. of good ground; acres of improved land; large farms—some farms contain from 40,000 to 60,000 acres of cultivated land, 40,000 acres of corn on a single farm; number of farmers; amount of wheat, corn, oats and honey produced; value of animals for slaughter; number of hogs; amount of pork; number of horses —three times as many as Kentucky, the horse State.

Illinois excels all other States in miles of railroads and in miles of postal service, and in money orders sold per annum, and in the amount of lumber sold in her markets.

Illinois is only second in many important matters. This sample list comprises a few of the more important: Permanent school fund (good for a young state); total income for educational purposes; number of publishers of books, maps, papers, etc.; value of farm products and implements, and of live stock; in tons of coal mined.

The shipping of Illinois is only second to New York. Out of one port during the business hours of the season of navigation she sends forth a vessel every ten minutes. This does not include canal boats, which go one every five minutes. No wonder she is only second in number of bankers and brokers or in physicians and surgeons.

She is third in colleges, teachers and schools; cattle, lead, hay, flax, sorghum and beeswax.

She is fourth in population, in children enrolled in public schools, in law schools, in butter, potatoes and carriages.

She is fifth in value of real and personal property, in theological seminaries and colleges exclusively for women, in milk sold, and in boots and shoes manufactured, and in book-binding.

She is only seventh in the production of wood, while she is the twelfth in area. Surely that is well done for the Prairie State. She now has much more wood and growing timber than she had thirty years ago.

A few leading industries will justify emphasis. She manufactures $205,000,000 worth of goods, which places her well up toward New York and Pennsylvania. The number of her manufacturing establishments increased from 1860 to 1870, 300 per cent.; capital employed increased 350 per cent., and the amount of product increased 400 per cent. She issued 5,500,000 copies of commercial and financial newspapers—only second to New York. She has 6,759 miles of railroad, thus leading all other States, worth $636,458,000, using 3,245 engines, and 67,712 cars, making a train long enough to cover one-tenth of the entire roads of the State. Her stations are only five miles apart. She carried last year 15,795,000 passengers, an average of 36½ miles, or equal to taking her entire population twice across the State. More than two-thirds of her land is within five miles of a railroad, and less than two per cent. is more than fifteen miles away.

The State has a large financial interest in the Illinois Central railroad. The road was incorporated in 1850, and the State gave each alternate section for six miles on each side, and doubled the price of the remaining land, so keeping herself good. The road received 2,595,000 acres of land, and pays to the State one-seventh of the gross receipts. The State receives this year $350,000, and has received in all about $7,000,000. It is practically the people's road, and it has a most able and gentlemanly management. Add to this the annual receipts from the canal, $111,000, and a large per cent. of the State tax is provided for.

THE RELIGION AND MORALS

of the State keep step with her productions and growth. She was born of the missionary spirit. It was a minister who secured for her the ordinance of 1787, by which she has been saved from slavery, ignorance, and dishonesty. Rev. Mr. Wiley, pastor of a Scotch congregation in Randolph County, petitioned the Constitutional Convention of 1818 to recognize Jesus Christ as king, and the Scriptures as the only necessary guide and book of law. The convention did not act in the case, and the old Covenanters refused to accept citizenship. They never voted until 1824, when the slavery question was submitted to the people; then they all voted against it and cast the determining votes. Conscience has predominated whenever a great moral question has been submitted to the people.

But little mob violence has ever been felt in the State. In 1817 regulators disposed of a band of horse-thieves that infested the territory. The Mormon indignities finally awoke the same spirit. Alton was also the scene of a pro-slavery mob, in which Lovejoy was added to the list of martyrs. The moral sense of the people makes the law supreme, and gives to the State unruffled peace.

With $22,300,000 in church property, and 4,298 church organizations, the State has that divine police, the sleepless patrol of moral ideas, that alone is able to secure perfect safety. Conscience takes the knife from the assassin's hand and the bludgeon from the grasp of the highwayman. We sleep in safety, not because we are behind bolts and bars—these only fence against the innocent; not because a lone officer drowses on a distant corner of a street; not because a sheriff may call his posse from a remote part of the county; but because *conscience* guards the very portals of the air and stirs in the deepest recesses of the public mind. This spirit issues within the State 9,500,000 copies of religious papers annually, and receives still more from without. Thus the crime of the State is only one-fourth that of New York and one-half that of Pennsylvania.

Illinois never had but one duel between her own citizens. In Belleville, in 1820, Alphonso Stewart and William Bennett arranged to vindicate injured honor. The seconds agreed to make it a sham, and make them shoot blanks. Stewart was in the secret. Bennett mistrusted something, and, unobserved, slipped a bullet into his gun and killed Stewart. He then fled the State. After two years he was caught, tried, convicted, and, in spite of friends and political aid, was hung. This fixed the code of honor on a Christian basis, and terminated its use in Illinois.

The early preachers were ignorant men, who were accounted eloquent according to the strength of their voices. But they set the style for all public speakers. Lawyers and political speakers followed this rule. Gov.

Ford says: "Nevertheless, these first preachers were of incalculable benefit to the country. They inculcated justice and morality. To them are we indebted for the first Christian character of the Protestant portion of the people."

In education Illinois surpasses her material resources. The ordinance of 1787 consecrated one thirty-sixth of her soil to common schools, and the law of 1818, the first law that went upon her statutes, gave three per cent. of all the rest to

EDUCATION.

The old compact secures this interest forever, and by its yoking morality and intelligence it precludes the legal interference with the Bible in the public schools. With such a start it is natural that we should have 11,050 schools, and that our illiteracy should be less than New York or Pennsylvania, and only about one-half of Massachusetts. We are not to blame for not having more than one-half as many idiots as the great States. These public schools soon made colleges inevitable. The first college, still flourishing, was started in Lebanon in 1828, by the M. E. church, and named after Bishop McKendree. Illinois College, at Jacksonville, supported by the Presbyterians, followed in 1830. In 1832 the Baptists built Shurtleff College, at Alton. Then the Presbyterians built Knox College, at Galesburg, in 1838, and the Episcopalians built Jubilee College, at Peoria, in 1847. After these early years colleges have rained down. A settler could hardly encamp on the prairie but a college would spring up by his wagon. The State now has one very well endowed and equipped university, namely, the Northwestern University, at Evanston, with six colleges, ninety instructors, over 1,000 students, and $1,500,000 endowment.

Rev. J. M. Peck was the first educated Protestant minister in the State. He settled at Rock Spring, in St. Clair County, 1820, and left his impress on the State. Before 1837 only party papers were published, but Mr. Peck published a Gazetteer of Illinois. Soon after John Russell, of Bluffdale, published essays and tales showing genius. Judge James Hall published *The Illinois Monthly Magazine* with great ability, and an annual called *The Western Souvenir*, which gave him an enviable fame all over the United States. From these beginnings Illinois has gone on till she has more volumes in public libaaries even than Massachusetts, and of the 44,500,000 volumes in all the public libraries of the United States, she has one-thirteenth. In newspapers she stands fourth. Her increase is marvelous. In 1850 she issued 5,000,000 copies; in 1860, 27,590,000; in 1870, 113,140,000. In 1860 she had eighteen colleges and seminaries; in 1870 she had eighty. That is a grand advance for the war decade.

This brings us to a record unsurpassed in the history of any age,

THE WAR RECORD OF ILLINOIS.

I hardly know where to begin, or how to advance, or what to say. I can at best give you only a broken synopsis of her deeds, and you must put them in the order of glory for yourself. Her sons have always been foremost on fields of danger. In 1832-33, at the call of Gov. Reynolds, her sons drove Blackhawk over the Mississippi.

When the Mexican war came, in May, 1846, 8,370 men offered themselves when only 3,720 could be accepted. The fields of Buena Vista and Vera Cruz, and the storming of Cerro Gordo, will carry the glory of Illinois soldiers along after the infamy of the cause they served has been forgotten. But it was reserved till our day for her sons to find a field and cause and foemen that could fitly illustrate their spirit and heroism. Illinois put into her own regiments for the United States government 256,000 men, and into the army through other States enough to swell the number to 290,000. This far exceeds all the soldiers of the federal government in all the war of the revolution. Her total years of service were over 600,000. She enrolled men from eighteen to forty-five years of age when the law of Congress in 1864—the test time—only asked for those from twenty to forty-five. Her enrollment was otherwise excessive. Her people wanted to go, and did not take the pains to correct the enrollment. Thus the basis of fixing the quota was too great, and then the quota itself, at least in the trying time, was far above any other State.

Thus the demand on some counties, as Monroe, for example, took every able-bodied man in the county, and then did not have enough to fill the quota. Moreover, Illinois sent 20,844 men for ninety or one hundred days, for whom no credit was asked. When Mr. Lincoln's attention was called to the inequality of the quota compared with other States, he replied, "The country needs the sacrifice. We must put the whip on the free horse." In spite of all these disadvantages Illinois gave to the country 73,000 years of service above all calls. With one-thirteenth of the population of the loyal States, she sent regularly one-tenth of all the soldiers, and in the peril of the closing calls, when patriots were few and weary, she then sent one-eighth of all that were called for by her loved and honored son in the white house. Her mothers and daughters went into the fields to raise the grain and keep the children together, while the fathers and older sons went to the harvest fields of the world. I knew a father and four sons who agreed that one of them must stay at home; and they pulled straws from a stack to see who might go. The father was left. The next day he came into the camp, saying: "Mother says she can get the crops in, and I am going, too." I know large Methodist churches from which every male member went to the army. Do you want to know what these heroes from Illinois did in the field? Ask any soldier with a good record of his own, who is thus able to judge, and he will tell you that the Illinois men went in to win. It is common history that the greater victories were won in the West. When everything else looked dark Illinois was gaining victories all down the river, and dividing the confederacy. Sherman took with him on his great march forty-five regiments of Illinois infantry, three companies of artillery, and one company of cavalry. He could not avoid

GOING TO THE SEA.

If he had been killed, I doubt not the men would have gone right on. Lincoln answered all rumors of Sherman's defeat with, "It is impossible; there is a mighty sight of fight in 100,000 Western men." Illinois soldiers brought home 300 battle-flags. The first United States flag that floated over Richmond was an Illinois flag. She sent messengers and nurses to every field and hospital, to care for her sick and wounded sons. She said, "These suffering ones are my sons, and I will care for them."

When individuals had given all, then cities and towns came forward with their credit to the extent of many millions, to aid these men and their families.

Illinois gave the country the great general of the war—Ulysses S. Grant—since honored with two terms of the Presidency of the United States.

One other name from Illinois comes up in all minds, embalmed in all hearts, that must have the supreme place in this story of our glory and of our nation's honor; that name is Abraham Lincoln, of Illinois.

The analysis of Mr. Lincoln's character is difficult on account of its symmetry.

In this age we look with admiration at his uncompromising honesty. And well we may, for this saved us. Thousands throughout the length and breadth of our country who knew him only as "Honest Old Abe," voted for him on that account; and wisely did they choose, for no other man could have carried us through the fearful night of the war. When his plans were too vast for our comprehension, and his faith in the cause too sublime for our participation; when it was all night about us, and all dread before us, and all sad and desolate behind us; when not one ray shone upon our cause; when traitors were haughty and exultant at the South, and fierce and blasphemous at the North; when the loyal men here seemed almost in the minority; when the stoutest heart quailed, the bravest cheek paled; when generals were defeating each other for place, and contractors were leeching out the very heart's blood of the prostrate republic: when every thing else had failed us, we looked at this calm, patient man standing like a rock in the storm, and said: "Mr. Lincoln is honest, and we can trust him still." Holding to this single point with the energy of faith and despair we held together, and, under God, he brought us through to victory.

His practical wisdom made him the wonder of all lands. With such certainty did Mr. Lincoln follow causes to their ultimate effects, that his foresight of contingencies seemed almost prophetic.

He is radiant with all the great virtues, and his memory shall shed a glory upon this age that shall fill the eyes of men as they look into history. Other men have excelled him in some point, but, taken at all points, all in all, he stands head and shoulders above every other man of 6,000 years. An administrator, he saved the nation in the perils of unparalleled civil war. A statesman, he justified his measures by their success. A philanthropist, he gave liberty to one race and salvation to another. A moralist, he bowed from the summit of human power to the foot of the Cross, and became a Christian. A mediator, he exercised mercy under the most absolute abeyance to law. A leader, he was no partisan. A commander, he was untainted with blood. A ruler in desperate times, he was unsullied with crime. A man, he has left no word of passion, no thought of malice, no trick of craft, no act of jealousy, no purpose of selfish ambition. Thus perfected, without a model, and without a peer, he was dropped into these troubled years to adorn and embellish all that is good and all that is great in our humanity, and to present to all coming time the representative of the divine idea of free government.

It is not too much to say that away down in the future, when the republic has fallen from its niche in the wall of time; when the great war itself shall have faded out in the distance like a mist on the horizon; when the Anglo-Saxon language shall be spoken only by the tongue of the stranger; then the generations looking this way shall see the great president as the supreme figure in this vortex of historv

CHICAGO.

It is impossible in our brief space to give more than a meager sketch of such a city as Chicago, which is in itself the greatest marvel of the Prairie State. This mysterious, majestic, mighty city, born first of water, and next of fire; sown in weakness, and raised in power; planted among the willows of the marsh, and crowned with the glory of the mountains; sleeping on the bosom of the prairie, and rocked on the bosom of the sea; the youngest city of the world, and still the eye of the prairie, as Damascus, the oldest city of the world, is the eye of the desert. With a commerce far exceeding that of Corinth on her isthmus, in the highway to the East; with the defenses of a continent piled around her by the thousand miles, making her far safer than Rome on the banks of the Tiber;

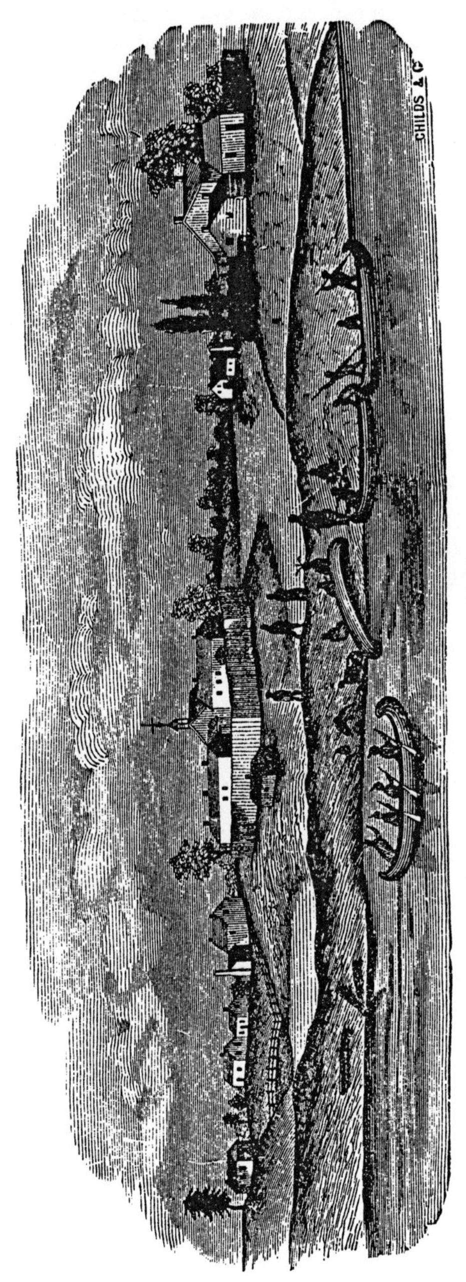

CHICAGO IN 1833.

with schools eclipsing Alexandria and Athens; with liberties more conspicuous than those of the old republics; with a heroism equal to the first Carthage, and with a sanctity scarcely second to that of Jerusalem—set your thoughts on all this, lifted into the eyes of all men by the miracle of its growth, illuminated by the flame of its fall, and transfigured by the divinity of its resurrection, and you will feel, as I do, the utter impossibility of compassing this subject as it deserves. Some impression of her importance is received from the shock her burning gave to the civilized world.

When the doubt of her calamity was removed, and the horrid fact was accepted, there went a shudder over all cities, and a quiver over all lands. There was scarcely a town in the civilized world that did not shake on the brink of this opening chasm. The flames of our homes reddened all skies. The city was set upon a hill, and could not be hid. All eyes were turned upon it. To have struggled and suffered amid the scenes of its fall is as distinguishing as to have fought at Thermopylæ, or Salamis, or Hastings, or Waterloo, or Bunker Hill.

Its calamity amazed the world, because it was felt to be the common property of mankind.

The early history of the city is full of interest, just as the early history of such a man as Washington or Lincoln becomes public property, and is cherished by every patriot.

Starting with 560 acres in 1833, it embraced and occupied 23,000 acres in 1869, and, having now a population of more than 500,000, it commands general attention.

The first settler—Jean Baptiste Pointe au Sable, a mulatto from the West Indies—came and began trade with the Indians in 1796. John Kinzie became his successor in 1804, in which year Fort Dearborn was erected.

A mere trading-post was kept here from that time till about the time of the Blackhawk war, in 1832. It was not the city. It was merely a cock crowing at midnight. The morning was not yet. In 1833 the settlement about the fort was incorporated as a town. The voters were divided on the propriety of such corporation, twelve voting for it and one against it. Four years later it was incorporated as a city, and embraced 560 acres.

The produce handled in this city is an indication of its power. Grain and flour were imported from the East till as late as 1837. The first exportation by way of experiment was in 1839. Exports exceeded imports first in 1842. The Board of Trade was organized in 1848, but it was so weak that it needed nursing till 1855. Grain was purchased by the wagon-load in the street.

I remember sitting with my father on a load of wheat, in the long line of wagons along Lake street, while the buyers came and untied the bags, and examined the grain, and made their bids. That manner of business had to cease with the day of small things. Now our elevators will hold 15,000,000 bushels of grain. The cash value of the produce handled in a year is $215,000,000, and the produce weighs 7,000,000 tons or 700,000 car loads. This handles thirteen and a half ton each minute, all the year round. One tenth of all the wheat in the United States is handled in Chicago. Even as long ago as 1853 the receipts of grain in Chicago exceeded those of the goodly city of St. Louis, and in 1854 the exports of grain from Chicago exceeded those of New York and doubled those of St. Petersburg, Archangel, or Odessa, the largest grain markets in Europe.

The manufacturing interests of the city are not contemptible. In 1873 manufactories employed 45,000 operatives; in 1876, 60,000. The manufactured product in 1875 was worth $177,000,000.

No estimate of the size and power of Chicago would be adequate that did not put large emphasis on the railroads. Before they came thundering along our streets canals were the hope of our country. But who ever thinks now of traveling by canal packets? In June, 1852, there were only forty miles of railroad connected with the city. The old Galena division of the Northwestern ran out to Elgin. But now, who can count the trains and measure the roads that seek a terminus or connection in this city? The lake stretches away to the north, gathering in to this center all the harvests that might otherwise pass to the north of us. If you will take a map and look at the adjustment of railroads, you will see, first, that Chicago is the great railroad center of the world, as New York is the commercial city of this continent; and, second, that the railroad lines form the iron spokes of a great wheel whose hub is this city. The lake furnishes the only break in the spokes, and this seems simply to have pushed a few spokes together on each shore. See the eighteen trunk lines, exclusive of eastern connections.

Pass round the circle, and view their numbers and extent. There is the great Northwestern, with all its branches, one branch creeping along the lake shore, and so reaching to the north, into the Lake Superior regions, away to the right, and on to the Northern Pacific on the left, swinging around Green Bay for iron and copper and silver, twelve months in the year, and reaching out for the wealth of the great agricultural belt and isothermal line traversed by the Northern Pacific. Another branch, not so far north, feeling for the heart of the Badger State. Another pushing lower down the Mississippi—all these make many connections, and tapping all the vast wheat regions of Minnesota, Wisconsin, Iowa, and all the regions this side of sunset. There is that elegant road, the Chicago, Burlington & Quincy, running out a goodly number of

OLD FORT DEARBORN, 1830.

PRESENT SITE OF LAKE STREET BRIDGE, CHICAGO, IN 1833.

branches, and reaping the great fields this side of the Missouri River. I can only mention the Chicago, Alton & St. Louis, *our* Illinois Central, described elsewhere, and the Chicago & Rock Island. Further around we come to the lines connecting us with all the eastern cities. The Chicago, Indianapolis & St. Louis, the Pittsburgh, Fort Wayne & Chicago, the Lake Shore & Michigan Southern, and the Michigan Central and Great Western, give us many highways to the seaboard. Thus we reach the Mississippi at five points, from St. Paul to Cairo and the Gulf itself by two routes. We also reach Cincinnati and Baltimore, and Pittsburgh and Philadelphia, and New York. North and south run the water courses of the lakes and the rivers, broken just enough at this point to make a pass. Through this, from east to west, run the long lines that stretch from ocean to ocean.

This is the neck of the glass, and the golden sands of commerce must pass into our hands. Altogether we have more than 10,000 miles of railroad, directly tributary to this city, seeking to unload their wealth in our coffers. All these roads have come themselves by the infallible instinct of capital. Not a dollar was ever given by the city to secure one of them, and only a small per cent. of stock taken originally by her citizens, and that taken simply as an investment. Coming in the natural order of events, they will not be easily diverted.

There is still another showing to all this. The connection between New York and San Francisco is by the middle route. This passes inevitably through Chicago. St. Louis wants the Southern Pacific or Kansas Pacific, and pushes it out through Denver, and so on up to Cheyenne. But before the road is fairly under way, the Chicago roads shove out to Kansas City, making even the Kansas Pacific a feeder, and actually leaving St. Louis out in the cold. It is not too much to expect that Dakota, Montana, and Washington Territory will find their great market in Chicago.

But these are not all. Perhaps I had better notice here the ten or fifteen new roads that have just entered, or are just entering, our city. Their names are all that is necessary to give. Chicago & St. Paul, looking up the Red River country to the British possessions; the Chicago, Atlantic & Pacific; the Chicago, Decatur & State Line; the Baltimore & Ohio; the Chicago, Danville & Vincennes; the Chicago & LaSalle Railroad; the Chicago, Pittsburgh & Cincinnati; the Chicago and Canada Southern; the Chicago and Illinois River Railroad. These, with their connections, and with the new connections of the old roads, already in process of erection, give to Chicago not less than 10,000 miles of new tributaries from the richest land on the continent. Thus there will be added to the reserve power, to the capital within reach of this city, not less than $1,000,000,000.

Add to all this transporting power the ships that sail one every nine minutes of the business hours of the season of navigation; add, also, the canal boats that leave one every five minutes during the same time—and you will see something of the business of the city.

THE COMMERCE OF THIS CITY

has been leaping along to keep pace with the growth of the country around us. In 1852, our commerce reached the hopeful sum of $20,000,000. In 1870 it reached $400,000,000. In 1871 it was pushed up above $450,000,000. And in 1875 it touched nearly double that.

One-half of our imported goods come directly to Chicago. Grain enough is exported directly from our docks to the old world to employ a semi-weekly line of steamers of 3,000 tons capacity. This branch is not likely to be greatly developed. Even after the great Welland Canal is completed we shall have only fourteen feet of water. The great ocean vessels will continue to control the trade.

The banking capital of Chicago is $24,431,000. Total exchange in 1875, $659,000,000. Her wholesale business in 1875 was $294,000,000. The rate of taxes is less than in any other great city.

The schools of Chicago are unsurpassed in America. Out of a population of 300,000 there were only 186 persons between the ages of six and twenty-one unable to read. This is the best known record.

In 1831 the mail system was condensed into a half-breed, who went on foot to Niles, Mich., once in two weeks, and brought back what papers and news he could find. As late as 1846 there was often only one mail a week. A post-office was established in Chicago in 1833, and the postmaster nailed up old boot-legs on one side of his shop to serve as boxes for the nabobs and literary men.

It is an interesting fact in the growth of the young city that in the active life of the business men of that day the mail matter has grown to a daily average of over 6,500 pounds. It speaks equally well for the intelligence of the people and the commercial importance of the place, that the mail matter distributed to the territory immediately tributary to Chicago is seven times greater than that distributed to the territory immediately tributary to St. Louis.

The improvements that have characterized the city are as startling as the city itself. In 1831, Mark Beaubien established a ferry over the river, and put himself under bonds to carry all the citizens free for the privilege of charging strangers. Now there are twenty-four large bridges and two tunnels.

In 1833 the government expended $30,000 on the harbor. Then commenced that series of manœuvers with the river that has made it one of the world's curiosities. It used to wind around in the lower end of the town, and make its way rippling over the sand into the lake at the foot of Madison street. They took it up and put it down where it now is. It was a narrow stream, so narrow that even moderately small crafts had to go up through the willows and cat's tails to the point near Lake street bridge, and back up one of the branches to get room enough in which to turn around.

In 1844 the quagmires in the streets were first pontooned by plank roads, which acted in wet weather as public squirt-guns. Keeping you out of the mud, they compromised by squirting the mud over you. The wooden-block pavements came to Chicago in 1857. In 1840 water was delivered by peddlers in carts or by hand. Then a twenty-five horse-power engine pushed it through hollow or bored logs along the streets till 1854, when it was introduced into the houses by new works. The first fire-engine was used in 1835, and the first steam fire-engine in 1859. Gas was utilized for lighting the city in 1850. The Young Men's Christian Association was organized in 1858, and horse railroads carried them to their work in 1859. The museum was opened in 1863. The alarm telegraph adopted in 1864. The opera-house built in 1865. The city grew from 560 acres in 1833 to 23,000 in 1869. In 1834, the taxes amounted to $48.90, and the trustees of the town borrowed $60 more for opening and improving streets. In 1835, the legislature authorized a loan of $2,000, and the treasurer and street commissioners resigned rather than plunge the town into such a gulf.

Now the city embraces 36 square miles of territory, and has 30 miles of water front, besides the outside harbor of refuge, of 400 acres, inclosed by a crib sea-wall. One-third of the city has been raised up an average of eight feet, giving good pitch to the 263 miles of sewerage. The water of the city is above all competition. It is received through two tunnels extending to a crib in the lake two miles from shore. The closest analysis fails to detect any impurities, and, received 35 feet below the surface, it is always clear and cold. The first tunnel is five feet two inches in diameter and two miles long, and can deliver 50,000,000 of gallons per day. The second tunnel is seven feet in diameter and six miles long, running four miles under the city, and can deliver 100,000,000 of gallons per day. This water is distributed through 410 miles of water-mains.

The three grand engineering exploits of the city are: First, lifting the city up on jack-screws, whole squares at a time, without interrupting the business, thus giving us good drainage; second, running the tunnels under the lake, giving us the best water in the world; and third, the turning the current of the river in its own channel, delivering us from the old abominations, and making decency possible. They redound about equally to the credit of the engineering, to the energy of the people, and to the health of the city.

That which really constitutes the city, its indescribable spirit, its soul, the way it lights up in every feature in the hour of action, has not been touched. In meeting strangers, one is often surprised how some homely women marry so well. Their forms are bad, their gait uneven and awkward, their complexion is dull, their features are misshapen and mismatched, and when we see them there is no beauty that we should desire them. But when once they are aroused on some subject, they put on new proportions. They light up into great power. The real person comes out from its unseemly ambush, and captures us at will. They have power. They have ability to cause things to come to pass. We no longer wonder why they are in such high demand. So it is with our city.

There is no grand scenery except the two seas, one of water, the other of prairie. Nevertheless, there is a spirit about it, a push, a breadth, a power, that soon makes it a place never to be forsaken. One soon ceases to believe in impossibilities. Balaams are the only prophets that are disappointed. The bottom that has been on the point of falling out has been there so long that it has grown fast. It can not fall out. It has all the capital of the world itching to get inside the corporation.

The two great laws that govern the growth and size of cities are, first, the amount of territory for which they are the distributing and receiving points; second, the number of medium or moderate dealers that do this distributing. Monopolists build up themselves, not the cities. They neither eat, wear, nor live in proportion to their business. Both these laws help Chicago.

The tide of trade is eastward—not up or down the map, but across the map. The lake runs up a wingdam for 500 miles to gather in the business. Commerce can not ferry up there for seven months in the year, and the facilities for seven months can do the work for twelve. Then the great region west of us is nearly all good, productive land. Dropping south into the trail of St. Louis, you fall into vast deserts and rocky districts, useful in holding the world together. St. Louis and Cincinnati, instead of rivaling and hurting Chicago, are her greatest sureties of dominion. They are far enough away to give sea-room,—farther off than Paris is from London,—and yet they are near enough to prevent the springing up of any other great city between them.

St. Louis will be helped by the opening of the Mississippi, but also hurt. That will put New Orleans on her feet, and with a railroad running over into Texas and so West, she will tap the streams that now crawl up the Texas and Missouri road. The current is East, not North, and a seaport at New Orleans can not permanently help St. Louis.

Chicago is in the field almost alone, to handle the wealth of one-fourth of the territory of this great republic. This strip of seacoast divides its margins between Portland, Boston, New York, Philadelphia, Baltimore and Savannah, or some other great port to be created for the South in the next decade. But Chicago has a dozen empires casting their treasures into her lap. On a bed of coal that can run all the machinery of the world for 500 centuries; in a garden that can feed the race by the thousand years; at the head of the lakes that give her a temperature as a summer resort equaled by no great city in the land; with a climate that insures the health of her citizens; surrounded by all the great deposits of natural wealth in mines aud forests and herds, Chicago is the wonder of to-day, and will be *the city of the future.*

MASSACRE AT FORT DEARBORN.

During the war of 1812, Fort Dearborn became the theater of stirring events. The garrison consisted of fifty-four men under command of Captain Nathan Heald, assisted by Lieutenant Helm (son-in-law of Mrs. Kinzie) and Ensign Ronan. Dr. Voorhees was surgeon. The only residents at the post at that time were the wives of Captain Heald and Lieutenant Helm, and a few of the soldiers, Mr. Kinzie and his family, and a few Canadian *voyageurs*, with their wives and children. The soldiers and Mr. Kinzie were on most friendly terms with the Pottawattamies and Winnebagos, the principal tribes around them, but they could not win them from their attachment to the British.

One evening in April, 1812, Mr. Kinzie sat playing on his violin and his children were dancing to the music, when Mrs. Kinzie came rushing into the house, pale with terror, and exclaiming: "The Indians! the Indians!" "What? Where?" eagerly inquired Mr. Kinzie. "Up at Lee's, killing and scalping," answered the frightened mother, who, when the alarm was given, was attending Mrs. Barnes (just confined) living not far off. Mr. Kinzie and his family crossed the river and took refuge in the fort, to which place Mrs. Barnes and her infant not a day old were safely conveyed. The rest of the inhabitants took shelter in the fort. This alarm was caused by a scalping party of Winnebagos, who hovered about the fort several days, when they disappeared, and for several weeks the inhabitants were undisturbed.

On the 7th of August, 1812, General Hull, at Detroit, sent orders to Captain Heald to evacuate Fort Dearborn, and to distribute all the United States property to the Indians in the neighborhood—a most insane order. The Pottawattamie chief, who brought the dispatch, had more wisdom than the commanding general. He advised Captain Heald not to make the distribution. Said he: "Leave the fort and stores as they are, and let the Indians make distribution for themselves; and while they are engaged in the business, the white people may escape to Fort Wayne."

RUINS OF CHICAGO.

Captain Heald held a council with the Indians on the afternoon of the 12th, in which his officers refused to join, for they had been informed that treachery was designed—that the Indians intended to murder the white people in the council, and then destroy those in the fort. Captain Heald, however, took the precaution to open a port-hole displaying a cannon pointing directly upon the council, and by that means saved his life.

Mr. Kinzie, who knew the Indians well, begged Captain Heald not to confide in their promises, nor distribute the arms and munitions among them, for it would only put power into their hands to destroy the whites. Acting upon this advice, Heald resolved to withhold the munitions of war; and on the night of the 13th, after the distribution of the other property had been made, the powder, ball and liquors were thrown into the river, the muskets broken up and destroyed.

Black Partridge, a friendly chief, came to Captain Heald, and said: "Linden birds have been singing in my ears to-day: be careful on the march you are going to take." On that dark night vigilant Indians had crept near the fort and discovered the destruction of their promised booty going on within. The next morning the powder was seen floating on the surface of the river. The savages were exasperated and made loud complaints and threats.

On the following day when preparations were making to leave the fort, and all the inmates were deeply impressed with a sense of impending danger, Capt. Wells, an uncle of Mrs. Heald, was discovered upon the Indian trail among the sand-hills on the borders of the lake, not far distant, with a band of mounted Miamis, of whose tribe he was chief, having been adopted by the famous Miami warrior, Little Turtle. When news of Hull's surrender reached Fort Wayne, he had started with this force to assist Heald in defending Fort Dearborn. He was too late. Every means for its defense had been destroyed the night before, and arrangements were made for leaving the fort on the morning of the 15th.

It was a warm bright morning in the middle of August. Indications were positive that the savages intended to murder the white people; and when they moved out of the southern gate of the fort, the march was like a funeral procession. The band, feeling the solemnity of the occasion, struck up the Dead March in Saul.

Capt. Wells, who had blackened his face with gun-powder in token of his fate, took the lead with his band of Miamis, followed by Capt. Heald, with his wife by his side on horseback. Mr. Kinzie hoped by his personal influence to avert the impending blow, and therefore accompanied them, leaving his family in a boat in charge of a friendly Indian, to be taken to his trading station at the site of Niles, Michigan, in the event of his death.

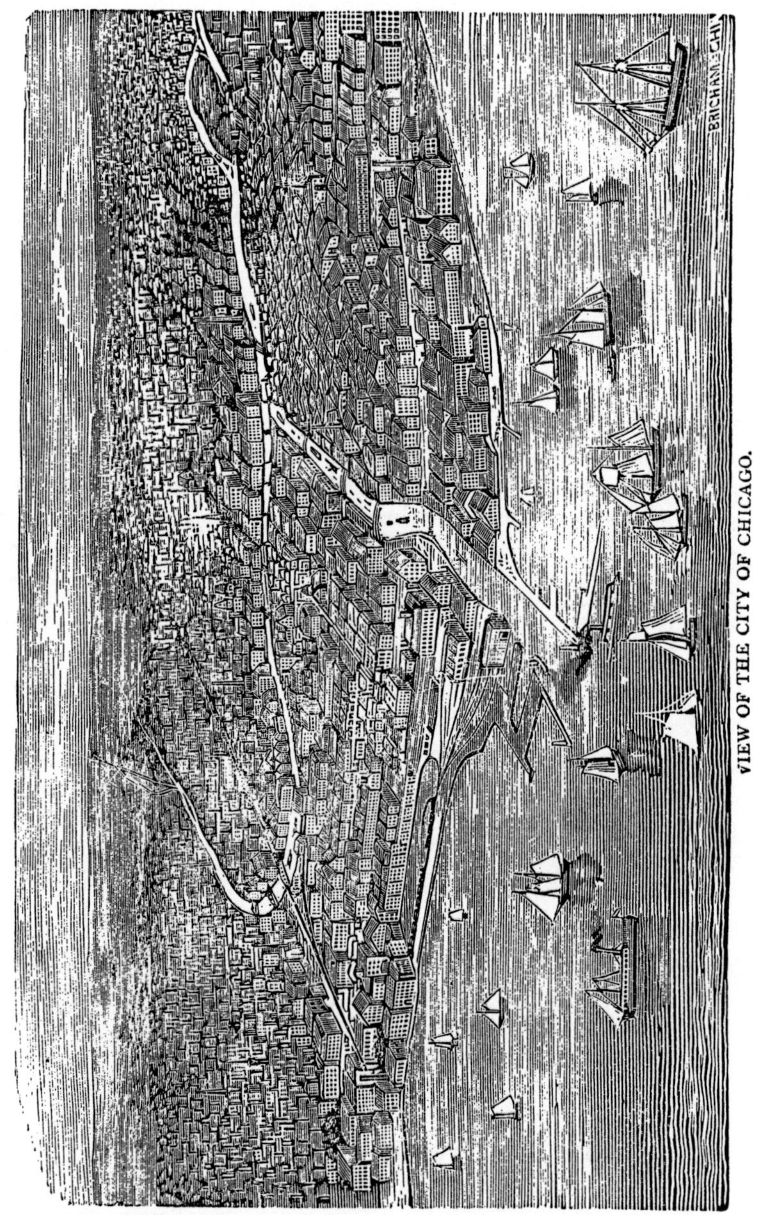

VIEW OF THE CITY OF CHICAGO.

The procession moved slowly along the lake shore till they reached the sand-hills between the prairie and the beach, when the Pottawattamie escort, under the leadership of Blackbird, filed to the right, placing those hills between them and the white people. Wells, with his Miamis, had kept in the advance. They suddenly came rushing back, Wells exclaiming, "They are about to attack us; form instantly." These words were quickly followed by a storm of bullets, which came whistling over the little hills which the treacherous savages had made the covert for their murderous attack. The white troops charged upon the Indians, drove them back to the prairie, and then the battle was waged between fifty-four soldiers, twelve civilians and three or four women (the cowardly Miamis having fled at the outset) against five hundred Indian warriors. The white people, hopeless, resolved to sell their lives as dearly as possible. Ensign Ronan wielded his weapon vigorously, even after falling upon his knees weak from the loss of blood. Capt. Wells, who was by the side of his niece, Mrs. Heald, when the conflict began, behaved with the greatest coolness and courage. He said to her, "We have not the slightest chance for life. We must part to meet no more in this world. God bless you." And then he dashed forward. Seeing a young warrior, painted like a demon, climb into a wagon in which were twelve children, and tomahawk them all, he cried out, unmindful of his personal danger, "If that is your game, butchering women and children, I will kill too." He spurred his horse towards the Indian camp, where they had left their squaws and papooses, hotly pursued by swift-footed young warriors, who sent bullets whistling after him. One of these killed his horse and wounded him severely in the leg. With a yell the young braves rushed to make him their prisoner and reserve him for torture. He resolved not to be made a captive, and by the use of the most provoking epithets tried to induce them to kill him instantly. He called a fiery young chief a *squaw*, when the enraged warrior killed Wells instantly with his tomahawk, jumped upon his body, cut out his heart, and ate a portion of the warm morsel with savage delight!

In this fearful combat women bore a conspicuous part. Mrs. Heald was an excellent equestrian and an expert in the use of the rifle. She fought the savages bravely, receiving several severe wounds. Though faint from the loss of blood, she managed to keep her saddle. A savage raised his tomahawk to kill her, when she looked him full in the face, and with a sweet smile and in a gentle voice said, in his own language, "Surely you will not kill a squaw!" The arm of the savage fell, and the life of the heroic woman was saved.

Mrs. Helm, the step-daughter of Mr. Kinzie, had an encounter with a stout Indian, who attempted to tomahawk her. Springing to one side, she received the glancing blow on her shoulder, and at the same instant seized the savage round the neck with her arms and endeavored to get hold of his scalping knife, which hung in a sheath at his breast. While she was thus struggling she was dragged from her antagonist by another powerful Indian, who bore her, in spite of her struggles, to the margin of the lake and plunged her in. To her astonishment she was held by him so that she would not drown, and she soon perceived that she was in the hands of the friendly Black Partridge, who had saved her life.

The wife of Sergeant Holt, a large and powerful woman, behaved as bravely as an Amazon. She rode a fine, high-spirited horse, which the Indians coveted, and several of them attacked her with the butts of their guns, for the purpose of dismounting her; but she used the sword which she had snatched from her disabled husband so skillfully that she foiled them; and, suddenly wheeling her horse, she dashed over the prairie, followed by the savages shouting, "The brave woman! the brave woman! Don't hurt her!" They finally overtook her, and while she was fighting them in front, a powerful savage came up behind her, seized her by the neck and dragged her to the ground. Horse and woman were made captives. Mrs. Holt was a long time a captive among the Indians, but was afterwards ransomed.

In this sharp conflict two-thirds of the white people were slain and wounded, and all their horses, baggage and provision were lost. Only twenty-eight straggling men now remained to fight five hundred Indians rendered furious by the sight of blood. They succeeded in breaking through the ranks of the murderers and gaining a slight eminence on the prairie near the Oak Woods. The Indians did not pursue, but gathered on their flanks, while the chiefs held a consultation on the sand-hills, and showed signs of willingness to parley. It would have been madness on the part of the whites to renew the fight; and so Capt. Heald went forward and met Blackbird on the open prairie, where terms of surrender were soon agreed upon. It was arranged that the white people should give up their arms to Blackbird, and that the survivors should become prisoners of war, to be exchanged for ransoms as soon as practicable. With this understanding captives and captors started for the Indian camp near the fort, to which Mrs. Helm had been taken bleeding and suffering by Black Partridge, and had met her step-father and learned that her husband was safe.

A new scene of horror was now opened at the Indian camp. The wounded, not being included in the terms of surrender, as it was interpreted by the Indians, and the British general, Proctor, having offered a liberal bounty for American scalps, delivered at Malden, nearly all the wounded men were killed and scalped, and the price of the trophies was afterwards paid by the British government.

Jno A Rawlins

(DECEASED)

LATE SECTY. OF WAR

SHABBONA.

This celebrated Indian chief, whose portrait appears in this work, deserves more than a passing notice. Although Shabbona was not so conspicuous as Tecumseh or Black Hawk, yet in point of merit he was superior to either of them.

Shabbona was born at an Indian village on the Kankakee River, now in Will County, about the year 1775. While young he was made chief of the band, and went to Shabbona Grove, now DeKalb County, where they were found in the early settlement of the county.

In the war of 1812 Shabbona with his warriors joined Tecumseh, was aid to that great chief, and stood by his side when he fell at the battle of the Thames. At the time of the Winnebago war, in 1827, he visited almost every village among the Pottawatomies, and by his persuasive arguments prevented them from taking part in the war. By request of the citizens of Chicago, Shabbona, accompanied by Billy Caldwell (Sauganash), visited Big Foot's village at Geneva Lake, in order to pacify the warriors, as fears were entertained that they were about to raise the tomahawk against the whites. Here Shabbona was taken prisoner by Big Foot, and his life threatened, but on the following day was set at liberty. From that time the Indians (through reproach) styled him "the white man's friend," and many times his life was endangered.

Before the Black Hawk war, Shabbona met in council at two different times, and by his influence prevented his people from taking part with the Sacs and Foxes. After the death of Black Partridge and Senachwine, no chief among the Pottawatomies exerted so much influence as Shabbona. Black Hawk, aware of this influence, visited him at two different times, in order to enlist him in his cause, but was unsuccessful. While Black Hawk was a prisoner at Jefferson Barracks, he said, had it not been for Shabbona the whole Pottawatomie nation would have joined his standard, and he could have continued the war for years.

To Shabbona many of the early settlers of Illinois owe the preservation of their lives, for it is a well-known fact, had he not notified the people of their danger, a large portion of them would have fallen victims to the tomahawk of savages. By saving the lives of whites he endangered his own, for the Sacs and Foxes threatened to kill him, and made two attempts to execute their threats. They killed Pypeogee, his son, and Pyps, his nephew, and hunted him down as though he was a wild beast.

Shabbona had a reservation of two sections of land at his Grove, but by leaving it and going west for a short time, the Government declared the reservation forfeited, and sold it the same as other vacant land. On Shabbona's return, and finding his possessions gone, he was very sad and broken down in spirit, and left the Grove for ever. The citizens of Ottawa raised money and bought him a tract of land on the Illinois River, above Seneca, in Grundy County, on which they built a house, and supplied him with means to live on. He lived here until his death, which occurred on the 17th of July, 1859, in the eighty-fourth year of his age, and was buried with great pomp in the cemetery at Morris. His squaw, Pokanoka, was drowned in Mazen Creek, Grundy County, on the 30th of November, 1864, and was buried by his side.

In 1861 subscriptions were taken up in many of the river towns, to erect a monument over the remains of Shabbona, but the war breaking out, the enterprise was abandoned. Only a plain marble slab marks the resting-place of this friend of the white man.

Abstract of Illinois State Laws.

BILLS OF EXCHANGE AND PROMISSORY NOTES.

No *promissory note*, *check*, *draft*, *bill of exchange*, *order*, *or note*, *negotiable instrument* payable at sight, or on demand, or on presentment, shall be entitled to *days of grace*. *All other bills of exchange*, *drafts or notes* are entitled to *three days of grace*. All the above mentioned paper falling due on *Sunday*, *New Years' Day*, *the Fourth of July*, *Christmas*, or any day appointed or recommended by the *President of the United States* or the *Governor of the State* as a day of *fast or thanksgiving*, shall be deemed as due on the day previous, and should two or more of these days come together, then such instrument shall be treated as due on the day *previous* to the first of said days. *No defense* can be made against a *negotiable instrument* (*assigned before due*) in the hands of the assignee without notice, *except fraud was used* in obtaining the same. To hold an *indorser*, due *diligence* must be used *by suit*, in collecting of the maker, unless suit would have been unavailing. Notes payable to *person named* or to order, in order to absolutely *transfer title*, must be indorsed by the *payee*. Notes payable to *bearer* may be *transferred by delivery*, and when so payable *every indorser* thereon is held as a *guarantor of payment* unless otherwise expressed.

In computing interest or discount on negotiable instruments, a *month* shall be considered a *calendar month or twelfth of a year*, and for less than a month, a day shall be figured a *thirtieth* part of a month. Notes *only bear interest* when so expressed, but after due they draw the legal interest, even if not stated.

INTEREST.

The *legal rate* of interest is *six per cent*. Parties *may agree in writing* on a rate not exceeding *ten per cent*. If a rate of interest greater than ten per cent. is contracted for, it works a *forfeiture of the whole of said interest*, and only the principal can be recovered.

DESCENT.

When *no will is made*, the property of a deceased person is distributed as follows:

First. To his or her children and their descendants in equal parts; the descendants of the deceased *child or grandchild* taking the share of their deceased parents in equal parts among them.

Second. Where there is no child, nor descendant of such child, and no widow or surviving husband, then to the parents, brothers and sisters of the deceased, and their descendants, in equal parts, the surviving parent, if either be dead, taking a double portion; and if there is no parent living, then to the brothers and sisters of the intestate and their descendants.

Third. When there is *a widow* or *surviving husband, and no child or children,* or descendants of the same, then one-half of the real estate and the whole of the personal estate shall *descend* to *such widow* or *surviving husband,* absolutely, and the other half of the real estate shall descend as in other cases where there is no child or children or descendants of the same.

Fourth. When there *is a widow or surviving husband* and *also a child or children,* or descendants of the latter, then *one third* of all the personal estate to the *widow* or *surviving husband* absolutely.

Fifth. If there is *no child, parent, brother or sister,* or descendants of either of them, and no widow or surviving husband, then in *equal* parts to the *next of kin* to the intestate in equal degree. Collaterals shall not be represented except with the descendants of brothers and sisters of the intestate, and there shall be no *distinction between kindred of the whole and the half blood.*

Sixth. If any intestate leaves a *widow or surviving husband* and *no kindred,* then to *such widow or surviving husband;* and if there is no such widow or surviving husband, it shall escheat to and vest in the county where the same, or the greater portion thereof, is situated.

WILLS AND ESTATES OF DECEASED PERSONS.

No exact form of words are necessary in order to make a will good at law. *Every male* person of the age of *twenty-one years,* and every *female of the age of eighteen years, of sound mind and memory,* can make a valid will; it must be in *writing,* signed by the testator or by some one in his or her presence and by his or her direction, and *attested by two* or more *credible witnesses.* Care should be taken that the *witnesses are not interested* in the will. *Persons knowing themselves to have been named in the will* or appointed executor, must within *thirty days* of the death of deceased cause the will to be proved and recorded in the proper county, or present it, and *refuse to accept;* on failure to do so are *liable* to forfeit the sum of *twenty dollars per month. Inventory* to be made by executor or administrator within *three months* from date of letters testamentary or of administration. Executors' and administrators' *compensation* not to exceed six per cent. on amount of personal estate, and three per cent. on money realized from real estate, with such additional allowance as shall be reasonable for extra services. *Appraisers' compensation* $2 per day.

Notice requiring all claims to be presented against the estate shall be given by the executor or administrator *within six months* of being qualified. Any person having a claim *and not presenting it* at the time fixed by said notice is required to have summons issued notifying the executor or administrator of his having filed his claim in court; in such cases the costs have to be paid by the claimant. *Claims* should be filed within *two years* from the time *administration* is granted on an estate, as after that time they are *forever barred*, unless *other estate is found* that was not inventoried. *Married women*, *infants*, *persons insane*, *imprisoned* or without the United States, in the employment of the United States, or of this State, have *two years* after their disabilities are removed to file claims.

Claims are *classified* and *paid out* of the *estate* in the following manner:

First. Funeral expenses.

Second. The *widow's award*, if there is a widow; or *children* if there are children, *and no widow.*

Third. *Expenses* attending the *last illness*, not including physician's bill.

Fourth. *Debts due* the *common school* or *township fund.*

Fifth. All expenses of *proving the will* and taking out letters testamentary or administration, and settlement of the estate, and the *physician's bill* in the last illness of deceased.

Sixth. Where the *deceased* has received *money in trust* for any purpose, his executor or administrator shall pay out of his estate the amount received and not accounted for.

Seventh. *All other debts* and demands of whatsoever kind, without regard to *quality or dignity*, which shall be exhibited to the court within *two years* from the granting of letters.

Award to Widow and Children, exclusive of debts and legacies or bequests, except funeral expenses:

First. The *family pictures* and *wearing apparel*, *jewels* and *ornaments* of *herself* and *minor children.*

Second. *School books* and the *family library of the value of* $100.

Third. *One sewing machine.*

Fourth. *Necessary beds*, *bedsteads* and *bedding* for herself and family.

Fifth. *The stoves* and *pipe* used in the family, with the necessary *cooking utensils*, or in case they have none, $50 in money.

Sixth. *Household and kitchen furniture to the value of* $100.

Seventh. *One milch cow and calf for every four members of her family.*

Eighth. Two sheep for each member of her family, and the fleeces taken from the same, and *one horse, saddle and bridle.*

Ninth. Provisions for herself and family for one year.

Tenth. Food for the stock above specified for six months.

Eleventh. Fuel for herself and family for three months.

Twelfth. One hundred dollars worth of other property suited to her condition in life, to be *selected by the widow.*

The *widow if she elects* may have in lieu of the said award, the same personal property or money in place thereof as is or may be *exempt from execution* or attachment against the *head of a family.*

TAXES.

The owners of real and personal property, on the *first day of May* in each year, are *liable for the taxes* thereon.

Assessments should be completed before the *fourth Monday in June*, at which time the town board of review meets to examine assessments, *hear objections*, and make such *changes* as ought to be made. The county board have also power *to correct or change assessments.*

The tax books are placed in the hands of the town collector on or before the tenth day of December, who retains them until the tenth day of March following, when he is required to return them to the county treasurer, who then *collects all delinquent taxes.*

No *costs accrue* on real estate taxes *till advertised*, which takes place the first day of April, when three weeks' notice is required before judgment. Cost of advertising, twenty cents each tract of land, and ten cents each lot.

Judgment is usually obtained at *May term* of County Court. Costs six cents each tract of land, and five cents each lot. Sale takes place in June. Costs in addition to those before mentioned, twenty-eight cents each tract of land, and twenty-seven cents each town lot.

Real estate sold for taxes may be *redeemed* any time before the *expiration of two years* from the date of sale, by *payment* to the *County Clerk* of the amount for which it was sold and twenty-five per cent. thereon if redeemed within six months, fifty per cent. if between six and twelve months, if between twelve and eighteen months seventy-five per cent., and if between eighteen months and two years one hundred per cent., and in addition, all subsequent taxes paid by the purchaser, with ten per cent. interest thereon, also one dollar each tract if notice is given by the purchaser of the sale, and a fee of twenty-five cents to the clerk for his certificate.

JURISDICTION OF COURTS.

Justices have jurisdiction in all civil cases on *contracts* for the *recovery of moneys for damages for injury to real property*, or taking, detaining, or *injuring personal property; for rent;* for all cases to recover damages done real or personal property by railroad companies, in actions of *replevin*, and in actions for damages for *fraud* in the *sale, purchase*, or *exchange of personal property*, when the amount claimed as due is not over $200. They have also *jurisdiction* in all cases for *violation* of the *ordinances* of *cities, towns* or *villages.* A *justice of the peace* may *orally* order an *officer or a private person* to *arrest* any one committing or attempting to commit a *criminal offense. He also* upon complaint can issue his warrant for the arrest of any person *accused of having committed a crime*, and have him brought before him for examination.

COUNTY COURTS

Have jurisdiction in all *matters of probate* (except in counties having a population of one hundred thousand or over), settlement of estates of *deceased persons*, appointment of *guardians* and *conservators*, and settlement of their accounts; all matters relating to *apprentices;* proceedings for the *collection* of *taxes* and *assessments*, and in proceedings of *executors, administrators, guardians* and *conservators for the sale of real estate.* In *law* cases they have concurrent jurisdiction with Circuit Courts in all cases where justices of the peace now have, or hereafter may have, jurisdiction when the amount claimed shall not exceed $1,000, and in all criminal offenses where the punishment *is not imprisonment in the penitentiary, or death*, and in all cases of appeals from justices of the peace and police magistrates; *excepting* when the county judge is sitting as a justice of the peace. *Circuit Courts* have unlimited jurisdiction.

LIMITATION OF ACTION.

Accounts five years. Notes and written contracts *ten years. Judgments twenty years. Partial payments* or new promise in writing, within or after said period, will *revive the debt.* Absence from the State deducted, and when the cause of action is barred by the law of another State, it has the same effect here. *Slander and libel, one year. Personal injuries, two years. To recover* land or make entry thereon, *twenty years. Action to foreclose mortgage* or trust deed, or make a sale, *within ten years.*

All persons in *possession of land*, and *paying taxes for seven* consecutive *years*, with color of title, and all persons paying taxes for seven consecutive years, with color of title, on vacant land, shall be held to be the *legal owners to the extent of their paper title.*

MARRIED WOMEN

May sue and be sued. Husband and wife not liable for each other's debts, either before or after marriage, but both are liable for expenses and education of the family.

She may contract the same as if unmarried, except that in a partnership business she can not, without consent of her husband, *unless he has abandoned or deserted her*, or is idiotic or insane, or confined in penitentiary; she is entitled and can recover her own earnings, but neither husband nor wife is entitled to compensation for any services rendered for the other. At the death of the husband, in addition to widow's award, a married woman has a dower interest (one-third) in all real estate owned by her husband after their marriage, and which has not been released by her, and the husband has the same interest in the real estate of the wife at her death.

EXEMPTIONS FROM FORCED SALE.

Home worth $1,000, *and the following Personal Property:* Lot of ground and buildings thereon, occupied as a residence by the debtor, being a householder and having a family, to the value of $1,000. *Exemption continues after the death* of the householder for the benefit of widow and family, some one of them occupying the homestead until *youngest child shall become twenty-one years of age, and until death of widow.* There is *no exemption from sale for taxes*, assessments, debt or liability incurred for the *purchase or improvement of said homestead.* No release or waiver of exemption is valid, unless in writing, and subscribed by such householder and wife (if he have one), and acknowledged as conveyances of real estate are required to be acknowledged. The *following articles of personal property* owned by the debtor, are exempt from *execution, writ of attachment, and distress for rent:* The necessary *wearing apparel*, Bibles, school books and family pictures of every person; and, 2d, one hundred dollars worth of other property to be selected by the debtor, and, in addition, when the debtor is the head of a family and resides with the same, three hundred dollars worth of other property to be selected by the debtor; provided that such selection and exemption shall not be made by the debtor or allowed to him or her from any money, salary or wages due him or her from any person or persons or corporations whatever.

When the head of a family shall die, desert or not reside with the same, the family shall be entitled to and receive all the benefit and privileges which are by this act conferred upon the head of a family residing with the same. No personal property is exempt from execution when judgment is obtained for the *wages of laborers or servants.* Wages of a laborer who is the head of a family can not be garnisheed, except the sum due him be in excess of $25.

DEEDS AND MORTGAGES.

To be valid there must be a valid consideration. Special care should be taken to have them signed, sealed, delivered, and properly acknowledged, with the proper seal attached. *Witnesses* are not required. The *acknowledgement* must be made in this state, before *Master in Chancery, Notary Public, United States Commissioner, Circuit or County Clerk, Justice of Peace, or any Court of Record having a seal, or any Judge, Justice, or Clerk of any such* Court. When taken before a *Notary Public, or United States Commissioner*, the same shall be *attested* by his *official seal*, when taken before a *Court or the Clerk* thereof, the same shall be attested by the *seal* of such *Court*, and when taken before a *Justice of the Peace* residing out of the county where the real estate to be conveyed lies, there shall be added a certificate of the *County Clerk* under his seal of office, *that he was a Justice of the Peace* in the county at the time of taking the same. A deed is good without such certificate attached, but can not be used in evidence unless such a certificate is produced or other competent evidence introduced. Acknowledgements made out of the state must either be executed according to the laws of this state, or there should be attached a certificate that it is in conformity with the laws of the state or country where executed. Where this is not done the same may be proved by any other legal way. Acknowledgments where the *Homestead* rights are to be waived must state as follows: "Including the release and waiver of the right of homestead."

Notaries Public can take acknowledgements any where in the state.

Sheriffs, if authorized by the mortgagor of real or personal property in his mortgage, may sell the property mortgaged.

In the case of the *death of grantor or holder of the equity of redemption* of real estate mortgaged, or conveyed by deed of trust where equity of redemption is waived, and it contains power of sale, must be foreclosed in the same manner as a common mortgage in court.

ESTRAYS.

Horses, mules, asses, neat cattle, swine, sheep, or goats found straying at any time during the year, in counties where such animals are not allowed to run at large, or between the last day of October and the 15th day of April in other counties, *the owner thereof being unknown, may be taken up as estrays.*

No person *not a householder* in the county where estray is found *can lawfully* take up an estray, and then only *upon or about his farm* or place of residence. *Estrays should not be used before advertised*, except animals giving milk, which may be milked for their benefit.

Notices must be posted up within five (5) days in three (3) of the most public places in the town or precinct in which estray was found, giving the residence of the taker up, and a particular description of the estray, its age, color, and marks natural and artificial, and stating before what justice of the peace in such town or precinct, and at what time, not less than ten (10) nor more than fifteen (15) days from the time of posting such notices, he will apply to have the estray appraised.

A copy of such notice should be filed by the taker up with the *town clerk*, whose duty it is to enter the same at large, *in a book* kept by him for that purpose.

If the *owner* of estray shall not have appeared and *proved ownership*, and taken the same away, first paying the taker up his reasonable charges for taking up, keeping, and advertising the same, the taker up shall appear before the justice of the peace mentioned in above mentioned notice, and make an affidavit as required by law.

As the *affidavit has to be made before the justice*, and all other steps as to appraisement, etc., are before him, who is familiar therewith, they are therefore omitted here.

Any person taking up an estray at any other place than about or upon his farm or residence, or *without complying with the law, shall forfeit and pay a fine of ten dollars with costs.*

Ordinary diligence is required in *taking care of estrays*, but in case they die or get away the taker is not liable for the same.

GAME.

It is *unlawful* for any person to kill, or attempt to kill or destroy, in any manner, any *prairie hen or chicken* or *woodcock* between the 15th day of January and the 1st day of September; or any *deer*, *fawn*, *wild-turkey*, *partridge* or *pheasant* between the 1st day of February and the 1st day of October; or any quail between the 1st day of February and 1st day of November; or any wild goose, duck, snipe, brant or other water fowl between the 1st day of May and 15th day of August in each year. Penalty: Fine not less than $5 nor more than $25, for each bird or animal, and costs of suit, and stand committed to county jail until fine is paid, but not exceeding ten days. *It is unlawful* to hunt with *gun*, *dog* or *net* within the inclosed grounds or lands of another *without permission*. Penalty: Fine not less than $3 nor more than $100, to be paid into school fund.

WEIGHTS AND MEASURES.

Whenever any of the following articles shall be contracted for, or sold or delivered, and no special contract or agreement shall be made to the contrary, the weight per bushel shall be as follows, to-wit:

	Pounds.		Pounds.
Stone Coal,	80	Buckwheat,	52
Unslacked Lime,	80	Coarse Salt,	50
Corn in the ear,	70	Barley,	48
Wheat,	60	Corn Meal,	48
Irish Potatoes,	60	Castor Beans,	46
White Beans,	60	Timothy Seed,	45
Clover Seed,	60	Hemp Seed,	44
Onions,	57	Malt,	38
Shelled Corn,	56	Dried Peaches,	33
Rye,	56	Oats,	32
Flax Seed,	56	Dried Apples,	24
Sweet Potatoes,	55	Bran,	20
Turnips,	55	Blue Grass Seed,	14
Fine Salt,	55	Hair (plastering),	8

Penalty for giving less than the above standard is double the amount of property wrongfully not given, and ten dollars addition thereto.

MILLERS.

The owner or occupant of every public grist mill in this state shall grind all grain brought to his mill in its turn. The *toll* for both *steam* and *water* mills, is, for grinding and bolting *wheat*, *rye*, or *other grain*, one *eighth part;* for grinding *Indian corn*, *oats*, *barley* and *buckwheat* not required to be *bolted*, one *seventh part;* for grinding *malt*, and *chopping* all kinds of grain, one *eighth part.* It is the duty of every miller when his mill is in repair, to *aid* and *assist* in *loading* and *unloading* all grain brought to him to be ground, and he is also required to keep an accurate *half bushel measure*, and an accurate set of *toll dishes* or *scales* for weighing the grain. The *penalty* for neglect or refusal to comply with the law is $5, to the use of any person to sue for the same, to be recovered before any justice of the peace of the county where penalty is incurred. Millers are accountable for the safe keeping of all grain left in his mill for the purpose of being ground, with bags or casks containing same (except it results from unavoidable accidents), provided that such bags or casks are distinctly marked with the initial letters of the owner's name.

MARKS AND BRANDS.

Owners of cattle, horses, hogs, sheep or goats may have *one ear mark* and one brand, but which shall be *different* from his *neighbor's*, and may be *recorded* by the county clerk of the county in which such property is kept. The *fee* for such record is fifteen cents. The *record* of such shall be *open* to examination free of charge. In cases of *disputes* as to marks or brands, such *record* is *prima facie evidence.* Owners of cattle, horses, hogs, sheep or goats that may have been branded by the *former owner*, may be re-branded in presence of one or more of his neighbors, who shall certify to the facts of the marking or branding being done, when done, and in what brand or mark they were re-branded or re-marked, which certificate may also be recorded as before stated.

ADOPTION OF CHILDREN.

Children may be adopted by any resident of this state, by filing a petition in the Circuit or County Court of the county in which he resides, asking leave to do so, and if desired may ask that the name of the child be changed. Such petition, if made by a person having a husband or wife, will not be granted, unless the husband or wife joins therein, as the adoption must be by them jointly.

The petition shall state name, sex, and age of the child, and the new name, if it is desired to change the name. Also the name and residence of the parents of the child, if known, and of the guardian, if any, and whether the parents or guardians consent to the adoption.

The court must find, before granting decree, that the *parents of the child*, or the survivors of them, have *deserted his or her family* or such child for one year next preceding the application, or if neither are living, the guardian; if no guardian, the next of kin in this state capable of giving consent, has had notice of the presentation of the petition and consents to such adoption. If the child is of the *age* of *fourteen years* or upwards, the adoption *can not* be made *without its consent.*

SURVEYORS AND SURVEYS.

There is in every county elected a surveyor known as county surveyor, who has power to appoint deputies, for whose official acts he is responsible. It is the *duty* of the *county surveyor*, either by himself or his deputy, to make *all surveys* that he may be called upon to make within his county as soon as may be after application is made. The necessary chainmen and other assistance must be employed by the person requiring the same to be done, and to be by him paid, unless otherwise agreed; but the chainmen must be disinterested persons and approved by the surveyor and sworn by him to measure justly and impartially.

The County Board in each county is required by law to provide a copy of the United States field notes and plats of their surveys of the lands in the county to be kept in the recorder's office subject to examination by the public, and the county surveyor is required to make his surveys in conformity to said notes, plats and the laws of the United States governing such matters. The surveyor is also required to keep a record of all surveys made by him, which shall be subject to inspection by any one interested, and shall be delivered up to his successor in office. A certified copy of the said surveyor's record shall be *prima facie* evidence of its contents.

The fees of county surveyors are six dollars per day. The county surveyor is also *ex officio inspector of mines*, and as such, assisted by some practical miner selected by him, shall once each year inspect all the mines in the county, for which they shall each receive such compensation as may be fixed by the County Board, not exceeding $5 a day, to be paid out of the county treasury.

ROADS AND BRIDGES.

Where practicable from the nature of the ground, persons traveling in any kind of vehicle, *must turn to the right* of the center of the road, so as to permit each carriage to pass without interfering with each other. The *penalty* for a violation of this provision is $5 for every offense, to be recovered by the *party injured;* but to recover, there must have occurred some injury to person or property resulting from the violation. The *owners* of any carriage traveling upon any road in this State for the conveyance of passengers who shall *employ* or continue in his employment as driver any person who is addicted to *drunkenness*, or the excessive use of spiritous liquors, after he has had notice of the same, *shall forfeit*, at the rate of $5 per day, and if any *driver* while actually engaged in driving any such carriage, shall be guilty of *intoxication* to such a degree as to *endanger* the safety of *passengers*, it shall be the duty of the owner, on receiving *written notice* of the fact, signed by one of the *passengers*, and *certified* by him *on oath*, forthwith to discharge such driver. If such owner shall have such driver in his *employ within three months* after such notice, he is liable for $5 per day for the time he shall keep said driver in his employment after receiving such notice.

Persons *driving* any *carriage* on any public highway are prohibited from *running their horses* upon any occasion under a *penalty* of a fine not exceeding $10, or imprisonment not exceeding sixty days, at the discretion of the court. Horses *attached* to any *carriage* used to convey *passengers* for hire must be *properly hitched* or the lines placed in the hands of some other person before the driver leaves them for any purpose. For violation of this provision each driver shall *forfeit twenty dollars*, to be recovered by action, to be commenced within six months. It is understood by the *term carriage* herein to mean any carriage or vehicle used for the transportation of passengers or goods or either of them.

The commissioners of highways in the different towns have the care and superintendence of highways and bridges therein. They have all the powers necessary to lay out, vacate, regulate and repair all roads, build and repair bridges. In addition to the above, it is their duty to erect and keep in repair at the forks or crossing-place of the most important roads post and guide boards with plain inscriptions, giving directions and distances to the most noted places to which such road may lead; also to make provisions to prevent thistles, burdock, and cockle burrs, mustard, yellow dock, Indian mallow and jimson weed from seeding, and to extirpate the same as far as practicable, and to prevent all rank growth of vegetation on the public highways so far as the same may obstruct public travel, and it is in their discretion to erect watering places for public use for watering teams at such points as may be deemed advisable.

The Commissioners, on or before the 1st day of May of each year, shall make out and deliver to their treasurer a list of all able-bodied men in their town, *excepting* paupers, idiots, lunatics, and such others as are exempt by law, and assess against each the sum of two dollars as a poll tax for highway purposes. Within thirty days after such list is delivered they shall cause a written or printed notice to be given to each person so assessed, notifying him of the time when and place where such tax must be paid, or its equivalent in labor performed ; they may contract with persons owing such poll tax to perform a certain amount of labor on any road or bridge in payment of the same, and if such tax is not paid nor labor performed by the first Monday of July of such year, or within ten days after notice is given after that time, they shall bring suit therefor against such person before a justice of the peace, who shall hear and determine the case according to law for the offense complained of, and shall forthwith issue an execution, directed to any constable of the county where the delinquent shall reside, who shall forthwith collect the moneys therein mentioned.

The Commissioners of Highways of each town shall annually ascertain, as near as practicable, how much money must be raised by tax on real and personal property for the making and repairing of roads, only, to any amount they may deem necessary, not exceeding forty cents on each one hundred dollars' worth, as valued on the assessment roll of the previous year. The tax so levied on property lying within an incorporated village, town or city, shall be paid over to the corporate authorities of such town, village or city. Commissioners shall receive $1.50 for each day necessarily employed in the discharge of their duty.

Overseers. At the first meeting the Commissioners shall choose one of their number to act General Overseer of Highways in their township, whose duty it shall be to take charge of and safely keep all tools, implements and machinery belonging to said town, and shall, by the direction of the Board, have general supervision of all roads and bridges in their town.

As all township and county officers are familiar with their duties, it is only intended to give the points of the law that the public should be familiar with. The manner of laying out, altering or vacating roads, etc., will not be here stated, as it would require more space than is contemplated in a work of this kind. It is sufficient to state that, the first step is by petition, addressed to the Commissioners, setting out what is prayed for, giving the names of the owners of lands if known, if not known so state, over which the road is to pass, giving the general course, its place of beginning, and where it terminates. It requires not less than twelve *freeholders* residing within three miles of the road who shall sign the petition. Public roads must not be less than fifty feet wide, nor more than sixty feet wide. Roads not exceeding two miles in length, if petitioned for, may be laid out, not less than forty feet. Private roads for private and public use, may be laid out of the width of three rods, on petition of the person directly interested; the damage occasioned thereby shall be paid by the premises benefited thereby, and before the road is opened. If not opened in two years, the order shall be considered rescinded. Commissioners in their discretion may permit persons who live on or have private roads, to work out their road tax thereon. Public roads must be opened in five days from date of filing order of location, or be deemed vacated.

DRAINAGE.

Whenever one or more owners or occupants of land *desire to construct a drain* or ditch across the land of others for *agricultural, sanitary or mining purposes*, the proceedings are as follows:

File a petition in the Circuit or County Court of the county in which the proposed ditch or drain is to be constructed, setting forth the necessity for the same, with a description of its proposed starting point, route and terminus, and if it shall be necessary for the drainage of the land or coal mines or for sanitary purposes, that a drain, ditch, levee or similar work be constructed, a description of the same. It shall also set forth the names of all persons owning the land over which such drain or ditch shall be constructed, or if unknown stating that fact.

No private property shall be taken or damaged for the purpose of constructing a ditch, drain or levee, without compensation, if claimed by the owner, the same to be ascertained by a jury; but if the construction of such ditch, drain or levee shall be a benefit to the owner, the same shall be a set off against such compensation.

If the proceedings seek to affect the property of a minor, lunatic or married woman, the guardian, conservator or husband of the same shall be made party defendant. The petition may be amended and parties made defendants at any time when it is necessary to a fair trial.

When the petition is presented to the judge, he shall note thereon when he will hear the same, and order the issuance of summonses and the publication of notice to each non-resident or unknown defendant.

The petition may be heard by such judge in vacation as well as in term time. Upon the trial, the jury shall ascertain the just compensation to each owner of the property sought to be damaged by the construction of such ditch, drain or levee, and truly report the same.

As it is only contemplated in a work of this kind to give an abstract of the laws, and as the parties who have in charge the execution of the further proceedings are likely to be familiar with the requirements of the statute, the necessary details are not here inserted.

WOLF SCALPS.

The County Board of any county in this State may hereafter allow such bounty on *wolf scalps* as the board may deem reasonable.

Any person claiming a bounty shall produce the scalp or scalps with the ears thereon, within sixty days after the wolf or wolves shall have been caught, to the Clerk of the County Board, who shall administer to said person the following oath or affirmation, to-wit: "You do solemnly swear (or affirm, as the case may be), that the scalp or scalps here produced by you was taken from a wolf or wolves killed and first captured by yourself within the limits of this county, and within the sixty days last past."

CONVEYANCES.

When the reversion expectant on a lease of any tenements or hereditaments of any tenure shall be surrendered or merged, the estate which shall for the time being confer as against the tenant under the same lease the next vested right to the same tenements or hereditaments, shall, to the extent and for the purpose of preserving such incidents to and obligations on the same reversion, as but for the surrender or merger thereof, would have subsisted, be deemed the reversion expectant on the same lease.

PAUPERS.

Every poor person who shall be unable to earn a livelihood in consequence of any *bodily infirmity*, *idiocy*, *lunacy* or *unavoidable cause*, shall be supported by the father, grand-father, mother, grand-mother, children, grand-children, brothers or sisters of such poor person, if they or either of them be of sufficient ability; but if any of such dependent class shall have become so from *intemperance* or other *bad conduct*, they shall not be entitled to support from any relation except parent or child.

FORMERLY OF GALENA

The children shall first be called on to support their parents, if they are able; but if not, the parents of such poor person shall then be called on, if of sufficient ability; and if there be no parents or children able, then the brothers and sisters of such dependent person shall be called upon; and if there be no brothers or sisters of sufficient ability, the grand-children of such person shall next be called on; and if they are not able, then the grand-parents. Married females, while their husbands live, shall not be liable to contribute for the support of their poor relations except out of their separate property. It is the duty of the state's (county) attorney, to make complaint to the County Court of his county against all the relatives of such paupers in this state liable to his support and prosecute the same. In case the state's attorney neglects, or refuses, to complain in such cases, then it is the duty of the overseer of the poor to do so. The person called upon to contribute shall have at least ten days' notice of such application by summons. The court has the power to determine the kind of support, depending upon the circumstances of the parties, and may also order two or more of the different degrees to maintain such poor person, and prescribe the proportion of each, according to their ability. The court may specify the time for which the relative shall contribute—in fact has control over the entire subject matter, with power to enforce its orders. Every county (except those in which the poor are supported by the towns, and in such cases the towns are liable) is required to relieve and support all poor and indigent persons *lawfully* resident therein. Residence means the *actual* residence of the party, or the place where he was employed; or in case he was in no employment, then it shall be the place where he made his home. When any person becomes chargeable as a pauper in any county or town who did not reside at the commencement of six months immediately preceding his becoming so, but did at that time reside in some other county or town in this state, then the county or town, as the case may be, becomes liable for the expense of taking care of such person until removed, and it is the duty of the overseer to notify the proper authorities of the fact. If any person shall bring and leave any pauper in any county in this state where such pauper had no legal residence, knowing him to be such, he is liable to a fine of $100. In counties under township organization, the supervisors in each town are ex-officio overseers of the poor. The overseers of the poor act under the directions of the County Board in taking care of the poor and granting of temporary relief; also, providing for non-resident persons not paupers who may be taken sick and not able to pay their way, and in case of death cause such person to be decently buried.

The residence of the inmates of poorhouses and other charitable institutions for voting purposes is their former place of abode.

FENCES.

In counties under township organization, the *town assessor* and commissioner of highways are the fence-viewers in their respective towns. In other counties the County Board appoints three in each precinct annually. *A lawful fence* is *four and one-half feet high*, in good repair, consisting of rails, timber, boards, stone, hedges, or whatever the fence-viewers of the town or precinct where the same shall lie, shall consider equivalent thereto, but in counties under township organization the annual town meeting may establish any other kind of fence as such, or the County Board in other counties may do the same. Division fences shall be made and maintained in just proportion by the adjoining owners, except when the owner shall choose to let his land lie open, but after a division fence is built by agreement or otherwise, neither party can remove his part of such fence so long as he may crop or use such land for farm purposes, or without giving the other party one year's notice in writing of his intention to remove his portion. When any person shall enclose his land upon the enclosure of another, he shall refund the owner of the adjoining lands a just proportion of the value at that time of such fence. The value of fence and the just proportion to be paid or built and maintained by each is to be ascertained by two fence-viewers in the town or precinct. Such fence-viewers have power to settle all disputes between different owners as to fences built or to be built, as well as to repairs to be made. Each party chooses one of the viewers, but if the other party neglects, after eight days' notice in writing, to make his choice, then the other party may select both. It is sufficient to notify the tenant or party in possession, when the owner is not a resident of the town or precinct. The two fence-viewers chosen, after viewing the premises, shall hear the statements of the parties, in case they can't agree, they shall select another fence-viewer to act with them, and the decision of any two of them is final. The decision must be reduced to writing, and should plainly set out description of fence and all matters settled by them, and must be filed in the office of the town clerk in counties under township organization, and in other counties with the county clerk.

Where any person is liable to contribute to the erection or the repairing of a division fence, neglects or refuses so to do, the party injured, after giving sixty days notice in writing when a fence is to be erected, or ten days when it is only repairs, may proceed to have the work done at the expense of the party whose duty it is to do it, to be recovered from him with costs of suit, and the party so neglecting shall also be liable to the party injured for all damages accruing from such neglect or refusal, to be determined by any two fence-viewers selected as before provided, the appraisement to be reduced to writing and signed.

Where a person shall conclude to remove his part of a division fence, and let his land lie open, and having given the year's notice required, the adjoining owner may cause the value of said fence to be ascertained by fence-viewers as before provided, and on payment or tender of the amount of such valuation to the owner, it shall prevent the removal. A party removing a division fence without notice is liable for the damages accruing thereby.

Where a fence has been built on the land of another through mistake, the owner may enter upon such premises and remove his fence and material within six months after the division line has been ascertained. Where the material to build such a fence has been taken from the land on which it was built, then before it can be removed, the person claiming must first pay for such material to the owner of the land from which it was taken, nor shall such a fence be removed at a time when the removal will throw open or expose the crops of the other party; a reasonable time must be given beyond the six months to remove crops.

The compensation of fence-viewers is one dollar and fifty cents a day each, to be paid in the first instance by the party calling them, but in the end all expenses, including amount charged by the fence-viewers, must be paid equally by the parties, except in cases where a party neglects or refuses to make or maintain a just proportion of a division fence, when the party in default shall pay them.

DAMAGES FROM TRESPASS.

Where stock of any kind breaks into any person's enclosure, the fence being *good* and *sufficient*, the owner is liable for the damage done; but where the damage is done by stock *running at large, contrary to law*, the owner is liable where there is not such a fence. Where stock is found trespassing on the enclosure of another as aforesaid, the owner or occupier of the premises may take possession of such stock and keep the same until damages, with reasonable charges for keeping and feeding and all costs of suit, are paid. Any person taking or rescuing such stock so held without his consent, shall be liable to a fine of not less than three nor more than five dollars for each animal rescued, to be recovered by suit before a justice of the peace for the use of the school fund. Within twenty-four hours after taking such animal into his possession, the person taking it up must give notice of the fact to the owner, if known, or if unknown, notices must be posted in some public place near the premises.

LANDLORD AND TENANT.

The owner of lands, or his legal representatives, can sue for and recover rent therefor, in any of the following cases:

First. When rent is due and in arrears on a lease for life or lives.

Second. When lands are held and occupied by any person without any special agreement for rent.

Third. When possession is obtained under an agreement, written or verbal, for the purchase of the premises and before deed given, the right to possession is terminated by forfeiture on con-compliance with the agreement, and possession is wrongfully refused or neglected to be giver upon demand made in writing by the party entitled thereto. Provided that all payments made by the vendee or his representatives or assigns, may be set off against the rent.

Fourth. When land has been sold upon a judgment or a decree of court, when the party to such judgment or decree, or person holding under him, wrongfully refuses, or neglects, to surrender possession of the same, after demand in writing by the person entitled to the possession.

Fifth. When the lands have been sold upon a mortgage or trust deed, and the mortgagor or grantor or person holding under him, wrongfully refuses or neglects to surrender possession of the same, after demand in writing by the person entitled to the possession.

If any tenant, or any person who shall come into possession from or under or by collusion with such tenant, shall willfully hold over any lands, etc., after the expiration the term of their lease, and *after demand made in writing* for the possession thereof, is liable to pay *double rent.* A tenancy from year to year requires sixty days notice in writing, to terminate the same at the end of the year; such notice can be given at any time within four months preceding the last sixty days of the year.

A tenancy by the month, or less than a year, where the tenant holds over without any special agreement, the landlord may terminate the tenancy, by thirty days notice in writing.

When rent is due, the landlord may serve a notice upon the tenant, stating that unless the rent is paid within not less than five days, his lease will be terminated; if the rent is not paid, the landlord may consider the lease ended. When default is made in any of the terms of a lease, it shall not be necessary to give more than ten days notice to quit or of the termination of such tenancy; and the same may be terminated on giving such notice to quit, at any time after such default in any of the terms of such lease; which notice may be substantially in the following form, viz:

To ——, You are hereby notified that, in consequence of your default in (here insert the character of the default), of the premises now occupied by you, being etc. (here describe the premises), I have elected to determine your lease, and you are hereby notified to quit and deliver up possession of the same to me within ten days of this date (dated, etc.)

The above to be signed by the lessor or his agent, and no other notice or demand of possession or termination of such tenancy is necessary.

Demand may be made, or notice served, by delivering a written or printed, or partly either, copy thereof to the tenant, or leaving the same with some person above the age of twelve years residing on or in possession of the premises; and in case no one is in the actual possession of the said premises, then by posting the same on the premises. When the tenancy is for a certain time, and the term expires by the terms of the lease, the tenant is then bound to surrender possession, and no notice to quit or demand of possession is necessary.

Distress for rent.—In all cases of distress for rent, the landlord, by himself, his agent or attorney, may seize for rent any personal property of his tenant that may be found in the county where the tenant resides; the property of any other person, even if found on the premises, is not liable.

An inventory of the property levied upon, with a statement of the amount of rent claimed, should be at once filed with some justice of the peace, if not over $200; and if above that sum, with the clerk of a court of record of competent jurisdiction. Property may be released, by the party executing a satisfactory bond for double the amount.

The landlord may distrain for rent, any time within *six months* after the expiration of the term of the lease, or when terminated.

In all cases where the premises rented shall be sub-let, or the lease assigned, the landlord shall have the same right to enforce lien against such lessee or assignee, that he has against the tenant to whom the premises were rented.

When a tenant abandons or removes from the premises or any part thereof, the landlord, or his agent or attorney, may seize upon any grain or other crops grown or growing upon the premises, or part thereof so abandoned, whether the rent is due or not. If such grain, or other crops, or any part thereof, is not fully grown or matured, the landlord, or his agent or attorney, shall cause the same to be properly cultivated, harvested or gathered, and may sell the same, and from the proceeds pay all his labor, expenses and rent. The tenant may, before the sale of such property, redeem the same by tendering the rent and reasonable compensation for work done, or he may replevy the same.

Exemption.—The same articles of personal property which are by law exempt from execution, except the crops as above stated, is also exempt from distress for rent.

If any tenant is about to or shall permit or attempt to sell and remove from the premises, without the consent of his landlord, such portion of the crops raised thereon as will endanger the lien of the landlord upon such crops, for the rent, it shall be lawful for the landlord to distress before rent is due.

LIENS.

Any person who shall by *contract*, express or implied, or partly both, with the owner of any lot or tract of land, furnish labor or material, or services as an architect or superintendent, in building, altering, repairing or ornamenting any house or other building or appurtenance thereto on such lot, or upon any street or alley, and connected with such improvements, shall have a lien upon the whole of such lot or tract of land, and upon such house or building and appurtenances, for the amount due to him for such labor, material or services. If the contract is *expressed*, and the time for the *completion* of the work is *beyond three years* from the commencement thereof; or, if the time of payment is beyond one year from the time stipulated for the completion of the work, then no lien exists. If the contract is *implied*, then no lien exists, unless the work be done or material is furnished within one year from the commencement of the work or delivery of the materials. As between different creditors having liens, no preference is given to the one whose contract was first made; but each shares pro-rata. Incumbrances existing on the lot or tract of the land at the time the contract is made, do not operate on the improvements, and are only preferred to the extent of the value of the land at the *time of making the contract*. The above lien can not be enforced *unless suit is commenced* within *six months* after the last payment for labor or materials shall have become due and payable. Sub-contractors, mechanics, workmen and other persons furnishing any material, or performing any labor for a contractor as before specified, have a lien to the extent of the amount due the contractor at the time the following notice is served upon the owner of the land who made the contract:

To ——, You are hereby notified, that I have been employed by—— (here state whether to labor or furnish material, and substantially the nature of the demand) upon your (here state in general terms description and situation of building), and that I shall hold the (building, or as the case may be), and your interest in the ground, liable for the amount that may (is or may become) due me on account thereof. Signature, —— Date, ——

If there is a contract in writing between contractor and sub-contractor, a copy of it should be served with above notice, and said notice must be served within forty days from the completion of such sub-contract, if there is one; if not, then from the time payment should have been made to the person performing the labor or furnishing the material. If the owner is not a resident of the county, or can not be found therein, then the above notice must be filed with the clerk of the Circuit Court, with his fee, fifty cents, and a copy of said notice must be published in a newspaper published in the county, for four successive weeks.

When the owner or agent is notified as above, he can retain any money due the contractor sufficient to pay such claim ; if more than one claim, and not enough to pay all, they are to be paid pro rata.

The owner has the right to demand in writing, a statement of the contractor, of what he owes for labor, etc., from time to time as the work progresses, and on his failure to comply, forfeits to the owner $50 for every offense.

The liens referred to cover any and all estates, whether in fee for life, for years, or any other interest which the owner may have.

To enforce the lien of *sub-contractors*, suit must be commenced within *three months* from the time of the performance of the sub-contract, or during the work or furnishing materials.

Hotel, inn and *boarding-house keepers*, have a lien upon the baggage and other valuables of their guests or boarders, brought into such hotel, inn or boarding-house, by their guests or boarders, for the proper charges due from such guests or boarders for their accommodation, board and lodgings, and such *extras* as are furnished at their request.

Stable-keepers and other persons have a lien upon the horses, carriages and harness kept by them, for the proper charges due for the keeping thereof and expenses bestowed thereon at the request of the owner or the person having the possession of the same.

Agisters (persons who take care of cattle belonging to others), and persons keeping, yarding, feeding or pasturing domestic animals, shall have a lien upon the animals agistered, kept, yarded or fed, for the proper charges due for such service.

All persons who may furnish any railroad corporation in this state with fuel, ties, material, supplies or any other article or thing necessary for the construction, maintenance, operation or repair of its road by contract, or may perform work or labor on the same, is entitled to be paid as part of the current expenses of the road, and have a lien upon all its property. Sub-contractors or laborers have also a lien. The conditions and limitations both as to contractors and sub-contractors, are about the same as herein stated as to general liens.

DEFINITION OF COMMERCIAL TERMS.

$—— means *dollars*, being a contraction of U. S., which was formerly placed before any denomination of money, and meant, as it means now, United States Currency.

£—— means *pounds*, English money.

@ stands for *at* or *to*. ℔ for *pound*, and bbl. for *barrel;* ℘ for *per* or *by the*. Thus, Butter sells at 20@30c ℘ ℔, and Flour at $8@12 ℘ bbl.

% for *per cent* and # for *number*.

May 1.—Wheat sells at $1.20@1.25, "seller June." *Seller June* means that the person who sells the wheat has the privilege of delivering it at any time during the month of June.

Selling *short*, is contracting to deliver a certain amount of grain or stock, at a fixed price, within a certain length of time, when the seller has not the stock on hand. It is for the interest of the person selling "short," to depress the market as much as possible, in order that he may buy and fill his contract at a profit. Hence the "shorts" are termed "bears."

Buying *long*, is to contract to purchase a certain amount of grain or shares of stock at a fixed price, deliverable within a stipulated time, expecting to make a profit by the rise of prices. The "longs" are termed "bulls," as it is for their interest to "operate" so as to "toss" the prices upward as much as possible.

NOTES.

Form of note is legal, worded in the simplest way, so that the amount and time of payment are mentioned.

$100. Chicago, Ill., Sept. 15, 1876.

Sixty days from date I promise to pay to E. F. Brown, or order, One Hundred dollars, for value received.

L. D. Lowry.

A note to be payable in any thing else than money needs only the facts substituted for money in the above form.

ORDERS.

Orders should be worded simply, thus:

Mr. F. H. Coats: Chicago, Sept. 15, 1876.

Please pay to H. Birdsall, Twenty-five dollars, and charge to

F. D. Silva.

RECEIPTS.

Receipts should always state when received and what for, thus:

$100. Chicago, Sept. 15, 1876.

Received of J. W. Davis, One Hundred dollars, for services rendered in grading his lot in Fort Madison, on account.

Thomas Brady.

If receipt is in full it should be so stated.

BILLS OF PURCHASE.

W. N. Mason, Salem, Illinois, Sept. 15, 1876.

Bought of A. A. Graham.

4 Bushels of Seed Wheat, at $1.50 - - - -	$6.00
2 Seamless Sacks " .30 - -	.60
Received payment,	$6.60

A. A. Graham.

ARTICLES OF AGREEMENT.

An agreement is where one party promises to another to do a certain thing in a certain time for a stipulated sum. Good business men always reduce an agreement to writing, which nearly always saves misunderstandings and trouble. No particular form is necessary, but the facts must be clearly and explicitly stated, and there must, to make it valid, be a reasonable consideration.

GENERAL FORM OF AGREEMENT.

THIS AGREEMENT, made the Second day of October, 1876, between John Jones, of Aurora, County of Kane, State of Illinois, of the first part, and Thomas Whiteside, of the same place, of the second part—

WITNESSETH, that the said John Jones, in consideration of the agreement of the party of the second part, hereinafter contained, contracts and agrees to and with the said Thomas Whiteside, that he will deliver, in good and marketable condition, at the Village of Batavia, Ill., during the month of November, of this year, One Hundred Tons of Prairie Hay, in the following lots, and at the following specified times; namely, twenty-five tons by the seventh of November, twenty-five tons additional by the fourteenth of the month, twenty-five tons more by the twenty-first, and the entire one hundred tons to be all delivered by the thirtieth of November.

And the said Thomas Whiteside, in consideration of the prompt fulfillment of this contract, on the part of the party of the first part, contracts to and agrees with the said John Jones, to pay for said hay five dollars per ton, for each ton as soon as delivered.

In case of failure of agreement by either of the parties hereto, it is hereby stipulated and agreed that the party so failing shall pay to the other, One Hundred Dollars, as fixed and settled damages.

In witness whereof, we have hereunto set our hands the day and year first above written.

JOHN JONES,
THOMAS WHITESIDE.

AGREEMENT WITH CLERK FOR SERVICES.

THIS AGREEMENT, made the first day of May, one thousand eight hundred and seventy-six, between Reuben Stone, of Chicago, County of Cook, State of Illinois, party of the first part, and George Barclay, of Englewood, County of Cook, State of Illinois, party of the second part—

WITNESSETH, that said George Barclay agrees faithfully and diligently to work as clerk and salesman for the said Reuben Stone, for and during the space of one year from the date hereof, should both live such length of time, without absenting himself from his occupation;

during which time he, the said Barclay, in the store of said Stone, of Chicago, will carefully and honestly attend, doing and performing all duties as clerk and salesman aforesaid, in accordance and in all respects as directed and desired by the said Stone.

In consideration of which services, so to be rendered by the said Barclay, the said Stone agrees to pay to said Barclay the annual sum of one thousand dollars, payable in twelve equal monthly payments, each upon the last day of each month; provided that all dues for days of absence from business by said Barclay, shall be deducted from the sum otherwise by the agreement due and payable by the said Stone to the said Barclay.

Witness our hands.

REUBEN STONE.
GEORGE BARCLAY.

BILLS OF SALE.

A bill of sale is a written agreement to another party, for a consideration to convey his right and interest in the personal property. The purchaser must take actual possession of the property. Juries have power to determine upon the fairness or unfairness of a bill of sale.

COMMON FORM OF BILL OF SALE.

KNOW ALL MEN by this instrument, that I, Louis Clay, of Princeton, Illinois, of the first part, for and in consideration of Five Hundred and Ten dollars, to me paid by John Floyd, of the same place, of the second part, the receipt whereof is hereby acknowledged, have sold, and by this instrument do convey unto the said Floyd, party of the second part, his executors, administrators, and assigns, my undivided half of ten acres of corn, now growing on the farm of Thomas Tyrrell, in the town above mentioned; one pair of horses, sixteen sheep, and five cows, belonging to me, and in my possession at the farm aforesaid; to have and to hold the same unto the party of the second part, his executors and assigns, forever. And I do, for myself and legal representatives, agree with the said party of the second part, and his legal representatives, to warrant and defend the sale of the afore-mentioned property and chattels unto the said party of the second part, and his legal representatives, against all and every person whatsoever.

In witness whereof, I have hereunto affixed my hand, this tenth day of October, one thousand eight hundred and seventy-six.

LOUIS CLAY.

BONDS.

A bond is a written admission on the part of the maker in which he pledges a certain sum to another, at a certain time.

COMMON FORM OF BOND.

KNOW ALL MEN by this instrument, that I, George Edgerton, of Watseka, Iroquois County, State of Illinois, am firmly bound unto Peter Kirchoff, of the place aforesaid, in the sum of five hundred dollars, to be paid to the said Peter Kirchoff, or his legal representatives; to which payment, to be made, I bind myself, or my legal representatives, by this instrument.

Sealed with my seal, and dated this second day of November, one thousand eight hundred and sixty-four.

The condition of this bond is such that if I, George Edgerton, my heirs, administrators, or executors, shall promptly pay the sum of two hundred and fifty dollars in three equal annual payments from the date hereof, with annual interest, then the above obligation to be of no effect; otherwise to be in full force and valid.

Sealed and delivered in
presence of GEORGE EDGERTON. [L.S.]
WILLIAM TURNER.

CHATTEL MORTGAGES.

A chattel mortgage is a mortgage on personal property for payment of a certain sum of money, to hold the property against debts of other creditors. The mortgage must describe the property, and must be acknowledged before a justice of the peace in the township or precinct where the mortgagee resides, and entered upon his docket, and must be recorded in the recorder's office of the county.

GENERAL FORM OF CHATTEL MORTGAGE.

THIS INDENTURE, made and entered into this first day of January, in the year of our Lord one thousand eight hundred and seventy-five, between Theodore Lottinville, of the town of Geneseo in the County of Henry, and State of Illinois, party of the first part, and Paul Henshaw, of the same town, county, and State, party of the second part.

Witnesseth, that the said party of the first part, for and in consideration of the sum of one thousand dollars, in hand paid, the receipt whereof is hereby acknowledged, does hereby grant, sell, convey, and confirm unto the said party of the second part, his heirs and assigns forever, all and singular the following described goods and chattels, to wit:

Two three-year old roan-colored horses, one Burdett organ, No. 987, one Brussels carpet, 15x20 feet in size, one marble-top center table, one Home Comfort cooking stove, No. 8, one black walnut bureau with mirror attached, one set of parlor chairs (six in number), upholstered in green rep, with lounge corresponding with same in style and color of upholstery, now in possession of said Lottinville, at No. 4 Prairie Ave., Geneseo, Ill.;

Together with all and singular, the appurtenances thereunto belonging, or in any wise appertaining; to have and to hold the above described goods and chattels, unto the said party of the second part, his heirs and assigns, forever.

Provided, always, and these presents are upon this express condition, that if the said Theodore Lottinville, his heirs, executors, administrators, or assigns, shall, on or before the first day of January, A.D., one thousand eight hundred and seventy-six, pay, or cause to be paid, to the said Paul Ranslow, or his lawful attorney or attorneys, heirs, executors, administrators, or assigns, the sum of One Thousand dollars, together with the interest that may accrue thereon, at the rate of ten per cent. per annum, from the first day of January, A.D. one thousand eight hundred and seventy-five, until paid, according to the tenor of one promissory note bearing even date herewith for the payment of said sum of money, that then and from thenceforth, these presents, and everything herein contained, shall cease, and be null and void, anything herein contained to the contrary notwithstanding.

Provided, also, that the said Theodore Lottinville may retain the possession of and have the use of said goods and chattels until the day of payment aforesaid; and also, at his own expense, shall keep said goods and chattels; and also at the expiration of said time of payment, if said sum of money, together with the interest as aforesaid, shall not be paid, shall deliver up said goods and chattels, in good condition, to said Paul Ranslow, or his heirs, executors, administrators, or assigns.

And provided, also, that if default in payment as aforesaid, by said party of the first part, shall be made, or if said party of the second part shall at any time before said promissory note becomes due, feel himself unsafe or insecure, that then the said party of the second part, or his attorney, agent, assigns, or heirs, executors, or administrators, shall have the right to take possession of said goods and chattels, wherever they may or can be found, and sell the same at public or private sale, to the highest bidder for cash in hand, after giving ten days' notice of the time and place of said sale, together with a description of the goods and chattels to be sold, by at least four advertisements, posted up in public places in the vicinity where said sale is to take place, and proceed to make the sum of money and interest promised as aforesaid, together with all reasonable costs, charges, and expenses in so doing; and if there shall be any overplus, shall pay the same without delay to the said party of the first part, or his legal representatives.

In testimony whereof, the said party of the first part has hereunto set his hand and affixed his seal, the day and year first above written.

Signed, sealed and delivered in
presence of
SAMUEL J. TILDEN.

THEODORE LOTTINVILLE. [L.S.]

LEASE OF FARM AND BUILDINGS THEREON.

THIS INDENTURE, made this second day of June, 1875, between David Patton of the Town of Bisbee, State of Illinois, of the first part, and John Doyle of the same place, of the second part,

Witnesseth, that the said David Patton, for and in consideration of the covenants hereinafter mentioned and reserved, on the part of the said John Doyle, his executors, administrators, and assigns, to be paid, kept, and performed, hath let, and by these presents doth grant, demise, and let, unto the said John Doyle, his executors, administrators, and assigns, all that parcel of land situate in Bisbee aforesaid, bounded and described as follows, to wit:

[*Here describe the land.*]

Together with all the appurtenances appertaining thereto. To have and to hold the said premises, with appurtenances thereto belonging, unto the said Doyle, his executors, administrators, and assigns, for the term of five years, from the first day of October next following, at a yearly rent of Six Hundred dollars, to be paid in equal payments, semi-annually, as long as said buildings are in good tenantable condition.

And the said Doyle, by these presents, covenants and agrees to pay all taxes and assessments, and keep in repair all hedges, ditches, rail, and other fences; (the said David Patton, his heirs, assigns and administrators, to furnish all timber, brick, tile, and other materials necessary for such repairs.)

Said Doyle further covenants and agrees to apply to said land, in a farmer-like manner, all manure and compost accumulating upon said farm, and cultivate all the arable land in a husbandlike manner, according to the usual custom among farmers in the neighborhood; he also agrees to trim the hedges at a seasonable time, preventing injury from cattle to such hedges, and to all fruit and other trees on the said premises. That he will seed down with clover and timothy seed twenty acres yearly of arable land, ploughing the same number of acres each Spring of land now in grass, and hitherto unbroken.

It is further agreed, that if the said Doyle shall fail to perform the whole or any one of the above mentioned covenants, then and in that case the said David Patton may declare this lease terminated, by giving three months' notice of the same, prior to the first of October of any year, and may distrain any part of the stock, goods, or chattels, or other property in possession of said Doyle, for sufficient to compensate for the non-performance of the above written covenants, the same to be determined, and amounts so to be paid to be determined, by three arbitrators, chosen as follows: Each of the parties to this instrument to choose one, and the two so chosen to select a third; the decision of said arbitrators to be final.

In witness whereof, we have hereto set our hands and seals.

Signed, sealed, and delivered
in presence of
JAMES WALDRON.

DAVID PATTON. [L.S.]
JOHN DOYLE. [L.S.]

FORM OF LEASE OF A HOUSE.

THIS INSTRUMENT, made the first day of October, 1875, witnesseth that Amos Griest of Yorkville, County of Kendall, State of Illinois, hath rented from Aaron Young of Logansport aforesaid, the dwelling and lot No. 13 Ohio Street, situated in said City of Yorkville, for five years from the above date, at the yearly rental of Three Hundred dollars, payable monthly, on the first day of each month, in advance, at the residence of said Aaron Young.

At the expiration of said above mentioned term, the said Griest agrees to give the said Young peaceable possession of the said dwelling, in as good condition as when taken, ordinary wear and casualties excepted.

In witness whereof, we place our hands and seals the day and year aforesaid.

Signed, sealed and delivered
in presence of
NICKOLAS SCHUTZ,
Notary Public.

AMOS GRIEST. [L.S.]
AARON YOUNG. [L.S.]

LANDLORD'S AGREEMENT.

THIS certifies that I have let and rented, this first day of January, 1876, unto Jacob Schmidt, my house and lot, No. 15 Erie Street, in the City of Chicago, State of Illinois, and its appurtenances; he to have the free and uninterrupted occupation thereof for one year from this date, at the yearly rental of Two Hundred dollars, to be paid monthly in advance; rent to cease if destroyed by fire, or otherwise made untenantable.

PETER FUNK.

TENANT'S AGREEMENT.

THIS certifies that I have hired and taken from Peter Funk, his house and lot, No. 15 Erie Street, in the City of Chicago, State of Illinois, with appurtenances thereto belonging, for one year, to commence this day, at a yearly rental of Two Hundred dollars, to be paid monthly in advance; unless said house becomes untenantable from fire or other causes, in which case rent ceases; and I further agree to give and yield said premises one year from this first day of January 1876, in as good condition as now, ordinary wear and damage by the elements excepted.

Given under my hand this day. JACOB SCHMIDT.

NOTICE TO QUIT.

To F. W. Arlen,

Sir: Please observe that the term of one year, for which the house and land, situated at No. 6 Indiana Street, and now occupied by you, were rented to you, expired on the first day of October, 1875, and as I desire to repossess said premises, you are hereby requested and required to vacate the same. Respectfully Yours,

P. T. Barnum.

Lincoln, Neb., October 4, 1875.

TENANT'S NOTICE OF LEAVING.

Dear Sir:

The premises I now occupy as your tenant, at No. 6 Indiana Street, I shall vacate on the first day of November, 1875. You will please take notice accordingly.

Dated this tenth day of October, 1875. F. W. Arlen.

To P. T. Barnum, Esq.

REAL ESTATE MORTGAGE TO SECURE PAYMENT OF MONEY.

This Indenture, made this sixteenth day of May, in the year of our Lord, one thousand eight hundred and seventy-two, between William Stocker, of Peoria, County of Peoria, and State of Illinois, and Olla, his wife, party of the first part, and Edward Singer, party of the second part.

Whereas, the said party of the first part is justly indebted to the said party of the second part, in the sum of Two Thousand dollars, secured to be paid by two certain promissory notes (bearing even date herewith) the one due and payable at the Second National Bank in Peoria, Illinois, with interest, on the sixteenth day of May, in the year one thousand eight hundred and seventy-three; the other due and payable at the Second National Bank at Peoria, Ill., with interest, on the sixteenth day of May, in the year one thousand eight hundred and seventy-four.

Now, therefore, this indenture witnesseth, that the said party of the first part, for the better securing the payment of the money aforesaid, with interest thereon, according to the tenor and effect of the said two promissory notes above mentioned; and, also in consideration of the further sum of one dollar to them in hand paid by the said party of the second part, at the delivery of these presents, the receipt whereof is hereby acknowledged, have granted, bargained, sold, and conveyed, and by these presents do grant, bargain, sell, and convey, unto the said party of the second part, his heirs and assigns, forever, all that certain parcel of land, situate, etc.

[*Describing the premises.*]

To have and to hold the same, together with all and singular the Tenements, Hereditaments, Privileges and Appurtenances thereunto belonging or in any wise appertaining. And also, all the estate, interest, and claim whatsoever, in law as well as in equity which the party of the first part have in and to the premises hereby conveyed unto the said party of the second part, his heirs and assigns, and to their only proper use, benefit and behoof. And the said William Stocker, and Olla, his wife, party of the first part, hereby expressly waive, relinquish, release, and convey unto the said party of the second part, his heirs, executors, administrators, and assigns, all right, title, claim, interest, and benefit whatever, in and to the above described premises, and each and every part thereof, which is given by or results from all laws of this state pertaining to the exemption of homesteads.

Provided always, and these presents are upon this express condition, that if the said party of the first part, their heirs, executors, or administrators, shall well and truly pay, or cause to be paid, to the said party of the second part, his heirs, executors, administrators, or assigns, the aforesaid sums of money, with such interest thereon, at the time and in the manner specified in the above mentioned promissory notes, according to the true intent and meaning thereof, then in that case, these presents and every thing herein expressed, shall be absolutely null and void.

In witness whereof, the said party of the first part hereunto set their hands and seals the day and year first above written.

Signed, sealed and delivered in presence of

JAMES WHITEHEAD, WILLIAM STOCKER. [L.S.]
FRED. SAMUELS. OLLA STOCKER. [L.S.]

WARRANTY DEED WITH COVENANTS.

THIS INDENTURE, made this sixth day of April, in the year of our Lord one thousand eight hundred and seventy-two, between Henry Best of Lawrence, County of Lawrence, State of Illinois, and Belle, his wife, of the first part, and Charles Pearson of the same place, of the second part,

Witnesseth, that the said party of the first part, for and in consideration of the sum of Six Thousand dollars in hand paid by the said party of the second part, the receipt whereof is hereby acknowledged, have granted, bargained, and sold, and by these presents do grant, bargain, and sell, unto the said party of the second part, his heirs and assigns, all the following described lot, piece, or parcel of land, situated in the City of Lawrence, in the County of Lawrence, and State of Illinois, to wit:

[*Here describe the property.*]

Together with all and singular the hereditaments and appurtenances thereunto belonging or in any wise appertaining, and the reversion and reversions, remainder and remainders, rents, issues, and profits thereof; and all the estate, right, title, interest, claim, and demand whatsoever, of the said party of the first part, either in law or equity, of, in, and to the

James G. Soulard

GALENA

above bargained premises, with the hereditaments and appurtenances. To have and to hold the said premises above bargained and described, with the appurtenances, unto the said party of the second part, his heirs and assigns, forever. And the said Henry Best, and Belle, his wife, parties of the first part, hereby expressly waive, release, and relinquish unto the said party of the second part, his heirs, executors, administrators, and assigns, all right, title, claim, interest, and benefit whatever, in and to the above described premises, and each and every part thereof, which is given by or results from all laws of this state pertaining to the exemption of homesteads.

And the said Henry Best, and Belle, his wife, party of the first part, for themselves and their heirs, executors, and administrators, do covenant, grant, bargain, and agree, to and with the said party of the second part, his heirs and assigns, that at the time of the ensealing and delivery of these presents they were well seized of the premises above conveyed, as of a good, sure, perfect, absolute, and indefeasible estate of inheritance in law, and in fee simple, and have good right, full power, and lawful authority to grant, bargain, sell, and convey the same, in manner and form aforesaid, and that the same are free and clear from all former and other grants, bargains, sales, liens, taxes, assessments, and encumbrances of what kind or nature soever; and the above bargained premises in the quiet and peaceable possession of the said party of the second part, his heirs and assigns, against all and every person or persons lawfully claiming or to claim the whole or any part thereof, the said party of the first part shall and will warrant and forever defend.

In testimony whereof, the said parties of the first part have hereunto set their hands and seals the day and year first above written.

Signed, sealed and delivered
in presence of
JERRY LINKLATER.

HENRY BEST, [L.S.]
BELLE BEST. [L.S.]

QUIT-CLAIM DEED.

THIS INDENTURE, made the eighth day of June, in the year of our Lord one thousand eight hundred and seventy-four, between David Tour, of Plano, County of Kendall, State of Illinois, party of the first part, and Larry O'Brien, of the same place, party of the second part,

Witnesseth, that the said party of the first part, for and in consideration of Nine Hundred dollars in hand paid by the said party of the second part, the receipt whereof is hereby acknowledged, and the said party of the second part forever released and discharged therefrom, has remised, released, sold, conveyed, and quit-claimed, and by these presents does remise, release, sell, convey, and quit-claim, unto the said party of the second part, his heirs and assigns, forever, all the right, title, interest, claim, and demand, which the said party of the first part has in and to the following described lot, piece, or parcel of land, to wit:

[*Here describe the land.*]

To have and to hold the same, together with all and singular the appurtenances and privileges thereunto belonging, or in any wise thereunto appertaining, and all the estate, right, title, interest, and claim whatever, of the said party of the first part, either in law or equity, to the only proper use, benefit, and behoof of the said party of the second part, his heirs and assigns forever.

In witness whereof the said party of the first part hereunto set his hand and seal the day and year above written.

Signed, sealed and delivered DAVID TOUR. [L.S.]
in presence of
THOMAS ASHLEY.

The above forms of Deeds and Mortgage are such as have heretofore been generally used, but the following are much shorter, and are made equally valid by the laws of this state.

WARRANTY DEED.

The grantor (here insert name or names and place of residence), for and in consideration of (here insert consideration) in hand paid, conveys and warrants to (here insert the grantee's name or names) the following described real estate (here insert description), situated in the County of —— in the State of Illinois.

Dated this —— day of —— A. D. 18——.

QUIT CLAIM DEED.

The grantor (here insert grantor's name or names and place of residence). for the consideration of (here insert consideration) convey and quit-claim to (here insert grantee's name or names) all interest in the following described real estate (here insert description), situated in the County of —— in the State of Illinois.

Dated this —— day of —— A. D. 18——.

MORTGAGE.

The mortgagor (here insert name or names) mortgages and warrants to (here insert name or names of mortgagee or mortgagees), to secure the payment of (here recite the nature and amount of indebtedness, showing when due and the rate of interest, and whether secured by note or otherwise), the following described real estate (here insert description thereof), situated in the County of —— in the State of Illinois.

Dated this —— day of —— A. D. 18——.

RELEASE.

KNOW ALL MEN by these presents, that I, Peter Ahlund, of Chicago, of the County of Cook, and State of Illinois, for and in consideration of One dollar, to me in hand paid, and for other good and valuable considerations, the receipt whereof is hereby confessed, do hereby grant, bargain, remise, convey, release, and quit-claim unto Joseph Carlin of Chicago, of the County of Cook, and State of Illinois, all the right, title, interest, claim, or demand whatsoever, I may have acquired in, through, or by a certain Indenture or Mortgage Deed, bearing date the second day of January, A. D. 1871, and recorded in the Recorder's office of said county, in book A of Deeds, page 46, to the premises therein described, and which said Deed was made to secure one certain promissory note, bearing even date with said deed, for the sum of Three Hundred dollars.

Witness my hand and seal, this second day of November, A. D. 1874.

PETER AHLUND. [L.S.]

State of Illinois, Cook County. } ss.

I, George Saxton, a Notary Public in and for said county, in the state aforesaid, do hereby certify that Peter Ahlund, personally known to me as the same person whose name is subscribed to the foregoing Release, appeared before me this day in person, and acknowledged that he signed, sealed, and delivered the said instrument of writing as his free and voluntary act, for the uses and purposes therein set forth.

[NOTARIAL SEAL.]

Given under my hand and seal, this second day of November, A. D. 1874.

GEORGE SAXTON, N. P.

GENERAL FORM OF WILL FOR REAL AND PERSONAL PROPERTY.

I, Charles Mansfield, of the Town of Salem, County of Jackson, State of Illinois, being aware of the uncertainty of life, and in failing health, but of sound mind and memory, do make and declare this to be my last will and testament, in manner following, to wit:

First. I give, devise and bequeath unto my oldest son, Sidney H. Mansfield, the sum of Two Thousand Dollars, of bank stock, now in the Third National Bank of Cincinnati, Ohio, and the farm owned by myself in the Town of Buskirk, consisting of one hundred and sixty acres, with all the houses, tenements, and improvements thereunto belonging; to have and to hold unto my said son, his heirs and assigns, forever.

Second. I give, devise and bequeath to each of my daughters, Anna Louise Mansfield and Ida Clara Mansfield, each Two Thousand dollars in bank stock, in the Third National Bank of Cincinnati, Ohio, and also each one quarter section of land, owned by myself, situated in the Town of Lake, Illinois, and recorded in my name in the Recorder's office in the county where such land is located. The north one hundred and sixty acres of said half section is devised to my eldest daughter, Anna Louise.

Third. I give, devise and bequeath to my son, Frank Alfred Mansfield, Five shares of Railroad stock in the Baltimore and Ohio Railroad, and my one hundred and sixty acres of land and saw mill thereon, situated in Manistee, Michigan, with all the improvements and appurtenances thereunto belonging, which said real estate is recorded in my name in the county where situated.

Fourth. I give to my wife, Victoria Elizabeth Mansfield, all my household furniture, goods, chattels, and personal property, about my home, not hitherto disposed of, including Eight Thousand dollars of bank stock in the Third National Bank of Cincinnati, Ohio, Fifteen shares in the Baltimore and Ohio Railroad, and the free and unrestricted use, possession, and benefit of the home farm, so long as she may live, in lieu of dower, to which she is entitled by law; said farm being my present place of residence.

Fifth. I bequeath to my invalid father, Elijah H. Mansfield, the income from rents of my store building at 145 Jackson Street, Chicago, Illinois, during the term of his natural life. Said building and land therewith to revert to my said sons and daughters in equal proportion, upon the demise of my said father.

Sixth. It is also my will and desire that, at the death of my wife, Victoria Elizabeth Mansfield, or at any time when she may arrange to relinquish her life interest in the above mentioned homestead, the same may revert to my above named children, or to the lawful heirs of each.

And lastly. I nominate and appoint as executors of this my last will and testament, my wife, Victoria Elizabeth Mansfield, and my eldest son, Sidney H. Mansfield.

I further direct that my debts and necessary funeral expenses shall be paid from moneys now on deposit in the Savings Bank of Salem, the residue of such moneys to revert to my wife, Victoria Elizabeth Mansfield, for her use forever.

In witness whereof, I, Charles Mansfield, to this my last will and testament, have hereunto set my hand and seal, this fourth day of April, eighteen hundred and seventy-two.

Signed, sealed, and declared by Charles Mansfield, as and for his last will and testament, in the presence of us, who, at his request, and in his presence, and in the presence of each other, have subscribed our names hereunto as witnesses thereof. PETER A. SCHENCK, Sycamore, Ills. FRANK E. DENT, Salem, Ills.	CHARLES MANSFIELD. [L.S.]

CODICIL.

Whereas I, Charles Mansfield, did, on the fourth day of April, one thousand eight hundred and seventy-two, make my last will and testament, I do now, by this writing, add this codicil to my said will, to be taken as a part thereof.

Whereas, by the dispensation of Providence, my daughter, Anna Louise, has deceased November fifth, eighteen hundred and seventy-three, and whereas, a son has been born to me, which son is now christened Richard Albert Mansfield, I give and bequeath unto him my gold watch, and all right, interest, and title in lands and bank stock and chattels bequeathed to my deceased daughter, Anna Louise, in the body of this will.

In witness whereof, I hereunto place my hand and seal, this tenth day of March, eighteen hundred and seventy-five.

Signed, sealed, published, and declared to us by the testator, Charles Mansfield, as and for a codicil to be annexed to his last will and testament. And we, at his request, and in his presence, and in the presence of each other, have subscribed our names as witnesses thereto, at the date hereof.
FRANK E. DENT, Salem, Ills.
JOHN C. SHAY, Salem, Ills.

CHARLES MANSFIELD. [L.S.]

CHURCH ORGANIZATIONS

May be legally made by *electing* or *appointing*, according to the *usages* or *customs* of the body of which it is a part, at any meeting held for that purpose, *two* or *more* of its *members* as trustees, wardens or vestrymen, and may adopt a *corporate* name. The chairman or secretary of such meeting shall, as soon as possible, make and file in the office of the recorder of deeds of the county, an affidavit substantially in the following form:

STATE OF ILLINOIS, }
——— County. } SS.

I, ———, do solemnly swear (or affirm, as the case may be), that at a meeting of the members of the (here insert the name of the church, society or congregation as known before organization), held at (here insert place of meeting), in the County of ———, and State of Illinois, on the —— day of ———, A.D. 18—, for that purpose, the following persons were elected (or appointed) [*here insert their names*] trustees, wardens, vestrymen, (or officers by whatever name they may choose to adopt, with powers similar to trustees) according to the rules and usages of such (church, society or congregation), and said ———

adopted as its corporate name (here insert name), and at said meeting this affiant acted as (chairman or secretary, as the case may be).

Subscribed and sworn to before me, this —— day of ——, A.D. 18—. Name of Affiant —— ——

which affidavit must be recorded by the recorder, and shall be, or a certified copy made by the recorder, received as evidence of such an incorporation.

No certificate of election after the first need be filed for record.

The term of office of the trustees and the general government of the society can be determined by the rules or by-laws adopted. Failure to elect trustees at the time provided does not work a dissolution, but the old trustees hold over. A trustee or trustees may be removed, in the same manner by the society as elections are held by a meeting called for that purpose. The property of the society vests in the corporation. The corporation may hold, or acquire by purchase or otherwise, land not exceeding ten acres, for the purpose of the society. The trustees have the care, custody and control of the property of the corporation, and can, *when directed* by the society, erect houses or improvements, and repair and alter the same, and may also when so directed by the society, mortgage, encumber, sell and convey any real or personal estate belonging to the corporation, and make all proper contracts in the name of such corporation. But they are prohibited by law from encumbering or interfering with any property so as to destroy the effect of any gift, grant, devise or bequest to the corporation; but such gifts, grants, devises or bequests, must in all cases be used so as to carry out the object intended by the persons making the same. Existing societies may organize in the manner herein set forth, and have all the advantages thereof.

SUGGESTIONS TO THOSE PURCHASING BOOKS BY SUBSCRIPTION.

The business of *publishing books by subscription* having so often been brought into disrepute by agents making representations and declarations *not authorized by the publisher;* in order to prevent that as much as possible, and that there may be more general knowledge of the relation such agents bear to their principal, and the law governing such cases, the following statement is made:

A subscription is in the *nature of a contract* of mutual promises, by which the subscriber agrees to *pay a certain sum* for the work described; the *consideration is concurrent* that the publisher shall *publish the book named*, and deliver the same, for which the subscriber is to pay the price named. *The nature and character of the work is described in the prospectus and by the sample shown.* These should be *carefully examined before subscribing*, as they are the basis and consideration of the promise to pay, and not the too *often exaggerated statements of the agent*, who is *merely employed* to *solicit subscriptions*, for which he is usually *paid a commission* for each subscriber, and has *no authority* to *change or alter* the conditions upon which the subscriptions are authorized to be made by the publisher. Should the *agent assume* to agree to make the subscription conditional or *modify or change the agreement of the publisher*, as set out by prospectus and sample, in order to *bind the principal*, the *subscriber* should see that such conditions or changes are stated *over or in connection with his signature*, so that the publisher may have notice of the same.

All persons making contracts in reference to matters of this kind, or any other business, should remember *that the law as to written contracts is*, that they can *not be varied, altered or rescinded verbally, but if done at all, must be done in writing.* It is therefore *important* that all *persons contemplating subscribing should distinctly understand that all talk before or after the subscription is made, is not admissible as evidence, and is no part of the contract.*

Persons employed to solicit subscriptions are known to the trade as canvassers. They are agents *appointed to do a particular business in a prescribed mode*, and *have no authority* to do it in any other way to the prejudice of their principal, nor can they bind their principal in any other matter. They *can not collect money*, or agree that payment may be made in *anything else but money.* They *can not extend* the time of payment *beyond the time of delivery, nor bind their principal* for the *payment of expenses* incurred in their buisness.

It would save a great deal of trouble, and often serious loss, if persons, *before signing* their names to any subscription book, or any written instrument, would *examine carefully what it is;* if they can not read themselves, should call on some one disinterested who can.

6

CONSTITUTION OF THE UNITED STATES OF AMERICA AND ITS AMENDMENTS.

We, the people of the United States, in order to form a more perfect union, establish justice, insure domestic tranquillity, provide for the common defense, promote the general welfare, and secure the blessings of liberty to ourselves and our posterity, do ordain and establish this Constitution for the United States of America.

ARTICLE I.

SECTION 1. All legislative powers herein granted shall be vested in a Congress of the United States, which shall consist of a Senate and House of Representatives.

SEC. 2. The House of Representatives shall be composed of members chosen every second year by the people of the several states, and the electors in each state shall have the qualifications requisite for electors of the most numerous branch of the State Legislature.

No person shall be a representative who shall not have attained to the age of twenty-five years, and been seven years a citizen of the United States, and who shall not, when elected, be an inhabitant of that state in which he shall be chosen.

Representatives and direct taxes shall be apportioned among the several states which may be included within this Union, according to their respective numbers, which shall be determined by adding to the whole number of free persons, including those bound to service for a term of years, and excluding Indians not taxed, three-fifths of all other persons. The actual enumeration shall be made within three years after the first meeting of the Congress of the United States, and within every subsequent term of ten years, in such manner as they shall by law direct. The number of Representatives shall not exceed one for every thirty thousand, but each state shall have at least one Representative; and until such enumeration shall be made the State of New Hampshire shall be entitled to choose three, Massachusetts eight, Rhode Island and Providence Plantations one, Connecticut five, New York six, New Jersey four, Pennsylvania eight, Delaware one, Maryland six, Virginia ten, North Carolina five, and Georgia three.

When vacancies happen in the representation from any state, the Executive authority thereof shall issue writs of election to fill such vacancies.

The House of Representatives shall choose their Speaker and other officers, and shall have the sole power of impeachment.

SEC. 3. The Senate of the United States shall be composed of two Senators from each state, chosen by the Legislature thereof for six years; and each Senator shall have one vote.

Immediately after they shall be assembled in consequence of the first election, they shall be divided as equally as may be into three classes. The seats of the Senators of the first class shall be vacated at the expiration of the second year, of the second class at the expiration of the fourth year, and of the third class at the expiration of the sixth year, so that one-third may be chosen every second year; and if vacancies happen by resignation or otherwise, during the recess of the Legislature of any state. the Executive thereof may make temporary appointments until the next meeting of the Legislature, which shall then fill such vacancies.

No person shall be a Senator who shall not have attained to the age of thirty years and been nine years a citizen of the United States, and who shall not, when elected, be an inhabitant of that state for which he shall be chosen.

The Vice-President of the United States shall be President of the Senate, but shall have no vote unless they be equally divided.

The Senate shall choose their other officers, and also a President *pro tempore*, in the absence of the Vice-President, or when he shall exercise the office of President of the United States.

The Senate shall have the sole power to try all impeachments. When sitting for that purpose they shall be on oath or affirmation. When the President of the United States is tried the Chief Justice shall preside. And no person shall be convicted without the concurrence of two-thirds of the members present.

Judgment, in cases of impeachment, shall not extend further than to removal from office, and disqualification to hold and enjoy any office of honor, trust, or profit under the United States; but the party convicted shall nevertheless be liable and subject to indictment, trial, judgment, and punishment according to law.

SEC. 4. The times, places and manner of holding elections for Senators and Representatives shall be prescribed in each state by the Legislature thereof; but the Congress may at any time by law make or alter such regulations, except as to the places of choosing Senators.

The Congress shall assemble at least once in every year, and such meeting shall be on the first Monday in December, unless they shall by law appoint a different day.

SEC. 5. Each house shall be the judge of the election, returns, and qualifications of its own members, and a majority of each shall constitute a quorum to do business; but a smaller number may adjourn from day to day, and may be authorized to compel the attendance of absent members in such manner and under such penalties as each house may provide.

Each house may determine the rules of its proceedings, punish its members for disorderly behavior, and, with the concurrence of two-thirds, expel a member.

Each house shall keep a journal of its proceedings, and from time to time publish the same, excepting such parts as may, in their judgment, require secrecy; and the yeas and nays of the members of either house on any question shall, at the desire of one-fifth of those present, be entered on the journal.

Neither house, during the session of Congress, shall, without the consent of the other, adjourn for more than three days, nor to any other place than that in which the two houses shall be sitting.

SEC. 6. The Senators and Representatives shall receive a compensation for their services, to be ascertained by law, and paid out of the treasury of the United States. They shall in all cases, except treason, felony, and breach of the peace, be privileged from arrest during their attendance at the session of their respective houses, and in going to and returning from the same; and for any speech or debate in either house they shall not be questioned in any other place.

No Senator or Representative shall, during the time for which he was elected, be appointed to any civil office under the authority of the United States, which shall have been created, or the emoluments whereof shall have been increased during such time; and no person holding any office under the United States, shall be a member of either house during his continuance in office.

SEC. 7. All bills for raising revenue shall originate in the House of Representatives; but the Senate may propose or concur with amendments as on other bills.

Every bill which shall have passed the House of Representatives and the Senate, shall, before it becomes a law, be presented to the President the United States; if he approve he shall sign it; but if not he shall return it, with his objections, to that house in which it shall have originated, who shall enter the objections at large on their journal, and proceed to reconsider it. If, after such reconsideration two-thirds of that house shall agree to pass the bill, it shall be sent, together with the objections, to the other house, by which it shall likewise be reconsidered, and if approved by two-thirds of that house, it shall become a law. But in all such cases the votes of both houses shall be determined by yeas and nays, and the names of the persons voting for and against the bill shall be entered on the journal of each house respectively. If any bill shall not be returned by the President within ten days (Sundays excepted), after it shall have been presented to him, the same shall be a law, in like manner as if he had signed it, unless the Congress, by their adjournment, prevent its return, in which case it shall not be a law.

Every order, resolution, or vote to which the concurrence of the Senate and House of Representatives may be necessary (except on a question of adjournment), shall be presented to the President of the United States, and before the same shall take effect shall be approved by him, or, being disapproved by him, shall be re-passed by two-thirds of the Senate and House of Representatives, according to the rules and limitations prescribed in the case of a bill.

SEC. 8. The Congress shall have power—

To lay and collect taxes, duties, imposts and excises, to pay the debts, and provide for the common defense and general welfare of the United States; but all duties, imposts, and excises shall be uniform throughout the United States;

To borrow money on the credit of the United States;

To regulate commerce with foreign nations, and among the several States, and with the Indian tribes;

To establish a uniform rule of naturalization, and uniform laws on the subject of bankruptcies throughout the United States;

To coin money, regulate the value thereof, and of foreign coin, and fix the standard of weights and measures;

To provide for the punishment of counterfeiting the securities and current coin of the United States;

To establish post offices and post roads;

To promote the progress of sciences and useful arts, by securing, for limited times, to authors and inventors, the exclusive right to their respective writings and discoveries;

To constitute tribunals inferior to the Supreme Court;

To define and punish piracies and felonies committed on the high seas, and offenses against the law of nations;

To declare war, grant letters of marque and reprisal, and make rules concerning captures on land and water;

To raise and support armies, but no appropriation of money to that use shall be for a longer term than two years;

To provide and maintain a navy;

To make rules for the government and regulation of the land and naval forces;

To provide for calling forth the militia to execute the laws of the Union, suppress insurrections, and repel invasions;

To provide for organizing, arming and disciplining the militia, and for governing such part of them as may be employed in the service of the United States, reserving to the states respectively the appointment of the officers, and the authority of training the militia according to the discipline prescribed by Congress;

To exercise legislation in all cases whatsoever over such district (not exceeding ten miles square) as may, by cession of particular states, and the acceptance of Congress, become the seat of the government of the United States, and to exercise like authority over all places purchased by the consent of the Legislature of the state in which the same shall be, for the erection of forts, magazines, arsenals, dock yards, and other needful buildings; and

To make all laws which shall be necessary and proper for carrying into execution the foregoing powers, and all other powers vested by this Constitution in the government of the United States, or in any department or officer thereof.

SEC. 9. The migration or importation of such persons as any of the states now existing shall think proper to admit, shall not be prohibited by the Congress prior to the year one thousand eight hundred and eight, but a tax or duty may be imposed on such importation, not exceeding ten dollars for each person.

The privilege of the writ of habeas corpus shall not be suspended, unless when in cases of rebellion or invasion the public safety may require it.

No bill of attainder or *ex post facto* law shall be passed.

No capitation or other direct tax shall be laid, unless in proportion to the census or enumeration hereinbefore directed to be taken.

No tax or duty shall be laid on articles exported from any state.

No preference shall be given by any regulation of commerce or revenue to the ports of one state over those of another; nor shall vessels bound to or from one state be obliged to enter, clear, or pay duties in another.

No money shall be drawn from the Treasury, but in consequence of appropriations made by law; and a regular statement and account of the receipts and expeditures of all public money shall be published from time to time.

No title of nobility shall be granted by the United States: and no person holding any office of profit or trust under them, shall, without the consent of the Congress, accept of any present, emolument, office, or title of any kind whatever, from any king, prince, or foreign state.

SEC. 10. No state shall enter into any treaty, alliance, or confederation; grant letters of marque and reprisal; coin money; emit bills of credit; make anything but gold and silver coin a tender in payment of debts; pass any bill of attainder, *ex post facto* law, or law impairing the obligation of contracts, or grant any title of nobility.

No state shall, without the consent of the Congress, lay any imposts or duties on imports or exports, except what may be absolutely necessary for executing its inspection laws, and the net produce of all duties and imposts laid by any state on imports or exports, shall be for the use of the Treasury of the United States; and all such laws shall be subject to the revision and control of the Congress.

No state shall, without the consent of Congress, lay any duty on tonnage, keep troops or ships of war in time of peace, enter into any agreement or compact with another state, or with a foreign power, or engage in war, unless actually invaded, or in such imminent danger as will not admit of delay.

ARTICLE II.

SECTION 1. The Executive power shall be vested in a President of the United States of America. He shall hold his office during the term of four years, and, together with the Vice-President chosen for the same term, be elected as follows:

Each state shall appoint, in such manner as the Legislature thereof may direct, a number of Electors, equal to the whole number of Senators and Representatives to which the state may be entitled in the Congress; but no Senator or Representative, or person holding an office of trust or profit under the United States, shall be appointed an Elector.

[* The Electors shall meet in their respective states, and vote by ballot for two persons, of whom one at least shall not be an inhabitant of the same state with themselves. And they shall make a list of all the persons voted for, and of the number of votes for each; which list they shall sign and certify, and transmit, sealed, to the seat of the government of the United States, directed to the President of the Senate. The President of the Senate shall, in the presence of the Senate and House of Representatives, open all the certificates, and the votes shall then be counted. The person having the greatest number of votes shall be the President, if such number be a majority of the whole number of Electors appointed; and if there be more than one who have such majority, and have an equal number of votes, then the House of Representatives shall immediately choose by ballot one of them for President; and if no person have a majority, then from the five highest on the list the said House shall in like manner choose the President. But in choosing the President, the vote shall be taken by states, the representation from each state having one vote; a quorum for this purpose shall consist of a member or members from two-thirds of the states, and a majority of all the states shall be necessary to a choice. In every case, after the choice of the President,

* This clause between brackets has been superseded and annulled by the Twelfth amendment.

the person having the greatest number of votes of the Electors shall be the Vice-President. But if there should remain two or more who have equal votes, the Senate shall choose from them by ballot the Vice-President.]

The Congress may determine the time of choosing the Electors, and the day on which they shall give their votes; which day shall be the same throughout the United States.

No person except a natural born citizen, or a citizen of the United States at the time of the adoption of this Constitution, shall be eligible to the office of President; neither shall any person be eligible to that office who shall not have attained the age of thirty-five years, and been fourteen years a resident within the United States.

In case of the removal of the President from office, or of his death, resignation, or inability to discharge the powers and duties of the said office, the same shall devolve on the Vice-President, and the Congress may by law provide for the case of removal, death, resignation, or inability, both of the President and Vice-President, declaring what officer shall then act as President, and such officer shall act accordingly, until the disability be removed, or a President shall be elected.

The President shall, at stated times, receive for his services a compensation which shall neither be increased nor diminished during the period for which he shall have been elected, and he shall not receive within that period any other emolument from the United States or any of them.

Before he enters on the execution of his office, he shall take the following oath or affirmation:

"I do solemnly swear (or affirm) that I will faithfully execute the office of President of the United States, and will, to the best of my ability, preserve, protect, and defend the Constitution of the United States."

SEC. 2. The President shall be commander in chief of the army and navy of the United States, and of the militia of the several states, when called into the actual service of the United States; he may require the opinion, in writing, of the principal officer in each of the executive departments, upon any subject relating to the duties of their respective offices, and he shall have power to grant reprieves and pardon for offenses against the United States, except in cases of impeachment.

He shall have power, by and with the advice and consent of the Senate, to make treaties, provided two-thirds of the Senators present concur; and he shall nominate, and by and with the advice of the Senate, shall appoint ambassadors, other public ministers and consuls, judges of the Supreme Court, and all other officers of the United States whose appointments are not herein otherwise provided for, and which shall be established by law; but the Congress may by law vest the appointment of such inferior officers as they think proper in the President alone, in the courts of law, or in the heads of departments.

The President shall have power to fill up all vacancies that may happen during the recess of the Senate, by granting commissions which shall expire at the end of their next session.

SEC. 3. He shall from time to time give to the Congress information of the state of the Union, and recommend to their consideration such measures as he shall judge necessary and expedient; he may on extraordinary occasions convene both houses, or either of them, and in case of disagreement between them, with respect to the time of adjournment, he may adjourn them to such time as he shall think proper; he shall receive ambassadors and other public ministers; he shall take care that the laws be faithfully executed, and shall commission all the officers of the United States.

SEC. 4. The President, Vice-President, and all civil officers of the United States, shall be removed from office on impeachment for, and conviction of, treason, bribery, or other high crimes and misdemeanors.

ARTICLE III.

SECTION I. The judicial power of the United States shall be vested in one Supreme Court, and such inferior courts as the Congress may from time to time ordain and establish. The Judges, both of the Supreme and inferior courts, shall hold their offices during good behavior, and shall, at stated times, receive for their services a compensation, which shall not be diminished during their continuance in office.

SEC. 2. The judicial power shall extend to all cases, in law and equity, arising under this Constitution, the laws of the United States, and treaties made, or which shall be made, under their authority; to all cases affecting ambassadors, other public ministers, and consuls; to all cases of admiralty and maritime jurisdiction; to controversies to which the United States shall be a party; to controversies between two or more states; between a state and citizens of another state; between citizens of different states; between citizens of the same state claiming lands under grants of different states, and between a state or the citizens thereof, and foreign states, citizens, or subjects.

In all cases affecting ambassadors, other public ministers, and consuls, and those in which a state shall be a party, the Supreme Court shall have original jurisdiction.

In all the other cases before mentioned, the Supreme Court shall have appellate jurisdiction, both as to law and fact, with such exceptions and under such regulations as the Congress shall make.

The trial of all crimes, except in cases of impeachment, shall be by jury; and such trial shall be held in the state where the said crimes shall have been committed; but when not committed within any state, the trial shall be at such place or places as the Congress may by law have directed.

SEC. 3. Treason against the United States shall consist only in levying war against them, or in adhering to their enemies, giving them aid and comfort. No person shall be convicted of treason unless on the testimony of two witnesses to the same overt act, or on confession in open court.

The Congress shall have power to declare the punishment of treason, but no attainder of treason shall work corruption of blood, or forfeiture, except during the life of the person attainted.

ARTICLE IV.

SECTION 1. Full faith and credit shall be given in each state to the public acts, records, and judicial proceedings of every other state. And the Congress may, by general laws, prescribe the manner in which such acts, records, and proceedings shall be proved, and the effect thereof.

SEC. 2. The citizens of each state shall be entitled to all privileges and immunities of citizens in the several states.

A person charged in any state with treason, felony, or other crime, who shall flee from justice and be found in another state, shall, on demand of the executive authority of the state from which he fled, be delivered up, to be removed to the state having jurisdiction of the crime.

No person held to service or labor in one state, under the laws thereof escaping into another, shall, in consequence of any law or regulation therein, be discharged from such service or labor, but shall be delivered up on the claim of the party to whom such service or labor may be due.

SEC. 3. New states may be admitted by the Congress into this Union; but no new state shall be formed or erected within the jurisdiction of any other state; nor any state be formed by the junction of two or more states, or parts of states, without the consent of the Legislatures of the states concerned, as well as of the Congress.

The Congress shall have power to dispose of and make all needful rules and regulations respecting the territory or other property belonging to the United States; and nothing in this Constitution shall be so construed as to prejudice any claims of the United States or of any particular state.

SEC. 4. The United States shall guarantee to every state in this Union a republican form of government, and shall protect each of them against invasion, and on application of the Legislature, or of the Executive (when the Legislature can not be convened), against domestic violence.

ARTICLE V.

The Congress, whenever two-thirds of both houses shall deem it necessary, shall propose amendments to this Constitution, or, on the application of the Legislatures of two-thirds of the several states, shall call a convention for proposing amendments, which, in either case, shall be valid to all intents and purposes as part of this Constitution, when ratified by the Legislatures of three fourths of the several states, or by conventions in three-fourths thereof, as the one or the other mode of ratification may be proposed by the Congress. Provided that no amendment which may be made prior to the year one thousand eight hundred and eight shall in any manner affect the first and fourth clauses in the ninth section of the first article; and that no state, without its consent, shall be deprived of its equal suffrage in the Senate.

ARTICLE VI.

All debts contracted and engagements entered into before the adoption of this Constitution shall be as valid against the United States under this Constitution as under the Confederation.

This Constitution, and the laws of the United States which shall be made in pursuance thereof, and all treaties made, or which shall be made, under the authority of the United States, shall be the supreme law of the land; and the Judges in every state shall be bound thereby, anything in the Constitution or laws of any state to the contrary notwithstanding.

The Senators and Representatives before mentioned, and the members of the several state Legislatures, and all executive and judicial officers, both of the United States and of the several states, shall be bound by oath or affirmation to support this Constitution; but no religious test shall ever be required as a qualification to any office or public trust under the United States.

Article VII.

The ratification of the Conventions of nine states shall be sufficient for the establishment of this Constitution between the states so ratifying the same.

Done in convention by the unanimous consent of the states present, the seventeenth day of September, in the year of our Lord one thousand seven hundred and eighty-seven, and of the independence of the United States of America the twelfth. In witness whereof we have hereunto subscribed our names.

GEO. WASHINGTON,
President and Deputy from Virginia.

New Hampshire.
John Langdon,
Nicholas Gilman.

Massachusetts.
Nathaniel Gorham,
Rufus King.

Connecticut.
Wm. Sam'l Johnson,
Roger Sherman.

New York.
Alexander Hamilton.

New Jersey.
Wil. Livingston,
Wm. Paterson,
David Brearley,
Jona. Dayton.

Pennsylvania.
B. Franklin,
Robt. Morris,
Thos. Fitzsimons,
James Wilson,
Thos. Mifflin,
Geo. Clymer,
Jared Ingersoll,
Gouv. Morris.

Delaware.
Geo. Read,
John Dickinson,
Jaco. Broom,
Gunning Bedford, Jr.,
Richard Bassett.

Maryland.
James M'Henry,
Danl. Carroll,
Dan. of St. Thos. Jenifer.

Virginia.
John Blair,
James Madison, Jr.

North Carolina.
Wm. Blount,
Hu. Williamson,
Rich'd Dobbs Spaight.

South Carolina.
J. Rutledge,
Charles Pinckney,
Chas. Cotesworth Pinckney,
Pierce Butler.

Georgia.
William Few,
Abr. Baldwin.

WILLIAM JACKSON, *Secretary.*

CHICAGO

(FORMERLY OF GALENA)

Articles in Addition to and Amendatory of the Constitution of the United States of America.

Proposed by Congress and ratified by the Legislatures of the several states, pursuant to the fifth article of the original Constitution.

Article I.

Congress shall make no law respecting an establishment of religion, or prohibiting the free exercise thereof; or abridging the freedom of speech, or of the press; or the right of the people peaceably to assemble, and to petition the Government for a redress of grievances.

Article II.

A well regulated militia being necessary to the security of a free state, the right of the people to keep and bear arms shall not be infringed.

Article III.

No soldier shall, in time of peace, be quartered in any house without the consent of the owner, nor in time of war but in a manner to be prescribed by law.

Article IV.

The right of the people to be secure in their persons, houses, papers, and effects against unreasonable searches and seizures, shall not be violated; and no warrants shall issue but upon probable cause, supported by oath or affirmation, and particularly describing the place to be searched and the persons or things to be seized.

Article V.

No person shall be held to answer for a capital or otherwise infamous crime, unless on a presentment or indictment of a Grand Jury, except in cases arising in the land or naval forces, or in the militia when in actual service in time of war or public danger; nor shall any person be subject for the same offense to be twice put in jeopardy of life or limb; nor shall be compelled in any criminal case to be a witness against himself, nor be deprived of life, liberty, or property, without due process of law; nor shall private property be taken for public use, without just compensation.

Article VI.

In all criminal prosecutions, the accused shall enjoy the right to a speedy and public trial, by an impartial jury of the state and district wherein the crime shall have been committed, which district shall have been previously ascertained by law, and to be informed of the nature and cause of the accusation; to be confronted with the witnesses against him; to have compulsory process for obtaining witnesses in his favor; and to have the assistance of counsel for his defense.

Article VII.

In suits at common law, where the value in controversy shall exceed twenty dollars, the right of trial by jury shall be preserved, and no fact tried by a jury shall be otherwise re-examined in any court of the United States than according to the rules of the common law.

Article VIII.

Excessive bail shall not be required, nor excessive fines imposed, nor cruel and unusual punishments inflicted.

Article IX.

The enumeration, in the Constitution, of certain rights, shall not be construed to deny or disparage others retained by the people.

Article X.

The powers not delegated to the United States by the Constitution, nor prohibited by it to the states, are reserved to the states respectively, or to the people.

Article XI.

The judicial power of the United States shall not be construed to extend to any suit in law or equity commenced or prosecuted against one of the United States by citizens of another state, or by citizens or subjects of any foreign state.

Article XII.

The Electors shall meet in their respective states and vote by ballot for President and Vice-President, one of whom, at least, shall not be an inhabitant of the same state with themselves; they shall name in their ballots the person to be voted for as president, and in distinct ballots the person voted for as Vice-President, and they shall make distinct lists of all persons voted for as President, and of all persons voted for as Vice-President, and of the number of votes for each, which list they shall sign and certify, and transmit sealed to the seat of the government of the United States, directed to the President of the Senate. The President of the Senate shall, in presence of the Senate and House of Representatives, open all the certificates, and the votes shall then be counted. The person having the greatest number of votes for President shall be the President, if such number be a majority of the whole number of Electors appointed; and if no person have such majority, then from the persons having the highest number not exceeding three on the list of those voted for as President, the House of Representatives shall choose immediately, by ballot, the President. But in choosing the President, the votes shall be taken by States, the representation from each state having one vote; a quorum for this purpose shall consist of a member or members from two-thirds of the states, and a majority of all the states shall be necessary to a choice. And if the House of Representatives shall not choose a President whenever the right of choice shall devolve upon them, before the fourth day of March next following, then the Vice-President shall act as President, as in the case of the death or other constitutional disability of the President. The person having the greatest number of votes as Vice-President, shall be the Vice-President, if such number be the majority of the whole number of electors appointed, and if no person have a majority, then from the two highest numbers on the list, the Senate shall choose the Vice-President; a quorum for the purpose shall consist of two-thirds of the whole number of Senators, and a majority of the whole number shall be necessary to a choice. But no person constitutionally ineligible to the office of President shall be eligible to that of Vice-President of the United States.

ARTICLE XIII.

SECTION 1. Neither slavery nor involuntary servitude, except as a punishment for crime, whereof the party shall have been duly convicted, shall exist within the United States, or any place subject to their jurisdiction.

SEC. 2. Congress shall have power to enforce this article by appropriate legislation.

ARTICLE XIV.

SECTION 1. All persons born or naturalized in the United States and subject to the jurisdiction thereof, are citizens of the United States, and of the state wherein they reside. No state shall make or enforce any law which shall abridge the privileges or immunities of citizens of the United States; nor shall any state deprive any person of life, liberty, or property, without due process of law, nor deny to any person within its jurisdiction the equal protection of the laws.

SEC. 2. Representatives shall be appointed among the several states according to their respective numbers, counting the whole number of persons in each state, excluding Indians not taxed; but when the right to vote at any election for the choice of Electors for President and Vice-President of the United States, Representatives in Congress, the executive and judicial officers of a state, or the members of the Legislature thereof, is denied to any of the male inhabitants of such state, being twenty-one years of age and citizens of the United States, or in any way abridged except for participation in rebellion or other crimes, the basis of representation therein shall be reduced in the proportion which the number of such male citizens shall bear to the whole number of male citizens twenty-one years of age in such state.

SEC. 3. No person shall be a Senator or Representative in Congress, or Elector of President and Vice-President, or hold any office, civil or military, under the United States, or under any state, who, having previously taken an oath as a Member of Congress, or as an officer of the United States, or as a member of any state Legislature, or as an executive or judicial officer of any state to support the Constitution of the United States, shall have engaged in insurrection or rebellion against the same, or given aid or comfort to the enemies thereof. But Congress may, by a vote of two-thirds of each house, remove such disability.

SEC. 4. The validity of the public debt of the United States authorized by law, including debts incurred for payment of pensions and bounties for services in suppressing insurrection or rebellion, shall not be questioned. But neither the United States nor any state shall pay any debt or obligation incurred in the aid of insurrection or rebellion against the United States, or any loss or emancipation of any slave, but such debts, obligations, and claims shall be held illegal and void.

SEC. 5. The Congress shall have power to enforce, by appropriate legislation, the provisions of this act.

ARTICLE XV.

SECTION 1. The right of citizens of the United States to vote shall not be denied or abridged by the United States, or by any state, on account of race, color, or previous condition of servitude.

SEC. 2. Congress shall have power to enforce this article by appropriate legislation.

ELECTORS OF PRESIDENT AND VICE-PRESIDENT.

NOVEMBER 7, 1876.

COUNTIES.	Hayes and Wheeler, Republican.	Tilden and Hendricks, Democrat.	PeterCooper Greenback.	Smith, Prohibition.	Anti-Secret Societies.
Adams	4953	6308	41	17	....
Alexander	1219	1280	....	....	....
Bond	1520	1142	17	....	....
Boone	1965	363	43	2	....
Brown	944	1495	183	1	....
Bureau	3719	2218	145	2	11
Calhoun	441	900	....	....	....
Carroll	2231	918	111	1	3
Cass	1209	1618	74	7	....
Champaign	4530	3103	604	....	1
Christian	2501	3287	207	1	6
Clark	1814	2197	236	....	9
Clay	1416	1541	112	....	....
Clinton	1329	1989	132	....	....
Coles	2957	2822	102	....	....
Cook	36548	39240	277	....	....
Crawford	1355	1643	38	....	....
Cumberland	1145	1407	129	....	....
De Kalb	3679	1413	65	....	3
DeWitt	1928	1174	746	10	3
Douglas	1631	1357	94	....	....
DuPage	2129	1276	25	....	8
Edgar	2715	2883	161	....	....
Edwards	970	466	61	....	....
Effingham	1145	2265	43	....	....
Fayette	1881	2421	57	....	....
Ford	1601	742	204	....	....
Franklin	966	1302	391	....	....
Fulton	4187	4669	89	....	1
Gallatin	703	1140	282	2	....
Greene	1695	3160	1	....	9
Grundy	1996	1142	108	....	....
Hamilton	627	1433	770	....	4
Hancock	3496	4207	....	....	....
Hardin	330	611	134	....	....
Henderson	1315	1015	1	....	....
Henry	4177	1928	340	4	6
Iroquois	3768	2578	249	14	1
Jackson	2040	2071	106	....	....
Jasper	....	....	....	....	....
Jefferson	1346	1667	647	....	....
Jersey	1345	2166	....	12	....
Jo Daviess	2907	2276	140	2	3
Johnson	1367	893	61	....	....
Kane	5398	2850	172	....	5
Kankakee	2627	1363	26	....	2
Kendall	1869	524	309	....	....
Knox	5235	2632	141	....	1
Lake	2619	1647	55	....	1
La Salle	6277	6001	514	....	15
Lawrence	1198	1329	27	....	....
Lee	3087	2080	100	2	6
Livingston	3550	2134	1170	....	3
Logan	2788	2595	37	....	....
Macon	3120	2782	268	16	....
Macoupin	3567	4076	114	....	....
Madison	4554	4730	39	1	....
Marion	2009	2444	209	....	....
Marshall	1553	1430	135	....	1
Mason	1566	1939	86	3	....
Massac	1231	793	20	....	....
McDonough	2952	2811	347	....	....
McHenry	3465	1874	34	....	3
McLean	6363	4410	518	8	7
Menard	1115	1657	10	....	....
Mercer	2209	1428	90	....	3
Monroe	845	1651	7	....	....
Montgomery	2486	3013	201	....	....
Morgan	3069	3174	109	....	3
Moultrie	1245	1672	28	....	....
Ogle	3833	1921	104	....	8
Peoria	4665	5443	95	....	....
Pope	1319	800	5	....	....
Perry	1541	1383	48	....	....
Piatt	1807	1316	117	....	....
Pike	3055	4040	35	1	4
Pulaski	1043	772	....	....	....
Putnam	646	459	14	....	....
Randolph	2357	2589	2	....	....
Richland	1410	1552	55	....	....
Rock Island	3912	2838	27	....	....
Saline	980	1081	641	....	....
Sangamon	4851	5847	29	....	....
Schuyler	1522	1804	115	....	....
Scott	910	1269	182	....	....
Shelby	2069	3553	341	....	....
Stark	1140	786	96	....	....
St. Clair	4708	5891	99	....	1
Stephenson	3198	2758	26	....	3
Tazewell	2850	3171	44	2	2
Union	978	2155	3	....	....
Vermilion	4372	3031	288	....	9
Wabash	650	936	207	....	....
Warren	2795	1984	138	....	1
Washington	1911	1671	39	....	....
Wayne	1570	1751	482	....	....
White	1297	2066	469	....	4
Whiteside	3851	2131	133	8	1
Will	4770	3999	677	....	....
Williamson	1672	1644	41	....	..
Winnebago	4505	1568	70	13	2
Woodford	1733	2105	237	1	4
Total	275958	257099	16951	130	157

PRACTICAL RULES FOR EVERY DAY USE.

How to find the gain or loss per cent. when the cost and selling price are given.

RULE.—Find the difference between the cost and selling price, which will be the gain or loss.

Annex two ciphers to the gain or loss, and divide it by the cost price ; the result will be the gain or loss per cent.

How to change gold into currency.

RULE.—Multiply the given sum of gold by the price of gold.

How to change currency into gold.

Divide the amount in currency by the price of gold.

How to find each partner's share of the gain or loss in a copartnership business.

RULE.—Divide the whole gain or loss by the entire stock, the quotient will be the gain or loss per cent.

Multiply each partner's stock by this per cent., the result will be each one's share of the gain or loss.

How to find gross and net weight and price of hogs.

A short and simple method for finding the net weight, or price of hogs, when the gross weight or price is given, and vice versa.

NOTE.—It is generally assumed that the gross weight of Hogs **diminished** by 1-5 or 20 per cent. of itself gives the net weight, and the net weight **increased** by ¼ or 25 per cent. of itself equals the gross weight.

To find the net weight or gross price.

Multiply the given number by .8 (tenths.)

To find the gross weight or net price.

Divide the given number by .8 (tenths.)

How to find the capacity of a granary, bin, or wagon-bed.

RULE.—Multiply (by short method) the number of cubic feet by 6308, and point off ONE decimal place—the result will be the correct answer in bushels and tenths of a bushel.

For only an approximate answer, multiply the cubic feet by 8, and point off one decimal place.

How to find the contents of a corn-crib.

RULE.—Multiply the number of cubic feet by 54, short method, or by 4½ ordinary method, and point off ONE decimal place—the result will be the answer in bushels.

NOTE.—In estimating corn in the ear, the **quality** and the **time it has been cribbed** must be taken into consideration, since corn will shrink considerably during the Winter and Spring. This rule generally holds good for corn measured at the time it is cribbed, provided it is sound and clean.

How to find the contents of a cistern or tank.

RULE.—Multiply the square of the mean diameter by the depth (all in feet) and this product by 5681 (short method), and point off ONE decimal place—the result will be the contents in barrels of 31½ gallons.

How to find the contents of a barrel or cask.

RULE.—Under the square of the mean diameter, write the length (all in inches) in REVERSED order, so that its UNITS will fall under the TENS; multiply by short method, and this product again by 430; point off one decimal place, and the result will be the answer in wine gallons.

How to measure boards.

RULE.—Multiply the length (in feet) by the width (in inches) and divide the product by 12—the result will be the contents in square feet.

How to measure scantlings, joists, planks, sills, etc.

RULE.—Multiply the width, the thickness, and the length together (the width and thickness in inches, and the length in feet), and divide the product by 12—the result will be square feet.

How to find the number of acres in a body of land.

RULE.—Multiply the length by the width (in rods), and divide the product by 160 (carrying the division to 2 decimal places if there is a remainder); the result will be the answer in acres and hundredths.

When the opposite sides of a piece of land are of unequal length, add them together and take one-half for the mean length or width.

How to find the number of square yards in a floor or wall.

RULE.—Multiply the length by the width or height (in feet), and divide the product by 9, the result will be square yards.

How to find the number of bricks required in a building.

RULE.—Multiply the number of cubic feet by 22½.

The number of cubic feet is found by multiplying the length, height and thickness (in feet) together.

Bricks are usually made 8 inches long, 4 inches wide, and two inches thick; hence, it requires 27 bricks to make a cubic foot without mortar, but it is generally assumed that the mortar fills 1-6 of the space.

How to find the number of shingles required in a roof.

RULE.—Multiply the number of square feet in the roof by 8, if the shingles are exposed 4½ inches, or by 7 1-5 if exposed 5 inches.

To find the number of square feet, multiply the length of the roof by twice the length of the rafters.

To find the length of the rafters, at ONE-FOURTH pitch, multiply the width of the building by .56 (hundredths); at ONE-THIRD pitch, by .6 (tenths); at TWO-FIFTHS pitch, by .64 (hundredths); at ONE-HALF pitch, by .71 (hundredths). This gives the length of the rafters from the apex to the end of the wall, and whatever they are to project must be taken into consideration.

NOTE.—By ¼ or ⅓ pitch is meant that the apex or comb of the roof is to be ¼ or ⅓ the width of the building **higher** than the walls or base of the rafters.

How to reckon the cost of hay.

RULE.—Multiply the number of pounds by half the price per ton, and remove the decimal point three places to the left.

How to measure grain.

RULE.—Level the grain; ascertain the space it occupies in cubic feet; multiply the number of cubic feet by 8, and point off one place to the left.

NOTE.—Exactness requires the addition to every three hundred bushels of one extra bushel.

The foregoing rule may be used for finding the number of gallons, by multiplying the number of bushels by 8.

If the corn in the box is in the ear, divide the answer by 2, to find the number of bushels of shelled corn, because it requires 2 bushels of ear corn to make 1 of shelled corn.

Rapid rules for measuring land without instruments.

In measuring land, the first thing to ascertain is the contents of any given plot in square yards; then, given the number of yards, find out the number of rods and acres.

The most ancient and simplest measure of distance is a step. Now, an ordinary-sized man can train himself to cover one yard at a stride, on the average, with sufficient accuracy for ordinary purposes.

To make use of this means of measuring distances, it is essential to walk in a straight line; to do this, fix the eye on two objects in a line straight ahead, one comparatively near, the other remote; and, in walking, keep these objects constantly in line.

Farmers and others by adopting the following simple and ingenious contrivance, may always carry with them the scale to construct a correct yard measure.

Take a foot rule, and commencing at the base of the little finger of the left hand, mark the quarters of the foot on the outer borders of the left arm, pricking in the marks with indelible ink.

To find how many rods in length will make an acre, the width being given.

RULE.—Divide 160 by the width, and the quotient will be the answer.

How to find the number of acres in any plot of land, the number of rods being given.

RULE.—Divide the number of rods by 8, multiply the quotient by 5, and remove the decimal point two places to the left.

The diameter being given, to find the circumference.

RULE.—Multiply the diameter by 3 1-7.

How to find the diameter, when the circumference is given.

RULE.—Divide the circumference by 3 1-7.

To find how many solid feet a round stick of timber of the same thickness throughout will contain when squared.

RULE.—Square half the diameter in inches, multiply by 2, multiply by the length in feet, and divide the product by 144.

General rule for measuring timber, to find the solid contents in feet.

RULE.—Multiply the depth in inches by the breadth in inches, and then multiply by the length in feet, and divide by 144.

To find the number of feet of timber in trees with the bark on.

RULE.—Multiply the square of one-fifth of the circumference in inches, by twice the length, in feet, and divide by 144. Deduct 1-10 to 1-15 according to the thickness of the bark.

Howard's new rule for computing interest.

RULE.—The reciprocal of the rate is the time for which the interest on any sum of money will be shown by simply removing the decimal point two places to the left; for ten times that time, remove the point one place to the left; for 1-10 of the same time, remove the point three places to the left.

Increase or diminish the results to suit the time given.

NOTE.—The reciprocal of the rate is found by **inverting** the rate; thus 3 per cent. per month, inverted, becomes ⅓ of a month, or 10 days.

When the rate is expressed by one figure, always write it thus: 3-1, three ones.

Rule for converting English into American currency.

Multiply the pounds, with the shillings and pence stated in decimals, by 400 plus the premium in fourths, and divide the product by 90.

U. S. GOVERNMENT LAND MEASURE.

A township—36 sections each a mile square.

A section—640 acres.

A quarter section, half a mile square—160 acres.

An eighth section, half a mile long, north and south, and a quarter of a mile wide—80 acres.

A sixteenth section, a quarter of a mile square—40 acres.

The sections are all numbered 1 to 36, commencing at the north-east corner.

The sections are divided into quarters, which are named by the cardinal points. The quarters are divided in the same way. The description of a forty acre lot would read: The south half of the west half of the south-west quarter of section 1 in township 24, north of range 7 west, or as the case might be; and sometimes will fall short and sometimes overrun the number of acres it is supposed to contain.

The nautical mile is 795 4-5 feet longer than the common mile.

SURVEYORS' MEASURE.

7 92-100 inches	make 1 link.
25 links	" 1 rod.
4 rods	" 1 chain.
80 chains	" 1 mile.

NOTE.—A chain is 100 links, equal to 4 rods or 66 feet.

Shoemakers formerly used a subdivision of the inch called a barley-corn; three of which made an inch.

Horses are measured directly over the fore feet, and the standard of measure is four inches—called a hand.

In Biblical and other old measurements, the term span is sometimes used, which is a length of nine inches.

The sacred cubit of the Jews was 24.024 inches in length.

The common cubit of the Jews was 21.704 inches in length.

A pace is equal to a yard or 36 inches.

A fathom is equal to 6 feet.

A league is three miles, but its length is variable, for it is strictly speaking a nautical term, and should be three geographical miles, equal to 3.45 statute miles, but when used on land, three statute miles are said to be a league.

In cloth measure an aune is equal to 1¼ yards, or 45 inches.

An Amsterdam ell is equal to 26.796 inches.

A Trieste ell is equal to 25.284 inches.

A Brabant ell is equal to 27.116 inches.

HOW TO KEEP ACCOUNTS.

Every farmer and mechanic, whether he does much or little business, should keep a record of his transactions in a clear and systematic manner. For the benefit of those who have not had the opportunity of acquiring a primary knowledge of the principles of book-keeping, we here present a simple form of keeping accounts which is easily comprehended, and well adapted to record the business transactions of farmers, mechanics and laborers.

1875. A. H. JACKSON. Dr. Cr.

1875.		A. H. JACKSON.	Dr.		Cr.	
Jan.	10	To 7 bushels Wheat.................... at $1.25	$8	75		
"	17	By shoeing span of Horses....................			$2	50
Feb.	4	To 14 bushels Oats.................... at $ .45	6	30		
"	4	To 5 lbs. Butter.................... at .25	1	25		
March	8	By new Harrow....................			18	00
"	8	By sharpening 2 Plows....................				40
"	13	By new Double-Tree....................			2	25
"	27	To Cow and Calf....................	48	00		
April	9	To half ton of Hay....................	6	25		
"	9	By Cash....................			25	00
May	6	By repairing Corn-Planter....................			4	75
"	24	To one Sow with Pigs....................	17	50		
July	4	By Cash, to balance account....................			35	15
			$88	05	$88	05

1875. CASSA MASON. Dr. Cr.

1875.		CASSA MASON.	Dr.		Cr.	
March	21	By 3 days' labor.................... at $1.25			$3	75
"	21	To 2 Shoats.................... at 3.00	$6	00		
"	23	To 18 bushels Corn.................... at .45	8	10		
May	1	By 1 month's Labor....................			25	00
"	1	To Cash....................	10	00		
June	19	By 8 days' Mowing.................... at $1.50			12	00
"	26	To 50 lbs. Flour....................	2	75		
July	10	To 27 lbs. Meat.................... at $ .10	2	70		
"	29	By 9 days' Harvesting.................... at 2.00			18	00
Aug.	12	By 6 days' Labor.................... at 1.50			9	00
"	12	To Cash....................	20	00		
Sept.	1	To Cash to balance account....................	18	20		
			$67	75	$67	75

INTEREST TABLE.

A Simple Rule for Accurately Computing Interest at Any Given Per Cent. for Any Length of Time.

Multiply the *principal* (amount of money at interest) by the *time reduced to days*; then divide this *product* by the *quotient* obtained by dividing 360 (the number of days in the interest year) by the *per cent.* of interest, and *the quotient thus obtained* will be the required interest.

ILLUSTRATION.

Require the interest of $462.50 for one month and eighteen days at 6 per cent. An interest month is 30 days; one month and eighteen days equal 48 days. $462.50 multiplied by .48 gives $222.0000; 360 divided by 6 (the per cent. of interest) gives 60, and $222.0000 divided by 60 will give you the exact interest, which is $3.70. If the rate of interest in the above example were 12 per cent., we would divide the $222.0000 by 30 (because 360 divided by 12 gives 30); if 4 per cent., we would divide by 90; if 8 per cent., by 45; and in like manner for any other per cent.

Solution.

```
         $462.50
             .48
         -------
          370000
6)360     185000
-----    -------
   60)$222.0000($3.70
        180
        ---
        420
        420
        ---
         00
```

MISCELLANEOUS TABLE.

12 units, or things, 1 Dozen.	196 pounds, 1 Barrel of Flour.	24 sheets of paper, 1 Quire.
12 dozen, 1 Gross.	200 pounds, 1 Barrel of Pork.	20 quires paper 1 Ream.
20 things, 1 Score.	56 pounds, 1 Firkin of Butter.	4 ft. wide, 4 ft. high, and 8 ft. long, 1 Cord Wood.

NAMES OF THE STATES OF THE UNION, AND THEIR SIGNIFICATIONS.

Virginia.—The oldest of the States, was so called in honor of Queen Elizabeth, the "Virgin Queen," in whose reign Sir Walter Raleigh made his first attempt to colonize that region.

Florida.—Ponce de Leon landed on the coast of Florida on Easter Sunday, and called the country in commemoration of the day, which was the Pasqua Florida of the Spaniards, or "Feast of Flowers."

Louisiana was called after Louis the Fourteenth, who at one time owned that section of the country.

Alabama was so named by the Indians, and signifies "Here we Rest."

Mississippi is likewise an Indian name, meaning "Long River."

Arkansas, from Kansas, the Indian word for "smoky water." Its prefix was really *arc*, the French word for "bow."

The *Carolinas* were originally one tract, and were called "Carolana," after Charles the Ninth of France.

Georgia owes its name to George the Second of England, who first established a colony there in 1732.

Tennessee is the Indian name for the "River of the Bend," *i. e.*, the Mississippi which forms its western boundary.

Kentucky is the Indian name for "at the head of the river."

Ohio means "beautiful;" *Iowa*, "drowsy ones;" *Minnesota*, "cloudy water," and *Wisconsin*, "wild-rushing channel."

Illinois is derived from the Indian word *illini*, men, and the French suffix *ois*, together signifying "tribe of men."

Michigan was called by the name given the lake, *fish-weir*, which was so styled from its fancied resemblance to a fish trap.

Missouri is from the Indian word "muddy," which more properly applies to the river that flows through it.

Oregon owes its Indian name also to its principal river.

Cortes named *California*.

Massachusetts is the Indian for "The country around the great hills."

Connecticut, from the Indian Quon-ch-ta-Cut, signifying "Long River."

Maryland, after Henrietta Maria, Queen of Charles the First, of England.

New York was named by the Duke of York.

Pennsylvania means "Penn's woods," and was so called after William Penn, its orignal owner.

Delaware after Lord De La Ware.

New Jersey, so called in honor of Sir George Carteret, who was Governor of the Island of Jersey, in the British Channel.

Maine was called after the province of Maine in France, in compliment of Queen Henrietta of England, who owned that province.

Vermont, from the French word *Vert Mont*, signifying Green Mountain.

New Hampshire, from Hampshire county in England. It was formerly called Laconia.

The little State of *Rhode Island* owes its name to the Island of Rhodes in the Mediterranean, which domain it is said to greatly resemble.

Texas is the American word for the Mexican name by which all that section of the country was called before it was ceded to the United States.

POPULATION OF THE UNITED STATES.

STATES AND TERRITORIES.	Total Population.
Alabama	996,992
Arkansas	484,471
California	560,247
Connecticut	537,454
Delaware	125,015
Florida	187,748
Georgia	1,184,109
Illinois	2,539,891
Indiana	1,680,637
Iowa	1,191,792
Kansas	364,399
Kentucky	1,321,011
Louisiana	726,915
Maine	626,915
Maryland	780,894
Massachusetts	1,457,351
Michigan	1,184,059
Minnesota	439,706
Mississippi	827,922
Missouri	1,721,295
Nebraska	122,993
Nevada	42,491
New Hampshire	318,300
New Jersey	906,096
New York	4,382,759
North Carolina	1,071,361
Ohio	2,665,260
Oregon	90,923
Pennsylvania	3,521,791
Rhode Island	217,353
South Carolina	705,606
Tennessee	1,258,520
Texas	818,579
Vermont	330,551
Virginia	1,225,163
West Virginia	442,014
Wisconsin	1,054,670
Total States	38,113,253
Arizona	9,658
Colorada	39,864
Dakota	14,181
District of Columbia	131,700
Idaho	14,999
Montana	20,595
New Mexico	91,874
Utah	86,786
Washington	23,955
Wyoming	9,118
Total Territories	442,730
Total United States	38,555,983

POPULATION OF FIFTY PRINCIPAL CITIES.

CITIES.	Aggregate Population.
New York, N. Y	942,292
Philadelphia, Pa	674,022
Brooklyn, N. Y	396,099
St. Louis, Mo	310,864
Chicago, Ill	298,977
Baltimore, Md	267,354
Boston, Mass	250,526
Cincinnati, Ohio	216,239
New Orleans, La	191,418
San Francisco, Cal	149,473
Buffalo, N. Y	117,714
Washington, D. C	109,199
Newark, N. J	105,059
Louisville, Ky	100,753
Cleveland, Ohio	92,829
Pittsburg, Pa	86,076
Jersey City, N. J	82,546
Detroit, Mich	79,577
Milwaukee, Wis	71,440
Albany, N. Y	69,422
Providence, R. I	68,904
Rochester, N. Y	62,386
Allegheny, Pa	53,180
Richmond, Va	51,038
New Haven, Conn	50,840
Charleston, S. C	48,956
Indianapolis, Ind	48,244
Troy, N. Y	46,465
Syracuse, N. Y	43,051
Worcester, Mass	41,105
Lowell, Mass	40,928
Memphis, Tenn	40,226
Cambridge, Mass	39,634
Hartford, Conn	37,180
Scranton, Pa	35,092
Reading, Pa	33,930
Paterson, N. J	33,579
Kansas City, Mo	32,260
Mobile, Ala	32,034
Toledo, Ohio	31,584
Portland, Me	31,413
Columbus, Ohio	31,274
Wilmington, Del	30,841
Dayton, Ohio	30,473
Lawrence, Mass	28,921
Utica, N. Y	28,804
Charlestown, Mass	28,323
Savannah, Ga	28,235
Lynn, Mass	28,233
Fall River, Mass	26,766

POPULATION OF THE UNITED STATES.

STATES AND TERRITORIES.	Area in square Miles.	POPULATION. 1870.	POPULATION. 1875.	Miles R. R. 1872.
States.				
Alabama	50,722	996,992	....	1,671
Arkansas	52,198	484,471	....	25
California	188,981	560,247	....	1,013
Connecticut	4,674	537,454	....	820
Delaware	2,120	125,015	....	227
Florida	59,268	187,748	....	466
Georgia	58,000	1,184,109	....	2,108
Illinois	55,410	2,539,891	....	5,904
Indiana	33,809	1,680,637	....	3,529
Iowa	55,045	1,191,792	1,350,544	3,160
Kansas	81,318	364,399	528,349	1,760
Kentucky	37,600	1,321,011	....	1,123
Louisiana	41,346	726,915	857,039	539
Maine	31,776	626,915	....	871
Maryland	11,184	780,894	....	820
Massachusetts	7,800	1,457,351	1,651,912	1,606
Michigan*	56,451	1,184,059	1,334,031	2,235
Minnesota	83,531	439,706	598,429	1,612
Mississippi	47,156	827,922	....	990
Missouri	65,350	1,721,295	....	2,580
Nebraska	75,995	123,993	246,280	828
Nevada	112,090	42,491	52,540	593
New Hampshire	9,280	318,300	....	790
New Jersey	8,320	906,096	1,026,502	1,265
New York	47,000	4,382,759	4,705,208	4,470
North Carolina	50,704	1,071,361	....	1,190
Ohio	39,964	2,665,260	....	3,740
Oregon	95,244	90,923	....	159
Pennsylvania	46,000	3,521,791	....	5,113
Rhode Island	1,306	217,353	258,239	136
South Carolina	29,385	705,606	925,145	1,201
Tennessee	45,600	1,258,520	....	1,520
Texas	237,504	818,579	....	865
Vermont	10,212	330,551	....	675
Virginia	40,904	1,225,163	....	1,490
West Virginia	23,000	442,014	....	485
Wisconsin	53,924	1,054,670	1,236,729	1,725
Total States	1,950,171	38,113,253	....	59,587
Territories.				
Arizona	113,916	9,658	....	....
Colorado	104,500	39,864	....	392
Dakota	147,490	14,181	....	....
Dist. of Columbia	60	131,700	....	*
Idaho	90,932	14,999	....	....
Montana	143,776	20,595	....	....
New Mexico	121,201	91,874	....	....
Utah	80,056	86,786	....	375
Washington	69,944	23,955	....	....
Wyoming	93,107	9,118	....	498
Total Territories.	965,032	442,730	....	1,265
Aggregate of U. S.	2,915,203	38,555,983	....	60,852

* Last Census of Michigan taken in 1874.

* Included in the Railroad Mileage of Maryland.

PRINCIPAL COUNTRIES OF THE WORLD;

POPULATION AND AREA.

COUNTRIES.	Population.	Date of Census.	Area in Square Miles.	Inhabitants to Square Mile.	CAPITALS.	Population.
China	446,500,000	1871	3,741,846	119.3	Pekin	1,648,800
British Empire	226,817,108	1871	4,677,432	48.6	London	3,251,800
Russia	81,925,400	1871	8,003,778	10.2	St. Petersburg	667,000
United States with Alaska	38,925,600	1870	2,603,884	7.78	Washington	109,199
France	36,469,800	1866	204,091	178.7	Paris	1,825,300
Austria and Hungary	35,904,400	1869	240,348	149.4	Vienna	833,900
Japan	34,785,300	1871	149,399	232.8	Yeddo	1,554,900
Great Britain and Ireland	31,817,100	1871	121,315	262.3	London	3,251,800
German Empire	29,906,092	1871	160,207	187.	Berlin	825,400
Italy	27,439,921	1871	118,847	230.9	Rome	244,484
Spain	16,642,000	1867	195,775	85.	Madrid	332,000
Brazil	10,000,000	......	3,253,029	3.07	Rio Janeiro	420,000
Turkey	16,463,000	......	672,621	24.4	Constantinople	1,075,000
Mexico	9,173,000	1869	761,526	......	Mexico	210,300
Sweden and Norway	5,921,500	1870	292,871	20.	Stockholm	136,900
Persia	5,000,000	1870	635,964	7.8	Teheran	120,000
Belgium	5,021,300	1869	11,373	441.5	Brussels	314,100
Bavaria	4,861,400	1871	29,292	165.9	Munich	169,500
Portugal	3,995,200	1868	34,494	115.8	Lisbon	224,063
Holland	3,688,300	1870	12,680	290.9	Hague	90,100
New Grenada	3,000,000	1870	357,157	8.4	Bogota	45,000
Chili	2,000,000	1869	132,616	15.1	Santiago	115,400
Switzerland	2,669,100	1870	15,992	166.9	Berne	36,000
Peru	2,500,000	1871	471,838	5.3	Lima	160,100
Bolivia	2,000,000	......	497,321	4.	Chuquisaca	25,000
Argentine Republic	1,812,000	1869	871,848	2.1	Buenos Ayres	177,800
Wurtemburg	1,818,500	1871	7,533	241.4	Stuttgart	91,600
Denmark	1,784,700	1870	14,753	120.9	Copenhagen	162,042
Venezuela	1,500,000	......	368,238	4.2	Caraccas	47,000
Baden	1,461,400	1871	5,912	247.	Carlsruhe	36,600
Greece	1,457,900	1870	19,353	75.3	Athens	43,400
Guatemala	1,180,000	1871	40,879	28.9	Guatemala	40,000
Ecuador	1,300,000	......	218,928	5.9	Quito	70,000
Paraguay	1,000,000	1871	63,787	15.6	Asuncion	48,000
Hesse	823,138	......	2,969	277.	Darmstadt	30,000
Liberia	718,000	1871	9,576	74.9	Monrovia	3,000
San Salvador	600,000	1871	7,335	81.8	Sal Salvador	15,000
Hayti	572,000	......	10,205	56.	Port au Prince	20,000
Nicaragua	350,000	1871	58,171	6.	Managua	10,000
Uruguay	300,000	1871	66,722	6.5	Monte Video	44,500
Honduras	350,000	1871	47,092	7.4	Comayagua	12,000
San Domingo	136,000	......	17,827	7.6	San Domingo	20,000
Costa Rica	165,000	1870	21,505	7.7	San Jose	2,000
Hawaii	62,950	......	7,633	80.	Honolulu	7,633

POPULATION OF ILLINOIS,

By Counties.

COUNTIES.	AGGREGATE.					
	1870.	1860.	1850.	1840.	1830.	1820.
Adams	56362	41323	26508	14476	2186	-------
Alexander	10564	4707	2484	3313	1390	626
Bond	13152	9815	6144	5060	3124	2931
Boone	12942	11678	7624	1705	-------	-------
Brown	12205	9938	7198	4183	-------	-------
Bureau	32415	26426	8841	3067	-------	-------
Calhoun	6562	5144	3231	1741	1090	-------
Carroll	16705	11733	4586	1023	-------	-------
Cass	11580	11325	7253	2981	-------	-------
Champaign	32737	14629	2649	1475	-------	-------
Christian	20363	10492	3203	1878	-------	-------
Clark	18719	14987	9532	7453	3940	931
Clay	15875	9336	4289	3228	755	-------
Clinton	16285	10941	5139	3718	2330	-------
Coles	25235	14203	9335	9616	-------	-------
Cook	349966	144954	43385	10201	-------	-------
						*23
Crawford	13889	11551	7135	4422	3117	2999
Cumberland	12223	8311	3718	-------	-------	-------
De Kalb	23265	19086	7540	1697	-------	-------
De Witt	14768	10820	5002	3247	-------	-------
Douglas	13484	7140	-------	-------	-------	-------
Du Page	16685	14701	9290	3535	-------	-------
Edgar	21450	16925	10692	8225	4071	-------
Edwards	7565	5454	3524	3070	1649	3444
Effingham	15653	7816	3799	1675	-------	-------
Fayette	19638	11189	8075	6328	2704	-------
Ford	9103	1979	-------	-------	-------	-------
Franklin	12652	9393	5681	3682	4083	1763
Fulton	38291	33338	22508	13142	1841	-------
Gallatin	11134	8055	5448	10760	7405	3155
Greene	20277	16093	12429	11951	7674	-------
Grundy	14938	10379	3023	-------	-------	-------
Hamilton	13014	9915	6362	3945	2616	-------
Hancock	35935	29061	14652	9946	483	-------
Hardin	5113	3759	2887	1378	-------	-------
Henderson	12582	9501	4612	-------	-------	-------
Henry	35506	20660	3807	1260	41	-------
Iroquois	25782	12325	4149	1695	-------	-------
Jackson	19634	9589	5862	3566	1828	1542
Jasper	11234	8364	3220	1472	-------	-------
Jefferson	17864	12965	8109	5762	2555	691
Jersey	15054	12051	7354	4535	-------	-------
Jo Daviess	27820	27325	18604	6180	2111	-------
Johnson	11248	9342	4114	3626	1596	843
Kane	39091	30062	16703	6501	-------	-------
Kankakee	24352	15412	-------	-------	-------	-------
Kendall	12399	13074	7730	-------	-------	-------
Knox	39522	28663	13279	7060	274	-------
Lake	21014	18257	14226	2634	-------	-------
La Salle	60792	48332	17815	9348	-------	-------
Lawrence	12533	9214	6121	7092	3668	-------
Lee	27171	17651	5292	2035	-------	-------
Livingston	31471	11637	1553	759	-------	-------
Logan	23053	14272	5128	2333	-------	-------

POPULATION OF ILLINOIS—Concluded.

COUNTIES.	AGGREGATE.					
	1870.	1860.	1850.	1840.	1830.	1820.
Macon	26481	13738	3988	3039	1122	....
Macoupin	32726	24602	12355	7926	1990	....
Madison	44131	31251	20441	14433	6221	13550
Marion	20622	12739	6720	4742	2125	....
Marshall	16950	13437	5180	1849	....	....
Mason	16184	10931	5921	....	....	....
Massac	9581	6213	4092	....	....	....
McDonough	26509	20069	7616	5308	(*b*)	....
McHenry	23762	22089	14978	2578	....	....
McLean	53988	28772	10163	6565	....	....
Menard	11735	9584	6349	4431	....	....
Mercer	18769	15042	5246	2352	26	....
						*21
Monroe	12982	12832	7679	4481	2000	1516
Montgomery	25314	13979	6277	4490	2953	....
Morgan	28463	22112	16064	19547	12714	....
Moultrie	10385	6385	3234	....	....	....
Ogle	27492	22888	10020	3479	....	....
Peoria	47540	36601	17547	6153	(*c*)	....
Perry	13723	9552	5278	3222	1215	....
Piatt	10953	6127	1606	....	....	....
Pike	30768	27249	18819	11728	2396	....
Pope	11437	6742	3975	4094	3316	2610
Pulaski	8752	3943	2265	....	....	....
Putnam	6280	5587	3924	2131	*c*1310	....
Randolph	20859	17205	11079	7944	4429	3492
Richland	12803	9711	4012	....	....	....
Rock Island	29783	21005	6937	2610	....	....
Saline	12714	9331	5588	....	....	....
Sangamon	46352	32274	19228	14716	12960	....
Schuyler	17419	14684	10573	6972	*b*2959	....
Scott	10530	9069	7914	6215	....	....
Shelby	25476	14613	7807	6659	2972	....
Stark	10751	9004	3710	1573	....	....
						*5
St. Clair	51068	37694	20180	13631	7078	5248
Stephenson	30608	25112	11666	2800	....	....
Tazewell	27903	21470	12052	7221	4716	....
Union	16518	11181	7615	5524	3239	2362
Vermilion	30388	19800	11492	9303	5836	....
Wabash	8841	7313	4690	4240	2710	....
Warren	23174	18336	8176	6739	308	....
Washington	17599	13731	6953	4810	1675	1517
Wayne	19758	12223	6825	5133	2553	1114
White	16846	12403	8925	7919	6091	4828
Whitesides	27503	18737	5361	2514	....	....
Will	43013	29321	16703	10167	....	....
Williamson	17329	12205	7216	4457	....	....
Winnebago	29301	24491	11773	4609	....	....
Woodford	18956	13282	4415	....	....	....
						*49
Total	2539891	1711951	851470	476183	157445	55162

PRODUCTIONS OF AGRICULTURE, STATE OF ILLINOIS, BY COUNTIES.—1870.

COUNTIES.	Improved Land.	Woodl'nd	Other unimproved	Spring Wheat.	Winter Wheat.	Rye.	Indian Corn.	Oats.
	Number.	Number.	Number.	Bushels.	Bushels.	Bushels.	Bushels.	Bushels.
Total	19.329.952	5,061.578	1.491.331	10.133.207	19.995.198	2.456.578	129.921.395	42.780.851
Adams	287,926	112,576	19,370	16,191	947.616	20,989	1,452,905	759,074
Alexander	13,836	17,761	....	....	42,658	30	244,220	21,627
Bond	145,045	42,613	1,915	700	368.625	6,240	1,064.052	461,097
Boone	137,307	29,886	2,658	241,042	599	35,871	466,985	579,127
Brown	57,062	35,491	25.608	13,276	117,502	4,742	337,769	70,852
Bureau	398,611	41,866	15.803	465,236	7[illegible]	43,811	3,030,404	987,426
Calhoun	37,684	63,443	2,754	75	221,2[illegible]3	186	234,041	26,234
Carroll	186,864	29,793	33,302	418,073	260	25,721	1,367,965	775,100
Cass	92,902	33,493	6,604	12,165	127,054	2.772	1,146,980	168,784
Champaign	419,368	16,789	58,502	102,577	123,091	45,752	3,924,720	721,375
Christian	241,472	19,803	19,173	18,360	504,041	10,722	1,883,336	383,821
Clark	118,594	102,201	5,420	....	195,118	7,308	614,582	212,628
Clay	146,922	80,612	5,225	1,894	85,737	3,221	1,019,994	269,945
Clinton	150,177	48,868	8,722	500	610,888	1,619	813.257	446,324
Coles	208,337	45,214	3,274	2,651	154,485	8,825	2,133,111	315,954
Cook	348,824	19,635	17,337	144,296	4,904	20,171	570,427	1,584,225
Crawford	105,505	78,350	27,185	60	212,924	15,497	581,964	136,255
Cumberland	75,342	40,334	5,604	550	84,697	14,798	403,075	171,880
DeKalb	334,502	17,722	6,551	398,059	190	21,018	1,023,849	1,087,074
DeWitt	168,539	29,548	17,633	106,493	11,695	11 540	1,311,635	216,756
Douglas	147,633	11,897	7,316	7,683	65,461	9,017	1,680,225	225,074
DuPage	164,874	17,243	3.851	106,096	693	7,532	331,981	860,809
Edgar	265,458	66,803	14,282	13,283	247,360	37,508	2,107,615	290,679
Edwards	58,912	57,585	830	....	122,703	528	352,371	129,152
Effingham	120,343	56,330	26,206	77	195,716	19,759	620,247	386.073
Fayette	187,196	93,460	16,786	....	351,310	25.328	962,525	497,395
Ford	141,228	2,996	63,976	42,571	1,008	11,577	565,671	154,589
Franklin	80,749	3,994	86,710	365	111.324	5.195	653,209	222,426
Fulton	228,132	123,823	4,076	193,669	223,930	131,711	1,508,763	261,390
Gallatin	49,572	68,750	2,565	....	83,093	512	509,491	27,164
Greene	175,408	93,242	29.653	....	577,400	415	1,051,313	64,029
Grundy	193,999	6,256	4,505	21,700	150	4,930	295,971	269,332
Hamilton	88,996	93,878	3,343	129	92,347	11,672	735,252	203,464
Hancock	311,517	43,385	18,480	181,378	232,750	133,533	1,510,401	579,599
Hardin	28,117	44,771	107	13	32,306	865	172,651	26,991
Henderson	140,954	34,705	14,243	161,112	69,062	96,430	1,712,901	229,286
Henry	265,904	12,620	31,459	462,379	445	35,766	2,541,683	668,367
Iroquois	322,510	22,478	63,498	57,160	10,480	23,259	799,810	430,746
Jackson	78,548	87,642	5,991	890	329,036	524	611,951	149,931
Jasper	90,867	67,023	12,250	....	87,808	9,165	461,345	149,214
Jefferson	118,951	94,888	778	....	100,553	5,934	887,981	285,949
Jersey	94,147	51,427	1,363	....	558,367	....	519,120	71,770
JoDaviess	156,517	82,076	45,779	282,758	555	7.185	1,286,326	874,016
Johnson	57,820	3	79,141	....	92,191	2,468	343,298	74,525
Kane	240,120	34,646	399	188,826	325	23,618	674,333	785,608
Kankakee	312,182	10,978	10,598	103,466	480	12,935	637,399	772,408
Kendall	164.004	14,244	2,283	90,681	1,249	5,163	681,267	468,890
Knox	330,829	41,566	25.155	267,764	7,654	113,547	2,708,319	787,952
Lake	207,779	21,072	24,399	168,914	221	5,870	517,353	699,069
LaSalle	533,724	48,117	2,356	271,181	2,193	48,308	3,077,028	1,509,642
Lawrence	87,828	72,738	3,273	....	264,134	1,121	656,363	131,386
Lee	322,212	12,071	7,409	450,793	2,260	14,829	1,656,978	903,197
Livingston	377,505	12,462	41,788	120,206	1,339	26,163	1,182,696	659,300
Logan	321,709	17,394	408	198,056	40,963	37,232	4,221,640	490,226
Macon	205,259	18,153	9,115	55,239	196,613	29,222	2,214,468	454,648
Macoupin	231,059	81,224	7,343	160	861,398	2.404	1,051,544	459,417
Madison	257,032	89,450	13,675	550	1,207,181	3.685	2.127,549	475,252
Marion	173,081	61,579	4,142	....	173,652	14,517	1,034,057	389,446
Marshall	166,057	28,260	2,976	106,129	900	36,135	1,182,903	362,604
Mason	209,453	31,739	31,013	73,261	125,628	49,182	2,648,726	272,660
Massac	25,151	33,396	30	....	72,316	544	133,126	22,097
McDonough	261,635	52,547	14,035	273,871	36,146	52,401	1,362,490	280,717
McHenry	230,566	53,293	57,998	401,790	270	29,264	1,145,005	910,397
McLean	494,978	40,366	49,087	211,801	10,955	39,824	3,723,379	911,127
Menard	134,173	34,931	13,952	36,152	45,793	4,288	1,973.880	235,091
Mercer	222.809	45,977	22,588	289,291	13,203	40,778	2,054,962	452,889
Monroe	92,810	83,369	666	....	651,767	1,425	543,718	152,251
Montgomery	276,682	47,804	8,495	59	744,891	3,296	1,527,898	668,424
Morgan	293,450	60,217	1,376	18,196	357,523	5,535	3,198,835	198,724
Moultrie	144,220	24,783	13,112	17,128	196,436	6,670	1,753,141	263,992
Ogle	316,883	43,643	14,913	497,038	5,580	157,504	1,787,066	141,540
Peoria	170,729	48,666	2,516	92,361	31,843	99,502	969,224	334,892
Perry	93,754	68,470	220	....	350,446	1,016	384,446	338,760
Piatt	94,454	5,978	13,897	26,382	39,762	9.248	1,029,725	130,610
Pike	233.785	128,953	9,302	130	1,057,497	25,303	1,399,188	161,419
Pope	55.980	87,754	....	....	70,457	2,309	315,958	67,886
Pulaski	19,319	12,516	....	....	44,922	222	195,735	16,511
Putnam	37,271	17,184	4.174	28,137	796	7,707	334,259	86,519
Randolph	140,764	162,274	1,170	450	1,031,022	3,235	510,080	414,487
Richland	75,079	50,618	2.025	....	150,268	3.401	482,594	204,634
Rock Island	155.214	31,239	20,755	243,541	2.279	20,003	1,459,653	276,575
Saline	72,309	70,393	809	200	83.011	568	531,516	69,793
Sangamon	421,748	51,085	19,932	89,304	247,658	23,073	4,388,763	397,718
Schuyler	96,195	62,477	21,294	56,221	165,724	20,841	440,975	119.359
Scott	85.331	44,633	1,610	18	266.105	930	752,771	13.462
Shelby	310,179	74,908	9,314	15,526	452,015	23,686	2,082,578	637,812
Stark	138,129	12,375	2,783	124,630	....	30,534	1,149 878	316.726
St. Clair	231,117	76,591	2,016	2,550	1,562.621	1,008	1,423,121	476,851
Stephenson	254,857	43.167	13,701	527,394	2,118	135,362	1,615,679	960.620
Tazewell	229,126	45,268	14,846	132,417	72,410	59,027	2,062,053	505,841
Union	75,832	83,606	5,300	....	180,231	1,737	679,753	124,473
Vermilion	360,251	53,078	31,122	44,806	249,558	52,476	2,818,027	436,051
Wabash	54,063	37,558	509	....	202.201	....	421,361	110,793
Warren	266.187	27,294	14,583	186,290	5,712	72,212	2,982,853	601.054
Washington	177.592	55,852	1.931	....	672,486	2,576	836,115	533,398
Wayne	147,352	146,794	10,486	266	164,689	8,665	1,179,291	404,482
White	92,398	78.167	869	....	184,321	418	870,521	119.653
Whitesides	239.809	21.823	37.310	457.455	264	31,658	2,162,943	880.838
Will	419,442	24,261	6,335	195,286	1,996	8,030	1,131,458	1,868,682
Williamson	128,448	116,949	1,648	176	170,787	6,228	655,710	180,986
Winnebago	241,373	37,238	15,237	408,606	2,468	137,985	1,237,406	868,903
Woodford	225,504	25,217	23,135	178,139	108,307	20,426	2,154,185	744,581

Geo. W. Girdon

GALENA

History of Jo Daviess County.

GENERAL HISTORY.

When the thirteen American colonies declared their independence of British rule, July 4, 1776, the magnificent valley of the Mississippi and its tributaries was under the jurisdiction of European powers. France had ceded to Great Britain that portion of the Province of Louisiana lying on the east side of the "Father of Waters." The first British Governor, Captain Sterling, took formal possession of Illinois and raised the English flag at Fort Chartres, ten years after the treaty of cession in October, 1765, and in 1766, by an act of Parliament known as the Quebec bill, the Illinois country was annexed to Canada, and this region remained under Canadian jurisdiction until 1778—a period of fourteen years.

In 1778, Col. George Rogers Clarke, a native of Virginia, who had won military fame in conflicts with the Indians of Kentucky, Ohio and elsewhere, conceived the idea of an expedition to capture the British posts in the Illinois country. Patrick Henry, then Governor of Virginia, favored the enterprise, and aided by the advice of Thomas Jefferson, George Mason and George Wythie, directed the expedition. Col. Clarke raised four companies of Virginians, and through his wonderful skill and heroism the expedition was completely successful. The Virginia Legislature voted the thanks of the people to Col. Clarke, his officers and men, for their brilliant achievements, and in October, 1778, by act of the House of Burgesses, established the country of Illinois, embracing all the territory northwest of the Ohio River, and making Col. John Todd, Jr., its civil commandant. "Thus," says Mr. Miller, "Patrick Henry became the first American Governor of Illinois." The proclamation to its inhabitants is dated June 15, 1779.

At the close of the Revolutionary War, Great Britain formally ceded to the United States all her territory east of the Mississipi River, and in 1784 Virginia ceded to the Federal Government all the territory northwest of the Ohio River, her claim to the Illinois country being through a grant from James I. of England, and by virtue of conquest in 1778.

By the ordinance of 1787, all this vast region was organized as the Northwestern Territory. General Arthur St. Clair was made its Governor, with the capital at Marietta, afterwards at Chillicothe, and in 1795, at Cincinnati; but from 1784 until 1790, when Gov. St. Clair organized the first county in Illinois (St. Clair), there was no executive, no legislature and no judicial authority exercised in the county. The people were a law unto themselves, and during these six years it is said that remarkable good feeling, harmony and fidelity to agreements prevailed. Previous to the division of the Northwest Territory, in 1800, there had been but one term of court having criminal jurisdiction in the three western counties of the territory, viz., Knox County, now in Indiana, and St. Clair and Randolph Counties, Illinois.

The ordinance of 1787 provided that not less than three nor more than five states were to be erected out of the territory northwest of the Ohio River. Three states were to include the whole territory, and these states were to be bounded on the north by the British possessions; but Congress reserved the right, if it should be found expedient, to form two more states of that part of the territory which lies north of an east and west line drawn through the southern extremity of Lake Michigan.

It is not necessary to trace the various changes of territorial jurisdiction to which Illinois, and especially its northwestern portion, was subjected, until the admission of the state into the Union in 1818. During all that time this section of the country was inhabited only by Indians, and this whole region was claimed by them. In 1804, the Sacs and Foxes, then a powerful tribe, by treaty made at St. Louis with Gen. Harrison, then Governor of the Territory of Indiana, ceded to the United States all their lands lying east of the Mississippi ; but Black Hawk and other chiefs who were not present at St. Louis, refused to be bound by it. All the territory north of the line drawn west from the southern extremity of Lake Michigan to the Mississippi was in the undisputed possession of the native tribes, when the state was erected, in 1818, except a tract five leagues square on the Mississippi, of which Fever River was about the centre, which, by treaty with various tribes in 1816, the United States Government had reserved ostensibly for a military post, but really to control the lead mines. The Government had had knowledge for many years of the existence of lead mines here, but their location was not known, and it was thought that all would be included within the limits of the reservation. The Government designed to own and hold exclusive control of these mines.

In January, 1818, the Territorial Legislature of Illinois, assembled at Kaskaskia, petitioned Congress for the admission of the territory as a sovereign state with a population of 40,000.

The petition was sent to Nathaniel Pope, the territorial delegate, by whom it was promptly presented, and it was referred to the proper committee, which instructed Mr. Pope to prepare and report a bill in accordance with its prayer. The bill, as drawn in accordance with these instructions, did not embrace the present area of Illinois, and when it was reported to Congress, certain amendments proposed by Mr. Pope were reported with it. It was generally supposed that the line established by the ordinance of 1787, namely, the line drawn through the southern part of Lake Michigan, west to the Mississippi, was to be the northern boundary of the new state. But this, if adopted, would have left the port of Chicago in the Territory of Michigan, as well as all the territory now embraced within the limits of fourteen rich and populous counties in northern Illinois. A critical examination of the ordinance, however, convinced Mr. Pope that Congress had the power and could rightfully extend the northern boundary of the state as far beyond the line provided in 1787 as it pleased. The principal amendments proposed by Mr. Pope, therefore, were, first, that the northern boundary of the new state should be extended to the parallel of 42 deg. 30 min. north latitude—this would give a good harbor on Lake Michigan; and secondly, more important than the boundary line, to apply the three per cent fund arising from the sale of public lands to educational purposes, instead of making roads, as had been the case in Ohio and Indiana. These amendments were adopted without serious opposition, and Illinois was declared an independent state.

These important changes in the original bill, says Mr. Ford in his History of Illinois, "were proposed and carried through both Houses of Congress by Mr. Pope on his own responsibility. The Territorial Legislature had not petitioned for them—no one had suggested them, but they met the general approval of the people." The change of the boundary line, however, suggested to Mr. Pope—from the fact that the boundary as defined by the ordinance of 1787, would have left Illinois without a harbor as Lake Michigan—did not meet the unqualified approval of the people in the northwestern part of the new state. For many years the northern boundary of the state was not definitely known, and the settlers in the northern tier of counties did not know whether they were in Illinois or Michigan Territory. Under the provisions of the ordinance of 1787, Wisconsin at one time laid claim to a portion of northern Illinois, "including," says Mr. Ford, writing in 1847, "fourteen counties embracing the richest and most populous part of the state." October 27, 1827, nine years after the admission of the state, Dr. Horatio Newhall, who had then recently arrived at the Fever River Settlement, wrote to his brother as follows:—"It is uncertain whether I am in the boundary of Illinois or Michigan, but direct your letters to Fever River, Ill., and they will come safely." In October, 1828, a petition was sent to Congress from the people of that part of Illinois lying north of the line established by the ordinance of 1787, and that part of the Territory of Michigan west of Lake Michigan and comprehending the mining district known as the Fever River Lead Mines, praying for the formation of a new territory. A bill had been introduced at the previous session of Congress for the establishment of a new territory north of the State of Illinois, to be called "Huron Territory," upon which report had been made, *in part*, favorable to the wishes of the petitioners, but they asked for the re-establishment of the line as ordained by Congress in 1787. They declared "that the people, inhabiting the territory northwest of the Ohio, had a right to expect that the country lying north of an east and west line passing through the southernmost end of Lake Michigan, to the Mississippi River, and between said lake, the Mississippi and the Canada line, would REMAIN TOGETHER" as a territory and state. They claimed that this was a part of the compact, unchangeably granted by the people of the original states to the people who should inhabit the "territory northwest of the Ohio." They declared that the change of the chartered limits, when Illinois was made a state, was open invasion of their rights in a body when they were unrepresented in either territory; that "an unrepresented people, without their knowledge or consent, have been transferred from one sovereignty to another." They urged that the present "division of the miners by an ideal line, separating into different governments individuals intimately connected in similar pursuits, is embarrassing." They asked for "even-handed justice," and the restoration of their "chartered limits." The *Miners' Journal*, of October 25, 1828, which contains the full text of the petition, says: "We do not fully agree with the memorialists in petitioning Congress again to dispose of that tract of country which has once been granted to Illinois; but we think that it would be for the interest of the miners to be erected, together with the adjoining county above, into a separate territory. And we firmly believe, too, that Congress departed from the clear and express terms of their own ordinance passed in the year 1787, when they granted to the State of Illinois nearly a degree and a half of latitude of the CHARTERED LIMITS of this country. Whether Congress will annex this tract to the new territory we much doubt, but we believe the ultimate decision of the United States Court will be, that the northern boundary line of the State of Illinois shall commence at the southernmost end of Lake Michigan." The petition was unavailing, and the northern line of Illinois remains unchanged, but the agitation of the subject by the people of this region continued. In 1840 the people of the counties north of the ordinance line sent delegates to a convention held at Rockford to take action in relation to the annexation of the tract north of that line to Wisconsin Territory, and it is said the scheme then discussed embraced an effort to make Galena the capital of the territory. Charles S. Hempstead and Frederick Stahl were delegates to the convention for Galena. At that convention, speeches were made by Messrs. Charles S. Hempstead, Martin P. Sweet, Jason P. Marsh, and perhaps others. Resolutions were adopted requesting the senators and representatives in Congress for Illinois to exert their influence in favor of the project. The labors of the convention produced no results, but until the admission of Wisconsin as a state, there was a strong feeling among the people of northwestern Illinois that they rightfully belonged to Wisconsin, and there was a strong desire to be restored to their chartered limits. Perhaps the heavy debt with which Illinois was burdened at that time may have had some influence in causing the feeling.

St. Clair County, organized April 28, 1809, included the whole territory of Illinois and Wisconsin, to the line of Upper Canada, north of Randolph County, these two being the only counties in the territory.

Madison County was erected from the St. Clair, September 14, 1812, and comprised all the territory north of the second township line south, to the line of Upper Canada. County seat, Edwardsville.

Bond County was organized out of part of Madison, January 4, 1817, and extended in a strip about 30 miles wide on each side of the third principal meridian to the northern boundary of the territory.

Pike County was erected January 31, 1821, from Madison, Bond, and other counties, and embraced all the territory north of the Illinois River and its south fork, now Kankakee River. This was the first county erected by the State of Illinois which embraced the present territory of Jo Daviess County. A Gazetteer of Illinois and Wisconsin, published about 1822, says that the county "included a part of the lands appropriated by Congress for the payment of military bounties. The lands constituting that tract, are included within the peninsula of the Illinois and Mississippi, and extend on the meridian line passing through the mouth of the Illinois, one hundred and sixty-two miles north. Pike County will no doubt be divided into several counties; some of which will become very wealthy and important. It is probable that the section about Fort Clark (now Peoria) will be the most thickly settled. On the Mississippi River, above Rock River, lead ore is found in abundance. Pike County contains between 700 and 800 inhabitants. It is attached to the first judicial circuit, sends one member to the House of Representatives and, with Greene, one to the Senate. The county seat is Colesgrove, a post town. It was laid out in 1821, and is situated in township 11 south, in range 2 west of the fourth principal meridian. Very little improvement has yet been made in this place or the vicinity. The situation is high and healthy, and it bids fair to become a place of some importance." This is all that is known of the Town of Colesgrove, the county seat of all this region in 1821.

Fulton County was formed from Pike, January 28, 1823, and included all the territory north of the base line, and west of the fourth principal meridian, which had been in Pike.

Peoria County was created from Fulton, January 13, 1825, and, with some exceptions, included the same territory that comprised Fulton. The county seat was Fort Clark, now Peoria, and the first election of which record exists, within the present limits of Jo Daviess County, was in Fever

River precinct of Peoria County, August 7, 1826. The election was held at the house of James Smith. This was the trading post then recently located by Amos Farrar and occupied by Smith as a tavern: a double log cabin that stood on the west bank of the river about half way between the foot of Perry and the foot of Franklin Streets, Galena. Water Street now passes over its site.

The following is a copy of a document found among the archives of Peoria County, at Peoria.

I hereby certify that Nehemiah Bates, T. W. Shull and Andrew Clamo, judges, and B. Gibson and Joseph Hardy, clerks of the election, were severally sworn before me as the law directs, previous to entering upon the duties of their respective offices.

Dated at Fever River, this 7th of August, 1826.

JOHN L. BOGARDUS,
Justice of the Peace of Peoria County.

[Poll Book Continued.]

Samuel C. Mure,	James Beck,	William Barton,	Edward Foster,
Thomas Nicholdson,	George E. Jackson,	Isaac Martin,	Benson Calvert,
Smith Moore,	Warren Town,	Little Walker,	William Kelley,
John Richardson,	Andrew Mowery,	John McDonald,	Israel Mitchell,
Martin Porter,	John S. Miller,	Richard Palmer,	Richard Kirkpatrick,
James M. Hayle,	Thomas Reynolds, Jr.	Thompson Homes,	William Kirkpatrick,
Atlas Moore,	Robert McGoldrick,	Johnathan Browder,	William Harvell,
James Taylor,	Isaac Hustow,	Alexander Mitchell,	George Middleton,
William Bridger,	John R. Nickerson,	Crawford Faudle,	John Ames,
Jeremiah Smith,	Charles Shargout,	Stephen Sweet,	George Weddling,
Martin Duke,	Seth Catlin,	Hillary Paden,	Elisha Kellogg,
Samuel Gouch,	Josiah Little,	Samuel Adams,	Bensan Hunt,
John Armstrong,	John Hosley,	Henery M. Willison,	John Love,
George Evans,	John Boyle,	Francis Webster,	John Ray,
Daniel Fowless,	John O'Neil,	Thomas Ray,	John Clewes,
James Read,	Mathew Fawcett,	Thomas Briggs,	James Moefett,
Thomas Drum,	David Sciley,	John J. Chandler,	John Moefett,
Ely Chaffin,	Charles Gear,	Enoch Long,	William Dalton,
Harbet Flewisland,	Thomas McKnight,	Thomas Alven,	John Williams,
Harrison H. Jordon,	Thomas J. Webb,	Josiah Fulton,	James Colligan,
William Riley,	James C. Work,	Charles Love,	Thomas McCrany,
James Williams,	Alexis Phelps,	William Mitchell,	Robert Clayton,
Andrew Arnett,	John Knight,	Isaac Hamilton,	Abner Eads,
Peter White,	John B. Dophant,	Levi Gilbert,	Joseph Clagg,
John M. Curtiss,	John O. Handcock,	A. P. Vanmeter,	Mathew Johnston,
George A. Reynolds,	Samuel S. Lawrence,	Thomas Bado,	Isaac Wisehart,
Levi McCormac,	James Harris,	James Duncan,	William Troy,
David Kirker,	John Marfield,	Hugh Walker,	Owen Callahan,
Henry Gratiot,	James H. Kirkpatrick,	Samuel Scott,	Francis Martin,
George Scott,	Thaddeus Hitt,	Robert D. Duke,	William Timmerahon,
Caleb Downey,	Felix Scott,	Benjamin Bird,	Focasson M. Donald,
Richard W. Chandler,	John Ellis,	Nathan Smith,	Aaron Crandall,
Jacob M. Hunter,	Stephen Howard,	Adams Hymer,	Jeremiah Goder,
John Philley,	Charles St. Vrain,	James Parmer,	John Barrett,
Stephen Thracher,	Thomas Davis,	Abraham Kinney,	Chandler Armstrong,
John Wood,	Andrew Clarmo,	John Brown,	Joseph Winett,
James Trimble,	Joseph Hardy,	Thomas Hymers,	Gotham Straiter,
Thomas Gray,	J. W. Shull,	John Finneley,	Michael Byrnes,
Samuel Atchison,	Nehemiah Bates,	Jacob Glass,	David Clark,
Moses M. Twist,	Barney Handley,	George M. Britton,	Thomas Harris,
Thomas Thornton,	John Furlong,	William D. Adams,	John Conley,
William Hitt,	Patrick Gorman,	Daniel Snider,	Michael Finley,
John Welmaker,	John Handley,	Peter Dumont,	James Browner,
Elias Addams,	William Hansley,	Ebenezer Owen,	Daniel McCaig,
T. R. Lurton,	Patrick Lawler,	William St. John,	James Smith,
Solomon Perkins,	Charley Guilegan,	Daniel Moore,	William McCloskey,
William Nickols,	B. Gibson,	William D. Johnston,	John Coray,
Thomas Connor,	John L. Bogardus,	Cyrus Hibbert,	Patrick Doyle,
Thomas Bennett,	James Foley,	Thomas Lumley,	Charles Larock,
Patrick Hogan,	Thomas Fitzpatrick,	Benjamin Skillimus,	
John R. Smith,	John Gibbin,	Burt Curtis,	

There is a tax-list of 1826 on file at Peoria, containing 204 names of men in the Fever River Settlement; but the deputy collector who undertook to collect the taxes reports that they openly defied him and refused to pay a cent.

Jo Daviess County was organized from Peoria, February 17, 1827, and was bounded as follows: Beginning on the Mississippi River at the northwestern corner of the state, thence down the Mississippi to the north line of the Military Tract, thence east to the Illinois River, thence north to the northern boundary of the state, thence west to the place of beginning. Galena was named as the county seat.

The earliest history and first occupation of the region of country now embraced within the limits of Jo Daviess County, are enshrouded in almost impenetrable obscurity. After the lapse of more than three quarters of a century, the almost total absence of records, and the fact that the whites who visited or lived in this region prior to 1820 have all passed away, render it impossible now to determine, with any degree of certainty, the name of him who is entitled to the honor of being recorded as first settler, or who first even temporarily sojourned on the banks of the Sin-sin-ah-wah (the home of the Eagle) and the Mah-cau-bee (the fever that blisters.)

Probably the first explorer of this region was Le Sueur, a French trader, who, on the 25th of August, 1700, while on an expedition to the Sioux on St. Peter's River (now the Minnesota,) discovered a small river entering the Mississippi on the right side, which he named "The River of the Mines." He describes it as a small river running from the north, but it turns to the northeast, and he further says, that a few miles up this river is a lead mine. Le Sueur was unquestionably the first white man who ever trod the banks of Fever River, and visited the mines *then known* and probably worked by the natives.

When Julien Dubuque first located near the present town of Dubuque, in 1818, he was accompanied by one D'Bois, who is said to have located on the east bank of the Mississippi a short distance below the present town of Dunleith, very nearly opposite his companion's location. But nothing further is known of him, and from that time until about 1810 or '11 no definite information can be obtained. It is said that traces of white occupants at a very early period were discovered on the Sinsinawa by the first settlers or miners. It would be strange, indeed, with the knowledge of the immense deposits of lead and the abundance of game in this region, as well as of the mining operations of Dubuque on the west side of the Mississippi, if no adventurers or traders ever visited the Riviere au Feve, now Galena River, or ventured among the Sacs and Foxes on the east side of the Mississippi from 1788 until about 1820. Roving traders and the agents of the American Fur Company could not have overlooked the value of this location as a trading post, even if they made only annual visits, remaining long enough to dispose of their goods and purchase the lead and peltries accumulated by the Indians. But thus far no records of such occupation have been discovered, and the only positive evidence of the occupation of any portion of the territory of Jo Daviess County after D'Bois, and prior to 1819-'20, is the testimony of Captain D. S. Harris, of Galena, the oldest surviving steamboat captain on the Mississippi, and the oldest known survivor of the immigration of 1823, who says that, about 1811, George E. Jackson, a Missouri miner, had a rude log furnace and smelted lead on an island then existing in the Mississippi River, on the east side of the main channel, a short distance below Dunleith, nearly opposite the mouth of Catfish Creek. Here the first smelting now known to have been done by white men, within the limits of Jo Daviess County, was done. Jackson built a flat boat to float his lead to St. Louis, and had much trouble with the Indians on his way down the river. "He was joined," says Capt. Harris, "probably about 1812 or '13, by John S. Miller, but soon after the island was abandoned; Jackson went to Missouri, and Miller went down the river and built the first cabin and blacksmith shop on the present site of Hannibal, Mo." It is also said that in 1818, Miller, with George W. Ash and another, ascended the Mississippi with a boat load of merchandize as far as Dubuque's mines, trading with the Indians, and he probably visited La Pointe and may have spent some time there. Both Jackson and Miller returned to Fever River in 1823. The island has now nearly disappeared, but in the Fall of 1823 two keel-boat loads of scoriæ and partially burned mineral were taken from the site of Jackson's old furnace, by Moses Meeker, brought to his furnace on Fever River and smelted.

The first permanent settlements by the whites in this county, and, in fact, in all Northwestern Illinois, of which any record or reliable knowledge now remains, existed about 1820 on the banks of the river now known as the Galena. This river was then known as Feve or Bean River. There is a tradition that the river took its name from one La Fevre, a Frenchman who first visited this locality, but there is no evidence to confirm it. The Indian name for the river was Mah-cau-bee—Macaubee, which, translated, means "fever," or, more literally, "fever that blisters," the Indian term for small pox. They gave it this name, it is said, because, in the early history of this county, when the extreme western frontier of the white settlements were many hundred miles eastward, some of the warriors from the populous Indian villages then existing on the present site of Galena, and on the banks of a small creek a little way southward, went to the assistance of their eastern brethren. On their return they brought with them the loathsome disease for which they had no other name than Mah-cau-bee, the fever that blisters. The larger one they called "Moshuck—Macaubee—Sepo," Big Small Pox River, and the smaller "Cosh-a-neush—Macaubee—Sepo," Little Small Pox River. Hundreds of the natives died, and the Indians named both streams Macaubee. The smaller one is still called Small Pox Creek, but the larger was changed by the whites to the rather more pleasant name of Fever, and the little frontier hamlet was known as "Fever River Settlement," or La Pointe, until 1826-7, when the name of Galena was substituted. The name "Bean," which was sometimes applied to Fever River in early days, came from the fact that the early French traders and adventurers, who were evidently familiar with this locality long before 1820, had changed the Indian name to "Riviere au Feve," which, translated into English, means "river of the bean;" hence the name "Bean River,"* applied to it in the early gazetteers.

*Since this was written, some additional light has been thrown upon the origin of the names "Bean" and "Fever." Mr. B. C. St. Cyr, one of the early merchants of Galena, on the authority of his uncle, who traded among the Indians in this region, more than a hundred years ago, states that the stream was then called by the French *Fielle*. from an old Indian chief, bearing that name, then living on its banks. This name, Fielle, signifying gall, was afterwards corrupted by later French visitors, or by the Indians themselves, to Feve, signifying bean, the pronunciation being somewhat similar. From Feve the transition was easy, to Fevre—Fever. The origin of the Indian name Macaubee appears to be more modern. In 1835, Wm. H. Snyder, Esq , of Galena, spent some time with Col. Geo. Davenport. Mr. Snyder had then recently opened one of the ancient mounds on the bluff near the Portage, and found an immense quantity of human bones, evidently of quite modern date. Mentioning the circumstance to Col. Davenport, that gentleman said that the Indians

This is but another indication pointing to the occupation of La Pointe, prior to the date of its first settlement, as now fixed by some historians. Certainly the names of the men who were first here, and applied the name "Riviere au Feve," have passed into oblivion.

As early as 1822, this extreme western frontier settlement had become sufficiently well known to have a place in the literature of that day. A rare copy of "The Gazetteer of Illinois and Missouri" (now many years out of print), published in 1822, and at present in the possession of William Hempstead, Esq., of Galena, contains the following:—

"BEAN RIVER (Riviere au Feve, Fr.,) a navigable stream of Pike County, emptying into the Mississippi three miles below Catfish Creek, twenty miles below Dubuque's mines and about seventy above Rock River. Nine miles up this stream, a small creek empties into it from the west. The banks of this creek, and the hills which bound its alluvian, are filled with lead ore of the best quality. Three miles below this on the banks of Bean River *is the Traders Village* consisting of ten or twelve houses or cabins. At this place the ore procured from the Indians is smelted and then sent in boats either to *Canada or New Orleans. The mines are at present extensively worked by Col. Johnson, of Kentucky, who during the last session of Congress (winter of 1821-2) obtained the exclusive right of working them for three years. The lands on this stream are *poor*, and are only valuable on account of the immense quantities of mineral which they contain."

In the same work Chicago is simply mentioned as "a village of Pike County, containing twelve or fifteen houses, and about sixty or seventy inhabitants." It is very evident that there was a "Traders Village" on or near the present site of Galena in 1822, and that it was a point of more importance, commercially, than Chicago, at that time. The statement of the gazetteer is confirmed by a letter from Capt. M. Marston, then Commander at Fort Edwards, to Amos Farrar, Fever River, dated April 12, 1822, in which occurs the following:—"The Johnsons of Kentucky have leased the Fever River lead mines and are about sending up a large number of men. It is also said that some soldiers will be stationed there. If this is all true, the Foxes, and *all the trading establishments* now there, must remove."

In 1803, when the United States purchased the province of Louisiana from Napoleon, of France, the existence of lead mines in this region was known. In 1807 Congress enacted that these mines should be reserved from sale, and held in fee simple, under the exclusive control of the government. Leases of three to five years were issued to various individuals to work them as tenants of the United States, but until about 1823, the most of the work being done in Missouri, the mining operations appear to have been carried on without much system. Miners throughout all the lead mining districts paid but slight attention to Congressional enactments. Lessees were not properly supported in their rights, and of course became constantly involved in disputes with claimants and trespassers, which often proved ruinous to their undertakings.

In November, 1821, when the charge of the lead mines was transferred from the General Land Office to the War Department, no mines were known to be worked in any of the mining districts, under leases or legal authority, although many were known to be worked without authority especially in Missouri.

living on the streams now called Fever River and Small Pox Creek had taken the small pox, and died in large numbers; the survivors fled, but while he (Davenport) lived at Portage, about 1816, they returned, gathered up the remains of the victims, and buried them in the the mound Snyder had opened. From that time the Indians called both streams "Macaubee," "the fever that blisters," hence the name Fever; the smaller stream being still called Small Pox.

* By way of Wisconsin River to the portage, then down the Fox River to Green Bay.

D. S. Harris

GALENA, ILLS.

Mr. Seymour, in his history of "Galena Mines," etc., published in 1848-49 states, on the authority of Jesse W. Shull, that previous to 1819 "the Sacs and Foxes, noted as warlike and dangerous tribes, had already killed several traders who had attempted to traffic among them," and adds: "It was a current report among the settlers at Prairie du Chien, that a trader was murdered in 1813, at the mouth of the Sinsinawa. His wife, a squaw, had warned him to leave the country, as the Indians meditated taking his life. Disregarding her friendly warnings, he remained, and was murdered the same night."

In 1816, by a treaty made at St. Louis with various tribes to settle the disputes that had arisen under the treaty of 1804, by which the Sacs and Foxes had ceded to the United States all the lands lying between the Illinois and Wisconsin River east of the Mississippi, all the lands north of a line running west from the southern extremity of Lake Michigan to the Mississippi River were relinquished to the Indians, except a tract one league square at the mouth of the Wisconsin, and another tract five leagues square on the Mississippi River, of which Fever River was about the center. These reservations were intended to be sufficient to embrace the lead mines known to be worked by the squaws and presumed to be valuable, although their location was not known to the government.

From the best information now accessible, it appears that the point of land lying between Fever River and the creek now known as "Meeker's Branch," at the junction of these streams, was called "January's Point," when the "first settlers" came in 1819 or '20. John Lorrain, in his History of Jo Daviess County, published in 1876, says: "In 1820 Jesse Shull and Samuel C. Muir opened a trading post near the present site of the City of Galena, *then* called "January's Point," and by this name it was known to the early settlers, as well as by the French name La Pointe—The Point—by which it was generally called by the traders and miners for years afterwards, until a Frenchman named Frederic Gros Claude settled near the site of January's old post, and then it was sometimes called Frederic's Point. The presumption is that Thomas H. January, a Pennsylvanian, occupied The Point as a smelter and trader long enough before the arrival of Shull and others to give his name to it, or "La Pointe," the name given to it by the French traders, familiar with the location and friendly with the Indians, perhaps, even before January located there. Captain Harris, previously quoted, however, thinks that January, who was from Pittsburg, was not permanently located here until about 1821 or 1822.

In the Spring of 1848, the Louisville *Courier* stated that one Henry Shreeve came up Fever River and obtained lead in 1810.

In February, 1810, Nicholas Boilvin, then agent for the Winnebagoes at Prairie du Chien, passed through this region on foot from Rock Island, with Indians for guides, and by them was shown a lead mine, which, from his memoranda, written in the French language, was near Fever River, and was probably what was afterward known to the early settlers as "the old Buck lead."

The veteran Capt. Harris says, that unquestionably Julien Dubuque operated on both sides of the Mississippi, and mined on Apple River, near the present villiage of Elizabeth, worked the old Buck and Hog leads, near Fever River, the Cave diggings, on what is now Vinegar Hill Township, and others, as early as 1805, and very probably at a still earlier date. The Indians were on very friendly terms with Dubuque, and when they reported a discovery to him he sent his assistants, Canadian Frenchmen and half-breeds, to prove them , and in some cases to work them. All over this region, when Capt. H. came to Fever River, a lad of fifteen, in 1823, traces of old mining operations existed, which were evidently not the work of the Indians. At what was called the Allenwrath diggings, at Ottawa, about two miles from the present City of Galena, a heavy sledge hammer was found under the ashes of one of these primitive furnaces, in 1826. This furnace had been worked long before the date generally assigned to the first white settlement in this region. This ancient hammer weighing from fifteen to twenty pounds, is still preserved by Mr. Houghton, for many years the leading editor of the Northwest. The Indians never used such an implement, and it was unquestionably left where it was found in 1826, by some of Dubuque's miners.

All these important considerations, in connection with the fact that the Mississippi River was the great highway of the pioneers of that day—that Prairie du Chien was a thriving French village, and had been a French military post as early as 1755, long before Dubuque located above the mouth of Catfish Creek—that a military and trading post existed at Fort Armstrong (Rock Island) previous to the later "first settlements" on the east side of the Mississippi, now Jo Daviess County, lead almost irresistably to the conclusion that "La Pointe" was well known to the earlier Indian traders, and that the lead mining region around Riviere au Feve had been visited and occupied, temporarily at least, by white men for many years prior to 1819–'20. But by whom? History is silent, and these hardy pioneers have left no footprints on the ever shifting sands of time.

It must be considered as reasonably certain, as previously stated, that the lead mining district now lying in both Jo Daviess County and in Wisconsin was more or less occupied by Dubuque's men before any permanent settlements were made in the territory. Dubuque, by his wonderful magnetic power, had obtained great influence among the Indians, then occupying this entire region. They believed him to be almost the equal of the Great Spirit, and they feared him nearly as much. They implicitly obeyed him, and it is not a mere chimera to presume that they reported to him the existence of leads on the east, as well as on the west, side of the Father of Waters, and it is reasonable to suppose when such reports were made to him, that he verified them by actual observations made by himself or his men. From the remembrances of the oldest residents of this county now surviving, and the traces of mining done by whites long before any permanent settlements were made, it seems more than probable that Dubuque and his men were the first whites who occupied the Fever River lead mining district, in common with the aboriginal inhabitants.

It must also be considered certain that La Pointe, as the present City of Galena was called by the French traders and miners, was familiar to them as a trading post or point for many years before the first settlements were made, of which meagre fragmentary and often confused and conflicting accounts have come down to the present day. These were favorite hunting grounds for the native tribes who had populous villages on the banks of the Macaubee and other streams in this county and it was undoubtedly a favorite resort for traders, who voyaged up and down the Mississippi on their periodical trafficking expeditions. That it was known as a good trading point for many years prior to Mr. Shull's location here in 1819 is beyond question. The total absence of records of the local events in these early days, however, renders it impossible now to determine who they were. Doubtless some of them were here after permanent settlements were made, and were among the first settlers.

In 1819, the historic diggings, known for more than half a century as the "Buck lead," were being worked by the Indians, the most of the work being done by the squaws. It was the largest body of mineral then ever discovered on Fever River, and an immense amount of Galena ore was taken out by the natives and sold to the traders before it was worked out by Johnson. Mr. Farrar estimated that several million pounds had been taken from this lead by the Indians, more, in fact, than was taken from it by white miners afterwards. This lead took its name from "the Buck," a Sac or Fox chief who was encamped, with his band, on Fever River, in 1819, and worked it. Its existence had been known to the Indians for many years, and unquestionably by Dubuque, previous to its working by Buck and his band. Close by it, and parallel with it, was a smaller lead, which was called the "Doe lead," in honor of Buck's favorite squaw. Before the arrival of Johnson, in 1820 or '21, the Indians took from this lead the largest nugget of mineral ever raised in the mines. It took all the force they could muster to raise it, and when they had safely landed it on terra firma the Indian miners wanted the traders to send it to Washington as a present to the "Great Father." As it never reached there, the presumption is that the traders preferred to purchase the mineral, at the rate of a peck of corn for a peck of mineral.

In 1816, the late Col. George Davenport, agent of the American Fur Company, trading with Sacs and Foxes, occupied the trading post at the Portage, on Fever River, and lived there, how long is not now known. He soon after left that point and went to Rock Island. The post was afterwards occupied, in 1821, by Amos Farrar, of the firm of Davenport, Farrar & Farnham, agents of the American Fur Company. This important fact in the early history of this region is given on the authority of Wm. H. Snyder, Esq., of Galena, who received it from the lips of Davenport himself, in 1835.

In 1819, when the "Buck lead" was being worked by the Indians, as above stated, Mr. Jesse W. Shull was trading at Dubuque's mines (now Dubuque) for a company at Prairie du Chien. That company desired him to go to Fever River and trade with the Indians, but he declared that it was unsafe—that the Sacs and Foxes had already murdered several traders—and declined to go unless he could have the protection of the United States troops. Col. Johnson, of the United States Army, was induced to summon a council of Sac and Fox nations at Prairie du Chien, and when the chiefs had assembled he informed them that the goods that Mr. Shull was about to bring among them were sent out by their Father, the President of the United States (it was not considered a sin to lie to the Indians even then), and told them that they must not molest Mr. Shull in his business. Having received from the government officers, and from the Indians assurances of protection, Mr. Shull came to Fever River late in the Summer of that year (1819), and erected a trading house on the bottom near the river, near the foot of Perry Street, probably. Mr. Seymour, in his history of Galena, published in 1848, fixes the location as "just below where the American House now stands," but as the "American House" has long since disappeared, this location is not now very definite. During that year (1848), Mr. Seymour had a personal interview with Mr. Shull, then residing in Green

County, Wisconsin, and gathered from his own lips the facts as stated above. At that interview Mr. Shull stated that himself and Dr. Samuel C. Muir were the first white settlers on Fever River, *at this point*, in 1819, that "during that year Dr. Muir commenced trading here with goods furnished by the late Col. Davenport, of Rock Island," a statement to which reference will be made in its proper place hereafter. Mr. Shull also stated that later in the same year Francois Bouthillier came and *occupied* a shanty at the bend, on the east side of Fever River, below the present limits of the City of Galena. It is to be regretted that Mr. Shull had not been more explicit, as it would be very interesting now to know whether Mr. Bouthillier built that shanty there, or whether it had been built by him or some other roving trader before that time, and whether it was *occupied* temporarily or permanently by him in 1819. Mr. Bouthillier was a French trader known at Prairie du Chien as early as 1812, when, it is said, he acted as interpreter and guide for the British troops. He undoubtedly knew of the Fever River trading point, and may have frequently visited it and "occupied a shanty," as probably others had, prior to 1819. Mr. Shull himself does not appear to have been a very permanent fixture *at this point* then, for during "the Fall he moved his goods to the mouth of Apple River, of the Maquoketa, and other places to suit the convenience of the Indians, as they returned from their Fall hunts." Mr. Shull does not appear as a trader after this year, although he may have been engaged in the Indian trade somewhat later, but he soon became interested in mining, and remained in the mining district, finally locating in Michigan Territory, now Wisconsin.

At that time all this region was a wilderness, occupied only by a few fur traders and roving tribes of Indians. The nearest settlements at the north were at Dubuque's mines and Prairie Du Chien, the latter an old town of great distinction and extensive trade, relatively of as much importance in the Mississippi Valley at that period as St. Paul and St. Louis are now. On the east the nearest village was Chicago, consisting of a few rude cabins inhabited by half-breeds. At Fort Clark (now Peoria), on the south, were a few pioneers, and thence a long interval to the white settlements near Vandalia.

Dr. Samuel C. Muir, mentioned by Mr. Shull as trading here in 1819, may have been here at that time, but whether before, after, or with Mr. S. does not appear. It is very probable that he was here, may have been here before 1819, but if he engaged in trade it was very temporary. It may be that he came here on a tour of observation, and took a few goods with him, like the provident Scotchman he was, "to pay expenses." But Dr. Muir was a physician. He had received his education at Edinburgh, and felt a just pride in his profession, a man of strict integrity and irreproachable character. He was a surgeon in the United States army previous to his settlement at La Pointe. When stationed with his regiment at some post in the northern country he married an Indian woman of the Fox nation. Of the marriage the following romantic account is given.

The post where he was stationed was visited by a beautiful Indian maiden, whose native name unfortunately has not been preserved, who, in her dreams, had seen a white brave unmoor her canoe, paddle it across the river, and come directly to her lodge. She knew, according the superstitious belief of her race, that in her dream she had seen her future husband, and came to the Fort to find him. Meeting Dr. Muir, she instantly recognized him as the hero of her dream, which she, with childlike innocence and simplicity, related to him. Her dream was indeed prophetic. Charmed with Sophia's beauty, innocence and devotion, the doctor honorably married her; but, after awhile, the sneers of his brother officers, less honorable, perhaps, than he, made him ashamed of his dark-skinned wife, and when his regiment was ordered down the river to Bellefontaine, it is said he embraced the opportunity to rid himself of her, and left her, thinking that she could never find him again, or, if she could, that she would not have the courage and power to follow him. But, with her infant child the intrepid wife and mother started alone in her canoe, and, after days of weary labor, at last reached him, but much worn and emaciated, after a lonely journey of nine hundred miles. She said, "When I got there, I was all perished away—so thin." The doctor, touched by such unexampled devotion, took her to his bosom, and, until his death, treated her with marked respect. She always presided at his table, and was respected by all who knew her, but never abandoned her native dress. In 1819–'20, Dr. Muir was stationed at Fort Edwards, now Warsaw, but threw up his commission, and in the Spring of 1820 built the first cabin erected by a white man on the present site of the City of Keokuk, Iowa, but leased his claim to parties from St. Louis, and, later in the same year, came to LaPointe to practice his profession, and was the first physician known to have located in Northern Illinois. He remained in practice here about ten years, and lived, it is said, on the east side of Bench Street, near the corner of Hill. He had four children, viz.: Louise (married at Keokuk, since dead), James (drowned at Keokuk), Mary, and Sophia. Dr. Muir died suddenly, soon after he returned to Keokuk, left his property in such condition that it was wasted in vexatious litigation, and his brave and faithful wife, left penniless and friendless, became discouraged, and, with her children, disappeared, and, it is said, returned to her people on the Upper Missouri.

Francois Bouthillier, the other and later occupant of that shanty in 1819, was a roving trader, following the Indians. Whether he remained here permanently from that time is very uncertain, but nothing further is known of him until Mr. J. G. Soulard, then on his way to Fort Snelling, found him here in 1821, still an Indian trader. "Mr. Bouthillier," says Mr. Shull, "after he occupied a 'shanty at the Bend,' in 1819, purchased a cabin then known as the cabin of Bagwell & Co., supposed to be situated near the lower ferry." But he says, "in 1824, and *previous* to Bouthillier's purchase, the house and lot had been sold for $80." Here Mr. Bouthillier engaged in trade, and established a ferry, which is the first permanent settlement made by him of which there is authentic account. Captain Harris says he remembers distinctly when Bouthillier built his trading house at or near that point.

In this connection, it is well to add that Mr. George Ferguson and Mr. Allan Tomlin, both early settlers and highly esteemed and reliable citizens of Galena, express the opinion that there was a trading post at the Portage, three and one-half miles below LaPointe, between Fever River and the Mississippi, even prior to the advent of either of those whose names have been mentioned. However this may be, it must be admitted that there were a large number of Indians encamped or living here at that time, whose women and old men were engaged in raising lead from the "Buck lead," and the fame of their rude and, for them, extensive mining operations must have naturally attracted the attention of traders, who came here to traffic with them. Probably others than Shull, Muir and Bouthillier were in this vicinity with their goods, and the surrounding circumstances would seem to corroborate and justify the opinion expressed by Messrs. Ferguson and Tomlin. The Portage was a narrow neck of land between the Fever River and the Mississippi, so named because the Indians and traders were accustomed to transport their canoes and goods across to save the journey down to the mouth of the Fever River, about two and one half miles, and up to the same point again, the distance across the neck being only a few rods. A furrow was plowed across this neck of land at its narrowest point, by Lieut. Hobart, in 1834, and now there is a deep channel, called the "cut-off." This location was very convenient for a trading post.

If the lead mines attracted traders, they attracted miners as well. Among the first, if not the first, to work the mines, of whom any definite account has been preserved, was James Johnson, of Kentucky, said to be a brother of Colonel R. M. Johnson, of historic renown as the slayer of Tecumseh. It has already been shown that "the Johnsons" of Kentucky were engaged in lead mining here in 1822. The date of Johnson's first arrival here must forever remain in obscurity, unless some records not now accessible, shall be found to show it. In a letter written by Dr. H. Newhall, dated Fever River, March 1, 1828, he speaks of the "Buck lead" as having been "worked out by Colonel Johnson while he was at these mines in 1820–'21." Mr. J. G. Soulard, who passed LaPointe in 1821, on his way to Fort Snelling, and stopped here a day or two, says that, on his way up, they met Johnson's boats going down, and that, while here, he understood that he was mining here, but did not see him. From the best information now at hand, it would seem that Mr. Johnson first visited this region as a trader, as early, perhaps, as 1819, possibly before, and that, in 1820–'1, he was mining here without authority from the government, under purchased permission of the Indians. It does not appear that the government exercised any especial jurisdiction here at that time, as the lead mining district was under the control of the general land office until 1821. It may be, also, that he was not mining, but simply smelting the mineral purchased from the Indians.

Some time during the Summer of 1820, Mr. A. P. Vanmeter — or Vanmatre, as the name is spelled in early records — is said to have located here, probably on the east side of the river, opposite the present woolen mill above Baker's Branch, as he was afterwards there, engaged in smelting.

It is more than probable that others came with him, or during the same year, but their names do not appear of record. Mr. D. G. Bates was associated with Vanmatre shortly afterwards in the smelting business, but whether he arrived here contemporaneously with Mr. Vanmatre is not known.

In August or September, 1821, Amos Farrar was managing a trading post on Fever River as agent for the American Fur Company, and was living here with his Fox wife. This fact is established beyond question by a letter addressed to him at the "Lead Mines, Fever River," from Major S. Burbank, commander at Fort Armstrong, dated October 14, 1821, "by favor of Mr. Music," presenting Mr. Farrar with "my old black horse, if he will be of any service to you." A letter dated Fort Armstrong, November 21, 1821, signed J. R. Stubbs, a blacksmith, addressed to Amos Farrar, Fever River, introducing to the latter the bearer of the letter, "Mr. Symmes, who was accompanied by Mr. Connor and Mr. Bates" — undoubtedly D.

Symmes and James Connor, and, perhaps, David G. Bates, who have always been considered among the earliest settlers in the mining region. These and other letters and papers belonging to Mr. Farrar were kindly placed at the disposal of the historians by Captain G. W. Girdon, of Galena, one of the oldest steamboat captains now in service on the Mississippi, and enabled them to fix the date of his permanent settlement on Fever River more accurately than can be done with some others. From these letters it appears that Mr. Farrar was, for at least two years before, and up to July 22, 1821, in the service of Louis Devotion as a trader on the Mississippi, located at Fort Armstrong, bringing his supplies *via* Green Bay from Canada. At that date he left the service of Mr. Devotion, and, immediately after, came to Fever River, as before stated. and probably located at the Portage. In 1823, he had a trading house on the bank of the river, near the centre of what is now Water Street, between Perry and Franklin Streets. On the 1st of June, 1825, Mr. Farrar received a permit, signed Charles Smith, acting sub-agent U. S. lead mines, permitting him to occupy five acres of United States land for cultivation, and to build a cabin thereon, situated near the Portage. He must comply with all regulations concerning cutting timber. Mr. Farrar had three children by his Indian wife (now all dead). About two years before his death he married Miss Sophia Gear, sister of Captain H. H. Gear, who still survives him. He died of consumption, at his residence within the stockade. July 24, 1832, beloved and respected by all who knew him. The following copy of a printed notice to the inhabitants will show the esteem in which he was held:

> Yourself and family are respectfully invited to attend the funeral of Mr. Amos Farrar this morning at ten o'clock, from his late residence within the stockade.
>
> GALENA, July 26, 1832.

That house is still standing on the southeast side of Perry Street, near the corner of Bench.

In Stubbs' letter to Farrar, it will be remembered, the name of Mr. Bates was mentioned. Whether this was David G. Bates, or Nehemiah, can not now be determined, but David G. Bates was here very early — Mr. Ferguson thinks as early as 1819 — on a trading voyage, but, like many other events of that period, there are no records left to fix the time of his first arrival.* Unquestionably, however, he was among the earliest permanent settlers, and was here, probably, in 1820.

Thomas H. January is another of the early pioneers, whose first arrival at the little Fever River settlement is enveloped in uncertainty. He is said to have come from Pittsburg, Pa., with a keel-boat, on a trading voyage, and is thought to have visited this locality as early as 1821, if not prior to

* Since the above was in type, among some old papers kindly placed at the disposal of the historians by Mr. W. O. Gear, of Iowa, was found the following paragraph, in one of a series of articles on the "Upper Mississippi Lead Mines," published in the *Galena Sentinel*, about 1843:—"In the Fall of the year 1819, our old friend, Capt. D. G. B., started from St. Louis, with a French crew, for Fever Riviere Upper Mississippi lead mines. His vessel was a keel, the only way of conveyance then of heavy burthens on the Upper Mississippi, and the boatmen, in those days, were. some of them, 'half horse and half alligator.' But the merry French, after arriving off Pilot Knob, commenced hunting for Fever River. After a search of three days, they found the mouth, and, on the 13th of November, after pushing through the high grass and rice lakes, they arrived safe at where Galena now stands, where they were greeted by some of the natives, from the tall grass, as well as by our old acquaintances, J. B. (W.) Shull and A. P. Vanmatre, who had taken to themselves wives from the daughters of the land, and were traders for their brethren. (A portion of the scrap is gone; others are evidently mentioned; Dr. Muir, for one.) Capt. B., after disposing of, or leaving his cargo in exchange for lead, fur, etc., returned to St. Louis for another cargo."

that time. It seems probable from all data at hand that he located on the point since known by his name, and erected a double log cabin and warehouse there about 1821, or even earlier. He was there in June, 1823, when Captain D. S. Harris arrived in this county, and had been there certainly for a year or two then.

In November, 1821, the jurisdiction of the lead mines was transferred from the general land office to the war department, and January 4, 1822, leases were granted to T. D. Carniel and Benjamin Johnson, and to Messrs. Suggett & Payne, all of Kentucky, for one hundred and sixty acres of land to each of the two parties, to be selected by them, in the northern part of Illinois or the southern part of Michigan Territory (now Wisconsin). Lieut. C. Burdine, of the U. S. Army, was ordered to meet them in the Spring at the Great Crossings of the Kentucky, proceed with them in exploring the country, assist them in the selection of their lands, protect them with an armed force, and make surveys of the ground for the information of the government. Subsequently, leases were granted to other parties. There are no records accessible at this point (Galena) now, to show the movements of Lieut. Burdine, but it may be considered as true that he was here in 1822, attending to the duties assigned to him. April 12, 1822, Captain Marston, at Fort Edwards, wrote to Mr. Farrar, at Fever River, that "the Johnsons of Kentucky have leased the Fever River Lead Mines, and are about sending up a large number of men." It is probable that under their lease they selected land to include the "Buck lead," and a little later in the same year James Johnson and a Mr. Ward, probably D. L. Ward, came from Kentucky, each with a large number of negro slaves. It is also said that they were accompanied by several young men, whose names can not now be recorded. Johnson had his furnace near where McCloskey's store now stands, on the levee. Johnson worked the "Buck lead" and raised a large amount of ore. David G. Bates and A. P. Vanmatre worked a vein of mineral on Apple River, near Elizabeth (Georgetown), but smelted their ore at Fever River. It would be interesting to know how many miners were engaged in this district at that time, but it is not possible to determine that fact.

During 1822, Dr. Moses Meeker visited the lead mining district on a tour of observation. Unquestionably others visited Fever River the same year for the same purpose, as the fame of the stupendous deposits of mineral awaiting discovery here had begun to reach the older settlements. About this time, although the date of his arrival can not now be determined, Major John Anderson, of the U. S. Topographical Engineers, was stationed here as government agent, and occupied a cabin on what was then called "Anderson's Slough" (now "Harris' Slough"), about two and one half miles from Galena.

In 1823, large and important accessions were made to the population of the then remote pioneer settlement on Fever River, and the history of the mining region begins to emerge from the obscurity and uncertainty heretofore surrounding it. The testimony of reliable living witnesses of the stirring events of that period, Capt. D. S. Harris and Hiram B. Hunt, the only known survivors here of the immigration of 1823, and a few others who came in 1824, renders the labors of the historian less arduous and more satisfactory. The actual settlement of this region may be said to have really commenced about this time.

Dr. Moses Meeker, of Cincinnati, O., who had prospected on Fever River

Frederick Stahl

GALENA.

during the previous year, organized a colony, and embarked on the 20th day of April, 1823, on the keel-boat* "Col. Bumford," with 30 men besides the women and children, and 75 tons of freight, consisting of a complete mining outfit, merchandize and provisions, sufficient to subsist the party a year after their arrival at the "mines."

Among the passengers, and all whose names can now be recorded, were—Dr. Moses Meeker, James Harris and his son, Daniel Smith Harris; then in his 15th year, Benson Hunt, his wife, Elizabeth Harris Hunt, his two daughters, Dorlesca and Dorcina, and son, Hiram Benson, aged six, four and two years respectively. (Dorlesca died in 1838; Dorcina married —— Johns, and now lives, a widow, in Kansas); John Doyle, wife and child; Maria Bunce (Mrs. Doyle's sister), and her two brothers, John and Hiram; Maria Rutherford; Thomas Boyce; Israel Garretson; John Whittington (the steersman); Wm. Howlett (a deaf man), and —— House.

At St. Louis James Harris left the boat, purchased a number of cattle for Dr. Meeker and drove them across the country to Fever River, arriving two or three weeks after the "Col. Bumford," which arrived on the 20th of June, having made the trip in sixty days, then regarded as a remarkably quick passage. The Mississippi was very high and had overflowed its banks, and the crew were often obliged to resort to warping and bushwhacking. At Grand Tower, below St. Louis, the "Col. Bumford" was passed by the steamer "Virginia," commanded probably by Capt. John Shellcross, on her way from Pittsburg to Fort Snelling, with supplies for the troops stationed there, and she was the first steamboat that ever ascended the Mississippi above the mouth of the Illinois River; certainly she was the first boat propelled by steam that ever parted the waters of Fever River, in June, 1823.

The "Col. Bumford" arrived on Sunday, June 20, 1823, run up the little creek now known as Meeker's Branch, a short distance, and made landing on the south bank.

The arrival of Dr. Meeker and his companions marks a new era in the history of the mining district, and gave impetus and growth to the little remote settlement, until then scarcely more than an Indian trading post, almost unknown except to roving traders and frontiersmen. It required enthusiasm, energy, bravery, perseverance and patient endurance of toil and privations, unknown in later years, to venture into the very heart of the Indian country, and make permanent settlement in the midst of a populous Indian village. Dr. Meeker possessed all these characteristics in a remarkable degree, as did also Mr. James Harris, his foreman, confidential counsellor and friend. These two men became the head and soul, so to speak, of

*A keel-boat was built something like a modern barge only its hull was lower. These boats were from 50 to 80 feet long, and from 10 to 15 feet beam, and from 2 to 2½ feet hold. On the deck was built the "cargo-box," which generally extended to within about ten feet of either end and set in from the gunwale about two feet on each side, leaving a gangway or "walking-board," as it was called, on each side the whole length of the boat. Sometimes on small boats these walking-boards projected over the hull. The rudder was a long sweep, some thing like a gigantic oar. The keel-boat was propelled by sails, by rowing, poling, bushwacking, cordelling and warping. When the water was high or the boat was running close in shore, the crew would grasp the bushes growing on the bank and pull the boat up river. This was "bushwhacking." Some times a long line or rope would be attached to the mast, and the crew walking on the shore with the other end, towed the craft up stream. This was "cordelling." At other times when cordelling was impracticable, in crossing rapids, a long line would be carried ahead, and made fast to a tree or rock, or to a small anchor and the crew in the boat, taking the line over their shoulders, would walk from bow to stern, drop the rope, then walking back on the other side to the bow, and take it up again, in the rear of the others, keep the boat in motion.

the new settlement, and to them, perhaps more than to any others, it owes its rapid development and growth, until, only six years after, on the spot where they landed, a town was laid off by the United States authorities. To these hardy pioneers and their worthy associates, fit representatives of "nature's noblemen," who first settled this country, belongs the honor of really leading the way where others were so soon to follow, and of laying the foundations for the permanent settlement of this, then extreme, western frontier. Mrs. Meeker died December, 1829, aged 39 years. Dr. Meeker removed to Iowa County, Wis., in 1833, and resumed the practice of his profession, and died there, July 7, 1865, aged 75 years. His remains were brought to Galena, and lie in the old cemetery on the hill. Mr. Harris lived but a few years to witness the results of his labors, as he died suddenly, in 1829, and he, too, lies near his old friend, in the midst of the scenes he loved so well, but how changed since he left for a higher and better settlement above! His children and descendants still live in the home he helped so largely to make for them, among the most honored and respected citizens of the country.

Dr. Meeker built a cabin on what was called Meeker's Bench, on the east side of Main street or Broadway, a short distance above "Whittam Row." Hunt built a cabin a little north, about where Mr. Bench's brick building now stands, near Duer's flouring mill. Directly across the road from Meeker's cabin, a well was sunk. This well, called "Meeker's Well," still remains, although unused, as an unerring landmark of that time. Fifteen or twenty feet north of that well, near the road, in what is now J. Moore's front yard, Benson Hunt built a little log blacksmith shop, and went to work at his trade; the first blacksmith known to have lifted a hammer in Jo Daviess County. (It is proper to add that Mr. Hunt lived in Galena until 1838, when he removed to Sand Prairie, remained there two years and then returned to Galena, where he continued to reside until a short time prior to his death). Harris and his son also built a cabin on Meeker's Bench, near Meeker and Hunt, and near the present Court House.

At this time there was a ford across Fever River, almost directly at the foot of Franklin Street, used in low water—there were no bridges then. Below the ford, to the mouth of the river, says Captain Harris, there was then, and for years afterwards, a depth of from twelve to sixteen feet at "dead low water." In fact, the water was always two or three feet deeper in the Fever River (which is really only an arm of the Mississippi to Galena) than it was in the channel of the "Great River." In after years, at high water, large boats steamed up the Fever River some distance above the town, and also up Meeker's Branch, now an insignificant rivulet.

When Dr. Meeker and his party arrived here in June, 1823, they found less than one hundred white men mining and trading with the Indians. Prominent among them were Dr. Samuel C. Muir (who was practicing medicine and stood high), Thomas H. January, Amos Farrar, Jesse W. Shull, Francois Bouthillier, A. P. Vanmatre, D. G. Bates, John Conley, John Ray, James Johnson, Nehemiah Bates, James Connor, B. Symmes, E. Rutter, John Barrell, Joseph Hardy, Robert Burton (not the smelter), Montgomery Wilson, Stephen P. Howard, Martin Smith, Israel Mitchell (a surveyor), John Armstrong, Cuyler Armstrong, —— Vanderslice, Wm. Thorn, and others.

Wm. Adney and wife were also here at that time. Adney had been a soldier, and arrived here that Spring; "and his wife," says Capt. Harris, "was the only white woman here when we arrived." Mr. Lorrain says "Mrs. Adney was the first white woman who came to the mines," but this does not appear to be absolutely certain. About three years later, in 1826, Thomas H. January is said to have exhumed the remains of his wife, who had been buried some years, certainly before 1823, somewhere near the junction of Bench and Diagonal Streets, and re-interred them elsewhere. If she was a white woman, as presumably she was, Mrs. January came to these mines before the arrival of Mrs. Adney, and in the absence of further knowledge must be considered the first white woman who settled in Jo Daviess County. Mr. Shull, subsequently, in 1827, went into Michigan Territory, now Wisconsin, and founded the Village of Shullsburg.

"When I arrived," says Capt. Harris, "there were six or eight cabins on and below the present site of the woolen mill, above Baker's Branch. Bates and Vanmatre had a smelting establishment on the east side of the river, opposite that point, obtaining their mineral mostly from Vanmatre's lead, on Apple River, near Elizabeth. Next above was the smelting establishment of James Johnson, consisting of a double log cabin, a log and an ash furnace, very nearly on the present site of H. F. McCloskey's store on the levee on the west side of Main Street, directly opposite the foot of Bouthillier Street. Amos Farrar had a trading post (a double log cabin), on the bank of the river, between the foot of Perry Street and of Franklin, about in the middle of Water Street. There was a little bayou or slough opening out of the river near the foot of Perry Street, and running up behind Farrar's post. Near by was a cabin built by Farrar, to accommodate his Indian customers. Thomas H. January also had a double log cabin and warehouse on the point bearing his name. Wm. Adney had a little cabin on the south side of "Buck-lead" branch, now Meeker's Branch, just below the first fork, on the second bench.

These few log cabins constituted the dwellings and places of business of the entire white population of all this region at that time, but the river bottoms, ravines and hillsides were thickly dotted with the wigwams of the Sacs and Foxes, who numbered at least 2,000 in this immediate vicinity. They were peaceable, and treated the white settlers kindly. They were engaged in hunting and fishing, and supplied the whites with a large portion of their meats, consisting of venison, game, fish, etc. The squaws and old men, too old to hunt, raised the most of the mineral which supplied the furnaces. Captain Harris remarks that for years they "felt quite as safe among these Indians as they do now," and this is the universal testimony of all the early settlers in this county, now living. The Winnebagoes and Menominees also came here to trade, but their home was then farther north, in Michigan Territory. The Menominees are represented as being the most pleasant and friendly, while the Winnebagoes were always the most insolent, irascible and turbulent. At this time a large pond existed where the De Soto House now stands, corner of Main and Green Streets, and extended some distance northward, east of Main Street. Here the boys, both white and Indian, used to come to fish for years afterwards. During the high water, in 1828, a catfish weighing 106 pounds was caught at the present site of the De Soto House. In August, following his arrival, Smith Harris and a young Sac boy, about his own age, sunk a hole, in search of mineral, on the north side of Franklin Street, about one fourth of a mile from the present court house, but were not very successful. At this time the white settlers were engaged in mining and smelting mineral dug by themselves and furnished by the Indians, and in trading, but with a spirit of enterprise, characteristic of the frontier at that time, they were prospecting and making claims in the vicinity for miles around, and commenced the work of making settlements elsewhere, the particulars of which will be found in the township histories in another part of this volume.

In September, 1823, according to reports to the War Department, the only persons engaged in mining or smelting at Fever River mining district under lease from the government were: James Johnson, James Connor, B. Symmes and E. Rutter. Dr. Meeker erected a furnace near the present site of Whittam Row, and being possessed of some capital, commenced business on a somewhat extensive scale. During the Fall of this year, James Harris commenced making a farm for Mr. Meeker, about two and one half miles north of the present city limits of Galena, at what has ever since been known as "Meeker's farm," and the next year, (1824) raised a crop on it, and, as accurately as can be ascertained, planted there the first orchard in the county in the same year.

In the Fall of 1823, Israel Garretson and Maria Bunce were married at the cabin of Dr. Meeker by an army officer, whose name can not be ascertained (possibly Maj. John Anderson, then stationed here as the government agent), as there was neither minister nor magistrate here. Miss Rutherford and William Hines were married at the same time. These, so far as is known, were the first marriages solemnized in this part of the country. About the same time, it is said that a General Schimerman died on Fever River, and was buried on Prospect Street, a short distance from Spring Street. This was the first death after the arrival of the Ohio immigrants.

John S. Miller and family also arrived at the mines in 1823, built a large, double log cabin in what is now called Oldtown, at the northwest corner of Branch and Dodge Streets, and kept a tavern and boarding house. George E. Jackson also returned to this region from Missouri.

1824. This year James Harris commenced making a farm on the Mississippi at Anderson's Slough, since known as Harris' Slough, and occupied the cabin abandoned by Major Anderson. This and the Meeker farm were the first farms known to have been cultivated in the mining district of Fever River, although at that time, and until about 1830, when lead was so low that the miners were compelled to plant or starve, the impression generally prevailed that this region was too far north to be an agricultural country, and that the soil was valuable only for the mineral it contained. This year witnessed still greater additions to the population of the settlement, now not confined to the banks of Fever River. Meeker's keel boat, the "Col. Bumford," came up the river again, loaded with immigrants. Among the passengers were the family of James Harris, consisting of his wife, Abigail Harris; sons, Robert Scribe (now living in Dubuque), Martin Keeler and James Meeker (now residing in Galena); and daughters, Selinda, Lucina and Electa; James Smith and his wife, Susan Harris Smith; Mrs. Mary R. Meeker, wife of Dr. Meeker; his sons, Jonathan, Henry, Warner and John, and a daughter, Eveline (who married —— Potts), William Colvin, and others. Selinda Harris married John Ray in 1825, and the young couple were obliged to go to Prairie du Chien to be married, as there was no person then authorized to solemnize marriages in the Fever River Settlements. Lucina Harris married Lieut. C. C. Hobart, of the army, a nephew of Gen. Dearborn. Her second husband was William Blair. Electa married William H. Hooper, since delegate to Congress from Utah Territory. Among the other arrivals at the mines in 1824 were Orrin Smith, James L. Langworthy (who soon afterwards removed to Dubuque), Mathew Fawcett, Barney Dignan, P. Hogan, Michael Byrne, John Furlong, James Bruner, John Clews, Thompson Humes, Daniel Dyer and John Dugan.

August 18, 1824, Lieut. Martin Thomas was appointed superintendent of the lead mines of the Upper Mississippi, and authorized to grant leases and permits to smelters and miners, and to farmers, provided they did not interfere with the mining interests.

In October, 1824, a son was born to Benson Hunt. The old family bible contains the following entry, now nearly effaced: "James Smith Hunt, born at 15 minutes past one o'clock P. M., on (day illegible) the 9th day of October, 1824." Soon after this event, Mary S. Miller, daughter of John S. Miller was born. Both these children were born within the limits of the present City of Galena, and, so far as is known, were the first white children born in Jo Daviess County.

1825. The immigration to the mines now became so large that only a few of the arrivals can be mentioned in the brief space allotted to this part of the work. John Foley, first sheriff of the county; Capt. James Craig, a surveyor and a prominent man, and Capt. William Henry came this year. Craig's wife was a grand-daughter of Daniel Boone. He afterwards settled in Hanover, at what is now called "Craig's Mills." Later in the Fall of this year, Col. Henry Gratiot and his brother, John P. B. Gratiot, came to the Fever River Settlement in a light wagon, with three hired men and their outfit. They struck some mineral and made their first settlement in the valley, between Hinckley's and Waddell's Mounds.

Subsequently the Indians made some large discoveries fifteen miles from Fever River, in Michigan Territory. The Gratiots purchased from them the right of settlement, and located there, naming the place "Gratiot's Grove."

1826. Among those prominent in the early history of this region, who arrived in 1826, are Maj. T. B. Farnsworth, M. C. Comstock, Charles Gear, his son William T. Gear, his sister Sophia Gear, John Turney, William Smith, John Dowling and his son Nicholas, Capt. Allenwrath, Capt. Abraham Hathaway, Lemon Parker, William P. Tilton, R. P. Gaylord, James H. Hammett, John Campbell, William Townsend, Louis Chetlain and many others. Charles Gear was an enthusiastic Mason, and was undoubtedly instrumental in organizing Strangers Union Lodge, No. 14, the first masonic organization in "the mines," under the jurisdiction of the Grand Lodge of Missouri. Sophia Gear, his sister, opened the first school taught by a female, in 1827, and subsequently married Amos Farrar. Allenwrath struck the lead called "Allenwrath Diggings," soon after his arrival. John Turney was a lawyer, said to be the first limb of the law to settle here. Hathaway was a butcher for some years, and then removed to Guilford, where he now resides. Lemon Parker, William P. Tilton, D. B. Morehouse and Robert P. Guyard organized the firm of Parker, Tilton & Co., or the "Galena Mining Company," and located at Ottawa (now Burton's), one and one half miles above January's Point, on the east side of the river, and for years this was a place of considerable importance. Steamboats ran up there, loaded with supplies, and to load with lead. The principal business of the company, says Mr. Lorrain, "was smelting lead ore, which was on an extensive scale. They used what were called 'log furnaces,' of which they had several. They also had a large building, filled with all kinds of miners' supplies, which they sold to the miners and took mineral in exchange. This firm continued to operate until the year 1829, when the partnership was dissolved. One of the parties, Lemon Parker, converted the premises into a factory for the purpose of manufacturing sheet lead and lead pipe. The article made was of superior quality. Not receiving sufficient patronage, however, the business was abandoned. Shortly after, the war department ordered ten thousand dollars' worth of sheet lead, but the order came too late to save the enterprise, as at that time the machinery had been taken out and sold." At Apple River (now Elizabeth), a large amount of mineral was raised and smelted, and the place was of some importance.

During this year a large number of Swiss arrived and settled here. These people had emigrated to the North Red River in 1821, under the auspices of Lord Selkirk. They soon became dissatisfied with their location and, in 1823, some of them (among whom was Louis Chetlain) left that region and went to St. Louis. Mr. Chetlain and others came to Fever River in the Spring of 1826, and nearly all the colony at Red River left there, came to the mines in the Autumn of the same year, and settled in various parts of the mining district. Their descendants still live here, among the most respected and reliable citizens of the county.

June 4, 1826, the first post-office was established in the mining district. It was called "Fever River," Crawford County, Illinois. As this was then Peoria County, the post-office department evidently labored under the impression that Crawford County, Michigan Territory, was in Illinois. Ezekiel Lockwood was appointed postmaster. The office was located at the northwest corner of Perry and Main Streets, and was to be supplied from Vandalia,* the mails being transported on horseback once in two weeks. December 17, 1829, the name of the post-office was changed to "Galena," Jo Daviess County, Ill.

In July, 1826, the upper street in the town was surveyed and staked off into lots, the surveying being done by Israel Mitchell and James Craig. The first mention of the "Town of Galena," so far as is known, occurs December 27, 1826. Several permits granted by Thomas McKnight, February 22, 1827, are dated Galeni.

August 7, 1826, occurred probably the first election held in the mining district. This was then the Fever River Precinct of Peoria County, which embraced all the settlers in the mining region, extending far up into Michigan Territory. The poll book contains two hundred and two names, as previously shown on page 225.

September, 1826, a school was opened in a little log building on the south side of Franklin, near Bench, and was taught by Dr. John O. Hancock. Dr. Hancock was employed by Mr. Meeker on salary for a year, but early in the Winter received intelligence of sickness in his family, and went East, employing Samuel S. Lawrence to take his place in the school. Lawrence taught until Hancock returned with his family, in the Spring of 1827. On his return, Hancock threw up his contract and engaged in the practice of his profession, and John G. Hughlett, then just arrived, took the school, in April, 1827, and continued it for some years.

* Regular mail service was not established until 1828.

In 1826, Thomas H. January. one of the earliest settlers, had a smelting establishment at Buncombe, and his diggings, known as "January's Patch Diggings," extended over a large part of the eastern portion of what is now Vinegar Hill Township. George E. Jackson had previously smelted here as early, probably, as 1825.

1827. The condition of the mining district at this time is graphically portrayed in the following extract from a communication signed "H," (supposed to be written by Dr. H. Newhall), published in the *Miners' Journal* of May 9, 1832:

> At the close of 1826 there were but few inhabitants in the country. About fifteen log cabins constituted what is now the City of Galena, and in the year ending 30th of September, 1826, there was manufactured, in the whole lead mining country, only 958,842 pounds of lead. In the Spring of 1827, vast numbers of persons immigrated to these mines. Buildings were raised, one after another, in rapid succession, and the town and county continued to flourish until July 1, when the Winnebago War (more extended reference to which will hereafter be made) commenced. All mining operations stopped, and thousands left the county. But in the Spring of 1828, immigrants began to arrive, and on the 14th of July of this year there were in the Village of Galena one hundred and ninety-five dwelling houses, warehouses and shops, and forty-six buildings were commenced, but not, at that time, finished. The number of inhabitants in the village was 669. The population at the mines was estimated at 10,000.

One peculiarity of the miners was to apply to the people from the various states, names suggested by some peculiarity of character or surrounding circumstances. Miners and others came in such large numbers from Missouri as to suggest to the fertile imagination of the hardy settlers the idea that the State of Missouri had taken an emetic, and forthwith all Missourians were dubbed "Pukes." The people of Southern Illinois had the habit of coming up here with their teams in the Spring to haul mineral and work in the mines, but regularly returned to their homes in the Fall. This suggested that they were like the fish called "suckers,' which run up the small streams in the Spring, and run down to deeper water at the approach of cold weather. All Illinoisans were called "Suckers," therefore, and here, in the lead mines of the Upper Mississippi, originated the term which is now applied to all residents of the "Sucker State." Kentuckians were called "corn-crackers;" Indianians, "Hoosiers;" Ohioans, "Buckeyes," etc.

Among those who have been prominent in the history of this county, who arrived in 1827, are, Dr. Horatio Newhall, Capt. H. H. Gear and family, John G. Hughlett, James G. Soulard, William B. Green, Harvey Mann, Charles Peck (of firm of Hooper, Peck and Scales), Solomon Oliver, Allan Tomlin, Gov. Thomas Ford, Col. James M. Strode, C. C. P. Hunt, Capt. John Atchison, Paul M. Gratiot, Nathaniel Morris. Moses Hallett, Lucius H. and Edward Langworthy, William Hempstead, D. B. Morehouse, and many others whose names are familiar in Jo Daviess County, and of whom want of space alone forbids mention.

Dr. Newhall arrived here March 31, 1827, 26 days from St. Louis, and engaged in mining and smelting, but abandoned it the next year and resumed the practice of his profession. Jan. 27, 1830, he married Elizabeth P. P. Bates, by whom he had six children, three sons and three daughters. In the Fall of 1830 he became a surgeon in the U. S. Army, and was stationed at Fort Winnebago, but retired from the service and returned to Galena in 1832. When the Black Hawk War broke out he volunteered his services, and, by order of Gen. Scott, established a military hospital at Galena, of which he had sole control until the end of the war, and was warmly complimented by Gen. Scott for its "neatness and good arrangement." Aug. 19, 1832, he wrote to his brother that he had received all of the wounded and most of the sick of an army of 5,000 men, and besides, he says, "I have not visited less than twenty per day for several weeks out of the hospital." With the army came the Asiatic Cholera, which prevailed in its most malignant form. It was the first time it had appeared in the United States. The disease was new and its treatment unsettled. Dr. Newhall soon formed a decided opinion as to the pathology of the disease and its proper treatment, and such was his success that his name was a household word from St. Louis to the Falls of St. Anthony. Dr. Newhall, in addition to his extensive practice, found time for much literary labor. The *Miners' Journal*, the first newspaper in the mining district, was under his editorial charge, as was also the Galena *Advertiser*, afterwards published by Newhall, Philleo & Co. He died on Monday, Sept. 19, 1870. Dr. Newhall was a man of marked character, stern integrity and superior ability. He largely moulded public opinion in this region, and at his death left in the hearts and memories of this people a monument more enduring than the marble that marks his last resting place.

Capt. Hezekiah H. Gear, who also arrived at the mines in April, 1827, was another man who exercised a powerful influence in this (then) new country. His brother, Charles, had removed to Buncombe, and he lived on Meeker's Bench, near where Benson Hunt lived, for three months, and then removed to Buncombe (or Bunkham, as it is shown on old maps) and located a mining tract about seven miles from Galena, near the Village of Old Council Hill, and called his place "Tower Hill" from a large rock, something in the form of a tower, on his claim. As showing the trials and hardships of the pioneer settlers at that time, Capt. Gear's daughter, Charlotte (who subsequently married Capt. George W. Girdon) relates that when her father built his cabin at Tower Hill, he cut his logs on a steep bluff on the banks of Fever River, rolled them into the water and towed them, one by one, up stream half a mile to the site he had selected, by tying one end of a rope around the log and the other end around his body, and walking up, sometimes in the water, sometimes on the bank. When he had thus collected a sufficient number of logs, the miners in the vicinity helped him raise his cabin. The roof of this cabin was thatched with long prairie grass and covered with sods. The floor of the cabin was the native earth, and as the roof was not water-tight, the situation of the inmates in a rain storm can be imagined. The next year Capt. Gear sawed some planks from pine logs with a whip-saw, and laid a floor. It was just after a heavy storm, when it rained indoors harder than it did out, and Mrs. Girdon (then a miss of ten years) says: "I never expect to be so happy again, this side of Heaven, as I was when that floor was laid." Capt. Gear soon after provided a better roof and the family was better housed; but such was pioneer life in the mines in 1827. Just after the close of the Black Hawk War, in which he participated, he discovered an immense deposit of mineral. Shortly before his death he declared that he had realized from the sale of 26,000,000 pounds of lead ore, all taken from that mine. He became one of the most wealthy and enterprising men of the Northwest, and at one time he was, perhaps, more extensively engaged in mining and smelting than any other person.

In connection with Godfrey, Gilman & Co., of Alton, and backed by the old State Bank of Illinois, he largely controlled the business of lead

Wm. T. Geary

GUILFORD TOWNSHIP

mining and gave a prodigious impetus to the mining interests by advancing largely to miners and inciting them to new discoveries. In the competition in the purchase of mineral at the time, it was said that in traveling over the country in the pursuit of his object, he used to carry his money in the top of his hat, ready to advance to any miner who pretended to have a reasonable "show" of mineral.

In 1847 Capt. Gear was a member of the State Senate. He was one of the original projectors of the Illinois Central Railroad; also of the Pacific. He was three times married, and left five children: Charlotte Maria (now Mrs. Girdon), Alexander H., John C., Clarissa E. and William O. Impetuous and indomitable energy, undaunted courage, unyielding firmness, strictest honesty and great generosity were the prominent characteristics of Capt. H. H. Gear. In the days of his prosperity he contributed liberally to all public and charitable enterprises. He gave to Galena the lots on which its public school building stands, and established the Episcopal Church in Galena. He was and is a part of the history of Jo Daviess County.

James G. Soulard, now an aged man, still lives amid the scenes of his earlier life. Of him Hon. E. B. Washburne says: "He still holds that high place in the esteem, respect and affection of all our people which a long life of probity and honor have secured to him. Is probably the only man living who ascended the Mississippi River from St. Louis to Fort Snelling as early as 1821. What he has lived to see in the development of this country, surpasses all that which could have been conceived by the wildest imagination."

Early in 1827 the name of the Village of Fever River was changed to Galena, and became generally known by that name. It is said that to Dr. Samuel C. Muir belongs the honor of giving it this name, suggested by the name applied to lead ore, but this is doubtful. A public meeting was held to select a name, in the Winter of 1826–'7, and at that meeting Richard W. Chandler is said to have suggested the name "Galena," which was adopted.

The first public religious services known to be held in the mines occurred in 1827, conducted, says Lorrain, by Rev. Revis Cormac. It is said, however, that an Episcopal clergyman, a chaplain of the Hudson Bay Company at York Factory, was here, weather bound, in 1826, and preached on Sunday in the log tavern then just built opposite the present site of the De Soto House.

In the Autumn of this year Hugh W. Shannon built a saw mill on Small Pox Creek, about one mile from its mouth, having received a permit dated July 17, 1827, from the superintendent of lead mines to occupy 80 acres of land there. This, says Mr. St. Cyr, is the first saw mill known to be built in this county. Mr. Seymour, in his "History of Galena," published in the first directory, 1847, says: "The first mill in this section of county, carried by water power, was a corn-cracker, erected on Spring Brook, near the northern limits of the city. The hopper held about a peck, and the building which sheltered it was a dry goods box." But singularly enough Mr. Seymour omitted to give the date of this primitive mill. It is now to be added, however, that this mill was put in operation by Hiram Imus in 1828. It was the corn-cracker of the pioneers, a cast iron mill, like a huge coffee mill. These mills were usually run by hand, but Imus contrived to run his machine by water.

During this year (1827), much sickness prevailed in the Mining District. Dysentery, diarrhœa, or flux, prevailed as an epidemic to an alarming extent. The few doctors in the county were constantly engaged, but there was much suffering for the want of medical attendance and proper nursing, and many deaths occurred in consequence.

In the Winter of 1826–'7 occurred the famous dispute, graphically described in Lorrain's "Centennial History." In the Summer or Fall of 1826, two boys had discovered a rich lead. Complying with the regulations to secure their claim, they concluded to let it rest for a while, and attend Mr. Lawrence's school. While doing this, an adventurer, who had lost, as the miners termed it, his "bottom dollar," came across their diggings, "jumped," and applied to the agent for a permit. Mr. McKnight, discovering that the boys made a prior claim, appointed J. Duncan and James Higley arbitrators in the case, who decided in favor of the boys. Lorrain says:

The defeated party, being a great athletic fellow, declared that he would not stand by the decision, but would resort to the law of might. Early the next morning the two lads, instead of going to school, armed themselves and went out to their claim. They had not been there long before their opponent also appeared, fully armed. The boys ordered him to stand and told him that now was the time to try the case by his code. He scanned their countenances for a few moments and then left, never disturbing them again. Both of these boys are now living, in the persons of Capt. D. S. Harris, of Galena, and his brother, R. S. Harris, of Dubuque, Iowa.

Better than any history compiled from the fragmentary statements of after years—better even than unaided memory, striving often in vain to recall the events of fifty years ago, are the letters and memoranda written at that time by intelligent men, who lived here, and knew whereof they wrote. Dr. E. G. Newhall has permitted the following copy of a letter, written by his honored father, Dr. Horatio Newhall, to his brother Isaac Newhall, Esq., of Salem, Mass., to be taken expressly for this work. It will be valuable to the people of this county, both on account of the information it conveys, and because the writer, now passed away, is tenderly enshrined in their memories.

GALENA, FEVER RIVER LEAD MINES,
UPPER MISSISSIPPI, SUPPOSED IN ILLINOIS,
Nov. 20, 1827.

Dear Brother:

I received, by the last mail brought here by steamboat "Josephine," a newspaper from you, on the margin of which were endorsed the following words: "Write a full account." I was rejoiced to see once more a Massachusetts paper, and presume you meant by the endorsement, a full account of "Fever River." This would puzzle me or any other person on the River. It is a nondescript. It is such a place as no one could conceive of, without seeing it. Strangers hate it, and residents like it. The appearance of the country would convince any one it must be healthy; yet, last season, it was more sickly than Havana or New Orleans. There is no civil law here, nor has the Gospel been yet introduced; or, to make use of a common phrase here, "Neither law nor Gospel can pass the rapids of the Mississippi." The country is one immense prairie, from the Rock River on the south to the Ouisconsin on the north, and from the Mississippi on the west, to Lake Michigan on the east. It is a hilly country and abounding with lead ore of that species called by mineralogists "galena," whence is derived the name of our town. The lead mines of the Upper Mississippi, as well as those of Missouri, are under the control of the Secretary of War. Lieutenant Thomas is superintendent. He resides at St. Louis: a sub-agent resides at this place. Any person wishing to dig gets a permit of the agent to do so, by signing certain regulations, the principal of which is that he will sell his mineral to no one but a regularly licensed smelter. He has all the mineral he can raise, and sells it at $17.50 per thousand (pounds), delivered at the furnaces. Any person who gets a permit stakes off two hundred yards square. This is his lot so long as he works it, and no one can interfere with his discoveries. Any person who will give bond to government for $5,000 can have half a mile square, on condition that he employs 20 laborers, and pays government ten per cent of lead made from mineral raised on his survey, or sells his mineral to a public smelter. The public smelters, of which I am one, give bond for $20,000 to pay government one tenth of all lead manufactured. They buy mineral of any person who has a permit to dig, manufacture it into lead, pay government one tenth, monthly, and are the *great men of the country*. The mineral, lead, and cash all go into their hands. H. Newhall & Co. got their furnace in operation 1st of Sept., 1827. I made, by the 15th, twenty tons of lead. My men became sick, and I made but 14,000 pounds until 1st of November, since which time I have manufactured about 17,000 pounds every week. I have a store of goods, in Galena, for the supply of those with whom I have dealings, and never sell anything for less than 50 per cent advance. My furnace is on the Sinsinawa River, three miles from Galena, a stream navigable for boats to my furnace. * * * The privilege of working these mines, you know, was first given by the government to Col. Johnson, of Kentucky, five years ago (in 1822). He did but little and sunk money. Not much lead was made here till last year. There were then four log buildings in Galena. Now there are one hundred and fifteen houses and stores in the place. It is the place of deposit for lead and provisions, etc., for all the mining country. There is no spot in America, of the same size, where there is one fourth of the capital, or where so much business is done. There was manufactured here, in the year ending September last, five million seven hundred and forty pounds of lead. The population consists mainly of Americans, Irish and French (that is, in the diggings). There are but comparatively few females. Hence, every female, unmarried, who lands on these shores, is immediately married. Little girls, fourteen and thirteen years old, are often married here. Three young ladies, who came, fellow passengers with me, in June, and the only ones on board, are all married months since. Du' Buque's Mines, on the opposite side of the Mississippi, are worked by the Fox Indians. They, however, merely skim the surface. The windlass and bucket are not known among them. Du' Buque's Mines is a delightful spot, particularly the Fox Village, on the bank of the Mississippi. But of all the places in the United States, which I have seen, Rock Island, at the lower rapids of the Mississippi, called the Rapids of the Des Moines, is by far the most beautiful. Fort Armstrong is on this island. At the mouth of Fever River is a trading house of the American Fur Company. Their trading houses are scattered up and down the Mississippi, on the River Des Moines, St. Peters, etc. Their capital is so large, and they gave such extensive credit to the Indians, that no private establishment can compete with them. An Indian debt is outlawed, by their own custom, in one year. The fur company credits each Indian hunter a certain amount from one to five hundred dollars, according to his industry and skill in hunting and trapping. If, when they return in the Spring, they have not furs and peltry enough to pay the debt, the trader loses it. But on the goods sold to the Indians there is a profit of two or three hundred per cent made, and a profit on the furs received in payment.

Dec. 7, 1827.

Fever River was closed with ice on the 21st of November, and, of course, navigation is ended, and I have not sent my letter. I now have an opportunity to forward it by private conveyance to Vandalia. We are now shut out from all intercourse with the world until the river opens again in Spring. We have no mail as yet, but shall have a mail once in two weeks to commence the 1st of January next. I have not received a letter from one of my friends since I have been in Fever River. I hope you will write me before 1st of January, or as soon as you receive this letter. Sincerely yours,

H. NEWHALL.

This letter was mailed at Vandalia Dec. 25, and by it is established the fact that although Fever River post-office was established in 1826, it was not regularly supplied, even once a fortnight, until the Spring of 1828. Mails were brought by steamboat in the Summer, and in the Winter the people had none.

In the Fall of 1827, Strader & Thompson brought a keel-boat load of general merchandise, including a quantity of flour and pork, from St. Louis. Mr. Bouthillier, whose trading house was on the east side of the river, near the present site of the railroad station, purchased the entire cargo to secure the flour, as that was scarce, even then. Winter set in without a sufficient supply of provisions to supply the wants of the miners. Nearly all the flour obtainable was held by Bouthillier. It was sour and hard. He chopped it out of the barrels with hatchets, pounded it, sifted it loosely into other barrels, filling two with the original contents of one, and then sold it for $30 per barrel. Even then, the settlers saw with alarm, that there was not enough to last until Spring. The Winter of 1827–'8 was mild and open until Jan. 6; the streets had been muddy, and "not freezing in the least, even at night"—but the river froze over then. Word had reached St. Louis that the people in the mines were destitute of provisions. The steamboat, "Josephine," Capt. Clark, was loaded with flour and started off to take her chances of getting as near as possible to the mines. Slowly she made her way up the Mississippi, and when she reached the mouth of Fever River, the warm weather had weakened the ice, and she made her way, unheralded, to Galena. The date of her arrival is fixed by the following entry in a memorandum book, kept by Dr. H. Newhall: "Feb. 25, 1828, arrived steamboat 'Josephine;' broke the ice to get up Fever River." Farther corroborated by a letter from Dr. Newhall to his brother, dated March 1, 1828, in which he says: "To our astonishment, on Monday last, a steamboat arrived from St. Louis." The people rushed to the bank, rejoiced and amazed to see a steamboat loaded with flour, except Bouthillier. The day before, Mr. Gratiot had offered him $25 a barrel for all the flour he had, and the offer was refused. Mr. Gratiot now asked him what he would take for his flour, and Bouthillier, with a shrug, replied: "Dam! hell! suppose, by gar! what man tinks one steamboat come up Fever River in mid de Wint?" Feb. 27, the river froze over, and March 5 the boat was still detained by ice, but arrived at St. Louis about March 14.

The following extracts from a letter from Dr. H. Newhall to his brother, dated March 1, 1828, will give some idea of social life in the mines 50 years ago:

> We have had but two mails this Winter. It has been pleasantly warm here during Winter, and the *heavy rains* caused the ice in the river to break. * * It has been extremely cold for four days; the river is closed with ice, and the boat (the "Josephine," which arrived on the 25th), consequently detained. We have been almost completely isolated from the rest of the world this Winter. We have received the President's Message and proceedings of Congress up to the 26th of December, since that time we have had nothing. We, in Galena, enjoyed ourselves well during the Winter. There have been ten or twelve balls, the last was on the 22d of February. At noon a salute was fired from the cannon received during the Winnebago War. In the evening a ball was given at the Cottage Hotel (the name applied by Dr. N. to the log tavern on the west side of Main Street, corner of Green), in a hall (building) sixty feet in length, ornamented with evergreens. * * There were sixty ladies and ninety gentlemen present. The ladies were elegantly dressed, and many of them were handsome. The ball was managed with a degree of propriety and decorum scarcely to be expected in this wild country. Had I been suddenly transported into the ball-room, I should have imagined myself in some eastern city, rather than in the wilds of the upper Mississippi. Little should I have dreamed that within five miles was the home of the savage, and that only twelve miles off is a large Fox village, where I have witnessed the Indian dance around a fresh taken scalp. March 5.—The steamboat ("Josephine") is still detained by ice. * * The *Miners' Journal*, a newspaper, will be commenced at Galena by 1st of May next. The proprietor, in his prospectus, calls it the *Northern Herald*. He altered the name at my suggestion. * * "Old Buck," the Fox chief, who discovered (?) the famous "Buck Lead," has been encamped all Winter within a mile of my furnace (on the Sinsinawa, three miles from town). Himself and sons often visit me in town.

The *Miner's Journal*, to which allusion is made, was not started at the time fixed. The first number was issued July 8, 1828, by James Jones, proprietor, under the editorial supervision of Dr. Newhall. The first printing in the first printing office established at Galena, by Jones, is said to have been an invitation to a ball and excursion, of which the following is a *fac simile* as to style, orthography and punctuation:

STEAM-BOAT INDIANA.

AMERICAN INDIPENDENCE.

M The pleasure of your company is respectfully solicited to a Party to be given on board the Steam-Boat Indiana, on Friday the 4th day of July, at 8 o'clock, A. M.

M. C. Comstock,
L. R. M. Morce,
W. P. Tillton,
D. B. Morehouse,
W. Hempstead,
G. H. M'Neair,
J. H. Lockwood,
H. Newhall.
} *Managers.*

Galena June 24th, 1828.

The date of the highest water in the Mississippi within the period of the occupation of this county by the whites, has been variously stated by historians, and men's memories differ. It has been fixed by Seymour, Lorrain and others as occurring in the Summer of 1826. Careful inquiry, however, seems to establish the fact that while the water in the river was high in 1826, it was still higher in 1827, and the highest flood occurred June, 1828. Capt. D. S. Harris, H. B. Hunt, Allan Tomlin, H. H. Gear, and others who were here at that time, agree on the statement that the highest water was in 1828, when, says Capt. H., "the Indians informed me that it was two feet higher than they had ever known it." Steamboats crossed the Portage in ten feet of water, passed along over the bottom where Main Street now is located (the street has been raised considerable since then), took on lead at Meeker's Point, near the present Court House, ran up Meeker's Branch and loaded lead at Miller's tavern, etc. The water backed up to Hughlett's furnace. Capt. Harris states that in "1826 there was a heavy freshet on the Wisconsin River, which submerged Prairie du Chien, but it did not extend to the upper Mississippi or to the other tributaries, hence was not felt here very much." He also states that the water was always higher in the Mississippi, and, of course, in Fever River, in those earlier years than it is now.

The arrivals at the mines during 1828 were very numerous. The Sucker trails were full of teams, and steamboats and keel-boats were loaded with emigrants. Among the numerous throng may be mentioned George Ferguson, B. C. St. Cyr. W. Townsend, Jesse Morrison, and hundreds of others. Daniel Wann, Frederick Stahl, Emily C. Billon (who subsequently married John Atchison), C. S. Hempstead, and Rev. Aratus Kent, are among the arrivals of 1829. Mr. Wann has been intimately connected with the history of this region from that day to the present. He was formerly largely engaged in trade and in river navigation, but for the last 25 years has been Surveyor of the Port of Galena, and, says Mr. Washburne, "has always performed his duty with so much satisfaction to the Government and the people, through all administrations, that, in all the desire for office, no man has ever sought to displace him." Mr. Kent organized the first Presbyterian Church, Oct. 23, 1831, with six members, as follows: Abraham Hathaway, Abraham Miller, Eliza Barnes, Ann Crow, Susan Gratiot and

Isabella McKibbins. Mr. Stahl engaged in trade, and, so far as known, took the first lead by wagon to Chicago, in 1833, at the time the Potawattomie Treaty was made. He loaded two eight-ox teams, belonging to Hiram Edes, with 3,500 pounds of lead each. The route was *via* Dixon, and, says Mr. Stahl, these teams made the first heavy wagon trail on that route, although some light government wagons had passed over the route in 1832.

Among those who came here prior to 1830, whose names have not been mentioned, were James Jones, who established the *Miners' Journal*, Dr. Addison Philleo, John L. Bogardus (1826), Benj. Mills, one of the most brilliant lawyers of his time, Dr. A. T. Crow, Samuel Scales, Robert Graham, the Gray brothers, Abner Field, the Argent family, and Gen. Henry Dodge.

In 1829, David G. Bates built a small steamboat at Cincinnati and called her the "Galena," to run between Galena and St. Louis. In the Spring or Summer of that year, Robert S. Harris went to Cincinnati and came up on her first trip as engineer. She run only a short time and was lost.

October 10, 1829, that sturdy pioneer, who had done so much for the infant settlement; who had made the first farm in Northern Illinois; who had seen the little hamlet on Fever River suddenly expand, in the short space of six years, into a town of no little commercial importance—JAMES HARRIS—died suddenly of cholera, the second victim, it is said, of that terrible scourge in the "mines," and the second to be borne to his final resting place under Masonic honors (Thomas H. January being the first, Dec. 1, 1828). Mr. Harris enjoyed the entire confidence of the people among whom he lived and died. He was one of the first commissioners of Jo Daviess County, and one of the first justices of the peace in the county. He was faithful to the interests confided to him by the people, and was the first man in the county who died in office. James Harris was born in Connecticut, October 14, 1777; married Abigail Barthrick, of Kinderhook, N. Y. (born March 24, 1782), November 9, 1797. Subsequently removed to Ohio, thence to Fever River. By the death of her husband Mrs. Harris was left with six children at home to rear and train, the eldest of whom was then but twenty years old. The brave women who accompanied their pioneer husbands to this wild country at that early day, of whom Mrs. Harris was one of the first, are entitled to a conspicuous place in history. They were indeed the mothers of the frontier, the worthy companions and counselors of those noble and fearless men—the advance guard of civilization destined ere long to occupy the whole country. Mrs. Harris was a woman of sterling worth, a consistent Christian, affable, charitable, and universally beloved and respected. She lived to see her children become useful and honored members of society, and died July 9, 1844.

In the Winter of 1832-'3, Captain D. S. Harris and his brother, R. S. Harris, built the first steamboat built on Fever River, at the Portage, and called her the "Jo Daviess." These men were among the earliest pioneers in Galena steamboating. No men on the Upper Mississippi were ever better known or more highly esteemed and respected. They were perfect masters of their profession, and as engineers, pilots and commanders, had no superiors. They run the "Jo Daviess" themselves, and prior to 1840 bought out the "Heroine," the "Frontier," the "Smelter," the "Relief," the "Pizarro," the "Pre-emption," and the "Otter."

Negro slavery existed in the mines for some years. Many of the early miners were from slave-holding states, and brought their slaves with them. In 1823, when Captain Harris arrived, there were from 100 to 150 negroes here. Under the ordinance of 1787, slavery was forever prohibited in the Northwestern Territory, but Illinois sought to evade this organic law by the enactment of statutes by which these slaves could be held here as "indentured" or "registered servants," and these statutes were known as the Black Laws. As late as March 10, 1829, the commissioners of Jo Daviess County ordered a tax of one half per cent to be levied and collected on "town lots, *slaves, indentured or registered servants*," etc.* There is now living in Galena a venerable old colored man, Swanzy Adams, born a slave, in Virginia, in April, 1796, who moved to Kentucky, and thence, in April, 1827, to Fever River, as the slave of James A. Duncan, on the old steamer "Shamrock." His master "hired him" to Captain Comstock, for whom he worked as a miner. He subsequently bought himself for $1,500 (although he quaintly says, "good boys like me could be bought in Kentuck for $350"), and discovered a lead on Sunday that paid it, but he was compelled to serve five years longer as a slave, and was once kidnapped and taken to St. Louis. "Old Swanzy," as he is familiarly called, is the sole survivor of the slaves held under the Black Laws of Illinois, then in force, but which have long since been swept from her statute books. It is pleasant to add that, by hard labor, industry and economy, since he owned himself, "Swanzy" has secured a comfortable home and competence against want in his declining years.

For many years, and as late as 1856-'7, the only money current in the mines consisted of British sovereigns and French five-franc pieces. The former were rated at $4.90—often passing for $5, and the latter were current at $1.00.

In 1832, just before the commencement of the Black Hawk War (to be noticed more at length hereafter), the whole mining district was in a prosperous condition. In 1829-'30, the price of lead went down, and for two or three years the miners labored under serious disadvantages, but in 1830 the government reduced the lead rent from 10 to 6 per cent, lead advanced until, in 1832, it commanded a fair price, and the condition of the county at that time is admirably summed up in an article published in the *Miners' Journal* of May 9, 1832, as follows:

> The miner, the smelter and the merchant all transact a *cash* business. Fine farms are to be seen in every part of the country. Mills are built on almost every stream. Machines are in operation for the rolling of lead and for the manufacture of leaden pipes. A shot tower is being built at Helena.† Laborers receive from $15 to $20 per month and their board. There are three churches in the town of Galena—a Catholic, a Methodist and a Presbyterian. There is a temperance society of seventy-five members, and a juvenile temperance society of forty-five members. Education is encouraged and promoted. Justice is regularly administered. Numerous crimes common in older settlements are here wholly unknown. Most persons sleep with unbarred doors, and sleep in safety. A jail has been finished three years, and during all that time has not been occupied a single week. The people of Galena are generally well dressed, polite and sociable, and if there is a place where a respectable stranger finds pure, unalloyed hospitality, it is at the Upper Mississippi

* Slavery existed in the mines for several years after this date, and was not finally abolished until about 1840.

† This was on what was called January's Point. The tower was never built, but the foundations were commenced, and the location is now called "Shot Tower Hill." Sheet lead was manufactured a short time by Parker, at Ottawa, but the enterprise was soon abandoned.

lead mines. One hundred and two steamboats* and seventy-two keel-boats have arrived in a single year, and the annual product of lead has increased to 13,343,150 pounds.

It is now necessary to return to a review of the early history and management of the lead mines under United States authority. Prior to the appointment of Lieut. Martin Thomas, as superintendent of United States lead mines, in August, 1824, there does not appear to have been an agent of the government here authorized to grant leases and permits to operate on United States lands. Leases of large tracts were obtained from the government, and on these lands small miners were permitted to enter and dig under the lessees. But their numbers were few. In 1823 the principal leads worked were all old Indian and French mines struck anew. There were diggings on January's Point, about six hundred yards above January's warehouse. On the school section just above were two leads. Next north was the "Hog" lead, beyond which were the "Doe" and "Buck" leads, the latter of which had been worked by French miners under Dubuque. Then there was the "Old Cave Diggings," on Cave Branch, in what is now Vinegar Hill Township, that had also been worked by Dubuque, and the old "Indian lead," west of the "Buck lead." On the east side of the river was the "Back-bone lead," about half a mile east of January's Point, and Vanmatre's lead, on the east side of Apple River, near the present Village of Elizabeth. On the west, near Anderson's (now Harris') Slough, were two old French leads, one of which was worked by —— McLanahan, and the old "Indian Diggings," west of Galena two miles. In 1824, John and Cuyler Armstrong struck a lead on the middle fork of Miller's Branch (now Meeker's), above the old Indian leads. North of this another lead was struck, near where the Comstock lead was afterward discovered. Mr. Vanderslice had made a discovery about two miles northwest of the settlement, and two new leads east of Vinegar Hill, were worked by J. Bruner, Michael Byrne and John Furlong. On Cave Branch, one and one quarter miles southeast of "Cave Diggings," John Armstrong had found a good lead, and "the only one," says Captain Harris, "where I ever saw native lead sticking to mineral." These were all the principal diggings known in what is now Jo Daviess County when Lieut. Thomas arrived, and they had all, or nearly all, been previously worked by the Indians and French.

Up to that time it is probable that the local agent, Major Anderson, had not been authorized to grant leases and permits. Johnson and others had obtained their leases at Washington. But the Fever River lead deposits were found to be richer than those of Missouri, and the greater facility with which the mines or "leads" were worked attracted a large number of miners from Missouri. The government of the United States had, by advertisements in the leading papers of the Union, called the attention of the people to these lead mines, and invited miners and settlers to the region. They were flocking hither, and it became indispensable to station a resident superintendent here, clothed with authority to grant permits and leases, issue regulations, settle disputes, etc. There was no other law at that time,

* It was nothing remarkable to see fifteen or twenty large Mississippi steamboats in the river at a time, and Captain Harris is sufficient authority for the statement that steamboats have arrived or departed in every month in the year. The channel of the river, which has very little current, has become filled up now, so that steamers can come up to Galena only in high water, but the people think, not without reason, that if the government would improve the channel by dredging—with the construction of a narrow guage railroad now in operation from this point into the mining districts of Wisconsin—some, at least, of the old prestige of Galena would return.

Diadamia Frentress

DUNLEITH.

and, as a rule, the inhabitants were quite as orderly and quite as mindful of each others' rights as they have been in later days. Property was safe, and doors needed no locks.

Lieut. Thomas arrived at Fever River in October (probably), 1824, and established his headquarters in a double log cabin which then stood on the bank of the river, in the middle of what is now Main Street, about sixty feet south of Gear Street. On the north side of Gear Street, close by the agency, was a little pond, fed by a large spring, and a little creek connected the pond with the river. Immediately after his arrival, Lieut. Thomas issued an order to all miners to suspend operations the next day, (the absence of records renders it impossible now to fix the precise date). William Adney, D. G. Bates, John Barrell and John Furlong were working the "Old Cave Diggings," and had just uncovered a sheet of mineral when the order came to stop the next day. They worked all night, and the next morning had raised 100,000 pounds. All mining operations stopped, but only for a short time. Within a week they were at work again, under direction to sell the mineral only to licensed smelters,* so that the government could collect the rent lead.

No records can be found of Major Anderson's transactions, and two old volumes marked "A" and "B," containing some of the transactions of Lieut. Thomas' agency during 1825-'6-'7, which are preserved in the archives of the county, are all of these records available for this work. Mr. Charles Smith was the sub-agent residing here, and came with Lieut. Thomas, who lived at St. Louis and visited Fever River occasionally.

The first established regulations of which record remains, and probably the first code promulgated by Superintendent Thomas, bear date "1825," but were undoubtedly issued very early in the Spring, and are as follows:

REGULATIONS FOR MINERS AT THE UNITED STATES MINES ON THE UPPER MISSISSIPPI.

First.—All miners shall forthwith report themselves to the agent, who will enter their names on a register and give them a written permit to mine on ground which is not leased.

Second.—Without such written permit, no miner shall dig or mine; he shall forfeit his discovery and all mineral he digs, and be prosecuted as a trespasser.

Third.—Any miner who gives false testimony in any dispute or arbitration, or before any magistrate, or who is convicted of stealing ore or any other thing, setting fire to the prairie or woods, cutting timber where it is prohibited, shall forfeit his permit to mine or dig, and no smelter shall purchase his ore or give him any employment.

Fourth.—When going to dig, two or more miners must work in company. They are permitted to stake off three hundred yards square, lines to be north and south and east and west.

Fifth.—A permanent post or stake shall be placed near every digging with marks designating ownership.

Sixth.—A discontinuance of work for eight days in succession shall cause a forfeiture of ground.

Seventh.—When a dispute shall arise respecting the right to ground, the matter shall be arbitrated among miners or smelters. On their failing to settle it, a reference to the agent, whose decision shall be final.

Eighth.—No person is permitted to build a cabin, cultivate land, cut timber, or settle in any manner, without written permission of the agent.

Ninth.—Whenever surveys of discovery are required, they will be surveyed twenty rods by forty, running to cardinal points, the length to correspond with the course of the lead, and the discoverer will be entitled to a certificate of survey.

* Miners could sell mineral only to licensed smelters, for which the government collected one tenth for rent, and paid them for smelting it. Miners were paid for only nine tenths of the mineral they delivered. It is said that in later years the smelters have received from the government the value of the lead thus paid, but it belonged to the miners, not to the smelters, and the money should have been expended in public improvements in the territory, in the absence of the rightful claimants.

Tenth.—No miner shall hold two discoveries at the same time, nor shall any miner be permitted to go on other ground until his lead is dug out or sold, or until he abandons it and renders up his certificate of survey.

Eleventh.—All miners must report to the agent the name of the smelter to whom they deliver their mineral, and the amount they deliver in each quarter.

Twelfth.—No certificate of survey shall be sold or transferred to any other than a miner who has a written permit, or to a smelter who has a license; and no survey or other diggings shall remain unwrought for more than eight days in succession on penalty of forfeiture.

Thirteenth.—All mineral raised *when searching* for discoveries or leads must be delivered to a licensed smelter, and *to no other person.*

Fourteenth.—Any miner who shall disobey or go contrary to any of these regulations, shall forfeit his permit to dig or mine; and should he attempt to cut timber, mine, farm, cultivate land or build cabins, without written permission from the agent, he will be prosecuted as a trespasser on United States land.

(*Signed*) M. THOMAS,
Lieut. U. S. A. and Superintendent of Lead Mines.

FORM OF PERMIT TO MINERS.

—— —— is hereby permitted to dig or mine on United States land which is not leased or otherwise rightfully occupied. He is not to set fire to the prairie grass or woods, and must deliver his mineral to a licensed smelter, and comply with all regulations.

FEVER RIVER, ——, 1825.

GENERAL REGULATIONS.

Smelters and lessees will have their ground on Fever River off two hundred yards in front on the river, and four hundred in depth, running in right lines perpendicular to the river.

No timber to be cut within one hundred yards of Fever River bank, from one mile above its mouth to and one mile above the *point* where January's cabins are situated.

M. THOMAS,
Lieut. U. S. Army and Supt. of Lead Mines.

Persons desirous of taking a lease are notified that Bonds in the penalty of $5,000, with two sureties, are required, when a lease for 320 acres, as usual, will be granted, provided the ground is not occupied. Blank Bonds may be had of the agent, who will make the survey when the bonds given.

[illegible]ULATIONS FOR SMELTERS.

This agreement, made and entered into this — day of ——, 1825, between Lieut. M. Thomas, Superintendent of the United States Lead Mines and —— ——, Lead Smelter.

Witnesseth:—That the said —— —— is hereby permitted to purchase lead ore at the United States Lead Mines on the Upper Mississippi, for one year from the date hereof, on the following conditions:

First.—No purchases of ore to be made from the location of any person without his consent in writing.

*Third.**—To smelt with a log furnace, or furnaces, at all times when one hundred thousand pounds of ore (or more) are on hand at any one furnace.

First.—No ore, ashes or zane to be purchased or otherwise acquired from any other person than an authorized miner or lessee.

Fourth.—To haul mineral to furnaces when fifty thousand pounds (or more) are dug at any one place of three hundred and twenty acres.

Fifth.—To run an ash furnace when four hundred (or more) thousand pounds of ore have been smelted at any one set of furnaces.

Sixth.—To comply with all general regulations for cutting timber.

Seventh.—To keep books which shall contain an accurate and true account of all lead ore, ashes or zane purchased or dug, of all smelted, and of the amount of lead manufactured or purchased; from whom purchases were made, and from whence the ore was dug. Said books to be open for the inspection of the U. S. Agent of Mines, and a monthly transcript of the contents to be furnished to him, to be verified on oath, if required.

Eighth.—To clean, or cause to be cleaned, all lead ore previous to smelting it, and to weigh a charge of the log furnace when required and the lead made from such charges.

Ninth.—To pay to the United States a tax of one tenth of *all* lead manufactured from ore, ashes or zane, to be paid monthly in clean, pure lead, to be delivered at the U. S. Warehouse (near the mines), free of expense.

* The record was so made.

Tenth.—To build a strong log warehouse twenty by sixteen feet, one story high; the logs to be squared as not to admit of a bar of lead being passed between them, to have a strong door with a good and sufficient lock, to have a log ceiling in the usual manner; said warehouse to be located at such place as the agent for mines shall direct, to be built free of expense to the United States.

Eleventh.—Not to employ in any manner whatever any *miner, lessee or smelter* who has forfeited his *permit to dig*, his *lease* or license, on written notice to that effect being given by the agent.

Twelfth.—A non-compliance or neglect of performance of any one of the foregoing articles to constitute a forfeiture of this license and of the Bond given for the faithful performance thereof, and on proof being offered to the Agent of the United States that such forfeiture has been incurred, his written notice to the smelter shall be sufficient to suspend the stipulations aforesaid.

Thirteenth.—No sale, transfer or shipment of lead is to be made by said smelter until all arrears or tax which are due are paid; nor any removal of lead from the place of manufacture, without the consent of the Agent of the United States. The said —— —— to be allowed wood and stone for smelting and furnaces, and to cultivate enough land to furnish his teams, etc., with provender and his people with vegetables.

It is distinctly understood that the Bond given for the performance of the Stipulation in this License is to be in full force and virtue until all arrearages of rent or tax are paid to the Agent of the United States, and a written settlement is made with him, on which a certificate that no such arrearages exist shall be given, when the Bond shall be null and void.

The earliest permit recorded is as follows :

John S. Miller, a blacksmith, has permission to occupy and cultivate U. S. land. He will comply with all regulations for the cutting of timber, etc. 20 acres. Dated May 16, 1825. (*Signed*) M. THOMAS, etc., etc.

The first recorded survey of mineral land was of "five acres of mineral land (a discovery lot), two acres in length by one quarter of an acre in breadth, lying and being on what is known as 'January's patch diggings,'" bounded by "beginning at a stake on the north side of a rocky bluff," running to stakes in mounds to the place of beginning. This was a survey for Patrick Dugan and Barney Handley, dated Fever River, May 28, 1825, and signed Charles Smith, Acting Sub-agent, U. S. Lead Mines.

There is also recorded, June 21, 1825, a survey of 320 acres of mineral land on Apple River, for David G. Bates, the original field notes being taken July 2, 1823. Signed, John Anderson, Major U. S. Top'l Engineers, on Ordnance duty.

A copy of a bill of lading of May, 1825, shows that lead was transported from the Fever River mines to St. Louis for forty cents per hundred pounds.

According to the Regulations, all disputes between the miners were settled by the U. S. agent. The earliest account of these of which record now exists is a "Record of Proceedings in the case of Dugan and Welsh and David Mitchell." Joseph Miller and Ebenezer Orne were witnesses for Dugan and Welsh, and Joseph Hardy, Stephen Thrasher and William H. Smith, for Mr. Mitchell. There were no lawyers to complicate matters. The witnesses stated what they knew in few words, and the case was summed up and adjudicated by Lieut. Thomas, who gave one half the mineral dug on the disputed claim to Mitchell, "and it is considered that the other half is an *ample* compensation to Dugan and Welsh for the labor they bestowed on digging it. Their conduct was violent and quarrelsome, which will be utterly discountenanced at these mines. Mr. Charles Smith, acting Sub-agent, will see this settlement carried into effect." Signed M. Thomas, Lieut. U. S. Army, Superintendent of Lead Mines, and dated May 21, 1825.

In the record of the proceedings in the case of Joseph Hardy *vs.* Ray,

Orne and Smith, on the same day, Israel Mitchell testified that Col. Anderson stated that "Mr. Hardy was the oldest applicant for survey on the river."

The following extracts from reports made by Charles Smith, to his superior officer, are valuable as showing the exact state of affairs at that time:

June 11, 1825. Hardy and Jackson are running an ash furnace. Meeker is smelting in his log furnace. Vanmatre's ash furnace will be in operation to-day. Perfect harmony exists among the diggers. The Regulations appear to give universal satisfaction. Every man appreciates the protection which they afford, and the security they give to their operations presents a stimulus to enterprise, and prevents encroachments upon the rights of others. The difficulty of borrowing or hiring a horse when wanted has rendered necessary the purchase of one. I have accordingly bought one—old, to be sure, but serviceable—the price $20. He will be worth as much, probably, a year hence.

June 11, 1825. I have just visited a discovery made by C. Armstrong and I. Thorn, about ¾ of a mile south of the cave diggings. They dug 20 or 30 feet before they struck mineral. 2,000 were taken out in three hours—6,000, at least, are in view on the west side of the digging, and I struck mineral over one half of the bottom. The hole is about five feet in diameter.

Lead was low, and Smith already begins to find that the miners appreciate the situation. The following extracts are significant, and indicate that the miners were not quite satisfied with the reign of Thomas, and were expecting a change. They were not delivering mineral to the licensed smelters with much alacrity.

July 4, 1825. The diggers generally are keeping back their mineral, some with the expectation of raising the price, and others in the belief that licenses will be obtained by smelters from below. I understand that Meeker offers $18, an increase of 50 cents on the former price.

July 22, 1825. Smith reported that in his opinion some regulation is necessary to enable the smelters to keep their furnaces in operation. The diggers are deluded with an expectation that mineral will rise, and as they are generally able to hold on, they refuse to make deliveries.

July 22, 1825. Lieut. Low is here with 25 men; arrived on the 11th inst.; he is encamped near the Agency's establishment for a few days and occupies the finished cabin, with my permission, until he can select a suitable *scite* for building barracks.

Lieutenant Low came here with his men to build barracks and remain to enforce the regulations and the collection of the lead rent, as well as to compel the miners to deliver their mineral to the licensed smelters, whether they desired to do so or not. Lieutenant Low selected as a suitable "scite" for barracks a point on the west side of Fever River, at about one and one half miles below the Agency establishment, cleared the ground, erected a flag staff, but before the barracks were commenced, the order was countermanded and Low left with his command. The point is still known as "Low's Point." Tholozan & Detandabaratz afterwards had their smelting establishment on the east side of the river, about half a mile below "Low's Point," or half way down the "Long Reach."

It is to be inferred that the orders of Lieutenant Thomas were not always obeyed with the promptness desired by military officers. The following is selected from a large number of similar orders on record at that time because Mr. Meeker was one of the prominent men at the mines, as well as to show that then, as in later days, such men sometimes took their own time.

FEVER RIVER, July 19, 1825.

To MR. MOSES MEEKER, Smelter,

Sir.—By an order of Lieut. Thomas, of the 18th of May, 1825, you were required to "erect the warehouse stipulated in your license as a smelter (at the place on Fever River where it will be designated to you), without delay, as it was required immediately. You have since, by consent, commenced the erection of a cabin in lieu of the storehouse, and made considerable progress in that building. You are now required to erect a storehouse (agreeably to the stipulation in your license) from the foundation on such ground as will be designated to you, or to *complete* the cabin, at your election. Should the order not be complied with within a reasonable time, the fact will be reported to the Principal Agent, and such measures adopted in the meantime as will be justified by the 12th Article of your license.

By order,

CHARLES SMITH, U. S. A.

The following orders indicate difficulty in securing obedience to established regulations:

Notice is hereby given to all the diggers of lead ore upon the public land in the vicinity of Fever River, Small Pox and Apple Creeks, that they must forthwith deliver to the licensed smelters all the mineral they have dug; and in future, the smelters, when guaranteeing the tax to the United States, will take measures to have the ore delivered at such times as may be convenient—*at least* once every month. A refusal on the part of any digger to comply with this order (which is in accordance with the true intent and meaning of the Regulations), will cause his permit to dig to be forfeited, and the ore already obtained will be taken possession of by the Agent for the use of the United States.

Sept. 5, 1825. (*Signed*) M. THOMAS, *Lieut. U. S. Army.*
Supt. of Lead Mines.

FEVER RIVER, Oct. 13, 1825.

M. MEEKER, ESQ.,

Sir:—Unless *immediate* provision be made for the hauling and smelting of mineral at the diggings, as well as for a satisfactory settlement therefor, notice will be given to diggers to deliver their mineral to licensed smelters, without regard to existing guarantees. It is necessary that the order of the 5th of September should be immediately complied with.

I am, Sir, CHARLES SMITH,
U. S. Lead Mines, Fever River.

The first recorded return of lead mineral received and on hand at the furnaces of M. Meeker and Bates & Vanmatre, the only licensed smelters at that date, from April 3 to May 31, 1825, shows that Meeker received from sundry persons 30,342 pounds, and Bates & Vanmatre 25,601 pounds. Total number of diggers who have permits, 69. June 30 the number of diggers had increased to 89; July 31, 96. In August the number of diggers permitted was 105. Five smelters reported in August, viz.: Meeker, Bates & Vanmatre, Hardy, Jackson and N. Bates. At the end of September there were 127 diggers, and the five smelters had manufactured during the month 154,323 pounds of lead. The name of Gratiot first appears in these monthly reports in December, 1825, but he made no return until June following. The number of diggers at the end of December is reported at 151, but the aggregate amount of lead manufactured was only 2,792 pounds.

January 31, 1826, the name of Gibson appears in the list of smelters; diggers number 163; 29,185 pounds of lead manufactured, but the amount of mineral at the diggings was estimated at 425,000 pounds.

In April, 1826, the number of diggers was 287; amount of mineral at the diggings, 900,000 pounds; lead manufactured, 78,528 pounds. May shows a rapid increase of the number of diggers, 350. Mineral at the diggings accumulates, but only 6,927 pounds of lead are reported as manufactured by licensed smelters. June, the first return of Gratiot appears; 406 diggers; 173,479 pounds of lead. July, 1826, Comstock's name appears among the licensed smelters; 441 diggers; 140,781 pounds of lead, and 1,400,000 pounds of mineral at the diggings. October, 1826, diggers, 548; smelters, 7; 269,405 pounds of lead; 1,500,000 pounds of mineral at the diggings. This is the last report to be found.

Although this region was then heavily timbered, it seems that lessees and smelters were favored by the government, and farmers and villagers had to go to the islands for their wood, as is shown by the following:

NOTICE.

Those persons who have received permission to occupy land in the vicinity of Fever River, are hereby informed that all timber for fuel, fencing, or building, must be obtained from the islands in the Mississippi, and from no other place in this vicinity, as the timber elsewhere is reserved for the purposes of smelters and lessees.

(*Signed*) M. THOMAS, *Supt. of Lead Mines.*

FEVER RIVER, June 5, 1826.

The following document will be interesting now, when people can own their land. Then, and for a long time afterwards, the only title to land was by permit. All the people were tenants at will, of the United States, liable to be ejected from their homes at any time, at the caprice of one man. It is proper to add that, in 1826 the people at the mines petitioned Congress for more permanent titles, but no attention was paid to their request:

It having been requested from the U. S. Agent for Lead Mines to grant us permission to build, and enclose in a small quantity of ground for our convenience, it has been granted upon the following conditions viz.:

That we will not claim any right, title or interest in the said lands (other than as tenants at the will of said agent, or such other agent as may be appointed for the superintendence of the mines), and we hereby bind and obligate ourselves to quit said premises upon one month's notice to that effect, being given by said agent—it being understood that these persons who have licenses or leases are not included in this arrangement, but are to occupy agreeably to their contracts. No transfer of said ground or improvement will be made without the consent of the agent, and will be subject to the aforesaid regulation.

FEVER RIVER, June 6, 1826.

A large number of names are attached to this Register, among whom are many of the leading settlers. The first name is R. W. Chandler. James Harris and Jonathan Browder, first Commissioners of Jo Daviess County, are among the first signatures. James Foley, Sam S. Lawrence, Geo. W. Britton, T. H. January, Thomas Ray, Wm. H. Johnson, N. Bates, Thomas Hymer, J. P. B. Gratiot, Sam. C. Muir, A. P. Vanmeter, Amos Farrar, J. W. Shull, F. Dent, B. Gibson, James Jones, Elijah Ferguson, Isaac Swan, David M. Robinson, E. F. Townsend, H. H. Gear, and R. H. Champion are among the signers of this unique document.

A report from Charles Smith, dated July 25,1826, says: "I have surveyed the upper street in the town, and staked off the lots 50 feet, 41 in number. There is a great itching for privileges, and a superabundant *measure* of *independence.* Complaints about right to ground, and *this*, *that* and the *other* right are accumulating every day, both from diggers and settlers, and God knows *what* and *when* will be the end of all things. The *dead* and the living both conspire to cause me a great deal of trouble. I am no prophet, but I will be mad enough to predict that not *many months* will elapse without the necessity of the intervention of military force (the only force that can be recognized in this county), to protect the interest of the mines, and to encourage their development. Every day adds proof of their immense importance, and justifies the employment of every possible means for their protection and support. The competition among smelters may, I dare say *will*, have a tendency eventually to injure the mines, by producing a reaction upon themselves, and exciting a rebellious spirit among the miners."

Mr. Smith's allusion to the *dead* and the living is explained by the fact that in earlier days the people buried their dead in various places along the bench where Bench Street is now. These remains had to be removed, of course, when the town was laid out, and caused the good-natured Smith a deal of trouble. His gloomy predictions, happily, were not fulfilled.

Thomas McKnight * arrived at Fever River as sub-agent November 15, 1826. His first report is dated November 28, 1826, in which he says: "I arrived here on the 15th inst., but did not receive the government papers until the 20th, in consequence of having a little house to repair for an office. Mr. Dent, the bearer, leaves here to-morrow morning. I am told that there is a great quantity of mineral lying, and will lie, all Winter unsmelted. There is a great scarcity of corn for feeding teams. A great many of the teamsters are sending their teams down to the settlements to winter."

The "little house" referred to by Mr. McKnight is still standing on the west side of Main Street, Galena, about one hundred and fifty feet north of the corner of Spring Street, on lot three. The stone "government house," built for a warehouse in which to store lead, in 1829, by Harvey Mann and others, is still standing a little further north, on lot six.

Here occurs a list of persons in whose favor the superintendent has notified his acceptance of bonds for leases. The list was evidently made and entered of record in November or December, 1826, and entries of dates of surveys made subsequently:

John P. B. Gratiot, survey made; John Cottle, survey made; Ira Cottle, survey made; George Collier, survey made; Jesse W. Shull, survey made; M. C. Comstock, survey made Jan 22, 1827; John Barrel, survey made Jan. 22, 1827; William Henry, survey made Jan. 22, 1827; P. Hogan, survey not made; —— Bouthillier, survey not made; —— Tholozan, survey not made; Charles St. Vrain, survey made April 5, 1827; David G. Bates (Cave), survey not made; John P. B. Gratiot, (section timber land), survey made.

The first mention of the "Town of Galena" occurs December 27, 1826, in a permit to Patrick Gray and Thomas Drum, to occupy lot No. 25 in the Town of Galena, fifty feet fronting on Hill or Second Street, running back to the bluff, but this permit is dated "Fever River."

January 23, 1827, a permit was granted to Gray and Drum to enclose fifty feet on First (or Front) Street, north of Davis, for the purpose of building a bake shop thereon.

There may have been, probably were, other permits to persons desiring to occupy "town lots" prior to the above, but these are the first that appear of record. The future City of Galena was laid off, and evidently named, in 1826, as these records show, but permits of the superintendent were the only titles the people could have to their lots, improvements and homes, and these they must vacate and abandon on thirty days' notice. The United States still retained ownership.

May 12 to 15, 1827, various permits were signed by "Wash Wheelwright, Lt. Artillery," probably acting in Mr. McKnight's absence.

Historians have given, as one of the causes of the "Winnebago War," which occurred in 1827, the fact that the Indians were dissatisfied because the miners were encroaching on their territory and digging mineral on the north side of the "Ridge," which they considered the boundary of the "five leagues square." In this connection, the following letter and orders will be of interest:

* Mr. McKnight succeeded Charles Smith as resident sub-agent, and remained until Lieut. Thomas was succeeded by Capt. Legate, in 1829. Chas. Smith died at Galena, March 3, 1829.

UNITED STATES LEAD MINING OFFICE,
FEVER RIVER, June 30, 1827.

To Mr. Elijah Ferguson, now mining on the Pecalotea,

SIR: It is doubtful whether you are within the limits of the country which the United States, by treaty with the Pottawattomies, etc., have a right to explore for mining purposes. Under this circumstance, you will not remove further towards Rock River. Should you prefer to remain where you now are, you are at present at liberty to do so, with the express understanding, however, that, should that part of the country be eventually decided to belong to the Winnebagoes, you remove when duly notified of the fact from this office.

I am, sir, your obedient servant,
(*Signed*) M. THOMAS.
Lieut. U. S. A., Superintendent U. S. Lead Mines.

CIRCULAR TO SMELTERS.

U. S. LEAD MINING OFFICE, GALENA, October 1, 1827.

Sirs: You are hereby directed to desist from working over the Ridge, and to employ no force whatever, either in hauling or smelting any mineral that may have been, or in the future may be, raised there. Also to make no purchases of said mineral from any digger.

CHARLES SMITH.

By order of LIEUT. THOMAS, *Superintendent of Lead Mines.*

On the same date miners were notified that they had no right to go beyond said ridge for the purpose of mining, and were ordered to suspend all further operations until further orders from the superintendent.

On the 8th of October, 1827, an order was issued directing all discoveries of lead to be reported to the lead mining office, Galena.

On the 15th of November, 1827, the following persons having struck leads prior to the 3d of July, 1827, beyond the ridge, were licensed to dig or work them out without interruption, "but no others were to be allowed to mine beyond the Ridge *under any circumstances whatever:*" Cabanae, for Ewing & Co.; Stevens, for Kirker & Ray; Riche, for Winkle; Elijah Ferguson; Hawthorn & Deviese; Carroll, for Dickson; Stevenson, transferred to Blanchard; Gillespie & Hymer; Stevens & Co.; George Ames' survey; Moore & Watson, sold to Blanchard; Foster & Hogan.

July 2, 1827, Lieut. Thomas granted a permit to M. C. White to burn one *lime of kiln* (kiln of lime) above the mouth of Small Pox. On the same day, Mr. Comstock had permission to cut fifty large trees for building logs, near the large mound south of Mr. Gratiot's survey. Arbitrations were ordered between McKnight and Ewen Boyce & Co., on Mackey's survey, and between Jacob Hymer and WillBaker, to take place on the 7th.

NOTICE.

There will not, for the present, be any town laid off at the Old Turkey Village, commonly called Grant River Town. All persons are hereby forewarned from building cabins or houses there, except such licensed smelters who may locate in that vicinity, and such smelters will first obtain a special permission.

M. THOMAS, *Lieut. U. S. Army,*
Supt. U. S. Lead Mines.

FEVER RIVER, July 13, 1827.

Aug. 14, 1827, a permit was granted to Messrs. D. G. Bates, and Jefferson and Hempstead to make a wharf, or landing, in front of their houses and lots, provided such landing is at all times free to public use: no building to be placed upon it.

On the 8th of August, 1827, Michael Dee was convicted by arbitrators of having stolen certain articles, the property of Thomas Williams, and all smelters and miners on Fever River forbidden to harbor said Dee, or give him any employment.

This is the first conviction for theft of which record remains.

J. A. Packard

CHICAGO.

(FORMERLY OF GALENA).

McKnight left no records except a few recorded permits, and except the two volumes from which the above extracts have been made there are no records of the transactions of the Lead Mines Agency accessible, unless they are preserved in the War Department at Washington, and a letter to that department, asking for information, has failed to elicit a reply.

The only entries to be found of date later than 1827 are a code of regulations for miners, dated April, 1833, and signed Tho. C. Legate, Captain Second Infantry, Superintendent U. S. Mines, and another and shorter code, dated October, 1840, signed by H. King, Special Agent U. S. Lead Mines, in which miners were required to pay not to exceed six per cent of the ore, or its equivalent in metal, to the United States.

Under Lieut. Thomas' administration, Charles Smith and Thomas McKnight were resident sub-agents, at Galena. About 1828, the agency was removed to a log building there recently erected under permit, by Barney Dignan, on the southwest corner of Main and Washington Streets. In 1829 the office was in the first building above Mr. Barnes' boarding-house on the upper (Bench) street, and in later time, and until discontinued, the office of the superintendent was in Newhall's building, southwest corner of Hill and Main Streets.

In 1829, Lieut. Thomas was succeeded by Capt. Tho. C. Legate, Second Infantry, under whom Capt. John H. Weber was assistant superintendent. Major Wm. Campbell, Col. A. G. S. Wight and R. H. Bell were also connected with the office. In November, 1836, Capt. Weber's signature as superintendent appears of record, and it is probable that he was appointed about that time.

As previously shown, under the old system, which generally prevailed until 1836, diggers were permitted to sell their mineral only to licensed smelters, and the government collected the rents (ten per cent until 1830, and six per cent, subsequently, delivered at the United States Warehouse, in Galena) of the smelters. The prices paid to miners were made with that fact in view. In 1827, as clearly indicated by the letter from Lieut. Thomas to E. Ferguson, and subsequent orders, the diggers and some of the smelters were operating on lands not owned or controlled by the United States, in some instances having the permission of the Indians and paying them for the privilege, and in more cases, probably, trespassing on their domain. It had begun to dawn upon the people that five leagues square comprised only a very small portion of the lands rich in mineral wealth, and it was not possible for the government agents to prevent digging for mineral outside the limits of the reservation, over which only could the United States exercise control. The superintendent of the United States Mines had no authority to grant permits on Indian territory. He could forbid such trespass, but it would require a military force to prevent mining beyond the limits of the reservation, provided the diggers obtained the consent of the native owners. It was plain that the government could rightfully collect rent only of those who obtained their mineral within the recognized limits of the "five leagues square." The agent could not justly demand any of the lead obtained beyond the limits of the reservation, and this led to difficulty. It was unjust to pay rent to the Indians and pay it again to the United States, nor could the agent collect rent even if it had been surreptitiously obtained. Some of the smelters, and especially those operating on Indian lands, either with or without the permission of the natives, or buying mineral from diggers operating beyond the jurisdiction of the agent, began to refuse to pay rent, alleging that as they obtained lead from Indian lands and were not protected by the government, they were under no obligation to pay. The agent was placed in an embarrassing position. They were obtaining mineral on U. S. lands, but they were also obtaining it on lands over which the United States exercised no control, he had no means of determining the amount actually due the government, and therefore could not enforce payment of any. This refusal became more general until the unauthorized sale of the mineral lands in Wisconsin, in 1834, and subsequently by the Register of the Land Office at Mineral Point, (called "Shake-rag" in early mining days), who in violation of his express instructions, permitted a large number of the diggings actually worked to be entered. Many miners were thus outrageously defrauded and their rights were disregarded. From that time they declined taking leases, and the lead office gradually fell into practical disuse. Captain Weber remained as agent until about 1840, but his agency was purely nominal. The regulations were not enforced. Smelters paid no rent, and there was a season of freedom from governmental supervision. In 1840, however, an attempt was made to revive the office. H. King, special agent, was sent to the mines, probably to investigate Weber's loose manner of doing business, or rather his neglect of business. "With Mr. King," says Mr. Houghton, "or very nearly the same time, came John Flanagan."* Mr. King remained but a short time. Weber was removed or superseded, and Flanagan left in charge, with instructions to enforce the regulations established by Mr. King. About the same time, Walter Cunningham, who, says Mr. Houghton, had been appointed to investigate the Superior copper mines, returned from a tour through that region and established himself here with Flanagan. From this time, the regulations required the miners to pay the rent "not to exceed 6 per cent of the ore, or its equivalent in metal," but in practice, it is said, the rent that was collected was generally paid through the smelters, as formerly. Flanagan, his associate, Cunningham, and a clerk named Conroddy, by their associations and habits rendered themselves exceedingly odious to the people. Flanagan commenced a large number of suits against individuals for arrears of rent, compromised them for what he could get in cash, but, it is said, made no returns to the government of his collections, defrauding the people and the government at the same time. He was accustomed to say to the people that the "government must be

*Since this was in type, a letter has been received from Captain W. B. Green, who was familiar with the events of that period, which contains the following: "The Lead Mine Agency was suspended for several years prior to 1841. After the inauguration of President Harrison, in 1841, the agency was revived and Flanagan appointed superintendent—revived, probably, to give Flanagan the appointment. Previous to the suspension of the agency, the royalty to the government was paid by the miners through the smelters. After the revival of the agency under Flanagan, the attempt was made to collect the royalty directly from the miners. The attempt was only a partial success, as the miners generally refused or evaded the payment. During the suspension of the agency, through affidavits gotten up (as affidavits can be to prove any thing when taken *ex-parte*), a bill was lobbied through Congress, giving one of the early smelters a large sum of money for royalty paid by him on mineral purported to have been taken from Indian lands outside the original purchase. This established a precedent of which most of the other smelters availed themselves, and in a similar manner had large sums voted them—in the aggregate, it may be, amounting to more than all the royalty received by the government from the mines. The truth is, there was but a very inconsiderable amount taken from the Indian lands prior to the purchase of the lands south of the Wisconsin River, in the Winter of 1827-'8. What little there was should, of right, have been paid to the Indians; or, ignoring their right, it should have been paid to the miners who *actually paid it*, as the smelters took the royalty into account when they purchased the mineral, and *deducted it* from the value thereof."

paid first," and his arrogant declaration to smelters and others that "I am the government," sufficiently indicates his character and the disposition he made of his collections. If he was "the government," there was no necessity of making returns to any body, and none were known to be made by him. Complaints of his high-handed proceedings reached Washington, and in 1843, Mr. Wann states, Captain —— Bell, stationed at St. Louis, was ordered by the Secretary of War to Galena, to investigate Flanagan's administration. He came, but remained but a few days, dismissed Flanagan and placed Maj. Thomas Mellville, of Galena, in charge of the office temporarily, until report could be made to the War Department, and a Superintendent should be appointed.* The next year, 1844, according to the best information to be obtained, John G. Floyd, of Virginia, was appointed to the office. Mr. Floyd made an effort to enforce the collection of rent and in some measure succeeded, but was removed, in 1845, at the instance of Hon. Joseph P. Hoge, then member of Congress for this (then Sixth) district, and James A. Mitchell was appointed as his successor, who remained until the office was finally discontinued about 1847, when the lands were thrown into the market. Practically, however, the office was little more than nominal after the resignation of Capt. Legate, in 1836. Under the pre-emption laws a large amount of mineral lands had been entered. Settlers were required to make oath that no mineral *was being dug* on the lands they desired to enter, and this requirement was easily evaded.

The people generally considered the Agency as an imposition, and it was impossible to secure the implicit obedience to the rule of the Superintendent that obtained in the days of Thomas and Legate. The experiment of reviving the office was not a success. The Government found upon trial that, instead of being a source of revenue, the management of the lead mines produced constant drafts upon the Treasury, and at last, after the settlers had petitioned in vain for years, early in the session of 1846–'7, Congress authorized the sale of the lands. A receiver was appointed, and by the 5th day of April, 1847, says Seymour, "land to the amount of $127,700 had been sold at minimum prices,† and the days of governmental supervision or ownership of the lead mines ended."

The amount of lead shipped from various ports on the Mississippi, principally from Galena, for nine years prior to the discovery of gold in 1849, and the estimated value thereof, is as follows:

1841—31,696,980 lbs., valued at $3 per cwt.	$950,909 40
" Small bars and shot valued at	31,433 50
Total	$982,342 90
1842—31,407,530 lbs., at $2.75@$3 per cwt.	$746,296 46
1843—39,461,171 lbs., at $2.37½ per cwt.	937,202 00
1844—43,722,070 lbs., at $2.82½ per cwt.	1,235,148 47
1845—54,492,200 lbs., at $3.00 per cwt.	1,634,766 00
1846—51,268,200 lbs., at $2.90 per cwt.	1,486,778 09
1847—54,085,920 lbs., at $3.00 per cwt.	1,622,577 60
1848—47,737,830 lbs., at $3.50 per cwt.	1,670,824 95
1849—44,025,380 lbs., at $3.62½ per cwt.	1,595,920 02

In 1849 the gold discoveries in California disturbed "the even balance of ordinary business operations" in the lead mining district. The tide of

* Later information renders it certain that Flanagan was not appointed until 1841, arriving at Galena July 9 of that year. Capt. W. H. Bell's report was printed in the Spring of 1844.

† $1.25 per acre for farming and $2.50 per acre for mineral lands.

immigration that had been directed to this region was diverted to the Pacific Coast, and a large number of miners and business men, dazzled by the glitter of California gold, left to seek their fortunes on the slopes of the Sierra Nevada. Large amounts of real estate covered by valuable improvements were forced into market and sold at nominal prices, to obtain the means wherewith to remove to California. Enormous rates were paid for money and a large amount of capital was withdrawn from the usual channels of trade; improvements, commenced or contemplated, were suspended or delayed, and the heavy emigration from the lead to the gold, mining region was seriously felt. A large number of men usually engaged in prospecting, and by whom new and important discoveries had been constantly made, were no longer here, and operations were principally confined for a time, to old "leads." But in compensation for this the price of mineral advanced to $28 per thousand (it had at some periods been as low as $8 or $9, and was seldom higher than $22) and this advance caused operations to be renewed in diggings that had been abandoned as too unproductive to be remunerative. Writing in 1850, in discussing the effect of the "gold fever," Mr. Seymour says: "Although lead is one of the baser metals, and does not strike the imagination like pure gold dug from the bowels of the earth, yet it immediately becomes gold in the pockets of the miner, for nothing but gold is given in exchange for it by the smelter, and it is always in great demand at the market price. If enterprising men were willing to undergo here half the privations and sufferings which they endure by a journey to California and hard labor in the gold mining, their happiness and prosperity would probably be as well promoted by their pecuniary success, saying nothing of the extreme perils thereby avoided, and the painful disruption of domestic ties, so common to this class of emigrants."

THE WINNEBAGO WAR.

The year 1827 is memorable in the history of Jo Daviess County as being the period of the first serious troubles with their Indian neighbors, experienced by the settlers, dignified now by the title of the "Winnebago War." All the territory north of the Ordinance line of 1787 was in the undisputed possession of the Indians, except the reservations at the north of the Wisconsin and on Fever River, and the mining district in Jo Daviess County and Michigan Territory, outside these reservations, was occupied largely by the Winnebagoes. Early in 1827, miners, settlers and adventurers flocked hither in great numbers, and inevitably extended their explorations for mineral beyond the "Ridge," recognized as the line of the "five leagues square," although it does not now appear that the limits of the reservation were ever accurately determined. Many rich leads were discovered on Indian lands, and miners persisted in digging there, in direct disobedience of the orders of the superintendent of the United States Lead Mines to desist and withdraw from lands on which the United States were not authorized to even explore for mineral. In exceptional instances the right to mine was purchased of the Indians, but in most cases the restless searchers for mineral wealth totally disregarded the orders of the superintendent and the rights of the Indians, who, according to the acts of the trespassers "had no right which a white man was bound to respect." Frequent disputes occurred in consequence between the miners and the Indians. Mr. Shull, who had discovered a fine lead and had erected a shanty near it, was driven off, and his cabin destroyed by the Winnebagoes, who, owning the land, did no more, and perhaps not as much, as whites would have done under similar circumstances, to protect and preserve their rights and property. The dissatisfaction and ill feeling engendered by these encroachments upon their territory was, perhaps, a minor cause of the outbreak, but had no other cause operated to further exasperate the Indians, the difficulties might, and probably would, have been amicably adjusted without bloodshed.

About this time, and while these disputes between the miners and Indians were occurring, two keel-boats, belonging to the contractor to furnish supplies for the troops at Fort Snelling, while on their way up the river stopped at a point not far above Prairie du Chien, where were encamped a large number of Winnebago Indians. John Wakefield, Esq., in writing from memory an account of the war, if it can be called such (and it must be admitted now, writing in a spirit of bitter prejudice against the Indians, who had been peaceable and friendly with the settlers here, until provoked beyond endurance) says that these boats were run by "Capt. Allen Lindsey, a gentleman of the first respectability in our country," and that he was with his boats on this particular trip, but it is to be hoped that Wakefield was in error, for no "respectable gentleman" could have permitted men under his command to indulge in such fiendish excesses, not only endangering their own lives, but imperiling the safety of all the frontier settlements as well.

Reynolds says that after stopping at the Winnebago camp "the boatmen made the Indians drunk—and no doubt were so themselves—when they captured six or seven squaws, who were also drunk. These captured squaws were forced on the boats for corrupt and brutal purposes. But not satisfied with this outrage on female virtue the boatmen took the squaws with them in the boats to Fort Snelling." Another version given by Harvey Mann, and others who were familiar with the events of that year, is that the boatmen and the Indians had a drunken frolic; that several squaws were kept on board the boats all night, and put ashore the next morning before any of the tribe had recovered from the effects of their "spree," and the boats continued on their voyage up the river. These accounts agree as to the main fact that the boatmen committed a gross outrage upon the Indians, and provoked an attack.

When the duped and injured Winnebagoes had slept off the effects of their debauch and became sober enough to comprehend the outrage committed upon their women, and the injury done them in "this delicate point," they were intensely exasperated, and resolved to wash out the stain upon their honor in blood. What white people would not have done the same, under similar circumstances? Runners were sent out in all directions summoning the warriors to the scene of action at once for an attack on the boats when they returned. A war party of the Winnebagoes went from Jo Daviess County, in the vicinity of Galena, to aid their northern brethren in avenging the insult they had received. Capt. D. S. Harris states that at this time a band of 15 or 20 of these Indians stopped at his father's house, on their way up the river and were very insolent. "Old Curley," a friendly Indian, had notified the family of the intended visit, and the younger members had sought refuge in the neighboring cornfield, leaving only Smith and Scribe in the house with their mother. "The Indians," says Smith Harris, "were very insolent, as was not unusual for that tribe. They offered no personal injury, for Scribe and I stood by our guns. They did attempt to take some articles of goods we had, but we told them if they didn't let things alone we should shoot, and they knew we meant it. They finally left without doing any harm, and we felt much relieved." This band went north, and, it is said, murdered a family near Prairie du Chien. Four Winnebago Chiefs called upon the Gratiots, at Gratiot's Grove, and informed them that on account of the action of the whites, they should be unable to restrain their young men from declaring war, and as they did not desire to harm the "Choteaus" (as the Indians always called the Gratiot family) they had come to tell them that they had better remove. But careful inquiry among those who were here during that year fails to develop any evidence that any outrages were committed by the Indians in the mining district at that time, either before or after the insult by those drunken keel-boatmen, and which the injured party intended to avenge upon the guilty parties themselves.

Wakefield says that some of the Indians "came aboard of Lindsey's boat on his way up and showed such signs of hostility that he was led to expect an attack on his return, and provided himself with a few fire arms so that in case of an attack by them he might be able to defend himself." Other accounts state that the boatmen anticipated an attack upon their return. Why, if they had done nothing to provoke an assault? The Indians were peaceable, and even in the mines where they had reason to complain of the encroachments of the whites upon their territory they had done nothing more than to drive off the trespassers.

Of course the boatmen expected an attack on their return trip, for they knew they deserved it, and the dispassionate judgment of humanity, after the lapse of half a century concurs in that opinion. Knowing this, they attempted to run by the Winnebago Village on their return, in the night. The watchful, vengeful Winnebagoes, however, were not to be eluded. The boats were forced to approach near the shore in the narrow channel of the river at that point, and there, says Reynolds, "the infuriated savages assailed one boat and *permitted the other to pass down*" unmolested. The presumption is that the boat assailed contained the offenders whom they wished to punish. Reynolds' account of the fight is as follows :—

> The boatmen were not entirely prepared for the attack, although to some extent they were guarded against it. They had procured some arms, and were on the alert to some degree. The Indians laid down in their canoes and tried to paddle them to the boat; but the whites, seeing this, fired their muskets on them in the canoes. It was a desperate and furious fight, for a few minutes, between a good many Indians exposed in open canoes and only a few boatmen protected, to some extent, by their boat. One boatman, a sailor by profession on the lakes and ocean, who had been in many battles with the British during the war of 1812, saved the boat and those of the crew who were not killed. This man was large and strong, and possessed the courage of an African lion. He seized a part of the setting pole of the boat, which was about four feet long and had on the end a piece of iron, which made the pole weighty and a powerful weapon in the hands of "Saucy Jack," as the champion was called. It is stated that when the Indians attempted to board the boat, Jack would knock them back into the river as fast as they approached. The boat got fast on the ground, and the whites seemed doomed, but with great exertion, courage and hard fighting, the Indians were repelled. ("Jack," unmindful of the shower of bullets whistling about, seized a pole, pushed the boat into the current and it floated beyond the reach of the assailants.) The savages killed several white men and wounded many more, leaving barely enough to navigate the boat. Thus commenced and thus ended the bloodshed of the Winnebago War. No white man or Indian was killed before or after this naval engagement.

The arrival of these boats at Galena and the report of their narrow escape created great alarm, intensified by the arrival, the same day, of a party who had fled to Galena for safety, anticipating war, and by the warning given to the Gratiots. All mining operations ceased;

the miners and scattered settlers hurried to Galena for safety, built stockades and blockhouses in their own neighborhoods, or left the country. A little fort was built at Elizabeth, another at Apple River, and still another in Michigan Territory. These forts, although not needed then, were afterwards found "very handy to have in the family."

Governor Edwards received information, on which he relied, that the Winnebago Indians had attacked some keel-boats, that the settlers and miners on Fever River were in imminent danger of an attack from a band of the same and other Indians (although the facts, as reported to him and upon which he acted, have never been made public), and called out the Twentieth Regiment Illinois Militia, under Col. Thomas M. Neale, who were to rendezvous at Fort Clark (Peoria), "and march with all possible expedition to the assistance of our fellow citizens at Galena." The brave citizens of Sangamon rallied to the rendezvous, and, with ten days' rations, marched to Gratiot Grove, and—finding no hostile Indians there, disbanded and went home.

Gen. Lewis Cass, Governor of Michigan Territory, who had been appointed by the government to hold a treaty with the Lake Michigan Indians, at Green Bay, arrived there about this time, but, finding but few there and hearing that the Lake Indians had received war messages from the interior, hastened to communicate the startling intelligence to the military commander at St. Louis. He ascended Fox River from Green Bay, descended the Wisconsin and Mississippi, and in nine days arrived at St. Louis. It is said that "among the Winnebagoes he discovered warlike preparations, but his sudden and unexpected appearance among them in a birch canoe, of larger size than that used by ordinary traders, filled with armed men, with the U. S. flag flying, led the Indians to suspect that he was accompanied by a superior force. To this fact and the rapidity of his movements may be attributed his safety and the men under his command." A single birch bark canoe, with armed men enough in it to overcome thousands of hostile savages for hundreds of miles, must have been worth seeing.

On his way down, Gen. Cass stopped at Galena, where Gen. Henry Dodge and Gen. Whiteside had raised a company of volunteers, ready to march against the terrible foe. An eye witness of his arrival says that in the midst of the alarm then prevailing the excited people heard singing, and thought the Indians were coming, but soon their fears were allayed, for they saw, gliding gracefully up the river, around the point below the village, a large canoe flying the United States flag and containing an American officer and six Canadians dressed in blue jackets and red sashes, with bright feathers in their hats, who were singing the "Canadian Boat Song" as they bent over their oars, and with measured strokes sent it flying to the bank, when Gen. Cass stepped ashore amid the cheers of the assembled population. "Armed men" were few and far between in that boat.

Immediately upon receipt of news from Governor Cass, General Atkinson marched with 600 men to the "seat of war," and formed a junction with the Galena Volunteers at Fort Winnebago. "Thus far they had marched into the bowels of the land without impediment." During all this period of alarm, excitement and feverish expectation of a descent of the hostile Indians upon the defenseless frontier settlements in the mining district, what were these Indians doing? They had had time enough to have swept the white settlers on Fever River out of the country, or out of existence, before the "imposing display of such a large number of troops in the heart of their country dampened their war spirit and induced them to surrender their chiefs," but it does not appear that they murdered a single settler or committed any serious depredations after they had punished the keel-boatmen who had so grossly insulted them.

Capt. D. S. Harris, who was a volunteer in the Galena company commanded by Gen. Dodge, says: "We marched to Fort Winnebago, where Red Wing was brought in a prisoner, and that was the end of it." The Winnebagoes surrendered Red Wing and We-Kaw, the two chiefs who had led the attack upon the keel-boats, when Gen. Atkinson made the imposing military display in "the heart of their country." Red Wing was imprisoned at Prairie du Chien, where he was to be kept as a hostage for the good behavior of his nation, but his proud spirit was broken by confinement that he felt was unjust, and he soon died.

Thus ended the Winnebago War, which was really only an attack upon some keel-boatmen, provoked by the outrages upon the Indians by the boatmen themselves. There was no war elsewhere, but the prosperity of the mining region was temporarily checked by the alarm and consequent suspension of mining and business.

Whether, had the Indians succeeded in their attempt to murder the offending crew of the boat they attacked while they permitted the other to pass down the river unmolested, they would have entered upon the war path against all the white settlements in this region, must forever be a matter of conjecture, and while there were and are differences of opinion, the most of the survivors of that period of excitement coincide in the belief that had not the Indians been stung to fury by these drunken boatmen there would have been no trouble. The mineral lands could have been bought, as they were, subsequently, by treaty. If the government, when it demanded the surrender of Red Wing and kept him as a hostage, had arrested those boatmen and imprisoned them for life, both for the outrage they committed and for recklessly disturbing the peace, and destroying for a time the prosperity of the frontier settlements, and causing so much damage to the innocent settlers, or had delivered them to the Indians to be kept as hostages for the good behavior of their class, it would have been only even-handed justice.

Soon after this disgraceful, and in some respects ludicrous, affair, a treaty was made with the Winnebagoes by which for twenty thousand dollars paid in goods and trinkets at fabulous prices, they were satisfied for the damages sustained by them in consequence of the trespasses on their lands, and relinquished a large tract of these lands to the miners.

THE BLACK HAWK WAR.

The great event of the year 1832 was the Black Hawk War. The reader is familiar with the general history of this war, but there are some incidents connected with it and some phases of it familiar to the survivors of the sturdy rank and file that participated in it, who had and still have their opinions relating to its causes and conduct, differing from most published accounts, that should be recorded. The war was commenced and most of the blood was spilt in what was then Jo Daviess County. Mostly confining this sketch to these events and to the causes of the war as received

H. S. Townsend.

WARREN

from the lips of the survivors, it may appear that, like the Winnebago affair of 1827, the whites were not entirely guiltless.

In 1831, Black Hawk and his band had crossed to their old homes on Rock River, but had negotiated a treaty and returned to the west side of the Mississippi, receiving liberal presents of goods and provisions from the Government, and promised never to return without the consent of the President of the United States or the Governor of Illinois. But on the 6th day of April, 1832, he again recrossed the Mississippi with his entire band and their women and children. The *Galenian*, edited by Dr. A. Philleo, of May 2, 1832, says that "Black Hawk was invited by the Prophet, and had taken possession of a tract about forty miles up Rock River, but that he did not remain there long, but commenced his march up Rock River." Capt. William B. Green, now of Chicago, but who served in Stephenson's Company of mounted rangers, says that "Black Hawk and his band crossed the river with no hostile intent, but to accept an invitation from Pittawak, a friendly chief, to come over and spend the Summer with his people on the head waters of the Illinois," and the movements of Black Hawk up Rock River before pursuit by the military, seems to confirm this statement. There seems to be no question of the fact that he came in consequence of an invitation from the Prophet or Pittawak, or both, as his people were in a starving condition.

Others who agree with Green, that Black Hawk did not come to fight and had no idea of fighting, say that he had retired to the west side of the Mississippi the previous year under treaty, receiving a large quantity of corn and other provisions, but in the Spring his provisions were gone, his followers were starving, and he came back expecting to negotiate another treaty and get a new supply of provisions.

There is still another explanation that may enable the reader to harmonize the preceding statements and to understand why Black Hawk returned in 1832. It is well known that in nearly all the treaties ever made with the Indians, the Indian traders dictated the terms for their allies and customers, and, of course, received a large share of the annuities, etc., in payment for debts due to them. Each tribe had certain traders who supplied them. George Davenport had a trading post at Fort Armstrong. His customers were largely the Sacs and Foxes, and he was held in high esteem by them, in fact his word was their law. It is said that Black Hawk's band became indebted to him for a large amount and were unable to pay. They had not had good luck hunting during the Winter and he was likely to lose heavily. If Black Hawk, therefore, could be induced to come on this side of the river again and the people could be alarmed so that a military force could be sent in pursuit of him, another treaty could be made, he might assist in making terms and get his pay out of the payments the government would make, and all would be well. Mr. Amos Farrar, who was Davenport's partner for some years, and who died in Galena during the war, is said to have declared, while on his death-bed, that the "Indians were not to be blamed, that if they had been let alone there would have been no trouble—that the band were owing Mr. Davenport and he wanted to get his pay and would, if another treaty had been made."

In a letter to Gen. Atkinson, dated April 13, 1832, Davenport says: "I have been informed that the British band of Sac Indians are determined to make war on the frontier settlements. * * * From every information that I have received I am of the opinion that the intention of the

British band of Sac Indians is to commit depredations on the inhabitants of the frontier."

Just such a letter as he or any other trader would have written to cause a pursuit, and consequent treaty. Black Hawk evidently understood the game. He was leisurely pursuing his way up Rock River, waiting for the first appearance of the military to display the white flag and negotiate as he had done the previous year.

Although Black Hawk's movement across the Mississippi, on the 6th of April, was at once construed into a hostile demonstration, and Davenport skillfully cultivated the idea, he was accompanied by his old men, women and children. No Indian warriors ever went on the war path encumbered in that way. More than this, it does not appear, from the sixth day of April until Stillman's drunken soldiers fired on his flag of truce, on the 12th of May, that a single settler was murdered, or suffered any material injury at the hands of Black Hawk or his band. In truth, Hon. H. S. Townsend, of Warren, states that in one instance, at least, where they took corn from a settler, they paid him for it. Capt. W. B. Green writes: "I never heard of Black Hawk's band, while passing up Rock River, committing any depredation whatever, not even petty theft." Frederick Stahl, Esq., of Galena, states that he was informed by the veteran John Dixon, that "when Black Hawk's band passed his post, before the arrival of the troops, they were at his house. Ne-o-Pope had the young braves well in hand, and informed him that they intended to commit no depredations, and should not fight unless they were attacked."

Whatever his motive may have been, it is the unanimous testimony of the survivors, now residing on the old battle-fields of that day, that except the violation of treaty stipulations and an arrogance of manner natural to an Indian who wanted to make a new trade with the "Great Father," the Sacs under Black Hawk committed no serious acts of hostility, and intended none, until after the alternative of war or extermination was presented to them by Stillman's men.

Certain it is that the people of Galena and of the mining district generally apprehended no serious trouble and made no preparations for war until Capt. Stephenson brought the news of Stillman's rout, on the 15th of May.

Some United States troops arrived at Galena from Prairie du Chien on the 1st of May, and about the same time Black Hawk commenced his march up Rock River, from the Prophet's Village, but there was no serious alarm among the inhabitants of the settled portions of Jo Daviess County, and the troops went to Rock Island (Fort Armstrong) on the 7th. About that time, J. W. Stephenson, John Foley and Mr. Atchison returned from a reconnoitering expedition, and reported that the Indians had "dispersed among the neighboring tribes." The *Galenian* of May 16th, printed before the tidings of Stillman's fiasco had reached Galena, said: "It is already proved that they will not attempt to fight it out with us, as many have supposed. Will the temporary dispersion of Black Hawk's band among their neighbors cause our troops to be disbanded?"

On Saturday, May 12, Gov. Reynolds was at Dixon Ferry, with about two thousand mounted riflemen, awaiting the arrival of Gen. Atkinson's forces from Fort Armstrong. A day or two previous, Major Isaiah Stillman, "with about four hundred well-mounted volunteers," says the *Galenian*, "commenced his march with a fixed determination to wage a war of extermination wherever he might find any part of the hostile band." Just before night, on the 12th of May, 1832, Stillman's forces encamped at White Rock Grove, in what is now Ogle County, about thirty-five miles from Dixon. He was in close proximity to Black Hawk's encampment but did not know it. Black Hawk was at that moment making arrangements to propose to treat for peace. Stillman's men were well supplied with whisky. Some authorities state that they had with them a barrel of "fire water," and many of them were drunk. They were all eager to get sight of an Indian, and were determined not to be happy until each had the gory scalp of a Sac dangling at his belt. Extermination was their motto, although the game they hunted had committed no depredations.

Soon after, becoming aware of the immediate presence of an armed force, Black Hawk sent a small party of his braves to Stillman's camp with a flag of truce. On their approach, they were discovered by some of the men, who, without reporting to their commander, and without orders, hastily mounted and dashed down upon the approaching Indians. These, not understanding this sudden movement, and apparently suspicious, retreated towards the camp of their chief. The whites fired, killed two and captured two more, but the others escaped, still pursued by the reckless volunteers. When Black Hawk and his war chief, Ne-o-pope, saw them dashing down upon their camp, their flag of truce disregarded, and, believing that their overtures for peace had been rejected, they raised the terrible war-whoop and prepared for the fray.

It was now the turn of the volunteers to retreat, which they did with wonderful celerity, after murdering their two prisoners, without waiting for the onslaught, supposing they were pursued by a thousand savage warriors. The flying rascals rushed through the camp, spreading terror and consternation among their comrades, but late so eager to meet the foe. The wildest panic ensued, there was "mounting in hot haste," and without waiting to see whether there was any thing to run for, every man fled, never stopping until they had reached Dixon's Ferry or some other place of safety, or had been stopped by the tomahawk or bullet. The first man to reach Dixon was a Kentucky lawyer, not unknown to fame in Jo Daviess County, who, as he strode into Dixon, reported that every man of Stillman's command had been killed except himself. Another man, named Comstock, never stopped until he reached Galena, where he reported that "the men were all drunk, as he was, got scared and made the best time they could out of danger, but that he didn't see a single Indian." All accounts concur in the main facts, however, that the men were drunk, and that the white flag displayed by Black Hawk was fired upon in utter disregard of all rules of warfare recognized, even among the Indians. The whites had commenced the work of murder, and the Indians, losing all hope of negotiation, determined that extermination was a game that both parties could play at. Gen. Whiteside, were in command at Dixon, at once marched for the fatal field, but the enemy gone, the main body having moved northward, and the rest scattered in small bands to avenge the death of their people upon unoffending settlers. Eleven of Stillman's men were killed, among whom were Captain Adams and Major Perkins. Their mutilated remains were gathered and buried, and the place is known as "Stillman's Run" to this day. This was the commencement of hostilities, and justice compels the impartial historian to record that the whites were the aggressors. Many of the volunteers appreciated the fact, too. It was not such grand sport to kill Indians when they found that Indians might kill them, and especially when war had been wantonly commenced by firing upon and killing the bearers of the flag of peace. They grumbled and demanded to be mustered out, and were dismissed soon after by Governor Reynolds. Another call was issued, and a new regiment of volunteers was mustered in at Beardstown, with Jacob Fry as Colonel; James D. Henry, Lieutenant Colonel, and John Thomas, Major. The late commanding general, Whiteside, volunteered as a private.

The fatal act of Stillman's men precipitated all the horrors of Indian border warfare upon the white settlements in Jo Daviess County, as it then existed, and in the adjoining portions of Michigan Territory. Nor is it certain that all the outrages were perpetrated by the "British Band." It is certain that young Pottawatomies and Winnebagoes joined Black Hawk, and after the war suddenly closed at Bad Axe, it was ascertained that many of the murders had been committed by these Indians. Among the first results of "Stillman's defeat" was the descent of about seventy Indians upon an unprotected settlement at Indian Creek, where they massacred fifteen men, women and children of the families of Hall, Davis and Pettigrew, and captured two young women, Sylvia and Rachel Hall. These girls, seventeen and fifteen years old respectively, were afterwards brought in by Winnebagoes to Gratiot Grove, and were ransomed by Major Henry Gratiot, for two thousand dollars in horses, wampum and trinkets, and came to Galena.

May 15, 1832, Capt. James W. Stephenson arrived at Galena with the startling intelligence of Stillman's disastrous defeat and the commencement of bloody hostilities by the Indians, creating intense excitement among the people. The ringing notes of the bugle called the settlers and miners together on the old race course on the bottom near the river, near the foot of Washington Street, Galena, and a company of mounted rangers was organized, with James W. Stephenson for captain. At 3 o'clock on the morning of Saturday, May 19, Sergeant Fred Stahl (now a respected citizen of Galena) and privates William Durley, Vincent Smith, Redding Bennett, and James Smith, started to bear dispatches to Gen. Atkinson at Dixon's Ferry, with John D. Winters, the mail contractor, for guide, but on Sunday, 20th, Sergeant Stahl returned and added to the alarm of the people by reporting that his party had been ambuscaded by the Indians just on the edge of Buffalo Grove, now in Ogle County, fifty miles from Galena, about 5 o'clock P. M. Saturday afternoon, and that Durley was instantly killed and left on the spot. Stahl received a bullet through his coat collar, and James Smith afterwards found a bullet hole in his hat and became intensely frightened. After the war, the leader of the Indians told Dixon that he could have killed the young fellow (Stahl) as well as not, but he had a fine horse, and in trying to shoot him without injuring the animal, he shot too high, as Stahl suddenly stooped at the same time.

The *Galenian* of May 23, 1832, says: "The tomahawk and scalping knife have again been drawn on our frontier. Blood of our best citizens has been spilt in great profusion within the borders of Illinois. * * The Indians must be exterminated or sent off."

In the same paper it is said that "fortifications for the defense of the town are rapidly progressing. On Saturday last (19th) a stockade * was com-

* A stockade was made by first digging a trench and standing upright in it timbers from 6 to 12 inches in diameter, from 10 to 14 feet long, and hewed to a point on the top end. These timbers were placed close together, so that when the trench was filled with

menced near the centre of the town." On the bluff above (near the corner of Perry and Prospect Streets), on a spot selected by Lieut. J. R. B. Gardenier, commanding the stockade and a large part of the town, a blockhouse was erected and a battery planted, manned by an artillery company, of which Lieut. Gardenier was captain. (On the northeast corner of Perry and Main Streets there stood a stone house occupied by Maj. Campbell; a little distance behind it was a well that is still in existence, and above the well, towards Bench Street, was a log house built by Dr. Hancock; a short distance west of Hancock's house was another log cabin that is still standing on the west side of Perry Street, and in the northwest corner of Perry and Bench Streets was another little cabin. The stockade included these houses and the well, extended from near the middle of Bench Street nearly to the rear of Campbell's stone house, and along Bench Street from a point nearly opposite Col. Strode's residence, east about 200 or 250 feet. A blockhouse was built at the northwest corner. Col. Strode lived on the northwest side of Bench Street, a little way west from Perry, and the gate of the stockade was directly opposite his residence.)

On Monday, May 21, *Col. J. M. Strode, commanding the 27th Regiment Illinois Militia, proclaimed martial law, and required every able bodied man to work on the stockade from 9 A. M. to 6 P. M. Strode's proclamation also prohibited the sale of spirits "at any of the groceries or taverns in Galena from 8 o'clock A. M. until 7 o'clock P. M.," and all persons were "positively prohibited from firing guns without positive orders, unless while standing guard to give an alarm."

The following is a list of the officers of the different companies then organized, as published in the *Galenian*, May 23:

"1st Mounted Rangers, J. W. Stephenson, Captain; J. K. Hammett, Alex. Kerr, Lieutenants.

2d Artillery, J. R. B. Gardenier, Captain; W. Campbell, 1st Lieutenant.

Independent Company of "Galena Volunteers Guards," M. M. Maughs, Captain; Moses Swan and R. Singleton, Lieutenants.

Capt. H. H. Gear's Company consists of 60 men. Capt. Beedle's Company of 40 or 50 men. Capt. Aldenrath's Company from East Fork is also in town.

A block house and stockade are built at Apple River (near Elizabeth) and a company of 46 men organized, commanded by Vance L. Davidson, James Craig and James Temple, Lieutenants.

At White Oak Springs, ten miles from Galena, a stockade was erected, and a company of 70 organized. Benj. W. Clark, Captain; John R. Shultz, J. B. Woodson, Lieutenants.

At the New Diggings, nine miles from Galena, was another company of 69 men under command of L. P. Vosburgh, Captain; P. Carr and H. Cavener, Lieutenants; and at Vinegar Hill a company of 52 men was commanded by Capt. Jonathan Craig, with Thos. Kilgore and R. C. Bourn, Lieutenants. There was also a large company of nearly 100 men at Gratiot's Grove."

The miners and settlers were thus able to protect themselves within a week after the news of Stillman's disaster reached them.

May 21, Indians fired on a Mr. Goss, near the mouth of Plum River.

earth there would be a solid wooden wall 8 to 10 feet in height. In the inside a platform was built on which the inmates could stand to fire over the top, and the walls were also pierced with loop-holes.

* Col. Strode was said to have been the first man to reach Dixon after Stillman's defeat.

May 23, Felix St. Vrain, Agent for the Sacs and Foxes, bearer of dispatches, left Gen. Atkinson's headquarters, on Rock River, accompanied by John Fowler, Thos. Kenney, Wm. Hale, Aquilla Floyd, Aaron Hawley, and Alexander Higginbotham. At Buffalo Grove they found the body of the lamented Durley, and buried it a rod from the spot where they found it. The next day (24th) they were attacked by a party of thirty Indians, near Kellogg's "old place." St. Vrain, Fowler, Hale and Hawley were killed. The other three escaped and arrived at Galena on the morning of the 26th.

From the time the first volunteers were mustered out by Gov. Reynolds on the 26th or 27th of May, until the new levies were organized on the 15th of June, numerous murders were committed by the Indians, and the only protection the people had were their own brave hearts and strong arms. The atrocities perpetrated by the Indians upon the bodies of their victims, aroused the vengeance of the settlers and miners, many of whom had previously felt that the Indians were not so much in fault, and had been needlessly provoked to bloodshed.

On the 30th day of May, 1832, a meeting of the citizens of Galena and vicinity, called by Col. Strode, to consider the perilous situation of the mining district and devise measures for security and protection, was held at the house of M. & A. C. Swan (standing then on the corner of Main and Green Streets, opposite De Soto House). William Smith, Esq., was called to the chair, and Capt. James Craig appointed Secretary.

On motion of Dr. Meeker, a committee of nine, consisting of Moses Meeker, William Hempstead, Michael Byrne, Robert Graham, Mr. Shears, James Craig, D. R. Davis, Mr. Thomas and David McNair, were appointed to deliberate and propose such measures as they may think best calculated to secure the object in view. This committee subsequently reported a series of resolutions, that the picketing and block houses be finished; that a garrison of 100 to 150 men be detailed, one third to be quartered in the garrison, and the others to be equally divided in the two extremities of the town, independent of the artillery and horse companies; that not less than 15 men belonging to the artillery company lodge in the block house every night; recommending that two companies be made of Capt. Stephenson's company and that they and Capt. Craig's company elect a major to command the squadron; that these companies shall be stationed in the vicinity of Galena, and shall keep out a sufficient number of spies or scouts to form a circuit of from 10 to 25 miles around Galena, and report every evening; that all persons subject to military duty be immediately enrolled, held in readiness for active service, and to parade with their arms and equipments every evening at four o'clock; that at least ten days provisions for one thousand men, with fifty barrels of water, be kept constantly in the stockade; that there must be unity of action between the forces under Gen. Dodge and the mounted men of this place, and that Dr. A. T. Crow, William Smith, Esq., and James Craig should prepare an address to the citizens of the mining district, in order to remove some existing misunderstanding * between the people of the town and country.

* The people of the country coming to Galena for safety were not provided for as they thought they ought to be. The people of the town were all excited, had their own business (the little that remained) to manage, and probably left their country neighbors to take care of themselves. Numbers of them were encamped on the bottom near the river for some time, no provision for them having been made within the stockade. Miners refused to come into town for this reason. They said, "We may as well remain at home as to go to the Point, where no arrangements have been made for us." A feeling of jealousy or bitterness sprang up in consequence, and to this the committee had reference.

The gentlemen named prepared and published the following:

ADDRESS.

To the Citizens of the Mining District, embracing the County of Jo Daviess in the State of Illinois, and the Western parts of the Territory of Michigan on the Upper Mississippi:

Inhabiting, as we do, a country isolated from our brethren both of the State and of the Union, to which we belong, surrounded by a savage and hostile enemy, who have raised both the tomahawk and scalping knife, alike on the defenseless inhabitants, as the soldier going forth to battle. Already have we witnessed the fall of a Durley, a St. Vrain, a Hale, a Fowler, and a Hawley on this side of Rock River, while the scalping knife is still reeking in the blood of our fellow-citizens between Rock River and Peoria, and two of our sisters (Sylvia and Rachael Hall) are groaning in captivity amongst a savage enemy—our communication cut off by land from the south and east. Prevented by Indian hostility from cultivating our farms and gardens, receiving but little succor from the State to which we belong, or from the General Government, receiving but scanty supplies by way of the Mississippi, which must every day become more precarious. Thrown as we are upon our defensive means and resources, let us rally to the standard of our country, and husband with the utmost care the means we can command for our preservation and protection. Our supplies of every kind are principally in this place; already are our means of security advancing rapidly to a completion, and here will be a place of security for our women and children; here also will be food and raiment for them. It is but too true that some of our citizens have been too remiss in their duty; the flame of patriotism does not burn alike in every bosom; and the soldier will look with pity and not with contempt at his less gifted neighbor. But when common danger threatens, let brethren unite the more closely, and while our enterprising men shall contend with an enemy in the open field, let those who remain at home do their duty in procuring and preparing all the means of defense and preservation in their power.

The time can not be distant when our situation must be known to our brethren abroad, and if we can defend our position but a short time, we may reasonably look for the succor which both the State and General Government are bound to give us. Let us do with alacrity the duty assigned to each of us, and forget our little bickerings and jealousies. Let us finish our stockading and block houses. Let us examine the country, watching the approach and movements of any hostile party that may be in our borders; meet and chastise them if we can; and when peace shall again gladden our ears, we will then settle our misunderstanding if any should then remain.

Signed on behalf of the meeting by

A. T. CROW,
WM. SMITH,
JAMES CRAIG.

GALENA, May 30, 1832.

On the 6th of June the *Galenian* says: "The stockade in Galena is nearly done, and those in the country are in a tolerable state of completion." But it is evident from the above address and from concurrent testimony that the people did not all rally to the work as earnestly as the commander wished. Perhaps they did not realize that they were in any immediate danger, and they had to attend to their own business affairs. To show them the importance of completing their defenses and of attending to duty as well as to give the citizens some practice in case the Indians should really make a night attack, some of the officers, including Col. Strode planned to have a false alarm, by firing the cannon by midnight the Monday night following the meeting. The date and results of the "scare" are given in a letter from Dr. Newhall to his brother, dated Galena, June 8, 1832, as follows:

"The Indian war has assumed an alarming character. On Monday night last (4th) we had an alarm that the town was attacked. The scene was horrid beyond description; men, women and children flying to the stockade. I calculated seven hundred women and children were there within fifteen minutes after the alarm gun was fired—some with dresses on and some with none; some with shoes and some barefoot; sick persons were transported on other's shoulders; women and children screaming from one end of the town to the other. It was a false alarm. Had there been an Indian attack, I believe the people would have fought well."

Many ludicrous incidents are related of this "big scare," ludicrous afterwards and now, but not then, when all save a few in the secret fully believed the Indians were upon them. Among these, it is said that the worthy postmaster didn't stop to put on his trousers, and rushed into the stockade wrapped in a sheet, calling wildly for somebody to bring him a pair of pants. A Mrs. Bennett was already there making cartridges, and as the P. M. was rushing about for some clothes, she handed him a musket, with the cool remark, "Here, take this gun, and don't be scared to death."

The next day, when the people learned how cruelly their fears had been played upon, their indignation knew no bounds. All business was suspended, Colonel Strode and his associates fled the town, an impromptu indignation meeting was held at Swan's tavern, at which strong denunciatory resolutions were passed and a committee appointed to investigate the matter, of which Rivers Cormack, the old Methodist minister, was chairman. After a few days, popular indignation subsided, and Colonel Strode returned. His motive was good, but the means adopted did not quite meet the approval of the citizens, and the experiment was not repeated.*

In Dr. Newhall's letter of June 8, quoted above, occurs the following :

> The Indians have already taken about forty scalps in the whole. News has this day arrived of one more man (Mr. Auberry) having been killed and scalped, near Blue Mound.†

June 8, Captain Stephenson's company of mounted rangers found the bodies of St. Vrain, Hale, Fowler and Hawley four miles south of Kellogg's Grove, and buried them.

Colonel Wm. S. Hamilton arrived in Galena with two hundred and thirty Indians, mostly Sioux, with some Menominees and Winnebagoes, on the 8th. These Indians left Galena on the 10th, to join General Atkinson at Dixon's Ferry, all anxious to obtain Sac scalps. Black Hawk's band reported moving slowly northward.

On the night of June 8, the Indians stole fourteen horses just outside the stockade on Apple River (Elizabeth), and on the night of the 17th ten more were stolen. The next morning, Captain J. W. Stephenson, with twelve of his men and nine from Apple River fort, started on the trail of the red thieves, and overtook them about twelve miles east of Kellogg's Grove, southeast of Waddam's Grove, and pursued them several miles, until a little northeast of Waddam's (in Stephenson County), the Indians (seven in number, says Captain Green,) took refuge in a dense thicket and awaited the attack. Stephenson dismounted his men, and, detailing a guard for the horses, led his men in a gallant charge upon the concealed foe, received their fire and returned it, returning to the open prairie to load. Three times the brave boys charged upon this fatal thicket, losing a man each time. Only one Indian was known to be killed. He was bayonetted by private Hood, and stabbed in the neck by Thomas Sublett. This Indian was scalped several times, and a piece of his scalp-lock is now (1878) in the possession of Wm. H. Snyder, Esq., of Galena. The three men killed were Stephen P. Howard, George Eames and Michael Lovell. Stephenson himself was wounded. After the third charge, Stephenson retreated, leaving

* Tuesday night, July 24, a fire broke out in Dr. Crow's stable in the stockade, and two horses were burned. It was said that there was powder stored in the stable, and there was another scare, but this time the stampede was *from* the stockade. Amos Farrar died at his house in the stockade the same night.

† At the close of the war it was discovered that Mr. Auberry was murdered by some Winnebago Indians.

COLLINSVILLE

MADISON COUNTY.

his dead where they fell, and returned to Galena, arriving on the 19th. Of this desperate battle, Governor Ford says: "This attack of Captain Stephenson was unsuccessful, and may have been imprudent; but it equalled any thing in modern warfare in daring and desperate courage."

On the evening of June 14, five men, at work in a cornfield at Spafford's farm, five miles below Fort Hamilton, on Spafford's Creek, and on the morning of the 16th Henry Apple, a German, were killed within half a mile of the fort. Gen. Dodge, with twenty-nine men, at once pursued them about three miles, when they were discovered, eleven in number, in open ground, but were not overtaken until they crossed the East Pick-e-ton-e-ka, and entered an almost impenetrable swamp, at Horse Shoe Bend. At the edge of the swamp, Dodge ordered his men to dismount and link horses. Four men were left in charge of the horses, four were posted around the swamp to prevent the escape of the savages, and the remainder, twenty-one in number, advanced into the swamp about half a mile, where they received fire of the Indians, and three men fell severely wounded. Gen. Dodge instantly ordered a charge. The Indians were found lying under the bank of a slough, and were not seen until the soldiers were within six or eight feet of them, when they fired. The whole hostile party were killed and scalped in one or two minutes, except one who swam the slough in an attempt to escape, and was shot down on the opposite bank. In this battle F. M. Morris and Samuel Wells were mortally, and Samuel Black and Thomas Jenkins severely, wounded. This was the first victory achieved over the murderous Sacs, and occasioned great rejoicing in the settlements.

On the 20th Stephenson's and Craig's companies, under command of Col. Strode, went to Waddam's Grove to bury the remains of Howard, Eames and Lovell, which they did, but left the dead Indian above ground. On their return they heard some suspicious sounds, but pushed on in the night to Imus's (in Rush Township) and returned to Galena in safety. Afterwards, says Capt. Green, who was with Stephenson's company, we learned that "a large party of Sacs were within a half-hour's march of us, when we left the graves of our dead comrades."

This party, which numbered about 150, had left the main body of Sacs on the Rock River, and, after following Strode's command, were, undoubtedly, the same who made a furious attack on the stockade at Apple River, on the night of the 24th, under the following circumstances: F. Dixon, Edmund Welsh, G. W. Herclerode and —— Kirkpatrick started to carry dispatches to Gen. Atkinson. They had passed Apple River Fort when they were fired upon by Indians, and Welsh was badly wounded. His companions told him to retreat to the fort, and to give him time, turned upon the foe and raised a yell. This temporarily checked them; Welsh reached the fort and gave the alarm. Their stratagem succeeded. Dixon dashed through the savages, and escaped to Galena. Kirkpatrick and Herclerode gained the fort; the gate was shut, and for three quarters of an hour the battle raged. The women and girls made cartridges and loaded the muskets. Herclerode was killed while taking deliberate aim at an Indian over the top of the pickets. The number of Indians killed was not known, but they were supposed to have lost several, and finally withdrew, after stealing a large number of cattle, and destroying considerable property.

On the 29th of June, three men at work in a cornfield at Sinsinawa Mound (Jones' Mound), ten miles from Galena, were attacked by a small party of Indians, and two of them, James Boxley and John Thompson, were killed. Major Stephenson with thirty men started immediately on receipt of the news to bury the murdered men and pursue the murderers. The bodies were shockingly mangled and both scalped, and Thompson's heart cut out. The Indians were followed to the residence of Mr. Jordan, on the Mississippi, where they had stolen a canoe and crossed the river. These Indians could hardly have been any of Black Hawk's band, unless they had deserted and were making their way back to the west side of the Mississippi.

On the 30th of June, all the inhabitants north of Galena and on the Mississippi, this side of Cassville, came into Galena for safety. It was not then considered safe to go a mile out of town without a strong guard.

Captain George W. Harrison, in command of Fort Hamilton, on the Pick-a-ton-e-ka, thirty miles from Galena, after vainly endeavoring to get a cannon, went to Colonel Hamilton's furnace and cast several lead pieces, intended for two-pounders, which were properly mounted at the stockade, and answered every purpose.

June 20, 1832, the ladies of Galena, represented by Mrs. Nancy B. Lockwood, Mrs. Sarah B. Coons, and Miss Elizabeth A. Dodge, committee, presented a stand of colors to Captain Jas. W. Stephenson's company. On the 21st, "The daughters of the lead mines" presented a flag "to our Father War Chief," General Henry Dodge. Afterwards, on the 15th of July, the ladies of the mining country, represented by Miss Margaret C. Brophy and Miss Bridget F. Ryan, presented a stand of colors to Captain Bazil B. Craig's company, and about the same time, Misses Catherine S. and Amelia G. Dyas presented colors to Captain Alex. M. Jenkins.

It must be remembered that Black Hawk's forces kept on their march up Rock River, with the evident intention of returning to the west side of the Mississippi, as the forces of General Atkinson below prevented their return by the way they came, and they as evidently believed, after the affair with Stillman, that no flag of truce or proposals for peace would be received by the whites. But various Indian signs were discovered on the Mississippi River. July 6, Lieutenant Orrin Smith was sent, with twenty men, to Jordon's farm, opposite Dubuque mines, to scour the country there. On the 9th, Indians were in the vicinity of Rountree's Fort (Plattsville), where they held a war dance around the scalp of a woman. On the 10th, the *Galenian* says: "To-day we learn that the trail of the Indians shows that they must have come from the west of the Mississippi, in a direction from Dubuque's mines."

These facts indicate very plainly that Black Hawk and his band were not responsible for all the outrages committed in the mining district, but that some of them, at least, are to be attributed to Indians from the west, while others, it is now known, were committed by young Winnebagoes.

July 14, Governor Reynolds, Colonel Field (Secretary of State), Judges Smith and Brown, Colonels Hickman, Grant, Breese and Gatewood, Captain Jeffreys and others arrived at Galena from the army. These gentlemen reported that the Indians were entirely destitute of provisions, and were endeavoring to reach and re-cross the Mississippi.

July 15, an express arrived at Galena, stated that Captain Harney, of the U. S. A., had found and pursued the trail of the Indians for thirty miles, passing four of their encampments in that distance, and that he found many signs of their want of provisions, "such as where they had butchered horses, dug for roots, and scraped the trees for bark," and it became evident that the military had concluded that Black Hawk was doing his best to escape to the west side of the Mississippi. Orders were sent to troops stationed on the banks of that River "to prevent or delay the Indians from crossing until the brigade sent by General Atkinson could come up with them." Indian outrages had now nearly ceased in Jo Daviess County, and a brief sketch of the movements of the troops from Dixon's Ferry to Bad Axe will close this part of the history.

On the 15th of June, 1832, the new levies of volunteers in camp at Dixon's Ferry were formed into three brigades. The first was commanded by General Alexander Posey; the second by General Milton R. Alexander, and the third by General James D. Henry.

June 17, Captain Adam W. Snyder, of Colonel Fry's regiment, sent to scout the country between Rock River and Galena, while encamped near Burr Oak Grove, in what is now the Township of Erin, Stephenson County, was fired upon by four Indians. He pursued and killed them, losing one man mortally wounded. Returning, he was attacked by seventy Indians, both parties taking positions behind trees. General Whiteside, then a private, shot the leader of the band, and they retreated, but were not pursued. Snyder lost two men killed and one wounded.

June 25, a detachment of General Posey's brigade, commanded by Major John Dement, and encamped at Kellogg's Grove, or Burr Oak Grove, as it was then called, was attacked by a large party of Indians and a sharp skirmish ensued. Major Dement lost five men and about twenty horses killed. The Indians left nine of their number stretched upon the field. General Posey, then encamped at Buffalo Grove, hastened to the relief of Dement, but the Indians had retreated two hours before he arrived. He returned to Kellogg's Grove to await the arrival of his baggage wagons, and then marched to Fort Hamilton, M. T.

Gen. Atkinson commenced his slow and cautious march up the river about the 25th of June, and finally reached Lake Kushkanong, where he was joined by Gen. Alexander's brigade, and then continued his march to White River or Whitewater, where he was joined by Posey's brigade and the Galena battalion under Maj. Dodge. Gen. Alexander, Gen. Henry and Maj. Dodge were sent to Fort Winnebago for supplies. Here they heard that Black Hawk was making his way toward the Wisconsin River, and, disobeying orders, Henry and Dodge started in pursuit (Gen. Alexander and his brigade returning to Gen. Atkinson), struck the broad, fresh trail of the Indians and followed them with tireless energy. Ever and anon they would find old men, women and children, who could not keep up and had been abandoned to their fate by the flying Indians; some were killed. One old man left to die was sitting against a tree, and was boldly shot and scalped by a surgeon, who afterwards exhibited the scalp as a trophy of his valor.

Black Hawk was overtaken at Wisconsin River, and his braves offered battle to enable the women and children to cross the river. The battle of Wisconsin Heights, at which the Indians were badly whipped by our troops, and "worse whipped by starvation," says Mr. Townsend, was fought on the 22d of July, 1832. Skirmishing commenced a little after noon, but the heaviest fighting was about sunset. The first Indian killed was discovered walking ahead of the troops with a pack of meat on his back. A soldier fired but missed him, when he turned and threw down his gun but was bayonetted after his surrender by Sample Journey. The fighting ceased about 10 o'clock P. M., and the men bivouacked for rest on their arms. "About daybreak," says Capt. D. S. Harris, then a lieutenant in command of Stephenson's Company, "the camp was alarmed by the clarion voice of the Prophet from a hill nearly a mile away. At first we thought it was an alarm, but soon found that the Prophet wanted peace. Although he was so far distant I could hear distinctly every word, and I understood enough to know that he did not want to fight. The interpreter said that he said that they 'had their squaws and families with them and were starving—that they did not want to fight any more, but wanted peace and would do no more harm if they could be permitted to cross the Mississippi in peace.'" Mr. P. J. Pilcher, now of Elizabeth, who was also there, says that they were awakened by the shrill voice of the chief, and that he plainly understood: "Ne-com, P-e—e-l—o-o-o;" "Friends, we fight no more." Mr. Pilcher says he told Henry what the Indian said, but Henry said "pay no attention to any thing they say or do, but form in line of battle." The Winnebagoes in camp also informed the officers of the meaning of the Prophet's message, and "early in the morning," says Pilcher, "they went with us to the spot where the Indian had stood, when he proclaimed peace, and there we found a *tomahawk buried*," an emphatic declaration that so far as Black Hawk and his band were concerned *hostilities were ended*. No attention was paid to this second attempt to negotiate peace. It is said that the officers had no interpreter and did not know what the Prophet said until after the war closed. This excuse is exploded by the direct and emphatic testimony of Capt. Harris and Mr. Pilcher, but the starved and dying Indians must be exterminated.

The next morning not an Indian remained on the east side of the Wisconsin. Gen. Henry pushed back for supplies and Gen. Atkinson's "bottled forces" coming up, the pursuit was renewed, and the battle of Bad Axe was fought August 2, 1832. "For eight miles," says Townsend, "we were skirmishing with their rear guard," and numbers of squaws and children were killed. Mr. Townsend says he passed one squaw that had been shot and fallen on her face. On her back was strapped a child. The same shot that killed its mother had broken its arm, but in spite of this it was sitting on the back of its dead parent gnawing in its ravenous hunger the raw flesh from a horse-bone.

The battle of Bad Axe terminated the war, and Black Hawk's surrender, subsequent visit to Washington, and return to his people in Iowa, are events familiar to the reader. After nearly half a century has passed since the stirring events narrated occurred, and the Indians have long since disappeared before the westward advance of civilization, it is but just that the truth should be recorded. Passion and prejudice have passed away, and it must be admitted that "when the tomahawk and scalping knife were drawn" in 1832, it was only after the whites had commenced the carnival of blood by first firing on the flag of truce at "Stillman's Run." The vindictive pursuit and murder of women and children after the Prophet had, in person informed his ruthless pursuers that "his people were starving and wanted peace," can not be justified. It was as savage an act as the savages themselves had committed. It must be added also that after Stillman's defeat, Black Hawk, then an old man, lost all control of his young braves, who were led by Ne-o-Pope. But for that fatal act of Stillman's drunken soldiers, in all human probability the subsequent acts of savage barbarity by both Indians and whites had remained undone. "Fire-water" was the active cause of the Black Hawk War, as it was of the Winnebago affair.

LOCAL HISTORY.

AN ACT ESTABLISHING JO DAVIESS COUNTY.

SECTION 1.—Be it enacted by the people of the State of Illinois, represented in the General Assembly, that all that tract of country lying within the following boundaries, to wit: Beginning on the northwest corner of the state, thence down the Mississippi River to the northern line of the military tract, thence east with said line to the Illinois River, thence north to the northern boundary of this state, thence west with said boundary line to the place of beginning, shall constitute a county, and to perpetuate the memory of Colonel Joseph Hamilton Daviess, who fell in the battle of Tippecanoe, gallantly charging upon the enemy at the head of his corps, the said county shall be called Jo Daviess.

Origin of the Name.—The singular name of Jo Daviess was not given to the county by its citizens. The name Ludlow was incorporated in the original bill, and was intended to honor and perpetuate the memory of the naval hero of that name. When the bill was under consideration in the House of Representatives, a member moved to strike out "Ludlow," and insert the name of "Daviess," in honor of Colonel Jo Daviess, a Kentuckian, who fell at the head of his regiment at the battle of Tippecanoe, Indiana. Another member moved to amend the amendment by inserting before Daviess the word "Jo," giving as a reason that as there was a member of the House of the name of Daviess, the people might think the honor was intended for him, and that it would be indelicate for the House, by any direct act, to transmit their names to posterity. This motion, made in jest, was carried by a large majority, and the name Jo Daviess was incorporated in the bill with the expectation that "Jo" would be struck out by the Senate. The Senate, however, passed the bill without amendment, and the name by common use has become as pleasant to the ear as the ordinary names of counties.

An old *Gazetteer* of Missouri and Illinois, published in 1822, now in the possession of William Hempstead, Esq., says the military tract referred to in the act creating Jo Daviess County, commenced at the mouth of the Illinois River, extended north 162 miles to a line running east from the Mississippi to the Illinois River, and included all that country between the two rivers, an area equal to 240 townships of six miles square, covering 8,640 square miles and embracing 5,529,600 acres.

This tract of land was appropriated by Congress to pay military bounties for the war of 1812, and hence its designation as the military tract. This *Gazetteer* is the only accessible authority for the extent of this tract, and it may or may not be exactly accurate or authentic. There must be some law of Congress on the subject, but the writer was unable to find it during the limited time assigned for the compilation of these pages.

SECTION 2 of the law creating Jo Daviess County further provided that the qualified voters residing within said county "shall meet at the Village of Galena, on the first Monday of June next (1827) and elect three County Commissioners, one Sheriff and one Coroner for said county; and Charles St. Vrain, David G. Bates and Patrick Hogan are hereby appointed judges of said election, who shall give notice, appoint two clerks, and conduct the said election as other elections for the same officers are now required by law to be published and conducted."

SECTION 3. That, for the present, until the true boundaries of the county be known and provision therefor be made by law, for establishing the permanent seat of justice for said county, all courts shall be held at the said Village of Galena.

SECTION 4 provided that Jo Daviess should be a part of the first judicial circuit, and that the justices of the peace of the county or any three of them, might hold court. Section five defined the duties of prosecuting attorneys, and section six declared that the county should vote in all general elections, in conjunction with Peoria, Fulton, Schuyler, Adams and Pike Counties.

The boundaries and regulations thus established were not disturbed in any essential particular until January, 1836, when the Counties of Winnebago, Whiteside, Kane and Ogle were organized.

In accordance with the provisions of section two of the law under which Jo Daviess County was erected, an election was held on the first Monday in June, 1827, for the officers named in that section. There are no records to be found in the archives of the county to show the number of voters in the county at that time. It is a lamentable fact that in nearly all the counties whose history we have attempted to write, there seems to have been an inexcusable carelessness or negligence about preserving official papers. For this carelessness no valid excuse can possibly be offered, and, in fact, none should be accepted. On the other hand, there ought to have been a heavy penalty imposed upon all officials who failed to preserve intact the official papers of the offices they filled. If this had been the practice in the early days of Jo Daviess, Carroll and other counties, to write their history would be a comparatively easy task. As it is, with many important documents unpreserved, the task is an arduous and difficult one. The loss of the pioneer poll-book of Jo Daviess County, with only one voting precinct within its boundaries, is an important link missing from its chain of history. To determine the number of votes polled at Galena on the first Monday in June, 1827, with any degree of accuracy, is an impossibility. To arrive at any thing like accuracy, the only recourse is to an old poll-book of *Fever River Precinct, Peoria County, under date of August* 7, 1826, which is probably a record of the first election held in the Galena section of Northwestern Illinois. At that election, as is already elsewhere stated, Nehemiah Bates, J. W. Shull and Andrew Clamo were judges or inspectors, and B. Gibson and Joseph Hardy, clerks. That poll-book bears the names of 202 voters—not one of whom is known to be alive now. In June, 1827, there must have been at least one hundred and fifty more voters, as under the laws in existence at that time no territory could be organized as a county with less than three hundred and fifty qualified voters. There may have been more than this number of voters in Fever River Precinct at the time of the first election for county officers for Jo Daviess County, but certain it is there was but one voting precinct in all of that territory now so densely populated.

This election was held on the first Monday in June. On the 5th day of that month, there seems to have been a session or meeting of two of the county commissioners elected—James Harris and Jonathan Browder. This meeting of the county commissioners was held at the "tavern" of Messrs. Abbott & Swan, on the site now occupied by Waggoner's book store, at the corner of Main and Green Streets. On the 11th and 18th days of June, special or called sessions were held, but no record of their proceedings seems to have been made until 1833, when the following transcript of them was entered of record by Moses Swan, County Clerk :

Transcript of the Proceedings of the Board of County Commissioners of Jo Daviess County, at the First Session, June 5, 1827.

STATE OF ILLINOIS, }
JO DAVIESS COUNTY, } GALENA, June 5, A. D. 1827.

This day James Harris and Jonathan Browder, two of the County Commissioners for said County, met at the house of Abbott and Swan, in the town of Galena, in said county, at which meeting the said two commissioners appointed Hugh R. Coulter to act as County Commissioners Clerk in and for said county. Said clerk, after appointed, as aforesaid, delivered a bond to the County Commissioners of said county for the use of the same in the penal sum of one thousand dollars, agreeably to the statute in such cases made and provided, with David G. Bates and John Ray his securities. The Court then organized itself and proceeded to business.

Stroder Inman was recommended to said Court as a proper person to fill the office of Constable in and for said county, who gave a bond as the law directs (after receiving his appointment), with John Foley his security. Said Constable then took the several oaths prescribed by law in open court, before entering on the duties of his office.

Ordered, That this Court adjourn till Monday, the 11th inst., at 11 o'clock A. M., then to meet at the above place.

GALENA, June 11, 10 o'clock A. M.

The County Commissioners Court met pursuant to their adjournment. Present, Jas. Harris and Jonathan Browden, as before. Ebenezer Orn, one of the commissioners elected for said county, appeared, received a certificate of his election, took the several oaths prescribed by law (which were administered by the clerk), all of which being done in usual form, said Commissioner took his seat, and the Court then proceeded to business.

Stroder Inman, constable, was appointed as an illisor to attend on said court and to perform the duties of Sheriff, according to the statute in such cases made and provided.

A petition was presented, signed by several of the inhabitants of said county, praying said Court to recommend John Foley and Hugh R. Coulter as suitable persons to fill the office of Justices of the Peace in and for said county, whereupon it was

Ordered, That John Foley and Hugh R. Coulter be recommended to the Governor of this state as suitable persons to fill the office of Justices of the Peace within and for said county, agreeable to the petition of P. Hogan and others.

A petition was presented by sundry citizens, praying said Court to recommend Geo. W. Lott, of said county, to the Governor of this state, to fill the office of Justice of the Peace in and for said county, whereupon it was

Ordered, That George W. Lott be recommended to the Governor of this state as a suitable person to fill the office of Justice of the Peace within and for said county, at the petition of P. Hogan and others.

Ordered, That this court adjourn *sine die*.

At a special term of the County Commissioners Court of Jo Daviess County, held at the house of Messrs. Abbott and Swan, in the Town of Galena, June 18, 1827—present, Ebenezer Orn and Jonathan Browder, county commissioners, and Hugh R. Coulter, clerk. Samuel Kain was appointed an illisor to attend on said court.

A petition was presented by Patrick Hogan, Esq., requesting said court to prepare a safe place of confinement for John Kelley, who stood committed for an assault and battery with an intent to murder, committed on the body of Elisha Eldredge; whereupon it was ordered that Stroder Inman, constable, is hereby authorized to provide a safe place of confinement for John Kelley, who now stands convicted of an assault and battery with an attempt to murder, on the body of Eldredge, and to provide for said Kelley comfortable board until he can be further dealt with according to law.

Ordered, That a tax of one fourth per cent be levied on all personal property (belonging to the citizens of said county) made taxable by law.

Ordered, That Martin Warren be, and he is, hereby appointed by this court an assessor to assess the tax of said county, agreeably to the statute in such cases made and provided.

Ordered, That this court adjourn till the next term in course.

It is hereby certified that the foregoing is a true copy, *verbatim et literatim*, from the loose papers in my office, and entered in this book by order of the court this 20th day of March, A. D. 1833, and of the Independence of the United States the fifty-seventh.

Attest: MOSES SWAN, *Clk.*

From this certificate there is no reason to doubt that the proceedings of these sessions of the first Board of County Commissioners of Jo Daviess County were kept on loose slips of paper, and that six years had passed before any attempt was made to preserve them as matters of record.

July 24, 1827, the commissioners selected the following named citizens to serve as the first grand jury:

P. Hogan, David G. Bates, John Foley, Benson Hunt, Jas. Craig, Richard Chandler, Amos Farrar, Michael Murphy, Chas. Gear, Frederick Hollman, Jas. Foley, Mitchel Coe, Thos. McCraney, Jesse W. Shull, Michael Finley, Jas. Lynch, Stanlus Hudd, Jno. Ewins, John W. McClintoc, William Morrison, H. Dodge, and Owen Riley.

From the reason that no term of the Circuit Court was held in Jo Daviess County until June, 1828, it is fair to presume that the above named citizens never qualified or served in the capacity for which they were selected.

July 23, 1827, a special session of the County Commissioners Court was held, when the county was divided into three election precincts—Galena, Centreville and Shullsburg. The Galena precinct was described as follows:

Commencing at Lockwood's furnace and running on a parallel line to James Foley's Vinegar Hill, thence due west to the Mississippi River; thence down said river to Apple Creek; thence up said river and embracing all settlements on said river to Vanmatre's furnace and its vicinity; thence to the place of beginning at Lockwood's furnace.

P. Hogan, John S. Miller and Moses Meeker were appointed to be judges of elections in this precinct.

Centreville precinct was described as follows:

Beginning at Vanmatre's old furnace, on Apple River; thence on a parallel line to White Oak Springs; thence to G. W. Lott's establishment; thence to Chandler's Fort; thence to intersect the Galena precinct line at the Mississippi River.

F. Hollman, Charles Gear and James L. Langworthy were named as judges of elections.

The Shullsburg precinct embraced all that territory defined by the following boundaries:

To embrace all that tract of country beginning at Vanmatre's old furnace, and running east to the county line; thence north on said line twenty miles; thence to J. (or I.) Boner's, intersecting Centreville precinct line.

Henry Gratiot, Jesse W. Shull and Michael Finley were designated to act as judges of elections in this precinct.

It may be of interest to the reader to know something of the territory embraced in these three precincts—to know the beginning and terminus of their several lines, and the location of the several places named in their boundaries. Fifty-one years, almost, have come and gone since these precincts were established. The ravages of these years have blotted out many landmarks once familiar to the people, and, while the names of such places as "Vanmatre's old furnace," "Lott's establishment," etc., are still familiar to them, of many with whom the writer talked, the fewest number could tell where they were located. To re-establish these old places in the minds of the public, and preserve them to posterity as a part of the history of Jo.

H. B. Hunt,

HANOVER TP.

Daviess County, especial labor and inquiry have been exerted to fix the locations that are almost lost.

Lockwood's furnace was situated at the junction of the east branch with Fever or Galena River.

Foley's place was in Vinegar Hill Township, near the Wisconsin state line.

Lott's establishment is supposed to have been on Wolf Creek.

Chandler's Fort was about ten miles beyond Gratiot's Grove (probably to the northeast), and about twenty-five miles from Galena.

Vanmatre's old furnace was on Apple River, near the present site of the village of Elizabeth, and probably at what was known in early times as Georgetown.

The same session of the Commissioners Court that erected the three original voting precincts also ordered an election to be held on the first Monday in August, 1827, for the choice of three justices of the peace and one constable in the Galena precinct; one justice of the peace and one constable in the Centreville precinct, and one justice of the peace and one constable in the Shullsburg precinct. The court also ordered that, in the Galena precinct, the election should be held at the house of John S. Miller, and in the Shullsburgh precinct at the house of Jesse W. Shull. The voting place in the Centreville precinct was not named. The polls were ordered to be opened at ten o'clock in the morning, and to be kept open until four o'clock in the afternoon.

A careful examination of subsequent entries on the commissioners' record fails to show who were elected justices of the peace at that election. Among the old bonds on file in the county clerk's office, there are three bonds made respectively by William T. Managan, George H. Eymer and William Troy, who were elected as constables at the August election—but not the scratch of a pen to show who were elected as justices of the peace.

Managan's bond, in the sum of $500, with Duke L. Smith and L. P. Vosburg, was filed October 30, 1827. George H. Eymer's bond, in the same sum, John S. Miller and John Foley, sureties, was filed October 11, 1827, and Troy's bond, in the same sum, with John Furlong and John Foley as bondsmen, was also filed October 11, 1827—the two last named being the first constables to qualify and enter upon a discharge of their duties as such officers.

From the fact that the first term of Circuit Court held in the county was held by justices of the peace—John Connolly, Hugh R. Coulter and Abner Field, as judges, we are led to the conclusion that these were among the five justices ordered to be elected by the County Commissioners Court at their session, July 23, 1827, the order regulating which has already been quoted. Mr. John Lorrain says in his "History of Jo Daviess County," prepared in the Centennial year:

> In 1828, John Connolly, H. R. Coulter, Abner Field and James Harris were elected justices of the peace; Wm. Risley, county treasurer; Abner Field, clerk, and John Foley, sheriff, but on account of his not getting his certificate of election to Vandalia in thirty days, according to law, he was not confirmed, but the records show that he acted as such.

The same authority says further that "the first circuit court held in the county commenced on the 20th day of June, 1828, and that John Connolly, Hugh R. Coulter and Abner Field, justices, presided 'as judges.'" If these "judges" were not elected on the first Monday in August, 1827, they must have been elected in the Spring of 1828. They were not elected in August,

1828, for they sat as circuit court judges in June, 1828. So we are left to the irresistible conclusion that they were elected on the first Monday in August, 1827, and not in 1828, as stated by Mr. Lorrain. This position is strengthened by the fact that in the early days of Illinois elections for county and state officers were held in August, as they are now held in August in the State of Kentucky, and on the second Tuesday of October in Ohio and Indiana.

July 24, 1827, John S. Miller was granted a license to keep tavern for one year, on the payment of $9, and James Craig was appointed county assessor, when the court adjourned.

On the 27th of July a special session of the court was held, when the office of county clerk was declared to be vacant, because Hugh R. Coulter, the clerk, did not keep his office at the county seat, as provided by law. At the last meeting of the court, on the 24th of July, they had entered an order directing the sheriff to call on Mr. Coulter and demand of him the records, books, papers, etc., belonging to the office. There is no entry of the return made by the sheriff, but from the fact that the court proceeded to appoint Abner Field as clerk it is fair to presume that Mr. Coulter "accepted the situation," and turned over the records, etc., without much reluctance.

The next entry on the record was the appointment of D. G. Bates to serve as judge of election in the place of Moses Meeker, who had been appointed when the precinct was first created.

This session of the court also established a schedule of prices to regulate the charges of tavern keepers. Saloons or places devoted exclusively to the sale of liquors were not so fashionable in those days as at present, but no tavern was a tavern without its bar of liquors. The first license granted for the sale of spirituous liquors appears to have been issued to P. Harkey. The standard of charges fixed by the County Commissioners Court was as follows:

For all foreign liquors	37½c	½ pint
Ale, domestic	17¾	do
Whiskey	12½	do
Each meal victuals	37½	cents
Horse, per night	50	do
Horse, per feed	25	do
Cider or porter per quart	25	do
Small beer, mead or Metheglin	12½	do
Lodging, per night	12½	do

Fifty-one years of time have brought about many changes, and if the Board of Supervisors (successors to County Commissioners) were to attempt to fix the rates of charges of "tavern" keepers and retail dealers in spirituous liquors, in 1878, the attempt would be regarded as an unconstitutional and intolerable infringement upon the rights of man.

Friday, July 27, 1827, Abner Field was appointed to the office of county clerk, and Saturday, the 28th, he gave bonds in the sum of $1,000 for a faithful discharge of the duties of the office. John Foley and George M. Egnew were his bondsmen.

The same day (Saturday) James Craig appeared before the court, and, stating his reasons (business engagements), declined to serve as county assessor, and George M. Egnew was appointed to the vacancy.

The first account allowed against the county was to Patrick Hogan, and was in the sum of $8.12½, for stationery furnished for the use of the county. John Foley was next allowed $10 for four days' services as county clerk, *pro tem*, and $2 for one day's services as election clerk, in June, when the first county election was held.

Strother Inman was allowed the sum of $50 for carrying the June election returns to the secretary of state at Vandalia, then the state capital. He was also allowed $16 constable fees, in the case of "The People of the State of Illinois *vs.* John Kelly, apprehended on a charge of attempt to murder." Each one of the commissioners was allowed the sum of $10 for official services up to date.

A session of the County Commissioners Court was held on the third and fourth days of September, but there was no business of any note to claim their attention. On the 18th of that month, the commissioners again met, and at this session passed sundry orders relating to the holding of the first term of the Circuit Court, and

Ordered, That the house of John S. Miller be selected as a fit place for holding Circuit Court for Jo Daviess County.

John S. Miller's house* was known as "Miller's tavern," and was situated on or near the corner of what is Branch and Dodge Streets, in that part of the city called "Old Town." On the same day the above order was entered, the following named citizens and voters were selected to serve as petit jurors: James Craig, John Chandler, Thomas Gray, Francis Kirkpatrick, John Barrell, James Smith, Thomas Drum, Joseph Hardy, John Ray, William Henry, James Langworthy, Samuel Whitesides, Martin Warren, Moses Eastman, James Cherry, James Kindall, Adam Hymer, Thomas Hymer, Peter Carr, George Ferguson, William H. Smith, James Brady, Enoch Wethers and William Brazier.

The next order was in the words following:

Ordered, That one half of one per centum be levied on all personal property in Jo Daviess County, to defray the expenses of this year.

John S. Miller was appointed treasurer and required to give bond in the sum of $500. It was also

Ordered, That the treasurer assess the tax ordered to be levied by this court of one half of one per cent, and that he make his return of said assessment to the clerk of this court on or before the first Monday of November next.

If Mr. Miller ever made a report of his services as assessor and treasurer, the records fail to show it, and there are no papers on file (at least, none can be found) to show the assessed valuation of the personal property of Jo Daviess County at that time, nor the amount of revenue derived from the assessment of one half of one per centum thereon.

The court next passed upon their claims for services as commissioners, and allowed themselves $1.50 per day, each, "for every day they served during the present term, and that John Foley be allowed $3 per day for his services."

In those days the commissioners appear to have been at the service of the public—that is, to have been very accommodating, for whenever any one wanted a license to keep a "tavern," all that was necessary was to

* Mr. Lorrain says in his Centennial History "the first court was opened in a building put up with rough boards, by Charles Peck, on the corner where the De Soto House now stands." If Mr. L. is correct in this statement, and there seems to be no good reason to doubt its authenticity, then Miller's house or tavern was never occupied for Circuit Court purposes. That the first term of the court was held in the building described by Mr. Lorrain is most reasonable, from the fact that there was a very large attendance, and it is not probable that there was a house in the village at that time large enough to hold one half of the spectators.

advise the county clerk of their wants, when the commissioners would be notified and a called or special session of the court would be held. In one instance, October 3, 1827, Barney Ferguson desired a license to keep a "tavern." The commissioners were called together, the desired license was granted, and, without the transaction of any other business, the court adjourned.

The last session of the court of 1827 was held on the 3d of December, which was devoted to "squaring up" the accounts of the officials, making allowances for sundry necessary articles furnished the county, etc.

The first session for 1828 was held on the 3d of March, when a "tavern" license was granted to Robert Duncan, and a second grand jury selected—no term of the Circuit Court having been held in 1827. The names drawn for this grand jury, as taken from the record, were Duke L. Smith, H. Flewellyn, William Carr, Jno. B. Campbell, A. P. Vanmeter, Patrick Hogan, D. G. Bates, Benson Hunt, Richard W. Chandler, George Ames, John D. Winters, Richard Murphy, Charles Gear, Frederick Holloway, James Foley, James Mitchell, Thomas McCrary, Jesse W. Shull, M. Finley, James Lynch, B. B. Lawless, John W. McClintick, Owen Riley, William H. Monson.

At the same session, the following named were drawn to serve as petit jurors: John Chandler, Thomas Gray, Francis Kirkpatrick, John Barrell, James Smith, Thomas Drum, James Hardy, John Ray, William Henry, James Langworthy, Isaac Martin, Willis St. Johns, Amos Farrar, Thomas Bennett, James Kindall, Adam Hymer, Thomas Hymer, Peter Carr, Robert Duncan, William H. Smith, H. H. Gear, Davison Parish, William Brazier, Elias Phelps.

At a called session of the County Commissioners Court, held on the 2d of May, 1828, an assessment of one half of one per centum was ordered to be levied upon the personal property owned in the county to meet the expenses of the county, and Hugh R. Coulter was appointed county treasurer, and ordered to give bond in the sum of $1,000. At this session Mr. Coulter was also licensed to keep "tavern."

According to Mr. Lorrain, "the first term of the Circuit Court was commenced on the 20th day of June, 1828, with John Connolly, Hugh R. Coulter and Abner Field, justices of the peace, as judges.

The grand jury consisted of the following named persons: Herbert Flewellyn, Patrick Hogan, Richard W. Chandler, Michael Murphy, Charles Gear, Frederick Hollman, James Foley, James Mitchell, Roland R. Holmes, Hugh W. Shannon, James Craig, John Ellis, John A. Wakefield, Joseph Conway, Joel Wright, Jesse W. Shull and A. P. Vanmeter, of which Richard Chandler was foreman.

The first indictment was filed on the second day of the term, and charged one Michael Dee with assault with intent to commit murder. He was tried and found guilty, but the records fail to show what penalty (if any) was imposed by the court.

The next term of the Circuit Court commenced on the 6th of October, 1828—John Connolly, Jas. Harris, Abner Field, Hugh R. Coulter and —— Burke, justices of the peace, serving as judges. This session lasted three weeks and three days, with 200 cases on the docket, all but twenty of which were cleared from the docket.

The first divorce case came up for trial at this term of the Circuit Court, and was entitled Mary Hall *vs.* John Hall—John Turney, plaintiff's attorney. The divorce was granted.

The lawyers who appeared at this term of the court, were Jno. Turney, Benjamin Mills, William Smith, and James M. Strode.

In 1828, Moses Meeker, James Mitchell, Moses Hallett, and F. Berry, were the only citizens regularly engaged in farming and raising crops. Every other person was either directly or indirectly engaged in mining.

In this year (1828), steamboats began to make regular trips between St. Louis and Galena, taking lead to St. Louis, and bringing back supplies. Merchants who bought goods at New York, Philadelphia, and other Eastern markets, had them shipped *via* New Orleans and the Mississippi River, to Galena. Among the boats engaged in this trade, were the "Josephine," Clark, master; "Missouri," Culver, master; and the "Red Rover," Throckmorton, master. There were others, of course, but their names and the names of their masters are buried out of memory.

The first Court presided over by a judge, commenced May 11, 1829, and was presided over by Hon. Richard M. Young.

This year, Charles S. Hempstead came to Galena as an attorney, from St. Louis, where he had commenced the practice of his profession as early as 1814. In the office of his son, William Hempstead, collector of U. S. revenue, may be seen the old square table that was made for his St. Louis office when he first opened a law office in that city. In its time it was considered a grand piece of office furniture, and Hempstead's office was regarded as the most gorgeously furnished of any in that city. But by the side of the furniture to be found in ordinarily furnished law offices of 1878, it is very plain and commonplace. Soon after his arrival here, Mr. Hempstead opened an office, from which time until the date of his death, December 10, 1874, he continued a permanent resident, and prominent and leading lawyer of the county. At the time of his death he was the oldest lawyer in practice in the state, and probably the oldest one in the United States.

Within one year from the time the county machinery was put in motion (June 5, 1827), there was a very rapid influx of immigrants, and at the June session (1828) of the County Commissioners Court, three additional voting precincts were established to accommodate the voters who had settled out in the different sections of the county. June 3, on petition of William R. McAdams and others, Menominee precinct was established with the following boundaries: "Beginning at the Sinsinawa, thence running north with the main stream of said Sinsinawa to a grove known by the name of Big Hickory Grove, on the head of the south fork of Little Platte; thence west down the Platte to the Mississippi River to a point opposite the Menominee Mound; thence east by said mound to the beginning."

The house of Mr. McAdams was designated as the voting place, and William R. McAdams, George Davidson, and Robert Henderson, were appointed judges of election.

The order next following related to the presentation, by Mr. Strode, of a petition in relation to a road district including Galena. The petition was received and put on file, and at a later period during the session, the district was declared established.

The Court next considered the erection of Apple River Precinct, which was established as follows: "Beginning at Major Ankeny's on Small Pox, running east to the Lewiston road; thence along the road to Plumb River; thence down said river to the Mississippi; thence up said Mississippi River within five miles of the mouth of Small Pox, and from thence to the place of beginning."

The voting place was ordered to be at the house of John D. Winters, and John D. Winters, George Ames, and Warner Lewis were appointed judges of election. This precinct was established on petition of John D. Winters and others.

"*Ordered*, That Stanislaus Mudd be allowed $48.25 (forty-eight dollars and twenty-five cents), for book case for clerk, and benches.

This was the first piece of office furniture provided for the use of the county clerk's office. Up to this time there was no place to keep either books or papers. Papers, such as petitions, accounts, etc., are said to have been "filed away in the hats or pockets of the officials, and the books carried from the office to the house of the clerk or others in charge of them, and then carried back to the office." When papers began to accumulate, and grew too numerous to file away in the bookcase referred to, and filled the hats and pockets of the officials, they were 'dumped' in barrels and boxes. And one official gentleman with whom the writer had frequent interviews during the progress of this work, said that in the winter seasons of those days, when kindling was scarce, the barrels and boxes of old county documents afforded ready means of starting fires. It must be remembered, however, that this gentleman is something of a wag, and that he was not born until a good many years after the county was organized. But it is beyond doubt that a good many of the early documents of the county that ought to have been preserved, are not to be found.

June 4, James B. Campbell presented a petition signed by himself and others, praying for the erection of Plattville precinct. The prayer of the petitioners was granted, and the following boundaries established: "Beginning at the mouth of the Platte River and running up the same to the Big Hickory Grove, on the head of the south fork of the Little Platte; thence east to the ridge dividing the waters of the Fever River from those of Platte River, and to include all the country of Jo Daviess County lying north of said line.

The house of Rountree & Campbell was designated as the voting place, and John Rountree, Frederick Hollman, and John Jones, were appointed to be judges of election.

June 6, 1828, the streets of Galena were declared to be public highways, and Lewis R. M. Morse was appointed supervisor.

The same day Hugh R. Coulter presented his bond as County Treasurer, with Isaac Chambers and Thomas McCraney as bondsmen. From subsequent entries in the Commissioners journal of proceedings it seems that Mr. Coulter's bond was not satisfactory to the tax-payers, for on the 12th of the same month D. G. Bates appeared before the Court and made complaint as to the insufficiency of Coulter's bond. The latter was cited to appear before the Commissioners and give additional security, etc. Rather than give additional security Mr. Coulter preferred to resign the office, and his resignation was accepted by the Court, and on the 13th William Risley was appointed to the vacancy.

Up to this time, and in fact up to March, 1829, there are no entries to be found showing an assessment of personal property for purposes of taxation. Neither are there any written evidences to show that any tax had been collected, and we are left to one of two conclusions—first, that if there had been an assessment and collection of taxes, the officials failed to make the proper record; and, second, if such record was made, it was made on loose paper and subsequently lost. The only source of revenue of which any trace can be found from the organization of the County up to this date appears to have been from "tavern" license. The charges for such license were from nine to sixteen dollars, and as almost every housekeeper aspired to be a "tavern" keeper, the sum derived from this source (including liquor license, or license for retailing liquors) was not inconsiderable.

The first trace of money derived from taxation of which there is any record appears under date of March 3, 1829. At a regular session of the County Commissioners Court on that day the following entry was made:

Ordered, That the Sheriff be charged with the sum of $833 for taxes assessed for county purposes on personal property for the year 1828, and that he be charged with all the fines in the Circuit Court that have been imposed, and other fines for which he may be accountable.

The Sheriff tendered and filed the Treasurer's receipt for the following sums paid into the treasury during the years 1828 and 1829, and it is

Ordered, That he be allowed a credit for the same. The sum paid is, as per Treasurer's receipt, $691.38.

There is no record to show the total valuation of the personal property in 1828, as found by the Assessor, but it is very clear that if a tax levy of one-half of one per cent returned $833 of county revenue, the total valuation must have been $166,000.

In 1825 the number of men working in the mines was 100; in 1826 the number had increased to a little over 400, and in 1827 the population was estimated at 1,600. Of this number 283 were credited to the *sixty* log cabins that made up the village of Galena. In 1830, according to the U. S. census report, the population was only 2,111, so that the increase from 1827 to 1830 was not very heavy, but it is to be presumed the population was not permanent—that the miners were coming and going—and that when the census of 1830 was taken, the business of the miners was at a "stand still," in consequence of the low price of lead, and that the operators were absent at their homes in other places, so that it is not unreasonable to suppose that the population in 1828 and 1829 was greater than it was in 1830.

June, 1828, the first road view was ordered. A petition was presented to the County Court asking for the location of a public or county road "commencing at Galena and to run by the nearest and best way, by the way of McDonald & Eams' furnace, so as to intersect the Lewiston road at Rush Creek." John D. Winters, John Thomas and John McDonald were appointed viewers. The petitioners were required to deposit $16 with the County Clerk to cover the cost of the view and survey, if the viewers reported unfavorably. If their report was favorable, the deposit was returned, and the expenses sustained by the county. Such was the established practice in all the counties.

Another road was petitioned for at the same time—from Galena to Shullsburg. [At that time the people of this part of the Galena section did not know whether they belonged to Illinois or the Michigan territory, which embraced all of the present State of Wisconsin. Jesse W. Shull, the founder of Shullsburg, Wisconsin, was at one time—from August, 1828, to 1829—one of the County Commissioners of Jo Daviess County, so that that part of Wisconsin was embraced within the jurisdiction of Jo Daviess County.] Joseph Hardy, Henry Gratiot, and Samuel Whitesides were appointed viewers. Their report was favorable, the deposit of sixteen dollars was returned to the petitioners, and the road established.

In those days the Commissioners Court had jurisdiction over the persons of orphan minors, and would "bind them out." The first exercise of this jurisdiction was in June, 1828, when the Court

Ordered, That Sarah Tessat, an infant minor, under fourteen years of age, be bound as an apprentice to Moses Meeker, to serve until she is eighteen years of age."

About this time the people began to agitate the necessity of building a county jail, and on the 12th of June the Court took the matter under consideration, and ordered that a jail be "built of two thicknesses of ten-inch square timber, with a vacancy between the two thicknesses to be filled with rock, as to the lower room, so that the lower room shall be fifteen feet square in the clear and eight feet high. The floors to be made of ten-inch square timber, covered with two-inch plank, to be put on bias and fastened down well with sufficient spikes; one door-way in the lower room, well cheeked—one shutter opening inwardly and the others outwardly—the shutters to be made of two thicknesses of one and a half inch oaken plank. The upper part to be composed of only one wall of ten-inch square timber, but to be well secured with strong rafters, heavy sheeting," etc. A site was selected in "Old Town," on or near the site now occupied by the Presbyterian Church, but the jail was not commenced until June, 1829, when a contract for its erection was awarded to Messrs. William Bennett and Eli S. Lattin. From some cause these contractors did not, as appears from the records, complete the jail, for January 20, 1830, John S. Miller was appointed by the Commissioners to complete it and "fix the same as to make it comfortable for the reception of prisoners." Until completed, some time in 1830, when a prison was needed, a room or building was rented wherever it could be found. Early in the Spring of 1828 a building on Bench Street, near the old Mansion House, was used for a jail, and in which a man was imprisoned on a charge of shooting another one in Vinegar Hill, but he managed to escape and fled the country before trial. In those days there was not as much need of prisons as there was a few years later, for the reason that there were not so many evil-doers. Merchants would some times leave their store doors open and unguarded over night. Piles of mineral would be left in exposed conditions, but it was never disturbed. But when the county was fully organized, courts established and lawyers came to settle here, then came frequent infractions and violations of law. Evil-doers grew bolder and had less fear of statute laws than they had of the laws made by the miners. Among them there was a strict regard for the rights of each other, and to feloniously invade their rights or dishonestly appropriate any of their property was sure to bring instant and speedy punishment. There were none of the delays known to statute laws—no changes of venue—but arrest and immediate trial and punishment (if found guilty) followed in quick succession after detection.

The jail was completed and ready for use in the season of 1830, and in September, 1836, when the right of claimants to the lots they held under permit from the general government was being passed upon by a commission appointed by an act of Congress for that purpose, was the subject of the following little episode:

The commission referred to was composed of three persons: Daniel Wann and John Turney, of Galena, and Samuel Leech, of Quincy—Daniel Wann, chairman. The commission was provided with a plat of the town, and when it met as a court of adjudication, the clerk, or some other one, commenced at lot No. 1, and asked, "Who claims lot No. 1?" The

Lot L. Dimmick
(DECEASED)
APPLE RIVER TP.

claimant would respond, "I claim that lot," and if there were no objections his claim was considered valid, and it was recorded in his name. Lot No. 2 was disposed of in the same way, and so on until the entire plat was disposed of. When they came to the lot on which the jail was built, "Lot No. —; who claims it?" there was no response, although the county authorities had occupied it for county purposes by permit from the government agent. There was no response. Silence reigned for some moments, which was finally broken by one George Madeira, who said: "I claim that lot. I am the first man that occupied it as a residence, and according to the rules that govern here I am entitled to possession." The pith of the joke flashed across the minds of the commission and the crowd in attendance in a moment, and then followed a roar of laughter that shook the building to its very foundations. Madeira had been the first man to occupy it—the jail—after its completion, on an indictment for some criminal offense, but the facts being presented to the governor, he ordered the attorney for the people to enter a *nolle prosequi* against the indictment, and he was released from imprisonment. Some years after the occurrence of the episode referred to, Mr. Madeira emigrated to California, where, at last accounts, he had become a wealthy, useful, influential and highly respected citizen.

In 1832, when the Black Hawk war broke out, this jail was seized by the government, torn down, removed to another place, and re-erected as a block house by the Twenty-seventh Regiment of Illinois Volunteers. September 8, 1832, immediately after the close of the war, the commissioners met, and among their first business caused the following entry to be made:

Ordered, That the clerk make out an account against the United States for the price of the jail of said county, which was taken for public use, together with the damages the county sustained by reason of said jail having been taken, and lay the same before the proper tribunal for adjustment.

March 9, 1833, the account had not been adjusted, and the clerk submitted to the commissioners court the following itemized bill, which was approved by the court, and ordered to be entered of record:

The United States:

To Jo Daviess County,	Dr.
For the cost of jail	$381.00
For damages sustained for want of jail	265.00
	$646.00

A certified copy of this bill was made out under seal of the court, properly attested and forwarded to the proper United States authorities. A subsequent order, entered on the 12th of March, indicates that the claim was favorably considered by the authorities of the general government, and that arrangements were made for its payment, for it was

Ordered, That whatever money the Government may allow for the jail and damages, be paid to H. Newhall (the county treasurer) and retained by him for the purpose of procuring suitable buildings for the county.

Whatever may have been the prospect for receiving pay, damages, etc., from the government when the above orders were passed, no records were found showing when or what amount was received. Some "old settlers" say the matter was referred to a member of Congress from this district at the time, and that to the best of their memory nothing ever came of it.

June 13, 1828, the County Court commenced to agitate the propriety of securing grounds for county buildings, and appointed David G. Bates, Samuel C. Muir, Mathew C. Comstock, J. S. Miller and Richard W. Chandler as commissioners to select suitable grounds, etc., with instructions to report their action in the premises to the County Court on the following Tuesday —June 20. At that time the committee appeared before the commissioners and *reported that they had nothing to report*—that they had made no selection of grounds, and asked to be discharged, which request was granted, and an order entered dismissing them from a further consideration of the subject.

Wednesday, the 21st, Samuel C. Muir, Mathew C. Comstock and D. G. Bates were appointed to the same duty, and on the 28th this committee also reported that they had been unable to find a suitable location, and were also discharged.

The commissioners then entered upon a general discussion of the subject, and finally

Ordered, That a court house be erected on the lot heretofore set apart by the agent for the erection of a school house, on the "bench" near the house of J. S. Miller; and that James Harris, Samuel C. Muir and D. G. Bates be authorized to contract for the building of the said court house and jail, and that they be authorized to pledge the revenue of the County of Jo Daviess for the payment of $2,000 on account of said buildings.

This order was not immediately carried out, as from Mr. Lorrain's Centennial History, and from other sources of information, it appears that (with the exception of the jail completed in 1830) all the buildings used by the county were rented or leased until the completion of the present court house and other county buildings.

Taking the business of the County Commissioners Court in regular order, we find, under date of March 10, 1829, the following entry:

Ordered, That a tax of one half of one per cent be levied and collected on town lots, *slaves*, indentured or registered servants, pleasure carriages, distilleries, stock in trade, horses, mules, mares, asses, neat cattle three years of age, watches and other appendages, and all other property not real in the possession of citizens."

At that date lands were not taxable. The title was still in the government, and could not be occupied except by permit from the general government. [Full reference to the conditions that withheld the lands in the Galena section from actual occupation by individuals and their consequent taxation, will be found in the preceding pages of this book.]

Under date of June 3, 1829, the following entry appeared, and from which it will be seen by reference to the maps, that the Rock Island precinct extended down below the present City of Rock Island, to the north line of the south tier of townships of Mercer County. The north line of the military tract commenced at the northwest corner of the southwest township of that county, and extended east to the Illinois River, a few miles below the present City of Hennepin, in Putnam County.

It appearing to the satisfaction of the court that a considerable portion of the Platteville election precinct is out of the bounds of Jo Daviess County, it is therefore ordered that said precinct be vacated and that such part thereof as does pertain to said county be attached to Menominee precinct.

Ordered, That the following be established as a district for the election of Justices of the Peace and Constables in Jo Daviess County, to be called the Rock Island precinct, to-wit: Beginning at the intersection of the Maria Dosia and Rock Rivers, thence along the said Maria Dosia to the middle of the Mississippi River; thence along the middle of said river to the northern boundary line of the military tract; thence east along the said line to a point due south from the place of beginning; thence due north to the place of beginning.

It is ordered that the elections in said precinct be held at Farnhamsburg, and that George Davenport, John Barrel and —— Casner be appointed judges of election.

June 9, 1829, Wm. Risley tendered his resignation as county treasurer, which was *excepted* (county clerk's orthography), and Horatio Newhall was appointed to the vacancy.

September 22, 1829, Charles D. St. Vrain was "allowed $76 in full payment of rent of court house and jail;" and it was further

Ordered, That William Bennett and Eli S. Lattin be allowed the sum of two hundred dollars in part pay for building a jail in Jo Daviess County.

December 7, 1829, Joseph Ogee, who had established himself on Rock River, at the crossing of the old Galena and Fort Clark (Peoria) state road, as a tavern keeper, made application for license to keep a ferry. The license was granted, and the following ferry rates fixed by the court:

Man and horse	$ 25
Horses or cattle per head, other than cattle yoked	37½
Road wagon	1 00
For each horse hitched to said wagon	25
Each two-horse wagon	75
Each two-wheeled carriage or cart	1 00
One-horse wagon	75
Each hundred weight of merchandise, etc.	6

At the same session of the court (Dec. 8), John Barrel was granted a license to maintain a ferry across the Mississippi River at Rock Island, and to charge the same rates as those established by George Davenport.

Before adjournment, the court directed its attention to fixing the rates of "tavern keepers" for the year 1830. We have heretofore incorporated within these pages the first standard of prices thus established for the government of landlords and saloon keepers, but as this one is a little more elaborate, we reproduce it from the musty old record:

Each meal	37½	cents
Horse feed	25	"
Horse per night at corn and hay	62½	"
Man per night	12½	"
Each half pint of French brandy or wine	25	"
" " " " whisky or other domestic liquors	12½	"
" " " " Holland gin	25	"
Each quart of porter, cider or ale	25	"

In January, 1830, the people began to manifest some anxiety to know where they lived, whether in the State of Illinois or the Michigan Territory, and on the 20th of that month the county commissioners

Ordered, That D. R. Davis be and he is hereby employed to run a random line from Galena, taking as his data the observation of Lieutenant Bourdine, and establishing a temporary line for the government of the officers of Jo Daviess, between the County of Jo Daviess and the Territory of Michigan.

As has already been stated, the miners at Gratiot's Grove, Shullsburg, Rountrees, and a half dozen other places, now known to be in Wisconsin, and extending away up towards Dodgeville (as is now), were included in Jo Daviess in the first establishment of election precincts. Jesse W. Shull was at one time a member of the County Commissioners Court, and the people up there bore their part of the early expenses of the county—their personal effects being taxed with the people in the immediate vicinity of Galena, the county seat. As late as 1840, as elsewhere noticed, the people here were not fully satisfied as to their personal whereabouts, or else were ambitious for state capital honors, and in the Fall of that year a meeting of the leading citizens of Jo Daviess and other counties, was held at Rockford, to agitate the subject. We have been unable to find any written or printed account of the proceedings of that meeting, and come to the conclusion that the people finally concluded to accept the situation, and make the most they could out of the advantages afforded by their galena-filled hills.

Immersed in the first records of the county, we had well nigh forgotten a very important enterprise—the commencement of the publication of a newspaper by James Jones, called the *Miners' Journal*. The first number of the *Journal* was issued July 8, 1828, and was received with pleasure and satisfaction by the people. It was, we believe, the first newspaper enterprise undertaken in any part of Northern Illinois, Chicago not excepted. The *Journal* was a four-page paper, with four columns to the page, printed in long primer and brevier type, and on coarse, heavy paper, now brown with age. Dr. Horatio Newhall, one of the earliest and best settlers at Galena, carefully preserved the files of this paper, and had them substantially bound, which—thanks to his son, Dr. E. G. Newhall—were placed at our service while writing up this history. The file is perfect from July 25, 1828, to June 12, 1830, and is the only file of that paper in existence. Unfortunately the first two numbers are missing, so that we are unable to present even a synopsis of the editor's salutatory or introductory address, but there is enough else in the two years the files cover to make the file a most interesting volume. Fifty years, lacking a few months, have passed since the *Journal* was commenced, but these fifty years have been so full of history—have worked so many changes—that an examination of the contents of this old file—this keep-sake of half a century ago—makes one almost believe that he is in another world.

Turning to number three of the *Journal*, dated July 25, 1828, we extract the following personal mention of one of the native representative men of that time:

WA-PO-NA, the principal chief of the Fox nation, remained several days in this town during the last week, on his return from a visit to the Indian village at Du Buque's mines. During his stay here he sat for his portrait at Mr. Berry's rooms. He was dressed in fine style, and Mr. Berry has succeeded with his usual happy talent in taking a very striking likeness of the "Prince." Wa-po-na resides on Rock River, is much respected by the Americans, and is universally revered by his nation. He was attended by ten or twelve of his principal braves. By his open address, the dignity of his manners, and by his unassuming deportment, he has gained the friendship of all who know him. He has once been at the City of Washington, and visited the President of the United States."

Then follows an item of general news that will show the extent of the fur trade of the West and Northwest at that time:

On the 10th inst., thirteen boats passed the City of Jefferson on their way to St. Louis, laden with FUR, from the Rocky Mountains, the property of McKenzey & Co., and is supposed to be the most valuable cargo ever collected from that quarter.—*Mo. Intel.*

In 1828 General Jackson was a candidate for president, and the *Journal* printed both the Jackson and administration Adams electoral tickets:

"*Jackson Electoral Ticket.*—John Taylor, of Sangamon County; John Huston, of Wabash County; R. M. Young, of Randolph County.

" *Administration Electoral Ticket.*—Elijah Iles, of Sangamon County; Sam'l H. Thompson, of St. Clair; George Webb, of White.

"*Representatives to Congress.*—Hon. Joseph Duncan, George Forquer, Esq.

" STATE LEGISLATURE.

"*Senator* for the district composed of the counties of Jo Daviess, Peoria, Schuyler, Fulton, Pike and Adams—R. W. Chandler, of Jo Daviess; John A. Wakefield, of do.; Henry J. Ross of Pike.

"*Representatives for same District.*—John Turney, Jas. Nagle, James Craig, of Jo Daviess; Ossian M. Ross, of Fulton; Abraham Pricket, of Adams; John Orendorff, of Fulton.

"*Sheriff for Jo Daviess County.*—John Foley, John Barrell, Samuel Burks, Thomas W. Thompson.

"*County Commissioner.*—James Harris, Hugh R. Coulter, George Davidson, Jesse W. Shull.

"*Coroner.*—George W. Carman."

The same number of the *Miners' Journal* that contained the above extracts had the following arrival and departure of steamboats:

STEAMBOAT REGISTER.

1828. ARRIVED.

July 18—Missouri, Culver, from St. Louis.
22—Red Rover, Throckmorton, St. L.
23—A Mackina boat from Green Bay, laden with Merchandise, in part from New York and Green Bay.
July 25—Rover, Carlysle, St. Louis.

DEPARTED.

July 15—Josephine, Clark, for St. Louis.
19—Missouri, Culver, St. Louis.
23—Red Rover, Throckmorton, St. L.

This issue of the *Journal* of fifty years ago also had the following announcements of marriages in high life:

MARRIED.—In England, *Francis Godolphin D'Arcy*, Marquis of Calmarthan, son of the duke of Leeds, and heir apparent, to Lady *Hervey*, daughter of Richard Caton, and granddaughter of Charles Carroll, of Carrollton.

——— In Bellville, Ill., *Jas. H. Lane*, of the house of Lane, Knox & Co., merchants of St. Louis, to Miss *Margaret*, daughter of his Excellency, N. Edwards.

But we can not copy into this history of Jo Daviess County all that we find of interest in Jones' *Miners' Journal*, for it is a great volume within itself, and full of historical information, all of which would be of interest. We will, however, have frequent occasion to draw on its columns hereafter, and will only copy one more item from its well-filled pages now. This extract is from the Buffalo (N. Y.) *Journal*, after receiving a copy of the *Miners' Journal*. The Buffalo editor wrote:

Miners' Journal.—During the past week we received the first number of a paper bearing this title, and published by Mr. *James Jones*, at Galena (*lead ore*), Fever River, to give which stream a "local habitation" proved no light tax upon our geographical stock of information. Any one could tell us what we well knew before—namely, that Fever River is among the lead mines, and in the vicinity of the Winnebago Indians; but all this did not locate the spot whence emanated the thrice welcome sheet we have mentioned. We resorted to all the Gazetteers within our reach, but no one recognized Fever River, and we searched some twenty different maps, including the last edition of Finly's great Atlas, with no better success. We then seated ourselves to read the entire sheet carefully through, in search of the place of its birth. By this process we learned that a court had been held in the County of Jo Daviess—but the map showed no such county, and we were again at fault. Persevering in our plan, we at length discovered that a "party of about one hundred ladies and gentlemen went on board the steamboat Indiana, at 9 o'clock A. M. (on the 4th of July), descended Fever River to its mouth and ascended the Mississippi about eighteen miles, to Fox Village or Dubuque's mines."

This was a great relief, but still we knew not upon which bank of the Mississippi to pursue our search. Finding there was a post-office at Galena, we resorted to the Postmaster General's list of these useful establishments, by which we learned that Galena is a post township, the capital of *Jo Daviess* County, and situated upon Fever River, in the extreme northwest corner of the State of Illinois, and, of course, upon the east bank of the Mississippi. The receipt of a newspaper from the heart of the boundless forests of the mining district is like that of news from a far-off country, and was as little expected by us as the *Lake of the Woods Herald* or *Columbia River Gazette.*

* * * * * * * * * * *

A history of Galena and the mining country around it, from its earliest settlement, is promised by a correspondent, to be given in future numbers of the *Journal.* This will require no *antiquarian*, we imagine, although the production will be full of interest, and will contain, we trust, facts by which the next compilers of maps and geographies will duly profit. It is stated in the sheet before us that the miners already occupy a territory of *one hundred square miles*, and that they are still extending their bounds, to make room for the flood of immigration that is constantly rolling in upon the settlement.

We strongly recommend that all anti-tariff lead dealers subscribe for the *Miners' Journal*, if they dare encourage a domestic article.

The Galena *Advertiser*, dated "Galena, Upper Mississippi Lead Mines, Illinois," was commenced July 20, 1829, by Newhall, Philleo & Co.—Horatio Newhall, Addison Philleo and Hooper Warren. Files of this paper from its first issue, July 20, 1829, to May 24, 1830, and of the *Galenian* from May 2, 1832, to January 2, 1833, were preserved by Dr. Newhall in the same volume with the *Miners' Journal*, and embrace a record of events of half a century ago that is invaluable.

The *Advertiser* of the 22d of February, 1830, referring to the random survey of the line between Jo Daviess County and the Territory of Michigan, as ordered by the County Court, quotes from the report of Mr. D. R. Davis, who was appointed to that duty, as follow :

Assuming as correct, the latitude of Galena 42 deg., 22 min., 55 sec., ascertained from numerous observations by Lieut. Burdine, they started from the lower block house and proceeded north 8 miles, 15 chains and 38 links. The line as surveyed by Mr. Davis, strikes the Mississippi about eight miles above Dubuque's mines. Going eastward, it passes Firman's (formerly Tompkins') house and furnace, running along the northern base of the Sinsinawa Mound, leaving the whole of it in this county. The line passes through the Hardscrabble Diggings, leaving R. R. Young's house about 30 yards south of it. It crosses Fever River at the head of the Natchez race track, leaving Natchez in the Michigan Territory, and including the principal part of the New Diggings in this state. The line thence passes through Gratiot's Grove, including Joseph Paine's house, and leaving all Gratiot's buildings in the territory. Bunkum and the White Oak Springs are, of course, in Jo Daviess.

Thus, almost three years after the county was organized, its north line was established, and the miners and other settlers advised of their whereabouts. Until that time no one knew how far north the county extended.

Thus far the historians have exercised great care in following the records of the County Court, in order that they might present to the readers of these pages a general summary of the labor necessary to put the machinery of the county in full, complete and successful operation. With a few more general quotations from the early records of the county, and their pen will only place on record the more important events of the county's history, such as the building of the Court House, the history of the Agricultural Society, Adoption of the Township System, the Educational Interests, War Record, etc., etc.

Among the more important duties of the early County Commissioners was the erection of voting and justices precincts. As the reader may see by taking a map and tracing the boundary lines of the original Jo Daviess County, heretofore given, the territory embraces a larger extent of country than is embraced in each of several States of the American republic. To regulate and manage the local affairs of so large an extent of territory, was not a very easy task, but was a duty that required a good deal of skill and judgment. However, there were men among the miners and mechanics that had graduated from the farms and shops and cabins and old log school-houses of states older than Illinois, that were just as competent to the task of organizing order out of the chaotic confusion of Indian wilds, as were the college graduates who came after the pioneers had established the customs of civilization and introduced in the wilderness of the Upper Mississippi that enterprise and industry that developed the great agricultural and mineral wealth that made for Galena and all the lead-producing region of the Northwest a name and a fame co-extensive with civilization. To the sturdy sons of toil—the hardy miners, the strong armed mechanics who accompanied them, and their brave, heroic wives, who bartered safety and comfort in their girlhood's homes, for Indian dangers and probable privation and want, and not to the sons of rich men, raised in affluence and wealth, schooled in colleges and fitted for the profession of law or politics, and who came here long after the dangers and privations and hardships were over, belongs the honor of reducing the primitive wilds to a condition of civilization that is second to no other part of a common country. But such observations aside, and we turn again to the official proceedings of the local legislators of Jo Daviess County—the County Commissioners.

March 3, 1830, Rock Island precinct was established, and thus defined:

"Beginning at the mouth of Maria O'gee and running due east to the eastern extremity of Jo Davièss Co., thence south to the County of Peoria, thence west to the southwest corner of said county of Jo Daviess, thence up the Mississippi to the place of beginning."

The same day Apple River precinct was established:

"Beginning at Shannon's mills and running due east to the east (?) corner of Jo Daviess County, thence south to the Rock Island precinct, thence due west to the mouth of the Maria O'gee, thence to the place of beginning."

The Galena precinct was changed as follows:

"To begin at Shannon's mills and run east to where the Apple River road crosses the east and west line; thence west to Lockwood's furnace (including the settlement at said furnace), thence on a west line to the Mississippi River; thence with the state line to the place of beginning."

The boundary lines of Centreville precinct were also changed as follows:

"Beginning at Meeker's farm and running to Lockwood's furnace; thence to Council Hill on the old road traveled; from thence with the New Diggings road to the state line; west to the Mississippi River to the line of the Galena precinct; thence east to the place of beginning."

A new precinct called White Oak Springs precinct was erected, the boundary lines being thus defined:

"Beginning at the Apple River road where the east and west line crosses said road from Shannon's mills; thence east to the eastern extremity of said county; thence north to the state line; thence west to the New Diggings (including the settlers on the east fork and on the head waters of Apple River); thence along the road to Council Hill; thence to Lockwood's furnace; thence to the place of beginning."

The wording of these orders is a little vague in some respects, and the location of some of the lines rather indifferently defined, but it must be borne in mind that a good deal of the territory included in these several precincts was entirely unsettled, so that it was a somewhat difficult matter to establish "landmarks," and so locate them that every body could follow the boundary lines in their mind and know just where they started, what particular points they passed, or precisely where they terminated. Roads, in those days, were little else than trails, perhaps first marked out by Indian feet and Indian ponies. The same lines could be established now so that every school-boy, almost, could readily locate every particular place within the precincts. Where then there were not more than twenty or thirty voters, there now are hundreds, and the waste places of March 30, 1830, are full of productive farms and the busy hum of industry.

June 8, 1830, John Campbell was licensed "to keep a ferry across the Mississippi River, opposite Dubuque's mines, on payment of eight dollars to the County Treasurer, and entering into bonds with good and sufficient security." He was permitted to charge fifty cents for crossing man and horse.

Then follows a long list of road orders, the granting of tavern license, etc. In fact, for several years a good deal of the time of the various sessions of the Commissioners Court was consumed in matters of this kind. Immigration was rapid, and there had to be places of entertainment. Provisions were scarce and high. The settlers could not afford, however hospitable and willingly inclined, to keep travelers scot free, and hence they were licensed to charge reasonable rates. These taverns were rude concerns—not grand structures like the De Soto House—but log cabins, and may be, had only one room. Or if they had more, they were low, side additions. Some times a cabin was built sufficiently high to permit sleeping quarters above. In such cases a common step ladder in one corner of the room afforded access to the room above, or just as like as any other way, the upper portion of the house was reached by a ladder on the outside in the "chimney corner." If tables in those days were void of elaborate bills of fare and the edibles to be found in "taverns" of more modern date, there was plenty of substantials, and what would now be called varieties. One old pioneer, Samuel Simpson, now in his eightieth year, and living in Elizabeth Township, who came to the state in 1832, told the historians that during the first fourteen years of his residence in Illinois there was no necessity for serving a single meal in his house without wild honey and either fresh or dried venison. All the streams abounded with fish of the choicest varieties; wild turkeys were to be found in large flocks in almost every forest, and prairie chickens, pheasants, etc., were to be found in plenty.

June 10, 1830, the County Commissioners Court

Ordered, That the sheriff be charged with the sum of $610.27, that being the amount of the tax list for the year A. D, 1829; and that he be credited by the delinquent list for the sum of $49.66, and that he also have a credit for the sum of $581.11, the amount of the taxes for the year A. D. 1829, and the fines of Jonas ($30), Furguson & Gear's ($5), as assessed at the November term, 1829, of the Circuit Court for said county.

The next day, June 11, they ordered that all the county orders previously issued and redeemed by the treasurer should be burned, which order was carried out, and orders representing $2,242.96¼ were committed to the flames. A subsequent order recited this fact, as well as the names of the parties to whom the orders had originally been issued, and their various amounts.

Slavery once existed in Illinois. This italicized declaration may sound a little harsh to the ears of some of the readers of these pages, but it is a fact, nevertheless. A full reference to this condition of affairs will be found in that part of this book devoted to the general history of the early settlement of the Galena section of the Upper Mississippi or Fever River country, so that an extended reference to this "twin relic of barbarism" in this connection is unnecessary. As late as 1839, and perhaps 1840–'1, taxes were assessed against *slaves* or *indentured apprentices*, and by "indentured apprentices" the authorities ordering the assessment of taxes

CHARLES S. HEMPSTEAD
(DECEASED)
GALENA

meant negro slaves. The subterfuge of "indentured apprentices" didn't remove the fact that they were as much slaves as were the negroes of the South, and that property was recognized in man. There yet lives in the City of Galena at least two (Swanzy Adams and his wife) representatives of this "indentured apprentice" class ("what a whipping of the devil around the stump!") against whom taxes were levied as upon so many cattle, and from whose earnings and industry the assessment was collected. At last, however, the foul blot and stain upon our boasted freedom was washed out, and negro slavery exists no more.

In Book A, the first volume of the records of the County Commissioners Court, under date of June 30, 1830, two instruments of writing are recorded that are transferred to these pages for preservation to posterity—not only as a part of the early history of the county, but as a part of the history of a government whose fathers claimed it to have been founded upon the principle of freedom to *all* men, because all men, in their opinion, were created free and equal.

On that day Arch, *alias* Arch Davis, an "indentured apprentice," caused to be entered of record the following document:

Col. A. Field to Arch.—Know all men by these presents, that Abner Field, of the County of Jo Daviess, Illinois, and by these presents do liberate and set free a certain black man now an indentured apprentice, named Arch *alias* Arch Davis, hereby releasing and exonerating the said Arch from all further service; *provided*, however, that the said Arch shall be compelled to work to the amount of at least two days in each week so long as he shall remain in the house of the said Field, and cohabit with his (the said Arch's) wife. The said Field is to furnish him with a sufficiency to eat, and to permit him to sleep in his kitchen, etc. ABNER FIELD. [Seal.]

January 12, 1829.
Recorded June 30, 1830. JAMES W. STEPHENSON, *Clerk, etc.*

The same day a female indentured apprentice named Cherry *alias* Chaney, caused a similar instrument of writing to be recorded, as follows:

Abner Field to Cherry.—Know all men by these presents, that I, Abner Field, do by these presents release and free an indentured woman of color now belonging to me, known and called Cherry *alias* Chaney, on condition that she, the said woman, will serve me for one year from the date of this writing, and permit herself to be taken to Kentucky or elsewhere by my giving bond and security for her return.

In testimony of the foregoing, I hereto set my hand and seal this 27th day of April, 1830. ABNER FIELD. [Seal.]

Recorded June 30, 1830.
J. W. STEPHENSON, *Clerk, etc.*

And so, one by one, where death or other causes did not intervene, were the "indentured apprentices" or *slaves* of Illinois emancipated from bondage and restored to the normal condition of all mankind. It is more than probable that the only survivors of this class of Illinois *slaves* are residents of Galena, where, overcome with years, they are watching and waiting for the summons to appear before that Master who is no respecter of persons.

September 8, 1830, the commissioners ordered that the next term of the Circuit Court be held at the house lately occupied by Hammett & Campbell, and that the sheriff cause the same to be prepared for that purpose, and that James K. Hammett be allowed the sum of thirty dollars for the use of the same. The house here referred to was a frame store room situated on Diagonal Street, not far from the present court house.

From September, 1830, until March, 1831, there was but little business to engross the attention of the commissioners, so that we find nothing in these months worthy of special mention. On the 9th of that month provisions for raising money to defray the year's expenses were considered, and it was ordered that an assessment of one half of one per cent be levied on slaves or indentured negro or mulatto servants, on pleasure carriages, on all horses, mares, mules, asses and neat cattle above three years of age, and on watches and clocks and their appendages, and on lead and hogs.

At a meeting held on Saturday, April 23, the following entry was ordered to be made:

It is considered by the court that the sheriff of the county be permitted to release from taxation such lead as has been assessed for taxes for the year 1830, as may appear on the oath of the merchant or person with whom the same is stored, to belong to non-residents of this state; *Provided*, That, if the merchant or persons aforesaid do not consent by their oath to partition their individual lead from that, they, or either of them, may have in storage, then this order shall not operate as a repeal of any former order on the subject.

On complaint of Thomas Jordan, made April 29, 1831, the license of John Campbell, as ferryman between the Illinois side of the Mississippi River and Dubuque's mines, was revoked, because of Campbell having abandoned the undertaking. The same day license was granted to Mr. Jordan to keep a ferry at his landing (now Dunleith), upon payment of five dollars to the county treasurer, and giving security for a lawful discharge of a ferryman's duties. Jordan's was the first licensed ferry at that point.

During the Summer, Fall and Winter of 1831, there was no business of an extraordinary nature to claim the attention of the local legislators. Settlements had extended to various parts of the county, and immigrants were coming in, selecting claims and settling down to their improvement. For the balance of the year the sessions of the County Court were taken up, for the most part, in the ordinary business of the county—granting road views, tavern licenses, selecting grand and petit juries, etc. In the Spring of 1832 the Indian War came on, and all kinds of business, public and private, was almost entirely suspended. That war was vigorously prosecuted, the Indians subdued and a permanent peace conquered. September 6, of that year, a part of the volunteer militia for the suppression of the Indian rebellion were mustered out of the service at Galena, and the army disbanded. On the 8th the commissioners were in session and the county business again taken up. Among the other business of that session, an order was entered allowing Dr. Newhall fifty cents for each visit to the poor and diseased, Dr. Newhall to furnish his own medicines. The other business of that session, as of the remaining sessions of that year and up to March, 1833, related solely to ordinary matters. On the 12th day of March, for the first time, so far as the records show, an assessment of taxes was ordered against ferries. At this time there appeared to have been only four ferries within the county—at what are now Dixon, on Rock River, Rock Island, Galena, and Jordan's (between the present sites of Dunleith and Dubuque). On Dixon's ferry a county tax of $15 was levied; on Foley's Galena ferry, $12; on Barrel's Rock Island ferry, $10.

The subjugation of the Indians, in 1832, removed all apprehension of Indian dangers, and the people settled down to earnest, hard work. New plans were marked out by those engaged in the mines, by those who were making farms and by those who were charged with the management of county affairs.

Early in 1833, six years after the county machinery had been set in motion, the necessity of permanent quarters for the county offices came to be considered by the Commissioners. On the 22d of March of that year they

Ordered, That the clerk of this court be, and is hereby, authorized to contract with Charles Peck for his house, if it can be obtained on the following terms, viz.: For one hundred and twenty dollars a year, for 3 years, payable in two equal payments, the first to be paid in June, and the other in December of each and every year, the house to be put in good repair by Mr. Peck; the said payments to draw six per cent interest from the time they become due until paid.

The Peck House here referred to, was a large frame structure and stood on the ground now occupied by the De Soto House, and with the exception of Comstock's storehouse, was the largest in Galena.

May 8 it was also

Ordered, That the house of Peck & Heath shall be the Court House for this county, during the continuance of the lease; also, that the several clerks are requested to keep their respective offices in the said house.

December 27, 1834, Messrs. Charles Peck, H. Newhall, and E. Charles submitted a plan and estimate for a jail, which was satisfactory to the Court, and it was ordered that public notice be given in the *Galenian* and Northwestern *Gazette*, inviting sealed proposals through the office of the county clerk (where plans and specifications could be seen), until the first Monday of March following, for building the said jail according to the plans proposed. The site for the proposed jail was on the southwest corner of the public grounds, between Main and Bench Streets, on the (then) late residence grounds of Amos Farrar. The jail was to be completed by the first of December, 1835, one half of the contract price to be paid when the building was put under roof, and the balance when the building was completed and accepted, good security to be given for a faithful performance of the contract. The building of the jail as contemplated by this order was never commenced. Some difficulty was experienced in the purchase of the necessary lot on which to build it, and it was not until the ground on which the county buildings were subsequently erected were secured, that a jail was completed.

The following is an itemized exhibit (and the first on record that we have been able to find), of the receipts and expenditures of Jo Daviess County, for the year ending Dec. 10, 1834.

RECEIPTS:

From ferries	$ 55 00
From merchants and tavern keepers	1,062 77
From fines	85 00
From county taxes	195 39
From orders of Peck	300 00
From county taxes current year not collected	472 72
From outstanding and doubtful accounts	325 23
Total	$2,496 11

EXPENDITURES:

For paupers	$ 681 75
For roads	251 00
For rent of court house and jail	225 12
For election expenses	134 42
For guarding prisoners	90 00
For constables	70 00
For sheriff	90 00
For treasurer	93 00
For county commissioners	68 25

EXPENDITURES—Continued.

For clerk commissioners court	$ 81 00
For clerk circuit court	57 00
For wood and stationery	75 00
For miscellaneous	46 61
For lot of orders current year	767 97
Total	$2,638 43

RECAPITULATION:

Expenditures	$2,638 43	
Receipts	2,496 11	
Excess of expenditures over receipts		$142 32

About this time the people and the county authorities began to agitate the question of purchasing grounds for public buildings, and on the 9th of March, 1835, the County Court

Ordered, That Abraham Hathaway and Elijah Charles (two of the County Commissioners at that time) be appointed agents, on the part of county to execute a note from the county to the commissioners appointed in a matter of petition between George Davenport and others for the payment of nine hundred dollars for a certain lot (of ground) in the town of Galena, bought for the purpose of erecting public buildings thereon.

The following day (March 10), an entry was made from which it appears that James Bennett, Rivers Cormack and W. B. Green had been duly authorized to purchase a lot of ground in Galena as a site for a court house and jail. Bennett had purchased a lot known as the "Connolly lot," for the use of the county, but had taken the deed in his own name and had given his note with security to James Craig, Horatio Newhall and David G. Bates, commissioners for the sale of the said lot, for the sum of nine hundred dollars, and it was ordered that Bennett be required to deed the said house and lot to Jo Daviess County, and in default thereof suit was directed to be commenced against him. The same day an order on the County Treasurer was directed to issue "to Charles Peck for what money he may have to advance on a note executed to James Craig, Horatio Hewhall and David G. Bates, commissioners appointed in a matter of partition between Davenport and others, of certain real estate," etc. On application, Bennett refused to deed the property as required in the order of the 10th of March, and suit was ordered to be commenced against him in the Circuit Court.

Some time subsequent to the adjournment of this session of the County Commissioners and prior to a session held on the 22d of April, a proposition was made to the Court by Charles Hempstead in regard to certain grounds for public buildings, which the court, at the date just quoted, agreed to take under advisement until the next term, June 13, when it was

Ordered, That a writ of injunction be applied for to stop proceedings of certain commissioners appointed at a late term of the Circuit Court to set off the dowry of Mrs. Sophia Farrar, in a certain lot of ground (recently purchased by the county at a Commissioners' sale), known as the Connolly lot, situate in the Town of Galena.

Suit against Bennett had been commenced, and the finding of the Circuit Court was adverse to the interests of the county, and on the 6th of September, 1836, it was

Ordered, That an appeal be taken to the Supreme Court from the decision of the Circuit Court at its late session (Jo. Daviess County *vs.* James Bennett), and the Clerk of the Commissioners Court is authorized to employ Jesse B. Thomas, William Thomas, and Henry J. Galewood, as counsel.

September 8, 1838, John W. Foster was appointed to take possession of the lot then in possession of Sophia Farrar, and on the 8th of December, 1838, a quit-claim deed was directed to be made to Sophia Farrar to lot No. 52, on Bench Street.

While these proceedings were going through the courts, the County Commissioners and public-spirited citizens were busy maturing plans, looking to the erection of a court house, jail, etc. After Colonel Strode seized, tore down and removed the jail erected in 1830, and re-erected it as a block house at the beginning of the Black Hawk war, in 1832, there was no place for the confinement and safe keeping of prisoners until the erection of the present brick jail on lot No. 17, block No. 24, in 1838. During these years rooms were rented, and men employed at the expense of the county to guard prisoners, the expenses of which were very heavy.

At a special term of the County Court, in October, 1835, a "petition was ordered to be forwarded to the Congress of the United States for the avails of the sale of 640 acres to be laid off into town lots at Galena, to go for the benefit of the county in lieu of pre-emption right to 160 acres granted to county seats located on Congress lands, and that a letter be addressed to the representative in Congress on the same subject." The county commissioners at this time were James Craig, Abraham Hathaway, and E. Charles. This petition seems to have been favorably considered by Congress, for in 1836 that body passed the following act relative thereto, entitled "An Act to amend an 'act authorizing the laying off a town on Bean River, in the State of Illinois, and for other purposes,' approved fifth February, eighteen hundred and twenty-nine."

Be it enacted by the Senate and House of Representatives of the United States of America, in Congress assembled, That all acts and duties required to be done and performed by the surveyor of the States of Illinois and Missouri, and the Territory of Arkansas, under the act to which this is an amendment, shall be done and performed by a board of commissioners of three in number, any two of whom shall form a quorum to do business; said commissioners to be appointed by the President of the United States, and shall, previous to their entering upon the discharge of their duties, take an oath or affirmation to perform the same faithfully and impartially.

SECTION 2. *And be it further enacted,* That the said commissioners shall have power to hear evidence and determine all claims to lots of ground arising under the act to which this is an amendment, and for this purpose the said commissioners are authorized to administer all oaths that may be necessary, and reduce to writing all the evidence in support of claims to pre-emption presented for their consideration; and when all the testimony shall have been heard and considered, the said commissioners shall file with the register and receiver of the land office at Galena, for the lot or lots to which such person is entitled, the receiver shall grant a receipt therefor, and issue certificates of purchase, to be transmitted to the General Land Office, as in other cases of the sale of public lands.

SECTION 3. *And be it further enacted,* That the register and receiver at Galena, after the board of commissioners have heard and determined all the cases of pre-emption under the act to which this is an amendment, shall expose the residue of lots to public sale to the highest bidder, after advertising the same in three public newspapers at least six weeks prior to the day of sale, in the same manner as is provided for the sale of the public lands in other cases; and after paying to the commissioners the compensation hereinafter allowed them, and all the other expenses incidental to the said survey and sale, the receiver of the land office shall pay over the residue of the money he may have received from the sale of lots aforesaid, by pre-emption as well as at public auction, into the hands of the County Commissioners of Jo Daviess County, to be expended by them in the erection of public buildings and the construction of suitable wharves in the Town of Galena.

SECTION 4. *And be it further enacted,* That the commissioners appointed to carry this act into effect shall be paid by the receiver six dollars each per day, for their services, for every day they are necessarily employed.

Approved, July 2, 1836. [See U. S. Statutes at Large, Vol. 5, p. 79.]

Having thus introduced the law and the means under and from which part of the money was derived to build the court house, we return to the

County Commissioners' record, to bring up some other important items which were omitted from regular chronological order.

From March, 1835, to March, 1836, a period of one year, there is nothing on the record out of the usual routine of county business. March 15, of the year last named, the following assessment was made against the several ferries within the county for county and road purposes:

Ferry.	*County Tax.*	*Road Tax.*
Dixon's	$20 00	$10 00
Wight, Galena	15 00	7 50
Jordan, Dunleith	50 00	15 00
Bush	15 00	7 50
Brophy, Dunleith	50 00	15 00
McClure	5 00	2 50
Bales	15 00	7 50
Kirkpatrick	15 00	7 50
L. H. Bowen, Savanna (Carroll Co.)	10 00	5 00
J. L. Brewster	10 00	5 00
John Phelps	15 00	7 50
Total	$220 00	$90 00
Grand total of taxes assessed against ferries		$310 00

September 10, 1836, the County Court offered a premium of one hundred dollars for the best plan for a court house, and thirty dollars for the best plan for a jail, to be presented at the December term of the court (first Monday in December, 1836), the probable cost of the court house to be $40,000, and of the jail, $10,000, and directed the county clerk to advertise for the same through the Galena newspapers and the St. Louis *Republican*, the advertisement to be inserted weekly in each of the above named papers for eight weeks.

A number of plans were presented to the commissioners at their December term (Thursday, the 8th) and after having examined and considered all of them carefully, the plans presented by Charles H. Rogers for court house and jail were thought to be superior to any others, and were consequently adopted, and the award offered in the advertisement was paid by an order drawn on the county treasurer.

April 19, 1837, the county clerk was directed to advertise through the columns of the *Northwestern Gazette* and *Galena Advertiser* for sealed proposals until June 1, for building a jail according to the plans adopted as above. This jail, as shown elsewhere, was completed in 1839.

This year (1837) a financial panic swept over the country and very materially interrupted the plans, purposes and undertakings of the people. There was a general cry of "hard times," and many promising business men were stranded by "shrinkage in values." Charles Peck, county treasurer, either out of his goodness of heart and mercy for tax payers, or for some other cause, failed to make an assessment, and on the 7th of September the county court ordered suit commenced against him on his official bond for such failure. Thomas Drummond, now a prominent U. S. Judge, but then a young lawyer of Galena, was retained on the part of the county.

The records of the Circuit Court show that the suit was commenced at the Fall term thereof, and that on the 19th of October the defendant (Peck) filed a demurrer to plaintiff's declaration. On the docket for the July term, 1838, under date of the 11th, this entry appears: "After argument by counsel, court takes time." There, so far as the judicial records show, the case terminates. Some of the surviving citizens of that period tell us that a compromise satisfactory to all parties was effected, and the case finally disposed of in that way.

As yet there was no way of raising money to defray the expenses of the county, except from taxes levied upon personal property. During the fiscal year ending on the first day of March, 1839, the legitimate expenses of the county were $11,408.16, and the receipts from all sources, $8,114.80, leaving a balance against the county of $3,293.36.

The following statement shows the real condition of the county from the first day of March, A. D. 1836 to the first day of March, A. D. 1839:

EXPENDITURES.

To amount paid on purchase of lots for court house	$ 296 22	
" " for paupers	1,539 34	
" " " roads	1,066 05	
" " " rent of court house	852 00	
" " " clerk of Circuit Court	173 25	
" " " " " County "	346 37	
" " " sheriff	838 10	
" " " county commissioners	671 00	
" " " guarding and boarding prisoners	1,169 61	
" " " miscellaneous	122 68	
" " " county treasurer	269 13	
" " " constables attending Circuit Court	84 00	
" " " stationery	110 37	
" " " elections	227 33	
" " " coroner	47 25	
" " " printing	9 00	
" " " stoves for court house	123 12	
" " " attorney's fees for attending suits in Circuit Court	508 75	
" " " court house	16,000 00	
" " " plans for and repairs on same	1,110 28	
Probable amount of county orders in circulation March 1, 1836	2,140 53	$27,704 38

RECEIPTS.

From merchants	$2,764 33	
" tavern keepers	2,267 58	
" auctions	100 00	
" ferries	495 00	
" sheriff for county taxes	628 60	
Due from sheriff for taxes 1838	1,015 31	
" " " interest on judgment	35 32	
" " fines in Circuit Court	720 00	
" " sheriff, July term, 1838	30 00	
" " justices of the peace	8 00	
From rent from basement of court house	50 66	$8,114 80

Amount of indebtedness from the organization of the county and first meeting of county commissioners in June, 1827 .... $19,589 80

The large excess of expenditures over the receipts, as shown in the above statement, is owing to the purchase of a part of the stone building on Main Street, known as the Dowling building, for the uses of a court house, etc. On Thursday, the 11th day of January, 1838, the county commissioners

Ordered, That for the purpose of providing a suitable court house and offices for the County of Jo Daviess, as required by law, the county commissioners of said county, on behalf of the same, having contracted with John Dowling for the purchase of a certain lot or piece of land in the town of Galena, being part of an extra lot of ground known and described on the town plat as lot No. 36, on the east side of Main Street, and containing thirty-three feet and two and a half feet of the adjoining lot, No. 37, together with a part of a stone building erected on the same, bounded northeast by the center of the wall dividing the entire building into two parts or tenements, under one roof; southwest by lot No. 35, owned by P. F. Scheimer; in front, by Main Street; and in the rear by Commerce Street, making the premises contracted for 35½ feet in front by 120 feet in depth, more or less.

And the said John Dowling, having given his obligation for certain additional improvements in the building, it is thereupon ordered by the court that, on said John Dowling and wife executing to the county a good and sufficient warranty deed for said premises, warrants, in sums as desired, on the county treasurer, to the amount of sixteen thousand dollars consideration for the premises, be issued in favor of said John Dowling, in the usual form, to bear six per cent interest from the first of March next.

At a special term of the County Commissioners Court, held on the 12th of September, 1837, an order was entered which shows that the building had already been used for holding a session of the Circuit Court, for it was

Ordered, That John Dowling be allowed $150 rent of house for Circuit Court, June term, 1837, and that W. H. Bradley be appointed agent to contract for the removal of the court room from the second to the ground floor.

The contract for the Dowling building was fully perfected as is shown by the following order under date of March 10, 1838:

Ordered, That W. B. Green be appointed agent for the County of Jo Daviess to lease such part of the Court House as was not needed for the uses of the Court or officers; also, that said Green take charge of the Court Room and offices, when the same shall be fitted up according to contract pending, and be authorized to contract for the use of the Court Room to the Episcopal Church at the rate of $200 per annum.

The Dowling building continued to be used as a court house until the building and completion of the present one. The counters, shelves, etc., that were in the building when it was purchased were disposed of by Thomas Drum, appointed to that duty by an order of the county court, also dated September 12.

At the same time the County Commissioners were contracting for the purchase of the Dowling property, it seems they were arranging to build a house for the same uses, for at a special meeting held on the 12th of September, 1838, it was ordered that W. B. Green "be allowed $225, for money paid C. S. Hempstead on note for court house lot." At was also

Ordered, That John L. Slaymaker and Samuel Mazzuchelli (a Catholic Priest) be appointed agents to superintend and oversee the architectural work which will be required in the building of a new court house for the county.

It is a little difficult for an ordinary mind to see the economy of paying $16,000 in county paper, for a house for county uses, while at the same time arrangements were being perfected for the erection of a court house building. The warrants paid to Dowling were not worth more than one third of their face value, and it is said they finally found their way into the hands of Pittsburg iron dealers, who, in after years, when the county had grown into good condition, financially, collected from the tax-payers their full face, together with the accumulated interest. This debt was not settled until some time in 1856, when, by order of the Board of Supervisors, and at the request of the holders of the warrants, smaller orders were issued in exchange for the larger ones. They subsequently fell into the hands of Nicholas Dowling, but were paid up in full.

Retrospective.—It is now necessary to go back a few years in order to bring up some details that have a bearing upon the grounds occupied by the county buildings. As previously stated Galena was laid off in 1836. The first act in relation to the matter was entitled "An Act to authorize the

E. A. Small

CHICAGO.

FORMERLY OF GALENA

laying off 'a town on Bean River, in the State of Illinois, and for other purposes,'" and was approved February 5, 1829. Section two of this act provided that it should be the duty of the "Surveyor to class the lots already surveyed, in the said Town of Galena, into three classes, according to the relative value thereof on account of situation and eligibility for business, without regard, however, to the improvements thereon, and previous to the sale of the said lots aforesaid, each and every person, or his, her or their legal representative or representatives, who shall heretofore have obtained from the agent of the United States a permit to occupy any lot or lots in the said Town of Galena, or who shall have actually occupied and improved any lot or lots in the said town, or within the tract of land hereby authorized to be laid off into lots, shall be permitted to purchase such lot or lots, by paying therefor, in cash, if the same shall fall within the first class, as aforesaid, at the rate of twenty-five dollars per acre; if within the second class, at the rate of fifteen dollars per acre; and if within the third class, at the rate of ten dollars per acre: *Provided*, That no one of the persons aforesaid shall be permitted to purchase by authority of this section more than one half acre of ground, unless a larger quantity shall be necessary to embrace permanent improvements already made."

July 2, 1836, an amendatory act (already published) went into effect, and on the 7th of July, 1836, under Van Buren's administration, appointments were issued to Daniel Wann and John Turney, of Galena, and General Samuel Leech, of Quincy, as commissioners provided for in the amendatory act of July 2, 1836. The following is the form and wording of the appointment:

TREASURY DEPARTMENT,
July 7, 1836.

SIR—I am instructed by the President to inform you that he has appointed you, in conjunction with Gen. Samuel Leech and John Turney, Esq., a Commissioner, under an "Act to amend an act entitled an act authorizing the laying off a town on Bean River, in the State of Illinois, and for other purposes, approved the 5th February, 1829"—a copy of which act I herein enclose you.

"The Commissioner of the General Land Office will be directed to give you all necessary instruction to enable you to proceed in the business of the appointment.

"I am, Sir, with respect, yr. ob't.,
LEVI WOODBURY,
Secretary of the Treasury.

DANIEL WANN, ESQ.,
Galena,
Illinois.

The instructions referred to above were very elaborate, and were as follows, as copied from the original:

GENERAL LAND OFFICE, 18th July, 1836.

GENTLEMEN:—By this day's mail there has been transmitted to you separate letters from the Secretary of the Treasury, notifying you that the President had appointed you Commissioners to carry into effect the provisions of the Act of the 2d instant, "to amend the Act entitled An Act authorizing the laying off a Town on Bean River, in the State of Illinois, and for other purposes, approved 5th February, 1829," and enclosing copies of the Act under which you are appointed, and which, in connection with the original Act of 1829, defines the duties required of you.

By the Act of 1829, it was provided that a tract of land not exceeding 640 acres, at and including "Galena," on Bean River, should be laid off, under the direction of the Surveyor General at St. Louis, "into town lots, streets and avenues, and into out lots, having regard to the lots and streets already surveyed, in such manner and of such dimensions as he may think proper," the town lots not to exceed one quarter of an acre each, and the out lots not more than two acres each. It being also provided that a strip of land of proper width on the River, and running therewith the whole length of the Town, should be reserved from sale for the public use and as a common highway. A plat of the survey, when it is completed, was to be returned to the Secretary of the Treasury. By the 2d Section of that law it was made the duty of the Surveyor General to divide the lots "*already surveyed*" into *three* classes, according to the relative value thereof, on account of situation and eligibility for business, without regard to the improvements made thereon, and previous to the public sale of the said lots, any person, or the Legal Representative of any person who had, previous to the date of that Act, obtained from the agent of the United States a permit to occupy any lot or lots in the Town of Galena, or who had previous to that date actually occupied and improved any lot or lots within the Town or within the limits of the tract so to be laid off, was permitted to purchase such lot or lots by paying therefor in cash if in the 1st class at the rate of $25 per acre; if in the 2d at $15 per acre; and if in the 3d at $10 per acre; provided, that no one person should be permitted to purchase by the authority of that section more than *one half* acre, unless a larger quantity was necessary to embrace the permanent improvements which had been made previous to the passage of this law. By the 1st Section, no Town Lot could be sold for less than $5. Under this law it appears to me:

1st. That in making the resurvey the Surveyor General was obliged to be governed "by the lots and streets already surveyed," or in other words, by the lines of the lots, streets, etc., which had been previously run under the restriction however of the first proviso that no Town Lot should exceed one quarter, nor no out lot more than two acres.

2d. That only such lots could be classed as had been actually surveyed previous to the date of the law.

3d. That the right of purchase prior to the public sale only vested in such persons or their Legal Representatives, as had previous to the date of the Act obtained from the Agent permits to occupy any lot or lots, or as had previous thereto occupied and improved any such surveyed and classed lots.

4th. That not more than one half acre can now be entered by any person or his Legal Representatives who obtained such permit, or who had so actually occupied and improved a lot or lots, unless an additional quantity is necessary to embrace the permanent improvements made previous to the date of the Act, and then only such quantity as may be necessary to include them.

5th. Where a permit was obtained for any Town Lot or lots exceeding a quarter of an acre, or for any out lot exceeding two acres, or where any such lots were occupied and improved, not exceeding two town lots of one quarter of an acre each, nor more than *one half* acre of any out lot can be entered, and the out lot must necessarily be subdivided so as to restrict the entry to that quantity, unless indeed, as before mentioned, it is necessary to exceed that area to embrace the permanent improvements, when such addition only is to be made to the half acre as may be required to include them.

6th. The Act specifies the minimum price at which any Town Lot, and the minimum rate per acre at which the classed lots are to be sold; for the out lots not so classed, no minimum is affixed, and therefore they are to be sold for whatever they will bring at auction.

By the Act of the 2d instant, the duties required to be performed by the Surveyor General by the Act of 1829 are to be performed by you as a Board of Commissioners, and in so doing you will be governed by the principles above mentioned, as well as the following instructions:

After taking the oath of office prescribed by the law, which is to be transmitted to this office, you will give public notice of the day upon which you will commence the investigation of claims under the 2d section of the Act, and you will keep a full and accurate record of all the evidence which may be offered in each case, and after having the Town surveyed in the manner required by the Act of 1829, designating the squares and lots by separate and regular series of numbers, you will file the evidence in each case, with your decision thereon, with the Register of the Land Office, accompanied by your joint certificate in favor of each person entitled to a pre-emption, designating the lot which he is to be permitted to purchase; these certificates should be regularly numbered and an abstract thereof transmitted to this office. In all cases where the right of entry is claimed under a permit from the Agent of the United States, the production of such permit, or of satisfactory evidence of its loss or destruction, and precise contents, must be required; and where the claim is based upon actual occupancy and improvement prior to the 5th February, 1829, satisfactory evidence of such actual occupancy and improvement prior to that time is indispensable. The affidavit of the claimant is in no case sufficient.

In making the survey of the Town, you will employ a competent and faithful person, who should be duly sworn, and you are authorized to allow him a fair and reasonable compensation for executing the work and making the required plats showing the designation, boundaries, and area of each lot. One copy of this plat is to be furnished, as required by the Act of 1829, to the Secretary of the Treasury, and another copy is to be furnished to the Register of the Land Office to guide him in selling the lots. The field notes of the survey must be deposited with the Register. Any reasonable contingent expenses (but not clerk hire) which may be incurred in carrying this Act into effect will also be allowed and paid by the Receiver. I send for your information and guidance a copy of the plan of the Town as laid out under the direction of the agent of the War Department.

The Act fixes your compensation at Six Dollars each, per day, for every day necessarily employed in the discharge of your duties, and you should therefore attach to your respective accounts a certificate that you were necessarily employed, in discharging your duties under the law, the number of days charged for. I am, very respectfully, your obt. servt.,

ETHAN A. BROWN,
Commissioner of the Gen'l Land Office.

Messrs. Daniel Wann, John Turney, and Samuel Leech,* Galena, Illinois.

August 20, 1836, two of the commissioners, Daniel Wann and John Turney, appeared before Samuel Smoker, a justice of the peace, at Galena, and subscribed to the oath of office as required by the law under which they were appointed. They then proceeded to business by notifying the commissioners of the General Land Office that they had organized, rented a room for the use of the commission, etc., and that the services of a clerk were indispensable, and that they had appointed Samuel Smoker, Esq., to that position. James Craig was appointed surveyor, he being in possession of the only field notes ever taken of the first survey in 1826–'7. August 25, the commission

Ordered, That notice be given by publication in the *Galenian* and *Northwestern Gazette*, that the commissioners have proceeded to survey the town of Galena, and that said notice be inserted for three weeks.

The commission also ordered "that suitable rocks, at least three feet in length, be procured, six inches of the top of them to be dressed and a hole half an inch deep drilled in the top as a point to measure from; these to be planted at least two and a half feet deep, with the top projecting above the ground at the commencement of each division of the town of Galena; and that at every station or change in the course of the streets, a rock shall be planted at least two feet in the ground, to perpetuate said angular point, and that each lot shall have wooden stakes drove at the corners, and that the front stakes on the streets to be marked with the appropriate number of the lot, and that all the measurements shall be horizontal, and with suitable leveling stones," etc., etc.

On the 26th, William B. Green, George W. White and John C. Bond were sworn to "faithfully measure and return a correct account of the measurement of the lots in the Town of Galena," etc. October 5, the commissioners (having adjourned on Saturday the 17th of September to Wednesday, October 5) "ordered that notice be given that the commissioners will be prepared to receive testimony on Monday the 17th instant, relative to claims to lots on the prairie from No. 1 to No. 46; on Monday the 24th instant, on all the lots between Main and Bench Streets, as far as Moses Meeker's garden, and on Monday the 31st, on all other lots included in the old survey, or within the limits of Galena, and that the Board of Commissioners would sit from day to day until the testimony was all taken."

Thus it will be seen that the first evidence of claimants of lots was heard on Monday the 17th of October, 1836. The commissioners journal of proceedings is preserved among the records of the Circuit Clerk's office. and an examination of its pages reveals some curious phases of human life. In many cases there were exciting contests between claimants, and all sorts of testimony was given. As claims were passed upon, certificates were issued to the rightful claimant, and were filed with the Register of the Land office of the district, where the land or lots were entered. As the net proceeds of the sales of lots, etc., were to be paid over to the county commissioners of Jo Daviess County to be used in the erection of public buildings,

*Mr. Leech did not qualify and appear as Commissioner until the 7th of February, A. D. 1838. Up to that time the business of the commission was conducted entirely by Messrs. Wann and Turney.

the improvement of wharves, etc., the order of the county commissioners requesting the Recorder of the Land Office to receive any money current in Illinois at the time, from the holders of pre-emption certificates to lots in Galena, is easily understood. At that time gold and silver was the standard currency at the U. S. Land Offices, and the object of the county commissioners was evidently to help the miners, mechanics, laborers and other citizens of the Galena of 1836 secure their homes with such money as might be in circulation here at the time.

The services of the pre-emption commissioners were continued from August 20, 1836, to March 29, 1838—about one year and seven months. Their last meeting was held at the date last written, when the following entry was made:

It appearing that all applications for the right of pre-emption have been decided, and the decisions entered of record, it is ordered that the board adjourn.

SAMUEL LEECH, }
JOHN TURNEY, } *Commissioners.*

In closing their official labors as commissioners for laying off the Town of Galena, etc., the undersigned state that they entered upon the discharge of their duties with much diffidence, arising from the novel and multifarious character of the claims they had to adjust and the rights they had to determine. They could find no precedent to guide them nor any general rules that could be applied to the cases arising under the law. Nor was it in their power to establish any. They consequently gave a liberal construction to the law and judged of every case according to its intrinsic merits, without regard to strictly legal technicalities. The course they have adopted, and the decisions they have made, they are proud to believe have met with the hearty appreciation of a great majority of their fellow citizens.

It is very evident the commissioners intended to append their signatures to this closing order, but for some reason unknown to the writer they failed to do so.

September 10, 1836, soon after the pre-emption commissioners entered upon a discharge of their duties, the county commissioners, being in session,

Ordered, That the commissioners for laying off the Town of Galena be requested to have reserved for public purposes that portion of ground on the prairie on the bottom between the cross streets running by Bernard Dignan's and Lawrence Ryan's, and in the rear of the tier of lots on Main Street, to the river; also any portion of the ground on what is called Meeker's Point, as may not belong to individuals.

This request appears to have been granted, for on page 40 of the pre-emption record the commissioners Wann and Turney say that "after mature deliberation, it is ordered that the lots on the prairie extend back from Main Street one hundred and twenty feet, and that a street of seventy feet wide, parallel thereto, be laid out, only making the angles on the cross streets, instead of the blocks, and that the residue of the ground between this street and Water Street be divided in its center, one half fronting on the street laid parallel to Main Street, and the other half fronting on Water Street, and that the square back of Benninger's and Ryan's be reserved for public uses, in conformity with the request of the County Commissioners Court of Jo Daviess County."

[The lots covered by the above order of the pre-emption commissioners are known as and described on the plat as No. 61, 62, 63 and 64. These lots were all entered by the president of the Board of Trustees of the Town of Galena, July 23, 1838. September 18, 1839, lot No. 62 was mortgaged by the Board of Trustees to William Tiernan for $200, which mortgage has never been satisfied, but remains unpaid, and, of course, is "outlawed." They are occupied by the market house.]

March 20 and 28, 1838, about the time the pre-emption commissioners were closing up the business of their appointment, and among the last business entries the following appears of record:

March 20, 1838. Present, Samuel Leech, John Turney, Daniel Wann. The County Commissioners of Jo Daviess County claim lot No. 64, above Meeker's, on behalf and for the benefit of said county, and in support of said claim produced a regular permit granting the same to the County Commissioners of said County, dated June 28, 1828, and signed by M. Thomas, Sup't U. S. lead mines. The Commissioners are therefore of the opinion that the County Commissioners of Jo Daviess County and their successors in office for the erection of public buildings are entitled to a pre-emption to said lot No. 64 above Meeker's for the use and benefit of the county aforesaid. Said lot fronting 134 feet on Gratiot Street, and running westwardly 217 8-12 feet, containing .669 of an acre of the first class. Certificate issued " March 28, 1838. Present, Samuel Leech and John Turney: The County Commissioners of Jo Daviess County claim lot No. 52, between Bench and Main Streets, and in support of said claim produced evidence that the same was occupied and improved in the years 1827, 1828 and 1829, by John Connelly, together with a deed from said Farrar dated May 22, 1829; also, an instrument of settlement between Amos Farrar, Russell Farnham and George Davenport, by which said Farnham and Davenport became joint owners of said lot with Farrar; also, a deed executed by James Craig, Horatio Newhall and D. G. Bates, Commissioners appointed by the Circuit Court of Jo Daviess County, at a public vendue ordered by said Circuit Court, for the sale of certain property belonging to the said Farrar, Farnham and Davenport, to James Bennett, dated January 7, 1834. It appearing, however, by a certified copy of the record of the County Commissioners Court of Jo Daviess County, filed in this case, that the said James Bennett "bid off" the same lot at the public vendue above mentioned by direction and under authority of the Commissioners of the said county, for the uses and purposes mentioned in said record—that said James Bennett received from said county one hundred dollars, it being the sum required to be paid down by the terms of said sale—that the said Commissioners have taken up the note given by the said James Bennett, to the said Craig, Newhall and Bates, Commissioners in "partition" aforesaid, for the balance of the purchase money (nine hundred dollars) for said lot.

The Commissioners are therefore of the opinion that the County Commissioners of Jo Daviess County are entitled to a pre-emption to lot No. 52, fronting 104½ feet on Bench Street, and running eastwardly 116 feet, containing .257 of an acre of the first class. Certificate issued.

Lot No. 51, center addition was entered by Thomas Fox, and by the administrator of the estate of Thomas Fox was conveyed to Thomas Drum.. September 29, 1838, Thomas Drum conveyed it to the commissioners of Jo Daviess County. Drum also conveyed to the county the lot (No. 17, block 24) on which the jail is situated. Lot No. 52 was entered by Nathaniel Head, and after one or two changes of ownership, was conveyed to the county.

Court House and Jail Redivivus.—Having traced up the origin of the title to the court house grounds, we return to the erection of the jail and court house. There were no records to show that the jail was built under contract, nor was there any person to be found who remembered the particulars attending its erection. There are several orders, however, made by the county commissioners that leave the inference that it was built by different mechanics, laborers, etc., under the direction of an agent appointed for that purpose by the county. For instance, September 13, 1838, a draft on the "cash fund of the county for $2,000 was ordered to issue to William H. Bradley, to be expended as required for the erection of the jail." The same day, W. B. Green was allowed "fifty dollars for his services as agent for erecting the county jail," and "Hughes & Co. were allowed $500 out of the cash fund for quarrying stone for jail foundation." At the same time "Thomas Drum, Abel Proctor and Elijah Charles were appointed to superintend the erection of the jail." This last order indicates the removal of W. B. Green as agent for the purpose. These several orders indicate pretty clearly that the jail was not built under contract. The plans presented by Rogers and approved by the court, as heretofore mentioned, were carried out, and the jail so far completed in 1839 as to be tenantable. It was not fully completed, however, as shown by an order of the Commissioners Court passed June 11, 1841, which provided for the appointment of Abraham Hathaway as agent "to complete the jail, now in an unfinished condition." No resident of Galena could be found by the historians who remembered the name of a single mechanic—stone mason, brick mason or carpenter—who was employed on its erection. Neither were any records to be found showing to whom money was paid for the purpose, or how much. The money ($2,000 already quoted) was directed to be paid to Bradley, and it is presumable that he paid it over to the workmen, and hence the fact that their names do not appear in the records.

The court house appears to have been built in like manner. March 9, 1839, it was "ordered (by the county commissioners) that Thomas Drum and Abel Proctor (now of Wright County, Iowa,) be appointed agents to superintend the erection of the court house, with full power to make and enter into contracts for the erection of the same, and to do all other acts and things which to them shall be deemed necessary for the prosecution and speedy completion of the said court house." The same day it was further "ordered by the court that William H. Bradley be appointed agent for the county to pay all bills certified by the agents of the county, of the laborers and contractors for work done in and about the erection of the court house, and to keep a correct account of all money paid, and all and every expense attending the erection of the same, and to make report of the same to the agents or to the court when it shall be required."

Of the many mechanics, laborers, agents, and others who bore a part in the erection of the court house, not many are now living. William H. Bradley, who was clerk of the County Commissioners Court at the time, and financial agent, is now clerk of the Circuit and District Courts for the Northern District of Illinois. Abel Proctor, one of the county commissioners mentioned, is a resident of Wright County, Iowa, and is in the eighty-third year of his age—hale, hearty and active, and as straight as an Indian. John L. Slaymaker, now an old man, lives near Albany, in this state. Richard Darigan, who, with John Hughes and Michael Gannan, made the excavation for the foundation walls of the court house, still lives in Galena and is court house janitor. He is an old man now, but hale, hearty, active and trustworthy. Hughes and Gannan are both dead. Andrew Telford (a brother of John Telford, who did the carpenter work) then a journeyman carpenter, helped to roof the building in the Spring of 1840—the year after he came here to join his brother John, and has ever since continued to make Galena his home. If the others of their associate workmen are alive, their whereabouts is unknown.

Messrs. Barrick & Russell are remembered by Mr. A. Telford as the stone masons who dressed the stone and laid up the walls.

It is remembered that there were some complaints from tax payers against what they conceived to be mismanagement and extravagance on the part of some of the managers or agents of the court house building. Rev. Father Mazzuchelli, who, with John L. Slaymaker, was appointed engineer to superintend and oversee the architectural work, was not backward, it is said, in his denunciation of the management of some of the authorities. Whatever grounds there may have been for these charges, it is certain that, notwithstanding the amount of money given to the county from the sales of the Galena town lots (amounting, as Mr. Daniel Wann thinks, to about

$18,000 * cash) the county treasury was so depleted that it became necessary to borrow money to complete the undertaking. December 4, 1839, the County Commissioners

Ordered, That the Senator and Representative of this district be requested to use their influence to have a special act passed by the legislature to authorize the County Commissioners of Jo Daviess County to mortgage real estate belonging to the county for the purpose of raising money in order to finish and complete the court house; and that the clerk forward to them a copy of this order.

An order of March 14, 1840, shows that the authority sought through the means of a special legislative enactment was granted, for on that day it was ordered that John Atchison be appointed an agent to negotiate a loan and to mortgage real estate belonging to the county as security therefor. From subsequent orders, it appears that the loan was effected, and the Dowling property so mortgaged as security. By an order made on the 14th day of May, 1840, Atchison was also authorized to mortgage lots numbered 51 and 52 (in so-called Centre Addition), fronting on Meeker and Bench Streets, and the new court house, in addition to the old court house. March 5, 1841, it was "ordered that John Atchison, commissioner, negotiate a loan for the completion of the court house, appointed by an order of this court at the March term, 1840, be requested to make a report to the next term of this court, of the amount of the loan effected by him, of the amount advanced by him from said loan, either to the order of the County Court or their agent, and of all his acts under said agency."

The "next term" of the court was held in June, the records of which show the following proceedings:

Friday Morning, June 11, 1841.

Court met pursuant to adjournment. Present, Messrs. Drum and Hathaway.

In pursuance of an order of this court at the March term thereof, 1841, John Atchison, Commissioner to negotiate a loan for the completion of the new court house, made his report, which is accepted by the court and ordered to be recorded, and is in the words and figures following, to-wit:

To the County Commissioners of Jo Daviess County, Illinois,

Gentlemen:—Under the authority of your court of the March term thereof, 1840, as commissioner to negotiate a loan for the completion of the new court house, I borrowed of Richard H. McGoon, on the 16th of May, 1840, seven thousand dollars, at ten per cent interest, payable annually, for which I mortgaged to Mr. McGoon lot No. thirty-six (36), part of lot No. thirty-seven (37), on Main Street, Galena, lots on which the old court house stands, and also lots fifty-one and fifty-two in Centre Addition, so called, on which the new court house is erected, of which sum I have paid out as per account rendered herewith, $3,427 02

I have accepted an order for	203 00
Balance in my hands at this date, say	3,369 98
	$7,000 00

With Respect, Your Ob't Servt.,

JOHN ATCHISON.

* A letter from Mr. Bradley, under date of "Office Clerk Circuit and District Courts, United States, Northern District of Illinois, Chicago, February 15, 1878," after referring to the fact of Congress providing for the "laying off a town on Bean River, in the State of Illinois, and for other purposes," the appointment of pre-emption commissioners, and their duties, etc., says: "The proceeds of the sale of lots, after the payment of the expenses of the commission, amounted to $35,000, which was paid over to the county commissioners by Col. John Dement, receiver of the land office then located at Galena." If this statement is correct, and Mr. Bradley ought to know, the people and tax-payers of 1878 will wonder why the necessity of borrowing money by mortgaging the Dowling property and the lots on which the court house stands, together with the new court house, to complete a building that ought not to have cost more than $25,000, at the most. If Mr. Bradley's figures are correct, the court house did not cost less than $60,000, or $65,000, as any one can see by following up the records and figures quoted.

Without attempting to follow up in detail all the orders, specifications, etc., of the county commissioners, their agents and others, in regard to the erection of the court house, suffice it to say, that, by the time the stone and mason work was completed, the money was all exhausted, and the building was left in an unfinished condition for several years. It was finished, however, in 1844. Captain Abner Eads, then a county commissioner, had been very active in his efforts to complete it, and personally superintended the removal of the offices from the old Dowling building.

The tablet over the entrance to the court house credits its erection to to the year 1839. It ought to be made to read "Commenced in 1839, and completed and occupied in 1844."

The McGoon loan, negotiated by John Atchison, by mortgaging the Dowling property, etc., was not fully settled until the year 1848. At a special meeting of the county commissioners held on the 24th day of January, of that year, the matter came up for consideration, and a final adjustment was effected. The debt was created by a special act of the Legislature, as heretofore mentioned, and another special enactment became necessary to help the commissioners out of the difficulty. The second special act authorized the imposition of a *special* tax for the payment of the mortgage held by McGoon, which mortgage was made under authority of an act of the Legislature, passed January 18, 1840.

On the 16th day of April, 1844, there was due on this mortgage $5,041.50, and there was to be issued in payment for the interest due or to become due on said mortgage, $504.15, which orders were to draw six per cent interest (subsequently increased to ten per cent). The commissioners ordered that the sum of $1,650 "at present collected under said special tax be paid over to said McGoon, in part payment of the principal sum of said mortgage," and the treasurer was further ordered to pay to the said McGoon the moneys to be collected under the special tax. McGoon agreed to continue to take orders in payment of the interest, and whenever the principal should be paid, McGoon agreed to release the mortgage and hold the orders for interest, merely like any other creditor. The county commissioners agreed, on the part of the county, "to pay such orders given, and to be given for payment of interest, with ten per cent interest on said orders, free from all objections of want of consideration, etc., etc.; it being expressly understood that this settlement is final and conclusive settlement forever, binding between the county and said McGoon. If the payment of the principal sum shall be made on said mortgage on or before the 16th of April, 1848, then the present year's interest is to calculated according to law, and an order for such sum is to be issued bearing ten per cent interest as heretofore. If the said principal sum is not so paid, as aforesaid, then the interest due on the principal which may not be paid at that time may be liquidated upon the same principle as heretofore laid down.

October 3, 1843, the county clerk was ordered to advertise for bids for furnishing the court house, according to plans on file, *to be paid in orders on the county treasurer at fifty cents on the dollar*. [See p. 212, County Commissioners' Record, No. 1].

November, of the same year, a contract for completing the joiners' work on the court house was let to John L. Slaymaker and John Lent.

March 6, 1844, Mr. Atchison made a final settlement, as loan agent, relative to which the following entry appears:

NEW YORK.

(FORMERLY OF GALENA).

On this day John Atchison rendered vouchers for payments made by him on account of the McGoon fund, amounting to the sum of $280.06, which were allowed by the court, and said Atchison is to be credited with interest thereon in final settlement on his account from the date of said payments respectively. Said allowances were as follows, to-wit:

Paid by J. A. to Slaymaker, Nov. 1, 1842	$181.50
Paid by J. A. to McNulty, Jan. 7, 1843	38.56
Paid by J. A. to McNulty, Jan. 7, 1843	60.00
Amount of vouchers	$280.06

July 6, 1844, a contract for plastering the court house was awarded to S. A. Rambo and J. B. Deneber, the contract to be completed "in time for the sitting of the next term of the Circuit Court, on the third Monday of October, 1844; and September 4, 1844, D. Hinkle was employed to paint the wood work of the court house, and have it in readiness by the next "term of the Circuit Court, on the third Monday in October next."

So endeth the court house chapter.

POOR HOUSE.

An examination of the records of the County Clerk's office reveals the fact, and a most commendable one, that from a very early period in the county's history, generous and humane provisions were made for the care of the poor, the sick, and the disabled, to whom fortune had denied her favors. In the earlier days their care and maintenance was secured under contract with suitable persons, who were governed or superintended by commissioners appointed by the County Commissioners Court. The records show that on the 6th of September, 1838, the following order was made:

For the purpose of affording relief to the sick and helpless individuals now in this county, the commissioners have this day contracted with Isham Hardin to furnish, on his part, house room in the dwelling now occupied by him for such persons as shall be directed or sent by the direction of a committee hereinafter mentioned, to the house of him, the said Hardin, and that he shall give such attention and assistance as shall be required by the persons thus sent or directed to his house, after being furnished by the committee aforesaid with the necessary provisions, etc., at the rate of one dollar and fifty cents a week for each person thus brought or sent to his house. And it is further ordered by the court that Philip Barry, R. W. Carson, George W. Fuller, P. F. Schimer and J. P. DeZoya be appointed a committee to attend, as often as necessary, at the house of said Hardin, for the purpose of furnishing provisions and other things which they shall deem necessary for the comfort and health of those in the care of Mr. Hardin aforesaid, and that they furnish the provisions necessary aforesaid, at the expense of the county.

Thomas Drum, Abel Proctor and James A. Mitchell were the county commissioners at this date.

An examination of the receipts and expenditures for different years, from 1836 to 1843, shows the following expenditures for poor purposes.

For the year ending March 1, 1836, $1,539.34; March 1, 1840, $4,257.60; March 1, 1841, $3,488.29; March 1, 1842, $1,160.69; March 1, 1843, $539.75.

A brief reference here to the financial condition of the county may not be out of place in this connection. On the first day of March, 1845, the indebtedness of the county over resources was $53,942.10; March 1, 1846, $63,392.66; March 1, 1847, $68,526.34; March 1, 1848, $67,776.55; March 1, 1849, $44,619.28. The indebtedness of the county was never fully paid off until 1875. During the war, time orders were issued by the board of supervisors, on which a loan of $229,000 was secured for war purposes. These orders bore eight per cent interest, but in 1875 the principal and interest and all other evidences of indebtedness were fully settled, and the county paper is now as good as gold.

June 9, 1848, notwithstanding there was an indebtedness of $67,776.55 hanging over the county, over and above its resources, the authorities took under consideration the purchase of a tract of land and the erection of buildings thereon for poor purposes. A tax of six mills on the dollar was ordered for general county purposes, and an additional tax of one half mill for poor purposes—that is, for the purchase of land for a poor farm and the erection of suitable buildings. In 1849 the poor tax was increased to one mill.

Thursday, July 5, 1849, W. B. Green, E. Graham, John Garner and John Lent were appointed a committee to devise plans for a poor house, with a view to building immediately. Sealed proposals for building the same had been invited by public advertisements, and July 19 the clerk was ordered to open the proposals deposited with him from contractors. The proposition of Messrs. Snyder & Willis was considered to be the most favorable, and was accepted, but at a subsequent meeting of the court it was

Ordered, That the building of the poor house be deferred until next Spring.

[December 3, 1849, the county commissioners were succeeded in the management of county affairs by a county judge and two associate justices, who continued to discharge such duties until the people of the county voted to adopt the township system in 1853.]

February 1, 1850, County Judge Bostwick, and R. Brown, as associate justice, sitting as a county court (in special session) for the transaction of county business, had the poor house under consideration. After the county commissioners had ordered that the building of the poor house be deferred, as in the above order, and some time during the month of December, 1849, or January, 1850, new bids for building the same had been invited. Under direction of Judge Bostwick the bids received were opened and severally recorded as follows:

Smith & Chambers	$5,975
H. J. Stouffer	6,000
A. Telford & Co.	7,050
O. Bardwell	6,998
Willis & Co.	6,890
John Rush	7,224
John L. Slaymaker	6,476

The contract was awarded to Chambers & Smith. March 4, 1850, they filed the required bond and made preparations to commence operations.

June 6, 1850, it was "ordered that all alterations from specifications and contracts for building poor house made and agreed upon by V. J. Blood with the contractors, to-wit: Chambers & Smith, be, and the same is, hereby approved." The building was completed as per contract, and a permanent home thus provided for the poor of Jo Daviess County.

The land upon which the poor house was built was bought of Matthew Fawcett, the deed bearing date January 30, 1849, and was described as follows: "The west half of the southeast quarter of section 27, town 28 north, range 1 east (excepting a small part thereof as not intended to be conveyed, of 8.50 acres), and also the east half of the southeast quarter of section 27, same town and range, containing eighty acres"—in all 151½ acres.

This farm and the poor house were successfully and satisfactorily managed until Saturday night, January 8, 1870, when the poor house proper was destroyed by fire. The inmates, forty in number, were at once transferred to a building known as the "Gratiot Building," at the fair grounds, where they were maintained until the completion of a new poor building in 1871.

In the meantime, the board of supervisors, February 23, 1870, voted to sell the old poor farm and purchase a new one. Messrs Switzer, Jones and Chapin were appointed as a committee to sell the old farm, and instructed not to sell it for less than $4,000. A new farm was looked up, and the Phillips place at Scales Mound selected and conditionally bargained for. The committee for the sale of the old farm found a purchaser in the person of James Roberts, and on the 22d of March, 1870, the supervisors, in consideration of the sum of $6,205, caused a deed to issue to him therefor,

The Phillips place at Scales Mound did not prove altogether satisfactory, and its purchase was given up, and the following described parcels of land (a part of it belonging to the old farm) purchased for $3,500. "Part of the northeast quarter of the southeast quarter ot section 28 and part of the northwest quarter of the southwest quarter of section 27, town 28 north, range 1, east of the 4th principal meridian, containing 38.03 acres; also, a strip of land 98 links in width off the west side of the northeast quarter of said section number 27, containing 1.97 acres." The deed from James Roberts to the County of Jo Daviess bears date January 2, 1871.

The new building was erected by Messrs. Stowe & Pepoon, and cost $5,560.80. It is a brick structure, built nearly upon the foundation walls of the old one, for the loss of which by fire the county received $5,000 insurance from the Underwriters of New York—almost enough to pay for the new one, without the loss involved in the sale of the whole of the old farm and the repurchase of a small part of it—about forty acres.

MISCELLANEOUS COUNTY COURT RECORDS.

The first will recorded in Jo Daviess County was made September 2, 1831, by Patrick Markey. He designated Robert Graham and Patrick Gray as his executors. He directed that his executors should endeavor to make such arrangement with his creditors that "what little personal property I possess and the house and lot on which I live, may not be sacrificed or sold for the payment of my debts, but wait for the payment of debts due me, and for rent arising from my said house, for the discharge of my debts. But if such arrangement can not be made with my creditors, then to sell only the personal property, and so soon as money sufficient can be collected, to pay, in the first place, a debt due to Mr. Edward McSweeney, amount not recollected." This will was signed in presence of John Turney, judge of probate, on the second, and recorded by him on the 8th of September, 1831.

The following marriage certificate was not the first, but is given for its literary style and the vein of humor running through it:

John Roberts
and
Elizabeth Davis. } *License issued 10th Dec., 1836.*

I, Samuel Smoker, a justice of the peace in and for the County of Jo Daviess and State of Illinois, do hereby certify that, according to the usages in such cases made and provided, and according to the ordinances of God in this behalf, I did join in holy and honored wedlock and in the bonds of everlasting love, the hearts and hands of the within named son and daughter of Adam, viz.: John Roberts and Elizabeth Davis; and consigning them to the blessing and protection of heaven, and to the enjoyment of long years of uninterrupted connubial felicity, I subscribe myself, SAM'L SMOKER, *J. P.*

License for the first ferry on Fever River at Galena was granted to John Foley and Abner Field, May 15, 1829.

The following is a memorandum of furniture belonging to the court house December 6, 1832: "One writing desk and case; one seal press; one table; four benches; judge's bench; two stationary benches in court house; one pigeon-hole desk."

March 7, 1833, it was

Ordered, That the present mail route from Galena to Farnhamsburg, at Rock Island, as marked by Daniel Fowler, Vance L. Davidson and John Kinney, be, and the same is, hereby declared a public highway—passing Rice's farm, the falls of Apple and Plumb Rivers, crossing the Marvais d'Ogee at the mouth, thence to Farnhamsburg.

TOWNSHIP ORGANIZATION.

Elijah M. Haines, in his "Laws of Illinois, Relative to Township Organization," says the county system "originated with Virginia, whose early settlers soon became large landed proprietors, aristocratic in feeling, living apart in almost baronial magnificence on their own estates, and owning the laboring part of the population. Thus the materials for a town were not at hand, the voters being thinly distributed over a great area. The county organization, where a few influential men managed the whole business of the community, retaining their places almost at their pleasure, scarcely responsible at all, except in name, and permitted to conduct the county concerns as their ideas or wishes might direct, was moreover consonant with their recollections or traditions of the judicial and social dignities of the landed aristocracy of England, in descent from whom the Virginia gentlemen felt so much pride. In 1834, eight counties were organized in Virginia, and the system, extending throughout the state, spread into all the Southern States, and some of the Northern States, unless we except the nearly similar division into 'districts' in South Carolina, and that into 'parishes' in Louisiana from the French laws.

"Illinois, which, with its vast additional territory, became a county of Virginia on its conquest by Gen. George Rogers Clark, retained the county organization, which was formally extended over the state by the constitution of 1818, and continued in exclusive use until the constitution of 1848. Under this system, as in other states adopting it, most local business was transacted by three commissioners in each county, who constituted a county court, with quarterly sessions. During the period ending with the constitutional convention of 1847, a large portion of the state had become filled up with a population of New England birth or character, daily growing more and more compact and dissatisfied with the comparatively arbitrary and inefficient county system." It was maintained by the people that the heavily populated districts would always control the election of the commissioners to the disadvantage of the more thinly populated sections—in short, that under that system, "equal and exact justice' to all parts of the county could not be secured. The township system had its origin in Massachusetts, and dates back to 1635. The first legal enactment concerning this system provided that, whereas, "particular towns have many things which concern only themselves, and the ordering of their own affairs, and disposing of business in their own town," therefore, "the freemen of every town, or the major part of them, shall only have power to dispose of their own lands and woods, with all the appurtenances of said towns, to grant lots, and to make such orders as may concern the well-ordering of their own towns, not repugnant to the laws and orders established by the General Court." "They might. also (says Mr. Haines), impose fines of not more than twenty shillings, and 'choose their own particular officers, as constables, surveyors for the highways, and the like.' Evidently this enactment relieved the * general court of a mass of municipal details, without any danger to the powers of that body in controlling general measures or public policy. Probably, also, a demand from the freemen of the towns was felt, for the control of their own home concerns.

"Similar provisions for the incorporation of towns were made in the first constitution of Connecticut, adopted in 1639; and the plan of township organization, as experience proved its remarkable economy, efficacy and adaptation to the requirements of a free and intelligent people, became universal throughout New England, and went westward with the emigrants from New England, into New York, Ohio and other Western States, including the northern part of Illinois."

Under these influences, the constitutional provision of 1848, and subsequent law of 1849 were enacted, enabling the people of the several counties of the state to vote "for" or "against" adopting the township system. This question was submitted to the people of the state on the first Tuesday after the first Monday in November, 1849, and was adopted by most of the counties north of the Illinois River—Jo Daviess being one of the exceptions.

February 12, 1849, the legislature passed a law creating a county court. Section one of this law provided "that there should be established in each of the counties of this state, now created and organized, or which may hereafter be created or organized, a court of record, to be styled the 'County Court,' to be held and consist of one judge, to be styled the 'County Judge.'" Section seventeen of the same act [see pp. 307–10, Statutes of 1858] provided for the election of two additional justices of the peace, whose jurisdiction should be co-extensive with the counties, etc., and who should sit with the county judge as members of the court, for the transaction of all county business, and none other.

The first session of this court in Jo Daviess County was held in December, 1849.

As previously noted, the question of township organization was voted on by the people of Jo Daviess County at the November election, 1849, but was defeated.

September 25, 1851, the County Court was petitioned to order another election in November on the same proposition. The election was so ordered, but the proposition was again defeated. The poll book for that year shows that 414 votes were cast for, and 746 against, township organization.

* The New England colonies were first governed by a "general court," or legislature, composed of a governor and a small council, which court consisted of the most influential inhabitants, and possessed and exercised both legislative and judicial powers, which were limited only by the wisdom of the holders. They made laws, ordered their execution by officers, tried and decided civil and criminal causes, enacted all manner of municipal regulations, and, in fact, did all the public business of the colony.

September 29, 1852, the County Court was again petitioned to order an election for the same purpose. The election was so ordered, and this time the proposition prevailed, but by what majority we are unable to state, from the fact that the poll book for the November (1852) election is not to be found. Neither is the poll book of the election held in November, 1849, on file among the other papers in the County Clerk's office.

Saturday, December 11, 1852, after the result of the election was known, the County Court, William C. Bostwick, County Judge, and Josiah Conlee and Richard Brown, Associate Justices, appointed Charles R. Bennett, George N. Townsend and David T. Barr to "divide the County of Jo Daviess into towns or townships.

February 15, 1853, this committee reported to the County Court that they had divided the county into townships, and established them as follows:

1. Fractional townships 28 and 29 north, range 5 east, to constitute one township, named Nora.

2. Fractional township 29 north, range 4 east, to constitute one township, named Courtland (now Warren).

3. Township 28 north, range 4 east, to constitute one township, named Rush.

4. Township 28 north, range 3 east, and fractional township 29 north, range 3, east, to constitute one township, named Thompson.

5. Fractional township 29 north, range 2 east, and that part of township 29 north, range 1 east, east of Fever (Galena) River, to constitute one township, named Scales (now Scales Mound).

6. That part of township 29 north, range 1 east, west of Fever River, and that part of township 29 north, range 1 west, east of the Sinsinawa River, to constitute one township, named Mann (now Vinegar Hill).

7. That part of fractional township 29 north, range 1 west, west of the Sinsinawa River, and fractional township 29 north, range 2 west, and fractional township 28 north, range 2 west, and that part of fractional township 28 north, range 1 west, west of the Sinsinawa River, to constitute one township, named Menominee.

8. Township 28 north, range 2 east, to constitute one township, named Gilford (now spelled Guilford).

9. That part of township 28 north, range 1 east, and that part of township 28 north, range 1 west, east of Fever River, and fractional township 27 north, range 1 east, and fractional township 27 north, range 1 west, to constitute one township, named East Galena.

10. That part of township 28 north, range 1 west, east of Sinsinawa River, and west of Fever River, and all that part of township 28 north, range 1 east, west of Fever River, to constitute one township, named West Galena.

11. Township 27 north, range 2 east, to constitute one township, named Elizabeth.

12. Township 27 north, range 3 east, to constitute one township, named Jefferson (changed to Woodbine).

13. Township 27 north, range 4 east, to constitute one township, named Stockton.

14. Fractional township 27 north, range 5 east, to constitute one township named Ward's Grove.

15. Township 26 north, range 4 east, and fractional township 26 north, range 4 east, to constitute one township named Pleasant Valley.

16. Township 26 north, range 3 east, to constitute one township named Derinda.

17. Township 26 north, range 2 east, and fractional township 26 north, range 1 east, to constitute one township named Hanover.

First Board of Supervisors, Elected April, 1853.—Harvey Mann, Mann Township, now Vinegar Hill; Beeri Serviss, Courtland, now Warren; Patrick McLeer, West Galena; Jonathan Hendershot, Derinda; C. C. Thompson, Thompson; James Findlay, Menominee; E. C. Hamilton, Stockton; M. Leekley, Council Hill; Samuel Knight, ———; James Harrison, Pleasant Valley; John W. Taylor, Guilford; Ambrose B. White, Woodbine; Halstead S. Townsend, Rush; S. K. Miner, Nora; Thomas B. Carter, Ward's Grove; John Lorrain, East Galena; W. J. Robinson, East Galena.

The first meeting of the board of supervisors was held on Monday, September 12, 1853. Harvey Mann, one of the old county commissioners, was chosen chairman. Richard Seal was county clerk.

At the June meeting of the board of supervisors, 1854, the following alterations were made:

Fractional section 18 and sections 19, 30 and the north half of section 31, in township 29, range 5 east, Township of Nora, be detached therefrom, and that the same be attached to the Township of Courtland, and to take effect from and after the fifteenth day of March, 1855.

18. The Township of Council Hill was created bounded as follows, to-wit:

Commencing at the northeast corner of section 17, on the state line in township 29, range 2 east; thence west along the state line five miles, to the northwest corner of section 15, township 29, range 1 east; thence due south on section line to the southwest corner of section 34, township 29, range 1 east; thence due east along the township line five miles to the southeast corner of section 32, township 29, range 2 east; thence north on the section line to the state line or place of beginning.

The Township of Mann was bounded as follows by order of the board of supervisors at the March term, in 1855, to-wit:

Commencing at the northeast corner of section 16, township 29, range 1 east; thence west along the state line to the northwest corner of section 15, township 29, range 1 west; thence due south on the section line to the southwest corner of section 34, township 29, range 1 west (which said section line is the division line between the Township of Menominee and the Township of Mann); thence due east along the township line to the southeast corner of section 33, township 29, range 1 east; thence due north to the state line or place of beginning.

The division line between Menominee and West Galena Townships was made as follows, by the board of supervisors at a meeting held in March, 1855, to-wit:

Commencing at the northeast corner of section 4, township 28, range 1 west; thence south on the section line one mile; thence west to the Sinsinawa River; thence down said river to the Mississippi River.

At the same meeting the following alterations were made in the Township of Woodbine, to-wit:

Sections 6, 7, 18, 19, 30 and 31 in township 27, range 3 east, Township of Woodbine, be detached therefrom, and that the same be attached to the Township of Elizabeth. (This was changed back, as originally, in June, 1855.)

19. At the February meeting of the board of supervisors, 1857, the following change was made in the Township of Pleasant Valley, to-wit:

All that part of fractional township 26, range 5 east, be struck off from the Township of Pleasant Valley and created a new township and established as such, by the name of Berreman.

20. At the September meeting, 1858, the following was erected, to-wit:

All of fractional township 29, north of range 3 east, being taken from the Township of Thompson, and the same be made a new and distinct township, and be named Apple River.

21. At the February meeting, 1859, the following township was created, to-wit:

All of fractional township 27, range 1 east, and all of fractional township 27, range 1 west, be taken from the Township of East Galena, and be made a new and distinct township, and be named by the name of Washington. (Changed to Rice.)

Since the changes as above noted, there have been a few others of minor importance. These are noted in the history of the townships they affect.

CIRCUIT COURT.

Previous to 1828 there was no court of adjudication on Fever River. The only written law in the mines was contained on a single page of foolscap, signed by the superintendents of the mines, and posted up at the most public place. These " regulations " provided for the settlement of disputes between miners, but in the ordinary business transactions, as in credits, the people were governed entirely by the laws of honor.

The fourth section of the act of February, 1827, establishing Jo Daviess County, constituted it a part of the first judicial circuit, and provided for terms of the Circuit Court to be held on the first Mondays in June and October, providing, also, that if the judge of the circuit was unable to attend at any regular term, he should notify the clerk, who thereupon should notify all the justices of the peace in the county, who should, or any three of them, attend and hold the court, and while sitting, were clothed with the same powers exercised by the judges, except as to capital offenses.

By another act of the same legislature, and approved the same day, the judge of the first circuit was required to hold a court in one of the counties below at the same time the court was to be held in Jo Daviess. Of course the judge could not preside in both counties on the same day, and left the new county of Jo Daviess to take care of itself and organize its own court. Both terms in 1828 were accordingly held by justices of the peace, in compliance with the law, but the people complained that they were not treated as well as the other counties were treated, and the justices' court failed to satisfy them.

The first term of the Circuit Court commenced on Monday, June 2, 1828, by three justices: Connolly, Coulter and Field. The attorney for the court was not present, either in person or by deputy, and the court appointed Jonathan H. Pugh " to prosecute at this term."

The first case of record was that of Andrew Arnett, James Arnett and Houston Barton, partners, doing business under the name and style of Andrew Arnett & Co., vs. Thomas Jordan and Kinchen Odom. " It appear-

Wm. H. Bradley

CLERK U.S. COURTS. N. DIST. OF ILLS.

CHICAGO

FORMERLY OF GALENA

ing to the court that 'the process in this case not having been served on the defendants, it is ordered that this case be continued till the next term of this court, and that an *alias* issue.'"

On the first day of this term James A. Clark, a Missouri lawyer, was permitted "to practice at this term, and until the next term of this court."

The first indictment returned was on the second day of the term against Michael Dee, for assault and battery, with intent to murder. Dee was arrested at once, brought into court, arraigned, and pleaded not guilty. A jury, consisting of William Tate, Alexis Phelps, William Brasure, John Barrel, Peter Carr, James Langworthy, James Smith, Dawson Parish, H. H. Gear, James Kindall, John Ray and William Henry, were "elected, tried and sworn." The defendant, by his attorney, "moved to exclude the testimony of Daniel Harrison and Warren Spears, and that they be sworn to answer whether they believed in a future state of rewards and punishments. The witnesses said they knew nothing about it, and they would not swear to any thing which they did not know." This answer was evidently satisfactory to the court, as the witnesses were sworn. The case was tried, and the jury brought in a verdict of "guilty."

Thus, the first case was commenced and completed in one day.

June 4, the jury brought in thirty-four bills of indictment, and the court ordered capiases to issue, returnable instanter.

June 5, Joseph Payne and James M. Strode were fined ten dollars each for contempt, and the sheriff was ordered to take their bodies and keep them in custody until the fines were paid.

Abbott & Swan were indicted for retailing spirits without a license. Moses Swan appeared, was tried and acquitted.

In a number of similar cases defendants pleaded guilty, and were fined ten dollars each and costs.

The first divorce case in the county was entered by Mary Hall against John Hall.

The first term adjourned June 12, after ordering a special term to be held on the third Monday in August, for the trial of chancery causes.

At the second term, commenced Monday, October 6, 1828, Justices Connolly, Harris and Field presided, and "P. H. Winchester presented an appointment from the attorney general to prosecute in this court at this term as his deputy."

Among others fined for contempt at this term was William S. Hamilton, who was fined $5. There was apparently no little contempt of court in those days, and the court was determined that it should be properly respected.

During the Winter of 1828–'9 the legislature changed the time of holding court in this county, and the third term commenced on Monday, May 11, 1829. Judge Richard M. Young presided.

A grand jury was impanelled in due form as follows: William P. Tilton, William Hempstead, Elisha Blanchard, William Bennett, Charles D. St. Vrain, Moses Hallett, H. H. Gear, David McNair, A. T. Crow, David G. Bates, D. B. Morehouse, A. R. Howe, Dennis Murphy, James Wanton, Horatio Newhall, Thomas K. Rice, Hiram Watson, James Bennett, Lewis Curtis. David G. Bates was appointed foreman, and the first court in Jo Daviess County held by a judge was in operation. Albion T. Crow and Horatio Newhall were discharged from the panel, as they were physicians, and John Ankeny and H. Smean were sworn in their places.

On the 12th of November, 1829, Robert B. Bartlett, a Scotchman, made declaration of his intention to become a citizen of the United States—the first act under the naturalization laws in the Circuit Court of Jo Daviess County.

At the circuit court begun and held at Galena April 6, 1835, Sidney Breese produced his commission as circuit judge of the Second Judicial Circuit.

Since April, 1835, the judges in regular order have been:

August term, 1835, Stephen T. Logan.

April 4, 1836, Thomas Ford, Sixth Judicial Circuit. [Mr. Ford was afterwards (in August, 1842) elected governor of the state, and served four years. He died at Peoria in 1850.]

April 10, 1837, Dan Stone.

March 2, 1841, Thomas C. Browne.

March 9, 1849, Benjamin R. Sheldon.

March —, 1870, William Brown.

CRIMINAL MENTION.

Considering that many of the early miners of the Fever River country were adventurers or fortune hunters, rather than settlers—that is, people who came to found homes—the criminal calendar of the circuit court has always been remarkably free from records of a very atrocious character. This fact is due, perhaps, more to the firm, unyielding, uncompromising and determined character—the honesty and sterling moral worth of the early permanent settlers, like the Harrises, Meekers, Newhalls, Proctors, Greens, Bates, Langworthys, the Gears and the Hempsteads, and others of their associates—who came to make homes in the mineral wilds of Fever River, than to any other cause. However determined and guarded as these pioneer fathers were, desperate characters—gambling adventurers—would often find their way to the mines, and, after a time, throw off all disguise and seek to over-awe and over-ride every one who, in any way, interfered with their plans and purposes. This has been the history of all mining regions—of all new countries. But as true as it may be, the history of Galena and of Jo Daviess County is freer from capital offenses—atrocious murders—perhaps, than almost any other county in the state, and it is a credit to the names of the people who pioneered the way to the wealth, population and intelligence of 1878, that, through all the changes—from chaos and absence of all written or statute law when the Johnsons came in 1821—to the present, so far as any positive knowledge exists, not a single case of lynch-law stains the name of Jo Daviess County. No other mining district, so far as the knowledge of the writer extends, can show the same record. Murders, it is true, have been committed, but these have been atoned through means provided by the law. There have been other criminal offenses, but in no case have the people taken the law into their own hands. In only one instance has the capital sentence been executed, and that was in the case of Taylor, who was hanged on the 19th of February, 1855, on the charge of murdering his wife. The circumstances in brief were as follows:

In the Galena *Gazette*, of December 7, 1877, we find a summary of the several murders and murder trials in the county, prepared by George W. Perrigro, Esq., associate editor of that paper, from which we make the following extracts. In his introductory to this *resume*, Mr. Perrigro says:

"The citizens of Jo Daviess County have been frequently shocked by foul and bloody tragedies which have occurred in their midst; yet this section has not been distinguished in this regard above others, for crime is the natural offspring of all localities, and will be so long as justice is a mockery and the statute books a dead letter."

Taylor Wife Murder.—The first notable crime which was committed within the borders of the county was the murder of Mrs. Taylor, by her husband, John I. Taylor, who suffered the death penalty as an atonement for the deed. Since that time murderers have got off with various terms of imprisonment, from three years to life sentences. The facts connected with the Taylor murder were briefly as follows: Taylor resided in the upper story of a dilapidated frame house in Old Town, near the bank of the creek. A man by the name of Rosenburg occupied the first floor, and is said to have been on too intimate terms with Taylor's wife. One night in the month of October, 1856, Taylor reeled home drunk, and began to abuse his wife. Rosenburg heard the disturbance overhead, and went up for the purpose of quelling it. Taylor, enraged at the sight of the man whom he imagined was criminally intimate with his wife, seized a gun and struck at Rosenburg, who had turned for the purpose of fleeing down stairs. At that instant Mrs. Taylor stepped between the two men, and received the blow on the side of her own head, crushing in the skull.

As already stated, Taylor was arrested, tried, found guilty, and sentenced to be hanged. The jury was made up of W. L. Waterman, Jonathan Hendershot, John Morgan, William Green, Thomas Thompson, Thomas Hamilton, Nicholas Shott, Joseph Hempstead, William Ball, Bazil Meek, Addison Philleo and John B. Hornell. The death sentence was rendered by Judge Ben R. Sheldon, before whom the case was tried, on Thursday, November 30, 1854, and Taylor was ordered to be hanged on "Friday, the nineteenth day of January next (1855), between the hours of ten o'clock in the forenoon and four o'clock in the afternoon of that day." The verdict of the law was carried out on the day above named by W. R. Rowley, sheriff. The scaffold was erected on the poor house farm, and the execution was open, and witnessed by as many as five thousand people. That was the first and last execution in Jo Daviess County. It has been said that one of the principal witnesses, and the only important one against Taylor, confessed on his death-bed that he was the one who killed Mrs. Taylor, and that Taylor was innocent. As to the truth or untruth of this rumor the people differ. But, true or false, the confession, if one was made, came too late to save Taylor's life, or to affect him for either weal or woe.

The Shay Case.—"In 1855, one Michael Shay, of Pleasant Valley, murdered a citizen of that place, whom he followed home from a saloon in which they had been drinking, and felled him to the ground with a club. Shay escaped from justice, and was never afterwards apprehended."

The Howe-McCarty Murder.—"A year later, a man named McCarty was stabbed to death by a blacksmith named Bat Howe, on his wedding day, and was taken home to his bride a corpse. McCarty was a currier, in the employ of Grant (Gen. Grant's father) & Perkins. He was married at the Four Mile House, now kept by Joseph Greibe. He returned to town with the priest who performed the ceremony, and on the way back was met by Howe, at the beginning of the plank road at Franklin Street, who charged him with having asserted that he (meaning McCarty) was a better man than Howe was. A fight ensued, during which McCarty fired a revolver at Howe twice. The first shot passed over his head, while the second entered his shoulder. Howe then whipped out a clasp knife and plunged it deep into the thigh of his antagonist, who died within two minutes after receiving the wound. Strange to say, the deed was witnessed by Circuit Clerk W. R. Rowley, Deputy Sheriff Wm. Pittam, and other officers, who were at that time searching in that neighborhood for an escaped prisoner, and the desperado Howe was arrested by the fearless Pittam and escorted to jail before the blood of his victim had fairly cooled. He was tried for manslaughter, convicted, sentenced to state prison for seven years, and died during his incarceration."

McCarty Wife Murder.—"The murder of Mrs. McCarty, in East Galena, by her husband, and the subsequent suicide of the latter, is well remembered by the older citizens. The tragedy occurred in 1859. McCarty lived with his wife, in a small frame house just back of the Normal School building. One night, maddened by drink, he went to his isolated home, dragged his wife out of doors by the hair, beat her to death with a club, carried the body into the house, and applied the torch to the building, to destroy the evidence of his guilt. The charred remains of the murdered woman were found, and McCarty was arrested and confined in jail. Shortly after the coroner's inquest had been concluded, McCarty obtained possession, in some unknown manner, of a razor, and drew the blade of the instrument across his neck, severing the windpipe. He lived eleven days without taking nourishment of any kind, and died a most horrible death, filling the grave of a murderer and suicide."

Zowar-Keller Murder.—"The next notable murder occurred in 1866, when Peter Zowar, frenzied by jealousy and a desire for revenge, repaired to the house of a Mr. Keller, residing in the Town of Guilford, armed with a revolver. Mrs. K. heard the desperado about the premises, and raised the window for the purpose of reconnoitering. She had no sooner put her head out of the window than Zowar fired at her, shooting her fatally through the body. Keller then rushed to the window, only to be a target for the murderer below, whose shot fortunately missed him. The former then ran down stairs, and, arming himself with a shot-gun, opened the front door and fired at Zowar, who was taken unawares. The latter received the contents in his breast, but, as the shots were small, they did not produce more than a slight wound. He fled the neighborhood that night, and was subsequently arrested in Northern Kansas by Sheriff Luke and S. K. Miner, Esq., and brought back to this city for trial. He was granted a change of venue to Stephenson County, was tried, convicted, and sentenced by Judge Sheldon to state prison for life. The incentive to the crime was hatred for the parents, who refused to permit him to visit their daughter."

The Ably Case.—The last murder trial that stains the criminal records of Jo Daviess County was concluded on Saturday, December 1, 1877. "Other crimes have been committed in Jo Daviess County, but for cold-bloodedness, premeditated design and systematic planning, the Ably murder of the 16th of last September ranks pre-eminent, as stated in the outset, above every other kindred crime that has transpired within the county. A son having assassinated his own father in a most cruel way, made it all the more shocking, and the deed will forever hereafter be pointed at as the blackest stain upon the annals of the county. Yet there are extenuating circumstances connected with the murder, which, in our history of the affair, ought not to be omitted, in justice to the wretched young man now confined in prison for the offense. These facts were brought to light by the officers during their untiring efforts to bring the guilty party to justice, and furnish a history of crime and mystery which will be perused with the greatest interest by our readers.

"Unveiling the past."--A portion of the land owned by Jacob Ably was originally entered by one Hiram N. Byers, who emigrated to this section before civilization had scarcely planted its banner in this part of the Great West. Byers' family consisted of his wife, one boy and a girl. The wife of Jacob Ably, the murdered man, then a young unmarried woman, was employed in the house of Byers as a servant, having emigrated to Council Hill from Chicago, One morning, Byers' wife died suddenly, and her rapid burial excited considerable comment on the part of the settlers. Soon after the death of the lady, the servant girl was advanced to the position of housekeeper and was subsequently married to Byers. Six months after this event, the girl by the first wife died suddenly, and, like its mother, was hurriedly buried. About that time Jacob Ably, who had just arrived in America from Switzerland, was employed on the farm of Byers, and became intimate with the latter's wife, who it is asserted, had a child by him, a girl, shortly after her marriage with Byers. One other girl was born, and soon after its entry into this world, the father of the child died in a mysterious manner. He retired to bed well and hearty at night, and before the dawn of the morrow, he was stiff in death. No investigation was ever had, and the story that Byers had died of cholera was generally credited, though some there were who shook their heads in doubt, believing that a foul murder had been committed. A few weeks after the death of Byers, his son, to whom he had secretly willed his property, left the house, transferring his interest in the estate to his step-sisters. No one knows where he went, nor has any one ever heard from him since his departure. In the course of time, Jacob Ably married the widow Byers, and shortly after their union the two girls, to whom had been transferred the estate, with the exception of a third interest, died within two weeks of each other, from causes which many regarded as unnatural. The property was inherited by the mother of the children, at that time the wife of Ably, and having been held in her name up to the time of her death, was the source of much trouble between them, and led to her melancholy suicide, and still later to the assassination of Ably. The latter vainly besought his wife in her lifetime to dispose of her farm and go to Nebraska. Refusing to accede to his wishes, Ably treated her in a brutal manner, and, as is claimed by the boys, beat her frequently. In February last, her body was found hanging to the limb of a tree in the back yard, and was dragged into the house by the husband, who had slept in a separate room that night. She was frozen stiff, and had died from strangulation. A jury was summoned, an inquest was held, and a verdict rendered to the effect that the unfortunate woman had committed suicide by hanging herself as indicated above. As soon as the grave closed over her remains, it began to be whispered about that she might have been murdered.

"There was but little evidence tending to criminate the husband, and it finally resolved itself into a dark suspicion which none dared to give utterance to except the boys of Jacob Ably, who openly charged their father with first having made way with the old lady, and then to cover up the crime, placed her in the position in which she had been found. They claimed that there were marks about her person, that they had had trouble the night before, and that their mother had been heard to moan and cry out with pain during the night. These stories may have been manufactured for the purpose of mitigating the awful crime which formed the sequel to the mysterious record detailed above.

"The circumstances attending the assassination of Jacob Ably are well remembered by our readers, and appear in detail in the voluminous report of the testimony adduced on the trial. * * * * Ably was a native of Glaris, Switzerland, was about 52 years of age, and a farmer by occupation. He was well known hereabouts, and regarded as an honest and industrious man. It has been stated, though not offered in evidence during the trial, that he informed parties in this city shortly before the murder, that he was afraid his boys would kill him. That they were dissatisfied, and would not remain at home, and that they wanted to get the farm into their own hands.

"The circumstances attending the arrest of the three Ably boys and Peter Miller, Sr., and Peter Miller, Jr., are also still fresh in the minds of all, and will not bear repetition here. It will be remembered that the elder Peter Miller was discharged, there being no evidence to criminate him. The remaining four boys were retained in custody, and at the recent session of the Grand Jury, Joseph, Henry, and Jacob Ably were severally indicted on the testimony of young Peter Miller, who had turned States evidence in the vain hope of saving his own head.

"Miller's story was to the effect that on the afternoon of the 16th of September, 1877, he accompanied Joseph Ably, then employed on the farm of John D. Brown, of the Town of Rush, across the country on foot, to the premises of the elder Ably, in Council Hill Township, eighteen miles away, for the purpose of stealing grapes from the latter's vineyard. That, during the journey over, Joseph Ably took from a corn shock, a musket, a revolver, and a box of cartridges. Arriving at the bottom in front of the house, they stopped to rest, when Miller asked young Ably to go up with him after the grapes. The latter replied: 'Wait a minute. I will go and see where the old man is.' This was about 8 o'clock in the evening. Young Ably, gun in hand, cautiously opened the barnyard gate, and, followed by Miller, crossed to the gate opening into the premises at the rear of the house. Miller testified that he remained at this second gate while Joseph entered the yard and passed around the back of the house. A moment after he had gone, Miller says he heard the report of fire-arms, and, rushing in the direction of the sound, he met Joe Ably fleeing toward him precipitately, and was by him urged to run, lest he be caught.

"The trial of this case came on at the September term of the Circuit Court, 1877, commencing on Monday, the 26th. Tuesday noon, the 27th, the following named jurors were obtained, after exhausting the regular panel and several special *venires:* Albert Stevenson, Dunleith, livery stable keeper; Joseph Gothard, Woodbine, farmer; John McFadden, Apple River, farmer; D. Mahoney, Vinegar Hill, farmer; G. Engles, Galena, shoemaker; W. Whippo, Galena, carpenter; T. E. Reynolds, Galena, dry goods clerk; L. Weisegarber, Galena, shoemaker; R. S. Bostwick, Galena, chair maker; E. A. Wilson, Galena, dry goods clerk; Conrad Bahwell, Galena, clothing merchant; W. H. Bond, Galena, painter.

"The people were represented by prosecuting attorney E. L. Bedford, and the prisoners by Messrs. Williams and Hodson, comparatively new practitioners at the Galena bar. The court room was crowded with spectators during the continuance of the trial, and the evidence of Peter Miller and Max St. Bar, who occupied a jail cell with Ably, was listened to with intense interest on the part of the court, the bar, the jury and the vast crowd of spectators.

"Joseph Ably, the principal figure in the trio, is a young man about nineteen years of age, with beardless face, brown, restless and sharp eyes, broad chin, firm-set mouth, high forehead, dark hair and florid complexion. He is about five feet eleven inches high, and during the whole of the trial manifested a nervousness and restless manner which was proof conclusive of his guilt. His brother Henry, strongly suspected of being accessory to the murder, is about five feet six inches in height, is a cripple, with piercing dark eyes, black hair and black mustache, and a defiant, careless look which militated more than a little against him, and which, in the absence of positive testimony, came very near sending him to a felon's cell. Jacob, the elder of the three, possessed a manly bearing, a frank, though sad, face, and impressed every one who saw him with his innocence. His acquittal was generally expected, and the verdict, so far as he was concerned, was, therefore, a surprise to no one.

"On Friday noon, the defense rested their case, and on the following day (Saturday), after lengthy and able arguments on the part of Messrs. Williams & Hodson for the prisoners, and E. L. Bedford, Esq., for the people, his honor charged the jury, and at half-past 2 o'clock, P. M., they retired to their room for consultation. At 6 o'clock they propounded the following query to his honor, Judge Brown:

"*To the Court:*

"Can the jury, if they find Henry Ably guilty, impose a sentence of less than fourteen years in the penitentiary?

"RICHARD S. BOSTWICK, *Foreman.*"

"In answer to the inquiry of the jury, the court instructs the jury that the least punishment it can inflict for murder is imprisonment in the penitentiary for fourteen years."

Having received the above instructions, the jury, at 7 o'clock, returned into court, with a verdict of not guilty as to Henry and Jacob, and guilty as to Joseph Ably, fixing his sentence at state prison for life. As soon as the verdict was announced, the wretched young man hung his head, while Mr. Williams, one of his attorneys, vainly sought to encourage him with words of cheer. The brothers, Jacob and Henry, were permitted to go free by his honor, the jail doors were locked upon the parricide, and he was left to ponder upon the awful crime he had committed and the dreadful future which awaited him.

"On Monday afternoon, October 3, at 3 o'clock, the motion for a new trial filed by his attorneys having been withdrawn, he was removed from his cell to the court house, for the purpose of having sentence pronounced upon him by the court, according to the requirements of the law. He had become in a measure reconciled to his doom, and was calm and apparently unmoved when brought into the presence of his honor and the large number of spectators who had assembled to witness the solemn scene. When asked if he had aught to say why sentence should not be pronounced upon him, he replied in a firm voice, 'No.' His honor, thereupon, in an eloquent and fervent manner, his voice tremulous at times with emotion which well nigh overcame him, addressed the prisoner, a death-like stillness pervading the court house the while."

Mr. Perrigo says of this address: "There was scarcely a dry eye in the court room during the address of his honor to the prisoner, and not one person within the sound of his voice who was not more or less affected by the solemn drama which had been enacted. Immediately after sentence had been pronounced, the prisoner was escorted to jail, where he was confined until evening, when he was put on board the 10 o'clock train, and, in company with six companions in crime, was conveyed to Joliet, under charge of Deputy Sheriffs Wm. Barner, of Galena, and M. S. Murphy, of Warren."

Ably's Confession.—On Monday forenoon, October 3, Mr. Perrigo visited the doomed Ably in his cell at the county jail, and succeeded in obtaining the confession from the parricide, of the terrible crime, which was subsequently sworn to before W. W. Wagdin, Master in Chancery. "The young man," says Mr. Perrigo, "told the story with remarkable nonchalence, though he seemed somewhat loth to come down to the real facts connected with the murder. The statement corroborated the testimony of St. Bar, and disclosed more fully than was shown during the trial, the circumstances connected with this most diabolical plot of Ably's to assassinate his own father."

Of the attorneys engaged in the trial of this case, the *Gazette* said: "We can not close our lengthy report of this, the most important criminal trial ever held in Jo Daviess County, without saying a word in commendation of Prosecuting Attorney Bedford, who managed the case on the part of the people with consummate skill, and in a manner highly creditable to him as a lawyer. The case was beset with almost insurmountable obstacles from the start, and had it not been for his untiring exertions, combined with the assistance rendered by Sheriff Barner, S. K. Miner, Esq., Detective Murphy and Deputy Sheriff Wm. Barner, a conviction could not have been secured.

"We also take pleasure in complimenting Messrs. Hodson & Williams, the attorneys for the defendants, for the ability shown by them in the management of their case. They are both graduates of the Ann Arbor Law University.

EDUCATIONAL.

The first schools taught in Jo Daviess County were private or subscription schools. Their accommodations, as may readily be supposed, were not good. Sometimes they were taught in small log houses, erected for the purpose. Stoves and such heating apparatus as are in use now were unknown. A mud and stick chimney in one end of the building, with earthen hearth, with a fire-place wide enough and deep enough to take in a four-feet back log, and smaller wood to match, served for warming purposes in Winter and a kind of conservatory in Summer. For windows, part of a log was cut out in either side, and may be a few panes of eight-by-ten glass set in, or, just as likely as not, the aperture would be covered over with greased paper. Writing benches were made of wide planks or, may be, puncheons, resting on pins or arms driven into two-inch augur-holes, bored into the logs beneath the windows. Seats were made out of thick planks or puncheons. Flooring was made of the same kind of stuff. Every thing was rude and plain, but many of America's great men have gone out from just such school-houses to grapple with the world and make names for themselves, and names that come to be an honor to their coun-

J. B. Brown

EDITOR GALENA GAZETTE

try. Among these might be named Abraham Lincoln, America's martyred President, and one of the noblest men ever known to the world's history. In other cases, private rooms and parts of private houses were utilized as school-houses, but the furniture was just as plain.

But all these things are changed now. A log school-house in Illinois is a rarity. Their places are filled with handsome frame or brick structures. The rude furniture has also given way, and the old school books—the "Popular Reader," the "English Reader" (the best school reader ever known in American schools), and "Webster's Elementary Spelling Book"—are superseded by others of greater pretensions. The old spelling classes and spelling matches have followed the old school-houses, until they are remembered only in name. Of her school system Illinois can justly boast. It is a pride and a credit to the adopted home of the great men this great state has sent out as rulers and representative men—men like Lincoln, Douglas, Grant, Shields, Lovejoy, Yates, Washburne, Drummond, and hundreds of others whose names are as familiar abroad as they are in the histories of the counties and neighborhoods where once they lived. While the state has extended such fostering care to the interests of education, the several counties have been no less zealous and watchful in the management of this vital interest. And Jo Daviess County forms no exception to the rule. The school-houses and their furnishings are in full keeping with the spirit of the law that provides for their maintenance and support. The teachers rank high among the other thousands of teachers in the state, and the several county superintendents, since the office of superintendent was made a part of the school system, have been chosen with especial reference to their fitness for the position.

The present superintendent of county schools is Robert Brand, Esq., who was first elected in November, 1873, and re-elected in November, 1877. From Mr. Brand's last report to the State Superintendent, the following statistics are compiled:

Number of males under 21 years of age	7,435
Number of females " " " "	7,363
Total	14,798
Number of males between 6 and 21 years	5,092
Number of females " " " "	5,002
Total	10,094
Number of school districts	121
Number having school five months or more	119
Average number of months school sustained	7.5-24
Number of male pupils enrolled	3,861
Number of female " "	3,516
Total	7,377
Number of male teachers enrolled	88
Number of female " "	153
Total	241

Grand total number of days' attendance, 607,110, being equal in school time (*i. e.*, nine months of four weeks each, and five days to a week) to 3,372 years, 7 months and 2 weeks.

Highest monthly wages paid to any male teacher	$111 11
" " " " female "	50 00
Lowest " " " male "	16 00
" " " " female "	15 00
Average " " " male "	47 17
" " " " female "	26 49
Value of school libraries	486 00

Total receipts during the year	$ 66,381 75
Total expenditures during the year	56,451 10
Balance in the hands of treasurers	9,850 65
Estimated value of school property	109,355 00
Estimated value of apparatus	2,134 00
Principal of township fund	51,126 47
Number of different places where examinations were held	13
Whole number of examinations held	35
Whole number of male applicants examined	16
Whole number of male applicants examined for second grade certificates	88
Whole number of female applicants examined during the year for first grade certificates	25
Whole number of female applicants examined during the year for second grade certificates	235
Total number examined	28
Total number of second grade certificates issued during the year	258
Number of male applicants rejected	20
Number of female applicants rejected	40
Total number rejected	65

During the year Mr. Brand visited seventy-seven different schools, nineteen of which were visited more than once. He failed to visit forty-two, and spent on an average of five hours in each of the schools he did visit. He spent ninety-six days in visitation, thirty-five in examinations, eleven in institute work, thirty-eight in office work, and seven in other official duties, making a total of one hundred and eighty-three days devoted especially to school work.

It is said that the "colored servants, or indentured apprentices," brought here by the Johnsons and others of the early miners, accumulated a good deal of property, which was subject to taxation. A friend to that people, believed to have been Hon. Thompson Campbell, secured the passage of an enactment by which the tax collected from them was set aside for their especial school benefit. In time, a sufficient sum accumulated to sustain a school a part of each year, but no one in Illinois at that time, either male or female, could be found who had courage enough to teach a negro school. Especial inquiry was made by the historians to learn the name of the public man of that time who was bold enough, philanthropic enough, generous enough, liberal enough, in the face of the then existing prejudice, to seek to educationally benefit the *emancipated Illinois slaves.* But no one could remember. Mr. Christopher, a representative man of the colored people of Galena, is of the opinion that the Mr. Campbell named above was the man, but does not state it as a fact. Neither could any one tell them what became of the money collected from that people in taxes and set apart for the support of a school for them.

Mr. Christopher does remember, however, that Captain H. H. Gear gave them a lot of ground for educational and religious purposes, which they utilized.

As late as 1866, the "color line" was so clearly defined in Galena, that a colored school was crushed out by public prejudice. A Miss Hannah Christopher (daughter of a Congregational minister of that name, who was located here) a woman of enlarged, humane, generous, liberal ideas, attempted to teach a colored school, but was forced to give it up. As soon as she commenced the school, she became an object of malice and malignity. Slander, abuse, traduction—every thing that prejudice could suggest or hatred of the blacks invent—were hurled at her with such merciless virulence that she was compelled to abandon the undertaking. She finally accompanied her family (that made up part of a colony) to Abilene, Kansas.

Gradually, however, the sober second thought, which is said to be always right, asserted itself, and about 1868 provisions were made for educating the children of that long-despised and down-trodden people. Separate schools were established. That was one step. But the prejudice still existed. The black scholars were objects of malice. The white scholars of the other schools seemed to think them natural enemies or natural objects for personal assault, and pitched battles were of not infrequent occurrence. But they learned rapidly, and soon demonstrated the fact that they were equally as apt as white scholars. They quickly reached a standard that entitled them to admission to the high school, and the demand for such admission was made by Mr. Christopher. Then came another "tug of war." Some of the authorities favored their admission to the high school, and, strange to say, some that had always professed to be friends of the colored people, opposed it. They assigned as a reason, that, if admitted to the high school, the white scholars would kill them. Mr. Christopher persisted in claiming equal rights and privileges for the children of his people, and finally told the opposition that he was willing to risk a trial. To quote his own words: "If there is any killing to be done, let them commence by killing some of my children. I am willing to make the sacrifice." There was an issue of right involved, and Christopher met it like a Roman hero. It was true, manly courage—a courage to be admired. He was contending for the rights of his people, and he triumphed. His children were admitted, and they were not killed. Others were admitted, and they were not killed. They now get along harmoniously, and are natural allies—offensive and defensive—the white and colored pupils of the high school against the scholars of the other schools. When an assault is made against one, it is an assault made against all. And scarcely any one is now to be found who was ever opposed to the education of the negroes, either in separate or mixed schools. So much for the advancement of civilization and intelligence. "John Brown's soul goes marching on."

The Northwestern German-English Normal School.—This institution was organized in 1868 by the German Methodist Conference, under whose auspices it still continues. This society purchased the building which was erected as a marine hospital, including eleven acres of ground, for six thousand dollars. The original cost to the government was $43,000.

The school was opened on September 23, 1868, with Professor Jacob Wernli, formerly assistant principal of the State Normal School at Platteville, Wisconsin, as principal; Professors Charles Zimmerman and B. F. Merten, assistants.

The objects of this school are to educate young ladies and gentlemen to become teachers in German, English or German-English schools; also, to prepare for college those desirous of a higher education.

In July, 1869, the school numbered 120.

In the Fall of 1869, Professor H. H. Oldenhage, of Milwaukee, assumed the chair of German, Latin and the natural sciences.

Mr. Oldenhage returned to Milwaukee in 1873, where, on December 20, 1877, he died, in the prime of life, amid the enjoyment of the highest esteem for his mental attainments, his ability as a teacher and his noble character.

His position in the school was filled by George P. Merten, A. B., until

June, 1876, who was in turn succeeded by Carl Hobe, A. B. Miss Addie Bonnell assisted as teacher from January, 1870, to June, 1871; Mr. Frederick Hirsch from 1871 to 1873.

In 1872 Prof. C. Zimmerman returned to Milwaukee, where he has for the last three years been superintendent of drawing in the public schools of Milwaukee. In 1873 Prof. J. Wernli resigned and was succeeded as principal by Professor B. F. Merton, who had been professor of mathematics, and who still holds the position of principal. Rev. B. Lampert and Miss Annie Tomlin taught from 1873 to 1875. Mrs. C. E. Anderson was connected with the school as teacher of instrumental music for six years. Since 1875 Jacob Boss, A. B., has assisted as instructor.

The school has done a valuable work for the educational development of this and other counties. Most of the schools of this county are taught by its graduates, of whom there have been forty-one. The school has a beautiful building and surroundings and excellent facilities for thorough education.

OLD SETTLERS' ASSOCIATION.

Oh! a wonderful stream is the river of Time,
  As it runs through the realm of tears,
With a faultless rhythm, and a musical rhyme,
And a broader sweep, and a surge sublime,
  As it blends in the ocean of years.

—*B. F. Taylor.*

Three quarters of a century has passed since white men first entered upon the occupancy of the fertile valleys and mineral lands of the extreme northwestern part of the great country of the *Illini*—erst the home of the Sacs, the Foxes, the Winnebagoes, the Menominees and kindred tribes of people native to American wilds. Since the time when the cabins of white men began to be reared upon the hillsides and within the valleys of the numerous streams that find their source in hill-side springs, and, flowing to the southwest, unite their waters with the mighty Mississippi, the Father of Waters, the years have been so full of changes that the visitor of to-day, ignorant of the past, could scarcely be made to realize that during these years a population of 28,000 has grown up within the limits of the county whose history we are writing. From a savage wild, marked only by bloody conflicts of Indian tribes and recorded only on rude, unspeaking tablets and dumb *mounds* of earth, the *galena* section has become a centre of civilization—the home and school of soldiers, great war ministers, congressmen, governors, grave senators, solemn judges, foreign ministers, presidents—men known and honored, not only at home, but among the crowned heads and titled courts of the old world. Schools, churches, colleges, busy manufactories, highly cultivated and remunerative farms, with their palatial-like dwellings, mark the camping places and battle-grounds of the wild men who once held dominion over these prairie-plains and forest-covered and mineral-filled hills. Cities, towns and villages occupy the places once dotted over with Indian wigwams. Iron bridges span the rivers where once bark canoes served as ferries for the wild men, their women and children, and railroads and telegraph lines—adjuncts and agencies of the highest type of civilization known to the world's history—mark the course of the trails they made when traveling from one part of the country to another. Of the land-marks of the "long ago," but few are left as the children of the forest and prairie wilds left them, except the prehistoric mounds to be found in almost every part of the county, *and they were fashioned by whom?*

It is not strange that among the pioneer settlers of any new country a deep-seated and sincere friendship should spring up, that would grow and strengthen with their years. The incidents peculiar to life in a new country—the trials and hardships, privations and destitutions—are well calculated to test not only the physical powers of endurance, but the moral, kindly, generous attributes of manhood and womanhood. They are times that try men's souls and bring to the surface all that there may be in them of either good or bad. As a rule, there is an equality of conditions that recognizes no distinctions. All occupy a common level, and as a natural consequence, a brotherly and sisterly feeling grows up that is as lasting as time, for "a fellow feeling makes us wondrous kind." With such a community, there is a hospitality, a kindness, a benevolence and a charity unknown and unpracticed among the older, richer and more densely populated commonwealths. The very nature of their surroundings teaches them to "feel each other's woe, to share each other's joy." An injury or a wrong may be ignored, but *a kindly, generous, charitable act is never forgotten.* The memory of old associations and kindly deeds is always fresh. Raven locks may bleach and whiten; full, round cheeks wither and waste away; the fires of intelligence vanish from the organs of vision; the brow become wrinkled with care and age, and the erect form bowed with accumulating years, but the *true* friends of the "long ago" will be remembered as long as life and reason endure.

The surroundings of pioneer life are well calculated to test the "true inwardness" of the human heart. As a rule, the men and women who first occupy a new country—who go in advance to spy out the land and prepare it for the coming of a future people—are bold, fearless, self-reliant and industrious. In these respects, no matter from what remote sections or countries they may come, there is a similarity of character. In birth, education, religion and language, there may be a vast difference, but imbued with a common purpose—the founding and building of homes—these differences are soon lost by association, and thus they become one people, united by a common interest, and no matter what changes may come in after years, the associations thus formed are never buried out of memory.

In pioneer life there are always incidents of peculiar interest, not only to the pioneers themselves, but which, if properly preserved, would be of interest to posterity, and it is a matter to be regretted that the formation of "Old Settlers' Associations" has been neglected in so many parts of the country. The presence of such associations in all the counties of our common country, with well kept records of the more important events, such as dates of arrivals, births, marriages, deaths, removals, nativity, etc., as any one can readily see, would be the direct means of preserving to the literature of the country the history of every community, that, to future generations, would be invaluable as a record of reference, and a ready method of settling important questions of controversy. As important as these associations are admitted to be, their formation has not yet become general, and there are many counties in the Western country whose early history is entirely lost because of such neglect and indifference. Such organizations would possess facts and figures that could not be had from any other source. Aside from their historic importance, they would serve as a means of keeping alive and further cementing old friendships, and renewing among the members associations that were necessarily interrupted by the innovations of increasing population, cultivating social intercourse, and creating a charitable fund for such of their members as were victims of misfortune and adversity.

Actuated by the purposes suggested in the preceding paragraph, the pioneers of Jo Daviess County organized a society in 1872, that was known as the Jo Daviess County Old Settlers' Association, which title was changed, in a meeting held June 14, 1873, to Jo Daviess Early Settlers' Association.

The first formal meeting was held at the office of the Gas Light Company at Galena, November 2, 1872, and a permanent organization effected at a subsequent meeting held at the County Court House two weeks later (on the 16th) when the following officers were elected:

President—James G. Soulard.

Vice Presidents—D. S. Harris and Samuel Tyrrell.

Secretary and Treasurer—John Lorrain.

Executive Committee—Henry Marfield, Edgar Bouton, John B. French, Wm. R. Rowley and Thomas O'Leary.

Committee on Constitution and By-Laws.—H. H. Houghton, John Lorrain, John B. French, Harvey Mann, and Richard Seal.

A residence in the county of thirty years, and the payment of one dollar fee, were the qualifications for membership, until October, 1874, when the Constitution was so modified that a residence in the lead mine region of thirty years, prior to application for membership, was required. The object of the society is thus defined by the Constitution:

> Feeling and knowing that many of our early settlers have passed away, and with them much valuable informtion has been lost, and now wishing to preserve, as much as possible, the early incidents attending the first settlement of Jo Daviess County, by gathering together her pioneer fathers; forming them into an association; cementing and renewing old friendships; bringing to light and recording old, and, in many cases, almost forgotten, reminiscences; thereby perpetuating and giving to our children and the world a true and reliable history of the first settlement of the northwest corner of the now great State of Illinois, do this day form ourselves into a permanent organization.

At a meeting held at the court house, June 14, 1873, Mr. D. S. Harris, the oldest pioneer settler in the county, was made President of the Association, *vice* J. G. Soulard, resigned, after which the following other officers were elected for the ensuing year:

Vice Presidents.—J. G. Soulard, Harvey Mann, and Samuel Tyrrell.

Secretary and Treasurer.—John Lorrain.

Historical Committee.—J. M. Harris, James G. Soulard, and J. C. Spare.

October 2, 1873, by invitation of the officers of Jo Daviess County Agricultural Association, the Association held a reunion on the Fair Ground, marching thereto in a body, with a flag, inscribed with their society name, floating above them, each member bearing a rosette of the National colors. Wm. R. Rowley was acting Marshal, and I. P. Stevens, Speaker of the day.

At the annual meeting held at the court house, June 20, 1874, the following officers were elected for the ensuing year:

President.—Daniel Smith Harris.

Vice Presidents.—Samuel Tyrrell, Samuel W. Hathaway, and Harvey Mann.

Secretary.—John Lorrain.

The following action was taken regarding the death of Brother John G. Potts:

"*Resolved*, That we each of us deeply sympathize with his bereaved family and many friends, knowing his sterling worth as an honest, upright and unimpeachable gentleman and citizen. As we honored him in life, we sincerely mourn him in death."

October 1, 1874, the Society visited the County Fair, under similar invitation to that of the year previous. Marshal, Thomas McNulty; Orator of the day, I. P. Stevens; Flag Bearer, P. M. McNulty.

The procession formed at the court house and marched to the ground. It was met by the Fair Marshal with the band, and by them escorted to the stand, where they were welcomed in the name of the society by Mr. R. Barrett. After music by the band, D. S. Harris, President, introduced I. P. Stevens, Orator of the day. After his address, in which he briefly spoke of the early local history, "Auld Lang Syne" was sung by the Association (standing). The band then rendered "The Star Spangled Banner," after which followed a general hand-shaking and reunion.

[The records of the association do not show that any meeting of the Society was held in 1875. There is, however, a long printed letter from Hon. E. B. Washburne to Captain Daniel Smith Harris, dated Paris, January 15, 1875, on the death of Mr. Charles S. Hempstead, that is preserved in the record in an appropriate place. In this letter Mr. Washburne pays a golden tribute of respect to the late Mr. Hempstead, as well as a general review of many of the incidents in which they (Washburne and Hempstead) were prominent actors.]

On the Fourth of July of the Centennial year (1876) the early settlers met in reunion, for which occasion a condensed paper was written by John Lorrain, on the History of Jo Daviess County, from which we have frequently quoted.

The next meeting of the Early Settlers was held at the court house on the 28th of October, 1876. This was a business meeting, for the election of officers, etc. Captain Daniel Smith Harris was chosen President, and Harvey Mann, A. M. Haines, G. H. Mars, I. P. Stevens, and G. W. Girdon Vice Presidents; John Lorrain, Secretary and Treasurer.

The regalia worn on the Centennial Fourth of July was adopted as the regular colors of the association.

James Wilson submitted the following resolution for the consideration of the meeting:

That we, the undersigned early settlers of Jo Daviess County, agree and obligate ourselves to form a permanent organization of the early settlers of said county, under articles and by-laws, etc., and, to make said organization binding, will pay to the treasurer of said association twenty-five cents per month, the fund so created to be used for sustaining the organization, and the burial of our dead.

The resolution was adopted, and John Lorrain chosen as special treasurer for this fund.

June 16, 1877, a meeting of the Association was held (at the call of the President) to make arrangements to celebrate the Fourth of July, 1877. At this meeting it was resolved to make a picnic excursion over the Narrow Gauge railroad to Benton, or vicinity, in Wisconsin.

In pursuance of the resolution, the Old Settlers and their families to the number of 130 met at the Narrow Gauge depot in Galena, on the morning of the Fourth of July, 1877, where they were greeted by a very large concourse of citizens. Taking passage on the cars of the Narrow Gauge, they were soon carried to their place of destination, where the following order of exercises were observed:

1. Prayer by Charles Potts, of Galena.
2. Singing by the Choir.
3. Reading of the Declaration of American Independence, by Miss Cottingham, of Benton.
4. Music and Song.
5. Address to Sunday School children, by Rev. S. S. Hellsby.
6. Dinner.

After dinner the excursionists and their Benton friends re-assembled at the speaker's stand, where the programme of the day was completed in the following order:

1. Music by the Choir.
2. Address by I. P. Stevens.
3. Music.

An Address by Mrs. Sarah C. Harris, on Woman Suffrage. She maintained that, while the Declaration of American Independence was broad and magnanimous, it was still unjust in its operations, as one half the people, the women, were not represented in the workings of the government. Soon after the delivery of this address, which is said to have been a most dignified and queenly effort, the excursionists adjourned to the cars that were in waiting to convey them back to Galena, whence they repaired to their respective homes.

With the Old Settlers of Jo Daviess County thus passed away the 4th day of July, 1877. That all of those who participated in this last reunion will be permitted to join in a similar meeting in 1878 is not to be expected, for one by one they are passing away—going to the everlasting shores of the Great Beyond—to join in an eternal reunion and pleasures and joys more perfect than any ever conceived in the mind of man.

It is a matter of regret that a complete registry of the names of the first settlers of every new county has not been kept. It would be an invaluable record—connecting and completing links in a country's history. Only in late years, however, has the importance of such a record suggested itself to the minds of men, and it is to be hoped that the spirit of the constitution of the Old Settlers Association of Jo Daviess will be carried out to the letter, and that the names, date of birth, date of arrival, etc., will be religiously preserved and handed down to those who will come in the not far distant by-and-by to fill the places now gladdened by the remaining pioneer fathers and mothers. Had this record been commenced when white men and white women first came to develop the great wealth that nature stored away in the galena hills, volumes of historical information would have been preserved, the want of which is now seriously experienced.

Many of the courageous men and women who were here from 1823, and up to and during the period of the Black Hawk War, have either passed from earth to brighter and happier existences, or removed to other scenes of labor and business conflict. Of those who remain, one hundred and fifteen names are entered of record on the Old Settlers' journal, and are herewith remitted to the descendants of those whose industry, enterprise, intelligence and patriotism have made for Jo Daviess County not only a national, but a world-wide, reputation.

Daniel Smith Harris, Delaware Co., N. Y., July 24, 1808. Arrived June 20, 1823.

S. W. Hathaway

GUILFORD TP.

Hiram B. Hunt, Green Co., O., 1822. Arrived June 20, 1823.

James M. Harris, Green Co., O., January 4, 1823. Arrived May 28, 1824.

Wm. T. Gear, Cleveland, O., October 19, 1816. Arrived May 18, 1826.

James G. Soulard, St. Louis, Mo., May 20, 1798. Arrived May 20, 1827.

*Thomas O'Leary, Ireland, December 3, 1817. Arrived October 27, 1827.

William B. Green, Knox Co., O., Nov. 6, 1806. Arrived April 1, 1827.

Harvey Mann, Aurelius, Cayuga Co., N. Y., October 21, 1805. Arrived June 15, 1827.

Solomon Oliver, Tenn., October 14, 1806. Arrived in May, 1827.

William Townsend, England, June 28, 1796. Arrived April 11, 1826.

Elias Bayliss, Fauquer Co., Va., August 6, 1806. Arrived in January, 1830.

Joseph Liddle, Northumberland, England, June 4, 1800. Arrived June 10, 1832.

John Lorrain, Germantown, Philadelphia Co., Pa., July 29, 1812. Arrived June 10, 1832.

G. P. Billon, Philadelphia, Pa., Feb. 29, 1812. Arrived in Aug., 1832.

* John P. De Zoya, De Gruson, Switzerland, August 21, 1792. Arrived April 8, 1833.

Johnstón Ginn, Ireland, 1798. Arrived May 18, 1834.

* Edward Irwin. Arrived in 1835.

Jas. Wilson, Baltimore, Md., Oct. 22, 1808. Arrived Aug. 14, 1836.

G. W. Fuller, Mass., October 4, 1807. Arrived in April, 1836.

James Gallagher, Frederick Co., Md., Aug. 15, 1811. Arrived in October, 1837.

W. G. Robinson, Donegal, Ireland, August 12, 1808. Arrived June 11, 1837.

R. S. Norris, Hartford Co., Md., Feb. 16, 1817. Arrived May 31, 1837.

J. C. Spare, Canticells Bridge, Newcastle Co., Del., March 7, 1819. Arrived May 11, 1838.

E. M. Bouton, West Chester Co., N. Y., September 16, 1817. Arrived in January, 1840.

*Thomas McNulty, Ireland, April 4, 1810. Arrived in May, 1836.

Wm. Ginn, Philadelphia, Penn., Nov. 30, 1827. Arrived in May, 1834.

William R. Rowley, St. Lawrence Co., N. Y. Arrived June 12, 1843.

George W. Girdon, Philadelphia, Penn., May 31, 1814. Arrived April 30, 1835.

Stewart Crawford, Monaghan, Ireland, March 30, 1815. Arrived in March, 1840.

Augustus Estey, Mt. Vernon, N. H., March 22, 1811. Arrived in July, 1836.

S. K. Miner, Ontario Co., N. Y., Dec. 17, 1820. Arrived in Oct., 1839.

* John G. Potts, Philadelphia, Penn., February 17, 1800. Arrived April 12, 1838.

Sam'l Roberts, Cornwall, Eng., Jan. 10, 1823. Arrived July 5, 1842.

W. W. Venable, Fluvanna Co., Va., March 8, 1817. Arrived March 8, 1842.

Benj. Christy St. Cyr, St. Louis, Mo., November 9, 1809. Arrived June 16, 1833.

Philip M. Wilmarth, Oneida Co., N. Y., June 19, 1816. Arrival unknown.

John W. New, Morgan Co., Ill., Feb. 8, 1831. Arrived in May, 1840.

Stephen Bastian, Cornwall, England, February 8, 1813. Arrived in May, 1840.

H. H. Houghton, Springfield, Vt., October 26, 1806. Arrived in April, 1835.

Richard Seal, England, July 15, 1807. Arrived November 19, 1836.

William Avery, Chenango Co., N. Y., August 15, 1807. Arrived in May, 1827.

William Rodden, Holywood, Ireland, March 2, 1806. Arrived in August, 1834.

H. A. Rice, Baltimore, Md., April 1, 1819. Arrived June 23, 1829.

Elliott T. Isbell, Warren Co., Ky., August 24, 1813. Arrived May 16, 1832.

I. N. Crumbacker, Green Co., East Tenn., June 12, 1816. Arrived July 5, 1835.

William Reed, Donegall Co., Ireland, March 25, 1822. Arrived in June, 1843.

John Brendel, Baden, Germany, November 16, 1815. Arrived March 18, 1842.

John Anton Burrichter, Lingerick-on-Walage, Hanover, July 13, 1822. Arrived in July 1840.

I. P. Stevens, Butler Co., O., March 20, 1814. Arrived April 14, 1836.

*Nicholas Stahl, Baltimore, Md., January 18, 1817. Arrived March 30, 1834.

Andrew Telford, Scotland, July 6, 1817. Arrived in July, 1839.

Nathaniel Morris, Logan Co., Ky., October 1, 1805. Arrived May 27, 1827.

Samuel West Hathaway, Otsego Co., N. Y., August 25, 1813. Arrived February 14, 1829.

Henry Bartell, Camtran, Cornwall, England, December 1, 1816. Arrived May 16, 1840.

Geo. Winters, Germany, July 14, 1827. Arrived August 13, 1843.

Beeri Serviss, Montgomery Co., N. Y., June 30, 1810. Arrived May 6, 1832.

Jno. Crummer, Ireland, February 23, 1816. Arrived in September, 1836.

Wm. W. Gillett, Hartford Co., Conn., June 10, 1810. Arrived July 7, 1836.

Jas. Blair, Green Co., Pa., January 23, 1813. Arrived January 1, 1836.

G. H. Mars, Philadelphia, Pa., Sept. 12, 1808. Arrived Sept. 12, 1836.

David Campbell, Donegal, Ireland, June 22, 1813. Arrived June 22, 1836.

Andrew Kilpatrick, Ireland, January 27, 1801. Arrived May 11, 1835.

Sam'l Scott, St. Clair Co., Ill., June 22, 1812. Arrived September 1, 1831.

David H. Heer, Germany, May 3, 1834. Arrived August 8, 1842.

Thos. Casper, Switzerland, January 17, 1823. Arrived in June, 1841.

H. V. W. Brown, Essex Co., N. Y., Sept. 3, 1815. Arrived in Oct., 1838.

Henry Goard, Cornwall, England, Oct. 12, 1814. Arrived in May, 1841.

N. Strott, Germany, July 15, 1815. Arrived in May, 1844.

Timothy Hallett, Fulton Co., Ill., November 7, 1826. Arrived in 1828.

C. F. Potts, Philadelphia, Pa., April 6, 1811. Arrived in July, 1838.

Jas. Edwards, Australia, February 8, 1810. Arrived in April, 1840.

Timothy Kennedy, Ireland, 1820. Arrived in April, 1842.

S. T. Napper, England, March 13, 1815. Arrived July 3, 1838.

Andrew M. Haines, Canterbury, N. H., January 1, 1820. Arrived August 13, 1839.

Frederick Stahl, Baltimore, Md., February 28, 1809. Arrived in April, 1829.

Jas. M. Day, Littleton, N. H., Sept. 9, 1819. Arrived April 6, 1828.

Stephen Jeffers, Broome Co., N. Y., September 21, 1821. Arrived in November, 1838.

Wm. Colvin, Washington Co., Pa., March 5, 1810. Arrived June 18, 1824.

Patrick McQullen, Ireland, April 10, 1825. Arrived in May, 1833.

Hiram DeGraff, Montgomery Co., N. Y., April 20, 1817. Arrived in December, 1836.

C. Pauzth, Prussia, January 6, 1815. Arrived in July, 1835.

Chas. Wenner, Germany, November 27, 1819. Arrived April 28, 1834.

Elihu B. Washburne, Livermore, Maine, September 23, 1816. Arrived April 1, 1840.

John Wenner, Lebanon Co., Pa., Jan. 21, 1819. Arrived April 24, 1841.

Christopher E. Sanders, Duchy of Oldenburg, August 8, 1809. Arrived July 5, 1835.

Frederick Chetlain, British Possessions, Selkirk, October 15, 1822. Arrived in May, 1826.

John Spratt, Township, Silver Lake, Pa., July 2, 1822. Arrived October 10, 1835.

John McDonald, Galley Co., Ohio, August 10, 1807. Arrived September 20, 1834.

Robert G. Ward, Cohoes Falls, N. Y., September 23, 1807. Arrived May 1, 1837.

John G. Eustice, Cornwall, Eng., Sept 23, 1806. Arrived in June, 1841.

G. A. Paige, Barnard, Vt., Oct. 16, 1817. Arrived Sept. 13, 1839.

Patrick McCarty, Longford Co., Ireland, June 18, 1807. Arrived June 20, 1834.

James McDonald.

John Shay, County of Cork, Ireland, November 1, 1818. Arrived November 15, 1839.

John B. French, Maryland, Dec. 12, 1820. Arrived Aug. 20, 1842.

Jno. Nesbitt, County Monaghan, Ireland, 1817. Arrived in May, 1842.

Louis F. Schaber, Jo Daviess Co., Ill., October 22, 1838.

* Thos. McNulty, Doneghan, Ireland, April 4, 1808. Arrived in October, 1832.

Thos. Annets, Monmouth, Eng., May 22, 1812. Arrived Aug. 1, 1842.

* Richard Dargin, Tipperary Co., Ireland. Arrived in September, 1836.

Adam Hoffman, Prussia. Arrived in September, 1836.

Frederick Gauss, Wurtemburg, Germany, September 26, 1817. Arrived in April, 1834.

Jacob Doxey, England, December 21, 1805. Arrived in June, 1839.

Christmann Brendel, Baden, Germany, Nov. 5, 1813. Arrived in 1846.

John Lupton, Yorkshire, Eng., Dec. 15, 1826. Arrived June 6, 1846.

John S. Crawford, Ireland, October 18, 1812. Arrived in 1841.

A. Reynick, County of Cork, Ireland, March 10, 1816. Arrived in 1825. Left, and returned in September, 1837.

Stephen Marsden, Winsten, Derbyshire, Eng., Dec. 26, 1810. Arrived in Galena in the Fall of 1834.

William Vincent, Cornwall, England, Jan. 19, 1823. Arrived June 3, 1837.

WAR RECORD.

If there is any one thing more than another of which the people of the Northern States have reason to be proud, it is of the record they made during the dark and bloody days of the War of the Rebellion. When the war was forced upon the country, the people were quietly pursuing the even tenor of their ways, doing whatever their hands found to do—working the mines, making farms or cultivating those already made, erecting homes, founding cities and towns, building shops and manufactories—in short, the country was alive with industry and hopes for the future. The people were just recovering from the depression and losses incident to the financial panic of 1857. The future looked bright and promising, and the industrious and patriotic sons and daughters of the Free States were buoyant with hope—looking forward to the perfecting of new plans for the ensurement of comfort and competence in their declining years, they little heeded the mutterings and threatenings of treason's children in the Slave States of the South. True sons and descendants of the heroes of the "times that tried men's souls"—the struggle for American independence—they never dreamed that there was even one so base as to dare attempt the destruction of the Union of their fathers—a government baptized with the best blood the world ever knew. While immediately surrounded with peace and tranquility, they paid but little attention to the rumored plots and plans of those who lived and grew rich from the sweat and toil, blood and flesh of others—aye, even trafficked in the offspring of their own loins. Nevertheless, the war came with all its attendant horrors.

April 12, 1861, Fort Sumter, at Charleston, South Carolina, Major Anderson, U. S. A., commandant, was fired upon by rebels in arms. Although basest treason, this first act in the bloody reality that followed was looked upon as a mere bravado of a few hot-heads—the act of a few fire-eaters whose sectional bias and freedom hatred was crazed by the excessive indulgence in intoxicating potations. When, a day later, the news was borne along the telegraph wires that Major Anderson had been forced to surrender to what had first been regarded as a drunken mob, the patriotic people of the North were startled from their dreams of the future—from undertakings half completed—and made to realize that behind that mob there was a dark, deep and well organized purpose to destroy the government, rend the Union in twain, and out of its ruins erect a slave oligarchy, wherein no one would dare question their right to hold in bondage the sons and daughters of men whose skins were black, or who, perchance, through practices of lustful natures, were half or quarter removed from the color that God, for His own purposes, had given them. But they "reckoned without their host." Their dreams of the future—their plans for the establishment of an independent confederacy—were doomed from their inception to sad and bitter disappointment.

Immediately upon the surrender of Fort Sumter, Abraham Lincoln—

America's martyr President—who, but a few short weeks before, had taken the oath of office as the nation's chief executive, issued a proclamation calling for 75,000 volunteers for three months. The last word of that proclamation had scarcely been taken from the electric wires before the call was filled. Men and money were counted out by hundreds and thousands. The people who loved their whole government could not give enough. Patriotism thrilled and vibrated and pulsated through every heart. The farm, the workshop, the office, the pulpit, the bar, the bench, the college, the schoolhouse—every calling offered its best men, their lives and fortunes in defense of the government's honor and unity. Party lines were, for the time, ignored. Bitter words, spoken in moments of political heat, were forgotten and forgiven, and, joining hands in a common cause, they repeated the oath of America's soldier statesman: "*By the Great Eternal, the Union must and shall be preserved!*"

Seventy-five thousand men were not enough to subdue the rebellion. Nor were ten times that number. The war went on, and call followed call, until it began to look as if there would not be men enough in all the Free States to crush out and subdue the monstrous war traitors had inaugurated. But to every call, for either men or money, there was a willing and a ready response. And it is a boast of the people that, had the supply of men fallen short, there were women brave enough, daring enough, patriotic enough, to have offered themselves as sacrifices on their country's altar. Such were the impulses, motives and actions of the patriotic men of the North, among whom the sons of Jo Daviess made a conspicuous and praiseworthy record. Of the offerings made by this people during the great and final struggle between freedom and slavery, it is the purpose now to write.

April 14, A. D. 1861, Abraham Lincoln, President of the United States, issued the following

PROCLAMATION.

WHEREAS, The laws of the United States have been, and now are, violently opposed in several states by combinations too powerful to be suppressed in the ordinary way, I therefore call for the militia of the several states of the Union, to the aggregate number of 75,000, to suppress said combination and execute the laws. I appeal to all loyal citizens to facilitate and aid in this effort to maintain the laws and the integrity of the perpetuity of the popular government, and redress wrongs long enough endured. The first service assigned to the forces, probably, will be to repossess the forts, places and property which have been seized from the Union. Let the utmost care be taken, consistent with the object, to avoid devastation, destruction, interference with the property of peaceful citizens in any part of the country; and I hereby command persons composing the aforesaid combination to disperse within twenty days from date.

I hereby convene both houses of Congress for the 4th day of July next, to determine upon measures for public safety which the interest of the subject demands.

ABRAHAM LINCOLN,
President of the United States.

WM. H. SEWARD,
Secretary of State.

The gauntlet thrown down by the traitors of the South was accepted—not, however, in the spirit with which insolence meets insolence—but with a firm, determined spirit of patriotism and love of country. The duty of the President was plain under the constitution and the laws, and above and beyond all, the people from whom all political power is derived, demanded the suppression of the rebellion, and stood ready to sustain the authority of their representatives and executive officers.

The first war meeting held in Galena convened at the court house on Tuesday evening, April 16, 1861. The meeting was called to order by

Charles Hempstead, on whose motion Mayor Robert Brand was chosen chairman. On taking the chair and acknowledging the honor conferred upon him, Mr. Brand said: "I am in favor of any honorable compromise that will again unite our whole country. I am in favor of sustaining the president so long as his efforts are for the peace and harmony of our whole country. I am in favor of a convention of the people, that an adjustment might be made, sustaining alike the honor, interest and safety of both sections of our country. I am in favor of sustaining our flag, our constitution and our laws, right or wrong. Yet I am opposed to warring on any portion of our beloved country, if a compromise can be effected."

The sentiments thus expressed, it seems from the *Courier* of the following evening (Wednesday, April 17) did not meet the views of Mr. E. B. Washburne then member of Congress from this district, and he immediately arose and denounced the address of the mayor, and moved that he vacate the chair, and that George W. Campbell, Esq., preside over the meeting. Mr. Brand put the motion, stating that as his sentiments did not appear to be to the taste of Mr. Washburne, he desired to withdraw. There was a slight response in the affirmative, and Mr. Brand was about leaving his chair, when he was called upon to put the negative. He did so, and the loud response which came from every part of the building was a significant rebuke to the gentleman who made the motion. The motion was renewed, and was again voted down by a large majority.

Hon. Frederick Stahl made some remarks to the effect that he had feared some such trouble would occur, regretting the exhibition of partisan feeling, and advising, if the meeting could not proceed harmoniously, an adjournment. * * * The remarks of Mr. Stahl had a happy effect, and Mr. Washburne seeing that his course was not sustained by the meeting, withdrew his motion (it had previously been twice voted down) and quiet was restored.

Mr. Washburne then introduced the following resolutions, which were unanimously adopted:

Resolved, 1. That we will support the government of the United States in the performance of all its constitutional duties in this great crisis, and will assist it to maintain the integrity of the American flag, and to defend it whenever and wherever assailed.

2. That we recommend the immediate formation of two military companies in this city to respond to any call that may be made by the governor of the state.

3. That we call on the Legislature, which is to assemble in extraordinary session on the 23d instant, to make the most ample provisions to respond to the call for troops now made, or that may hereafter be made, by the president of the United States.

4. That, having lived under the stars and stripes, by the blessing of God, we propose to die under them.

"Speeches were then made," continued the *Courier*, "by E. B. Washburne, Charles S. Hempstead, B. B. Howard, John A. Rawlins, Judge Platt, J. M. Shaw and I. P. Stevens, all of the gentlemen avowing their determination and calling upon all good citizens to rally around the flag, and to sustain the government of their country."

Thus was evoked the war spirit in Jo Daviess County.

The first meeting to organize a military company was held at the court house on Thursday evening, April 18, and twenty men enrolled their names. A movement was also on foot at the same time to organize a cavalry company, and some thirty names had been enrolled. We quote from the *Courier* of Saturday evening, April 20:

"*Galena Volunteers.*—The Volunteer Company of this city is now nearly full. Adjutant General Mather has signified his acceptance of the company, and requests that they report themselves at once. It is believed the company will be ready to leave here for Springfield on Monday evening next. The following persons have enrolled themselves as members of the company, the list including all that had enlisted up to four o'clock this afternoon:

Galena's First Offering.

A. L. Chetlain,
J. Bates Dickson,
Wallace Campbell,
M. E. Howard,
Nicholas Roth,
W. W. Pringle,
W. H. Bahne,
G. Godat,
H. Voss,
John Dietrich,
W. B. McMaster,
Charles Farr,
George W. Davis,
John Barton,
William Turnbull,
Henry Korpfen,
Gideon Stoddard,
Herman Meyer,
G. S. Avery,
John Eberhard,
Isaac Hewett,
William Peters,
F. Schmidmayer,
Samuel Starr,
Charles Kœnne,
Henry Bauer,
Charles W. Foster,
Edward R. Kræmer,
Joseph Mitsch,
Charles A. Wagener,
George L. Payson,
Frederich Brands,
John S. Cookson,
James Edwards,
Christian Doran,
Andrew Frank,
George Grosgans,
John Ferguson,
Anton Bahrœl,
Robert McLaren,
M. P. Wolf,
C. Miller,
John Wilson,
Charles Seitzberg,
George Beebe,
William H. Kent,
Frederick Ehman,
Ed. M. Schank,
William Hartnick,
Edward Quinton,
Joseph Clark,
Andrew Dish,
W. S. Phillips, musician,
Washington Fullen,
W. B. Phillips,
William Schearer,
Constantine Glookner,
John Clink,
George Gilmore,
George Scott,
D. H. Dildine,
J. C. Glenot,
O. L. Spaulding,
Squatz Klein,
John Brown,
Charles Simper,
S. Metzgar,
George Salzer,
Francis Kemley,
William Price,
William Rueckert,
James Houlehan,
John McLean,
J. T. Smith,
George Lawke,
Henry Shanck,
John Horman,
Edward T. Miller—78.

By Monday evening, the 22d, the following additional names were added to the roll:

John B. Saillet,
James Stone,
E. Kramer,
Francis Smith,
H. Ludwig,
F. A. Lanstead,
George Smith,
Henry F. Langdon,
Fred Reber,
A. Rochter,
M. Callahan,
J. B. Wise,
Albert Razel,
John McCrea,
W. H. Bryant,
George La Bucht,
John Craig,
E. Hellman,
Elias Whitney,
G. H. Dye,
F. J. Robinson,
Charles Mayers,
A. Kock,
James McDonald,
R. P. Bell—25.

This additional twenty-five increased the number to 103 men, good and true, of whom ninety-five, including the officers and two musicians, were uniformed and mustered into the service. An election for officers had been held on the Saturday evening previous, with the following result:

Captain, A. L. Chetlain; First Lieutenant, Wallace Campbell; Second

Lieutenant, J. Bates Dickson; First Sergeant, Nicholas Roth; Second Sergeant, Gideon Stoddard; Third Sergeant, D. H. Dildine; Fourth Sergeant, Fred. Ehman; First Corporal, Chas, Klœnne; Second Corporal, Henry Schanck; Third Corporal, Wm. McMaster; Fourth Corporal, Mark Howard; Ensign Bearer, Augustine Godat.

Thus officered, the first company raised in Jo Daviess in response to the country's call for volunteers to suppress the rebellion, were ready to march away to the field of battle. Saturday evening (the 20th), advices were received from the Adjutant-General's Office that the company should be uniformed at home. The uniform consisted of blue frock coat, dark gray pants, with blue cords. N. Corwith & Co., bankers, offered to make the necessary advances to fit out the company, and Messrs. Eberhardt & Klett and H. P. Corwith undertook the contract of having the uniforms ready by Wednesday (the 24th) at noon. The ladies of the city, in the meantime, were not idle, but were visiting among the business men, soliciting subscriptions of money to purchase a suitable flag, etc.

Thursday, the 25th, this company left for Springfield, escorted to the depot by the fire companies, the German Benevolent Society and citizens *en masse*, the procession forming in the following order:

Galena Brass Band.
Liberty Fire Company, No. 1.
The Guards, flanked on the right by Neptune Fire Company, No. 2, and on the left by Relief Hook and Ladder Company, No. 4.
Galena Fire Company, No. 3.
Schreiner's Brass Band.
German Societies.
Mayor and City Council.
Young Men's Volunteers.
Citizens.

At the depot a flag was presented to the company by E. A. Small, on behalf of the ladies, accompanied by an appropriate speech. He also presented to Captain Chetlain a package containing $70, the surplus of the money subscribed for the purchase of the flag, to be expended as the company desired. The flag presentation was made in the presence of a crowd of 5,000 people, and was received by Captain Chetlain with appropriate thanks and fitting remarks. After these exercises, and when the guards had formed in front of the depot, Mayor Brand presented the ensign bearer with a beautiful revolver (Colt's pattern), accompanied with the following remarks:

Friends and Soldiers:—The last links on which hung all my hopes of a reconciliation without a resort to arms is now broken. Virginia, dear old Virginia! the land of my father, has deserted us in this trying hour. We have nothing now left but to unfurl the "Star-Spangled Banner," and to defend it with our lives. Soldiers! our Union is in danger! Let no one falter now—that "Star-Spangled Banner" must wave in triumph over the *whole Union* as long as there is one drop of blood in our veins to protect it. Soldiers! Go—your country calls you to duty, and in the hour of battle let your war-cry be, "The Union, the whole Union, now and forever!"

Standard Bearer! On you all eyes will be turned, to see that "our flag is still there." Take this; it is all I have. Use it in defense of that noble flag you have the honor to bear."

Rev. J. H. Vincent followed in an affecting, eloquent and patriotic address. The cars soon drew up, and but a short time was left "to sever the ties that bound the members of the Guards to the hearts and hearth-stones of near and dear friends. Many a mother parted from a dear

Stephen Jeffers

HANOVER

son—many a wife from her beloved husband—many a sister from a fond brother. Then came the train, the hurried 'Good-byes,' the shaking of hands, the filling of the cars, and, although many hearts were sad, as the whistle sounded the moment of departure and the train moved off, thousands of hats and 'kerchiefs waved, and cheer upon cheer for the Guards and the Union they went to uphold, rang out on the evening air."

And so went out from among the people of Galena the gallant Chetlain and his brave company.

While this first company was being organized, uniformed and sent out to join in freedom's battle against treason and slavery, others were forming. In the Galena papers of the 20th of April, there appeared the following call:

Attention, Company! All those that are willing to volunteer, and are in favor of the Union, the enforcement of the laws, protection to our flag, and of responding to the call of the President of the United States, in suppressing rebellion, repressing invasions, dispersing mobs, and in re-capturing and protecting government forts, property, etc., to form a company for that purpose, and will hold themselves in readiness subject to a call by the Governor, are requested to enroll their names at my office. Said company, when formed, may elect its own officers. B. B. HOWARD.

In a few days Captain Howard's company was full, and on the evening of the 25th of April proceeded to the election of officers.

Captain, B. B. Howard; First Lieutenant, Thaddeus B. Drum; Second Lieutenant, Orrin Smith, Jr.; Sergeants, First, George Richardson; Second, James S. Charles; Third, William Kamphouse; Fourth, William Pittam; Corporals, First, Conrad Schlosser; Second, A. J. Brace; Third, John C. Leek; Fourth, John S. Jolly.

April 24, the *Courier* had the following: "*Captain Howard's Company*—Capt. Howard received a dispatch from the Adjutant-General at Springfield, last evening, informing him that they were full under the first call, but advising him to keep up his organization, as he thinks another call will be made soon."

Thursday, May 2, Captain Howard advertised as follows:

Attention, Anti-Beaure Guards!—You will report at headquarters (Jackson Hall), at 9 o'clock A. M. and 4 o'clock P. M., of each and every day, until further orders.
By order of B. B. HOWARD, Captain.
JAMES S. CHARLES, Sergeant.

Thus it will be seen that Captain Howard and his "boys in blue" were not only ready but waiting for the summons to march against the enemy. They were soon ordered to march, and were escorted to the depot as the first company had been, with music, banners, and thousands of citizens.

While these and other companies were being raised in Galena, other parts of the county were not idle.

The people of Morseville assembled at their school-house on Friday evening, the 19th of April, to take counsel together, and give expression to their sentiments. S. Tyrrell, Esq., was called to the chair, and S. Church chosen as secretary. A committee on resolutions was appointed, who reported the following:

WHEREAS, It becomes American citizens to know no political law but their country's welfare; and whereas, the flag of our country has been insulted, and the laws set at defiance by formidably organized bands of lawless men whose avowed purpose and overt acts are high treason against the government, therefore,

Resolved, That in the present endangered state of our country we will ignore all party differences and distinctions and will unite in rendering all the aid within our power, to the Federal Executive in executing the laws and defending the honor of our national flag.

2. That we recognize the form of government formed by our fathers—and baptized in their blood—as the best in the world; the birthright of American citizens, and to be given up but with our lives.

3. That we are unalterably for the *Union of the States, one and inseparable, now and forever.*

4. That the Secretary of this meeting forward a copy of these proceedings and resolutions to be published in the Warren *Independent*, Galena *Courier* and Galena *Gazette*.

Speeches full of patriotism were made by several gentlemen, when the meeting adjourned to be heard from again.

The citizens of Nora were actively at work. P. F. Parks, writing from that place to the *Courier*, under date of the 25th of April, said:

"On Sunday, in our church, the state of our country was presented. A telegraphic report at noon that Washington was actually attacked raised the feeling to the highest pitch of excitement; men, women and children were ready to enlist all their energies, in any form possible, to save our country. Never before have I seen such an outbreak of enthusiasm.

"A call was made on Monday evening to form a body for home protection, or to be ready to repel invasion. Mr. Lucius Blackman was chosen chairman. Patriotic speeches were made by G. F. Bennett, J. P. Harriman, Rev. Mr. Luke, Rev. Mr. Coolly, Lucius Blackman and others. A committee of three, Captain Stanchfield, Rev. O. W. Coolly and L. Blackman, was chosen to draft a constitution and by-laws for the company, and report on the next evening.

"On Tuesday evening the committee reported. The constitution was adopted, and *sixty* men immediately responded with their names. They proceeded to organize under the name of the "Nora Home Guards." This company was officered as follows:

"Captain, George B. Stanchfield; First Lieutenant, Charles T. Sisson; Second Lieutenant, Lucius Blackman; Clerk and Orderly Sergeant, P. F. Parks; Second Sergeant, W. E. Harriman; Third Sergeant, Ezra Turner, Fourth Sergeant, Alfred Stevens; Corporals, First, Thomas H. Leland; Second, Henry Lawrence; Third, Alexander Boileau; Fourth, H. J. Harriman."

So spake the patriotic people of Nora.

Wednesday evening, the 24th (April), the people of Elizabeth and vicinity assembled at the school-house to discuss the situation. The meeting was called to order by Dr. W. A. Little, on whose motion Stephen R. Elwell was made chairman. H. Green was chosen secretary. Mr. Elwell stated the object of the meeting, after which short, sharp, stirring speeches were made by Messrs. Cummings and Hicks, of Galena, which elicited hearty responses from the audience. As expressive of the sense of the people of that vicinity, the following resolutions were adopted:

Resolved, 1. That we, the people of Elizabeth, in view of the contest now pending in our country, involving our existence as a nation, and the existence of constitutional freedom, will hereafter know no party save that of patriot and of traitor.

2. That we will, as one man, give our support to the national administration in its endeavors to defend the national honor, execute the laws and maintain the perpetuity of the Union.

3. That the policy of the administration in the endeavor to maintain the integrity of the government, the possession of the forts and public property of the United States, meets with our hearty approval.

4. That we are filled with indignation when we think that the flag of our country has been torn down and trampled under the feet of traitors; and we pledge our lives and fortunes to the service of our country to vindicate that flag.

Information having been received that the companies called for by the governor had reported themselves ready for orders, and that no more could be received at that time, it was resolved to form a company for drill practice, in order to be prepared to respond to any future call. A call was made for volunteers for such company, and forty-four persons immediately responded.

Up to Saturday evening, the 27th, eighty-three men had enrolled their names, when they proceeded to an election of officers, as follows:

Captain, John Barker.

First Lieutenant, John Calvert.

Second Lieutenant, Charles Oversteel.

Sergeants, First, Stephen R. Elwell; Second, John Atchison; Third, John G. Byers; Fourth, Wayne Milligan.

At Millville, on the 28th, the people held a meeting to receive a flag from the ladies of that hamlet and neighborhood—an emblem of loyalty and devotion to the whole Union. A flag staff eighty-seven feet in height was raised, from the top of which the flag was unfurled. Guns were fired—one for each state and territory, after which the following sentiments were read:

1. Our motto is union and the preservation of the national flag, or death on the field of battle in its defense.
2. We regard all repudiators of the Constitution of the United States as rebels, and will treat them as such.
3. May the flag of our country be a terror to all rebellious or invading forces.
4. May the flag of our country float triumphantly over land and sea.

At Warren, Scales Mound, Apple River, Dunleith, Hanover—in fact, in almost every school-house and church building in the county—meetings were held, resolutions of patriotism adopted, and measures inaugurated for the enlistment of volunteers. The people spoke as if with one voice. There was no halting between two opinions, but all "rallied around the flag," and solemnly declared, as Andrew Jackson, America's soldier president declared—"*The Union must and shall be preserved.*"

A company was fully organized at Warren on Tuesday, the 23d of April, by the election of the following officers:

Captain, James Raney.

First Lieutenant, D. J. Benner.

Second Lieutenant, John W. Luke.

Third Lieutenant, A. T. Barnes.

This company was accepted under the second call for volunteers, and went into camp at Freeport a few days after its election of officers. On the morning of their departure for Freeport, they were escorted to the depot by a large concourse of citizens, where, on behalf of the ladies of Warren, Rev. Mr. Probst presented the company with a very handsome flag, accompanied by an appropriate address. The flag was received for the company by Dr. Marvin, who responded to the remarks of Mr. Probst in an easy, graceful manner, and pledged the men of the company to return the flag unsullied and unstained by any act of cowardice or dishonor to the fair hands of the ladies who made it, or to die in its defense. Soon the train bore them away to the camp of Freeport, and from thence they were soon assigned to regiments and ordered forward to meet the enemy, at the outposts of danger.

Our pen could be employed for months in sketching the uprising of the people, the formation of companies, and telling of the deeds of valor and heroism of the "Boys in Blue" from Jo Daviess County. There is material here for volumes upon volumes, and it would be a pleasing task to collect and arrange it, but no words our pen could employ would add a single laurel to their brave and heroic deeds. Acts speak louder than words, and their acts have spoken—are recorded in pages already written. The people of no county in any of the states of the freedom and Union-loving North made a better record during the dark and trying times of the great and final struggle between freedom and slavery—patriotism and treason—than the people of Jo Daviess. Monuments may crumble; cities may fall into decay; the tooth of time leave its impress on all the works of man, but the memory of the gallant deeds of the army of the Union in the war of the great rebellion, in which the sons of this county bore so conspicuous a part, will live in the minds of men so long as time and civilized governments endure.

Leaving these companies and others organizing and to be organized, to follow to the field of danger, we turn back to take up some other matters of local importance as forming a part of the war record we are seeking to preserve.

Thursday, April 25, there was a great powder excitement at Galena. On that day the steamboat "La Crosse," bound for St. Louis, had an order to ship 224 kegs of blasting powder from the Platteville Powder Mills, ostensibly for Pike's Peak. A number of Galenians, fearing the powder might fall into the hands of the secessionists, either at Hannibal or St. Louis, requested Mayor Brand to forbid the captain of the "La Crosse" from taking it. The mayor complied with their request, and also telegraphed to the governor to know if he should allow the powder to be shipped, to which Governor Yates replied, "*Detain it by all means.*" The powder was thereupon taken back to the powder house, and the Pike's Peakers never saw it, nor did it fall into the hands of those who would have used it to *blast* the union. Plattsville powder was not made for such purposes.

The people were liberal, as well as patriotic, and while the men were busy enlisting, organizing and equipping companies, the ladies were active in taking up subscriptions and making arrangements to secure the families of volunteers against want. Committees were appointed, and right nobly did they do their duty. The first fund raised was in the interest of the Jo Daviess Guards—Captain Chetlain's company. Friday evening, April 27, the sum of $1,600 was reported subscribed and subject to the order of the relief committee, and, it having been ascertained that some of the families were in need, an assessment of ten per cent was immediately made, and promptly paid and distributed "where it would do the most good." And so the good work went on. As the war continued, and more volunteers were needed, the county authorities came to the assistance of the people. The several townships were equally generous, and in most of them large sums were raised—not only by taxation, but by voluntary contributions. What these sums were, as provided by the authorities of the several townships, we could not ascertain. Each one of the town clerks was written to for information upon this subject, but for some cause unexplained, only a very few of them responded, much to our regret.

As an evidence of the liberality of the Galenians, the following incident was related to the writer, by Captain D. S. Harris: When a company of one-hundred-day men was being raised, Captain Harris started out to raise some money for the benefit of the company. He went up on one side of Main Street, and down on the other, and in one hour's time secured in cash a sum equal to $50 to each man of the company. When the company was ordered to Dixon, he and Mr. John Lorrain accompanied it to camp, and as soon as the men were all mustered in, paid over to each of them fifty dollars as the patriotic offering of the business men along Main Street, Galena.

The *Courier*, of April 30, contained the following personal announcement:

"AT SPRINGFIELD.—Capt. U. S. Grant, of this city, a graduate of West Point, and a Captain in the regular U. S. Army at the time of the Mexican War, is now absent at Springfield, where, it is understood, he will act as a drill officer for the soldiers at Camp Yates. Captain G. is said to be an excellent tactician, and the Governor, no doubt, considers himself fortunate in securing the aid of such an experienced man to assist in drilling the forces of the state."

May 11, the same paper made this additional personal mention:

"CAPT. GRANT.—Capt. U. S. Grant, of this city, who has been detailed by Governor Yates to muster the regiment for the Seventh Congressional into camp, was at Mattoon on the 9th inst., engaged in that service."

It was not supposed at this time that the war between the states would last long—not more than a few months, at the longest; and no one dreamed that the retiring, unassuming Captain U. S. Grant, assigned to drill service by order of Governor Yates, would, in less than two years' time, be made Commander-in-Chief of the United States Army, or that in less than ten years he would rise to a distinction and confidence that would command the highest office within the gift of the American people; or that in less than twenty years he would be the honored and courted guest of the crowned heads and titled courts of the Old World. Yet time has brought all these things about. No man in all the world has now brighter honors, or is more honored and respected than Captain Grant, once an humble leather dealer of Galena.

May 10, 1861, Daniel Wann, Surveyor of Customs at the port of Galena, caused to be published in the Galena papers the following

OFFICIAL NOTICE:

CUSTOM HOUSE, GALENA, May 10, 1861.

Notice is hereby given, to all whom it may concern, that under instructions received at this office, under date of May 2, 1861, in relation to the proclamations of the President of the United States, of the 19th and 27th of April, A. D. 1861, declaring the ports of South Carolina, Georgia, Florida, Alabama, Louisiana, Mississippi, Texas, Virginia, and North Carolina under blockade, a careful examination of the manifests of all steamers or other vessels arriving and departing from this port with cargoes whose destination I have reason to believe is for any port or place in control of insurrectionary persons or parties, will be made by me and compared with the cargoes on board. I will also make a careful examination of all flat boats, and other water craft without manifest, and of railroad cars, and other vehicles arriving at or leaving this port loaded with merchandise, the ultimate destination of which I may have satisfactory reason to believe is for any port or place under the control of insurrectionary parties now opposing the constituted authorities of the United States; and that if any arms, munitions of war, provisions, or other supplies are found on board such vessel, railroad car, or vehicle, having such destination, the same will be seized and detained, to await the proper legal proceedings for confiscation or forfeiture.

All persons are cautioned against furnishing arms, munitions of war, provisions, or other supplies to persons or parties now in insurrection to the constituted authorities of the United States, and are hereby notified that I will use all diligence to prevent the shipment of such arms, munitions of war, provisions, or other supplies to any port or place under the control of such insurrectionary parties, and that I shall use all the care and diligence in my power to bring to punishment any person or persons engaged in furnishing arms, munitions of war, provisions, or supplies, to parties now in open insurrection against the government of the United States.

In carrying out my instructions, I shall endeavor to make as little interruption or delay as possible of the lawful commerce of the country from this port.

DANIEL WANN, *Surveyor of Customs.*

Such were some of the more important events connected with the war history of Jo Daviess County. There were others, but, as previously stated, they can not all be taken up in detail. It has only been our purpose to do justice to the spirit and patriotism of this people, by showing the spirit that prompted them to action in the early days of America's great and bloody internecine conflict. It is a proud record—a record rendered doubly proud by reason of the fact that from their midst great leaders and military chieftains, like Grant and Rawlins, went out to lead the patriot hosts on to victory and the maintenance and perpetuity of the Union.

"A union of lakes, a union of lands—
A union that none can sever—
A union of hearts, a union of hands,
The American Union forever."

The world never witnessed such an uprising of the masses—such a unamimity of sentiment—such willingness to sacrifice men and money.

As we have before remarked, when the first companies were being raised measures were inaugurated and carried out to raise money by subscription for the support of the families of volunteers. But there were so many calls for men, that the needs of families increased so rapidly it became an impossibility for private purses, however willing their holders, to supply the demand, and at last the county authorities were petitioned to make an appropriation for the support of such of the families of the volunteers as needed help. The petition was granted, and the sum of $6,000 appropriated for that purpose. Some of the townships were equally liberal, and besides large sums raised for bounty purposes, sundry amounts were raised and applied to the support of wives and little ones whose husbands and fathers were in the army fighting for their homes. This money was raised in the midst of the war excitement, when the exigencies of the times demanded it, and the people never took the thought to inquire how much they were giving. Nor will it ever be known how much was given. Aside from the sums appropriated by county and township authority, no account was ever kept. Had there been, the sums would now seem almost fabulous.

We have sought by every possible means to arrive at the actual amounts appropriated by the county and its several townships for bounty and other war purposes, but for reasons already stated have failed to obtain the desired information. Only a part of the townships responded to our letters of inquiry. But so far as reports were received, the following is the showing:

Total bounty paid by Jo Daviess County from 1862 to the close of the war	$229,120 00	
Relief by county for soldiers' families, in the same time	6,471 47	—$235,591 47
Dunleith Township, for bounties, etc.	9,500 00	
Menominee " " " "	2,200 00	
Thompson " " " "	3,750 00	
Derinda " " " "	7,800 00	
Ward's Grove " " " "	2,454 00	
Rush " " " "	4,000 00	
Rush Township for relief of families	700 00	
Warren " " " " "	1,000 00	
Elizabeth " " bounties	3,960 00	— $35,364 00
It is fair to presume that the other twelve townships not named appropriated at least	40,000 00	
To which may be added, for voluntary contributions, etc., at least	50,000 00	— $90,000 00
Grand total, from all sources, for war purposes, according to the best sources of information		$361,955 47

The reports from Ward's Grove and Rush Townships are not official, but are believed to be correct. Mr. J. G. Mitchell, clerk of the Township of Ward's Grove, wrote, under date of February 14: "The record in my hands does not show the whole amount paid for bounties to soldiers. It does show $2,454 paid soldiers' bounties, but afterwards there was a tax of one and one half per cent levied for the purpose of liquidating the balance of the war debt. How much that amounted to, my books do not show."

The amount credited to Rush Township was not raised by taxation, but by voluntary contributions.

July 22, 1862, a paper was circulated among the people of Galena, of which the following is a copy, and which is worthy of preservation:

The Union—it must be Preserved. For the purpose of encouraging and assisting in the organization of a new company from Galena, the undersigned offer to contribute the sums attached to our names, to be paid to persons who shall regularly enlist in such company, and be mustered into the service of the United States, under the late call of President Lincoln for volunteers. The sum of $50 is offered to each person who shall enlist from the City of Galena, to be paid when the company is accepted by the Governor of the State of Illinois. *Provided,* That the undersigned shall not pay such subscription should the bounty be provided for by the Board of Supervisors of Jo Daviess County.

Name	Amount	Name	Amount
Henry Corwith	$250 00	R. S. Harris	$ 50 00
Samuel Hughlett	150 00	Jas. Rood	50 00
Augustus Estey	150 00	Benj. R. Sheldon	50 00
N. Corwith	150 00	E. C. Ripley	25 00
B. H. Campbell	150 00	T. H. Gilson	25 00
J. A. Packard	125 00	H. McNeill	25 00
Foster & Stahl	100 00	Wm. Carey	25 00
W. and J. M. Ryan	100 00	Henry Fricke	25 00
W. and J. Fiddick	100 00	S. S. Lorrain	20 00
L. S. Felt	100 00	S. O. Stillman	20 00
John Bennett	50 00	D. Le Better	20 00
Wm. C. Bostwick	50 00	A. Philleo	15 00
Gordon & Willis	50 00	R. Barrett	15 00
Jas. B. Young	50 00	R. Butcher	15 00
D. B. Morehouse	50 00	H. Strohmeyer	10 00
Joseph N. Waggoner	50 00	Jacob Thorworth	15 00
A. H. Davis	50 00		
Total			$2,130 00

The above was not an isolated case of the readiness and willingness of the more affluent people of Jo Daviess County to contribute largely of their means to help carry on the war for the Union. There were many such cases. As long as the war continued, money was ready—men were ready. Men of wealth furnished the former; the less affluent filled the ranks—furnished the brawn, the muscle and the bravery. Sometimes the former furnished not only their share of money, but shouldered their muskets and followed the flag, as well.

Having noticed the financial sacrifices and readiness of the wealthier part of the people to sustain the Union, we come now to the volunteer soldiery. And of these, what can we say? What words can our pen employ that would do justice to their heroic valor—to their unequalled and unparalleled bravery? Home and home comforts—wives and little ones—fathers, mothers, sisters, brothers—were given up for life and danger on the tented fields of battle—for exposure, disease and death at the cannon's mouth. But they reckoned none of these, but went out with their lives in their hands to meet and conquer the foes of the Union, maintain its supremacy, and vindicate its honor and integrity. We can offer no more fitting tribute to their patriotic valor than a full and complete record, so far as it is possible to make it, that will embrace the names, the terms of enlistments, the battles in which they engaged and all the minutiæ of their soldier lives. It will be a wreath of glory encircling every brow, and a memento which each and every one of them earned in defense of their country.

Jo Daviess County Volunteers.

ABBREVIATIONS.

Adjt	Adjutant
Art	Artillery
Bat	Battalion
Col	Colonel
Capt	Captain
Corpl	Corporal
Comsy	Commissary
com	commissioned
cav	cavalry
captd	captured
desrtd	deserted
disab	disabled
disd	discharged
e	enlisted
excd	exchanged
inf	infantry
kld	killed
Lieut	Lieutenant
Maj	Major
m. o	mustered out
prmtd	promoted
prisr	prisoner
Regt	Regiment
re-e	re-enlisted
res	resigned
Sergt	Sergeant
trans	transfered
vet	veteran
wd	wounded
hon discd	honorably discharged

History of 12th Infantry.

The Twelfth Infantry was called into the service under the proclamation of the President, April 6, 1861; was mustered into the service for three years, August 1, 1861. It was stationed at Cairo, Ill., Bird's Point, Mo., Paducah and Smithland, Ky., until February, when it embarked for Fort Henry, being present at its bombardment and surrender. It fought nobly at the memorable battle of Fort Donelson. Loss—19 killed, 58 wounded, 10 missing. It then moved to Clarksville and Nashville, Tenn., on steamer Glendale, and thence on some boat down Cumberland River, and up Tennessee to Pittsburg Landing, participating in that battle. Loss—109 killed and wounded, and 7 missing. It was in the siege of Corinth, and October 3 and 4 in the battle of Corinth, where it performed a very brilliant part. Total engaged—225; loss—17 killed, 80 wounded and 15 missing. The Twelfth was constantly doing active duty, but space forbids us to here follow in detail. It marched across the country to Pulaski, Tenn.; it was in Sherman's March from Chattanooga to Atlanta; took an active part in the battle of Allatoona Pass, and was there commanded by Capt. Robt. Kohler, of Rock Island, although this term of service had expired. In action—161; loss—57 killed and wounded. The Twelfth was in Sherman's March to the Sea, and up through the Carolinas to Washington, and thence to Louisville, where it was mustered out, July 16, 1865.

12th Infantry (3 mos.)

Lieutenant Colonel Augustus L. Chetlain, com. captain Co. F, April 7, 1861. Promoted lieutenant colonel May 3, 1861. Re-entered 3 years' service.

Company F.

Captain Wallace Campbell, com. April 27, 1861. Re-entered 3 years' service.
First Lieutenant J. Bates Dixon, com. second lieutenant April 27, 1861. Promoted first lieutenant May 11, 1861. Re-entered 3 years' service.
Second Lieutenant G. S. Avery, com. May 11, 1861.

12th Infantry (3 years.)

Colonel Augustus L. Chetlain, com. lieutenant colonel May 3, 1861. Promoted colonel April 1, 1862. Promoted brigadier general Dec. 29, 1863. Brevet major general June, 1864.
Adjutant J. Bates Dixon, com. Aug. 1, 1861. Promoted General McArthur's Staff.

Company F.

Captain Wallace Campbell, com. Aug. 1, 1861. Promoted colonel Second Alabama A.D., Dec. 26, 1863.
Captain Chas. Mayer, e. as corporal Aug. 3, 1861. Re-enlisted as veteran Jan. 1, 1864. Promoted sergeant, then second lieutenant Dec. 26, 1863. Promoted captain April 11, 1865. Mustered out July 10, 1865.
First Lieutenant Chas. Farr, e. as sergeant Aug. 3, 1861. Promoted second lieutenant June 20, 1862. Promoted first lieutenant Dec. 26, 1863. Died June 24, 1864.
Second Lieutenant Nicholas Roth, com. Aug. 1, 1861. Resigned June 20, 1862.
Second Lieutenant Geo. Lauk, e. as corporal Aug. 3, 1861. Re-enlisted as veteran Jan. 1, 1864. Mustered out July 10, 1865, as sergeant.
First Sergt. Chas. G. Lutmann, e. July 12, 1861, disd. June 20, 1862, disab.
Sergt. Fred. Ehman, e. Aug. 3, 1861, kld. at Shiloh April 6, 1862.
Sergt. John Eberhart, e. Aug. 3, 1861, disd., term ex.
Sergt. Washington Fuller, e. Aug. 3, 1861.
Corpl. Lewis Hoppe, e. Aug. 3, 1861, vet., kld. at Allatoona, Oct. 5, 1864.
Corpl. Henry Voss, e. Aug. 3, '61, disd. Apl. 22, '65, wd.
Corpl. Wm. H. Dean, e. Aug. 3, 1861, kld. at Atlanta, Ga., Aug. 14, 1864.
Corpl. Wm. H. Langdon, e. Aug. 3, 1861.
Corpl. Wm. H. Bahn, e. Aug. 3, 1861, disd., term ex.
Corpl. Wm. Rockhart, e. Aug. 3, '61, disd. Dec. 6, '62, wd.
Musician Chas. Seitsburg, e. Aug. 3, 1861, vet., trans. to non-com. staff as Prin. Mus'n.
Musician Aug. Richter, e. Aug. 3, 1861, disd., term ex.
Wagoner Leonard Esser, e. July 20, 1861, died March 22, 1862.

A. L. Chetlain

CHICAGO

(FORMERLY OF GALENA)

A L Chetlain

CHICAGO

(FORMERLY OF GALENA)

Brown Jno. e. Aug. 3, 1861, vet., m. o. July 10, 1865, as corpl.
Bahwell Anton, e. Aug. 3, 1861, disd., term ex.
Breigle Jno. e. July 13, 1861, disd. Sept. 7, 1862, disab.
Beckert Chas. A. e. July 13, 1861.
Boardway Wm. e. Aug. 15, 1861, vet., m.o. July 10,'65.
Beebe Geo. e. Aug. 3, 1861.
Bateman Jas. e.Aug.15,'61, vet., m.o. July 10,'65,sergt.
Ball Jas. W. e. Aug. 15, 1861, died June 22, 1862.
Daily Daniel, e. Aug. 3, 1861, kld. at Shiloh Apr.6,'62.
Dawson Wm. e. Aug. 3, '61, died or disd. May 28, '62.
Deitrich John, e. Aug. 3,'61, vet., drowned June 24,'64.
Dutcher Sol. R. e. Aug. 3, 1861, died Dec. 8, 1862.
Ferguson John, e. Aug. 3, 1861, disd., term ex.
Frus John, e. Aug. 10, 1861.
Godet Aug. e. Aug. 3, 1861.
Glookner C. e. Aug. 3, 1861, vet., m. o. July 10, 1865.
Gillmore Geo. e. Aug. 3, 1861, died. Oct. 8, 1862.
Gouschalk Jno. e. Aug. 3, 1861, disd., term ex.
Gault David M. e. Aug. 3, 1861.
Hardwick Wm. e. Aug. 15, 1861, vet., m. o. July 10, 1865, on detached service.
Hamilton Myron, e. Aug. 15, 1861, vet., kld. at Atlanta, Ga., July 28, 1864.
Hoguy Henry, e. Aug. 15, 1861, kld. at Allatoona, Oct. 5, 1864.
Kerfner Chas. e. July 21, 1861, disd., term ex.
Kline Ignatz, e. Aug. 3, 1861, disd., term ex.
Koch Aug. e. Aug. 3, 1861, vet., m. o. July 10, 1865,
Kroemer Ezekiel, e. Aug. 3,'61, died Aug. 18, '61, wds.
Kroemer Ed. R. e. Aug. 3, 1861, vet., m. o. July 10, 1865, absent, sick.
Kloenne Chas. e, Aug. 3, 1861, disd. July 29,1862.
Limper Chas. e. Aug. 3, 1861, disd., term ex.
Langenbach Wm. e, July 14, 1861, m. o. Aug. 29, 1864.
Leightner Jas. R. e. July 17, 1861, disd., term ex.
Myer Chas. R. e. July 21, 1861, disd., term ex.
Myers Herman, e. Aug. 3, '61, disd. Sept. 26,'62,disab.
Miller Samuel. e. Aug. 15, 1861, died Feb. 26, 1862.
Miller Chas. H. e. Aug. 3, 1861, disd., term ex.
McDonald Jas, e. Aug. 3, 1861, disd., term ex.
McCrae John, e. Aug. 3, 1861, vet., kld. at Atlanta, July 22, 1864.
Mitsch Jos. e.Aug. 3,'61, vet., m.o. July 10, '65, corpl.
Nevrill J. E. C. e. July 12, '61, disd. July 29,'62,disab.
Otten Henry, e. July 20, 1861, disd. Dec. 6, 1862.
Pfund John, e. July 13, 1861, vet., m. o. July 10, 1865.
Palmer L. H. e. Aug. 3,'61, vet.,m.o. July 10,'65, sergt.
Pringle Wm. W. e. Aug. 15, 1861.
Powers Chas. e. Aug. 3, 1861, disd., term ex.
Quinton Ed. e. Aug. 3, 1861, died Aug. 4, 1862.
Raik Christ. e. July 15, 1861, disd., term ex.
Rogers John, e. July 23, 1861, disd. July 9, 1862.
Starr Samuel, e. Aug. 3, 1861, vet., m. o. July 10, 1865.
Smith Frank, e. Aug. 3, 1861, vet., kld. at Atlanta, July 22, 1864.
Solzer Geo. e. Aug. 3, 1861, disd., term ex.
Seigenfuss Christ. e. Aug. 3, 1861, disd., term ex.
Sneider Geo. e. Aug. 3, 1861, disd., term ex.
Schneider Chas. e. Aug. 3, 1861, disd. June 14, 1862.
Scheerer Wm. e. July 13, 1861, disd., term ex.
Speth Andrew, e. Aug. 3, 1861, disd. July 29, 1862, wd.
Suter Burkhart, e. July 21, 1861, kld. at Atlanta, July 22, 1864.
Sager Wm. e. July 13, 1861, vet., m. o. July 10, 1865.
Stibbins Jacob, e. July 15, 1861.
Spalding O. L. e. July 22, 1861.
Stewart Chas. B. e. Aug. 3, 1861, disd. April 3, 1862.
Scofield Josiah, e. Aug. 15, 1861, vet.
Wilson John, e. Aug. 15, 1861, disd., term ex.
Wilkins Henry H. e. Aug. 3, 1861.
Williams R. A. e. Aug. 12, 1861, vet., m.o. July 10, '65.
Young Wm. e. Aug. 15, 1861, disd., term ex.
Zitha Frank, e. July 15, 1861, disd. June 26, 1862.
Zeiler Henry, e. July 20, 1861, vet., m. o. July 10, 1865.
Austine Philip, e. Feb. 14, 1864, m. o. July 15, 1865.
Budden Henry, e. Feb. 12, 1864, m. o. July 10, 1865.
Budden John, e. Feb. 17, 1864, m. o. July 10, 1865.
Bauer Jos. e. Feb. 17, 1864, m. o. July 15, 1865.
Buman John, e. Sept. 12, 1862, m. o. July 15, 1865, absent, wd.
Brunson John, e. Sept. 3, 1862, m. o. July 15, 1865.
Bettinger N. e. Feb. 14, 1864, died Nov. 23, wd.
Caille Louis, e. Sept. 15, 1862, m. o. July 10, 1865.
Clifford Jas. H. e. Oct. 31, 1863, disd. May 19, '65, disab.
Dinger Leonard, e. Feb. 17, 1864, m. o. July 10, 1865.
Dempsey Bate, e. Feb. 18, 1864, m. o. July 10, 1865.
Delannay M. F. e. March 4, 1864, m. o. July 10, 1865.
Godat G. A. e. Feb. 18, 1864, m. o. July 10, 1865, sergt.
Gavigan Jas. e. Feb. 20, 1864, m. o. July 10, 1865.
Gruenewald John, e. Feb. 3, 1864, disd. April 3, 1865.
Houy Geo. e. April 13, 1865, m. o. July 10, 1865.
Kirk Jas. e. Feb. 20, 1864, m. o. July 10, 1865.
Kelly Daniel, e. Feb. 24, 1864, m. o. July 10, 1865.
Kippenham Henry, e. Sept. 9, 1862, m. o. July 10, 1865, sick, absent.
Kain Chas. e. Sept. 12, 1862, m. o. July 10, 1865.
Kurth Chas. e. Sept. 3, 1862, m. o. July 10, 1865.
Mack Barnard, e. Feb. 24, 1864, m. o. July 10, 1865.
Murphy Thomas, e. Feb. 27, 1864, m. o. July 10, 1865.
McCormick John J. e. Feb. 27, 1864, m. o. July 10, '65.
McKinney Ed. e. Jan. 20, 1864, m. o. July 10, 1865.
Mahony L. B. e. Feb. 18, 1864, trans. to Vet. Reserve Corps.
O'Neil David, e. Oct. 1, 1864, m. o. July 10, 1865.
O'Neil John, e. March 6, 1865, m. o. July 10, 1865.
Prill John, e. Feb. 18, 1864, m. o. June 28, 1865.
Rippen Wm. e. Feb. 29, 1864, m. o. July 10, 1865, absent, wd.
Rourke John, e. Feb. 19, 1864, m. o. July 10, 1865.
Russington John, e. April 13, 1865, m. o. July 10, 1865.
Schlurer John, e. Feb. 25, 1864, m. o. July 10, 1865.
Seeger Wm. e. Feb. 10, 1864, m. o. July 10, 1865.
Starr Robt. e. Feb. 18, 1864, m. o. July 10, 1865.
Starr Geo. e. Oct. 7, 1864, m. o. July 10, 1865.
Sincock Thos. e. Feb. 17, 1864, died Oct. 15, 1864, wd.
Schultz F. e. Sept. 27, 1864, m. o. June 1, 1865.
Van Court R. D. e. Sept. 13, 1862, disd. Jan. 7, 1865.
White Robt. e. Feb. 26, 1864, m. o. July 10, 1865.
Williams P. e. Oct. 7, 1864, m. o. July 10, 1865.

15th Infantry.

The Fifteenth Regiment Infantry Illinois Volunteers was organized at Freeport, Illinois, and mustered into the United States service May 24, 1861—being the first regiment organized from the state for the three years' service. It then proceeded to Alton, Ill., remaining there six weeks for instruction. Left Alton for St. Charles, Mo.; thence by rail to Mexico, Mo. Marched to Hannibal, Mo.; thence by steamboat to Jefferson Barracks; then by rail to Rolla, Mo. Arrived in time to cover Gen. Siegel's retreat from Wilson's Creek; thence to Tipton, Mo., and thence joined Gen. Fremont's army. Marched from there to Springfield, Mo.; thence back to Tipton; then to Sedalia, with Gen. Pope, and assisted in the capture of 1,300 of the enemy a few miles from the latter place; then marched to Otterville, Mo., where it went into winter quarters Dec. 26, 1861. Remained there until Feb. 1, 1862. Then marched to Jefferson City; thence to St. Louis by rail; embarked on transports for Fort Donelson, arriving there the day of the surrender.

The regiment was then assigned to the Fourth Division, Gen. Hurlbut commanding, and marched to Fort Henry. Then embarked on transports for Pittsburg Landing. Participated in the battles of the 6th and 7th of April, losing 252 men, killed and wounded. Among the former were Lieutenant-Colonel E. T. W. Ellis, Major Goddard, Captains Brownell and Wayne, and Lieutenant John W. Puterbaugh. Captain Adam Nase, wounded and taken prisoner. The regiment then marched to Corinth, participating in various skirmishes and the siege of that place, losing a number of men killed and wounded.

After the evacuation of Corinth, the regiment marched to Grand Junction; thence to Holly Springs; back to Grand Junction; thence to Lagrange; thence to Memphis, arriving there July 21, 1862, and remained there until September 6. Then marched to Bolivar; thence to the Hatchie river, and participated in the battle of the Hatchie. Lost fifty killed and wounded in that engagement. Then returned to Bolivar; from thence to Lagrange; thence, with Gen. Grant, down through Mississippi to Coffeeville, returning to Lagrange and Memphis; thence to Vicksburg, taking an active part in the siege of that place. After the surrender of Vicksburg, marched with Sherman to Jackson, Miss.; then returned to Vicksburg and embarked for Natchez; Marched thence to Kingston; returned to Natchez; then to Harrisonburg, La., capturing Fort Beauregard, on the Washita River. Returned to Natchez, remained there until Nov. 10, 1863. Proceeded to Vicksburg and went into winter quarters. Here the regiment reenlisted as veterans, remaining until Feb, 1, 1864, when it moved with Gen. Sherman through Mississippi. On Champion Hills had a severe engagement with rebel Carney. Marched to Meridan; thence south to Enterprise; thence back to Vicksburg. Was then ordered to Illinois on veteran furlough. On expiration of furlough joined Seventeenth Army Corps and proceeded up the Tennessee River to Clifton; thence to Huntsville, Ala.; thence to Decatur and Rome, Ga.; thence to Kingston; and joined Gen. Sherman's army, marching on Atlanta.

At Allatoona Pass the Fifteenth and the Fourteenth Infantry were consolidated, and the organization was known as the Veteran Battalion Fourteenth and Fifteenth Illinois Infantry Volunteers, and numbering 625 men. From Allatoona Pass it proceeded to Ackworth, and was then assigned to duty, guarding the Chattanooga and Atlanta Railroad. Whilst engaged in this duty, the regiment being scattered along the line of road, the rebel Gen. Hood, marching north, struck the road at Big Shanty and Ackworth, and captured about 300 of the command. The remainder retreated to Marietta, were mounted and acted as scouts for Gen. Vandever. They were afterwards transfered to Gen. F. P. Blair, and marched with Gen. Sherman through Georgia.

After the capture of Savannah, the regiment proceeded to Beaufort, S. C.; thence to Salkahatchie River, participating in the various skirmishes in that vicinity —Columbia, S. C., Fayetteville, N. C., battle of Bentonville—losing a number wounded; thence to Goldsboro and Raleigh. At Raleigh, recruits sufficient to fill up both regiments were received, and the organization of the Veteran Battalion discontinued, and the Fifteenth re-organized. The campaign of Gen. Sherman ended by the surrender of Gen. Johnson. The regiment then marched with the army to Washington, D. C., via Richmond and Fredericksburg, and participated in the grand review at Washington, May 24, 1865; remained there two weeks. Proceeded, by rail and steamboat, to Louisville, Ky.; remained at Louisville two weeks. The regiment was then detached from the Fourth Division, Seventeenth Army Corps, and proceeded by steamer to St. Louis; from thence to Fort Leavenworth, Kan., arriving there July 1, 1865. Joined the army serving on the Plains. Arrived at Fort Kearney, August 14; then ordered to return to Fort Leavenworth, Sept. 1, 1865, where the regiment was mustered out of the service and placed en route for Springfield, Ill., for final payment and discharge—having served four years and four months.

Number of miles marched	4299
Number of miles by rail	2403
Number of miles by steamer	4310
Total miles traveled	11,012
Number of men joined from organization	1963
Number of men at date of muster-out	640

Lieutenant Jas. Rany, commissioned captain Co. E, April 24, 1861. Promoted major, April 7, 1862. Promoted lieutenant colonel, Nov. 2, 1862. Resigned Jan. 16, 1864.

Company E.

Captain Daniel J. Benner, commissioned first lieutenant, April 24, 1861. Promoted captain, April 7, 1862. Resigned April 18, 1863.
Captain Jno. W. Luke, commissioned second lieutenant, April 24, 1861. Promoted first lieutenant, April 7, 1862. Promoted captain, April 18, 1863. (See Co. E, Veteran Battalion.)
First Lieutenant Allen P. Barnes, e. as first sergeant, May 24, 1861. Promoted second lieutenant, April 7, 1862. Promoted first lieutenant, April 18, 1863. (See Co. E, Veteran Battalion.)
Sergt. Geo. N. Townsend, Jr., e. May 24, 1861, m. o. May 24, 1864.
Sergt. James R. Hastie, e. May 24, 1861, kld. at Shiloh, April 6, 1862.
Sergt. Wm. D. Lathrop, e. May 24, 1861, died April 22, 1862, wd.
Corpl. Rufus B. Tucker, e. May 24, 1861, vet., m. o. July 20, 1865.
Corpl. Cyrus Tilton, e. May 24, 1861, disd. July 2, '63.
Corpl. Wm. Parkinson, e. May 24, 1861, kld. at Shiloh, April 6, 1862.
Corpl. Lycurgus A. Haskel, e. May 24, 1861, died April 9, 1862, wd.
Ashkettle Wm. C. e. May 24, 1861, disd. Jan. 22, 1862.
Ashkettle Horace, e. May 24, 1861, kld. at Shiloh, April 6, 1862.
Belden H. S. e. May 24, 1861, vet., disd. Sept. 13, 1865.
Barnes Robt. R. e. May 24, 1861, vet., prmtd. corpl., m. o. Sept. 16, 1865.
Bates Richard, e. May 24, 1861, died Dec. 6, 1861.
Brininger B. e. May 24, 1861, disd. Aug. 17, 1862, disab.
Buckley W. L. e. May 24, 1861, disd. Jan. 7, 1864, disab.
Christian John V. e. May 24, 1861, died March 4, 1862.
Clancey M. e. May 24, 1861, m. o. May 24, 1864.
Clock Chas. L. e. May 24, '61, disd. April 28, '63, disab.
Conarty John, e. May 24, 1861, vet., m.o. May 20, 1865.
Cowan E. H. e. May 24, 1861, kld. at Shiloh, Apl. 6, '62.
Curry Jas. e. May 24, 1861, disd. Jan. 18, 1862, disab.
Dunkel A. K. e. May 24, 1861.
Davis D. W. e. May 24, 1861, kld. at Shiloh, Apl. 6, '62.
Flack Marion, e. May 24, '61, kld. at Shiloh, Apl. 6, '62.
French Horace H. e. May 24, '61, vet., disd. May 5, '65.
Fulton Ira, e. May 24, 1861, vet., m. o. Sept. 16, 1865, as corpl.
Foreman Alfred, e. May 24, 1861, vet., m.o. Sept. 16, '65.
Foss L. W. e. May 24, 1861, died Nov. 30, 1861.
Grice Isaiah, e. May 24, 1861, died Oct., 1861.
Godfrey S. W. e. May 24, '61, kld. at Shiloh, Apl. 6, '62.
Galt Hugh, e. May 24, 1861, died Aug. 5, 1863.
Helsby Chas. W. e. May 24, 1861, died Apl. 9, 1862, wd.
Horn Elias, e. May 24, 1861, vet., m. o. Sept. 16, 1865.
Huet John, e. May 24, 1861, kld. at Shiloh, Apl. 6, '62.
Huet Andrew, e. May 24, 1861, m. o. May 24, 1864.
Hart C. T. e. May 24, 1861, vet., m. o. May 30, 1865.
Isner Hiram, e. May 24, 1861.
Jerman John, e. May 24, 1861, kld. at Shiloh, Apl. 6, '62.
Kahler Wm. e. May 24, 1861, m. o. May 24, 1864.
Leet Jno. L. e. May 24, 1861.
Newton Wallace, e. May 24, 1861, m. o. May 24, 1864.
Neal Benj. F. e. May 24, 1861, vet., m. o. May 30, 1865.
Parkinson Jas. e. May 24, 1861, died Oct. 20, 1861.
Robbins Walter S. e. May 24, 1861, died Oct. 20, 1861.
Ruble Jas. P. e. May 24, 1861.
Rollison M. e. May 24, 1861, disd. Aug. 17, 1862.
Spencer A. L. e. May 24, 1861, vet., m. o. May 30, 1865.
Smith John J. e. May 24, 1861, m.o. May 24, 1864.
Shaw John W. e. May 24, 1861, disd. Aug. 23, 1863, wd.
Tucker H. Z. e. May 24, 1861, m. o. May 24, 1864.
Wiley Silas, e. May 24, 1861, died of wd. received at Shiloh.
Woodworth Wm. H. e. May 24, 1861, disd. May 12, 1863, disab.
Wier Jas. J. e. May 24, 1861, disd. Aug. 12, 1862, disab.
Yates Chas. H. e. May 24, 1861, disd. Oct. 15, '61, disab.
Allen E. F. e. Sept. 1, 1861, vet., on detached service.
Byors John T. e. May 25, 1861.
Braninger Peter, e. Sept. 12, 1861, vet., m.o. Sept. 16, '65.
Case Geo. W. e. Sept. 5, 1861, vet., m. o. Sept. 30. 1865.
Clark L. P. e. Sept. 12, 1861, vet., no report.
Edwards Aug. e. May 25, 1861, disd. Dec. 16, '62, disab.
Ewing John, e. April 1, 1864, m. o. May 30, 1865.
Griffiths John H. e. July 8, 1861, trans. as fife major.
Holmes Meric, e. June 3, 1861, died Oct. 18, 1862.
Jelly John S. e. June 4, 1861, m. o. May 24, 1864.
McClanion D. e. June 3, 1861, died May 6, 1862.
Munngar Geo. e. Sept. 12, 1861.
Reed Chas. B. e. Sept. 12, 1861, disd. Dec. 17, 1861, worthlessness.
Rodgers Wm. A. e. March 10, 1862, died July 7, 1862.
Sullivan M. e. Dec. 25, 1863, died at Andersonville, Jan. 18, 1865.
Ward Geo. W. disd. Aug. 17, 1862, disab.

Company K.

Holms Ed. P. e. March 10, 1862, disd. Sept. 15, 1863.
Thompson Wm. F. e. April 28, 1864, m. o. May 30, 1865.

14th and 15th Inf. Vet. Bat.

Company B.

Clark Cornelius, e. April 19, 1864, died Aug. 9, 1864.

15th Regt. Re-organized.

Company A.

Sergt. H. F. Caverly, e. Feb. 24, 1865, m.o. Sept. 16, '65.
Sergt. Leonard Kinsell, e. Feb. 22, 1865, m. o. Sept. 16, 1865.
Corpl. R. W. Isbell, e. Feb. 18, 1865, m.o. Sept. 16, 1865.
Corpl. Martin Binzler, e. Feb. 24, '65, m. o. Sept. 16, '65.

Wagoner S. A. Guild, e. Feb. 13, '65, m.o. Sept. 16, '65.
Barnes Jos. e. Feb. 23, 1865, m. o. June 28, 1865.
Dillon Thos. E. e. Feb. 22, 1865, m. o. Sept. 16, 1865.
Graten Peter, e. Feb. 22, 1865, deserted July 22, 1865.
Gilmore Patrick, e. Feb. 23, 1865, deserted June 30, '65.
Heckeismiller Adam, e. Feb. 24. 1865, m.o. July 19, '65.
Hubocker N. e. Feb. 24, 1865, m. o. Sept. 16, 1865.
Hipp Conrad, e. Feb. 24, 1865, m. o. July 19, 1865,
Holman John H. e. March 2, 1865, m. o. Sept. 16, 1865.
Jordan Henry, e. March 2, 1865, m. o. July 3, 1865.
Klett Julius, e. Feb. 24, 1865, m. o. Sept. 16, 1865.
Kammerer D. e. Feb. 24, 1865, m. o. Sept. 16, 1865.
Kurtz F. e. Feb. 24, 1865, m. o. Sept. 16, 1865.
McCormack P. e. March 2, 1865, deserted July 22, '65.
Read David, e. Feb. 22, 1865, m. o. Sept. 16, 1863.
Read Jas. e. Feb. 23, 1865, m. o. July 19, 1865.
Smith Chas. e. Feb. 1, 1865.
Schreitmuller J. M. e. Feb. 22, 1865, m. o. Sept. 16, '65.
Shaller Henry, e. Feb. 22, 1865, m. o. Aug. 14, 1865.
Stadell Wm. e. Feb. 17, 1865, m. o. July 31, 1865.
Vogit Jacob, e. Feb. 24, 1865, m. o. July 5, 1865.
Ward John, e. Feb. 23, 1865, m. o. Sept. 16, 1865.
Wolf John, e. Feb. 23, 1865, deserted March 26, 1865.

Company E.

Captain John W. Luke, commissioned April 18, 1863. Mustered out Jan. 9, 1864.
First Lieutenant Allen P. Barnes, commissioned April 18, 1863. Honorably discharged May 15, 1865.
Corpl. Jesse Fenn, e. Jan. 1, 1864, m. o. May 30, 1865.
Corpl. A. L. Spenser, e. Jan. 1, 1864, m. o. May 30, '65.
Blodgett E. A. e. Jan. 1, 1864, m. o. May 30, 1865.
Wilson Robt. B. e. Jan. 1, 1864, vet., prmtd. corpl. and sergt.

19th Infantry.

The 19th was enrolled June 4, 1861; mustered in for three years' service, at Chicago, June 17. Part of the regiment first moved to Cairo, where their duty was chiefly guarding railroad property. John B. Turchin was appointed Colonel; Jas. R. Scott, Lieutenant Colonel; Frederick Harding, Major; C. C. Miller, Adjutant; and H. W. Wetherell, Quartermaster. The officers of the Chicago companies had been members of the renowned Ellsworth Zouaves. The regiment left Chicago July 5, for Palmyra, Mo., where they received some notoriety on account of foraging on the enemy. In August they joined Pope's Command, and moved to Pilot Knob; thence to Cape Girardeau; thence toward Columbus, Ky. September 15 were ordered to join Army of the Potomac. On the way, about eighty-four miles west of Cincinnati, on Ohio & Mississippi R. R., a bridge gave way, after the engine and two cars had passed. The six following passenger coaches were precipitated a distance of sixty feet. In this disaster the regiment lost more than in their severest battle. Detained by this accident, the regiment joined Mitchell's Division, Sherman's Army, Colonel Turchin commanding brigade, and operated in Kentucky. At the time of the battle in Shiloh, Mitchell's Division marched to Nashville, and thence to Huntsville, Ala., where they captured a large amount of rolling stock and commissary stores. The command was then scattered around, guarding important points. At Athens, Ala., the 18th Ohio was driven out by Scott's rebel cavalry. General Turchin, with balance of brigade, recaptured the place. As many prominent citizens had derided our troops as they were being driven out of Athens, on their return they demolished a large part of the business portion of the place. General Buel soon after visited Athens, and was easily influenced by stories of citizens, to the effect that great improprieties had been practiced by the soldiers during the sacking of the place. A court martial was convened and Colonel Turchin dismissed from the service. Two days before the findings of the court martial, Colonel Turchin had been appointed Brigadier General by the President. The 17th, as a mark of disgrace, was cut up into small squads and assigned to guarding bridges. It then moved to Nashville and placed under General Negley's command. At the memorable battle of Stone River, in a critical juncture, General Negley cried: "Who will save the left?" "The Nineteenth!" said Colonel Scott; and forward dashed this heroic regiment, capturing four pieces of artillery, and, many say, saved the day. This command were from this time actively moving over the country, principally after Bragg, ending in the battle of Chicamauga, and then Mission Ridge, in both of which the 19th distinguished itself. Thence they proceeded toward Atlanta until their term of service expired, when they returned to Chicago and were mustered out.

Company I.

Captain Bashrod B. Howard, commissioned July 30, 1861. Killed by railroad accident.
Captain John R. Madison, commissioned second lieutenant, July 30, 1861. Promoted first lieutenant Oct. 20, 1861. Promoted captain March 24, 1862. Resigned Dec. 19, 1862.
Captain Jas. Longhorn, e. as private June 17, 1861. Promoted first lieutenant March 24, 1862. Promoted captain Dec. 19, 1862. Term expired July 9, 1864.
First Lieutenant Thaddeus G. Drum, commissioned July 30, 1861. Resigned Oct. 31, 1861.
First Lieutenant Wm. Quinton, commissioned second lieutenant Oct. 20, 1861. Promoted first lieutenant Dec. 19, 1862. Resigned Sept. 10, 1864.
Second Lieutenant D. B. Morehouse, e. as sergeant, June 17, 1861. Promoted second lieutenant Dec. 19, 1862. Term expired July 9, 1864.
First Sergt. Thomas J. French, e. June 17, 1861, disd. July 29, 1861, disab.
Sergt. Wm. Camphouse, e. June 17, 1861, m. o. July 9, 1864, as private.
Sergt. Wm. Pittham, e. June 17, 1861, disd. Feb. 25, 1862, disab.
Sergt. Conrad Schlosser, e. June 17. 1861, died at Chicago, July 4, 1864.
Corpl. H. Simons, e. June 17, 1861, sergt., died April 29, 1863.
Corpl. R. M. Lyons, e. June 17, 1861, m. o. July 9, 1864, as first sergt.
Corpl. Jerr Ingraham, e. June 17. 1861, kld. Sept. 17, '61.
Anton Nicholas, e. June 17, 1861, m. o. July 9, 1864.
Archer E. A. e. June 17, 1861, disd. July 2, 1861, disab.
Barras Henry, e. June 17, 1861, kld. Sept. 17. 1861.
Boston J. W. e. June 17, 1861, disd. Feb. 27, '63, disab.
Brown John, e. June 17, 1861, kld. Sept. 17, 1861.
Barton Jno. R. e. June 17, 1861, corpl., died Oct. 10, 1863, wd.
Bird Jesse W. e. June 17, 1861, disd. July 14, '61, disab.
Bartholow Robt. L. e. June 17, 1861, deserted Aug. 1, '61.
Coleman Jacob, e. June 17, 1861, kld. Sept. 17, 1861.
Cramer John, e. June 17, 1861, disd. Feb. 6, '62, disab.
Clark Samuel, e. June 17, 1861, kld. Sept. 17, 1861.
Carroll L. M. e. June 17, 1861, trans. to Signal Corps as sergt., Oct. 22, 1863.
Carroll L. e. June 17, 1861, kld. Sept. 17, 1861.
Craig Thos. e. June 17, 1861, m. o. July 9, '64, as corpl.
Connor Henry, e. June 17, 1861, kld. Sept. 17, 1861.
Deniken V. e. June 17, 1861, disd. Nov. 19, 1861, disab.
Davis Geo. W. e. June 17, 1861, m. o. July 9, 1864.
Dowling Stephen, e. June 17, 1861, m. o. July 9, 1864.
Dennis Henry, e. June 17, 61, disd. Nov. 19, '61, disab.
Donnelly John, e. June 17, 1861, deserted June 10, '62.
Doering Richard, e. June 17, 1861, m. o. July 9, 1864.
Douglas John, e. June 17. 1861, kld. Sept. 17, 1861.
Fowler Daniel, e. June 17, 1861, m. o. July 9, 1864.
Fox Richard M. e. June 17, 1861, disd. to enlist in 4th U. S. C.
Franks Andrew, e. June 17, 1861, m. o. July 9, 1864.
Gand John, e. June 17, 1861, m. o. July 9, 1864, was wagoner.
Harwick Jas. e. June 17, 1861, disd. to enlist in 4th U. S. C.
Harwick Wm. e. June 17, 1861, kld. Sept. 17, 1861.
Hogan W. T. e. June 17, 1861, m. o. July 9, 1864.
Harmes Henry, e. June 17, 1861, m. o. July 9, 1864.
Irvine Samuel C. e. June 17, 1861, disd. June 14, 1862, disab.
Judy Rodolf e. June 17, 1861, m. o. July 9, 1864.
Leinberger E. e. June 17, 1861, dishonorably disd. Aug. 26, 1861.
Lamb Thos. e. June 17, 1861, died at Nashville, Tenn., Oct. 4, 1862.
Lesh Jas. e. June 17, 1861, disd. Aug. 6, 1861, disab.
Linn Jas. e. June 17, 1861, deserted May 7, 1862.
Mensel F. e. June 17, 1861, died at Nashville, Tenn., July 23, 1862.
Matt Jcs. e June 17, 1861, m. o. July 9, 1864.
Metzger John, e. June 17, 1861, disd. Nov. 11, '63, disab.
Morrison Thos. e. June 17, 1861, died at Nashville, Tenn., Feb. 22, 1864.

Maloney M. e. June 17, 1861, deserted Oct. 3, 1862.
Morrisey Jno. e. June 17, 1861, m. o. July 9, 1864.
Michael J. M. e. June 17, 1861, m. o. July 9, 1864.
Noble Robt. e. June 17, 1861, m. o. July 9, 1864.
Nolan Wm. T. e. June 17, 1861, m. o. July 9, 1864.
Painter A. H. e. June 17, 1861. kld. Sept. 17, 1861.
Pugh W. H. e. June 17, 1861, disd. July 14, 1861, disab.
Palmer H. H. e. June 17, 1861, m. o. July 9, 1864.
Petree John, e. June 17, 1861, m. o. July 9, 1864.
Roffner A. e. June 17, 1861, kld. Sept. 17, 1861.
Ripin Alford, e. June 17, 1861, disd. to enlist in 4th U. S. C.
Streif Henry, e. June 17, 1861, m. o. July 9, 1864.
Smith Jos. e. June 17, 1861, kld. Sept. 17, 1861.
Scholtz Chas. e. June 17, 1861, disd. Mch. 17, '63, disab.
Snyder Daniel, e. June 17, 1861, m. o. July 9, '64, corpl.
Schermerhorn C. e. June 17, 1861, m. o. July 9, 1864.
Smith Wm. C. e. June 17, 1861, m. o. July 9, '64, corpl.
Tyler Wm. P. e. June 17, 1861, disd. Nov. 19, '61, disab.
Thorp Wm. D. e. June 17, 1861, disd. Aug. 7, '62, disab.
Vickers Wm. H. e. June 17, '61, disd. July 31, '62, disab.
Wirth Aug. e. June 17, 1861, disd. Nov. 19, '61, disab.
Waldner C. e. June 17, 1861, died Feb. 3, 1862.
Wepps Wm. e. June 17, 1861, disd. Dec. 4, 1861, disab.
Wilson John, e. June 17, 1861, disd. Aug. 1, 1861, disab.
Walker Richard, e. June 17, 1861, m. o. July 9, 1864.
Walker Abram, e. June 17, 1861, m. o. July 9, 1864.
Winterstein M. e. June 17, 1861, disd. Nov. 5, '61, disab.
Weinshorner H. e. June 17, 1861, disd. Nov. 5, '61, disab.
Waulthour D. B. e. June 17, 1861, deserted Jan. 6, '62.
Baldwin Jno. H. e. Oct. 2, '61, disd. Sept. 13, '62, disab.
Bruce A. J. e. Oct. 22, 1861, trans. to headquarters 14th A. C.
Barnhart John, e. Oct. 22, 1861, died at Louisville, Jan. 10, 1862.
Bruce Robt. e. July 3, 1861, kld. Sept. 17, 1861.
Cookson John S. e. Oct. 2, 1861, trans. to 14th A. C.
Cook Chas. e. Oct. 1, 1861, trans. to 14th A. C.
Connelly M. e. July 5, 1861, kld. Sept. 17, 1861.
Dawson Jas. W. e. July 2, 1861, disd. Nov. 29, '61, disab.
Ellis E. N. e. Sept. 7, 1862, m. o. June 4, 1865.
Gilmore Wm. e. July 1, 1861, deserted Aug. 2, 1862.
Hardy Frank, e. July 5, 1861, disd. Aug. 7, 1862, disab.
Honyer Leopold, e. July 4, 1861, m. o. July 9, 1864.
Koley Earnest, e. Oct. 3, 1861, disd. Apl. 12, '63, disab.
Keenan Frank, e. June 17, 1861, deserted Aug. 6, 1861.
McManners Thos. e. July 4, 1861, deserted Aug. 1, '61.
Plean C. e. July 4, 1861, disd. Nov. 9, 1861, disab.
Rhine John, e. July 5, 1861, kld. Sept. 17, 1861.
Ringer Wm. e. July 1, 1861, kld. Sept. 17, 1861.
Speck Aug. e. July 5, 1861, trans. to 14th A. C.
Stacey Wm. e. July 7, 1862, trans. to 14th A. C.
Thistlethuaite C. e. Oct. 1, 1861, trans. to 14th A. C.
Trittean John, e. June 17, 1861, kld. at Stone River, Dec. 31, 1862.
Winser Henry, Oct. 3, 1861, trans. to 14th A. C.
Walker S. H. e. June 17, 1861, m. o. July 9, 1864.

21st Infantry.

The Seventh Congressional District Regiment was organized at Mattoon, Ill., on the 9th of May, 1861. On the 15th of May it was mustered into the state service for 30 days, by Capt. U. S. Grant. On the 28th of June, it was mustered into United States' service for three years, by Capt. Pitcher, U. S. A., with Capt. U. S. Grant as colonel. Col. Grant was commissioned brigadier general Aug. 6, 1861, and was succeeded by Lieutenant Colonel J. W. S. Alexander, who was killed Sept. 20, 1863, at Chicamauga. On the 4th of July, 1861, the regiment marched for Missouri; 22d, arrived at Mexico, where it remained until Aug. 6, when it proceeded, by rail, to Ironton, Mo. Oct. 20, marched from Ironton, and on 21st participated in battle of Fredricktown. Remained at Ironton until Jan. 29, 1862. Marched, with Gen. Steele's expedition, to Jacksonport, Ark., when it was ordered to Corinth *via* Cape Girardeau. Arrived at Hamburg Landing, May 24, 1862. On evacuation of Corinth, pursued enemy from Farmington, Miss., to Booneville. Returning from the pursuit, it formed a part of an expedition to Holly Springs. On the 14th of Aug., 1862, was ordered to join Gen. Buell's army in Tennessee. Marched *via* Eastport, Miss., Columbia, Tenn., Florence, Ala., Franklin, Murfreesboro and Nashville, Tenn., and arrived at Louisville, Sept. 27, 1862. Engaged in battle of Perryville, Oct. 8th, and Chaplin Hill. Company F, Capt. David Blackburn, was the first in Perryville. From thence, marched to Crab Tree Orchard and Bowling Green, Ky., and to Nashville, Tenn. When the army marched from Nashville, Dec. 26, 1862, this regiment formed a part of the Second Brigade, First Division, Twentieth Army Corps, and was in the skirmish at Knob Gap. December 30, in connection with Fifteenth Wisconsin, Thirty-eighth Illinois, and One Hundred and First Ohio, it had a severe engagement with the enemy near Murfreesboro, where it charged the famous Washington (Rebel) Light Artillery, twelve Parrott guns, and succeeded in driving every man from the battery, when it was compelled to fall back by a division of Rebel Infantry. During the battle of Murfreesboro it was fiercely engaged and did gallant duty, losing more men than any other regiment engaged. The Twenty-first was with Gen. Rosecrans' army from Murfreesboro to Chattanooga; was engaged in a severe skirmish at Liberty Gap, June 25, 1863; was engaged in the battle of Chicamauga, Sept. 19 and 20, where it lost 238 officers and men. Col. Alexander being killed, and Lieut. Col. McMackin being wounded, Capt. C. K. Knight took command of the regiment. After the battle of Chicamauga, the Twenty-first was attached to First Brigade, First Division, Fourth Army Corps, and remained at Bridgeport, Ala., during October, November and December, 1863. Mustered out Dec. 16, 1865, at San Antonio, Texas. Arrived at Camp Butler, Jan. 18, 1866, for final payment and discharge.

Colonel Ulysses S. Grant, commissioned June 15, 1861. Promoted brigadier general Aug. 5, 1861. Promoted major general Feb. 16, 1862.

Company B.

Able John, e. Oct. 3, 1864, trans., m. o. Oct. 15, 1865.
Bingham Geo. e. Mch. 24, 1864, trans., m.o.Dec. 16, '65.
Bryson Robt. e. Mch. 3, 1864, trans., m. o. Dec. 16, '65.
Bennett E. R. e. Mch. 13, 1864, trans., m.o. Sept. 4, '65.
Collins Wm. H. e. Mch. 16, '64, trans., m.o. Dec. 16, '65.
Delaney Jas. e. Oct. 14, 1864, trans., died Aug. 2, 1865.
Davis Henry A. e. Jan. 4, 1864, trans., m.o. Dec. 16, '65.
Ebby Chas. e. Mch. 3, 1864, trans., m. o. Dec. 16, 1865.
Gayetty Wm. e. Apl. 13, 1864, trans., m. o. Dec. 16, 1865, as corpl.
Hull Balaam, e. March 3, 1864, trans., m.o. Dec. 16, '65.
Higley A. T. e. March 13, 1864, trans., died Aug. 21, '65.
Hefty John, e. March 3, 1864, trans., m.o. Dec. 16, '65.
Kuntz Chris., trans., m. o. Dec. 16, 1865.
Maller Robt. e. March 24, 1864, trans., m.o. Dec. 16, '65.
McCoy John, e. March 3, 1864, trans., m. o. Dec. 16, '65.
Oliver Wm. e. April 13, 1864, trans., m. o. Dec. 16, '65.
Radeke Herman, e. April 13, 1864, trans., m. o. Dec. 16, 1865.
Reed David, e. Oct. 14, 1864, trans., absent on furlough.
Skenif Chas. e. March 20, 1864, trans., never reported to Co.
Thistlewait C. e. March 20, '64, trans., m. o. Dec. 16, '65.
Tiffit Wm. H. e. March 20, 1864, trans., absent, sick, at m. o. of regt.
Virtue Robt. e. Oct. 14, 1864, trans., m. o. Oct. 15, '65.
Wohlfart Frederick, e. March 20, 1865, trans., m. o. Dec. 16, 1865.
Wayman Henry, e. Oct. 15, 1864, trans., m.o. Oct. 15, '65.
Weamers F. e. Oct. 14, 1864, trans., absent, sick, at m.o.
Wartzenaker G. e. March 24, 1865, trans., m. o. Dec. 16, 1865.
Woodward Geo. e. March 3, 1865, trans., corpl., died Oct. 16, 1865.
Winters Thos. e. April 10, 1865, trans., m. o. Dec. 16, 1865, as corpl.

Company E.

Bonham Homer, e. April 10, 1865, m. o. Dec. 16, 1865.
Curtis Jas. M. e. May 22, '64, m. o. Dec. 16, '65, corpl.
Farr Geo. e. Oct. 8, 1864, m. o. Oct. 12, 1865.
Grice Thos. e. April 3, 1865, m. o. Dec. 16, 1865
Grice W. e. April 3, 1865, m. o. Dec. 16, 1865.
Hawks Peter, e. Aug. 15, 1862, m. o. Dec. 16, 1865.
Jones Nat. e. Oct. 8, 1864, m. o. Oct. 12, 1865.
Jacobs John O. e. Oct. 7, 1864, m. o. Oct. 12, 1865.
Muller F. e. Oct. 8, 1864, m. o. Oct. 12, 1865.
Newmon M. M. e. April 10, 1865, absent, sick at m. o.
Potter P. D. e. April 10, 1865, m. o. Dec. 16, 1865.
Root R. L. e. Oct. 11, 1864, m. o. Oct. 12, 1865.
Sanford L. B. e. Oct. 8, 1864, m. o. Oct. 12, 1865.
Thain Nicholas, e. Feb. 8, 1865, m. o. Dec. 16, 1865.
Westwick Jas. e. Oct. 8, 1864, m. o. Oct. 12, 1865.

Company H.

Allendorf Wm. e. Oct. 7, 1864, trans. from 96th I.V. I., m. o. Oct. 6, 1865.
Bastian Thos. e. April 13, 1865, trans. from 96th I.V. I., m. o. Dec. 16, 1865.
Bahr Henry, e. Oct. 10, 1864, trans. from 96th I. V. I., m. o. Nov. 1, 1865.
Barr Wm. e. Oct. 11, 1864, trans. from 96th I. V. I., m. o. Oct. 11, 1865,
Brown Edmund, e. Oct. 8, 1864, trans. from 96th I. V. I., m. o. Oct. 11, 1865.
Durrstein Chris. e. Oct. 8. 1864, tran. from 96th I.V.I., m. o. Oct. 11, 1865.
Deal Jas. e. Oct. 8, 1864, trans. from 96th I. V. I., died Sept. 2, 1865.
Evans Geo. e. Oct. 7, 1864, trans. from 96th I. V. I., m. o. Oct. 11, 1865.
Echart Lewis, e. Oct. 8, 1864, trans. from 96th I. V. I., m. o. Oct. 11, 1865.
Fablinger Lewis,e. Feb. 23,1865, trans. from 96th I.V.I., m. o. Dec. 16, 1865.
Fablinger Nicholas, e. Feb. 23, 1865, trans. from 96th I. V. I., m. o. Dec. 16, 1865.
Fritz John, e. Oct. 8, 1864, trans. from 96th I. V. I., m. o. Oct. 11, 1865.
Gordon Wm. E. e. Oct. 8, 1865, trans. from 96th I.V.I., absent, sick.
Grube V. e. Oct. 8, 1864, trans. from 96th I.V. I., m. o. Oct. 11, 1865.
Hagus Edw. e. Oct. 8, 1864, trans. from 96th I. V. I., m. o. Oct. 11, 1865, as corpl.
Harinstreet A. e. Oct. 10, 1864, trans. from 96th I.V.I., m. o. Oct. 11, 1865.
Hoffman Godfrey, e. Oct. 9, 1864, trans. from 96th I.V. I., m. o. Oct. 11, 1865.
Irwin Wm. J. e. Oct. 11, 1864, trans. from 96th I.V. I., m. o. Oct. 11, 1865.
Kostenbader —, e. Oct. 8, 1864, trans. from 96th I.V.I., m. o. Oct. 11, 1865.
Kelmer Solomon, e. Oct. 8,1864, trans.from 96th I.V.I., m.o. Oct. 11, 1865.
Lankan Chas. e. Oct. 8, 1864, trans. from 96th I. V. I., m. o. Oct. 11, 1865.
Lee Wm. e. Oct. 7, 1864, trans. from 96th I.V. I., m. o. Oct. 11, 1865.
Pharo Lewis, e. Oct. 8, 1864, trans. from 96th I. V. I., m. o. Oct. 11, 1865.
Romhilt Geo. C. e. Oct. 8, 1864, trans. from 96th I. V. I., m. o. Oct. 11, 1865.
Schmitt —, e. Oct. 10, 1864, trans. from 96th I. V. I., m. o. Oct. 11, 1865, as sergt.
Sager Chas. e. Oct. 8, 1864, trans. from 96th I. V. I., m. o. Oct. 11, 1865, as corpl.
Spore John, e. Oct. 7, 1864, trans. from 96th I. V. I., m. o. Oct. 11, 1865.
Schroeder John, e. Oct. 8,1864, trans. from 96th I.V.I., m. o. Oct. 11, 1865.
Stidworthy Wm. e. Oct. 10,1864, trans.from 96th I.V.I., m. o. Oct. 11, 1865.
Scott Wm. H. e. Oct. 7, 1864, trans. from 96th I. V. I., m. o. Oct. 11, 1865.
Scott Warren A. e. Aug. 13, 1862, trans. from 96th I. V. I., m. o. Oct. 11, 1865.
Sanderson Samuel C. e. Oct. 11, 1864, trans. from 96th I. V. I., m. o. Oct. 11, 1865.
Treseder M. e. April 13, 1865, trans. from 96th I. V. I., m. o. Dec. 16, 1865.
Trevarthan John,e. Oct. 7,1864, trans.from 96th I.V.I., m. o. Oct. 11, 1865.
Toler Frank, e. Oct. 7, 1864, trans. from 96th I. V. I., m. o. Oct. 11, 1865.
Williams Wm. e. Oct. 10, 1864, trans. from 96th I.V.I., absent, sick.
White Geo. H. e. Oct. 8, 1864, trans. from 96th I.V. I., m. o. Oct. 11, 1865.
Weirch Bernard, e. Oct. 8, 1864,trans.from 96th I.V. I., m. o. Oct. 11, 1865.
Webber Sebastian, e. Oct. 10,1864, trans.from 96th I.V. I., m. o. Oct. 11, 1865.

Company I.

Calvert Wm. e. Oct. 10, 1864, m. o. Oct. 12, 1865.
Carson Samuel, e. Oct. 3, 1864, m. o. Oct. 12, 1865.
Fielding Jas. e. Oct. 10, 1864, m. o. Dec. 16, 1865.
Irwin Wm. T. e. Feb. 23, 1865, disd. Aug. 5, 1865.
Johnson H. H. e. Feb. 8, 1865, m.o. Dec. 16, 1865.
Jackson J. B. e. Oct. 10, 1864, m. o. Oct. 12, 1865.
Kilpatrick Robt. e. Feb. 23, 1865, m. o. Dec. 16,1865.
Lowry Henry, e. Oct. 11, 1864, m. o. Oct. 12, 1865.
Moore Robt. e. Feb. 23, 1865, m. o. Dec. 16, 1865.
Moore Chas. T. e. Feb. 24, 1865, absent. sick.
Miller Jas. e. Oct. 11, 1864, m. o. Oct. 12, 1865.
Miller Geo. F. e. Oct. 11, 1864, m. o. Oct. 12, 1865.
Reese Moses, e. Oct. 11, 1864, m. o. Oct. 12, 1865.
Reynolds Robt. e. Oct. 7, 1864, m. o. Oct. 12, 1865.
Skillie Wm. e. March 16, 1865, absent on furlough.
Scott John D. e. Oct. 11, 1864, absent, sick.
Stone John D. e. Oct. 10, 1864, m. o. Oct. 12, 1865.
Williams Edw. e. Feb. 8, 1865, m. o. Dec. 16, 1865.
Wright Robt. e. Feb. 23, 1865, m. o. Dec. 16, 1865.
Williams Wm. J. e. Oct. 10, 1864, m. o. Oct. 12, 1865.
Wilson Wm. F. e. Oct. 10, 1864, m. o. Oct. 12, 1865.

Company K.

Bates H. N. e. Oct. 7, 1864, m. o. Oct. 13, 1865.
Claypool N. B. e. Feb. 8, 1865, m. o. Nov. 13, 1865.
Dreyer John, e. April 10, 1865, m. o. Dec. 16, 1865.
Deroff Henry, e. April 3, 1865, m. o. Dec. 16, 1865.
Drier Fred'k, e. April 3, 1865, died July 24, 1865.
Feist Bernard, e. April 3, 1865, m. o. Dec. 16, 1865.
Groebel Harmon, e. April 10, 1865, absent, sick.
Hambrecht F. e. April 10, 1865, m. o. Dec. 16, 1865.
Kelly John, e. March 16, 1865, m. o. Dec. 16, 1865.
McKinley J. J. e. Feb. 8, 1865, m. o. Dec. 16, 1865.
Russell Jas. D. e. Oct. 7, 1864, m. o. Oct. 13, 1865.
Stein Geo. e. April 3, 1865, m. o. Dec. 16, 1865.
Turner Ezra, e. Oct. 3, 1864, m. o. Oct. 3, 1865.
Yerington John P. e. Oct. 3, 1864, m. o. Oct. 3, 1865.

45th Infantry.

The Washburne Lead Mine Regiment was organized at Chicago, Ill., Dec. 25, 1861, by Col. John E. Smith, and mustered into the United States service as the Forty-fifth Infantry Illinois Volunteers. January 15, 1862, moved to Cairo, Ill.; February 1, assigned to Brigade of Col. W. H. L. Wallace, Division of Brig. Gen. McClernand; February 4, landed below Fort Henry, on the Tennessee, and on the 6th marched into the fort, it having been surrendered to the gun-boats. February 11, moved toward Fort Donelson, and during the succeeding days bore its part of the suffering and of the battle. The flag of the Forty-fifth was the first planted on the enemy's works. Loss—2 killed and 26 wounded. March 4, moved to the Tennessee River, and 11th, arrived at Savannah. Was engaged in the expedition to Pin Hook. March 25, moved to Pittsburg Landing, and encamped near Shiloh Church.

The Forty-fifth took a conspicuous and honorable part in the two days' battle of Shiloh, losing 26 killed and 199 wounded and missing—nearly one-half of the regiment. April 12, Col. John E. Smith, of the Forty-fifth, took command of the Brigade. During the siege of Corinth, the regiment was in the First Brigade, Third Division, Reserve Army of the Tennessee, and bore its full share of the labors and dangers of the campaign. June 4, the regiment was assigned to Third Brigade, and moved towards Purdy, fifteen miles. On the 5th, marched to Bethel; 7th to Montezuma, and on the 8th to Jackson, Tennessee, the enemy flying on its approach.

During the months of June and July, engaged in garrison and guard duty. August 11, assigned to guarding railroad, near Toon's Station. On the 31st, after much desperate fighting, Companies C and D were captured. The remainder of the regiment, concentrating at Toon's Station, were able to resist the attack of largely outnumbering forces. Loss—3 killed, 13 wounded and 43 taken prisoners. September 17, moved to Jackson; November 2, to Bolivar, and was assigned to First Brigade, Third Division, Right Wing, Thirteenth Army Corps. November 3, 1862, marched from Bolivar to Van Buren; 4th, to Lagrange, and were assigned to provost duty; 28th, marched to Holly Springs; December 3d, to Waterford; 4th, to Abbeville; 5th, to Oxford, to Yocona River, near Spring Dale.

Communications with the north having been cut off, foraged on the country for supplies. December 17, notice received of the promotion of Col. John E. Smith to brigadier general, ranking from November 29; December 22, returned to Oxford; 24th, moved to a camp three miles north of Abbeville, on the Tallahatchie River, where the regiment remained during the month.

Mustered out July 12, 1865, at Louisville, Ky., and arrived at Chicago July 15, 1865, for final payment and discharge.

Colonel John Eugene Smith, commissioned July 23, 1861. Promoted brigadier general.
Colonel Jasper A. Maltby, commissioned lieutenant colonel Sept. 17, 1861. Promoted colonel Nov. 29, 1862. Promoted brigadier general Aug. 4, 1863.
Colonel John O. Duer, commissioned second lieutenant Co. D, Sept. 3, 1861. Promoted first lieutenant March 1, 1862. Promoted captain April 6, 1862. Promoted major June 25, 1863. Promoted lieutenant colonel Jan. 10, 1865. Promoted colonel May 11, 1865. Mustered out (as lieutenant colonel) July 12, 1865. Promoted brevet brigadier general July 12, 1865.
Major Lattan J. Cowan, commissioned captain Co. B, Aug. 30, 1861. Promoted major Nov. 29, 1862. Killed in battle May 22, 1863.
Major Joshua Van Devert, e as sergt. Co. B, Aug. 30, 1861. Promoted first lieutenant June 1, 1862. Promoted captain Nov. 29, 1862. Promoted m jor July 13, 1865. Mustered out (as captain) July 12, 1865.
Surgeon Edward D. Kittoe, commissioned Aug. 30, 1861. Promoted surgeon of volunteers Dec. 4, 1862, by president.

Company A.

Second lieutenant David Williams, e. as corporal Aug. 30, 1861. Promoted second lieutenant May 1, 1862. Resigned Aug. 7, 1863.
Bradford Thos. e. Aug. 30, 1861, m. o. Sept. 29, 1864, term ex.
Ballow S. A. e. Aug. 30, 1861, vet., disd. June 9, 1865, disab.
Bruce Wm. e. Nov. 2, 1861, vet., m. o. July 12, 1865.
Crummer W. F. e. Aug. 30, 1861, m. o. Sept. 8, 1864, as first sergt., wd.
Chapman T. C. e. Aug. 30, 1861.
Carson Solomon, e. Nov. 13, 1861, m. o. Jan. 16, 1865, term ex.
Edwards A. M. e. Aug. 30, 1861, disd. Nov. 3, 1862, wd.
Ferrell Andrew, e. Aug. 30, 1861, vet., m. o. July 12, '65.
Felix Albert, e. Aug. 30, '61, wd., disd. Nov. 24, 1862.
Gray Wm. H. H. e. Aug. 30, 1861, m. o. Sept. 29, 1864, term ex.
Harrison John B. e. Aug. 30, 1861, kld. at Vicksburg, June 4, 1863.
Hars John G. e. Aug. 30, 1861, dropped Aug. 18, 1862.
Kehl Wm. e. Aug. 30, 1861, died May 18, 1862.
Middagh Wm. e. Aug. 30, 1861, dropped Aug. 18, 1862.
Patterson Roscoe, e. Aug. 30, '61, dropped Aug. 18, '62.
Rawlings Jas. C. e. Aug. 30, 1861, m. o. Sept. 29, 1864, term ex.
Rawlings Jos. M. e. Aug. 30, 1861, m. o. Sept. 29, 1864, term ex.
Randecker C. e. Nov. 11, 1861, disd. June 13, 1862.
Shannon J. B. P. e. Aug. 30, '61, vet., m.o. July 12, '65.
Streckel Jas. e. Aug. 30, 1861, m. o. Sept. 29, 1864, term ex.
Summy Joel, e. Aug. 30, 1861, died May 12, 1862.
Thomas J. M. e. Aug. 30, 1861, died Feb. 13, 1863.
Venable John T. e. Aug. 30, 1861, vet., sergt., sick at m o.
Deichman E. e. Aug. 30, 1862, m. o. June 3, 1865.
Ellinor John, e. Aug. 30, 1862, died Nov. 28, 1862.
Ferrell James, e. Aug. 26, 1862, m. o. June 3, 1865.
Goodmiller J. e. Aug. 30, 1862, m. o. June 3, 1865.
Harris Geo. e. Aug. 30, 1862, m. o. June 3, 1865.
Hackett Dwight, e. Aug. 26, 1862, m. o. June 3, 1865.
Pulley Wm. e. Aug. 30, 1862, died March 25, 1863.
Roggenthine Frank, e. Oct. 8, 1864, sick at m. o.
Strickle Jno. e. Sept. 15, 1862, m. o. June 3, 1865.
Venable Jas. e. Aug. 26, 1862, m. o. June 3, 1865.
Williams Wm. e. Aug. 26, 1862, died in hands of enemy.
Williamson Wm. e. Aug. 26, 1862, m. o. June 3, 1865.

Company B.

First Lieutenant Daniel W. Cowen, e. as sergeant Sept. 11, 1861. Promoted second lieutenant June 4, 1862. Promoted first lieutenant Nov. 29, 1862. Term expired Dec. 25, 1864.
Second Lieutenant Samuel H. Townsend, commissioned Aug. 30, 1861. Resigned June 4, 1862.
Second Lieutenant Ephraim Graham, e. as private Sept. 11, 1861, Re-enlisted as veteran Jan. 3, 1864. Mustered out (as sergeant) July 12, 1865. Commissioned second lieutenant, but not mustered.
Sergt. John B. Laillet, e. Aug. 30, 1861, disd. July 23, 1862, disab.
Sergt. Nelson Blineberry, e. Sept. 5, 1861, kld. at Shiloh April 6, 1862.
Corpl. Robert Scott, e. Aug. 30, 1861, m.o. Sept. 29, '64.
Corpl. Geo. W. Hayden, e. Aug. 30, 1861, vet., m. o. July 12, 1865.
Corpl. Montgomery A. Anderson, e. Aug. 30, 1861, vet., m. o. July 12, 1865.
Corpl. Jeremiah Lohr, e. Aug. 30, 1861, drowned Aug. 1, 1862.
Corpl. E. Olds Kingsley, e. Aug. 30, 1861, vet., m. o. July 12, 1865, 1st sergt., com. 2d lieut., not mustered.
Corpl. Axel J. Espring, e. Aug. 30, 1861, sergt., kld. June 25, 1862.
Anger John G. e. Sept. 4, 1861, vet., m. o. July 12, '65.
Barnes Geo. W. e. Sept. 5, 1861, vet., m.o. July 12, '65.
Blackmore F. M. e. Aug. 30, '61, vet., m. o. July 12, '65.
Bush Villroy L. e. Sept. 5, 1861, disd. May 2, '62, disab.
Cain John, e. Aug. 30, 1861, m. o. Sept. 3, '64, term ex.
Calvin Jas. e. Oct. 10, 1861, disd. July 23, 1862, wd.
Conely Jas. e. Aug. 30, 1861, disd. May 6, 1862, disab.
Crissey Byron, e. Aug. 30, 1861, disd. July 23, '62, disab.
Dimmick H. M. e. Oct. 2, 1861, died near Corinth, May 19, 1862.
Dittman E. e. Sept. 21, 1861, wd. April 7, 1862, m. o. July 12, 1865, vet.
Estes Jas. M. e. Sept. 4, 1861, died May 9, 1862.
Finley Samuel P. e. Aug. 30, '61, disd. May 12, '62, disab.
Foss A. B. e. Sept. 21, 1861, disd. May 9, 1862, disab.
Hawks Peter, e. Aug. 30, 1861, disd. by order of Col. Smith.
Hagarity Martin, e. Sept. 11, 1861, dropped, sentence G. C. M.
Harding Jas. L. e. Aug. 30, 1861, captured while carrying dispatches, supp sed to be kld.
Honlihan John, e. Aug. 30, 1861, supposed disd.
Jones O. A. e. Aug. 30, '61, m.o. Sept. 29, '64, term ex.
Lohr Israel, e. Sept. 21, 1861, died May 5, 1862, wd.
Martzell Solomon, e. Aug. 30, '61, disd. July 23, '6 , disab.
Mason Jesse, e. Sept. 4, 1861, disd. May 12, 1862, supposed died.
McElhannon Wm. J. e. Aug. 30, 1861.
McGill Wm. H. e. Sept. 4, '61, disd. July 30, '62, disab.
Morgan Alfred, e. Aug. 30, '61, vet., m.o. July 12, '65.
Nugent Jas. e. Aug. 30, 1861, disd., since died.
Patterson Thos. e. Aug. 30, 1861, died, 1862.
Powell John, e. Aug. 30, '61, disd. Nov. 10, '62, disab.
Powell Jos. e. Sept. 4, 1861, vet., m. o. July 12, 1865.
Rue Chas. W. e. Sept. 5, 1861, vet., m.o. July 12, 1865.
Ryan Walter S. e. Aug. 30, '61, vet., m. o. July 12, '65.
Sanford Noble, e. Sept. 27, 1861, disd. July 23, '62, disab.
Sanford E. A. e. Sept. 27, 1861, m. o. Nov. 20, 1864.
Spur John M. e. Aug. 30, '61, vet., m. o. July 12, 1865.
Stephens Wm. H. e. Sept. 21, 1861, vet., m.o. July 12, 1865, as sergt.
Tuffs Jas. M. e. Sept. 11, 1861, m. o. Sept. 29, 1864, as sergt., term ex.
Walker Henry, e. Sept. 4, 1861, vet., m.o. July 12, '65.
White Francis T. e. Aug. 30, 1861, died March 4, 1864.
Wilkins Wm. L. e. Aug. 30, 1861, m. o. Sept. 29, 1864, term ex.
Williams Wm. A. e. Aug. 30, '61, disd. Nov. 10, '62, disab.
Wood Holoway, e. Aug. 30, 1861, kld. at Shiloh April 6, 1862.
Coltrin Wm. H. e. Dec. 19, 1862, m. o. Dec. 4, 1864, term ex.
Eaton Henry, e. April 11, 1864, m. o. July 12, 1865.
Elston Geo. e. April 1, 1864, m. o. July 12, 1865.
Geddis Robt. J. e. Dec. 16, '61, disd. Sept. 2, '62, disab.
Graham Andrew, e. Dec. 24, 1861, vet., m. o. July 12, 1865, as sergt.
Graham Geo. E. e. Feb. 27, 1864, m. o. July 12, 1865.
Honlilian John, e. Oct. 29, 1863, died Dec. 8, 1863.
Irmscher Aug. e. Sept. 24, 1864, m. o. June 3, 1865.
Matthews Wm. T. e. Dec. 19, 1861, died Feb. 2, 1862.
Murphy Thos. e. Aug. 21, 1862, m. o. Oct. 30, 1863, sentence G. C. M.
Newton Eber, e. April 11, 1864, m. o. July 12, 1865.
Robail Vincent, e. Nov. 21, '61, vet., m. o. July 12, '65.
Richards Thos. e. Dec. 14, '61, vet., m. o. July 12, '65.
Reynolds A. H. e. Dec. 15, '61, vet., m. o. July 12, '65.
Smith A. J. e. Nov. 21, 1861, dropped at muster, Aug. 18, 1862.
Sanford N. e. Feb. 27, 1864, vet., m. o. July 12, 1865, as corpl.
Trevethan M. e. Dec. 16, '61, vet., m. o. July 12, 1865.

Wheeler Wm. e. Dec. 29, '61, vet., m. o. July 12, '65.
Williams Geo. e. April 11, '64, desrtd. June 12, 1864.
Zuck Francis, e. April 11, 1864, m. o. July 12, 1865.

Company C.

Captain Thos. Burns, com. Sept. 2, 1861. Resigned May 5, 1862.
Captain Jas. Rouse, com. first lieutenant Sept. 2, 1861. Promoted captain May 5, 1862. Mustered out Nov., 1864.
Captain Jos. Vincent. e. as first sergeant Sept. 2, 1861. Promoted first lieutenant May 9, 1862. Promoted captain April 20, 1861. Mustered out (as first lieutenant) May 29, 1865.
Captain Jas. Clifford, e. as sergeant Sept. 2, 1861. Promoted second lieutenant June 1, 1862. Promoted adjutant Sept. 22, 1864. Promoted captain July 9, 1865. Mustered out (as adjutant) July 12, 1865.
First Lieutenant Samuel P. Adams, e. as sergeant Sept. 3, 1861. Re-enlisted as veteran Jan. 5, 1864. Mustered out (as first sergeant) July 12, 1865. Com. first lieutenant, but not mustered.
Second Lieutenant John Byrne, com. Sept. 2, 1861. Resigned May 16, 1862.
Second Lieutenant John B. Annetts, e. as private Sept. 2, 1861. Re-enlisted as veteran Jan. 5, 1864. Mustered out July 12, 1865, as sergeant. Com. second lieutenant, but not mustered.
Sergt. Thos. Redford, e. Sept. 10, 1861, m. o. Sept. 20, 1864, term ex.
Corpl. Matthew Shannon, e. Sept. 3, 1861, m. o. Sept. 29, 1864, term ex.
Corpl. Jas. W. Gear, e. Sept. 2, '61, disd. July 14, '62, wd.
Corpl. Sterling L. Parker, e. Sept. 2, 1861, disd. June 4, 1862, disab.
Corpl. Wm. Philpot, e. Sept. 17, 1861, died at Hanover, Ill., April 3, 1862.
Corpl. Jas. M. Day, e. Sept. 20, 1861, m. o. Sept. 29, 1864, term ex.
Corpl. David Walsh, e. Oct. 20, 1861, disd. May 30, '62.
Musician John Callaghan, e. Sept. 2, 1861, trans. to V. R. C. April 29, 1864.
Musician J. Paul, e. Sept. 2, 1861, vet., m.o. July 12, '65.
Atkins Jas. e. Sept. 17, 1861.
Beldin Wm. W. e. Sept. 2, 1861, died May 4, 1862.
Bailey Edw. e. Sept. 2, 1861.
Borland Jas. R. e. Sept. 26, 1861, trans. to Inv. Corps, Sept. 15, 1863.
Brown Henry, e. Sept. 2, 1861.
Bourke Michael, e. Sept. 2, 1861, m. o. Sept. 29, 1864, term ex.
Bastian John, e. Sept. 2, '61, m.o. Sept. 29, '64, term ex.
Bowden N. e. Sept. 6, 1861.
Belknap F. L. e. Sept. 10, 1861, kld. at Mendon, Tenn., Aug. 31, 1862.
Conroy Jas. e. Sept. 2, 1861, died May 20, 1862.
Cloran John, e. Sept. 2, 1861, trans. to Inv. Corps Sept. 15, 1863.
Coughlin Nicholas, e. Sept. 2, 1861, trans. to Inv. Corps Sept. 15, 1863.
Calgy John, e. Oct. 1, 1861, enlisted in Co. D, 1st Ill. Lt. Art., vet.
Casey John, e. Oct. 2, 1861, kld. at Shiloh April 7, '62.
Callahan Peter, e. Oct. 8, 1861, m. o. July 12, 1865.
Delaney Michael, e. Sept. 10, 1861, m. o. Sept. 29, 1864, term ex.
Gray Jas. e. Oct. 9, 1861, died March 8, 1862.
Hughes Thos. e. Sept. 2, 1861, disd. Dec. 19, '63 disab.
Hanly Wm. e. Sept. 2, 1861.
Hill David, e. Sept. 2, 1861, kld. at Shiloh April 7, '62.
Hellmand E. T.G. e. Sept. 4, '61, disd. April 4, '62, disab.
Henry Jas. e. Sept. 19, 1861, died June 4, 1862.
Houlihan Jas. e. Nov. 3, 1861, trans. to 23d I. V. I. Dec. 7, 1861.
Hynds John, e. Oct. 21, 1861, disd. May 18, 1862.
Jerome Jas. e. Sept. 2, 1861, died April 3, 1862.
Juda John, e. Sept. 2, 1861, m.o. Sept. 29, '64, term ex.
Kelly Chris. e. Sept. 2, 1861.
Linnane M. e. Sept. 2, '61, disd. Oct. 18, '62, disab.
Louis Henry, e. Sept. 24, 1861.
Metcalf Wm. M. e. Sept. 2, 1861, disd. May 30, 1862.
Marshall Jas. e. Sept. 5, 1861, m. o. Sept. 29, 1864 term ex.
Mock Geo. e. Sept. 10, 1861, disd. Oct. 24, 1862.
Morris S. e. Sept. 19, 1861.
Malia Robt. e. Oct. 3, 1861, died at Paducah, May 20, 1862, wd.
Miller Henry, e. Oct. 7, 1861.
Metz Jno. B. e. Sept. 2, 1861, kld. at Shiloh, Apl. 7, '62.
Murphy Michael, e. Nov. 7, 1861, vet., m.o. July 12, '65.
Nalion Michael, e. Sept. 2, 1861, m. o. July 12, 1865.
Owens Hugh, e. Nov. 11, 1861, disd. May 7, 1862.
Peacock J. R. e. Sept. 5, 1861.
Quirke Wm. e. Sept. 2, 1861, deserted Oct. 3, 1864.
Retzman John, e. Sept. 2, 1861, vet., m. o. July 12, 1865, as sergt.
Savage Geo. e. Sept. 2, 1861, vet., m. o. July 12, 1865.
Scofield John, e. Oct. 1, 1861, m. o. Nov. 21, 1864.
Taylor Canby, e. Sept. 6, 1861.
Taylor Henry H. e. Sept. 5, 1861, m. o. Sept. 8, 1864.
Trainer Jas. H. e. Sept 2, 1861, deserted May 12, 1862
Towle O. H. e. Oct. 4, 1861, died April 15, 1862, wd.
Wales Jas. e. Sept. 10, 1861, disd. July 29, 1862.
Wales David, e. Sept. 2, '61, m.o. Sept. 29, '64, term ex.
Young Allison, e. Sept. 9, 1861.
Bell Arthur, e. Dec. 16, 1863, m. o. July 12, 1865, sergt.
Chase Geo. W. e. Oct. 8, 1864, m. o. July 12, 1865.
Crowley Jas. e. April 10, 1865, m. o. July 12, 1865.
Dwire Michael, e. Dec. 29, 1863, m. o. July 12, 1865.
Dobson Jos. e. April 10, 1865, m. o. July 12, 1865.
Eckhart Ernst, e. April 10, 1865, m. o. July 12, 1865.
Fogle Robt. B. e. Jan. 1, 1862, disd. Nov. 4. 1862, disab.
Gross Jos. e. Dec. 19, 1863, m. o. July 12, 1865.
Gause Philip, e. Oct. 5, 1864, m. o. July 12, 1865.
Jones M. B. e. Oct. 7, 1864, m. o. July, 12, 1865.
Kavoon John, e. Jan. 15, 1862, vet., m. o. July 12, 1865.
Klough Wm. e. Jan. 18, 1862.
Lawson Geo. C. e. March 28, 1864, m. o. July 12, 1865.
Leckley Jas. T. e. April 14, 1864, absent at m. o. regt.
Long David, e. April 10, 1865, m. o. July 12, 1865.
Miller M. M. e. Jan. 10, 1862.
McCarty John E. e. April 10, 1865, m. o. July 12, 1865.
Ostrander Jerome, e. Feb. 15, 1864, m. o. July 12, 1865.
Ross John E. e. Dec. 10, 1861, m. o. May 12, '65, sergt.
Rouse Caleb H. e. Jan. 18, 1862, died April 12, 1862.
Rourke Peter, e. April 10, 1865, m. o. July 12, 1865.
Stiles Samuel, e. Dec. 16, 1863, m. o. July 12, 1865.
Smith James, e. April 10, 1865, m. o. July 12, 1865.
Schrader Henry, e. April 10, 1865, m. o. July 12, 1865.
Simmons Hiram, e. April 10, 1865, m. o. July 12, 1865.
Thompson Wm. e. April 10, 1865, m. o. June 30, 1865.
Borland Wm. H. e. Jan. 5, 1864, m. o. July 12, 1865.
Miller John H. e. Jan. 5, 1864, died March 27, 1865.
Paul John, e. Dec. 19, 1863, m. o. July 12, 1865.
Webber Valentine, e. Jan. 5, 1864, m. o. July 12, 1865.

Company D.

Captain Thomas D. Conner, commissioned Sept. 3, 1861. Killed at Shiloh.
Captain Jos. W. Miller, e. as first sergeant Sept. 21, 1861. Promoted second lieutenant March 1, 1862. Promoted first lieutenant April 6, 1862. Promoted captain June 25, 1863. Promoted by president.
Captain Otto C. Hager, e. as private Sept. 3, 1861. Promoted sergeant, first sergeant, then second lieutenant, May 1, 1862. Promoted first lieutenant June 25, 1863. Promoted captain June 25, 1863. Mustered out July 12, 1865.
First Lieutenant Wm. R. Rowley, commissioned Nov. 13, 1861. Promoted Gen. Grant's staff.
First Lieutenant John R. Dawson, e. as private Sept. 3, 1861. Promoted sergeant, first sergeant and first lieutenant.
Second lieutenant E. O. Hammond, e. as private Oct. 23, 1861. Veteran. Promoted corporal, first sergeant and second lieutenant.
Musician Peter W. Bellingall, e. Nov. 3, 1861., vet., m. o. July 12, 1865, as first sergt.
Bennett Chas. F. e. Nov. 21, 1861, disd. May 12, 1862.
Bisson E. R. e. Nov. 3, 1861.
Brown Jas. D. e. Nov. 3, 1861, disd. May 12, 1862.
Bryson Wm. e. Nov. 3, 1861, kld. April 6, 1862.
Black Wm. W. e. Nov. 21, 1861, died Sept. 8, 1862.
Carson Wm. J. e. Sept. 20, 1861, vet., m. o. July 12, '65.
Chapman Anderson, e. Sept. 3, 1861, trans. to Invalid Corps, Sept. 15, 1863.
Chapman John, e. Sept. 11, 1861, died May 14, 1862.
Chapman Wm. e. Sept. 3, 1861.
Chapman Jos. e. Sept. 3, 1861, vet., m. o. July 12, 1865, as sergt.
Chapman Geo. e. Sept. 21, 1861, vet., m. o. July 12, '65.
Craig David, e. Sept. 3, 1861, disd. Jan. 1, 1864, disab.
Curtiss Geo. P. e. Sept. 10, '61, disd. Sept. 26, '62, disab.
Cutis Wm. H. e. Sept 20, 1861, trans. to Invalid Corps Sept. 15, 1863.
Dawson John R. e. Sept. 3, 1861.
Dawson Jas. D. e. Sept. 3, 1861, vet., m. o. July 12, 1865, as sergt.

Dye Geo. H. e. Sept. 21, 1861, vet., accidentally kld. Feb. 29, 1864.
Edwards John, e. Sept. 3, 1861, vet., m. o. July 12, '65.
Entwhistle Robt. e. Sept. 19, 1861, disd. May 12, 1862.
Evans Chas. e. Sept. 3, 1861, vet., m. o. July 12, 1865.
Garland John, e. Sept. 3, 1861, died April 8, 1862.
Goss Wm. B. e. Sept. 5, 1861, disd. May 12, 1862.
Green Ephraim, e. Sept. 11, 1861, disd. in 1862, disab.
Hammond E. O. e. Oct. 23, 1861, vet.
Kuntz John G. e. Oct. 17, 1861, disd. Jan. 1, '64, disab.
Lemaster Jas. N. e. Sept. 7, 1861, vet., m. o. July 12, 1865, as corpl.
Leekly John T. e. Sept. 21, 1861, vet., m. o. July 12, 1865, as corpl., was prisr.
Lindsay Benj. J. e. Sept. 11, 1861, disd. Apl. 4, '62, disab.
Lamb John R. e. Nov. 21, 1861, vet., m. o. July 12, 1865, as sergt.
Morehead Wm. e. Sept. 9, 1861, died at St. Louis, March 24, 1862.
Morehead Thomas, e. Sept. 9, 1861, m. o. Dec. 30, 1864, term ex.
Murray Francis, e. Sept. 5, 1861, vet., m. o. July 12, '65.
McCall David, e. Oct. 10, 1861, m. o. Dec. 30, 1864, term ex.
McCrary John, e. Sept. 3, 1861, died at St. Louis, May 24, 1862.
McKenley John, e. Sept. 11, 1861, musician.
Oliver Jas. E. e. Sept. 3, 1861, vet., m. o. July 12, '65.
Patterson N. e. Sept. 3, 1861, vet., m. o. July 12, 1865.
Reed John, e. Oct. 12, 1861, died at Jackson, Tenn., Aug. 21, 1862.
Reed Francis, e. Sept. 30, 1861, died April 2, 1862.
Rodenbaugh Jacob, e. Oct. 19, '61, disd. July 23, '62, disab.
Rogers Wm. e. Sept. 20, 1861, vet., m. o. July 12, 1865, as corpl.
Scott Thos. e. Sept. 10, '61, m. o. Dec. 30, '64, term ex.
Secord David, e. Sept. 3, 1861, vet., m. o. July 12, 1865, as corpl.
Sherrill Jno. E. e. Sept. 3, '61, m. o. Dec. 30, '64, term ex.
Stone Jas. e. Nov. 20, 1861, disd. Oct. 12, 1862, disab.
Thornberry Thornton, e. Sept. 7, '61, died May 24, '62.
Wanney Jerod, e. Oct. 11, '61, disd. Jan. 26, '64, disab.
Wanney J. B. e. Sept. 11, '61, m. o. Dec. 30, '64, term ex.
Willard F. M. e. Sept. 10, 1861, disd. Oct. 26, 1861, disab.
Weinsheimer A. e. Sept 3, '61, m. o. Dec. 30, '64, term ex.
White S. D. e. Sept. 20, 1861, m. o. Dec. 30, 1864, term ex.
Wilson Jno. e. Sept. 1, 1861, disd. Jan. 31, 1863, disab.
Young Robert, Sept. 3, 1861, died Tenn. April 16, 1862.
Anders Lewis, e. Feb. 26, 1864, died July 26, 1864.
Argent John, e. Feb. 29, 1864, m. o. June 5, 1865.
Arnold S. N. e. Jan. 2, '62, disd. or died Sept. 5, '62, wd.
Allen Robt. e. March 6, 1865, m. o. July 12, 1865.
Bayles Robert, e. Nov. 21, 1861, vet., m. o. July 12, 1865.
Bell Arthur, e. Dec. 4, 1863, m. o. July 12, 1865.
Blair Andrew, e. Oct. 8, 1864, m. o. July 12, 1865.
Brown Mark W. e. Oct. 5, 1864, m. o. June 24, 1865.
Clause Joseph, e. Dec. 29, 1861, vet., m. o. July 12, 1865.
Consalus John J. e. Feb. 25, 1864, m. o. July 12, 1865.
Curley B. e. Feb. 25, 1864, m. o. July 12, 1865.
Creegan John, e. Oct. 3, 1864, m. o. July 12, 1865.
Cogan Henry, e. Oct. 7, 1864, m. o. July 12, 1865.
Callahan P. Oct. 8, '64, trans. to Co. C. March 27, '65.
Conklin R. e. Oct. 8, 1864, m. o. June 3, 1865.
Calanan Wm. e. Oct. 8, 1864, m. o. July 12, 1865.
Clark Geo. R. e. Oct. 7, 1864, m. o. July 12, 1865.
Drone A. C. e. Nov. 28, 1863, m. o. July 12, 1865.
Doyle Jas. e. Dec. 11, 1863, absent without leave at m. o.
Duffey Thomas, e. Oct. 7, 1864, m. o. July 12, 1865.
Dawson Eugene, e. Oct. 5, 1864, m. o. July 12, 1865.
Estey A. M. e. Oct. 5, 1864, m. o. July 12, 1865.
Frickie Chris. e. Oct. 8, 1864, m. o. July 12, 1865.
Friesner Levi, e. Sept. 15, 1862, returned to 54th I. V. I. as deserter Oct. 1, 1864.
Friesner Lewis, e. Sept. 15, 1862, returned to 54th I. V. I. as deserter Oct. 1, 1864.
Fisher Wm. e. Oct. 5, 1864, disd. April 26, 1865.
Goss Leonard, e. Feb. 25, 1864, m. o. July 12, 1865.
Hollan Chas. H. e. Dec. 15, 1863, m. o. July 12, 1865.
Hammett John, e. Oct. 8, 1864, m. o. July 12, 1865.
Hunter Edward, e. Oct. 8, 1864, m. o. July 12, 1865.
Hocking R. N. e. Oct. 5, 1864, m. o. July 12, 1865.
Haines John K. e. Oct. 5, 1864, m. o. July 12, 1864.
Haines Patrick, e. Sept. 30, 1864, m. o. July 12, 1865.
Klein Lewis, e. Oct. 11, 1864, m. o. July 12, 1865.
Law Joseph, e. Nov. 30, 1863, absent, sick at m. o.
Linsey Thomas, e. Oct. 8, 1864, m. o. July 12, 1865.
Logan Hugh, e. Oct. 8, 1864, died April 17, 1865.
Metzker M. e. Oct. 7, 1865, m. o. July 12, 1865.
Medary Wm. J. e. Oct. 5, 1864, m. o. July 12, 1865.
Murphy Edward, e. March 22, 1864, m. o. July 12, 1865.
Norris Wm. E. e. Oct. 5, 1864, died March 19, 1865.
O'Connor M. e. Mar. 6, 1865, died in N. Y. Mar. 29, '65.
Patterson Andrew, e. Feb. 25, 1864, m o. July 12, 1865.
Peatt Thos. e. Feb. 29, 1864, died April 9, 1864.
Patterson John, e. March 31, 1864, m. o. July 12, 1865.
Rawlibs Jas. S. e. Aug. 28, 1862, m. o. June 3, 1865.
Swift Isaac W. e. Feb. 28, 1864, m. o. July 12, 1865.
Swift A. O. e. Sept. 26, 1864, m. o. June 3, 1865.
Spensley J. R. e. Oct. 5, 1864, m. o. May 23, 1865.
Simon Peter, e. Oct. 7, 1864, m. o. July 12, 1865.
Sharpe Wm. H. e. Oct. 4, 64, m. o. July 12, 1865.
Sharpe John W. e. Oct. 5, 1864, m. o. July 12, 1865.
Sherrill Samuel, e. Aug. 28, 1862, disd. in Jan., 1864.
Taylor Obadiah, e. Oct. 7, 1864, m. o. July 12, 1865.
Tomlin Edward A. e. April 10, 1865, m. o. July 12, '65.
Upton Wm. B. e. March 6, 1865, desrtd. June 12, 1865.
Welch Thomas, e. Oct. 3, 1864, m. o. July 12, 1865.
Wilcox Thos. A. e. Oct. 5, 1864, m. o. July 12, 1865.
Westenhaver A. e. Sept. 30, '64, died at Cin. Feb. 2, '65.

Company E.

Captain Charles K. Erwin, e. as sergt. Oct. 22, 1861. Promoted first sergeant, then second lieutenant, Nov. 4, 1862. Promoted first lieutenant May 22, 1863. Promoted captain April 20, 1865. Mustered out July 12, 1865.
First Lieutenant Charles D. Overstreet, commissioned Sept. 14, 1861. Resigned Nov. 4, 1862.
First Lieutenant John D. Spragins e. as corporal Sept. 18, 1861. Re-enlisted as veteran Jan. 5, 1864. Mustered out as first sergeant July 12, 1865. Commissioned first lieutenant but not mustered.
Sergt. David McGrath, e. Sept. 14, '61, disd. April 5, '62.
Corpl. Jas. M. Herring, e. Sept. 14, 1861.
Corpl. Saml. F. Clark e. Sept. 18, 1861, vet., m. o. July 12, 1865, as sergt.
Corpl. Elias Venable e. Sept. 14, '61 died Mch. 23, '62.
Bowden Daniel, e. Sept. 14, 1861, died Jan. 28, 1862.
Bowden Wm. e. Sept. 18, 1861.
Buck A. H. e. Sept. 14, 1862, vet., m. o. July 12, 1865.
Bonney J. e. Sept. 18, 1861.
Bucker Andrew, e. Sept. 18, '61, vet., m. o. July 12, '65.
Bucher Jacob, e. Sept. 24, 1861, disd. Dec. 14, 1863, to receive promotion in colored regt.
Bucher Jacob 2d, e. Oct. 7, 1861, vet., m. o. July 12, '65.
Bain Hugh R. e. Oct. 17, 1861, vet., m. o. July 12, 1865.
Bohn Frank, e. Oct. 25, 1861, vet., m. o. July 12, 1865.
Clark Wm. F. e. Sept. 18, 1861, vet., m. o. July 12, 1865.
Clevenger H. C. e. Oct. 2, 1861, vet., m. o. July 12, '65.
Costillo M. e. Oct. 25, 1861, m. o. Nov. 8, '64, term ex.
Gott Sutton, e. Nov. 18, 1861, disd. July 25, 1862.
Gault Matt. e. Sept. 14, '61, m. o. Sept. 29, '64, term ex.
Gillett C. S. e. Oct. 17, 1861, disd. July 25, 1862, wd.
Glattaar J. J. e. Oct. 7, 1861, disd. term ex.
Herring John W. e. Sept. 14, '61, vet., m. o. July 12, '65.
Hazell Robt. e. Nov. 1, 1861, disd, term ex.
Kidd Wm. H. e. Sept. 24, 1861, died at Memphis Feb. 23, 1863.
Lamb Michael, e. Oct. 25, 1865.
Miller J. e. Sept. 18, 1861, m. o. Sept. 29, 1864, term ex.
Machamer I. e. Sept. 14, 1861, vet., m. o. July 12, 1865.
Machamer T. J. e. Sept. 14, 1861, disd. July 10, 1862, wd.
McQuay John, e. Sept. 18, 1861, disd. May 21, 1862.
Patterson L. e. Sept. 24, '61, m. o. Sept. 29, '64, term ex.
Rock Geo. M. e. Sept. 24, 1861, vet., m. o. July 12, 1865.
Steffens Wm. e. Sept. 18, 1861, vet., m. o. July 12, 1865.
Skeene Geo. e. Sept. 18, 1861, died April 10, 1862.
Spittler Henry, e. Oct. 4, '61, m. o. Nov. 8, '64, term ex.
Shepard J. e. Oct. 25, 1861, m. o. Nov. 8, 1864, term ex.
Machamer M. e. Dec. 12, 1861, disd, July 26, '62, disab.
Steffins Fred. e. April 6, 1865, m. o. July 12, 1865.
White Allen, e. Sept. 11, 1862, m. o. June 3, 1865.
Butler Jas. E. e. Oct. 5, 1864.
Burton Wm. e. March 6, 1864.
Hendricks John S. e. Dec. 24, 1863.
Terry M. D. e. May 2, 1864.

90th Infantry.

The Ninetieth Infantry Illinois Volunteers was organized at Chicago, Illinois, in August, September and October, 1862, by Colonel Timothy O'Meara. Moved to Cairo, November 27, and to Columbus, Ky., 30th. From thence proceeded to Lagrange, Tenn., where the regiment arrived December 2. On the 4th, ordered to Coldwater, Miss., where it relieved the Twenty-ninth Wisconsin Infantry. On the morning of the 20th of December, a detachment of Second Illinois Cavalry ar-

J. C. Smith

CHICAGO

FORMERLY OF GALENA

rived at Coldwater, having cut their way through Van Dorn's forces, out of Holly Springs. Soon after, four companies of One Hundred and First Illinois came in, and were followed by the enemy to our lines. The demonstrations made by the Ninetieth deterred the enemy from making any severe attack, although he was 4,000 or 5,000 strong, and, after some skirmishing, he withdrew. The regiment was mustered out of service June 6, 1865, at Washington, D. C., and arrived at Chicago June 12, 1865, where it received final pay and discharge.

Company B.

Captain Michael W. Murphy, com. Sept. 6, 1862. Mustered out June 6, 1865.
First Lieutenant Thos. Gray, com. Sept. 6, 1862. Mustered out June 6, 1865.
Second Lieutenant Chas. Bellingdale, com. Sept. 6, 1862. Resigned April 7, 1862.
Sergt. W. H. Jones, e. Aug. 14, 1862, disd. Aug. 8, '64.
Sergt. Jas. McCabe, e. Aug. 12, 1862, kld. at Mission Ridge Nov. 25, 1863.
Sergt. John McDonald, e. Aug. 12, 1862, m. o. June 6, 1865 as private.
Sergt. Thos. Fitzpatrick, e. Aug. 12, '62, m.o. June 6, '65.
Corpl. F. E. Bale or Ball, e. Aug. 14, 1862, m. o. June 6, 1865, as private.
Corpl. W. J. Burns, e. Aug. 14, 1862, m. o. June 6, 1865, as private.
Corpl. Thos. Long, e. Aug. 12, 1862, m. o. June 24, 1865, as sergt., prisr. war.
Corpl. Daniel Harnet, e. Aug. 14, 1862, m. o. June 6, 1865, as private.
Corpl. J. Quinan, e. Aug. 14, 1862, died at Chicago April 15, 1864.
Corpl. Jas. Wales, e. Aug. 14, 1862, m. o. June 6, 1865, as private.
Corpl. Hugh Calaghan, e. Aug. 14, 1862, m. o. June 6, 1865, as private.
Musician Edw. Clark, e. Aug. 5, 1862, m. o. June 6, 1865, as private.
Musician John Shanan, e. Aug. 14, 1862, deserted Aug. 30, 1864.
Wagoner Cornelius Lynch, e. Aug. 14, 1862, drowned June 9, 1863.
Bell Henry, e. Sept. 1, '62, died at Memphis Oct. 18, '63.
Bejjan Patrick, e. Aug. 20, '62, deserted Nov. 25, 1862.
Burn or Breen P. e. Aug. 18, 1862, m. o. June 6, 1865, as corpl.
Burns John, e. Aug. 15, 1862, trans. to V. R. C. March 15, 1865.
Clancy Thos. e. Aug. 29, 1862, trans. to Sig. Corps Jan. 25, 1863.
Connors Pat. e. Aug. 13, 1862, kld. at Mission Ridge Nov. 25, 1863.
Calaghan D. e. Aug. 14, 1862, m. o. June 6, 1865.
Carry Michael, e. Aug. 29, 1862, m. o. June 6, 1865.
Calaghan Bernard, e. Sept., '62, desrtd. Nov. 30, 1862.
Donejan Thos. e. Aug. 15, 1862, m. o. June 6, 1865.
Daily Pat'k, e. Aug. 20, 1862, disd. March 20, 1865.
Fitzpatrick John, e. Aug. 18, 1862, trans. to V. R. C. June 18, 1864.
Flynn Daniel, e. Aug. 10, 1862, died Oct. 19, 1863.
Galvin Daniel, e. Aug. 14, 1862, disd. Sept. 10, 1863.
Grady P. e. Aug. 14, 1862, m. o. June 6, 1865.
Gavin Jos. e. Aug. 14, 1862, m. o. June 6, 1865.
Galvin P. I. e. Aug. 12, '62, disd. May 17, '65, as sergt.
Galagher Neill, e. Aug. 12, 1862, m. o. June 6, 1865, prisr. war.
Gavin John, e. Aug. 12, 1862, disd. May 3, 1865.
Gavin John, e. Aug. 14, 1862, corpl., desrtd. Nov. 25, '62.
Griffith Jos. e. Aug. 14, 1862, m. o. June 22, 1865.
Grace John, e. Aug. 18, 1862, m.o. June 6, '65, as sergt.
Hailey John, e. Aug. 13, '62, died Miss. Sept. 19, 1863.
Hynes Jas. e. Aug. 12, 1862, died Ind. Dec. 5, 1864.
Hynes Jno. e. Aug. 12, 1862, m. o. June 6, 1865.
McKenna Jas. e. Aug. 14, 1862, desrtd. Nov. 30, 1862.
Mahan Pat'k, e. Aug. 14, 1862, m. o. June 6, 1865.
McKarney P. e. Aug. 14, 1862, m. o. June 6, 1865.
McCardle John, e. Aug. 14, '62, absent, wd. at m.o. regt.
McKenna Thos. e. Aug. 30, 1862, desrtd. Nov. 30, '62.
McCormack D. e. Aug. 12, 1862, m. o. Nov. 3, 1865, to date June 6, 1865.
McCabe Luke, e. Aug. 14, 1862, died at Camp Sherman, Sept. 19, 1863.
McIntosh Jos. e. Aug. 14, 1862, m. o. June 6, 1865.
McKernan Jas. e. Aug. 18, 1862, desrtd. Nov. 1, 1864.
McDonald Alex. e. Aug. 14, 1862, m. o. June 6, 1865.
Mann Jas. e. Aug. 14, 1862, m. o. June 6, 1865.
Monaghan M. e. Aug. 30, 1862, desrtd. Nov. 30, 1862.
McNeary Jas. e. Sept. 1, 1862, desrtd. Sept. 2, 1862.
O'Halonan Edw. e. Aug. 18, 1862, m. o. June 6, 1865.
Powers John, e. Aug. 9, 1862, m. o. June 6, 1865.
Quinn Jas. e. Sept. 1, 1862, m. o. June 6, 1865.
Ryan Thos. L. e. Aug. 12, 1862, died at Chattanooga, of wounds.
Roberts M. e. Aug. 18, 1862, m. o. June 6, 1865, wd.
Sutter Lanty, e. Aug. 18, '62. m. o. June 6, '65, corpl.
Short John, e. Aug. 18, 1862, died N. C. March 26, '65.
Snell Wm. e. Sept. 11, 1862, died N.C. Feb. 17, 1865.
Todd Henry, e. Aug. 13, 1862, died Sept. 19, 1863.
Welch Chas. e. Aug. 9, '62, absent, wd. at m. o. of regt.
Norton John, e. Aug. 13, 1862, m. o. June 6, 1865.
Larkin John, e. Sept. 27, 1864, m. o. June 6, 1865.

96th Infantry.

The Ninety-sixth Regiment Illinois Infantry Volunteers was recruited in July and August, 1862, and mustered into the United States' service at Camp Fuller, Rockford, Ill., Sept. 6, 1862.

This regiment was recruited largely from Jo Daviess County, six of its companies, A, E, F, H, J and K, being composed entirely of Jo Daviess County men, while companies B, C, D and G were from Lake County, thus forming a union of the northeast and northwest counties of this state, counties so long united in the old First Congressional District.

The Rebel forces, under Gen. Bragg, being on the march toward Louisville, while those under Kirby Smith were threatening Cincinnati, October 8 the Ninety-sixth was ordered to the latter place, taking position in the defences in front of Covington and Newport, Ky. October 19 the regiment moved in two detachments to Lexington, where, uniting, they proceeded to Harrodsburg, there employed in scouting and guarding Rebel prisoners. November 28, marched toward Lebanon Junction after Gen. John H. Morgan, returning to Danville two days later, Morgan having escaped.

Jan. 26, 1863, marching orders were received for Nashville, Tenn., to join the forces under Gen. Rosecrans.

Reached Louisville, Ky., January 31, when the Third Division, Army of Kentucky (the 2d Brigade to which the Ninety-sixth was attached) embarked on board steamers, and arrived in Nashville, February 7. Disembarked on the 8th and went into camp south of the city, where they remained until March 5, when they proceeded to Franklin, Tenn., to reinforce the First Brigade of the division under Col. Coburn, who was then engaged at Spring Hill.

March 9 to 12, skirmished with the enemy under Van Dorn, and drove him south of Duck River, then returned to camp at Franklin.

March 27, proceeded to Brentwood, and fortified, and again returned to Franklin, April 8.

On the 10th, Van Dorn attacked our lines and drove in the Grand Guard, but was repulsed. The regiment moved, on the 2d of June, to Triune, and on the 11th skirmished with the Rebels under Gen. Wheeler.

June 14, the Army of Kentucky was re-organized and attached to the Reserve Corps of the Army of the Cumberland. The Ninety-sixth I. V. I. was assigned to the First Brigade, First Division of said corps.

On the 23d, joined the forces moving against Bragg. Marched to Salem and joined the right wing of the army. Reached Walnut Grove Church, where the Ninety-sixth Regiment was detached to guard prisoners (who were captured at Liberty Gap) back to Murfreesboro.

Having re-joined their command, they reached Shelbyville on the 30th, and July 3 marched to Wartrace; there performed garrison duty until August 12, when the line of march was taken up for Elk River. Here engaged in scouting until September 7, when tents were once more struck, and the Ninety-sixth, together with all the troops of the Reserve Corps, were hastened forward to reinforce Gen. Rosecrans, now south of the Tennessee River.

On the 12th of September, reached Bridgeport, Ala., crossed the Tennessee, and camped on the south side. September 13 and 14, crossed Lookout Mountain to Rossville, Ga. On the 18th moved out on a reconnoissance toward Reid's Bridge, and skirmished with the enemy. SEPTEMBER 19 AND 20, BATTLE OF CHICAMAUGA. LOSS OF THE NINETY-SIXTH I. V. I. IN KILLED, WOUNDED AND MISSING, 220. On the 21st and 22d, fell back to Chattanooga.

From September 23 to October 26, lying on Moccasin Point, under Lookout Mountain, canonading and skirmish firing daily.

At this time, weather bad, reduced to one fourth rations; men without proper clothing; camp and garrison equipage *none;* and on the morning of the 26th the only rations issued were *one ear of corn per man!* About this time the army was re-organized, the Reserve Corps abolished, and the Ninety-sixth Regiment attached to the Second Brigade, First Division, Fourth Army Corps.

October 27, crossed the river to reinforce Gen. Hooker in the Wauhatchie Valley, and returned to bivouac on the Point. Re-crossed on the 29th to support Hooker, in which engagement the regiment lost several men. Again returned to the Point, and November 1, 2 and 3 crossed to the south side of Tennessee, and marched down the river to Shell Mound; there placed on outpost duty in Nickajack Cove, Ga. The troops were more comfortable than when at Moccasin Point, being in receipt of full rations and an abundance of clothing.

November 20, six days' rations being issued, reconnoitered the enemy's lines, and returned to camp. Marched, on the 23d, to the Wauhatchie and joined the column under Gen. Hooker, for the storming of Lookout Mountain.

On the 24th, crossed Lookout Creek at daylight, ascended the mountain, and moved forward, driving the enemy. The Ninety-sixth was then ordered to the extreme right, on the front line, climbing up the mountain side to where it rises perpendicularly, the regiment rapidly advanced; flanking the enemy's works, they poured a destructive fire down the rifle pits, which caused the Rebels to give way and fall back to the mountain point near Craven's house.

Night coming on, a heavy firing was kept up, under cover of which the enemy evacuated the mountain. November 20, the Ninety-sixth Illinois and Eighth Kentucky advanced and occupied the mountain, where they remained until December 1, when orders were received to return to out post duty at Nickajack Cove, and here camped until Jan. 26, 1864. The Ninety-sixth was then ordered to cover the working party repairing the East Tennessee R. R. Reached Blue Springs February 7, where the regiment reconnoitered until the 22d, and then joined the column operating against the enemy in front of Dalton. Moved to the extreme left of the army on the 25th, and took position in fr nt line, and were heavily engaged all day in the action known as "Buzzard Roost," after which skirmished until the 28th, when the regiment returned to camp at Blue Springs. March 1, ordered to Cleveland, to fortify and garrison, where they remained until April 23, when camp was broken, and the Ninety-sixth again joined to its command, preparatory to commencing the Atlanta campaign.

May 3, 1864, the regiment moved with command; engaged the enemy on the 9th at Rocky Face, losing heavily; entered Dalton on the 13th; engaged again at Reseca on the 14th and 15th, with heavy loss; skirmished with the enemy on the 19th, and drove him to Kingston, where the army rested until the 24th. Engaged at New Hope Church on the 25th, and again, from the 27th to June 5, in the rifle pits in front of Dallas, between Lost and Pine Mountains. Skirmished on the 10th and 11th of June; in action at Pine Mountain on the 14th, where the rebel, Gen. Bishop Polk, was killed; marching and fighting from the 15th to the 19th; 20th and 27th, assault on Kenesaw Mountain, and again the Ninety-sixth lost heavily. July 3 and 4, skirmishing, and in action at Smyrna camp ground; crossed the Chattahoochie River on the 12th; in action on the 19th and 20th at Peach Tree Creek; from the 22d to August 25, continuous fighting in front of Atlanta; again in action, at Rough and Ready, on the 31st; September 1 and 2, engaged in battles of Jonesboro and Lovejoy Station, and skirmished until the 6th. Atlanta having been captured, the regiment returned to camp near city, where it remained until October 3, when the march back to the Tennessee River was commenced, camping on the many battle-fields of the campaign. From Chicamauga, the command crossed to Pulaski, Tenn., which place was reached November 3. On the 23d, Hood appeared before Pulaski, and the march for Nashville began. Franklin was reached on the 30th, when the regiment was again engaged in a desperate battle.

Falling back December 1, to Nashville, the Ninety-sixth was in front of the enemy, doing picket duty, until the 15th, when the battle of Nashville began, and continued two days, during which time the regiment behaved gallantly, carried the enemy's line near the Franklin Pike, planted the first colors on his earth works, and captured a battery of 12-pounds Napoleons, together with prisoners far exceeding their own number. Joining in pursuit of the remnant of Hood's command to the Tennessee, the Ninety-sixth exchanged the last infantry shots with that army.

The regiment reached Athens Jan. 4, 1865. From thence, marched to Huntsville, Ala., where it camped until March 15, when the march to Bull's Gap and Shields' Mills, in East Tennessee, commenced. The regiment scouted until the surrender of Lee's army, when the command was ordered to Nashville, *en route* for Texas, to operate against the rebels under Kirby Smith; but, he having surrendered to Gen. Canby, thus ending the war, on the 11th of June, the Ninety-sixth Regiment was ordered to Camp Douglas, Ill., for final pay and muster out of the United States' service, where it arrived on the 14th. Received pay on the 29th and 30th day of June, 1865, the Ninety-sixth Regiment Illinois Infantry Volunteers had passed into history, after an eventful existence of three years, rendered historic by deeds written in blood on many a battle-field. The sufferings and privations of the brave men who conposed that organization can be best understood when the casualties they met, the battles in which they were actively engaged, and the number of miles traveled are made known, and not even then can their devotion and sacrifice to their country be sufficiently estimated.

A careful estimate of the marches made, including the distance transported by rail, shows that the regiment traveled over five thousand miles in their three years' service.

The following were the casualties of the regiment:

COMMISSIONED OFFICERS.

Resigned on account of disability	20	
Transferred by order	2	
Died of disease	1	
Killed in action	1	
Died of wounds	5	
Missing in action	3	—32

ENLISTED MEN.

Discharged for disability	165	
Died of disease	92	
Killed in action	59	
Died of wounds	33	
Missing in action	75	
Transferred by order	283	
Deserted	30	—737
Total		769

The following were the principal actions and battles in which the Ninety-sixth Regiment was engaged:

Spring Hill, Tenn., March 10, 1863; Franklin, Tenn., April 10; Triune, Tenn., June 11; Liberty Gap, Tenn., June 28; Chicamauga, Ga., Sept. 19 and 20; Lookout Mountain, Tenn., Nov. 24 and 25; Buzzard Roost, Ga., Feb. 25, 1864; Rocky Face Ridge, Ga., May 8 and 9; Dalton, Ga., May 13; Resaca, Ga., May 14 and 15; Kingston, Ga., May 19; New Hope Church, Ga., May 25; In front of Dallas, Ga., May 26 to June 5; Pine Mountain, Ga., June 14; Kenesaw Mountain, Ga., June 20; Kenesaw Mountain, Ga., June 27; Smyrna Camp Ground, Ga., July 4; Peach Tree Creek, Ga., July 20; Atlanta, Ga., July 22 to August 25; Rough and Ready, Ga., August 31; Jonesboro, Ga., September 1; Lovejoy Station, Ga., September 2; Franklin, Tenn., November 30; Nashville, Tenn., December 15 and 16.

In addition to the above general engagements, the Ninety-sixth Regiment Illinois Infantry Volunteers was engaged in many of the skirmishes and all the movements and marches of the Fourth Army Corps of the Army of the Cumberland, from the date of its organization until muster out, in the month of June, 1865.

Colonel Thomas E. Champion, com. Sept. 6, 1862. Hon. disd. June 7, 1865.

Lieutenant Colonel John C. Smith, com. Major Sept. 6, 1862. Prmtd. Lieut. Col. Sept. 20, 1863. M. o. June 10, 1865. Prmtd. Brevet. Brig. Gen. June 20, 1865.

Major George Hicks com. Capt. Co. A Sept. 6, 1862. Prmtd. Maj. Sept. 20, 1863. M. o. June 10, 1865.

Quartermaster Stephen Jeffers, com. Sept. 6, 1862. Prmtd. by president.

Quartermaster George W. Moore, com. 2d lieut. Co. I, Sept. 6, 1862. Prmtd. 1st lieut. Oct. 6, 1863. Prmtd. Q. M. April 16, 1864. M. o. June 10, 1865.
Surgeon Charles Martin, com. Sept. 6, 1862. Res. Feb. 6, 1863.
Surgeon Byron G. Pierce, com. Jan. 6, 1863. M. o. June 10, 1865.
Chaplain J. M. Clendenning, com. Sept. 8, 1862. Res. Jan. 23, 1863.
Sergt. Maj. Francis Quinn, e. Aug. 5, 1862, wd. drowned Feb. 19, 1864.
Q. M. Sergt. W. S. Bean, e. Aug. 4,'62, kld. Sept. 20,'63.
Q. M. Sergt. Geo. Jeffers, e. Aug. 15,'62, m.o. June 9,'65.
Q. M. Sergt. Benj. F. Shepard e. Aug. 11, 1862, m. o. June 10, 1865.
Gom. Sergt. J. E. James e. Aug. 5, 1862, m. o. June 10, 1865.
Principal Musician Niles Carver, e. Sept. 4, 1862, disd. Jan. 20, 1863.

Company A.

Captain Wm. Vincent, com. 1st. lieut. Sept. 6, 1862. Prmtd. Capt. Sept. 20, 1863. M. o. June 10, 1865.
First Lieutenant Robert Pool, com. 2d lieut. Sept. 6, 1862. Prmtd. 1st lieut. Sept. 20, 1863. Hon. disd. June 10, 1865.
Second Lieutenant F. A. Weir, e. as sergt. Aug. 2, 1862, wd., prmtd. 1st sergt. then 2d lieut. May 19, 1865. M. o. June 10, 1865.
First Sergt. I. G. Shaefer e. July 29, 1862, kld. Sept. 20, 1863.
Sergt. David Rogers, e, Aug. 2, 1862, disd. April 6, 1863, disab.
Sergt. I. L. Pringle, e. July 29, 1862, m.o. June 10, '62.
Sergt. Wm. S. Holmes, e. July 30, 1862, m.o. June 10, 1865, as private.
Corpl. W. S. Bean, e. Aug. 4, 1862, prmtd. Q. M. sergt.
Corpl. C. H. Berg, e. July 30, 1862, m.o. June 10, 1865, as 1st sergt.
Corpl. I. Vincent, e. July 30, 1862, m. o. June 10, 1865, as sergt.
Corpl. Wm. Price, e. Aug. 5, 1862, kld. Sept. 20, 1863.
Corpl. John R. Taylor, e. Aug. 4, 1862, m. o. June 10, 1865 as private.
Corpl Henry Peeper, e. Aug. 4, 1862, trans. to engineers corps.
Corpl. I. E. Shipton e. Aug. 5, 1862, disd. Feb. 13, 1863, disab.
Corpl. Jason B. Isbell, e. Aug. 8, 1862, m. o. June 10, 1865, as sergt., wd.
Musician B. F. Fox, e. Aug 4, 1862, m. o. June 10,'65.
Musician G. Bowman, e. Aug. 4, 1862, m. o. June 10, 1865, as private.
Wagoner John Strong, e. Aug. 2, 1862, disd. Sept. 13, 1863, disab.
Allison A. M. e. Aug. 5, 1862, m. o. June 10, 1865.
Barthold E. e. July 30, 1862, m.o. June 10, '65, as sergt.
Binninger J. A. e. July 30, 1862, m. o. June 10, 1865.
Beck G. e. July 31, 1862, m, o. June 10, 1865, wd.
Buys John, e. Aug. 2, 1862, disd. Jan. 25, 1863, disab.
Beall Jas. M. e. Aug. 5, 1862, died Feb. 1, 1863.
Beall Josiah, e. Aug. 5, 1862, died April 11, 1863.
Barrett Chas. e. Aug. 2, 1862, disd. April 3, 1863, disab.
Buck O. J. e. Aug. 4, 1862, disd. Dec. 22, 1863, disab.
Bastin John, e. Aug. 2, m. o. June 10, 1865.
Burgess Alfred, e. Aug. 8, 1862, m. o. June 10, 1865.
Ball D. R. P. e. Aug. 8, 1862, disd. in Feb., 1864, disab.
Campbell H. M. e. July 31, 1862, desrtd. Jan. 28, 1863.
Consolus J. E. e. Aug. 4, 1864, m. o. June 10, 1865.
Connor Jno. W. e. Aug. 5, m.o. June 10, 1865, wd.
Campbell P. D. e. Aug. 22,'62, trans. to engineer corps.
Dish Andrew, Jr., e. Aug. 5, 1862, kld. Lovejoy Station, Ga., Sept. 2, 1864.
Dish A., Sr., e. Aug. 15, 1862, disd. Jan. 25, 1863, disab.
Einhart M. R. e. Aug. 1, 1862, disd. Jan. 25,'63, disab.
Einsweild John, e Aug. 2, 1862, m.o. June 10, 1865, wd.
Erskine R. L. e. Aug. 2, 1862, disd. Jan. 19,'63, disab.
Fletcher I. C. e. Sept. 1, 1862, disd. Feb. 16, '63, disab.
Fleck C. B. e. Aug. 5, 1862, disd. Dec. 2, 1863, disab.
Funstan Adam, e. Sept. 3, 1862, trans. to invalid corps Sept. 25, 1863.
Godat Edward, e. Aug. 2,'62, m.o June 10,'65, as corpl.
Gault Samuel C. e. Aug. 4, 1862, m. o. May 16, 1865.
Greenwold Jno. e. Aug. 6, 1862, disd. Feb. 13,'63, disab.
Gayetty W. S. e. Aug. 6, 1862. disd, Feb. 23,'63, disab.
Geyer Wm. e. July 31, 1862, m. o. June 10, 1865.
Goatrea L. C. G. e. Aug. 4, 1862, died at Cleveland, Tenn., April 12, 1864.
Glover Milton, e. Aug. 22, 1862, m. o. June 10,'65, wd.
Holden John H. e. Aug. 4, 1862, m. o. June 10, 1865.
Hopp Theo. e. Aug. 2, 1862, m. o. June 10, 1865.
Hesse Conrad, e. Aug. 6,'62, m.o. June 10,'65, as corpl.
Hoch John, e. Aug. 20, 1862, m. o. June 10, 1865.
Isbell David, e. Aug. 2, 1862, corpl., missing in action at Chicamauga, Sept. 20, 1863, wd.
James J. Ed. e. Aug. 5, 1862, prmtd. com. sergt.
Keiburg F. J. e. Aug. 4, 1862, disd. Mch. 10,'63, disab.
Kaufman Chris. e. Aug. 5, 1862, died Sept. 24, 1863, wd.
Kunz Clemens, e. Aug. 5, 1862, disd. June 17, 1863.
Langdon E. B. e. Aug. 5, 1862, disd. April 7, 65, wd.
Lewis Wm. e. Aug. 1,'62, kld, Atlanta, Ga., Aug. 19,'64.
McMaster Wm. B. e. Aug. 4, 1862, disd. for promotion in 7th Ky. Heavy Art.
Metcalf J. e. Aug. 5, 1862, m.o. June 10, 1865, as corpl.
Marsden S. R. e. Aug. 2, 1862, disd. Sept. 13,'63, disab.
Miller R. K. e. Aug 4, 1862, m. o. June 10, 1865.
Menzimer Chas. C. e. Aug. 5, 1862, died June 16, 1864.
Menzimer Harrison, e. Aug. 5, 1862, m. o. June 10, 1865.
McKinley Jno. I. e. Aug. 4,'62, disd April 5, '63, disab.
Neal Robt. e. Aug. 2, 1862, disd. March 22, 1863.
Robinson F. I. e. July 29, 18 2, m. o. June 10, 1865.
Rausch C. e. Aug. 6, 1862, disd. Feb. 20, 1863, disab.
Reubeno Edward, e. Aug. 9, 1862, m. o. June 10, 1865.
Saulsbury Wm. e. Aug. 4, 1862, died at Chicago, Jan. 9, 1865.
Simpson Ed. e. July 31, 1862, m. o. June 10, 1865.
Turner Calvin, e. Aug. 5. 1862, disd. Apl. 5,'63, disab.
Treftz Theo. e. Aug. 4, 1862, m. o. June 10, 1865.
Tate E. e. Aug. 5, 1862, m. o. June 10, 1865.
Utrecht Frederick, e. July 31, 1862, disd. April 24, 1863, disab.
Virtue Wm. e. Aug. 8, 1862, m. o. June 10, 1865, corpl.
Vickers Thomas, e. Aug. 4, 1862, m. o. June 10, 1865.
Willard W. H. H. e. Aug. 4, 1862, m. o. June 10, 1865, as corpl.
Wearmouth N. e. Aug. 4, 1862, m. o. June 10, 1865.
Witman John H. e. Aug. 5, 1862, died Oct. 30, '63, wd.
Weber Gottlieb. e. July 31, 1862, m. o. June 10, 1865.
Wilson Harvey G. e. Aug. 22, 1862, disd. July 23, 1863, disab.
Young Jos. e. Aug. 8, 1862, m. o. May 30, 1865, wd.
Allendorf Philip, e. Sept. 19, 1864, m. o. June 10, 1865.
Bryson John, e. Oct. 1, 1864, m. o. June 10, 1865.
Bray Thos. e. March 2, 1865, died April 26, 1865.
Daves Noah N. e. Sept. 21. 1864, m. o. June 10. 1865.
Metcalf Thomas, e. March 2, 1865, died at Nashville, May 16, 1865.
Richards James, e. March 2, 1865, died at Nashville, May 16, 1865.
Tutin Nicholas, e. Sept. 27, 1864, m. o. June 10, 1865.
Tippit Wm. H. e. March 20, 1865, died at Nashville, May 3, 1865.
Wheeldin John, e. Sept. 27, 1864, m. o. June 10, 1865.
Weir John T. e. Oct. 1, 1864, m. o. June 10, 1865.
Wilcox I. M. e. Oct. 14, 1864, died April 16, 1865.
Yontz Mathias, e. Sept. 27, 1864, m. o. June 10, 1865.

Company E.

Second Lieut. Edward E. Todd, e. as private Aug. 7, 1862. M. o. as 1st sergt. June 10, 1865. Com. 2d lieut. but not mustered.
Sergt. Jos. N. Lindsay, e. July 26, 1862, private, trans. to Engineer Corps, July 18, 1864.
Corpl. Wm. McDonald, e. July 26, 1862, disd. April 14, 1863, disab.
Corpl. D. W. Dimick, e. Aug. 10, 1862, m. o. June 10, 1865, as sergt.
Corpl. Edgar Warner, e. Aug. 14, 1862, kld. Sept. 20,'63.
Musician Jas. M. Cole, e. Aug. 14, 1862, disd. May 22, 1863, disab.
Wagoner Samuel Barber, e. Aug. 2, '62, m.o. June 10,'65.
Allison Robert C. e. Aug. 26, 1862, died at Nashville, Oct. 12, 1863, wd.
DeGraff Wm. F. e. Aug. 5, 1862, sergt., died at Chattanooga, May 16, 1864, wd.
Dimick Geo. W. e. Aug. 22, 1862, wd. and captd. Sept. 20, 1863.
Edgar Wm. e. Aug. 15, 1862, kld. Sept. 20, 1863.
Frisby Calvin, e. Aug. 11, 1862, m.o. June 10, '65, sergt.
Fleming Peter, e. Aug. 7, 1862, m.o. June 10, '65, sergt.
Gowing Jos. B. e. Aug. 4, 1862, wd., trans. to V. R. C. April 10, 1865.
Griburg Simon, e. Aug. 1, 1862, m. o. June 10, 1865.
Gunn Jas. e. Aug. 11, 1862, died in Ky. Feb. 21, 1863.
Harrison Richard, e. Aug. 4, 1862, m. o. June 10, 1865.
Harrington D. e. Aug. 9, 1862, kld. Sept. 20, 1863.
Harding John, e. Aug. 4, 1862, died Dec. 24, 1863.

Hubbard Wm. e. Aug. 15, 1862, died in Ky. June 25,'63.
Jellison Wm. W. e. Aug. 9, 1862, m. o. June 10, 1865, prisr. war.
Jennings Geo. W. e. Aug. 14, 1862, m. o. June 10, 1865.
Jellason Marcus, e. Aug. 11, 1862, m. o. June 10, 1865.
Junken Jas. e. Aug. 11, 1862, corpl., died June 23, 1864, wd.
King Andrew, e. Aug. 11, 1862, m. o. June 10, 1865.
Keyes Thos. e. Aug. 22, '62, died in Tenn., Mch. 5,'63.
Lewis Jas. e. Aug. 14, 1862, disd. March 31, 1863, disab.
Lamberton David H. e. Aug. 15, 1862, m.o. June 10,'65.
Martins Thos. e. Aug. 9, 1862, died at Nashville, Dec. 19, 1863, wd.
Mack Henry, e. Aug. 12, 1862, died at Chattanooga, Oct. 12, 1863, wd.
Mathew Wm. e. Aug. 7, 1862, died at Chattanooga, Oct. 14, 1863, wd.
Montgomery Wall W. e. Aug. 21, 1862, m. o. June 10, 1865, prisr. war.
Moore Thos. e. Aug. 15, 1862, m. o. June 10, 1865.
Noogles Isaac, e. Aug. 11, 1862, trans. to Engineer Corps, July 24, 1864.
O'Leary Dennis, e. Aug. 10, 1862, died Oct. 26, '63, wd.
Oberlin Wm. e. Aug. 12, 1862, m. o. June 10, 1865.
Power Newton, e. Aug. 15, 1862, m. o. June 10, 1865, as corpl.
Pooly John H. e. Aug. 17, 1862, corp., trans. to V. R. C., wd.
Pool Frank, e. Aug. 11, 1862, died in Ky. Nov. 30, '62.
Phippin O. e. Aug. 11, 1862, m. o. June 10, 1865.
Patch Duane, e. Aug. 7, 1862, disd. March 8, '63, disab.
Poston Richard, e. Aug. 7, 1862. m. o. June 10, 1865.
Shay James, e. Aug. 22, 1862, deserted Feb. 3, 1863.
Strong Brainard E. e. Aug. 15, 1862, died in Ky. Jan 10, 1863.
Sage John, e. Aug. 12, 1862, died March 30, 1863.
Sprague Wm. e. Aug. 9, 1862, m. o. June 10, 1865.
Smith Jno. e. Aug 6, 1862, m. o. June 10, 1865.
Stott Thos. e. Aug. 9, 1862, m. o. June 10, 1865.
Trummond Harry, e. Aug. 7, 1862, disd. July 12, 1863, disab.
Thomas James, e. Aug. 11, 1862, kld. at Chicamauga, Sept. 20, 1863.
Trusty Ed. e. Aug. 22, 1862, dishon. disd. May 5, 1865.
Teal Geo. e. Aug. 21, 1862, m. o. June 10, 1865, wd.
Tinkley Jos. e. Aug. 22, 1862, kld. at Chicamauga, Sept. 20, 1863.
Williams John, e. Aug. 11, 1862, m. o. June 10, 1865.
White Jabes, e. Aug. 7, 1862, disd. Nov. 20, '64, disab.
Wollam Jas. e. Aug. 10, 1862, m. o. June 10, 1865.
Woodell Lloyd, e. Aug. 2, 1862, m.o. June 10,'65, corpl.
Grabham John, m. o. June 10, 1865, as corpl.
Muller F. e. Oct. 8, 1864, trans. to Co. E, 21st I. V. I.

Company F.

Captain Thomas A. Green, com. Sept. 6, 1862. Res. Nov. 24, 1862.
Captain Charles E. Rowan, com. 1st. lieut. Sept. 6, 1862. Prmtd. capt. Nov. 24,'62. M.o. June 10,'65.
First Lieut. Nelson R. Simms, com. 2d lieut. Sept. 6, 1862. Prmtd 1st lieut. Nov. 24, 1862. Died Sept. 29, 1863.
First Lieut. Wm. Dawson, e. as sergt. Aug. 11, 1862. Prmtd. 1st sergt., then 2d lieut., Nov. 24, 1862. Prmtd. 1st lieut. Sept. 29, 1863. M. o. June 10,'65.
Second Lieut. Franklin W. Pierce, e. as corpl. Aug. 12, 1862. Prmtd. sergt., then 2d lieut., Sept 29, 1863. M. o. June 10, 1865.
First Sergt. J. B. Leekley, e. Aug. 12, 1862, died in Andersonville Prison, Sept. 25, 1864.
Sergt. Chas. G. Luttman, e. Aug. 13, 1862, m. o. June 10, 1865, as private, reduced at his own request.
Sergt. Hiram L. Bostwick, e. Aug. 14, 1862, as private, kld. Sept. 20, 1863.
Sergt. Augustus Wirth, e. Aug. 13, 1862, trans. to Vet. Res. Corps Feb. 8, 1864.
Corpl. John C. Lee, e. Aug. 14, 1862, as sergt., trans. to Engineer Corps, July 18, 1864.
Corpl. Robert A. Fowler, e. Aug. 11, 1862, kld. May 11, 1864, wd.
Corpl. Henry Frefz, e. Aug. 12, 1862, died Mch. 31,'63.
Corpl. John McCarty, e. Aug. 11, 1862, m. o. June 10, 1865, as private.
Corpl. John R. Oatey, e. Aug. 13, 1862, kld. at Chicamauga Sept. 20, 1863.
Corpl. Wm. Irvine, e. Aug. 11, 1862, m. o. June 10, 1865, as private.
Wagoner L. A. Guild, e. Aug. 15, 1862, disd. Feb. 15, 1863, disab.
Armbruster A. e. Aug. 11, 1862, as corpl., died Oct. 7, 1863, wd.
Bastion Sampson, e. Aug. 11, 1862, m. o. June 10, 1865.
Bailey Geo. W. e. Aug. 12, 1862, m. o. June 10, 1865.
Brown James, e. Aug. 11, 1862, m. o. June 10, 1865, wd.
Bonjom Thos. e. Aug. 14, 1862, m. o. June 10, 1865.
Calvers R. e. Aug. 11, '62, trans. to V.R.C. Jan. 16, '65.
Clark W. P. e. Aug. 11,'62, trans. to 3d Mo. Cav. Oct. 7,'62.
Conway P. e. Aug. 15, 1862, m. o. June 10, 1865, wd.
Craig John, e. Aug. 11, 1862, disd. May 26, 1865, disab.
Calvert Wm. e. Aug. 15,'62, died in Ga. Sept. 4, '64, wd.
Edgerton W. I. e. Aug. 13, 1862, died March 13, 1863.
Elberth Jacob, e. Aug. 15, 1862, died Sept. 25, 1863.
Fablinger P. e. Aug. 11,'62, m.o. June 10,'65, as corpl.
Garrow Frank, e. Aug. 15, 1862, m. o. June 10, 1865.
Graham Thos. e. Aug. 12, 1862, m.o. June 10, 1865, as corpl., wd.
Goodwin W. E. e. Aug. 13,'62, disd. Sept. 15,'63, disab.
Holtkamp H. e. Aug. 11, 1862, disd. June 12,'63, disab.
Hocking John, e. Aug. 11, 1862, m. o. June 10, '65, wd.
Hallarter Jacob, e. Aug. 11, 1862, m. o. June 10, 1865.
Handley Wm. e. Aug. 15,'62, disd. June 20,'63, disab.
Holtkamp B. e. Aug. 13, 1862, died Sept. 13, 1864.
Hancock Edward, e. Aug. 11, 1862, m.o. June 10, 1865.
Jelly W. A. e. Aug. 15, 1862, died Sept. 10, 1864, wd.
Kramer Gottlieb, e. Aug. 11, 1862, m.o. June 10, 1865.
Kearnaghan E. e. Aug. 11, 1862, m.o. June 10, 1865.
Kimmins Thos. e Aug. 14, 1862, m.o. June 10, 1865.
Kneebone John, e. Aug. 14, 1862, m. o. June 10, 1865.
Lawrence T. H. e. Aug. 11,'62, disd. Jan. 25,'63, disab.
Mahood Edwd. e. Aug. 15, 1862, m.o. June 10, 1865.
Metcalf Rigdon, e. Aug. 14, 1862, m. o. June 10, 1865.
Munson B. F. e. Aug. 12, 1862, m. o. June 10, 1865.
Miller John, e, Aug. 12, 1862, m. o. June 9, 1865.
Nash Wm. G. e. Aug. 15, 1862, m. o. June 10, 1865.
Perkins Jos. e. Aug. 15, 1862, trans. to Engineer Corps July 25, 1864.
Pinley Jas. e. Aug. 15, 1862, kld. Sept. 20, 1863.
Romer L. e. Aug. 14, 1862, m.o. June 10, 1865, as sergt.
Reed Walton, e Aug. 12, 1862, kld. Sept. 20, 1863.
Rogers Jos. e. Aug. 11, 1862, disd. April 24, 1863, disab.
Robinson Q. e. Aug. 15, 1862, m.o. June 10,'65, as musn.
Sturges Wm. e. Aug. 11, 1862, died March 18, 1863.
Stewart Jas. e. Aug. 11, 1862, m.o. June 10,'65, as sergt.
Shannon J. e. Aug. 11,'62, trans. to V.R.C. Mch. 15, '65.
Sidner Wm. e. Aug. 12, 1862, disd. Sept. 18,'63, disab.
Sullivan M. e. Aug. 15, 1862, as sergt., died in Ky. Jan. 10, 1865, wd.
Spencer R. e. Aug 15, 1872, disd. March 19, 1865, wd.
Sincock John, e. Aug. 15, 1862, m. o. June 10, 1865.
Scott Jas. M. e. Aug. 11, 1862, kld. April 16,'63, Tenn.
Shannon Thos e. Aug. 12, 1862, disd. Jan. 9, 1865, as corpl., disab.
Spencer S. e. Aug. 11, 1862, m.o. June 10, 1865, as corpl.
Sidner Geo. e. Aug. 14, 1862, died at Nashville, Tenn., Nov. 12, 1863.
Trudgian W. e. Aug. 11,'62, died in Tenn., Sept. 14,'63.
Telford James, e. Aug. 11, 1862, died Nov. 6, 1864.
Trevorthen Thos. e. Aug. 13, 1862, m. o. June 10, 1865.
Vanalstine Wm. e. Aug. 12,'62, disd. Feb. 28,'63, disab.
Wakefield C. e. Aug. 12, 1862, corpl., died Mch. 23,'63.
Warus F. H. e. Aug. 13, 1862, m. o. June 10, 1865.
Williams Hugh. e. Aug. 11, 1862, absent, sick at m. o.
White Andrew, e. Aug. 15,'61, disd. April 11,'63, disab.
Wright Wm. e. Sept. 4, 1862, m. o. June 10, 1865.
Bailey F. S. e. Oct. 8, 1864, died Dec. 17, 1864, wd.
Buckner Henry, e. Oct. 8, 1864, m. o. June 1, 1865.
Damson Robt. e. Sept. 26, 1864, m. o. June 10, 1865.
Golden John, m. o. June 10, 1865, as musician.
Grotjohn C. e. Oct. 10, 1864, m. o. May 25, 1865.
Hammond C. W. trans. to Engineer Corps July 25, '64.
Pinley Robt. m.o. June 10, 1865, as corpl.

Company H.

Captain Alexander Burnette, com. Sept. 6, 1862. Res. May 27, 1863.
Captain Joseph L. Pierce, e. as 1st sergt. Aug. 9, 1862. Prmtd. 2d lieut. Feb. 6, 1863. Prmtd. 1st lieut. April 28, 1863. Prmtd. capt. May 27, 1863. M. o. June 10, 1865.
First Lieut. Samuel H. Bayne, com. Sept. 6, 1862. Res. April 28, 1863.
First Lieut. George F. Barnes, e. as sergt. Aug. 13, 1862 Prmtd. 2d lieut. April 28, 1863. Prmtd. 1st lieut. May 27, 1863. Died Oct. 2, 1863.
First Lieut. Chas. H. Yates, e. as sergt. Aug. 11, 1862. Prmtd. 2d lieut. May 27, 1863. Prmtd. 1st lieut. Oct. 2, 1863. Commission canceled.

Second Lieut. Reuben L. Root, com. Sept. 6, 1862. Res. Feb. 6, 1863.
Sergt. A. J. Francisco, e. Aug. 15, 1862, disd. July 23, 1864, as 1st sergt., wd.
Sergt. M. J. Carpenter, e. Aug. 15, 1862, disd. April 27, 1863, as private, disab.
Corpl. M. J. Penwell, e. Aug. 15, 1862, m.o. June 10, '65.
Corpl. Michael Hileman, e. Aug. 15, 1862, m. o, June 10, 1865, as sergt.
Corpl. Chester J. Rees, e. Aug. 22, 1862, m. o. June 10, 1865, as 1st sergt.
Corpl. M. M. Bruner, e. Aug. 15, 1862, disd. Jan. 22, 1864, as sergt, wd.
Corpl. Horace Gray, e. Aug. 15, 1862, disd. April 1, 1863, as private, disab.
Corpl. John A. Boothby, e. Aug. 6, 1862, died in prison in Richmond, Va., Dec. 25, 1863.
Musician Niles Carver, e. Sept. 4. 1862, prmtd. principal musician.
Addudle Isaac, e. Aug. 15, 1862, died at Estelle Springs, Aug. 31, 1863.
Andrews Wallace, e. Aug. 15, 1862, m. o. June 10, '65.
Andrews Geo. W. e. Aug. 3, 1862, m. o. June 10, 1865, prisr. war.
Briggs Frederick, e. Aug. 15, '62, deserted Sept. 9, '63.
Bryan Wm. B. e. Aug. 15, 1862, m. o. June 10, 1865.
Bryan A. C. e. Aug. 15, 1862, m. o. June 10, 1865, corpl.
Bryan Geo. e. Aug. 15, 1862, died at Lexington, Ky., Nov. 13, 1863.
Burbridge Robt. e. Aug. 18, 1862, kld. June 23, 1864.
Bunce Chas. D. e. Sept. 1, 1862, m. o. June 10, 1865.
Cressey H. W. e Aug. 22, 1862, disd. June 8, '63, disab.
Curry J. J. e. Aug. 6, 1862, died Oct. 1, 1863, wd.
Chown R. B. e. Aug. 14, 1862, m. o. June 10, 1865.
Crowell L. C. e. Aug. 15, 1862, died at Chattanooga, Nov. 3, 1863.
Cullen Richard, e. Aug. 14, 1862, m. o. June 10, 1865.
Conley Wm. e. Aug. 14, 1862, died at Nashville, Tenn., April 22, 1863.
Crocker W. W. e. Aug. 9, 1862, trans. to V. R. C., Dec. 12, 1863.
Dunton Oscar W. e. Aug. 22, '62, disd. Feb. 4, '63, disab.
Davis J. P. e. Aug. 15, 1862, died March 18, 1863.
Dowd Daniel W. e. Aug. 14, 1862, m. o. May 27, 1865, prisr. war.
Davidson Peter, e. Aug. 9, '62, m. o. May 30, '65, corpl.
Edwards Thos. J. e. Aug. 15, 1862, trans. to V. R. C.
Farly Albert, e. Aug. 6, 1862, kld. at Chicamauga, Sept. 20, 1863.
Forsyth James, e. Aug. 15, 1862, kld. at Chicamauga, Sept. 22, 1863.
Farrell Patrick 1st, e. Aug. 13, 1862, m.o. June 10, 1865.
Farrell Patrick 2d, e. Aug. 15, 1862, m. o. June 1, 1865, as corpl.
Flanery Patrick, e. Aug. 15, 1862, corpl., died in prison at Danville, Va., Dec. 8, 1863.
Foss Alvin B. e. Aug. 14, 1862, m. o. June 10, 1865.
Foster John H. e. Aug. 11, 1862, m. o. June 24, 1865, prisr. war.
Flanders Francis L. e. Aug. 9, 1862, m. o. June 8, 1865.
Graham Chas. W. e. Aug. 15, 1862, absent, sick at m.o.
Gates Edward W. e. Aug. 6, 1862, trans. to V. R. C.
Howard Chas. P. e. Aug. 11, '62, m. o. June 10, '65, as sergt., wd.
Ingersoll Wm. e. Aug. 15, 1862, died at Danville, Va., Jan. 17, 1864.
Johnson Thos. e. Aug. 15, 1862, died Nov. 10, '63, wd.
Marshall A. e. Aug. 22, 1862, corpl., died in Andersonville Prison, Aug. 18, 1864.
Moore Hensen, e. Aug. 15, 1862, disd. May 17, '65, wd.
McWain Nathaniel, e. Aug. 21, 1862, m. o. June 24, 1865, was prisr.
Metts Chas. e. Aug. 9, 1862, m. o. June 10, 1865, wd.
Morton W. S. e. Aug. 9, 1862, corpl., kld. at Chicamauga, Sept. 20, 1863.
McGinnis Ed. e. Aug. 9, '62, disd. May 6, 1865, wd.
Millett Hiram P. e. Aug. 15, 1862, trans. to Engineer Corps, July 29, 1864.
Nelson H. W. e. Aug. 15, 1862, m. o. May 20, '65, wd.
Post Ranselaer, e. Aug. 15, '62, disd. June 24, '63, disab.
Pettibone Theopholis, e. Aug. 22, 1862, trans. to Engineer Corps, July 25, 1864.
Rees James, e. Aug. 22, 1862, disd. June 25, 1864, wd.
Richards Ransom, e. Aug. 15, '62, disd. Sept. 19, '63, disab.
Stanchfield Geo. H. e. Aug. 15, 1862, died in Andersonville Prison, June 26, 1864.
Smith Finley, e. Aug. 15, '62, disd. July 30, 1863, disab.
Sallee Jas. M. e. Aug. 11, 1862, absent, sick at m. o.
Vroman Adam, e. Aug. 15, 1862, m. o. June 10, 1865, prisr. war.
Vandyke Edwin, e. Aug. 11, 1862, m. o. July 22, 1865, was prisr.
Vick Jos. T. e. Aug. 15, 1862, disd. Dec. 29, 1862, disab.
Wilkirson John V. e. Aug. 16, 1862, m. o. June 24, 1865, prisr. war.
Wilson John E. e. Aug. 15, '62, disd. Apl. 30, '63, disab.
Whelock Alberto, e. Aug. 15, 1862, died in Andersonville Prison, May 10, 1864.
Ward Norman P. e. Aug. 15, 1862, m. o. June 29, 1865.
Zuke S. H. R. e. Aug. 15, 1862, trans. to V. R. C. Jan. 18, 1864.
McCafferty James, m. o. June 10, 1865.

Company I.

Capt. John Barker, com. Sept. 6, 1862. Resigned Oct. 6, 1863.
Capt. John P. Tarpley, com. 1st lieut. Sept. 6, 1862. Prmtd. capt. Oct. 6, 1863. M. o. June 10, 1865.
First Lieut. Thos. J. Smith, e. as sergt, Aug. 5, 1862. Com. 1st lieut., not mustered. Died of wd. June 9, 1864.
First Lieut. Geo. W. Marshall, e. as corpl. Aug. 8, 1862. Prmtd. sergt., 1st sergt., then 1st lieut. June 9, 1864. M. o. June 10, 1865.
Second Lieut. John Long, e. as corpl. Aug. 4, 1862. Prmtd. sergt., 1st sergt., then 2d lieut. Feb. 21, 1865. M. o. June 10, 1865.
First Sergt. J. M. Woodruff, e. Aug. 6, 1862, disd. Oct. 26, 1864, for promotion in U. S. C. T. as 1st lieut.
Sergt. W. C. Woolsey, e. Aug. 5, 1862, disd. March 7, 1863, disab.
Sergt. Francis P. Quinn, e. Aug. 5, 1862, prmtd. sergt. maj.
Sergt. J. B. Hamilton, e. Aug. 23, 1862, disd. May 26, 1863, private, disab.
Corpl. Jno. Reynolds, e. Aug. 4, 1862, m. o. June 10, 1865, as sergt
Corpl. G. W. Roberts, e. Aug. 8, 1862, died at Nashville, Tenn., April 26, 1863.
Corpl. Arthur Spare, e. Aug. 9, 1862, m. o. June 10, 1865, as 1st sergt.
Corpl. Henry Bonitell, e. Aug. 4, 1862, reduced at his own request, missing since battle of Chicamauga.
Corpl. Wm. B. Goss, e. Aug. 6, 1862, m. o. June 10, 1865, as private.
Corpl. Geo. Dawson, e. Aug. 9, 1862, m. o. June 10, 1865, as sergt.
Abbe Christian, e. Aug. 20, 1862, m. o. June 10, 1865.
Adams John, e. Aug. 8 1862, missing since battle of Chicamauga.
Beck Wm. P. e. Aug. 6, 1862, disd. Sept. 20, '63, disab.
Bell Wm. e. Aug. 7, 1862, m. o. June 10, 1865.
Bennett John, e. Aug. 7, 1862, died at Nashville, Tenn., March 25, 1863.
Bennett Truman F. e. Aug. 8, 1862, kld. at Chicamauga, Sept. 20, 1863.
Bevard Wm. H. e. Aug. 5, 1862, died at Nashville, Tenn., Aug. 6, 1864.
Bowman John, e. Aug. 7, 1862, missing since battle of Chicamauga.
Bray Thos. B. e. Aug. 7. 1862. trans. to Engineer Corps, July 18, 1864.
Brower Almon, e. Aug. 6, 1862, m.o. June 10, 1865.
Byers John, e. Aug. 4, 1862, m. o. June 10, 1865.
Crowley D. e. Aug. 20, 1862, absent, sick at m. o.
Conley Wm. e. Aug. 6, 1862, disd. Dec. 29, 1862, disab.
Darr John C. e. Aug. 20, 1862, m. o. June 10, '65, sergt.
Daly Wm. e. Aug. 5, 1862, disd. May 18, 1863, disab.
Damphouse Peter, e. Aug. 4, 1862, m. o. June 10 1865.
Dunberger Jos. e. Aug. 5, 1862, desrtd. Feb. 9, 1863.
Edwards Jas. e. Aug. 5, 1862, disd. Jan. 1, 1864, disab.
Evans Jno. E. e. Aug. 8, 1862, m. o. June 10, 1865.
Evans George, e. Aug. 10, 1862, m. o. June 10, 1865.
Foster A. B. e. Aug. 8, 1862, m.o. June 10, 1865, as corpl.
Furlong M. e. Aug. 14, 1862, m.o. June 10, '65, as sergt.
Forbes Wm. J. e. Aug. 20, 1862, died at Pleasant Valley, Ill., Nov. 20, 1863.
Gage H. e. Aug. 8, 1862, m. o. June 10, 1865, as corpl.
Gerome John, e. Aug. 4, 1862, m. o. June 10, 1865.
Goddard Abram, Aug. 8, '62, disd. March 1, 1865, disab.
Goodburn Henry, e. Aug. 8, 1862, m. o. June 10, 1865.
Gray Joseph, e. Aug. 11, 1862, m. o. June 10, 1865.
Green Geo. e. Aug. 6, 1862, disd. June 26, 1863, disab.
Harvey C. e. Aug. 8, 1862, trans. V.R.C. July 29, 1864.
Heck L. e. Aug. 5, 1862, m.o. June 10, '65, as wagoner.
Hewitt Patrick, e. Aug. 14, 1862, kld. Lovejoy Station, Ga., Sept. 2, 1864.
Hobson Thos. e. Aug. 6, '62, trans. V.R.C. Sept. 12, '63.

Holland Thos. e. Aug. 8, 1862, trans. to Engineer Corps July 25, 1864.
Hill John, e. Aug. 8, 1862, corpl., died Atlanta, Ga., Sept. 23, 1864.
Hughes Hugh R. e. Aug. 8, 1862, m. o. June 10, 1865.
Hughes Owen, e. Aug. 15, 1862, m.o. June 10, 1865.
Hutchinson Jas. e. Aug. 8, 1862, m. o. June 10, 1865, wd.
Hopkins Freeman, e. Aug. 20, 1862, m.o. June 10, 1865.
Johnson Jasper M. e. Aug. 15, 1862, m. o. June 10, '65.
Koontz Francis S. e. Aug. 5, 1862, m. o. June 10, 1865, as corpl., wd.
Leslie Humphrey, e. Aug. 6, 1862, died at Nashville, Tenn., April 9, 1863.
Long Wm. H. e. Aug. 5, 1862, disd. Nov. 23,'63, disab.
Ma one Daniel, e. Aug. 15, 1862, m.o. June 10, 1865.
McDonald Wm. e. Aug. 7, 1862, m. o. June 10, 1865.
McDonough T. e. Aug. 6,'62, m.o. June 10,'65, as corpl.
McGregor Jas. e. Aug. 8, 1862, m. o. June 10, 1865.
Meres Michael, e. Aug. 10, 1862, died at Bridgeport, Ala., Feb. 15, 1864.
Morris Otho, e. Aug. 15, 1862, m. o. June 10, 1865.
Moore T. e. Aug. 9, 1862, m. o. June 10, 1865, as corpl.
McNeill T. L. e. Aug. 20,'62, trans. V.R.C. July 29, '64.
Noble John, e. Aug. 8, 1862, m. o. June 10, 1865.
Parker Chas. e. Aug. 6, 1862, m. o. June 10, 1865.
Perry Oliver H. e. Aug. 5, 1862, m. o. May 18, 1865.
Perry Wm. M. e. Aug. 5, 1862, m. o. June 10, 1865.
Perrin Wm. e. Aug. 9, 1862, disd. Oct. 8, 1863, disab.
Pogue F. M. e. Aug. 6, 1862, disd. Aug. 7, 1864, wd.
Ranson John A. e. Aug. 15, 1862, m. o. June 10, 1865.
Reynolds Thos. e. Aug. 30, 1862, m. o. June 10, 1865.
Schaible John, e. Aug. 6, 1862, disd. Feb. 9, '63, disab.
Shaw Chas. e. Aug. 6, 1862, m.o June 10,'65, as corpl.
Stremle Aug. e. Aug. 9, 1862, m.o. May 17, 1865, wd.
Spittler Joseph, e. Aug. 16, 1862, m. o. June 10, 1865.
Tarpley R. D. e. Aug. 7,'62, m. o. June 10,'65, as corpl.
Tarpley A. C. e. Aug. 5, 1862, died at Bridgeport, Ala., May 11, 1864.
Tippart Chas. R. e. Aug. 7, 1862, m. o. June 10, 1865.
Topping Geo. e. Aug. 8, 1862, m.o. June 10,'65, as corpl.
Travis W. C. e. Aug. 6, 1862, disd. May 30, 1865, as corpl., disab.
White Samuel, e. Aug. 6, 1862, m.o. June 10, 1865.
White Robert, e. Aug. 5, 1862, m. o. June 10, 1865.
White Mathew, e. Aug. 5, 1862, m. o. June 10, 1865.
Williams John, e. Aug. 20, 1862, died at Danville, Ky., Feb. 18, 1863.
Williams Hugh, e. Aug. 8, 1862, died at Florence, S.C., Nov. 29, 1864, while a prisoner of war.
Wilson B. B. e. Aug. 7, 1862, m. o. June 10, 1865, wd.
Wright Thos. e. Aug. 8, 1862, m. o. June 10, 1865.
Young David, e. Aug. 5, 1862, m. o. June 10, 1865.
Young Gains W. e. Aug. 16, 1862, kld. at Chicamauga, Sept. 20, 1863.
Craig Thos. e. Sept. 17, 1862, m.o. June 10, 1865.
Crummer Jos. e. Sept. 17, 1862, disd. Mch. 18,'63, disab.
Endress Andrew, e. Sept. 23, 1864, m. o. June 10, 1865.
Johns Nathan, e. Sept. 17, 1864, m. o. June 10, 1865.
King Geo. W. e. Sept. 17, 1864, m.o. June 10, 1865.
Lane Edwin, e. Sept. 17, 1864, m. o. June 10, 1865.
Nicholas Thos. P. e. Sept. 17, 1864, m.o. June 10, 1865.

Company K.

Captain Timothy D. Rose, com. Sept. 6, 1862. Res. March 21, 1864.
Capt. Ed. E. Townsend, com. 1st lieut. Sept. 6, 1862. Prmtd. capt. March 21, 1864. M. o. June 10, 1865.
First Lieut. Geo. W. Pepoon, com. 2d lieut. Sept. 6, 1862. Prmtd. March 21, 1864. M. o. June 10, 1865.
Second Lieut. Garrett W. Luke, e. as sergt. Aug. 6,'62. Prmtd. 1st sergt., then 2d lieut.. May 5, 1865. M. o. June 10, 1865.
First. Sergt. C. C. Cowen, e. Aug. 6, 1862, trans. to V. R. C. Jan. 27, 1864, wd.
Sergt. Wallace Tear, e. Aug. 4, 1862, disd. Nov. 9,'63, for promotion in 14th U. S. colored regt.
Sergt. H.R. Earley, e. Aug. 6,'62, disd. Oct. 16,'63, disab.
Sergt. W. W. Abbey, e. Aug. 4, 1862, trans. to V.R.C. July 7, 1863.
Corpl. C. N. Elston, e. July 29, m. o. June 8, 1865, as sergt., wd.
Corpl. Thos. S. Leland, e. Aug. 6, 1862, as sergt., kld. at Reseca, Ga., May 14, 1864.
Corpl. A. W. Conlee, e. Aug. 5, 1862, m. o. June 10, 1865, as private.
Corpl. Wm. E. Tilton, e. Aug. 4, 1862, m. o. June 10, 1865, as private, wd.
Corpl. C. M. Kinney, e. Aug. 6, 1862, trans. to Engineer Corps July 18, 1864.
Corpl. Thos. J. Carlton, e. Aug. 8, 1862, m. o. June 10 1865, as private.
Corpl. Albert F. Wood, e. Aug. 5, 1862, m. o. June 10, 1865, as private.
Corpl. Daniel Sullivan, e. Aug. 5, 1862, m. o. June 10, 1865, as sergt.
Arnold Chas. A. e. Aug. 6, 1862, m. o. June 10, 1865.
Appleby Leonard, e. Aug. 9,'62, m.o. June 10,'65, sergt.
Barton Ira, e. July 25,'62, trans. to V.R.C. Jan. 15,'62.
Brinkerhof A. e. Aug. 6, 1862, kld. at Chicamauga Sept. 20, 1863.
Buser Ellis W. e. Aug. 6, 1862, m. o. June 10, 1865.
Black Jas. E. e. Aug. 6, 1862, m. o. June 10, 1865, wd.
Bowker Joseph S. e. Aug. 6, 1862, kld. at Chicamauga Sept. 20, 1863.
Buser Henry, e. Aug. 6, 1862, m. o. June 10, 1865.
Brown Thomas, e. Aug. 6, '62, disd. April 1, '63, disab.
Buser Samuel, e. Aug. 6, 1862, m. o June 10, 1865.
Benton A. E. e. Aug. 7, 1862, kld. at Dallas, Ga., May 30, 1864.
Burthwick S. S. e. Aug. 6, 1862, m. o. June 10, 1865.
Baird Geo. e. Aug. 22, 1862, disd. Jan. 20, 1863, disab.
Bates John, e. Aug. 22, 1862, m. o. June 10, 1865.
Blackman F. e. Sept. 4, 1862, kld. at Atlanta, Ga., Aug. 19, 1864.
Chaddock M. R. e. July 26, 1862, m. o. June 10, 1865.
Champlin J. F. e. Aug. 4, 1862, m. o. June 10, 1865.
Clendenning J. M. e. Aug. 5, 1862, disd. Dec. 8, 1862, for promotion as Chaplain.
Courter Chas. L. e. Aug. 6, 1862, kld. at Reseca, Ga., May 14, 1864.
Conlee Thos. A. e. Aug. 6, 1862, m.o. June 10,'65, wd.
Cowen O.W. e. Aug. 6, 1862, m.o. June 10,'65, as corpl.
Carlton C. W. e. Aug. 6,'62, trans. to V.R.C. May 1,'64.
Chambers Geo. e Aug. 6, 1862, m. o. June 10, 1865.
Crane H. D. e. Aug. 6, 1862, died at McMinnville Oct. 10, 1863, wd.
Dean H. S. e. Aug. 4, 1862, m. o. June 10, 1865.
Dunbar M. e. Aug. 6,'62, kld. Chicamauga Sept.20,'63.
Dalrymple Geo. e. Aug. 6,'62, disd. Dec. 16,'63, disab.
Eaton Parley, e. Aug. 5, 1862, m. o. June 10, 1865.
Edwards Wm. J. e. Aug. 9, 1862, m.o. June 10, 1865.
Fox M. e. Aug. 5, 1862, kld. Chicamauga Sept. 20, 1863.
Foss Phineas, e. Aug. 5, 1862, m. o. June 10, 1865.
Graves T. C. e. Aug. 6.'62, m.o. June 24,'65, was prisr.
Graham Edw. e. Aug. 6, 1862, m o. June 10, 1865, wd.
Godding H.W. e. Aug.5,'62, m. o. June 10,'65, 1st sergt.
Ghelston Jno. e. Aug. 5, 1862 disd. Jan. 2, 1863, disab.
Heydon W. P. e. Aug. 5, 1862, disd. Jan. 1, 1864, disab.
Hughes Wm. W. e. Aug. 6, 1862. m. o. June 10, 1865.
Hamilton H. H. e. Aug. 6,'62, m. o. June 10,'65, corpl.
Harriman H. J. e. Aug. 8, 1862, sergt., kld. at Dalton, Ga., Feb. 25, 1864.
Hover W. W. e. Aug. 6, '62, m o. June 10, '65, as corpl.
Hay John, Jr., e. Aug. 6, 1862, died at Chattanooga Aug. 4, 1864, wd.
Haggerty C. e. Aug. 6, 1862, m. o. June 10, 1865.
Hull N. B. e. Aug. 4, 1862, disd. April 15, 1863, disab.
Hicks James, e. Aug. 9, 1862, m. o. June 10, 1865.
Jenkins B. J. e. Aug. 6, 1862, m. o. June 10, 1865.
Jennings Chas. e. Aug. 6, 1862, died Aug. 20, 1863.
Kish Wm. e. Aug. 1, 1862, trans. to V.R.C. Jan. 15,'64.
Kennedy D. W. e. July 29, 1862, kld. at Chicamauga Sept. 20, 1863.
Lester J. D. e. Aug. 1, 1862, died Jan. 11, 1863.
Morgan Thos. e. Aug. 4, 1862, m. o. June 10, 1865.
Morse Geo. C. e. Sept. 2,'62, m. o. June 10,'65, as corpl.
Newton J. A. e. Aug. 6, 1862, disd. May 21,'63, disab.
Newton Butler, e. Aug. 5, 1862, died at Nashville, Tenn., Nov. 7, 1863.
Nadeg Jacob, e. Aug. 7, 1862, m. o. June 10, 1865.
Pritchard Wm. e. Aug. 6, 1862, disd. Sept. 4,'63, disab.
Porter Thomas, e. Aug. 5, 1862, corpl., died in Tenn., Oct. 12, 1863, wd.
Payne J. P. e. Aug. 5,'62, m. o. June 10, '65, furlough.
Pruner O. H. e. Aug. 5, 1862, trans. to Engineer Corps, July 18, 1864.
Pomeroy C. e. Aug. 4, 1862, disd. Jan. 16, 1864, wd.
Pollard R. e. Aug. 4,'62, died Danville, Ky., Dec. 19,'62.
Rose Tim. D. e. Aug. 5, 1862, prmtd. capt. Sept. 5, '62.
Rayne R.P. e. Aug.5,'62, kld. Kenesaw Mt., June 23, '64.
Richardson C. e. Aug.6,'62, m.o. June 10,'65, sergt., wd.
Sherk T. J. e. Aug. 6, 1862, m. o. June 10, 1865.
Schultz Henry, e. July 29, 1862, m. o. June 10, 1865.
Smith Jesse, e. Aug. 4, 1862, m. o. June 10, 1865.
Sommers Daniel, e. Aug. 4, 1862, m. o. June 10, 1865.
Shick P. e. Aug.5,'62, trans. Engineer Corps, July 29, '64.
Southerland B. e. Aug. 5, 1862, disd. Feb. 7, '63, disab.
Servis Beri, e. Aug. 5, 1862, disd. Oct. 26, 1864, wd.
Simmons John C. e. Aug. 6, 1862, m. o. June 10, 1865.

Smith Charles, e. Aug. 6, 1862, m. o. June 10, 1865.
Tucker J. e. Aug. 4, 1862, m.o. June 10, 1865, as corpl.
Torrey Geo. e. Aug. 6, 1862, disd. Dec. 29, 1862, disab.
Taylor J. L. e. Aug. 6, 1862, disd. July 30,'63, disab.
Vroman John J. e. Aug. 5, 1862, kld. at Reseca, Ga., May 14, 1864.
Vaughn James, e. Aug. 22, 1862, kld. at Rocky Face Ridge May 16, 1864.
Watson Franklin, e. July 26, 1864, m. o. June 10, 1865.
Woodworth B. B. e. Aug. 6, 1862, m. o. June 10, 1865.
Westfall J. M. e. Aug. 7, 1862, disd. Jan. 3, 1863, disab.
Williams P. e. Aug. 8, 1862, disd. Jan. 12, 1863, wd.
Weaver Samuel C. e. Aug. 9, 1862, m. o. June 10, 1865.
York Delos P. e. Aug. 6. 1862, m. o. June 10, 1865.
Bates Wm. N. e. Oct. 7, 1864, died at Huntsville, Ala., Feb. 16, 1865.
Kimble Wm. e. Oct. 1, 1864, died at Nashville, Tenn., Jan. 12, 1865.
Bahr John, e. Feb. 24, 1864, died at Camp Butler, Ill., March 20, 1864.
Gunn Samuel, e. Sept. 30, 1864, rejected by board.
King Christian.
Moore Josiah, e. Feb. 24, 1865.
Reynick Alexander M. e. March 13, 1865.
Selby Henry, e. Sept. 17, 1864.

140th Infantry (100 days.)

Adjutant General's report gives no history.

Major. Wm. O. Evans, com. June 18, 1864. Mustered out Oct. 29, 1864.

Company C.

Capt. Jos. A. Bockiens, com. June 18, 1864, m. o. Oct. 29, 1864.
First Lieut. Ed. A. Tomlin, com. June 18, 1864, m. o. Oct 29, 1864.
Second Lieut. David McGrath, com. June 18, 1864, m. o. Oct. 29, 1864.
First Sergt. Wm. H. Metcalf, e. May 9. 1864, m.o. Oct. 29, 1864.
Sergt. Arthur V. Rankin, e. May 12,'64, m.o. Oct.29,'64.
Sergt. Thos. J. Root, e. May 9, '64, m. o. Oct. 29, '64.
Sergt. Thos. H. Lawrence, e. May 16,'64, m.o. Oct.29,'64.
Sergt. Lemuel F. Eib, e. May 10, '64, m.o. Oct. 29, '64.
Musn. Geo. Reynolds, e. May 9, '64, m. o. Oct. 29,'64.
Musn. John Adams, e. May 17, '64, m. o. Oct. 29, '64.
Wagoner Jonathan Landon, e. May 14, 1864, m.o. Oct. 29, 1864.
Allenstein Christoph, e. May 30,'64, m. o. Oct. 29, '64.
Bockiens F. B. E. e. May 23, 1864, m. o. Oct. 29,1864.
Bergman Chas. W. e. May 7, 1864, m. o. Oct. 29, 1864.
Brown Robt. e. May 13, 1864, m. o. Oct. 29, 1864.
Brady Chas. H. e. May 9, 1864, m. o. Oct. 29, 1864.
Burns Hugh, e. May 26, 1864, m. o. Oct. 29, 1864.
Beck Wm. P. e. May 10, 1864, m. o. Oct. 29, 1864.
Brown Chas. e. May 9, 1864, m. o. Oct. 29, 1864.
Collings Wm. H. e. May 9, 1864, m. o. Oct. 29, 1864.
Childers John F. e. May. 13, 1864, m. o. Oct. 29, 1864.
Childers David J. e. May 13, 1864, m. o. Oct. 29, 1864.
Dean Jas. e. May 11, 1864, m o. Oct. 29, 1864.
Drum Thad. G. e. May 10, 1864, prmtd. sergt. maj.
Delannay M. G. e. May 12, 1864, m. o. May 29, 1864.
Davis Henry A. e. May 9, 1864, m. o. Oct. 29, 1864.
Farrell Jas. e. May 11, 1864, m. o. Oct. 29, 1864.
Froggatt Thos. e. May 12, 1864, m. o. Oct. 29, 1864.
Fablinger Louis, e. May 4, 1864. m. o. Oct. 29, 1864.
Farrell Thos. e. May 16, 1864, m. o. Oct. 29, 1864.
Farrell Wm. e. May 13, 1864, m. o. Oct. 29, 1864.
Fablinger Nicholas, e. May 7, '64, m. o. Oct. 29, 1864.
Holland Bernard, e. May 14, 1864, m. o. Oct. 29, 1864.
Henry Jas. J. e. May 11, 1864, m. o. Oct. 29, 1864.
Haynes Martin, e. May 11, 1864, m. o. Oct. 29, 1864.
Hawthorn H. H. e. May 12, 1864, m. o. Oct. 29, 1864.
Isenhour Wm. e. May 10, 1864, m. o. Oct. 29, 1864.
Kearns John, e. May 10, 1864, m.o. Oct. 29, 1864.
Keithly John, e. May 11, 1864, m. o. Oct. 29, 1864.
Kuentzel Leonard, e. May 5, '64, m. o. Oct. 29, 1864.
Lange Chas. e. May 12, 1864, m. o. Oct. 29, 1864.
Layhan Timothy, e. May 23, 1864, m. o. Oct. 29, 1864.
Lynch Francis M. e. May 11, 1864, m. o. Oct. 29,1864.
Manly Pat'k, e. May 31, 1864, m. o. Oct. 29, 1864.
McCarty John E. e. May 2, 1864, m. o. Oct. 29, 1864.
Martell Jos. e. May. 14, 1864, m. o. Oct. 29, 1864.
Mencimer Christ. e. May 13, 1864, m. o. Oct. 29, 1864.
Martineau A. e. May 10, 1864, m. o. Oct. 29, 1864.
Newton Allen, e. May 10, 1864, m. o. Oct. 29, 1864.
Noble John, e. May 12, 1864, m. o. Oct. 29, 1864.
Pitcher Robt. e. May 25, 1864, m. o. Oct. 29, 1864.
Pugh Wm. H. e. May 9, 1864, m. o. Oct. 29, 1864.
Rogers Thos. e. May 11, 1864, m. o. Oct. 29, 1864.
Rogers Wm. e. May 11, 1864, died at Memphis, Aug. 9, 1864.
Rouse Jacob, e. May 9. 1864, m. o. Oct. 29, 1864.
Simpson Wm. H. e. May 11, 1864, m. o. Oct. 29, 1864.
Smith John F. e. May 13, 1864, m. o. Oct. 29, 1864.
Senter Jas. e. May 10, 1864, m. o. Oct. 29, 1864.
Steinmetz Peter, e. May 12, 1864, m. o. Oct. 29, 1864.
Smith Gabriel, e. May 7, 1864, m. o. Oct. 29, 1864.
Simmons Hiram, e. May 12, 1864, m. o. Oct. 29, 1864.
Smelser Obed, e. May 13, 1864, m. o. Oct. 29, 1864.
Sidner H. M. e. May 12, 1864, m. o. Oct. 29, 1864.
Sauers Augustus, e. May 13, 1864, m. o. Oct. 29, 1864.
Schmidt Chas. H. e. May 16, 1864, m. o. Oct. 29, 1864.
Schrader Henry, e. May 12, 1864, m. o. Oct. 29, 1864.
Thomas Richard G. e. May 15, 1864, m. o. Oct. 20,'64.
Tuttle Geo. G. e. May 9, 1864, m. o. Oct. 20, 1864.
Vincent Chas. e. May 10, 1864, m. o Oct. 29, 1864.
William John, e. May 13, 1864, m. o. Oct. 29, 1864.
Wilcox Isaac, e. May 11, 1864, m. o. Oct. 29, 1864.
Wannamaugher Jas. E. e. May 12,'64, m.o. Oct.29,'64.
Weinsheimer H. e. May 31, 1864, died at Memphis Sept. 9, 1864.
Young Wm. B. e. May 30, 1864, m.o. Oct. 29, 1864.
Zimmer Nathan, e. May 13, 1864, m. o. Oct. 29, 1864.

Company D.

First. Sergt. Benj. H. Campbell, e. May 5, 1864, m. o. Oct. 29, 1864.
Sergt. J. Eugene Smith, e. May 11,'64, m.o.Oct.29,'64.
Corpl. Geo. G. Greene, e. May 5,'64, m.o. Oct. 29,'64.

142d Infantry (100 days.)

The One Hundred and Forty-second Infantry Illinois Volunteers was organized at Freeport, Illinois, by Col. Rollin V. Ankey, as a battalion of eight companies, and ordered to Camp Butler, Ill., where two companies were added and the regiment mustered June 18, 1864, for 100 days. On 21st of June the regiment moved for Memphis *via* Cairo and Mississippi River, and arrived on the 24th. On 26th moved to White's Station. 11 miles from Memphis, on the Memphis & Charleston Railroad, where it was assigned to guarding railroad. Mustered out of United States service Oct. 27, 1864, at Chicago, Ill.

Chaplain Ruel Cooley, com. June 18, 1864. M. o. Oct. 27, 1864.

Company B.

First Lieut. Abel F. Boileau, com. June 18, 1864. M. o. Oct. 27, 1864.
First Sergt. Wm. E. Judson, e. May 10, 1864, m. o. Oct. 26, 1864.
Sergt. Wm. Tinkler, e. May 10, 1864, m.o. Oct. 26, 1864.
Corpl. Manlove Way, e. May 10, 1864, m.o. Oct. 26, '64.
Corpl. David Mackey, e. May 10, '64, m.o. Oct. 26, '64.
Corpl. David S. Farley, e. May 10, '64, m.o. Oct.26,'64.
Corpl. H. H. Lawrence, e. May 10, '64, m.o. Oct.26,'64.
Corpl. Lester C. Turner, e. May 10, 1864, m. o. Oct. 26, 1864.
Musician Frank H. Warner, e. May 10, 1864, m. o. Oct. 26, 1864.
Andrews Ralzy S. e. May 10, 1864, m. o. Oct. 26, 1864.
Backers Reuben, e. May 10, 1864, m. o. Oct. 26, 1864.
Blackman Nathan G. e. May 10, '64, m. o. Oct. 26, '64.
Bell John, e. May 10, 1864, m. o. Oct. 26, 1864.
Bennett Albert, e. May 10, 1864, m. o. Oct. 26, 1864.
Crowell Marvin, e. May 10, 1864, m. o. Oct. 26, 1864.
Crowell Hiram, e. May 10, 1864, m. o. Oct. 26, 1864.
Dickson Jos. F. e. May 10, 1864, m. o. Oct. 26, 1864.
Davey Thos. e. May 10, 1864, m. o. Oct. 20, '64, to re-e.
French D. e. May 10, 1864, m. o. Oct. 26, 1864.
Foss John, e. May 10, 1864, m. o. Oct. 26, 1864.
Farley Wallace, e. May 10, 1864, m. o. Oct. 26, 1864.
Harrington C. e. May 10, 1864, m. o. Oct. 26, 1864.
House John, e. May 10, 1864, m. o. Oct. 26, 1864.
Hagarty Daniel, e. May 10, 1864, m. o. Oct. 26, 1864.
Kelly John, e. May 10, 1864, m. o. Oct. 26, 1864.
Lichtenberger E. L. e. May 10, 1864, m.o. Oct. 26, '64.
Lichtenberger A. e. May 10, 1864, m. o. Oct. 26, 1864.
Lovin Henry R. e. May 10, 1864, m. o. Oct. 26, 1864.
Morris John E. e. May 10, 1864, m. o. Oct. 26. 1864.
Mayheu Duane, e. May 10, 1864, m. o. Oct. 26, 1864.
Marshall Chas. A. e. May 10, 1864, m. o. Oct. 26, 1864.

Norton Frank, e. May 10, 1864, m. o. Oct. 26, 1864.
O'Leary John, e. May 10, 1864, m. o. Oct. 26, 1864.
Rogers John, e. May 10, 1864, m. o Oct. 26, 1864.
Smith Levi, e. May 10, 1864, m. o. Oct. 26, 1864.
Snyder W. H. H. e. May 10, 1864, m. o. Oct. 26, 1864.
Stanchfield S. e. May 10, 1864, died at Memphis, Aug. 21, 1864.
Stebbins John D. e. May 10, 1864, m. o. Oct. 26, 1864.
Thompson Riley, e. May 10, 1864, m. o. Oct. 26, 1864.
Van Blaricome S. e. May 10, 1864, m. o. Oct. 26, 1864.
Williams John, e. May 10, 1864, m. o. Oct. 26, 1864.

153d Infantry (one year.)

The One Hundred and Fifty-third Infantry Illinois Volunteers was organized at Camp Fry, Ill., by Col. Stephen Bronson, and was mustered in Feb. 27, 1865, for one year. On March — moved by rail *via* Louisville and Nashville to Tullahoma, reporting to Major General Millroy. The regiment was assigned to the Second Brigade, Defenses of Nashville and Chattanooga Railroad, Brigadier General Dudley commanding brigade. In the latter part of March, Maj. Wilson, with three companies, went on a campaign into Alabama and returned. On July 1 moved *via* Nashville and Louisville to Memphis, Tenn., and was assigned to the command of Brevet Major General A. L. Chetlain. Was mustered out Sept. 15, 1865, and moved to Springfield, Ill., and Sept. 24 received final pay and discharge. Col. Bronson received appointment as brevet brigadier general.

Company D.

Second Lieut. Thos. F. Whitmore, com. June 12, 1865. M. o. Sept. 21, 1865.
Sergt. Geo. W. Houseman, e. Feb. 10, 1865, m. o. Sept. 21, 1865.
Corpl. Jefferson Blackmore, e. Feb. 10, 1865, m.o. Sept. 21, 1865.
Corpl. John Davis, e. Feb. 14, 1865, m. o. Sept. 21, '65.
Musician James Hall, e. Feb. 14,'65, m. o. Sept. 21, '65.
Arnold Jos. C. e. Feb. 10, 1864, m. o. Sept. 21, 1865.
Clay Jeremiah, e. Feb. 14, 1864, m. o. Sept. 21, 1865.
Dittmar John, e. Feb. 14, 1864, m. o. Sept. 21, 1865.
Dittmar Kasper, e. Feb. 14, 1864, m. o. Sept. 21, 1865.
Donahue Daniel, e. Feb. 14, 1864, m. o. Sept. 21, 1865.
Donovan Michael, e. Feb. 14, 1864, m. o. Sept. 21, 1865.
Eacker John, e. Feb. 15, 1864, m. o. Sept. 21, 1865.
Holland Herman, e. Feb. 13, 1864, died at Indianapolis, Ind., July 7, 1865.
Jordan W. V. e. Feb. 17, 1864, m. o. June 13, 1865.
Kent John A. e. Feb. 13, 1864, m. o. Sept. 21, 1865.
Leibard Andrew, e. Feb. 14, 1864, m. o. Sept. 21, 1865.
Mullen Geo. W. e. Feb. 14, 1864, m. o. Sept. 21, 1865.
Pingle Chas. e, Feb. 17, 1864, m. o. July 18, 1865.
Pulfrey Chas. e. Feb. 13, 1864, m. o. Sept. 21, 1865.
Patterson Geo. e. Feb. 13, 1864, m. o. Sept. 21, 1865.
Patterson J. F. e. Feb. 13. 1864. m. o. Sept. 21, 1865.
Sass Johann, e. Feb. 14, 1864, m. o. Sept. 21, 1865.
Stick Mathias, Feb. 17, 1864, m. o. Sept. 21, 1865.
Shipman W. H. e. Feb. 13, 1864, disd. Aug. 20,'65, disab.
Shumny A. F. e. Feb. 14, 1864, disd. June 18, '65, disab.
Staley Wm. e. Feb. 13, 1864, m. o. Sept. 21, 1865.
Staley Henry, e. Feb. 13, 1864, m. o. Sept. 21, 1865.
Winter A. e. Feb. 14, 1864, died at Memphis July 20,'65.
Winter Michael, e. Feb. 17, 1864, m. o. Sept. 21, 1865.

Company I.

Sergt. Edwin Thomas, e. Feb. 20,'65, m. o. Sept. 21,'65.
Corpl. Wm. Thompson, e. Feb. 20,'65, m.o. Sept. 21, '65.
Creighton John, e. Feb. 20, 1865, m. o. Sept. 21, 1865.
Dunnegan M. e. Feb. 20, 1865, m. o. Sept. 21, 1865.
Gardner F. M. e. Feb. 19, 1865, m. o. June 5, 1865.
Morrison Alex. e. Feb. 20, 1865, m. o. Sept. 21, 1865.
Schoman Mathias, Feb. 20, 1865, m. o. Sept. 21, 1865.
Walkinshaw H. e. Feb. 20, 1865, m. o. Sept. 21, 1865.

Miscellaneous Infantry.

9th Consolidated Infantry.

Cassaday Peter, e. Jan. 1, 1864, m. o. July 13, 1865.
Long Owen, e. Jan. 1, 1864, m. o. July 9, 1865.
Parkhurst J. C. e. Jan. 1, 1864, m. o. July 9, 1865.

11th Infantry.

Shaw W. C. e. Sept. 1, 1861, died. Sept. 4, 1864.
Walker Joseph, e. July 3, 1861, kld. at Ft. Donelson, Feb. 15, 1862.

27th Infantry.

Beam Wm. C. e. Aug. 20, 1861, m. o. Sept. 20, 1864.
Bostwick R. S. e. Aug. 20, 1861, trans. to 4th. U. S. Cav. Nov. 26, 1862.
Entwhistle T. e. Aug. 20, 1861, m. o. Sept. 20, 1864.
Entwhistle Jno. e. Aug. 20, 1861, trans. to 4th U.S. Cav. Nov. 27, 62.
McDonald R. e. Aug. 20,'61, m.o. Sept. 20, '64, as sergt.
Paul Willis, e. Aug. 20, 1861, disd. Feb. 28, 1862, disab.
Riley Pat. e. Aug. 20, 1861, disd. July 18, 1862, disab.
Vanvaltingberg Louis, e. Aug. 20, 1861, disd. July 17, 1862, disab.
Vanaltingberg Daniel, e. Aug. 20, '61, died Dec. 5,'61.
White Robt. e. Aug. 20, 1861, captd., failed to report after exchange.

1st Artillery.

Battery F.

Brink Walton C. e. Sept. 19, 1864, died at Nashville, Tenn.
Fink Jos. e. Oct. 13, 1864, m. o. July 26, 1865.
Groff Lewis, e. Oct. 13, 1864, m. o. July 26, 1865.
Gordon Jos. e. Oct. 10, 1864, died at Nashville, Tenn.
Levitt Jeremiah, e. Oct. 10, 1864, m. o. June 5, 1865.
Morgan Edw. e. Oct. 13, 1864, m. o. July 26, 1865.
Sauce Nicholas, e. Oct. 13, 1864, m. o. July 21, 1865.
Thomas Wm. J. e. Oct. 10, 1864, m. o. July 26, 1865.
Williams Rich. e. Oct. 10, 1864, m. o. July 26, 1865.

Battery H.

Boynton Albert, e. Sept. 19, '64, desrtd. March 15, '62,
Gruener Chas. e. Jan. 28, 1862, died at Memphis Aug. 14, 1862.
Godie Seth, e. March 2, '62, disd. Oct. 20, 1862, disab.
Ruf Fabian, e. Feb. 27, 1364, absent, wd. at m. o. regt.

Battery I.

McCarty Jonas, e Feb. 9,'62, vet., m. o. July 26, 1865.
Smith Simeon, e. Feb. 8, 1862, disd. Nov. 13, 1862.
Williams Geo. or J. W. e. Feb. 9, 1862, m. o. July 26, 1865, as 1st sergt.

2d Artillery.

Battery A.

Addleman Andrew, e. Oct. 13, 1864, m. o. July 27, '65.
Apfeld Edw. e. Oct. 13. 1864, m. o. July 27, 1865.
Conrad Chas. e. Oct. 13, 1864, m. o. July 27, 1865.
Dish Xavier, e. Oct. 13, 1864, m. o. July 27, 1865.
Gubser Mechoir, e. Oct. 13, 1864, m. o. July 27, 1865.
Kuch Jacob, e. Oct. 13, 1864, m. o. July 27. 1865.
Letch Peter, e. Oct. 13, 1864, m. o. July 27, 1865.
Reeber Fred'k, e. Oct. 13. 1864, m. o. July 27, 1865.
Staudenmeyer J. e. Oct. 13, 1864, m. o. July 27, 1865.
Schrempf Lewis, e. Oct. 13, 1864, m. o. July 27, 1865.

Battery C.

Beverly Dwight C. e. Oct. 3, 1864, m. o. Aug. 3, 1865.
Bute Lewis H. e. Oct. 3, 1864, m. o. Aug. 3, 1865.
Hollister Frank, e. Oct. 3, 1864, m. o. Aug. 3, 1865.
Moulton Philander, e. Oct. 3, 1864, m. o. Ang. 3, 1865.

Battery G.

Nail John A. e. Sept. 27, '61, disd. April 17, '62, disab.

Battery H.

Archer Thos. e. Oct. 4, 1864, m. o. July 29, 1865.
Arnot Daniel, e. Oct. 4, 1864, died at Nashville, Tenn., Feb. 9, 1865.
Bowden John E. e. Oct. 4, 1864, m. o. July 29, 1865.
Eva Henry, e. Oct. 4, 1864, m. o. July 29, 1865.
Handley John, e. Oct. 4, 1864, m. o. July 29, 1865.
Laird Wm. e. Oct. 4, 1864, m. o. July 29, 1865.

Philip A. Hoyne

CHICAGO

FORMERLY OF GALENA

Luckley Thos. C. e. Oct. 4, 1864, m. o. July 29, 1865.
Pearce Wm. e. Oct. 4, 1864, m. o. July 29, 1865.
Temperley Vickers, e. Oct. 4, 1864, m. o. July 29, 1865.
Thompson Jos. e. Oct. 4, 1864, m. o. July 29, 1865.
Yellard Albert, e. Oct. 4, 1864, m. o. July 29, 1865.
Madison John, e. Oct. 4, 1864.

Chicago Board of Trade Battery.

Smith Alex. e. Dec. 29, 1864, m. o. June 30, 1865.

42d Infantry.

Druthick Otis, e. Aug. 1, '61, disd. Feb. 2, '62, disab.
Eberle Wm. e. March 28, 1865, m. o. Sept. 25, 1865.
Hess Casper, e. March 28, 1865, m.o. Dec. 16, 1865.
Hoffman Henry, e. March 28, 1865, m.o. Dec. 16, 1865.
Hoffman John, e. April 12, 1865, m. o. Dec. 16, 1865.
Hemberger Jacob, e. April 12, 1865, died Nov. 4, 1865.
Wurster Andrews e. March 28, '65, desrtd. June 18, '65.
Clark Benj. R. e. Oct. 17, 1864, m. o. Oct. 16, 1865.
Parks Sam'l, e. Oct. 5, 1864, disd. May 3, 1865.
Polker Lewis, e. Oct. 5, 1864, died July 28, 1865.
Spaulding Lyman, e. Oct. 5, 1864, kld. Franklin, Tenn., Nov. 30, 1864.
Schubert F. e. Oct. 5, 1864, m. o. Oct. 4, 1865.
Wurster Albert, e. Oct. 18, '64, sub., m.o. Oct. 16, '65.

58th Infantry (consolidated.)

Quartermaster Francis Widmer, com. 1st lieut. Co. F Sept. 8, 1862. Prmtd. capt. Feb. 1, 1864. Prmtd. capt. Co. C (consld) Sept. 8, 1862. Prmtd. Q. M. May 19, 1865. M. o. Apr. 1, 1866.

92d Infantry.

Flack Wm. M. e. Aug. 11, 1862, died at Lexington, Ky., Nov. 22, 1862.
Furgason D. H. e. Aug. 11, '62, disd. July 9, '63, disab.
Giddings H. M. e. Aug. 14, '62, m.o. June 21, '65, corpl.
Johnson M. C. e. Aug. 11, 1862, m. o. June 21, 1865.
Oberheim D. L. e. Aug. 14, 1862, m. o. June 21, 1865.
Plummer P. D. e. Aug. 15, 1862, died at Danville, Ky., —— 5, 1863.
Plummer R. F. e. Aug. 13, 1862, died at Danville, Ky., —— 5, 1863.
Robinson Clark, e. Aug. 11, 1862, m. o. June 21, 1865.
Whitson Chas. W. e. Aug. 12, 1862, m. o. June 21, '65.
Corpl. Hosea Dale, e. Aug. 11, '62, m. o. June 21, '65.
Bishop Wm. e. Aug. 11, '62, m.o. July 3, '65, prisr. war.
Edgerton Chas. e. Aug. 11, 1862, m. o. June 21, 1865.
Fox Wm. e. Aug. 9, 1862, m. o. June 21, 1865.
Harpster Henry H. e. Aug. 9, 1862, m. o. June 24, 1865, prisr. war.
Mader Jno. e. Aug. 11, '62, m.o. June 24, '65, prisr. war.
Plotner John F. e. Aug. 9, 1862, m. o. June 2, 1865.
Plotner Wm. McHenry, e. Aug. 9, 1862, m. o. June 2, 1865.
Peterson Thos. B. e. Aug. 9, 1862, disd. Feb. 3, 1865.
Rice Jas. H. e. Aug. 9, 1862, m. o. June 21, 1865.
Spence John, e. Aug. 9, 1862, m. o. Feb. 3, 1866, as sergt., prisr. war.
Wade John A. e. Aug. 6, '62, absent, sick at m. o. regt.
Allison Jas. e. April 6, '65, trans. to Co. G, 65th I.V.I.
Cullens Wm. H. e. Dec. 1, 1863, trans. to Co. G, 65th I. V. I.
Bartlett Thos. H. m. o. June 21, 1865.
Hayward Robert, disd. Feb. 23, 1863, disab.
O'Brine John, e. April 6, 1865.

17th Cavalry.

The Seventeenth Cavalry Regiment Illinois Volunteers was organized under special authority from the War Department, issued Aug. 12, 1863, to Hon. John F. Farnsworth. The rendezvous was established at St. Charles, Kane County, Illinois. By the approval of the governor of the state, the coloneley of the regiment was offered John L. Beveridge, then major in the Eighth Illinois Cavalry, who assumed the work of recruitment and organization, and opened the rendezvous Nov. 15, 1863. Eight companies were mustered in Jan. 22, 1864. Four other companies were mustered in, and the organization of the Regt. completed Feb. 12, 1864. The regiment was sent to Jefferson Barracks, Mo., where 1,100 sets of horse equipments were received. From there it moved to Alton, Ill., and relieved the Thirteenth Illinois Cavalry in guarding the Military Prison at that place.

Early in June following, the First Battalion was ordered to St. Louis, and the Second Battalion followed immediately. Both being fully mounted, were ordered at once to North Missouri District. The First Battalion, Lieutenant Colonel Dennis J. Hynes commanding, proceeded to St. Joseph, Mo., where the commanding officer reported in person to General Fisk, commanding District of North Missouri. The Second Battalion, Major Lucius C. Matlack commanding, was assigned by General C. B. Fisk to the post of Glasgow, Mo. From this period, for four months, the three battalions were separate and remote from each other, and so extended were their movements, that it is impossible to follow them in this brief sketch. They seem to have been all over Missouri after Price's and Jeff. Thompson's Guerilla Bands, following them into Kansas and Arkansas, doing most efficient service.

Company F.

Capt. Reuben Baker, com. Jan. 8, 1864. On detached service at m. o. of regt.
First Lieut. Wm. W. Black, com. Jan. 8, 1864. M. o. Dec. 18, 1865.
Second Lieut. E. M. Backus, com. Jan. 8, 1864. Res. Feb. 12, 1865.
Second Lieut. Joel G. Ball, e. as private Dec. 25, 1863. Prmtd. 1st sergt., then 2d lieut., March 13, 1865. M. o. Dec. 18, 1865.
First Sergt. Clinton A. Bamber, e. Nov. 25, 1863, m. o. Dec. 18, 1865, as Co. comsy. sergt.
Q. M. Sergt. Wm. H. Stock, e. Nov. 25, 1863, m. o. Dec. 18, 1865, as sergt.
Comsy. Sergt. Philo J. Cowen, e. Dec. 1, 1863, m. o. Dec. 18, 1865, as sergt.
Sergt. Ambrose A. Snyder, e. Dec. 1, 1863, m. o. Dec. 18, 1865, as private.
Sergt. Edwin A. Carpenter, e. Dec. 1, 1863, m. o. Dec. 18, 1865, as private.
Sergt. Byron Crissey, e. Dec. 1, 1863, m. o. Dec. 18, 1865, as 1st sergt.
Sergt. Allen Cornelius, e. Nov. 25, 1863, m. o. Dec. 18, 1865, as private.
Corpl. Jos. W. Townsend, e. Dec. 10, 1863, m. o. Oct. 3, 1865, as private.
Corpl. Samuel Mawney, e. Dec. 1, 1863, private, deserted Sept. 24, 1865.
Corpl. Jas. M. Westfall, e. Dec. 10, 1863, m. o. Dec. 18, 1865, as private.
Corpl. Geo. P. Foster, e. Dec. 1, 1863, disd. Nov. 13, 1865, as private.
Corpl. Jabes H. Vroom, e. Dec. 25, 1863, m. o. Dec. 18, 1865, as sergt.
Corpl. Reuben Holcomb, e. Dec. 1, 1863, m. o. Dec. 18, 1865, as private.
Gorpl. Benj Bennett, e. Dec. 1, 1863, m. o. Dec. 18, 1865, as sergt.
Corpl. Robert B. Renwick, e. Dec. 1, 1863, m. o. Dec. 18, 1865, as Co. Q. M. sergt.
Farrier John F. Strong, e. Dec. 1, 1863, m. o. Dec. 18, 1865, as private.
Farrier Stanton C. Way, e. Dec. 1, 1863, m. o. Dec. 18, 1865, as corpl.
Bugler Frank Dove, e. Dec. 1, 1863, desrtd. Sept. 26, '65.
Bugler Jas. J. Tarplay, e. Dec. 1, 1863, m.o. Dec. 18, '65.
Sadler Jno. W. Williams, e. Nov. 25, 1863, m. o. Dec. 18, 1865, as bugler.
Wagoner Griffin D. Way, e. Dec. 1, 1863, m. o. Dec. 18, 1865, as private.
Arnold Adam, e. Dec. 22, 1863, m. o. Dec. 18, 1865.
Barton Eli A. e. Dec. 1, 1863, m. o. Dec. 18, 1865.
Bateman Sam'l, e. Dec. 10, 1863, m. o. Dec. 18, 1865.
Benton Wm. W. e. Dec. 25, 1863, m. o. Dec. 18, 1865.
Bowden John, e. Jan. 4, '64, desrtd. Sept. 26, 1865.
Clark C. e. Dec. 25, 1864, m. o. Dec. 18, 1865.
Dewell W. e. Dec. 1, 1864, m. o. Dec. 18, 1865, corpl.
Deeds Geo. W. e. De. 10, 1864, m. o. Dec. 18, 1865.
Eby Joel R. e. Dec. 1, 1864, m. o. Dec. 18, 1865.
Eastwood Wm. H. e. Dec. 1, 1864, m. o. Dec. 18, 1865.
Felt Francis M. e. Dec. 1, 1863, m. o. Dec. 18, 1865.
Gott Richard M. e. Dec. 10, 1863, m. o. Dec. 18, 1865.
Gochez F. M. e. Dec. 1, 1863, m. o. Dec. 18, 1865.
Holcomb Wm. H. e. Dec. 1, 1863, m. o. Dec. 18, 1865.
Howell John H. e. Dec. 1, 1863, m. o. Dec. 18, 1865.
Hicks John G. e. Dec. 1, 1863, m. o. Dec. 18, 1865.
Herrington Jas. B. e. Dec. 10, 1863, m. o. Dec. 18, '65.
Herrington John T. e. Dec. 10, '63, m. o. Dec. 18, 1865.
Jordon Daniel, e. Dec. 1, 1863, m. o. Dec. 18, 1865.

Judd Jas. M. e. Dec. 1, 1863, m. o. Dec. 18, 1865.
Jagger Geo. e. Dec. 25, 1863, m. o. May 17, 1865.
Judd Ashley H. e. Jan. 13,'64, m.o. Dec. 18,'65, corpl.
Kneebone Henry, e. Jan. 11, 1864, m. o. Dec. 18, 1865.
Lawhorn R. J. e. Dec. 1, '63, m. o. Dec. 18, '65, sergt.
Middaugh Wm. e. Jan. 4, 1864, m. o. Dec. 18, 1865.
Noble Peter, e. Dec. 10, 1863, m. o. Dec. 18, 1865.
Phelps Oscar W. e. Dec. 15, 1863, disd. March 20, '64.
Pomeroy H. C. e. Dec. 10, 1863, m. o. Dec. 18, 1865.
Petty Ira E. e. Dec. 1, 1863, died at Rush, Ill., May 24, 1864.
Stambrough Sam'l, e. Dec. 31,1863, m. o. Dec. 18,1865.
Smith J. R. e. Dec. 29, 1863, m. o. Nov. 13, 1865.
Starner Elias W. e. Dec. 1,'63, sick at m.o. regt., abs't.
Teal Eugene B. e. Dec. 15. 1863, m. o. Dec. 18, 1865.
Tenyck Hamilton, e. Jan. 4, 1864, desrtd. Sept. 27, '65.
Wright Geo. W. e. Dec. 10, 1863, drowned at Glasgow, Mo., July 31, 1864.
Wilder Newton, e. Dec. 1, 1863, m. o. Dec. 18, 1865.
Wilson John S. e. Dec. 25, '63, m.o. Dec. 18,'65, corpl.
Brock Geo. e. Sept. 24, 1864, disd., term expired.
Backus Robt. O. e. Oct. 7, 1865, m. o. Oct. 25, 1865.
Coon Wm. A. e. Feb. 24, 1864, m.o. Dec. 18,'65, as corpl.
Isbell Hope H. e. Sept. 24, 1864, m. o. May 15, 1865.
McAllister Jason S. e. Oct. 13, 1864, m. o. Aug. 8, 1865.
Myers Nathan, e. Oct. 21, 1864, m. o. Oct. 25, 1865.
Morris Nathan, e. Oct. 21, 1864, m. o. Oct. 25, 1865.
Rannels John F. e. Oct. 6, 1864, m. o. Oct. 25, 1865.
Stanton H. B. e. Oct. 3, 1864, m. o. Oct. 25, 1865.

Miscellaneous Cavalry.

7th Cavalry.

Sergt. Charles E. Welty, e. Sept. 5, 1861, m. o. Oct. 15, 1864, as private.
Hogan Richard, e. March 27, 1865, m. o. Nov. 4, 1865.
Hill Peter F. e. Feb. 10, 1864, m. o. Nov. 4, 1865.

8th Cavalry.

Edwards Thos. e. Oct. 10, 1864, m. o. July 17, 1865.
Kofmehe Jos. e. Oct. 13, 1864, m. o. June 22, 1865.
Kuntz Chas. e. Oct. 12, 1864, m. o. July 17, 1865.
Still Rollin, e. Oct. 10, 1864, m. o. July 17, 1865.
Theurer Henry, e. Oct. 10, 1864, m. o. July 17, 1865.
Young Peter, e. Oct. 11, 1864, m. o. July 17, 1865.

13th Cavalry Consolidated.

Bacon Wm. F. e. Jan. 3, 1864, prmtd. sergt. maj.

14th Cavalry.

Welch Benj. F. e. March 30, 1864, missing in action since Aug. 3, 1864.

The war ended and peace restored, the Union preserved in its integrity, the sons of Jo Daviess who had volunteered their lives in defense of their government, who were spared to see the army of the Union victorious, returned to their homes to receive grand ovations and tributes of honor from friends and neighbors who had eagerly and jealously followed them wherever the fortunes of war called. Exchanging their soldiers' uniforms for citizens' dress, most of them fell back to their old avocations—on the farm on the mines, at the forge, the bench, in the shop, and at whatever else their hands found to do. Some of them were called to higher honors, and their names have become as familiar to the people and governments of the Old World as their noble deeds in the hour of their country's peril are dear to the hearts of the people whom they so faithfully served. Brave men are honorable always, and no class of citizens are entitled to greater respect than the volunteer soldiery of Jo Daviess County, not alone because they were soldiers, but because in their associations with their fellow-men their walk is upright, and their honesty and character without reproach.

> Their country first, their glory and their pride;
> Land of their hopes—land where their fathers died;
> When in the right, they'll keep their honor bright;
> When in the wrong, they'll die to set it right.

The deeds of daring and glorious achievements of the army of the Union during the Great War of the Rebellion will always be dearly cherished by patriotic hearts. But there were scenes and incidents, and accidents, the memory of which will shade with sadness the bright reflections engendered by the contemplation of a heroism, devotion and sacrifice, the like of which the world never knew before. To die on the field of battle, in face of an enemy's guns, is a crowning earthly glory. To die or be maimed for life by accident or *treachery*, when one is seeking to serve his country, is pitiable and lamentable. That there were such instances of commiseration, the pages of history amply verify. The memory of at least one of these deplorable occurrences is familiar to the present people of Jo Daviess County, but fifty years hence, in the "sweet by-and-by," when the fathers and mothers of to-day will have been gathered in an eternal home, they will be remembered by their posterity more as matters of tradition than absolute, written history. And it is only an act of justice—a tribute of respect to the memory of the killed and the sufferings of the maimed, that a record should be made in these pages of a treacherous accident that deprived the country of the services of a number of as brave men as any that ever faced an enemy. We refer to an accident that occurred at Beaver Creek bridge, on the Ohio & Mississippi Railroad, one hundred and forty miles west of Cincinnati, on the night of September 17, 1861, by which Captain B. B. Howard, of Galena, and a number of his company were hurried into eternity. September 18, 1861, the telegraph wires bore to all parts of the patriotic North the following sad announcement:

"CINCINNATI, September 18, 1861.—Last night, at half-past eight o'clock, a train on the Ohio & Mississippi Railroad, containing a portion of Col. Turchin's 19th Illinois Regiment, while passing over a bridge near Huron, Indiana, 140 miles west of Cincinnati, fell through, killing and wounding over one hundred soldiers.

"Intelligence of the disaster reached here last night, when a special train was dispatched to their assistance.

"Circumstances indicate that the bridge had been weakened by malicious or *traitorous* persons.

The bridge where this accident occurred is known as bridge No. 48, is of sixty feet span, 10 feet high, over a depth of three feet of water.

Captain Howard's Galena Company, known here as the "Anti-Beaure-Guards," formed a part of the 19th, and the intelligence of the catastrophe fell like a death pall upon the community from which the company had mostly been made up. Captain Howard and seventeen of his men—Corporals Samuel Clark, Jerry Ingraham, and A. Painter, William Frost, L. Carroll, Isaac Coleman, Henry Conners, John Brown, Joseph Smith, —— McConnolly, Robert Bruce, H. C. Burroughs, William Hardwick, Antoine Raffner, Peter Fowler, William Ringer, John Douglas, and Henry Hunt—were either instantly killed or died immediately after being recovered from the wreck. Seventy-one were wounded and crippled.

As soon as the people sufficiently recovered from the shock occasioned by the sad telegraphic news to act intelligently, communication was opened with Cincinnati, and measures inaugurated for the recovery and burial of the Galena dead. A meeting of the City Council was held on the 20th of September, and under resolution thereof, Mayor Robert Brand was directed to proceed immediately to Cincinnati and receive the bodies of the dead and bring them home for burial. He left on his sad mission on the evening train of that day, and returned early in the next week with his charge. Wednesday, September 25, a meeting of the City Council and a committee of citizens was held at the custom house for the purpose of making further arrangements for the burial of the dead. At that meeting a resolution was adopted requesting Mayor Brand to furnish a report of his mission for publication. In compliance with that request he prepared the following, which was published in the city newspapers:

"TO THE HONORABLE CITY COUNCIL OF GALENA, AND COMMITTEE OF CITIZENS,

"*Gents:*—In pursuance to a resolution of the council, under date of the 20th inst., requesting me to proceed immediately and receive the bodies of the dead of Company I, of 19th Ill. Volunteers, and bring them to this city for a public burial, I started the same evening for Cincinnati, where I learned the bodies, with the wounded, had been conveyed after the accident of the 17th inst. Before starting, I telegraphed the Mayor of Cincinnati, advising him of my coming, and requested he would withhold the burial of the dead belonging to Galena. On my arrival, I was met by the Hon. Geo. Hatch, Mayor of Cincinnati, who showed me every attention, and introduced me to Brig. Gen. O. M. Mitchell, who at once issued the following order:

SPECIAL ORDERS, No. 158. HEAD QUARTERS DEPARTMENT OF THE OHIO, CINCINNATI, O., Sept. 23, 1861.

I.—The General Commanding this Department takes this occasion to express his heartfelt sympathy with the bereaved friends of the members of the 19th Illinois Regiment, U. S. Volunteers, killed by the accident on the night of the 17th inst., on the Ohio & Mississippi Railroad.

The patriotic men so suddenly snatched away from the service of their country now rest among the nation's honored dead.

Of the surviving wounded, he is happy to say that they are doing well, and trust that very soon they will be able to rejoin their comrades, to battle with the enemy.

II.—His Honor, Mayor Robert Brand, and six citizens of Galena having arrived at Cincinnati for the purpose of conveying back to their homes the remains of thirteen of the dead, the General Commanding directs that Captain J. H. Dickenson, Asst. Quartermaster, U. S. A., will provide suitable metallic coffins to contain the bodies, and will also furnish transportation to Galena for His Honor, the Mayor, his escort and the remains.

By command of BRIG. GEN. O. M. MITCHELL,
N. H. MCLEAN, *Asst. Adj't General.*

"I was also introduced to Capt. N. H. McLean, U. S. A.; Capt. J. H. Dickenson, U. S. A.; Lieut. Col. A. E. Jones, U. S. A., and Bro. Charles Stevens, Chairman of the Relief Committee of the I. O. O. F., who were each unremitting in their attentions, and rendered me essential services in accomplishing the object of my visit.

"I found that the body of Captain B. B. Howard had been taken charge of by the Odd Fellows, and was carefully preserved in a metallic coffin and deposited in the Arsenal. I found fifteen other bodies of our dead, enclosed in coffins, carefully identified and marked, and deposited in the vault of Spring Grove Cemetery, all awaiting my arrival.

"Three of the bodies—Bruce, Carroll and Conley, were claimed by their relatives, and I was induced to give them up to them for burial. Bruce was taken by his brother and buried in the cemetery there; the other two were taken by their friends and buried in the Catholic cemetery. Those I was permitted to return with I had carefully prepared for transportation, in air-tight coffins, under the superintendence of J. P. Eppy, Esq., to whose kindness and attention I am under many obligations. Indeed, the kindness, consideration and attention shown me, and the facilities extended, without money and without price, in accomplishing my sad mission, induced me, as an act of justice, to make the following public acknowledgment there in the Cincinnati *Daily Enquirer*, of the sympathy and attention everywhere extended to me:

CARD TO THE PUBLIC.

The undersigned would do injustice to his own feelings if he omitted, on his return from the peculiarly sad mission with which he has been charged, to return his sincere and heartfelt acknowledgments for the kindness, care and consideration which has been extended to the Galena (Illinois) victims of the unfortunate accident upon the Ohio & Mississippi Railroad, by the Mayor and other municipal authorities, charitable institutions and the people generally of Cincinnati. If any thing could in the least alleviate the keen pangs of sufferings of the friends and relatives of the unfortunate deceased, it will be their consciousness that every thing which humanity could dictate, or charity conceive, was done in their behalf.

Those whom I represent are under special obligations to the Hon. Geo. Hatch, Mayor of your city; to Chas. Stevens, of the Relief Committee of the I. O. O. F.; to Captain N. H. McLean, and to the Managers and Directors of the Marine Hospital, who have been most unremitting and assiduous in their devotion to the cause of humanity. I shall return to Galena, the city of my residence, with the strongest emotions of gratitude toward Cincinnati, the memory of whose noble conduct will never be effaced from the tablets of recollection.

Gen. Mitchell, Commander of the United States Army at this point, has very kindly placed at my disposal passes, with the dead bodies of Company I, over the different roads to the place of their final interment in Illinois, and has acted in a manner worthy of his high reputation, and becoming the government he so worthily serves.

ROBERT BRAND, *Mayor of the City of Galena, Ill.*

"I not only found attention, aid and sympathy from all the citizens I came in contact with, but S. S. L'Hommidue, President of the Hamilton & Dayton R. R., presented me with free passes over his road, and the conductor, H. O. Hoyt, Esq., delayed the train in advancing our interests. At Chicago, H. D. Colvin, Superintendent of the U. S. Express Co., without charge, conveyed the bodies to the Galena & Chicago Union R. R. Depot, where Dr. Edward Williams, the Superintendent, not only furnished a special car, but in like manner passed us free over his road. I am also under many obligations to John Drew, Esq., of Chicago, for his attention and assistance; and the officers of the Ill. Central R. R., and their gentlemanly conductor, J. A. Poland, and Geo. Blanchard, General Freight Superintendent of the Ohio & Mississippi R. R.; each and all did every thing in their power to facilitate the sad duty I was engaged in—of bringing our dead to rest among us.

"I can not close this report without a just tribute to the ladies of Cincinnati for the manner in which they garlanded the dead, and their attention to our wounded—such attention as only women know how to bestow, and men to appreciate. The coffins in the vault of the cemetery were literally covered with flowers, placed there by the kind hands of fair women, attesting their sympathy at the sad bereavement. On visiting the Marine Hospital, I found some fifty of our brave boys, more or less injured from the same accident. The wounded were the objects of special attention, not only from the kind managers and directors of the hospital, but from the overflowing kindness of the citizens. No comfort that money could purchase, or sympathy that the purest love and charity could offer, was withheld. The hospital was attended by the best surgical skill, and every thing that would add to the comfort of the afflicted was extended without stint or price, while the fair ladies covered with wreaths and bouquets, and cheered and comforted by words of affection the mangled heroes that laid on their couches of affliction. Such kindness tends to bring forth all the best feelings of the human heart, and in this instance it was every where overflowing.

This report would be incorrect were I to omit the names of Colonel Turchin and his heroic wife. To the Colonel, for his care and attention in providing for his soldiers, and the facilities he extended in the performance of my sad duties to the dead. But to hear the wounded men speak of the heroic conduct of the brave Mrs. Turchin when the accident occurred! When the dead, dying and mutilated lay in one mass of ruin—when the bravest heart was appalled, and all was dismay, this brave woman was in the water rescuing the mangled and the wounded from a watery grave, and tearing from her person every available piece of clothing as bandages for the wounded, stamps beyond all question that she is not only the right woman in the right place, but a fit consort for the brave Turchin in leading the gallant sons of Illinois to battle. Such misfortunes bring forth heroic women, whose services may be frequently needed if this fratricidal war shall continue to the bitter end.

"In conclusion, allow me to add that the city officials, the Odd Fellows' Lodges, military men, and all men and women with whom I came in contact, seemed to have but one object—the doing of some act of kindness for the wounded men and the friends of the dead. Such noble conduct elevates humanity and places our city under a deep debt of gratitude that will not soon be forgotten. Yours, with respect,

"ROBERT BRAND, *Mayor.*

"At the final meeting of the committee appointed on the part of the City Council and the citizens of Galena, held at the custom house on the 1st day of October, A. D. 1861, to express their feelings of profound gratitude and admiration for the eminently kind manner in which the Hon. Robert Brand, Mayor of the City of Galena, and a delegation of our citizens were treated by the several individuals and corporations which they came in contact with, in the discharge of the melancholy duty imposed on them in recovering the bodies of our dead soldiers from the accident of the 17th of September, slain in the discharge of their duty as citizen soldiers hastening to defend the Capital of our late happy and prosperous nation against the attacks of the enemy, the following resolutions were read and unanimously adopted:

Resolved, That the thanks of the citizens of Galena are hereby tendered to the Hon. Geo. Hatch, Mayor of the City of Cincinnati; Brig. Gen. O. M. Mitchell, U. S. A.; Capt. N. H. McLean, U. S. A.; Capt. J. H. Dickenson, U. S. A.; Lieut. Col. A. E. Jones, U. S. A.; Chas. Stevens, Esq., Chairman of the Relief Committee of the I. O. O. F.; the Managers and Directors of the Marine Hospital; J. P. Eppy, Esq., of Cincinnati; and John Drew, Esq., of Chicago; and each of them, for the many attentions and acts of kindness rendered on their part to our Mayor and the delegation of our citizens in the performance of the sad duty imposed upon them.

Resolved, That the thanks of the citizens of Galena are hereby tendered unto S. S. L'Hommidue, President of the Hamilton & Dayton R. R.; H. O. Hoyt, Esq., conductor on the same; H. D. Colvin, Esq., Superintendent of the U. S. Express Co., Chicago; Dr. Edward Williams, Superintendent of the Galena & Chicago Union R. R.; the officers of the Illinois Central R. R., and J. A. Poland, Esq., the gentlemanly conductor on the same; and George Blanchard, Esq., General Freight Agent of the Ohio & Mississippi R. R.; and each of them for their kind and disinterested attention on the sad occasion.

Resolved, That the citizens of Galena are under a deep debt of gratitude to the ladies of Cincinnati for the cordial sympathy and kind attention bestowed on our wounded and dead; and that to Col. Turchin and his heroic wife we tender our most profound regard.

Resolved, That the foregoing resolutions be printed, and a copy be forwarded by the Mayor to the several parties above named.

Resolved, That this joint committee could not adjourn and do justice to their feelings without tendering to his Honor, Robert Brand, Mayor of this city, the thanks of our community for the very efficient and kind manner in which he discharged the onerous duties devolving on him in his recent trip to Cincinnati and return. We also commend to the grateful remembrance of our citizens the magnanimous manner in which the members of Schreiner's Band tendered their aid. And to the livery stables and citizens who furnished carriages and conveyances for the use of the friends of the deceased and conveyance of the dead to their final resting place, on the day of the funeral, free of charge, we tender the thanks of a grateful people.

S. CRAWFORD,	C. R. PERKINS,
H. H. GEAR,	WM. FIDDICK,
J. C. SMITH,	J. EBERHARDT,
R. SEAL,	J. WELDON,
N. CORWITH,	J. PAUL,
Committee of Citizens.	*Committee of City Council.*

W. W. HUNTINGTON, *Secretary.* STEWART CRAWFORD, *Chairman.*

Of the killed, the remains of fourteen were delivered to Mayor Brand for interment at their homes. One of the bodies was left in the vicinity of

Dixon to be delivered to friends. Thirteen other bodies were brought to Galena. From here the remains of William Frost were taken to Bellevue, Iowa, for burial. Two others, Henry Connor and ——— ——— were buried in the Catholic cemetery, and the remains of the following named ten—Captain B. B. Howard, Samuel J. Clark, Jerry Ingraham, H. H. Painter, H. C. Barras, John Douglas, Joseph Smith, William Ringer, Antoine Raffner and John Brown—were buried in the new Galena Cemetery, their remains being followed there with imposing funeral ceremonies and sincere demonstrations of respect.

Of Captain Howard the Chicago *Tribune*, about the date of the accident, said:

> Capt. Howard was a leading democrat in Jo Daviess County, and during Buchanan's administration was Postmaster of Galena. At the breaking out of the rebellion he warmly espoused the popular and patriotic cause, and was made Captain of the fine company that Galena sent to fight the battles of the country. He had served with great gallantry in the Mexican war, and was a popular and efficient officer. His death will be greatly lamented in the western part of the state, where he was so well and favorably known.

SWORD PRESENTATION TO GENERAL GRANT.

In the Summer of 1863 the people of the county inaugurated a measure for the purchase of a costly sword to be presented to General Grant. A petition was prepared and numerously signed, asking the Board of Supervisors to make an appropriation from the county funds for that purpose. On the 15th of September the Board of Supervisors being in session, the petition was called up for action, when the following preamble and resolution were offered and unanimously adopted :

> WHEREAS, The people of the County of Jo Daviess, in the State of Illinois, being desirous of manifesting to Major General U. S. Grant, a citizen of said county, their appreciation of his inestimable services to the country in the suppression of the rebellion; and particularly in opening to the people of the valley of the Mississippi their great pathway of commerce to the ocean; and also, their regard for him as a man and a citizen; be it therefore
>
> *Resolved*, That an appropriation be and is hereby made of ONE THOUSAND DOLLARS for the purpose of procuring a sword to be presented to Major General U. S. Grant, and that the clerk be authorized to pay the same when required by the Committee of the Board, appointed to procure said sword.

Messrs. Packard, Napper and Townsend were then named as the committee to purchase the sword. This committee entrusted the order for its manufacture to the Ames Manufacturing Works, Chicopee, Massachusetts. It was very elaborate in design, the grasp and guard ornamented with classical designs representing highly finished heads of Jupiter, Mars, Mercury and Minerva. The grasp inlaid with tortoise shell, held in place by gold studs—the pommel handsomely finished and encircled by a ring of diamonds, costing $1,400, which were set in pure gold. Underneath the circle of diamonds was a shield bearing the motto "*Sic Floret Republica.*" On the cross guard, surrounding General Grant's name is the following inscription : Jo Daviess County, Illinois, to Major General Ulysses S. Grant, the hero of the Mississippi." The sword also bears the names and dates of the battles in which the recipient bore a part, as follows;

Palo Alto, May 8, 1846.
Resaca de la Palma, May 9, 1846.
Monterey, September 19, 20, and 21, 1846.
Vera Cruz siege, March 7 to 27, 1847.
Cerro Gordo, April 18, 1847.
San Antonio, August 20, 1847.

Cherubusco, August 20, 1847.
Moline del Rey, September 8, 1847.
Chepultepec, September 13, 1847.
Goula San Cozana, September 14, 1847.
City of Mexico, September 14, 1847.
Belmont, November 8, 1861.
Fort Henry, February 16, 1862.
Fort Donelson, February 13, 14, 15, and 16, 1862.
Shiloh, April 6 and 7, 1862.
Corinth, siege, April 23, to May 30, 1862.
Iuka, September 19, 1862.
Hatchie, October 5, 1862.
Corinth, October 3 and 4, 1862.
Tallahatchie, December 1, 1862.
Port Gibson, May 1, 1863.
Raymond, May 12, 1863.
Jackson, May 14, 1863.
Champion Hill, May 16, 1863.
Black River Bridge, May 17, 1863.
Vicksburg, July 4, 1863.
Chattanooga, November 23, 24, 25 and 26, 1863.

These battles embraced a list of all in which General Grant had participated from his first battle at Palo Alto, Mexico, May 8, 1846, up to the time the sword was completed and ready to be presented. It was received here the first day of March, 1864, and was carried South by Messrs. S. T. Napper and H. S. Townsend, and presented to General Grant at Nashville, Tennessee, on Friday, March 18, 1864.

In his visit to the capitols of the old world and at the receptions tendered him by the titled courts of the European people, this sword, the gift of the people of Jo Daviess County, is at his side, a cherished *souvenir* of the confidence and respect entertained for him by the people among whom he lived and moved only a few short years ago without ostentation or vanity—characteristics that have always and under all circumstances marked his public, as well as his private life.

In making the appropriation for the purchase of the sword above described and presented, the supervisors also ordered that the proceedings in relation thereto "be engrossed on parchment, and that the same be presented to General Grant with the sword." These instructions were carried out by the county clerk, and a copy of the engrossed order, handsomely framed, may be seen in the office of the county clerk.

All is Well that Ends Well.—During the war, party and political feeling ran high, and, as a natural consequence, many things were done in hours of excitement that, looked upon now, when the smoke of battle has cleared away and passions cooled off, seem harsh, if not unnecessary and inexpedient. When the life of the nation was at stake, men did not always stop to inquire about justice or expediency, but bowed to the popular feeling without stopping to think of future results. Justly maddened at the attempted destruction of the Union, the dominant party looked only to the strength of the war power for support. The right of Americans to criticise the acts of their public servants was considered as treasonable and free speech of doubtful and dangerous propriety. Friends of long standing became alienated, and many an outspoken man brought vengeance and

James D Rawlins

GUILFORD TP.

death upon himself for the expression of honest convictions and criticisms. Such has always been the case in all countries in times of war, and such, in all human probability, will always be the case. During the war with Mexico, Thomas Corwin, of Ohio, as true a patriot as ever drew freedom's breath, brought political ruin to himself when he made that famous speech in which he declared that, if he were a Mexican, as he were an American, he would welcome the American soldiers with bloody hands to hospitable graves. Many years passed before he recovered from the political disaster the honest convictions of his heart brought upon himself. Had his words and their meaning been properly understood and interpreted, they would have been received as harmless and ineffective. So in many cases in the American Union's great struggle against treason and rebellion. But *when men are not understood, their motives are misinterpreted.* Misunderstandings and misinterpretations brought arrest and imprisonment to many northern men in the years of the war. Some of these arrests were made in the county whose history we are writing, and naturally form a part of that history. We would that it were otherwise, but truth to history directs our pen to the following record:

On the 28th day of August, 1862, David Sheean was arrested in Galena, without warrant or process of law, or charge of offense, on a *telegram* from Edwin M. Stanton, Secretary of War, at Washington, and taken from thence to Fort Lafayette, in New York, where he was detained until December 13 following, when he was unconditionally released. No charge of any offense was ever made; he was not informed why he was arrested and detained, nor at whose instance it was done. Borrowing money sufficient to pay his own expenses back to Galena, he determined to vindicate himself and the law violated in the acts against him, by a suit for false imprisonment against the guilty parties concerned in his arrest. He suspected that the influence of the Hon. E. B. Washburne, then the member of Congress from this district, was procured, through Daniel S. and Robert S. Harris, to induce the Secretary of War to send the telegram, and accordingly his suit was brought against those three persons, and against J. Russell Jones, United States Marshal at Chicago, and his deputy, Geo. L. Webb, the officers making the arrest. In the progress of this suit, it was disclosed, in the deposition of Maj. L. C. Turner, Judge Advocate, taken in Washington by the defendants, that the reason for his arrest was, that, as the attorney of one Bernard Donnelly, he brought suit in the Circuit Court of Jo Daviess County, Illinois, for false imprisonment against Daniel S. Harris, Robert S. Harris and John C. Hawkins—the Harrises making the affidavit for that purpose. Before this was done, they assaulted him at the court house for commencing the suit, and Robert S. Harris threatened him with the arbitrary proceedings that were soon after visited upon him. The facts in the Donnelly case were, that, while intoxicated, he declared his purpose of not enlisting in the army unless he received the county bounty in advance—citing instances where his acquaintances, who had enlisted, had not received it. For this he was assaulted and beaten by Daniel S. Harris, and taken to jail, without any warrant or complaint made against him, and there detained for several weeks. Donnelly employed Mr. Sheean as his attorney to procure his release, and, after several ineffectual attempts to do so, Mr. Sheean finally brought the suit that the Harrises made affidavit to as a pretense for his own arrest. While he was confined in Fort Lafayette, the defendants in this Donnelly suit succeeded in getting it dismissed, for want of prosecution; but on Mr. Sheean's return he again renewed the suit, and on the final trial, Robert S. Harris and John C. Hawkins were found guilty, and a judgment of $510 and costs was rendered in favor of Donnelly for falsely imprisoning him.

In the suit commenced by Mr. Sheean for his own vindication, he charged the defendants with falsely procuring his arrest and detention without cause. The defendants, Jones and Webb, defended on the ground that, under the war power, the telegram of the Secretary of War, issued by authority of the President of the United States, was a sufficient authority to them to take the plaintiff into custody to New York; and they also set up other matters in their pleas against the plaintiff. On this issue the case went to the Supreme Court of Illinois, where it was decided, by a unanimous court, that the defense set up was unlawful, "without constitutional support, and inconsistent in every principle of liberty and free government." In passing upon the questions, the Supreme Court, after referring to the Constitutional provisions in favor of liberty, say, "It can not be denied, that when this plaintiff was arrested without writ or warrant, and conveyed by the marshal to the City of New York, and there delivered, not into the custody of the law upon a criminal charge, but to a military officer, to be imprisoned in a military fortress, without judicial investigation, and without even the charge of crime, the letter and spirit of all the foregoing provisions of the constitution were plainly violated." * * "If the President could rightfully arrest him, by military force, and consign him, without process or trial, to a fortress in the harbor of New York, he could do the same thing to any other person in the State of Illinois. * * As no charge is made, no judicial investigation had, it is left entirely to the caprice of Government to determine what persons shall be seized. The power to thus arrest being once conceded, every man in the state, from the Governor down to the humblest citizen, would hold his liberty at the mercy of the military officer in command." * * "This theory, then, pushed to its logical results, is this: That whenever the government is engaged in suppressing a rebellion in Florida, or waging war on the frontiers of Maine, martial law may be enforced in Illinois, where there is neither war nor public enemy, and where the courts are daily administering justice; and every citizen of the state shall hold his liberty and his property at the whim and discretion of the military officer in command. The proposition thus stated in its nakedness, may well startle us, when we remember how liable we are to be involved in war. *But it is not true*, for it is utterly at variance with the most cherished objects of the constitution and its most solemn prohibitions." One of the Judges in giving his opinion, says: "I do not suppose pecuniary considerations influenced the plaintiff to bring this action, but rather to vindicate the constitution and the laws so grossly violated in his person. This he has effectually done, by the unanimous judgment of this court, in holding that the proceedings of which he complains were without any warrant, and in direct and palpable violation of the letter and spirit of the constitution." The case is reported in the 44th volume of Illinois Reports, at page 167. After the decision of the Supreme Court the case came back for trial in the Circuit Court of Jo Daviess County, where the following final judgment was rendered, as appears from its proceedings, taken from book "U," of Court Records, page 541, viz:

"David Sheean, *plaintiff*, *vs.* J. Russell Jones, Daniel S. Harris,

Robert S. Harris, Elihu B. Washburne, and George L. Webb, *defendants*. Trespass for false imprisonment.

And now come the said defendants, Jones and Webb, and admit that the said pleas, heretofore filed by them in said case, and the matters and things therein set forth against said plaintiff, are untrue in substance and in fact; and the defendants ask leave of the court to withdraw the same, which is granted by the court. And the said defendants further confess the wrongful trespass and imprisonment set forth in said declaration; and that the said defendants are guilty in manner and form as therein stated and set forth; and that said plaintiff has sustained great damage thereby, as is alleged in said declaration. And said defendants further confess that the said seizure and imprisonment of said plaintiff was wrongful, unjustifiable, and without cause, and that said plaintiff was innocent of the violation of any law, or of doing any act inimical to the government of the United States; and that said plaintiff did no act, used no expression, or exercised any influence, to the knowledge of said defendants, that was not in support of the government of the United States, its constitution, and laws. And inasmuch as said suit was brought by said plaintiff for the purpose of a personal vindication of his character and conduct as a citizen, he releases the said damages, except as to the sum of one thousand dollars, for expenses incurred by said plaintff on account of said wrongful seizure and imprisonment. It is thereupon considered by the court that the said plaintiff have and recover of and from the said defendants the said sum of one thousand dollars and costs of suit, and that execution issue therefor.

AGRICULTURAL SOCIETY.

In the month of August, 1855, a call was made through the columns of the Galena newspapers for a meeting of the farmers and others interested to consider the advisability of organizing an agricultural society. The meeting was held at the court house on the 13th of September of that year. F. A. Tisdall, Sr., of Courtland, now Warren, Township, presided, and W. B. Green, of West Galena, acted as secretary. After some discussion, it was resolved to organize an agricultural society, to be called the "Jo Daviess County Agricultural Society," and H. Newhall, S. S. Brown, Joseph Finley, William B. Green and E. B. Washburne were appointed a committee on Constitution and By-Laws. At a subsequent meeting the constitution was accepted and adopted.

The first officers were: S. S. Brown, President; F. A. Tisdall, Sr., A. Edgerton and Joseph Finley, Vice Presidents; John E. Smith, Treasurer; W. W. Huntington, Corresponding Secretary; R. S. Norris, Recording Secretary.

These gentlemen at once entered upon their respective duties for the furtherance of the object desired by the organization of the society. Feeling that their success depended, in a great measure, upon the holding of an annual fair, and also the importance of controlling some suitable piece of ground for that purpose, and the society being financially weak, it was determined to apply to the Board of Supervisors for assistance, in the purchase of the same, who generously agreed to pay for the same (ten acres), providing the society would fence and make suitable improvements thereon.

It was determined that at or near the City of Galena would be for the best interests of the society, presuming that gate fees would be the principal source of revenue. Some difficulty was experienced in fixing upon a site, and the question of selecting the ground was finally left to the Board of Supervisors, with a request that a committee be appointed from that body to confer with the Executive Committee of the society in locating the grounds. In accordance with this request, Messrs. M. Claypool, J. D. Champion and J. W. White were appointed as such committee from the Board of Supervisors. After examining several pieces of ground, they finally recommended the purchase of ten acres of ground at Horse Shoe Mound, two miles east of the City of Galena. Funds were raised to fence the grounds with a tight board fence, and also to make sheds and buildings necessary for the accommodation of stock and articles sent in for exhibition. The most of the money needed for this purpose was raised among the business men of Galena, and the City Council contributed very handsomely, which enabled the committee to fully prepare for the first annual fair of Jo Daviess County Agricultural Society, which was held on the 23d, 24th, and 25th of September, 1856. The financial report of the fair is as follows:

Whole number of entries for exhibition, 286.

RECEIPTS.		
Received from Board of Supervisors for premiums	$225.00	
Received from State of Illinois	50.00	
Received from City of Galena	390.50	
Received on subscription in Galena	481.69	
Received at gate and from members	721.85—	$1,869.04
EXPENDITURES.		
Paid for fencing and sheds	$1,188.23	
Paid incidental expenses	109.15	
Paid premiums	231.50—	$1,528.88
Leaving a balance in treasury		$340.16

The report says the weather was favorable, and the fair well attended.

The second board of officers were: S. S. Brown, President; H. S. Townsend, Joseph Finley and A. Edgerton, Jr., Vice Presidents; John E. Smith, Treasurer; W. W. Huntington, Corresponding Secretary; and R. S. Norris, Recording Secretary. The election for these officers was held at the annual meeting, in December, 1856.

The second annual fair and exhibition was held October 1 and 2, 1857. Whole number of entries for competition, 301.

FINANCIAL EXHIBIT.

RECEIPTS.		
On hand from 1856	$340.16	
Received from State of Illinois	100.00	
Received on subscription, Galena	55.00	
Received at gate and from members	638.70—	$1,133.86
EXPENDITURES.		
Paid printing and diplomas	$85.00	
Paid seal and press	10.00	
Paid lumber, improving grounds, and incidental expenses	287.46	
Paid premiums for 1856	17.50	
Paid premiums for 1857	642.50—	$1,042.46
Leaving balance in Treasury of		$91.40

At the annual meeting in December, 1857, the following board of officers were elected:

N. Dowling, President; M. Claypool, William Logan, J. Robson, Vice Presidents; J. E. Smith, Treasurer; E. H. Beebe, Corresponding Secretary; R. S. Norris, Recording Secretary.

Enlarged grounds were deemed a necessity, and the new board of officers inaugurated and carried out measures for the purchase, from James Roberts, of 4 71-100 acres, which were enclosed with the other grounds, and increased its area to 14 71-100 acres.

The third annual fair and exhibition was held on the 6th, 7th, and 8th days of October, 1858. Whole number of entries for competition, 292.

FINANCIAL EXHIBIT.

RECEIPTS.

Cash in treasury, 1857	$90 42	
Received from State of Illinois	100 00	
Received from Jo Daviess County	112 50	
Received from gate and members	894 50	
		$1,197 42

EXPENDITURES.

Paid lumber for fencing, building booths, etc., nails and labor,	$415 92	
Paid printing and diplomas	122 25	
Paid incidental expenses	197 10	
Paid premiums	361 50	
		$1,096 77
Leaving a balance in treasury of		$100 65

The following officers were elected for 1859: E. M. Bouton, President; John B. Reynolds, Thomas Prouse and J. Bryan, Vice Presidents; Kittoe, Corresponding Secretary; R. S. Norris, Recording Secretary.

The fourth annual fair was held on the 21st, 22d, and 23d days of September, 1859. Whole number of entries for competition, 376.

FINANCIAL EXHIBIT.

RECEIPTS.

Cash in Treasury from 1858	$100 65	
Received at gate and from members	1,088 20	
		$1,188 85

EXPENDITURES.

Paid premiums, 1858	$5 50	
Paid premiums, 1859	505 90	
Paid for printing, etc.	70 50	
Paid incidental expenses	166 57	
Leaving a balance in Treasury of		$748 47

The officers elected for 1860, were, E. D. Kittoe, President; Thomas Prouse, H. S. Townsend, and E. H. Beebe, Vice Presidents; E. M. Bouton, Treasurer; A. Philleo, Corresponding Secretary; R. S. Norris, Recording Secretary.

Mr. Bouton declined to accept the office of treasurer, and Mr. T. Hallett was appointed to the vacancy.

Such were the beginnings of the Jo Daviess Agricultural Society. It has been carefully and judicially managed from the time of its organization, and it is one of the very few societies of the kind that has always "paid its way."

The old grounds at Horse Shoe Mound were occupied until 1866.

They were sold, and the present grounds purchased and fitted up. The society was "first organized," says the last report, "on the membership basis of annual payments, but finding this plan hardly adequate to furnish a liberal premium list, its managers, in 1866, conceived the plan of a stock company, and so organized under the state laws, and have been successfully running since that time, holding annual fairs and paying liberal premiums, but never as yet paying dividends from earnings, to its stockholders, the object of its organization not being as much for the profit of dividends on its stock as to furnish the annual holiday to the citizens in the district, and for the advancement of the interests of the agriculturist, the mechanic, and the artist. Hence, all gate fees and earnings have been paid back to the successful competitors at its fairs. And the executive committee earnestly hope that all those who feel an interest in such enterprises will continue to aid it by their presence at the fair to be held September 24 to 27, 1878; and the committee would respectfully suggest that the merchants of Galena fix a day for the closing of their stores, so that all may have an opportunity to attend the fair, thus insuring the receipt of gate fees sufficient to pay the large and liberal premium list offered by them, as the gate alone is the source from which arises the funds to pay expenses and premiums."

FINANCIAL EXHIBIT, 1877.

RECEIPTS.

Balance in treasury, 1877	$ 25	
Received from E. Kuhn, 1876	80	
" loan of R. Brand	350 00	
" for pic-nics	25 00	
" from state board	100 00	
" from ground rent	50 00	
" from proceeds of fair, 1877	2,547 05	
Balance in treasury overpaid	17 85	
		$3,090 95

EXPENDITURES.

Paid premiums, 1876	$57 05	
" interest on loan mortgage	120 00	
" D. A. Taylor, for advance	50 00	
" D. A. Taylor, interest on same	1 10	
" fire insurance	25 20	
" Union Agricultural Society, Warren	50 00	
" loan, R. Brand	350 00	
" interest on same	17 50	
" expenses of fair	710 45	
" repairs, 1877	99 80	
" premiums awarded	1,614 80	
	$3,095 90	
Less premiums unpaid	4 95	
		$3,090 95

LIABILITIES.

For loan on mortgage	$1,100 00
For interest on same, due February, 1878	100 00
For balance due treasurer	17 85
For unclaimed premiums	4 95
For stock issued, total	11,500 00

Present Officers.—Ralph S. Norris, President; Henry B. Chetlain, Vice President; Frank Bostwick, Secretary; David N. Corwith, Treasurer.

Directors.—Edgar M. Bouton, Fred. Chetlain, West Galena; William Vincent, Moses Annetts, East Galena; Charles Speer, Hanover.

Patrons of Husbandry.—The following brief sketch of this organization has been furnished by a prominent and active member:

The first grange organized in this county was at the house of J. Tear, in Warren, Nov. 25, 1872, when G. W. Curtiss was elected Master, and J. Bird, Secretary. The latter was the first county deputy, and organized nearly all the granges in the county. The office of state chaplain was awarded to this county at the Champaign session of State Grange in 1875, in the person of L. F. Farnham. At the Peoria session in 1878, G. W. Curtiss was elected a member of the executive committee. There existed at this time seven, out of seventeen, originally chartered granges in this county. Outside of these are several hundred ancient patrons (members of granges which have fallen by the way), who are still in sympathy with the organization. As elsewhere, so in this county, there were too many granges (one township had four,) chartered, for that healthy growth, essential to its success. While among the objects sought by the patrons are amusements, education, and pecuniary profit, of which the last should be the least essential, still many thought in the pathway of the grange was the rapid road to sudden wealth, with but little, if any, exertion on their part, and in which they were very properly disappointed. Others looked for easily acquired political preferment, and having reckoned without their host, very suddenly lost all interest in the grange, and departed from its gates. The granges remaining in good standing in the order, with the later additions of members, are on a more permanent basis than the last granges, and are silently but effectually doing much towards accomplishing the objects and work for which they were organized.

HORTICULTURAL SOCIETY.

James G. Soulard, Esq., the first president of the Jo Daviess County Horticultural Society, planted the first vineyard in this county, in 1832, on his old homestead, one and one-half miles northwest of Galena. He planted about one and one half acres with the Catawba and Isabella varieties. In 1834 he commenced the first nursery for the growth of apple, pear, plum and other fruit trees, and was the leading nurseryman of the Northwest until about 1858.

Mr. Soulard was born in 1798, first visited Galena in 1821 and 1822, and made his permanent home here in 1857. His tastes led him to engage in horticulture, in which he has been enthusiastically engaged nearly all his life. He is one of those noble, generous, whole-souled men who aided in the development of this country. He is now an old man, who, ere long, will be gathered to his fathers, but let it be inscribed on the stone that shall mark his last resting-place: "He did not live in vain." Mr. Soulard imported stocklargely from Europe, in addition to his own growth, introducing many valuable varieties of fruits now generally cultivated, among which may be mentioned the Elvira grape. There are sample trees now growing on his old grounds that he imported, and that are not to be found elsewhere. He also experimented largely in efforts to produce new varieties of fruits. Among the results of his experiments are the "Soulard Apple" and the "Soulard Crab." The former is now rated first in the list of Fall apples. The tree is hardy, and the fruit is esteemed for its superior flavor, size and general good qualities. The "Soulard Crab Apple" he produced by hybridizing the wild crab of the country with the common, grafted apple.

The variety thus produced is valued for its peculiar aroma, for preserving and for the manufacture of cidar and vinegar.

In connection with this part of the history of the county, it will not be out of place to mention that the Hallett orchard, on the old Hallett farm, in the Township of Rice, is from seeds planted by Moses Hallett, in 1832. It is still thrifty and fruitful.

There are now standing on the Soulard homestead, and on the "Chetlain place," about a quarter of a mile distant, some venerable old seedling pear trees, about sixty feet in height. There are others at Savanna, Carroll County, and they are found scattered in the pathway of the Jesuits who early visited this region, from Detroit to St. Louis. It is not known by whom these trees in Galena were planted, but it is supposed by some that the seeds were planted by the Jesuit priests in some of their visits to the Indians here, or by the early Swiss and French settlers. They were certainly planted a long time before 1832.

The "Miner Plum," now well known throughout the West, originated here. It is said the trees were brought to this region in 1831, by a man from Ohio, who planted them on the Townsend farm, in Rush Township, but the next year, when the Black Hawk War commenced, he took them up and brought them here, left them with Major Hinckley, and left the country. Major Hinckley planted them and they still stand, about twenty-five in number, on the old Hinckley farm, now owned by Captain Porter. At a little distance they resemble an old New England apple orchard. The trees are large, measuring, two feet from the ground, four or five feet in circumference, branching out about six feet from the ground, and spreading from thirty to thirty-six feet. They are hardy and fruitful. It is a singular fact that, although the trees are said to have been brought from Ohio, no trees of the kind are to be found there except those originated from the old Hinckley farm.

There is also a singular variety of the elm, now propagated by tree-growers, which can be found native in no other locality in this part of the country. This is called by Mr. Scott the "Weeping Elm," and the original tree stands about one quarter of a mile east of the Hinckley plum orchard also mentioned, on a high, bleak point of land, where it has probably been growing for at least 150 years. The first settler who cleared the land was thoughtful enough to leave it standing on account of its singular appearance. It is about forty-five feet high, and two feet in diameter near the ground. When engrafted on the American elm, its branches grow directly downward, and in grafting, young stocks, unless supported for several years until the trunk becomes self-supporting, it runs about on the ground like a vine.

The Lieb cherry, now a favorite, originated in Galena. Mr. John Lieb re-visited his native Germany about twenty years ago, and while there found under a favorite cherry tree four little sprouts, which he supposed sprang from the roots of the tree, and were the same. He brought them with him when he returned to Galena, but they did not prove to be the same as he supposed. Three of them were worthless, but one which he planted himself produced fruit of a new and superior variety. Although some experts in vegetable physiology declare such a result impossible, the Lieb, says Mr. Scott, is unquestionably a hybrid between the Morello, or sour, and the Heart, or sweet, types of the cherry. The fruit is about three times the size of the Early Richmond, with very small pits or stones, deliciously pulpy

Harvey Mann

VINEGAR HILL.

and juicy, partaking of the Heart, being almost as sweet, while the tree inclines strongly to the Morello type. There is nothing like the Lieb cherry in this country or in Europe, and it is either a hybrid or a new creation.

About the time Mr. Soulard relinquished the nursery business, Mr. D. W. Scott started in it, in 1858, notice of which is given elsewhere.

Mr. Jacob Zins came from Germany in the employ of Mr. Soulard, but about 1845 started a nursery and vineyard on his own account, in East Galena, having about six acres in each department.

Mr. Herman Gronner, florist, of Galena, connected a nursery with his green-house about 1870, and makes a specialty of the "Lieb Cherry" and the Weeping Elm.

Mr. C. Vandervate, who had been employed for some years by Mr. Scott, as a florist, started a small nursery in 1874. Dr. W. S. Caldwell and —— Benworth commenced a nursery in Woodbine a few years ago, but it is being closed out now. Another one at Warren, commenced in 1868, by Allen & Cole, is also being closed out. Some others have started, but run only a short time.

Although there were many interested in horticulture in this county, there was no organization, or none is known, until 1868. Mr. Soulard had done more than any other man to develop the horticultural interest in the county, and next to him, perhaps, ranks Mr. Scott, but there were many others who were interested in it and its kindred interests. Among them were Dr. Horatio Newhall and his wife, Dr. Edward D. Kittoe, Mrs. Sarah C. Harris, Captain E. H. Beebe and others.

On Saturday, February 29, 1868, a meeting of the friends of horticulture was held in the sheriff's room at the court house in Galena, to organize the Jo Daviess Horticultural Society. There were present J. G. Soulard, Dr. Newhall, Dr. Kittoe, D. W. Scott, R. S. Norris, J. W. Robson, Timothy Hallett, John Harney, E. H. Beebe, F. Chetlain, J. M. Harris, Jacob Zins, H. Gronner, A. L. Cumings and others. Mr. James G. Soulard was elected chairman, and D. W. Scott secretary of the meeting.

On motion, a committee to select officers for permanent organization was appointed by the chair, who reported as follows: For President, James G. Soulard; Vice Presidents, E. D. Kittoe, E. H. Beebe, J. W. Robson, Harvey Mann, A. Mougin, T. Hallett; Corresponding Secretary, Horatio Newhall; Recording Secretary, D. Wilmot Scott; Treasurer, F. Chetlain.

On motion, A. L. Cumings, J. G. Soulard and D. Wilmot Scott were appointed a committee to draft a constitution and by-laws, and report at next meeting.

The membership fee was fixed at one dollar, and it was voted that no fruit should be added to the list for cultivation without a two-thirds vote of the members present.

The early records of the society are not accessible, and the historians are, therefore, unable to give the history of this society and its valuable labors as fully as they would like. Its meetings have been held monthly, and many valuable papers have been read.

James G. Soulard was succeeded as president by A. L. Cumings, Esq., probably in 1869 or 1870. In 1871 J. W. Robson was secretary, but in November of that year he resigned, as he was about to remove to Kansas, and Robert Brand, Esq., was elected secretary. It is supposed that all the records kept by Mr. Scott, and by Robson to that date, were carried away by the latter when he went to Kansas. The society may be willing to suffer the loss of its records, but it creates a chasm in its history that can not be filled. Mr. Cumings remained president until ——, when Timothy Hallett succeeded him. The present officers are understood to be Timothy Hallett, President; Robert Brand, Secretary. The last election is not recorded, and there are probably some other officers whose names should appear. In closing this article, it is proper to suggest that if the reader will undertake to search among any old records for information, he will appreciate the importance of a good clerk or secretary for any organization. Records constitute history, and if they are imperfect, the continuous chain is broken.

THE PRESS.

The *Miners' Journal* was the first newspaper published in Jo Daviess County, and, indeed, the first in the northwest. The first number was issued July 8, 1828, by James Jones, who was here in 1827. In his prospectus Mr. Jones proposed to call the newspaper the *Northern Herald*, but changed the name on the suggestion of Dr. H. Newhall, who is said to have assisted him in the editorial department. The *Miners' Journal* was a small five-column paper, neutral in politics, and was furnished to subscribers for $3.50 a year, in advance, payable in smelter's acceptances, lead or cash. It was issued (not always regularly, for paper was not always obtainable) probably until the death of Mr. Jones by cholera, in 1833. Jones struggled hard to make an honest living, but the support he received was but meagre and inadequate. He was an honest man, of excellent character, but peculiar in his religious ideas. Mr. Jones labored hard to prepare a book of legal forms, and was assisted in the preparation of the forms by Judge Young. He expected to obtain an appropriation from the Legislature to help him out and enable him to place his book in the hands of lawyers and justices, but the judge did not recommend the work to the Legislature. Jones was deprived of the expected aid, and could not obtain paper to make the book as large as he desired. Most of the forms printed by Jones are still in use in this state. Mr. Abel Proctor, now residing in Wright County, Iowa, was a printer, and helped "set up" and "work off" the concluding pages of "Jones' Form Book," in 1829.

The *Galena Advertiser*, same size and price of the *Miner's Journal*, was started July 20, 1829, by Dr. Horatio Newhall, Dr. Addison Philleo and Hooper Warren, under the firm name of Newhall, Philleo & Co. Warren was the printer of the concern (from Rutland, Vermont), and for two or three months was assisted by Abel Proctor. How long the *Advertiser* was continued can not be determined. A file of the paper in the possession of Dr. E. G. Newhall ends with May 24, 1830. Dr. Newhall and Warren were Whigs. Dr. Philleo was a Democrat, and it is possible that the combination was unable to harmonize. Warren afterwards went to Chicago.

The *Galenian* was established May 2, 1832, by Dr. Addison Philleo. In the first number the editor said: "No principles other than republican (Democratic) will ever receive our support. To enter into a discussion of the political concerns of the nation at this period, further than pertains to our local interest, we deem altogether out of place." The *Galenian* was published until September, 1836 certainly, as a Democratic paper, but subsequently Dr. Philleo associated with himself Mr. Geo. N. Palmer, and the name of the paper was changed, probaby in 1836 or '7, to the *Galena Democrat*, which was running in 1838. The only file of the *Galenian* known to be in existence is owned by Dr. E. G. Newhall, and this embraces only a part of the first volume.

The *Northwestern Gazette and Galena Advertiser* was commenced November 29, 1834, with Loring & Bartlett, editors and publishers. The *Galenian* was the only paper in the county then. It was pretty strongly Democratic—party lines were strictly drawn, and the Whigs were determined to have an organ. Twelve prominent gentlemen subscribed $100 each, sent to St. Louis for material, and Sylvester M. Bartlett and Charles E. Loring came from that city to run it, with the understanding that the money raised by the citizens was in the nature of a bonus. They were to run the paper, and have all they could make, but could call on the subscribers to the fund for no more. Loring soon became disgusted and returned to St. Louis. Benjamin Mills, an able and brilliant lawyer, became editor December 20, 1834, and remained until May 23, 1835, when he retired, having disappointed himself and his friends as an editorial writer, leaving Mr. Bartlett alone. Mr. Horace H. Houghton, a son of the Green Mountain State, came here in April, 1835, and engaged in mining at New Diggings during the Summer, but returned in the Fall to Galena, and was employed by Bartlett for a year. Soon after, he purchased one half of the paper, Bartlett, in the meantime, had been challenged by John Turney to mortal combat. Bartlett accepted, but the affair was compromised. Perhaps they found that Bartlett wouldn't scare. But one shot was fired, and that accidentally. Bartlett was afterward elected to the legislature. In the Spring of 1838, Houghton purchased Bartlett's interest for $1,500, and became sole owner, as he thought, but now came forward the men who had furnished the money in 1834, and demanded of Mr. Houghton the money they had put in, with interest, and he paid it, thus buying the office twice. Bartlett went to New Orleans, but subsequently returned to Quincy, Illinois, and started the Quincy *Whig*. In March, 1838, immediately after he became sole proprietor, Mr. Houghton started the *Tri-Weekly Gazette*.

In 1843, Mr. Houghton sold the *Gazette* office to W. C. E. Thomas, receiving a mortgage on it for a part of the purchase money, but in 1845, he was back in it again as editor, and in 1847 was again sole owner. During a part of the time that Mr. Thomas published the paper Mr. I. B. Gara was associated with him.

January 1, 1848, the first number of the *Galena Daily Advertiser* was issued by Mr. Houghton, and he remained the leading Whig editor of the Northwest (becoming Republican when that party was organized) until he retired in 1863.

In 1857, W. W. Huntington, Esq. (for twelve years postmaster at Galena), who had learned the printer's trade in Mr. Houghton's office in Middlebury, Vermont, purchased of Houghton & Foster the job printing office and book-bindery connected with the *Gazette*.

In 1858 Mr. D. W. Scott purchased one third of the paper, and the next year Mr. Nesbitt Baugher became connected with it with one third interest, Mr. Houghton retaining the editorial control of its columns. At the commencement of the war, in 1861, Mr. Baugher entered the service of the United States, and fell mortally wounded at the battle of Pittsburg Landing, having been shot seven times. His remains were taken to Gettysburg and interred in the cemetery there, a short time before the battle of Gettysburg. Mr. Baugher was the son of President Baugher, of Gettysburg College, and was a very highly educated and talented young man. In 1863, the office and paper were sold to James B. Brown, Esq., and George K. Shaw. The latter remained only a short time, when he retired; Mr. Brown became sole proprietor and editor, changed the name to the Galena *Gazette* (daily and weekly) and has managed it very successfully ever since. The "Old *Gazette*," through all its mutations, has been continuously published on its regular days, without missing a single issue, from the time it started, in 1834, to the present time.

Mr. Houghton, so long and so completely identified with the *Gazette*, it is but just to say in this connection, claims to be the first to conceive the idea of printing the first sides of newspapers at some central point, and sending the sheets so partly printed to be published in other places, and in that way published the *Vermont Statesman*, the *Rutland Herald*, the *Voice of the People*, at Springfield, the *American*, at Middlebury, and the *Gazette* at Vergennes—all in his native state, Vermont. In 1834, he took a power press to New York, the first ever seen in that city so arranged as to throw off the sheets after they were printed, by means of fingers, now universally used. "By that device," says Mr. Houghton, "the Adams power press became a complete book press, and the Hoe machine and other cylinder presses greatly improved." In New York he became discouraged. Others took advantage of his invention, and he came West, to exercise a powerful influence in moulding the destiny and making the history of this new country. Without money, except a dollar borrowed from a friend, he traveled to Philadelphia, thence to Marietta, Ohio, by way of Baltimore and Harper's Ferry, several hundred miles, on foot, with his pack on his back. At Marietta he had money enough to pay his passage to Cincinnati, where he worked at the trade until Spring, when he went to St. Louis, Missouri, thence to Galena. Such was the man who, by his patience, perseverance and unflagging industry, successfully conducted the Galena *Gazette* for nearly thirty years.

Mr. Brown, who has conducted the *Gazette* with signal skill and ability for the last fifteen years, is a native of New Hampshire, and is a splendid specimen of a Westernized New Englander. Born in New Hampshire, and educated at Gilmanton, he came West and settled in Dunleith in 1857, but removed to Galena when he became proprietor of the *Gazette*. Under Mr. Brown's management the *Gazette* was greatly improved. He appreciated the importance of making the paper a full and complete record of passing events *at home*, as well as abroad, a department of journalism that editors, outside of the great news centres, too often overlook. Had the conductors of the first newspapers in the county realized the importance of recording local events, the historian would have had a full and invaluable source of information relating to the early history, now entirely beyond reach. The *Gazette*, under Mr. Brown's admirable management, has become one of the best and most valuable local papers in the state, and in this respect, at least, it has no superior in the country. Fifty years hence the future historian will find in the files of the *Gazette* since 1863 ample materials for a complete history of Jo Daviess County, from that time to the present.

The *Galena Journal* was started in 1838, by a sort of stock company, who it is understood purchased or *inherited* the *Democrat*. W. C. Taylor and John Stark were the editors. In 1840, the parties interested found themelves considerably in debt, and suspended publication.

The Galena *Star* twinkled a short time in 1840 or 1841, under the management of Beriah Brown, printed on the old *Journal* type, but it soon went out. The material passed into the hands of Major John Dement, and was purchased by Mr. Houghton, who moved it to Dubuque and published a paper there called the *Transcript* for a short time, after he sold the *Gazette* to Mr. Thomas.

The Galena *Sentinel*.—In 1840, two men, named McGrew, brought an outfit for a printing office from St. Louis, and established the Galena *Sentinel* as a Democratic paper. After running a short time, the McGrews are said to have sold to —— Sweeney and his son, Charles Sweeney, by whom it was continued for several years, until 1845 or 1846. The *Sentinel* was the organ of Joseph P. Hoge.

The Galena *Jeffersonian*, weekly and semi-weekly, was established in September, 1845, by Horace A. and Henry W. Tenney, from Elyria, Ohio. It was Democratic in politics; was very ably conducted and liberally supported, but the proprietors and nearly all the workmen were attacked with fever and ague, and they sold to Charles Sweeney, who became editor and proprietor January 1, 1847. The *Jeffersonian*, under the management of the Tenneys, achieved the reputation of being the best and ablest paper in Illinois. In 1852 it passed into the hands of Randall, Sanford & Co. Randall remained but a few months and sold his interest to Dr. Charles H. Ray, and it was published a while by Ray & Sanford, but in December, 1853, D. W. Scott having previously purchased Sanford's interest, it was published by Ray & Scott until December, 1854, when Mr. Scott became sole proprietor. Dr. Ray afterwards went to Chicago; became interested in the Chicago *Tribune*, and subsequently started the Chicago *Post*. After running the *Jeffersonian* a few months, Mr. Scott sold two thirds of the office to L. F. Leal and Charles Crouch, and the *Jeffersonian* disappeared.

The *Courier*, which took the place of the *Jeffersonian*, was commenced in November, 1855, by Leal, Crouch & Co., Mr. D. W. Scott being the "Co." Soon after, Mr. Scott retired, and in 1860 Mr. Crouch also retired. In May, 1861, Mr. Leal sold the *Courier* establishment to E. R. Paul, of the Dunleith *Advertiser*, who discontinued the daily and continued the weekly for a while, when he sold to —— Bristol, of Kankakee, who run it until the next year, when the *Courier* was sold to a company.

The Galena Democrat.—The purchasers of the *Courier* establishment organized a stock company, and the shares were taken by leading Democrats who were anxious that an organ of their party should be maintained here, and were ready to contribute money to accomplish the purpose. This company revived the paper about December 1, 1862, under the name of the Galena *Democrat*, with L. S. Everett as editor. But the company soon after found itself considerably in debt, and made an arrangement with H. H. Savage by which they relinquished to him the entire establishment, on condition that he should pay the debts standing against it. Everett retired and Savage run the paper until it was closed out, about 1868, by a sale under chattel mortgage given by Savage to secure the debts which he assumed.

The Commercial Advertiser, Galena. Monthly; devoted mainly to horticulture. Established in 1863, by D. W. Scott. Mr. Scott came to Galena in 1853 and opened a printers' furnishing warehouse in connection with the *Jeffersonian*. He sold to Gov. Gorman, in that year, the material for the first Democratic printing office in St. Paul, Minnesota, and the next year fitted out the first printing office established in La Crosse, Wisconsin, by Lord, Rodolph & Ladue. He became connected with the press of Galena in 1853. He had sold his interest in the *Gazette* in 1863 on account of ill health, but recovering, he established, late in the same year, a small job printing office, for which he had a portion of the material, and started the *Commercial Advertiser*, originally designed for a mercantile and business paper, but being engaged in tree growing and horticulture, the paper gradually became devoted to his favorite topics. The little job office of 1863, by his energy and capacity, rapidly expanded to mammoth proportions. In 1872 he admitted as a partner Alonzo L. Cumings, Esq., a gentleman of sterling worth and a lawyer of ability (now editor of the *Industrial Press*), and their large and increasing business since that time has been conducted by D. W. Scott & Co., who have now the largest and best appointed job printing office in Northern Illinois (Chicago excepted), having a book-bindery and stereotype foundry connected with it. Scott & Co. have made a specialty of printing for nurserymen. Mr. Scott is himself one of the leading nurserymen of the state, and the firm have been enabled to build up an immense business, filling orders for printing from all the Western states and territories. This is the only steam printing establishment in Jo Daviess County, and the enterprising proprietors thoroughly understand their business.

The Galena *Sun*, weekly, rose in 1868, edited and published by S. W. Russell. It was printed on the old *Democrat* press and type obtained for the purpose, with the option of purchase if the paper succeeded, but its support did not meet the expectations of its projector, and after a brief existence it ceased to shine in 1869.

The Spirit of the Press, Galena, weekly, was established on October 9, 1871, by H. H. Houghton, Esq., and was printed by D. W. Scott & Co. After publishing it a little more than two years Mr. Houghton sold his subscription list to J. B. Brown, Esq., and the paper was, in January, 1874, merged in the Galena *Gazette*.

The Industrial Press, Galena, weekly: "Independent in every thing, neutral in nothing," was established February 6, 1874, by A. L. Cumings and James W. Scott, firm name Cumings & Scott, and was printed by D. W. Scott & Co. At the end of the first year James W. Scott (now proprietor of the *Hotel Reporter*, Chicago), retired, and his father, D. W. Scott, purchased his interest, but no change was made in the firm name. *The Industrial Press* is a large, handsomely printed and ably edited paper of eight pages, six columns to the page, and has a large circulation in Jo Daviess and adjoining counties.

The Galena *Correspondent* (German) was issued from the office of the Galena *Jeffersonian*, about 1851, and was continued for about a year and a half. Then a number of leading Germans contributed for the purchase of materials, and the *Correspondent* was continued under the management of ——— Stybold until about 1854 or '5, when he abandoned it and suddenly left town. Stybold was succeeded by Messrs. Wuertenburg & Beckert, who continued the publication of the paper until about 1862, when they sold to Mr. Pingel, who changed the name to the Galena *Deutsche Zeitung*, and continued it until the Spring of 1868, when he sold the office to Von Kettler.

The Galena *Volksfreund*. In 1868, Von Kettler purchased the material on which the *Deutsche Zeitung* had been printed, and started the Galena

Volksfreund, and continued it until November, 1872, when he sold it to J. Voss and M. Witt, by whom it is now published. Two years ago the paper was enlarged, and is now a large, well-printed and well-edited eight-column folio sheet, and has a large circulation in this and the other northern counties in Illinois. Mr. Voss, the editor, is a highly educated gentleman who instructs a class in the German language in the Galena High School in addition to his editorial duties. The *Volksfreund* is the only German newspaper in Jo Daviess County.

Warren Republican was started at Warren in 1855, by Charles Blaisdell, but was discontinued after running about a year. On the 23d day of September, 1857, a newspaper called the Warren *Independent* was started by Freeman A. Tisdell, Sr., and Thomas E. Champion—Geo. E. Randall, editor. After several changes Herst C. Gann, Esq., became editor and proprietor. In July, 1866, the name was changed to Warren *Sentinel.*

Dunleith *Commercial Advertiser* started June, 1857, died 1861, when it was transferred to the Galena *Democrat.*

OFFICIAL RECORD.

The following list, prepared by W. F. Crummer, County Clerk, shows a *partial* record of county officers from 1836 to 1840, and a complete official record from 1840 to the present—February, 1878:

Nov. 7, 1836, special election, Moses Hallett, Sheriff, County.

Aug., 1836, J. Craig, E. Charles, Representatives to General Assembly, County.

Aug. 3, 1840, H. W. Thornton, Thomas Drummond, Representatives to Legislature, Galena.

Aug. 5, 1844, Joseph P. Hoge, Member of Congress, Galena. Cyrus C. Aldrich, Representative to Legislature, Galena. Harvey Mann, County Commissioner, Vinegar Hill. Alexander Young, Sheriff, Galena. John Wood, County Treasurer, Galena. William P. Millard, County Coroner, Galena.

Aug., 1845, Isaac S. Horr, County Commissioner. W. C. Bostwick, School Superintendent, Galena. Richard Seal, County Clerk, Galena. Thomas Allinson, Coroner, Scales Mound. Thomas Prouse, County Treasurer, Scales Mound.

Aug. 3, 1846, Wm. P. Millard, Sheriff, Galena. John R. Smith, County Commissioner, Galena. Robert Starr, Coroner, Galena.

Aug. 11, 1848, Marshall B. Pierce, Sheriff, Galena. Wilmot Cady, Coroner, Galena. Wm. H. Bradley, Clerk Circuit Court, Galena. John Winner, County Commissioner.

Nov. 9, 1850, C. E. Sanders, Sheriff, Galena. Thomas McNulty, Coroner, Galena.

Nov. 4, 1851, Joseph O. Martin, County Commissioner, Galena. J. P. DeZoya, County Treasurer, Galena. John C. Gardner, County Surveyor, Galena.

Nov. 2, 1852, Wm. H. Brown, Prosecuting Attorney, Rockford. Wm. H. Bradley, Clerk Circuit Court, Galena. Wm. Meighan, Sheriff, Galena. Thomas McNulty, Coroner, Galena.

Nov. 4, 1853, Geo. M. Mitchell, County Judge, Galena. Richard Seal, County Clerk, Galena. J. P. DeZoya, County Treasurer, Galena. John C. Gardner, County Surveyor, Galena. J. N. Waggoner, County School Commissioner, Galena.

Nov. 7, 1854, W. R. Rowley, Sheriff, Galena. Freeman A. Tisdell, Coroner, Warren.

Nov. 6, 1855, John D. Platt, County Judge, Warren. Geo. M. Mitchell, Clerk Circuit Court, Galena. Fleming C. Maupin, County Treasurer, Galena. John C. Gardner, County Surveyor, Galena. Geo. W. Ford, School Commissioner.

Nov. 4, 1856, U. D. Meacham, Prosecuting Attorney, Freeport. W. R. Rowley, Clerk Circuit Court, Galena. Simeon K. Miner, Sheriff, Galena. James C. H. Hobbs, Coroner, Galena.

Nov. 3, 1857, John D. Platt, County Judge, Warren. Richard Seal, County Clerk, Galena. Thomas J. Maupin, County Treasurer, Galena. John C. Gardner, County Surveyor, Galena. Joseph Adams, County Commissioner, Galena. Samuel Tyrrell, Nicholas Mertes, Associate Judges, Ward's Grove.

Nov. 2, 1858, John H. Conlee, Sheriff, Galena. B. F. Fowler, Coroner, Galena.

Nov. 8, 1859, John E. Smith, County Treasurer, Galena. Geo. Hicks, School Commissioner, Galena. Luther H. Cowan, County Surveyor, Warren.

No. 6, 1860, Smith D. Atkins, Prosecuting Attorney, Freeport. W. R. Rowley, Clerk Circuit Court, Galena. Simeon K. Miner, Sheriff, Nicholas Roth, Coroner.

Nov. 5, 1861, Mathew Marvin, County Judge, Warren. Richard Seal, County Clerk, Galena. Ralph S. Norris, County Treasurer, Galena. Milton Wadleigh, County Surveyor, Galena. John C. Hawkins, County Coroner, Galena.

Nov. 4, 1862, John C. Hawkins, County Sheriff, Galena. A. M. Jones, County Coroner, Warren.

Nov. 3, 1863, R. S. Norris, County Treasurer, Galena. Milton Wadleigh, County Surveyor, Galena. James B. Brown, County Superintendent of Schools, Dunleith.

Nov. 8, 1864, William R. Rowley, Circuit Clerk, Galena. William Farrar, County Sheriff, Galena. Ernst Frowine, County Coroner, Galena.

Nov. 7, 1865, Mathew Marvin, County Judge, Galena. Milton Wadleigh, County Surveyor, Galena. Richard Seal, County Clerk, Galena. R. S. Norris, County Treasurer, Galena.

Nov. 5, 1867, R. S. Norris, County Treasurer, Galena. Milton Wadleigh, County Surveyor, Galena.

Nov. 2, 1869, Richard Seal, County Judge, Galena. Wilbur F. Crummer, County Clerk, East Galena. Ralph S. Norris, County Treasurer, Galena. George W. Pepoon, County Superintendent of Schools, Warren. Milton Wadleigh, County Surveyor, Galena.

Nov. 8, 1870, William Pittam, Sheriff, Dunleith. William Vincent, Coroner, East Galena.

Nov. 7, 1871, Ralph S. Norris, County Treasurer, Galena. Milton Wadleigh, County Surveyor, Galena.

Nov. 5, 1872, John W. Luke, States Attorney, Galena. William R. Rowley, Circuit Clerk, Galena. William Pittam, Sheriff, Galena. George Houy, Coroner, Galena.

Nov. 4, 1873, William Speasley County Judge, Galena. Wilbur F. Crummer, County Clerk, Galena. Ralph S. Norris, County Treasurer, Galena. Robert Brand, County Superintendent of Schools, Galena.

W. Hunkins

GALENA

Nov. 3, 1874, John Sheean, Sheriff, Galena.

Nov. 2, 1875, H. Davis, County Treasurer, Galena. James H. Murphy, County Surveyor, Rush.

Nov. 7, 1876, Edward L. Bedford, States Attorney, Galena. George S. Avery, Clerk Circuit Court, Guilford. Christov Barner, Sheriff, Galena.

Nov. 6, 1877, William R. Rowley, County Judge, Galena. Wilbur F. Crummer, County Clerk, Galena. C. M. Gregory, County Treasurer, Warren. Robert Brand, County Superintendent of Schools, Galena.

ROLL OF HONOR.

In closing this History of Jo Daviess County, the historians offer, as a tribute of respect to the intelligence of the people among whom they labored for so many weeks, and whose acquaintance and hospitality they so pleasantly enjoyed, the following as a Roll of Honor that has been made up from among them:

First on the Roll is the name of *U. S. Grant*, the successful leader of the Union Army, and for eight years—from March 4, 1868, to March 4, 1876, President of the United States.

E. B. Washburne, Member of Congress eighteen years, Secretary of State, and now Minister to France.

John A. Rawlins, Brigadier General, chief on Grant's staff, and afterwards Secretary of War. Reared a farmer's boy, educated in a log cabin, and, by his inherent talent and indomitable energy, a leading lawyer.

Joseph P. Hoge, Member of Congress four years.

Thompson Campbell, Member of Congress four years, Judge U. S. Land Court, California.

Edward D. Baker, Member of Congress two years. Afterwards United States Senator from Oregon, and killed at the battle of Bales' Bluff.

Thomas Drummond, Judge U. S. Court.

Joseph B. Willis, Lieutenant Governor of Illinois.

J. R. Jones, Minister to Belgium.

A. L. Chetlain, Brigadier General, U. S. Consul to Brussels.

Gratiot Washburne, Secretary U. S. Legation to France.

Stephen Hempstead, Governor of Iowa.

W. H. Hooper, Delegate to Congress from Utah.

Moses Hallett, Judge of the Supreme Court of Colorado.

Thomas Ford, Governor of Illinois.

Hugh R. Coulter, County Judge in Wisconsin over twenty years.

H. Van Higgins, Judge Superior Court of Chicago.

S. L. Richmond, Judge Circuit Court 23d Circuit.

Dan Stone, Judge Circuit Court.

Thos. C. Browne, Judge Circuit Court.

O. C. Pratt, Judge of Superior Court, San Francisco.

Benj. R. Sheldon, Judge Superior Court of Illinois.

Thos. Hoyne, United States District Attorney of Illinois.

Wm. H. Bradley, Clerk U. S. Circuit Court.

B. H. Campbell, U. S. Marshal of Northern Illinois.

A. G. S. Wight, Member of the State Senate.

G. W. Harrison, Member of the State Senate.

L. P. Sanger, Member of the State Senate.

B. B. Howard, Member of the State Senate.

H. H. Gear, Member of the State Senate.

John H. Gear, Speaker of the House of Representatives, Iowa.

H. H. Houghton, oldest editor in the State of Illinois, U. S. Consul to Sandwich Islands.

Thomas Springer, Public Printer of California.

John A. Clark, Surveyor General of New Mexico.

Edward Breath, printer of the first newspaper in the Persian language.

Richard M. Young, first Judge Jo Daviess County, U. S. Senator and Commissioner General Land Office.

Alexander Field, Secretary of State of Illinois and afterward of Wisconsin.

Col. James W. Stephenson, a prominent member of the Legislature of Illinois.

Jesse B. Thomas, Judge of the Supreme Court of Illinois.

Benj. Mills, one of the keenest wits and most brilliant lawyers in the state.

James Craig, Member of the Legislature of Illinois, and whose wife was a grand-daughter of Daniel Boon.

Samuel Wilson, the best civil lawyer on the Pacific coast.

Dr. A. T. Crow, who at the age of sixty, raised a company of volunteers in Galena for the Mexican war, who was selected by General Taylor at the terrible battle of Buena Vista to defend the most dangerous position, supposed to be killed on that battle ground. He was a veteran soldier in 1812.

J. M. Douglass, a leading lawyer in Galena, President Illinois Central Railroad.

J. T. Mills, for many years Circuit Judge in Wisconsin.

W. R. Rowley, on staff of General Grant.

John E. Smith, Brigadier General in the Union army, now Colonel in the regular army.

Jasper A. Maltby, Captain in the Mexican War, Brigadier General in the Union army.

John C. Smith, Brigadier General Union army.

Gen. John O. Duer, now of Iowa.

J. N. Jewett, State Senator from Chicago.

Col. Charles B. Atchison, U. S. Army, now dead.

E. A. Small, prominent lawyer in Chicago.

Henry Corwith, one of the most successful bankers in the West, now in Chicago.

D. S. Harris, the oldest and one of the most successful steamboat owners and Captains on the Mississippi River.

S. M. Bartlett, publisher of the first Whig paper in Galena, and founder of the Quincy *Whig*.

Bates Dixon, Colonel of the Union army, now commander of the military forces of the Hawaiian Government.

Cyrus Aldrich, member of Congress from Minnesota.

Wm. Cary, U. S. District Attorney, Utah.

Mr. McDougal, U. S. Senator, from California.

Rev. James Lynch, at one time pastor of the M. E. Church, Galena, and afterward Secretary of the State of Mississippi.

A TABULAR STATEMENT

Showing the Totals of Real and Personal Property Assessed for Taxation in Jo Daviess County, for the Year 1877.

Compiled by W. F. Crummer, County Clerk.

PERSONAL PROPERTY.	Number	Average Value.	Assessed Value.
Horses of all ages	9,307	$33 25	$309,511
Cattle of all ages	26,324	9 44	248,633
Mules and Asses af all ages	248	36 96	9,167
Sheep of all ages	8,704	1 45	12,691
Hogs of all ages	39,795	2 29	91,319
Steam Engines, including Boilers	29	258 70	7,480
Fire or Burglar-Proof Safes	59	56 94	3,360
Billiard, Pigeon-Hole, Bagatelle or other similar Tables	22	37 27	820
Carriages and Wagons, of whatsoever kind	3,588	23 08	83,826
Watches and Clocks	2,769	4 08	11,309
Sewing and Knitting Machines	1,571	16 01	25,162
Piano Fortes	179	81 95	14,670
Melodeons and Organs	344	31 82	10,948
Franchises	------	------	510
Patent Rights	3	------	55
Steamboats, S'l'ng Ves'ls, Wharf Bts., Barges, or other water craft	1	------	550
Merchandise	------	------	254,634
Material and Manufactured Articles	------	------	16,720
Manufacturers' Tools, Implements and Machinery	------	------	7,368
Agricultural Tools, Implements and Machinery	------	------	50,460
Gold and Silver Plate and Plated Ware	------	------	1,215
Diamonds and Jewelry	------	----	120
Moneys of Banks, Bankers, Brokers, etc	------	------	1,000
Credits of Banks, Bankers, Brokers	------	------	14,700
Moneys of other than Bankers, etc	------	------	221,812
Credits of other than Bankers, etc	------	------	152,900
Bonds and Stocks	------	------	3,000
Prop. of Corporations not before enumerated (incl'd'g R. R. prop.)	------	------	10,800
Property of Saloons and Eating Houses	------	------	610
Household and Office Furniture	------	------	109,363
All other Personal Property	------	------	7,262
Investments in Real Estate and Improvements thereon	------	------	225
Shares of Stock, State and National Banks	------	------	162,500
Total Assessed Value of Personal Property	------	------	$1,844,700
REAL ESTATE.			
Improved Lands	204,605	13 77	2,816,566
Unimproved Lands	171,097	5 55	950,340
TOWN AND CITY LOTS.			
Improved Town and City Lots	4,496	152 02	703,505
Unimproved Town and City Lots	4,587	11 18	51,296
Total Assessed Value of Real Estate	------	------	$4,521,707
Total Value of all Taxable Property Assessed in County	------	------	$6,366,407

Acres of Wheat, 7,054; of Corn, 70,614; of Oats, 37,464; of Meadows, 37,580; other Field Products, 7,532; of Inclosed Pasture, 56,629; of Orchard, 2,233; of Woodland, 120,846. Number of Towns in County, 22.

STATEMENT OF THE ASSESSMENT OF PROPERTY BY TOWNSHIPS IN JO DAVIESS COUNTY AND THE TAXES LEVIED THEREON FOR THE YEAR 1877.

TOWN.	Total Assessed Value.	Total Equalized Value by Co. Board.	Total Equalized Val. by State Board.	Corporation Tax.	State Tax.	County Tax.	Town Tax.
Apple River	$216,591	$216,591	$183,224		$659 59	$883 19	$254 02
Berreman	73,084	97,732	81,372		292 77	391 93	128 24
Council Hill	152,934	138,453	114,412		412 43	551 23	76 57
Dunleith	331,267	331,267	273,953	$4,030 43	985 50	1,319 59	199 41
Derinda	248,694	245,101	203,935		734 10	982 71	128 85
East Galena	305,857	275,428	233,957		842 74	1,127 23	594 01
Elizabeth	459,310	159,310	392,566		1,412 81	1,892 46	251 32
Guilford	222,857	227,526	187,472		674 73	903 64	204 51
Hanover	401,428	361,378	303,396		1,092 01	1,463 09	175 00
Menominee	146,734	149,854	122,008		439 06	587 91	251 02
Nora	322,754	322,754	268,051		965 49	1,291 30	202 75
Pleasant Valley	220,735	242,816	201,994		726 99	973 36	175 75
Rush	308,848	308,848	251,884		906 87	1,213 75	151 62
Rice	134,250	134,250	110,540		398 08	532 50	149 34
Stockton	354,858	395,780	332,750		1,197 19	1,603 55	152 43
Scales Mound	176,790	182,296	151,857		546 51	731 68	275 41
Thomson	227,789	222,255	183,138		658 97	882 48	274 81
Vinegar Hill	104,710	115,079	93,663		337 23	451 37	124 89
Woodbine	335,916	323,058	266,947		960 29	1,286 37	101 39
Warren	526,933	491,929	431,038	381 87	1,550 56	2,077 89	175 02
Ward's Grove	171,302	184,475	151,751		545 89	731 21	75 07
West Galena	921,407	928,279	838,362		3,018 44	4,041 67	996 59
Railroad Tax (Mineral Point R.R.)	3,000	3,000	21,684	3 66	78 06	104 47	22 41
Grand total	$6,368,048	$6,357,450	$539,954	$4,423 96	$19,436 31	$26,024 58	$5,140 43

STATEMENT OF THE ASSESSMENT OF PROPERTY BY TOWNSHIPS IN JO DAVIESS COUNTY AND THE TAXES LEVIED THEREON FOR THE YEAR 1877.—*Continued.*

TOWN.	District School Tax.	District Road Tax.	Road and Bridge Tax.	Int. Regr. Bond Tax.	Municipal Tax.	Back Tax.	Total Tax.
Apple River	$1,455 00	$23 38	$301 71				$3,633 24
Berreman	628 51	56 35	405 44			$4 40	1,874 41
Council Hill	912 27	23 12	187 52			62 03	2,202 05
Dunleith	2,766 69		1,094 94			254 91	10,659 47
Derinda	689 93	29 13	815 86				3,380 58
East Galena	1,335 40	115 84	1,396 51	$807 43	$866 03	363 15	7,448 34
Elizabeth	2,331 58	45 09	1,202 08			783 52	7,918 86
Guilford	1,030 61	55 38	325 39			99 85	3,294 11
Hanover	1,489 99	760 01	607 14			229 16	5,816 40
Menominee	966 06	88 70	755 60			6 87	3,095 22
Nora	2,126 03	168 06	1,072 31			15 52	5,841 46
Pleasant Valley	1,558 71	58 90	676 10			48 39	4,213 20
Rush	2,539 34	121 28	650 16			174 74	5,757 76
Rice	576 80	143 71	504 39			99 20	2,404 02
Stockton	1,600 80	82 38	800 64			7 27	5,444 26
Scales Mound	1,495 18	24 77	604 72				3,678 27
Thomson	1,352 55	62 66	803 55			21 94	4,056 96
Vinegar Hill	738 85		101 59			29 00	1,782 93
Woodbine	1,681 88	55 89	400 23			13 73	4,499 78
Warren	5,677 76	26 99	793 87			44 67	10,728 63
Ward's Grove	911 22	41 46	173 27			2 30	2,480 43
West Galena	1,242 77	112 14	2,480 27	8,407 24	9,036 08	2,060 56	31,395 76
Railroad Tax (Mineral Point R. R.)	283 66		55 22	67 23	72 37		687 08
Grand total	$35,391 59	$2,095 24	$16,208 51	$9,281 90	$9,974 48	$4,316 22	$132,293 22

OFFICIAL VOTE OF JO DAVIESS COUNTY, ILLINOIS, NOVEMBER 7, 1876.

NAMES.	Apple River.	Berreman.	Council Hill.	Derinda.	Dunleith.	East Galena.	Elizabeth.	Guilford.	Hanover.	Menominee.	Nora.	Pleasant Valley.	Rush.	Rice.	Stockton.	Scales Mound.	Thompson.	Vinegar Hill.	Woodbine.	Warren.	Ward's Grove.	West Galena, Dist. 1.	West Galena, Dist. 2.	TOTAL.
President—																								
Hayes	108	65	107	85	117	184	228	101	163	12	122	72	172	64	138	91	90	53	144	316	37	211	227	2,907
Tilden	98	27	17	46	113	205	83	111	80	126	53	62	29	40	87	62	58	113	48	56	40	371	351	2,276
Cooper	5	----	1	9	1	----	1	2	5	----	19	34	15	----	20	2	6	----	3	13	1	2	1	140
Total	211	92	125	140	231	389	312	214	248	138	194	168	216	104	245	155	154	166	195	385	78	584	579	5,323
Governor—																								
Cullom	109	65	107	86	116	186	229	103	164	12	121	71	173	64	139	91	90	53	144	321	37	214	234	2,929
Steward	102	27	17	54	115	202	83	111	84	126	71	86	39	40	106	63	61	113	51	66	41	370	347	2,375
Lieutenant Governor—																								
Shumann	108	65	107	86	117	184	229	103	164	12	121	71	172	64	138	91	90	53	144	316	37	214	230	2,916
Glenn	98	27	16	46	113	205	83	110	80	126	53	62	29	40	87	61	58	113	48	57	40	369	248	2,169
Pickwell	5	----	1	9	1	----	----	1	4	----	20	34	14	----	20	2	6	----	3	14	1	2	1	138
Secretary of State—																								
Harlow	108	65	107	86	117	184	229	101	163	12	121	71	172	64	138	91	90	53	144	316	37	215	231	2,915
Thornton	98	27	16	46	113	205	83	111	80	126	53	60	29	40	87	61	58	113	48	57	40	367	348	2,266
Hooton	5	----	1	9	1	----	----	2	5	----	20	34	15	----	20	2	6	----	3	14	1	3	1	142
Auditor Public Acc'ts—																								
Needles	108	65	107	86	117	184	229	101	163	12	121	71	172	64	138	91	90	53	144	316	37	221	234	2,924
Hise	103	27	17	55	114	204	83	113	85	126	72	89	41	40	87	63	63	113	50	71	41	363	346	2,366
Treasurer of State—																								
Rutz	108	65	107	86	117	184	229	103	163	12	121	71	172	64	138	91	90	53	144	316	37	215	231	2,917
Gundlach	98	27	16	46	113	205	83	110	80	126	53	62	29	40	87	61	58	113	48	57	40	368	348	2,268
Aspena	5	----	1	9	1	----	----	1	5	----	20	34	14	----	20	2	6	----	3	14	1	2	--	138
Attorney General—																								
Edsall	108	65	107	86	117	184	229	101	163	12	121	71	172	64	138	91	90	53	144	318	37	215	233	2,919
Lynch	98	27	16	46	113	205	83	110	80	126	53	62	26	40	87	61	58	113	48	56	40	368	356	2,265
Coy	5	----	1	9	1	----	----	3	5	----	20	34	14	----	20	2	6	----	3	13	1	2	1	140

OFFICIAL VOTE OF JO DAVIESS COUNTY, ILLINOIS, NOVEMBER 7, 1876.—*Continued.*

NAMES.	Apple River.	Berreman.	Council Hill.	Derinda.	Dunleith.	East Galena.	Elizabeth.	Guilford.	Hanover.	Menominee.	Nora.	Pleasant Valley.	Rush.	Rice.	Stockton.	Scales Mound.	Thompson.	Vinegar Hill.	Woodbine.	Warren.	Ward's Grove.	West Galena, Dist. 1.	West Galena, Dist. 2.	TOTAL.
Fifth Congress'nl Rep.—																								
Burchard	109	66	102	83	119	183	228	101	162	12	117	70	173	64	137	91	90	54	144	318	37	205	225	2,890
Patterson	102	26	22	56	112	203	84	113	85	126	77	96	39	40	109	63	62	112	48	69	42	375	350	2,411
State B'd Equalization—																								
Warner	108	65	107	86	117	185	229	104	163	12	117	74	172	64	138	91	90	53	144	321	37	212	230	2,916
Johnson	98	27	16	46	113	205	83	110	80	126	53	62	28	40	87	61	58	113	48	52	40	371	349	2,266
Buell	5	....	1	9	1	....	....	....	....	....	20	34	15	....	20	2	6	....	3	14	2	2	1	140
State Senator, 10th Dis.—																								
McClellan	106	66	105	86	118	187	229	97	164	12	117	73	172	64	138	91	89	53	143	305	37	218	227	2,897
Stahl	105	26	20	57	113	203	84	117	82	125	72	95	38	40	107	63	64	113	53	72	42	366	345	2,402
Represent'ves, 10th Dis.—																								
Tyrrell	282	210	18	249	339	549	687	294	492	36	360	216	522	192	490½	258	270	159	426	945	111	642	691	8,738½
Hammond	315	63	57	174	354	615	252	348	252	378	219	258	123	120	310½	191	192	324	177	216	123	1110	1044	7,125½
County Attorney—																								
Bedford	108	65	107	85	117	184	230	101	163	12	117	71	172	64	138	92	90	53	144	317	37	214	231	2,912
Clerk Circuit Court—																								
Avery	107	67	103	85	115	166	231	108	163	12	110	76	172	63	141	89	88	53	141	316	37	213	222	2,878
Rockey	104	25	22	56	115	224	82	106	85	126	81	91	43	41	104	65	67	113	55	71	42	371	355	2,444
Sheriff—																								
Barner	105	66	84	85	112	155	217	73	159	17	115	71	172	55	137	82	87	56	141	303	37	207	243	2,779
Sheean	106	26	41	57	118	231	96	141	89	120	78	96	43	49	108	73	68	110	55	83	42	376	337	2,543
Coroner—																								
Passmore	106	65	118	86	117	174	229	97	164	12	119	73	172	63	138	102	100	54	143	317	37	202	215	2,903
Weirich	105	27	5	55	114	216	84	117	84	126	75	95	43	41	107	53	55	112	53	70	42	381	366	2,426

GALENA.

Galena is situated on both sides of Galena River, generally called Fever River, six miles from its junction with the Mississippi, in township 28 north, of ranges 1 east and 1 west of the 4th principal meridian, which runs through the city. Fever or Galena River was formerly navigable for any class of boats that could ascend the Mississippi. Steamboats often ascended the river two or three miles above Galena, and up the creek now known as Meeker's branch. But since the completion of the Illinois Central Railroad, the river has become so filled up from the deposit of soil washed from the bluffs on either side, broken by the picks of the miners, that now it is not navigable except when the water in the Mississippi is very high. In 1847 the west side of Main Street was about thirteen feet above the ordinary stage of water.

The ground on which the city is built rises abruptly from the river, except a narrow strip of bottom land below Bouthillier Street on the east side, and extending above Warren to Commerce Street on the west side. The highest point in the city is on High Street, near the cemetery, where the bluff is nearly 210 feet above the river. This high bluff is composed of limestone, and encircles the whole city, pierced by Meeker's branch on the north, and by two ravines extending westward from the river, one near the center and the other near the south side. The city is literally built on hills, although not the classic number—seven.

The history of the early settlement of Jo Daviess County is the early history of Galena, and as this has been given as fully as can now be gathered, in the General History, a brief review is all that is required here.

Prior to 1820, the present site of Galena was occupied by the Indians, mostly Foxes, and was a favorite trading post for the migratory traders. It is more than probable that it had been temporarily occupied by these traders for many years. Until this town was laid off by Lieut. Thomas, and named Galena by the settlers in 1826, the place was called Fever River in official documents, but was generally called La Pointe by the French, or "The Point" by the Americans. Among the earliest permanent settlers was Thomas H. January, a trader from Kentucky, who built a cabin and warehouse on the high bluff, on the point between the Fever River and Buck Lead branch, (now called Meeker's branch), and the point was known as "January's Point" by the early miners for some years, until a Frenchman named Frederic Gros Claude settled there, when it was sometimes called "Frederic's Point." But the settlement was generally known as "The Point," even after the name "Galena" had been applied to it by the miners and settlers.

It seems to be settled that Jesse W. Shull was here trading with the Indians in 1819. Also that others were here in that year, among whom were Dr. Samuel C. Muir and F. Bouthillier. It is also admitted that others may have been here at that date, or even earlier. Some accounts state that Mr. A. P. Vanmatre was here trading about that time, and, it is said, had married a Fox woman, who showed him a rich lead on Apple River. Captain David G. Bates is said to have come to "La Pointe" on a trading voyage from St. Louis in 1819, and that he found Shull and Van-

W. H. Huntington

POSTMASTER

GALENA

matre, with their Indian wives, both here at that time. It is unquestionably true that this point was well known to traders at that time, and had been well known for some years. In 1817 Stephen Hempstead, brother of Chas. S. Hempstead, went from Missouri up the Mississippi as far as Prairie du Chien, and it is said that he came to " La Pointe " at that time or soon after. He bought a quantity of furs of the Indians between here and Dunleith, probably at the Portage, in that year.

In 1820 Dr. Muir was permanently located here, practicing his profession. Mr. Vanmatre was also here, and, perhaps, Captain D. G. Bates, although he did not permanently locate until 1823, and his family came in 1826. "The Johnsons," it is said, also came about that time. Johnson left the place in 1823.

THE FIRST WHITE FAMILY.

In the general history of the mining region and sketch of its early settlement, the name of Thomas H. January occurs, and it is said he came from Pittsburgh, Pennsylvania. Since that portion of the work went to press, the authors have received a letter from Dr. J. R. Hereford, of Ferguson, Missouri, enclosing a note from Mr. C. P. Hanly, of Florissant, Missouri, whose father, now a very old man, still living, worked for Mr. January here in 1821–'2, prospecting and mining. The elder Hanly says that "January was a wealthy man in Maysville, Kentucky, but having lost the bulk of his property, came to Fever River, "La Pointe," with his family, consisting of his wife and only son, in 1821, hoping to retrieve his fortune by mining, but failed in that. Soon after his arrival his wife died, and some time afterwards her remains were sent to Kentucky for burial." (This confirms the former statement that Mr. January exhumed the remains of his wife in 1826.) "Mr. January," says Mr. Hanly, "was the best man I ever worked for." His son went to California. Mr. Hanly thinks that January "was an editor of a paper at Galena." It may be possible that Mr. January may have assisted in establishing the *Miners' Journal.* He was here at that time, but he died in Galena on Saturday, November 29, 1828, after a few days' illness, and, says the *Miners' Journal*, "was on Monday, December 1, 1828, interred with Masonic honors, in presence of a numerous assemblage." Mr. Hanly is the only known survivor of those who were here in 1821, and his testimony, in connection with facts already recorded, lead to the inevitable conclusion that Mr. January settled on the Point that bore his name, *with his family*, in 1821, and while it may not be safe to say that Mrs. January was the "first white woman who came to these mines," it is safe to conclude that she is the first white woman known to have settled here, two years at least before the arrival of Mrs. Adney, to whom that honor has heretofore been given. Whether any white family preceded Mr. January's arrival is a problem that probably must remain forever unsolved, but in the light of present knowledge it may be considered that Thomas H. January's family was the first white family who settled in Galena, or, indeed, in all northwestern Illinois.

In 1821 La Pointe was well known to the traders and voyageurs on their way up and down the Mississippi, and had become a regular stopping place for them. In 1822, the government having transferred the supervision of the Lead Mines from the General Land Office to the War Department, the previous year, began to grant leases of mineral lands, and miners from Missouri and other places began to flock to the new El Dorado.

The first arrival of any considerable number of permanent settlers, however, was in 1823, and it may be said that the real settlement of Galena dates from the arrival of Dr. Moses Meeker and James Harris, with their large colony in June of that year, and the first farm was commenced soon after. Prior to that time "The Point" could hardly be called more than an Indian trading post. The Sacs and Foxes were in possession of the whole country, and had a large and populous village on the present site of the city.

The progress of the infant settlement has been pretty fully shown in the general history of the county, and it is needless to repeat it here.

THE FIRST SURVEY.

In July, 1826, the upper street of the town was laid off into lots, by order of Lieut. Thomas, Superintendent of the Lead Mines. Whether the entire survey was completed in that year, or the Spring of 1827, does not appear of record. It was not generally called Galena until the latter date. It is said that the name "Galena" was given to it at a meeting of the settlers held probably in 1826, at which thirty-three persons were present. At this meeting it is said that it was first proposed to call the new town "Jackson," but this was lost by one vote. A proposition to call it "Jo Daviess" was rejected by a majority of eight. Mr. R. W. Chandler proposed the name of "Harrison," and this was accepted by only three majority, but in view of the differences of opinion, Mr. Chandler afterwards suggested the name "Galena" as being one upon which all could agree, as well as being very appropriate, and that name was unanimously adopted. Until this time the little cluster of cabins had been called "Fever River," or "The Point," and the first mention of the Town of Galena in official records occurs in December, 1826, but documents were dated Fever River until February, 1827. The survey of the original town is said to have been made by James Craig and Israel Mitchell, and the principal streets, with some slight changes, remain as they established them.

In June, 1827, the following regulations for the occupation of "town lots" were established by Lieut. Thomas, and signed by those who received "permits" from the Superintendent of Lead Mines, their only title until 1836 and 1837:

> It having been requested from the United States Agent for Lead Mines to grant us permission to build and enclose a small quantity of ground for our convenience, it has been granted upon the following conditions, viz.:
>
> That we will not claim any right, title, or interest in the said land other than as tenants at the will of said agent, or such other agent as may be appointed for the superintendence of the mines, and we hereby bind and obligate ourselves to quit said premises upon one month's notice to that effect being given by said agent, or other agent, it being understood that those persons who have licenses or leases are not included in this arrangement, but are to occupy agreeably to their contracts.
>
> No transfer of said ground, or improvements will be made without the consent of the agent, and will be subject to the aforesaid regulation. That we will abide by all regulations which may be made with respect to directions of streets, etc.; also to commence to build upon said ground within sixty days from the date of our permits to occupy, and not to sell or transfer the lot or piece of ground without consent and through the office of said superintendent.
>
> GALENA, June, 1827.

Appended to this document are the signatures of over three hundred of those who received permits and occupied lots in the Town of Galena, as surveyed under the direction of the superintendent in 1826–'7. The first to sign was Dr. Albion T. Crow, June 22, 1827; Dr. Addison Philleo, June

23d; James Jones, the printer, 24th; James G. Soulard, 26th. On the roll among others are the names of James Craig, Abner Field, Thomas H. January, Moses Bates, C. C. Hobart, Horatio Newhall, F. Dent, J. M. Strode, Charles Peck, J. E. Tholozan, Frederic Gros Claude (from whom January's Point was called Frederic's Point), John Henry, John Foley, James Harris, Geo. W. Jones, Nicholas Dowling, C. S. Hempstead (Jan. 6, 1829), Jesse B. Thomas, John G. Hulett (Hughlett), J. H. Lockwood. The last signatures, made in the Spring of 1829, are Geo. M. Richards, D. S. Harris and John Shackford.

Nearly all the names are the signatures of the settlers, only twenty-eight having been signed by "his X mark," and photo-engraved, this roll would furnish a valuable souvenir for the numerous descendants of the early settlers now living as well as for future generations.

The first school was opened September, 1826, by Dr. John O. Hancock.

Until 1827, the only government was that of the United States, administered by the Superintendent of Lead Mines, who settled all disputes among the people and sometimes decided in civil cases. This year, however, the County of Jo Daviess was organized, county commissioners elected, a circuit court established, and the power of the Superintendent began to wane.

1827 is also noted for the occurrence of some difficulties with the Winnebago Indians, recorded elsewhere in this volume (on page 274). It is sufficient to say here that during the continuance of the "scare," the people from the surrounding country flocked to Galena for safety. All mining operations were suspended, hundreds left the country, and business was seriously interrupted.

The 4th day of July, 1828, "Independence Day," was celebrated by the citizens of Galena by an excursion and ball on the steamer Indiana.

The first newspaper, the *Miners' Journal*, was commenced by James Jones, July 8, 1828.

1828 is noted for the flood in the Mississippi. The water was higher than it has ever been known before or since. The *Miners' Journal* of July 25, 1828, contains the statement that "the Mississippi and Fever Rivers still continue high."

Rattlesnakes were plenty in this region in the early times. The following item from the *Miners' Journal* of August 23, indicates that some of them were of respectable size:

> We are informed that a gentleman in this vicinity a few days ago killed a rattlesnake which measured 6 feet 2½ inches long, and he had within him a *badger* of nearly full size. It had 23 rattles.

Whether it was the snake or the badger that had the rattles the paper does not state distinctly. Great numbers of these venomous reptiles were killed in the Spring on the bluffs in and around the town. When they first came out in the Spring they were torpid and sluggish and were killed without difficulty.

From the 25th to the 30th, inclusive, of August, 1828, the mercury stood at 90 to 93 degrees, but on the night of September 1 there was a frost; on the 2d a heavy frost destroyed all vegetation, and on the 3d, ice one quarter of an inch thick was formed.

In September of this year there were no steam or keel-boats in the port of Galena, and several flat boats were built to transport lead to St. Louis.

In October, 1828, a subscription paper was circulated among the citizens of Galena for raising a fund for the establishment of a seminary of learning to be called the Galena Academical School. Subscribers bound themselves to pay the sum set against their respective names, and the subscription paper contained a constitution the first article of which provided that "the payment of ten dollars per annum constitutes any person a member of this society, and a donation of fifty dollars a member for life." There was to be a board of nine directors.

October 25, 1828, the *Miners' Journal* said: "Farmers are daily settling in our vicinity. The medical corps is strong and respectable, and the bar of Jo Daviess, in point of numbers, may vie with any in America." This evidently did not quite please the lawyers, for the next week the editor took pleasure in remarking "that the bar of Galena is equally respectable in point of *talents* and numbers."

During October several town meetings were held to consider the uncertain titles of the citizens to lots, and a memorial to Congress was prepared on the subject.

In the Summer of 1828 a Sabbath-school was opened and maintained for some weeks by the united efforts of Messrs. John Shackford, of St. Louis, and C. R. Roberts, of New York.

In February, 1829, a bill was passed by Congress authorizing the laying off of a town on Bean River, in the State of Illinois, and for other purposes, the full text of which will be found in Local History of the County (page 325). While the bill was pending, the *Miners' Journal* of February 7, in its comments on it, said:

The bill commences, "That a tract of land in the State of Illinois, at, and including 'Galena,' on Bean River, shall," etc. It may be that "*Galena*, BEAN RIVER" is in the State of Illinois, but if it is, the citizens of this town have no knowledge of, nor interest in *it*. But we have no doubt that Mr. Kane meant "Galena, on *Fever River*" (in the mining district).

March 17, 1829, St. Patrick's Day was celebrated in grand style under the auspices of "The Association of the Friends of Ireland in the Town of Galena and in the Mining District." (Organized December 18, 1828.) A meeting of friends of Ireland and of civil and religious liberty was held at the house of Mr. Dowling, after which the company moved off in procession, accompanied with music to Washington Hall (on Franklin, above Bench) where a sumptuous dinner was prepared by Mr. Oldenburg, the proprietor. The president of the day was Dr. Samuel C. Muir; orator of the day, Dr. Horatio Newhall; marshal, Daniel Murphy. Thirteen regular toasts were read, the last of which was as follows:

The Fair of the Lead Mines.—It needs not the *paints* of lead to give lustre to their cheeks, nor its *gravity* to add weight to their characters—9 cheers. Air—*Kiss me Sweetly.*

A large number of volunteer toasts were read by Dr. S. C. Muir, President of the day; Col. Abner Field, President of the Association; Dr. H. Newhall, orator of the day, who gave "*The British Lion.*—He roared under the lash of the HICKORY. May he tremble in fear of the *Shillalah.*" Dr. A. Philleo, Michael Byrne, J. Connolly, Patrick Gray, Daniel Murphy, Walter Dillon, John Furlong, Patrick Markey, John Foley, M. Faucette, Lt. Abercrombie, D. B. Morehouse, Dr. A. T. Crow, L. R. M. Morse, F. S. Clopton, Thos. Davis, Jas. Miller, S. Smoker, J. A. Clark, Eli S. Lattin, R. W. Chandler, Wm. Troy, Owen Riley, B. Dignan, B. M. Foley, Jas. Jones, John Dempsey, Wm. Earl, W. M. Wilson, Bernard Brady, Philip Byrne,

Jas. Doyle, Walter Furlong, John Pierce, Dennis Byrne, J. Dowling, Bernard Gray, D. G. Bates, S. Mudd and John Reed. At the close of the exercises, Ninian Edwards, Governor of Illinois; A. P. Field, Secretary of State; Judge R. M. Young and Chief Justice William Wilson were admitted as honorary members of the Association.

March 26, 1829, Fleet S. Clopton, of the firm of Clopton & Vanmatre, of Galena, was shot at Mineral Point, by H. Richardson and —— Wells, on account of a quarrel about a lead mine. Richardson fired at Vanmatre, the shot passing through the latter's thigh and entering the body of Clopton. A second shot, from Wells, entered Clopton's back above his hip, and he fell. He lived sixteen hours.

During the Winter of 1828–'9, probably, Rev. Aratus Kent applied to the American Home Missionary Society "for a place so hard that no one else would take it." About the same time, forty-four citizens of Galena subscribed and pledged the sum of $530 to "to any clergyman who shall come and discharge the duties of his sacred order for the space of one year, or to pay in proportion for a shorter period." This pledge was sent to the American Home Missionary Society, with an application for a minister. That society, probably concluding that Galena was just the place Mr. Kent wanted, appointed him on the 21st of March, 1829, and he arrived here in April following. On the 10th of May he preached his first sermon, in an unfurnished frame house, then being erected by Mr. William Watson, on Bench Street. His congregation was composed entirely of young people, as there were no old people here then. Mr. Kent was born in Suffield, Conn., January 15, 1794, graduated from Yale College in 1816, devoted four years to theological studies in New York, and was licensed to preach by the Presbytery of New York April 20, 1820. He was well known and much beloved, not only by the people of Galena, but of Northern Illinois, for many years.

May 1, 1829, weekly mail service ordered from Vandalia to Fever River by the Postmaster General.

Galena News Room, opened by James Jones, May 9, 1829. Mr. E. Coleman opened a select school on Monday, May 18, 1829. Thos. K. Rice was also teaching a select school at the same time.

In May, 1829, the people of Galena were much excited by a case of small pox on the steamer "Red Rover." Doctors Crow, Muir, Newhall, and Philleo certified that they had "examined Mr. Wilson, mate of the steamboat 'Red Rover,' and were satisfied that he had small pox," and a notice from these physicians urged upon the people the necessity of vaccination, as they had visited the boat in large numbers. It does not appear that the disease prevailed here to any extent.

In 1829 (probably, although, it may be a little a earlier), a regimental organization was effected, and J. M. Strode, a lawyer, who thought "Yankee" was spelled "Yanky," was the colonel.

On the 22d of August, 1829, Col. Strode issued a regimental order, notifying "all persons subject by law to military duty in Jo Daviess County that on the fifth day of September next, there will be election held in the first and second battalions for three captains, three first lieutenants and three second lieutenants, in each battalion in their respective company bounds."

The first company was bounded as follows:

Beginning at the ford of the Sinsinawa River where the road leading from Galena to Menominee crosses the same, including all persons living on the southeast side of said stream from that point to its mouth; thence down the Mississippi River to the mouth of Fever River; thence such a course as shall include Shannon's Mill on the Small Pox; thence such a course as will include Hempstead's furnace, Cottle's furnace and all the settlements on both sides of the Small Pox as high up the same as when a due north line will strike the northeast corner of Col. Mitchell's garden on Fever River; thence up the southeast side of Fever River to Lockwood's furnace, including it and the settlements at it; thence such a course as to include Meeker's farm, to the place of beginning. The place of holding election for officers in the first company shall be at Harris' grocery, Main Street, in the Town of Galena.

The other companies were as particularly bounded, and the order was signed "By order of J. M. Strode, Colonel of the Jo Daviess regiment, 3d brigade, 1st Division Illinois Militia; Stanislaus Mudd, Adj."

In accordance with the order, the militiamen of the first company met at Harris' grocery on Main Street, on the 5th of September, 1829, and elected Jesse B. Thomas, Jr., Captain; Milton M. Maughs, 1st Lieutenant; Daniel S. Harris, 2d Lieutenant.

The new steamboat Galena, Capt. D. G. Bates, was advertised to leave St. Louis August 22, 1829, but the following extract shows the date of her arrival at Galena, on the 29th day of October:

The new and long-looked-for steamboat GALENA, *D. G. Bates*, Master, arrived here on Thursday morning last. Much benefit has already been witnessed by her first arrival; for flour fell from ten dollars to eight dollars per barrel within two hours after she came to this port—*Galena Advertiser*, Nov. 2, 1829.

In the general history of the county it is stated that, so far as is known, the first wagon loaded with lead from Galena to Chicago was in 1833. This is incorrect. That was probably the first ox-wagon, but in August, 1829, Mr. J. G. Soulard's wagon and mule team took a load of lead (3,000 pounds) "to Chicago near the southernmost bend of Lake Michigan." The Galena *Advertiser* of Sept. 14, 1829, says: "This is the first wagon that has ever passed from the Mississippi River to Chicago. The route taken from mines was to Ogee's Ferry on Rock River, eighty miles; thence east course sixty miles to the Missionary establishment on the Fox River of the Illinois; and thence in a northeasterly course sixty miles to Chicago. Making the distance from this place to Chicago, as traveled, 200 miles. The trip out was performed in eleven, and the return trip in eight days."

The first frost in 1829 occurred on the 3d day of September.

Sept. 14, 1829, fresh butter was selling in Galena at 37½ cents per pound.

Monday evening, February 1, 1830, a meeting of the citizens of Galena was held at the house of Moses Swan, on the corner of Main and Green Streets, for the purpose of organizing for protection against fire.

Moses Meeker was called to the chair, and J. B. Brown appointed Secretary. At this meeting it was

Resolved, That there be a company formed, styled the Galena Fire and Protection Company.

Col. J. M. Strode, Capt. M. C. Comstock, and Capt. C. D. W. Johnson were appointed a committee to solicit subscriptions from the citizens for the purpose of procuring forthwith fire-hooks, ladders, axes, etc. Robert Graham, M. M. Maughs, and John Atchison were appointed a committee "to examine forthwith all stoves, fire-places, and chimneys in this town," and to request proprietors to keep on hand a number of buckets equal to the number of their stoves and fire-places, with the further request "that they will, on any alarm of fire being given, repair immediately to the place with said buckets," and aid in extinguishing the fire. The meeting adjourned to meet again on Thursday, at four o'clock P. M. As the citizens were groping their way home in the darkness, a fire was discovered emerging from the roof of a drinking-house kept by Major T. B. Farnsworth, near the corner of Main and Green Streets. Here was an opportunity for these primitive firemen to exhibit their prowess in fighting the fiery fiend, and the "b'hoys" scampered to the scene of action, mounted the roof, and cutting away a portion of the shingles and boards, discovered the position of the fire, and extinguished it with a few well aimed buckets of water. The Major was absent on a fishing excursion, and the jolly firemen helped themselves to "sperets."

There are no records of subsequent meetings, but the company was duly organized, Mr. Wann says, by the choice of C. D. W. Johnson as Captain, succeeded afterwards by Captain H. H. Gear. The town was divided into four fire wards, and a notice in the Galena *Advertiser* of Feb. 22, contains the following:

Inasmuch as the "Fire Implements" will be distributed in the several wards, and to avoid difficulty in the event of fire, the following arrangement is deemed necessary, viz.: For the First Ward, D. R. Davis, Director; M.C. Comstock, L. R. M. Morse, James G. Soulard, R. M. Brush, N. T. Head, Lewis Oldenburg, J. B. Brown, Daniel Wann, John Atchison, W. P. Tilton, Leonard Goss, William Hempstead, Frederick Stahl, B. M. Foley, Philip Byrne, Harvey Mann, John Foley, and A. Baker, Esqs.

For the Second, B. Dignan, Director; A. T. Crow, John Reed, E. S. Lattin, H. Rolette T. B. Farnsworth, Moses Meeker, Moses Swan, D. S. Harris, H. Newhall, D. G. Bates, J. F. O'Neil, Owen Riley, Samuel Reed, Garey White, William Boggess, Jentry McGee, William Townsend, and Charles R. Bennett, Esqs.

For the Third, Major John Campbell, Director; J. M. Strode, E. McSweeney, Addison Philleo, Robert Graham, J. R Vineyard, J. K. Hammett, James Jones, G. C. Parker, Patrick Gray, John Turney, James Bennett, William Campbell, James Poland, Patrick Markey, James Campbell, Thomas Bennett, N. Dowling and Z. Bell, Esqs.

For the Fourth, Matthias Shears, Director; T. S. Smith, Benson Hunt, John S. Miller, Daniel Harrison, Joseph Bartroe, Mason Taylor, Esqs., and others names not reported.

Axemen, M. M. Maughs, Director; Sylvester Baker, Michael Byrne, A. C. Swan, S. D. Carpenter, John Howe and Alfonzo Delauney, Esqs. Property Guards: Benjamin Mills James Barnes, William Bennett and R. M. Young, Esqs.

This was the first fire organization in Galena, and embraced nearly all the leading men of the town—judges, lawyers, doctors and merchants—all ran with their buckets and axes when a fire occurred.

The following item shows what was considered a remarkable feat of traveling in 1832:

Rapid Traveling.—Two gentlemen arrived at this place on the steamboat Enterprise, in twenty days from the City of New York, out of which they were detained, in waiting for conveyance, *five* days.—*Galenian, July* 18, 1832.

On Saturday, May 26, 1832, Simeon Kelsey was shot in Main Street, Galena, by Charles McCoy. They were both miners, residing about ten miles from town. McCoy surrendered himself to the civil authorities, was examined and discharged. This was the first event of the kind that ever occurred in Galena.

The Galena Academy was in operation in the Summer of 1832, during the Black Hawk War, under the superintendence of Mr. J. Wood, assisted by Mrs. Wood and Mr. Robinson. The first quarterly examination occurred on Monday, July 30, 1832, and the *Advertiser* of that date spoke highly of the skill of the teachers and the proficiency of the pupils.

The cholera prevailed to a fearful extent in 1832. The steamboat Warrior, with a detachment of soldiers from Fort Armstrong, arrived at Galena

August 31 with quite a number of cases on board; several had died. It was a gloomy time for the settlers, and there was mourning and sorrow in many a household, for the terrible scourge added to the horrors of the Indian war. The disease did not finally subside until November.

Adulteration of articles of food is supposed to be a modern invention. The following announcement in the *Galenian* of December 19, 1832, shows that the custom may date back farther than is generally supposed. The *Galenian* says: "Fine yellow corn meal has been brought to this place and sold for London ground mustard."

The citizens of Galena held a public meeting at the Court House on Monday, Dec. 22, 1834, to consider the subject of fires. William Smith, Chairman, Dr. H. Newhall, Secretary. At this meeting the town was divided into four districts, and four committees appointed to examine stove-pipes, chimneys, etc. It would seem from this that the organization in 1830 had failed to accomplish its purpose, or had become extinct.

1st District—From Abner Edes' tavern to Meeker's furnace. Committee, Moses Hallett, Matthias Shears and Abner Edes.

2d District—From Meeker's furnace to the street running north of Dr. Newhall's dwelling house (Hill Street). Committee, A. L. Crow, John Dowling and James Bennet.

3d District—From Newhall's house to Cross Street between Atchison's store and Baldwin's coffee house (Warren Street). Committee, B. Dignan, P. F. Schimer and H. Newhall.

4th District—From Baldwin's to the lower end of town. Committee, Col. A. G. S. Wight, M. Byrne and D. B. Morehouse.

T. B. Farnsworth, Wm. Townsend and Leonard Goss were appointed a committee to collect the fire hooks, ladders, etc., heretofore prepared and deposit them in some convenient place for use in case of fire.

A resolution was adopted requesting the Senator and Representative from this district to procure the passage of a special act authorizing the citizens to incorporate the Village of Galena.

Another meeting was held at the Court House August 25, 1835, to consider the question of procuring fire engines and forming a fire company. Dr. H. Newhall, Chairman, Daniel Wann, Secretary. Capt. H. H. Gear, William Waddell and Daniel Wann were appointed a committee to circulate a subscription paper for that purpose. The meeting adjourned to Wednesday evening, Aug. 26, when the committee reported that the sum of $1,557 had been subscribed, and that they thought that the further sum of $215 could be secured, making $1,772, which the committee thought would be sufficient to procure an engine of the first class.

The same committee was instructed to purchase an engine.

The subject of incorporating the town of Galena was then taken up; addresses were made by Col. J. W. Stephenson, Capt. H. H. Gear and John Turney, Esq., when it was unanimously resolved that the town ought to be incorporated. John Turney was requested to give the necessary notice for calling a town meeting of the citizens to take a vote on the matter.

Notice was given accordingly, and on the 7th of September a town meeting was held at the Court House; Benjamin Mills was chosen president and Geo. W. Campbell, clerk. Sixty-five votes were thrown for incorporation. One against. Record of this meeting was filed with the county commissioners Oct. 2, 1835.

September 15, 1835, a meeting was held for the election of Trustees of the Town of Galena, which resulted in the election of M. C. Comstock, Dr. H. Newhall, Reuben W. Brush, John Howe and John S. Miller.

Edwd. L. Bedford
STATES ATTORNEY
GALENA

Until 1827 the only government exercised was administered by the superintendent of lead mines. At that date the County of Jo Daviess was organized and civil authority was exercised by the County Commissioners Court, while the superintendent still exercised some authority. The only attempt at local self-government by the people of Galena seems to have been repeated efforts to protect themselves against fire, and this had now resulted in a town or village organization.

October 3, 1835, the newly elected trustees held their first meeting in the court house, and organized by the election of M. C. Comstock, president, and William B. Green, clerk. H. H. Gear was elected town treasurer, and James Kemp, town constable and collector.

At the next meeting of the trustees, on the second day of December, 1835, present, Comstock, Miller, Howe and Newhall.

The president and trustees of the Town of Galena ordained as follows:

The limits of the town shall extend from the house built by Mr. Snyder, and now owned by H. H. Gear (then standing in the continuation of Main Street, a little south of Green Street) to the house built by J. S. Miller (on Branch and Dodge Streets) and now owned by Abner Eads, and extending due east and west from the above mentioned houses one half a mile and including said buildings.

It was also ordained:

The town shall be divided into four districts, the first to include all that part lying south of the cross street which passes Farnsworth & Ferguson's and Atchison's stores (Warren Street); the second shall extend from said cross street to Perry Street; the third from Perry Street to Meeker's old furnace (near Franklin Street), and the remaining part of the town shall constitute the fourth district.

At this meeting stringent ordinances were passed for the protection of the town against fire. Stove pipes must not be passed through roofs or partitions unless properly protected. No hay, straw, chips or shavings could be burned in town within forty feet of any building on penalty of five dollars. Any person occupying any shop or other building wherein shavings or other combustible material may be contained, shall, under penalty of five dollars, remove the same at least twice a week by Wednesday and Saturday. No person in removing chips, shavings, etc., shall scatter or throw them into the streets or alleys or permit the same to be done under penalty of five dollars. No person shall carry any fire in, into, or through any street or lot except the same be placed or carried in some close or safe vessel, under penalty of five dollars. The same penalty was attached to firing any squib, cracker, gun powder or fire works or any gun or pistol in said town.

A fire warden was ordered to be appointed in each district, whose duty it was made to visit and examine once within the first week of each of the months of October, November, December, January, February, March and April of each year, every house, store and shop in his district, and ascertain and report to the board of trustees all violations of these ordinances.

There does not appear to have been any further use for the board of trustees. Having provided regulations for the prevention of fires, their duties apparently ended. The appointment of fire wardens, if any were made, was not recorded, and the next meeting of record was held August 30, 1836, at which the only business transacted was the passage of the following order:

Ordered, That an election be held at the court house in Galena on Thursday, September 15 next, for Trustees for the Town of Galena. Polls of election to be opened at eight o'clock A. M. and to continue open until six o'clock P. M., and that John Campbell, N. T.

Head, and Matthias Shears be appointed Judges of said election, with power to fill any vacancy and to appoint clerks.

Thus, from the records now accessible, and the files of the *Northwestern Gazette*, it would seem that the united efforts of the citizens had been directed since 1830, principally toward providing protection against fire, and the first municipal organization had confined itself entirely to legislating against fire.

On the 2d day of July a bill passed by Congress entitled "An Act to amend an act entitled an act authorizing the laying off a town on Bean River, in the State of Illinois, and for other purposes, approved February 5, 1829," was approved. The full text of this bill will be found in the Local History (pp. 325). Under its provisions Samuel Leech, of Quincy, and Daniel Wann and John Turney, of Galena, were appointed Commissioners, and entered at once upon their duties. James Craig was appointed Surveyor, and for the second time the Town of Galena was surveyed by United States authority. This important matter is fully treated in the Local History.

The second meeting for the election of Trustees for the Town of Galena was held on the 15th day of September, 1836, and N. T. Head, Dickinson B. Morehouse, Philip F. Schirmer, Abraham Hathaway and Robert B. McDowell were elected. There is no record to show the number of votes thrown, but the *Gazette* says, "great apathy existed, and not more than half the votes in town were polled.

The new board met and organized September 19, 1836. Abraham Hathaway, President; W. B. Green, Clerk; Dr. H. Newhall, Treasurer; Robert M. Miller, Town Constable and Collector of Fines. This board proceeded at once to business, and immediately after perfecting its organization, passed an ordinance entitled "A Law appointing and prescribing the duties of certain officers therein named." Chapters I. and II. established the office of Street Commissioner, and defined his duties. To him was committed the custody of all real estate belonging to the corporation; the collection of rents due it; the location of streets under direction of the Trustees; the repairing of streets and wharves, paving, Mac-adamizing streets, etc., and he was made Surveyor by virtue of his office.

Chapter III. defined the duties of the Town Treasurer. This officer was to recover all moneys belonging to the corporation, and deposit them in the Branch Bank of the State of Illinois, at Galena.

Section 4 of Chapter III. appointed W. B. Green Street Commissioner.

Chapter IV., passed on the 20th, defined the duties of the Clerk.

Chapter V. created the office of Town Inspector, who was to be appointed each and every year, whose principal duties appeared to be to abate nuisances.

September 21, the following orders were passed:

It is hereby ordained that the survey of the Town of Galena, made by James Craig in 1836, by authority of the United States, under the superintendence of the Commissioners appointed by the President of the United States, shall be, and the same is hereby declared to be, the survey of the Town of Galena, and that the map of the same furnished by him shall be carefully preserved in the clerk's office, together with the field notes of said survey.

The town was divided into three street or road districts, as follows:

All that part lying below Cross Street (Morrison's alley) was the first district, and Jesse Morrison appointed Supervisor. The second district was between Cross Street and Diagonal Street, S. D. Carpenter, Supervisor. The third district was above Diagonal and Cross Streets, George Madeira, Supervisor.

September 27, the Trustees passed "An ordinance for the appointment of Assessors," specifying the number (two) and prescribing their duties.

The same day an order was passed "for the graduating of Main Street, and paving sidewalks in the Town of Galena. This order provided for "graduating the west side of Main Street, at the expense of the corporation, sufficient for one track from the sidewalk." When this was done the owners of lots on the west side of Main Street, from United States Warehouse to Franklin Street were required to pave the sidewalk in front of their premises, "with good strong bricks or flag-stone, said pavements to be six inches wide." This is the first known provision for sidewalks in Galena.

October 7, 1836, Main Street was ordered to be graded. October 24, George W. Campbell and R. W. Brush were appointed Assessors for the corporation for the present year.

November 3, 1836, *Ordered*, That the corporation of Galena assume the payment of balance due on engines, and that orders issue on the Treasurer to H. H. Gear and Daniel Wann for the same, with interest until paid.

This is the first order involving present or future payment of money made by the Trustees, and in this the amount is not specified. It will be remembered that in August, 1835, the citizens of the town had subscribed liberally for the purchase of a fire engine, and the committee, consisting of Messrs. Wann, Gear and Waddell, instructed to make the purchase. It appears, however, that the committee decided it to be advisable to order two from the builders. They were small engines, known as the "Selye"* and arrived here probably in September, 1836.

June 25, 1836, the committee notified the public that "the engine was shipped from Rochester and arrived in Buffalo last Fall, and in all probability has reached Chicago ere this, and is expected here daily." They desired the subscriptions to be paid up. On the 9th of September a call was published in the *Northwestern Gazette* for a meeting of citizens on the 10th to select suitable candidates for Trustees, and to organize two fire companies. The following notice explains the order of the board, and also determines the fact that the engines had arrived prior to September 17, and explains why they reached here *via* Green Bay.

The undersigned committee appointed by the citizens of Galena to raise, by subscription, funds to procure two fire engines, beg leave to report, that the sum of $1,794 was subscribed for that purpose, and about a year since the committee ordered the engines, the cost of which was $2,431.76, including the sum of $235.56, being costs and charges of transportation. The committee have received from the subscribers the sum of $1,494, leaving a balance due on the subscription of $300. The committee is bound to the engine builder for the balance due, say $937.76—which amount they are liable to be called on for. Capt. Gear, one of the committee, has advanced the sum of $117.78 on account of freight and charges on the engines; this amount, with the sum due the builder, in all, say $1,055.54, remains to be provided for. The committee therefore most respectfully ask of the citizens to place them in funds to meet their engagements. The engines have arrived in good order, with the necessary apparatus, subject to the inspection of the subscribers. When they were ordered the builder was instructed to forward them to Buffalo, and from thence to Chicago;

* Selye manufactures his engines at Rochester, New York. They were warranted to throw water from 100 to 150 feet, according to size. His prices, including drag-ropes, suction hose, wrenches, axe, torches, pilot, etc., were: For these designed for twenty men, discharging 200 gallons of water per minute, $700; sixteen men, 140 gallons per minute, $600; twelve men, eighty gallons, $400. The committee purchased the largest, and hose and extra, made up the sum paid.

but when they arrived at Buffalo the house who received them departed from the instructions, and shipped them to Green Bay, and from thence to Fort Winnebago, which accounts for the great delay in getting them, and also for the charges for transportation.

DANIEL WANN,
H. H. GEAR,
GALENA, Sept. 17, 1836. WM. WADDELL.

Although the engines, the Cataract and the Neptune arrived early in September, 1836, it does not appear that they were manned until nearly two months later, and not until after the corporation had assumed the payment of the money advanced by the committee. The inference is that the committee very wisely refused to allow them to be used until some provision was made for paying for them. Tuesday, Nov. 8, two fire companies were organized—Galena Fire Association No. 1 and No. 2. The *Gazette and Advertiser* of Nov. 12 contained the following:

We congratulate our citizens upon the organization of two fire companies. The meeting on Tuesday night last was well attended and great unanimity of feeling prevailed in the election of officers, etc. Both engines are well manned, and by men, too, that can be depended upon in case of fire.

Unfortunately, the *Gazette* made no report of the meeting, and the names of the officers and men were not considered of sufficient importance to be recorded. Every body in town then, knew who they were, and why publish any thing that every body knew? Nobody remembers who they were now, and it is only known that of No. 1—the Cataract—George M. Mitchell, and of No. 2—the Neptune—William H. Hooper, were the secretaries.

Nov. 15, the following fire wardens were appointed: Ward One, John C. Smith; Ward Two, Charles Peck; Ward Three, George Madeira; Ward Four, Matthias Shears.

The same day Samuel D. Carpenter was appointed Town Inspector, and Michael Byrne, collector of tax. An ordinance was passed prohibiting burning coal-pits, brick or lime kilns, or smelting lead within the limits of the town under penalty of five dollars for every day's offense, "and the same are hereby declared public nuisances," and turned over to the Inspector.

Thus far no provision had been made for raising money except by fines, but on the same day the following order is recorded:

Ordered, That P. F. Schirmer and D. B. Morehouse be authorized to borrow on account of the Corporation of Galena three hundred dollars.

Nov. 24, in order to repair the streets the Trustees ordained that every male inhabitant of the town over twenty-one years old should labor on the streets not less than three days in each year.

The first assessment of tax in Galena was made on the 5th of December, 1836, as follows:

The list of assessments having been presented by the Assessors: The President and Trustees of the Town of Galena do ordain, That a tax of one half per cent be collected on the assessment for the year 1836.

During the Winter of 1836–'7 the Legislature of Illinois passed "An act to change the corporate powers of Galena." This act required that an election should be held on the first Monday in April, 1837, for the election of Town Trustees, and on that day seven Trustees were elected, viz.: H. H. Gear, Daniel Wann, John L. Slaymaker, D. B. Morehouse, R. W. Brush, J. L. Kirkpatrick and P. F. Schirmer. On the 10th of April the board organized by unanimously electing D. B. Morehouse, President, and W. B. Green, Clerk.

The first act of the board was to pass an ordinance regulating the harbor in the Town of Galena, and appointed S. D. Carpenter Wharf and Lumber Master. Geo. W. Campbell was elected Treasurer, and Martin Haines appointed Town Constable, Charles Peck, Collector, W. B. Green, Street Commissioner.

May 3, 1837, the following order was passed:

Ordered, That Martin Haines be, and he is hereby, allowed one hundred and fifty dollars per annum, to be paid quarterly, from 1st inst., as compensation for extra services as Town Constable.

The constable was the first salaried officer in Galena.

At a special meeting, May 10, 1837, John Stark, Esq., was appointed attorney and counselor for the corporation.

May 22, 1837. The trustees passed an ordinance for providing a corporation seal and fixing the device therefor, as follows:

SECTION 1. The device of the Common Seal of the Corporation of the Town of Galena shall be a steamboat. Shall be so engraved as to represent by its impression the device aforesaid, surrounded by a scroll inserted with the words, "Corporation Town of Galena, Illinois." Said seal shall be circular, and not more than one and seven eighths inches in diameter.

July 12. The town was divided into five wards, and the following persons appointed fire wardens: 1st, J. C. Smith; 2d, Geo. Ferguson; 3d, John Turney; 4th, M. Shears; 5th, M. Faucette.

August 16. The collector was ordered to proceed forthwith to collect last year's tax, and the following order was passed, which is commended to officials of later day:

It is hereby ordained that in case any member of the Board of Trustees shall omit to attend any stated or special meeting of the trustees, he shall forfeit and pay to the treasurer, for the use of the corporation, the sum of one dollar; and it is made the duty of the clerk to report all such absentees to the treasurer, who shall thereupon collect the fines. Provided, that the absence from town of any member at the time said meeting is called, shall excuse such member from the payment of such fine.

This does not appear to have been remarkably effective, however, as at the two meetings immediately following the passage of the order, no quorum was present.

August 31. J. L. Kirkpatrick having resigned, Abraham Hathaway was elected to fill the vacancy, and George Ferguson was elected in place of P. F. Schirmer declined to serve.

October 4. Daniel Wann, R. W. Brush, A. Hathaway and Geo. Ferguson were fined one dollar each for non-attendance. Several others were fined from time to time, but afterwards all fines were remitted, on account of faithful services.

Money was scarce in the town treasury, and on the 5th of October, 1837, the town fathers unanimously passed the following order, on motion of Mr. Morehouse:

Ordered, That the clerk prepare orders on the treasurer, with the seal of the corporation plainly impressed upon them, and signed by him in the usual way, and of the following denominations, viz.: Of five dollars each, one hundred orders; of seven dollars and fifty cents each, forty orders; and of ten dollars each, twenty orders, making in all the amount of one thousand dollars, which shall, as soon as prepared, be delivered to the treasurer, who shall be charged with the same. The treasurer shall issue the above orders in exchange for the larger orders now issued or hereafter to be issued by the clerk, who shall continue to issue orders in the usual way upon all accounts allowed and passed by the Board of Trustees.

This was the commencement of the issue of town scrip, afterwards more abundantly issued, and which was bought up, some of it as low as six cents on the dollar and funded by the city as its face. A very large amount of corporation paper was issued.

At this meeting, William Bennett was appointed assessor, and a Fourth Road district created on the east side of Fever River, with A. G. S. Wight, supervisor.

January 16, 1838, a tax of a half per cent was levied on the amount of real estate and personal property returned by the assessor.

About this time the building of a public market house was agitated, and on the 19th day of February, 1838, Daniel Wann, J. L. Slaymaker and George Ferguson were appointed a committee to select a suitable site for a market house, and report at the next meeting.

A committee consisting of Daniel Wann, H. H. Gear, and D. B. Morehouse, was also appointed to correspond with the Commissioners of Public Works, in relation to building a bridge across Fever River.

March 19, 1837, *Ordered*, That the report of the committee for selecting a market square, designating lots Nos. 65, 64, 63, 62 and 61, between Hill and Perry Streets, fronting on Commerce Street, be, and the same is, hereby received.

Ordered, That Messrs. H. H. Gear and D. B. Morehouse be appointed a committee to attend at commissioners meeting, for laying off the Town of Galena, and request them to declare the lots designated by the committee on the subject of market house, to be left as public property.

The clerk was ordered to make out a complete account of the fiscal concerns of the corporation from September 1, 1836, to March 20, 1838, which he subsequently did, as follows:

A Complete Statement of the Fiscal Accounts of the Galena Corporation, from 1*st September*, 1836, *to the* 20*th March*, 1838.

Mar. 20,	RECEIPTS.		
1838.	To amount received for building walls	$320 25	
	" " making sidewalk	777 16	
	" " from wharf and lumber master	925 36	
	" " " merchant, tavern, and dray lic'ns's	2,680 00	
	" " " fines and circus licenses	70 00	
	" " " tax, 1836 and '7, on real and personal property	5,048 77	
	Whole amount of actual receipts		$9,821 54
	Add small orders given treasurer for change		3,000 00
	Balance orders outstanding		4,718 90
			$17,540 44
	Amount due and in hands of collector for collection, to wit:		
	For sidewalk	$454 00	
	For walls	390 12	
	For balance tax on real and personal property, for 1836 and 1837	3,100 57	
	Whole amount in hand of collector for collection		$3,944 69
	Amount for sidewalk and walls unfinished and not yet assessed, to wit:		
	For sidewalks	$500 00	
	For walls	150 00	
	Whole amount not yet assessed		$650 00
	Balance against corporation		124 21
			$4,718 90

Mar. 20. EXPENDITURES.

For excavating and filling in Main and Cross streets	$5,455 40	
" " Franklin, Bench, and Diagonel streets	2,150 25	
For building walls	2,341 39	
" making sidewalks	1,731 16	
" fire engine	1,078 00	
" amount expended on wharf	324 36	
" " paid for printing	120 00	
" " " street commissioner	400 00	
" " " treasurer	153 06	
" " " clerk	200 00	
" " " wharf master and inspector	124 00	
" " " collector	59 19	
" " " assessor	45 00	
" " " attorney	150 00	
" " " constable	37 50	
" " refunded on licenses	60 00	
Miscellaneous expenses, hook, ladders, etc.	111 13	
Whole amount expenditures		$14,540 44
Small orders issued and left with treasurer for change		3,000 00
		$17,540 44
Balance orders unredeemed		4,718 90
By balance		$124 21

I, W. B. Green, Clerk of Board of President and Trustees of Galena Corporation, do hereby certify the foregoing to be a correct account of the fiscal concerns of the said corporation, from the commencement of its operations up to the 20th of March, 1838.

W. B. GREEN, Clerk.

On the 2d day of April, 1838, a new board of trustees was elected, as follows: John L. Slaymaker, Dickinson B. Morehouse, Daniel Wann, John Dowling, John Campbell, Hezekial H. Gear, and Dudley Simmons. On the 3d the board organized by the election of D. B. Morehouse, President, and W. B. Green, Clerk. W. B. Green was appointed Street Commissioner; George W. Campbell, Treasurer; J. W. Foster, Town Constable and Collector; S. D. Carpenter, Wharf and Lumber Master; John Stark, Attorney.

Messrs. Slaymaker, Morehouse, and Dowling, were appointed a committee to report a plan and estimate for a market house, and the probable expense of filling Market Square. At the next session, April 9, the committee reported a plan, which was unanimously adopted, and Messrs. Dowling, Morehouse, and Slaymaker, were constituted a committee to enter into arrangements for building the same, but there is no record to show that anything was done.

May 14, 1838, the location of the northern terminus of the Central Railroad was felt to be of such "deep and vital interest and importance to the inhabitants of the Town of Galena," and the people felt that "they had a right to be heard in the matter," that the board directed its clerk to call a meeting of the citizens, on Saturday the 19th, to consider the matter. On the 21st, on motion of H. H. Gear, the following preamble and resolution was adopted:

WHEREAS, The opening of the "Central Railroad" at Galena is an event of immense importance and interest to the citizens of this place; therefore,

Resolved, That the citizens of this town be requested to meet to-morrow at 5 o'clock, P. M., to take measures to notice the event in a becoming manner.

The location evidently was not eminently satisfactory, for on the 28th, at a session of the board, Mr. Gear moved that the Board of Public Works be requested to cause a resurvey of the termination of the Central Railroad to be made, and this matter was laid over until night, at "early candle light." In the evening, on motion of Mr. Gear, the following was adopted:

WHEREAS, In the opinion of this Board the present location of the northern termination of the Central Railroad, on the east side of Fever River, is a measure hostile to the interest of this town, and in violation of law; now, therefore, we, the Trustees, in Town Council convened, do hereby protest against the present location of said northern termination of the Central Railroad, and request the Board of Public Works to order a new survey of the line to Galena, in such way as to fully redress the wrong. This protest to be forwarded to the Board of Public works under the seal of the corporation.

The following order, passed June 8, 1838, provided for the issue of an indefinite amount of town scrip:

Ordered, That the President procure a sufficient number of blank orders, properly engraved or printed on bank note paper, and that, when obtained, all orders issued, either in exchange for these now outstanding or otherwise, shall bear interest at the rate of six per cent per annum from date thereof until redeemed.

Subsequently, on the 7th of August, the following appears of record:

Ordered, That the blank orders received, bearing interest at six per cent, shall be signed by the president as President of the Board of Trustees, and by the clerk, and they be authorized to exchange said orders for any previously given out, and for all debts due by the corporation.

The constable, who was chief of police, was, on the 8th day of June, directed to find a place suitable for a jail or lock-up, and reported that the under story of the house on Main and Diagonal Streets, owned by G. W. Harrison, would answer the purpose by putting in a floor.

There was a strong effort made to induce the receiver, Col. John Dement, who sold the lots and out-lots in the Town of Galena, in accordance with the provisions of the act of July 2, 1836, to receive corporation paper or "town scrip" in payment, and it was argued that inasmuch as the money was to be expended for public buildings here, the scrip could be paid over to the local authorities as so much money. In anticipation that this paper might be taken by the receiver, the Board of Trustees passed the following ordinance on the 18th of July, 1838:

July 18, 1838. *Be it ordained by the President and Board of Trustees of the Town of Galena*, That all orders for the payment of money issued by this corporation, and which shall be taken by the land office as payment for lots and out-lots in the town of Galena, to be sold by the United States, shall bear interest from the day of sale at the rate of six per cent per annum, and shall be redeemed in current bank paper in three equal payments—first in 12 months, second in 15 months, and third in 18 months—and that to the faithful performance of this the faith of the corporation is hereby pledged.

Be it further ordained, That the President of the Board is hereby empowered and directed to execute, in the name of the corporation, under the seal thereof, a bond covenanting for the faithful performance of all stipulations contained in this ordinance.

Be it further ordained, That the President of this Board proceed forthwith to make arrangements to procure orders of the corporation to the amount of seven thousand dollars, to be taken in payment by the land office under conditions and stipulations contained in this ordinance.

The sale took place, but the corporation paper, although backed by the foregoing pledges, was not current at the counter of the Receiver. It had become depreciated, and subsequently became almost worthless. It was issued in large quantities; the stuff was, it is said, at one time kept in an old shoe-box under the clerk's counter, and persons so disposed could easily help themselves. Whether any of it that was subsequently funded by the City of Galena was obtained without consideration or not, it is certain that

C Barner

SHERIFF

GALENA

it was paid out by the town authorities to all who would take it in payment at the rate of about three dollars for one, and it was hawked about the streets at twenty, fifteen, ten, and even six per cent of its face. As before stated, after the city was organized, this paper was funded at par in city bonds, and a considerable portion of the present city debt springs from this source.

After the sale, the town fathers became exercised lest the money, if it should be paid over to the county commissioners, should not be expended to suit them and the people of the town, and on the 30th day of July the board adopted the following resolution:

Resolved, That the Receiver of Public Moneys be and he is hereby requested to withhold moneys received from the sale of town lots from the county commissioners, until such time as the trustees of the town shall have security, and be notified that said money will be properly appropriated according to law, and that a copy of this resolution be signed by the clerk, and forwarded to Col. Dement, Receiver of Public Moneys.*

Whether this resolution deferred the payment of the money to the Commissioners is doubtful, but there seemed to be a lingering suspicion to that effect in the minds of the County Court, and they probably concluded that the money would be forthcoming if an amicable arrangement could be made with the town, for, on the 8th of September, 1838, the trustees received a communication from the county commissioners, concerning certain public moneys arising from the sale of town lots, now in the hands of the receiver, and the following order was passed:

Ordered, That a committee of three be appointed from this board to make such arrangement with the county commissioners, with respect to these funds, as to them may seem right, and any arrangement they may make shall be binding and in full force on the part of the Town of Galena.

On the 10th, this committee reported that the commissioners and trustees had agreed mutually to proceed forthwith to expend said fund in building a jail and market house in the Town of Galena, in such manner as to them may seem most beneficial to the public.

On the 11th, on motion of Mr. Gear, a committee was appointed to meet with the county commissioners for the purpose of making necessary arrangements for the erection of a jail and market house with all possible expedition, and Gear, Slaymaker and †John Atchison were appointed.

There is no subsequent record to show that any further action was taken in the market house matter. The commissioners received the money and appropriated it to building a court house. Later in this history, the reply of the commissioners to the mayor and aldermen of the city will be found, which should be read with the above record of their action in view.

July 23, 1838, the following entry appears of record: "On motion of Mr. Dowling, ordered that P. B. Cook be and he is hereby appointed Clerk of the Board of President and Trustees of the Town of Galena."

September 8, 1838. The first circus license recorded was issued on this date to Mr. Miller, for $20.

October 17, 1838. A draft of a city charter prepared by John Stark, the corporation counsel, was read, and referred to a committee consisting of the trustees, and Wm. Smith and John Stark. On the 25th, the committee reported, approving the charter, and it was ordered to be sent to Hon. G.

* John Dowling's protest against this resolution is entered of record.

† John Atchison had been elected a member of the board in place of D. B. Morehouse, resigned.

W. Harrison, senator at Vandalia, with the request that he should secure its enactment by the legislature.

On the same day, the trustees took measures to prevent the wash of mud into the river at McKnight's Point, as there was danger that the navigation of Fever River might be seriously injured.

December 3, 1838. The first recorded license for a theatre was granted on this date to McKenzie & Jefferson, for one year; license fee, $75.

In February, 1839, it is evident that intelligence of the passage of the city charter, drafted by Stark, had reached Galena, and on the 18th of that month the trustees passed the following resolution:

Resolved, That whenever the new charter of Galena shall be received, the President of this body shall cause the same, together with the proceedings of this board thereon, to be published.

It required money, or its equivalent, to run a town government. The trustees began to feel the necessity of providing funds. The Galena Chamber of Commerce had suggested to them the idea of making a loan. The board received the suggestion kindly, and on the 25th of February, 1839, Daniel Wann, H. H. Gear and John Dowling were appointed to negotiate a loan with some of the Eastern banks for a loan of not exceeding $50,000 for the corporation, for a term of three years or longer.

The committee was not successful; at least, the records do not indicate that such a loan was effected.

The lots set aside for public uses by the United States Commissioners, and called the "market house lots," had been awarded to the county commissioners, and they had paid for them. It was desirable that the town should possess them, and an arrangement was made by which the county authorities transferred them to the town, as will be seen from the following:

March 4, 1839, Messrs. Gear, Slaymaker and Simmons were appointed a committee to obtain funds sufficient to pay the county commissioners the amount of money paid by them for the Market House lots.

The following order of March 11, 1839, affords some light on the manner in which business was done by the town authorities. Sometimes it happened that their creditors did not want "corporation paper," and then they had to trade it off for "good money."

Resolved, That Messrs. Dowling and Gear be a committee to solicit an exchange of $92.25 corporation paper for good money to pay Daniel Sweeney for rock put on Levee.

On the 27th day of March the board received a communication from Hon. G. W. Harrison, state senator, informing the trustees that the city charter had been passed by the late legislature, but it was on the eve of a new election, and the communication was laid on the table.

April 1, 1839, Daniel Wann, John L. Slaymaker, Matthew Faucette, John P. DeZoya, Michael Murphy, Jesse Morrison and F. W. Schwatka were elected trustees. On the 2d Daniel Wann was elected president. On the 3d R. F. Barry was elected clerk; Geo. M. Mitchell, treasurer; John Stark, attorney; Milton M. Maughs, street commissioner and inspector; H. Marfield, town constable and collector; R. F. Barry, wharf master.

A communication was received from Hon. G. W. Harrison enclosing a copy of the city charter, which was referred to Corporation Counsel Stark for his opinion. April 29 Mr. Stark made his report, and the following somewhat singular preamble and resolution was adopted, on motion of Mr. Murphy:

WHEREAS, This board has been informed by G. W. Harrison, state senator from this district, that an act passed the legislature of this State at its late session entitled "An Act to amend the several acts incorporating the Town of Galena," an unauthenticated copy of which act has been furnished to this board by the said Harrison; and, whereas, this board is advised, and is of the opinion that the act in question has no validity or obligation as a law by reason of sundry provisions therein contained *in contravention to and in violation of the constitution of this state* and the law of the land, and in derogation of the rights of a portion of our citizens;

Resolved, That this board will not and does not recognize said act as a law, and that this board will not take any steps to carry the same into effect.

Stark had drafted the charter, but the legislature had seen fit to make some amendments that did not suit him. One of the objections, it is said, was that the bill, as passed, provided that none but American citizens should vote under its provisions. The preamble and resolution were evidently prepared by Stark; by its adoption the town board of Galena assumed the prerogative of the supreme court and undertook to decide a question of constitutional law, while they placed themselves in open rebellion against state authority.

Little of interest to the historian was done by the board in 1839, except to issue corporation paper.

July 13, 1839, a committee was appointed to count, register and burn all the *old* corporation paper.

September 30, 1839, Mr. Barry resigned as clerk, and Samuel Smoker was elected to succeed him.

November 26, M. M. Maughs and John G. Potts were appointed assessors.

The attitude of the board under the lead of the revolutionary Stark in the city charter matter had not been permitted to pass unnoticed. Early in May notice was served upon the contumacious trustees that application for a writ of mandamus would be made at the circuit court, by leading citizens, who were determined to know which was subordinate, the state or the Board of Trustees of the Town of Galena, and the suit was brought as an agreed case.

On the 10th of October, the corporation counsel, who had brought them into the difficulty, submitted to the board a draft of return to the mandamus rule against it. This was read, and on motion of A. T. Crow,

Resolved, That the president sign the said return and cause the seal of the corporation to be affixed, and the return to be made to the rule by the counsel of the board.

Among the last acts of this board at their last session was the adoption, on the 3d day of April, of the following:

Ordered, That the sum of $1,500 be issued to meet the wants of the corporation.

Similar orders frequently occur in the town records. It didn't matter if it took three dollars to pay one; scrip was easily printed and easily issued.

On the same day licenses were granted to keep tippling shops to Hugh Wilson, Philip Byrne and John Dowling.

April 6, 1840, John L. Slaymaker, J. P. DeZoya, Wm. H. Hooper, J. Turney, N. Dowling, Abraham Hathaway, P. F. Schirmer, were elected trustees. Organized on the 7th. John L. Slaymaker, president; Samuel Smoker, clerk; G. M. Mitchell, treasurer; John Stark, attorney.

May 4 Mr. Smoker resigned as clerk, and James Rice was elected in his place.

July 6, 1840, Mr. Stark reported that the application for mandamus against the late trustees was still pending in the circuit court, and had not reached final decision.

September 7, 1840, the trustees received a proposition from the county commissioners to apply the revenue to accrue from the sale of grocery licenses within the corporation of Galena to the erection of a bridge across Fever River. Mr. Stark, attorney, and Mr. Rice, clerk, were appointed a committee to confer with the commissioners and to take the necessary steps to carry the arrangement into effect.

Sept. 21, 1840, a resolution to license tippling houses was carried by ayes and noes as follows: Ayes, Slaymaker, Dowling and DeZoya—3. Noes, Schirmer and Hathaway—2.

On the same day the following communication was received from the Attorney of the Corporation:

To the President and Trustees of the Town of Galena:

In the matter of the application for a mandamus, the Circuit Court, on Saturday last ordered that an alternative mandamus issue against your board commanding you within thirty days from the date of the order to carry into effect the 45th Section of the City Charter; or to show cause why you do not so, next term.

JOHN STARK,
Corporation Attorney.

October 26, on motion of Mr. Hooper, it was ordered that the sum of $5,000 in the notes of this corporation be issued.

Nov. 16. A writ of mandamus was served on the President of the Board of Trustees by the Sheriff of Jo Daviess County, commanding the Trustees to carry into effect the 45th section of the City Charter, or show cause why they do not so, at the next term of the Circuit Court. Mr. Hathaway offered a resolution that the 45th section of said City Charter be complied with according to the order of the court, and that the election be held on the 7th day of December next. Lost. Ayes: Hathaway and Schirmer—2. Noes: Slaymaker, Dowling and Hooper—3. The Corporation Attorney was then instructed to show cause at the next term by a vote of 3 to 2.

While the Board of Trustees were thus defying the laws of the state they were not backward in issuing corporation paper, for on the same day that they determined to "show cause," they ordered, on motion of Mr. Hooper, that $3,000 on the notes of the corporation be issued.

Nothing of particular importance was done by the board except to issue corporation paper, and on the 5th of April, 1841, a new board was elected, consisting of Abraham Hathaway, Wm. H. Hooper, Nicholas Dowling, John Dement, John L. Slaymaker, R. W. Brush and Charles S. Hempstead. On the 6th, Abraham Hathaway was elected President, J. Rice, Clerk *pro tem.*

It would seem that the City Charter question was practically decided by the people at this election, for immediately after the election of President, on motion of Mr. Hempstead, the following resolutions were adopted:

Resolved, That the act of the Legislature of this state, entitled an "An act to amend the several acts incorporating the Town of Galena," approved Feb. 15, 1839, be immediately submitted to the inhabitants of said town for *acceptance* or *rejection*, pursuant to the 45th section of said act.

Resolved, That we do now proceed to take all the steps required of us to perform by said 45th section.

Resolved, That the 26th day of April instant, be fixed upon as the day on which said city charter shall be presented to the citizens of Galena for their acceptance or rejection.

Resolved, That the clerk give notice of the time of laying the charter before the inhabitants of the town, according to the 45th section of the act, and that he cause the said act to be published in the *Northwestern Gazette and Advertiser*, being the only paper published in said town, at least ten days before the election.

Resolved, That W. B. Green, Daniel Wann, and G. W. Campbell, be appointed judges of election, as aforesaid.

On the 26th of April, the charter was accepted by a vote of 196 for accepting and 34 for rejecting, the charter.

May 3, at a meeting of the trustees, Henry Marfield, William B. Green, and John Woods, were appointed to take the census of the town.

May 10, the board divided the town into three wards:

First, All that portion of the town on the west side of Fever River, which lies south of the southern line of Warren Street, and westwardly with said street to West Street, thence, so as to include block 60, to the western line of the town; and on the east side of Fever River, all south of Van Buren Street, from the river to the eastern and southern line of the town.

The second to embrace all that portion of the town on the west side of Fever River, from the northern side of Warren Street to West Street, up that street to Green, and with said street to the western line of the town; and from the north side of Warren and Green Streets to the south side of Elk Street and Perry Street, and by a direct line between said streets, running through lots 49 and 50, between Bench and Prospect Streets.

The third ward to comprise all the remaining parts of the town, lying north of Elk and Perry Streets, and the line through lots 49 and 50, before mentioned, and on the east side of Fever River, all the blocks lying north of Van Buren Street, to the northern and eastern line of the town.

The persons appointed to take the census, reported 1,900 inhabitants in the town. The 24th day of May, 1841, was fixed as the day for the election of mayor, and two aldermen for each of the wards of the city under the charter. Judges of election were appointed as follows:

First Ward—James Johnson, John Campbell, and T. B. Farnsworth; voting place, the office at the corner of Morrison Alley and Bench Street.

Second Ward—Daniel Wann, M. M. Maughs, and O. S. Johnson; voting place, Scott's Warehouse.

Third Ward—Michael Murphy, Geo. M. Mitchell, and W. B. Green; voting place, the court house.

The election was held, as ordered, on the 24th day of May. The whole number of votes for Mayor, 356. Charles S. Hempstead had 185, H H. Gear 95, and Daniel Wann 76 votes; Charles Hempstead was declared elected. The aldermen elected were: First Ward, Henry J. Morrison; Second Ward, R. W. Brush and Samuel S. Crowell; Third Ward, Michael Dowling and Elijah Charles. In the First Ward T. B. Farnsworth and J. G. Potts each had 72 votes, consequently neither was elected, and a special election was ordered in that ward on the 7th day of June, to fill the vacancy.

Saturday, May 29, 1841, was fixed upon as the day on which the mayor and aldermen elect should organize the city government; and the board of trustees of the Town of Galena, having performed its last act, adjourned *sine die*.

It is worthy of note that while there were 356 votes cast for mayor at the first city election in 1841, there had been nearly 200 votes cast at the first election for town trustees in 1835, and more than 200 votes were registered in Fever River precinct in 1826.

The Galena Branch of the State Bank of Illinois was established in 1835, and in August the following officers were appointed:

President, Daniel Wann; Cashier, David Prickett (who did not accept, and Wm. C. Bostwick was appointed in his place); Directors, A. G.

S. Wight, M. C. Comstock, J. Morrison, Geo. W. Campbell, Thomas C. Legate, John Atchison, Charles Peck, and Patrick Gray. Although the officers were appointed in August, the bank did not go into operation until December, as appears from the following notice printed in the *Northwestern Gazette:*

BRANCH OF THE STATE BANK OF ILLINOIS,
GALENA, December 5, 1835.

This bank will be opened to-day for the transaction of business. Discount days, Tuesday of each week. Banking hours daily from 9 o'clock A. M. to 1 o'clock P. M.

By order of the board,
WM. C. BOSTWICK, *Cashier.*

Mr. Wann was succeeded as president by Frederick Stahl. Mr. Bostwick was cashier until 1838, when E. W. Turner was appointed. The bank ceased active business in 1842.

The Galena Library Association was organized in 1835. The following appears in the county records of that year:

State of Illinois, Jo Daviess County:

I do hereby certify that on the tenth day of this month, being the second Tuesday of said month, a number of gentlemen of Galena (exceeding ten) assembled at the Methodist Church, a place previously agreed on, having subscribed over one hundred dollars for the purpose of a library, and organized themselves by appointing John Turney Chairman of the meeting. Whereupon it was resolved that the name and style of said association shall be "The Galena Library Association." The meeting then proceeded to the election of five trustees for the ensuing year, when the following named gentlemen received a plurality of votes and were declared duly elected, to wit: Horatio Newhall, Jacob Wyeth, Wm. Smith, Benjamin Mills and John Turney.

(Signed) JOHN TURNEY,
Chairman.

Nov. 11, 1835.

The Board of Trustees, Wm. Smith, Chairman, adopted a code of by-laws and regulations Dec. 29, 1835.

In the Summer of 1836 the first lot of books was purchased, and at the third annual meeting in November, 1838, the library contained about 825 volumes. The number of shares that had then been sold was one hundred and twenty-eight. The society had $240 in the treasury, had due for taxes or annual dues from members $416, and owed for books, etc., $410. Until this time the trustees had found it impossible to secure either a suitable room or a competent person to act as librarian, but now had made arrangements to have the library kept in the reading-room of the Chamber of Commerce, and engaged Mr. P. B. Cook for librarian. At this meeting William Smith, Dr. H. Newhall, G. W. Campbell, C. S. Hempstead, John Turney, T. Drummond and Dr. J. Wyeth were elected trustees. The library was maintained for some years, but the membership was not maintained, and at last it came into the sole possession of H. H. Houghton, Esq., by whom it was donated to the Literary Institute or Galena Seminary, and it was finally burned with the building about 1854.

Dr. Jacob Wyeth, one of the originators of the Galena Library, was one of the historical characters of Galena. Born in Cambridge, Mass., January 8, 1800, he graduated at Harvard College; came to Galena and commenced the practice of medicine in 1833; was connected with Dr. Colord in the drug business, and had an extensive practice. Married June, 1834, Mary C. Brady. Two children, both dead. He died Aug. 24, 1841. Mrs. Wyeth died in Chicago July 25, 1864. "Dr. Wyeth," says his intimate friend, Mr. Houghton, "was a character by himself. He was the soul of principle and integrity, and was as courageous as he was honest. There was not a mean or unmanly flaw in his composition. His clearness of thought and independent decision of character made him a leading man in the community. The history of Galena would not be perfect with his name omitted."

Francis Bouthillier, one of the earliest habitues of Galena, when it was only an Indian trading post, died in the Summer of 1835. The corner-stone of the Catholic Church was laid Sept. 12, 1835.

J. D. Carson and Jonathan Haines built a steam sleigh in the Fall of 1835, designed to run between Galena and Dubuque. It was covered, provided with doors, windows, seats, stoves, etc., and was as comfortable as the saloon of a steamboat. It was run on the ice on Fever River, but the engine, says Capt. Girdon, was too small, it had not sufficient power, and it was pronounced a failure. The *Gazette* of that date, however, expressed the opinion that the steam sleigh was "destined to come into general use," but that was before the day of railroads.

Dec. 28, 1835, Thomas Drummond, Samuel T. Cluff, W. H. Snyder, R. M. Briggs, W. A. Jordan, J. A. Dean, Philip P. Bradley, J. P. Hoge, W. B. Dodge, Hamilton Norton, Frederick Stahl, S. M. Bartlett and others, organized a Young Men's Society for moral and intellectual improvement; S. M. Bartlett, Secretary.

This organization afterwards became the Galena Lyceum.

On Saturday, Feb. 13, 1836, John B. Smith, who shot and killed Woodbury Massey in Dubuque the previous year, was shot in Main Street by Henry L. Massey, who was provided with a horse by some of the citizens and left town for a few days but soon returned.

In May, 1836, Col. Henry Gratiot died in Baltimore. On the 14th the citizens of Galena held a meeting to express their respect for the deceased. Dr. A. T. Crow was Chairman, and Joseph P. Hoge Secretary of the meeting, John Turney, D. B. Morehouse and Daniel Wann, committee to prepare resolutions.

In June, 1836, Capt. G. W. Girdon, of the steamer Heroine, ran his boat up the now insignificant creek called Meeker's branch, to Gear's furnace, and took on lead. The creek was then, in ordinary stages of water, eight or ten feet deep at the mouth. The slow but continuous process of filling up Fever River that has been in operation, certainly since the occupation of the country by the whites, is worthy of note. There is but slight current in the river; it is really little more than a bayou or slough of the Mississippi rising and falling with that. Consequently when the storms of Spring and Fall wash large quantities of earth into the river where it is held in suspension, before the water reaches the Mississippi the suspended substances settle to the bottom and remain. In a few years longer, unless the channel is dredged and the constant arrival and departure of steamboats prevent the mud from settling permanently to the bottom, Fever River will become simply a ravine, with perhaps a little creek, like Meeker's branch, running through it.

N. A. Drummond and G. W. Fuller patented an "Improved Air Furnace" for smelting lead in August, 1837. This furnace, known as the "Drummond," was an improvement on the "Cupola," and superseded it in a great measure.

The Galena Temperance Society was organized on Monday evening, January 22, 1838, at a large meeting at Dowling's new building, of which Dr. H. Newhall was Chairman, and H. H. Houghton Secretary. A constitution was adopted on the total abstinence platform, and the following officers elected, viz.: Charles S. Hempstead, President; Wm. C. Bostwick, A. G. S. Wight, Geo. W. Harrison, George Ferguson, S. M. Jackson, Vice Presidents. John Stark, Secretary; Geo. W. Fuller, Frederick Stahl, James Johnson, Nelson Stillman, D. Campbell, Executive Committee.

The Galena Chamber of Commerce was organized at a meeting of the merchants on the 2d day of February, 1838, when the following officers were elected, viz.: President, Daniel Wann; Vice President, Samuel McLean; Treasurer, Geo. W. Campbell; Secretary, Thomas Melville; Committee of Appeals, D. B. Morehouse, H. H. Gear, John Atchison, G. W. Fuller, John Campbell, and W. C. Bostwick. The next year, 1839, the following were elected: Dr. H. Newhall, President; R. W. Carson, Vice President; G. W. Fuller, Treasurer; Frederick Stahl, Secretary; Committee of Appeals, G. W. Campbell, J. Atchison, R. W. Brush, H. H. Gear, H. W. Morrison, F. B. Farnsworth. In 1840 R. W. Brush was President; H. H. Gear, Vice President, and Thomas Melville, Secretary.

For several years the Chamber of Commerce exercised a powerful and beneficial influence on the business interests of Galena. It had elegantly furnished rooms on the west side of Main Street, below Green, near where Burrichter's store now stands, and had a very superior reading room attached Many important controversies were settled through its instrumentality, without recourse to the courts, and it was perhaps unfortunate that it did not become a permanent institution.

In February, 1838, the subscription books of the Galena Railroad and Transportation Company were opened, at the store of Farnsworth & Ferguson. Geo. Ferguson, John Stark, Frederick Stahl, John Reed, Jacob Wyeth, Commissioners.

A meeting of the citizens of Galena was held at the court house March 10, 1838, to consider the expediency of introducing the common school system of education. John Turney was called to the Chair, and A. B. Campbell appointed Secretary. John Turney, Joseph P. Hoge, Capt. H. H. Gear, Maj. T. Melville, Rev. A. Kent, Rev. E. T. Gear, and John Stark were appointed a committee to consider the practicability of introducing the system in Galena.

On Saturday, April 7, 1838, a large number of mechanics assembled at John Dowling's new stone building (on Main Street) and organized the "Mechanics' Association and Galena Beneficial Society," and subsequently procured a charter from the Legislature. Its records are not accessible, and its first officers can not be given, but in April, 1839, its officers were John L. Slaymaker, President; James Johnson and M. Gorman, Vice Presidents; J. B. Spare, Secretary, and P. F. Schirmer, Treasurer.

This Association was very prosperous for ten or fifteen years; built a hall near the market house, but finally, like many other enterprises, died out, and its property was partitioned among the remaining members.

During the Winter and Spring of 1838 the Galena Lyceum was flourishing. R. F. Barry was the Secretary.

Two early settlers who had been prominently identified with Galena since 1825–'6, died in the Spring of 1838, viz.: Capt. M. C. Comstock, in April, and William Smith, Esq., in May. Capt. Comstock died in the South (some of his cotemporaries say Cuba) and his remains were brought to Galena for interment. His funeral was largely attended.

A public meeting was held at the court house June 4, 1839, to consider the question of erecting a hotel suitable for the wants and demands of

B. F. Fowler, M.D.

GALENA

Galena. Charles S. Hempstead presided, and Allen Tomlin was Secretary. Samuel McLean, T. C. Legate, M. F. Truett, R. W. Brush, and E. W. Turner were appointed a committee to draft a plan for a joint stock company to erect a hotel, to report at a subsequent meeting. On the 8th the committee reported, recommending the formation of a company with a capital of $30,000, in shares of $50 each, and Miers F. Truett, George Ferguson and R. W. Brush, Esqs., were appointed to open subscription books. A committee was also appointed to ascertain what lots suitable for a site for the hotel could be obtained, and at what price. No further report appears, and the enterprise fell through, to be revived more successfully some years later.

October 31, 1838, Mr. McKenzie and Joseph Jefferson opened a theatre in "Mr. Dowling's large room" (new stone building). Their first performance was "Wives as they were and Maids as they are," "Tickets $1, to be had at the bars of the Eagle Saloon and the Galena Hotel." The company was very popular and were liberally patronized during the Winter, but left and went to Chicago the next Spring. Mr. Jefferson's son, Joseph, of Rip Van Winkle fame, then a lad of ten or twelve years, was here with his father and mother during the Winter and attended school. Among the members of the company were Mr. and Mrs. Jefferson, Mr. and Mrs. McKenzie, Mrs. Ingersoll, Mr. William Warren, Mr. and Mrs. Germon and Mr. Wight. Mr. Warren, who played in Galena in 1838, is the same William Warren who has been for so many years so popular at the Boston Museum.

July 22, 1839, Capt. H. H. Gear informed the people through the *Gazette* that "our internal improvement system would have a tendency to fill up the river," and he lived to see the prediction fulfilled.

The Galena Colonization Society was organized Sept. 9, 1839, President, C. S. Hempstead; Vice Presidents, Elijah Charles and H. H. Gear; Managers, Thomas Melville, James Johnson, P. F. Schirmer, T. B. Farnsworth and A. G. S. Wight; Treasurer, E. W. Turner; Secretary, Geo. W. Campbell.

A public meeting was held at the Court House pursuant to public call, signed by one hundred and eighteen citizens, on Saturday, Feb. 1, 1840, to "express an opinion in relation to the Boundary question between the State of Illinois and the Territory of Wisconsin." C. S. Hempstead was called to the Chair and O. S. Johnson appointed Secretary. Dr. A. T. Crow, H. H. Gear, John Atchison, T. B. Farnsworth, John Dowling, C. S. Hempstead and O. S. Johnson were appointed a committee to collect facts in relation to the question at issue, which was the annexation of Northern Illinois to Wisconsin. Thomas Melville, Frederick Stahl and M. M. Maughs were appointed to correspond with the people in the various districts of the "Disputed Territory," and ascertain their views and feelings. A resolution was adopted, on motion of H. H. Gear, recommending the people in the several districts to hold meetings for the expression of their views.

A similar meeting was held at Belvidere, Boone Co., on the 11th of Feb. Hon. N. Crosby presided, and at which the meeting resolved in favor of being annexed to Wisconsin. A full report of the meeting was published in the *Northwestern Gazette* of Feb. 21, 1840. At Elkhorn precinct, Samples M. Journey presided at a similar meeting on the 15th. In Deerfield precinct, Boone Co., a meeting was held at Amesville, on the 17th. Marcus White, president. At this meeting the citizens resolved "that though nominally subject to the State of Illinois, we consider ourselves virtually citizens of Wisconsin." Other meetings were held in various parts of the county.

On Saturday, March 7, another meeting was held at the Court House in Galena, C. S. Hempstead in the Chair. Mr. Hempstead, from the committee to collect facts, made a long and exhaustive report on the subject in favor of annexation to Wisconsin. Mr. Melville, from the Corresponding Committee, reported that they had heard from Boone, Mercer, Winnebago, Stephenson, Carroll, Fulton and Whiteside Counties, favorably to the project. A series of resolutions were adopted, among which was one recommending a convention of delegates to be chosen by the people, to assemble at Rockford on the 6th day of July, and another, under which John Stark, Thomas Melville, Davis Divine, A. L. Holmes, Jacob Wyeth and George W. Campbell were appointed a committee to address a circular letter to the people in all parts of the disputed territory, calling the convention. Galena sent several delegates to the convention, elected in April; among them were Charles S. Hempstead and Frederick Stahl, Esqs., Nelson Stillman, and Capt. H. H. Gear. James Craig was also a member of the convention. Brief allusion to the convention at Rockford is made in the general history (pp. 224), but it is proper to add that Josiah C. Goodhue, of Winnebago County, was its President; John Howe, and Orris Crosby, of Boone, and E. G. Nichols, of Whiteside, Vice Presidents; Hamilton Norton, of Ogle, and William E. Dunbar, Secretaries. James Craig, H. H. Gear and C. S. Hempstead were members of the Committee on Resolutions, and Hempstead, Gear, Craig, Nelson Stillman and Thomas Melville, constituted the Central Corresponding Committee.

In April, 1840, the Galena Literary Institute was established by A. B. Campbell. In May the United States Land Office for the Northwestern Land District of Illinois was removed from Galena to Dixon.

June 17, 1840, the public were informed by notice that the mail stage from Chicago to Galena, *via* Rockford—Frink, Walker & Co., proprietors, —would, through the Summer and Fall, be run "*through in one day*," to Rockford, three times a week, fare $5. J. D. Winters was the proprietor of the line from Rockford to Galena—fare $8—making $13 from Chicago to Galena.

In the Summer of 1840 Dr. Burhans delivered a course of private lectures on Phrenology to the excitable Galenians, who, following the custom of the town, forthwith organized a Phrenological Society on the 10th of August. Dr. Wyeth was chairman of the meeting, and E. H. Snow, secretary. Resolutions were in order, of course, and Messrs. Turney, Rice and Stevens were entrusted with the important duty of drafting them, which duty they performed admirably, and John Turney, I. P. Stevens, James Rice, W. C. E. Thomas and Moses Hallett were deputed to convey the aforesaid resolutions to Dr. Burhans. Turney, Stevens, Rice, Hallett and Dr. P. B. Crossman were appointed to draft rules and regulations, and the meeting adjourned. Nothing further is known of the society. Perhaps it followed in the wake of some other organizations.

Before proceeding with the history of the City of Galena, brief mention should be made of some local celebrities, who, although walking in the humbler ranks of life, were, nevertheless, somewhat prominent features in Galena social life. Mention has already been made of "Uncle Swanzy," as he is called in Galena—Swanzy Adams, who is the last survivor of the slaves of Illinois, an aged colored man who still drives his water cart and supplies his old friends with spring water, as he has done for two-score years and more. No resident of Galena since 1827 will ever forget honest old Uncle Swanzy.

And what Galenian can ever forget Barney Norris? Genial, courteous Barney! who came to Galena as servant for Captain Thomas C. Legate, superintendent of lead mines, in August, 1834. He was footman for John Quincy Adams, President of the United States, from 1826 to 1828. The following sketch from the pen of Captain G. W. Girdon will be read with interest when all now living shall have passed away:

Upon the occasion of the "wedding feast" this whitened head has reigned supreme at every wedding of Galena's belles; ever attentive to the guests, with light steps and dignified presence, seeking those who are most congenial to sit together and enjoy the feast. What wedding would be perfect without Barney Norris, the prince of caterers? There is a gifted and talented lady among us, who, when at those wedding feasts, says that he reminds her of a "butler of ye olden time." And when spring-time comes, and house-cleaning is the order of the day, the ever dreaded time when we, "lords of creation," are banished from "the old arm chair," the mother tells us that Barney Norris is coming to paper and whiten the parlor. And she has no anxiety, for Barney handles his brush with as fine a touch as a Landseer. Do you want to go fishing? Tell Barney that at break of day you will be ready, and it will not be his fault if you do not bring home a heavy string of finest pike and bass. There is a trio of friends, fishermen of old, who for many years have made up a fishing party. Of that party, one is a great banker, who once claimed home here (Henry Corwith) and who still comes in the golden summer-time, to go fishing with Barney. Another, that genial "gentleman of the olden school," whose presence commands respect from all (Daniel Wann). Every one knows him, and the younger and happier he on returning from one of those day's fishing down at the "cut-off" with Barney. The other, whose hair has been whitened by the touch of old Time's ever busy fingers—the veteran "Izaak Walton" of the party (George Ferguson, Senior) but who would rather Barney would catch all the fish than not, so that he has a good day's recreation. These are all old friends, old settlers; the busy cares of life have made them old, but they all go back to youth again and Barney with them, when they go down the river for a day of sport.

For full thirty years has Barney Norris rang that old church* bell, calling together the faithful flock to hear their honored shepherd read from Holy Writ, and in strains of eloquence divine soothe their sad and anguished hearts. Full many a bereaved heart—a mother or a daughter, or perhaps a father or a son, has found hope and consolation there where Barney rings the bell. Yes, full thirty years has the faithful Barney tolled the bell for some loved one who has gone, never more to return.

"Silence whilst he marks the hour
By the bell of yonder tower."

Many whose willing feet have hastened to the House of God when Barney rang the bell, have gone to the higher house above. Some who have occupied that pulpit have gone to their reward; others to other fields of labor; but Barney still remains faithful at his post, in sunshine or storm, opening the doors of God's house alike to rich and poor, neglecting no duty, and beloved by all. No Galenian will ever forget him. He still lives among us, hale and hearty, although the frosts of many winters rest upon his faithful head. "Faithful to duty" has been his motto ever, and ever will be, until he tolls that bell no more.

And then, old "Uncle Isaac" and "Aunt Edy," with faces of ebony hue, but with hearts as white as the clothes they always wore, who, in the days of trial and fearful foreboding in the days long ago, when the fearful war-whoop of the Indian rang over the prairie, did the washing for the defenders of the fort at Galena. They have gone, with many another busy actor in those stirring scenes, but they are not forgotten by those who remain.

And "old Tom Jasper" and his old roan horse; an old, old negro, whose highest ambition was to sit in the sunshine and sleep, beside his old nag as sleepy as he. What old settler will ever forget him?

Another peculiar character was Leopold De Mussier, the first baker of

*Barney Norris has been sexton of the First Presbyterian Church for more than thirty years.

Galena, who claimed to have been one of Napoleon's old guard. He was a character in Galena, penurious and miserly, and was the butt of the town. When he died he left his property to St. Mary's Church.

Still another familiar character was Jack O'Neal, who had been a soldier in the United States service, and came here from Prairie du Chien prior to 1829. A native of the Emerald Isle, he was naturally a man of superior ability, finely educated, and possessed poetic talent, contributed for the newspapers, and was the author of a song well known in those days, entitled "The beautiful Maiden of Prairie du Chien." But he was the slave of the cup, and was frequently seen lying drunk in the gutter, guarded by his faithful dog. He afterwards reformed somewhat, taught school in Carroll, and subsequently returned to Ireland, where, it is said, he inherited a title and an estate.

Of the many who were here prior to 1828, but few remain now to tell the story of their early trials. The young men and maidens, the boys and girls of fifty years ago, are now nearly all gone. Those who still remain on "this side of the river" are rapidly nearing the end of their long and toilsome journey of life. Among those whose names are not on the roll of the Early Settlers' Association may be mentioned Daniel Wann, Esq., Allen Tomlin, Esq., George Ferguson, Esq., Mrs. Sophia Farrar, Mrs. Charlotte M. Girdon, of Galena; Gen. A. L. Chetlain, Capt. Orrin Smith, Mrs. Adile (Gratiot) Washburne, wife of Hon. E. B. Washburne, of Chicago; Captain Robt. S. Harris, of Dubuque; Abel Proctor, Esq., Alexander H. Gear and Wm. O. Gear, of Iowa; Samuel Warner, of Apple River; James S. Hunt, of Hanover; Mrs. Susan Rouse, of Guilford; —— Hanly, of Florissant, Mo.; Mrs. Dorcina (Hunt) Johns, of Kansas; Captain Abraham Hathaway, of Guilford; Andrew J. Harris, and Edward and Solon M. Langworthy, of Dubuque; Mrs. Orrin Smith (Mary Ann Langworthy), of Chicago.

THE CITY OF GALENA.

On the 29th day of May, 1841, the first mayor elect, Charles S. Hempstead, and the first alderman elect, took and subscribed the oath of office, and the first city government of Galena was duly organized. Elsewhere will be found the list of officers. June 6, Capt. H. H. Gear was elected to fill the vacancy in the first ward.

June 23, 1841, the Finance Committee made a report in relation to funding the debt of the Corporation of Galena, which was referred to a special committee consisting of Aldermen Brush, Charles and Morrison. On the 28th this committee reported an "Ordinance for the funding and payment of the corporation debt of the Town of Galena," which was passed at the next session. This ordinance provided that for all those debts (which include of course the depreciated corporation paper), the City Council "shall and will, issue promissory notes in sums not less than one hundred dollars," payable in ten years with interest at six per cent, per annum, payable annually. The ordinance took effect on the 1st of September, 1841, and the work of funding commenced immediately.

July 17, an ordinance was passed for the collection of assessments of taxes due to the Corporation of Galena.

The work of funding the old corporation debt continued for several years, and amounted in February, 1847, to $82,579.13, of which there had been paid and cancelled $1,212.36.

Feb. 3, 1849, there had been $4,775.07 of these promissory notes paid, leaving $77,844.06 outstanding. At that date the city authorities commenced re-funding them, and up to 1857 had re-funded $62,806.85.

At this date (March, 1878) there are, of the original promissory notes issued in 1841-'2-'3-'4-'5, $1,019.28 still outstanding, and of the bonds issued for them subsequently, $19,427.47, making $20,446.75 of the debt of the town in 1841, still outstanding against the city.

The total amount of old and matured bonds at this date is $45,000. In 1872 the City of Galena issued its bonds, in aid of the Galena & Southern Wisconsin Railroad (narrow gauge), amounting to $57,000. Since July 3, 1873, under a funding ordinance of that date, city bonds amounting to $49,-532.77 have been issued. The total city debt, therefore, in March, 1878, amounted to $151,532.77, of which $20,446.75 is the balance of the old town debt assumed by the city in 1841, and still remaining unpaid. In thirty-seven years this amount alone (saying nothing of the balance that has been paid after running from ten to thirty years), at simple interest, has amounted to $65,838.53, and at compound interest to $175,000 in round numbers. The accrued interest on the $20,446.75 has been $45,391. A careful compilation of the interest paid on the original amount, $82,579.13 until $62,-132.38 of the principal was paid, would show the people a somewhat startling amount of interest paid on the old corporation paper which was issued for 33⅓ per cent of its face. The annual interest paid on the whole amount was nearly $5,000 a year. In 1857 the city had re-funded $62,806.85 of the promissory notes first issued, on which had been paid annually $3,768 interest. In fifteen years they had paid $56,500 interest on that sum alone. Taking into consideration the statement confidently made by the old citizens conversant with the matter, that the town authorities issued three dollars of their paper to pay one, which would show an actual debt of only about $27,526, instead of $82,579 as paid by the city, the good people of Galena can imagine what a burden that debt has been to them. The interest on the present debt at 6 per cent amounts to over $9,000 a year. With interest compounded at that rate the city debt in ten years will amount to about $300,000. In time the American people will learn that a public debt is a public calamity.

Until the necessities of the people demanded the erection of a market house, there was nothing out of the usual routine of business to demand the attention of the city legislators, nor to distract the minds of the people from their ordinary business pursuits. The grading of streets, granting of licenses, wharf improvements, assessment and collection of taxes, for city purposes, were the principal subjects of aldermanic attention, so that up to the time when it was determined to build a market house, city hall, etc., there is nothing worthy of historic mention.

At a stated meeting of the City Council, held on the 28th of January, 1845, the market house question was taken up, and the following proceedings and ordinance in relation thereto entered of record:

WHEREAS, sundry citizens have expressed a wish and earnest desire to the City Council, to have a public market house erected on Market Square, comprising lots 61, 62, 63, and 64, as described on the plat of this city, and have signified their willingness to advance to the city, by way of a loan, funds sufficient to erect said market house, and to await the return, and reimbursement of such advance, till the same can be realized from the rent of said market house.

AND WHEREAS, The City Council being desirous of carrying into effect the wishes of those public-spirited individuals, and to secure them in the repayment of their advances of money to the city for the purpose aforesaid; therefore,

Be it Ordained, by the Mayor and Aldermen of the City Council of Galena, in Council:

SECTION 1. That books be prepared by the City Clerk of the city, for the subscription of stock to build a market house on Market Square, in the City of Galena, and to be opened immediately after the passage and publication of this ordinance, and to be kept open until the stock is all taken.

SEC. 2. That said stock shall consist of the sum of two thousand and five hundred dollars, to be divided into shares of five dollars each, to be paid in installments, as follows, to-wit.: one fifth part thereof to be paid at the time of subscribing, and the same proportion when the City Council shall, by resolution, require the same, and give ten days' notice of such requirement in the newspaper which publishes the proceedings of the City Council; that upon the final payment of the stock subscribed, the City Clerk shall issue a certificate thereof to the person entitled thereto, stating the number of shares; which certificate shall be transferable by assignment, drawing eight per centum interest, and be redeemable at the pleasure of the City Council: And should any subscriber fail or refuse to pay his, her, or their installments, in pursuance of this section, he, her, or they shall forfeit to the city the amount already paid.

SEC. 3 That to secure the subscribers of said stock in the repayment of their advances to the said city, the stockholders shall have and enjoy all the rights and advantages, and the same lien on the said market house and square, for the term of ten years, as mechanics and others have under, and by virtue of an act of the legislature of this state, entitled "An act to provide for securing to mechanics and others, liens for the value of labor and material," in force from the 10th December, 1844.

SEC. 4. So soon as the stock shall all be taken, the City Council shall commence the erection of said market house, and shall complete the same within six months thereafter.

SEC. 5. That ordinance No. 65, passed October 1, 1843, entitled an ordinance to enable the City Council to build a market house on Market Square, and all other ordinances coming within the purview of this ordinance, are hereby repealed.

Passed January 28, 1845.

On the 4th of February, 1845, the superintendent of ways and bridges was directed to advertise for sealed proposals for bids for the erection of a market house, according to the plans and specifications on file in the office of the city clerk. On the 17th of February the bids offered were opened, and the bid of H. J. Stouffer considered to be the lowest and best, and the contract for its erection was awarded to him—the building to be completed within six months, which contract was faithfully performed. It was built on lots No. 61, 62, 63 and 64, as described on the city plat.

The law of Congress, approved July 2, 1836, entitled "An Act to amend an 'act authorizing the laying off a town on Bean River, Illinois, and for other purposes,' approved 5th February, 1829," and published elsewhere in full, provided in the last clause of section three, that the receiver of the land office, after paying all expenses incidental to the survey, should pay over the residue of the money to the County Commissioners of Jo Daviess County, to be expended by them in the erection of public buildings and the construction of suitable wharves in the Town of Galena.

This law was very plain, but as shown in the local history of the county, it seems there was a clear violation of the provisions quoted in the last paragraph above, in that they appropriated the entire amount so received to the erection of the court house, jail, etc., and that they never gave a single dollar to the improvement of wharves, or any other city undertaking. Several attempts were made by the city authorities to recover part of the money, but they were never successful. The last effort of this kind was made about the first of September, 1842, when a resolution was passed by the city council "instructing the city attorney and solicitor to call upon the County Commissioners of Jo Daviess County and require them to comply with certain acts of Congress," etc. This resolution was presented to the County Commissioners while in session on the 9th of September. "The court, after considering (see county commissioners record of that date) the same, takes further time for answering the demand, until the next special term of this court to be holden on the 19th day of September, instant."

The commissioners did meet on the 19th, but the matter was not taken up until the 20th, when the following order and learned legal decision was rendered:

The court having sufficiently considered and being fully advised upon the demand made by the Mayor and Aldermen of the City of Galena, by their attorney and solicitor, at the last regular term of the court, requiring this court to comply with the laws of Congress passed in the years 1829 and 1836 appropriating the moneys arising from the sale of town lots in the Town of Galena for the erection of public buildings and the construction of suitable wharves in the said town, are of the opinion that they can not comply with said demand.

And although the court conceive that their predecessor, in not appropriating any part of the proceeds of said sale of town lots to the construction of suitable wharves in Galena, have not complied with the letter of the acts of Congress above referred to, yet they believe that so far as said money has been expended in the erection of public buildings the spirit as well as letter of said acts of Congress have been complied with.

The last amended act of Congress, approved July 2, 1836, was passed upon application by petition of the County Commissioners of Jo Daviess County, and two of the petitioners who made the application and were then county commissioners, constitute at this present date a majority of the board of county commissioners, and whatever might have been the intention of Congress in passing said act, it was the intention of the county commissioners, upon whose petition the said last named act was passed, to appropriate the proceeds of said sale of town lots to the erection of public buildings of a similar character to those in the erection of which said money has been expended. And under that impression and with that view the county commissioners relinquished all claim to any other quarter section of land, which under a law of Congress they would otherwise have had a right to insist upon to enable them to erect suitable public buildings, the court are further of the opinion that had it been the intention of Congress to appropriate the proceeds of said sale of town lots exclusively to the benefit of the Town of Galena, they would have made the president and trustees of Galena the trustees or agents for its expenditure, but as Congress expressly made the County Commissioners trustees or agents for the performance of specific duties, they believe they are responsible for the discharge of those duties alone to the power that delegated to them that authority.

So ended all attempts to secure to the city a part of the money arising from the sale of the lands at Galena—money to which the city was as clearly entitled as the county.

The building of the market house, the school-houses, bridges, etc., etc., embrace about all the enterprises undertaken and completed by the city. A fire department has been maintained from an early day, but this is properly noticed under the caption of "The Fire Department." With a reference to the bridges, a list of city officers from 1841 to the present, and our history of Galena will close.

BRIDGES.

The first means of crossing Galena River was by a ferry boat, established by Bouthillier. This he continued to manage until the coming of A. G. S. Wight, who purchased and run it until about 1842, when he, by subscription, secured the erection of a wooden bridge at Bouthillier Street, another bridge being built at Franklin Street, by John L. Slaymaker & Co. These were carried away by an ice flood, and in 1847 Darius Hunkins and John Lorrain built two draw bridges, at Spring and Meeker Streets, having obtained permission from the city to use them as toll bridges. But the city soon after purchased and made them free bridges. These remained until they were condemned, when the present bridges replaced them.

The iron draw bridge at Spring Street was built by Thomas F. Gaylord, for $14,180, and completed April 25, 1859. It was, when new, a bridge of much credit to the City of Galena, having a fine iron railing, and, in all parts, showing a beautiful and skillful construction. It is no longer used, except for foot passage. The King truss, iron bridge, at Green Street, was erected in 1875, at a cost of $6,500, one half of which was borne by the county.

In 1867 a small iron bridge, costing $700, was erected at the Meeker Street crossing of Hughlett's Branch.

FIRE DEPARTMENT.

November 8, 1836, the first fire company of Galena was organized with a roll of sixty-six members, many of whom have since been prominent in Galena's history. This company was called the "Galena Fire Association No. 1." At the next meeting recorded, the Association is termed the "Cataract Engine Co. No. 1." Meetings were held on the first Saturday of each month, the Secretary being Geo. W. Mitchell. At a meeting held at the Engine house on Bench Street, on February 4, 1837, a committee was appointed to act with a similar committee from "Neptune Fire Co. No. 2," which was then organized, to solicit subscriptions for their use. May 6, the joint committee reported $188.50 as having been received on subscriptions in aid of the companies.

Among the officers elected for 1838, were, Captain, Robert W. Carson; 1st Lieut., F. Stahl. In January, 1838, a fireman's ball was given, from the proceeds of which a hose carriage was procured. At this ball the members were designated by a blue ribbon in the button-hole. This, according to Capt. Girdon, was the grandest social affair that had ever been given in Galena. In February, 1839, Neptune Fire Company No. 2, disbanded and handed their books and accounts over to the Cataract Company. In this month, a Fireman's Benefit Hop was given, but, notwithstanding the assistance received, it was not sufficient to maintain the organization, and in November, 1839, the company disbanded. The association was reorganized May 17, 1842.

On July 26, 1843, this company held a joint meeting with the Neptune and Mechanics' Fire Companies, at which time all companies disbanded. At this time there were in the city the Cataract, the Neptune, and a Hook and Ladder Company; the latter was probably the "Mechanics'."

On October 28, 1851, Liberty Fire Company No. 1, was organized and the constitution of the old Neptune Company adopted. Of this, John Lorrain was elected Foreman. The Neptune Fire Company No. 2, was soon after reorganized and the companies purchased two first-class engines, costing $1,600 each, of Agnew, Philadelphia, and one thousand feet of double-riveted leather hose, of Adam Dialogue, Philadelphia. G. H. Mars as their agent went to Philadelphia and made these purchases. The engines arrived in Galena on January 5, 1855. In 1854, Galena Fire Company No. 4, was organized and took possession of the old "St. Louis" side-brake engine, which Capt. H. H. Gear purchased in St. Louis, in an early day. This they transformed into a double-brake engine. In November, 1860, Relief Fire Company No. 4 was organized, having a hook and ladder truck and a side brake engine for use on the hill.

By an ordinance of the City Council, July 6, 1875, these four companies were placed under the general direction, at fires, of a Chief and Assistant Marshal. These offices were filled by the election of John Adams, Chief, and John F. Brendel, Assistant. Mr. Adams soon resigned, leaving Mr. Brendel the chief officer. August 1, 1876, John H. Hellman was made

J C Spare

GALENA

Chief Director and John Adams, Assistant. The present Directors are John H. Hellman, Chief; John F. Brendel, Assistant.

The present officers of Liberty Fire Co. No. 1, are:

Foreman, Edward Donahoe; Assistant do., Edward Cawthorn; Secretary, J. F. Donahoe; Treasurer, C. L. Butcher; Engineer, H. F. Bergmann; Assistant do., E. M. Pendegast; Chief Hose Director, Chas. Bergmann; 1st Assistant do., John Spoor; 2d do., do., M. Fitzpatrick; 3d do., do., Ben Jackson; 4th, do., do., Wm. Caille; 5th, do., do., Arthur Green; 6th do., do., George Caille; 7th do., do., John Weimer.

Trustees—W. S. Metzger, Isaac Kelly, T. W. Gorman.

Officers of Neptune Fire Company are:

Frank Kratochvil, Foreman; Thomas Casserly, Assistant Foreman; Wm. F. O'Hara, Secretary; P. W. Maxciner, Treasurer; Thomas Scott, Engineer; George Starr, Assistant Engineer; John Brehany, Chief of Hose; Thomas Metzger, Wm. O'Hara, John Casserly, Wm. Jeffrey, Assistant Hose Directors.

Finance Committee—John Brendel, Jr., John Casserly, John Brehany.

The officers of Galena Fire Company are:

Foreman, M. McGee; Assistant do., Thos. Murray; 2d do., do., Hugh Sweeny; Secretary, Will Brown; Treasurer, Wm. Kloth; Chief Engineer, P. McCormack; Assistant do., Simeon Brown; Pipeman, John Taylor; Assistant do., James Rooney.

Trustees—Thos. Ryan, John Hayes and Frank Komisky.

The officers of Relief Fire Company No. 4, also Hook and Ladder Co., are:

Foreman, L. Griner; Assistant do., Chas. Hahnemann; Secretary, Jno. Tashaller; Treasurer, G. Reide; Steward, J. Klein; Engineer, H. Meurer. Hook and Ladder Director, Chas. Steinmetz; Bucket and Axe Directors, John Buhman, Nic Schroeder.

CITY OFFICERS.

Commencing with the first election, May 24, 1841, the following is the official city record, revised and corrected by City Clerk French:

1841—Mayor, Charles S. Hempstead; Aldermen, Henry J. Morrison, 1st ward;* S. S. Crowell, and R. W. Brush, 2d ward; Elijah Charles, and Nicholas Dowling, 3d ward.

The following were elected *pro tem* to the offices designated:

Clerk, James Rice; Marshal, Henry Marfield; Superintendent Ways and Bridges, Wm. B. Green; Harbor and Lumber Master, J. L. Slaymaker.

June 14, 1841, the following officers were elected:

Assessor, Jeremiah Bettis; Marshal, John Woods; Superintendent Ways and Bridges, Wm. B. Green; Collector, W. P. Millard; Treasurer, Jeremiah Bettis; Attorney, Daniel Stone; Harbor Master, S. D. Carpenter.

1842—Mayor, Albion T. Crow; Aldermen, Henry J. Morrison and T. B. Farnsworth, 1st ward; Daniel Wann and Henry C. Park, 2d ward; Nicholas Dowling and Wm. W. Chase, 3d ward; Clerk, John Campbell; Marshal, Henry Marfield; Superintendent Ways and Bridges, W. C. Taylor; Treasurer, Geo. M. Mitchell; Collector, James A. Gallagher; Attorney, John Turney.

* In June, 1841, Hezekiah H. Gear was elected alderman from 1st ward.

1843—Mayor, Nicholas Dowling; Aldermen, Thomas Drum and Richard Barry, 1st ward; E. A. Collins and G. H. Mars, 2d ward; W. W. Chase and Michael Gorman, 3d ward; Clerk, John Campbell; Collector, Richard Seal; Marshal, James A. Gallagher, Harbor Master, J. L. Slaymaker; Treasurer, Geo. M. Mitchell; Attorney, John Turney; Superintendent Ways and Bridges, M. Faucette; Sexton, Thomas Whitely.

In May, Mayor Dowling and Ald. Collins resigned, and Daniel Wann was elected mayor and Zephaniah Bell was elected alderman from the 2nd ward.

1844—Mayor, Orrin Smith; Aldermen, John Lorrain and H. J. Morrison, 1st ward; John E. Smith and R. S. Norris, 2d ward; Michael Gorman and Ebenezer Graham, 3d ward; Clerk, John Campbell; Collector, Richard Seal; Marshal, James A. Gallagher; Harbor Master, S. H. Haines, Treasurer, G. M. Mitchell; Attorney, Daniel Stone; Superintendent Ways and Bridges, Wm. B. Green; Sexton, Thomas Whitely.

1845—Mayor, Geo. M. Mitchell; Aldermen, Thomas Blish and Henry Marfield, 1st ward; M. M. Maughs and Wm. Montgomery, 2nd ward; Geo. C. Rice and John L. Slaymaker, 3d ward; Clerk, John Campbell; Collector, Richard Seal; Marshal, John Byers; Superintendent Ways and Bridges, W. B. Green; Sexton, Thomas Whitely; Treasurer, Hugh Boyd, who resigned, and E. W. Turner elected; Attorney, O. C. Pratt; Harbor Master, W. A. Slaymaker.

1846—Mayor, Michael Gorman; Aldermen, Henry Marfield and A. G. S. Wright, 1st ward; G. H. Mars and R. W. Carson, 2d ward; David Smith and D. K. Hinkle, 3d ward; Clerk, John Campbell; Marshal, J. A. Gallagher; Superintendent Ways and Bridges, Edward Grace; Harbor Master, W. A. Slaymaker; Sexton, Thomas Whitely; Treasurer, A. M. Haines; Attorney, D. A. Holmes; Collector, Richard Seal; Market Master, J. P. DeZoya.

In December John Campbell removed, and A. J. Jackson was appointed clerk.

1847—Mayor, Michael Gorman, who resigned in June, and Henry B. Truett elected mayor; Aldermen, H. Marfield and A. G. S. Wight, 1st ward; Osee Welch and Wm. H. Bradley, 2d ward; David Smith and D. K. Hinkle, 3d ward; Clerk, A. J. Jackson; Collector, Richard Seal; Superintendent Ways and Bridges, Edward Grace; Harbor Master, J. A. Gallagher, Sexton, Thomas Whiteley; Treasurer, A. M. Haines; Attorney, J. Churchman; Marshal, Robert Starr; Market Master, J. P. DeZoya.

Ald. Hinkle resigned in June, and J. L. Slaymaker was elected alderman of the 3d ward. Ald. Bradley resigned in November, and Leopold De Messuir was elected alderman of the 2d ward. Ald. Messuir resigned in December following.

1848—Mayor, Henry B. Truett; Aldermen, Henry Marfield and M. Byrne, 1st ward; R. S. Norris and J. C. Harkelrodes, 2d ward; J. L. Slaymaker and David Smith, 3d ward; Clerk, Alexander J. Jackson; Collector, Richard Seal; Marshal, Thomas McNulty; Market Master, J. P. DeZoya; Street Commissioner, M. Wadleigh; Treasurer, A. M. Haines; Attorney, T. Campbell; Harbor Master, J. J. Cruikshank; Sexton, Thomas Whitely.

1849—Mayor, John G. Potts; Aldermen, Wm. Hempstead and Allan Tomlin, 1st ward; D. A. Barrows and Philip M. Howse, 2d ward; James Bloomer and David Smith, 3d ward; Clerk and Collector, A. J. Jackson; Marshal, I. C. Robe; Market Master, P. Stemler; Street Commissioner, M.

Wadleigh; Treasurer, G. W. Campbell; Attorney, J. M. Douglas; Harbor Master, J. J. Cruikshank; Sexton, Thos. Whitely. In January, 1850, the seat of Ald. Howse was declared vacant.

1850—Mayor, John G. Potts; Alderman, Zephaniah Bell and Henry Marfield, 1st ward; R. S. Norris and V. J. Blood, 2d ward; D. Smith and H. W. Foltz, 3d ward; Clerk, A. J. Jackson; Marshal, I. C. Robe; Street Commissioner, M. Wadleigh; Sexton, Thos. Whitely; Treasurer, Jas. Connolly; Attorney, M. Y. Johnson; Harbor Master, J. L. Slaymaker; Market Master, F. W. Schwatka.

1851—Mayor, Nicholas Dowling; Aldermen, H. Marfield and Henry Corwith, 1st ward; H. Newhall and R. S. Norris, 2d ward; John Adams and H. V. W. Brown, 3d ward; Clerk, A. J. Jackson; Marshal, I. C. Robe; Street Commissioner, M. Wadleigh; Sexton, T. Whitely; Treasurer, John Eddowes; Attorney, Van H. Higgins; Harbor Master, J. L. Slaymaker; Market Master, F. W. Schwatka.

1852—Mayor, Nicholas Dowling; Aldermen, H. Marfield and Henry Corwith, 1st ward; Samuel P. Smith and George McCully, 2d ward; John Adams and H. V. W. Brown, 3d ward; Clerk and Collector, A. J. Jackson; Street Commissioner, M. Wadleigh; Marshal, John Byers; Sexton, T. Whitely; Treasurer, John Eddowes; Attorney, B. B. Howard; Harbor Master, J. L. Slaymaker; Market Master, F. W. Schwatka. Ald. Smith resigned in June, and Geo. Tyler elected to succeed him.

1853—Mayor, John G. Potts; Aldermen, H. Marfield and H. Corwith, 1st ward; C. R. Perkins and D. A. Barrows, 2d ward; H. V. W. Brown and John Adams, 3d ward; Clerk and Collector, Geo. W. Woodward; Street Commissioner, M. Wadleigh; Marshal, John Byers; Harbor Master, J. L. Slaymaker; Treasurer, John Eddowes; Attorney, John W. Campbell; Market Master, F. W. Schwatka; Sexton, Wm. Davies.

1854—Mayor, Geo. M. Mitchell; Aldermen, H. Marfield and H. Corwith, 1st ward; C. R. Perkins and D. A. Barrows, 2d ward; W. W. Chase and Adam L. Telford, 3d ward; Clerk, A. J. Jackson; Street Commissioner, Wm. Shea; Marshal, Robt. Starr; Market Master, Patrick Moore; Treasurer, John Eddowes; Attorney, H. B. McGinnis; Harbor Master, J. L. Slaymaker; Sexton, Wm. Davies.

1855—Mayor, John Adams; Aldermen, Henry Marfield and J. Russell Jones, 1st ward; Chas. R. Perkins and S. W. Swift, 2d ward; Adam L. Telford and Ebenezer Graham, 3d ward; Clerk, A. J. Jackson; Street Commissioner, C. Rousch; Marshal, D. L. Miller; Market Master, J. Ryder; Treasurer, John Eddowes; Attorney, J. M. Jewett; Harbor Master, A. J. Harris; Sexton, Wm. Davies. Marshal Miller resigned, and Robt. Starr appointed Marshal.

1856—Mayor, Fred. A. Strockey; Aldermen, H. Marfield and J. P. De Zoya, 1st ward; D. A. Barrows and L. S. Felt, 2d ward; H. V. W. Brown and Edward Grace, 3d ward; Clerk, A. J. Jackson; Collector, H. W. Foltz; Marshal, J. A. Gallagher; Street Commissioner, M. Faucette; Sexton, Wm. Davies; Treasurer, John Eddowes; Attorney, B. B. Howard; Harbor Master, A. J. Harris; Market Master, H. Kamphaus. In July Alds. Felt and Barrows resigned, and Drs. McKenny and Jones elected Aldermen from 2d ward.

1857—Mayor, F. A. Strockey; Aldermen, H. Marfield and J. P. De Zoya, 1st ward; E. H. Beebe and Thos. Foster, 2d ward; James Temple and Amos E. Brenter, 3d ward; John G. Potts and Jas. Thompson, 4th ward;

Jas. H. Sampson and Wm. Shea, 5th ward; Clerk, Geo. M. Mitchell; Collector, H. W. Foltz; Street Commissioner, Jas. M. Walsh; Treasurer, D'Arcy A. French; Attorney, John A. Rawlins; Marshal, Jas. A. Gallagher; Sexton, Wm. Davies; Harbor Master, J. F. Woodward; Market Master, Thos. Grove; Auditor, John W. Campbell.

1858—Mayor, Robert Brand; Aldermen, H. Marfield and Dennis Galvin, 1st ward; Wm. Dixon and Thomas Foster, 2d ward; John A. Rawlins and John A. Packard, 3d ward; W. W. Chase and Thomas O'Mara, 4th ward; James Weldon and Wm. Shea, 5th ward; Clerk, G. M. Mitchell; Collector, Hiram W. Foltz; Street Commissioner, Chris. Rousch; Marshal, J. A. Gallagher; Market Master, Patrick Moore; Treasurer, D. A. French; Attorney, Thos. H. Robertson; Harbor Master, J. F. Woodward; Sexton, Wm. Davies; Auditor, E. W. Turner.

1859—Mayor, Frederick Stahl; Aldermen, Dennis Galvin and Henry Marfield, 1st ward; Thomas Foster and E. H. Beebe, 2d ward; J. A. Packard and H. Nelson, 3d ward; James Barrach and A. M. Sackett, 4th ward; John Lorrain and Edwin Johns, 5th ward; Clerk, G. M. Mitchell; Collector, H. W. Foltz; Street Commissioner, Patrick Byrne; Marshal, John New; Auditor, John G. Potts; Treasurer, D. A. French; Attorney, T. H. Robertson; Harbor Master, Wm. Graham; Market Master, Thos. Grove; Sexton, Wm. Davies.

Marshal New resigned in June and John G. White elected.

1860—Mayor, Robert Brand; Aldermen, Darius Hunkins and James Weldon, 1st ward; H. Marfield and D. Galvin, 2d ward; J. A. Packard and Stewart Crawford, 3d ward; John C. Spare and Thomas O'Leary, 4th ward; M. Gorman and H. V. W. Brown, 5th ward; Clerk, George M. Mitchell; Collector, Jasper A. Maltby; Street Commissioner, Thomas Cavanaugh; Marshal, Thomas McNulty; Sexton, M. Faucette; Treasurer, D. A. French; Attorney, David Sheean; Harbor Master, Wm. Graham; Market Master, Thomas Grove; Auditor, Joseph Adams.

Ald. Spare resigned in May, and C. R. Perkins was elected in his place. Treasurer French died in August. He was succeeded by H. W. Foltz.

1861—Mayor Robert Brand; Aldermen, James Weldon and John Paul, 1st ward; H. Marfield and C. E. Sanders, 2d ward; Jacob Eberhardt and Wm. Fiddick, 3d ward; C. R. Perkins and Thomas O'Leary, 4th ward; John Adams and Wm. Shea, 5th ward; Clerk, G. M. Mitchell; Street Commissioner, Fred Kemler; Collector, B. C. St. Cyr; Marshal, T. McNulty; Sexton, M. Faucette; Treasurer, H. W. Foltz; Attorney, B. B. Howard; Harbor Master, H. Kamphaus; Auditor, J. G. Potts.

1862—Mayor, Robert Brand; Aldermen, James Weldon and Leo Knoble, 1st ward; Henry Marfield and J. Adams, 2d ward; J. Eberhardt and John Heinlein, 3d ward; T. O'Leary and C. R. Perkins, 4th ward; Benj. Britton and Wm. Shea, 5th ward; Clerk, G. M. Mitchell; Collector, L. F. Leal; Street Commissioner, F. Kemler; Marshal, F. Burke; Sexton, M. Faucette; Treasurer, H. W. Foltz; Attorney, A. L. Cumings; Auditor, J. H. Barry; Harbor Master, W. Graham; Market Master, H. Kamphaus.

1863—Mayor, Robert Brand; Aldermen, James Weldon and Leo Knoble, 1st ward; Henry Marfield and John Galvin, 2d ward; John Heinlein and Fred'k Frey, 3d ward; C. R. Perkins and Geo. Sanders, 4th ward; Wm. Shea and Patrick Byrne, 5th ward; Clerk, G. M. Mitchell; Collector, J. H. Barry; Marshal, Thos. O'Leary; Street Commissioner, J. McQueeney;

Market Master, H. Kamphaus; Treasurer, H. W. Foltz; Attorney, D. Sheean; Harbor Master, R. P. Morrissey; Auditor, Louis Zeoller; Sexton, M. Faucette.

1864—Mayor, Robert Brand; Aldermen, Conrad Metzger and Leo Knoble, 1st ward; Henry Marfield and John Galvin, 2d ward; Cephas Foster and J. A. Meusel, 3d ward; Chas. E. Duer and Joseph Haser, 4th ward; Clerk, G. M. Mitchell; Collector, J. H. Barry; Marshal, Thos. O'Leary; Street Commissioner, F. Kemler; Sexton, John Hanft; Treasurer, H. W. Foltz; Attorney, Wm. S. Metzger; Harbor Master, R. P. Morrissey; Market Master, Felix McCarty; Auditor, John G. Potts.

1865—Mayor, David Sheean; Aldermen, Philip Bollinger, 1st ward; Henry Marfield, 2d ward; Herman DeJager, 3d ward; Jos. Haser, 4th ward; Jos. H. Barry, 5th ward; Clerk and Collector, John McHugh; Street Commissioner and Surveyor, Chas. R. Gray; Marshal, T. O'Leary; Sexton, John Hanft; Treasurer and Assessor, Geo. Ferguson; Harbor and Lumber Master, Peter Kline; Market and Weigh Master, F. McCarty; Auditor, L. Zeoller.

1866—Mayor, Louis Shissler; Aldermen, P. Bollinger, 1st ward; Henry Marfield, 2d ward; Samuel Snyder, 3d ward; Jos. Haser, 4th ward; Jos. H. Barry, 5th ward; Clerk and Collector, John McHugh; Street Commissioner, Patrick Byrne; Marshal T. O'Leary; Sexton, John Hanft; Treasurer and Assessor, Geo. Ferguson; Harbor Master, Peter Kline; Market Master, Michael Courtrade; Auditor, L. Zeoller.

October, 1866, Ald. Snyder resigned and A. S. Miller elected.

1867—Mayor Louis Shissler; Aldermen, P. Bollinger, 1st ward; Henry Marfield, 2d ward; H. DeJager, 3d ward; Peter Dax, 4th ward; J. H. Barry, 5th ward; Clerk, John McHugh; Street Commissioner, Patrick Byrne; Marshal, T. O'Leary; Sexton, Michael Shissler; Treasurer, Geo. Ferguson; Harbor Master, Peter Kline; Market Master, M. Courtrade; Auditor, L. Zeoller.

1868—Mayor, H. H. Savage; Aldermen, B. McQuirk, 1st ward; Henry Marfield, 2d ward; Herman DeJager, 3d ward; Peter Dax, 4th ward; Jos. H. Barry, 5th ward; Clerk, John McHugh; Street Commissioner, Thomas McIntyre; Marshal, T. O'Leary; Sexton, M. Shissler; Treasurer, Geo. Ferguson; Harbor Master, Wm. Shea; Market Master, M. Courtrade; Auditor, Louis Zeoller. Mr. McHugh resigned in February, 1869.

1869—Mayor, Robert Brand; Aldermen, Otis S. Horton, 1st ward; Henry Marfield, 2d ward; John C. Spare, 3d ward; John H. Hellman, 4th ward; C. Bench, 5th ward; Clerk, A. V. Richards; Street Commissioner, Thomas McIntyre; Marshal, T. O'Leary; Sexton, E. Berthold; Treasurer, Geo. Ferguson; Harbor Master, W. F. O'Hara; Market Master, Xavier Willy; Auditor, John G. Potts. Mr. Richards resigned in November, 1869. Alderman Hellman resigned in February, 1870, and Wm. W. Venable was elected in place.

1870—Mayor, Joseph Haser; Aldermen, John Lorrain, 1st ward; Henry Marfield, 2d ward; B. F. Fowler, 3d ward; John C. Dubler, 4th ward; Joseph H. Barry, 5th ward; Clerk, Robert Brand; Street Commissioner, Chas. Spoor; Marshal, Thomas O'Leary; Sexton, Ernest Berthold; Treasurer, John B. French; Harbor Master, Wm. F. O'Hara; Market Master, James Crowley; Auditor, John G. Potts. Mr. Brand resigned in May, 1871.

1871—Mayor, Joseph Haser; Aldermen, Otis S. Horton, 1st ward;

Henry Marfield, 2d ward; B. F. Fowler, 3d ward; Mat Hilgers, 4th ward; Joseph H. Barry, 5th ward; Clerk, ———; Street Commissioner, Xavier Kammerer; Marshal, T. O'Leary; Sexton, Ernest Berthold; Treasurer, John B. French; Harbor Master, Wm. Shea; Market Master, Thomas McIntyre; Auditor, John G. Potts.

1872—Mayor, Joseph Haser; Aldermen, Otis S. Horton, 1st ward; Henry Marfield, 2d ward; Edward Claussen, 3d ward; Peter Dax, 4th ward; Joseph H. Barry, 5th ward; Clerk, ———; Street Commissioner, X. Kammerer; Marshal, T. O'Leary; Sexton, Ernest Berthold; Treasurer, J. B. French; Harbor Master, Wm. F. O'Hara; Market Master, Xavier Willy; Auditor, Robert Brand. Aldermen Barry and Horton resigned early in June, 1872, and D. Wilmot Scott, of 1st ward, and Abraham Ringer, of 5th ward, were elected.

1873—Mayor, Thomas J. Sheean; Aldermen, Louis Uhlrich, 1st ward; Henry Marfield, 2d ward; M. M. Wheeler, 3d ward; Peter Dax, 4th ward; C. Bench, 5th ward; Clerk, ———; Street Commissioner, Thos. McIntyre; Marshal, T. O'Leary; Sexton, E. Berthold; Treasurer, J. B. French; Harbor Master, W. F. O'Hara; Market Master, Martin F. Munchrath; Auditor, Robert Brand. Mr. Berthold died in March, 1874, and John Berthold was elected sexton for balance of term.

1874—Mayor, Thos. J. Sheean; Aldermen, Louis Uhlrich, 1st ward; James M. Harris, 2d ward; Ed Claussen, 3d ward; John J. Jones, 4th ward; C. Bench, 5th ward; Clerk, ———; Street Commissioner, Thos. McIntyre; Marshal, T. O'Leary; Sexton, Jos. Sorgenfrey; Treasurer, J. B. French, Harbor Mastor, Wm. F. O'Hara; Market Master, F. M. Munchrath; Auditor, F. J. Uhlrich.

1875—Mayor, Thomas J. Sheean; Ald. D. Wilmot Scott, 1st ward; Henry Marfield, 2d ward; B. F. Fowler, 3d ward; J. J. Jones, 4th ward; C. Bench, 5th ward; Clerk, ———; Street Commissioner, Chas. Spoor; Marshal, T. O'Leary; Sexton, J. Sorgenfrey; Treasurer, John B. French; Harbor Master, W. F. O'Hara; Market Master, F. M. Munchrath; Auditor, ———.

1876—Mayor, Ed. G. Newhall; Aldermen, D. W. Scott, 1st ward; Daniel Ryan, 2d ward; John C. Spare, 3d ward; Solomon Hatherell, 4th ward; Thomas Burton, 5th ward; Clerk, ———; Street Commissioner, Patrick Bell, Jr.; Marshal, Wm. Ginn; Sexton, J. Sorgenfrey; Treasurer, J. B. French; Harbor Master, Wm. Graham; Market Master, Xavier Willy; Auditor, G. Ferguson, Jr.

1877—Mayor, Ed. G. Newhall; Aldermen, Geo. O. Howard, 1st ward; Henry Marfield, 2d ward; Chris. Hornung, 3d ward; John J. Hassig, 4th ward; Anton Homrich, 5th ward; Clerk, J. B. French (Aug. 1877); Street Commissioner, P. Bell, Jr.; Marshal, John Sheean; Sexton, Leopold Heit; Treasurer, David N. Corwith (Aug. 1877); Harbor Master, Jos. H. Barry; Market Master, Anton Krengel; Auditor, G. Ferguson, Jr.

Ald. Hassig resigned in November, 1877, and Enos C. Ripley was elected Alderman from the 4th ward in his place.

THE GALENA BAR.

There is not, perhaps, a town or city in Illinois, or any other one of the Western States, that has given to the country and its interests so many distinguished attorneys and jurists—statesmen and soldiers—as Galena. Of this fact Galenians may well be proud.

Tuesday evening, October 16, 1877, a grand reception was tendered to Hon. E. B. Washburne by his old friends and neighbors at Galena. The invitation to him had been signed by over one thousand of his old friends, and the welcome was a spontaneous tribute of their respect for that gentleman. After the introductory exercises, speeches of welcome, etc., Mr. Washburne addressed the assembled thousands at length. Towards the close of his speech he referred to the early Bar of Galena, from which the following extracts are made. He said:

I was admitted to the Galena Bar in April, 1840. The members of the Galena Bar at the April term of court, 1840—Hon. Dan. Stone, presiding judge—were: John Turney, Charles S. Hempstead, Joseph P. Hoge, Thomas Drummond, Thompson Campbell, John Stark, David Divine, Allan Tomlin and Artemus L. Holmes. Among the lawyers who had lived at Galena previous to that time, but who had then left or had died, were James M. Strode, Jesse B. Thomas, afterwards judge of the Supreme Court of the State, and Thomas Ford, subsequently Governor of the State. William Smith, a man of fine talents and an excellent lawyer, but of intemperate habits, who came to Galena in 1827, was dead. Benjamin Mills, one of the most gifted men in the State of his time, as much distinguished for his ability as a lawyer as for his eloquence as a speaker, was obliged to leave Galena on account of ill health before my arrival here, and went back to Massachusetts, where he died some years afterwards. Of the Galena lawyers who were present at that April term of the court in 1840, Mr. Hempstead, Mr. Stark, Mr. Campbell, Mr. Turney and Mr. Holmes are dead. Mr. Tomlin and myself are the only residents of Galena, members of the Bar at the present time, who were members of the Bar then. I regret that it is impossible for me now to pay a just and fitting tribute to my associates of the Bar in Galena in 1840—the living and the dead. I need not speak of Mr. Hempstead, who was a man without reproach.

John Turney, a Tennesseean, who came to Galena in 1827, and who successfully practiced his profession here until his death in 1844 or '45. John Stark emigrated from Massachusetts to Galena in 1836. He was a highly educated and a highly cultivated man, and well read in his profession, but his *penchant* for literary pursuits and political discussions (for he was the editor of the Democratic paper at that time) interfered with his professional success. He returned to Massachusetts and died at Cambridge many years ago. Thompson Campbell made an impress upon his time by his talent, genius, wit and eloquence, and for a few years few men filled a larger space in the public attention in the State. Practicing law at Galena, and in the northern counties of the State, and before the supreme court at Springfield, and afterwards at Ottawa, he stood acknowledged in the front rank of his profession. As Secretary of State under the administration of Governor Ford, and a member of Congress from 1851 to 1853, he distinguished himself in the field of politics and acquired an influence and consideration in his party in the State second to no one. Going to California in 1853 as Judge of the United States Land Court, he made that State substantially his residence until his death there in the Winter of 1868. Artemus L. Holmes emigrated, when a young man, from New Hampshire to Galena in 1839. He was a man of liberal education and a sound and well read lawyer—industrious, careful, vigilant, and faithful to his clients. In a few years he abandoned his profession for mercantile pursuits. He left Galena in 1849, and died in New York some years since. I need not speak here of Thomas Drummond, who was taken from the Galena Bar and appointed Judge of the United States District of Illinois by President Taylor, in 1849. His record for nearly thirty years as such judge and Judge of the Circuit Court of the United States is known far beyond the limits of this state. A profound jurist, an honest man, and an incorruptible judge, he has adorned the high position he has so long occupied. Joseph P. Hoge is remembered by all who knew him at the bar, as one of the ablest lawyers we ever had in the State. It was the professional reputation which he acquired as a member of the Galena Bar which led to his nomination and election to Congress from the old Sixth District in 1842 and in 1844. Though taking no very leading part in the discussions in the House of Representatives, he was yet regarded by all who knew him as one of the ablest members of that body. Emigrating to California in 1853 he has added much to the high reputation which he here enjoyed, as a lawyer, and for years has stood in the very first rank of the California Bar, second in point of ability to no bar in the United States.

RELIGIOUS.

"You raised these hallowed walls; the desert smiled,
And Paradise was opened in the wild." —*Pope.*

As the transformation of any country from a condition of barbarity to one of civilization is the work of long time, so that branch of civilization, Religion, must be of slow development.

For many years after the cabins of mining emigrants began to dot the hillsides and valleys, religious worship was known only at the home firesides of those who, in distress and privation, had not forgotten their devotion to Him who had provided their dwelling place. The earliest public worship of which trace remains in history was conducted in 1826, by a weather-bound preacher, *en route* to the East from the Selkirk settlement, north of Minnesota.

In 1827 lay readings of the Episcopal Church were held by Mr. Gear at his house.

In the same year, religious meetings were held by Rivers Cormack, a settler who remained many years.

The first regularly appointed preacher to Galena is a matter of some dispute. By reference to the sketches of the Methodist and Presbyterian societies, it will be seen that Revs. John Dew and Aratus Kent were appointed to this station at about the same time; that Mr. Kent arrived on the first of April, 1829, and Mr. Dew one week later. If, as Mr. Field claims, Mr. Dew made a preliminary trip to Galena in the Fall of 1828, he was doubtless here before Mr. Kent, but he was, at all events, not a regular preacher at this station until April, 1829.

At the present time, Galena has twelve churches, of which five are situated on Bench Street. Being of tasty construction and located on terraced bluffs, these edifices are shown to good advantage, and, as a visitor remarked, Galena might well be termed the "City of Churches."

The Methodist Church—In 1826, Peter Cartwright was Presiding Elder of Sangamon, and was also Superintendent of the Pottawattomie Mission, which is supposed to have included the whole Northwest Territory. No record, however, is made to indicate that a missionary of this district ever came to Galena. A sketch of the life of the first laborers in the field at Galena, is considered meet.

Rev. John Dew was born on the 19th day of July, 1789, in the State of Virginia. In early life he embraced religion and attached himself to the Methodist Episcopal Church, of which he remained a constant member and laborer through life. He was received on trial, as preacher, in the Ohio conference and was stationed as follows: 1813, Salt River circuit; 1814, Jefferson circuit; 1816, Guyandotte circuit. He then located; and in 1824 was re-admitted into the traveling connection in the Missouri Conference and was appointed as follows: 1824–'5, Illinois circuit; 1826, Missouri district; 1827, St. Louis station; 1828, Conference Missionary; 1829, Galena mission.

From a letter written by A. D. Field, of Apple River, to the Galena *Gazette*, Dated Dec. 10, 1869, it appears that Mr. Dew made his first trip to Galena to examine the territory in the Fall of 1828, which is probable, as he was then "Conference Missionary."

B. H. Campbell

CHICAGO.

FORMERLY OF GALENA.

The following is an extract from the letter: "The Illinois Conference, which met at Madison, Indiana, in [the Fall of] 1828, appointed Rev. John Dew to Galena. Galena was to be the rallying point, but Mr. Dew's work included the whole lead mine region. The new preacher lived in Southern Illinois. He at once set out for Galena, and remained long enough in the Fall to explore the country and to preach several times. He preached at Gratiot's Grove among other places, and baptized a daughter of Mr. Clyma, who (Mr. Clyma) now resides at Apple River. It was the custom of many people, especially teamsters, to return south when Winter set in, and Mr. Dew returned with the tide, to his family to spend the Winter. In the Spring he returned, arriving at Galena one week later than Mr. Kent.

* * * * * * * * *

"John Dew organized a Methodist Class at Galena during the Summer of 1829, consisting of six members. The names of this first Methodist Society north of Peoria, were Rivers Cormack, (a local preacher who was in Galena as early as 1827), Mr. Cormack's wife, George Davidson and wife, and a blind daughter, Sally, who came up in 1827, and one or two others. From that day, for forty years, there has never ceased to be a Methodist Society in Galena."

These facts are important, simply because they record the first religious history in the great Northwest. The first society organized in Chicago was in 1831. Mr. Kent first preached, as will be seen, in a house on Bench Street, which he purchased, fitted up for the purpose, and used for many years. The Methodists built a church during the Summer of 1833, which was dedicated by John Sinclair, in the Fall of 1833. This was the first regular church building in Northern Illinois. The second was a Methodist church, dedicated in Chicago in 1834. The carpenter, H. Whitehead, who built this church, was in 1870, a clerk in the Methodist Book room, Chicago.

The Galena station was created in the Illinois district, of which Peter Cartwright was Presiding Elder, in 1829, with John Dew, preacher, as stated. After that year Mr. Dew returned to other fields of labor. In 1837 he was made President of McKendree College. He died after a noble life of indefatigable labor for his Master, on the 5th of September, 1840.

In 1830, Benjamin C. Stephenson was appointed preacher of Galena Mission, in Sangamon district, at which time there were twelve members of the society.

In 1831 and 1832, Galena Mission had a membership of seventy-five, and was in charge of Smith L. Robinson.

The membership in 1833 was twenty-two, John T. Mitchell being preacher. Membership in 1834, fifty; preachers, Barton Randle and J. T. Mitchell, who also had charge of "De Buke" Mission. The two missions contained, in 1835, 130 members, and at that time was formed *Galena Mission District*, with Hooper Crews, Superintendent, who was also preacher of Galena Station. It embraced Galena, Iowa, Dubuque, Rock Island, and Buffalo Grove Stations. The membership of the district was 252, and of the station, 32.

In 1836 and 1837, Alfred Brunson was made Superintendent of Galena Mission and Missionary to the Indians on the Upper Mississippi. The station preacher during these two years was Wellington Wiehley, now Attorney-at-Law in Galena.

In 1837 the Methodist Church, a frame building situated on Bench, between Washington and Green streets, on the site of the I. O. O. F. hall, was burned. A new church of brick was commenced immediately and completed during the following year, on the same site. It is now used as the Odd Fellows' Hall. The membership of Galena Station in 1837 was 28; Bartholomew Weed, P. E., Wm. W. Mitchell, preacher, both of whom continued during 1838. Membership in 1838, 84. At this time Apple River Station is first mentioned in the reports, being probably the present "Elizabeth" charge. The preacher in 1839, was Washington Wilcox. In 1840, Galena district was made a portion of Rock River Conference, and had a membership of 1,692. In the same year the district was discontinued and Galena became a station of the Mount Morris District, Josiah W. Whipple preacher. The preacher in 1841 was Robert Y. McReynolds, membership being 80. The preacher in 1842 was Henry W. Reed; membership 99. 1843, Silas Bolles, preacher; membership 124. 1844, Francis T. Mitchell, preacher; membership, 330. 1845, F. A. Savage, preacher; membership, 250. 1846, Philo Judson, preacher, Rev. Henry Crews, presiding elder. 1847, November, R. A. Blanchard, preacher. 1848, October, and 1849, Z. Hall preacher. 1849-'51, Asahel E. Phelps; 1851-'2, Matthew Sorin; 1852-'4, Hooper Crews; 1854-'5, Charles M. Woodward; 1855-'7, Francis A. Reed; 1857-'9, E. M. Boring; 1859-'61, John H. Vincent; 1861-'3, Henry Whipple; 1863-'6, J. F. Yates; 1866-'8, N. H. Axtell; 1868-'71, S. A. W. Jewett; 1871-'3, C. E. Mandeville; 1873-'5, I. F. Yates. James Baume is the present pastor.

The first Sabbath School Superintendent was William A. Jordan, and the present officer, Wilbur F. Crummer. In 1852 the present parsonage was built at a cost of $1,800.

In 1855-'6, the old church was sold and the present commodious edifice was built at the corner of Washington and Bench Streets, at a cost of $23,000. It was dedicated January 18, 1857.

The Presbyterian Church.—An interesting sketch of the life and ministerial labors of *Rev. Aratus Kent* was written by Dr. Horatio Newhall, and printed in the Galena *Gazette* of November 23, 1869, which necessarily includes the history of the First Presbyterian Church of Galena, and from which the following liberal extracts have been taken:

Rev. Aratus Kent, son of John Kent, a merchant of Suffield, Connecticut, was born on the 15th of January, 1794, and belonged to the same branch of the family from which Chancellor Kent, of New York, came. He was fitted for college at Westfield Academy, Massachusetts, and at the age of nineteen entered the Sophomore class at Yale College. He united with the church under President Dwight, August 15, 1815, and was graduated in 1816.

He spent the next four years in theological studies in the City of New York. He was licensed to preach by the Presbytery of New York on the 20th day of April, 1820. From November 21, 1822, until April 11, 1823, he was a regular student of the Theological Seminary at Princeton. He was ordained January 26, 1825, at Lockport, New York.

After being licensed, he spent one year, 1821, as a missionary in what was then the wilds of Ohio, one in Massachusetts and Connecticut, three in Lockport, New York, and one in Connecticut with his aged father.

In 1828 Capt. John Shackford, of St. Louis, spent several months in the Village of Galena. Through his representations of the situation of the people, without churches, without a clergyman of any denomination, the American Home Missionary Society determined to send out a missionary to occupy the field. Just at this time Mr. Kent applied to to the society "for a place so hard that no one else would take it," and he was sent by way of the Ohio and Mississippi Rivers to this place, the metropolis of the lead mines.

The following document has come into my possession: "We, the subscribers, feeling desirous for the improvement, welfare and morals of society of Galena, and believing the best step to the accomplishment of this important object is to have among us a clergyman of talents, education, and piety to promote an object so desirable, we agree to pay the several sums set against our respective names, to a committee to be appointed to receive and collect the same, and to pay it over to any clergyman who shall come and discharge the duties of his sacred order, for the space of one year, or to pay in proportion for a shorter period." This was signed by forty-four of the leading citizens, guaranteeing the sum of five hundred and thirty dollars. This subscription paper accompanied the application to the Home Missionary Society. As Mr. K. applied for a hard place, it might be inferred that Galena was remarkable for its wickedness. The above document speaks well for her citizens. Although they were non-professors of religion, and without religious privileges, many of them had pious parents, were liberally educated. The writer, who was personally acquainted with the forty-four gentlemen above referred to, think it would puzzle any one to find in the present population an equal number of more enterprising, intelligent, high-minded men.

The appointment of Mr. Kent was dated March 21, 1829; he arrived at Galena in April of the same year. Above St. Louis there was not another Protestant minister on the river; none in Northern Illinois. Iowa, Wisconsin, and Minnesota were occupied by Indians. Mr. Kent at that time was thirty-five years of age, a strong, healthy man, except a weakness of the eyes. He immediately made himself known as a missionary. But where should he hold forth? Where preach to the multitude who came into the village on the Sabbath to do business? Mr. Kent was not a man to be discouraged. He knew the power of Him on whom he leaned. Although there was no church, no public hall of any description, yet "where there is a will there is a way." Mr. William Watson was building a frame house on Bench Street, two lots south of the present Young Ladies' school-house. The house was inclosed, but no floor laid. A few enterprising young men laid some boards upon the sleepers at one end of the building, on which was placed a borrowed pine table, and after considerable search, a Bible and Watt's hymn-book were found. Notice was given in the *Miners' Journal* of the 9th of May that Mr. Kent would preach the next day, Sunday, 10th. The congregation was composed wholly of young people, there were no old ones here, occupying the sleepers for seats, very conveniently resting their feet upon the ground, there being no cellar under the house. The whole congregation sung the good old tunes of St. Martin's, Mear and Old Hundred. Here was preached Mr. Kent's first sermon.

* * * * * * * * * *

In November he purchased with his own money the house and lot next south of the present First Presbyterian Church. It contained two rooms, separated by a pine partition. The smallest was occupied as a study and bed-room, and the largest being supplied with long wooden benches, was used for a church and Sabbath School. Mr. Kent was unceasing in his labor in Galena and the vicinity, and in the Spring of 1830 had a Sabbath School* with ten teachers and from sixty to ninety scholars. He also commenced a day school, education being with him a matter next of importance to religion. He taught the school through the week and preached on Sundays, until October, when he was laid by with remittent fever, and the day school was turned over to Samuel Smith, a brother of Capt. Orrin Smith. Having performed a very large amount of labor in preaching and teaching, at the end of two and a half years, October 28, 1831, he organized the First Presbyterian Church of Galena, consisting of six members: Abraham Hathaway, Abraham Miller, Eliza Barnes, Ann Crow, Susan Gratiot, and Isabella McKibben; two only, and those females, resided in the village, the others lived at various distances, from five to forty miles.

In 1832 was the Indian war, known as the Black Hawk War. The village was crowded with people from the country. Block houses and stockades were built for defense, and the place was under martial law. The church was occupied by soldiers, and Mr. Kent took this opportunity to visit the East, and on the 4th of September, 1832, was married to Miss Caroline Corning, a daughter of Daniel Corning, who was the son of Ezra C., of Hartford, Connecticut. He returned to Galena in November with his wife, and other assistance, and soon after recommenced his labors, with uncommon zeal, being very much aided by the efficient help he brought with him.

In January, 1833, he had collected a church of twenty members, and held a communion for the second time in Galena. The room in which services were held had become too small to accommodate all who wished to attend, and in February the partition was removed, and the whole house thrown into a single room.

* * * * * * * * * * *

Mr. Kent continued to labor as a missionary and stated supply of the First Presbyterian Church from 1829 until the 6th of April, 1841, when he received a call to become pastor of the church, with the promise of a salary of six hundred dollars per annum. The call was accepted, and he was installed April 28.

His labors as a pastor were constant. All knew him to be a man of God. In zeal and self-sacrifice he was rarely, if ever, surpassed.

Did space permit we should gladly give the entire account of this great man's Herculean labors. He was active in the organization of three

* Probably the first Sabbath School in Northern Illinois. The first one in Chicago having been organized in 1833.

colleges and two seminaries, now all in a prosperous condition. He labored without cessation until his death, on November 8, 1869. To him this great country owes a debt of gratitude. No man has lived in the Northwest who has so left the impress of his life, and influenced so many minds. May not the humble minister who has spent his energies in gathering disciples on the frontier, and training them and their children for usefulness on earth and glory in Heaven, be regarded as having accomplished as much for his country's weal as the Senator whose thrilling speeches have electrified the Nation?

The present First Presbyterian Church building was erected in 1838. It is a large stone edifice, seating 350 persons. A tower was added in 1854. The location is Bench, between Hill and Franklin Streets.

In September, 1845, a portion of the society colonized, forming the Second Presbyterian Church, with Rev. George F. Magoun, now President of Iowa College, at Grinnell, Iowa, as pastor. This church again consolidated with the old one in November, 1860. In December, 1848, Mr. Kent closed his pastorate of the church, and was succeeded by Rev. S. G. Spees, who continued until November, 1855.

April, 1856, Rev. Arthur Swazey was elected pastor, which charge terminated in April, 1860.

No regular pastor was then called until 1863, although the pulpit was filled in 1861 by Rev. W. Bray, and in 1862–'3 by Rev. David Clark. In May, 1863, Rev. A. K. Strong was elected pastor.

August 18, 1866, Rev. John McLean was made pastor, who remained six years, and was followed, in 1872, by Rev. G. W. Mackie. He remained until July, 1874, when the First and South Presbyterian Churches met for a time together, the pastor being Rev. A. C. Smith, of the South Church. In July, 1877, the First Presbyterian Church returned to worship in its own house, and in December Rev. Lewis J. Adams was called as pastor, who still remains. The present membership is 123. The Sunday-school membership is 242, its superintendent being Joshua Brooks.

Episcopal Church.—The first lay service at the Episcopal Church was established in 1827, at which time the first Sabbath-school was also instituted, at the residence of Captain H. H. Gear. The church was first organized in October, 1834, in a frame building, formerly used as a stable, but repaired for a court house, on the site of the De Soto House. Services were here conducted by Rev. Henry Tullige, rector, who received his support from Captain H. H. Gear.

In the Spring of 1835 the parish was organized under the name of Grace Church. The first vestry was composed of H. H. Gear, as Senior Warden, D. B. Morehouse and Joseph A. Dean. In 1836 the rectorship was succeeded in by Rev. E. Gear, who became known in the annals of the Northwest by the *soubriquet* of "Father Gear."

A chapel was erected in the Summer of 1838, on the northeast corner of the block, at the junction of Bench Street and Comstock's Alley, which was consecrated in August of that year, by the Rt. Rev. Jackson Kemper, who was the first missionary bishop of the church for the Northwest.

In the same year (1838), a pipe organ was purchased for the church, the first and only one that was in the city for many years. The Rev. James De Pui succeeded Father Gear in 1847, and was in turn succeeded by Rev. Alfred Sonderback. During the rectorship of this reverend gentlemen, the present Grace Church was erected, and consecrated by the Rt. Rev. Philander Chase, D.D., on the 28th day of April, 1850. The corner stone was laid April 5, 1848.

In 1849 Rev. John B. Calhoun became rector of the church, and was followed by Rev. Thos. N. Benedict; then Rev. Hugh Miller Thompson, in August, 1859, and from January 20, 1861, Rev. John H. Eagar held the rectorship until 1863, when Rev. Wm. H. Roberts succeeded him, who was followed by Rev. Samuel Edson, in 1865.

The present pastor, Rev. E. H. Downing became rector October 31, 1869, and has occupied the pulpit longer already than any previous clergyman.

The Free German Evangelical Protestant Church was organized in October, 1873, by Chas. Claussen, preacher, at the court house. A good number of persons became interested in the organization, who purchased the building which they now occupy and fitted it for church purposes. A school was opened in the basement, with Henry Zimmerman as teacher, who still holds forth. The entire cost of the building was $2,700.

Mr. Claussen was followed by Rev. Mr. Henrichs; then Rev. Julius Keohler, who was replaced by the present pastor, Rev. Paul Lorenzsen. The present officers are Geo. Caille, President; Geo. C. Biesman, Vice President; August Thode, J. Wiemer, Edward Claussen, Hans Ehmson, Wm. Siebert, Trustees; Theodore Schaefer, Secretary; Martin Geiger, Treasurer.

The present membership is 95.

St. Matthew's Evangelical Lutheran Church was organized on September 22, 1858, in the building on Hill Street, now used as a school and pastor's residence, by Rev. John Klindworth, who has been its pastor from that time to the present. Services were held in the building referred to, which was purchased by the society, until 1863, when the present church, 32 by 60 feet in size, on High, between Hill and Washington Streets, was erected at a cost of $3,500. In 1874 the roof of this church was blown off by a tornado, after which it was rebuilt, with an addition of twenty-five feet. This was done within seventy days, at a cost of $2,000.

Day-school has been kept, by Mr. Klindworth, in the lower story of his residence, from the time of organization. There are now one hundred pupils.

The first trustees of the church were: Ernest Sanders, Fred Henke, Charles Kraseman, and Fred. Peters. The present trustees are: Peter Lehnhardt, August Habick, John Kastner, Wm. Beckner, Charles Gammelin, and John Hartig.

The present membership is eighty families.

First German Presbyterian Church.—The organization of this church was effected in 1854, by Rev. A. VanVliet, of Dubuque. Preliminary meetings were held in the South Presbyterian Church, which church donated the lot on which the German Presbyterian Church was built. The church was a frame building, on the corner Washington and West Streets, and was built in 1855, at a cost of about $2,000.

The first trustees were: John Armbruster, Rudolph Geselbracht, and Andrew Uhren.

The first pastor was Rev. Andrew Kolb, who was followed by Revs. John Bantley, F. C. Schwartz, John Schaible, John Leirer, J. A. Steinhardt, and Jacob Conzet, the present preacher.

Sunday-school was organized in connection with the church, by John Armbruster, as Superintendent. The present Superintendent is Andrew

Uhren. Its membership is forty, while that of the church is sixty. The present church trustee is Jacob Nagle. There is a good parsonage, which was erected by the society about 1867.

The church is under the regular Presbyterian Board, differing only from others in that its services are held in the German language.

St. Mary's German Catholic Church was organized in 1851, under the name of "St. Joseph's Catholic Church," in the old Catholic Church. The first church was of frame, built in 1852, on the corner of Franklin and High Streets. The first to preach in the church was Father Heimerling, who remained until the present church was built.

In 1860, the old church was sold, moved away, and the present large brick church, 40 by 80 feet in size, was built on the same site, at a cost of about $8,000. In 1867, an addition of 32 by 65 feet was made on the rear end, at an equal cost.

From the time of the erection of this church, Father Herderer presided until the coming of Father Fisher, who was followed by the present priest, Father Bally. Under the guidance of the last named priest, many improvements and much general advancement have been made.

In 1865, the present brick German school-house, of two stories with basement, was built on the same lot with the church. There had been a two-story frame school-house built about two years after the first church.

The first priest's residence was situated where the school house now stands, when the first church was built. A brick house, near the church, was afterwards bought for the priest's use. In 1876, this house was torn away and the present, elegant, two-story brick residence of the priest, erected. At the same time the church tower was added. The entire value of this property is estimated at $50,000.

African Methodist Episcopal Church—This society was organized in 1843 by Rev. Byrd Parker, pastor. The first trustees were John Barton, Nelson Monroe and Preston Story. Their church was erected at the same time, 43 by 44 feet in size, situated in the rear of the High School building. The membership at that time was twelve. The following pastors have officiated in the years noted: Baker Brown, 1845; Henry Cole, 1846; James Curtis, 1847; George W. Johnson, 1848; Wm. Dove, 1850; Wm. Jackson, 1851–'2; Charles C. Doughty, 1853; Turner Roberts, 1854; Charles Epps, 1855; Frederick Meyers, 1856; John Nellson, 1857; Horace B. Smith, 1858; Levi Evans, 1859; James Lynch*, Charles Henderson, Henry Brown, John McSmith, and William Ward, George W. Benson, 1870; Wm. Valentine, 1874; George W. Peyton, 1875; Henry Willett, 1876; Thomas Cheek, 1877–'8.

The names to which no dates are attached, are of ministers who held occasional services in the church during the war of the Rebellion; during which time, 1860–'70, no regular pastor could be procured.

In 1851 the church had forty-one members; it has now but thirteen.

The present trustees are: C. H. Gross and H. Christopher; Stewards, James Drayden and John Duffin.

German Methodist Church was organized in 1846 by Thomas Schulz as pastor. The Sabbath-school was organized in the year following, with N. Strott as Superintendent. At present the Sabbath-school is presided over by George Wichmann, with E. Haas as Vice Superintendent; Conrad

* James Lynch afterwards found his way to the State of Mississippi, where he was elected Secretary of State.

Haas, Librarian; John Haas, Secretary. It has 20 teachers and a membership of 140.

The church building, which was situated on Hill Street between High and Dodge Streets, was erected in 1847. Its first officers were: N. Strott, F. Schneider and H. Bopp. The following pastors have officiated in succession: Revs. Thomas Schulz, Wm. Schreck, H. Dryer, H. Nuelson, W. Ellers, Ch. Hollmann, A. Korfhage, H. Fiegenbaum, H. Roth, L. Kunz, W. Fiegenbaum, C. Wenz, J. L. Schaefer, F. Heinz, G. Haas, Ch. Hollmann, W. Schreiner, E. R. Jamscher, F. Klinkhohn, W. Schreiner, and F. Schmidt, who is the present minister. Present officers: J. Haas, N. Strott, G. Wichman, M. V. Berg, N. Seubert, A. Duer, F. Scheel, J. Boss, H. Aushutz, F. Schaup.

In 1853 a new brick church was erected, 40 by 60 feet in size, costing $3,000. In this the congregation still continue to hold religious services in a pleasant and prosperous condition.

The First Baptist Church of Galena was organized at the residence of A. G. S. Wight in 1836, or '7, by Rev. Mr. Carpenter of Dixon, and Rev. Mr. Powell of Davenport. The first year a small house was rented in which prayer meetings were held. At the end of that time they built a small frame church, 25, by 35 feet, just across the street from the present South Presbyterian Church. In this church, Rev. Mr. Morey first served as regular pastor. He was followed by Revs. Wheeler, Hackett, King and Brown, who was the last pastor under the old organization. The church was dissolved about 1850.

On March 17, 1851, a meeting was held to organize a new Baptist Church, at which J. B. Branch was Moderator and James H. Russell Clerk. The society met for recognition May 10, 1851, as the Union Baptist Church of Galena, at which meeting there were present Elder Clark and Brother Brackenbridge of the Rockford Baptist Church and Elder Scofield of the Freeport Baptist Church.

The members at the time of recognition were: W. Bailey, Wm. Shannon, James H. Russell, J. B. Branch, C. H. Blanchard, Richard Evans and Sisters H. B. Blanchard, Frances C. B. Adams, Hannah Evans, Caroline Peck and Elizabeth Burton. The first Trustees were Wm. Bailey, C. H. Blanchard and Richard Evans. Meetings were first held in other chapels, in the Court House, and in Davis Hall. The first pastor was Rev. A. Chapin, from Holyoke, Mass. On April 22, 1855, the present church was dedicated, having been erected at a cost of $6,000. The pastors in succession were Revs. F. Ketcham, S. A. Este, H. R. Wilbur, Asa Prescott and J. Wassall. For the last two or three years the society has not been able to support a pastor.

Sabbath-school has always been held in connection with the church of which John G. Baker is the present Superintendent.

The South Presbyterian Church of Galena.—This church was organized on the 5th day of January, 1846, with twenty-one members, by the Rev. Ithamar Pillsbury and the Rev. John Stocker.

In the following April it was received under the care of the Presbytery of Schuyler.

The officers in the original organization were:

Elders—William Hempstead, Thomas Foster.

Deacons—Philip F. Schirmer, Thomas Hoge.

Trustees—Edwin Ripley, William Strawbridge, James Campbell, Thomas H. Beebe, Andrew Dodds.

For the first two years, until the completion of the present church, the congregation worshiped in a building rented from the Baptists, just opposite. The present edifice was first occupied in 1847, in an unfinished state. It was completed in 1848, and was dedicated upon the 10th of September of that year, Rev. John M. Smith, of Pittsburgh, officiating.

In 1855, the church was enlarged. The cost of original building and enlargement was about $15,000.

During the first three years of its existence, the church was without a settled pastor. But the pulpit was regularly supplied by the Revs. Ithamar Pillsbury, David Kelly, P. D. Young and others.

From the Spring of 1847, and for about one year, the pulpit was occupied by the Rev. E. W. Larkin, greatly to the satisfaction of the congregation. The Rev. H. B. Gardiner was the first pastor, who entered upon his duties in June, 1849, and remained until the pastoral relation was dissolved, May 2, 1851. During the ministry of Mr. Gardiner a large number were added to the church—the last year, 50—mostly on profession of faith.

After this, the church was temporarily supplied by different ministers, who remained only for a few Sabbaths, until the Fall of 1852, when the Rev. H. I. Coe was called to the pastorate. He remained until September, 1855, when he resigned to accept the secretaryship of the Church Extension Committee. Rev. Charles Axtell was then called to the pastorate in the Fall of 1855, and remained until April, 1860, when he resigned on account of ill health, but is now filling the pastorate at Tipton, Iowa. He was succeeded by Rev. D. S. Gregory, who was elected pastor October 9, 1860; ordained and installed February 12, 1861, and resigned August 17, 1863, his health being such that he could not remain. Rev. H. G. Blinn was chosen pastor in the Fall of 1863, and resigned in March, 1866. Rev. Ambrose C. Smith was called to the pastorate September 10, 1866; was ordained and installed January 18, 1847, and remains at this date (February, 1878) the honored and beloved pastor of the church.

The whole number of communicants in connection with the church has been about 400, and the amount of money contributed to benevolent objects outside of the expenses of the organization has been about $30,000.

Those who have served in the eldership, in addition to those elected at the organization, are: Edwin Ripley, Geo. W. Fuller, H. L. Crookes, Nicholas Stahl, Lyman Husted and Wm. Hempstead. Of these, Wm. Hempstead, Edwin Ripley, H. L. Crookes and Nicholas Stahl are deceased.

In addition to the first board, the following persons have served as trustees:

R. H. McClellan, James Temple, Lyman Husted, Nicholas Stahl, J. A. Bishop, John E. Corwith.

The officers of the church at present are:

Pastor—Rev. Ambrose C. Smith.

Elders—Thomas Foster, Geo. W. Fuller, Lyman Husted.

Trustees—John E. Corwith, S. O. Stillman, James B. Young.

At the time of organization of the church a Sabbath-school was commenced and has continued to this time. The first superintendent was Thomas Foster, who was succeeded by George W. Fuller, George G. Johnson and the present pastor of the church, Rev. Ambrose C. Smith.

The Union Endeavor Sunday-School, of School District No. 2, West Galena, was organized July 29, 1877. There were about twenty present. Superintendents, teachers and officers were appointed. Mr. R. Barrett, Sr.,

G. W. Pepoon

WARREN

was unanimously elected superintendent; Miss Lucy Norris, now a resident of Chili, South America, assistant superintendent. The following teachers were appointed to their respective classes: Mrs. R. S. Norris, Bible class; Miss Julia Brown, an intermediate class of girls, and Miss Jennie Barrett, a class of boys. Officers were as follows: Mr. Dan. Mann, librarian. He resigned, and Mr. Will. Barrett has taken his place. Miss Jennie Mann, chorister; Miss Lucy Norris, black-board artist, and Miss Beccie Norris, secretary. Average attendance, twenty-nine. Has been kept up during the Winter, though most of the time the roads have been bad.

HISTORY OF MASONRY IN GALENA.

Strangers' Union Lodge, No. 14.—The history of Jo Daviess County would be incomplete without a brief sketch of masonry in Galena and other towns in the county, more especially as it embraces the names of many of the earliest and most prominent settlers of the lead mining district, who were active in masonry while they were shaping the destinies of this region. Especially is this true of the craft in Galena, where a lodge was organized before the "village" of Galena was surveyed and plotted, and was working two years before the publication of the first newspaper in this the then northwest.

Strangers' Union Lodge, No. 14, was the first lodge of F. and A. M. north of Fulton County and west of Lake Michigan.

The records of its early meetings are not now in existence; all its members have joined the Grand Lodge above, and the destruction of the archives of the Grand Lodge by fire, by which many important facts in connection with the early history of masonry in this state were lost to the craft, and it is now impossible to fix the date of the organization of the first lodge in Galena, but it was regularly at work in 1826, having been chartered probably in that year by the Grand Lodge of Missouri.

The first officers of Strangers' Union Lodge, No. 14, were as follows: Lemon Parker, W. M.; Moses Meeker, S. W.; Benson Hunt, J. W.; L. P. Vausburg, treasurer, and James Harris, secretary. The first authentic record of this lodge is dated April 21, 1827. At this meeting Charles Gear, W. M.; James Harris, S. W. *pro tem.;* Benson Hunt, J. W.; L. P. Vausburg, treasurer; G. W. Britten, secretary; M. Meeker, S. D.; M. Faucette, J. D.; W. Spear, tyler, and Daniel Moore, were reported present, and the petition of John J. Chandler was presented. A committee was appointed to "revise the by-laws and report amendments," which indicate that the lodge had been some time at work. The fact that no record of the old Grand Lodge of Illinois has been found of later date than January 10, 1826, renders it tolerably certain that Strangers' Union, No. 14, must have been chartered at that time, although it does not so appear in the records now in existence.

In the records of the next stated communication, held May 11, 1827, the names of two visitors appear who have since taken an active part in the affairs of the City of Galena, viz.: Dr. A. T. Crow and Captain H. H. Gear, who died in 1877, aged 86 years. On the 23d of June, 1827, the following officers were elected, viz.: Charles Gear, W. M.; Benson Hunt, S. W.; James Smith, J. W.; James Harris, treasurer; Joseph Hardy, secretary.

May 29, 1828, officers were elected as follows: Moses Meeker, W. M.; Daniel Murphy, S. W.; M. Faucette, J. W.; James Harris, treasurer; J. J. Chandler, secretary. June 3d these officers were installed and F. S. Clopton appointed S. D., and R. R. Holmes, J. D. At this time the lodge was evidently prosperous, as it had rented a room for "*four* months, or even *one year*," and ordered 200 copies of the by-laws printed, for which it paid $25, and here, says the historian, Gen. J. C. Smith, "is the first record of a printing office in Galena."

On the 13th of December, 1828, the W. M., Moses Meeker, read an address upon the propriety of surrendering the charter, but the Lodge resolved to retain its charter and pay G. L. dues for 1827–'8. December 20, —— Fields, James Harris and Charles Gear, were appointed a committee "to make arrangements for celebrating the 27th, by providing a dinner, and obliging some brother to deliver an address. The 27th was celebrated in due and ancient form." It does not appear of record what brother was "*obliged* to deliver the address," or the precise mode of the celebration, although it *is* recorded that, on the motion of Bro. Chandler, seconded by Bro. Hunt, two brothers, guests of the lodge, were prohibited from walking in the procession. They were probably too tired to participate in the parade. It is worthy of note that Strangers' Union Lodge did general work and conferred degrees on the Sabbath. As the members were scattered, it is probable that Sunday was the only day they could meet, and certainly the work of a Masonic Lodge could not be a violation of the Sabbath.

January 2, A. D. 1829, A. L. 5829, D. B. Morehouse, for many years well known in Galena as "Captain" Morehouse was initiated. On the 3d, T. B. Farnsworth was raised. On the 4th, the Lodge was in session. On the 7th, James Craig was elected on demit. Sunday, January 11, Captain Morehouse was crafted. On the 12th, L. R. M. Morse was crafted. On the 13th, E. Block crafted, and a petition received from William Hempstead, "an active business man and prominent citizen, whose generous liberality as a Mason during the remainder of his life, was only equalled by his love for the church with which he was connected." On the 14th, Mr. Hempstead was elected and initiated. The 16th, E. Block raised. The 18th, D. B. Morehouse raised. These almost daily communications clearly indicate a period of unusual prosperity as well as the wonderful devotion of the members to their sublime work.

About February 15, James Craig became the Secretary. Mr. Craig afterwards settled in Wapello, now Hanover, and died there. March 22d, Wm. Hempstead and Peter Prim were examined in open lodge on the first two degrees and raised. This is the first record of any examination.

On the 11th of June, A. L. 5829, A. D. 1829, a resolution was adopted providing that all officers should hold over, a certain sign of approaching dissolution, for at the same communication less than six months after the lodge had been at work almost daily, another resolution was presented, "That we return our charter to the G. M. or D. G. M. of Illinois, and apply to the G. L. of Missouri for another one," but its consideration was postponed until the 18th, one week. But what action if any was taken upon it is unknown. No further records can be found, and Strangers' Union Lodge

No. 14, ceased to be. Whether it collapsed because of its failure to elect officers, or because the G. L. of Illinois had ceased to exist, can not now be determined. It is probable, however, that it yielded to the fierce storm of Anti-Masonic fanaticism then sweeping over the country.

The names of the men who fifty years ago conducted the affairs of the first Lodge of Masons in Galena, so far as they can be compiled from the imperfect records now remaining, will complete this brief sketch of Strangers' Union Lodge, No. 14.

Names of Members.—Lemon Parker, Benson Hunt, M. Faucette, Dan'l Moore, Thomas H. January, A. T. Crow, John Colter, James Craig, Charles Gear, L. P. Vausburg, W. Spear, —— Clayne, Jos. Hardy, Jas. A. Clark, W. F. Maneen, Samuel Smoker, Horatio Newhall, James Harris, Moses Meeker, G. W. Bretton, James Smith, R. R. Holmes, John O. Hancock, F. S. Clopton, E. Welch.

Initiated—R. P. Guyard, Saml. Jamison, J. R. Vineyard, Jesse B. Williams, J. P. B. Gratiot.

Initiated and Passed—A. C. Caldwell, Israel Mitchell, John Barrell, Lieut. Christopher C. Hobart, U. S. A.

Initiated, Passed and Raised—John J. Chandler, E. Block, Daniel Murphy, T. B. Farnsworth, J. R. Hammett, Peter Prim, L. R. M. Morse, D. B. Morehouse, William Hempstead, J. H. Rountree.

Among the visitors were: Capt. H. H. Gear, and C. C. P. Hunt, Gov. John Wood, and many others from other lodges—Illinois, Missouri, Kentucky, Ohio, and New Jersey. Although this was Strangers' Union Lodge No. 14, the names of several visitors from Lafayette Lodge No. 14, also under the jurisdiction of the G. L. of Illinois, at that time, appear of record, and in Reynolds' History of Masonry in Illinois, it is asserted that Lafayette No. 14 was chartered at the session of the G. L. of Illinois held January 10, 1826. If this is true it may be possible that Strangers' Union was organized under another jurisdiction, especially since it is known that its immediate and ephemeral successor worked under a dispensation from the G. L. of Missouri.*

Galena Lodge U. D., 1830.—If Strangers' Union Lodge ceased to work because of the Anti-Masonic excitement, the brethren of Galena and vicinity were not disposed to give up the ship without another trial, for on the 17th of July, 1830, the date of the first record of Galena Lodge U. D., it is stated that that lodge was working under dispensation from the Grand Lodge of Missouri. Officers and members present: Benjamin Mills, W. M.; Daniel Wann, S. W.; Moses Meeker, J. W. *pro tem;* William Hempstead, S. D.; Samuel Smoker, Secretary. Visitors, Jas. A. Clark, James Burns and Lewis M. Morse. Another meeting was held July 22, entirely taken up with the consideration of by-laws. On the 29th of July another meeting is recorded, in which the name of T. D. Farnsworth appears as J. D. One petition for initiation and one for membership on demit were read and referred. No further records of this lodge can be found. Doubtless its members found it wise to bow to the fierce tempest of Anti-Masonic hate that for some years prevailed at that period. Galena Lodge U. D. ceased to exist, and for eight years no Masonic organization existed in Galena, but those who had gathered around the altar of Masonry did not forget its teachings and cherished its sublime principles in their hearts.

* Since the above was in type, the authors have become satisfied that the Strangers' Union was under the jurisdiction of the Grand Lodge of Missouri.

Far West Lodge U. D. and No. 29, 1838 to 1846—After the lapse of eight years, during which the bitter persecutions to which the Masonic fraternity of the country had been subjected, had spent its fury and the fires of hate had burned out, on the 27th day of December, 1838, pursuant to public notice, the following Master Masons assembled at the Chamber of Commerce: Charles Gear, H. H. Gear, S. McLean, A. T. Crow, M. Faucette, John Sherman, T. B. Farnsworth, E. W. Turner, John E. Smith, R. Pattison and James A. Clark.

At this meeting officers were elected as follows: Charles Gear, W. M.; E. W. Turner, S. W.; S. McLean, J. W.; T. B. Farnsworth, treasurer; John E. Smith, secretary; A. T. Crow, S. D.; H. H. Gear, J. D.; M. Faucette, tyler. On the 29th a petition was drawn and signed by all present to the Grand Lodge of Missouri for a Dispensation, and before it was forwarded was also signed by Daniel Wann, George M. Mitchell and Samuel Smoker. One well known citizen and member was prevented from signing by a resolution "that, owing to the atheistical opinions as publicly expressed he is unworthy of being taken by the hand as a Mason." Meetings were held regularly every two weeks until March 23, 1839, when the Dispensation from the Grand Lodge of Missouri was received, read and accepted. E. L. Ogden, who had obtained the document, was thanked for that service and admitted without payment of the regular fee. C. P. Burrows and T. C. Legate also became members, and from this date the work of Far West Lodge U. D. commenced. On the 6th of April of that year William H. Hooper and A. J. Jackson were elected and initiated. The first has since been a member of Congress and the second for many years the efficient clerk of the City of Galena. Regular work was continued until October 18, when Bro. Geo. M. Mitchell returned from the Grand Lodge of Missouri and presented the lodge with its charter as "Far West Lodge, No. 29." The years 1841 and 1842 were prosperous ones for "Far West." Meetings were well attended and a large amount of work done. December 26, 1844, a resolution was adopted making application to the Grand Lodge of Wisconsin for a charter under the name of Galena Lodge. A dispensation was granted, and Galena Lodge appears to have worked on the 2d of January, 1845, composed of the same members as 29, which, however, did not cease to exist until June 22, 1846, when M. W. G. M., Rev. Wm. F. Walker, visited the lodge, and it was resolved to accept a charter from the Grand Lodge of Illinois and return the one held under the Grand Lodge of Missouri, and the following officers were elected: M. Y. Johnson, W. M.; W. C. Bostwick, S. W.; Daniel Wann, J. W.; M. P. Silverburgh, treasurer; D. H. Moss, secretary. These officers were installed on the 26th, when Far West Lodge, No. 29, closed its labors. Charles Gear was W. M. in 1839–'40–'41–'42–'43–'44; H. H. Gear in 1845, and M. Y. Johnson, 1846.

Far West Lodge, No. 5.—June 29, 1846, William F. Walker, Grand Master of Illinois, granted a Dispensation to the brethren, giving them the same name but changing the Missouri number to five, and on the 8th of October a charter was granted by the Grand Lodge of Illinois to Far West Lodge, No. 41, of Galena. The record shows that on the 9th of October the lodge held its meeting in a building owned by Geo. Roddewig. August 30, 1847, a motion was made to surrender the charter and a committee was appointed to assist the officers in settling the affairs of the lodge, but the lodge appears to have gone along with its work until September 1, 1848, when its records terminate. The causes leading to its death, and how it died, do not appear of record.

Phœnix Lodge U. D.—From September 1, 1848, to February 9, 1854, nearly six years, there is no record of any masonic body working in Galena. At the latter date the record of "Phœnix Lodge U. D." appears, which shows the following officers and members:

E. R. Hooper, W. M.; L. J. Germain, S. W.; W. R. Rowley, J. W.; T. M. Wilcox, treasurer; J. E. Smith, secretary; G. W. Woodward, S. D.; Jacob Davis, J. D.; A. Lovenstein, tyler. H. H. Gear, Geo. M. Mitchell, Geo. G. Gould, George Houy, Nathan Meyer. Visitor Jesse R. Grant. This lodge worked under dispensation from the Grand Lodge of Illinois, held a number of meetings, and did some work for a year and a month, and then as suddenly disappeared as it came in March, 1855, and the sound of the gavel was heard no more in Galena until 1858.

Miners' Lodge, No. 273, 1858.—A meeting of the Masons of Galena and vicinity was called at the De Soto House February 20, 1858, but no records are preserved until April 17, 1858, when the record of Miners' Lodge U. D. shows Ely S. Parker, W. M.; Geo. G. Gould, secretary, and on this day the corner-stone of the new custom house was laid with Masonic honors by Ely S. Parker as proxy for the G. M. October 15, 1858, Miners' Lodge, No. 273, received its charter and was duly consecrated. June 24, 1859, the new hall on Bench Street, formerly known as Mitchell's Hall, was dedicated, and at the banquet following, at the De Soto House, Hon. E. Washburne, M. C., Hon. C. B. Denio and other prominent citizens were present as invited guests. December 27, 1859, St. John the Evangelist's Day, a grand Masonic and citizens' dress ball at the De Soto House, under the auspices of Miners' Lodge, the great feature of the occasion being the entrance of Bro. Ely S. Parker clothed in the full uniform of a Knight Templar. June 7, 1861, a Lodge of Sorrow was held in memory of Stephen A. Douglas, who died in Chicago June 3, 1861, at which the following resolution was adopted:

Resolved, That the memory of Stephen A. Douglas will be cherished in the precious recollections of his brother Masons, and the bright light of his deeds will assure and encourage posterity to emulate his noble example as a law-giver, as a citizen and as a Mason.

During the war, from 1861 to 1865, the lodge continued to work, although so many of its active members were absent in the military service of the United States that it was often difficult to secure a quorum. Among those who were absent were Gen. Ely S. Parker, the talented Indian chief, afterwards commissioner of Indian affairs; Gen. John A. Rawlins, secretary of war; Generals John C. Smith, John E. Smith and W. R. Rowley, Capt. Geo. W. Felt and others. Gen. Rawlins died in Washington September 6, 1869, and the following entry was made on the records of the lodge:

"His work was not done, yet his column is broken. The silver chord is loosed, the golden bowl is rent in twain; the dust has returned to the earth as it was, and the spirit to God who gave it."

Nov. 25, 1873, the building on Main Street near Warren Street, owned by Henry Corwith and Charles H. Rogers, was purchased, and after having been changed in plan to adapt them to Masonic purposes under direction of W. M., J. C. Smith, assisted by W. R. Rowley, J. B. Young and S. O. Stillman, and the work completed, was finally dedicated June 15, 1874. On the same day the various Masonic bodies of the city, assisted by all the lodges from the surrounding county, laid the corner-stone of the new public Hall of the Galena Social Turner Society with Masonic ceremonies. W. M., J. C. Smith, as proxy of the G. M. officiated, assisted by J. C. Spare,

D. G. M.; M. Coleman, S. G. W.; A. Reynolds, J. G. W.; Geo. Broderick, G. Treasurer; Daniel LeBetter, G. Secretary; B. Yerrington, G. S. D.; A. J. Louchheim, G. J. D.; A. H. Simpson and John Eiseman, Grand Stewards, and J. A. Berryman, S. Tyler.

The Committee of Arrangements for the dedication consisted of S. K. Miner, R. H. Fiddick, D. LeBetter, C. S. Merrick, J. R. Davidson, David N. Corwith, Jesse Crooks, Richard Keller, S. Hunkins, H. H. Browning and Daniel Stewart.

The venerable H. H. Gear was Master of Ceremonies. In his admirable address on this enteresting occasion, Acting Grand Master John C. Smith said: "The Masons of Galena have a record of which they may well be proud. A lodge was formed here when this city was but a frontier post. The venerable brother and illustrious Sir Knight, Capt. H. H. Gear, now presiding, who has resided in this city from time immemorial; certainly so long that 'the memory of man runneth not to the contrary,' informs me that he found a lodge at work here in May, 1827, and knows it had been at work for one or two years previous. Records are in my possession of earlier meetings, and in them I find Bro. Gear recorded as a 'visitor' at the time he speaks of. This was the Strangers' Union Lodge, which was afterwards succeeded by 'Far West', 'Galena', and 'Phœnix;' from the ashes of which arose our own loved Miners' Lodge No. 273, and its three higher bodies. There are many pleasant memories clustering about these old lodges, it would be so interesting to speak of but more eloquent than words of mine are the living witnesses who are present with us on this occasion."

The speaker alluded to Capt. H. H. Gear who was raised to the sublime degree of a Master Mason in Mystic Lodge, Berkshire, Mass., in March, 1815, immediately after the close of the war of 1812, in which he had borne a gallant part. Also to Daniel Wann and M. Y. Johnson, of Far West.

The first board of officers of Miners' Lodge was constituted as follows, serving in 1858: Ely S. Parker, W. M.; E. W. Turner, S. W.; M. Y. Johnson, J. W.; M. P. Silverburgh, Treasurer; Geo. G. Gould, Secretary; Samuel Frazer, S. D.; Geo. M. Mitchell, J. D.; S. H. Helm, Tyler.

Masters from 1858 *to* 1878.—Ely S. Parker, 1858–'9–'60; J. C. Spare, 1861; Samuel Snyder, 1862–'3–'4–'5–'6–'7; T. R. Bird, 1868; A. Campbell, 1869; John C. Smith, 1870–'1–'2–'3–'4; S. O. Stillman, 1875–'6–'7; R. H. Fiddick, 1878.

Secretaries.—Geo. G. Gould, 1858; M. F. Burke, 1859–'60–'1; J. C. Smith, 1862; S. O. Stillman, 1863–'4–'5–'6–'7–'8–'9–'70–'1–'2; Daniel LeBetter, 1873–'4; D. N. Corwith, 1876-'7-'8.

Treasurers.—M. P. Silverburgh, 1858-'9-'60-'1-'2-3-'4- 5; J. M. Spratt, 1867-'8-'9-'70-'1-'2-'3-'4-'5-'6-'7; S. O. Stillman, 1878.

Jo Daviess Chapter, No. 51, 1859.—Jo Daviess Chapter, No. 51, of Royal Arch Masons, was organized at Galena under Dispensation June 9, A. D. 1859, by D. G. H. P., William Mitchell. Present: Rev. E. M. Boring, Capt. H. H. Gear, Ely S. Parker, George Thompson, M. D. Chamberlain, J. M. Shermerhorn, Daniel Wann, William Spaulding, William Bulger, Dr. J. A. Scroggs and Geo. M. Mitchell. Charter granted November 24, 1859.

First Board of Officers, 1859.—Ely S. Parker, H. P.; Daniel Wann, K.; Geo. M. Mitchell. S.; John E. Smith, C. H.; Wm. Spaulding, P. S.;

W. R. Rowley, R. A. C.; Darius Hunkins, G. M. 1st V.; Jonathan W. Woodruff, G. M. 2d V.; John A. Scroggs, G. M. 3d V.; Madison Y. Johnson, Treasurer; S. O. Stillman, Secretary; M. Faucette, Tyler.

High Priests from Organization.—Ely S. Parker, 1859-'60-'1; Darius Hunkins, 1862; Samuel Snyder, 1863-'4-'5-'6-'7; John C. Smith, 1868-'9-'70-'1-'2-'3-'4; Simeon K. Miner, 1875-'6-'7; S. O. Stillman, 1878.

Secretaries.—S. O. Stillman, 1859-'60-'1-'2-'3-'4-'5-'6-'7-'8-'9-'70-'1-'2-'3; Daniel LeBetter, 1874; J. Fawcett, 1875; D. N. Corwith, 1876-'7-'8.

Treasurers.—Madison Y. Johnson, 1859; W. R. Rowley, 1860-'1; Daniel Wann, 1862-'3; S. O. Stillman, 1864-'5-'6-'7-'8-'9-'70-'1-'2; J. M. Spratt, 1873-'4-'5-'6-'7-'8.

Ely S. Parker Council, No. 60—*Royal, Super-Excellent and Select Masters.*—Ely S. Parker Council, No. 60, was constituted under a Dispensation from the T. I., George E. Loumsburg, G. P. of the Grand Council of Illinois, July 9, 1873. It received its name from the first master of Miners' Lodge, and High Priest of Jo Daviess Chapter, Gen. Ely S. Parker, the accomplished Indian chief and grandson of Red Jacket. The organization of a Council of Cryptic Masonry drew together a large number of distinguished masons, among whom were Hon. H. C. Burchard, M. C.; Gen. Smith D. Atkins, Hon. Robert Little, W. S. Best and others. Charter granted October 29, 1873.

Members Under Dispensation.—John C. Smith, Loyal L. Munn, William Young, L. J. Turner, Robert Little, W. J. McKinn, J. S. Gates, E. C. Warner, George Thompson, James S. McCall.

Officers, U. D., 1873.—John C. Smith, T. I. G. M.; Robert Little, D. I. G. M.; Loyal L. Munn, P. C. of W.; Gerhard H. Mars, Chaplain; Daniel LeBetter, Recorder; Richard H. Fiddick, Treasurer; Jacob Fawcett, Con.; Simeon K. Miner, Capt. of G.; A. J. Souchheim, Steward; Daniel Stewart, Sentinel.

Officers Under Charter, 1873-4.—John C. Smith, T. I. G. M.; R. H. Fiddick, D. I. G. M.; Jacob Fawcett, P. C. of W.; G. H. Mars, Chaplain; D. LeBetter, Recorder; A. J. Louchheim, Treasurer; J. P. Williams, Con.; J. R. Davidson, C. G.; D. Stewart, Steward and Sentinel.

R. H. Fiddick, T. I. G. M., 1875-'6-'7-'8; J. Fawcett, Recorder, 1875; D. N. Corwith, Recorder, 1876-'7-'8; S. K. Miner, Treasurer, 1875-'6-'7-'8.

*Galena Commandery No.*40, *Knights Templars*, Galena Commandery, U. D., was organized September 29, 1871, under dispensation issued by D. G. C. Wiley M. Egan. Galena Commandery, No. 40, chartered October 24, 1871.

Members U. D.—John Carson Smith, Samuel Cook, Simeon Kingsley Miner, John Minot Daggett, Mortimer Marcus Wheeler, John Olinger, Charles Silas Burt, Robert Little, Smith D. Atkins.

Officers U. D. 1871—John Carson Smith, E. Commander; Samuel Cook, Generalissimo; Simeon Kingsley Miner, Captain-General; John Minot Daggett, Prelate; Mortimer Marcus Wheeler, S. W.; John Olinger, J. W.; Charles S. Burt, Treasurer; Daniel LeBetter, Recorder; Robert Little, Standard Bearer; Smith D. Atkins, Sword Bearer; Daniel Stewart, Captain of the Guard.

First Officers Under the Charter 1872—John C.Smith, Eminent Commander; Wm. R. Rowley, Generalissimo; Simeon K. Miner, Captain-General; Daniel LeBetter, Prelate; Mahlon Coleman, S. W.; M. M. Wheeler, J. W.; Wm. R. Burkhard, Treasurer; Daniel LeBetter, Recorder; Richard

Henry Fiddick, Standard Bearer; Edward James, Sword Bearer; Daniel Stewart, Captain of the Guards.

Eminent Commanders—John C. Smith, 1874; W. R. Rowley, 1875, 1876, and 1877; J. C. Calderwood, 1878.

Recorders—Daniel LeBetter, 1874; E. C. Ripley, 1875; D. N. Corwith, 1876, 1877, and 1878.

I. O. O. F.

On April 26, 1819, Thomas Wildey founded this great organization in America, by instituting at Baltimore the first lodge in the New World. That same great worker in this brotherhood visited the City of Galena in July. 1838, at the solicitation of P. G. M., J. G. Potts; Brothers Daniel Wann, Richard Pattison, John Turney, Archibald McGinnis, James H. Sheldon, Joseph A. Dean, F. W. Schwatka and Edward W. Turner, and established the first lodge of Odd Fellows in the great Northwest, July 28, 1838. The lodge was called *Wildey Lodge No.* 5, and was placed under the guidance of the venerable Patriarch, Past Grand Master John G. Potts, who, as D. D. Grand Sire of the Grand Lodge of the United States, was given charge of Illinois, Iowa, Wisconsin and Minnesota, a man whose name has ever been intimately connected with this Association in the Western States.

To his industry the lodge at Galena owes much of its prosperity and success. March 29, 1847, the members of the lodge, in testimony of the respect in which they held him, and in consideration of the valuable services which he had rendered the order, presented to him a beautiful and elegant encampment regalia. He was elected their first representative to the Grand Lodge of the State, May 24, 1847.

He organized a large number of lodges in Iowa, Wisconsin, Minnesota and Illinois. He was a prominent member of Galena society, being for two years mayor of the city, where he lived more than thirty years. When he died, February 10, 1874, he was buried, with imposing ceremonies, by the Odd Fellows' Associations of Galena.

As the lodge had no suitable room to meet in, no regular meetings were held until January 2, 1839, at which time the first quarter commences.

The lodge continued to work under the warrant granted by the Grand Lodge of the United States until the third quarter, when the lodge acknowledged, and has since remained under, the jurisdiction of the Grand Lodge of the State of Illinois, the charter from which is dated August 1, 1840, and under which charter it still continues to work. The lodge, having received its charter from the Grand Lodge of the United States before the Grand Lodge of the State was instituted, at first refused to acknowledge the authority of the State Grand Lodge, upon the ground that she owed allegiance only to that power whence she derived her charter, and having received her charter, which required obedience to the Grand Lodge of the United States, previous to the institution of the State Grand Lodge, that therefore the Grand Lodge of the State held no authority over this lodge. The difficulty was, however, amicably and satisfactorily settled by the lodge receiving a charter from, and acknowledging the authority of, the Grand Lodge of the State, to whom, in the third quarter, she made her first report including the percentage and work of the two preceding quarters.

The first presiding officer of the lodge was Brother Daniel Wann, who at the close of his term, at the request of the Lodge, presented to them his

Hert C. Gann.

EDITOR & PROPRIETOR WARREN SENTINEL

WARREN.

portrait in the regalia of a P. G., which was ordered to be placed in the lodge room in remembrance of his having been its first presiding officer. It is a beautiful painting, the work of Brother Stanley. An elegant medal was presented to Brother Wann on Sept. 21, 1839, as a testimony of esteem.

The meetings of the lodge were first held in the counting room of Daniel Wann, until the latter part of January, 1839, when the lodge removed to a room in what was then called the Court House.

July 19, 1839, Charles R. Bennett, who afterwards became a member of the society, presented it with a lot on Prospect Street, between Green and Washington Streets where the lodge built their first hall, at a cost of $2,208.22. This hall was dedicated on the anniversary of the institution of Odd Fellowship in America, April 27, 1840, at which time a grand celebration was held, with addresses by P. G., Wm. C. E. Taylor and Brother Divine.

Wildey Lodge was first represented in the Grand Lodge of the State by proxy, by P. G., J. E. Starr, of Alton.

February 3, 1840, the State Legislature passed an act of incorporation, for the benefit of the lodge, which gives it all the privileges and powers of a body politic and corporate. The lodge has had many celebrations, which have always been distinguished for elegance and fine display. At the celebration of April 26, 1839, A. T. Crow delivered the address; at the celebration of April 27, 1840, W. C. Taylor; April 26, 1841, John Turney; April 26, 1845, P. G., A. D. Robertson; April 26, 1846, A. F. Savage; July 4, 1849, Thompson Campbell.

In the thirty-first quarter (September, 1846), a number of the brothers withdrew, for the purpose of establishing a new lodge, to be called Galena Lodge No. 17, which was subsequently instituted and is now in a prosperous condition.

Wildey Lodge holds its meetings every Monday evening.

A few years ago they sold their old hall and purchased a church building on Bench Street, between Green and Washington Streets, which they have fitted up in an elegant manner, as their hall. Both the Lead Mine Encampment and Galena Encampment hold their meetings here.

The officers of Wildey Lodge No. 5 are:

Jr. P. G.—Wm. J. Bailey.

N. G.—Geo. F. Keeling.

V. G.—Anton Beil.

Secretary—Robert Brand (for twenty-five years).

Treasurer—Henry Marfield.

Trustees—F. K. Uhlrich, Wm. F. O'Hara and Frank Kratochoil.

District Deputy Grand Master and Grand Lodge Representative—Lewis Grimm.

Galena Lodge No. 17, was an offshoot of Wildey Lodge No. 5, and received its charter August 25, 1846. The charter members were, Daniel Wann, R. W. Carson, W. C. Thomas, John Cumberland, E. E. Leeke, T. A. Livermore, James McCleary, P. H. Lesher, J. M. Maugh, John Q. Charles, D. H. Hinkle, D. Hunkins, Peter Marsden, E. H. Chambers, John Stickel and William Whitham. Meetings were held in Coatsworth's building until 1866.

May 6, 1862, the lodge disbanded and gave up its charter, but, upon petition, the charter was restored, May 26, 1862, to the following members: P. G., John C. Smith, J. Y. Wonderly, T. J. Smith, D. Stewart, J. C. Spare, J. W. Newburgh, C. E. Duer, C. H. Merrick, A. L. Rodgers, John New, Charles Manning, Jones Worden, George Snyder, Wm. Fisher, John Strossler and J. B. Young.

The following officers were elected:

N. G.—J. C. Smith.

V. G.—D. Stewart.

Secretary.—J. W. Newburgh.

Representative to the Grand Lodge.—J. C. Spare.

Trustees.—J. C. Smith, A. L. Rodgers, J. W. Newburgh, D. Stewart, and C. E. Duer.

In the year of 1866 the Lodge purchased the three-story brick building of which they now occupy the upper story. It is situated on the west side of Main, between Warren and Green Streets.

The present officers are:

N. G.—James Hudson.

V. G.—Edward Ross.

Secretary.—Eugene O. Spare.

Treasurer.—John C. Spare.

Meetings are held on every Tuesday evening. The present membership is 77.

Steuben Lodge No. 321, was organized on Sept. 27, 1865, by Past Grand Master John C. Smith. The following were chartered members:

Edward Haase P. G.; John D. Brendel, P. G.; Chrstopher Barner, P. V. G.; John Philip Hoffmann, Edward Claussen, John Eiseman, John Thode, John Weinberger, Henry Weimer, Conrad Bahwell. These had been members of Wildey and Galena Lodges and separated to form a German lodge. The first officers were: N. G., Christopher Barner; V. G., John Thode; Secretary, Edward Claussen; Treasurer, John P. Hoffmann. The first Representative to the Grand Lodge of Illinois, was Edward Haase, P. G. At that that time meetings were held in the hall of Wildey Lodge, until June, 1866, when the lodge furnished a hall in Dr. A. Wierich's building on Bench Street, between Green and Washington Streets, where meetings are still held. The membership at present is 108.

The present officers are:

N. G.—Charles Geiger.

V. G.—Michael Bader.

Secretary.—Edward Claussen.

Treasurer.—Conrad Bahwell, who is also Representative to the Grand Lodge.

The lodge has a capital of $3,879.

Lead Mine Encampment No. 5, was organized May 7, 1846, upon petition to the Grand Lodge for a dispensation for that purpose, by the following brothers; C. P., John G. Potts; P. H. P., A. D. Robertson; Patriarch, D. K. Hinkle; Patriarch, F. G. Schwatka; Almon Leach, Henry Marfield, G. H. Mars, John P. DeZoya, James McCleary, and George C. Rice.

On June 2, Patriarchs A. D. Robertson and A. D. Boyce, exalted the following brothers to the Royal Purple Degree, to wit: A. Leach, H. Marfield, G. H. Mars, and on the eighth day of the same month, Jas. McCleary was also exalted, when the petitioners, being in readiness, proceeded to elect the following officers:

C. P., A. D. Robertson.
H. P., F. G. Schwatka.
S. W., A. Leach.
J. W., H. Marfield.
Scribe, D. K. Hinkle.
Treasurer, J. G. Potts.
Sentinel, James McCleary.

Other members were soon after exalted and made members. Meetings have always been held in Wildey Lodge Hall.

Its present officers are:
C. P., H. A. Uhren.
H. P., Richard Seal.
Sr. Warden, John Edwards.
Scribe, Robert Brand.
Treasurer, Henry Marfield.
Jr. Warden, Jas. B. Ginn.
Trustees, F. J. Uhlrich, Dan'l H. Dildine, Richard Seal, John F. Brendel, James B. Ginn.
D. D. G. P. and Representative, Louis Grimm.

Galena Encampment No. 132, is a German organization. It was established January 26, 1872, by P. G. Patriarch, John C. Smith, and is an offspring of Lead Mine Encampment. The charter members were, P. C. Patriarch, George Caille; P. C. Patriarch, Peter Simon; Patriarchs, Edward Claussen, Charles Scheerer, Rudolph Speier, John Eisemann, Conrad Bahwell, Stephen Yunker, Christian Hornung. The first officers were, Peter Simon, C. P.; George Caille, H. P.; John Eisemann, S. W.; Edward Claussen, Scribe; Rudolph Speier, Treasurer; Charles Scheerer, J. W. Meetings have always been held in the hall of Wildey Lodge.

The present membership is 46. The Encampment has a capital of $216.30.

Present officers:
C. P.—John Speier.
H. P.—Peter Simon.
S. W.—Christian Hornung.
Scribe.—Edward Claussen.
Treasurer.—Rudolph Speier.
J. W.—Joseph Bensch.

The Odd Fellows' Union Protective Association.—This society is an outgrowth, as its name implies, of the I. O. O. F., which was established February 10, 1870. Its object and workings can best be understood by reference to its constitution, from which the following articles are extracts:

Article 1, Section 1. This society shall be known as the "Odd Fellows' Union Protective Association of Jo Daviess County, Illinois." Its object is to provide a fund for the immediate relief of the widows and orphans of deceased members of the Association.

Article 3, Section 1. Qualification for membership shall be membership in good standing of a subordinate Lodge of the I. O. O. F. and residence in Jo Daviess County, State of Illinois, Provided, That if a member should remove out of the county, his membership in this Association shall not be affected by such removal, so long as he remains a member in good standing of a Lodge of the I. O. O. F. in this county, and pays all assessments made upon him by the Association.

The applicant must be in good health, not over fifty years of age, of good moral character, and pay an initiation fee of one and a quarter dollars, of which one dollar shall be devoted to the protection of widows and orphans, and the remaining be for contingent expenses.

Article 4, Section 1. To retain membership in this Association, the member must retain membership in good standing in the lodge, and at the death of each member of this Association, he shall pay to the secretary the sum of one dollar and twenty-five cents, as provided for in section 3, article 3, within ten days after being notified.

Section 2. Should a member be dropped, suspended or expelled from his lodge, his membership immediately ceases in this Association, and one dollar shall be refunded to him; nor is this Association bound to his widow, orphans, heirs, or assigns, for any pecuniary protection.

Section 3. Should a member be re-instated in his lodge, he may be re-instated in this Association by a proper certificate, the same as a new member.

Section 4. Should a member withdraw from his lodge by final card or otherwise, his membership in this Association is not effected thereby, so long as there remains an assessment to his credit upon the books, and for ten days thereafter, after which time no new assessment can be made upon a member holding a final card.

Article 5. At the decease of a member, who at the time of his death, was entitled to benefits from his lodge and to all the rights and privileges of this association, or who had to his credit one assessment in advance, the widow, orphans, or heirs of such deceased member, shall receive from the funds of the Association, an amount in cash equal to one dollar, for each and every surviving member of the association.

Officers of the Association for 1878, are:

Dr. Benj. F. Fowler, of Wildey Lodge No. 5, President.

Manley Rogers, of Ridgley Lodge No. 259, Vice President.

Henry Marfield, of Wildey Lodge No. 5, Secretary.

F. J. Uhlrich, of Wildey Lodge No. 5, Treasurer.

Board of Trustees.—Henry Marfield, of Wildey Lodge No. 5; John C. Spare and F. Stryker, of Galena Lodge No. 17; Edward Claussen and Edward Haase, of Steuben Lodge No. 321; E. R. Smith, of Hardin Lodge No. 33; John Buckley, of Reliance Lodge No 533.

Finance Committee.—E. H. Marsh, George Beasman, and Charles Sheerer.

KNIGHTS OF PYTHIAS.

Saxon Lodge, No. 62, K. of P., owes its origin to the efforts of Geo. W. Perrigo, its first presiding officer (by whom it was named), and John H. Walsh, Past Chancellor. It was instituted on the night of November 22, 1875, by Past Grand Chancellor, H. W. Rice, in the hall of Galena Lodge No. 17, I. O. O. F., on Bench Street. The following is a list of its charter members:

Geo. W. Perrigo, John H. Walsh, Jacob Fawcett, B. F. Fowler, John F. Brendel, Wm. R. Rowley, Charles Scheerer, S. K. Miner, Richard H. Heller, Geo. O. Howard, Wm. Spensley, H. D. Howard, F. Buckdorf, Wm. Buckdorf, E. C. Ripley, D. F. Barrows, J. C. Glenat, Wilbur F. Crummer, F. B. Newhall, S. P. Comstock, Frank LeBron, S. S. Tobey, H. B. Chetlain, Brougham Thompson, Wm. Davis.

Its original officers were: P. C., J. H. Walsh; Chancellor Commander, Gen. W. Perrigo; Vice Chancellor, J. Fawcett; Prelate, B. F. Fowler; Master of Exchequer, Wm. Spensley; Master of Finance, W. F. Crummer; K. of R. & S., Geo. O. Howard; Master-at-Arms, John F. Brendel; Inner Guard, Frank LeBron, Outer Guard, Wm. Buckdorf. Since November 29, 1875, the Lodge has held its meetings in Harmonia Hall on Bench Street. It has twice been represented in the Grand Lodge by Past Chancellor, George W. Perrigo, who, at the last session of the Grand Lodge convention held in the city of Springfield, was made Grand Master-at-Arms, and now holds that position. Its members are nearly all uniformed and well drilled in the tactics of the

John Tear

WARREN.

Order. Saxon Lodge took part in the Centennial celebration of the 4th of July, 1876, in Galena, and appeared in the imposing procession, mounted and in full uniform, making a magnificent display and exciting the admiration of the vast crowds of spectators, with which the streets of the city were thronged. The lodge meets in its Castle Hall every other Tuesday, pays weekly benefits to sick members, and carries out in other respects the objects of the Order. Its present officers are as follows: P. C., Chas. Scheerer; C. C., John F. Brendel; V. C., H. B. Chetlain; Prelate, Frank LeBron; K. of R. & S., Geo. W. Perrigo; M. of E., B. F. Fowler; M. of F., G. H. Miller; M.-at-A., D. N. Reed; Inner Guard, S. P. Comstock; Outer Guard, Henry Kastner; Representative to the Grand Lodge, J. Fawcett; Alternate, Frank LeBron. Since the institution of the lodge, the office of Deputy Grand Chancellor has been held by George W. Perrigo, P. C.

OTHER SOCIETIES.

St. Joseph's Benevolent Association.—This is also a society for benevolent purposes, similar to those mentioned. It was organized October 14, 1869. The first officers were:

President—Sebastian Maybrunn; *Vice President*—Gerhardt Paar; *Secretary*—Christopher Schreiner; *Assistant Secretary*—Paul Lemper; *Treasurer*—Valentine Dietz.

Meetings have always been held in St. Mary's Church school-house. The present membership is eighty, and the cash capital about $2,000. The present officers are:

President—Anton Lemper; *Vice President*—Paul Nelles; *Secretary*—Christopher Schreiner; *Assistant Secretary*—Arnold Becker; *Treasurer*—John Tasshaller; *Trustees*—Adam Nack, H. Loheinrich, S. Maybrunn, V. Dietz, H. Strohmeier.

The Irish-American Benevolent Association, was organized in 1874, for same purposes as those above mentioned, although no charter has been the secured, and their actions are entirely independent. The present membership is 150. In 1875, they purchased the two-story brick building on the corner of Franklin and Bench Streets, which was built for a Catholic Convent. This property is valued at $2,000, and is still used as their hall. The present officers are:

President—John Leader; *Vice President*—John Hart; *Secretary*—John McHugh; *Treasurer*—Thomas Harney.

The German Benevolent Society, of Galena was first organized in 1840, but no permanent institution was effected until February 10, 1844. It is an independent society, acting under a state charter, as a benevolent institution, its objects being to relieve its members who are in sickness, to bury the dead, and to assist widows and orphans. In 1853 they built their present brick hall, on Prospect Street, on the southwest side of the High School. It has continued its commendable labors to the present time, and now has a membership of 141.

It has property to the value of $1,667.50, and a cash capital of $4,613.37. Its officers at this time are:

President—Joseph Meller; *Vice President*—Xavirous Kammer; *Secretary*—Edward Claussen; *Assistant Secretary*—Louis Sanders.; *Treas-*

urer—John Kucherman; *Trustees*—Philip Brunner, Mathias Friesenecker, and Theodore Schaffer.

The Harmony Benevolent Society was originally organized as Harmony Lodge, No. 18, D. O. H., a German lodge, of the order of "Deutcher Orton Harugari," similar to the Odd Fellows in its purposes. The date of incorporation was July 22, 1849. John Eberhardt being the first Ober Bardi; Henry Fricke the first Secretary, and Frederick Bergman the first Treasurer.

In 1862 the meetings of the society were moved to the present location on Bench Street, in Wierich's Hall. This Association instituted a system of insurance among its members on July 31, 1871. In August, 1873, the Grand Lodge decided to begin a similar system, and requested this society to join in it, and transfer their funds ($6,369.72) to the treasury of the Grand Lodge. The local association thought this to be a one-sided bargain, and gave up its charter.

August 21, 1873, its members reorganized themselves under the name of Harmony Benevolent Society, an independent organization, with the following officers:

President—Edward Haase.

Vice President—Rudolph Speier.

Secretary—Conrad Recht.

Corresponding Secretary—Theodore Schaffer.

Treasurer—Edward Claussen.

Trustees—John Weinberger, Martin Geiger, George Caille, John Kucherman, and Casper Klett.

Meetings of the society are held every Thursday evening. They now have a cash capital of $6,009.73, and a membership of 112.

Galena Sociale Turner Gemeinde.—The aims and objects of the Turner societies, of which there are in the United States about two hundred *Vereines*, possessing property valued at $3,000,000 and a membership of nearly 15,000, are not generally understood by the American people, and as the order has been brought into prominence in Galena, we will give a brief synopsis of their origin. The Turner *Vereine*, or lodge, is an auxiliary to the General Assembly or Turnerbund, meaning Grand Lodge, from which body charters are obtained, the same as in the organization of other bodies. Numerous *vereines*, however, are in existence which claim no allegiance to the Turnerbund, and are, therefore, independent of that body. To this class the Galena Sociale Turner Gemeinde belongs, though the rules by which it is governed, as well as the objects of the Society, are exactly the same as those deriving their charters from the General Assembly.

The original object of the Turner Unions is the development of scientific gymnastics, which object has seemed to languish somewhat among young German-Americans, and the Association becomes one of social intercourse, while the exercises become a means of occasional amusement. The history of the order in this city has been marked with several reverses. The first organization dates back to 1851, when it was composed of many of our adopted citizens, whose names have since stood high upon the roll of honor. Their meetings were then held in Harmonia Hall, where they had valuable scenery belonging to the dramatic company, which was an auxiliary of the Association.

The society continued until the outbreak of the civil war, when it disbanded, and the majority of its members, inspired by love for the flag of their chosen country, left their homes to assist in maintaining its honor and the perpetuity of the States.

April 6, 1872, the present Galena Sociale Turner Gemeinde was organized at Wierich Hall, when the following named gentlemen were duly elected officers of the society:

C. Barner, First Sprecher; H. Marfield, Second Sprecher; P. Simon, Secretary; R. Heller, Treasurer; F. Kratochoil, First Turnwalt; T. Hassig, Second Turnwalt; C. Heller, Zeugwart.

The members of this new organization were composed of the very best portion of the German population. Their numbers rapidly increased, which suggested the need of more commodious quarters. It was then that the project of erecting a hall was agitated, which resulted in the building of an edifice not only for their, but for the public benefit. Turner Hall is now the place of holding the majority of public entertainments which visit Galena. It is a large stone building, with a hall on the first floor, which cost $15,000. It is furnished with a large stage, 46 by 22 feet, piano, costly scenery, and is considered by the traveling entertainment companies to be one of the finest in Northwestern Illinois.

At the time of laying the corner-stone (in 1874) of this building, a grand celebration and procession was made, embracing sixteen societies of Galena and a host of citizens. The procession formed at 10:30 A. M. on Bench Street, and marched through Bench, Meeker, Main and Gear Streets, concluding by passing up Bench Street to the Public Hall, where appropriate exercises were the order of the day. The Chief Marshal was Col. M. M. Wheeler; Aid-de-Camp, Geo. W. Perrigo.

The present officers of the society are:

President, Christopher Barner.
Vice President, Mat. Meller.
Secretary, Charles Miller.
Treasurer, Charles Scheerer.
First Turnwart, Charles Grimm.
Second Turnwart, Louis Hornung.
Zeugwart, E. F. Hille.

SCHOOLS.

Galena High School.—June 5, 1860, the number of members of the School Board was changed from three to five. The first board under this act was J. N. Waggoner, Thomas Foster, S. W. McMaster, H. W. Foltz and John Adams. One member of the board, Mr. McMaster, was chosen to act as superintendent.

At this time the erection of the High School building was begun, with John Adams and Mr. McMaster as building committee. Oliver Marble was hired to superintend the completion of the building, who reported it finished on December 8, 1860. It is a fine, large, brick structure of three stories, on Prospect Street. The contractor, D. Farr, received $11,219.35, and a bill of $1,712.92 was allowed for furniture.

At this time seventeen teachers were enrolled, and the school population was 4,262. A. F. Townsend, now of Waterloo, Iowa, was principal, at $60 per month. On August 8, 1862, H. H. Miller was made principal, at $90 per month, who held the position until August 14, 1866, when he resigned. August 24 Sterne Rogers was elected principal, at $100 per month, who continued until September 6, 1869, when the present efficient principal, Mr. Samuel Hayes, was employed.

The present Board of Education consists of Dennis Galvin, President; D. N. Corwith, Treasurer; Wm. Hempstead, M. Munchrath, Dennis Galvin, C. L. Butcher and Andrew Telford.

The present teachers are: S. Hayes, Jr., Superintendent and Principal High School; Alice Luke, Assistant, High School; Annie Tomlin, Second Assistant, High School; John McHugh, room No. 26; Emma Gorman, room 28; Anna Delahunt, room 25; Katie McHugh, room 20; Louie Foltz, room 16; Era Brand, room 3; Maggie Gardner, room 17; Sarah Jones, room 2; Sarah Henry, East Galena District No. 3; Paulina Willy, East Galena District No. 3; Fanny Obuchon, Gear Street School; Mary Donahue, Seminary Hill; Maggie Murphy, Seminary Hill; Katie Burke, Gratiot School.

THE CUSTOM HOUSE AND MARINE HOSPITAL

At Galena were built under an appropriation of an Act of Congress for the year 1856. The buildings were commenced in June, 1857, and finished in the Fall of 1859. Messrs. Geiger & Joice, of the City of Washington, being the contractors, Ely S. Parker, Superintendent; and Daniel Wann, Disbursing Agent. The Custom House cost $78,529; the Marine Hospital, $43,430.

POST-OFFICE.

The post-office at Galena is the oldest in the northern part of the state; established June 4, 1826, as Fever River P. O., *Crawford* Co., Illinois, and changed to Galena, December 17, 1827. Until 1828 there was no regular mail service, and the office was supplied by steamboat in Summer, and during the Winter the postmaster was idle. In 1828 it was supplied from Vandalia once in two weeks, the mail being carried on horseback. Weekly mail service was established May 1, 1829. Notwithstanding the woful lack of mail service, the office early became one of great importance, as it was for some time the only post-office in the lead mining district. In the third number of the *Miners' Journal*, the list of letters remaining in the post-office July 1, 1828, numbered 350.

The following are the names and dates of appointment of the postmasters at Galena: Ezekiel Lockwood, June 4, 1826; Samuel Smoker, 1830; James G. Soulard March 5, 1835; Albion T. Crow, June 10, 1836; Philip P. Bradley, 1837; Allen Tomlin, August 23, 1839; Robt. W. Carson, 1841; John L. Slaymaker, August 25, 1845; Wm. P. Millard, 1849; Bernard Gray, 1853; Bushrod B. Howard, April, 1857; Warren W. Huntington, March 5, 1861; Horace H. Houghton, May 4, 1873; Warren W. Huntington, May, 1877,—took possession July 1, 1877.

Of these, the only ones known to be living are J. G. Soulard, A. Tomlin, W. W. Huntington and H. H. Houghton, all residing in Galena, and J. L. Slaymaker, residing near Albany, Ill. Howard left Galena, as Captain of Co. I, 19th Regiment Illinois Volunteers, and was killed at the fatal railroad disaster near Cincinnati, while his regiment was *en route* to the seat of war. Mr. Huntington served continuously from March, 1861, to May, 1863, and is probably the oldest postmaster of his class in the state. During Mr. Houghton's term, he was Special Agent of the Post-office Department until his re-appointment in 1877.

James Allan

SCALES MOUND

BANKING AND INSURANCE.

The Galena Branch of the State Bank of Illinois went into operation Dec. 5, 1835. Daniel Wann, President; Wm. C. Bostwick, Cashier. Mr. Wann was succeeded by Frederick Stahl about 1840. E. W. Turner was cashier in 1838–'9, and was succeeded by ——— Campbell. This bank ceased the transaction of banking business in 1842, and its affairs were wound up by the president and cashier about 1846 or '7.

The Galena Insurance Company was organized originally in 1851, with William Hempstead, President and Nicholas Stahl, Secretary, simply to preserve the charter. So continued until March 19, 1857, when it was reorganized by the election of Frederick Stahl, Nicholas Dowling, Chas. L. Stephenson, M. Y. Johnson, G. W. Campbell and John Lorrain, Directors; Frederick Stahl, President; and William H. Snyder, Secretary. The company transacted a banking business in connection with insurance, but abandoned the insurance business after two or three years. April 14, 1865, its stockholders having decided to take stock in the Merchant's National Bank, voted to discontinue banking business on and after the evening of the 15th, except in liquidation, that the deposits and other trust funds should be transferred to the bank, and that the assets should be divided as soon as realized. This company was successful, and at its close its stockholders received $14 for every $1 invested.

The Merchants National Bank of Galena, capital $125,000, was organized March 7, 1865, by the election of Augustus Esty, Frederick Stahl, L. S. Felt, Thomas Foster, J. H. Hellman, S. Crawford, J. M. Ryan, R. S. Norris and P. Klingle, Directors; Augustus Esty, President; Wm. H. Snyder, Cashier. Present officers: Augustus Esty, President; Wm. H. Snyder, Cashier.

The Bank of Galena.—The house of Rogers & Corwith were largely in the clothing business and dealing in lead in Galena at an early period, gradually became engaged in banking business; were known as bankers in 1842. In 1847 the firm sold their clothing business to E. H. & H. P. Corwith, and Henry Corwith, Nathan Corwith and Charles H. Rogers became known as the house of N. Corwith & Co., bankers. In 1853, the Bank of Galena was organized by these gentlemen under the laws of the State of Illinois, with Henry Corwith, President, and C. C. P. Hunt, Cashier. Nathan Corwith was afterwards President, succeeded in 1864 by R. H. McClellan. The Bank of Galena was succeeded by the National Bank of Galena.

The National Bank of Galena was organized in March, 1865. Its first directors were: Henry Corwith, Nathan Corwith, R. H. McClellan. T. B. Hughlett and John E. Corwith. President, R. H. McClellan; Cashier, E. C. Ripley. Present officers: R. H. McClellan, President; E. C. Ripley, Cashier; capital, $200,000.

THE GAS LIGHT COMPANY OF GALENA.

On the 25th day of July, 1855, E. H. Beebe, M. Y. Johnson, H. H. Gear, D. B. Morehouse, Frederick Stahl, Benj. Coombe, S. S. Lorrain, and G. W. Woodward, organized the Galena Gas Company, under the general laws approved Feb. 10, 1849, and elected a board of five trustees, viz.: E. H. Beebe as President, G. W. Woodward, Secretary, and M. Y. Johnson, Benj. Coombe and D. B. Morehouse. Aug. 10, 1855, the trustees made a contract with Samuel Ross to build for the company complete gas works, including mains and all the appliances for $80,000. Mr. Woodward resigned and Samuel Ross took his place in the board. In 1857, the company accepted the act of incorporation by the Legislature, and John Lorrain was elected director in the place of Samuel Ross. July 22, 1859, the property of the company was sold by the Sheriff. John Lorrain was the purchaser, and on the 24th day of October, 1859, the Gas Light Company of Galena was organized under the general laws, by John Lorrain, Darius Hunkins, Shewell S. Lorrain and O. O. Phillips. John Lorrain, D. Hunkins and S. S. Lorrain, Trustees; John Lorrain, President, Secretary and Treasurer. The Gas Light Company of Galena was incorporated by special act of the Legislature approved March 30, 1869. The charter was accepted by the old company which was reorganized May 1, 1869. John Lorrain, D. Hunkins and William J. Anderson, Directors. O. O. Phillips was elected in place of Anderson, March 5, 1872, and there has been no change since. Capital stock of the company, paid up, $63,000.

THE GALENA AND SOUTHERN WISCONSIN RAILROAD

Is purely a Galena enterprise. It was chartered by the Legislature of Illinois by act approved January 26, 1853. The original corporators were: Henry Corwith, James Carter, Alexander C. Davis, Daniel A. Barrows, Lucius S. Felt, Eli A. Collins, Wm. H. Bradley, Madison Y. Johnson, John Lorrain, Edward Hempstead, Nicholas Dowling and Halstead S. Townsend. Daniel A. Barrows, A. C. Davis, E. Hempstead, Fred. Stahl, James Carter and Henry Corwith, were made Commissioners, until a board of directors were chosen, for receiving subscriptions to the capital stock of the company. This charter authorized the building of a railroad from Galena to the line of Wisconsin in Jo Daviess County. By act approved March 2, 1857, the Legislature of Wisconsin incorporated the Galena and Southern Wisconsin Railroad Company. Nicholas Dowling, Edward H. Beebe, M. Y. Johnson, Sylvester McMasters, Daniel A. Barrows, L. S. Felt and Wellington Weigley, corporators, and authorized them to continue the construction of their railroad from a point on the state line in Jo Daviess County to a point of intersection with the line of the Milwaukee and Mississippi Railroad Company, west of Monroe. Having obtained the necessary legislation in both states, the company procured one hundred thousand dollars of the bonds of Jo Daviess County and an equal amount of the bonds of the City of Galena, but the Milwaukee company finally abandoned the line from Monroe to the Mississippi, and the G. & S. W. R. R. surrendered the bonds but maintained its organization until the charter could be used under more favorable circumstances. In 1871, Darius Hunkins, Madison Y. Johnson, James M. Ryan, Geo. R. Melville and Richard Barrett were the Directors of the Company. Madison Y. Johnson, President; James M. Ryan, Vice President; Robert Brand, Secretary; Wm. H. Snyder, Treasurer; Edward Harding, Chief Engineer; Louis Shissler, Attorney. In August, 1871, the directors having determined to adopt the narrow gauge for the contemplated road, and the president appealed to the citizens of Galena to subscribe for the stock. In October of the same year the engineer reported that the route had been surveyed. In 1872 the City of Galena issued its bonds for $57,-000 to aid in the construction of the road.

Work on the road was immediately commenced, and nearly all the grading completed in 1873. Then, failing to negotiate their bonds, work was suspended until 1874, when a reorganization was effected by the election of a new board of officers. In July of that year bonds to the amount of $200,000 were negotiated; work was resumed, and the road ironed to Plattville on the 31st day of December, 1874.

In consequence of some misunderstanding, the expected Plattville aid was withheld, and from the further fact of a snow blockade, the road was not operated that Winter. In the early Spring of 1875, another organization became necessary because of the resignation of some of the old managers. The new company went to work at once to put the road in condition to be operated. In the Fall of 1874, the company commenced running trains from Galena to Benton, fifteen miles. In the early Summer of 1875, trains commenced running to Plattville, since when there has been no interruption except by a "washout" by heavy rains, July 4, 1876, after which the traffic was suspended for a period of three months, when the damage was repaired and traffic resumed. Since then the earnings of the road have been gradually increasing, until they are now a little in excess of the expenses. In 1877, the road was extended from Phillips' Corner, four miles east of Plattville, *via* Belmont to McCormick's Corners, ten miles. This part of the road will be in operation early this Spring (1878). As fast as the means of the company will permit, the road will be continued to Wingville, in the centre of the zinc region of Wisconsin. These mines are the richest zinc discoveries ever made in the U. S. From Wingville it will be extended to Muscoda or vicinity, on the Wisconsin River, as soon as possible. When completed that far, the pine and lumber regions will be reached and made accessible and available to the country between Galena and Muscoda.

The following is the present organization of the company:

Directors—R. Barrett, Galena; Matt. Murphy, Benton, Wis.; D. Hunkins, W. H. Blewett, D. Rochford, Galena.

Officers—R. Barrett, President; Matt. Murphy, Vice President; S. O. Stillman; Secretary; E. C. Ripley, Treasurer; W. H. Blewett, Superintendent; A. W. Bell, Attorney, Plattville, Wisconsin.

The stations along the road after leaving Galena, are: Millbrig, Buncombe, Benton, Cuba City, St. Rose, St. Elmo, and Platteville, on the old route. On the extension, the only station named is Grand View (old Belmont). Trains make one trip per day from Galena to Plattville and return. An additional train will be established this Spring. From the time the road was first completed to the present, there has been no accident or injuries to passengers or employes, of any kind—a record that can not be shown by every railroad.

GALENA TURNPIKE COMPANY.

May 12, 1868 the Galena newspapers contained the following:

"NOTICE OF ORGANIZATION.

"Notice is hereby given that the books will be opened on Saturday, May 30, 1868, at 10 o'clock, A. M., at the Court House in Galena, for subscription to the capital stock of a turnpike or macadamized road from Galena to the Wisconsin State line, at or near John Miller's place, at which meeting the organization will be fully completed under the general laws of the State of Illinois. All interested are invited to be present.

"JACOB DOXEY,
"R. S. NORRIS,
"HARVEY MANN,
"GEORGE SANDERS,
"J. M. HARRIS."

This road was designed to take the place of a plank road that had been built by a company known as the Mineral Point Plank Road Company, which was organized about 1856 or 1857. The plank road was built but did not prove to be a profitable investment. In times when the roads were good, the road was avoided by farmers and others to save toll. When planks in one part of the road would rot away, their places would be supplied with planks taken up and removed from another part. With this kind of management, says Mr. R. S. Norris, teams were kept busy all the time transferring planks from one part of the road to another. The road was never in good condition, and at last came to be almost universally condemned and travel over it abandoned. Under this condition of affairs, a few of the enterprising men of Galena and vicinity, conceived the idea suggested in the advertisement quoted above.

The capital stock of the Turnpike Company was fixed at $37,500. July, 1868, W. Weigley, S. S. Brown and James M. Ryan were elected directors. S. S. Brown was chosen as president of the company, and R. S. Norris, secretary and treasurer.

The building of the road was commenced in July, 1868, and completed and put under toll to the Four Mile House by the 1st of November, of that year. The remainder of the road to the State line was completed in 1869. Twenty-two thousand dollars of the capital stock was paid in, with which the road was undertaken and completed to the Four Mile House. The balance of the road was completed from its earnings. At the beginning of the undertaking, the company issued bonds bearing eight per cent interest per annum, on which a loan of $15,500 was negotiated. After the completion of the road, stock dividends were declared every six months and the earnings of the road applied to the payment of the bonds which were all all taken up in 1873. Since the payment of the bonds, the dividends have averaged about seven per cent per annum.

When the company was organized the county authorities gave them the right of way and control of the old free road, sixty feet in width, for thirty years from 1868. The charter will expire in 1898.

HOTELS.

De Soto House.—In 1852 a stock company was organized for the purpose of erecting a hotel building which would be in keeping with the general prosperity and growth of Galena, and, as a result, the present De Soto House was completed in 1853, at a cost of $85,000. It was planned to be of five stories, but, deciding to add another, the company borrowed $13,000 on mortgage, for that purpose. The hotel was furnished at a cost of $15,000, and first occupied by John C. Parks. But, as is often the case, the mortgage ultimately caused the sale of the building. It was then held under foreclosure until 1874, when the present proprietor, Wm. H. Blewett, re-opened and has since managed it in commendable style. It is a six-story brick building, 100 by 110 feet in size, containing 240 rooms.

The principal hotels of Galena now are the De Soto House, by Wm. H. Blewett; European Hotel, by L. Van Embden; Mississippi House, by Joseph Dittenburg; Lawrence House, by John Hassig; Logan House, by Henry Logan; United States Hotel, by James Ingram; Hornung House, by John Hornung; Broadway House, by Wm. Cloth; Union House, by W. Ivey; Bethel House, by Wm. Hoey.

MISCELLANEOUS.

Adjustment of Land Claims.—It may seem somewhat strange to the people of the present, that there were not more serious differences between the conflicting interests of the early settlers—miners and farmers—than there were. When the first settlers came, in 1819, and up to the organization of the county in 1827, it may be said there were no written or statute laws to govern the people in any of their transactions. The agent representing the interests of the U. S. government issued certain *pronunciamentos* for the government of the miners. Those engaged in other pursuits governed themselves, and it is said by the surviving settlers of the early days that there was less of theft, larceny and kindred crimes in those days than there is now. The settlers were governed entirely by the laws of honor.

To give the young people an idea of how the pioneer settlers protected the claims of each other, we make the following extracts from the proceedings of a Settlers' Meeting, called to devise "ways and means" for that purpose:

"Pursuant to public notice, a meeting of the settlers on the public lands in Township 28 N., R. 2 E. (Galena), was held at the school-house on Saturday, the 2d day of January, 1847. On motion of James D. Rawlins, Samuel W. Hathaway was called to the chair, and E. Baldwin chosen Secretary.

"Mr. G. M. Hallett offered a resolution pledging the meeting to concur in the resolutions adopted at a Settlers' Meeting held in Galena, on the 5th of December, 1846, which was adopted. [No written proceedings of the meeting referred to in this resolution were to be found.]

"M. Hallett, S. Snyder, F. Stahl, J. Hawkins and J. Holman were appointed a committee to report regulations for the government of claimants in the township. The committee reported, recommending the election of a board of arbitrators, consisting of five persons, authorized to settle all disputes between conflicting claimants, on principles of equity and justice, their decisions to be final. If any claimant objected to either arbitrator, and a majority of the board sustain the objection, the member objected to should retire during that trial, and that his place be filled by a good and suitable citizen. The board to appoint their own clerk, who, at his own expense, shall provide books, paper and plats. The clerk was directed to provide for the registry of claimants before the first day of February next, and to receive a fee of ten cents for each claim presented for registry.

George Troxell, David Matlack, H. Willard, H. Singer, and John Crumbellick, were appointed arbitrators, and the gentlemen present pledged themselves to each other to "use all just means in our power to sustain the decisions of the arbitrators for this township, and to abide by such decisions in all cases in which we are interested."

The meeting adjourned to meet at Dixon on the morning of the first day of the land sales, prepared for two weeks active service.

The claimants of the public lands in township 28 north, range one, east of the 4th principal meridian, held a meeting at Mount Hope Meeting House on Tuesday, the 5th day of February, A. D. 1847, and adopted a constitution and by-laws similar to the provisions above quoted. The arbitrators chosen under the proceedings of that meeting, were Samuel Hughlett, A. Snyder, Michael Byrne, R. S. Norris, Charles G. Thomas, Patrick McAllen, and S. M. McMaster. The following was their written pledge:

"We hereby pledge ourselves to each other, that we will use all just means in our power, to sustain the decisions of the arbitrators for this township; and that we will abide by such decisions as they shall make, in all cases in which we are interested."

To this pledge ninety-two signatures were attached, only three of which were by "his X." In no case was the pledge violated. No appeal was taken from the decision of the arbitrators—no "motion made for a new trial." Many of the ninety-two whose names grace the book from which the pledge is copied, still remain in the county, and have always been useful and influential citizens.

Fires.—Galena has never suffered seriously, but once, from fires. On 3 o'clock on the morning of April 1, 1854, a fire broke out in M. O. Walker's stage stable, situated on Commerce Street, in the rear of the next block north of the De Soto House. The fire extended northward across Main, Washington, and Bench Streets. Thirty-two buildings were burned, comprising a large part of the business part of the town, and including St. Michael's Church, on the opposite side of Bench Street. Among the buildings destroyed was the office of the *Courier*. The total loss estimated at $300,000. The *Gazette* of that date attributes the fire to an incendiary.

River Improvements.—In 1854, various projects were discussed for improving the navigation of Fever River, and it was seriously proposed to construct a dam and lock of seven feet lift, at, or near, its mouth. It ended however, as it began—in talk.

The present winter (1877-'8), Congress was petitioned and strongly urged to include Galena River in the appropriations for harbor and river improvements, with some hopes of success. M. Y. Johnson was sent by the Galenians, as a delegate, to present the subject, and urge it upon the attention of Congress. He labored earnestly and faithfully, and received many assurances that the appropriation would be made.

Casualties.—On the 18th day of August, 1868, a sad and melancholy accident occurred on the Illinois Central Railroad, that brought sorrow and death to several homes in Galena. The particulars of this terrible event, we gather from a pamphlet published a few days after its occurrence, the facts of which were compiled from the Galena *Democrat:*

At about 8 o'clock on the morning aforesaid, Conductor James Woods started out from Galena with his ditching train, consisting, at the time, of two dirt cars, destined for Apple River. He had some thirty workmen on the train, most of whom occupied the second car from the engine. The train was "backing up." When rounding a curve, within about half a mile of Council Hill, and going, at the time, at a full rate of speed, they collided with two detached cars, which were approaching from the opposite direction, at a rate, it was thought, of thirty miles per hour. They were both heavily loaded; the first with railroad iron, the second with a cast iron wheel, of 4,500 pounds weight. Owing to the curve in the road, the detached cars were not perceived by the men, until they were within two or three rods, and as the larger number were old men, the instinct of self-preservation had not time to take any definite action. A horrible crash—the heavy, iron rails were pushed forward—the large iron wheel rolled forward, and Thomas Boyd and Michael Niland were still in death. Mr. Boyd with his head crushed to jelly. Patrick Maghan, a young man of twenty-one years, had his skull fractured, and an arm horribly mutilated. He survived but a few hours. Mr. Thomas Mulligan, Cornelius Howe, and Mr. McClann, were also injured, it is feared fatally. The others, by jumping, managed to escape fatal injuries, but were more or less hurt. Master M. Birmingham, one of the injured, who escaped with the loss of five teeth, said that he had no thought of jumping from the car, but rushed to the forward brake of the rear car, thinking that with that support he could stand the shock. He was picked up after the collision in an insensible condition, close by the engine, having been thrown more than the length of the car. So soon as the engine could be run back to Galena, Drs. Hempstead, Campbell and Newhall, accompanied by Father Power, were brought to the relief of the wounded. But one, only, of the three first fatal cases, then needed their help, and that was young Maghan. Upon consultation, it was decided to amputate his fractured arm, but his sufferings were ended by death before they were ready to commence the operation. He died calling on his mother, but his last audible words were: "lay me down to die." A jury was summoned and an inquest held, by two Aldermen of Council Hill. The jury rendered a verdict in accordance with the facts herein stated.

At half past nine, the morning after the catastrophe, three hearses, carrying the bodies of three of the victims, were slowly driven up Main street, and came to a stand before the Church of St. Michael. On either side of the hearses were the pall-bearers—those by the body of the young man were youths, and some of them fellow-companions of the deceased, when he was in life but yesterday. The chief mourners were driven in carriages, and a long retinue of sympathizing friends were in attendance. The scene, as the three bodies were carried in close succession into the church, was profoundly impressive. The poor widow of one of the aged victims, borne, almost fainting up the long steps of the church; the blanched countenances of all those nearest kin to the dead; and the hundreds of spectators, moving slowly up, with the bearing of deep sympathy, all tended to produce a sensation which will not soon be forgotten.

The deceased were all members of the St. Michael's Church, and hence their funeral rites were served at one and the same time, in that church, Father Power officiating.

The solemn and impressive ceremonies were concluded with an address by the Rev. Pastor, in which he spoke eloquently and feelingly.

The Blue Ribbon Movement.—The tidal wave of the Blue Ribbon. Temperance Reform Movement reached Galena the first days of October, 1877. Under the labors and directions of Messrs. Hoofstetter and Rowell, a reform was inaugurated that promises to result in great good. As showing the effect of this movement, the following figures are presented, showing the falling off in the consumption of beer in Galena from October 1, 1877, as compared with the same period in 1876:

In October, 1876, 456 barrels were consumed; in November do., 382; in December do., 424. Total in three months, 1,262 barrels.

In October, 1877, 250 barrels were consumed; in November, 198; in December, 266. Total, 714—a falling off of 548 barrels. Reduced to gallons, the falling off was equal to 17,536 gallons. Reduced to glasses, and estimating twenty glasses to the gallon, the cash falling off in the beer trade for the three months named was equal to $17,536.

A Reform Club was organized October 11, 1877, and continues in good working order.

FINALE.

The Buffalo—When Did They Disappear?—When the first settlers came to the Fever River region, there was but little underbrush in any part of the country. Its growth had been kept down by the Indians, who started fires for that purpose, that their hunting grounds might be the less obstructed. Forty years ago this Winter (1877–'8), says Captain D. S. Harris, I was out hunting with an old Indian, and we came to an open prairie or plain, to one portion of which my attention was particularly directed because of its circular form and the heavy growth of old weeds and grass within it. I applied to my Indian companion for an explanation, and he gave me this traditionary solution:

"Seventy years ago this Winter (1838) was the coldest ever known. During the Winter a heavy, deep snow came on, and the buffaloes were snowed in. The snow fell so deep they could not travel, and in making the attempt they went round and round, just like a white man when he becomes lost on the prairies or in the woods. The snow was so deep and remained so long, that they fell exhausted and starved or froze to death. Their carcasses decayed and enriched the ground where they died, and so the weeds and grasses, different from those natural to the prairie, came to grow over their bones. After that Winter the buffalo left—crossed the Mississippi, and none have ever been seen on the east side of the great river since."

Captain Harris says within the circle and beneath the old grasses, and weeds, and mould, there were a few remnants of bones, and that he has every reason to believe the Indian's traditionary narrative to have been correct. If true, the disappearance of the buffalo from this part of the country may be fixed at one hundred and ten years ago, or in 1768, as any one can determine by the application of a little arithmetic.

Any one who has noticed the fact that on a wild spot of ground where an animal has died and decayed, a new growth of grass and weeds, different from those natural to the ground, will spring up, will see the reasonableness of Harris' Indian companion's theoretic explanation for the growth of weeds in the circle to which his (Harris') attention was called, while on a hunt "forty years ago," whatever of credit may be given to the remainder of the tradition.

The Weather.—The Winter of fifty years ago—1827-'8—was so mild and open that, on the 25th of February, 1828, the steamer Josephine arrived at Galena from St. Louis, bringing a cargo of flour—an incident related elsewhere. The present Winter seems to be equal to that one in temperature. At no time has the Mississippi been closed with ice for more than a few days at a time. For the greater part of the time it has been as open and as free to navigation as in the summer months. The roads to the country have remained almost impassable from the time Winter commenced, while the streets of Galena have either been dry or sloppy nearly every day from the first of December to this, the 28th day of February. Only on one or two occasions was there a sufficient fall of snow to justify an attempt at sledding or sleigh-riding, and that for but a few hours. The ice harvest is a failure—in fact the Winter of 1877-'8 may be set down as a season of ice famine to the people of Galena.

DUNLEITH

DUNLEITH.

A correct history of Dunleith can not be written without going back to the period when white people first disturbed the primitive condition of the towering bluffs and the narrow valley that nestles down between their base and the great Mississippi River. Although a French Indian trader named D'Bois is known to have maintained a trading post on the land now owned by Augustus Switzer, two and a half miles east of Dunleith, and almost directly opposite the Iowa bluffs where Julien Dubuque (after whom the City of Dubuque was named) was buried, no data can be found to fix the time when this trading post was established, or how long it was continued. The best sources of information indicate that Dubuque and D'Bois came at the same time, and that, while Dubuque stopped at the mouth of Cat Fish Creek, on the Iowa side, D'Bois (or Dubois) chose the Illinois side as his field of operations. When the first permanent settlers came, in 1832, the old cabins erected by D'Bois were still standing, and although they had fallen into partial decay, one of them was refitted and made to serve as a school house for the first school ever taught in the territory now embraced within Dunleith Township. The site of that old cabin is enclosed in the beautiful farm residence grounds of Augustus Switzer, and within a few feet of his summer house. That these cabins were allowed to remain so long after D'Bois abandoned them can only be attributed to the friendly disposition of the Menominee Indians, and the respect and friendship they entertained for their builder and first occupant.

Some authorities say that the island (now nearly gone) just below Dunleith, and almost directly between the Dubuque and D'Bois interests, was occupied by white men long before settlements were made at Galena—that rude (log) smelting works had been erected there by a Missouri miner named George E. Jackson as early as 1811. The island on which these smelting works were operated has been well-nigh washed away, and consequently the last remnant of Jackson's cabin and his log furnaces has disappeared with the island on which they were built. There are no data to be found to show how long Mr. Jackson occupied this island or the extent of his operations, but it is known that he built a flat boat on which the product of his furnaces was carried to St. Louis, and that he experienced a good deal of trouble with the Indians in making his trips to St. Louis. Neither is it known when Jackson abandoned the island, or the causes that induced him to give up his undertaking, but in the Fall of 1823 he returned to the mining district and settled at or near Galena.

Some authorities say that D'Bois and Dubuque came to the country together, but separated on their arrival, as already shown—the former opening an Indian trading place on the Illinois side, and Dubuque on the Iowa side of the Mississippi. While there are no records to be found showing the time when D'Bois built his trading cabin at the site already described, it is known that Dubuque was here as early as 1788, hence it is reasonable to suppose that D'Bois commenced his operations simultaneously with Dubuque, and there is but little reason to doubt that the first cabin built by a white man in the territory of Jo Daviess County was built by D'Bois, in what is now Dunleith Township, many years before white men began to work the lead mines at Galena. Add the further well authenticated statement that George E. Jackson occupied the island already indicated, and engaged in smelting lead ore as early as 1811, and the fact is pretty well established that the first white men to claim an abiding and business place within the present territory of Jo Daviess County were D'Bois and Jackson; and that within the territory now embraced in this township, the primitive stillness of a region now so full of life and business was first disturbed by the innovations of white men.

When D'Bois took his departure, either for other wilds, or the fancied happy hunting grounds of the Indians, among whom he traded, and Jackson and his associates (if he had any) abandoned the island, the country relapsed into its natural condition, and left the Menominee people "monarchs of all they surveyed," until the early Winter of 1831–'2, when Eleazer Frentress, a native of North Carolina, came into the township, and selected a claim of 320 acres at the site of the present Frentress homestead, and immediately set about the erection of a double log cabin. Mr. Frentress and his family, consisting of his wife and children, had emigrated from Wood River, in Madison County, near Alton, to the Galena district in the Spring of 1827. They took passage at Alton on board the steamboat "Indiana," and on the 7th day of April, of that year, were landed at the present site of the City of Galena. At that time, says Mrs. Frentress, there were not more than a half dozen cabins in the place, and entertainment in any of them impossible to be secured. There was a keel-boat tied up at the landing, and that afforded all the shelter possible to be obtained, and that was placed at the service of the new comers. At that time there were glowing reports of the discovery of rich leads of galena in the vicinity of what is now Cassville, Wisconsin, and not finding things at Galena to his liking, and the keel-boat in which they had found shelter since their arrival on the 7th, being bound for Cassville, Mr. Frentress determined to go on there in pursuit of fortune. A man named Camp and his wife, who had also found shelter and a resting place on the keel-boat, accompanied the expedition, if it may be called such, and there is a very strong probability that Mrs. Frentress and Mrs. Camp were the first white women to venture into the untamed wilds of Wisconsin—especially in that part of it around Cassville. At this time Mrs. Frentress was the mother of two children—Thomas, aged four, and Lucy, aged two years—and it will require no very great stretch of imagination to recognize in Mrs. F. a courage amounting to heroism, when she assumed the risk of placing her babes and herself beyond the pales of civilization and at the mercy of hordes of Indians. The boat landed its passengers at a mining camp, very nearly where Cassville has been built, and there they were left to find shelter from the elements of the weather in the rude tents of the miners, and where they remained for a period of three weeks. At the end of that time they found their way to Grant River, and settled down to mining life in the near vicinity of Beetown. Here a company was formed, and active operations commenced, and successfully prosecuted until the 4th of July, 1827, when there came an Indian scare, and the camp was hastily abandoned. On the morning of that day the men of the camp had gone to Cassville, and when they arrived there they found that a keel-boat descending the river had been attacked by the Winnebago Indians, one man killed and another one wounded. The cargo box had three hundred bullet holes within it, while the hull of the boat probably had as many more. At Cassville all was excitement and alarm. The Beetown miners hastily returned to their camp, and prepared to leave immediately for Galena. The women quickly packed what few bed-clothes, wearing apparel, etc., they had in boxes and trunks, which were secreted in a dense thicket near by; a few provisions—a little bread and a little meat—put into a basket or sack for the children, and hurried arrangements made for a forced march to Galena. The camp possessed two horses—two women, two children and one sick or disabled man out of the fifteen who composed the male part of Beetown. The two women and one of the children were mounted on one of the horses and the sick man on the other. The cooking dinners were left over the fire, and at four o'clock the flight to Galena was commenced, and kept up until far into the night, when they reached a windfall, where the fallen timber, thick undergrowth, etc., so impeded their progress that, in the darkness they found it impossible to proceed further until daylight, and they went into camp—or rather, they halted until morning. As soon as it became sufficiently light to enable them to find their way out of the fallen *debris*, the flight was resumed, and a little after twelve o'clock, July 5, 1827, the party arrived at Galena, and Mr. Frentress and his wife stopped at the house and home of her father. The distance traveled, said Mrs. Frentress to the writer, was from fifty to sixty miles, every step of which was full of dreadful apprehension and terrible suspense.

When the Indian scare had somewhat subsided, Mr. Frentress went down to Peoria, where he remained about one month, when he returned to Galena, and soon after went back to the mines at Beetown, where he remained undisturbed until he sold out his interests for $700 in the Winter of 1828–'9. The sum thus realized enabled him to fit himself out with a team of horses, a cow or two, and the necessary implements to engage in farming pursuits, and he leased or rented a farm on Fever River, about four miles above Galena, where he remained until he commenced the improvement of the claim already mentioned.

The Frentress Cabin was a double one, built out of round logs, and then "scutched" down. There was a hall, or entry, between the two parts, and, for many years it was regarded as the grandest farm house in all this region of country. Its doors were always open, and its beds and its table always free and welcome to every one who claimed its hospitality. Although Mrs. Frentress now occupies a very handsome brick residence, the "old log cabin" is still preserved as a memento of pioneer days.

The old cabin was finished in the Winter of 1831–'2, but was not occupied by the family until the 7th of September, 1832—after the close of the Black Hawk War.

In the Spring of 1832, as soon as the frost was out of the ground, Mr. Frentress commenced breaking the prairie sod with a view to making a crop. Potatoes, corn, etc., were planted, and the foundation of a home in the wilds of the Menominee and Sinsinawa Valleys commenced in goodly earnest. While Stephen D'Bois built the first cabin in this region, to Mr. Frentress belongs the honor of turning over the first furrow of prairie sod.

While the making of this pioneer farm was under way, the Indians were concentrating their forces with a view to negotiating a new treaty, the Black Hawk War was precipitated, and for a time the industries of the mines and farms were interrupted—in fact, almost entirely suspended. May 14, of that year (1832), while Frentress was busily at work on his claim, plowing and planting, his wife sent a runner to him with the information that the Indians were reported to be marching on Galena with the threatened purpose of destroying every man, woman and child in the settlement. He unhitched his team from the plow, left it standing in the middle of a furrow, and hastened to Galena to join the forces that were being mustered to resist the apprehended invasion, and, joining Captain Vosburgh's Company, which was made to form a part of Colonel Strode's regiment, he continued with that command until a peace was conquered by the subjugation of the Indians. September 6, 1832, he was mustered out of service, and on the 7th, the goods of the family were packed and loaded into wagons and the journey to the new home commenced. There were neither roads nor crossing places on the streams. Trackways for the wagons had to be cut out and the banks of the streams dug away to afford crossings, and two days were consumed in making the trip of less than ten miles. On the afternoon of the 8th of November, 1832, the family moved in and took possession of their new home—a house built the Winter previous. Thus was commenced the settlement of that part of Jo Daviess County, which, in later years, came to be known as Dunleith.

About the same time that Frentress made his claim, Thomas Jordan made a claim on the banks of the Mississippi River, and to which he removed his family the same day that Frentress moved to his claim. For a number of years Jordan maintained a canoe ferry to the west shore of the Mississippi River to accommodate the little trade and the large number of mining explorers from Illinois and Wisconsin (then Michigan Territory), who looked forward to the time when they might have a legal right to occupy the lead mines which had been worked by Julien Dubuque from about 1788 to the time of his death in 1810. The occupancy of a claim at the present site of the City of Dunleith by the Jordan family, in September, 1832, establishes the fact that they were the pioneer settlers and the first white people to claim a permanent abiding place in a locality now so full of intelligence, business activity and manufacturing industries, and the site of a city that is known throughout the civilized world for its production of labor-saving machinery.

The Jordan cabin was built very nearly on the site now occupied by Sutter's livery stable, and the well in the street in front of that stable was dug by the Jordans soon after they occupied their pioneer cabin.

In the Spring of 1833, the Mattox family came in and settled about half a mile east of the Frentress family, and one by one settlers continued to come in and make claims, and build cabins and settle in the neighborhood, until there was quite a community.

In the Spring of 1832, two men named Boxley and Thompson made claims in the Callagan bottom, north of the Frentress place, broke some land and planted a few acres of corn. It seems that they paid no attention to the alarm that called Frentress from his claim on the 14th of May, and that they remained to cultivate their fields. While engaged in plowing their corn, they were fired upon and killed by the Indians. The exact date of these Indian murders, Mrs. Frentress does not remember, but thinks it must have been some time in the month of June, by reason of their bodies being found between two rows of corn where they were plowing.

This much by way of a history of the pioneer settlement of the Dunleith district, and we now take up some of the later events, although they are among the occurrences of half a century ago.

Emsley H. Frentress was the first male child born in the settlement, his birth occuring on the 10th of February, 1833. [He died on the 21st day of November, 1876.]

The first female child, according to Mrs. Frentress' best recollection, was Lydia Ann Mattox, now the wife of Duncan Cameron, of Oakland, California. The date of her birth is not remembered.

The first marriage was in 1836, when the rites of matrimony were solemnized between Hayden Gilbert and a Miss Jordan.

The first school was taught in one of the D'Bois cabins, before mentioned. It was a subscription school and was taught by a man named Kennedy. The next school was taught in a small plank house, erected for the purpose on the Frentress place by the Frentress and Mattox families. These parties also employed the teacher and became responsible for his salary, although the children of the other families of the neighborhood were admitted.

The first religious meetings were held in this school house, under the auspices of the Methodist Episcopal Church, in 1838–'39. Revs. J. Crummer and James, who had been commissioned and sent to this part of Illinois, by the Conference district, of which it formed a part, as Circuit Riders. They held services alternately, and every body in the neighborhood were regular attendants. Services were not held regularly every Sabbath—sometimes once in two weeks, and sometimes not more than once a month.

The first deaths within the territory designated as Menominee Township, of which Dunleith formed a part until March, 1865, were the decease, by Indian murder, of Boxley and Thompson, in the Callagan bottom, in June, 1832. The first from natural causes, was the death of Zachariah Hoffman, who died of cholera, in 1833.

The first orchard in the township was planted by Mr. Frentress, in 1837. The trees were bought at Montague's nursery at Waddam's Grove, in what is now Stephenson County. To some readers it may seem a little strange that no orchard should be started until 1837, while the settlement of the township was commenced almost five years before, but this is explained by the fact that the Fever River Country was regarded by many people as only a mining country, and entirely unsuited to agricultural or horticultural purposes, and that the early settlers were almost exclusively mining adventurers and speculators, who, when they first came, did not expect or intend to become permanent residents, nor to engage in any business not directly connected with mining.

The incidents so far related cover the early settlement of Menominee and Dunleith Townships. After the Indian troubles were permanently settled, in 1832, there was not much to disturb the conditions of pioneer life. For several years straggling Indians would come along, but the only annoyance they occasioned was in persistent begging and petty thefts. Claim hunters and settlers kept coming in, new cabins were built, new farms opened from year to year, until within ten years all the available land was claimed, and for the most part occupied. By-and-by the old cabins gave way to a better class of buildings, and thus, without the occurrence of any thing of historical interest, the country continued to improve and prosper, until the building of railroads came to be considered a measure of commercial necessity. Among the early railroad enterprises of Illinois, was the Galena and Chicago Union. January 7, 1846, a meeting of the representative men of the several counties along the line of the proposed road between the Mississippi River and Chicago, was held at Rockford, to consider the feasibility of buying out the interests of a New York company, who had obtained a charter under the name and style of the Galena & Chicago Union Railroad Company. This company had also obtained a tract of 1,000 acres of land on Dupage River, and, in 1838, had done some work on the prairie west of Chicago. This much being accomplished, the undertaking was left in abeyance. Some time in the latter part of 1845, Messrs. Ogden and Jones, of Chicago, negotiated with Messrs. Nevins and Matteson, for the purchase of the charter and franchises of the Galena & Chicago Union Railroad Company, for $20,000. When the Rockford meeting of January 7, 1845, had assembled and organized, Mr. Jones, of Chicago, introduced the following resolution, which was adopted:

Resolved, If a satisfactory arrangement can be made with the present holders of the stock of the Galena & Chicago Union Railroad Company, that the members of this convention will use all honorable measures to obtain subscriptions to the stock of said company.

This recitation covers the history of the beginning of that railroad, the completion of which, in later years, connected the Mississippi, at Dunleith, with Lake Michigan, at Chicago.

In 1850, Mr. Douglas, then a member of Congress, secured the passage of a law, making a large grant of government land to aid in the construction of the Illinois Central Railroad, the managers of which had become possessed of that part of the Galena & Chicago Union Railroad between Galena and Freeport. And while the building of the last named road was well under way between Freeport and Chicago this large grant of land to the Illinois Central Railroad Company gave a new impetus to every enterprise of the country adjacent to Dunleith. In June, 1855, this road was completed to the eastern bank of the Mississippi River, at the present site of Dunleith.

In 1849, there was but one house and one fishing shanty, at Dunleith, but by the time the road was completed, June 1, 1855, as many as fifty substantial buildings, many of them graceful brick structures, had been erected and were in waiting for the business the road was expected to bring.

The land on which the city was laid out was entered from the government by Augustus Gregoire, at the land sales at Dixon, in the Spring of 1847. By the death of Augustus Gregoire, Charles Gregoire, a brother, succeeded to the ownership of the land, fifteen acres of which he sold to the Railroad Company for railroad purposes—freight house, depot buildings, etc. In 1853, a town company, composed of George W. Sanford, Jonathan Sturges, Morris Ketchum, George W. Jones, George Griswold and Charles Gregoire, was formed, who were known as the Proprietors of the Town of Dunleith, to which company Charles Gregoire conveyed the northwest quarter of section 29, the southwest quarter of section 20 and fractional sections of 19 and 30, all in town 29 north, range 2 west of the 4th principal meridian, which was laid off into lots, blocks, streets, avenues and alleys, and named upon the plat and records, as Dunleith, in honor of Dunleith, Scotland. The plat was filed in the office of the County Clerk (W. H. Bradley, clerk), duly acknowledged by Charles Gregoire, December 14, 1853. The plat was made by John C. Goodyear, County Surveyor, certified and approved March 16, 1854, and recorded March 18, 1854. The first public sale of lots was had in the Summer of 1855, although some lots had been sold and occupied soon after the town was laid out. Frederick Jessup and Charles Gregoire were general managers for the proprietors, and Jessup the ruling spirit. In making sales of lots, Jessup imposed the condition that all purchasers of lots in Sinsinawa* Avenue should erect thereon nothing but three-story brick buildings, and that no spirituous liquors should ever be sold therein. Under these conditions, what is now the Commercial House and Post-Office building, at the corner of First Street and Sinsinawa Avenue, was built by Colonel James Robinson, for storage and commission purposes. A man named John Monti, of Galena, bought a lot on the corner of Second Street and Sinsinawa Avenue, and in 1855, erected thereon a three-story brick building for a general store. This building was destroyed by fire in the Fall of 1877.

The first building erected on the town plat, after the town was laid out, was built by Charles Gregoire, for hotel purposes, and occupied a position on Wisconsin Avenue, a short distance above Sinsinawa Avenue. It was a two-story brick, erected in 1853, and at one time was known as the Bates House.

The first store, or trading place, was opened in 1854, by Charles Wheeler. Wheeler occupied a small frame shanty that stood on Wisconsin Avenue, almost opposite the hotel building erected by Gregoire, and which was first called the Dunleith House, but afterwards the Bates House, as already stated. In 18— John Clise opened a store in the Monti building, and where he continued in business up to 185–. Holdorff was also a merchant during the same period, and in 1857 Augustus Switzer, who had engaged in farming in Menominee Township for several years (the earlier part of his life having been spent in mercantile persuits), purchased property in Dunleith, remained here and opened a store at the corner of Third Street and Sinsinawa Avenue, his present place of business. From that time forward until the bridging of the Mississippi between Dunleith and Dubuque, business was good. Dunleith's star was in the ascendant. Lots ran up to almost fabulous prices. A number of grand enterprises were projected and some of them commenced, but the beginning and completion of the tunnel† and bridge, in 1868, resulted in the derangement of many plans, threw many men out of employment and the means of making a living at Dunleith, and hence they were compelled to seek remunerative engagements elsewhere. The transfer of passengers and freight between Dunleith

* Menominee for Home of the Eagle.

† The tunnel is 972 feet in length, and the bridge about 3.960 feet, or three-quarters of a mile in length.

and Dubuque was of itself sufficient to employ fifty or more men and a number of teams. But their occupation vanished when the first train of cars passed through the tunnel, and crossed the bridge to the Dubuque side, and thence onward toward the setting sun, to the lands of the Nebraskas and Dakotahs. From the time the railroad was completed, in 1855, up to the opening of the bridge, in 1868, the transfer business was heavy, and it is said that the gentleman who managed the business for the transfer company (and the company was really composed of railroad officers who were prevented by statutory provisions from being known in its management), who was the ostensible president and owner of the stock, wagons and other appurtenances necessary to the business, realized, in clear cash, in the twelve or fifteen years the transfer traffic was continued, the handsome fortune of $182,000! Certain it is that from an employe in a Galena store, a few years before, he accumulated at least money enough to build one of the handsomest residences in Dunleith, and to venture on several undertakings that promised large returns, but all of which proved disastrous failures.

Among the other grand undertakings of the friends of Dunleith—of those who saw a bright future and a great city in the near advance of years—was the Argyle House, named after the Duke of Argyle, Scotland, a relative of the Jessup already mentioned as agent and manager for the proprietors of the town of Dunleith. The Argyle was built in 1855. It was a four-story brick, with stone basement, with a front of 145 feet on the railroad track, and 50 feet deep, covering an area of 7,250 feet. The object in building it was to accommodate the railroad and river passenger traffic, and there is a strong suspicion that transit affairs were so managed as to detain travelers here over night, and thus "make it pay." But like the transfer business, when the bridge was completed the Argyle's glory departed. It has gone into decay. Its walls are dingy and brown. A few of its lower rooms are occupied as shops; and some of the upper rooms are occupied as residences by families, but for the most part it is unoccupied and tenantless. When first opened, it was managed by a hotelier from Chicago, named Luce, and in its almiest days had no psuperior on the Upper Mississippi. For ten years or more it was the pride and glory of Dunleith, but now its walls are blackened and weak, and its unoccupied rooms cheerless and dark.

Pro Bono Publico.—A Market House, with City Hall, was built in 1865. A Fire Company was organized about the same time, of which Augustus Switzer was foreman for a long time. A Fire Engine, Hose Cart and Apparatus, Fire Bell, Fireman's Silk Flag, etc., were purchased, without cost to the city, through a series of entertainments and balls, under the supervision and management of the Company's foreman.

EDUCATIONAL.—The original part of the present graded school building was erected in 1858. In 1864 an addition was made of sufficient size to afford ample room for fine, well conducted departments. This building is a plain, unpretentious brick structure costing only about $5,000. School is maintained about nine months of the year, during which the best educational talent to be had in the country is employed. There are 400 scholars (between six and twenty-one years of age) in the district (No. 1) entitled to school benefits. Of these, 250 are enrolled. Out of this number there is an average daily attendance at this time (Jan., 1878), of 220. Robert A. Hayes is principal, assisted by H. P. Caverly, Grammar Department; Carmie Daggett, Intermediate; Kate Paul, Second Primary, and Julia Joy, First Primary.

School Board.—C. S. Burt, President; John Buckley, Secretary; John B. Chapman, Director.

CHURCHES.—The Presbyterians erected a small frame church in 1855, which was also used as a school house. This building gave way some years ago, and is now known only in name.

The Congregationalists commenced work here in 1861, and built a brick church edifice near the present school house. They occupied it until about 1870 or 1871, when they ceased, and sold their church building to the Methodists, who kept up regular services for about four years, when the society became too weak to maintain a pastor, and gave way before decreasing membership. The building is now occupied by the German Lutherans, who have regular preaching every Sabbath. They also maintain a well organized Sabbath-school The services and Sunday-school are conducted in the German tongue.

The Catholic Church edifice was erected under the management of Rev. Fathers Jarboe, Fortune and Bernard, in 1857, at a cost of $3,500. The contractor was William Melvin, a carpenter. He sub-let the stone work to James Muldowney, and the brick work to a man named Morrison. The church is a plain, substantial one, in which services are conducted every alternate Sabbath by the Rev. Father McMahan. The society has a membership of about 70 families.

NEWSPAPERS.—Dunleith had a weekly newspaper from June, 1857, to May, 1861—four years. The first few (5) numbers were printed in Dubuque, by the Flaven Bros., who named their paper the *Dunleith Commercial Advertiser*. In August following the first issue, Mr. E. R. Paul, then of Potosi, Wisconsin, became interested in the publication, and removed hither a press and material, so that the sixth number, dated August 12, 1857, was printed entirely in Dunleith. In a brief time the Flaven Bros. retired, Mr. J. R. Flynn taking their interest. Flynn also withdrew in a few months, leaving M. Paul alone in its management. He continued to publish *The Dunleith Advertiser* until its discontinuance in May, 1861. At that time its patronage was transferred, as was also its proprietor, to the *Galena Courier*. No one has since ventured to establish a paper in Dunleith. The printing material was afterwards (in 1863 or '64), sold to parties in Lanark, Carroll County, this state.

MANUFACTURING INDUSTRIES.

Burt Machine Works.—The leading manufacturing industry is known and designated as above. They are not only the most extensive in Dunleith, but among the best known in the West, and are really the saving interests of the city in which they are maintained. This establishment was commenced in 1856, by D. R. Burt, father of C. S. Burt, as a manufactory of combined reapers and mowers, and were continued in that interest until destroyed by fire in 1863, which involved a loss of $50,000. Soon after the fire, the business was resumed in an old building near by, and during the early part of 1864 new buildings (the ones now occupied), were erected at a cost of $10,000, and supplied with the latest styles of machinery at an additional cost of $25,000. When operations were commenced in the new buildings, they added the manufacture of shingle-machines to that of reapers and mowers, and the combined industries were continued up to 1869, when the manufacture of reapers and mowers was abandoned, with the intention of making the manufacture of shingle machines a specialty, but there came a demand from Dubuque parties for large numbers of the Julien Churn, and the Burts entered into a contract to supply the demand, and turned out about 10,000 of these domestic machines. This additional industry did not interfere with their other machine operations, or cripple their capacity for other work. When the demand for the Julien Churn was supplied, the shops were employed almost exclusively, up to 1876, in the shingle machine business. At that date they added facilities and machinery for the manufacture of the McDermott Riding and Walking Cultivator, which line of business is still continued. The shops, as now managed, can turn out 3,000 of these cultivators per year, a little less than ten per day of ten hours, or nearly one cultivator per hour.

SCALES MOUND

Although so largely engaged in the manufacture of cultivators, there has been no falling off in the manufacture of shingle machines, but, on the contrary, there has been a steadily increasing demand for them, which demand has been promptly met by the addition of new machinery and enlarged capacity from time to time. These machines are made of different sizes and capacity, the Evarts Patent Rotary, Twelve Block Machine, being the largest and fastest, and is acknowledged to be the best large shingle machine in the world. It has two circular saws located on opposite sides of the machine, and a circular carriage way to deliver the blocks to the saws without interruption. Its capacity in ordinary cypress and pine timber, is about 150,000 shingles per day of ten hours, or 75,000 to each saw; 7,500 per hour, or 125 per minute, or two and 1-12 shingles per second. With such capacity, it is no wonder that there is a demand for these machines in all parts of the civilized globe—in Austria, Russia, Prussia, Sweden, Norway, New Zealand, South America, and, in fact, wherever else shingle timber grows and is used. It can be operated by one man.

Smaller machines are also made that will turn out from 25,000 to 30,000 per day. In addition, machines are made for bunching shingles that command admiration for simplicity and labor-saving facilities.

The manufacture of these machines is a specialty, but they do not include all the work done at the Burt shops, but they have become so universally popular, and have received such high awards of praise, at home and abroad, that, in compliment to the county in which the shops in which they are made have been built up—a county, the history of which is being written—that a somewhat extended notice seemed deserved. Add to this the fact that, at the Centennial Exhibition at Philadelphia, in 1876, they received a Medal Award, Diploma and Special Mention, and the people of Jo Daviess County have special cause to be proud that such machines are the result of the enterprise and handiwork of their fellow-citizens.

In the Centennial Report of Awards, the following entry appears of record:

PHILADELPHIA, Feb. 7, 1877.

The undersigned having examined the product herein described (to-wit: SHINGLE MACHINES), respectfully recommend the same to the United States Centennial Commission for Award for the following reasons, viz: GREAT SIMPLICITY OF DESIGN, SOLIDITY OF CONSTRUCTION, GREAT POWER OF PRODUCTION, and GREAT ORIGINALITY.

F. REIFER, Judge.

Approval of Group of Judges:—John Anderson, Geo. H. Blelock, John A. Anderson, Augt. Gobert, *fils*, F. Perrier, W. F. Durfee, C. A. Augustrom.

A true copy of the Record, FRANCIS A. WALKER,
Chief of Bureau of Award.

Given by authority of Centennial Commission.

[SEAL.] A. T. GOSHORN,
Director General.

J. L. CAMPBELL, J. R. HAWLEY,
Secretary. Director General.

In February, 1877, these works also commenced the manufacture of the Frentress Barbed Fence Wire, and during that year turned out 115 tons thereof. This year (1878), they will make 300 tons. They have ten machines for making this wire, all of which were made at their own works, and are of superior quality. Fence wire makers say these machines are far superior to any thing of the kind yet introduced in any part of the country. The employment of these ten machines will give them a capacity of three tons per dav, or 339 tons per year, of one hundred and thirteen uninterrupted working days.

The Burt Machine Works cover one entire block and are conveniently arranged in all their various departments. The machinery employed is all of the latest and most improved patterns, and selected with a view to capacity, adaptability and durability. The company is composed of C. S. and S. Burt, and R. E. Odell—all industrious, practical men, and thoroughly devoted to the interests of their business, and to the welfare and prosperity of the county and city of their home. These works now employ thirty men regularly, whose earnings go to the support of the grocers, merchants and other dealers of Dunleith. In 1876 the number of employes was not so large as during 1877, but large enough to involve a labor account of $6,000. The labor account of 1877 shows an outlay of $10,000—a very handsome outlay, but which will be increased to about one-half more during 1878.

Nail Mill.—Nail works were commenced in 1873 or 1874, by L. & J. C. Holloway, of Lancaster, Wisconsin. This mill was supplied with six nail machines, two sets of rolls, and all the appliances peculiar to the business of nail making. The mill had a capacity of 100 kegs per day, but the enterprise was not continued many months until operations were suspended and the mill closed up. The mill and its machinery are now owned by G. T. Walker, of Lancaster, Wisconsin.

Cultivator Works.—E. Children's cultivator works were commenced in 1867. He manufactures his own patent, and turns out both riding and walking machines, making about 300 per year. His machinery is now driven by steam power.

Novelty Grain Separator Works—These works are located in the Argyle building. The manufacture of these machines was commenced by Messrs. Redd & Sanford, in 1876. This is a machine that commends itself to all practical millers, and can be best described in the manufacturers' own words: "The machine consists of two suction fans, oat and cockle extractor. The grain enters the first suction spout in a thin sheet, through a peculiar feed box, where it is met by a strong upward current of air, which removes the dust, light screenings, chaff, etc. The wheat then passes upon a series of zinc screens that effectually remove all oats, straws, sticks, weeds, and any thing larger than a grain of wheat. The wheat next passes upon the large cockle screen, which takes out all cockle, small seeds, and sand. After the wheat leaves the cockle extractor, it enters, in a thin sheet, another suction spout, where it passes through a strong upward current of air, that removes all unsound grains of wheat, light oats, smut balls and every thing lighter than a grain of wheat. The suction blasts are regulated by a valve in the top of the machine. Prominent among the new features of this machine is the cockle extractor, which consists, first, of a large screen, with a peculiar arrangement for keeping it clean, which takes out all cockle and also some small grains of wheat. The cockle and small wheat are gathered on a smaller perforated sheet iron screen, with a stationary cover, the wheat and cockle passing under the cover, which holds the wheat down flat and prevents it from turning up and passing through the holes, but forces the cockle through, the wheat passing over the end and entering the suction spout with the wheat from the first screen. This makes it the best separator ever invented. It makes no dust or dirt and can be placed in any part of the mill. The arrangement of the fans and suction spouts is such that it gives the strongest and best blast for separating grain, with the least power, of any other machine. It occupies less room than any other separator and does better work than any two others. In fact, it is two machines combined—a separator and a cockle extractor.

MISCELLANEOUS.

The City of Dunleith was first incorporated under the general laws of the state in 1856. The first election for town officers was held on Wednesday, April 8, of the same year, when the following named citizens were chosen to the several offices:

Trustees.—Charles Bogy (brother of the late U. S. Senator Bogy, of Missouri), James A. Campbell, John Smith, William E. Boone, and James Currie.

At the first meeting of the Board of Trustees, Mr. Bogy was chosen president; Charles Wheeler, clerk; James Garnick, treasurer and assessor, and William Pittam, marshal and collector.

Up to 1865, the City of Dunleith belonged to Menominee Township, which covered an area of forty-five sections of land. On the 2d day of March, of that year, a petition was presented to the Board of Supervisors, signed by numerous citizens of Menominee Township, praying for a division of the township, and the erection of the Township of Dunleith out of the western part of Menominee. The petition provided that the dividing line should commence at the state (Wisconsin) line at the corner of fractional sections 14 and 15, town 29 north, range 2 west, thence running due south on section lines to the Mississippi River, at the southeast corner of section 3, town 28 north, range 2 west, and that all that part of Menominee lying east of that line should continue to be called Menominee, and that all west of that line, to the Mississippi River should be known and designated as Dunleith Township.

The petition was accepted, when Mr. Marfield moved to lay the petition on the table until the afternoon session, but the motion was lost. Mr. Gear then moved that the prayer of the petitioners be granted. The ayes and nays being called, the vote stood as follows:

Ayes.—Messrs. Bennett, Duffy, Heinlen, Stratt, Lorrain, Brendel, Switzer, Furlong, Napper, Jewell, Woodworth, Mars, Gear, Tyrrell, Haws, Wier, Deeds, Campbell, Edgerton Ginn—20.

Nays.—Messrs. Gray, Marfield, Luning, Laird, Morse, Townsend, Green, Wingart—8.

So the prayer of the petitioners was granted, and the Township of Dunleith established.

From the date of the completion of the railroad to Dunleith, June 1, 1855, to the completion of the tunnel and bridge in the Fall of 1868, there was a pretty steady increase of population, and the citizens—those interested in business—felt the need of a better system of local government than that provided by the general laws of the state for the incorporation of towns and villages. Public meetings were held, and the matter thoroughly discussed. Finally, in pursuance of a resolution of the Board of Trustees, A. Switzer, with the legal assistance of Attorney Weigley, of Galena, drafted a charter which was submitted to the Legislature through Representative Platt, and in February, 1865, the charter was approved and granted, since when the city has been subject to its provisions, Mr. Switzer being chosen first mayor thereunder. He was re-elected in 1866, and again elected in 1868—serving, in all, three terms. He was also the first supervisor elected from Dunleith Township after it was set off from Menominee in 1865.

Dunleith Land Company.—What was known as the Dunleith Land Company succeeded the Proprietors of Dunleith in 1863, their articles of incorporation being filed July 20, of that year. This company was composed of Jonathan Sturgis, E. Bement, John H. Thompson, George Griswold, Theodore A. Neal. Theodore A. Neal, president, and R. E. Odell, secretary. The old company, known as the Proprietors of Dunleith, had been dissolved, and the property (unsold) divided. Four members of the new company had been members of the original Town Company, and when the new company was organized the remaining property was divided into six equal shares, four shares of which were held by the four members of the old company. The other two shares were held by Dubuque parties—one of whom was Charles Gregoire, who transferred his interest to R. E. Odell and C. S. Burt. The other one sixth interest was held by Hon. George W. Jones, who has since sold off the larger share thereof, and now owns but a very small interest. In February, 1868, the Dunleith Land Company sold their entire interest to C. S. Burt, who retains the property and its management.

When the town was first laid off, the Proprietors of Dunleith failed to record that part of the town plat north of Sinsinawa avenue, but made sales of sundry lots along the base of the bluffs, as well as upon their sides and summits, a negligence that involved the proprietors in some litigation, in 1856, when the corporate authorities brought suit against them for a violation of the laws in such cases made and provided, resulting in a finding and heavy costs against the company.

FLOODS.—Dunleith has been three times visited by disastrous floods. Wisconsin Avenue comes down a narrow ravine from the north, which, in times of heavy rains, quickly becomes a rapid, roaring current. About four o'clock on the afternoon of September 9, 1875, a tremendous rain storm passed over this section, falling in torrents, and quickly filling every little channel upon the hillsides, these little channels, or sluice-ways, carried the water into Wisconsin Avenue, which soon became a resistless sea. Gathering force from the steep bluffs, it dashed on, sweeping every thing before it, and plunging into Switzer's store room, filled the interior above the counters, tearing down the shelves, overturning boxes, sweeping down packages and piles of goods and threatening general destruction. Maguire's store, on the opposite side of Sinsinawa Avenue, at the corner of Wisconsin Avenue, and the stores above, on the west side of the last named thoroughfare, shared in the same visitation of destruction. By this flood and a subsequent one in 1876 Switzer lost about five thousand dollars' worth of goods, wares, etc., and Mayor Maguire lost very nearly the same amount.

March 10, 1876, another calamity of the same character was visited upon Dunleith, doing serious damage to every thing within its reach. At Hazel Green, Wisconsin, a few miles north of east from Dunleith, this rain storm was accompanied by a terrific hurricane or tornado, that killed nine persons, besides doing incalculable damage to property. Houses were lifted from the ground, carried up into the air and then dashed to pieces against the earth. A wagon and a pair of horses were taken up and carried high into the air, almost out of sight, and hurled to the earth a mass of *debris* and lifeless carcasses.

The night of July 4, 1876, a third flood rolled down upon the city and startled the people from their slumber and rest. The same night, Rock Dale, on Catfish Creek, Iowa, only a few miles to the southwest of Dunleith, was overwhelmed by a rush of waters, forty-two lives destroyed and many houses washed away, and many others dashed to pieces. On the morning of the 5th, desolation and mourning filled the little valley village, which, on America's Centennial Day, had been so full of life and bustling activity.

These three floods have seldom had their counterpart or equal in volume and destruction in any part of the country, and never in Northwestern Illinois.

School Directors of Different School Districts in Dunleith Township, Town 29, Range 2 West of the fourth Principal Meridian, 1877—School Dist. No. 1, John Buckley, Charles S. Burt, John B. Chapman; Dist. No. 2, Sylvester Long, Harmon Brummer, Renier Schermann; Dist. No. 3, Francis Kruse, David Foltz, Sterns D. Platt; Dist. No. 4, Henry N. Frentress, Henry Lutters, John Shulting.

Teachers Employed in Township, 1877—Robert Hayes, Dist. No. 1; H. P. Caverly, Carmine Daggett, Katie Paul, Julia Joy, Philip Maguire, Dist. No., 2; James Maguire, Dist. No. 3; Maria E. Culton, Dist., No. 4.

School Treasurer, 1877—Thomas Maguire.

Dunleith Township Officers, 1877—Supervisor, Charles S. Burt; Town Clerk, Charles Mayer; Assessor, Henry Smith; Collector, James Farnan; Commissioners of Highways, Merritt Platt, Henry N. Frentress, Herbert Rees; Constables, John Buckley, Anthony Dames; Justices of the Peace, John Staudenmayer, Henry Smith.

Dunleith City Officers, 1877.—Mayor, Thomas Maguire; Aldermen, George

Most, William Quinlan, Joseph Whatmore, Anthony Thielen; Marshal, John D. Clise; City Treasurer, William P. Ennor; Street Commissioner, Theophilus Dames, Sr.

SCALES MOUND.

In 1826, when the tide of immigration was drifting towards the lead mines of northwestern Illinois, a party of men, consisting of two brothers, named Watson, Joshua Streeter and three sons, John Wood, a Mr. Brigham, Mr. Blane and a few others, discovered the mines of the upper East Fork. They stopped there, built cabins and mined for four or five years. These men can not properly be considered as settlers of Scales Mound Township, as they left their families at other places, to which they would make frequent trips, and seemed to regard these mines as but a temporary location.

In 1827, Mr. Conrad Lichtenburger came from Pennsylvania, with his family, and settled in that vicinity. In 1828, the second permanent settler, Elijah Charles, also with a family, built a house at the base of the mound.*

The first agricultural pursuits were followed in this township by these two pioneers. Among other early settlers were Wm. McMath and Abel Proctor, who built cabins near Mr. Lichtenburger, in 1827. Mr. Proctor was one of the prominent residents of the county for many years, holding at times the offices of County Commissioner and Justice of the Peace. He is now a resident of Iowa.

The first child known to have been born in this frontier settlement was Mary M. Lichtenburger, on April 4, 1828, and the first death occurred in the same family, March 29, 1831, when Harriet Lichtenburger died at the age of seventeen years.

In 1830, Samuel H. Scales purchased the claim and cabin of John L. Sole, who had lived there nearly two years, and built a public house near the base of the mound, which is now known by his name. This tavern was on the historical "Sucker Trail" over which, afterwards, passed the Chicago & Galena stage line, and it was kept, in succession, by Scales, Moffett, Cowgill and Moppin. For many years after the *village* of Scales Mound was built, on the railroad, nearly a mile from the old tavern, the mound was generally distinguished by the name of "Maupin's Mound." It has now, however, reverted to its old title.

The name of Jesse W. Shull is prominent in the record of this county. He came to the mining regions in 1819, and roamed with Indians for many years. In 1831, Mr. Shull settled on a farm near the mound and continued to live there, raising a large family of boys. Though he had for years been on the most intimate terms with the Indians, he proved a true friend to his white brethren when the settlement was obliged to seek protection in the fort, during the Black Hawk War.

MINES.—In June, 1835, Mr. Lichtenburger discovered a rich vein of lead which soon became of considerable note in the county. On account of the gambling miners who flocked there, they were soon known as the "Black Leg Diggings," a name which they continued to carry. This, with the East Fork leads are the only mines which have been successfully worked in the township. In the Summer of 1836, one range of the Black Leg Diggings yielded nearly two million tons of mineral. A small village soon sprang up at this place, to which was given the high-sounding name of "Veta Grand." A tavern was opened by a Mr. Bonus; goods were sold by Mr. Hovey and Mr. Dixon, although Bennett & Shin started the first store. In 1845, a school house was built and afterwards a Methodist Church. With the decline of the mines the village became depopu-

* This mound was ascertained by the civil engineers of the Illinois Central Railroad, to be the highest point of land in the state.

lated, though the Scales Mound minister has continued to hold services in the church. Hon. H. S. Magoon now operates the East Fork mines, which yield about 5,000 pounds of mineral per month.

But to return to an account of the pioneer farmers. They soon found need for a school house, and in 1831 the first one was built near the state line, and was opened to the children by George Cubbage, as teacher. In the same year divine services were held at the house of Elijah Charles, by Rev. Thomas, of New Diggins, Wisconsin, who thereafter preached occasionally in the new school house.

Before the adoption of the township system, the precinct elections were held at the house of F. C. Maupin. When the township system came into operation, the voting place was changed to the village.

In the Fall of 1852, the people of Jo Daviess voted to adopt the township system. At a subsequent session of the county court, Messrs. Charles Bennett, G. N. Townsend and David T. Barr, were appointed Commissioners, for the purpose of dividing the county into townships and defining their several boundary lines. At a meeting of the Board of Supervisors, in 1855, some alterations were made in certain boundary lines, and a new township created, called Scales Mound, in honor of Samuel H. Scales, who was an enterprising and influential citizen, and who died in the Fall of 1877. The boundaries of this township were defined as follows:

> Commencing on the state line at the northeast corner of section 13, town 29, range 2 east, thence west along the state line four miles to the northwest corner of section 16; thence due south on the section line, to the southwest corner of section 33; thence east, along the township line four miles, to the southeast corner of section 36; thence due north to the state line, or place of beginning, to be called Scales Mound.

The first supervisor elected in this township was F. C. Maupin, Esq.

SCALES MOUND VILLAGE.—In 1848, a man named Dunning entered the land on which the village stands. It was laid out in September, 1853, by Josiah Conlee and B. B. Provost. When the railroad passed through, in 1854, Sherman Eddy established a store for the supply of railroad employes, miners and farmers. This was followed by a few houses, among them a blacksmith shop, by Thomas Davy. In 1854 and 1855, the Methodist Church was built, and in the next year the school house was erected. In 1859, George Allan started a general store, which was continued until his death, in 1864, and has since been continued by his brother, James Allan, who also does a produce shipping business. In 1873, Joseph Tangye established a general store, and in 1875 another one was opened by Thomas McNulty. These constitute the principal stores of the village.

The first hotel was built in 1856, at a cost of $6,000, by Dunston, Pryor & Roberts, and was managed by Henry Roberts. There are now three hotels. In 1857, Joseph Conlee erected, just northwest of the village, a tall, round, stone wind-mill, but it proved a poor speculation and has been vacant for many years.

July 14, 1877, a meeting was held to consider the propriety of incorporating the village under the general law of the state, at which 38 votes were cast for, and 4 against, the proposed incorporation. The village was consequently incorporated.

The following officers were elected at a meeting held soon after:

Trustees—George Hawk, President; James Allan, James A. Adams, James Carey, Moses Bushby and H. M. Fowler.

The first Clerk was Edgar Wilkins; Treasurer, A. J. Hawkins.

These officers are still in power, except Mr. Hawkins, who recently removed. The vacancy thus created was filled by the election of Mr. Wilkins.

The present Postmaster is H. M. Fowler, the first one having been F. C. Maupin.

The township organization is as follows:—Supervisor, Thomas Knucky; Assessor, Robert Robson; Collector, Thomas Allinson, Commissioners of Highways, James Carr, Benj. Lyon and Wm. Gummo; Notary Public and Justice of the Peace, John Moore.

Schools, Churches, Etc.—The first school was taught by Joshua Hawkins in 1855. The house in which it was held was of that primitive kind which is aptly described by the term "shanty." The present two-story brick building was built in 1855-'6. It embraces two departments which are taught by J. W. Wilcox and Robert Lindsey.

The Methodist Church was built, as has been stated, in 1854-'5. It is of stone, seats about 200 persons, and cost $1,800. Rev. John L. Williams officiated at its dedication, though the first regular pastor was Rev. Summersides. The following is a list of pastors, in their order: Rev. James Lawson, Rev. Avermill, Rev. Kellogg, Rev. Devinan, Rev. Cooley, Rev. McCutchin, Rev. Joseph Crummer, Rev. J. T. Cooper, Rev. T. H. Helliwell, Rev. Isaac Springer, Rev. Henry Springer, Rev. Benj. Close, and Rev. F. F. Farmiloe, the present minister. H. Martin was first Superintendent of the Sabbath-school, which was organized in 1855. The present Superintendent is Joseph Tangye. It has a membership of 65, while the church membership numbers 125. There is a good parsonage, costing $600, in connection with the church.

The German Presbyterian Church was purchased in 1860, from a society of Americans, who were unable to longer support and maintain a pastor. Its value at that time was about $1,000. The first elders of the new organization were Geo. Rittweger and John Reteldorf. Its ministers have been, Rev. Kolb, Rev. John Schwartz, Rev. Jacob Liesveld, Rev. J. Funk, concluding with the present pastor, Rev. F. Schwabe.

Their Sabbath-school was organized in 1871, by John Boell, who still remains its Superintendent.

The Catholic Church organization was effected in 1853, and continued to be held in private houses until 1868, when a brick store-room, built by Mr. Covey, was purchased and used until 1874. At that time the present brick church was erected on the old site. Father Balley, of Galena, has officiated for them during the past fifteen years.

The organizations of Scales Mound are concluded with their Lyceum, which was established in 1856, by George Allan, John Conlee, J. M. Conlee and Silas Corey. Though it was for a time suspended, its long existence entitles it to a place in history. Its present officers are: Prest., John Allan; Vice Prest., Henry Roberts, Secretary, J. W. Wilcox.

NORA.

The first settler was Garrett Garner, who located a claim on section seven, which is now included in the farms owned by Samuel and Tilman H. Dobler. The following year Garner sold his claim to Asher Miner, and removed to Wisconsin, where he died a few years ago. To Asher Miner, the second permanent settler, belongs a large meed of credit for many of the undertakings of the township and the high character it has always sustained. He was a man of sterling worth, and highly esteemed by his neighbors and acquaintances for his clear sense of honor. In early life he was a resident of Ontario County, New York, but subsequently removed to Alleghany County in that state, and after a few years' residence there, emigrated to Jo Daviess county and settled in this township. He died in the village of Nora, October 11, 1867.

To Sarah B. Miner, daughter of the pioneer above named, belongs the honor of teaching the first school in the township. It was a subscription school, and was taught in the log house of her father in the Fall of 1846. This house was the first one built in the township, and a portion of it is still standing at this date, January, 1878.

The first marriage in the township was between Miss Jane Miner, another daughter of Asher Miner, and Sylvanus Crowell. They were married April, 1841.

"Aunt Jane Crowell" (as by that name she is best known in Nora, where she resides) is now sixty-two years of age, and beloved and highly respected by all who know her, and to her the writer is largely indebted for the early history of the township. Her memory is remarkably clear and accurate as to incidents and dates, and her mind well informed upon what has transpired since her girlhood days.

A Mr. Shaw and Seth Post came to the county in the Fall of 1836. Post made a claim in the town of Rush, but Shaw did not select a claim until after they had gone back to Alleghany County, New York, and he returned with his family. When they started back to New York, Mr. Post left his two sons, Alonzo and Joseph, in charge of his claim and other property here, and during his absence "the boys" were very industrious in settling the house in order against the coming of their father, mother and the rest of the family, a coming they were destined never to realize.

When the two families were ready to leave New York for new homes in the west, they hired their passage on a lumber raft from Olean Point, which was bound for Cincinnati *via* Pittsburg. This raft not only conveyed the two families, but all their household goods, and one span of horses and wagon belonging to Mr. Shaw. Shaw was to come overland with his team from Cincinnati, while Post was to come by water to Galena. Arriving in Cincinnati, Post took passage on the steamer Moselle, and just as they were rounding the outer pier, the boiler exploded, killing Mr. Post, his wife and two children. This caused Mr. Shaw to remain until the goods belonging to the two families (which had been shipped on the steamer) could be saved. This delayed Mr. Shaw so that he did not arrive here until late in the Spring, and the duty of imparting to the Post brothers, who were "watching and waiting" for father, mother and little ones, the sad intelligence of the terrible calamity that rendered them parentless, was one that he would gladly have had imposed upon others. But there was no other to discharge that duty, and with a heavy heart and in trembling accents, he related to the griefstricken sons and brothers a full account of the terrible scenes attending the fatal boiler explosion.

After Shaw's arrival, he selected a claim on section 18, now the beautiful and attractive home of his son, J. P. Shaw. Alonzo and Joseph Post, the two sons of Seth Post, made a claim on section 19, just opposite that selected by Mr. Shaw. They have since pushed on "out West," and their whereabouts are unknown.

George W. Wiley, a Tennessean, came to the county in 1827, and after drifting around a while and participating in the Black Hawk War in 1832, made a claim on section 21, in the northeast part of the township, in 1836. The same season he commenced breaking and improving his claim, and in 1838 moved to and occupied it, and has made it his permanent home ever since.

Another economical, prudent old settler is Fordice M. Rogers, who located a claim in section 33, on 1841, built a little log cabin, but which long since gave way to a large and palatial like dwelling. Mr. Rogers was the first supervisor after the adoption of the township organization system, and is now township treasurer, an office he has held for twenty-seven consecutive years.

The four Simmons brothers and their families came to the township almost simultaneously with Mr. Rogers, and settled in the southwestern corner of the township. These brothers have always proven themselves honest, industrious, pushing farmers; their farms are adjoining each other, and for several years past they have raised large crops of tobacco, which is the principal product of the township.

S. K. Miner

NORA TOWNSHIP.

From 1845 to 1849, immigration was heavy, and however willingly we would give the names of each successive settler, we find it impossible to do so, hence we mention only a few—not because there are none others equally as worthy of public mention, but because we have not the requisite space. There were Austin Warner, father of George and Goodwin Warner, and Cyrus Puckett, father of most of the Puckett families of the township. Captain George B. Stanchfield, was also among the early settlers, and was the founder of the Village of Nora. Not only has Captain Stanchfield been a warm supporter of the public enterprises of the village, but has always taken an active part in all matters pertaining to the advancement of the township of his home. His, to guide, and other kindred spirits to co-operate, has made Nora one of the best townships in the county. Although Mr. Stanchfield has retired from active participation in public affairs, his many good deeds and valuable services are not forgotten.

Among the active political and educational workers, may be mentioned the names T. Clarkson, Puckett, S. K. Miner, Robert M. Wilson and Alfonso E. Ricker. The acknowledged excellence of the high school and the public schools in general, and the brilliant success of the Nora Lecture course, is attributed to the energy, intelligence and enterprise of these gentlemen. Mr. Forest Turner, another citizen, has also had the honor to represent this people in the lower branch of the State Legislature, having been elected in 1874.

The first hotel built in the township was what was known as the One Mile House, and was on the stage route from Dixon to Galena. It was a little, low frame building, but has been enlarged and improved until it is a respectable dwelling house, and is occupied by a pioneer settler from Wisconsin, Mr. James Hood.

War Record.—There was no draft in this township. The people were too full of patriotism and love of the Union for that. One full company was raised and sent out to fight against treason and traitors. This company was made to form a part of Hurlbut's Fifteenth Regiment, which was organized at Freeport, and mustered into the United States service May 24, 1861, and was the first regiment organized from the state for the three years' service. A full record of this regiment, and a brief history of the engagements in which it took part, will be found in another chapter, together with the names of the " brave boys " that Nora offered as a sacrifice for the cause of freedom and unity. Not only were the people liberal in their offer of volunteers, but of money as well, and, we are glad to be able to place within these pages the sum provided by the tax-payers, for the benefit of the soldiers and their families. These figures will be found in the War Record.

Village of Nora.—June 4, 1849, George B. Stanchfield and Samuel Stanchfield entered 320 acres of land in sections four and five. A part of this land is now occupied by the Village of Nora. The town site was laid out by George B. Stanchfield, John C. Gardner, County Surveyor. The plat was duly acknowledged before William C. Bostwick, County Judge, and Joseph Conlee. Associate Justice, June 20, 1853. Three additions have been made to the original plat, as follows: by Brigam, Binneson and the Illinois Central Railroad Company.

George B. Stanchfield built the first dwelling house, and Elijah Winslow the first store building, and kept the first store. The second store, but really the first in importance, was kept by a Mr. Leland. Mr. George B. Stanchfield is responsible for the story, that during the first Summer Leland kept this store, several barrels of eggs accumulated on his hands, because there was no market at which they could be sold. Some of the eggs rotted causing a bad odor to arise, when he hauled them out on the prairie in order to remove the stench, and where he might assort them at his leisure. Some little boys found the barrels and opened them, and every day or two would bring eggs to Leland, who readily bought them at from one to two sticks of candy per dozen. For some days there was a remarkably large supply of eggs, and Leland thinking he was driving a good bargain, took occasion one day to boast to Mr. Stanchfield, how cheap he was buying eggs from boys who purloined them from their parents. The offering of eggs continued until several bushels accumulated on Leland's hands, before the trick was discovered. The "joke" leaked out and the laugh was at Leland's expense. *Leland had been buying his own rotten eggs.*

The dry goods trade is represented by W. F. Rockey and G. W. Messick.

Walter Stickney is a heavy dealer in grain whose annual shipments are very large.

Messrs. Young & Waddington represent the hardware trade.

J. H. Hines is the pioneer agricultural implement dealer, doing a business the first year of $1,000.00, which has increased to $8,000.00 per year.

Henry R. Lovin started the first meat market, with a capital of $50.00. He now pays out about $5,000.00 per year for stock for his market.

Walter L. Wasson represents the harness manufacturing business in a small way.

R. M. Rockey keeps the drug store and news depot, while A. Stevens and D. S. Farley are dealers in live stock, their aggregate business amounting to nearly $300,000.00 per year.

I. L. Cutler, M. D., is the physician.

Robert M. Wilson is the Village Blacksmith, and the present supervisor of the township.

Besides the above named business men and business houses, there are a large number of others—mechanics, etc.—who carry on business in a small way, but all of which goes to make Nora a village of no mean importance in a commercial sense.

RELIGIOUS.—The Nora M. E. Church is the outgrowth of the labors of Rev. James McKean, who came up from Vermilion County in 1835 by consent of the Illinois Conference. In the Fall of that year he organized a class at Waddam's Grove, Stephenson County, about six miles east of Nora. At that time this settlement was the largest one between Freeport and Galena. Luman and Rodney Montague were then the only Methodists at the Grove. Luman Montague left a written statement of these facts which the Nora Church has preserved, and from which this early history is gathered.

This territory then belonged to Waddam's Grove class, and to the Pecatonica Mission. In 1837 it was embraced in Pecatonica Circuit, with Rev. James MeKean as its pastor. In 1840 it was in Freeport Circuit, with Rev. Richard A. Blanchard in charge. In 1850 it was embraced in Cedarville Circuit. In 1854 Rev. Joseph Hartman, from Warren Circuit, came to Nora and formed a class consisting of eight members, to-wit: Cornelius Judson, Lucy Judson, Wyman Stephens and Deborah Stephens, Silas Hill and Ruth Hill, John Cowan and Mariah Cowan. The first services were held in a brick store now owned and occupied by Wm. B. Leach as a wagon shop. In this building and in the school house, services were held until 1868, when their present Church edifice was completed at a cost of $3,200.00. In 1855 this station was embraced in Lena Circuit with Rev. G. F. Gage in charge, but there were no services this year, as the people were too poor to raise the required amount. In 1865 Nora Circuit was established. The church now has a membership of fifty-five. The average attendance at the Sunday Sunday is sixty, with O. T. Spencer as superintendent.

Rev. Bertram Dickens is the present pastor.

Wesleyan Methodist.— This branch of the Christian church of America dates its separate and independent organization from 1842. In November of that year, Revs. O. Scott, J. Horton and L. R. Sunderland, three eminent divines of the Methodist Episcopal Church, who had long been dissatisfied with the indifference of that society towards the institution of American slavery, as well as with the arbitrary rules of its church government, withdrew from that organization, and inaugurated measures for the establishment of a church body in opposition to slavery, and with a greater degree of liberality in government. Another source of objection entertained by these eminent divines against the present church was its quasi endorsement of Masonic and other secret societies. The old discipline of that church emphatically denied permission to its followers, especially its ministers, to become members; but as the country and the church grew older, this forbidding clause ceased to be enforced, and seemed likely to become a dead letter in their faith and practice. Claiming to be true Methodists—disciples of Wesley, the founder of Methodism—Scott, Horton and Sunderland, when they took the decisive step of secession, because, in their way of thinking, the true spirit of Methodism and its teachings were being prostituted and violated, found many followers, and succeeded in establishing what is now known as the Wesleyan Methodist Church Organization. They retained the anti-Masonic clause of the old discipline, and rigidly enforced it; they discarded bishops, and introduced a system of lay preachers in their annual and general conferences, that makes their church thoroughly republican in form. Their government recognizes no distinctions, as between elders, pastors or people. They are all equal in their church relations as they are equal in the sight of God.

In 1848, six years after Scott, Horton and Sunderland had withdrawn from the parent society, a general division of the Methodist Church occurred on the question of slavery. The General Conference was held at Louisville, Kentucky, that year, and its proceedings were marked with national interest and importance, resulting in a separation, or complete and, so far, irrevocable division. Northern Methodists had, in six years, come to regard slavery as a relic of barbarism unholy and ungodly—a league with hell, and a covenant with death—and were as bold in their denunciations of the evil as they had formerly been meek, submissive and acquiescent. Southern Methodists believed it to be a divine institution, and that it was a religious duty to uphold and sustain it. After the separation they came to be known as the Methodist Episcopal Church South. The separation is still maintained, although several meetings of the representative men of the Northern and Southern Methodists have been held with a view of fixing a way for a reunion.

From this brief reference to the Louisville division of the M. E. Church in 1848, it will be seen that the Wesleyans were the pioneer Methodists in opening war upon the system of American slavery.

A society organization of Wesleyans, known as the Chelsea Church, is maintained in this township. The early records of the society have been lost, however, so that we are unable to fix the date of organization, but it is remembered that Rev. Morrison Delap was the first Wesleyan Methodist minister to preach in Nora Township. He came in the Fall of 1849 and organized the society, which held meetings in the school-houses of the neighborhood for twelve years, during which time the office of pastor was filled by Revs. Mr. Morgan, W. W. Steward, H. R. Will and his wife Mary A. During the charge of the latter minister, in 1861, their church was built on the township line road five and one half miles south of Warren. Since that time the following ministers have officiated: Revs. R. Baker, F. Mastin, D. W. Bond, Wm. Cummings, J. P. Spaulding, and the present minister—D. W. Bond. The present membership numbers about thirty-five. The Sunday school was organized in connection with the church at the time of the erection of their building. Its first superintendent was Rev. H. R. Will. At present Rev. D. W. Bond acts in that capacity. The Sabbath-school has a membership of fifty.

The German Baptist Church.—The members of this organization are noted for their industry and integrity, being nearly all farmers of thrifty and economical habits. Unbelievers in worldly show or display, they wear clothes of the plainest kind, discarding entirely jewelry or ornaments of any description. The exact date of their church organization at Nora could not be obtained, but in the Fall of 1874 they erected a house of worship, a plain but neat structure 32 by 40 feet, at a cost of $1,400, on section 16, two and three quarter miles due south of the village of Nora. This church is a branch of the Waddam's Grove District in Stephenson County, and among its first preachers were one Mr. Fry and B. H. Kepner, who officiated as early as 1850, and held services in a store basement in what was known as the Chelsea School District. Mr. Kepner still lives in Nora, and is actively engaged in the church, and in conjunction with Wm. K. Moore, has placed the Sunday-school in a flourishing condition, with an average attendence of about sixty scholars. The church proper has a membership of 35 persons, and an attendance of upwards of 150.

LECTURE ASSOCIATION.—The Nora Lecture Association was organized in the Fall of 1875, with the following officers: *President*, T. C. Puckett; *Secretary*, A. E. Ricker; *Treasurer*, R. M. Rockey.

Four lectures were given for the first course, as follows:

1. Prof. E. C. Hewett, of Normal, Illinois.
2. Hon. William Parsons, Dublin, Ireland. Subject, "George Stephenson."
3. Prof. David Swing, Chicago. Subject, "The Novel of the Future."
4. Mrs. Mary E. Livermore, Chicago. Subject, "What shall we do with our daughters?"

The Association now has $150.00 at interest, which it has earned and saved above expenses since its organization. Among the Lecturers this Winter (1878) was Wendell Phillips, one of America's greatest orators.

The present officers of the Association are T. C. Puckett, president; H. B. Lathe, secretary; A. J. Young, treasurer.

APPLE RIVER.

The oldest living resident of Apple River Township is Mr. William Colvin, whose intimate connection with the early history of the County has already been mentioned. Mr. Colvin came to Galena June 18, 1824, on the keel boat "Col. Bumford." After mining near there until 1828, he settled on the farm where he now lives, four miles west of the village of Apple River. At that time Lot L. Dimick, Wm. Hudson and Adam Vroman had already settled in the township as farmers. In 1829, Samuel Warner came from Ontario County, New York, and settled near Mr. Colvin where he has resided up to the present time.

For five years after the township organization, Apple River was incorporated in the Township of Thompson. The name of the township and village were derived from a river of that name by which the land is watered.

In 1854 the Illinois Central Railroad was built through the northern townships, and soon after, the village was established. Ebenezer Baldwin, a civil engineer on the road, J. W. Webster and Charles H. Lamar purchased the ground north of the railroad and laid out the town plat. The railroad company owned the land south of the track and formed it into a town addition. F. A. Strockley also made an addition on the east side of the original plat. The north line of the village is identical with the state line.

The first house on the site of Apple River was built of logs about 1832, by Daniel Robbins—the first settler at that place. He sold out to Francis Redfern, who came West about 1850, from Ohio. A large family of rough characters, named Daves, settled on a branch of the Apple River about the year 1835, which received, on account of their residence there, the name of "Hell Branch." In 1837 they had a dispute with a man named Alexander McKillips regarding his claim, which resulted in the Daves brothers waylaying McKillips, at night—tieing him to a stump and whipping him until almost dead. Such acts were among the lawlessness of frontier life. It may be added that a just retribution overtook these brothers, several of whom were hung, one killed by a falling mineral tub, and another chopped to pieces with an ax.

In 1842 Melzer Robbins, a brother of Daniel, settled in Apple River and became a prominent man in its progress. School was first taught by Edward Town, at the site of the village, in a log cabin situated where the residence of Thos. H. Maynard now stands. Soon after, school was kept by John Hartwell in the old historical cabin built by Daniel Robbins. The location of this house was across the railroad track just opposite the present Robbins Hotel. Mr. Redfern built the third house at the village on the site of Capt. John Maynard's present residence. In 1854, Francis Cosgrove built the first boarding house and saloon for the accommodation of railroad hands. The first hotel was built in 1854 by William Hoskins where the Robbins House now stands. It was originally 28 by 32 feet in size but was enlarged and owned for many years by J. B. Robbins, a son of Melzer, who, in 1877, built the present and only hotel of Apple River. In the Spring of 1854, J. M. Irvin built the first general store in the village and has continued in business on the same location to the present time. A little later in the same year David Black built a store room and sold goods there for a few years. In 1855, James Powers opened a store, and the following year another was added by George Frost, who continued in business until 1864, then, after eleven years' absence in Chicago, he established the first and only Bank of Apple River.

The first local election remembered was in 1856 when Chauncey Hutchings and E. B. Downes were nominated for the office of Justice of the Peace. The night before election a gravel train was run into town, bringing about sixty men (more than the entire number of residents) and, being of Downes' nativity (Irish), they gave him an overwhelming majority. However, Mr. Downes, who is still living at Apple River, declined to serve and Mr. H. S. Russell was made Justice.

After the adoption of the township system in 1853, and up to September, 1858, Apple River Township was included in Thompson Township, and C. C. Thompson was the first Supervisor. At that date, however, a new township was created, and called Apple River. It was created out of fractional township 29, north of range 3 east, and was taken from the Town of Thompson. Wm. F. Taylor was the first Supervisor. At a later period, a mile strip of territory was taken from Warren Township and attached to Apple River, including the Village of Apple River. After this change, Hiram DeGraff was the first Supervisor. Another change was made about 1864, by taking a strip of one mile and a half from Apple River, including the Village of Scales Mound, and attached to Scales Mound Township. At the election of 1859, held at Hudson Mound School-house, 80 votes were cast.

July 22, 1868, a vote was taken on the propriety of incorporating Apple River as a village, resulting in 35 votes for, and 33 against, incorporation. Incorporation under the general laws of the state followed immediately. The following Trustees were elected: J. A. Funk, Rob't Irvine, James M. Irvine, S. Woolan and Melzer Robbins. February 19, 1870, it was re-incorporated under special charter. The population of Apple River Township in 1860 was 508, and in 1870, 1,108 persons.

The assessed valuation of the township for 1877 was:—

Real Estate	$125,700	
Lots	38,245	
Personal	92,646	
		$216,591 00

Its present officers are: Joseph Roberts, Supervisor; P. A. Easley, Town Clerk; John Barry, Assessor; D. W. Christy, Collector; Patrick Murphy, John Hume and C. Lichtenburger, Commissioners of Highways; Geo. Frost, T. J. Birmingham, Hugh Williams, Henry Smith, Joseph Robbins and Robert Parkins, Trustees; Thomas Scott and William Levitt, Justices of the Peace; John Bush and C. Teppert, Constables.

SCHOOLS.

The schools held in cabins have already been referred to. The first building erected for school purposes was in 1857, on lot one, block nine of the railroad addition, which was donated, for the purpose, by the railroad company. On it was built a one-story stone house, to which a second story was afterwards added. As the village grew, more school room was found necessary, and in 1873, a frame building of two stories was erected on the opposite side of the railroad track, to be used as a high school. Professor Brown first acted in the capacity of teacher in this building. The present principal is Thomas Bermingham, while Misses Ada Rivenburg and Selina Woodward officiate in the stone building. Twelve hundred dollars is appropriated annually for teachers' salaries.

CHURCHES.

Rev. J. Hartwell preached, in a log cabin, the first sermon in Apple River, in 1855. The first regular mission preacher, of whom record remains, was William Taylor, now Postmaster at Nora, who, in connection with school teaching, directed the devotions of the scattered settlers as early as the year 1857.

In the year 1858, the people gathered in the school-house to listen to the teachings of Rev. S. S. Guyer, a Methodist circuit-rider, and in the same year, a Methodist Sunday-school was organized, by T. F. Hastie, in the railroad office. This was soon transferred to the school-house. Two years after, the Methodist Church, a good frame building, was erected, costing about $2,000, and seating three hundred persons. At present, Hans Lamont is the Sabbath-school Superintendent. The church was dedicated by Rev. Peter Cartwright, a pioneer of Methodism in Illinois. The ministers in succession have been: Revs. J. Clendenning, E. B. Russell, J. M. Clendenning, J. Odgers, H. U. Reynolds, S. O. Foster, T. L. Olmsted, A. D. Field, Joseph Crummer, Joseph Caldwell, Thomas Cochrane, concluding with the present pastor, Rev. D. W. Linn.

Catholic.—Church services were held for several years in private houses. In 1858, Rev. Father P. Corcoran superintended the building of their church, which was originally 26 by 36 feet in size, but was enlarged in 1872 by an addition of 30 by 26 feet. It now seats about five hundred persons, and the church has a membership of one hundred families. Rev. Fathers Shilling, Michael El Heren, Joseph Kindekins and M. Zara have, in succession, officiated as their priests, Father Zara having just taken the position.

The Presbyterian Church was organized by Rev. John Reynard, in April, 1861, at the residence of Mr. Vroman, when Joseph C. Jellison was made elder. From this time, the association took no action until 1864, when Rev. J. W. Cunningham came, reorganized the society, and caused the church to be built. Rev. Rufus King was their first permanent minister. He was followed by Rev. G. M. Jenks, then John Cook, D. B. Gordon and E. B. Miner, who remained until 1876, since which time the church has been unable to maintain a regular pastor.

INDEPENDENT ORDERS.

Masonic.—Apple River Lodge, No. 548, A. F. and A. M., was organized October, 1868, with M. Maynard, W. M.; J. P. Black, S. W., and H. J. D. Maynard, J. W. The present officers are: Geo. Frost, W. M.; Thos. White, S. W.; Hugh Williams, J. W.; E. M. Funk, Secretary; Geo. Kleeburger, Treasurer. Meetings are held on the first and third Saturdays of each month. Membership, forty-five.

I. O. O. F.—The Reliance Lodge, No. 533, was organized Nov. 9, 1873. Its first officers were: John Buche, N. G.; John Sieber, V. G.; Wm. Uhren, Treasurer, and D. P. Emery, Secretary. The first four named, with R. Buche and Thomas Gelaspie, constitute the charter members. The present officers are: Hans Lamon N. G.; Nemiah Rowlston, V. G.; John Sieber, Treasurer; G. L. H. Kleeburger, Secretary.

BUSINESS INTERESTS.

In the southeastern part of town is situated a large three-story stone building, erected at a cost of $10,000 by Black, Irvine & Co. as a plow factory. This business was sold, in 1876, to the Grand Detour Plow Factory, of Dixon, Ill., since when it has been occupied as a planing and sawing mill.

The leading business firms of Apple River at present are given below, together with the date of their establishment:

General Store.—J. M. Irvine, 1854; G. L. H. Kleeburger, 1870; Malachi Maynard, 1860; Nicholas Murphy, 1873; W. D. Ennor, 1876; S. H. Shoop, 1875.

Drugs.—R. L. Hall, 1870.

Hardware.—M. Maynard, 1877.

Jewelry.—T. Y. Maynard, 1870.

Lumber.—T. J. Bermingham, 1873.

Millinery.—Misses B. A. & L. Hall, 1864.

Wagon Making.—Hugh Williams, 1869.

Harness Making.—C. F. Spofford, 1877.

Banker.—George Frost, 1875.

Physicians.—Daniel Sheffield, 1859; Charles Carey, 1866.

The first postmaster was J. M. Irvine; the present one is Beeri Serviss, who has held the position since Mr. Irvine resigned. The village has a general appearance of prosperity; is well supported by a good farming community, and does a large amount of mineral, stock and produce shipping. It is the shipping point for several zinc and lead mines in Wisconsin.

WARREN.

To Captain Alexander Burnett is due the honor of first entering upon the lands of Warren for permanent residence. In the Spring of 1843 he emigrated from Ohio; made his claim and built a cabin, where now stands Mr. B. Servis' brick building at the corner of Water and Main Streets, upon section 24, of this Township.

Mr. Burnett continued to be the only settler in this immediate vicinity until the Fall of 1845, when Freeman A. Tisdel, of Michigan, came in and bought one half of Mr. Burnett's claim—about 120 acres.

At that time the surveyor had not defined the section lines, and the small branch running south through the town was made the line of division between the two farms—Mr. Burnett's being on the east, and Mr. Tisdel's on the west side. At this time, Mr. Kingsley Olds and family, living about a mile south,

Mr. Cowen, a mile west, and Mr. Newville, a mile east, constituted their only civilized neighbors.

The land upon which these people had settled still belonged to the government and did not come into the market until 1847, when they became legal owners by purchase, at the Land Office in Dixon. Mr. Burnett being located upon the old "Sucker trail," kept a public house for many years, and by the crossing of two roads near his house, the place received the title of "Burnett's Corners."

In the Fall of 1845, Mr. Burnett gave Mr. Tisdel possession of the log house, and built for himself a frame dwelling on the site of the present Burnett House. He still resides at Warren. The post-office was first established at Mr. Tisdel's house, in 1847.

In the Fall of this year, Mr. E. T. Sandoe made his *debut* at "The Corners," and started a blacksmith shop. William, a son of Mr. Sandoe was the first white male child known to have been born in the settlement; although the date of his birth has not been left on record.

A Mr. Baldwin opened a little store in a frame building opposite the log hotel soon after the arrival of Mr. Sandoe.

In 1851, Mr. Tisdel completed a large stone building known as the "Warren House," to which he removed, making room in the log house for a store which was opened by J. W. Parker, who was soon after joined by Manly Rogers, under the firm title of "Parker & Rogers."

The settlers now had a habitation, but no name. A meeting was called to decide upon a title for the settlement, and, after much discussion, "Courtland" was selected as the name which should supersede the common-place "Corners."

In the Spring of the same year, Mr. John D. Platt opened a store in a wing of the Warren House, to which firm Mr. A. L. Brink was soon made partner. Soon after (1853), the firms of "S. H. Clark & Co." and "Jackson & Son," were established. Until the advent of these stores, the wants of the settlers were supplied chiefly by peddlers.

At the time of Mr. Rogers' arrival, among the prominent citizens not yet mentioned, were Charles Cole (who removed to and died at Salem, Nebraska), G. A. Smith, and Dr. Thomas E. Champion, (afterwards Colonel of the 96th Illinois Volunteers. He died at Knoxville, Tenn). Judge Platt continued his store until 1858, since which time he has engaged in general business pursuits, always being a prominent, public-spirited citizen.

A daughter of Mr. Platt, Eva, now Mrs. W. C. Thompson, was the only "baby" known in the neighborhood, except the son of Mr. Tisdel, for many years, although she was born in McHenry County, soon before removing to Jo Daviess.

By this time the farming lands were generally occupied, and Courtland began to assume the appearance of a village. Among others, George W. Pepoon and John Tear had settled in the neighborhood, both of whom are still residing on their original farms having, with the lapse of years, accumulated valuable properties.

The chief mines of the vicinity are the "Babel" and "Pepoon" diggings, the latter of which received the name of its owner. They were, at one time valuable mines, but at present not much mineral is being raised.

April 30, 1852, Mr. Tisdel had a portion of his land, located on the southeast and southwest quarters of the northeast quarter of section 24, township 29, surveyed by J. C. Gardner, and subdivided into town lots, he and Mr. Burnett conceiving the idea of making a town in what seemed the middle of the prairies. The streets then established were: Washington, Main and Catlin, running south, 63 deg. east; Long, Centre and Warren, running south, 27 deg. east, and Railroad Street running south, 57 deg. east. It is evident from the last named street that the Illinois Central Railroad had already established its route and that the building of the road stimulated the formation of a village at that place.

A. M. Jones

At the township organization, February 15, 1853, fractional township 29 north, range 5, east of the fourth principal meridian, was called "Courtland." November 24, of this year, Sylvester and Alexander Burnett laid out the first addition to the town, under the name of "Burnett's Addition."

In the Summer of 1853, the Illinois Central Railroad was completed to this place, when the name of the village was changed to Warren, the Township, however, retaining its former name until March 2, 1865, when it, also, was changed to Warren.

March 15, 1855, fractional section 18, sections 19, 30 and 31 and the north half of section 31, township 29, north range, 5 east, were taken from the Township of Nora and added to Courtland, on account of the village of Warren being located on this territory; and December 14, 1864, fractional sections 17 and 18, sections 19, 20, 29, 30, 31 and 32, of Courtland were detached therefrom and added to Apple River, throwing the Village of Apple River in its proper township.

In 1853–'4 work was begun on the Mineral Point Railroad, which was laid out from Warren to Mineral Point, Wisconsin, but it was not completed until 1858. This road has always been well supported, furnishing, as it does, an outlet for the products of lower Wisconsin.

The year 1854 was the saddest one in the history of Warren. At this time its people suffered a visitation of the cholera, and more than fifty of these pioneer settlers succumbed to its attacks. Among them were George A. Smith, Asa Saxton, John Whitmore, Rollins Ballard, Mrs. Charles Cole, Lewis C. Gann, Allen Gates and a Mr. Hutchinson, whose first name has been forgotten.

On the evening of February 11, 1857, a meeting was held to consider the propriety of incorporating Warren as a village, at which thirty-four votes were cast for, and nine against, incorporation. At this meeting John D. Platt presided, and Thomas E. Champion acted in the capacity of secretary.

The rapid growth of Warren dates from 1853—the year when the Central Railroad terminated there, for a season. Soon a number of additions was made to the village, which have been recorded in the following order: Sylvester Burnett's 2d and 3d addition, Tisdel's addition and Sherk's addition, all June 15, 1854; Burnett's addition, June 5, 1855; Linkfield's addition, May 21, 1855; besides these, there are additions by Thomas York, D. A. Tisdel, J. D. Platt, D. Sinclair, F. A. Tisdel, Sr., F. and D. A. Tisdel, M. D. Rising, O. Jackson, M. M Yeakle, M. Y. Johnson, Wm. Cain, A. L. Brink, Jas. Bayne, A. M. Jones and J. Wright.

Being situated within a mile of the state line of Wisconsin, Warren is a great resort of criminals, who wish to get out of that state, and of eloping couples, who wish to take advantage of forbidding parents and the marriage laws of Wisconsin.

RELIGIOUS.

Religious interest was manifested in Warren at a very early stage of its history. Meetings were held among its first settlers by a traveling minister named George W. Ford, in the various private houses.

The Methodist organization was first effected in the village in 1854, though a class had existed two miles south for several years. The first church was erected (24 by 40 feet in size), in the same year by Rev. J. Sherk. Rev. Joseph Hartman acted as their pastor for two years. Among the leading members at the organization were, J. F. H. Dobler and wife, L. F. Farnham and wife, Thomas Hicks and wife, Joseph Sherk and wife, Samuel Phelps and wife, Joseph Graves, George Jamison, Mrs. Eunice Cobb, Mrs. Whitmore and a few others.

A Sabbath school was organized soon after the church, Joseph Graves acting as superintendent. In 1860 the prosperity of the society demanded an enlargement of the building, and an addition of 20 by 24 feet was made.

The erection of the present fine brick building was commenced in 1864, (on the site of the old one), under the pastorate of Rev. George Richardson, and completed under the charge of Rev. Joseph Odgers.

The following pastors have officiated at Warren successively: Revs. J. Hartman, J. Wallace, Wm. Keegan, Wm. Cone, C. F. Wright, T. L. Olmsted, Wm. Keegan, Geo. Richardson, Joseph Odgers, C. French, Geo. Richardson, G. L. S. Stuff, J. Linebarger, Wm. Burns, H. J. Huston, C. Brookins and Joseph Crummer, who is the present minister. John Bird is now superintendent of the Sunday school. The church and Sabbath school have each a present membership of about two hundred and fifty.

The Free Will Baptist Church was organized a little later in the same year, at a meeting held at the Burnett House. Their church was built in 1855. Professor Dunn, now of Hillsdale College, Michigan, took the active management of organization and dedication, although Rev. Horace G. Woodworth was the first regular pastor. A Sabbath school was organized in connection with the church; Charles Cole being the first superintendent. Rev. R. W. Bryant is the present pastor, and Mr. A. M. Jones, superintendent of the Sabbath school.

The Presbyterian Church was organized August 8, 1864, in the Baptist Church, where meetings were held for some time by Rev. John W. Cunningham, who preached their first sermon. Their church was built in the same year, being superintended by their first regular pastor, Rev. E. H. Avery. After six years Mr. Avery was superseded by Rev. H. P. Thayer; then Rev. G. H. Coit, then Rev. E. B. Miner, who was followed by the present pastor, Rev. S. S. Cryer. In 1877, an addition was made to the church, giving it a commodious auditorium. It is entirely free from debt. The first Board of Elders consisted of D. C. Allen, Manley Rogers and Thomas J. Graham. At present, the session is composed of Manley Rogers, E. H. Morris, J. N. Parker, G. W. Pepoon, L. E. Morris and W. R. Colburn. Junius Rogers first acted as Sabbath-school superintendent, which office is now filled by Manley Rogers. The school has a membership of about 160, while the number of church members is estimated at 135.

In 1859, by the personal endeavors of Mr. M. M. Yeakle, a large stone building was erected for a Lutheran Church, but as Mr. Yeakle failed before its completion, it was never dedicated to the use of that branch of the Christian church.

SCHOOLS.

Among the important duties of any people is to provide for the instruction of their children. Several years before the railroad was completed to the Village of Warren, the scattered pioneers had provided a means of education for their little ones.

About 1848 a school-house was built one half mile west of the site of Warren, in which Charles Cole first gave instruction. For some years after the settlement began to assume the character of a village, a school was maintained in a small cabin. About 1864, a brick school building was erected at a cost of $3,500. This was superseded by the present one in 1872, which is also of brick, fifty feet square with a wing, thirty by forty feet, and of two stories. It cost nearly $10,000.

The schools are taught by D. E. Garber, Principal; E. E. Grigsby, Assistant; Miss Josie McHugh, Grammar School; Miss Cora Harrower, Intermediate; Miss Maud Goodfellow, Secondary; Mrs. Rosa Parker, Primary.

In 1870 a small brick school-house was built on the east side of the railroad, which is under the charge of Miss L. A. Field. Three thousand dollars is appropriated annually for the teachers' salaries. The present directors are, H. V. Brown, Dr. A. F. Bucknam, W. C. DeLong.

Such is the past and present of Warren's schools. Its people appreciate the power of education, and have provided an ample fountain in their midst from which all the youth may freely drink.

LODGES AND ASSOCIATIONS.

A. F. & A. M.—In 1858 the Jo Daviess Lodge No. 278, A. F. & A. M., was organized. Its charter members were: S. H. Clark, Thos. E. Champion, N. B. Hull, E. Huntington, T. D. Rose, C. S. Hussey, J. C. Barnard and Chas. Francisco.

First officers: S. H. Clark, W. M.; T. E. Champion, S. W.; N. B. Hull, J. W.

Present officers: S. A. Clark, W. M.; W. S. Benson, S. W.; W. L. Gale, J. W.; John Tear, Treasurer; W. M. Capron, Secretary. Their meetings are held the first and third Saturdays of each month. Membership 100.

Olive Chapter No. 167, R. A. M., was organized October 28, 1875.

Charter Members.—J. D. Platt, A. C. Schadle, M. H. Luke, W. S. Benson, John Tear, J. C. Woodworth, W. L. Gale, C. A. Robey, F. W. Byers, S. A. Clark, A. Holcomb, L. E. Kessler.

First Officers. —J. D. Platt, H. P.; A. C. Schadle, K.; M. H. Luke, S.

Present Officers.—A. C. Schadle, H. P.; W. S. Benson, K.; B. F. Crummer, S. Regular convocations the first and third Mondays of each month. Membership, forty-one.

The societies own their society hall—a large and well-furnished building—which alone is sufficient evidence of their prosperity.

I. O. O. F.—The Odd Fellows' organization was effected in 1858, under the name of Ridgley Lodge, No. 259. Their first N. G. was Daniel Ransom.

Present Officers.—George Binns, N. G.; B. F. Crummer, V. G.; James Bayne, Secretary; J. A. Platt, Treasurer. Membership, 53.

North Star Encampment No. 83, was organized on Oct. 13, 1868.

First Officers.—H. H. Peckham, C. P.; J. L. Code, S. W.; Thomas M. Blake, H. P.; J. S. Morrell, J. W.

Present Officers.—H. S. Francisco, C. P.; T. D. Thornton, S. W.; Thos. M. Blake, H. P.; George Binns, J. W.; J. A. Platt, Scribe; John S. Morrell, Treasurer. Membership, 40.

A. O. U. W. Warren Lodge No. 27 was formed November 30, 1876. There are thirty-three charter members. Their officers are: A. C. Schadle, P. M. W.; G. H. Wilcox, M. W.; J. M. Hussey, G. F.; Charles Morten, O.; John Fraser, Recorder; W. L. Gale, F.; M. Rogers, R. Regular meetings on the second and fourth Mondays of each month. Membership, 40.

The Union Agricultural Society is one of the old established associations of Warren. It was first located on lands belonging to the Rising estate, about one quarter of a mile northwest of the village, in 1860. In 1872 it was removed to the present grounds, one half mile east of the village.

The grounds include twenty acres of land; are beautifully laid out and nicely ornamented.

Its officers are: President, Robert Hawley; Vice President, David Young; Secretary, Joseph Hicks; Treasurer, Wm. L. Gale; Directors, M. Lynch, G. W. Pepoon and Wm. Young. It includes in the Association the Counties of Jo Daviess, Stephenson and Lafayette (Wis.)

BUSINESS INTERESTS.

The Press.—Among the prominent features of every community are its newspapers. Very early in the history of Warren, the type and press were introduced to share the privations and fortunes of its people. In 1855, Charles Blaisdell published the *Warren Republican*. After a trial of one year it was discontinued, and, September 23, 1857, the first number of the *Warren Independent* was issued, which has continued, with one change of name, to the present time. It was published by Freeman A. Tisdel, Sr., and Thomas E. Champion, and edited by George A. Randall. April 2, 1858, Lewis and Baugher, who had come there to practice law, purchased the paper and continued its publication until Jan. 31, 1860, when M. P. Rindlaub (now editor of the Platteville, Wis., *Witness*), bought Lewis out, and in July of the same year, he purchased the remainder of the office. Mr. Nesbitt Baugher then became connected with the Galena *Gazette* until the outbreak of the war, at which time he enlisted in and was made a Lieutenant in Company B, 45th, or Lead Mine Regiment, and was mortally wounded at the battle of Pittsburg Landing. In December, 1860, D. J. Benner became a partner of Mr. Rindlaub. In May, 1861, Mr. Benner enlisted in the army, and was made First Lieutenant of Company E, 15th Illinois Volunteers. Mr. Herst C. Gann came to Warren with his parents at the age of ten years, in 1854, from Pennsylvania. His father became a victim of the cholera about three weeks after his arrival.

In 1857 Mr. Gann commenced learning the "art preservative," in the *Independent* office, and has had almost continuous connection with the paper since that time. March 10, 1864, he purchased the office, and has been its editor to the present time, except during an enlistment in the army of ten months, when it was managed by Steve. R. Smith, who decreased its circulation nearly one half. From 1866 to 1868, Mr. J. W. Leverett held an active interest in the paper, and, on account of the bad repute into which Smith had thrown it, Messrs. Leverett and Gann changed the name, in July, 1866, to its present title, the *Warren Sentinel*. Such is Warren's history, in brief, of that watchful, public guardian—the Press.

Banking Interests.—Something was done in the banking business by J. D. Platt in 1858, but his intentions of forming a permanent bank were interrupted by ill health and he returned to the East for a time.

In October, 1864, Manley and Junius Rogers established the first regular Bank of Warren. In March, 1865, the Farmers National Bank was organized with Manley Rogers, President; N. B. Richardson, Vice President, and Junius Rogers, Cashier. S. A. Clark became Cashier in January, 1873, and in May, 1875, the bank surrendered its charter. The business is now continued by Rogers, Richardson & Co., S. A. Clark being a member of the firm.

INDUSTRIES.

In 1859, M. M. Yeakle built a large, stone, steam grist-mill and grain elevator in the northern part of the town, at a cost of about $20,000. Mr. Yeakle, who has already been referred to as failing in the midst of his public-spirited endeavors, disposed of the mill to Messrs. Bird, Bridge & Co., who employ five men, and are doing a good, steady business.

A Planing Mill was established in Warren by N. Boothby & Co., in 1858. This business was carried on until 1871, when they began the manufacture of parquet flooring or wood carpet. They employ twelve men. Their sales are made principally by agents; large orders coming from Chicago, San Francisco, and other cities.

A Flax Tow-Mill was built in the eastern part of the town in 1870, by Col. John Dement, of Dixon, Ill., at a cost of $10,000. It employs twenty men, and works up about two thousand tons of straw annually. The tow is shipped to Dixon, where it is manufactured into bagging. It is superintended by Jacob Spielman.

Hotels.—Though it was of the pioneer character, Alexander Burnett kept the first public house of Warren. The house was the historical old "log cabin," which was built in 1843, though it was followed many years later by a hotel on the site of the present Burnett House, which is now kept by Charles Phillips.

Five years ago, at an expense of $20,000, the Barton House was erected by Major Barton, who came to Warren in 1853, when the railroad terminated there for the season, and followed the livery business until within three years. The Barton House is a large, three-story brick building, with basement, and containing the Public Hall. It is an ornament to the village, which is appreciated by the citizens, who may well regard Mr. Barton as a public benefactor.

The Jo Daviess Co-operative Association was organized in 1877, for the purpose of furnishing to its members, household and other supplies without the intervention of a "middle-man" between producer and consumer. It has a capital stock of $2,500. P. E. Enery, Agent. Directors: E. Farnham, B. F. Watson, G. W. Curtiss, R. Russell, G. S. Wing, L. F. Farnham and Charles Boone.

The following is a list of the principal business houses of Warren, at present, giving the business and date of establishment:

General Stock—H. M. Carlton, 1863; Wilcox Bros., 1872; A. B. Conyne, 1877. Hardware—W. C. DeLong, 1864; Carlton Bros. & Woodworth, 1872. Drugs—J. J. Knapp, 1867; L. E. Kessler, 1867; E. S. Baldwin. Groceries—Wm. Hoefer, 1861; L. T. Ziegle, 1862; Seth Bedell, 1871. Books and Jewelry—Geo. Richardson, 1873. Dry Goods—Wm. Thompson, 1875. Lumber—C. F. Taylor & Co., 1877. Produce Shipper—H. S. Van Derwort, 1865. Agricultural Implements—Foss & Bucknam, 1877; Furniture—Albert Totten, 1876. Machine Shop—Platt & Phillips, 1876. Carriage Maker—Charles Murray, 1877. Physicians—B. G. Pierce, 1854; A. F. Bucknam, 1870; B. F. Crummer, 1876; A. C. Tuttle, 1875. Dentist—Dr. A. C. Schadle.

The Township Officers are:

Supervisor—C. M. Gregory.

Township Clerk—Wm. L. Gale.

Assessor—Geo. W. Pepoon.

Collector—H. W. Godding.

Constables—John Stanton and M. S. Murphy.

Justices of Peace—James Bayne and C. L. Giles.

The Village Officers are:

Board of Trustees—Wm. S. Hicks—President—George Richardson, Walter C. Wells, C. M. Gregory, Martin L. Canfield, Ralph Dawson.

Clerk—John Bird; *Treasurer*—James Payne; *Postmaster*—Arthur Fanin.

In 1877 the Township of Warren had 8,284.86 acres of improved land and 3,388.80 acres of unimproved land, the assessed value of the former being $151,510, and of the latter, $20,980; besides these there are 1,704 lots, valued at $180,545. The assessed valuation of personal property for the same year was $263,024. As it is customary to assess at about one third the true value, the total wealth of the township may be placed at a much larger figure.

RUSH.

In the month of August, 1828, a Mr. Kirker erected the first house that was ever built in the Township of Rush on the old Sucker Trail, running along a branch of Apple River. Mr. Kirker built the house for the purpose of keeping a tavern, but as there was no travel in Winter, the business did not pay, and the would-be landlord left the house to take care of itself. In 1830, he sold his house to Hiram Imus, Jr., who with his wife moved into it.

In the Summer of 1831, Charles Imus, a brother of Hiram, and Henry Rice with his wife, came from Galena and settled at the mouth of Wolf Creek. The claim of Henry Rice was, at the time of the Township organization, included in Stockton Township. The next Spring they were driven back to Galena for protection by the Black Hawk War.

In the Spring of 1833, these families returned to the homes from which they had been driven by the Indians, and became permanent settlers. They were accompanied by Philip Rice and wife, who settled there. At this time Hiram Imus, Sr., with wife, son, Alfred, and daughter, Nancy, lived in Galena. In 1834, Nancy, while visiting her brother Hiram, died; this being the first death in Rush Township. In 1835 the balance of the Imus family moved to Rush Township, where Alfred died in the same year. In 1845, Charles Imus, with a son of Hiram Imus, Jr., also named Charles, went to California. In 1849 they were followed by the remainder of the family, and the Rice family.

In 1835, Thomas Burbridge and his two brothers, Rollin and Jackson, accompanied by John R. Smith, built a house on Apple River, at a place afterwards called Millville, and moved into it. In the Spring of 1836, they built a saw mill at that place, which was the first saw mill built on Apple River, with the exception of one built by Mr. Craig, at a place then called Wappello, but now known as Hanover. In this saw mill the Burbridges cut a vast amount of lumber, which they sold very readily to the new settlers who were then coming into the country. The Burbridges were all young men. Their mother kept house for them many years. She was a type of the pioneer women of America, and was highly respected by all who knew her. She died in 1874, in the 97th year of her age.

In 1835, Mr. Absalom Power settled about two miles west of Millville, near a Mound, which in honor of him was called Power's Mound. He had a large family—some eight or nine boys and two or three girls. The old gentleman and his wife died at their residence near the Mound.

In the Spring of 1836, George N. Townsend, Ira L. Townsend and Holstead S. Townsend, settled in the Township of Rush, about four miles south of Millville, near the Bald Mound. They built houses that Summer, purchasing their lumber of the Messrs. Burbridge. In the Fall they moved on and became actual settlers of the town. They quite naturally settled near together, and the place was known as the Townsend Settlement for many miles around.

The following extracts are from a paper written by H. S. Townsend, one of the oldest settlers:

"At this time the tide of emigration had fairly set in. Mr. Asher Miner came on in the Fall of 1836, from the State of New York, his family following him in the Fall of the next year. They settled in the Township of Rush, in what is known as Miner's Grove, about one and one half miles below Millville. Mr. Miner lived in the Townships of Rush and Nora for many years, and died in Nora in 1867, very much respected.

"RANSON Miner, son of Asher Miner, moved in at the time his father's family did, and settled in the Townsend Settlement, where he lived until his death in 1855. His wife yet lives on the old homestead.

"In 1837 Jasper Rosencrans moved into the Township of Rush, and settled in Townsend's Settlement, where he lived until 1850, when he went to California. Mr. Ira L. Townsend also went to California the same year. In September, 1850, they started home together, but were never heard of afterwards.

"Mr. Ira Bowker moved into the Township of Rush in 1837, and settled in Townsend Settlement, at what was known as Brushy Grove. He also went to California in 1850, and died while on his journey home, in Green County, in this state. His wife and most of his family are now living in Rush Township

"In 1837 Seth Post came to this county from New York, and in company with Mr. Charles Imus, erected a saw mill on Apple River, about two miles above Millville. This mill did a great deal of work, until the timber was exhausted, but it has now disappeared. Mr. Post returned to New York for his family, and was on his way back by way of the Ohio River, when at Cincinnati himself and wife were killed by the blowing up of the steamboat Mozelle, upon which they had taken passage. His two sons came on and resided here a number of years, when they sold their mill and removed to the State of Wisconsin. Joseph, the younger son, entered the army during the great Rebellion, and was elected Captain. He was wounded at the battle of Shiloh, from the effects of which he died. Lorenzo, the elder brother, is still living at Wayouaga, Wisconsin.

"Mr. Adam Arnold moved into the township in 1839, and settled near the old Kirker place, then occupied by the Imus family, where he died in 1850. He had a large family, most of whom yet reside in the Township of Rush.

"In 1839 Mr. George Renwick came on from the State of New York, and settled in Townsend Settlement, Brushy Grove. He died in 1871, leaving quite a large estate. The widow yet resides at the old homestead. He was highly esteemed and raised thirteen children, most of whom yet reside in this town.

"Such were the early settlers of Rush, and we might, even now, profit from the contemplation of their humble virtues, hospitable homes, and spirits noble, proud and free.

"Settlers were now coming in quite numerous, too much so to attempt to make special mention of them.

"Various as may have been the objects of our people in emigrating, no sooner had they come together, than there existed in each settlement a unison of feeling. In their intercourse with each other and with strangers, they were kind, beneficent and disinterested, extending to all the most generous hospitality which their circumstances could afford—their latch-string was always out. They were kind for kindness' sake, and sought no other recompense than the never-failing reward of an approving conscience.

"At the time of the first settlement of this township, the Indians were here, and for a time shared the country with us. They were of the Winnebago tribe, were generally friendly and did us but little harm.

"Game was plentiful, such as deer, turkeys, and a few bear. The game was all that brought the Indians here, and both soon disappeared.

"Mills were scarce and of rude construction, but we had no use for them until we had something to grind. If you had visited one of these settlers, you would have been made heartily welcome, and would have been received in the most friendly manner. In their log cabins a bountiful meal would have been set before you, of venison and corn bread, or mush, the meal for which was ground on a tin grater. This was the best that could be had short of Galena. To purchase luxuries, we needed money, and that was an article we did not possess.

"At this day fancy fashions and foolish pride had not reached us. Then we had no regular mail in this part of the country. We received our mail from Galena, Shullsburg, or wherever we went to trade. We received a newspaper about once in two weeks, and such was the interest produced by its advent that no one would think of sleep until every word of the paper had been read aloud.

"Galena was the largest place in northern Illinois, and Jo Daviess County the greatest county. The county was divided into election precincts soon after—the precinct embracing the whole of the northeastern part of the county, including what is now the Towns of Thompson, Apple River, Warren, Nora, Stockton, Ward's Grove and Rush. Elections were held at the house of Hiram Imus, at the old Kirker place. At that time the elections were held on the first Monday in August; but for many years they were lightly attended. Other matters occupied too much time and attention.

"The business of the county was done by three men called county commissioners. Those three men appointed three others in each election precinct, who managed the elections. But in 1838 there were two justices elected in the precinct. One lived in the Town of Rush. His name was Jedediah P. Miner. (He was a brother of Asher Miner, heretofore mentioned.) He came into the country about 1837, and on the first Monday in August, 1838, he was elected a Justice of the Peace in what was afterward the Township of Rush. He was the first justice ever elected in the town, and we all felt that we were rising in the world—and truly we were, for we then had a court of justice in our own town. However, we had but little use for our newly-elected justice. Any difficulty was generally settled by arbitration; there were no deeds to be made out, for our land was not yet in the market. As for marrying, there was very little of that to be done, for marriageable parties were about as scarce as money in old Jo Daviess County.

"What we needed most just now was a post-office, as we had become tired of receiving our mail but once in two or three weeks; so we got up a petition, directed to the Postmaster General, asking him to appoint John R. Smith Postmaster, and give us a mail once a week. Our worthy Postmaster General granted our petition, but required us to furnish a name for our post-office—a thing we had not before thought of. But that was easily supplied, and as there was but one mill in the town, with a strong probability that more would soon be built there, we named our post-office Millville; a name that the place yet bears. This post-office was of great value to us; we all began to take the weekly papers, and began to look a little into the affairs of our county, state and national government. With the increase in knowledge, came an increase in population and wealth. We had opened up our farms; our land produced bountifully; we raised cattle and hogs in abundance."

But now other wants were pressing upon the people. Children were growing up uneducated, and it was necessary to have school-houses.

In 1838, near the late residence of G. N. Townsend, the first school-house in the eastern end of the county was built. Pupils came to it from long distances. The late Gen. John A. Rawlins attended school here, also Joseph Moore. The second school-house built in the Township of Rush was erected in 1842. Miss Abigail Tyrrell—afterwards Mrs. Benjamin Parker—was engaged to teach the pupils of this school, which consisted of the three children, each, of Henry Rice, Philip Rice and H. S. Townsend and two of a Mr. Duncan. Both schools were continued for a number of years, or until the settlement demanded a larger house and different locality. At that time there were no school laws, or at least none were in force.

In April, 1847, the public land sale took place at Dixon. Until that time the people were but "squatters" on the public domain. There was, of course, considerable trouble among the settlers to procure enough ready money to purchase the lands to which they had laid claim. But those who were able to secure money sent it by a committee composed of Ira L. Townsend, Ira Bowker and Halstead S. Townsend, to Dixon, where the committee purchased the lands.

As there had been no surveys made there were many disputes as to the boundaries, so that the people of the township appointed a committee consisting of John D. Brown, George N. Townsend and John R. Smith, who were chosen arbitrators to settle such disputes.

In 1847, a grist mill was built in Millville by the owners, Messrs. Burbridge and Smith, and the old saw mill was torn down.

April 14, 1846, Millville was laid off on the southeast and southwest quarters of section 4, township 28, north of range 4, east of the 4th principal meridian, and bid fair to become a large town. A Mr. Dean built a blacksmith shop; John W. Marshall started a dry goods store; Mr. Eldridge Howard erected quite a large house, and opened a very good tavern there. Frink & Walker ran their stage line through the place, and Millville became quite a

John D Brown

RUSH TOWNSHIP

thriving village. Major Davenport and a Mr. Easley also started quite an extensive store in the place; a Mr. Dorn also had a store there for a short time.

Millville was on the shortest route from Galena to Chicago, and considerable travel passed through the town. For a number of years it was the only town of any importance between Freeport and Galena. But when the Illinois Central Railroad was completed, the trade all went to towns along the line of the railroad, giving to Millville a stunning blow, from which it never recovered.

"But now the sounds of population fail;
No busy murmurs fluctuate the gale,
No busy steps the grass-grown footway tread,
But all the blooming flush of life is fled.
*　*　*　*　*　*
One only master grasps the whole domain,
And half a tillage stints the smiling plain."

It is said that the love of money is the root of all evil: Be that as it may, we know that men will run greater risks for it than they will for anything else, and as proof of this we need only refer to the discovery of gold in California, which was made in 1848. Quite a large number of people went there in 1849, but in 1850 the tide seemed to break loose, and every body appeared to have contracted the gold fever. A great many went, and the Town of Rush furnished at least her full share of gold-seekers. The number of men who went from the Township of Rush can not now be given, nor the amount of money it took to fit them out. It was a great detriment to the township and county in general. As a rule the gold hunters did not get as much of the precious metal as it had cost to buy their outfits. Many returned to their homes broken down in constitution from the hardships they were forced to endure. The worst of all was the loss of life. The Township of Rush lost three of her best citizens, all of whom left families, and two of them leaving large families of children to mourn their loss. They were Ira Bowker, Ira L. Townsend, and Jasper Rosenkrans.

When George N. Townsend came to Rush Township in 1836, his half brother, Sherod B. Townsend, aged fourteen years, came with and lived with him until he was twenty-one years of age. On attaining his majority he bought a tract of land and made a farm in the neighborhood of his brothers. September 14, 1846, he was married to Miss Matilda Durnan. Industrious and economical, they acquired a handsome property, but not being blessed with children, in the Spring of 1863, Sherod B. concluded to go to Montana and try his luck in the gold mines, but before going he made a will, dividing his property equally between his wife and an adopted son. He did not find things in the mines as he expected, and at once determined to return home. He sold his team and provisions, bought a light wagon, a pair of mules and a riding-horse, and started for Illinois. He came as far as Nevada, Iowa, in safety, but there he was murdered by a man named McMullen, the murder being committed in November or December, 1863. The murderer was a man whom Sherod B. Townsend had found destitute about the time he was starting home from Montana, and had given him free passage to Nevada, Iowa, where the murder was committed. He was subsequently arrested, indicted, etc., for the murder, and, we believe, was tried, found guilty, and sentenced to be hanged, but died in jail, before the time fixed for his execution.

Sherod B. Townsend's widow remained single until 1871, when she married Ambrose Campbell, and still lives on the old homestead.

But those days are numbered with the past, and although the country has outgrown the loss of life and money, yet the memory of the dead will never be forgotten until the present generation shall have passed away.

The Legislature had provided that the county might adopt Township Organization, provided a majority of the people would vote in favor of it. In 1851 the question was brought before the people of the county, and by vote decided against Township organization. The following year G. N. Townsend and H. S. Townsend attended a Whig convention held at Elizabeth, where a resolution was passed favoring the Township organization, and at the next election the system was adopted. Hence the Township of Rush was organized by the committee appointed, in January, 1853.

On the first Monday in April, 1853, the Township meeting was held in the Township of Rush, when Halstead S. Townsend was elected Supervisor, and was re-elected for a number of years afterwards.

In 1870, the Township of Rush had a population of 1,037. It is out of debt, and the total assessed valuation of property in 1873 was $534,020. The assessed value is always below the real value.

In 1858, the Township of Rush had the honor of furnishing a Representative in the State Legislature—Hon. H. S. Townsend being that Representative.

In 1861, our country was thrown into that terrible Rebellion which filled the land with widows and orphans. For that war the Township of Rush furnished 116 men, and the blood of many of her sons watered those Southern battle-fields. At the close of the war it was ascertained that the Township had furnished thirty-seven more men than had been required by law or the rules of war.

In 1853, George N. Townsend was appointed Postmaster at Rush, and retained the office until his removal to Warren, in 1875. Mr. Chas. McCowen was appointed in his place.

In 1872 or '73, J. L. Cox and brother erected a very fine flouring mill about one half mile north of Millville, an enterprise deserving the patronage of the entire community.

At present the Township is one of the foremost, agriculturally, in the County. Its public interests are maintained in keeping with its development, and its people are continuing in a course of steady, even prosperity and happiness.

ELIZABETH.

Including a Sketch of Elizabeth and Woodbine Townships.

The Village of Elizabeth is situated near the township line, between the Townships of Elizabeth and Woodbine. The historical fort of the Black Hawk War was situated near the same line; and, in fact, the history of the two townships maintain, throughout, such intimate connection that it is thought advisable to unite them in our historical sketch.

The valley probably had no white visitor until the coming of A. P. Van Matre, in 1825. The legend is current that Mr. Van Matre was asked by an Indian girl whom he met, what he was seeking for. Upon replying that he was prospecting for mineral, he received the proposal, that if he would marry her, she would show him a good lead of mineral. He, doubtless, considered the bargain a very good one, and accepted it, when he was made acquainted with the diggings in the hollow, near Elizabeth, which have received his name. Here, on the bank of the river, he built the first smelting furnace in that part of the county, and also built a house on the opposite side of the river, where he continued to live and mine. The diggings were not exhausted for more than a dozen years.

The next earliest accounts of a civilized visitor to the rich valley of Apple River point to Henry Van Volkenburg, who is reputed to have passed through the territory now called Elizabeth, as early as 1827, on a trapping and prospecting excursion. Mr. Van Volkenburg afterwards returned to Ohio, then came back, and settled in Woodbine Township, where he lived until 1875, when he moved to Mitchell Co., Iowa.

In 1826, Jefferson Clark, John McDonald, and —— Rogers came to this vicinity for mining purposes. Mr. McDonald soon erected a smelting furnace, and followed that business for some years.

Between this time and 1830, a large number of men came, being attracted by the rich mines.

Thaddeus Hitt came to Galena in 1825, and soon went to Elizabeth, where in 1831, he married his wife, Rebecca, who is still living near the village, where Mr. Hitt died, in June, 1877, at the age of eighty-three. Mrs. Hitt is the oldest living resident of Woodbine Township.

In 1827 Nathaniel Morris settled on his farm, four miles northwest of Elizabeth, where he still resides with his family, being the oldest living resident of Elizabeth Township.

Thomas Killion, a mulatto, with his family and a white man named Lee, settled about this time on a farm three fourths of a mile northeast of the village (in Woodbine Township).

A smelting furnace was built near the site of the fort, one half mile east of northeast from the village site (Woodbine Township) in 1827, by Labaum and St. Vrain,* who also opened the first store of the vicinity in a cabin situated where Mr. Mathew's residence now stands. The furnace was managed by Charles Tracy until the Black Hawk War, after which it was not used.

James Flack settled in the southeastern part of Woodbine in 1828.

John D. Winters and family, settled on the Apple River at the site of the iron bridge, in Elizabeth Township. He and Captain Clack Stone owned the claim on which the village of Elizabeth is located and was for many years a prominent resident of this vicinity. His two children, Martha and Theodore, were the first white children born in Elizabeth Township.

James Flack, John D. Winters and others came west in 1827 and raised the first corn in Elizabeth Township.

"Uncle Ben" Tart, as he is called, the oldest settler now living in the Village of Elizabeth and the second oldest resident of the township, came up the Mississippi on the steamer "Dove" and landed at Galena in April 1832, where, before getting off the boat, he hired out to Charles Bowers and came with him, on an ox wagon, to his farm three miles southwest of Elizabeth. Here he worked until in May of that year, when rumors of an Indian War frightened the scattered pioneers and brought them together at Labaum and St. Vrain's store for consultation. They did not remain long inactive, but before night had constructed a rude fort for their protection. Trees were felled, split, and about one hundred feet square of ground was enclosed by driving these rough posts down, close together, leaving them above ground about twelve feet. One corner of the fort was formed by the log house in which one of the settlers had lived. In the opposite corner, was built a "block house," of two stories, with the upper story projecting over the other about two feet, so that the Indians could not come up near to the building for the purpose of setting it on fire, without being exposed to the guns of the settlers, from above. On one side of the yard were built two long cabins, for dwelling purposes, and in the two corners not occupied by houses, benches were made to stand upon and reconnoitre.

On the first day there were but twenty-two men and twenty-three women and children in the fort. Among them the following names have been remembered:

Ambrose White, Captain Clack Stone, Samuel Hughlett, Robert Johnson, and family, including his son, then a young man, James and John Flack, Jesse

* A Frenchman, known as "Savery;" killed in the Black Hawk War.

Van Buskirk, Jefferson Clark, Wm. Lawhorn, Nathaniel Morris and family, Henry Van Volkenburg and family, Thaddeus Hitt and family, John Armstrong and family, Benj. Tart, Charles Tracy, Mrs. Winters (her husband being at Galena)—Killion and family—Lee—Jamison and family, including son, John Murdock and family. Charles Bowers, arrived that evening from Galena. These people continued to live here for some time without being molested. Here the first marriage of white persons occurred; Jane, a daughter of John Murdock was wedded to Jefferson Clark, the ceremony being performed by Mr. McDonald.

The people made use of lead, at the furnace of which Mr. Tracy had charge, to make a cannon; but this, says Mr. Tart, "proved useless until the capture of Black Hawk at the battle of Bad Axe, in Wisconsin, when it was loaded to the muzzle and fired, in celebration of the event; it then burst, killing a soldier—probably the only person it killed during the war."

After moulding bullets and making all due preparations for an attack, the settlers began to have thought for the crops, which required attention. One man, Stephen H. Howard, returned to his farm, in Hanover Township, and was afterwards killed while endeavoring to regain horses which the Indians had stolen from his barn, a more complete account of which appears in the history of Hanover Township.

On a Sabbath of June, the 24th, four messengers—F. Dixon, G. W. Herclerode — Kirkpatrick, and Edmund Welch—who were en route from Galena to Dixon, were attacked by Indians while passing through the gap near the fort, and one of them, Mr. Welch, was wounded in the thigh. Mr. Dixon rode on, and reached Dixon in safety, but the others, including the wounded man, hurried to the fort.

The settlers there had just made up a gooseberrying party, and were starting out when the alarm was given, all hastened within the fort.

The Indians soon made an assault, but were repulsed. The women and children loaded guns for the men, by which they were enabled to keep up a rapid firing. This deceived the Indians as to the number of men within the fort, and they soon withdrew from the range of muskets. The attack lasted three quarters of an hour. The only life lost among those in the fort was that of George W. Herclerode, who was shot in the neck and instantly killed, as he was standing on one of the benches, looking over the pickets, to try his, the only percussion-lock gun in the fort. It is not known how many, if any, Indians were killed, as they conceal their dead, although some blood was afterwards seen in a deserted cabin.

After the assault upon the fort, the Indians rifled the houses of the settlers, and destroyed much valuable property. Elijah McDonald has now a large, black walnut book-case which was in his father's house during that siege, showing the marks of an Indian tomahawk.

No other attack was made on the fort, and in August the settlers returned to their homes.

With whomsoever the aggression may have been at the beginning of the Black Hawk War, these people acted only on the defensive, and their bravery and courage, in protecting the lives of their families, were the subjects of much comment.

The *Galenian* of June 25th says: "The women were all occupied as well as the men—girls of eight years took their part, some made cartridges, some run bullets, some loaded muskets, all were engaged, and God grant that America may never have greater cowards in her armies than the ladies in Apple River Fort."

Immediately after the war, John D. Winters moved to the hill just east of the site of Elizabeth, in the edge of Woodbine Township, where he established a tavern, and continued to direct the stage line. Here, also, the post-office was first established. Captain Clack Stone soon opened a store across the road, opposite the house of Mr. Winters.

In 1842, Horr and Smith built a saw mill west of Elizabeth, on the Apple River, which they continued to run until 1848, when Henry Glessner became a partner, after which the style of the firm was "H. Glessner & Co." In 1852, Mr. Smith sold his interest to Joseph Watson. The mill was changed to a carding, and afterwards to a yarn mill. In 1857, Mr. Glessner purchased the interest of Mr. Watson, and Isaac Horr died, although the estate of Mr. Horr continued to hold a one third interest until 1867, when it was sold, together with one third interest, belonging to Mr. Glessner, to Eby and Hefty, who purchased the remaining one third interest of Mr. Glessner in January, 1870, since which time the firm name has been "Eby & Hefty." They work seven months of the year, turning out 8,000 pounds of yarn. They have a dam one hundred and twenty feet long and five feet high, furnishing a power equal to twenty horses.

The first building erected within the site of Elizabeth was a saloon by Mr. Knack, a year or two after the war. Mr. Knack took the liberty of chopping logs for his cabin from the claim of Henry Van Volkenburg, during his absence. The first tavern was built by John Gates, and now forms a portion of Robert Scott's residence, on Main Street. Rev. Aratus Kent, who came to Galena in 1829, first gave religious instruction to the miners of this vicinity in 1830. Mr. Kent has been mentioned by the earliest members of many settlements in Jo Daviess County as a man who bravely bore the hardships of those years, and labored with a stern integrity to soften the characters and maintain the religious devotion of those men whom the wild surroundings had a tendency to make harsh and rough. From Mrs. Gates, now a resident of Woodbine, who settled there in the Fall of 1834, we learn some of the names of residents, at that time, on Jewell's Prairie—so-called from one of its first settlers, Mr. Jewell. Among them were: John McDonald, Henry Van Volkenburg, John Murdock, A. B. White, Johnson Young, George Harper, Milton Claypool, William Higgins, William Lawhorn, Francis Graham, Royal Daniels, Thaddeus Hitt, and Mr. Jewell.

The first birth was R. B., son of Edmund Gates, on December 19, 1836; John F. Childer was born in the same year.

The first death in Woodbine Township after the Black Hawk War was of the wife of Royal Daniels, in 1837.

Mrs. Hitt and Passingfair Gates are all who remain living in Woodbine of the early settlers of '36.

In 1835, a school-house was built, in which Rev. Schunk both taught school and preached.

In 1844, A. B. White and Solomon Shore organized the school districts and built two school houses—one on Jewell's Prairie and another on Tarpen Ridge. The former was taught by —— Perry, and the latter by Henry Wolcott. At that time there was another school-house in the township, located near Elizabeth.

A blacksmith shop and store were established on Jewell's Prairie in 1867; also a post-office called "Woodbine."

Religious services were held in the school-houses for a number of years, until in 1868 the Methodist Church was erected. J. F. Yates is believed to have preached the first sermon, although the first regular pastor of the church was James Rogers. Cyrus Carpenter and John Wixson were then leading members. At present Rev. William Liverton officiates.

The German Methodist Church of Woodbine is situated on Jewell's Prairie, on the farm of Leonhard Bastian. It was erected in 1871 and dedicated October 29. The first trustees for five years were: George Hermann, William Hildebrand, John Andrus, Henry Schultz and Erhard Dittmar. The present trustees are: Leonhard Bastian, Fredrich Steffens, George Krall, Samuel Horsch and John Andrus. Their ministers have been John Schnieder, for two years; John Schaad, one year; Henry Sauer, two years; Philip Hummel, one year, and Carl Miller, two years, the present pastor.

In 1837, Bird and Gomer built a saw mill near the forks of Apple River, which they continued to operate until 1847, when it was sold to James DeGraff, who transformed it into a grist mill. It was first operated by Hiram Tyrrell. He afterwards disposed of this to James B. Watts, by whose name it has since been known, although Roberts & Co. became its proprietors, and it is now owned by Mr. Sampson.

In 1856–'7, John Eustace built Mitchell's Mill, now known as Elizabeth Mill.

The Village of Elizabeth was laid out in 1839 by Charles R. Bennett, surveyor, on the land of John D. Winters and Captain Clack Stone, in the southeast quarter of section 24, township 27, range 2 east. It is one hundred and seventy feet above the water of Apple River. Its streets were: Madison, Main, Washington and Illinois Streets, running south, 35 deg. east; West, Vine and Catlin Streets, running north 8 deg. east; Myrtle, Sycamore, Poplar, Orange and East Streets, running north 55 deg. east.

John D. Winters afterwards laid out an addition which received the name of "Reynolds' Addition," in honor of Abram Reynolds, an early settler and the agent of the citizens in 1847 to purchase, at the Dixon land sale, all the lands of section 24, on which the village was located.

An election was held May 4, 1868, at the school-house, with D. Robinson, president, and W. H. Eustace, clerk, to ascertain the feeling of citizens regarding the incorporation of Elizabeth, as a village, at which seventy-four votes were cast for, and thirty-two against, incorporation.

After the Black Hawk War, Mr. Tart was absent from Elizabeth until 1843. Before his return Mr. P. J. Pilcher came (in 1841) and settled there with his family during the following year. Hence, Mr. Pilcher, who is still living there, is the oldest (continuous) living resident in the village. At the time of his arrival, James B. Watts and Samuel Nye had opened their store, the first one of prominence in the village.

James W. White opened a store, and in the Fall of 1843 Robert Barker, who still resides at the edge of town, built a store room and opened a general stock of goods.

After Watts & Nye opened their store, the post-office was moved there from the tavern of Mr. Winters, in Woodbine Township, and Samuel Nye was made postmaster.

In 1864, Mr. Barker sold out to Mr. Fraser, who, with his son, is still doing business there under the firm title of Fraser & Son. There are at present eighteen stores, among the prominent ones being those of Fraser & Son, D. Robinson, Goldsworth & Rankin, and Weir & Barrett, each of whom keep a general stock of goods. There is one hotel—the "Union Hotel"—of which Thomas B. Shaw is proprietor. There are four physicians: Drs. Kittoe, Wm. Howarth, and the firm of Hutton & Beebe.

Schools.—At the time of Mr. Barker's arrival, school was kept by Mr. Quigley in an old log building, bought by the people, which had been a dwelling. In this house meetings were also held by Rev. McKane. When the Presbyterian Church was completed, in 1846, it was used for school purposes until the present school-house was erected.

Mr. Packard, now a prominent educational worker of Chicago, first taught in the church, followed by Mr. Coleman. Mr. Eberhart opened the school in the new school building.

As the village grew, more school room was found necessary, and the Odd Fellows' Hall, situated just north of the school-house, was rented for school purposes. This school is now taught by Miss Amelia Davis, while the teachers in the school-house proper are Henry McKay, principal, assisted by Miss Abbie Linn.

Churches.—The first Presbyterian preaching was, as has been already stated, by Rev. Aratus Kent, in Ames' house at Rocky Point, in 1830.

From this time to the date of organization of the society, February 9, 1844, there was occasional preaching in private houses by Rev. Kent and Rev. Osias Littlefield, the latter of whom organized the church. At the organization the following trustees were elected: Wm. P. Warwick, James B. Watts, Wm. Bothwell and John Rees. A stone building was purchased in 1846, and fitted for church use. In this services were conducted until the erection of the present frame building in 1875, at a cost of $2,500.

The following pastors have officiated in their respective order: Revs. Calvin Gray, J. W. Downer, E. D. Neil (now an active educational and religious worker in Minnesota), —— King, W. W. Harsha (occasional), A. Kent (occasional), A. C. Childs, A. B. Peffers, J. R. Smith, Mr. Dillon, J. W. Stone, D.D., concluding with the present minister, Rev. J. R. Smith.

The present Trustees are: D. McKenzie, A. H. Weir, and John Hutchinson.

The Methodist Church.—The Methodist Association of Elizabeth is the oldest one, except that of Galena, in Northwestern Illinois; but owing to the fact that no records were made previous to the coming of Hon. Henry Green, in 1842, the facts regarding the Church previous to that date can not be obtained. At that time the Elizabeth Circuit extended north into Wisconsin, and south to include Savanna, Carroll Co. It is thought to have been organized in 1837. They first met in the old log school-house. The first Methodist Church was erected in 1845-'6; size 26 by 40 feet. The present one was built in 1871. Its size is 40 by 60 feet, seating 450 persons.

The following list of preachers who have been stationed on the Elizabeth charge since 1842, has been kindly furnished by Mr. Green:

Revs. —— Pillsbury, 1842; James McCain and M. Decker, 1843; James McCain and —— Thomas, 1844; Isaac N. Lehy, 1845; R. Blanchard, 1846; —— Parks, 1847; —— Wilmot, 1848; G. L. S. Stuff, 1849; George Lovsey, 1850; Boyd Lowe, 1851; William Tasker, 1852; William McKaig, 1853; William McKaig, 1854; Aaron Wolf, 1855; S. Guyer, 1856; S. Guyer (removed, and appointment filled by —— Aldrich), 1857; William Tasker, 1858; W. D. Atchison, 1859; W. D. Atchison, 1860; W. D. Skelton, 1861; W. D. Skelton, 1862; G. L. Wiley, 1863; Aaron Cross, 1864; Joseph Wardle, 1865; Fredrick Curtiss, 1866; C. R. Ford, 1867; Richard Donkersley, 1868; Richard Donkersley, 1869; S. S. Helsby, 1870; —— Anderson, 1871; —— Anderson, 1872; P. C. Stire, 1873; P. C. Stire, 1874; D. W. Linn, 1875; Samuel Cates, 1876; Samuel Cates, 1877.

The present membership of the Church is fifty, and of the Sabbath School, two hundred.

The Village Trustees are: George H. Green, Thomas Goldsworthy, Thomas Eustace, Charles Banworth, and Leopold Hessig. Clerk, E. R. Smith.

There is a post-office in Section 4, near the north line of the township, called "Avery," where there was at one time a tavern.

The bridge spanning Apple River, west of Elizabeth, was built originally of wood, in 1859. An iron bridge was built on the same abutments, by the township and county, regarding which the following resolution appears on the Board of Supervisors' Record, dated September 13, 1871:

"*Resolved*, That the sum of $2,134, or one half the cost of building an iron bridge over Apple River, in the Town of Elizabeth, be, and is hereby appropriated; the County to be at one half the cost of the bridge; provided said cost does not exceed $4,268; the appropriation to be paid when the bridge is completed and accepted; said bridge to be built under the supervision of the

County Bridge Commissioners in conjunction with the Commissioners of Highways of said Town."

The bridge was accordingly built in 1871–1872.

About 1842, Horr and Smith built a saw mill on the Apple River, west of Elizabeth, on Section 23. A few years thereafter Glessner, Horr and Smith put in machinery, and started a carding-mill, which was again changed to a yarn-mill. The present proprietors are Charles Eby and John Hefty.

WESTON.—In 1842 and '3, the mines two miles west of the Village of Elizabeth, gained considerable notoriety and, naturally, a large number of miners flocked to the vicinity. Many small patches of mineral were found, generally distributed with some fine bodies of ore.

In 1843, Green, Tart, Hughlett and Estey started the first smelting furnace. At that time there were but three cabins at that place, George Williams owned one—Vandyke another; the proprietor of the third has been forgotten. Many cabins sprung up in rapid succession and in 1844, "Green, Goldthorp & Co." (Estey having sold out to Wm. Goldthorp), started a general store, and post-office. O. A. Bennett was first postmaster, then Mr. Goldthorp managed the store and post-office while Mr. Green attended to the smelting. A Methodist Church was soon erected there in which Rev. Father McKane first preached. Its pulpit has been generally occupied by the Elizabeth pastor. Mr. A. B. Lewis soon opened school in the church building, which was continued until the erection of the school house in 1862. Mr. Lewis taught seven successive years. The teacher now is Mr. Wenner.

March 8, 1847, the Village of Weston was laid out and platted by John C. Gardner on the land of Benjamin Tart, in the west half of the southeast quarter of section 22.

But the village was not destined to prosper. As one of its proprietors remarked, "It sprung up like Jonah's gourd and died in the same manner." When the pockets of the earth were exhausted the miner shouldered his pick and sought other fields. The store was closed and in 1859 the post-office was discontinued. At present Mr. Wm. Goldthorp is the principal proprietor. Mr. Henry Green has a smelting furnace between Elizabeth and Weston, is one of the capitalists engaged in manufactures at Hanover, and lives on his farm near Elizabeth, where his beautiful residence and grounds are generally admired. At the time of the land sale at Dixon, in April 1847, Mr. Green was made the agent of the township residents and bid off their lands *en masse*.

In 1844, occurred the "Stone's field excitement," as it was called. Captain Stone owned land adjoining the Weston property on which he forbade prospecting. John Bennett, a German, and associates who were in the employ of Green, Goldthorp & Co., urgently requested permission to examine the land; but being refused, they went on the land at night and, before morning, mineral had been struck in three places. Then followed intense excitement. Mr. Stone endeavored to raise a company of armed men to protect his property, while miners flocked to the field in large numbers, all "armed to the teeth" with pistols, guns and knives. A bloody conflict was at one time imminent but Mr. Stone decided to accept the usual percentage, one sixth of all the mineral raised.

The third noted mines of Elizabeth Township were discovered by Martin Wishon and John Allen, about one and a half miles northwest of the village. They are still being worked though not so successfully as soon after they were opened, when, in two years, they yielded nearly 2,000,000 pounds of ore. The mines wlll be referred to more specifically in an article on that subject.

The officers of Elizabeth Township are:

Supervisor—John S. Young; *Assessor*—Thomas Cubbon; *Collector*—George Green; *Commissioners of Highway*—James Virtue, Thomas Cubbon, and Richard Eustace; *Justices of Peace*—E. R. Smith and J. Q. Robinson; *Constables*—James H. Bateman and John Price.

RUSH TP.

The population of the Township in 1850 was 1,805; in 1860 it had decreased to 1,460, and in 1870 it numbered 1,618.

The Township of Woodbine, which was originally called "Jefferson," had 935 inhabitants in 1860, and 959 in 1870.

The officers of Woodbine Township are:

Supervisor—Donald McKenzie; *Assessor*—Mark Thomas; *Collector*—Adam Long; *Commissioners of Highway*—John Old, John McCoy.

Kavanaugh Lodge, No. 36, A. F. & A. M., was first organized under the Grand Lodge of Wisconsin, June 16, A. D. 1845, with the following officers:

William Vance, W. M.; D. A. Main, S. W.; W. P. Warwick, J. W.; Roland Madison, Secretary; W. B. Whiteside. S. D.; William Rogers, J. D.; Jas. B. Goble, Tyler.

It continued under the jurisdiction of the Grand Lodge of Wisconsin until October 6, A. D. 1846, when it received its present charter from the Grand Lodge of Illinois, with the following as charter members:

Robert Barker, W. M.; August S. Mitchell, S. W.; W. P. Warwick, J. W.; P. G. Ames, Treasurer; William C. Smith, Secretary; William B. Whiteside, S. D.; Theodore Winters, J. D.; J. B. Goble, Tyler. Besides these officers there were William Vance, Isaac S. Horr, D. C. Berry, John Cadman, John McKie, and E. Marsh.

The present officers are: John Bowden, W. M.; John Long, S. W; John Martin, J. W.; John Hefty, Treasurer; W. H. Eustace, Secretary; T. W. Eustace, S. D.; John Goble, J. D.; Richard Bryant, Tyler. The present membership is fifty.

Hardin Lodge No. 33, I. O. O. F.—This Lodge was instituted September 15, 1847, by dispensation of the Grand Lodge of the State of Illinois. The charter members were James Thompson, William R. Bennett, Abram Wilcox, J. B. Watts, and Joseph Shipton.

The present officers are Alonzo Pierce, N. G.: W. J. Adams, V. G.; Wm. J. Davy, Secretary; T. B. Bray, Treasurer, and E. R. Smith, D. G. Master.

The Woodbine Mutual Fire Insurance Company.—This company was organized under the law providing for such associations, a portion of which is quoted in the Ward's Grove sketch. It was incorporated (by filing charter in the office of the Clerk of the County Court,) on February 23, 1874, and commenced business April 6, 1874, with the following officers:

Directors—Andrew Wand, Solomon Shore, Donald McKenzie, Amos H. Weir, Edward Mitchell, Sr., John Crawford, Ignatz Goldhagen, James Rogers, J. Steele Weir; *President*—D. McKenzie; *Treasurer*—Andrew Wand; *Secretary*—J. Steele Weir; *Agent*—A. H. Weir.

For the year ending December 31, 1874, the number of policies issued was fifty-six, and the whole amount of risks taken, $51,290. From April 6, 1874, to February 19, 1878, there have been ninety-nine policies issued, with a total amount of risks taken, $90,440.

This company having been organized nearly four years, is now in a prosperous condition, although it has not suffered any losses by fire as yet. The company feels able to meet any loss that may occur among its members, having a good amount of capital in the treasury. All business matters have been transacted thus far, with entire satisfaction. The members work harmoniously together, and the inhabitants of the township are becoming more and more interested in the advantages of township insurance companies. Each person insuring is a member, and is entitled to a seat in the regular meetings. The present number of members is 71. Officers are elected annually; the following are the present (1878) officers:

Directors—D. McKenzie, Amos H. Weir, Andrew Wand, Solomon Shore, E. Mitchell, Sr., Ignatz Goldhagen, Robert B. Gates, James Phillips, Joseph J. Artman; *President*—D. McKenzie; *Treasurer*—Andrew Wand; *Secretary*—Sampson R. Reed; *Business Agent*—Ignatz Goldhagen.

Jewell's Prairie appointment (now the head of the Woodbine Circuit) of the Methodist Episcopal Church, was first organized with the Pleasant Valley Circuit, December 22, 1855, with Rev. C. C. Best, Presiding Elder; Rev. W. D. Atchison, Pastor. Since that time the following Elders have presided: Revs. C. C. Best, 1855; D. Cassady, 1859; W. F. Stewart, 1862; R. A. Blanchard, 1864; F. A. Reed, 1868; W. H. Tibbals, 1873; J. H. Moore, 1877.

A parsonage was built at Jewell's Prairie in the Autumn of 1867, during the pastorate of Rev. J. M. Conlee. The M. E. Church was built on the same premises during the Summer of 1869; Rev. C. E. Smith, pastor. Both buildings are frame: the former costing $400, and the latter $1,200.

The title of the circuit has undergone several changes. It was, in 1855, called the Pleasant Valley Circuit, under which Rev. W. D. Atchison served as pastor. The Plum River Circuit was organized December 5, 1857, under which the following pastors served: Revs. W. H. Hunt, 1857; C. Furst, 1858; W. Tasker, 1859. The name of the circuit was then changed to "Elroy and Plum River," with Rev. J. C. Stover, pastor; J. Buss, assistant.

The Rush Creek Circuit was established January 4, 1862. The following pastors had charge: Revs. J. Buss, 1862; A. H. Ellis, 1863; M. W. Goodsell, 1863; S. P. Lilley, 1864; C. Coombes, 1865; J. M. Conlee, 1866; C. E. Smith, 1868; A. G. Smith, 1869; F. R. Mastin, 1870; J. L. Roberts, 1871; R. Brotherton, J. A. Gready, assistant, 1872; J. H. Kennedy, 1873. About this time the style of the circuit again changed to Woodbine Circuit, with the following pastors: Revs. A. Perry, 1874; S. W. Richards, 1875; J. H. Soule, 1877; W. J. Liberton, 1877.

At the present time there are three churches in this circuit: Jewell's Prairie Church, Salem Church (frame) which was built at a cost of $1,000, and Long Hollow Church, of brick. Three other appointments are held in school-houses.

James Rogers, of Jewell's Prairie, now the oldest resident official member of Woodbine Circuit, was, in 1875, appointed lay delegate to the Rock River Annual Conference, held at Joliet, Illinois, by which conference Hon. Henry Green, of Elizabeth, was appointed lay representative to the General Conference held at Baltimore in 1876.

About 1851 the first Sabbath School was held at Jewell's Prairie, in a school-house, conducted by the Baptists; Mrs. C. Carpenter and Mr. White, Superintendents. The Sunday School was afterwards taken up by the Methodists, who came to settle in the neighborhood, and has since been carried on by that denomination.

HANOVER.

The Township of Hanover forms the southwest corner of the county. It is consequently out of the lead mining region, except, perhaps, its northwestern border. Geographically, the township presents a great variety of natural beauty. On the western side lies a low prairie of nine by two miles in size, which, from its barren nature, has been named the "Sand Prairie." This is washed on the west by the "Father of Waters," while on the opposite side rises the high bluffy chain of hills which extends up the river bank to Galena, broken only by the valleys of the Small Pox and Galena Rivers. A tradition was current among the noble red men of the forest that the bed of the Mississippi once passed on the eastern side of the prairie near the bluffs, and an examination of this location tends to confirm the story. It is known that, in the flood of 1828 the supposed river bed was filled with water from the Mississippi.

Beyond the range of hills lies the beautiful valley of Apple River. Up this river, in the Fall of 1827, rowed Daniel Fowler and Charles Ames—two adventurers and the first "pale faces" whom the inhabitants had seen in that locality.

At the place where the Village of Hanover now stands, the voyagers encountered the Apple River Falls, and were obliged to carry their canoe around on the land. At this time, remarks our droll informant, there was here a large city called Wapello—inhabited by a tribe of Sacs and Foxes, and named after their chief. Appreciating the value of this location as a mill site, Fowler and Ames marked it with a claim stake, and proceeded up the river. The next Spring they returned, took up the claim and engaged in farming.

At this time this region was reserved as mineral land, though it was out of the mining region, and in 1827 a purse of $1,000 was made up by settlers of the county to defray the expenses of some person in going to Washington and securing a release of that portion of the land outside of the mineral region. Mr. James Craig was selected for that purpose, and returned the following Spring with the desired permission. He, also, had the Falls of Apple River in view as a location, and going there in 1828 he and his son Daniel compromised with Fowler and Ames, and secured one half of the land, including the falls. Here he dammed the river and erected a saw mill and a grist mill on the site of the present factory. The following year the family of Mr. Craig moved down from Galena.

A number of settlers soon entered farms in the valley. Among them were John Armstrong, Samuel Jamison and Stephen H. Howard. When the Black Hawk War began the pioneers hurried their families to the forts for protection.

But they had left crops which must be looked after or lost. One brave man, Stephen H. Howard, determined to return to his farm and risk discovery by the Indians. While he was plowing in the field, he saw a band of Indians approach his house and drive off with four horses which had been left in the barn. He jumped on his only remaining horse and fled to the fort. A body of men were there gathered to follow the thieves, whom they overtook near Waddam's Grove. A severe fight ensued in which Mr. Howard was killed.

Those were indeed dark days of hardships and bitterness to the resolute men who established the beautiful, and now, peaceful homes of Hanover. After peace and confidence had been restored, settlers began to fill up the valleys more rapidly. In 1835, Wm. R., son of James Craig, opened the first general store at the village, in a log house, but in the ensuing year he built a store-room, which now forms a part of Nathan Craig's residence. There was no other general store established until that of James W. White in 1845. Mr. Craig kept a public house from the time of his settlement but the first and only regular hotel was not built until 1847, by Joseph E. Milligan. It is called the "Hanover Hotel," and now owned by George W. Clark. In 1835, Mr. Craig erected a chair factory between the two mills he had already built. He found the water power sufficient to drive the machinery of the three establishments. At this point the river is about 200 feet wide, having a natural fall over a rocky bed of eleven feet. The dam is two hundred and forty feet long and five feet high, securely bolted to the rock, making a head and fall of sixteen feet, with a reservoir or flowage extending nearly ten miles and affording, probably, the best and most secure water power in northwestern Illinois.

Mr. Craig hired a man named Shunk, at twelve dollars per month, to teach school during the winter of 1835, in a rough cabin on the present site of the Hanover Hotel. After four weeks the pupils claimed to have exhausted their resource of instruction and the institution was suspended. The first school house in the township was built during the following year on the claim of Mr. Glisson, in section 21. John Yancey first gave instruction therein. No house was built especially for school purposes until 1848; in this building Miss

Phœbe Vaughn was the first school teacher. The house, which is a substantial brick building of one story, was built by subscription and is now used for a Town Hall. The present school building was erected in 1863. It is a neat two-story brick structure, with two apartments, accommodating 200 pupils. In this school Mrs. Julius A. Hamilton first taught. Wm. Gardner and Miss Ella Aldrich have management of the two departments.

A minister of Galena, Rev. Aratus Kent, delivered the first sermon ever uttered in Hanover Township at the house of James Craig, which was always open for religious devotion.

Benson Hunt, who was intimately connected with the early history of Galena, settled in the Fall of 1836, with his family, in the extreme southwestern corner of the township.

This was a good point on the Mississippi for shipping, and the Illinois Central Railroad Company was then grading a road along its bluffs to Galena, promising another outlet to the markets. Hence Mr. Hunt decided to locate there a village, named Huntsville, which was laid out and platted the following year, by Israel Mitchell. But the sandy soil proved an objection to settlers, and the parties who were building the railroad, exhausted their means, and were compelled to dispose of the road to a company who changed its location. Influenced by these facts, Mr. Hunt returned to Galena, leaving his farm under the management of one Smith, who proved to be a member of a notorious band of thieves which was scattered through this country. This band first disposed of the two teams, which Mr. Hunt had left, and then came with a barge and boldly carried away three thousand bushels of corn. Many similar depredations were committed among the scattered pioneers, and a system for protection was soon organized. The outlaws carried on their operations in a bold, defiant manner for many years, but were finally entrapped in a house at Bellevue, a village in Iowa, on the Mississippi, where seven of them were shot. Many years later, Thomas Parks made an attempt to establish a village on the site of Huntsville, calling it Parksville. He started a ferry there in 1849, and in the ensuing year Charles Jeffries opened a general store, which was followed by the stores of Daniel McIntire and a Mr. Jackson. But, as insufficient support was received, the village was again depopulated, and at present is devoid of all business interests. The Village of Hanover has been more successful. In 1837 it was laid out on the land of James Craig. Additional stores were opened, and, in 1840, Mr. Craig tore down the old grist mill and erected a large flouring mill, having two stories of stone, surmounted by two and a half stories of wood. The process of building such a mill was, in those days, slow and costly, but it was completed in 1842, and, after running only six weeks, was burned to the ground. Mr. Craig had invested all his means in the mill, and it proved a heavy misfortune, not only to the founder of the village, but to the town itself. The water power was idle until 1845, when James W. White purchased it; built a new dam, saw mill and flouring mill. The saw mill was afterwards torn down. The flouring mill, which was built on the site of the present factory, was a large stone building of four and one half stories, containing five runs of burrs. In 1857, the rear end of the mill fell in, after which all the walls were removed and rebuilt, as it now stands, of stone, three stories in height. At the time the flouring mill was established, wheat was one of the principal products in this vicinity, but, in 1858, the wheat crop began to fail, and much of it was transported on the railroad to other mills. In 1864, the Hanover Manufacturing Company was organized, with a capital of $60,000, and purchased the water power and mill of Mr. White. Its officers were: J. W. White, Manager, Secretary and Treasurer; Board of Directors—Henry Green, President; R. H. McClellan, H. S. Townsend, and James Martin. For the reasons above noted, the company removed a portion of the flouring machinery, and put in two sets of woolen machinery. The capital stock was increased, in 1865, to $80,000. In 1874, the company erected the present two-story frame flouring mill, and added two more sets of machinery to the woolen mill.

The cloth now manufactured is all of the finer quality of cassimere, and finds ready market among the wholesale houses of Chicago, St. Louis, and other cities.

The present officers are: J. W. White, Manager, Secretary and Treasurer; Board of Directors—Henry Green, President; R. H. McClellan, H. S. Townsend and John E. Corwith. Superintendent of Woolen Mill, A. C. Huntington.

In 1839, Craig (W. R.) and Laswell started a distillery one mile and a half east of the village, but soon discontinued it.

In 1875, a company was organized and incorporated for establishing a wood-pulp manufactory, four and a half miles south of the village, on Apple River. The pulp is made from the white portion of the cotton-wood, or aspen tree, and used for making paper, by mixing it with one half to three fourths parts of straw and rag paper.

The manufactory is run by water power, the river being controlled by a dam, ten feet in height and two hundred feet long. The water has a head and fall of eleven feet.

The capital of the company is $16,000. Officers: R. H. McClellan, President; J. W. White, Secretary and Treasurer.

From this brief sketch, it can be seen that the manufacturing interests of Hanover are of prime importance to its prosperity. Indeed, a visitor to the village is much surprised to find, so far from the railroad and outer world, a busy little village, nestled down among the hills, turning out a large quantity of fine cloths such as, but a few years ago, were known only as "English cassimeres."

CHURCHES AND LODGES.

The Methodist Episcopal Church of Hanover was organized in 1847, by Samuel McGrath, John McKinley, Walter Dean, Myron S. Hill, E. A. Chase and others.

Since that time, Hooper Crews, Richard Haney, C. C. Best, D. Cassidy, W. F. Stewart, R. A. Blanchard, F. A. Reed, W. H. Tibbals, and G. H. Moore (the present incumbent), have served the church in the capacity of elders.

In 1862, the present church building was erected, at a cost of $2,100; seats 180 persons. It was dedicated the following year, by Rev. Mr. Eddy, of Chicago. Following is a list of the pastors who have served this church: Thomas North, John F. Hill, P. Judson, John Crummer, S. B. Smith, M. L. Averill, A. M. Earley, C. H. Richie, Wm. Keegan, G. F. Gage, Robt. Brotherton, U. Eberhart, S. G. Havermill, J. A. Hammond, C. M. Webster, S. P. Lilly, M. Goodrell, J. M. Clendenning, A. Cross, M. G. Sheldon, J. J. Tobias, J. H. Soule, G. H. Wells, Z. S. Kellogg, D. W. Linn, J. H. Soule, who is the present incumbent.

The Trustees of the church at present are: A. Chase, Geo. Robinson, J. A. Hammond, J. P. Huntington, J. R. Chapman, Joseph Wiley and C. N. Hammond. Stewards—Walter Dean, Geo. Robinson, J. A. Hammond, J. R. Chapman, and C. N. Hammond. Class Leaders—Joseph E. Milligan and James Parker. Superintendent of Sabbath school—J. P. Huntington.

The Presbyterian Church of Hanover was organized with twenty-four members, April 22, 1858, by Rev. Charles Axtel and Elder Thomas Foster—a committee of Rock River Presbytery. Among those who manifested an active interest in the church at this time were John Miller, John Campbell, Andrew Kilpatrick, and George Miller, the first three mentioned being made elders. In July of the same year Rev. Alex. F. Lackey, was secured as pastor, who continued until February 1859, when Rev. Adam Craig assumed charge. In 1860, the church, a frame building, was erected at a cost of $2,000, affording 250 seats. It was dedicated September 23. After Mr. Craig the following ministers officiated in respective order: Samuel K. Dillon, September, 1865; Jared M. Stone, September, 1872; Henry Aurand, December, 1873; John Gilmore, who is now pastor.

The present session consists of John Miller, John Campbell, Wm. Davidson and John I. Miller.

Trustees—John Dawson, W. N. Miller and R. H. Campbell. There is a membership of fifty-five.

The Sabbath school was commenced soon after the church organization. Its present officers are: Superintendent—W. N. Miller; Treasurer—George Jeffers; Secretary—J. I. Miller; Librarian—Thomas Cobine.

The United Presbyterian denomination was constituted in 1858, by union of the "Associate Presbyterian," with the "Associate Reformed Presbyterian" denomination, hence, the present denominational name of this church.

The First United Presbyterian congregation of Hanover, was constituted by the merging together in a somewhat informal manner, of the "Associate Presbyterian Congregation of Apple River," organized in September, 1841, and a part of the "Associate Presbyterian Congregation of Galena," organized November, 1845.

The prime movers in securing the organization of the "Apple River" Church, were Mr. Charles Moore, Mr. John Miller, and Mr. Woods.

The first officers of the "Galena" organization, were Charles Moore, James Gamble and Robert Henry, Elders; James Gamble, Session Clerk.

The first officers of the Apple River Church, were James Gray and John Miller, Elders; James Gray, Session Clerk.

The present officers of the First United Presbyterian Church, are: Elders, James Gray, Thompson Weir, John Nesbitt, Daniel Gamble, Robert Wright, and James R. Speer; Session Clerk, John Nesbitt; Treasurer, Daniel Gamble; Superintendent of the Sabbath school, James Moore.

The following pastors have officiated during the years attached: Rev. Thomas Ferrier, 1841–'53; Rev. Wm. Willet Harsha, 1846–'54; Rev. Robert Atchison, 1857–'58; Rev. Walter Pinkerton Currie, 1858–'66; Rev. Jas. D. Smith, 1870 to the present time (1878). The membership numbers 124.

The church buildings are two: one of logs, erected in 1839, in the southwest part of Elizabeth Township, and the other of brick, in the Village of Hanover, 34 by 44 feet in size, which was erected in 1851–'52.

Hanover Lodge, No. 300, *A. F. and A. M.*, was organized October 30, 1858. Its first officers were:

Wm. O. Smith, W. M.; Stephen Jeffers, S. W.; Jas. Stewart, J. W.; Samuel Clements, Treasurer; B. F. Fowler, Secretary.

Present Officers.—A. B. White, W. M.; Stephen Jeffers, S. W.; Abram Reynolds, J. W.; Thomas E. Moore, Treasurer. H. N. Upson, Secretary; A. C. Huntington, S. D.; J. L. Phillips, J. D.; J. White, Jr., Tyler.

Present membership, 23. Meet first and third Saturdays of each month.

The Village of Hanover was laid out and platted on October 25, 1836, on the land of James Craig, being located on the south half of section 9, township 26 north, range 2 east of the fourth principal meridian. It was at that time called "Wapello" and a post-office established under that name, which was changed in 1849 to Hanover. Two additions have been made by White and Jeffers.

A petition was made to the Board of Supervisors April 9, 1877, for the privilege of incorporation. On the 28th day of the same month a meeting was held at the town hall to ascertain the wishes of the people on that issue, which resulted in fifty-seven votes being cast for, and three against, incorporation. June 9, the following trustees were elected: J. W. White, President; S. Jeffers,

Henry Chapman, Robert Dawson, Abram Reynolds and L. J. Phillips; Clerk, A. B. White.

In 1860, Hanover Township had a population of 969, and in 1870, 1,191. At its first organization Wm. J. Robinson was elected Supervisor. The present officers are:

Supervisor, Charles Spear; *Town Clerk*, Joseph Limage; *Assessor*, Julius Hammond; *Collector*, Augustus Chase; *Commissioners of Highways*, Cyrus Steele, Kelso White and Charles Hammond.

COUNCIL HILL.

The hill from which this township and village are named, received its appellation from the Indian Councils which were held there in olden times. The land is high, rolling, and, in some parts, very broken. Being within the mining region, it was inhabited by white men at a very early date. Much difficulty has been experienced in securing accurate and reliable information concerning the scattered inhabitants before the year 1828.

Patrick Hogan, who had been engaged in mercantile business at St. Louis, came to the lead mines in 1825, and laid out a claim near Council Hill Diggings, which had then been known for many years to the Indians and a few white miners. In 1826, Ezekiel Lockwood built there a furnace—the first one in the township. Mr. Lockwood afterwards (1828) engaged in business at Galena with his brother, J. H., going from there to Dubuque.

Being near Galena, Council Hill had very few permanent settlers until 1835. It is inferred from a review of the *Miners' Journal* of 1828–'9, that the miners went there for mining purposes but still considered Galena as their headquarters. Among these earlier inhabitants were Jonathan Hilliard, William Williams, Hiram Garrett, John Bowles, —— Barrows, and —— Hughes. There were many others, but this list embraces nearly all who remained to become permanent settlers.

Before the Black Hawk War Mr. Bowles had built a cabin at Horse Shoe Bend (on the Galena River), just below the present Millbrig Mill. At the same time he erected a saw mill on the Small Pox River, on land that is now included in Rice Township. In 1832, but three cabins stood on the site of Council Hill Village. Mr. Hilliard and Mr. Hughes first established saloons where Council Hill now stands, soon after the Black Hawk War. At this time saloons seem to have been very profitable investments. Mr. Barrows added one to the number, and in 1838, Mr. Brenton and Richard Arthur opened saloons, in connection with which some other goods were sold, but no regular store was operated until 1849, when Simon Alderson established a store, which was purchased in 1856 and is still continued at the same place by William Harvey. For some years after purchasing it, Mr. Harvey had a partner—Wm. Birkbeck. In 1837, Richard Arthur came with D. Harris, but they did not locate there for some time after. In the meantime (1838) George Redfern arrived. He still remains at Council Hill—the earliest, living permanent settler.

The chief mines of this township are the Council Hill, Grant Hill and Drummond Diggings. These have in the past been very prolific, but are not in a very prosperous condition at present. Nearly twenty million pounds of mineral have been taken from them.

The Village of Council Hill was laid off and platted on October 22, 1853, by J. C. Gardner, on the southeast and southwest quarters of section twenty-four and the northeast and northwest quarters of section twenty-five, township 29, N. R. E. The owners of the land were William Williams and Simon Alderson. There was but one street—"Mineral," running north 32 degrees west. The village was never incorporated.

The first, and only regular hotel, dates from 1840. It has always been kept by members of the Brenton family. The present school-house of Council Hill was erected in 1856 and enlarged in 1867. It is now a two-story building, containing two departments which are taught by G. W. Hickman and wife. Previous to the erection of this building and just south of the present site, stood for many years a little log school-house, in which church was also held. There is no one now resident at the village who is able to tell the date of erection of this house, although it within for fifteen or twenty years.

Church services were held in 1841 by Rev. W. Woods, followed by Revs. Pillsbury, E. Springer, J. Searles, J. W. Putnam and by John L. Williams, under whose pastorate the first and only church was built, in 1849. It is of brick, 30 by 40 feet in size. Since that time the following ministers have officiated: E. S. Grumley, William Summersides, James Lawson, S. G. Havermill, Z. S. Kellogg, John L. Williams, H. Ely, A. H. Ellis, G. L. Wiley, C. Perkins, Samuel Ambrose, A. Newton, Wm. Cross, F. Maston, W. S. Young, S. Cates, A. Perry, Z. S. Kellogg, George Wells and H. W. Record, who is the present minister.

The Sabbath school was organized in 1845. It now has a membership of 118. Present Superintendent, B. J. Ewing.

Simon Alderson was first made postmaster at the village, followed in 1856 by John McAllister. The present officer is William Harvey.

John Beatty, whose wife still lives at Council Hill Station, was one of the early settlers, not yet mentioned. In 1832, under his supervision, lead was smelted in a "blast furnace" for about the first time in America. Log and ash furnaces had been used prior to this time, but only fifty per cent of lead was extracted from the ore with them, while the ore, when smelted in a blast furnace, yielded seventy to eighty per cent. In 1833, a company was organized, with "Uncle John" Beatty, as he was called, at the head, who started four blast furnaces, as follows: One on East Fork, in Council Hill Township; one near Platteville, Wis.; one at Mineral Point, Wis.; and one at Catfish, near Dubuque, Iowa. The company, which afterwards divided into four associations, consisted of John Beatty, Major Legate, Daniel Wann, Robt. Shaw, Robt. Waller, Richard Waller, Richard Bonson, Robt. Bonson, Major J. H. Rountree, George Snowden, Henry Snowden and —— Snowden.

In 1837, a blast furnace was erected by Stahl, Leakley & Co., near the township line, between Vinegar Hill and Council Hill. This they continued to use until 1860, and in the meantime a settlement grew around it, part of which is in each township. In 1862, a large, four-story stone grist mill, containing three runs of stones, was built there, by Wm. Bell, Thos. B. Leakley, Nicholas and Frederic Stahl. This mill is run by water power from the Galena River, from which a head and fall of seventeen feet are secured.

In 1853, there was built, beside the cemetery on the hill, the Primitive Church, and in 1870 a second church (Methodist Episcopal) was erected in the valley below—both, however, in Council Hill Township.

In 1873, the narrow-guage railroad was laid through the settlement, past the mill, and a side track built, though there is no regular station.

In 1877, the post-office was first established in the mill, with William Bell as postmaster.

When the Illinois Central Railroad was built through the township, in 1854, a station was established one and one half miles south of Council Hill Village, which has received the name of Council Hill Station. There is much confusion caused by the similarity of the names of the two villages.

Andrew Conway opened a store at the station soon after the railroad was built, but at the present time there is none, although a few goods are kept at private houses. Anthony Roe at one time kept a public house, but the patronage did not justify its continuance.

Wm. Passmore.

COUNCIL HILL

A small frame school-house was built in 1857, which was torn down and a new one built in 1875.

The first postmaster was Simon Alderson, soon after the station was established. It is at present kept by Wm. Passmore. The church there was built in 1860; repaired and re-opened in 1877.

The station was laid off and platted by J. C. Gardner, on December 6, 1855, on the northwest quarter and a small portion of the southwest quarter of section 31, on the land of Wm. Williams, Simon Alderson, John Bethel and John Alston. It has never been incorporated.

At the township organization, in 1853, the territory of this township was incorporated in Scales Mound and Mann (now Vinegar Hill) Townships, the dividing line being Fever (now Galena) River.

At the June meeting (1854) of the Board of Supervisors, the Township of Council Hill was created, bounded as follows:

"Commencing at the northeast corner of section 17, on the state line in township 29 N., R. 2 E.; thence west along state line five miles, to the northwest corner of section 15, township 29 N., R. 1 E.; thence due south on section line to the southwest corner of section 34, township 29 N., R. 1 E.; thence due east along township line five miles to southeast corner of section 32, township 29 N., R. 2 E.; thence due north on section line to state line or place of beginning."

The population of Council Hill Township was, in 1850 (then a precinct) 628; in 1860, 850, and in 1870, 725.

After the township organization in 1853, an election was held at Rocky Point school-house, where Mark Leakley was elected Supervisor; Robert Shaw and John McAllister, Justices of the Peace, and Wm. Harvey, Township Clerk.

The present officers are:

Supervisor, Wm. Passmore; *Town Clerk*, Wm. Harvey; *Assessor*, Wm. Bell; *Collector*, Charles W. Leakley; *Commissioners of Highways*, Charles Smart, Wm. Lupton and Henry Goodbern; *Justices of Peace*, B. J. Ewing (at village), and R. T. James (at station).

DERINDA.

Robert Campbell made the first claim known in the Township of Derinda, in January, 1836, on section 7. Mr. Campbell had come to Illinois from Scotland by the unusual route of Hudson's Bay and the Red River of the North, having become an employe of the Hudson's Bay Company, at the Selkirk Settlement. After making his claim, Mr. Campbell returned to Galena until 1838, when he removed with his family to his land. In the meantime other settlers had been attracted to that vicinity by the fertile valleys and rolling prairies along Big and Little Rush Creeks. In the Spring of 1836, William and Thomas Oliver entered claims on the western border of the township, but built their houses across the line, in Hanover Township, so that the first house built in Derinda Township, except a cabin of Mr. Cook on section 1, was by Samuel McGrath, who came, with his family, in October of the same year. Jonathan Hendershot, Absalom Roberts, Jacob Handel and others soon followed.

In 1836, David Barr purchased the claim of Mr. Cook, to eighty acres, forming the northeast corner of the township, and, as the farms began to develop, he started a store. Mr. Barr * was one of the first justices of the town-

* At an election held for the purpose of choosing a name for the township, the votes were very nearly tied between the name of "New Germany," and Rush. This name, however, had been already taken by another township, so that it was reported back to the officer of this township—Mr. Barr. He decided the matter by reporting the name of his wife, "Derinda," which name was accepted.

ship, and was made postmaster in 1853, his house being on a stage route between Galena and Dixon. The post-office is now called "Derinda," and is kept by Mrs. John Leonard. Another post-office has been established in section 17, called "Derinda Centre," at a store which was opened by Joseph Pettit in 1867, and is now kept by Robert McGrath.

A large majority of the settlers are German and Irish, some of whom at the time of the land sale in 1847, were unable to pay in money for the claims which they had labored to cultivate. Consequently many of them accepted the offer of a banker of Dixon, to purchase the land in his name, and deed it to them when they were able to pay the usual price and an additional 33⅓ per cent as his commission.

School was first kept in the township by John McKinley, in his own house, on section 8. The first school-house was built in the south part of section 5, in 1839. There are now seven school districts, each having a good, substantial school-house.

The first preaching in the township was by Samuel McGrath, at his residence, where, afterwards, Mr. Schunk, a young circuit rider, held occasional meetings. The first church was one which the German Methodist Church members purchased at Galena, in 1855, took apart and brought to this township in wagons, erecting it again on section 21. Rev. Philip Funk occupied the pulpit of this church as first regular pastor. At present the membership is not large enough to support a pastor.

The Albright Evangelical Church.—Many Germans were converted to the Methodist Episcopal belief in Ohio and elsewhere, as early as 1830. About that time a German, named Albright, received permission from the M. E. Conference to labor in the ministry. In order to reach many of his countrymen, who did not understand English, he began preaching in the German language. To this the Conference made repeated objections, so that those people organized the Albright Evangelical Church, embracing the Methodist religion, but permitting worship in either language. To-day it is a permanent and comparatively strong denomination.

Such a society was organized at an early day in Derinda Township. They held meetings in the school-house for many years, and built their church on Section 27, in 1856. Rev. Mr. Sendlinger acted as first pastor in the church. At present, the minister is Rev. Mr. Riemenschneiter.

The First German Lutheran Church was organized by Rev. Mr. List, in 1856. A number of other ministers had preached occasionally in private houses. Their church was erected in 1858, on Section 22. At present, Rev. Theodore Seilor is their pastor. It is a strong, progressive society.

The Second German Lutheran Church was organized about the same time, and has been directed by the same pastors. Its church was built on Section 16, in 1872. Meetings were held for some years in the school-house and the old Methodist Church.

The Methodist Episcopal Church (English) has held services in the Derinda Centre School House since 1857. The Hanover pastor, Rev. Mr. Soule, now officiates.

In 1860, the population of the Township was 818; in 1870 it numbered 804.

No alteration has been made in its boundaries since the time of organization, in 1853.

The first officers of the township were: Supervisor, William McGrath; Clerk, William Jordan; Road Commissioners, Thomas Oliver, Alexander Molison, and Jacob Buck. The present officers are: Supervisor, William Logan; Clerk, Albert Dittmar; Road Commissioners, Joseph Khiel, Michael Gouse, and William Skene; Justices of the Peace, Ehrhardt Dittmar and John Rogers.

STOCKTON.

This name was suggested by Alanson Parker, who desired it named after a town in the East, and, also, as suggestive of the future development of the township, as one devoted to the raising of stock. The prophetic eye which foresaw this, was not in error, for to-day the farmers of this township are nearly all exclusive stock-raisers, and the beautiful prairies through it are devoted to pasturage or meadows; and stacks of hay are far more numerous than piles of straw, while the stubble is that of grass and corn, rather than of oats and wheat.

The first settler of the township was Henry Rice, who moved from Galena to Section 3 in 1832 with Philip Rice and others, who have been referred to more at length in the history of Rush Township. John Hayes moved to this township in 1836, from Indiana, where soon after his little daughter died—this being doubtless the first death of a white person in Stockton Township. Discouraged by the hardships of Western life, Mr. Hayes sold his claim and cabin, in 1837, to Elisha C. Hamilton, and returned to Indiana. Mr. Hamilton continued to live there until the time of his death, gaining a large circle of friends and being elected the first Supervisor of his township.

The fourth settler of this beautiful valley was Nathaniel Morris, who built a cabin on section 24, in 1838. He afterwards sold out to Mr. Jesse Wilson, and moved to Missouri, where he died. Mr. Wilson still resides in the original log house erected by Mr. Morris.

The next resident was John Wilkins, who settled in 1838, on the north part of section 28, where he died. After 1839 the country became more rapidly inhabited. In that year Alanson and Benjamin Parker settled on section 24. Then followed Whipple C. Ward, Wm. Richards, Fred Tucker, and J. R. Patridge.

School was first taught by Sarah Miner, who afterwards married Aratus Haskell, one of the early settlers of Nora.

The first school-house was built in 1843, of logs, on section 23. In this building Ben. F. Parker was the first teacher.

In the north half of the township the Wilsons were prominent among the early settlers. They took up large tracts of lands, and made extensive farms. Wm. Stayner was also an early settler. Ashael Morse came in 1841, and settled in the southeast corner of the township, on the site of Morseville. George L. Dow, Chester Parker, Orange Gray, the Lyons', and Stephen Johnson soon followed. A school-house was built where Morseville now stands in the year 1846, where Betsy Lyon first taught. In 1855 a stone school-house was built on the same lot, and in 1871 a new two-story wooden building was erected, the stone structure being sold for a residence. Here C. C. Waldo first gave instruction. At present the teacher is J. Hamilton.

The first school records were made in 1843, when E. C. Hamilton, J. R. Patridge and B. F. Parker were appointed trustees by the Commissioners Court. An enumeration of school children was made that year and it was found that there were seventy-five in the township. In 1868 there were 670, and at the present time there are 559. In 1843 the township was divided into two districts; now there are eight school-houses and a number of joint districts with other townships. The early history of Stockton and Ward's Grove Townships is intimately connected, and many men who are now residents of Stockton Township, came to Ward's Grove as early as 1835 to '38. The Tyrrells came in 1838; Miles and Frank are now living in Stockton Township. James Blair was also an early settler of Ward's Grove, although now living in Stockton. The vicinity of Morseville has been a trading point for a great many years; a blacksmith shop in 1851 by Jonathan Parker, and store, was one of the early institutions. In 1852, Miles Tyrrell purchased the business of Talbot, and has since been continually connected with the business interests of the place. In 1866, Ashael Morse had the Village of Morseville platted and recorded. In 1871 he built his hotel there, and, during the same year, the greater part of the buildings in the village were erected. In an early day the people were poorly provided with post-offices, although the township now has five. There was a post-office in the south part of the township known as West Plum River, but that was abandoned in 1842. Another office was established at or near the same place about 1849. During Buchanan's administration it was removed to Morseville, and Miles Tyrrell made postmaster. R. Strickland at present manages the office. In the Spring of 1862 another office was established, known as Yankee Hollow, and G. L. Dow made postmaster. He held the office until 1865, when B. F. Parker took it and held it until his death in 1874. His daughter was commissioned in Feb., 1875, and now holds the office. At quite an early day an office was established near the centre of the township known as Stockton, and Fred. Tucker was made postmaster. He went to California several years ago, when his wife took charge of the office, and continued to discharge the duties until May, 1875, when it was removed to Geo. Justus', and he was made postmaster. A post-office called Pitcherville was established in the northeast part of the township in 1868, and Mr. Pitcher officiated as postmaster. S. T. Eade now has charge of the office. In 1874 an office named Winters was established near the centre, with Henry Winter as postmaster. He still acts in that capacity. There are two church buildings in the township; one at the centre, and one at Morseville. The centre church nominally belongs to the Free Will Baptists, but the organization is very weak, and maintains no regular services. It was built in 1868. The church at Morseville is a Union church which was erected in 1870, and any denomination is welcome to the use of it. The Winebrenarians have a feeble organization, but do not hold regular services.

In 1875, an insurance company, known as the "Stockton and Ward's Grove Mutual Fire and Lightning Insurance Company," was organized under the act of 1874. The present officers are M. K. Hammond, President, Geo. Justus, Secretary, and Samuel Tyrrel, Treasurer. The company has had only one loss, which amounted to $425. They now have 135 policies in force, and $150,000 liable to assessment. There is a Masonic Lodge at Morseville, known as Plum River Lodge No. 554. It was chartered Oct. 1, 1867. The present officers are Francis Tyrrell, Master; A. B. Byrum, S. W.; C. Tiffany, J. W.; Wm. Farrell, S. D.; S. E. Waldo, J. D.; J. N. Sharp, Chaplain; Samuel Tyrrell, Treasurer; F. S. Tyrrell, Secretary; Millard Johnson and W. H. Starkey, Stewards; Jno. F. Tyrrell, Tyler. When the lands came into market the north half of this township was held as a mineral reserve, but the south half has proven the most valuable in mineral. More or less has been taken out since the country was first settled, but about 1871 the greatest quantity was found, and Morseville bid fair to become a lively mining town. But the lead suddenly gave out, and but very little has been done at it since. The manufacture of cheese was commenced, and two factories built. The work was abandoned, however, after a short time. At Morseville, H. F. Hastings has been in business in a general store for a number of years. He has always lived in the West, and is a thorough Western man. There are two blackmith shops in Morseville, also two wagon shops, one harness shop, one tin shop, one drug store, and one hotel. The latter was originated by Ashael Morse, who was killed about a year ago by being thrown from a wagon. Geo. A. Bixby now runs the hotel business. At the centre, Winter & Johnson are engaged in a general country store, and at Pitcherville, S. T. Eade is likewise engaged.

Stockton Centre Church is situated in the centre of the Town of Stockton. It was erected in the year 1868, by a Baptist organization then numbering about 100.

It is a beautiful and substantial structure, size 34 by 44 feet, and cost $2,500. It has 56 seats, capable of seating 280 people. Elder Torrey was their pastor. Unfortunately, however, the Baptist organization proved to be short lived. The work of erecting the building having been done during an excitement created by a revival, the members retreated from the ranks one after another, until there remain but few members.

The Township of Stockton has never been modified since its organization in 1853. It had, in 1860, a population of 1,044, and in 1870, 1,214.

Township Officers.—Supervisor, A. B. Byrum; Town Clerk, Joel G. Ball; Assessors, Wm. H. Starkley; Collector, Ira T. Benton; Commissioners of Highways, Chester Parker and Martin T. Carpenter, the third place being vacant since the decease of Mr. John Phelps.

WARD'S GROVE.

The first claimant of Ward's Grove Township is a matter of some doubt. It is understood that a few claims were made from 1834 to 1836. There is, however, no question but that Mr. Bernard Ward, after whom the township received its name, was its first permanent settler. Mr. Ward is still residing in single blessedness at the old location, where he is an influential citizen and large property holder.

It is learned from Joseph Moore that Homer and Charles Graves came west from Ohio in 1836, and made a claim in Ward's Grove Township in the Summer of the same year, near the head-timber of Yellow Creek, where they broke five acres of ground, but soon returned to Ohio, where they remained until 1838, when they again came to this township with their mother, brother William, sister Emily (now Mrs. F. M. Rogers) and half-brother Joseph Moore. These brothers became prominent residents of the township. Homer and William Graves and Mr. Moore still reside there, where the latter owns 1,527 acres of land.

James Blair came to Ward's Grove Township in the Fall of 1836, and settled there. Mr. Blair moved into Stockton Township in 1876, with his family, where he now resides. His marriage to Catherine Marsh, 1837, was the first in the township, and his daughter Margaret, born March 4, 1838, was the first white child born in the township.

Jabez Giddings came to the township in 1836, and his brother, Smith, in the next year, and to the former Mr. Blair and Arthur Tyrrell hired out to work in the same year. Mr. J. Giddings afterwards (1840) sold out to Jacob Reber.

Among other early settlers were Asa Hutton (1838), whose infant son was the first person who died (1839) in the township; Dr. Bratton, the first physician; Ezra Latham, who built a saw mill at the head-waters of Yellow Creek, in the northeastern part of the township, in 1839; George W. Flack, who came in April, 1837, and is now a resident of Iowa; John Flack, who came with his family in 1839, and died in 1842; Samuel, Charles and Miles Tyrrell, the former two of whom came in November, 1837, and the latter in November, 1838; Charles died in 1860; Samuel is still an influential citizen of Ward's Grove, while Miles is now living in Morseville, Stockton Township; H. A. Perry, who came in June, 1839, and is now a farmer of Stockton; Samuel Tyrrell, Sr., who came in October, 1841, with his family of four daughters and a son, of whom Mrs. Benjamin Parker, of Stockton, is the only daughter now residing in the county; Mr. Samuel Tyrrell, Sr., died in 1845; Hiram Tyrrell, who came in May, 1843, and now lives in Iowa. There are many other early settlers of the township, equally worthy of mention, many of whose biographies appear in another portion of this work.

Schools.—Bernard Ward first taught school by permitting the children of his neighbors to come to his house, where he gave them instruction, but the first organized school was taught by Mary R. Tyrrell, now Mrs. Isaac Lyons, in a cabin built in 1843, by Mr. Giddings, and owned by Jacob Reber. The first school-house was built in 1845, on section 29, and taught by Mary Tyrrell. The first Trustees of School Lands were James Blair and Samuel Tyrrell; school organization was effected at the house of Mr. Tyrrell just before building the school-house. The Directors were Charles B. Tyrrell, William Blair, Jr., and David Earlewine. There are now four school-houses in the township.

In almost all neighborhoods a substantial sympathy is usually extended to a citizen whose property is destroyed by fire. Many, of course, insure their property at high rates, so that much more money is taken from the neighborhood for insurance during a term of years than has been destroyed in value within the same limits. Investigate where you may, this will be found true. Hence, a number of the residents of Stockton and Ward's Grove Townships resolved to form an association within themselves by which they should pay all the losses of their members and each be insured against loss, without being obliged to support a large retinue of officers and agents at high salaries. Rush and the south fifteen sections of Nora Township were afterwards included. It is called the "Stockton and Ward's Grove Mutual Fire and Lightning Insurance Company, of Jo Daviess County, Illinois," and was organized and incorporated under the act approved March 24, 1874, entitled: "An Act to revise the law in relation to Township Insurance Companies," from which the following are extracts:

SECTION 1. *Be it enacted by the People of the State of Illinois, represented in the General Assembly*, That any number of persons, not less than twenty-five, residing in any congressional or political township, or in one or more adjoining congressional or political townships in this state, not exceeding six in number, and without regard to county lines, who, collectively, shall own property of not less than $50,000 in value, which they desire to have insured, may form an incorporated company for the purpose of mutual insurance against loss or damage by fire or lightning.

SECTION 2. Such persons shall file with the Auditor of Public Accounts a declaration of their intention to form a company for the purposes expressed in the preceding section, which declaration shall be signed by all the corporators, and shall contain a copy of the charter proposed to be adopted by them. Such charter shall set forth the name of the corporation, which shall embrace the name of the township in which the business office of such company is to be located, and the intended duration of the company, and if it is found conformable to this act and not inconsistent with the laws and constitution of this state, the Auditor shall thereupon deliver to such persons a certified copy of the charter, which, on being filed in the office of the County Clerk of the county where the office of such company is to be located, shall be their authority to organize and commence business. Such certified copy of the charter may be used in evidence for or against said company, with the same effect as the original: *Provided*, That such charter so obtained shall be subject to control of and modification by the General Assembly.

SECTION 8. Such company may issue policies only on detached dwellings, barns, (except livery, boarding and hotel barns), and other farm buildings, and such property as may properly be contained therein, for any time not exceeding five years, and not to extend beyond the limited duration of the charter, and for an amount not to exceed $3,000 on any one risk. All persons so insured shall give their obligation to the company, binding themselves, their heirs, and assigns to pay their *pro rata* share to the company of the necessary expenses and of all losses by fire or lightning which may be sustained by any member thereof, during the time for which their respective policies are written; and they shall, also, at the time of effecting the insurance, pay such percentage in cash, and such other charge as may be required by the rules or by-laws of the company.

The required members having been obtained, a charter was secured on April 17, 1875.

Officers.—M. K. Hammond, President; George Justus, Secretary; E. E. Byrum, Treasurer.

Directors.—George S. Wing, Samuel Tyrrell, M. K. Hammond, Simon Polker, George Justus, Wm. L. Lawhorn, John D. Brown, Ebenezer Backus nd E. E. Byrum.

Religious.—The first preaching in the township was by Rev. Fleeharty, a Methodist minister, who held occasional services in Hutton's cabin. He afterwards organized a class, and, after meeting for four years at Mr. Hutton's, the place of holding service was changed to Morseville, Stockton Township.

The first regular preaching of the Presbyterian denomination was in 1844, by Rev. Littlefield, at private houses. He was followed by Rev. Powell.

The first Free Will Baptist sermon was at Mr. Flack's, by Rev. Wm. Johnson, who was followed in 1842 by Rev. Norton, at Mr. Tyrrell's. Since the Union Church, spoken of in the Stockton sketch, was built, the residents of Ward's Grove generally attend divine worship at that place.

The only town attempted was by Wm. Johnson, who laid out a village on the southwest quarter of section 19, now on the farm of Joseph Moore, but as he received no encouragement, the plan was abandoned.

In 1848, a post-office was established at the residence of Samuel Tyrrell, after which the following gentlemen were made postmasters in succession: Orange Gray, Joseph Moore, Thomas B. Carter, and Eliab Meyer; after about ten years the office was discontinued.

This township, being the west half of township 27, range 5, was originally a portion of the Imus precinct, afterwards of Ward's Grove precinct, and at the time of township organization, 1853, it was given its present boundaries. The first officers elected were:

Supervisor—Thomas B. Carter; Town Clerk—B. Ward; Samuel Tyrrell was the first Justice of the Peace, and has continued until the present time. He was first elected in 1839, in the Imus precinct.

Present officers:

Supervisor—Samuel Tyrrell (chairman of County Board); Town Clerk—Isaac G. Mitchell; Assessor—Joseph Moore; Collector—Homer A. Tyrrell; Commissioners of Highways—Homer Graves, Wm. Blair, and John Heilman; Justices of the Peace—S. Tyrrell and I. G. Mitchell.

In 1860, the population of Ward's Grove Township was 425, and in 1870, it was 530.

GUILFORD.

Elias P. Avery first made claim, on section 33 of this township, in 1827. In April or May of the year following, he moved there with his sons, William, Azel, David and Elias, Jr., of whom the two former took claims; the latter, being a young man, lived with his father, while David took a claim across the present township line, in Elizabeth Township. Elias P. and Azel Avery continued to reside there until the time of their death. Elias, Jr., and William, who married in 1834, still reside in the vicinity, although William resides in Elizabeth Township.

Mr. E. T. Isbell came from Missouri in 1832, and mined at New Diggings and other places until the Spring of 1834, when he settled at his present location on section 25, in Guilford Township.

At that time, the following persons are remembered as residents there: John W. Taylor, on section 20, who afterwards moved to Clay County, Kansas, where he died. His remains were brought back in the Fall of 1877 for interment. His son, Obadiah, still lives on the old place; another son, Thomas, is dead; and two others, John and Henry, reside in Kansas. S. W. Hathaway, who is still a resident, settled on section 17, and married a daughter of Mr. Taylor. William Johnson, or "Uncle Billy," as he was called, settled on section 35, and furnished the only religious direction that the settlers received for some time. He had two sons and a daughter, all of whom are now gone.

Henry Williard settled in the township, on section 13, a short time before Mr. Isbell, and still lives there with his family. James D. Rawlins, father of John A., settled near the claim of Mr. Isbell, and built his house a little before him, where he still lives. Further mention is made of John A. Rawlins in another portion of this work.

School was taught in the house of William Avery, in 1837, by Mr. Swinburn. Abner Hodgins taught a school in the same year, near Mr. Isbell's farm, and soon after, a school-house was built on the south part of section 25, by Mr. Isbell. A school-house is believed to have been built a short time before this one, on the farm now owned by Robert Carson. Another school-house was built in 1851, in which Mrs. Phœbe Wait first taught. The school-house on section 25 was afterwards torn down, when a new and larger one was erected on section 26. There are now school-houses on sections 8, 11, 17, 26 and 32.

In 1835, Mr. Isbell opened a small stock of groceries, and continued to keep some goods for fifteen years.

Preaching was first held in the school-houses. The first regular preacher was David Matlock, Baptist. There is now a Methodist Episcopal Church, on the line between sections 10 and 11. The first Methodist Church was on the southwest corner of section 6.

The first post-office, called "Avery," was established on section 33, October 30, 1850, by William Avery, postmaster. The present postmaster is George S. Avery. A post-office was once kept at the house of J. D. Rawlins, called "Guilford," but it is now discontinued.

In 1837, Fuller & Lee built the only smelting furnace of the township, which was sold to Augustus Estey, who discontinued it about 1839.

At the time of township organization, in 1853, the name of the township was given in as "Gilford"; it is now spelled "Guilford." Among the first township officers were: John W. Taylor, Supervisor; John A. Rawlins, Clerk; Wm. Avery and Samuel W. Hathaway also held offices.

The first election was held at the Taylor school-house. E. T. Isbell was elected the second Supervisor, at which election about 150 votes were polled.

The present officers are: Supervisor—Wm. T. Gear; Town Clerk—Wm. Sinclair; Assessor—John Baus; Collector—James Henry; Commissioners of Highways—Simon Singer, H. Belden and James Sheean; Justices of Peace—Francis Varing and E. Schoenhardt; Constables—Philip Bausman and Frank Ehler.

Considerable mineral has been raised in this township. On the land of H. Bartell, J. W. Taylor and J. Hellman, in the western part of the township, valuable mines have been worked. C. A. Monnier and others have rich leads in the southwestern corner of the township, the principal part of which, however, lies across the line, in Elizabeth Township.

MENOMINEE.

Dudley Simmons and Philip settled in the Township of Menominee and built cabins on section four, in 1828.

About the same time Mr. Simmons built the first grist mill in the township. Soon after the Black Hawk War, Simmons and Shipton moved over on the Little Menominee, near the western edge of the township, where Mr. Shipton lived until the time of his death. Mr. Simmons afterwards moved to Iowa. Jacob Drablebis broke land and built a cabin, in 1833, on a claim in the southeastern part of the township which he afterwards sold to Harvey Mann, and moved to Iowa. James Hughlett, Benoni R. Gillett and Adolphus Hamlin were the first mineral smelters in this township. Their furnace was located near the

L P Woodworth

WARREN TP.

Sinsinawa River, on the lower Dubuque road, section 4, and was started in the Spring of 1833.

The second smelting was done by Harvey Mann, in the Spring of the year following. His location was about one half mile south of the other furnace, on the northwest quarter of section 8.

In 1838, Gratiot and Purdivil built a blast furnace south of Mr. Simmons' farm, using the water-power of the Menominee River. This continued but a short time.

In 1836, S. D. Carpenter took up a claim on the land known as the Buena Vista Farm. He sold out to Godfrey Shissler.

In the same year, John Shipton moved to the township, but soon sold out and went to Iowa, and Thomas Prouse settled on the lower Dubuque road. From this time settlers appeared more rapidly, so that Menominee, may be considered among the older townships of the county. It had a population, in 1850, of 720, and in 1860, of 853, while the inhabitants in 1870, numbered 593.

The Excelsior Mills were built on section 28, in 1860, by John Moore and John R. Gray. Mr. Moore afterwards moved to Iowa, since which time Gray has been sole proprietor. The mill was originally run entirely by water-power of the Sinsinawa River, but an engine has since been put in, both powers being now used. A post-office has been established in the mill for many years, Mr. Gray being postmaster. About 1860, a post-office was established at the house of Thomas Prouse, called "Alvina," but it continued only a few years.

When the railroad was built from Galena to Dubuque, along the river, a side-track and flag-station was established in the township, on section 18, called Menominee.

The first preaching remembered was about 1840, at Mr. Morton's house, on Buena Vista Farm, by a minister from Galena. There is now a school-house and Catholic church on the northeast part of section 30.

The first school-house was on section 6. At present there are school-houses on sections 5, 23 and 28.

Mining has always been carried on in this township to some extent, the land, however, is rich, productive and well watered by numerous springs and streams.

The present officers are:

Supervisor—John A. Gaffney; Town Clerk—B. Monneman; Assessor and Collector—Henry Arts; Commissioners of Highways—B. H. Wubben, Wm. H. Mann and Wm. Kanol; Constables—John Monneman and Wm. Rooney; Justices of Peace—Bernard H. Wubben and William Powers.

BERREMAN.

Thomas and John Deeds, referred to in the sketch of Pleasant Valley, probably made the first claim, erected the first cabin, and broke the first ground in this township. Of them the earliest permanent settler, N. C. Tenney, a cousin of the Tyrrells, of Ward's Grove, purchased his claim in October, 1836, in the northwestern part of the township. Here he remained until 1842, when he went to Nauvoo, and is now a Mormon Bishop in Utah.

In September, of the year 1837, the stepfather of Mr. Tenney, John Gates, Phebe, his wife, and S. B. Gates, his son, settled in the township, where John Gates afterwards died, leaving his wife and son the two oldest residents of the township.

In November, 1839, James Parkinson, with his family and brother, Isaac W., came to this vicinity and purchased a cabin and claim of a man whose name has been forgotton. James afterwards died; his children and brother, a bachelor, still live there, and are prominent residents. Dr. Peckham and wife, both of whom are now dead, came in November, 1839, bringing Mrs. Peckham's son, Delson Tiffany, still a resident of the township, who has served it in the capacity of Supervisor, and, in many other ways, been a highly useful citizen. Jacob Troxel settled, about 1839, on land in both Berreman and Pleasant Valley Townships, although his house was in the one last named. He built the first school-house, on the bottom road, near the township line, on section 7, afterward entered by S. B. Gates. There are now school-houses on sections 16, 5, and a combined church and school-house on section 29.

The first death remembered was of Dr. Peckham, who was mortally injured while building his house, by falling from a beam, in 1840. His funeral sermon was preached at the house of John Gates, by Elder Giddings, who lived on Yellow Creek, in Stephenson County. Mr. Giddings preached the first sermon in the township, although there was about that time some preaching by Lyman Clark, afterwards "one of the chosen twelve" at Salt Lake, and by other Mormon advocates.

Religious instruction was also dispensed by "Uncle Billy Johnson," a settler who paid his traveling expenses by retailing, after the sermon, thread, pins, and other notions.

The first church building erected was the Methodist, a substantial frame chapel, of tasty appearance, on section 5. No response has been received to an inquiry concerning the date of erection of the United Brethren Church, situated on the northeast corner of section 5.

The first birth in Berreman Township was a daughter of Mrs. James Parkinson, now Mrs. Jacob Klump. As before stated, the only post-office established was by Isaac W. Parkinson, who is now postmaster, although there have been several changes. The office is called "Willow," and located in Peter Bishop's store, which was the first general store opened in the township. There is now another near by, kept by Israel Solt, since 1876.

After the township was separated from Pleasant Valley, at the February meeting of the Board of Supervisors in 1857, Arthur Mahorney was made the first Supervisor. He named the township after a friend in Tennessee.

The present officers are:

Supervisor, Isaac W. Parkinson, Jr.; Town Clerk, George W. Schmeck; Assessor, Delson Tiffany; Collector, Charles Robinson; Commissioners of Highways, N. W. Calhoun, George Ray, and Taylor Williams; Justices of the Peace, Jacob B. Klump and Lafayette Wagner; Constables, Columbus Tiffany and Henry Collins. The population of Berreman Township in 1860 was 415, and in 1870, 559.

RICE.

Among its early settlers are Messrs. Rice, Lane, Schurl, Robinson, and Virtue, after the first of whom the township received its name.

This land, which is less used as farming land, is still very valuable, furnishing, as it does, some of the richest leads in the lead mining region. Passing along beside the river on the bluff road, which was graded for railroad purposes, in 1837, by the old Illinois Central Railroad Company, a beautiful view is presented, extending many miles up and down the river valley. All along the road, above and under it, drift leads penetrate far into the bluffs, marked on the outside by rows of clay dumps, which extend out into the river bayous. On each of these is a trainway, on which a dirt cart plies to and fro. Occasionally an engine is stationed at the mouth of one, for the purpose of pumping out the water. The largest mine now in use is that of Captain D. S. Harris, among the New California diggings, nine miles below Galena. Of it and the Marsden mines more is said in the special chapter relative to the mining interests.

There is a Methodist Episcopal Church on the northwestern part of section 5. The school-houses of the township are located on sections 11 (near the centre), and 9 (northeast part), and 27 (eastern part).

The present officers of Rice Township are:

Supervisor, James Ginn; Town Clerk, W. H. Dick; Assessor, Anthony McAllister; Collector, David Virtue; Commissioners of Highways, Bernard Lampa, John Funston, and John Bouch; Constable, Nelson Mougin; Justices of the Peace, David Virtue and John Spratt. The population was, in 1860, 539, and in 1870, 570.

PLEASANT VALLEY.

Alexander S. Smith, who with his family, consisting of Alexander, Jr., Mary and Ellen, came to Galena in 1824, on the steamer "Eclipse." The daughter, Mary, married John Love, and died at Galena in 1827. In 1828, Mr. Mitchell went to New Orleans. In the following year, Colonel James Mitchell, a brother of Alexander, who came to Galena in 1826 and had been living one and a half miles north of there, moved down on the Galena and Dixon road, in the rightly-named Pleasant Valley. His house, which was removed from the road several rods, was burned during the Black Hawk War, and its location has received the name of the "old camp." Alexander, Jr., and Ellen Mitchell went down to live with their uncle, but Alexander soon (1829) went South, where he remained until 1846.

After the war, Col. Mitchell rebuilt his house nearer the road, and established a tavern which he continued to keep for many years.

In 1837, Ellen Mitchell married Joseph Edwards. She now resides with her brother, Alexander, who, as stated, returned in 1846. They are the two oldest settlers of Pleasant Valley Township.

In 1834, Thomas and John Deeds, two brothers, settled on a claim which is still owned by their descendants; they were young men, and were somewhat transient in their location. They took up several claims in Berreman and Pleasant Valley Townships, on which they built cabins, broke a few acres of ground and then sold to others. Their father, Jacob Deeds, with his family, came to Pleasant Valley in 1837. They kept the first post-office and a stage station on the Galena and Dixon route.

About the same time, Mr. Kellogg and Mr. Williams settled in Pleasant Valley, and in 1835, also, James Venable. These men became permanent settlers. Mr. Kellogg went to California at the time of the gold fever, in 1849, but Mr. Williams remained until the time of his death. Thomas Deeds and James Venable married daughters of Mr. Williams. Mrs. Deeds is still living in the township.

Joseph Edwards, previously referred to, came in 1836, and lived there until his death.

Eli Thomas, G. Miller and Darius Myers were also early settlers of the township, the latter having come from New York to Galena in 1843. When passing through this valley, he was attracted by its fertility and general appearance, and after a trip back to New York, he bought a farm in this township, where he still resides. His brother, Solomon, came in 1844.

Jacob Troxel came about 1839, with his sons, Jacob, Edward and William, still here, and Henry, who went to California.

The first school-house was built of logs, by Thomas Deeds near his farm. The second was built on Darius Myers' land, on section 9. There are now nine school districts partly within the township, all having good, comfortable buildings. There are school-houses on sections 9, 14, 16, 20, 26 and 32. There are within the township Catholic, Winebrenarians, Presbyterian, Methodist and

Age-to-come Adventist Denominations, of whom only the Winebrenarians have a building. It is located on section 27. The remaining denominations hold meetings in the school-houses.

In an early day, a saw mill was built near the farm of Mr. Deeds, which has long since been torn away.

At the time of township organization, in 1853, the township of Pleasant Valley included Berreman. It was named by Thomas Deeds, who was the first supervisor.

The present officers are: Supervisor—J. D. Crowley; Town Clerk—Geo. W. Thomas; Assessor—John Sughroue; Collector—George M. Rock; Justices of Peace—George Winters and J. C. Ruble; Commissioner of Highways—Aaron Davis; Constables—John W. Ruble and John R. Buckley; School Trustee—E. D. Thomas.

The population of the township, in 1860, was 767, and in 1870, 943.

VINEGAR HILL.

The mines of Vinegar Hill Township were known and worked at a very early period of this country's settlement. Dubuque worked at the Cave Diggings as early as 1805; John Furlong worked there in 1823, more complete accounts of which appear in the General History.

The first saloon and store was opened there in 1826, by Michael Burns.

Moses Meeker made the first claims in the township with agricultural pursuits in view. He broke fifteen acres of land on the Mineral Point road, near the south line of the township, in 1827, and planted it to corn, although he continued to live in Galena.

In 1830, Harvey Mann broke twenty-five acres of land on the same road, five miles north of Galena, and also planted corn. Permanent settlers soon made claims to all the farming land, although the entire township is considered as mineral territory. As these claims were taken and improved before a survey had been made, they are in fractional parts of sections. All disputes regarding claims and boundaries were settled by arbitrators agreed upon. At the time of general land sales at Dixon, Harvey Mann was elected to "bid in" large tracts from the government, and then deed to the claimants according to the decisions of the arbitrators.

John Furlong was the father of the first child, William, born in the township. The date was August 30, 1829.

In 1836, Charles Olmstead and Seth Taylor, in this township, for the first time at the lead mines, scraped together the dirt which was taken out from around bodies of mineral, and which it was customary to throw away after picking out all the pieces of mineral visible, hauled it to a stream of water, made a sluice box, and washed the mineral dirt, thereby saving ore. This practice soon became customary, and is now done by all miners. The mining history of this township is referred to more specifically in a special chapter on the subject.

In 1845, Mr. Carrington located a store in the north hollow. Wm. Bennett opened another between the north and south hollows in 1853, and in 1857 Jonathan Bolton established a store near the mines in south hollow; the two latter named stores are still doing business at this date (February, 1878).

In 1851, a post-office was established, with F. B. Sidner postmaster, but it was afterwards discontinued.

In 1838, the first election in Vinegar Hill precinct was held at the house of Fielder Parish, located on the Mineral Point road. Since that time elections have been held in the Rock school-house, in district No. 2.

The derivation of the name Vinegar Hill was, probably, from a town of the same name near Wexford, Ireland, from which a number of miners emigrated to this vicinity. Michael Burns afterwards told Mr. Harvey Mann, that he himself, Jno. Furlong and Thos. Carroll, with others, while in a state of "spiritual hallucination" at Burns' saloon, christened an Indian mound near there, by pouring whisky over it and declaring that "henceforth and forever, this place shall be called Vinegar Hill."

At the time of township organization, a meeting was held at the house of John Cragen, for the purpose of choosing a name for the township, at which Mr. Mann proposed the name of "Meeker," Mr. Meeker having made the first permanent claim, but Colonel Cox proposed the name of "Mann," Mr. Mann being the oldest resident still living in the township, which name was adopted and so recorded. But the sons of the Emerald Isle were not satisfied, and the name was afterwards changed to "Vinegar Hill."

The first smelting furnace and grist mill were located at a settlement now known as Millbrig, a part of which is in Vinegar Hill, and a portion in Council Hill Township.

A number of Indian mounds, relics of ancient inhabitants, are still in existence in Vinegar Hill, of which the native Indians could give no account. There are two large, distinct mounds, about two rods in diameter at the base, and seven feet high, located on land belonging to John Welch, near the road leading from the turnpike to the Council Hill road, from which human bones have been extracted. These are supposed by some to be burial vaults erected in honor of eminent personages.

Schools.—In 1842, G. C. Shattuck taught a school in his own house. This is believed to be the first one opened in the township. When the school districts were established, in 1849, Harvey Mann, Caleb M. Eggleston, and Fielder Parish, were elected directors of district number two. Here the second school was taught by J. Phillips. The first school-house was built in 1850, and is located on the turnpike near the north boundary of Mr. Mann's farm. There are now two other school districts, numbers four and five, each having schools.

Churches.—The Catholic church was the first to be built in the township; the year of its erection was 1843. It is located at the head of the north hollow. Its first priest was Rev. Father James McCauley, who was followed, in succession, by Revs. Dunne, Smith, Powers, O'Connel and Father McMahan, the present pastor.

Methodist.—In 1844, the Methodist Episcopal church was built, in south hollow, near the cabin occupied by Jonathan Craig, before he sold his claim to Daniel Wann & Co., on section 27. The officiating ministers have been as follows:

Revs. Wm. Palmer, Mark Leakley, Wm. Birkbeck, Jonathan Clendenning, John Williams, Anthony Williams, Isaac Springer, Jesse T. Bennett, John L. Williams, Isaac Searles, William Tasker, S. L. Leonard, E. S. Grumley, Wm. Summersides, J. T. Prior, James Lawson, G. L. Wiley, Charles Perkins, S. G. Avermill, Z. S. Kellogg, J. Nibs, Wm. Sturges, M. Dinsdale, A. W. Cumins, P. E. Knox, Wm. Haw and A. J. Davis, the present pastor.

In 1850, Vinegar Hill Township had a population of 759, in 1860 there were 872, and in 1870, 693.

The township officers are:

Supervisor—John E. Furlong; Town Clerk—Richard Seward; Assessor—Clement Temple; Collector—Jeremiah Butler; Commissioners of Highways—Clement Temple, Leonard Slatts, Tom. McGuire; Justices of Peace—Anthony McGuire and A. McMennis; Constables—Joseph Thompson and John Liddle.

THOMPSON.

Not being within the principal mining district and of not very inviting appearance to settlers agriculturally disposed, on account of the roughness of its territory, Thompson Township was not settled at so early a date as many other portions of the county. An old county directory places the date of the first settlement at 1830, but does not state who inhabited at that time. Soon after the Black Hawk War, Robert Johnson and family settled on section 20, but removed to Missouri about 1840.

Among those who were permanent settlers at the time of the arrival of C. C. Thompson in 1839, were John Soule and family, who settled on section 5 or 6, and Gilbert Soule, his brother, who settled on section 8; two brothers named Keenan; John Isabel and wife, section 30; Wm. Isabel, section 28; Robert Johnson and family; Mr. Bird; and Marcus Hodgins, who settled on section 17, afterwards married a daughter of John Soule, and is believed to be the oldest living settler of the township. About the time of Mr. Thompson's arrival, — Walbridge and Whitfield Conlee put in an appearance, but soon removed.

As above stated, Christopher Columbus Thompson, with his brother Hiram and cousin Ichabod, settled on section 24, in 1839. There they erected a saw mill, for which they got out all the timbers by hand, after which they sawed the materials for a grist mill, 40 by 70 feet in size, of two stories, and containing two runs of stones. This they completed in 1842, and both mills were in successful operation until 1868. It was run by water power from the Apple River.

In 1845, the death of Hiram occurred, followed by Ichabod's death in the next year, thus leaving C. C. Thompson alone. He built, in 1856, a large, three-storied, stone grist mill, 30 by 50 feet in size, with three runs of stones, which he continued to manage until 1868, when he sold out for $10,000, to Eustace (John) and Schenouth. In 1872, they sold to Barrett and another John Eustace. In 1869, Mr. Thompson put in a steam saw mill, a half mile northeast of the grist mill, which in 1874 he moved to about seventy rods southwest of the mill. It was sold, in 1877, to Wm. Miller, who moved it down near the mouth of Apple River.

Schools.—In 1857, C. C. Thompson employed Ervina Earley, and afterwards Etta Jewett, to teach the children of the three families in the neighborhood. The schools were taught in his house. A stone school-house was afterwards built near the house of Mr. Thompson, in which Miss A. Wells first taught. This was the second school-house in the eastern half of the township, the first one having been erected near the north line on the Apple River Road. There are now school-houses in sections 2, 5, 23 and 27.

Churches.—There was preaching at Mr. Thompson's house in 1844, after which occasional services were held there and in the school-house. A circuit rider named Bennett had previously preached a few times in the township, though the first regular circuit preacher was Mr. McGee, from New York, who embraced a circuit of over forty miles, receiving but $200 per annum for his services.

The Salem M. E. Church.—This church, located on a picturesque rural spot at the junction of the roads leading from Thompson's Mills to Schapsville, and from Apple River to Elizabeth, on section 23, was erected in 1869. It was the first built in the township, Christopher Columbus Thompson and William Witham being the active men to whose zeal, exertions and influence the Methodists are indebted for its erection, George Westaby donating the land (one acre) on which it stands. It is a commodious frame building, 28 by 44 feet; cost $1,600, and is clear of debt. It was dedicated by Rev. S. A. W. Jewett. Rev. Archibald Smith, of the Rock River Conference, was the first pastor. He died in 1869, and was succeeded by Rev. F. R. Mastin, Messrs. Roberts, Brotherton and Kennedy, in the order as mentioned. W. J. Liberto at present holds service fortnightly, the pulpit on alternate Sundays being filled by Mr. William Witham and other local preachers. The congregation numbers forty members, and has a large attendance at Sunday services. The people of all denominations (Catholic included), and many of no religious belief, subscribed towards its erection. Henry Evans, William Witham, Ichabod Sampson and George Westaby were the first trustees. The present ones are William Sincox, William Witham, Charles Westaby, John Bastian and William Chapman.

The German Presbyterian Church, called Zion Church, was organized in the year 1854, with fifty members, with Elders G. Stadel and C. Winter, and Deacons John Wenzel and Ehrhard Dittmar. They erected a house of worship in 1860, 20 by 30 feet in size. The first pastor was Rev. A. Kolb, for three years, then the Rev. Rensker, for one year. After this the Rev. A. Kolb was their pastor, serving for four years. In 1864 the Rev. Jacob Schwartz was his successor until the Summer of 1865. A call as pastor was then extended to the Rev. J. Liesveld. Under his ministration the membership increased. In 1875, a call was given to Rev. J. E. Funk, of the Nazareth Church of Gasconade Co., Mo., who is the pastor at present. The present membership is one hundred. The Elders are G. Stadel C. Winter, J. Dittmar, J. Weiss and George Gruby.

There is on section 29 a Methodist Episcopal Church, of which no sketch has been furnished for this work.

The Thompson and Guilford Mutual Fire and Lightning Insurance Company was chartered and organized in April, 1877, to endure twenty-five years, its object being to protect its members against loss by fire and lightning. Officers and Directors are: Philip Parkins, President; Jeremiah Leavitt, Secretary; Charles Cable, Treasurer, and Edwin Rogers, E. T. Isbell, Anton Shap, J. G. Dittmar, G. A. Page, and Edward Sweeney, Directors.

The first post-office was established, with Peter Scofield as postmaster, in 1855, but it was kept by Mrs. Thompson, at the Mills, as deputy, until 1858, when C. C. Thompson became postmaster. In 1869 Philip Parkins took the office, moved it to his residence, in section 29, and it was changed to "Houghton," the former name having been "Thompson's Mills."

At the time of township organization in 1853, Thompson Township extended to the state line. At a meeting held to decide upon a name, James McAllister made a motion to call it after the oldest resident, which was carried, and the name of "Thompson" decided upon in honor of C. C. Thompson, although Mr. Hodgins is now known to be the older resident.

Mr. Thompson was elected the first Supervisor, an office which he continued to hold for five successive years. The first Township Clerk was Gilbert Soule.

The present officers are:

Supervisor—Philip Parkins; Town Clerk—Edward Sweeney; Assessor—Conrad Winter; Collector—Gottleib Stadel; Commissioner of Highway—Geo. Bell; Justices of the Peace—James N. Gallagher and Philip Parkins; Constables—Francis Keenan and A. P. Ketterer.

In 1860 the population of the township was 647, and in 1870 it numbered 800.

BIOGRAPHICAL DIRECTORY

OF

JO DAVIESS COUNTY.

NON-RESIDENTS, FORMERLY LIVING IN JO DAVIESS CO.

WM. HENRY BRADLEY (now of Chicago), was born in Ridgefield, Fairfield Co., Connecticut, Nov. 29, 1816. His grandfather, Philip Burr Bradley, was also a native of Ridgefield, a lawyer by profession and a graduate of Yale. During the War of the Revolution he was a Colonel in active service, and his Commission is still preserved. He was a warm and trusted personal friend of Washington, and was appointed by him, when President, Marshal for the District of Connecticut, an appointment renewed in Washington's second term, and also under President Adams. His son, and the father of the subject of this sketch, Jesse Smith Bradley, was also a graduate of Yale, and highly esteemed as a classical scholar. He was elected by the legislature one of the Judges of Fairfield Co., an office which he retained until his death in May, 1833. His wife, Elizabeth Baker, was also a native of Ridgefield, the daughter of a physician of note, Dr. Amos Baker.

The fifth son of these parents, William Henry Bradley, pursued his studies at home in Ridgefield Academy, and at the time of his father's death, was prepared to enter Yale College. Soon after that event, he went to New Haven and was employed as teller in the City Bank. At the end of four years, in the Fall of 1837, he removed, at the suggestion of an elder brother, to Galena, Ill., then the most considerable town of the Northwest.

There he was offered the position of Clerk of the County Court. He accepted the appointment and thus decided his future, for since that time he has been almost constantly connected with courts in a clerical capacity. In 1840, while discharging the duties of his position, and studying law in the office of Hon. Thomas Drummond, then a prominent lawyer in Galena, he was appointed Clerk of the Circuit Court of Jo Daviess Co. On the adoption of the new Constitution of Ill., in 1848, he was elected to the same office, and again re-elected in 1852. The large majorities by which he was successively elected, notwithstanding the intensity of partisan feeling occasioned by a Presidential campaign, and the nearly equal political division of the County between the two parties, and his active identification with one of them, sufficiently attest the public appreciation of him as a man, and a faithful and efficient officer. When Congress created a Second Judicial District in Ill., the Hon. Thomas Drummond, then Judge of the United States District Court for Ill., having been assigned to the Northern District, with the concurrence of Justice McLean, called Mr. Bradley to be Clerk of the new Courts. He accepted, and resigning his clerkship at Galena, removed to Chicago, and entered upon his duties March 22, 1855. He was, upon the usual examination, admitted to the bar, but has never been actively engaged in the practice of his profession.

For about twenty-three years he has performed the duties of his position, as clerk, with quiet and unfailing industry and exemplary fidelity, winning in this, as in other previous connections with the Courts, a rare and honorable measure of respect and trust, for readiness and accuracy as well as efficiency and skill in discharging the large and increasing business that has employed his energies and occupied his time. Still he has never been indifferent to other public interests, having taken an active part in the Young Men's Association of Chicago, and being elected its president in 1860.

Of the West Side City Railway Co., he has been a Director since its organization; was Vice President several years, and President for six years, which last position he resigned in 1875, owing to the laborious and exacting duties incident to the position.

In June, A. D., 1871, he was appointed, under the will of the late Walter L. Newberry (deceased), one of the Trustees of said estate, to fill the vacancy occasioned by the resignation of the Hon. Mark Skinner, and with his associate, E. W. Blatchford, Esq., continues to discharge the duties of that trust.

In his religious relations, he is a Congregational Christian, having united with a church of that order at Ridgefield, in 1831, and with another in New Haven, in 1833. In 1839, there being no Congregational Church in Galena, he transferred his connection to a Presbyterian Church in which, for eleven years, he served as Ruling Elder, then, removing to Chicago, he united with the New England Church, of which he is now a Deacon.

He married, in May, 1842, Miss Idea Sophronia Strong, of Roxbury, Litchfield Co., Connecticut.

RICHARD BROWN (now of New York), was born in London, Eng., May 10, 1825, the eighth of twelve children. When young Richard was seven years of age, in 1832, his father immigrated to America, settled in Brooklyn, N. Y., and engaged in business as Superintendent of Raymond's fur factory in that city, but in 1836 removed to Mobile, Ala., and engaged in the manufacture of brick; here the family remained until 1840, when they removed to Fort Madison, Iowa. Richard's educational advantages were very limited.

He attended public school during the residence of his father in Brooklyn (four years) only, for at Mobile and at Fort Madison he assisted his father in his business, and had no opportunity to attend school. By his own efforts, however, at leisure moments, he has acquired a good business education. It is worthy of note that, twenty-five years after he attended school in Brooklyn, he visited the same school to secure the admission of his son, and found his old teacher, Mr. White, still in charge. In 1842, his father died at Fort Madison. The death of his mother occurred in the following year, and Richard found himself, at the age of eighteen years, an orphan, dependent upon his own exertions for success in life. On the 6th day of November, 1844, he married Miss Hannah Aiken Bailey, of Boston, Mass.; settled in St. Louis, and engaged in brick making. Here he remained until June, 1846, when, becoming dissatisfied with his location, he visited Galena, Elizabeth, and other townships in Jo Daviess Co., with a view of changing his residence and establishing himself in a new country. The future prosperous merchant had then a capital of $100 in gold, and after a careful survey of the field, decided to locate at a little settlement near Elizabeth, called Georgetown, and bought of William Henry a little shop built of logs, which is still standing, or was two years ago, near Apple River Bridge. Here our young merchant removed with his wife, arriving at their new home about the 1st of July, 1846, and commenced business in a small way, selling provisions to the miners. The young man's strict integrity and attention to the business soon attracted the favor of his neighbors. His trade steadily increased, and he was soon able to add a few dry goods, groceries, etc., to his little stock, until 1848, when his little log store no longer sufficed, and he built a brick store near the old place. During these two years, in addition to his store he had started a brickyard, finding a ready market for his bricks at Elizabeth. In 1849, when gold was discovered on the Pacific Coast, he fitted out his brother-in-law, Joshua Bailey, and sent him to California, and the venture proved partially successful. In 1849 he was elected an Associate Justice of the County Court, and held the office four years, discharging his official duties with marked fidelity to the interests of the people. Prudent and economical in his own business, he carried the same characteristics into his official life, and it was a saying of his associates that "any bill that Brown would approve ought to be paid." In the Spring of 1850 he removed to Elizabeth, and opened a store in the old hotel building known as the "Marshall House," which he purchased the next year. Here he became deeply interested in the common schools, and for several years served as School Director. A new school was needed; the old one had become so dilapidated that it was a reproach. The County School Commissioner condemned it strongly in a newspaper article, but there was a strong opposition to the levy of a tax to build a new one. Mr. Brown was very active in his efforts to secure a respectable and comfortable schoolhouse, and it was largely due to his energy and perseverance that the Directors finally decided to levy the necessary tax. Mr. Brown advanced ten thousand dollars from his own pocket, and the house was built. After considerable delay the tax was collected, and he was reimbursed. He had effected his purpose, and a creditable school building took the place of the tumble-down concern dignified by that name. Mr. Brown was, and is, a man of great energy of character. He was popular with the people, and while he paid strict attention to his business, he took an active part in the politics of the Co., originally as a Whig, and afterward as a Republican; was active and influential in conventions, and some years was a member of the Co. Committee of his party. In 1855 he was nominated for Co. School Commissioner, and while the rest of his ticket was defeated by a majority of 400 to 500 votes, he came within 55 votes of an election. He was also a prominent member of the I. O. O. F. of Elizabeth; was a member of the Grand Lodge for several years, serving as Grand Marshal in 1850. In April, 1860, his wife died, leaving one child, Orville Alonzo, now residing in Brooklyn, N. Y. Later in the same year he sold his business and property in Elizabeth to his clerk, James H. Frazer, and Davis Robinson, and removed to New York, where, in the Spring of 1862, he purchased the scale factory of John L. Brown & Co., prosecuting this new business with his accustomed energy and success for six years. November 16, 1864, he married Miss Emma West, a very superior and amiable young lady, daughter of Samuel C. West, Esq., a highly respectable citizen of Philadelphia. Five children are the fruits of the marriage, viz.: Charles West, Mary Hazzard, Laura, Samuel Coffin, and Albert Oldfield, of whom Charles W. and Laura are no longer living. In 1868 he disposed of his scale manufactory, and early in 1870 Mr. John A. Packard, formerly of Galena, but then of Chicago, and President of the Frazer Lubricator Company, tendered to him the position of Manager of the affairs of the Company in New York, which he accepted, and was soon after elected Vice President of the Company, which position he still holds acceptably to his associates. Mr. Brown now resides in Elizabeth, N. J., honored and respected by all who are acquainted with his sterling worth. He is a devoted Episcopalian, and is a vestryman in Christ Church, Elizabeth.

BENJAMIN H. CAMPBELL was born in King William Co., Va., in 1816. He came to Galena in the Fall of 1835, being at that time 19 years of age. The steamer "Winnebago" (Capt. Laferty), upon which he arrived, was 13 days making the passage from St. Louis. He was first employed in the house of Campbell & Morehouse (George W. Campbell and D. B. Morehouse composing the firm). This store was situated in a log house on the lot which Wm. Hempstead and Edward H. Beebe afterwards occupied as a commission house, and which now stands empty on the levee. Mr. Campbell was married in July, 1837, at Sinsinawa Mound, Wis., at the then residence of Gen. Geo. W. Jones, by the venerable Father Mazzuchelli, to Miss Eliza H. Scott, niece of Gen. Jones, and daughter of Judge Andrew Scott, the first U. S. Judge of Ark., with whom he lived for more than 47 years. Mrs. C. died in Chicago, March 19, 1874, leaving eight children: Annie E., now wife of Gen. O. E. Babcock; Augustus S., Benjamin H., Jr., Mary L., Emily I., A. Courteney, Russella and Jessie. In 1839, Mr. C. purchased an interest in the house of Campbell & Morehouse, with Le Grand Morehouse, and the firm was then changed to Campbell, Morehouse & Co., and consisted of Geo. W. Campbell, D. B. Morehouse, B. H. Campbell and Le Grand Morehouse. In 1841, this firm sold out their entire stock of goods, and closed business, Le Grand Morehouse going on the river as Captain of the steamer "Iowa," running between St. Louis and Galena, and Mr. C. entered into the commission business. Soon after he took in as a partner Myers F. Truett, when the firm took the name of Campbell & Truett. This firm lasted but a short time. Mr. C. changed his business and commenced the wholesale grocery trade, with Capt. Orrin Smith as a partner, under the firm name of Campbell & Smith. This firm was in existence about two years, and after its dissolution Mr. C. carried on the business for a short time on his own account, when he entered into co-partnership with his brother-in-law, J. Russell Jones, who was then his chief clerk and book-keeper. This partnership continued until the business was finally closed up, the trade having been directed to Chicago.

About the year 1850 the old Minnesota Packet Co. was organized by Mr. C., the steamer "Argo," Capt. Wm. Ludwick, being its first boat. The running of the boats of this company proved to be a success financially, not only to the company, but it opened up a large and profitable trade with the river and interior towns of Iowa and Wis., above Galena, and the entire State of Minn. The company also contributed very largely to the development of these states, and was a source of wealth to the merchants of Galena. It was afterwards called the Galena, Dubuque, Dunleith & Minn. Packet Co; then the Northwestern Packet Co., and, a few years later, was merged into the Keokuk and Northern Line Packet Companies, now styled the Keokuk Northern Line Packet Co., running between St. Louis, Keokuk and St. Paul.

On the opening of the Milwaukee & Prairie du Chien R. R., the wholesale business of Galena rapidly changed to Chicago, and several of Galena's heaviest dealers retired from and changed their business. In 1861 the firm of B. H. Campbell & Co. closed out, Mr. Jones having been appointed Marshal of the U. S. for the Northern Dist. of Ill.

On retiring from the grocery trade, Mr. C. purchased the "Jennie Whipple," "Keokuk" and "Kate Cassell," and established a daily line between Davenport and Keokuk, carrying the U. S. mails. He afterwards built the steamers "Keithsburg" and "New Boston," and added them to the line. After operating this line for several years, he sold out to the Northern Line and Keokuk Packet Co., for the sum of $95,000. Mr. Campbell also built in 1859 the first and only steamer ever built in Dubuque. She was called the "Dexter." He also built two barges, the "Annie" and the "Jessie."

Mr. C. was appointed by President Grant, in 1869, U. S. Marshal for the Northern Dist. of Ill., which position he held for eight years. After receiving the appointment Mr. C. moved with his family to Chicago, where he now resides. At present he is one of the largest stockholders in the West Division Horse Railroad Co., of which he is Vice President. He is also a Director of the National Bank of Illinois at Chicago, and of the Union Hide and Leather Co.

Mr. C. was very successful in business in Galena, is a genial, pleasant gentleman, and while he resided in Galena was foremost in all plans tending to advance the interests of the city.

GEN. AUG. L. CHETLAIN (now of Chicago). The subject of this sketch was born in St. Louis, Mo., Dec. 26, 1824, of Franco-Swiss parents, who, three years previous to his birth, had emigrated from Neuchatel, Switzerland, the place of their nativity to St. Louis, *via* the Red River of the North. In 1826 his father moved to the lead mines in the vicinity of Galena, where he engaged in mining and smelting lead ore, following at the same time, to some extent, farming. He received from his parents a common school education. In 1851 he engaged in mercantile business in Galena; sold out in 1859 and went to Europe, where he remained one year. Upon his return he entered actively into the exciting political campaign of 1860, supporting with earnestness the claims of Mr. Lincoln for the Presidency. He was a ready debater, with the rare ability of presenting the grave issues involved in that canvass in a clear and intelligent manner. On the breaking out of the war, and but a few days after the bombardment of Fort Sumter, he enlisted for the war, being one of the first to do so in the Northwest. He assisted in raising a company of volunteers, of which he was elected Captain, and when the 12th Regt. I. V. I. was organized at Springfield, he was commissioned by Gov. Yates its Lieutenant Colonel. In Sept., 1861, he was placed by Gen. C. F. Smith in command of Smithland, Ky., where he remained till Jan., 1862, when he rejoined his regiment and accompanied it as its commander, with Gen. Smith's Division, in the expedition up the Tennessee River. He led the 12th at Fort Donelson, where it acquitted itself with great valor, and sustained a heavy loss in dead and wounded in that battle. For gallantry displayed in this action, Lieut. Col. Chetlain was promoted to the Colonelcy of the regiment, and commanded it at Shiloh, where it was in the thickest of the fight, and lost nearly one fourth of its men in killed and wounded, including several officers. At Corinth his command made a brilliant assault on a much superior force of the enemy, and received very honorable mention from its brigade commander, Gen. Oglesby. In October, 1862, Col. Chetlain was placed in command of the post at Corinth, and remained there until May, 1863, and upon being relieved, was complimented by Gen. G. M. Dodge, District Commander, in general orders, for his faithfulness and efficiency. While there he assisted in raising the first regiment of colored troops organized in the West, north of New Orleans. He was early convinced that the black man could fight, and of necessity must fight before the rebellion was crushed. In Dec., 1863, he received his well-earned promotion to the position of Brigadier General, and at the suggestion of Gen. Grant, the War Department placed him in charge of the movement for the organization of colored volunteers in Tennessee. In 1864 his labors in the fulfillment of this responsible duty extended over the State of Kentucky, and in Jan., 1865, he had in his command 17,000 colored troops. Of this force, one brigade did heroic fighting at Nashville, clearly proving the bravery and efficiency of the black man as a soldier. For his success in this service Gen. Chetlain received the rank of Major General by brevet. Gen. Lorenzo Thomas, Adjutant General of the United States army, in the Summer of 1865, when making his general report to the War Department, speaks of Gen. Chetlain as follows: "Brig. Gen. Chetlain reported to me, and I assigned him as Superintendent of the Recruiting Service in Tennessee and West Kentucky. He proved a most valuable officer, for I found him to possess both intelligence and zeal, with a rare qualification for the organization of troops. He never failed in any duty he was assigned, either as Superintendent or as Inspector, to which latter duty I assigned him, and I am gratified that he was subsequently rewarded by a Brevet Major General." From Feb. to Oct., 1865, Gen. Chetlain commanded the post and defenses of Memphis. From Oct., 1865, to Feb., 1866, he commanded the District of Talladega, Ala., and closed here an honorable and highly meritorious service under the national flag. In the Spring of 1867 he was appointed Assessor of Internal Revenue for the District of Utah, with headquarters at Salt Lake City. After filling this office for two years, he was appointed by President Grant as United States Consul to Brussels, Belgium, repairing thither in June, 1869. He remained in Brussels three years, and resigned the Consulate. Returning home, he took up his residence in Chicago. In the Autumn of 1872 the "Home National Bank" of Chicago was organized, and commenced business with Gen. Chetlain as its President. His career has been a remarkably varied and honorable one. His soldierly qualities, his ability as a tactician, his valor in action, his excellence as a disciplinarian and an administrator, could not fail to achieve for him a high distinction in the profession of arms. He is a gentleman of culture and of most pleasing address.

PHILIP A. HOYNE (now of Chicago), was born in New York City Nov. 20, 1824. He attended public and private schools until 1838, when at the age of fourteen he was apprenticed to the book-binding business with Colton & Jenkins, 144 Nassau Street—in the neighborhood of the newspaper publishing houses at that time. His apprenticeship lasted only about three years. In addition to his book-binding, he gained some knowledge of printing. In May, 1841, he emigrated to Chicago and commenced the study of law with his brother, Thomas Hoyne, who was practicing in that city, and who was City Clerk at that time. [Chicago at that time had only a population of 4,500—smaller than Galena.] Business was so dull in Chicago that on the 19th day of July, 1842, Mr. Hoyne went to Galena and put up at the old Illinois House on Franklin Street. He immediately obtained a situation as book-keeper for Wm. Montgomery, Auction and Commission

Merchant. At the time of the high water in the Mississippi, in 1844, Alexander Montgomery, a brother of William, induced Mr. Hoyne to go with him to St. Louis and take charge of the Wholesale Tea Business, where he remained only six weeks, he having been confined to his bed with sickness soon after his arrival, and which continued all the time he was there. He returned to Galena and again resumed his situation with Montgomery, which he filled until 1845, when he went into the Auction and Commission house of Wright & Sleeper and was afterward and until 1852 a partner of Nathaniel Sleeper, whom all the old citizens of Galena will recollect. Mr. Hoyne returned to Chicago in the early part of 1852, and entered into the real estate business with J. B. F. Russell, in which vocation he continued until March, 1853, when the Recorder's Court was created and he was elected its first clerk. Before the expiration of his clerkship he was appointed by Judge Drummond, in January, 1855, United States Commissioner for Illinois. At that time the whole state was embraced in one district. Mr. Hoyne has continued to hold this position ever since. He was married at Sinsinawa Mound, April 29, 1849, to Teresa C., daughter of the late D. A. French (and sister of John B. French and Mrs. George B. Melville, of Galena). His father-in-law, D'Arcy A. French, will be recollected by our old settlers as a finely educated and pleasant gentleman. Mr. Hoyne has two children living—Wm. A., with Culver, Page, Hoyne & Co., and John T., with J. V. Farwell & Co., and two grand children, Philip A. Hoyne and William M. Hoyne.

Mr. H. was admitted to the practice of law in 1855, but his other duties as United States Commissioner, Member of the Board of Trade, Member of the Board of Education of Chicago, Commissioner of Deeds for all the states in the Union, has been as much as he could well attend to and faithfully, which he has always done. Mr. Hoyne is one of the most genial and popular men in Chicago. He has been for four years and is now member of the Republican State Central Committee, belongs to the Masonic fraternity, is an Odd Fellow, and what is better than either, is regarded by all who know him as a kind-hearted, noble gentleman, and always remarks to Galenians whom he may chance to meet, that he entertains a deep love for the Galena Lead Mine City, where he lived about ten years—the most pleasant period of his life. He weighs about 225 pounds. "May his shadow never grow less."

JOSEPH RUSSELL JONES (Now of Chicago), was born at Conneaut, Ashtabula Co., Ohio, Feb. 17, 1823. His father, Joel Jones, was born at Hebron, Conn., May 14, 1792, and after marrying Miss Maria Dart, the daughter of Joseph Dart, of Middle Haddam, Conn., removed with his young family to Conneaut, Ohio, in 1819.

Joel Jones was the sixth son of Captain Samuel Jones, of Hebron, Conn., who was an officer in the French and Indian war, and also in the Revolutionary war. The latter held two commissions under George II. of England. He returned from the wars and settled in Hebron, where he married Miss Lydia Tarbox, by whom he had six sons and four daughters. Nine out of the ten lived to reach maturity.

From another brother descended the late Hon. Joel Jones, the first president of Girard College; the late Samuel Jones, M. D., of Philadelphia, and Matthew Hale Jones, of Easton, Pa. From a third brother descended Hon. Anson Jones, second President of the Republic of Texas.

The family are now in possession of a letter written by Captain Samuel Jones to his wife at Ft. Edward, dated Aug. 18, 1758. One hundred and ten years previous to the date of this letter, his ancestor, Colonel John Jones, sat at Westminster as one of the judges of King Charles I. Colonel John Jones married Henrietta (Catherine), the second sister of Oliver Cromwell, in 1623, and was put to death Oct. 17, 1660, on the restoration of Charles II. His son, Hon. William Jones, survived him, and one year before his father's death, married Miss Hannah Eaton, then of the Parish of St. Andrews, Holden, Epenton. He subsequently came to America with his father-in-law, the Hon. Theophilus Eaton, first Governor of the Colony of New Haven, Conn., where he occupied the office of Deputy Governor for some years, and died Oct. 17, 1706. Both himself and wife are buried at New Haven, under the same stone with Governor Eaton.

From the foregoing it will be seen that the subject of this sketch is connected by direct descent with the best blood of the Puritan fathers, and came honestly by the virtues which have characterized and adorned his private and official life. His father died when he was but an infant, leaving his mother with a large family and but slender means for their maintenance. At the age of 13 young Jones was placed in a store in Conneaut—his mother and other members of the family at the same time removing to Rockton, Winnebago Co., Ill. This, his first clerkship, gave to his employers great satisfaction. He remained with them for two years, when he decided to follow his family, and seek fortune in the West.

Taking passage on board the schooner "J. G. King," he made his first landing at Chicago on the 19th of August, 1838. From thence he proceeded to Rockton, where he remained with his family for the next two years, rendering such service to his mother as his tender years and slight frame would permit. In 1840 he went to Galena, then the largest and most flourishing city in the Northwest, determined to better his condition, but as his entire available capital amounted to only one Illinois State Bank dollar, his first appearance upon the scene of his future successes was not encouraging. He was glad to accept, at a mere nominal salary, a clerkship, which he filled for about six months, after which he entered the employment of Benjamin H. Campbell, one of the leading merchants of the city, and late United States Marshal for the Northern District of Illinois. His employer, perceiving his superior qualifications, his ready adaptability to the requirements of his position, his imperturbable good nature, self-possession, foresight and sagacity, advanced him rapidly to the position of book-keeper, and finally to a partnership in the business, which was continued successfully and profitably until 1856, when the co-partnership was dissolved. In 1846, while still engaged in the mercantile business, he was appointed Secretary and Treasurer of the Galena and Minnesota Packet Company. In 1860 he was nominated by the Republican party and elected member of the twenty-second General Assembly from the Galena District, composed of the Counties of Jo Daviess and Carroll. He soon became one of the most active and influential members of the Legislature, and was prominently identified with many measures of great public interest, so that his conduct as a representative received the high approval, not only of his own district, but of the whole state.

In 1861 Mr. Jones was appointed by President Lincoln to the office of United States Marshal for the Northern District of Illinois. This appointment required him to change his residence to Chicago, and brought him in contact with other and larger interests than those which had previously claimed his attention. Investing a portion of his means in the Chicago West Division Railway, he was elected president of that company, which position he occupies at the present time. In the midst of his exacting official duties, he found time to take part in various other commercial and manufacturing enterprises, all of which added to his ample fortune, and brought him into notice as one of the most successful and influential men of Chicago. Withal, he discharged his duties as marshal so efficiently and with such satisfaction to the government that, upon the commencement of Mr. Lincoln's second term, he was re-appointed, and held the office till Gen. Grant called him to fill a higher and much more conspicuous position. Mr. Jones was one of Mr. Lincoln's most trusted friends and enjoyed his fullest confidence.

Immediately after Gen. Grant's election, four years later, he nominated Mr. Jones to the senate as Minister Resident at Brussels, in grateful appreciation of his patriotic support of the government's policy during the civil war, in recognition of his services as a member of the National Republican Executive Committee during the political contest which had just terminated, and of his high qualities as a gentleman and citizen. He was confirmed in due time, proceeded quietly to his post accompanied by his family, took posession of the legation on the 21st of July, 1869, and addressed himself at once, unostentatiously but industriously, to the mastery of the situation. One of his first duties was to make an elaborate report upon the cereal productions of Belgium, by order of the state department, and the manner in which he did this left nothing to be required. Shortly afterwards he was called upon to interpose his good offices in behalf of an American citizen who had been unjustly condemned to imprisonment. He did so, quietly and without display, and succeeded speedily in effecting the release of his injured countryman.

When the difficulty arose with Great Britain with reference to the construction of the treaty of Washington, no minister was more active than he in disseminating correct information, and in giving public opinion a turn favorable to our interests. In the final extinguishment of the Scheldt dues he served the government with marked capability and intelligence. He also materially assisted in bringing about an understanding between Belgium and the United States, which enabled them to agree upon the terms of an extradition treaty, and he also furnished for the use of the senate committee on transportation, an admirable report upon the Belgian railways and canals.

Mr. Jones resigned the position of Minister to Belgium, and returned to Chicago in August, 1875. In September of that year he was tendered by President Grant the position of secretary of the interior, which he declined, and was appointed collector of the port of Chicago.

In 1848 Mr. Jones married Miss E. A. Scott, the sister of Mrs. B. H. Campbell, and the daughter of the late Judge Andrew Scott, of Arkansas. She is a most excellent and accomplished lady, and, with her interesting children, gave to the American legation at Brussels an enviable reputation for elegance and hospitality.

JOHN ARNOLD PACKARD (now of Chicago), was born in Denmark, Lewis Co., N. Y., Sept. 2, 1817. His father, Jared Packard, was an honest and industrious farmer, of more than ordinary ability, who left Mass. in 1802, and settled in what was called the "Black River Co.," in York State. He was a lineal descendant of Samuel Packard, who came from England in 1638, and settled in Hingham, Mass., but subsequently removed to Bridgewater. The subject of this sketch received his education in the public schools of his native town, and like most farmer's boys, labored on the farm in Summer and attending school about three months in Winter, until at the age of 18 years he attended two terms of High School at Watertown, and one term at Denmark. In the Winter of 1836, at the age of 19, young Packard left the paternal roof and went to Canada, where he taught his first school at Haldimand, but returned the next Spring and spent the Summer on his father's farm. From this time until 1844 he taught school in Winter and labored on the farm every Summer, except one, which he spent in the school-house.

In the Spring of 1844 he came to Galena, arriving May 6, and engaged in peddling, traveling on foot and carrying a pack and a large tin box, but returned to N. Y. early in Sept. On the 9th of April, 1845, he married Miss Mary Ann Tozer, a very estimable and accomplished young lady of Farmersville, Cataraugus Co., N. Y., and on the 13th of the same month, with their earthly effects packed in a blue chest, an heirloom in the bride's family, started with his wife on their tedious journey to Galena—from Buffalo to Cleveland by steamer, thence by canal to Portsmouth on the Ohio River. Here they took a steamer to St. Louis, and from there to Galena on the steamboat, "Sarah Ann," of which Wm. H. Hooper, since a delegate to Congress from the Territory of Utah, was Captain. On board was a young lady who was on her way to Prairie du Chien to be married, with whom Capt. Hooper fell in love and offered himself in marriage, but his proposal was respectfully declined, and he probably never knew that she was then on her way to meet her intended husband. On the 9th of May, after a tedious journey of four weeks, Mr. Packard arrived the second time in Galena, and settled in the part of the town called Oldtown, nearly opposite the "Old Cooper Shop," where preacher Haines hauled hoop-poles on Sunday thinking it was Saturday, and he engaged in supplying peddlers, sending out four wagons. His entire capital at the time was $350, $50 of which belonged to his wife and was invested in furniture, and his household expenses for the first year amounted to $320, a sum that would hardly suffice to maintain a family a year in these later days. The next year he removed to a small cabin near Hughlett's furnace, and beside supplying peddlers, taught school in that neighborhood. His business increased so rapidly that during the Summer of 1846, he went to New York and purchased a stock of goods on credit. During his absence of nine weeks his wife taught the school, and it is to be remarked that she was the first female teacher employed in that neighborhood. On his return, he made his house serve the double purpose of dwelling-house and store.

In the Autumn of 1847, he moved back to "Oldtown," occupying a new brick building, owned by William Parnell, near "The Convent," and living in the second story. Two years later he opened a store under the old American House, that was burned about 1858, and which stood on the corner of Hill and Main Streets, where Mr. Pratt's store now stands.

Here he engaged more extensively in the wholesale trade, supplying a large number of peddlers and jobbing to the country traders, gradually curtailing his retail business until 1851, when he removed to No. 105 Main Street, a building then just erected by Henry Corwith, and confined himself exclusively to the jobbing business. In 1855 he admitted his clerk, Mr. B. F. Ray, to an interest in his now extensive business, and in 1856 occupied the large new store on the opposite side of the street, built by Peter Marsden. In June, 1859, during his absence in Minnesota, his store was burned, and on his return he reoccupied No. 105 with the remnant of his stock saved from the fire, until the Marsden store was rebuilt, when he returned to it and remained until he retired from mercantile business in 1861, his partnership with Ray terminating in 1860. During the last two years he remained there his business amounted to about $250,000 annually.

In 1863 he went South and rented a large cotton plantation on the Yazoo River, eight miles from Vicksburg. That year cotton was largely destroyed by worms, and his crop was only 300 bales, which he shipped to New York and sold for 80c per pound, the capture of Savannah by Sherman having thrown a large quantity of this staple on the market, and the price fell from $1.50 to 70c and 80c. In March, 1864, the high water prevented planting, and he abandoned the plantation. During all this time armed men guarded the place against rebel foragers. In Feb., 1864, the Confederates made a raid down the Yazoo River and visited Packard's plantation, killing two negroes, stealing ten mules, and capturing a deserter from the rebel army, who was employed by Mr. Packard. The free and somewhat reckless use of Henry rifles in the hands of the little garrison, however, compelled the marauders to retreat with the loss of one of their leaders.

In 1865, Mr. Packard rented another large plantation eighteen miles from Vicksburg, near Haines' Bluff Landing, on the Yazoo River. Employed 300 hands, but it was not a good year for the cotton crop, prices ruled low, and he lost heavily. Becoming disgusted with cotton planting, he returned to Galena in the Fall of that year, rich in experience, and desiring no more of that particular kind.

Early in 1865, in connection with Chas. R. Perkins, he purchased the Grant interest in the Galena Leather Store, and in Feb., 1870, sold his interest in the leather business to Samuel Frazer in exchange for his interest in the Frazer Lubricator Company, and in May following removed to Chicago, where he now resides; acquired a controlling interest in the Company, became its president, and engaged largely in the manufacture of the Frazer Lubricator. Established a factory in Chicago and another in Jersey City, supplying the whole country with axle-grease and exporting large quantities to foreign nations.

Mr. Packard, during his long residence and business career in Galena, was an excellent citizen, and a quietly, energetic business man, enjoying the marked respect and esteem of his neighbors and townsmen. He was never actively engaged in politics, but was elected Alderman from the Third Ward, Galena, in 1858, and re-elected in 1859, serving both terms as Chairman of the Finance Committee, discharging the delicate and responsible duties of the position with credit to himself and the city. In 1861 he was elected one of the Board of Supervisors and served his fellow-citizens acceptably two years in that capacity. Mr. Packard was one of the Trustees of the Methodist Church in Galena, of which his wife was an earnest, consistent and valued member for twenty-five years. During their residence in Galena, eight children were born to this worthy family: George Chester, Felicia Marie, Frank, Ellen Eugenia, Mary Alice, John Elwood, Wm. Howard, and Clara Lillian. Of these only two are now living: Felicia Marie, who married Henry C. Norris and resides in California, and John Elwood, now in Florida.

ABEL PROCTOR (now of Wright Co., Iowa,) Farmer; was born in the Town of Cavendish, Windsor Co., Vermont, March 31, 1800; spent the first fourteen years of his life on a farm, going to school during the winter months; Sept. 14, 1814, he entered the office of the Rutland (Vt.) *Herald*, as an indentured apprentice to the printing business; he remained in that office until March 31, 1821, when he went to school for six months at Chester, Vt., Academy; leaving the Academy, he went to Boston and found a situation in the office of the *Patriot and Chronicle*, remaining there nearly two years, and then went to Richmond, Va., and engaged as a clerk in a boot and shoe store, and on the 5th of July, 1825, started across the mountains for Huntsville, Ala., arriving there some time in the latter part of August; at Huntsville, he made an engagement with the managers of the steamboat Nashville, as clerk, and was filling that position when the boat sunk on the 22d of Feb., 1826, about 60 miles above New Orleans; he returned to New Orleans and went as clerk on the steamboat Tuscumbia, and made one trip to the mouth of the Ohio, where the boat remained until Fall, when it returned to New Orleans, and Mr. Proctor engaged as receiver and accountant of cotton delivered there, having the cargoes of about thirty steamboats to look after; June 16, 1827, he left New Orleans for Galena, and arrived here on the 16th of July, following, and commenced mining, which he continued until 1834, when he commenced farming upon a claim he made near Scales Mound, and where he continued to reside until April, 1868, when he sold his farm there and removed to Wright Co., Iowa; during his residence in Jo Daviess Co., he served the people of his Tp. as Justice of the Peace for two years, and as Co. Commissioner two terms of one year each, in 1836 and 1837; he was also Assessor and Collector for the eastern district of the Co., during 1847 and 1848; he was married Dec. 23, 1831, to Miss Mary Moffat, who was born in Maine in 1806; his wife died May 14, 1865; had ten children, seven of whom are living: Emily, Charles, Catherine, Elizabeth, Mary Ann, George and Henry; has 21 grandchildren at this date (Jan. 30, 1878); his present home and P. O. is Fryeburgh, Wright Co., Iowa.

EDWARD A. SMALL (now of Chicago) was born in Rumford, Oxford Co., Me., Jan. 29, 1829. His ancestors for six generations were natives of the same state, except the first, bearing the same name, who came from England in 1635, and settled at Kittery, Me. All of these generations were tillers of the soil, and the subject of this sketch was, so far as known, the only one of the name and family who became a lawyer. At an early age he was left, by the death of his father, dependent upon his mother for his education and training, and through her aid he was fitted for college, at the age of sixteen. Here his school days ended, and at the age of seventeen he entered a store as a clerk, and thereafter, for ten years, was engaged in mercantile pursuits. In Sept., 1852, he settled in Galena, with no thought of any different vocation; but after four years' experience of its vicissitudes, he abandoned trade, and after a little more than one year's study, was admitted to the bar as a lawyer. From 1858 to 1861 he was associated as junior partner with Hon. W. Weigley, and during that period few, if any, of his most hopeful friends predicted the success he has since so remarkably achieved. But in 1861, his association with Mr. Weigley having expired by limitation, he was cast upon his own resources, and speedily came forward to a leading position at the bar. During the following eight years, and prior to his removal to Chicago, where he has since resided, his success in the profession was unprecedented, even at a bar which then and always had many able members. Intensely laborious in his profession, and devoted to the interests committed to his care, he is now, after twenty years' undeviating pursuit of its exacting duties, in the enjoyment of a practice second to none in the state. Mr. Small has achieved his success in the presence of obstacles which only the most indomitable energy and courage could have surmounted, and these qualities, coupled with excellent judgment and a thorough mastery of his profession, have given him his present position. He is now, and for a number of years past has been, the attorney for several railway and express companies of Chicago, whose large interests require his constant attention. The people of Jo Daviess Co. claim him with pride as one of the many distinguished graduates of the lead mine city, and we have no doubt he regards his former home and friends with an equal affection. Mr. Small was married Aug. 10, 1852, to Mary C. Roberts, of Portland, Me., and has five children, viz.: Mrs. Clara Rebecca Smith, wife of A. P. Smith, Esq., of Chicago; Adelia W., Edward A., Jr., Lora J., and Bessie C. Small.

JOHN CORSON SMITH (now of Chicago), the son of Robert and Sarah Smith, was born at Philadelphia, Feb. 13, 1832. His father is of Scotch descent, and possesses the shrewd, patient industry and sterling integrity of the typical Scotchman. His mother is of the English race, and is a woman of excellent judgment and affectionate disposition. Until his majority the son continued with his parents in Philadelphia, where he acquired such education as circumstances and a busy life would permit, and at the same time served an apprenticeship as a carpenter and builder, and worked diligently at his vocation. After about a year spent in New York and Cape May, he came, in the Spring 1854, to Chicago, whence he removed, a few months later, to Galena, where he fixed his residence. Engaging in business there, he erected many of the most substantial public and private buildings in that city. In 1859 Mr. Smith entered the employ of the government, in the capacity of assistant superintendent of the custom-house building, then in the process of erection at Dubuque, Iowa, which position he retained until 1861, when he resumed business in Galena. In 1862, impelled solely by patriotic motives, he abandoned several large and important contracts, at a great loss, and enlisted as a private in Co. I, 96th I. V. I.; was elected its captain, and subsequently, at an election by the rank and file of the entire regiment, he was chosen major. In October, of the same year, the Regt. was ordered to the defense of Cincinnati, which was then threatened by the confederate forces, where Major Smith was assigned to the command of several batteries. Early in 1863, the 96th was ordered to the relief of Rosecrans, and participated in the second battle of Ft. Donelson; thence was ordered to Nashville, whence, in March following, it marched to Franklin, and engaged Van Dorn. Soon after Maj. Smith was assigned to duty on the staff of Brig. Gen. Beard, a brave and gallant soldier of the regular army, where he served with distinguished ability until he was transferred to the staff of Maj. Gen. Steedman, where he served with conspicuous bravery through the battle of Chicamauga, the storming of Lookout Mountain and Mission Ridge. Generals James B. Steedman and Gordon Granger complimented him for gallant conduct at Chicamauga, and thereupon he was commissioned Lieut. Col., in recognition of eminent services. Assigned to duty by Gen. Rosecrans, upon falling back to Chattanooga, Col. Smith proceeded, in the night, to plant batteries upon Moccasin Point, immediately under the guns of Longstreet, who occupied Lookout Mountain. These batteries were so well placed that, opening fire at daybreak, they soon silenced the guns on the point of Lookout, the second shot of the 10th Ind. Bat., under command of Capt. Naylor, carrying away the rebel signal flag, and making their position untenable. After the battle of Mission Ridge Col. Smith, at his own request, was relieved from staff duty, and took command of his Regt. and the troops on outpost duty at Nickajack Cove, Ga. In Feb., 1864, he commanded the advance in the movement to East Tenn., and was in the action at Buzzard Roost. Subsequently, he was placed in command of the post, and made president of a board of claims at Cleveland, Tenn., which duty he continued to discharge until the opening of the Atlanta campaign, participating in the battles of Rocky Face Ridge, Resaca, New Hope Church, and all others, until, in the battle of Kenesaw Mountain, while in command of the brigade, in repelling a night assault, he was severely wounded, and compelled for a time to seek quiet and recruit his exhausted energies. Though wholly unfit for active duty, he returned to the field in Oct., and took part in the battle of Nashville, after which he was assigned to duty as president of a court martial, and, soon thereafter, of a military commission at Nashville, where he remained until the close of the war. While performing these important duties with marked ability and conscientious fidelity, Col. Smith's urbane manners and kindness of heart won for him warm and devoted friends, not only among the Union people, but among those who, while sympathizing with the fortunes of the South, were competent to appreciate honorable and chivalrous devotion to duty. In Feb., 1865, he was breveted Col. by President Lincoln "for gallantry," and soon thereafter promoted to the full rank of Col., and in June following he was breveted Brig. Gen. by President Johnson "for meritorious services." Patriotism seems to have been a family trait. The father, at fifty-five years of age, shouldered his musket and fought through the entire rebellion as a private soldier. The three brothers entered the army about the same time. Robert fell at Duck River, Tenn., and sleeps in a soldier's grave. Thomas was slain on the bloody field of Resaca. Of the three, Gen. Smith alone survives, and bears in manly silence the constant pain of injuries which nature can never repair. Immediately upon being mustered out of service, at the close of the war, the soldier was assigned to duty as a civilian in the department of internal revenue, with headquarters at Galena, in which department he continued to serve until the Summer of 1872, when the assessor's department, with which he was then connected, was abolished by act of congress. Relieved from the exercise of public trust, he engaged in business in Chicago. Here, again, he was sought out, and Gov. Beveridge appointed him, unsolicited, to the office of chief grain inspector of the City of Chicago, which important and responsible place he filled for several years, discharging its functions with remarkable discrimination, and to the satisfaction of the entire grain trade and the board of railroad and warehouse commissioners, from whom he received the following well merited certificate:

"*General J. C. Smith, Chicago, Ill.:*

"DEAR SIR—Your most excellent official report as chief inspector of grain for the City of Chicago was presented to the board at its session yesterday. It was entirely satisfactory to the board, and I esteem it a privilege, and also a great pleasure to inform you that the commissioners direct me to convey to you their thanks for the able and faithful manner in which you discharged the arduous duties of chief inspector, and to furnish you with a copy of the following resolution adopted by the board:

"On motion of Commissioner Oberly, the secretary was instructed to address a communication to Gen. Smith, formerly chief inspector of grain, embodying the statement that the commission had carefully examined his report, the accompanying documents, accounts and vouchers, and that the same were found to be correct; and, further, that the examination of said accounts show that the said Smith is free from all liabilities or indebtedness to this commission. Yours respectfully,

"M. H. CHAMBERLIN,

"*Sec'y R. R. and Warehouse Comm'n.*

"Springfield, Ill., Nov. 9, 1877."

Upon the expiration of his term of office as chief inspector of grain, Gen. Smith engaged in business as a commission merchant in Chicago. Of the many flattering notices given him by the press, the following, from the *Evening Journal* of Dec. 29, 1877, shows the estimation in which he is held by those who know him best:

"Gen. J. C. Smith, late chief grain inspector in Chicago, has recently commenced business as a commission merchant and opened an office at room 10, 156 Washington Street. Gen. Smith's record as chief inspector is a most enviable one. He brought to the discharge of the duties of that responsible position, not only integrity, industry and a high standard of personal and official honor, but also a rare faculty of clear perception, just discrimination and excellent judgment, and by his administration won the respect and esteem of the entire board of trade. At the close of his term of office, the board of railroad and warehouse commissioners, after a rigid scrutiny, pronounced Gen. Smith's accounts and vouchers correct in every particular, and ordered it so entered upon the records of the board. Gen. Smith's experience and personal qualifications fit him eminently for the prosecution of this business, and he deserves abundant success."

Gen. Smith was also one of the Centennial commissioners from Illinois, and as secretary of the state board of managers contributed largely toward the success of the state exhibit at the Philadelphia Exposition of 1876.

He was married in March, 1856, to Charlotte A. Gallaher, eldest daughter of James A. Gallaher, now living in the Town of Thompson, Jo Daviess Co., who, for many years, held the position of city marshal in Galena. Five children have blessed their union, four of whom still survive—three sons and one daughter.

Politically, Gen. Smith has been, and is, in full sympathy with the principles of the republican party, and an active participant in state and national politics. He was a delegate to the conventions which nominated Gen. Grant for the second term, and President Hayes for his present term. Gen. Smith has been an active and prominent member of the Masonic fraternity, and also of the Odd Fellows. In the former he is a past officer of all the bodies, is an officer of the Grand Commandery, and has received the thirty-third degree, and last degree of Masonry. In the order of Odd Fellows he has received the highest honors. He has filled the chair of Grand Patriarch of the Grand Encampment, Grand Master of the Grand Lodge, and has been three times chosen representative to the Grand Lodge of the United States, and is now Grand Scribe and Grand Treasurer of the Grand Encampment of Illinois, which position he has held for several years. He occupied the position of Grand Master at the time of the great fire in Chicago, and afforded invaluable assistance to the relief committee of that order, and won the highest encomiums of the fraternity, by his energy, zeal and devotion to the administration of that memorable manifestation of charity and fraternal sympathy.

In every position which, in his eventful life, he has been called to fill, Gen. Smith has been successful in the highest sense. He has left an untarnished record and unspotted reputation. As a business man he has been upright, reliable and honorable; as a soldier, brave and chivalrous, yielding cheerful obedience to authority, and exacting strict discipline from subordinates; as a public official, attentive and obliging, but inflexible and unswerving in the discharge of duty. In all places, and under all circumstances, he is loyal to truth, honor and right, justly valuing his own self-respect and the deserved esteem of his fellow men, as infinitely more valuable than wealth, fame or position. In those finer traits of character which combine to form that which we term friendship, which endear and attach man to man in bonds which nothing but the stain of dishonor can sever—which triumph over disaster and misfortune, and shine brightest in the hour of adversity—in these qualities he is royally endowed. Few men have more devoted friends than he. None excel him in unselfish devotion and unswerving fidelity to the worthy recipients of confidence and friendship.

E. B. WASHBURNE (now of Chicago) came to Illinois in the Spring of 1840, arriving in Galena on the first day of April in that year. He had graduated from the law school of the Harvard University in February previous, and had been admitted to the bar of the Commonwealth of Massachusetts. Taking up his residence in Galena, he entered actively into the practice of his profession. In 1844 he was a delegate to the Whig National Convention at Baltimore, which nominated Gen. Scott as the Whig candidate for President. In 1845, though of opposite politics, he was appointed by Gov. Ford Prosecuting Attorney for the "Jo Daviess Co. Court," presided over by the Hon. Hugh T. Dickey, of Chicago. In the same year he formed a law partnership with Charles S. Hempstead, Esq., then, and for a long time previous, the oldest member of the Galena bar. This partnership continued till the election to Congress of Mr. Washburne, in 1852. Mr. Washburne was a member of the Whig National Convention at Baltimore in the Summer of 1852, and was subsequently nominated as the Whig candidate for Congress for the First Congressional District of Illinois. On the 2d day of November in that year he was elected a member of Congress over Hon. Thompson Campbell, his Democratic competitor, by a majority of 286 votes. He was eight times re-elected, making nine terms in all, and for a longer period than any member of Congress has ever been elected in the State of Illinois. His majority in 1860 was 13,511, which was the largest majority received by any member of that Congress. He was for twelve years a member of the Committee of Commerce of the House of Representatives, and Chairman of the Committee for ten years. He was Chairman of the Committee on Appropriations of the 40th Congress. He was the author of the bill reviving the grade of Lieutenant General in the United States Army, and also the bill creating the grade of General in the army, both of which grades were conferred upon Gen. Grant. He was also the author of the bill establishing the National Cemeteries. On the incoming of Gen. Grant's administration he was appointed Secretary of State. After serving in that position for a short time, he was compelled to relinquish it on account of his health, and was thereupon appointed Minister of the United States to France. On the breaking out of the Franco-German War in 1870, at the request of the German Government, and with the consent of his own Government and the acquiescence of that of France, he was charged with the protection of the subjects of the North German Confederation, Saxony, Darmstadt, and Hesse-Grand Ducale in France during the Franco-German War. He was also during that period charged with the protection of the subjects of eleven other nationalities finding themselves in France. For his services to the Germans he received the formal thanks of the German Government, and after his retirement from office the Emperor William honored him by presenting to him his full-size portrait, which Prince de Bismark supplemented by his own portrait, which was painted by the distinguished American artist, Healy. After a service of eight years and a half, and for a longer period than the position was ever held by any American Minister to France, he was recalled by President Hayes, at his own request, in September, 1877, then entering into private life after a continuous public service of a quarter of a century.

ULYSSES SIMPSON GRANT.

Was born April 27, 1822, at Point Pleasant, Clermont County, Ohio. His father was of Scotch descent, and a dealer in leather. At the age of seventeen he entered the Military Academy of West Point, and four years later graduated 21st in a class of 39, receiving the commission of brevet Second Lieutenant. He was assigned to the Fourth Regular Infantry, and remained in the army eleven years. He was engaged in every battle of the Mexican war except that of Buena Vista, and received two brevets for gallantry.

In 1848, he married Julia, daughter of Frederick Dent, a prominent merchant of St. Louis, and in 1854, after having received the grade of captain, he resigned his commission in the army. For several years he was engaged in farming near St. Louis. In 1860 he entered his father's leather store at Galena, Ill. When the civil war broke out in 1861, he was thirty-nine years of age. President Lincoln's first call for troops was made on the 15th of April, and on the 19th Grant was drilling a company of volunteers at Galena. He was immediately employed by the Governor of Illinois in the organization of volunteer troops. In five weeks he was appointed Colonel of the 21st Illinois Infantry.

His first operations were in Missouri. On August 7, he was commissioned a Brigadier General of Volunteers without his knowledge, on account of his peculiar qualifications for the position. On September 1, he was placed in command of the district of Southeast Missouri. November 7, he fought his first and indecisive battle with the enemy, at Belmont. In 1862 he opened the campaign by capturing Fort Henry February 6, and Fort Donelson, with 14,623 prisoners, on the 14th — successes which compelled the confederates to evacuate Nashville and Columbus. General Grant's next success was at Shiloh, April 7, where he defeated Generals Beauregard and Johnson. Then, after inflicting a series of defeats, he drove the enemy into Vicksburg, to which he laid siege, capturing it July 4, 1863, with 31,600 men and 172 cannon—at that time the largest capture of men and material ever made in war. In October, having now become Major General in the regular army, he was entrusted with the command of the military department of the Mississippi, on account of his unprecedented victories in the West. Having driven the enemy almost entirely out of his department, he was appointed Lieutenant General by Congress, March 12, 1864, and was given the chief command of the Union armies.

He proceeded to the Army of the Potomac. On May 5, commenced the sanguinary and undecided battle of the Wilderness, the prelude to an almost daily series of engagements, until June 3, when he was defeated at at Cold Harbor, with heavy loss. He also failed in an assault on Petersburg, on July 30. On the 2d of April, 1865, Gen. Grant compelled Lee to evacuate that city, and followed up his success by bringing about the Confederate Commander-in-Chief's surrender at Appomattox Court House, on the 9th. In reward for his distinguished services he was specially created General of the Army of the United States, and acted as Secretary of War from Aug. 1, 1867, to June 14, 1868. He was nominated Republican candidate for the Presidency May 21, and was elected the following November. Was re-nominated and elected again in 1872. He is now making a tour of the Old World, where he is everywhere received by the Courts of Europe with distinguished honors, due alike to the nation he served so long and so faithfully and to his own wonderful ability as a military and civil leader.

Biographical Directory.

ABBREVIATIONS FOR TOWNSHIP DIRECTORY.

Co	company or county	P. O	Post Office
farm	farmer	prop	proprietor
I. V. I	Illinois Volunteer Infantry	S or Sec	section
I. V. C	Illinois Volunteer Cavalry	st	street
I. V. A	Illinois Volunteer Artillery	supt	superintendent
mkr	maker	treas	treasurer

WEST GALENA.

ABEL JOHN G. wood sawyer.

Abele Geo. farmer.

Adams Frank, plow maker.

Adams Isaac, book-keeper.

ADAMS MRS. SARAH M. Widow of John Adams; residence on High Street, between Franklin and Meeker; she was born in Tyrone, Huntingdon Co., Pa., March 28, 1825; married John Adams in Peoria, Ill., Nov. 7, 1843; Mrs. Adams' maiden name was Sarah M. Evans; John Adams was born in Washington Co., Pa., Jan. 6, 1813, and died in Galena Sept. 30, 1877; he established his plow works in 1847, although he came to Galena in 1845; his sons, Isaac M. and Walter, now conduct the business.

Adams Wm. D. plow maker.

Adams Swansey, supt. Galena water works.

Ahern David, drayman.

Allen Alex. miner.

Allen Samuel, laborer.

Allen Thos. laborer and miner.

Allendorf Phil. miner.

Altona Chas. saddler.

Altona Geo. saddle and harness maker.

Amon Conrad, laborer.

Angling John, farmer.

Annettes Thos. laborer.

Anschutz Henry, laborer.

ARMBRUSTER HENRY, of the firm of Scheerer, Armbruster & Co., Manufacturers and Dealers in Furniture, Upholsterers, Undertakers, etc., 183 Main Street; resides on Dodge Street, between Franklin and Hill; born in Baden, Germany, Aug. 3, 1831; came to Wheeling, Va., when 17 years of age; lived there one year, then went to Cincinnati, O., where he remained one year; came to Galena in May, 1850; Mr. Armbruster learned cabinet maker's trade when but a little over 14 years of age; he married Mary Elizabeth Cawthon in April, 1853; she was born in England; they have three children: Ellen F., Mary L. and Henry C.; they lost one daughter, Elizabeth, who died in 1860, aged 5 years; the family attend the Episcopal Church.

Armbruster John, lead miner.

Armitage Isaac, retired.

Asmus John, wood sawyer.

AVERY GEORGE S. Circuit Clerk; office in the Court House; resides in Guilford Tp., Sec. 33; born in that Tp., where his house now stands, April 16, 1835; engaged in farming until elected to present office in 1876, and still carries on his farm; served 3 years and 11 months; 3 months' service Co. F, 12th I. V. I. in 1861; re-enlisted in Co. I, 3d Mo. Cav.; elected First Lieutenant of same company, promoted to Captaincy of Co. H, same Regt., then Major of Regt.; mustered out as Major March 19, 1865; in all battles participated in by that Regt.; married Miss Elizabeth Little in June, 1863; they have five children: Wm. C., Geo. Wynne, Agnes, E. Florence and Alexandria; the Major is also P. M. of Avery P. O. Guilford Tp.

BACHELOR ROBERT, tinsmith.

Bader Michael, farmer.

BAHWELL ANTON, Prop. of Beer, Wine and Liquor Hall, Franklin Street, near High; resides at same No.; born in Germany, Jan. 17, 1835; came to Galena

May 28, 1857; engaged in present business since 1864; married Eliza Balback Oct. 24, 1866; she was born in Germany; they have five children: Emma B., George A., Edward C., Gustav A. and Bertha; they have lost two children; Mr. Bahwell served 3 years and 4 months in Co. F, 12th I. V. I.; he is a member of Steuben Lodge I. O. O. F. No. 321, and Galena Encampment No. 132.

BAHWELL CONRAD, Merchant Tailor and Dealer in Ready-made Clothing, Gents' Furnishing Goods, Hats and Caps, etc., 144 Main Street; resides on Bench Street, between Hill and Perry; born in Germany Dec. 26, 1822; came to Galena, May 18, 1857; has been engaged in present business ever since—for the last 12 years for himself; married Anna Schauck; she was born in Germany; they have five children living: Anna B. Johnnetta, G. L. Theodore, C. Barbara, and Ida; lost five children; Mr. B. is a member of Harmonia Benevolent Society, Humboldt Monie Steuben Lodge I. O. O. F., No. 321, Galena Encampment, No. 132, Miners' Lodge A. F. & A. M., No. 273, Jo Daviess Chapter, No. 51, and Commandery; he is also a member of the Turner Society.

Baker John, blacksmith.

Baker J. G. clerk.

Baker Matt, wagon maker.

Baker Wm. merchant.

Barker Wm. drayman.

Bardwell O. carpenter.

Barilani Jos. saloon.

BARNER CHRISTOV, Sheriff of Jo Daviess Co.; residence on Prospect Street, between Spring and Gear Streets; born in Germany Sept. 13, 1820; came to New York City Aug. 20, 1850; spent a short time there and at Hartford, Conn., and then went to St. Louis, arriving in that city Nov. 14, 1850; lived there until 1852, when he came to Galena, stopping a short time at Fort Madison; arrived in Galena, June, 1852; carried on merchant tailoring business here until he was elected Sheriff in 1876; he married Lisette Barner July 9, 1851, in St. Louis; they have two children living, William and Louisa; lost three daughters: Lisette, who died in infancy; Amelia, died aged two years and six months; Ottillia, died aged nearly three years.

Barner W. artist and deputy sheriff.

BARRETT RICHARD, Wholesale Grocer, 179 Main Street; residence on Turnpike, one mile from city limits; born in England Dec. 8, 1828; came to Eagle Harbor, Mich., in 1854; lived there until he came to Galena in 1855; engaged in the grocery business in 1856; he has been engaged in the wholesale trade since 1867; was Alderman of the Fifth Ward in 1864; is now President of the Galena & Southern Wisconsin Railway Co.; married Elizabeth J. Truscott Dec. 25, 1853; she was born in England in 1825; they have five children: Thos. T., Mary J., Honor V., Richard J., and Wm. G.; lost one daughter, Lillie, who was born Feb. 7, 1865, died Jan. 13, 1870; Mr. and Mrs. Barrett are members of the M. E. Church.

Barrett Thos. clerk.

Barry J. H. police magistrate.

Barth Jacob, miner.

Barrows D. A. lumber merchant.

Bastian John, plasterer.

Bastian John, farmer.

Bastian John, Jr., farmer.

Bastian Stephen, retired.

Bastian Stephen, Jr., farmer.

Bauer Anton, farmer.

Bauman John, laborer.

Baumberger M. shoemaker.

Baume James, pastor M. E. Church.

Baumgardt John, Sr., bricklayer.

Baumgardt John, Jr., bricklayer.

Beadle John, clerk.

Beaton Matt, merchant.

Beck George, stone mason.

BEDFORD EDWARD L. Attorney at Law; office cor. Main and Warren Streets, over National Bank of Galena; resides on Bench Street, over 93 Main Street; born in Lyne, Jefferson Co., N. Y., Sept. 15, 1844; came to Howardsville, Jo Daviess Co., in the Spring of 1855; in 1857 he removed to Warren, in this Co.; resided there till Nov. 10, 1873, when he came to Galena; he is a graduate of the Law Department of Michigan University, Ann Arbor; was Justice of the Peace while living at Warren; Master in Chancery in Galena previous to election as State's Attorney for this District in 1876; he married Ellie Evans Nov. 8, 1871; she was born in Steuben Co., N. Y.; they have one son, Claude Evans, who was born Sept. 20, 1872.

Beil Anton, merchant.

Beihl Chas. porter.

BELL P. Street Commissioner; office in Market House; resides on Morris Avenue, between Dodge and West Streets; born in Ireland March 17, 1838; came to New Jersey when 5 years of age; lived there two years, then came to Chicago, and lived there until he removed to Galena, in 1854; was engaged in the business of stone and brick mason about eighteen years; has been Street Commissioner two years.

Bench C. wagon maker.

Bench Jos. wagon maker.

BENNET CHAS. R. Resides at Collinsville, Madison Co., Ill.; born in New Jersey Nov. 1, 1807; came to Galena in 1830; was Co. Surveyor fifteen years, Supervisor ten years; Co. Commissioner of Schools two years; one of the Tp. Commissioners who laid off the town; married Maria W. Watson in 1827; she died in 1861; four children living, two sons and two daughters.

Bennet James, miner.

Bennett John, plasterer.

Bennett John C. merchant.

Benninger Fred. clerk.

Benrath Peter, miner.

Berger Anton, farmer.

Bergman C. W. cabinet maker.

Bergmann F. E. retired.

Bergman F. H. cabinet maker.

Bergman H. R. constable.

Berry Thos. farmer.

BERTSCH JOHN, Merchant Tailor and Dealer in Ready-made Clothing, Gents' Furnishing Goods, Hats and Caps, etc., 162 Main Street; resides on Division Street, between Franklin and Hill; born in Germany April 20, 1849; came to this country in 1870; came to Galena in 1872; engaged in present business ever since he came here; married Emma Able in Galena June 1, 1875; she was born in Galena; they have had one daughter, who died in infancy; Mr. B. is a member of St. Joseph Society Galena Sængerbund; Mr. and Mrs. B. are members of St. Mark's Catholic Church.

Bestler Frank, clerk.

Betts John, cabinet maker.

Billon G. P. retired.

Biessmann Ernest, brewer.

Biesman George C.

Birkbeck William, insurance agent.

Birkenmeyer Chas. barber.

Birkenmeyer Fred. brush maker.

Birmingham John, merchant.

BLEWETT WM. H. Prop. De Soto House and General Supt. of the Galena & Southern Wisconsin Railway Co.; born in England Sept. 12, 1835; came to Mineral Point, Wis., with his parents, in 1837; in 1838 they came to Galena; in April, 1851, Mr. Blewett went to California; he was engaged in mining there until 1857; returned to Galena in 1858; married Gramberss Tethers Sept. 12, 1859; in 1860 Mr. B. commenced freighting from Omaha to California; continued in that business until 1871; made twelve round trips across the Plains; he became interested in mining operations here in 1866, during the time he was freighting on the Plains, and has been considerably interested in same business for several years since that time.

Bock Bernhard, carpenter.

Bodell George, laborer.

Boesen Louis, miner.

Bohlen Conrad, gardener.

Bond C. J. plasterer.

Bond H. C. plasterer.

Bond William, painter.

Bonton Aug. farmer.

Bonton A. F. farmer.

Bonton E. M. farmer.

Bostwich F. Dept. Co. Clerk.

Bracken Andrew, R. R. engineer.

Brand Robt. auctioneer and Co. superintendent of schools.

Breen Pat. teamster.

Brehany John, clerk.

Brendel John, Jr., merchant.

RRENDEL JOHN, Merchant Tailor and Dealer in Ready-made Clothing, Gents' Furnishing Goods, etc., 136 Main Street; resides on Seminary Hill; born in Baden, Germany, Nov. 16, 1815; came to this country April 26, 1836; resided one year in New England; in 1838 he walked from N. Y. to Pittsburg, Pa.; went to Cincinnati in 1838; resided there until he came to Galena, March 18, 1842; married Margaret Miller in Cincinnati, Oct. 29, 1839; they have six children: Elizabeth, now Mrs. Joseph Newbergh, of Dubuque; Louisa, now Mrs. Ernst Barthold, of Marshalltown, Iowa; John, Jr., Julia, Hermann, and Rosa; Mr. and Mrs. B. are members of the First Presbyterian Church; Mr. Brendel has been engaged in merchant tailoring and manufacture of clothing ever since he came here; he is a member of Wildey Lodge, No. 5, I. O. O. F.

BRENDEL JOHN F. Dealer in Hats, Caps, Furs, Gloves, etc., 197 Main Street; residence same No.; born in N. Y. City Nov. 16, 1839; parents moved to St. Louis in 1840; his father, John D. Brendel, was engaged in the manufacture of hats and caps there for several years; in 1850 he removed with his family to Galena. where he was engaged in the hat and cap business until 1868; he died in Galena, Dec. 5, 1870; J. F. Brendel has carried on the business alone since 1868; he is a member of Wildey Lodge, I. O. O. F., No. 5, Lead Mine Encampment, No. 5, Saxon Lodge, K. of P., No. 62, and Turner Society; he has been a member of Liberty Fire Company 20 years—two years Fire Director or Marshal; he married Lena Beil, Jan. 19, 1865; she was born in St. Louis.

Brendel Mich. ice dealer.

Briegel John, saloon.

Brinkers John H. retired.

Britton Ben. police magistrate.

Bronk Charles, marble worker.

Brooks J. G. book store.

Brookes J. stationery and book store.

Brown Charles, wagon maker.

Brown Henry, clerk.

Brown H. V. W. wagon manufacturer.

BROWN JAMES B. Editor and Proprietor of the Galena *Gazette*, office cor. Main and Washington Sts.; born in Gilmarton, Belknap Co., N. H., Sept. 1, 1833; is the son of Jonathan and Mary Ann (Clough) Brown; his father represented his Dist. in the Legislature of N. H. for two terms, and was one of the Selectmen of Gilmarton for seven years; he was educated at the Gilmarton Academy, and studied medicine for some time under the preceptorship of the celebrated anatomist, Dr. Wright, but eventually relinquished his studies, and did not graduate; in 1857 he removed to Dunleith, Jo Daviess Co., Ill., and became principal of the school in that town; in 1861 he was elected Co. Supt. of Schools of Jo Daviess Co., and served three years; in 1863 he purchased the Galena *Gazette*, daily, tri-weekly and weekly, and removed to Galena; married Elizabeth Shannon, of Gilmarton, in 1858; they have one child, Abbie M.; Mr. B. is an honored citizen of Galena, a man of recognized ability and energy, and takes a just pride in his profession and in the *Gazette*.

Brown Joseph, U. S. mail carrier.

Brown Simon, blacksmith.

Brown S. S. farmer.

Brown Walter S. farmer.

Brinkmann J. retired.

Brunner P. P. soap and candle manufacturer.

Buhman Henry, upholsterer.

Burgdorf Fred. cabinet maker.

Burgdorf William, laborer.

Burk Michael, laborer.

Burke B. T. teamster.

Burke Francis, teamster.

Burke William, speculator.

BURKHARD JACOB J. Dealer in Guns, Cutlery, etc., 143 Main St.; born in Germany, June 23, 1830; came to Cincinnati, O., in 1852; came to Galena in 1853; has been engaged in present business ever since he came here; is a member of Steuben Lodge, I. O. O. F., No. 321.

BURNS CAPT. THOMAS W. Pilot; Galena; res. on Green St.; born in Boston, Mass., June 11, 1836; his parents emigrated to this Co. in 1842, and Galena has been his home since that; has been on the river as pilot and in charge of boats for 21 years; served as Capt. of Co. C, 45th I. V. I.; did the first recruiting for that Regt., in June, 1861; remained with his command through the sieges of Ft. Henry, Ft. Donelson, Shiloh and the evacuation of Corinth, when ill health compelled him to resign his position; was honorably discharged in 1862; was married to Miss Eliza C. Woodward Dec. 23, 1863; she was born in Pa., Jan. 28, 1843; they have two children: Blanche and Flora W.

BURRICHTER JOHN A. Wholesale and Retail Grocer, 84 Main St.; residence on High St., bet. Hill and Perry; born in Germany, June 13, 1822; came to Galena in 1839; was employed as a clerk until 1844, when he engaged in the grocery business for himself, and has continued in the same business ever since; married Mary Niemann; she died Jan. 20, 1850; present wife was Mary Strothman; married April 27, 1851; she was born in Germany; they have nine children living: Lizzetta, Mary, George, Harry J., John A., Jr., Frank, Adelle, Willie and Louisa; lost three children; Mr. B. was Supervisor one year; he is now largely interested in lead mining with Capt. D. S. Harris.

Burton B. F. miner.

BUTCHER CHARLES L. Dealer in Stoves and House Furnishing Goods, 194 Main St.; res. on Franklin St., near Bench; born in Galena; has been engaged in present business since he was 13 years of age; the business house which he now owns and conducts was established by his father, Robert Butcher, in 1837; Charles L. became proprietor of the business in 1870; he married Lu Emma Holmes, Sept. 1, 1867; she was born in Ohio; they have five children: Myrtle A., Zula E., Blanche L., and Garnett L. and Ruby H. (twins); Mr. B. is a member of the School Board from the 4th ward; Mr. and Mrs. B. are Episcopalians.

Buxton William, clerk.

Byrnes John, bricklayer.

Byrnes Pat. stone mason.

Byrnes Wm. H. lumberman.

CAILLE GEORGE, baker and confectioner.

CALDERWOOD JOHN C. of the firm of J. C. Calderwood & Co., Props. of Livery Stable, 60 Commerce Street; he is also Prop. of Wood and Coal Yard on Commerce Street, north of De Soto House; resides on Bench Street, near Spring; born in Birmingham, Huntingdon Co., Pa., Oct. 11, 1826; came to Galena in May, 1850; in 1851 he went to California, where he was engaged in mining and speculating until 1854, when he returned to Galena; engaged in the livery business in 1855; married Mary L. Laungett Dec. 27, 1856; she was born in Galena; they have nine children living, and have lost two; Mr. C. is a member of Miners' Lodge, A. F. & A. M., No. 273; Blue Lodge, Jo Daviess Chapter No. 51, Galena Commandery K. T. No. 40.

Callanan William, potter.

Campbell Andrew, teamster.

Cannon Pat. farmer.

Campbell James, smelter.

Canthorne George, plasterer.

Carey Thomas, saloon keeper.

Carrol John, grocer.

Cary Edw. traveling salesman.

Cashing Aug. cabinet finisher.

Casserly John, grocer.

Casserly Michael, teamster.

Casserly Michael, Jr., teamster.

CASSERLY N. & T. Grocers and Liquor Dealers, cor. Spring and Main Streets; Nicholas, senior member of the firm, was born in Ottawa, Canada, in 1842, and Thomas, born in same place in 1848; they came to Galena in 1851, accompanied by their parents, three brothers and two sisters; their father was born in Ireland in 1797, he died in 1872; their mother was born in Ireland in 1800, she died in 1875; the eldest brother died in 1877; they are members of the Catholic Church; N. & T. Casserly have been engaged in business here since 1868.

Casserly Peter, laborer.

Casserly Wm., Jr, laborer.

CHANDLER HORATIO H. Dealer in Dry Goods, Boots and Shoes, Hats, Caps, Millinery, etc., 154 and 156 Main Street; residence west side of Mars Avenue, north of Dodge Street; born in England Dec. 4, 1831; came to Galena Sept. 27, 1852; engaged in mercantile business ever since he came here; first wife was Annie Holder; she died July 19, 1874; seven children by this marriage, all living; their names are: Emma A., Frank H., Fanny H., Alice E., Mary E., Edith G. and Grace E.; Mr. C.'s present wife was Emma Shaw; Mr. C. is a member of the M. E. Church; Mrs. C. belongs to the Baptist Church.

Chapin H. M. porter.

Chetlain Fred. farmer and huckster.

Chetlain H. farmer and teamster.

CHETLAIN LOUIS (Deceased) was born in Switzerland Oct. 14, 1795; was married in 1820 to Julia Ombard Droz; she was born in Switzerland Dec. 5, 1799; they came to the U. S. in 1823; settled on the Red River of the North; lived there until 1826, when they came to this Co.; have six children living: Frederic, Augustus L., Adell, Julia, Cecelia and Henry B.; lost four: Louisa, Charles E., Emily and Louis; Mr. C. died Aug. 17, 1872; Mrs. C. still resides on the old homestead where they settled over forty years ago; owns 240 acres of land; P. O. Galena.

Childs A. S. insurance agent.

Childs Irving.

Childs L. W. insurance agent.

CHRISTOPHER HENRY, City Porter; res. cor. Dodge and Wight Sts.; born a slave in Richmond, Va., May 25, 1826; came from Va. to Bellville, Ill., with his master, Samuel Mitchell, in 1831; remained there with Mitchell until about 1839, when he removed to Platteville, Wis., where he remained until 1847; Mr. Mitchell emancipated him when he came to Ill., but he lived with his old master until he was 21 years old; came to Galena in 1847, and engaged with Frink, Walker & Co., stage proprietors; worked steamboating with Capt. Orrin Smith and others from 1849 to 1853; afterwards engaged in the confectionery business; is now a teacher of music and paper hanger; married July, 1848, Mrs. Corinda Howard; they have five children: Margaret, Richard, Virginia, William and Louis.

Clark Joseph, laborer.

Clarke Luke, stonecutter.

Clancey Thomas, laborer.

CLAUSSEN EDWARD, Merchant; Galena; was born in Holstein, Germany, Sept. 11, 1827; March 31, 1853, was married to Julia Seivers; she was born in Holstein July 8, 1829; they came to this city in 1858; was engaged in the grocery and provision trade ever since until last year; have five children living: Agnes, Willie, Conrad, Julia and Caroline; lost four; was Alderman two years; has been Secretary of Steuben Lodge, I. O. O. F., 13 years, Dist. Dept. Grand 6 years, Sec. Galena Encampment 6 years, and Dist. Grand Patriarch 5 years.

Claussen Jacob C. grocer.

Clay Gross, laborer.

Cloran John, grocer.

Cloran John, Jr., merchant.

Cloran John, Jr., grocer.

Clune Dennis, grain merchant.

Clymo Henry, retired.

Coddingham Thomas, miner.

Cogan Henry M. cigar maker.

Coleman C. H. retired.

Collins G. R. farmer.

Comstock, John E.

Comstock Samuel, livery.

COOK CHAS., with L. S. Felt, Estate Management, Dry Goods, etc., 155 Main Street; resides on Bench Street, between Hill and Franklin; born in Philadelphia, Pa., Feb. 23, 1836; was dry goods salesman in Philadelphia until he came to Galena in 1855; has been with L. S. Felt ever since he came here; married Agnes L. Brown, March 23, 1862; she was born in Oneonta, Otsego Co., N. Y., March 23, 1838; they have two children: Frank B., born May 30, 1863; Chas. I., Nov. 14,

1867; Mr. and Mrs. Cook are Episcopalians.

Connors B. F. laborer.

Connors Jerry, cabinet maker.

Cooney Anthony, laborer.

Cooney Mich. laborer.

Corey D. W. agent Singer Sewing Machine Company.

Corrigan Chas. wood sawyer.

Corrigan John, shoemaker.

CORWITH DAVID N. Dealer in Furniture, 258 Main Street; residence on Prospect Street, between Green and Washington; born in Plattsburg, N. Y., April 9, 1834, came to Galena in June 1852; married Celia Chetlain Jan. 18, 1866; she was born in Galena; they have five children: Nettie, Celia, Phœbe, Augusta, Louisa, and John Ross; during the Rebellion, Mr. C. was in Quartermaster Department about four years, nearly the whole time with the army of the Cumberland; he is now City Treasurer; Mrs. Corwith is a member of the First Presbyterian Church.

Corwith H. P. clothing.

CORWITH JOHN E. Vice President of the National Bank of Galena; residence on Prospect Street, between Spring and Gear; born in Bridgehampton, Long Island, N. Y., June 25, 1835; came to Galena in 1857; has been connected with the Bank of Galena ever since; he has also been largely interested in lead mining, shipping and smelting, which business he still carries on.

CRAWFORD JOHN S. Physician and Surgeon, office Main Street; residence on Bench Street, near First Presbyterian Church; born in Ireland, Oct. 18, 1812; spent five years at Dublin College, graduated from that institution; has diplomas also from the St. Louis University of Medicine, and Western Reserve College of Cleveland; came to Warwick, Orange Co., N. Y., in 1837; was engaged in the practice of his profession and drug business there and at Schenectady, N. Y., until 1841, when he came to Galena, where he has been engaged in practice ever since; for 28 years he was a member of the School Board here; he organized the Public Schools in 1844, also organized the City Medical Society in the same year; he was County Physician eight years, several years Health Officer of the city; he is the oldest resident physician now living in the city; he married Mary H. Breed in Sept., 1846; she was born in Boston, Mass.; they have three sons and four daughters; lost one son and one daughter.

CRAWFORD STEWART, Druggist, 131 Main Street; residence Second Street, between Monroe and Jackson; born in Ballibay, Ireland, March 30, 1815; came to N. Y. City in 1837; lived there and at Schenectady, N. Y., in Warwick, Orange Co., N. Y., until he came to Galena in 1840; he was engaged in farming on Sand Prairie, Rice Tp., until 1846, when he went into partnership with his brother, Dr. J. S. Crawford, under the firm name of S. Crawford & Co., and carried on the drug business together until about three years ago, when Dr. Crawford withdrew from the firm, and Isaac F. Moore became a partner, the firm name continuing as before; Mr. Crawford was Alderman of the Third Ward one term; he is a Director of the Merchants' National Bank; he married Jane Ritchie Oct. 26, 1842; she was born near Ballibay, Ireland; they have four children: Agnes, now Mrs. Isaac F. Moore; Letitia Jane, John S., and Wm. R.; lost one son, who died May 12, 1850, aged five years; Mr. and Mrs. Crawford are members of the South Presbyterian Church.

Crawford Thos. H. laborer.

Crawford W. S. doctor.

Cresswell Jas. dentist.

Cromiller Geo., Sr., cabinet maker.

Cromiller George, Jr., cabinet maker.

Crumbacker J. N. painter.

Crumbacker Vincent, artist.

CRUMMER W. F. County Clerk; office in Court House; res. High St., bet. Washington and Green Sts.; born in Sycamore, DeKalb Co., July 23, 1844; came to Pleasant Valley, this Co., when about ten years of age; lived there until Aug., 1861, when he enlisted in Co. A., 45th I. V. I., then being only 17 years of age; served three years in the same Co.; was engaged in all the battles participated in by the 45th Regt. until he was wounded at Vicksburg, July 2, 1863; mustered out in Sept., 1864, as 1st Lieut.; married Martha M. Olney, of Mt. Carroll, in July, 1868; they have one child, Mabel W.; he has served eight years as Co. Clerk.

CUMINGS ALONZO LEE (D. W. Scott & Co.), Editor *Industrial Press*, office 105 Main, res. cor. Prospect and Washington; born in Thetford, Vt., Feb. 21, 1820; removed with his parents to Oberlin, O., then a wilderness, in 1833, and lived there until 1845; was educated at Oberlin; read law in the office of Joseph Olds, Centreville, O., and was admitted to the bar in that state; removed to Savannah, Tenn., in 1845, and engaged in teaching and in the practice of law; married in Iowa, April 12, 1853, Miss Rebecca Chambers; she was born in Va. in 1822; removed to Galena in the Fall of 1854, and practiced law until 1872, when he entered into partnership with D. W. Scott in the printing business, and in 1874 became the editor of the *Industrial Press*; his wife died in Galena Dec 5, 1876.

Currier H. steamboat hand.

Curley Aug. livery stable keeper.

Curley Bernard, farmer.

DARRIGAN RICHARD, porter at court house.

Darst A. C. peddler.

Davis William, carpenter.

Davies William, retired.

DAX PETER, Blacksmith, Franklin St., near German Catholic Church; res. on Franklin bet. Hickory and Division; born in France, Nov. 16, 1831; came to Galena in 1853; worked at blacksmith's trade since he was 16 years of age; is a member of the German Catholic Church, St. Joseph's Society and German Benevolent Society; married Anna Watry; she was born in Germany; they have seven children: Hermann, John, Frank, Christina, Mary, Anna and Emma; have lost three children.

Degnan Michael, farmer.

Deitz Frank, cigar maker.

Deitz Henry, clerk.

DeJeager H. retired; justice of the peace.

Delauney Frank, carpenter.

Delauney Marshall, laborer.

Dellabella Frank.

Demka Mart. laborer.

Dempsey Anthony, laborer.

Dempsey Michael, laborer.

Denio Charles C. mason.

Denny D. M. carpenter.

DeVRY & HOGAN, Grocers; 186 Main St.

Desmond D. B. laborer.

Desmond Daniel, Sr., retired.

Desmond James, laborer.

Desmond John, laborer.

Desmond William, pilot.

Derry Fred. grocery and saloon.

Derry Maurice, grocery and saloon.

Dickson William, retired.

DIETZ VALENTIN, Dealer in Groceries, Provisions, Liquors, Woodenware, etc., also Fire Insurance Agent, 211 Main St.; res. Hill St., bet. High and Dodge; born in Undenheim, Hesse-Darmstadt, Germany, Nov. 14, 1822; married Christina Schnier, Dec. 25, 1851; she was born in Amt Friern, Hanover, Germany, Sept. 9, 1832; they have ten children: Henry V. J., Frank P. S., Benedict A., Mary Ann, Ann Lena, Mary Amelia C., Bertha, Anna J. and Franciska Philomenia; have lost one son, John J.

Dilldine Daniel, carpenter.

Dillon Lawrence, farmer.

DIRNBERGER, JOSEPH, Proprietor of the Mississippi House, 59 and 61 Main St.; born in Bavaria, Germany, July 4, 1830; came to Milwaukee, Wis., in 1848; went to Madison, Wis., in 1850, and in the Fall of 1850 came to Galena; in 1863 went to Col.; to Montana in 1864; to British Columbia in 1865; in 1866 returned to Montana, and remained there until he returned to Galena, Dec. 20, 1873; married Margaretta Gentz in March, 1874; she was born in Germany.

Disch Andrew, scavenger.

Dodds Andrew, carpenter.

Dolan James, deputy city marshal.

Dolan Thomas, teamster.

Donelly Patrick, farmer.

Donnavan J. H. farmer.

Donohue Ed. painter.

Donohue John, Sr., chair maker.

Donohue John, Jr., laborer.

Donovan D. carpenter.

Donovan James, laborer.

Donovan Jerry, laborer.

Donovan Patrick, laborer.

Doolan James, deputy city marshal.

Doolan Pat.

Doolan Tim. farmer.

Doran William, Sr., marble cutter.

Dotschman Louis, farmer.

Douck Fred, farmer.

Downing E. H. rector Episcopal Church.

DOWLING JOHN (son of Nicholas Dowling, deceased, one of the oldest merchants of Galena), born in Galena Jan. 13, 1853; educated at St. Louis University, St. Louis, Mo.

Doyle Owen.

Dreves Louis, laborer.

Drum Simon, chair maker.

Drynen James, bricklayer.

Dubler John C. insurance agent.

Dubois Wm. chair maker.

Duer Anton, flour mill.

Duffin Jno. laborer.

Dufour Aug. gardner.

Dunn John, blacksmith.

Dwyer John, laborer.

Dwyer Michael, laborer.

EBERHARD BERNARD, cooper.

Eckhardt Louis, lead miner.

Edwards G. R. accountant.

Edwards Jas. fisherman.

Edwards R. J. lumber dealer.

Ehles Mich. harness maker.

Ehles Peter, laborer.

Einsen Hans, clerk.

Eiseman Jacob, blacksmith.

Eiseman John, American Express agent.

Eisennacher A.

Engels G. shoe maker.

Engels John, cooper.

Erbe Charles, shoemaker.

Erner Fred, lead miner.

Erner Jos. shoemaker.

Ess John, blacksmith.

ESTEY AUGUSTUS, President Merchants National Bank; residence corner Green and High Streets; born in Mt. Vernon, Hillsboro Co., N. H., March 22, 1811; came to Galena in July, 1836; engaged in lead mining business principally until 1869; has been president of the Merchants National Bank since its organization in 1865; married Julia Monier March 20, 1840; they had five children; have lost three.

Etherly G. W., Sr., painter.

Etherly G. W., Jr., painter.

Etherly Wm. H. painter.

EVANS ISAAC, Retired; residence on High Street near Franklin.

Evans John W. harness maker.

Evans Rufus, plow maker.

Evans Thomas, miner.

Evans Walter, miner.

Evans W. P. merchant tailor.

Eye Christian, teamster.

Eye Louis, teamster.

FABER L. P. cooper.

Faber Matt, cooper.

Fagan John, laborer.

Fagan Patrick, saloon.

Fasseler John, grocer.

FAWCETT JACOB, of the firm of Spensley & Fawcett, Attorneys, Horton Block; residence S. W. corner Bench and Washington Streets; born in Benton, Lafayette Co., Wis., April 9, 1847; came to Galena, Nov. 16, 1869; studied law with Judge Spensley; admitted to the Bar in 1874; served three years and ten months in Co. I, 16th Wis. V. I.; enlisted when but a little over 14 years of age; was wounded at battle of Shiloh and at Atlanta; married J. Doxie April 16, 1868; she was born in this Co.; they have three children; Mr. and Mrs. F. are members of the First M. E. Church.

Fehlenser P., Sr., laborer.

Fehlenser P., Jr., laborer.

Fehlenser Wm.

FELT BENJAMIN F. Wholesale and Retail Grocer, 153 Main Street; residence Prospect Street, between Washington and Green; born in Plattsburg, Clinton Co., N. Y., Jan. 3, 1821; came to Galena in June, 1842; was employed as a clerk in his brother's store until 1846, when he engaged in grocery business for himself, and has continued in same trade ever since; he also buys wool and dressed hogs, which he has been doing for fifteen years; he is a Director of the Merchants National Bank; married Ann Elizabeth Platt Sept. 11, 1854; she was born in Plattsburg in March, 1830; they have four children: Zeph Chas., Ann Elizabeth, Mary B., and B. F., Jr.; they have lost three children, who died in infancy; Mr. Felt and family are members of the First Presbyterian Church.

Felthauer Martin, laborer.

Ferguson George, Sr., retired.

Ferguson George, Jr., grain buyer.

Fickbohm Wm. farmer.

FIDDICK JOHN, of the firm of J. & R. H. Fiddick, Dealers in Dry Goods, Carpets, Boots and Shoes, Furs and Feathers, 156 & 158 Main Street; resides on Prospect Street, between Washington and Green; born in England Feb. 22, 1826; came to Galena in 1841; engaged in mercantile business ever since he came here; in 1850 he went to California and spent two years there; interested in mining there until he returned to Galena in 1852; married Mary Bastian Feb., 1850; she was born in England, and is a member of the M. E. Church.

Fiddick R. H. dry goods. (J. & R. H. Fiddick.)

FIDDICK WM. Retired Merchant; residence on corner of High and Washington Streets; born in England Oct. 16, 1813; came to Galena Nov. 2, 1835; in 1839 he engaged in mercantile business here, which he continued until Jan. 1, 1869; married Phillippi Bastian; she was born in England, and is a member of the M. E. Church; Mr. Fiddick has been a Director of Galena Woolen Mills, and Alderman of the Third Ward.

Figgie Henry, tailor.

Fisher W. S. cloth merchant.

Fisk Steph, sawyer.

Fitzgerald Mich. drayman.

Fitzpatrick Frank.

Flick Chas. chair maker.

Floyd Samson.

Foecke Anton, grocer.

Foecke Wm., Sr., milk dealer.

Foltz Geo. druggist.

Ford Walter, Teller Nat. Bank of Galena.

Foster C. insurance agent.

FOSTER THOMAS, Secretary Galena Woolen Mills; residence corner

Second and Lafayette Streets; born in Carlisle, Pa., Oct. 17, 1817; in 1834 went to Montgomery Co., Tenn.; lived there until 1840, when he moved to St. Louis; remained there until 1843, then came to Galena; was a partner from that time until 1852 with Wood, Howse & Co.; then entered into partnership with Nicholas Stahl, and they continued together until the death of Mr. Stahl in 1876; Mr. F. was Alderman from 1857 to 1860; for three years thereafter he was president of the School Board; he has been an Elder in the South Presbyterian Church from the time of its organization, in 1846, to date; his first wife was Mary Campbell, of Albany, N. Y.; they were married Feb. 27, 1845; died in Aug. of same year; second wife was Cynthia Torode, of St. Louis; married Aug. 31, 1848; she died April 4, 1855; they had three children; lost one son; the living are: Annie H. and Geo. T.; present wife was Mary Lisa Hamstead, daughter of William Hamstead, one of the first merchants of Galena; married June 23, 1861; six children by this marriage; lost one daughter; the names of those who are living are: Mary, Manuel, Augusta H., William H., Jessie M. and Alfred T.

Foster Wm. cabinet maker.

Foster Wm. A. cabinet maker.

FOWLER BENJ. F., M.D. Office in Merchants Bank Building; residence corner High and Wight Streets; born in Steuben Co., N. Y., April 2, 1825; he was educated at Genesee Wesleyan Seminary, at Lima, N. Y.; graduate of Geneva Medical College, class of 1850; practiced in Geneseo, N. Y., from 1850 to 1856; he then removed to Hanover, Jo Daviess Co., Ill., and practiced there until he came to Galena in 1861; was Alderman of the Third Ward three terms, 1872, 1873 and 1875; was Pension Surgeon here from 1862 to 1865, when he resigned; was reappointed in 1874, and still acts in that capacity; he is also County Physician, has held that position for several years—about ten years in all; married Ann A. La Salle Oct. 19, 1853; she was born in Birdsall, Allegany Co., N. Y.; they have five children: Allie M., Annie L., Chas. A., Benjamin F., Jr., and Jennie P.; Mr. F. and family are members of the South Presbyterian Church.

Foyt Geo. plaster.

Fraser Sam, miner.

Frantzer Wm. brewer.

Freel James, grocer.

FRIESENECKER M. Dealer in Groceries, Provisions, Wines, Liquors, Cigars, Tobaccos, etc., 120 Main Street; resides on corner Decatur and Third Streets; born in Germany, Sept. 5, 1834; came to Galena in 1852; he is Supervisor of East Galena Tp.; he is a member of German Catholic Church and of the German Benevolent Society; married Margaret Yunker Nov. 12, 1861; she was born in Germany; they have four children living: Philip, Josephine, Anna and Paul; lost one daughter.

FRENCH JOHN B. City Clerk; born in Charles Co., Md., Dec. 12, 1820; he taught school in Maryland five years, and was engaged in mercantile business there one year; came to Galena in May, 1849; from June, 1849 to 1860 he was with Nicholas Dowling in hardware business; after the death of Mr. Dowling, in 1860, he continued to assist the estate in conducting the business until 1862, when he engaged in same business for himself and carried it on until 1871; in 1870 he was elected City Treasurer, and held that position until Aug., 1877; he also acted during the same period as City Clerk, *pro tem*, with the exception of two or three short intervals; in Aug., 1877, he was appointed City Clerk; married Mary L. Jones, Feb. 9, 1847; she was born in St. Mary's Co., Md.; she died Sept. 12, 1863; they have five children living: Wm. T., Eugene E., Mary H., Josephine C. and Walter H.; lost three; Mr. French's present wife was Mary J. Delahunt; they were married Jan. 18, 1865; she was born in Ireland; two children by this marriage, Caroline M. and Chas. H.; Mr. and Mrs. F. are members of the Catholic Church.

French Henry.

Fricke Chris, miller.

Fricke Henry, retired.

FRITZ JOHN, Proprietor of Sash, Door and Blind Factory, corner Perry and Water streets; residence on Third Street, corner Adams; born in Germany Feb. 4, 1823; came to Galena in 1846; worked at cabinet making business twenty-three years; engaged in present business in 1873; married Regula Blumer Oct. 14, 1847; she was born in Switzerland; they have three children: Susan Louisa, John, Jr., and Mary; lost two children; Mr. Fritz is a member of Harmonia Benevolent Society.

Fuchs John, Sr., cigar maker.

Fuchs John, Jr., cigar maker.

Fuchs Peter, cooper.

Fuller G. W. retired.

Furry Phil. fisherman.

GARNER JOHN, carpenter.

Garner Robert, retired.

Gallagher John, Sr., merchant tailor.

Gallagher John, Jr., clerk.

Gallagher Wm. farmer.

Galvin Dennis, school trustee.

Gehinnger Anton, farmer.

Geiger Chas. stone mason.

Geiger Gottleib, clerk.

Geiger John, cooper.

Geiger Martin, carpenter.

Geigler Martin, saloon keeper and carpenter.

Genty Henry, farmer.

Genz Geo. merchant.

Genz John, cigar maker.

Gibson Wm. saddler.

Ginn James, farmer.

Ginn Johnson, retired.

Ginn Wm. smelter.

GIRDON CAPT. GEO. W. Chairman of the Local Board of U. S. Inspectors of Steam Vessels, office in Custom House; residence on Bench Street; born in Philadelphia (of Prussian parentage) May 31, 1814; educated in Philadelphia as a physician; came to Galena in April, 1835; clerked for Col. A. G. S. Wight a few months; then became Captain of the steamboat Heroine, running between Galena and St. Louis; was commander of various steamboats for many years; he is the oldest living steamboat man on the Upper Mississippi, having been in that service forty-three years; he has been fourteen years in government service at this point; was for many years considerably interested in mining business in this vicinity; married Charlotte Maria Gear, daughter of H. H. Gear, June 14, 1838, at house of Hon. Edward Langworthy, in Dubuque; ceremony performed by Chief Justice Dunn of Wisconsin; they have five children: Mary Catherine (now Mrs. Edward Tomlin), Charlotte Augusta (now Mrs. J. Q. Gilbert of Sioux City, Iowa), Maria Therese, Erzsie and Ann Elizabeth; Capt. Girdon and family are members of the Episcopal Church.

Gladden Douglas, fruit and groceries.

Gloeckner Constantine, tailor.

Godat G. A. miner.

Gorman John.

Gorman Thomas, grocer's clerk.

GORMAN THOMAS W. (of the firm of Isaac Kelly & Co.), Dealer in Groceries, Provisions, Flour and Feed, 190 Main St.; res. Bench St., cor. Morrison's Alley; born in Galena Sept. 12, 1841; is a member of the Catholic Church.

Grace James, laborer.

Graham William, cabinet maker.

GRATIOT HENRY (deceased). Among the earliest and most prominent and enterprising early settlers of the Upper Mississippi Lead Mines was Colonel Henry Gratiot. Though born in St. Louis, he was of Huguenot descent, his ancestors having been driven out of France at the time of the Revocation of the Edict of Nantes. His father, Col. Chas. Gratiot, was born in Neuchatel, Switzerland, and emigrated to the United States before the revolution. Early espousing the cause of the colonists, he embarked his services, influence and large fortune in their cause. After the close of the war the American Government granted to him a large tract of country in the State of Ky., but to which he never made any claim. Settling subsequently in the little French Village of St. Louis, he became one of the band of enterprising Frenchmen who laid the foundations of that wonderful city, now numbering a half a million of people. His son, the subject of this notice, Col. Henry Gratiot, arriving at manhood, and revolting at the institution of human slavery which had been fastened upon the State of Missouri, determined to seek a home for himself and family in a state where that baleful institution did not exist. The discovery of lead ore which had been made at Fever River, had brought the Upper Mississippi country into notice, and, in 1826, he determined to move thither. He commenced smelting in the ravine, a short distance from Galena, through which the Savanna road now runs. Interesting himself afterwards in the mineral lands in the region of where Shullsburg, Wis., now stands, and purchasing from the Indians the right to mine for lead ore in their country, in company with his brother, John P. B. Gratiot, he established himself in smelting at what soon became known as "Gratiot's Grove," Wis. Territory, and some fifteen miles northeast of Galena. Here, for several years, the two brothers did an immense business in mining, smelting and merchandizing. At one time they had no less than nine log furnaces in operation, and did nearly all the smelting for the whole mining country. No men in the Upper Mississippi Lead Mines were ever more respected than the Gratiots, and their names were everywhere the synonym of probity, honor and business integrity. Uniting to the frankness and generosity of Western men the intelligence, suavity and polish of the highest type of the French gentleman, their names and their careers will ever be associated with all that is most agreeable in the early settlement of the Galena mines. Col. Henry Gratiot died suddenly at Baltimore in 1835. Two of his sons, Col. Charles H. Gratiot and Lieut. Col. Edward H. Gratiot, late paymaster in the volunteer service of the United States Army, live in Wis. Another son, Henry Gratiot, resides in Cal. His only surviving daughter is the wife of Mr. E. B. Washburne, ex-Member of Congress for eighteen years from the Galena district, ex-Secretary of State and ex-Minister to France. John P. B. Gratiot emigrated from Galena to the Richwood lead mines in Missouri in 1842, and died a few years since, when a member of the lower house of the Missouri State Legislature.

Graves J. laborer.

Gray Charles, farmer.

Green John E. painter.

Green William, carpenter.

Griffith Geo. G. engineer.

Griffith James G. retired.

Grimm Chas. wagon maker.

GRIMM LOUIS, of the firm of L & C. Grimm, Manufacturers of Wagons, Carriages, Buggies, Sleighs, Cutters, etc., Franklin Street corner High; resides on Dodge Street near Meeker; born in Prussia July 11, 1844; came to Galena in 1853; he has worked at wagon maker's trade since he was fourteen years of age; married Louisa C. Judd Sept. 22, 1870; she was born in Germany; they have two children; Frederick M. and Bertha C.; they have lost one son; Mr. G. was in Quartermaster's Department, Army of the Cumberland, about ten months; he is a member of Wildey Lodge I. O. O. F., No. 5., and of Galena Encampment No. 5.

Gross Chas. carpenter.

Gross Richard, laborer.

Gross Richard, Jr., butcher.

Gronner Fred, farmer.

Grunner Louis, farmer.

Grumme Chas. saddler.

GRUMME JULIUS, Harness Maker, 246 and 248 Main Street, corner Franklin; residence same numbers; born in Germany April 6, 1826; came to Philadelphia in 1847; went to Pittsburg the same year; lived there about one year and a half; went to Virginia then, and came to Galena in 1850; he has been in harness business since 1852; he married Olive Stebbins March 23, 1852; she was born in Mantua Tp., Portage Co., Ohio, April 28, 1833; they have six children: Almira Inez, Charles J., Wm. Fred, Frank, Arthur and Harry; they have lost two daughters; Mr. and Mrs. G. are members of the M. E. Church.

Guitter Christian, tailor.

Gundry Wm. retired miner.

HAASE JOHN, stone mason.

HAASE EDWARD, Dealer in Dry Goods, Boots and Shoes, etc., 172 Main Street, corner Hill; residence on High Street between Washington and Warren; born in Germany Jan. 29, 1835; came to Galena in the Spring of 1850; he has been engaged in his present business for the last ten years; married May A. Schaefer in Aug., 1857; she was born in Germany; they have four children: Gilbert E., Henry C., John Wesley and Eva M.; they have lost two sons; Mr. H. is a member of the German Methodist Church, Harmonia Benevolent Society, Steuben Lodge I. O. O. F. No. 321, and Lead Mine Encampment No. 5.

Habich Aug. grain buyer.

Hagus Jos. tailor.

Haele A. C. brick layer.

HAINES ANDREW M. Fourth son of Joseph and Martha G. (Dwinnell) Haines; was born in Canterbury, N. H., Jan. 1, 1820, and is the sixth in lineal descent from Deacon Samuel Haines the emigrant ancestor of the "New Hampshire family of Haines," who came from England in 1635, and settled at Portsmouth, N. H.; he received his education first in the District Schools and Gilmanton Academy, N. H., and lastly at the Salem, Mass., High School; in the year 1832, at the age of twelve years, he entered as a clerk the counting room of Charles C. Currier, Esq., a Salem merchant and ship owner, engaged in the trade of the West Indies, where he received the rudiments of mercantile life; on Aug. 13, 1839, he arrived from Lynn, Mass., at Galena where his elder brother, Sylvester Henry, had preceded him, and on the 11th of May, 1840, commenced business and was in active mercantile business for over twenty years, the last eight of which were engaged in the up-river wholesale trade, and during the past thirteen years has been connected with the Lead Smelting House of Hughlett & Co.; was Treasurer of the city for three years, 1846–'9; in Religion is a Presbyterian, and a member of the First Presbyterian Church since 1844; in 1866 was elected a corresponding member of the "New England Historical Genealogical Society," at Boston, Mass., and in 1869 a member of the "State Historical Society of Wisconsin;" was married at Lynn, Mass., Aug. 17, 1842, to Angeline Elizabeth, daughter of John and Sarah (Allen) Woodbury of Lynn, Mass., who was born at Ludlow, Vt., May 15, 1822, and by whom he has had seven children, of whom four survive: Flora A., born Aug. 18, 1852, and married Nov. 4, 1874, to Geo. E. Woodbury of Cambridge, Mass.; Sam'l A., Jan. 16, 1854, now of Boston, Mass.; Andrew M., March 9, 1861; Martha D., July 26, 1864.

Halbig C. wagon maker.

Hale Chas. E. bookkeeper.

Hanbery Thos. laborer.

Hand Cyrus, shoemaker.

Hanft Andrew, retired.

Hanft Casper, miner.

Hanlon John, laborer.

Hanneman Chris, farmer.

Hansen M. W. farmer.

Hart Alex. plow maker.

Harney Daniel, drayman.

Harney Patrick, Sr., farmer.

Harney Thomas, grocer and saloon.

Harrington Patrick, laborer.

HARRIS CAPT. DANIEL SMITH, Capitalist; son of James Harris, who was born in Conn., Oct. 14, 1777, and died in Galena, Ill., Oct. 10, 1829; his mother, Abigail Bathrick, was born in Delaware Co., N. Y., March 24, 1782, and died at Galena, Ill., July 9, 1844; these two were married in Delaware Co., N. Y., Nov. 9, 1797; he was born in Courtright, Delaware Co., N. Y., July 24, 1808; parents moved to Cincinnati in 1816; the Capt. and his father, James Harris, left Cincinnati April 20, 1823, on a keel-boat, (the "Col. Bumford") and came to Galena, the entire distance with that boat, which was loaded with provisions and mining outfits to the extent of 75 or 80 tons; they arrived here June 20, 1823; the Capt. married Sarah Maria Langworthy in Galena, May 22, 1833; she was born in the State of N. Y. Feb. 17, 1811, and died on the Island of Cuba Jan. 25, 1850; she was a daughter of the late Dr. Stephen Langworthy, of Dubuque, Iowa; they had five children, all now living: Lorinda Maria, born in Galena Jan. 9, 1835, and married Jonathan Dodge Feb. 22, 1855; Amelia, born in Galena Aug. 10, 1837, and married I. Francis O'Farrell, in Galena, Dec. 8, 1857; Mary Ann, born in Galena Sept. 20, 1839, and married Thomas J. Maupine, in Galena, March 7, 1861; Medora, born in Galena, Sept. 3, 1841, and married, in the same place, Charles T. Trego, of Chicago, May 14, 1863; Daniel Smith Harris, Jr., born in Galena, Sept. 13, 1843, and married Miss Kittie Ott, Eureka, Nev., April 19, 1874. Capt. Harris' present wife was Sarah Coates, daughof Samuel and Margaret Cherington Coates; she was born in Calu Tp., Chester Co., Pa., March 7, 1824; they were married Aug. 25, 1851; have had seven children, two of whom died in infancy; those now living are: Wenona, born Nov. 5, 1853, and married in Galena to John V. Hellman, Sept. 12, 1872; Ernestine, born in Galena Jan. 22, 1857; Irene, born same place Jan. 15, 1860; Anna, born same place Dec. 20, 1865, and Paul Cherington, born same place Aug. 11, 1868; Capt. Harris was a Lieut. in the U. S. A. at the time of the Black Hawk War, and commanded a company at the battle of Wisconsin Heights; is the oldest living settler in this section of the western country.

Harris Ed. miner.

HARRIS JAMES M. Wholesale and Retail Grocer, No. 177 Main St., Galena; born in Xenia, O., Jan. 4, 1823; came to this Co. in 1824; has been a permanent resident of this Co. since; his education was commenced at the age of six in a select school, where he spent ten years; he was then sent to Kemper College, St. Louis, Mo., where he finished his education; returned to Galena and entered the wholesale grocery and boat store business with the firm of D. S. & R. S. Harris; remained one year, when the firm dissolved, and he entered into a partnership with the junior member of the old firm, under the name of R. S. Harris & Co.; was the oldest house of the kind in Galena; was in the business from 1845 to 1864; had the credit of having the finest boat store on the Mississippi River, from New Orleans to St. Paul; the firm dissolved in 1864, and he retired to his farm, where he resided till 1872; returned to his residence in Galena, living in the retirement of his home in the city till 1877, when he resumed the wholesale and retail grocery business at his present location; was married in 1847 to Miss Louisa F. Stouffer; have two children living: Lyndley I. and Belle; lost two children in infancy, and a daughter at the age of 16; Mr. H. has always been a practical business man, enjoying the confidence and respect of all with whom he has been associated; is no aspirant to office, but was brought out and elected Alderman in the place of a very worthy and popular gentleman who had not been defeated for 29 years; was appointed by the City Council to go to Washington in the interests of the Galena River improvement, and succeeded in getting a survey by the government; was interested in the first line of boats that made regular trips up the Wisconsin River; also the first that ascended the Minnesota as far as Mankato, and the first that carried the mail to St. Paul.

Harris Lynn I. book-keeper.

Harris Sam.

Harris Stephen, photographer.

Harris William, laborer.

HART JOHN, Dealer in Wines and Liquors, 213 Main St., resides at same No.; born in Toronto, C. W., March 20, 1838; came to Galena in May, 1865; married Mary A. Harrington, Jan. 31, 1872; she was born in Galena; they have three children: Alice A., Ellen and James P.; Mr. H. and family are members of the Catholic Church.

Hartig John, chair maker.

Hartwig August, shoe maker.

Hartwig Charles, laborer.

Hartwig William F. farmer.

Haser Jacob, retired.

Haser Joseph, brewer.

Haslin Jo. farmer.

HASSIG JOHN J. Proprietor Lawrence House, cor. Commerce St. and Market Square; born in Germany Nov 26, 1838; came to Galena in 1845; has been Alderman of the 4th Ward; married Mary

Hewey, March 18, 1869; she was born in Galena; they have two children living: George and William; lost one child.

Hatherell Solomon, insurance agent.

Hawkings William, farm laborer.

Hayes Samuel, principal high school.

HEID FRANK, Superintendent Gas Works; resides at the Works; born in Bavaria, Germany, Feb. 24, 1824; came to America in 1852; lived in Louisville, Ky., until 1856; then moved to Rock Island, and lived there until 1862, when he came to Galena; married Louisa Schrader, Jan. 1, 1855; she was born in Hanover, Germany; they have seven children living: John, Mary, Frank, Joseph, August, Cleary and Francis; lost one daughter; Mr. H. and wife are members of the German Catholic Church.

Heit Leopold, city sexton.

Heider John, wood boatman.

Heller Chas. cigar maker.

Heller Richard, cigar manufacturer.

HELLER & BIESMAN, Wholesale and Retail Dealers in Cigars and Tobacco, Main Street.

Hellman August, conductor G. & S. W. R. R.

HELLMAN JOHN H. Wholesale Grocer, 130 Main Street; residence on Prospect Street, between Hill and Perry Streets; born in Hanover, Germany, Sept. 23, 1823; parents came to Lee Co., Iowa in 1835; Mr. H. removed to Galena in April, 1842; he has been in the grocery business since the Spring of 1844; married Christina Repohl April 23, 1845; she was born in Prussia; they have six children: Mary F., now Mrs. Wm. Stoltebehn, of Dubuque; John B., August J., Lena, now Mrs. J. H. Swartz, of Fort Madison, Iowa; Henry B. and Frank.

Hellman John V.

Hellstern Thos. saloon.

Hellstern Val, tinner.

HEMPSTEAD CHARLES S., Born Sept. 10, 1794; died Dec. 10, 1874. For the leading events in the life of Charles S. Hempstead, liberal extracts have been made from an "historical and biographical sketch," prepared by Mr. E. B. Washburn, dated Jan. 15, 1875, and addressed to the President of the Early Settlers' Association of Jo Daviess Co. Mr. Washburn had known Mr. H. for a period of about 35 years, and during all that time, somewhat more than a generation, the relations existing between them were of marked personal esteem, respect, and steadfast confidence in each other's integrity and ability. During eight of those years they were associated as partners in the practice of the law, and in professional business as well as social relations, no one was more intimately acquainted with Mr. H., and no one so well qualified to pay the tribute of respect and esteem which Mr. Washburn has so ably and faithfully placed on record in the historical annals of Jo Daviess County.

Chas. S. Hempstead was born at Hebron, Tolland Co., Conn., Sept. 10, 1794. He was the son of Stephen Hempstead, whose life deserves to be noticed as a worthy preface to that of his son. The ancestors of Stephen were among the first settlers of New London, Conn. On the breaking out of the Revolutionary War, Stephen, then only 22 years of age, joined the Patriot Army, and was with the first troops assembled at Boston, after the battle of Lexington. He served with arduous zeal, until, being incapacitated by the numerous wounds received in battle, he retired to private life shortly before the surrender of Cornwallis. Long ere he was restored to the robust health with which he entered the service, a new era had opened. His country was free; his blood had contributed to make her so; and now his care was to provide for a young family, with the only means within his power, viz.: the labor of a body enfeebled and broken by a multitude of wounds. An ordinary man would have called to his aid each successive son, as he became old enough, to the labor of the farm. But a noble resolution had been formed in the mind of him who had fought for liberty. In the successful issue of the struggle he saw the field of honor and of preferment thrown open under that banner. Talent, industry, and integrity, and not hereditary right were now to claim the highest prizes in the Republic. To acquire any of the great gifts which were within the grasp of all who labored and sought for them, Knowledge must be the lever, the power, to elevate, and Education the fulcrum on which the lever was to be placed. With this object in view, he determined that each nerve should be strained, economy practiced, and every force brought to bear that his children should accumulate all the advantage which carefully directed study would bring to them, and nobly he carried out his idea by giving to each of his children the very best educational advantages that New England afforded. Charles S. Hempstead attended the New London Academy until his 16th year, receiving all the advantages it could bestow. Then feeling that there was a larger sphere of usefulness for him beyond the limits of his native state, he resolved to seek a new field of labor—to go to that great West to which his elder brother, Edward, had emigrated in years before—to the new land that the Louisiana purchase had brought in, with so much of future promise. His brother had been successful, was honored, appreciated and rewarded with every gift within the bestowal of the people. He invited Charles to join fortunes with him. Accordingly, with his brother Thomas, he left New London in a schooner bound for Alexandria, Va., and reached there in the latter part of August, 1809. From this point they traveled by wagon through Winchester and Romney to Clarksburg, W. Va., thence to Marietta, Ohio. This was before the day of the steamboat or the railroad car—then, the Ohio was navigated by keel, flat-boat, or canoe. The river was too shallow in this season for either of the two former, so the latter was the only alternative. The brothers bought a canoe at Marietta, laid in the necessary supply of provisions, and started for Shawneetown, Ill., which was the landing point for foot passengers bound for St. Louis. Here they arrived in October, and being unable to obtain conveyance of any kind, they walked by way of Kaskaskia to their point of destination, over 150 miles, and reached their brother's residence, tired, weary, and footsore. Mr. H. at once entered his brother Edward's office, as a law student. At that time St. Louis had a population of only about 1,500 souls, of whom not more than sixty families were English speaking. There was not a house or chimney of brick in the town. The habits, manners, and language were all as thoroughly French as those of any provincial village in France. After pursuing his studies until Sept. 13, 1814, he was admitted to the practice of law in the Territory of Missouri, by a license dated at St. Charles, Mo., signed by Alex. Stewart and John D. Lucas, Judges of the Supreme Court of Mo. Ter. About the same time he received his license to practice law in the Territory of Illinois, signed by J. B. Thomas and Stanley Griswold, Judges of the District Court of said territory. One year after his admission to the Bar he was appointed Attorney for the Southern Circuit Court of Missouri by the then Governor of Missouri Territory, and removed to St. Genevieve, and entered there upon the practice of his profession. St. Genevieve was as completely a French settlement as St. Louis, with all its characteristics as to inhabitants and social life. Here he remained until 1817, when, in consequence of the death of his brother Edward, he returned to St. Louis to take charge of his legal business and the settlement of his estate. In 1818 he was elected to fill a vacancy in the Missouri Legislature, which was the only legislative position he ever held—not from want of opportunity, but from a decided aversion to political life. He could not and would not stoop to the means which make political preferment easy, but preferred to hold his honest opinions unbiased and untrammeled, rather than sacrifice his dignity, independence and honesty of character for the temporary success which a short hour of office would bring.

During his residence in Missouri he was the associate of many of the most distinguished men of his time, all of whom respected and esteemed him in the highest degree. In the year 1829 he was induced to remove to Galena. Large discoveries of lead ore had been made, and the tales of the fabulous mineral wealth in that vicinity were attracting thousands of emigrants. To a man of his ability, character and business habits it offered a splendid opportunity. From that time until his decease he was a resident of Galena.

In the Summer and Fall of 1829 he was secretary of the commission composed of Gen. John McNeill, U. S. A., Caleb Atwater and Col. Pierre Menard, which treated with the Pottawattomie and Winnebago Indians at Prairie du Chien, then in the Territory of Michigan. In the same year he was appointed by Gov. Cass of Michigan Territory District Attorney for the Eleventh District of said territory. He was re-appointed to the same office in 1834 by Gov. T. Mason, but he declined the appointment. The courts he then attended were held at Prairie du Chien and Mineral Point. The journey over the circuit was made on horseback, the hotel accommodations meagre and uncomfortable; hardships many; fees few and not at all commensurate with the labor and dangers of the journey.

In 1833 he was present at Chicago when the treaty was made by Gov. Porter of Michigan with the Pottawattomies; an occasion long to be remembered for the thousands of Indians there assembled at the treaty grounds on the north side of the river, near what is now Rush and Illinois Streets.

In 1841 Galena was incorporated as a city, and Mr. H. was honored by being elected the first mayor. Desiring to be useful to his country in its hour of peril, at the outbreak of the Rebellion he accepted the office of Paymaster in the army, voluntarily tendered by his old-time friend Mr. Lincoln, who knew and appreciated his sterling merit. No officer ever served more faithfully or more satisfactorily than he did up to the close of the war. He was one of the most public-spirited of men, always first and foremost in every enterprise which affected the general interest, and ever ready to contribute time and money to advance public prosperity. He was one of the most prominent in that great pioneer enterprise, the Galena & Chicago Union R. R., of which he was Director in the first board, and served in that capacity for many years.

At the Bar Mr. H. was regarded as an able lawyer; a man of sound legal judgment and the highest professional honor. He was not a fluent speaker, but his addresses to the jury were always effective, for his high and dignified character added to his forcible presentation of the case. His intercourse with the Bar and Bench was always marked by the utmost dignity and courtesy; and no man ever saw him betrayed into any wrangle with the opposing counsel or the court when trying a case. He was never a promoter of litigation, never made the court of justice an engine of oppression, or used it as a weapon to further his own ambition and gratify personal malice or spite; but on the other hand he endeavored, whenever it was possible to harmonize disputes without resorting to the courts.

But it was as a citizen and in private life that the virtues of Mr. H. shone out most conspicuously. Associating himself early with the Presbyterian Church, he was during his whole life an example of the highest type of the Christian gentleman under every circumstance, either in the society of the most cultivated or in the midst of the roughest characters of that early day, he invariably preserved the bearing, dress and manner of a gentleman. His evenness of temper was remarkable, and was scarcely ever ruffled or disturbed. He was scrupulously exact in his dealings. No man was more kind to the poor. No one had more consideration for the lowly.

Mr. Hempstead was twice married, first to Miss Rachel Will of Philadelphia, who died in St. Louis, Mo., leaving two sons, Edward and Charles W. Hempstead, who now reside in Chicago; second to Mrs. Eliza Barnes of Galena, a most estimable lady, who is now residing with her only surviving child, Wm. Hempstead, at the homestead in Galena.

Hempstead Wm. Int. Rev. assessor and col.

Henke Fred K. shoemaker.

Henke Henry, painter and musician.

Henning Conrad, baker.

Henning J. laborer.

Herron A. E. clerk *Gazette.*

Hess Conrad.

Hickman Geo. stock breeder.

Hilgers Wm. miner.

Hilgerts Jacob, shoemaker.

HILGERT JOHN P. Manufacturer of Fashionable Dress Boots and Gaiters; the best of custom work and repairing neatly done, No. 181 Main Street; resides at same No.; born in Prussia, Sept. 21, 1829; came to Galena June 24, 1854; commenced working at his trade when 13 years of age; established his present business in 1861; married Catherine Wagner Sept. 21, 1865; she was born in Bavaria; they have four children: John P., Jr., Catherine, Matthias, and Heinrich; they have lost two sons and two daughters; Mr. Hilgert is a member of the German Benevolent and St. Joseph Societies; he was president and secretary of both; he and his family are members of the German Catholic Church.

Hilgerts Jos. shoemaker.

Hins Delter, tailor.

Hirst Wm. clerk.

Holfer F. hostler.

Hoffman Dan, drug clerk.

Hoffman Jos. laborer.

HOFFMANN J. P. Druggist, 108 Main Street; resides on Branch Street between Green and Washington; born in Germany, Jan. 15, 1839; came to Galena in 1854; he has been in drug business since 1855; has been considerably interested in mining enterprises; in 1867 he was one of the firm of Geo. Paul & Co., proprietors planing mill and manufacturers of sash, doors and blinds; married Ann Caroline Sanders Nov. 5, 1863; she was born in Galena; they have five children: Amelia, Philip J., Augusta W., Chas. H. and Harry; Mr. H. is a member of Miners' Lodge, No. 273, A. F. & A. M., and two other Masonic bodies; member of Steuben Lodge 321, I. O. O. F. and Harmonia Benevolent Society.

Hogen Thos. merchant.

Holder Wm. R. retired grocerman.

Holmes D. A. retired.

Homrich A. Alderman Fifth Ward Galena.

Honahan John, farmer.

Hope Wm. retired.

Horning Charles, baker.

Horning Christ. hotel.

HORTON O. S. of the firm of Barrows, Taylor & Co., Lumber Dealers; residence Second Street between Jefferson and Madison; born in Littleton, Mass., May 8, 1831; parents moved to Herkimer Co., N. Y., when he was about ten years of age; resided there and in Oneida Co. until he came to Galena in 1853; he has been engaged in lumber business here fifteen years; was Alderman of First Ward; married Delia Crist in May, 1851; she was born in Herkimer Co., N. Y.; they have one child, Annie.

HORNUNG CHRISTIAN, Proprietor of the Hornung House, foot of Green Street; born in Wittenberg, Germany, Sept. 15, 1828; came to this Co. in 1849; he married Wilhelminie Kimble in 1853; she was born in Saxony Oct. 2, 1837; they have eight children: Louis, Adelia, Albert, Augusta, Edward, Christian and Minnie; Mr. H. was Supervisor one year; he is now serving first term as Alderman; family belongs to the Presbyterian Church.

Hostetter A. miner.

Houghton H. H. retired newspaper editor.

Houy Wm. hotel keeper.

HOWARD GEORGE O. Dentist, office 129 Main Street; residence Second Street; was born in Tionesta, Pa., July 6, 1845; his father emigrated to Wisconsin in 1845, remained but a short time; removed to Maine, thence to Massachusetts, where George received a common school education and graduated from the Clinton High School in 1860; he then studied dentistry in Clinton until 1863, when he enlisted in the 3d Regt. Mass. Cav., as a private; was in Banks' Campaign in Louisiana; participated in the battle at Alexandria, La., and was wounded at Pleasant Hill; as Gen. Emery's orderly was wounded in the head while carrying dispatches from Morganzia to Port Hudson; was shot in the knee in a skirmish near Winchester, and a week later was shot through the right lung at Winchester; discharged as Orderly Sergeant at the close of the war; came West and settled at Keithsburg, Ill., for a few months; traveled extensively in the Western States, and settled in Chicago and engaged in the practice of dentistry; in August, 1868 removed to Galena; married March 30, 1869, Miss Josephine Wheeler of Waterford, N. Y., born July, 1845; they have four children, all born in Galena: Horatio Hudson, Josephine Virginia, Clara Louise and Edna Regina; Dr. Howard is an active, consistent and influential member of the Temperance Reform Club of Galena, a man of liberal, charitable disposition, and a heart and hand ready to help his fellow men when they most need help.

Howard H. D. clerk.

Howe Wm. miner.

Hubbing Henry, tailor.

Huber Aug.

Huber Jos. shoe maker.

Huber Max, tailor.

Hudson James, miner.

Hughes Geo. laborer.

Hughlett Telford, laborer.

HUGHLETT THOS. B. Proprietor Smelting Works, Gratiot Street; residence on Council Hill Road, one quarter of a mile north of city limits; he was born March 22, 1839; married Emma M. Fiddick Oct. 15, 1873; she was born in Galena; thev have three children: Samuel J., Frank H. and Alice May; Mrs. Hughlett is a member of the M. E. Church; Mr. H. has been engaged in the smelting and mining business since 1861.

Hughlett Wm. laborer.

HUNKINS DARIUS. Capitalist; residence Second Street, near Decatur; born in Sanbornton, Strafford Co., N. H., April 29, 1812; moved to Baltimore; first wife was Ann McCarthy; they were married June 28, 1840; she was born at Silver Lake, Pa., Feb. 13, 1820, and died July 18, 1861; they had five children: Miriam Amelia, born in Sanbornton, N. H., March 14, 1841; she married Edward T. Greene Dec. 21, 1861; Charles McCarthy was born in Galena Feb. 1, 1843, and died March 12, 1843; Robert Stuart was born in Galena June 30, 1844, died Sept. 17, 1846; Sidney Cassius was born in Galena Aug. 2, 1847; he married Phenie Mills January 5, 1872; Frank Pierce was born in Galena July 15, 1850; married Fannie Blaetterman Oct. 18, 1877; Col. Hunkins' present wife was Maria F. Greene; they were married April 10, 1867; she was born at Napierville, Ill., Nov. 19, 1838; one child by this marriage, Kate Virginia, born in Galena Dec. 21, 1870; since 1832 the Colonel has been largely interested in the construction of railroads in various parts of this country; in 1832 he superintended the construction of a part of the Baltimore & Ohio Railway; afterwards contractor on the Allegheny & Portage R. R., in Pa., and Sandy & Beaver Canal, Ohio; in 1836 he took contract of the Louisville & Lexington Ry., from Louisville to Middleton; in 1837 engaged on the New Albany & Vincennes Ry.; in Spring of 1838 came to Galena; from 1838 to 1840 he was engaged as contractor in construction of the Illinois Central Ry.; in 1840 he went to N. H., where he was engaged in building the Concord & Nashua Railroad; in the Fall of 1842 he returned to Galena and engaged in mining and smelting; in 1845 he took the contract for the construction of the Government Military Road from Dubuque to the Des Moines River; completed this contract in 1846; in 1847–'48 he built the Spring and Meeker Street bridges in Galena; in 1851 he took the contract for building the Pacific Ry., from St. Louis to Jefferson City, Mo.; he completed that contract in Nov., 1855; he was attending a steamboat convention at New Orleans, when the first decided demonstrations of of the War of the Rebellion were made; in 1862, he went to the headwaters of the Missouri River, Washington Territory, taking with him the first steam engine which had ever been transported to that region; he took quartz mills to the territory in 1863, having to transport every thing by teams from the mouth of Milk River to Bannack City, a distance of 600 miles; from that time until the Fall of 1865 he was engaged in that region mining and quartz milling; in the Fall of 1865 he returned to St. Louis; in 1868 he took a contract for the construction of a portion of the Iron Mountain Ry.; in 1872–'73 he graded the Galena & Southern Wisconsin Ry. from Galena to Plattville, Wis.; in 1874 he took charge of the Keokuk Northern Line Packet; he was president and superintendent of the Galena & Southern Wisconsin Railway Co. in 1875; since then he has not been engaged in active business; our country has produced few men who have displayed greater energy and business sagacity than Col. Hunkins.

Hunkins S. livery stable.

HUNTINGTON WARREN W. born in Burlington, Vt., Oct. 10, 1820; educated at Middlebury, Vt., Academy; entered the printing office of H. H. Houghton, at Middlebury, as an apprentice, in the Spring of 1833; in 1835 was employed by Jewett & Barber, publishers of the Middlebury *Free Press*; Wilbur F. Storey, of the Chicago *Times*, was a fellow apprentice, and Oliver Johnson, of the *Christian Union*, foreman in the office at that time; in 1838 Mr. Huntington removed to Buffalo, N. Y., and entered the employ of E. R. Jewett & Co., publishers of the *Daily Commercial Advertiser* of that city, remaining with them until 1851, when he was induced by H. H. Houghton, his first employer, to emigrate to Galena; on his arrival here he entered into partnership with H. H. Houghton and Cephas Foster in the publication of the *Daily Advertiser and Galena Gazette*; in 1857 he sold out his interest in the paper, and purchased the job office and book-bindery connected with the establishment, and carried on the business until 1862; March 5, 1861, he was appointed Postmaster at Galena by President Lincoln, which position he held through the administrations of Lincoln, Johnson and Grant, until May 4, 1873, when he was appointed Special Agent of the Post-office Department; he continued in that capacity until May 27, 1877, when he was again appointed Postmaster at Galena by President Hayes; he holds five commissions as Postmaster, and is one of the oldest officers of the Post-office Department in the State of Illinois, having been almost continually in service for seventeen years; he was Superintendent of the M. E. Sunday School in Galena for twenty-two years; has been prominently identified with the Republican party since its organization; was an ardent Union man during the Rebellion, and was foremost in raising troops during the war, and devising means for the maintenance of the families of soldiers; in 1871 he was commissioned by Secretary Chase an agent to negotiate the Patriotic Loan, and filed with the Treasury Department bonds to the amount of $200,000; he has been frequently complimented by the heads of the Post-office Department for his valuable services and efficiency as an officer, and was specially delegated by President Grant in 1875 to investigate the political troubles in Mississippi under the administration of Gov. Ames, receiving, soon after filing his report, a letter of thanks from the Department for his impartial and thorough investigation; he is one of the representative men of his state, is a generous, thoroughly honest man, and is highly esteemed and greatly respected wherever he is known; he was first married May 1, 1843, in Buffalo, N. Y., to Eliza A., daughter of Henry Jeudevine, Esq.; his first wife died Oct. 11, 1876; he was again united in marriage to Minta C., daughter of Horace Birdsall, Esq., of Lockport, N. Y., Nov. 1, 1877; by his first wife he had a son, Henry J., who died Sept. 4, 1854, aged 10 years.

Hurley Wm. butcher.

Hurst Geo. miner.

Hurst Henry, miner.

Hurst John W. lead miner.

HUSTED LYMAN, Retired Merchant; resides on Prospect Street, between Warren and Morrison's Alley; born in Stamford, Conn., May 5, 1810; came to Chicago in 1838; lived on a farm eleven miles west of Chicago for about three years; came to Vinegar Hill Tp. in 1841, and engaged in mining until 1843, when he came to Galena and engaged in mercantile business, which he continued until the Spring of 1874; he has spent a portion of the time since then at Sheldon, O'Brien Co., Ia., where he has a son living; married Sarah Ann Scofield in Oct., 1836; she was born in Stamford, Conn., Jan. 15, 1818; they have two children living: Ellen S. (now Mrs. Gen. J. W. Bishop, of St. Paul, Minn.), and Albert W.; lost two daughters, who died in infancy; Mr. and Mrs. Husted are members of the South Presbyterian Church.

INGRAM JAMES, hotel keeper.

Ivey Patrick laborer.

JACKSON ALEX C. retired.

Jahnke Wm. carpenter.

James Angling, farmer.

James Ed. photographer.

Jennings Andrew, porter.

JOHNSON MADISON Y. Attorney at Law, office 87 Main Street; residence cor. of Bouthillier and Water Streets, East Galena; born in Xenia, Ohio, Jan. 7, 1817; came to Galena in 1844; in 1839 he was admitted to the Bar at Louisville, Ky.; Mr. Johnson has been engaged in the practice of his profession ever since he came to Illinois; he married Ann Eliza Wight; they have three children: Madison Leslie, Henrietta Pauline and Neville Lee; Mrs. Johnson's father was Augustus G. S. Wight, who came to Galena in an early day as the agent of the U. S. Government, for the purpose of supervising and leasing the lead mines at this point.

Jackson R. M. painter.

JONAS JOSEPH, Saloon Keeper, under the De Soto House; born in Prussia, Aug. 29, 1840; emigrated to Cincinnati, Ohio, in 1845; came to Galena in 1852; was married to Eliza Selby, June 17, 1860; she was born in this Co. Jan. 13, 1841; they have five children: Francis J., Anna, Carrie, Lydia and Josie; Mr. J. was foreman of the Neptune Fire Company from 1866 to 1871; family attend the M. E. Church.

Jones Abner, farmer and miner.

JONES JOHN J. Attorney at Law and Money Loaner, office over Newhall's Drug Store, corner Main and Hill Streets; resides on south side of Hill St. near West; born near Dubuque, Iowa, Sept. 26, 1846; his parents removed to Galena in 1847; Mr. Jones is a graduate of the Galena High School; he read law with D. & T. J. Sheean; was admitted to the bar at Ottawa Oct. 21, 1874; was Alderman of the Fourth Ward two terms, served from June, 1874, to June, 1876.

Jordan Ed. lead miner.

Jordan River, shoemaker.

Jordan Wm. machinist.

KAEGI CHAS. shoemaker.

Kamerer X. stone mason.

Kaster Jno. drayman.

Kastner John, sausage maker.

Keefe Daniel, laborer.

Kehl Adam, miner.

Keller Geo. planer.

Kelly Chris. laborer.

Kelly Daniel, watchman.

Kelly Daniel, Jr., bridge tender.

KELLY ISAAC, of the firm of Isaac Kelly & Co., Dealers in Groceries, Flour, Feed and Provisions, 190 Main Street; resides on Bench Street, corner Warren; born in Galena; married Jennie Dean Oct. 2, 1877; she was born in Galena; Mr. and Mrs. Kelly are members of the Catholic Church.

Kelly Jno. P. agricultural implement dealer.

Kelly Pat, laborer.

Kelly Thomas, laborer.

Kelly Thomas J. laborer.

Kempter Ernest, music teacher.

KEMPTER FRANK, Manufacturer of Best Sheet Iron Pumps for Miners, and Tin, Copper and Sheet Iron Ware, and Dealer in Parlor and Cooking Stoves for wood or coal, latest patterns, Crockery, Glassware, Lamps and House Furnishing Goods, No. 112 Main St., nearly opposite De Soto House; res. over store; entrance to residence on Bench St.; born in New Bavaria, Germany, Jan. 10, 1834; came to Galena in 1852; in present business ever since he came here; established in business for himself in 1858; married Bertha Brunner in Galena, Aug. 9, 1866; she was born in New Bavaria, Germany; they have two children, Philip and Ernest W.; Mr. and Mrs. Kempter are members of the German Catholic Church.

Koehler Fred. teamster.

Knack Herman, wood sawyer.

Kern Christian, laborer.

Kern William, mason.

Kerwin Richard, Sr., turner.

Kerwin Richard, turner.

Kestern Aug.

Kincade John, miner.

King George, laborer.

King John Henry, farmer.

Kirch Joseph, laborer.

Kirschbaum Anton, tailor.

Kittoe E. D. physician.

Klein A. shoemaker.

Klien Jacob, shoemaker.

Klingel Martin, farmer.

Kloekow Fred. retired.

Kloekow Henry, brickmaker.

Kloekow John, brickmaker.

Kloth William, merchant.

Kluth Gottleib, laborer.

Knobel Henry, waterman.

Koehler Charles F. teamster.

Koehler J. P. laborer.

Kohlbauer Frederick, farmer.

Kraft George, res. Fulton St., south of Oak.

Kramer Ed. laborer.

Kratochvil Frederick, cigar maker.

Kringel Anton, miner.

Kripp C. wood sawyer.

Kripp Henry, mason.

Kripps John, Sr., wood sawyer.

Kripps John, Jr., cabinet maker.

Krohling Louis, shoemaker.

Krossman Charles, carpenter.

Kruse Frank, farmer.

Kruser Henry.

Kucheman John, grocer.

Kuempel Ernest, wood turner.

Kuempel Frederick, shoemaker.

Kuempel John G. laborer.

Kuhlman Henry, cabinet maker.

Kuhn Ernest, meat market.

Kuntz C. saloon.

Kuntz John, miner.

Kurtz John, laborer.

LANDON JOHN, drayman.

Larsch James, shoemaker.

Larsch Lewis, laborer.

Lawrence M. E. clerk.

Leader John, railroad man.

Leahy P. A. boot and shoemaker.

LeBron Leo M. jeweler and watch maker.

LeBron Frank, jeweler.

Leekley George, smelter.

Leekley Tom K. miner.

LEEKLEY THOS. B. President Galena Woolen Mills; residence corner Second and Jackson Streets; born in County of Durham, England, Nov. 19, 1809; came to Pa. in 1829; lived at Pottsville until 1830; Oct. 12, 1830, went to Charlotte, N. C., as the agent of the London Co. attending to their mining interests; remained there until May, 1832, when he returned to the coal mining region of Pa., where he remained until he came here April 8, 1834; was engaged in smelting business here until about eight years ago; he married Sarah Wilde, Jan. 10, 1843; she was born in the County of Yorkshire, Eng., Jan. 26, 1823; they have had eleven children; only four now living; their names are: James F., Thos. M., John M., and Mary; Mr. and Mrs. Leekley are members of the South Presbyterian Church.

Leib John A. tailor.

Leib John, tailor.

Leinhardt Peter, Sr., miner.

Lemper A. G. cooper.

Lemper B. farmer.

Lempers H. tailor.

Leinberger Eugene, laborer.

Lenhard John, laborer.

Lester M. P. laberor.

Lewis Morgan, tailor.

Lichtenberger R. miner.

Liddle Jos. B. shoemaker.

Limper Chas. clerk.

Linenfelser Isadore, teamster.

Logan Henry, proprietor Logan House.

Lohenrich H. H. clerk.

Longette Chas. farmer.

Longdon John, clerk.

Longdon John W. clerk.

Loose Chas. laborer.

LORRAIN JOHN, President Gas Company, 82 Main Street; residence corner Jackson and Third Streets; born in Germantown, Pa., July 29, 1812; was engaged while quite young in the survey of large tracts of land in Pa., surveying one year (1831) 61,000 acres for Stephen Girard, and 67,000 acres for Paul Beck; laid out the Beaver Meadow Ry.; was Assistant Engineer of the Germantown Ry., which was the second road built in the U. S.; was Superintendent of coal mines at Pottsville, Pa.; came to Galena June 10, 1832; spent a few weeks here then went to Wis.; in 1833 went to Dubuque; clerked there one year, then went to Prairie du Chien, where he remained until 1836, when he went to Potosi, Wis.; Oct. 14, 1838, he came to Galena again and has remained here ever since; started the first wholesale grocery in Galena in 1855; he sold out to George R. Melville, and in 1859 bought the Gas Works, and has controlled and carried them on ever since; has been Supervisor and Alderman; married Virginia Little Dec. 4, 1844; she was born in Bel Air, Md.; they have four children: Madison J., Celestine F., now Mrs. Wm. P. Hazard, of St. Louis; John, Jr., and Maude; they have lost four children; Mr. L. has been interested in mining enterprises 44 years.

LOUCHHEIM ABRAHAM J. Dealer in Ready-made Clothing, Gents' Furnishing Goods, Hats, Caps, Trunks, etc., 148 Main Street; resides on Prospect Street near Hill; born in Germany July 25, 1840; came to Philadelphia in 1856; engaged in clerking there until 1859, when he went to Holly Springs, Miss.; was in clothing and dry goods business there until 1863, when he came to Galena; he has been engaged in present business ever since he came here; he is a member of Wildey Lodge, I. O. O. F., No. 5, Encampment same Order; he is also a member of Miners' Lodge, A. F. & A. M. No. 273, and Jo Daviess Chapter, No. 51; married Hanna Weinman, in Philadelphia, March 15, 1871; they have three children: Carrie, Samuel and Bertha.

Louhardt Peter.

Loveland D. F. retired.

Lowber A. M. traveling salesman.

Lowrey Mich. farmer.

Luberger Geo., Sr., tailor.

Luberger Geo., Jr., chair maker.

Luning Anton F. saloon.

Luning A. F., Jr., insurance agent.

Luning Henry, lead miner.

Luning Herman, farmer.

Luther Hartman, saddler.

McAVOY JAMES, miner.

McBreen Phil, teamster.

McCabe James, laborer.

McCafferty Antoney, farmer.

McCafferty Edward, farmer.

McCarty Chas. laborer.

McCarty Dan, horse trainer.

McCarty Jas. teamster.

McCarty John, teamster.

McCarty John E. teamster.

McCarthy Wm. laborer.

McCLELLAN HON. ROBT. H. President National Bank of Galena; resides on Second Street, East Galena; he was born in Hebron, Washington Co., N. Y., Jan. 3, 1826; graduated from Union College, Class of 1847; read law with Hon. Martin I. Townsend, of Troy, N. Y.; admitted to the Bar of New York State at Albany in 1850; came to Galena in 1850 and engaged in the practice of his profession, which he has continued to the present time; he has been attorney for the Illinois Central Railway at this end of the road ever since it was surveyed; he has been President of the National Bank of Galena ever since its organization; he is Director of Hanover Manufacturing Co., and Hanover Pulp Co.; one of the original Directors in both companies; was a member of the State Legislature in 1861, and was elected State Senator from this District in 1876; married Miss C. L. Sanford in Boston, Mass.; she was born in Albany, N. Y., and died in Galena Feb. 14, 1875; Mr. McC. has five children; he is a member of the South Presbyterian Church.

McCloskey H. F. retired merchant.

McCloskey Pat, lead smelter.

McDonald B. farmer.

McDonald Hugh, laborer.

McDonald Thos. milk dealer.

McDonald Thos., Jr., well borer.

McDonald Thos. laborer.

McFarlan Jno. shoemaker.

McGee Mich. shoemaker.

McGinn Pat, laborer.

McGough, P. D. grocer.

McGuire Mich. laborer.

McGuire Mich., Jr., farmer.

McIntyre Mich. watchman.

McHugh Jno. teacher.

McLoughlin A. laborer.

McKeegar Jas. carriage trimmer.

McKinley Jno. retired.

McMahon Roger, scavenger.

McMaster Walter S. clerk post-office.

McMaster S. P. book-keeper.

McManus Jno. residence corner Elk and Barry.

McManus Wm. stone cutter.

McNeil H. retired merchant.

McNEIL THOMAS, Druggist, 174 Main Street; resides on Bench Street between Green and Washington; born in Galena March 18, 1851; he has been engaged in drug business for ten years; married Nora A. Miner Jan. 25, 1877; she was born in Galena; Mr. McN. is a member of the First Presbyterian Church; Mr. McN.'s father is one of the old settlers of this Co., having come here in 1841; he lived two or three years at Plattville, Wis., previous to removal to Galena.

McMullen Jacob, carpenter.

Maguire Hugh, farmer and miner.

Maguire Thos. D. grocer.

Magby Mich. farmer.

Magor R. C., Jr., traveling salesman.

Mahoney Edward, laborer.

Mahoney Jr., Sr., lead miner.

Mahoney John, Jr., clerk.

MAHONEY & ROCHFORD, Pork Packers, Wholesale Liquor Merchants and Dealers in Grain, 38, 41, 42, 43 & 45 Main Street.

Maloy Jno. clerk.

Manuell Jno. marble dealer.

Manuell Richard, marble dealer.

Marfield Edward, grain dealer.

Marfield Frank, laborer.

Marfield Geo. laborer.

MARFIELD HENRY, Justice of the Peace, office corner Main and Green Streets; residence on Dodge Street between Gear and Spring; born in Baltimore, Md., Sept. 12, 1814; came to Galena in July, 1837; worked at cabinet making when he first came; was Constable fourteen years; Deputy U. S. Marshal four years; excepting three years he has been Alderman since 1843 to the present time; several times Acting Mayor; he is quite largely interested in mining in this section.

Marfield John H. laborer.

MARS GERHART H. Merchant Tailor and Dealer in Gents' Furnishing Goods, 126 Main Street; resides at same No.; born in Philadelphia, Pa., Sept. 12, 1808; removed to Lancaster, Pa.; carried on the tailoring business there and in Philadelphia; came to Galena in Sept., 1836; lived in Dubuque part of 1836 and 1837; carried on tailoring business until 1857, when he carried on his farm in Thompson Tp., Sec. 16, until 1867; during the Rebellion he was Supervisor of Thompson Tp. four years; was Assessor and Collector of same Tp. two years; was Commissioner for taking census of the Co. in 1865; was Alderman of Third Ward, Galena, for four years; married Charlotte J. Schwatka March 21, 1839; she was born in Baltimore, Md., July, 18, 1819; they have two sons living, Robt. R. and Gerhart C.; lost four daughters and two sons; Mr. Mars and family belong to the M. E. Church.

Marsden Samuel, captain steamboat.

Marsden Stephen, retired miner.

Martin B. farmer.

Martin John, farmer.

Martin James, farmer.

Masterson A. laborer.

Matt M. huckster.

May D. M. book-keeper.

MAYBRUN SEBASTIAN, Wholesale and Retail Dealer in Groceries, Liquors, etc., 201 Main Street; resides on Hill Street, between High and Dodge; born in Baden, Germany, Jan. 4, 1830; came to New York City Aug. 1, 1853; lived there three months, then moved to Newark, N. J., where he resided until April, 1855, when he went to Greenville, Darke Co., Ohio; from there he came to Galena, arriving here in Feb., 1856; he established his present business in April, 1861; he is a member of the German Benevolent Society and St. Joseph's Society; married Margaret Dietz Oct. 11, 1857; she was born in Germany; they have seven children, five sons and two daughters; they have lost one child.

Maybanks Wm. lead smelter.

Maxeiner P. W. tailor.

Maxeiner Wm. baker.

Melarkey Michael, farmer.

MELLER MATHIAS, Prop. Fulton Brewery, cor. Spring and Prospect Streets; born in Germany April 9, 1827; came to Galena in 1849; went to California in 1853; returned to Galena in 1857; married Louisa Brendel Nov. 1, 1860; she was born in St. Louis; they have four children: Augusta E., Julia L., Edward and Bertha C.; lost two children, who died in infancy; Mr. Meller was engaged in brewery and bakery business before leaving Germany; is at present time member of Board of Supervisors; belongs to the order of I. O. O. F. and two German benevolent societies —Turners' and Singers' Societies.

MELLER & HASER, Props. of Franklin Brewery, cor. Hickory and Elk Streets, near Franklin. Joseph Meller, born in Germany Sept. 21, 1829; came to Galena in 1849; engaged in brewing in 1853; married Teresa Haser in April, 1855; she was born in Germany; they have six sons and seven daughters. Joseph Haser, born in Germany Oct. 8, 1824; came to Galena in 1845; in 1846 he enlisted and served in the Mexican War; returned to Galena in 1848; went to California in 1849; engaged in mining there until 1853, when he came back to Galena; in 1854 went to California again, returning in 1858; engaged in brewery business in 1860; married Margaret Hanft in April, 1859; she was born in Davenport, Iowa; their children are: M. T. Josephine, J. August, F. Albert, J. Adolph, L. Lizzie, P. Louis; lost one son and one daughter; he has been Mayor, Supervisor, Alderman several terms; is a member of the German Catholic Church.

Melvill Geo. R. speculator.

Menegan Z. F. S. painter.

Menzemir Stephen, miner.

Merrick C. S. teller Merchants Nat. Bank.

Merrick J. B. book-keeper.

MEUSEL JOHN A. Mfg. of Copper, Tin and Sheet Iron Work, and Dealer in Stoves, Hardware, Crockery, Glassware and House Furnishing Goods, 203 Main Street; residence on cor. Spare and West Streets; born in Bavaria, Germany, Jan. 2, 1828; came to New York May 3, 1848; came to Galena May 24, 1850; he has been engaged in present business ever since he came here; married Louisa Frowein July 31, 1851; she was born in Prussia; they have six children: John A. W., Caroline, Benjamin Franklin, Albert, Clara and Hermann; they have lost four children; Mr. Meusel was Alderman from the Fourth Ward in 1864.

Metzger Aug. laborer.

Metzger Geo. laborer.

Metzger Jacob, laborer.

Metzger Jno. teamster.

Metzger Jas. carpenter.

Metzger Theobald, clerk.

METZGER WM. S. Justice of the Peace; office on Hill St., rear of Newhall's Drug Store; resides over office; born in Galena, Sept. 3, 1843; at the age of 21 years he was City Attorney; engaged in the practice of law here several years, having studied law with Gen. John A. Rawlins; graduate of University of Albany, class of 1862; admitted to the Bar in 1863; he has been Justice of the Peace about five years; married Mary E. Beil Sept. 10, 1868; she was born in St. Louis; they have one son, Wm. S., Jr.; lost three children; Mrs. M. is a member of the First Presbyterian Church; Mr. M. is a Democrat and a strong temperance advocate.

Meyer Chris. miner.

Meyer Henry, ornamenter.

Meyer Herman, chair maker.

Meyer Herbert, boots and shoes.

Meyer Jacob, miner.

Meyer Peter, laborer.

Miller A. S. teamster.

Miller A. W. laborer.

MILLER CHARLES, Saloon Keeper, corner Main and Green Sts.; born in Berlin, Prussia, Aug. 30, 1835; emigrated to New Orleans, La., in 1857; came to Galena in 185–; enlisted April, 1861, in 12th I. V. I.; was discharged Aug., 1864, at expiration of term of service; married Elizabeth Siewers Nov. 19, 1864; she was born May 15, 1845; they have four children: Annie, Sophia, Amanda and Willie; Mr. and Mrs. M. are members of the Free Evangelical Church, Galena.

Miller Fred. farmer.

MILLER GEORGE H., M. D., office in Horton Block; resides on Dodge St., between Gear and Spring Sts.; born in Galena, Nov. 23, 1840; was educated at Sinsinawa Mound College, Wis., Christian Brothers' College, St. Louis; attended medical lectures at Michigan University, Ann Arbor, Mich., and graduated from Rush Medical College, Chicago, in Feb., 1874; he has been engaged in the practice of his profession here ever since; was a teacher in the public schools of Galena six years; is a member of Wildey Lodge No. 5, I. O. O. F., and Saxon Lodge No. 62, Knights of Pythias.

Miller Jacob, teamster.

Miller Jno.

Miller Jas. butcher.

Miller Wm. boatman.

MINER SIMEON K. Gauger and Deputy U. S. Collector Internal Revenue; office in Custom House; family resides in Nora Township; born in Canandaigua, N. Y., Dec. 17, 1820; came to Jo Daviess Co. in 1839; was among the first farmers in the Co.; engaged in farming in Nora Tp. until 1855; represented that Tp. in the Board of Supervisors nearly the entire time until he took charge of the County House in 1855; in 1856 he was elected Sheriff of the Co.; re-elected in 1860; during the Rebellion he was Deputy Provost Marshal of the 3d district; served about two years; he has made all the revenue collections in this Co.; married Angeline Crowell Dec. 3, 1845; she was born in Angelica, Allegany Co., N. Y., June, 1820; they have three children living: Flora L., now Mrs. A. V. Richards, Henry B. and Nora A., now Mrs. Thomas McNeill; lost one son, Bruce, who died aged about five years.

Mochow John, laborer.

Mochow William, Jr., shoemaker.

Moegle Conrad, saloon.

Moegle Jacob, saloon.

Mohr John, cooper.

Molitor John, shoemaker.

Molitore Joseph, Sr., lead miner.

Molitore Joseph, Jr., lead miner.

Moore John, grocer.

Moore Patrick, retired.

Monniea James, saloon keeper.

Moran Peter, lime burner.

Morrisey Frank, furniture dealer.

Morrissey R. P. furniture dealer.

Morrison William, farmer.

Muchow William, laborer.

Muhlhaus John.

Munchrath M. res. cor. Clay and Division.

Murley John, cabinet maker.

Murphy Edw. laborer.

Murphy John, laborer.

Murray James, laborer.

Myer Joseph, laborer.

Myers William H. engineer.

NACK JOHN A. boots and shoes.

Nagle John, shoemaker.

Nelles Paul, farmer.

Newel James, laborer.

New John; steamboat man.

NEWHALL EDWARD G., M. D., Mayor of the City of Galena, office cor. Main and Hill Sts.; res. north side Bench St., two doors north of First Presbyterian Church; the Doctor was born in Galena, Feb. 18, 1844, and has been elected Mayor twice, without opposition; is a graduate of Beloit College, class of 1866; is also a graduate of the Medical Department of Harvard College, class of 1869; has been engaged in the practice of his profession in Galena since 1869; his father was Dr. Horatio Newhall, who was, at the time of his death, in 1870, the oldest practicing physician in Ill., having settled at Greenville, Bond Co., in 1821; in 1827 he came to Galena; in 1828 and 1830 he was editor of the *Miners' Journal* here; during his life time he was prominently identified with the public interests of the state and city in which he resided; was Surgeon in the U. S. A. at the time of the Black Hawk War; established the U. S. Hospital here in 1832. Mayor Newhall married Mary S. King, daughter of Lieut. Col. Edward A. King, of the regular army, June 27, 1872; she was born in Dayton, O.; they have two children: Horace Greer, born May 27, 1873, and Miriam Alice, Sept. 26, 1874.

Newhall F. B. druggist.

Nickle Richard, Jr., farmer.

Nichols John, farmer.

Nichols W. M. farmer.

Nolan H. res. cor. Franklin and Hickory.

Nolan M. res. cor. Franklin and Hickory.

Nolan Thomas, laborer.

NORRIS R. S. Farmer.

Norton John, shoemaker.

Notterman Aug. shoemaker.

Notterman Aug. cooper.

O'BRIEN MICHAEL, turner.

O'Day Michael, water man.

O'Halloran James, laborer.

O'Malley Thomas, laborer.

O'Neil D. laborer.

OATES & UEHREN, Wholesale and Retail Dealers in Shelf and Heavy Hardware, they also keep a stock of

Shovels, Forks, etc., for farmers' use, 188 Main Street. James Oates resides on Dodge Street, corner Washington; he was born in Eng. May 24, 1839; came to Wis. in 1852; lived in that state until he came to Galena in 1877; married Sarah Frygatt; she was born in Eng.; they have two sons and two daughters; Mr. Oates is a member of Wildey Lodge I. O. O. F., No. 5; Mr. and Mrs. Oates are members of the M. E. Church; Henry A. Uehren was born in Galena April 10, 1854; he married Amelia Musselman Aug. 27, 1877; she was born at Scales Mound, this Co.; Mr. Uehren is a member of Wildey Lodge I. O. O. F., No. 5, and Lead Mine Encampment No. 5.

Obermiller Louis, wagon maker.

Obey Benj. farmer.

Obey Chas.

Obuchon Frank, Sr., miner.

Obuchon Frank, miner.

Oetter Anton, soda water manufacturer.

Ohara Wm. F. carpenter.

Oldenburg Christ. farmer.

Oldenberg Fred, farmer.

Ostendorf E. shoemaker.

Ostendorf Fred, wood sawer.

Owens Jno. S. miner.

Owens Richard, livery.

PAAR GERHARDT, tailor.

Paar Herman, blacksmith.

Paar Joseph, tailor.

Packer Henry, shoemaker.

Pallett Leo. miner.

Pallet W. W. laborer.

Parker Henry, blacksmith.

Patridge Seth. farmer.

Patton Charles, laborer.

Paul Wm. H. bricklayer.

PEIN AUGUST, Superintendent of the Illinois Zinc Company; resides on West Street, Block 19, Galena; born in Germany Feb. 1, 1830; came to U. S. in 1851; lived in Wisconsin twenty-one years; came to this Co. in 1872; has been engaged in the mining business all the time; has been interested in the Illinois Zinc Co. since Jan., 1877; was married to Miss Augusta Michaelis in 1856; she was born in Germany Aug. 6, 1833; have four children: Charles, Lucy, Anna and Theodore.

Peoples Hugh, laborer.

Perkins C. R. leather and shoe findings.

Perrigo Chas. H. cigar dealer.

PERRIGO GEO. W. Associate Editor Galena *Gazette*; residence, De Soto House; born in Lockport, N. Y., Sept. 18, 1843; was educated at the Lockport (N. Y.) Union School, and at the Baptist University in Hastings, Minn.; served in the U. S. N. as Mate and Ensign during the last years of the Rebellion, and was attached to the West Gulf Blockading Squadron; was an officer on board the ill-fated U. S. steamer Milwaukee at the time that vessel was sunk by a torpedo, at the mouth of Blakely River, in, Mobile Bay, March 29, 1865; discharged from the naval service Oct. 30, 1866; was commissioned First Lieutenant Co. B, 66th N. Y. I.; admitted to the Bar May 7, 1868, at Buffalo, N. Y.; adopted the journalistic profession in 1869, as a member of the editorial staff of Buffalo, N. Y., *Courier*; was editor of Galesburg, Ill., *Free Press* in 1871; publisher of the *Liberal Union* (tri-weekly) during the Grant and Greeley campaign; was afterward, and until Nov. 5, 1873, one of the editors of the Galesburg, Ill., *Press;* since last mentioned date has been connected with Galena, Ill., *Gazette;* married Emma Birdsall, youngest daughter of Horace and Dorcas Birdsall., of Lockport, N. Y., Nov. 27, 1866; two daughters: Morna M., born Sept. 28, 1867; Emma D., died Aug. 19, 1871, aged 9 months.

Peters Conrad, carpenter.

Peters Fred, Sr.

Peters Fred, carpenter.

Pfeffer Henry, tailor.

Pfeffer John, tailor.

Fiehley Wm. teamster.

Pierce Frk. res. cor. Hill and Dodge.

Piffner Jacob, miner.

Pilling H. miner.

Pittam Thos. H. clerk in post-office.

PITTAM CAPT. WM. Ex-Sheriff; resides on Perry Street, between Main and Bench; born in Onondaga Co., N. Y., Aug. 13, 1831; came to this Co. in the Fall of 1853; lived in Dunleith until he was elected Sheriff, in 1870; served as Sheriff two terms; while living at Dunleith, he served as Marshal, Constable, Street Commissioner, Tp. Collector, Wharfmaster, etc.; he served in Co. I, 19th I. V. I. one year; was Orderly Sergeant; married Catherine J. Crawford Dec. 6, 1854, at Hazel Green, Wis.; she was born in Madison Co., Ill.; they have three children: Thos. H., Alice J. (now Mrs. A. L. Thorp) and Willie C.; lost three children.

Pohl Bernard, janitor High School.

Poole Robert, confectioner.

POOLEY JOHN H. Photographic Artist; gallery in Merchants National Bank Building; residence on Second Street, east side; born in England Aug. 12, 1843; parents removed to Council Hill, Jo. Daviess Co., Ill., in 1848; lived there four years, then removed to Scales Mound Tp.; Mr. Pooley served about 3 years in Co. E, 96th I. V. I.; mustered out

June 18, 1865; he was engaged in battles of Chicamauga, Kenesaw Mountain, Dallas, Resaca, Tallahoma, Tenn., etc.; came to Galena in the Fall of 1874; married Esther Vipond Oct. 7, 1874; she died Jan. 31, 1877; one son living, Wm. V., born Feb. 14, 1876.

Pryor Frk. res. Dodge bet. Meeker and High.

PUCKEY WALTER, Farmer; Sec. 3; P. O. Galena; born in Cornwall, Eng., July 11, 1849; came to this Co. in 1867; owns 160 acres of land; was married in 1873 to Inez A. Grumme; she was born in Galena May 16, 1853; they have one child, Charles W., born Nov. 7, 1874; they are members of the M. E. Church.

RAIN JOHN E. chair maker.

Rain Thos. shoemaker.

Rapp John, tailor.

Rastners Henry, shoemaker.

Rausch Christian, stone mason, res. West, bet. Elk and Hill.

Reardon Maurice, laborer.

Reardon Michael, brakeman.

Reed David N. agricultural implements.

Reed G. D. blacksmith.

Reed John, farmer.

Reed William, farmer.

Reger Andrew, butcher.

Reger Jos. laborer.

Reil Patrick, laborer.

Rellis James, pilot.

Remakel Michael, saloon.

Rerig Adam, farmer.

Reynolds Thos. E. clerk.

Rhoton B. W. dealer in clothing, etc.

Ridd Thos. farmer.

Riede Gottfried, blacksmith.

Rieske A. B. C. paper hanger.

Riesner Florian, Sr., tailor.

Rigdon Jos. C. engineer.

Riley Jno. farmer.

Riley Wm. laborer.

Ringer Abraham, carpenter.

Ringer Jos. carpenter.

RIPLEY ENOS C. Cashier of the National Bank of Galena, residence corner Hill and West Streets; born in Nichols, N. Y., Jan. 8, 1831; came to Galena Nov. 21, 1839; was for six years Deputy Circuit Clerk; four years engaged in the Crockery business; for the last seventeen years he has been with N. Corwith & Co., and the Bank of Galena; Cashier of the bank since it was organized under the National Banking Act in March, 1865; Mr. R. is Alderman of the Fourth Ward; married Lucy M. Newhall, Jan. 8, 1854; she was born in Galena; they have one child living: Edwin; they have lost five children.

RIPPIN WM. Deputy Circuit Clerk; office in the Court House; residence, Dodge Street, near Wight; born in England June 27, 1846; parents came to Galena in 1849; graduate of Illinois Soldiers' College, at Fulton, Ill., 1871; enlisted in 1862; served in Co. F, 12th Regt. I. V. I., a little over two years; engaged in battles of Shiloh, Corinth, and in all which the 12th Regt. participated in; wounded and lost left arm at the battle of Altoona Pass, Ga., Oct. 5, 1864; married Mary A. Baker, Jan. 5, 1876; she was born in Rome, N. Y.; one child: Winnie Mabel, born Oct. 5, 1876; Mr. R. is an attorney at law.

Ritter Martin, cooper.

Rittenger Geo., saloon keeper.

Roach Thos., teamster.

Roach Pat., teamster.

ROBERTS SAMUEL, of the firm of T. M. & S. Roberts, proprietors of City Market, located in Market House; resides near city limits on the Elizabeth road, one mile east of Court House; born in England, Jan. 10, 1823; came to Galena in 1842; Mr. Roberts was engaged in farming for several years in Dodgeville, Wis.; In 1862 he went to Oregon; spent three years in Oregon and Idaho; then returned to Dodgeville, arriving there Nov. 10, 1865; came to Galena in 1866; he married Mary Symons, May 1, 1847, at Elizabeth, in this Co.; she was born in England, March 1, 1830; they have eight children: Mary S., Phillippa A., Catherine J., Sarah G., Adda A., Frank S., Mildreth, William Henry; they have lost two sons and three daughters; Mr. and Mrs. R., and three of their children are members of the M. E. Church.

ROBERTS THOMAS M. of the firm of T. M. & S. Roberts, proprietors of the City Market, located in the Market House; resides on High street, between Washington and Green; born in England, July 7, 1830; came to Galena with his father, Henry Roberts, in 1842; until 1848 he was interested in farming and butchering; in 1848 he became interested in mining and gave his attention principally to that until 1855, a portion of the time in Michigan (Lake Superior copper mines); since Jan. 1, 1855, he has been engaged in the market business and dealing in live stock for shipment; he married Mary Catherine Gallaher, Jan. 24, 1860; she was born in Galena; they have five children, Helen C., Mary C., Frederick Grant, Henry T., and Lulu; Mrs. Roberts is a member of the M. E. Church.

Robinson Thos., painter.

Robinson Wm. G.

RODDEWIG ADAM, Harness Maker, 225 Main Street; resides on Franklin street between Dodge and West; born in Galena, Nov. 26, 1848; he has been engaged in the harness business three and a half years; married Jane Bastian, Sept. 5, 1871; she was born in this Co.; they have three children: George, Caroline and Mabel.

Roeffel Martin, farmer.

Rochford Dennis, grocer.

Rogers James, laborer.

Rohr John, upholsterer.

Rosemeir Anton, farmer.

Rosenthal Fred.

Ross Edward, miner.

ROSS JOHN, Agent for Henry Corwith and of the firm of Ross & Scott Wholesale Lumber Dealers; resides on Prospect Street; born in the Co. of Durham, Eng., Dec. 9. 1815; came to Galena in 1838.

Rossemeyer Henry, grocer.

Roth A. res. Dodge bet. Green & Wright.

Rottler G. H. confectioner.

Roltler John, porter.

Rowe James, farmer.

Rowe James, marble cutter.

Rowley Louis A. real estate broker and abstract maker.

ROWLEY GEN. WILLIAM R. County Judge, office 129 Main Street, residence Second Street, between Adams and Jefferson; born in Gouverneur, St. Lawrence Co., N. Y., Feb. 8, 1824; parents removed to Evans, Erie Co., N. Y., in 1832; at the age of seventeen years he went to Brown Co., Ohio, where he taught school for three years; in 1843 he came to Scales Mound, Jo Daviess Co.; taught school there several years; in 1849 he was appointed Assessor and Collector of District No. 1 of this Co.; he held this position for four years; he became Deputy Circuit Clerk under Wm. H. Bradley in 1853; Nov., 1854, he was elected Sheriff; after serving one term he was elected Circuit Clerk, which position he held continuously for twenty years; in Nov., 1861, he enlisted as First Lieutenant of Co. D., 45th Regt. I. V. I.; after the Battle of Fort Donelson he was commissioned as Captain and Aide de Camp on the staff of Gen. U. S. Grant; after the Battle of Shiloh commissioned as Major and Aide de Camp on same staff; after the capture of Vicksburg was detailed as Provost Marshal General of the Department of Tennessee and Cumberland, which position he held until the promotion of Gen. Grant as Lieut. Gen. of the army, when he was promoted to Lieut. Col. and Military Secretary to Gen. Grant; held that position until Oct., 1864, when in consequence of ill health he resigned; was breveted successively to the ranks of Col. and Brig. Gen.; served as Circuit Clerk until 1876, since which time he has been engaged in practice of law; in Nov., 1877, was elected County Judge; he married Elizabeth I. Miller in Sept, 1847; she was born in Springfield, Ill.; they have three children: Louis A., Louise R. (now Mrs. J. C. Glenat), and Estelle M.

Rubinan Edward, farmer.

Ruprecht Frank, residence Elk opposite Prospect.

Ryan Daniel, pork buyer.

Ryan Dennis, drayman.

RYAN JAMES M. Pork Packer and Dealer in Pig Lead, office 206 Main Street; resides two miles north of the city on the Turnpike; born in Zanesville, Ohio, Oct. 8, 1828; came to Galena in April, 1846; engaged in wholesale grocery and packing business until 1868, when he engaged in pork packing exclusively; married Catherine McNulta Oct., 1854; she was born in St. Louis; they have eight children: Charles L., Mary, Katie, James W., Oswald E., John M., Cecelia and Albert; lost three children, who died in infancy; Mr. and Mrs. R. are members of the Catholic Church.

Ryan John, bridge tender.

Ryan T. P. shoemaker.

Roger Salmon, laborer.

SALZER GEORGE, laborer planing mill.

Sanders A. F. E. traveling salesman.

Sanders B. H.

Sanders C. E. miner.

Sanders Geo. confectioner.

Sanders Herman, miner.

Sanders Henry H. lead miner.

Sanders Louis, baker and confectioner. (Sanders & Henning.)

Sauer Aug. tinner.

SAUER MICHAEL, Undertaker and Dealer in Furniture, 118 Main Street; resides on Bench Street, between Hill and Washington; born in Germany Aug. 15, 1815; came to Philadelphia, Pa., in 1840; worked there one year; came to St. Louis in 1841; worked one year there, and in 1842 came to Galena; has been engaged in present business ever since; married Lena Bergmann, in St. Louis, in Dec., 1841; she was born in Germany; they have two children living: August and Louisa; have lost one daughter and three sons; Mrs. Sauer is a member of the Lutheran Church.

Savage John P. traveling salesman.

Schader Aug. W. clerk.

Schader Chas. shoemaker.

Schaefer Aug. cigar maker.

Schaefer Theodore, insurance agent.

Scherrad Andrew, farmer.

Scherrad Jas. farmer.

Scherrad Scott, farmer.

SCHEERER CHARLES, of the firm of Scheerer, Armbruster & Co., Manufacturers of and Dealers in all kinds of Furniture, Upholsterers and Undertakers, 183 Main Street; resides on Franklin Street near Bench; born in Westphalia, Prussia, May 31, 1844; came with his parents to Galena in June, 1853; married Miss Emma Lebron Oct. 9, 1864; she was born in Galena; Mr. Scheerer is a member of Galena Lodge I. O. O. F., No. 17, Galena Encampment, No. 132; he is Chancellor Commander of Saxon Lodge K. of P.; he is also Treasurer of Turner Society.

SCHEERER HERMANN, of the firm of Scheerer, Armbruster & Co., Manufacturers of and Dealers in Furniture, Upholsterers, Undertakers, etc., 183 Main Street; resides on Hill Street, between High and Dodge; born in Prussia May 14, 1837; came to Galena in 1853; in 1854 engaged in cabinet making, and has continued in that business ever since; he married Phillippine Schmidt in May, 1867; she was born in Germany; they have four children: Louisa, Amelia, Mena, and Charles John; Mr. Scheerer is a member of Steuben Lodge I. O. O. F., No. 321, Galena Encampment, No. 132, and of the Turner Society.

Scheerer Wm. chair maker.

Schieber Mich. farmer.

Schilling Wm. laborer.

SCHILDWACHTER HENRY, Proprietor of Centennial Market, corner Green and Commerce Streets, opposite the Post-office; boards at Hornung House; he was born in Germany Jan. 5, 1853; came to New York in 1872; came to Galena in 1873; engaged in present business ever since he came here.

Schmidt Lenhard, cabinet maker.

Schmidt Herman, barber.

Schneider Geo.

Schneider John, butcher.

SCHREINER CHRISTOPH, Proprietor Schreiner Hall, Franklin, corner High Street, opposite German Catholic Church; born in Germany Feb. 9, 1820; came to Galena June 24, 1854; he has been a teacher of music ever since he came here; he is leader of Schreiner's Band; married Barba Hauth Oct. 20, 1848; she was born in Germany; they have four children: Nicholas, Cecelia, Louise, Gertrude; lost two daughters and three sons; Mr. and Mrs. S. are members of the German Catholic Church; Mr. Schreiner is a member of the German Benevolent Society and St. Joseph Society.

Schreiner Nicholas, cabinet maker.

Schreiner Seb. tailor.

Schreiner Wm. pastor Ger. Meth. Church.

Schroeder Henry, laborer.

Schroeder John.

Schuber Wm.

Schushardt Francis, clerk.

Schutz Casper, cigar manufacturer.

Schwab Lorenz, wines and liquors, saloon.

Schweitzer Christian, Jr., farmer.

SCOTT DAVID WILMOT (D. W. Scott & Co., Printers), Nurseryman and Florist; office No. 105 Main St.; res. Fourth St., E. G.; born July 6, 1830, in Unadilla, Otsego Co., N. Y.; his father, David Scott, was a steelyard manufacturer before the days of patent scales and balances; his grandfather Scott was Grand Master of N. Y. Grand Lodge, A. F. and A. M., at the time Morgan disappeared; at the time of his birth, his father was engaged in building the Chenango Canal, with a partner, Wilmot Roberts, and he received the name David Wilmot in consequence; his parents removed to Bainbridge, Chenango Co., N. Y., in 1831; here he attended a select school until 13 years of age, then entered Norwich Academy, where he pursued his studies three years, and then entered the printing office of the Chenango *Telegraph* as an apprentice, serving three years; after learning the printer's trade, he attended the Academy for a year; taught his first school in Preston in the Winter of 1848–'9, and the next Spring went to Janesville, Wis., and engaged in the publication of the Janesville *Free Press*, a Free Soil, Democratic paper; in 1852 he purchased an interest in the Galena *Jeffersonian*, but remained in the *Free Press* until the next year, when he removed to Galena, and, associated with Dr. Charles H. Ray, published the *Jeffersonian* and opened a furnishing warehouse for printers; in the Winter of 1853–'4 his office was partially destroyed by fire; in Dec., 1854, he became sole owner of the *Jeffersonian* establishment, but the next year sold two thirds to L. F. Leal and Charles Crouch, and in Nov., 1855, the *Courier* took the place of the *Jeffersonian*, published by Leal, Crouch & Co., and soon after he sold his interest in the concern to his partners, and took a contract to print the *Northwestern Gazette;* subsequently he purchased one third of the *Gazette*, and remained until early in 1863, when he was prostrated by paralysis, and sold his interest to James B. Brown, Esq.; in 1858 Mr. Scott started a nursery and greenhouses in East Galena, on Fourth St., where he now resides, and became widely known as one of the leading and enterprising nurserymen of the Northwest; this pursuit was congenial to his tastes, and he has continued it to the present time in addition to the printing business; he recovered from his illness in 1863 sufficiently to engage, in that year, in connection with his son, James W., in establishing a small job-printing office in the De Soto Block, and started, at the same time, the *Commercial Advertiser*; in 1872 he admitted as a partner A. L. Cumings, and still continues with him in the printing business under the firm name of D. W. Scott & Co.; Mr. Scott married March 9, 1848, Miss Mary Catherine Thompson, born March 17, 1831, eldest daughter of Dr. James Thompson, of Norwich, N. Y.; one child was the fruit of this union, James Wilmot; Mary C. Scott died in Galena April 9, 1861; married second time, the year following, Miss Ann Eliza Saxe, born in Catskill, N. Y., in 1829, eldest daughter of John P. Saxe, of Bainbridge, N. Y., had three children: Clara, Chenango and Mary Catherine; Ann Eliza Scott died Oct. 15, 1876; Mr. Scott holds the responsible position of Secretary of the American Association of Nurserymen, Florists, Seedsmen and other kindred interests.

Schweitzer Leopold, farmer.

Scovill M. A. laborer.

Seals Hon. R. ex-county judge.

Seegar Charles, plasterer.

Seubert Fred., Jr., tinner.

Seitzberg Charles, watch maker.

Seubert Fred. laborer.

Seubert Matthias.

Seubert Nicholas, stoves and house furnishing goods.

Shea Ed. railroad man.

SHEEAN DAVID, of the firm of D. & T. J. Sheean, Attorneys; office cor. Main and Hill Sts., boards at the De Soto House; born in Boston, Mass., July 3, 1834; his parents removed to Galena in 1837; was admitted to the bar in Jan., 1858; was City Attorney in 1859, and has been Counsel for the City of Galena for the last five or six years; was Mayor in 1865; married Miss Cora L. Spare Sept. 21, 1876; she was born in Ohio, and is the daughter of John C. Spare, one of the leading business men of Galena, and who was one of the early settlers.

Shecan John, city marshal.

SHEEAN THOMAS J. of the firm of D. & T. J. Sheean, Attorneys; office cor. Main and Hill Sts.; born in Guilford Tp., this Co., Dec. 15, 1838; he was Supervisor of that Tp. two terms, 1867–1868; in 1868 he removed to Rockford and engaged in the practice of law with his brother, David, having been admitted to the Bar the same year; he has served as Mayor of Galena three terms, from June, 1873, to June, 1876; Dec. 25, 1865, he married Miss Frances Delehunt.

Sheel Fred. butcher.

Sheerer Herman, carpenter.

Shefflin Pat. tailor.

Sheridan Jas. farmer.

SHISSLER LOUIS, A native of Delaware; born in Wilmington, Del., on the 30th of June, 1834; came to Galena in 1841; entered the Western Military Institute at Georgetown, Ky., in Nov., 1849; studied law with Hon. Thomas B. Monroe, U. S. District Judge, during the senior year in college; graduated in June, 1853, with the degrees of A. B. and L.L B.; entered Harvard University in Sept., 1853, and graduated in the law department in June, 1854; pursued the study of law at Harvard University in 1855, and in the office of Sohier & Welch, in Boston, in 1856; commenced to practice law at Galena, Ill., in January, 1857; married on the 25th day of June, 1861, to Rose Porter, of Lancaster, Pa., daughter of the late Gov. George B. Porter, of Michigan; Mayor of Galena in 1866 and 1867; in active practice of his profession up to the present time.

Shultz Chas. laborer.

Shuster Jacob, laborer.

Sidner F. R. farmer.

Sidner F. W. farmer.

Sidner John J. farmer.

Simmons Henry, watchman.

Simmons Edw. miner.

Simon A. farmer and miner.

Simon Peter, cigar maker.

Simpson A. H. miner.

Siniger John, candy maker.

Sievers Fred. clerk.

Slattery Michael, teamster.

Smith Bradner, capitalist.

Smith C. M. organ manufacturer.

Smith James, farmer.

Snow Robert, res. cor. Jackson and Gratiot.

SNYDER WM. H. Cashier Merchants National Bank; residence cor. Decatur and Third Streets, east side; born in Utica, N. Y., Jan. 1, 1814; came to Galena in 1835; for several years he was engaged in mercantile pursuits; has been in the banking business for the last twenty-five years; married Lucretia H. McLean; she was born in Alexandria, Va.; they have three children: Wilson M., Fanny and Alice L.; Mr. and Mrs. Snyder are Episcopalians.

SOULARD JAMES G. (whose portrait appears in this work), was born in St. Louis July 15, 1798, and resided there until he was 23 years of age, when he went to Fort Snelling, and was engaged as a sutler during the years 1821 and 1822; returned to St. Louis, and turned his attention for two or three years to surveying; in 1827 he moved to Galena, and became actively employed in mercantile business and smelting; in 1832, having gone out of business, he was appointed

Recorder, Co. Surveyor and Postmaster, which positions he held at one and the same time, until his resignation on account of ill health, which occurred two or three years afterwards; he then turned his attention to farming and dealing in real estate, and continued so up to 1860; from that time to 1870 he became engaged in the cultivation of the grape, which had always been a work of great interest to him, and he was the first to introduce it in the county; since 1870 he has lived in retirement, enjoying at a ripe old age the fruits of a well spent life; married Eliza M. Hunt, daughter of Col. Thomas Hunt, U. S. A., an officer of the Revolutionary War., in St. Louis, March 20, 1820; she was born in Detroit, Dec. 1804; they had eleven children, four of whom died: James, Henry, Emma and Henrietta; seven are living: Antoinette (widow of E. B. Kimball, of New Orleans), Isabel (wife of Henry Corwith, Chicago), Octavia (wife of J. D. Jennings, Dubuque), Theresa (wife of H. F. McCloskey, Galena), Adele (wife of Capt. E. V. Holcombe, St. Paul), Julia (wife of R. J. Tomkins, Mt. Carroll, Ill.), and Harriet (widow of W. W. Webb, St. Paul).

Sorgenfry J. res. Elk bet. Dodge and West.

Spare E. O. attorney at law.

SPARE JOHN C. Dealer in all kinds of Agricultural Machinery, Hides and Pelts, 209 Main St., res. Dodge St. cor. Morris Av.; born at Cantwell's Bridge, Newcastle Co., Del., March 7, 1819; came to Galena May 11, 1838; worked at carpenter's trade until 1856, then engaged in lumber business, which he carried on until 1870, excepting for an interval of three or four years; when he was on his farm, on Sec. 16, Thompson Tp., in 1873, he became manager of the Galena *Gazette*, which position he held until 1875, when he engaged in present business; was Alderman three terms, Supervisor one term, and Tp. Collector one year; is now Treasurer of the Jo Daviess Co. Agricultural Society; married Esther Gallagher, Nov. 12, 1840; she was born in Carlisle, Pa.; they have three children: S. Arthur, Cora L. (now Mrs. David Sheean), and Eugene O.; Mrs. S. is a member of the Presbyterian Church.

Specht Peter, miner.

Speir John, brewer.

SPEIER RUDOLPH, Proprietor City Brewery, Spring St., block 12, lots 1 to 7; res. same; born in Germany, Dec. 12, 1829; came to Galena in 1849; was in grocery until 1853, when he went into Fulton Brewery; in 1856 he established the City Brewery, and has carried it on ever since; married Maria Weitzel in 1856; she was born in Germany; have five children living: John, Mary D., Theodore, William W. and Bertha; lost two children; Mrs. Speier died Feb. 26, 1875; Mr. S. is a member of the Free Evangelical Protestant Church, and the following societies: Steuben Lodge I. O. O. F., No. 321; Galena Encampment No. 132, German Benevolent Society, Harmonia Benevolent Society, Turners' Society, Humboldt and Singers' Society, Humboldt Monie, and Liberty Fire Co.

Spensley William, attorney at law.

Spohr John, mason.

Spoor Charles, laborer.

Spoor Chris. stone mason.

Spoor Jno., stone mason.

SPRATT JAMES M. Dry Goods Merchant, cor. Main, Hill and Commerce Sts.; residence cor. Bench and Green Sts; born in Binghamton, N. Y., March 20, 1825; came to Galena in the Fall of 1839; engaged in mercantile pursuits ever since he came here in business for himself since 1849; first wife was Amelia Marshall of Plattsburg, N. Y.; present wife was Eliza Johnson; married in N. Y. City; she was born in Binghamton, N. Y.,; they have six children.

Sproul Jno. J., farmer.

SPROUL ROBT. Farmer; Sec. 10; P. O. Galena; born in Ireland in 1802; came to the U. S. in 1827; lived in Philadelphia 11 years; came to Galena in 1838; was married in 1839 to Mary Kirkpatrick; she was born in Ireland in 1822; they have four children living: Andrew R., Ann E. (now Mrs. Wilson), resides in Scott Co., Iowa, John J. and Saml. W.; lost three: Henrietta, George Alex. and Wm. H.; owns 215 acres of land; Mr. Sproul is among the oldest settlers now living here; they are members of the M. E. Church.

STAHL FREDERICK, Insurance Agent and Director of Merchants National Bank; office in bank; residence on Bench St. bet. Warren and Magazine Sts.; born in Baltimore, Md. (of German parentage), Feb. 28, 1809; came to Galena in April, 1829; clerked for A. L. Johnson until the first of June, 1831, when he became a partner with Mr. Johnson in general mercantile business; in 1833 dissolved partnership with Mr. J. and engaged in same business alone; in 1838 he took his brother Nicholas into partnership with him, and they continued the business until 1852; Mr. S. added smelting and lead shipping to his other business in 1837, and carried that on until he retired from mercantile trade in 1852; he became a Director of the Galena Branch of the Illinois State Bank in 1837; became President of the same bank in 1840, and continued to hold that position until its close; Mr. S. was a Sergeant in Col. Stephenson's Regt. during the Black Hawk War; after retiring from mercantile business in 1852, he was not engaged in active business again until 1857, when he became President of the Galena Marine Insurance Company, which position he held until its assets were merged into the Merchants National Bank in 1865; he then became Director in the bank, and has ever since held same position; was Mayor in 1859; married Alice L. McLean Dec. 1, 1839; she was born in Alexandria, Va.; they have three daughters: Susan S., now Mrs. A. N. Lawver, Alice B. and Mary E.; Mr. S. and family are members of the Episcopal Church; Mr. S. having served as Senior Warden over 25 years.

Starr Saml., laborer.

St. Cyr B. C., retired.

Stein Garnett, farmer.

Steinle, Wm. laborer.

Steinmetz Chas., carpenter.

Steinmetz Peter, laborer.

Steinmetz Wm., carpenter.

Stellenberg Ed., blacksmith.

Stephenson Wm., clerk.

Stewart Daniel, carpenter.

Stierman Theodore, miner.

Stillman S. O., hardware dealer.

Stitt R. P., bridge builder.

Stoddard Gideon, river captain.

Strief Fred., shoemaker.

STROHMEYER HENRY, Manufacturer and dealer in Boots and Shoes, 180 Main St.; born in Germany April 28, 1828; came to New Orleans in 1855; lived there 8 months, then came Galena, arriving here in June, 1856; Mr. S. commenced working at shoemaker's trade when he was 14 years of age; he married Paulina Keller, April 11, 1857; she was born in Germany; they have six children living: Joseph, Anton, Henry, Elizabeth, Catherine and Johanna; they have lost one daughter, Paulina; Mr. and Mrs. S. are members of the German Catholic Church; Mr. Strohmeyer is a member of the St. Joseph Society, German Benevolent Society and Relief Fire Company No. 4.

Strott Ed. stone mason.

Strott Leonidas, stone mason.

Strott Nich. mason.

Stott Wm. N. justice of the peace.

Strickland R. D. shoemaker.

Stryker F. dentist.

Sweeney Hugh, mason.

TASSAHALER JOHN, grocer.

TAYLOR DANIEL A. of the firm of Barrows, Taylor & Co., Lumber Dealers; yard foot of Franklin; residence cor. Turney and Muir Streets, School Section; born in Otego, Otsego Co., N. Y., March 9, 1829; came to Galena Feb. 5, 1855; engaged in present business since 1857; became a member of present firm in 1863; married Cordelia S. Norris in 1851; she was born in Erie Co., Pa.; they have three children: Charles Franklin, D. Webster and Nellie; lost two children; Mr. and Mrs. Taylor are members of the M. E. Church.

Taylor Frk. book-keeper.

Taylor Sam. laborer.

Thode Aug. retail grocer.

Thode Edw. grocer.

Tobin James, cigar maker.

Tobin John, teamster.

Toepper F.

Toggin John, farmer.

Tomlin Allen, wood merchant.

Townsend Wm. gardener.

Treller John B.

Tressel Adam, miner.

Tressel John, clothing.

Tresslin Robert, steward.

Trevarthen Joseph, Galena.

Trewartha Peter, livery.

Tripp Jos. vine dresser.

Tshude John, saloon.

Tuttle D. R. spinner.

UHLRICH EMILE, laborer.

UHLRICH FRANCIS J. Dealer in all kinds of Coal and Wood, and Agent of several leading Steamship Lines; office cor. Main and Warren Streets; residence on South Street, between High and Dodge; born in Alsace, France, Oct. 1, 1834; came to Allegheny City, Pa., in 1853; lived there three years, then removed to Rock Island, where he resided four years; then came to Galena; during his residence in this country he has been engaged almost the entire time in the gas business, being connected with the gas companies in all the places mentioned; was with the Galena Gas. Co. until 1871; has carried on coal and wood business since 1863; he was City Auditor in 1874 and 1875; married Teresa Heid Nov. 25, 1858; she was born in Bavaria; they have eight children: Mary F. Josephine, Teresa M., Emily, Emil J. L., Celestine, Bertha L., Frank A. and Flora J.; Mr. U. is a member of Wildey Lodge No. 5, I. O. O. F., Lead Mine Encampment No. 5, Harmonia Benevolent Society, and Humboldt Benevolent Society.

Uhren Andrew, clerk.

Uhren Chris. tailor.

Uhren Henry A. hardware dealer.

Unkapher Mich. ship carpenter.

Unkapher M. T. telegrapher.

VANDERWELDEN JACOB, proprietor Three Mile House.

Van Embden L. European Hotel.

Vaneyck Chas.

Vaughn Philip, laborer.

Venable Marion, harness maker.

Venable W. W. saddles and harness.

Virtue Adams, farmer.

Vogel B. baker.

Vogel Caspar, baker.

Vogt Christian, miner.

VOSS JOHN, of the firm of Voss & Witt, publishers of the *Galena Volksfreund*, corner Main and Franklin Streets; Mr. Voss was born in Germany Oct. 15, 1834; came to Galena Oct. 1, 1869; he was educated at Mecklenburg, Germany; for three years he taught in the German English Normal School of Galena; for five years he has been editor of the *Volksfreund*; he is also teacher of German language in the Galena High School.

WAGGONER HENRY S.

WADLEIGH MILTON, Deputy County Surveyor; P. O. Galena; born in Merrimac Co., N. H., Feb. 13, 1811; went to Chicago and from there to Galena in 1837; was engaged in the survey of the old Illinois Central R. R.; returned to his native state in 1840; came to Savanna, Carroll Co., in 1841; to this Co. in 1843; was married in Oct., 1852, to Mrs. Elizabeth Oliver, whose maiden name was Griffith; she was born in England, and came to this country in 1848; they have three children; Ben, Frank and Grace; served as Co. Surveyor fourteen years; re-surveyed the City of Galena in 1846, being appointed City Surveyor at this time, a position he held for fifteen years; was Assessor of West Galena one year; City Assessor five years and Street Commissioner five years; owns 300 acres of land.

WAGDIN WM. W. Attorney at Law and Master in Chancery, office over Newhall's Drug Store, corner Main and Hill Streets; born in Grant Co., Wis., July 16, 1847; came to Galena when four years of age; read law with Miller & Small and Wellington Weigley; admitted to the Bar Feb., 1871.

Walker Thos. carpenter.

Wallace H. gents' furnisher.

Wallace Pat, laborer.

Wallace W. J. book-keeper.

Walsh Jas. miner.

WALSH JOHN H. Flouring Mill; corner Claude and Meeker Streets; born in Canada Aug. 18, 1844: moved to Cedar Falls, Iowa, in 1865; went to Iowa Falls soon after; in 1868 went to Waterloo, Iowa; came to Galena in 1870; Mr. Walsh has been engaged in the milling business 18 years.

Walters Geo. saddler.

WANN DANIEL, Surveyor of Customs; born in Bel Air, Harford Co., Md., April 3, 1800; he was engaged in mercantile business in Bel Air until 1829, when he came to Galena, bringing with him a stock of goods; immediately engaged in mercantile business here; he continued in mercantile trade until 1851; two years thereafter he devoted to the closing of the affairs of the business of former years; in 1853 he was appointed Surveyor of Customs, and has held that position uninterruptedly ever since; served one year as Mayor, and was Alderman several terms; he was President of the Gov't Board of Commissioners, who laid off the City of Galena, and adjusted the titles to all the lots in the city.

Ward Pat, teamster.

Ward Thos. shoemaker.

Ward Thos., Jr., shoemaker.

Warneke Louis, shoemaker.

Waters J. H. miner.

Watery Mat. miner.

Watts John, machinist.

Weber Ben, teamster.

Weber Geo. teamster.

Weber Engelbat, grocer.

Weber Sebastian, laborer.

Webster D. E. shoemaker.

Weigley W. attorney at law.

Weiland Robt. cabinet maker.

Weinshank John, teamster.

Weinsheimer John, laborer.

Weinschenk F. X. teamster.

Welk Gerhard, farmer.

Welsh Henry, miner.

Welsh Nick. miner.

Welsh Pat. laborer.

Welsh Wm. lead miner.

Wenz C. F. peddler.

West Arkansas, carpenter.

WESTWICK JAMES, General Foundry and Machine Shops, Meeker Street, opposite Barrows, Taylor & Co.'s saw mill; born in Stocksley, Eng., Oct. 13, 1815; came to Galena in 1850; married Eliza Attwell in Nov., 1850; she was born in Ireland; they have nine children: James, Jr., Ann Eliza, Mary Jane, Ellen and Robert (twins), Harriet Josephine, George, John and Martha Matilda; lost two children.

WESTWICK JOHN, Prop. Foundry and Machine Shops, Claude Street, near Meeker; residence cor. Prospect and Elk Streets; born in Yorkshire, Eng., March 30, 1822; came to Galena in May, 1852;

married Mary Emmerson Nov. 20, 1845; she was born in Yorkshire, Eng.; they have seven children living: John Wm., Thos. E., Sarah A., Eunice, Mary, Charles and Emma; they have lost three children; Mr. and Mrs. W. are members of the Baptist Church.

Westwick Thomas, machinist.

Westwick William, machinist.

Whalen James, laborer.

White J. D. grocer.

Whitely T. traveling agent.

Whittam Emanuel.

Whittam Jos. baker.

Wichman F. lead miner.

Wichman Geo. clerk.

Wichman Henry, boatman.

Wichman John.

Wiemer Fred. tailor.

Wiegers Jos. saloon.

WIERICH AUGUSTUS, Physician and Surgeon; office 102 Main Street; resides at same No.; born in Galena Nov. 17, 1843; the Doctor was educated at the University of Berlin, University of Gottenberg, Hanover, Germany, and at the University of Pennsylvania in Philadelphia; he has been engaged in the practice of his profession in Galena eleven years; was Co. Coroner in 1875 and 1876; his father, Augustus Wierich, Sr., practiced medicine here for thirty-eight years previous to his decease, May 6, 1875.

Wilcox Wm. H. wagon maker.

Wilkins George, lead miner.

Williams Calvin, tailor.

Williams C. P. tailor.

Williams George, shoemaker.

Williams Wm. H. cigar maker.

Wilson C. H. clerk.

Wilson Robert.

Wintz Christov, laborer.

Wintz Fred, laborer.

Wippo Charles, laborer.

Wippo William, carpenter.

Wirsching, John, stone mason.

Wittenberger E. M. carpenter.

Wittenberger Martin, carpenter.

Wondelly J. Y. clerk.

Woolweber Henry, saloon.

Wright A. R. painter.

Wright T. F. carpenter.

Wurtenberger L. carpenter.

YEAGER WILLIAM, farmer.

Yelland Almand.

Young Christian, farmer.

Young George, painter.

Young James B. retired.

YUNKER CAPT. STEPHEN, Planing Mill and Manufacturer of Sash, Doors and Blinds; born in Germany Oct. 6, 1829; came to Buffalo, N. Y., in Dec., 1851; lived there until May, 1852, when he came to Galena; he was Captain of steamboats on the Mississippi River for over ten years; established present business in 1869; married Matilda Gerlich Dec. 10, 1853; she was born in Germany; they have five children: Stephen, Jr., John, Matilda, Christina and Katie; Mr. Yunker and family belong to the Catholic Church; Mr. Y. is a member of Steuben Lodge, No. 321, I. O. O. F., Galena Encampment, German Benevolent Society, Singers' Society, Turner Society, and Reliance Hook and Ladder Co.

Yunker Stephen, Jr., planing mill.

ZIMMERMON J. H. school teacher.

Zipter Rudolph, cigar maker.

EAST GALENA.

ADAMS John, farmer.

Albert Lorenz, laborer.

Annet John B., night watchman.

ANNETTS MOSES, Farmer; Sec. 36; P. O. Galena; born in Monmouth Co., Eng., Dec. 4, 1816; came to this country and Mass. in 1842; settled on his present farm in May, 1848; he has 160 acres of land in Sec. 36, and 80 acres in Sec. 1, Rice Tp.; married to Miss Sarah Lougue in 1847, from Ireland; they had two children, Thomas J. and Sarah A.; his wife died in 1851; he was married to Annie J. Nichol, from Ireland, in 1852; they had one child, Mrs. M. J. Berryman of Scales Mound; Mr. Annetts has held a prominent position in connection with the Glen Hollow M. E. Church, which was organized some twenty years ago; services being held in the school-house near where now stands their new and beautiful house of worship, which was erected in 1868; they have services once in two weeks, conducted by Rev. J. H. Soule, who is connected with the Hanover Circuit Rock River Conference; Mr. A. held the office of road commissioner ten years, and school director twelve years.

Annetts Thomas, miner.
Anguin R., retired.
Archer Thomas, farmer.
Aronson A C., junk dealer.

BACKUS E. T. farmer.

Baldwin John, farmer.
Barber Albert, laborer.
Bastian John, laborer.
Bastian Stephen A. farmer; Sec. 12.
Bastian Thomas, farmer; Sec. 13.
Bean Thomas, book-keeper.
Beehan Murty, laborer.
Bell John, teamster.
Beninger A. miner.
Beninger John, miner.
Bermingham Michael, school teacher.
Bermingham Thad. school teacher.
Bethel Landers, farmer; Sec. 2.
Bigwood Math. gardner.
Bolitho John, farmer; Sec. 13.
Bollinger Philip, railroad employe.
Boss Jacob, school teacher.
Bostwick R. S. chair manufacturer.
Bradey Hugh, railroad employe.
Bradey John, harness maker.
Bradey Patrick, shoemaker.
Brandt, Deitrich, butcher.
Breen David, laborer.
Breen John, retired.
Brendel Christ., Sr., farmer.
Brenigan Arthur, farmer; Sec. 24.
Bridgman H. N. news depot.
Brodrecht Martin, laborer.
Brunner Jacob, boarding house.
Brunner, Wm. tinsmith.
Bruer Wm. farmer.
Brown Daniel, laborer.
Brown Edward, teamster.
Brown John, laborer.
Brown John S. laborer.
Brown J. B. editor *Galena Gazette.*
Brown Phil., Jr., laborer.
Brown Wm. miner.
Budden Henry, cooper.
Budden Jacob, cooper.
Budden John, blacksmith.
Buckley Wm., laborer.
Burns John, farmer; Sec. 2.
Burns Wm. farmer; Sec. 15.
Burton Alonzo, miner.
Burton B. F. miner.
Burton Benjamin, miner and farmer; Sec. 15.

BURTON JOHN, Miner and Smelter; Sec. 15; P. O. Galena; born in Derbyshire Co., England, 1822; came to this country and Philadelphia, Pa., March, 1828; was engaged in smelting until 1831, when he moved to Galena; settled on his present site in 1834; has been engaged in mining and smelting in this Tp. since that time; in 1836 he hauled lead to Chicago with ox teams, it taking him three weeks to make the round trip; was married to Miss H. E. Watts, of Pa., in 1858; had one child: Annie E., born July, 1869; owns a flour mill near his smelting furnace; lived with his father for several years in the first frame house built in the County.

CALAHAN JOHN, farmer.

Cavey Michael, laborer.
Chapman Wm. farm laborer.
Cleine Joseph, shoemaker.
Colman Carroll, drayman.

COLMAN MRS. SARAH A. farmer; Sec. 23; P. O. Galena; born in Maryland April 27, 1834; parents came to this Co. and Tp. in 1835, and settled on the farm that she now occupies, known as the Kirkby estate; was married to Mr. M. Colman, of Philadelphia, Pa., March 3, 1858; he was born Nov. 21, 1822; they had six children: Mary E., born Oct. 27, 1858; Clara R., Sept. 10, 1863; James E., Oct. 16, 1865; Nathan G., Oct. 5, 1867; Wm. H., Aug. 16, 1870; Jennette A., Feb. 27, 1875; Mrs. C. has 200 acres of land; Mr. Colman died Jan. 27, 1877.

Collins John, Sr., farmer.
Collins John, farmer; Secs. 14 and 23.
Commins Ed. laborer.
Coners Ed. laborer.
Conley Thos. farmer.
Conklin Chas. cooper.
Conklin George, cooper.
Conklin Harris, cooper.
Conklin R. cooper.
Cortate John, tinsmith.
Cortate Oliver, tinsmith.
Corwith Henry, capitalist.
Cortney Ed. section boss I. C. R. R.
Costenbader Phil. laborer I. C. R. R.
Crawford J. S., Jr., clerk.
Crawford Stewart, druggist.
Crawley Joseph, laborer.
Crumbellick Thos. farmer, Sec. 1.

DAMPHOUSE PETER, miner.

Dean, Melville, telegraph operator.
De Bord W. H. laborer.
Deeds Bennett, farmer.

Degnan John, farmer; Sec. 13.
Deininger Michael, farmer.
Deininger Wm. farmer.
Davis Henry, ex-County Treasurer.
Davis Wm. farmer.
Davis Z. T. Deputy Surveyor of Customs.
Detters Joseph, Jr., farmer.
Detters Joseph, Sr., farmer.
Donley Bernhard, laborer.
Dower James, farmer; Sec. 24.
Dower Samuel, farmer; Sec. 2.
Dower Thomas, farmer; Sec. 24.
Draydon James, miner.
Driscoll John, laborer.
Duffey Peter, laborer.
Duggen Thomas, laborer I. C. R. R.
Dunigan Daniel, farmer; Sec. 1.
Dunigan Owen, clerk.

EASTWOOD Wm. farmer.
Edwards John, fireman G. & S. W. R. R.
Einsweiller Christ. miner.
Einsweiler H. miner.
Einsweiler John, miner.
Enor Wm. farmer.
Erwin James, farmer.
Evens Richard, miner; Sec. 15.
Exstein John, teamster.

FARECY John, laborer.
Fitzpatrick Pat. laborer.
Foster George G. book-keeper.
Foster Thomas, capitalist.
Friesmecker Mat. groceries and saloon.
Frietz John, Sr., sash and door maker.
Frietz John, Jr., clerk.

GAFFNER John, Sr., miner.
Gallagher John, laborer.
Gear Charles E., school teacher.
Gerlick B. laborer.
Gerlick John, laborer.
Gerlick Peter, bridge tender.
Gilson Jas. farmer.
Gleason Andrew, miner.
Gleason Richard, raft pilot.
Gleason Walter, fireman I. C. R. R.
Gleason Wm. mate on steamboat.
Glenatt Jos. book-keeper.
Gluck Henry, farmer.
Glynn Jno. miner.
Golden Ed. laborer.
Golden Thos. bridge tender.
Golden Wm. laborer.
Goodburn Henry, farmer.
Goss L. miner.
Grady Jno. blacksmith.
Grant U. S. ex-President.
Graney F. stone cutter.
Green E. T. telegraph operator.
Green Jacob, farmer.
Green Wm. laborer.
Grove Fred, butcher.
Gunn Pat, laborer.
Gunn Thos. laborer.

HALL JOHN, laborer.
Hallett Tim, farmer.
Hanley Wm. laborer.
Hanson Nicholas,
Hansing Al. fisherman.
Hansing Chas. drayman.
Hanning N. baker.
Hare D. H. farmer; Sec. 14.
Hamilton Campbell, farmer.
Harthman Luther, harness maker.
Hatter Chas. teamster.
Heckelsmiller W. farmer.
Heer David, farmer.
Hemler Wm. farmer.
Henner Chas. cooper.
Hemler Mike, Jr., farmer.
Hickman G. W. horse raiser.
Hines Pat. laborer.
Hocskings Frank, farmer, Sec. 13.
Holland B. F. painter.
Holland B. G. painter.
Holtkamp Henry, cigar maker.
Hottcamp John, laborer.
Horton O. lumber merchant.
Hony Daniel, laborer.
Hony Geo., Jr., brewery.

HOUY PHILIP S. Farmer; Sec. 28; P. O. Galena; born in Prussia Aug. 22, 1822; came to this country and Missouri in 1840; came to West Galena March, 1845; came to East Galena in 1847; settled on his present farm in 1864; married to Catherine Houy Aug. 1, 1851; she was born in Prussia May 19, 1824; they have had four children: Catherine, Laura, Caroline and Katie; Catherine and Katie are dead; Laura, born April 14, 1854; Caroline, born Jan. 28, 1857; Mr. H. owns 118 acres of land in Secs. 21, 22 and 28; value, $6,000; held the office of School Director six years; Mr. H. suffered the loss of all his property in the great flood that occurred in 1844 on the Mississippi and Missouri Rivers.

Howard G. O. dentist.

Hummel Pat. drayman.
Hunkins D. railroad contractor.
Hurst Jacob, laborer.
Hurt M. miner.
Huschar John, farmer.

IVEY EDWARD, farmer, Sec. 1.

JACKSON JAMES, bricklayer.

Jacobs W. H. farmer.
James J. E. photographer.
Jeffery Wm. drayman.
Johnson David, farmer; Sec. 35.
Johnson Hugh, farmer.
Johnson M. Y. lawyer.
Jones Edwin, farmer.
Jose John, farmer.

KAISER Christ. farmer.

Keef Wm. laborer.
Keif Pat. laborer.
Keif Wm. laborer.
Kelleher Daniel, farmer; Sec. 25.
Kelleher James, farmer; Sec. 35.
Kelleher Mike, farmer.
Kenny Thomas, carpenter.
Kirtz Paul, steamboat captain.

KETTLER JOHN H. Farmer and Miner; Sec. 33; P. O. Galena; born in Prussia; he came to this country and Galena in 1868; he published the *Volksfreund*, of Galena, from 1869 to 1874; he settled in East Galena Tp. in 1874; he was married in 1868 to Mrs. Wilmina Karrmann, of Galena; he practiced law in Prussia six years prior to coming to this country; he was in the Prussian army three years; he has 56 acres of land; he suffered the loss of his dwelling by fire November last.

Kline Ignatus, shoemaker.
Korte Henry, farmer.
Koule B. farmer.
Koule Henry, farmer.
Krews Conrad, engineer.
Kurtz John, steamboat man.
Kurtz Paul, steamboat captain.

LANE Daniel J. farmer.

Larkins James, laborer.
Larken Peter, laborer.
Leavens Mat. farmer; Sec. 35.
Lee James, laborer.
Leehan Jerry, farmer and collector National Bank.
Leenke B. farmer.
Levens James, farmer.
Leonhardt S. E. engineer.
Lenzing Andrew, milk dealer.
Lewis E. S. farmer.
Liddle George, miner.
Liddle Joseph, merchant.
Liddle Jno. W. shoemaker.
Liddle Wm. merchant.
Liddle Wm. shoemaker.
Lillig Peter, laborer.
Lobb Wm. laborer.
Lorrain John, president Gass Company.
Lorrain Mat, clerk.
Lucy Pat, farmer.

LUKE REV. GARRETT, Clergyman and Farmer; Sec. 21; P. O. Galena; born in Albany Co., N. Y., 1813; he came to this state and Boone Co. in 1854; he moved to this Co. and Nora Tp. in 1859, where he spent his time farming and preaching until 1869, when he moved to Iowa; in 1871 he returned to this state and Co., and settled on his present farm near Galena; he was married in 1837 to Miss Maria Hotaling from Albany, N. Y.; they have had eight children: John W., Garrett W., Moses H., Kate M., Jennie, Elmira, Allie, Elizabeth; Jennie and Elizabeth are dead; he has held the office of Tp. Treasurer three years; School Director ten years; Mr. Luke has held the position of local preacher for the M. E. Church for the past forty years; aside from his other labors on his farm he has filled vacancies in the Co. where he has lived; for the past two years he has given his services to the Colored M. E. Church of Galena; and during all these years of labor for destitute churches he has not received $40 in money; when the call was made for soldiers in our late war his three sons volunteered; John W. in the 15th Regt. I. V. I., Garrett W. in 96th Regt. I. V., I. Moses H. in the 17th Regt. I. V. C., and filled the position as dispatch bearer for Col. Beveridge; John W. held the office of Co. Sheriff two years; Garrett W. elected as Deputy for same.

LUPTON JOHN, Farmer; Sec. 13; P. O. Galena; born in England Dec. 15, 1824; came to this country and Council Hill Tp. in 1846; moved to Thompson Tp. in 1849; settled on his present farm in 1868; married in 1845 to Miss Mary J. Jackson from England; she was born June 3, 1823; they have two children: John G., born Aug. 16, 1845; Martha M., Jan. 6, 1862; John G. died March 8, 1847; Mr. L. owns 63 acres land valued at $4,000; he held office of School Director in Thompson Tp. one year; School Director eight years; in religion, Methodist, and is now class leader in the Union M. E. Church on north line East Galena Tp.

Lynch Jno. porter.

Lynch Thos. laborer.

McCARTY JOHN, laborer.

McCarty Pat, farmer; Sec. 34; P. O. Galena.

McClellan R. H. president National Bank.

McDermot Thos. collector I. C. R. R.

McDermot Thos. station agent I. C. R. R.

McGann James, laborer.

McGoldrich Peter, baggage man I. C. R. R.

McIntyre Thos. lime burner.

McLaughlin Pat.

McMahon Barney, laborer.

McMahon Wm. laborer.

McMuller Wm. laborer.

McNulty Jas. laborer.

McNulty Pat, laborer.

Maas John, laborer.

Mackey Michael, retired.

Madden Martin, in poor house.

Mahood Jno. school teacher.

Mars Geo. tailor.

Martin C. W. farmer.

Martin Henry, farmer.

Martin Richard, lumber merchant.

Maybanks Nat, shoemaker.

Menzimer Geo. laborer.

Mellvile A. C. merchant.

Menzimer Chas. laborer.

Menzimer Philip, laborer.

Merton B. F. superintendent North Western Normal School.

Merton Geo. P. professor in Normal School.

Metcalf Thos. farmer.

Metzger Louis, constable and harness maker.

Metzger Mike, brewer.

Miller Anton, butcher.

Miller Jos, butcher.

Moore Isaac, druggist.

Moore John, laborer.

Morello Frank, locksmith and merchant.

Morris Douglas, miner.

Moser John, brewer.

Murphy Ed. farmer; Sec. 2.

Murray Nicholas, laborer.

NEW JOHN, steamboat man.

Neuchwauger Christ. farmer.

Nolan Pat, laborer.

Norris Barney, sexton Presbyterian Church.

O'NEIL John, farmer; Sec. 1.

Oeding Frederick, farmer.

ORTSCHEID FRANCIS J. Farmer and Miner; Sec. 11; P. O. Galena; born in Alsace Co., France, May 21, 1832; came to this country and Racine, Wis., in 1855, moved to Cassville, Wis., 1856; came to Galena in 1858; settled on his present farm 1867; married to Miss Eliza Dieger, from Galena, in 1857; she was born in Baden, Germany, 1834; they have ten children: Jasper, Elizabeth, Mary, John, Fritz, Rubert, Augustus, Caroline, Rasea, Anna; Mr. O. has 203 acres of land in Sections 10 and 11 valued at $5,000; held office of Commissioner of Highways three years; he struck an East and West range on his farm March 29, 1877, and took out 300,000 pounds mineral.

Owens Jonathan, Sr., farmer.

Owens J., Jr., farmer.

PASCOE WM. farmer.

Petetgout Mike, farmer.

Plath Chris. saloon keeper.

PORTER SERENO E. Farmer; Sec. 28; P. O. Galena; born in Conn., Feb. 5, 1827; came to St. Louis 1832; moved to La. Dec. 28, 1843; from that time he was engaged in steamboating, as clerk and captain, for 34 years on the Red and Mississippi Rivers, except the years '57–'58 when he held the office of freight and ticket agent for the G. D. D. and Minn. Packet Co., at Galena; the year 1872 he spent on the government boat, "J. C. Coffery," as clerk; settled on his present farm 1857; married to Miss N. Hinckley, 1857, of East Galena Tp.; they had one child, Russell E.; born Nov. 17, 1858; Mrs. S. E. Porter died Sept. 7, 1866; he was married to Mrs. M. A. Crowell, of Vt., 1867; he has held the office of School Director six years; has 97 acres of land.

Pouder John, miner.

Potts C. F. book-keeper.

Potts Frank, clerk.

Price Wm. broom maker.

Price Wm. H. farmer; Sec. 36.

Pruitt G. W. laborer.

QUEMBY A. laborer.

Quillam Wm. miner.

REED JAMES, farmer; Sec. 25.

REED MRS. JOHN, Farming; Sec. 24; P. O. Galena; born in Ireland Oct. 4, 1811; came to this country and St. Louis in 1820; moved to Galena in 1828; was married to Mr. John Reed in 1829; he was born in Tyrone Co., Ireland, in Feb., 1797; he came to this country and Indiana in 1824; he came to Galena same year; he made the journey on foot, through deep snow, with his brother, before any roads were laid out, with only the compass as their guide; he purchased property here when the present site of the city was government land; he enlisted and served during the Black Hawk War; he was engaged in merchandizing several years; they settled on the estate in 1845; they have three children living: Elizabeth, Emma and Josephine; he died Feb. 12, 1870; Emma was married to Dennis Keleher, of Ia., Feb 29, 1876; Elizabeth married F. Campbell, of Chicago, Sept. 1, 1856; the estate consists of 168 acres of land on Secs. 24 and 25; also property in Galena.

Richard Wm. butcher.

Ridd Wm. clerk.

Reed Wm. farmer.

REDFEARN WM. Farmer; Sec. 33; P. O. Galena; born Jan. 7, 1849, in Council Hill Tp.; settled on his present farm in April, 1875; married Miss Nellie E. Virtue Jan. 7, 1875; she was born May 4, 1851, in West Galena Tp.; they have two children: Catherine A., born Nov. 27, 1875; Ida E., Nov. 11, 1877; he has 138 acres land, valued at $5,000.

Reitz Peter, cooper.

Reger Chas. miner.

Renwick Alex. tinsmith.

Renwick Jas. tinsmith.

Renwick Thos. tinsmith.

Runsacher Geo., Sr., cooper.

Rensacher Geo., Jr., cooper.

Reynolds George.

Reynolds Thos. smelter.

Richards Pierce, farmer.

Rigdon Howard, laborer.

Ripplinger Nicholas, farmer.

Ritter Geo. farmer.

RITTER ISAAC, Farmer; Sec. 14; P. O. Galena; born Sept. 21, 1819, in Pa.; moved to Ohio in 1824; came to this state in 1839; settled in Galena in 1842; was engaged in mercantile business until 1875, when he settled on his present farm; he was married to Miss R. Whitaker, from Del., Sept. 18, 1850; she was born July 25, 1824; they have five children: Mary E., born July 10, 1851; Emma, Oct. 20, 1853; Wm. A., May 6, 1856; Rebecca A., June 4, 1858; Charles J., Nov. 28, 1861; he has 180 acres land, valued at $5,000.

Ritter William, farmer.

ROBERTS HENRY, Farmer; Sec. 22; P.O. Galena; born in Cornwall Co., England, Dec. 21, 1817; came to this country in 1842; settled on his present farm in 1853; married Miss Grace Rowe, from England, Nov. 14, 1845; they have five children: Grace, Emma J., Naomi J., Leslie C. and Mabel; Grace was married to B. Magor Feb. 25, 1868; Emma J. was married to C. Brown Sept. 20, 1871; Naomi J. was born Aug. 6, 1857; Leslie C., Feb. 24, 1861; Mabel M., Sept. 24, 1868; Mr. Roberts has held office of School Director 6 years; has a beautiful farm of 240 acres of land, in Secs. 22 and 27.

ROBERTS JAMES M. Farmer; Sec. 22; P. O. Galena; born in Cornwall Co., England, April 2, 1820; came to this country and Tp. in 1842; settled on his present farm same year; married Feb. 12, 1846, Miss Mary Prisk, from Cornwall, England; she was born Feb. 23, 1824; had two children, Phillipa and Joseph; Joseph died Sept. 29, 1856; their daughter, Phillipa was married to R. G. Smith, April 2, 1865, and lives on the same farm; Mr. Roberts has 375 acres land in Secs. 22 and 27; he held the office of Supervisor two years, and School Director eleven years; has always taken a prominent part in the general interests of his Co. and Tp.; his father, Henry Roberts, Sr., came to this country at the same time; he died Aug. 10, 1872; Mr. R. is a Republican in politics, and a Methodist in religion.

Roberts Samuel, butcher.

Robinson Frank J. farmer; Sec. 35.

Rodewick E. farmer and miner.

Rodewick William, farmer and miner.

Rooney Wm. laborer.

Rosenthal Frank, painter.

ROWE JAMES, Farmer; Sec. 2; P. O. Galena; born in Cornwall, Eng., Feb. 2, 1826; came to this country and to East Galena Tp. in 1842; settled on his present farm same year; was married to Miss Mary Conley, from Ireland, in 1850; they have seven children: John, born June 20, 1852; James, Dec. 25, 1853; George, June 13, 1860; Joseph, May 13, 1862; Catherine, Sept. 20, 1855; Ellen, Aug. 15, 1857; Virginia, June 9, 1864; Mr. Rowe has 440 acres land in Secs. 1 and 2.

Rowe James, Jr., farmer; Sec. 1; P.O. Galena.

Rowe John A. laborer.

ROUSE GEORGE, Farmer; Sec. 26; P. O. Galena; born in Canada, Sept. 18, 1821; came to Louisa Co., Ia., in 1837, and to East Galena Tp. in 1843; settled on his present farm, the Kirkby estate, in 1870; married Miss Harriet Kirkby in 1851; she was born in Lincolnshire, Eng., March 26, 1819; she came to this country in 1832; Mr. Rouse has 365 acres land in Secs. 25 and 26; he enlisted in the 7th I. V. C. Feb. 14, 1865; mustered out in Nov., 1865; they had four children: Sarah A., Wm. A., Eliza W., Horace K.; Mrs. Rouse's father, Wm. Kirkby, died in 1854; her mother, Sarah Kirkby, died in 1869.

Rowley L. A. real estate and insurance.

Rowley W. R. county judge and lawyer.

Ryan Pat. laborer.

Ryan Philip, shoemaker.

Ryan Thomas, shoemaker.

SALE MARTIN S.

Samson James, retired.

Sampson James H. retired.

Sampson Yeno, clerk.

Schaffer Martin, boarding house.

Scheel Charles, farmer.

Scheller U. G. proprietor Scheller's vineyard.

Schmidt Charles, farmer.

Schmidt Christ. farmer.

Schmidt George, barber.

Schmidt Valentine, barber.

Schneider Conrad, stone cutter.

Schneider Frank, butcher.

Schneider Trany, retired.

Schuman Matt, cooper.

Scott D. W., editor *Industrial Press*.

Scott Thos., engineer.

Seck Geo., Jr., farmer.

Seck J. C., farmer; Sec. 14.

Shannon John., miner and farmer; Sec. 24.

Shannon Silas, miner.

Shannon Thos,. miner and farmer.

Shea Morris, laborer.

Sheean James, farmer.

Sincock Ben., farmer.

Sincock Edw., miner and farmer.

SINCOCK SAMUEL, Farmer and Hotel Keeper; P. O. Galena; born in Cornwall, Eng., Dec. 22, 1828; came to this country and Galena 1842; moved to Michigan in 1850; spent five years in the copper mines; went to California in 1855; spent 1858 in the British Possessions; settled in this Co. 1869 and in Glen Hollow in 1870; married to Miss Mary Ann Morris, of Elizabeth Township; she was born in Canada, Dec. 25, 1835; they have three children: Eldora, Douglas, Florence M.; Mr. S. has 80 acres of land in connection with his hotel.

Sincock Wm., miner.

Smith A. C., pastor S. Presbyterian Church.

Smith Edward, farmer.

Smith James, farmer.

Smith Michael, farmer; Sec 24.

Smith Robert G., stock buyer.

Smith W. H., farmer.

Sneider John, shoemaker.

SNYDER FRANK, Farmer; Sec. 36; P. O. Galena; born Town Elsice, France; came to this country and Shawneetown, Ill., 1822; moved to Galena in 1829; he lived with his father on the homestead, farming and mining until 1844, when he settled on his present farm; he was married in 1845 to Miss Emma Abram, from England; they had five children: Augustus, Catherine, Henry, Mary and Kate; Augustus and Catherine are dead; his wife died May 2, 1863; his youngest daughter, Katie, keeps house for him; his son, Henry, living with him, was born 1846, was married in 1870 to Miss Alice Ivey, East Galena Tp.; they have two children: Emma and Maud; Mr. Snyder enlisted in Major Stevenson's Company in 1832, and served during the Black Hawk War; he has 240 acres land valued at $5,000.

Snyder W. H., cashier Merchants N. Bank.

Snyder W. H., bank book-keeper.

Soulard James G., retired.

Speice Andrew, farmer.

Stafford Thos., farmer.

Stafford Thos. Sen., farmer.

Stafford Richard, farmer.

Stafford Robert, farmer.

Starr George, laborer.

Steinmetz Peter, laborer.

Stephens J. P. miner.

Stevenson C. L. U. S. inspector of steamers.

Stoner Stephen, farm laborer.

TAYLOR JOHN W., Jr., laborer.

Taylor Joseph, laborer.

Taylor William B., Sr., laborer.

Telford Andrew; builder.

Thompson Samuel, town clerk.

Tippett Benjamin, farmer; Sec. 12.

Tippett Joseph, farmer.

Tippett William H. farmer.

Tracy Thomas, boat hand.

Tregsloan Joseph, farmer.

Tresslin Walter, saloon keeper.

Trezedder Richard, farmer; Sec. 13.

Tresseder William, farmer.

TURNER ALEXANDER, Farmer; Sec. 34; P. O. Galena; born in Tyrone Co., Ireland, in Feb., 1822; came to this country and Baltimore in 1836; settled on his present farm in 1842; married Miss Mary Campbell, of Galena, Jan. 23, 1855; she was born in Aug., 1827; they have three children: Martha J., born Nov. 20, 1855; Alexander L., Jr., Dec. 28, 1862; Lillie H., Dec. 23, 1868; owns 200 acres land, valued at $5,000; held office of School Director three years.

Turner Ezra, clerk office I. C. R. R.

TURNER JOSEPH, Farmer; Sec. 34; P. O. Galena; born in Tyrone Co., Ireland, March 11, 1809; came to this country and Baltimore May 8, 1833; went to New Orleans in 1840; settled in this Tp. in 1841; married Miss Maria Sanders of Baltimore, in 1836; she died in 1839 married Miss B. Wise, from Germany, Jan. 13, 1857; they have five children: James, born Dec. 16, 1857; Joseph T., in 1859; Josephine, in 1861; Lena, in 1863; Lizzie, in 1865; he lives on 80 acres land in Sec 34, E. Galena Tp., which he holds in trust during life, and owns 160 acres in Rice Tp.

ULRICH LEWIS, clerk.

UNDERBURG FRANZ, Farmer; Sec. 33; P. O. Galena; born in Prussia, April 2, 1815; came to this country and Co. in 1844; settled on his present farm in 1845; was married May 12, 1847, to Miss Mary Brand, from Galena; she was born in Prussia in 1819; they have had six children, five of whom died; their daughter, Mary F., was born April 18, 1849; she was married May 1, 1867, to Henry Hiem; they live with her father; Mr. U. has 74 acres land; held office of Supervisor in 1844 and 1845; was Road Commissioner six years, School Director nine years; has always taken a prominent part in the interests of his Co. and Tp.

Underburg William, farmer.

Upson O. B. watch repairer.

VAHON JAMES, laborer.

Vahon John, laborer.

Vanderwate C. farmer.

Vaughn John, laborer.

VERRAN WM. Farmer; Sec. 28; P. O. Galena; born in England, Feb. 25, 1823; came to this country and Virginia in 1833; settled on his present farm 1849; he has 72 acres land valued at $5,000; married to Miss Mary Hinckley, from Maine, 1850; had four children: Mary E., born May 31, 1852; Virginia C., Oct. 3, 1855; Elizabeth N., March 7, 1857, and Catherine, May 1, 1859; Elizabeth died 1864; his wife died Aug. 22, 1870; he has held office of School Director four years, Overseer of the Poor five years.

VINCENT JOSIAH, Farmer; Sec. 26 and 27; P. O. Galena; born on the old homestead which he now occupies Oct. 11, 1841; the original estate was pre-empted by his father, Henry Vincent, in 1837, who purchased it from the government in 1844; he was married, in 1864, to Miss Eliza Coade, from Racine Co., Wis.; they have had six children: Myron L., born March 14, 1866; Laura, Feb. 5, 1867; Lettie B, Feb. 28, 1869; Charles R., April 20, 1871; Wm. U., June 3, 1872; Lillie May, Aug. 5, 1874; Myron L. died Aug. 15, 1866; Chas. R. died Aug. 22, 1871; he has 100 acres of land in Sections 26 and 27 valued at $3,000; he has held the office of School Director three years; his father, H. Vincent, took a trip across the plains to California in 1851 and died shortly after he reached the Golden Land at the age of 52; his mother died in 1866, at the age of 72 years.

VINCENT CAPT. WM. Farmer; Sec. 26; P. O. Galena; born in Cornwall Co., Eng., Jan. 19, 1823; he came to this country in the Spring of 1837; settled on his present farm in 1846; it is a part of the estate which his father, Henry Vincent, purchased from the government in 1844; he was married in 1848 to Miss Eliza Bray from England; they have had seven children: Henry, Eliza, Emily, Milton, Minnie, Annie, and Willie; Henry and Eliza are dead; he has 138 acres of land in Sections 26 and 34, and 80 acres in Elizabeth Tp.; he now holds the office of Supervisor; he has held the office of Coroner six years, Assessor and Collector two years, School Director eight years, Road Commissioner six years; he enlisted in 1862 in Co. A, 96th I. V. I. as Lieutenant; he was severely wounded Sept. 20, 1863, in the battle of Chicamauga and was permitted a furlough for four months; on his return he was promoted to Captain of his Company; he was actively engaged in 20 hard-fought battles, under command of Gens. Sherman and Thomas; he was breveted Major in 1864; he was prompt to step forth to the defense of his country in her hour of need; he is still active in the interests of his county and township.

VIRTUE ADAM B. Farmer; Sec. 27; P. O. Galena; born in Apple River Tp. April 15, 1843; came to Rice Tp. in 1852; settled on his present farm April 11, 1871; married to Miss Jennie E. Virtue in Rice Tp., April 4, 1871; they have three children: John A., Margaret E., Wilbur J.: John A. died June 29, 1872; he has 149 7-100 acres of land, valued at $5,000.

Voltz John, shoemaker.

WACKENHEIMER CONRAD.

Wadleigh Milton, deputy Co. surveyor.

Ward Pat. teamster.

Wamsley Richard, farmer.

Waterle John, laborer.

Weine Anton, farmer.

Weine Henry, farmer.

Weise Christ. farmer; Sec. 13.

Weiss Anton, farmer.

Weisman John, raftsman.

Weinseck John, farmer; Sec. 36.

Wessgerber, Louis, shoemaker.

Wheldin John, farmer.

Whitmore James, farmer.

Whitmore Henry, farm. and engineer; S. 13.

Williams Chester, laborer.

Willey Davis, blacksmith.

Willey Otto, blacksmith.

Wilson Jas. justice of peace.

Wilcox J. W. farmer.

Wise John, farmer and miner.

Wolfred Fred. farmer; Sec. 11.

Woods Ed. laborer I. C. R. R.

Woods James, laborer I. C. R. R.

Wright Paul, cooper.

YERINGTON BENJAMIN, Keeper of Co. Asylum and Alms House; P. O. Galena; was born in Oswego Co., N. Y., in Aug., 1822; he moved to Michigan in 1834; he settled in Nora, this Co., in 1855, where he now owns a homestead; he was married in 1843 to Miss Harriet A. Parks, from Cayuga Co., N. Y.; she was born in Oct., 1824; they have had five children: Sarah A., John P., Lester E. 1st, Lester E. 2d, Charles Scott; Lester E. 1st died in Sept., 1850; John P. enlisted in Co. K, 96th Regt. I. V. I. in Oct., 1864; he contracted disease while in the army, from which he died April 2, 1869; Mr. Yerington came to his present position in 1868.

Yerrington Lester, law student.

Yohn John, laborer.

Younker Adam, steamboat man.

Major Barton

PROPRIETOR OF BARTON'S HOTEL

WARREN

WARREN TOWNSHIP.

ADWARDS R. farmer; Sec. 23; P. O. Warren.

Aikens E. farmer; P. O. Warren.

Aikens Lawrence, engineer; Warren.

Alders James, laborer; Warren.

ALDERSON T. Retired; Warren.

Anderson Eric, laborer; Warren.

Avery A. H. Warren.

AVERY HENRY M. Warren.

BACKUS T. Sec. 14; P. O. Warren.

Baker Joseph, teaming; Warren.

Baker Solomon, farmer; P. O. Warren.

Baldwin E. S. druggist; Warren.

Baldin L. H. merchant; Warren.

Ballard L. K. farmer; P. O. Warren.

BALLARD W. P. Farmer; Sec. 30; P. O. Warren; born in Cortland Co., N. Y. Nov. 24, 1815; came to this Co. in 1852; Republican and Liberal; owns 340 acres of land; he married Emma Thompson, Sept. 16, 1868; she was born in Wis.; have two children: Nellie and Bernice.

Barnes A. T. tailor; Warren.

Barnard A. T. farmer; P. O. Warren.

Barrows James.

Barry Patrick.

BARTON MAJOR, Warren, whose portrait appears in this work, was born in Rochester, N. Y., Aug. 13, 1822. At the age of five his parents moved to Sandy Creek, west of Rochester, remaining there three years, when they removed to near "Daw's Corners," four miles north of Batavia, N. Y. In the year 1832 they again moved to near North East, Erie Co., Pa., where his father died. The subject of this sketch in the year 1839 went to Watertown, Canada, and was engaged for three years as a millwright. In 1842 he went to Lockport, N. Y., and carried on the grocery business until he moved to Chicago, in 1845, where he followed the auction business. In the Spring of 1849, a freshet having carried off all the bridges there, Mr. Barton started a ferry across the river where the Lake Street Bridge now stands. The city soon purchased the ferry, when Mr. Barton went to Rockford, and was proprietor of a hack line between that city and Elgin, then the terminus of the Chicago & Galena Union R. R. He followed up the terminus of the railroad and settled at Warren, in the livery business, in the year 1853, where he has since remained for a quarter of a century. In 1873 he built the well-known and popular hotel, the "Barton House," of which he still remains proprietor. As a public spirited citizen, he has always been ready to help any enterprise that would benefit Warren. It is to the enterprise and energy of such men that this Western country owes its advancement and prosperity. He married Harriet A. Stowell, in Warren, Sept. 5, 1859. She was born in Paris, Me., May 16, 1832. They had six children; three dead, Jessie and Bessie (twins) and Belle; three living: Lola B., Josephine S. and Major Arthur.

Bayne Chas. student; Warren.

Bayne Jas. Justice of the Peace; Warren.

Bayne R. J. clerk freight office I. C. R. R.; Warren.

Bedell Seth, grocer; Warren.

Bedford J. W. retired; Warren.

Benson W. S. station agt. I. C. R. R.; Warren.

Biggs Geo. laborer; Warren.

Biggs J. D. grocer; Warren.

Bird James, renter; P. O. Warren.

Bird J. W. cooper; Warren.

Bird John, miller; Warren.

Binz Geo. H. engineer; Warren.

Black James, laborer; Warren.

Black Perry, farmer; Sec. 14; P. O. Warren.

Black William, laborer; Warren.

Blackmore Frank, laborer; Warren.

Blackmore J. R. laborer; Warren.

Blackmore Jeff, teamster; Warren.

Blackstone B. agent; Warren.

Blake T. M. salesman; Warren.

BOONE CHAS. Farmer; Sec. 26; P. O. Warren; born in Somersetshire, Eng., Sept. 29, 1831; came to this Co. in 1854; Independent, Greenbacker and Liberal; owns 174 acres of land; was a member of the Nat. Guards, Nev. Ter., in 1863-4; married Sarah Leverett, of Adams Co., Ill., in 1859; have six children: two boys and four girls.

BOOTHBY N. Manufacturer of Inlaid Floors; Warren, Ill.; born in Ohio, Sept., 1832; came to this Co. in 1858; Republican and Liberal.

Boothby O. mechanic; Warren.

Brant William, engineer; Warren.

Brandes Henry, boots and shoes; Warren.

Bridge W. H. miller; Warren.

Brink Ead.

BRINK ABRAM L. Bakery and Confectionery; Warren; was born in Marathon, Cortland Co., N. Y., Jan. 23, 1829; came to this Co. in 1852; Republican and Episcopal preferred; has held the office of Town Clerk, and a member of the

Town Board; married Rocklette P. Knapp in 1853; she was born in Chautauqua Co., N. Y.; she died Aug. 12, 1869; present wife was Catherine Williams; born in Wales, May 15, 1837; married Nov. 22, 1870; have four children: Earl C. and Henry Jay by first marriage; Chester A. and Messena by present marriage.

Brown H. V. farmer; P. O. Warren.

Buckley John, farm; Sec. 27; P. O. Warren.

Buckman A. F. physician; Warren.

Burch Senica.

Burd George, laborer; Warren.

Burk William, laborer; Warren.

BURNETT ALEX. Miner; Warren; born in Franklin Co., N. Y., Oct. 15, 1810; Democratic and Liberal; Mr. Burnett was the first settler in the Town of Warren; laid out the town, and built the first house; built the Burnett House in 1854; Alex. Burnett came to this Co. in July, 1839, and first settled near what was known as "Cowers Mound," on Apple River; he was one of the first Trustees (for two years) of Warren after township organization, serving one year as President of the Board; he held office of Constable from 1857 to 1860, also Deputy Sheriff; some time in year 1850 he went to Minn. and spent two years building a saw mill 100 miles north of St. Paul; also built one in St. Paul; then returned to Warren; was captain of Company H., 96th I. V. I.; served one year; married Sarah A. Barlow, born in Florence, N. Y., March 24, 1841; have four children living: Warren, Phidelia, Nellie and Walter.

Buser S. L. artist; Warren.

BUTLER SELENUS J. Livery man and dealer in Agricultural Implements; Warren; born in Trumbull Co., O., Aug. 5, 1837; came to this Co. in 1876; has lived in the adjoining Co. since 1845; Republican and Methodist; married Frances Galvin Aug. 5, 1857; she was born in Trumbull Co., Ohio, May 20, 1838; she died July 11, 1875; present wife was Martha E. Lewis, born April 2, 1847, in Smithfield, Penn.; married Feb. 29, 1876; have two children, E. Grace, born Oct. 30, 1863; S. Erwin, Oct. 20, 1870.

CALDWELL W. S. physician and surgeon; Warren.

Campbell Chas. traveling agent; Warren.

CAMPBELL GEO. Farmer; Sec. 36. P. O. Warren; born in Ireland in 1803; came to this Co. in 1848; Republican and Methodist; owns 40 acres of land; married Elizabeth Montgomery in 1830; they have five children living, Eliza Jane, Robert, Henry, Wm., George, Maxwell, Scott, Sarah Ann; lost two.

Campbell M. S. Sec. 6; P. O. Warren.

Campbell W. G. blacksmith; Warren.

Capron W. W. express agent; Warren.

Carlton C. W. salesman; Warren.

Carlton H. M. merchant; Warren.

Carpenter E. farmer; P. O. Warren.

Carr J. H. farmer; P. O. Warren.

Canfield A. J. traveling agent; Warren.

Canfield M. L. butcher; Warren.

Chapman Jerrie, merchant; Warren

Charter E. A. renter; P. O. Warren.

Charter L. A. clerk; Warren.

Chaster Chas. W. retired; Warren.

Cheney Joseph, carpenter; Warren.

Clark Fred L. grain dealer; Warren.

Clark S. A. banker; Warren.

CLAYPOOL MRS. ROSAN, Warren; she was born in Byron Co., Ky., in 1819; was married to Milton Claypool in Sangamon Co., in this state, in 1835; they moved to this Co. in 1847; Mr. Claypool was born in Ohio in 1814; came to this state with his parents when nine years old; he represented this town as Supervisor, and has held various other offices; had three sons in the army: William, Newton and James, all of whom served until the close of the war, and were honorably discharged; Mr. Claypool raised the first wheat in this Co.; he died at his residence, in this place, on the 27th Dec., 1869.

Clendenning Jonathan, retired; Warren.

Clock Eugene, farmer; P. O. Warren.

Colburn W. R. miller; Warren.

Cole Fred, nursery; Warren.

Coltrin Alonzo, mason; Warren.

Coltren E. C. retired; Warren.

Conlee T. A. traveling salesman; Warren.

CONYNE A. V. Dealer in General Merchandise; Warren; born in Montgomery Co., N. Y., Jan. 1, 1829; came to Lafayette Co., Wis., in 1857, and to this Co. in 1867; Republican and Presbyterian; married Sarah Fox, of Montgomery Co., N. Y., Feb. 4, 1857; she was born Oct. 8, 1834; have two children, Charles D., born July 19, 1858; William F., Jan. 24, 1860.

Cooley B. shoemaker; Warren.

Coppernoll N. retired farmer; Warren.

Coppernoll Z. G. blacksmith; Warren.

Coverly E. farmer; Sec. 32; P. O. Warren.

Coverly James.

COWEN MRS. HARRIET, Warren, Ill.; was born in Chautauqua Co., N. Y., in 1821; came West in 1844; was married to Luther H. Cowen Nov. 13, 1847; have three children living. Maj. Luther H. Cowen, the subject of this sketch, was born in Clay Co., Ill., March 11, 1822; he resided the most of his life in this Co.; his parents settling in Galena in 1828; in his youth he evinced a strong desire for mental culture, and intellectual pursuits; notwithstanding the disadvantages for education incident to a new country, he succeeded, by his own efforts, in acquiring a liberal education, and particularly succeeded in the science of mathematics, and was skilled as a surveyor; modest and unassuming in his manner, he continued the pursuits of a private citizen, mostly engaged in farming, until the Fall of 1859, when he was nominated for the office of Co. Surveyor and was elected by a large majority, which office he held until he went in the army; he volunteered as a private soldier in Aug., 1861; was elected Capt. of Co. B, 45th Regt. I. V. I.; he distinguished himself at the battle of Fort Donelson by his cool and daring courage under the hottest fire during that terrible battle; he was in some other battles prior to his Regt. being ordered to Vicksburg, where he always exhibited the greatest skill and courage; he was promoted to the office of Major, for meritorious conduct on the battle-field, which office he held during the time that his Regt. was attached to Gen. Grant's department; he was engaged in a succession of battles fought near Vicksburg, up to the 22d of May, when he fell at the head of his Regt., bravely leading his men against the fortifications of the enemy in the face of a murderous fire; thus fell a noble and brave man in the discharge of his duty to his country; what higher tribute can be paid him? what greater eulogy can be pronounced, or worldly honors conferred upon him—he died in defense of his country.

Cowan R. V. constable; Warren.

Crandall S. butter and egg dealer; Warren.

CROPPER W. H. Stock Dealer; Warren; was born in Nottinghamshire, Eng., in 1831; came to this country in 1851 and settled in N. Y., where he remained one Summer; from there he went to Milwaukee, in which place he followed the business of milling for a number of years; married Miss M. Helena Gilden, in Iowa Co., Wis., in 1857; she was born in Lincolnshire, Eng., in 1841; they moved to this Co. in 1870, and it has since been their home; their children are: Eliza, born in 1858; Ann, in 1861; W. H., in 1864; Gracie, in 1870; Mr. Cropper has been engaged in stock dealing 15 years.

CRUMMER DR. BENJ. F. Warren; son of James Crummer; was born at Elizabeth, Sept. 18, 1848; was educated at Michigan University, and graduated from the medical department in 1869; also graduated from University of New York City, in 1875; practiced medicine at Elizabeth from 1869 to 1876, when he removed to Warren; married May Louise Donkersley, of Rockford, in 1871.

Crummer Jos., Meth. clergyman; Warren.

Cummings Alex. S. 21; P. O. Apple River.

Cummings M. laborer; Warren.

Cunningham A. miller; S. 33; P. O. Warren.

Cutiss G. W. retired; Warren.

DALRYMPLE S. L. traveling man; Warren.

Dawson Frank W.

Dawson J. C. farmer; P. O. Warren.

Dawson R. farmer; P. O. Warren.

Dean D. H. blacksmith; Warren.

DeBeque, R. laborer; Sec. 33; P. O. Apple River.

Delong R. R. retired; Warren.

De Long W. C. hardware dealer; Warren.

Dersham John, retired; Warren.

Dick A. C. carpenter; Warren.

Dick Byron, brakeman; Warren.

Dobler A. harness mkr. and dealer; Warren.

Dobler J. F. H. retired; Warren.

Dobler L. F. Sec. 25; P. O. Warren.

DOBLER PETER H. Retired; Warren; born in Lycoming Co., Pa., Feb. 19, 1823; came to this Co. in 1857; Republican and a member of the M. E. Church; has held the office of Town Trustee for several terms; Mr. Dobler has been engaged in milling, grain and general merchandising; also has followed farming; married Rebecca Follmer in 1847; she was born in Lycoming Co., Pa., Dec. 11, 1824; she died Nov. 7, 1866; his present wife was Harriet Young, born in Warren, Knox Co., Maine, Jan. 18, 1826; married in Oct. 1867; have four children: Jonathan A. Lewis F., Mary and Charles W.

Donkersley Jay H. hotel clerk; Warren.

Dodd Chas. laborer; Warren.

Dugan Wm. laborer; Sec. 21; P. O. Warren.

Duncan Frederic, sexton; Warren.

EASLEY H. D.

Easton B. F. laborer; Warren.

Eastman Amos, retired farmer; Warren.

Eckman D. lab.; S. 33; P. O. Apple River.

Eckman T. laborer; S.33; P.O. Apple River.

EDWARDS MRS. MARY, Farmer; Sec. 14; P. O. Warren; born in Cornwall, Eng., Jan. 31, 1827; came to this Co. in 1849; have four children: Anna, now living in England, Mary, William and Alice Jane. Richard Edwards, father-in-law of Mrs. Edwards, and now residing with her, was born in Cornwall, England, Jan. 14, 1788; came to this Co. in 1842; Republican and Methodist.

Edwards R. retired; Warren.

Elston G. farmer; Sec. 27; P. O. Warren.

Emery David P. agent of Jo Daviess co-operative association; Warren.

Emry Wm. farmer; Sec. 22; P. O. Warren.

FANNIN A. postmaster; Warren.

Farnham L. F. farm; Sec. 25; P.O. Warren.

Fleharty W. H. farm; S. 17; P. O. Warren.

Flower E. W. carpenter; Warren.

Fogerty M. laborer; Warren.

Foley John, laborer; Warren.

Ford W. A. clerk; Warren.

Foss H. W. dealer in agr. imp.; Warren.

Francisco H. S. mason; Warren.

Freeman R. retired; Warren.

Frisbie J. C. carpenter; Warren.

Frysley, E. H. shoemaker; Warren.

GALE W. L. lumberman; Warren.

GANN HERST C. Editor and Proprietor of Warren *Sentinel*; born in Lycoming Co., Pa., Jan.25, 1844; came to this Co. in 1854; Republican; Free Will Baptist preferred; was in Co. M, 11th Regt. I.V.C.; served 8 months; married Sada E. Haynes Nov. 5, 1868; she was born in Rushford, Alleghany Co., N. Y., April 20, 1849; have three children living, Herst C., born Aug. 11, 1871, Louis R., Nov. 14, 1873, Libbie Ella, Jan. 15, 1875; lost two.

Gardner John, mason; Warren.

Gardner Thomas, farmer; P. O. Warren.

Gates W. H. laborer; Warren.

Gower D. E.

Geeting W. H. fruit and confectionery store; Warren.

Giles C. L. Justice of the Peace; Warren.

Glover Milton, laborer; Warren.

Godding H. W. renter; P. O. Warren.

Godding Luther, laborer; Warren.

Godding M. laborer; Warren.

Graham W. H. laborer; Warren.

Gray S. A.

Greenbough E. laborer; Warren.

GREGORY CHARLTON M. Co. Treasurer; Warren; born in Cayuga Co., N. Y., Jan. 21, 1838; came to this Co. in 1867; Republican and Liberal; Mr. Gregory is Superintendent of the North America & Ophir Silver Mining Co., of Wyoming Territory; is an experienced miner, having been in Nevada four years; married Julia Surprise, born in Lockport, N. Y., Sept. 4, 1850; married Oct. 24, 1867; have three children: Charlton L., Myron S. and Francis W.

HARPER V. laborer; Sec. 33; P. O. Apple River.

Hart D. W. carpenter; Warren.

Hawks John, laborer; Warren.

Hawk Samuel, laborer; Warren.

Hawk Wm. laborer; Warren.

HAWLEY ROBERT, Farmer and Stock Raiser; Warren; was born in Lafayette Co., Wis., Nov. 26, 1829, and was engaged in farming and stock raising; he was one of the Board of Supervisors and Assessor; in the Spring of 1877 he moved to Warren and resides upon a farm of 300 acres, still owning his farm of 240 acres in Lafayette Co.; he married Theresa E. Way in Freeport, Ill., Oct. 20, 1854; she was born in Lewis Co., N. Y., Oct., 1832; they had five children, two dead, Stella and Alice; three now living: Elsie B., Dillie I., and May E.; Mr. H. is now largely engaged in buying and shipping stock; his father, Aaron Hawley, with five others, was waylaid by Indians during the Black Hawk War, while on their way home to Lafayette Co. from Sangamon Co., where they had been to purchase cattle, and only two of them escaped, Mr. Hawley's body was never found; his horse was afterward seen in the possession of Black Hawk, and ridden by that Indian Chief.

Hazen M.

Hewett Andrew, carpenter; Warren.

Heydon Geo. retired; Warren.

HICKS GEORGE, Farmer; Sec. 36; P. O. Warren; born in Cornwall, Eng., in 1810; came to this Co. in 1850; owns 160 acres of land; married Jane Osborne in 1831; she was born in England; have five children living.

Hicks J. W. farmer; P. O. Warren.

Hicks Joseph, cattle buyer; P. O. Warren.

Hicks Patrick, laborer; Warren.

Hicks Peter W. Sec. 36; P. O. Warren.

Hicks Samuel, option dealer; Warren.

Hicks T. H. farmer; Sec. 31; P. O. Warren.

Hicks Thomas S. butter buyer; Warren.

Hicks W. farmer; P. O. Warren.

High M. laborer; Warren.

HILEMAN MICHAEL, House Mover; Warren; born in Huntingdon Co., Pa., Jan. 22, 1820; came to this Co. in 1852; Republican and Liberal; has held the offices of Town Clerk and Constable; was Sergt. in Co. H, 96th Regt. I. V. I.; served three years, and was 15 months in the following rebel prisons: Libby, Danville, Andersonville, Charleston and Florence; married Amanda R. Backus, of Erie Co., Pa.; she died the 9th of March, 1867; present wife was Phœbe A. Willots; married Jan. 9, 1869; have five children by former marriage and one by present: MaryL., Joseph M., Thomas B., Martha E., Georgetta and Lottie.

Hinckly Lewis.

Hoefer Wm. grocery and provision store; Warren.

HODSON THOMAS, Farmer; Sec. 21; P. O. Apple River; born in England,

Jan. 28, 1848; Ind. Republican, and Meth.; has held the offices of School Director and Path Master; was in the 15th Regt. I. V. I., Co. E; served two years; was in Andersonville prison 7 months; captured at the battle of Kenesaw Mountain; married Alice Wright; she was born in Wis., May, 1848; married 17th of March, 1869; have two children: Henry Rollin and Sadie Bell.

Holland John, laborer; Warren.

House Peter, laborer; Warren.

HUETT GEORGE, Renter; Sec. 32; P. O. Apple River; born in Beaver Co., Pa., Aug. 4, 1827; came to this Co. in 1846; Republican and Liberal; married Sarah Ann Noyes of Pa., Oct. 11, 1857.

Huett Wm. laborer; Warren.

Hussey J. M. clerk lumber yard; Warren.

Hutchinson H. J. farm; S. 18; P. O. Warren.

Hutchinson J. H. salesman; Warren.

INMAN HENRY, mason; Warren.

Isabelle J. T. laborer; Warren.

JACKSON LEBRON, laborer; Warren.

Jefferson Thomas, laborer; Warren.

Jenkins J. B. agricultural dealer; Warren.

Jewell John, laborer; Warren.

Jewell Wm. retired; Warren.

Johnson Chas. laborer; Warren.

Johnson J. E. printer; Warren.

Johnson John, retired; Warren.

Jones A. S. retired; Warren.

Jones E. E. laborer; Warren.

Jones Sylvester, carpenter; Warren.

Jones Wm. mason; Warren.

Jones A. M. real estate dealer; Warren.

Judd Cyrus, teamster; Warren.

KEELER JOHN, carpenter; Warren.

Kellam Cuthbert, farmer; P. O. Warren.

Kellam L. M. baggage master, I. C. R. R.; Warren.

Kellogg O. laborer; Warren.

Kenney James, farmer; P. O. Apple River.

Kessler L. E. druggist; Warren.

Kevern Samuel.

King Frank W. laborer; Warren.

King J. B. teamster; Warren.

Kenne E.

Kirkendall John, laborer; Warren.

Knapp C. E. blacksmith; Warren.

KNAPP JAMES J. Druggist; Warren; born in Holland, Feb. 12, 1843; came to this Co. in 1867; married Miss E. Corning Sept. 1, 1867.

Knight Irvin, mason; Warren.

Knight K. mason; Warren.

Knight T. mason; Warren.

LAW J.

Lane John, farmer; P. O. Warren.

Leach Henry, Sec. 35; P. O. Warren.

LEVERETT JOSEPH, Retired; Warren; born in Mass. Sept. 4, 1804; Republican; Liberal; has held offices of Town Clerk and Road Commissioner; married Mary Tanner, of Mass., Feb. 19, 1828; have three children: Charles, Mary and Edith.

Lewis T. O. farmer; P. O. Warren.

Lindsley A. D. watch maker; Warren.

Lieb J.

Lovin Stephen B. harness maker; Warren.

Long Charles, laborer; Warren.

Long F. D. renter, Sec. 26; P. O. Warren.

Luke M. H.

Lynch James, laborer; Warren.

Lynde I. P. retired; Warren.

McCARTY P. Sec. 28; P.O. Apple River.

McCauley John, farmer; Sec. 21; P. O. Warren.

McCauley Sam'l, Sec. 21; P.O. Apple River.

McClatchy Wm. laborer; Warren.

McCORMICK ANDREW, Farmer; Sec. 34; P.O. Warren; born in the Co. of Tyrone, Ireland, Sept. 4, 1836; came to this Co. in 1872; Republican and Presbyterian; owns 230 acres of land; has held the office of School Director; married Elizabeth McCormick, of Ireland, in 1867; have five children, four girls and one boy.

McFarland P. grain dealer.

McIntee M.

McJairssey Rob't, Sec. 22; P. O. Warren.

McKinney J. farmer.

Marsh John, retired; Warren.

Martin Kent, laborer; Warren.

Martgall Daniel, teamster; Warren.

Matthews L. B. coal and cement dlr.; Warren.

Matthews W. C. retired; Warren.

Mears John, laborer; Warren.

Menzemer Geo. farmer; P. O. Warren.

Menzemer Geo. A. farmer; P. O. Warren.

Menzemer W. farmer; P. O. Warren.

Messersmith J. W. wagon maker; Warren.

Messersmith Z. T. wagon maker; Warren.

Metz Samuel, farmer; P. O. Warren.

Meyers C. G. laborer; Warren.

Mills H. S. sewing machine agent; Warren.

Miller A. fruit and candy store; Warren.

Miller Geo. W. clerk; Warren.

Miller L. farmer.
Miller O. B. restaurant and bakery; Warren.
Miller T. T. tailor; Warren.
Miner E. B. laborer; Warren.
Moran Wm. laborer; Warren.

MORRILL JOHN S. Retired Miner; Warren; born in Monmouth, Kennebec Co., Maine, Dec. 6, 1816; came to this Co. in 1841; Republican and Spiritualist; Mr. Morrill was engaged in mining in Shullsburg, Wis.; married Mary E. Wilcox in 1852; born in N. Y. in 1832; have had two children, one living: Henry Albert.

Morris E. H. provision dealer; Warren.
Morris J. H.
Morris L. E. provision dealer, Warren.
Morris W. E. retired; Warren.
Morse C. C. laborer; Warren.
Morse R. C. salesman; Warren.
Morse Watts, laborer; Warren.
Morton C. E. farmer; Sec. 30; P. O. Warren.
Morton Gus. farmer; P. O. Warren.
Morton G. A. farmer; Sec. 25; P. O. Warren.

MORTON MRS. RUTH J. Farming; Sec. 30; P. O. Warren; born in Lincoln Co., Maine, March 30, 1825; came to this Co. in 1853; owns 80 acres of land; married Ward L. Morton May 8, 1853; he was born in Maine; was in Co. H, 96th I. V. I.; killed in the battle of Chicamauga; have one child, Chas. E. Morton, born Sept. 21, 1855.

Murphy John A. liveryman; Warren.
Murphy Mort. liveryman; Warren.
Murphy M. S. detective; Warren.
Murphy T. yard master I. C. R. R; Warren.
Murray Chas. carriage maker; Warren.

NEUSUS JOHN, tailor; Warren
Newton Wilford.
Northan A. J. retired farmer; Warren.

O'NEIL ARTHUR, renter; Sec. 28; P.O. Apple River.
Osterout Peter.

PARSENS JOHN, retired; Warren.

PARKER JUSTIN N. Shoemaker and Dealer; Warren; born in Chittendon Co., Vermont, Nov. 16, 1825; came to this Co. in 1846; Republican and Presbyterian; was Second Lieut. in 92d I. V. I., Co. G; married Hannah Edwards June 14, 1849; she was born in Johnson, LaMoille Co., Vt., Sept. 22, 1826; have three children living: Gideon H., born Oct. 6, 1850, Ida M., Oct. 6, 1857, Alice C., March 19, 1859; Eugene N., April 9, 1854, died Dec. 17, 1856, Frank Eugene, April 28, 1861, died Sept. 12, 1862.

PELLETT DAVID, Retired Farmer; Warren; was born in Windsor Co., Conn., in 1787; he removed from this place to N. Y. when he was 25 years of age; came from there to this Co. in 1866; married Polly Jones, of N. Y., in 1837; she was born in 1802; Mr. Pellett's son William was in the army.

Pepoon A. Sec. 35; P. O. Warren.

PEPOON G. W. Farmer; Sec. 26; P.O. Warren; born in Painesville, Ohio, Nov. 4, 1832; came to this Co. March 19, 1850; Republican and Presbyterian; owns 186 acres of land; has held the office of Superintendent of Schools eight years; also, the offices of Collector and Assessor; holds the last mentioned office at the present time; was First Lieut. in Co. K, 96th I. V. I.; served three years; also, was Provost Marshal of second brigade, first division, fourth army corps; married Miss Mary A. Abbey April 7, 1857; she was born in Painesville, Ohio, Aug. 26, 1835; have three children: Wm. A., born Jan. 25, 1858, Herman S., Jan. 21, 1860, Mary A., July 15, 1868.

Pepoon M. carpenter and builder.
Perry John, Sec. 13; P. O. Warren.
Pettibone T. carpenter; Warren.
Phillips A. E. blacksmith; Warren.
Phillips Chas. prop. Barnett House; Warren.
Phillips J. H. salesman; Warren.
Phillips N. P. blacksmith; Warren.
Pierce B. G. physician and surgeon; Warren.
Platt J. A. machinist; Warren.

PLATT JOHN D. Warren; born in Otsego Co., New York, Nov. 28, 1824; worked with his father on the farm till 21 years of age; came West in 1849, and located in McHenry Co., Ill., and engaged in merchandising; married Sept. 30, 1850, to Julia E. Carpenter, only daughter of Dr. Joseph Carpenter, of Otsego Co., N.Y.; came to Warren Nov. 21, 1851, and started the first business house in town; was appointed Postmaster in Warren in 1852; elected County Judge to fill a vacancy in 1855; re-elected in 1857 for a full term; was a member of the celebrated Charleston Convention in 1860.

Powell Albert, laborer; Warren.
Powell John, farmer; Warren.
Powell S. laborer; S. 33; P. O. Apple River.
Power N. laborer; Warren.
Prescott Chas. teamster; Warren.
Pritchard Wm. retired soldier; Warren.
Propp Fred. laborer; Warren.

RANDALL A. switchman Mineral Point R. R.; Warren.
Redfeam F. retired; Warren.
Reed D. T. farmer; Warren.
Reed J. Sec. 29; P. O. Apple River.

Reed Wm. S. renter; Sec. 22; P. O. Warren.

Rembe Fred.

Rembe Phillips.

Reynolds J. W. laborer; Warren.

Richards E. J. laborer; Warren.

Richards Wm. miner; Warren.

Richards W. R. laborer; Warren.

Richardson Geo. merchant; Warren.

Richardson N. B. banker; Warren.

Robbins A. painter; Warren.

Robbins Geo. farmer; Sec. 17; P. O. Warren.

Robinson C. retired; Warren.

Robinson Hugh, laborer; P. O. Warren.

ROGERS MANLEY, Banker; born in Mt. Morris, Livingston Co., N. Y., Aug. 2, 1833; came to this Co. in Feb., 1852; Republican and Presbyterian; Mr. Rogers was engaged in the mercantile business from 1852 to 1863; organized banking house of M. Rogers & Co. in the Fall of 1864; this was succeeded by the Farmers Nat. Bank of Warren; was President of this for 10 years; in 1874 the business was again changed to that of Rogers, Richardson & Co., as at present; married Miss Maria Abbey in 1859; she was born in Painesville, Ohio, in 1842; have four children: James Hervey, Wm. Eugene, Jennie A. and Lucius Henry.

Roper J., S. 21; P.O. Warren and Apple River.

SAMPSON G. A. feed store; Warren.

Sanford D. drayman; Warren.

Sanford E. A. carpenter; Warren.

Sawdey Stewart, teamster; Warren.

Schadle A. C. dentist; Warren.

Schuster Jno. retired; Warren.

Seace Edgar, farmer; Sec. 24; P.O. Warren.

SERVISS BERI, Farmer; P. O. Warren; born in Montgomery Co., N.Y., June 30, 1810; came to this Co. in 1832; Republican and M. E.; has held the office of Justice of Peace several years; also, Supervisor; was a soldier in the Black Hawk War; married to Lydia A. Morton, of Maine, Oct. 2, 1846; have six children.

Serviss Orlando, laborer; Warren.

Serviss Wm. laborer; Warren.

Sherk Joseph, undertaker; Warren.

Sherk Joseph A. painter; Warren.

Sherk Thos. J. farmer; Warren.

Shroeder A. A. tinsmith; Warren.

Spofford C. F. harness and carriage dealer; Warren.

Spofford H. W. harness and carriage dealer; Warren.

Spofford M. teamster; Warren.

Spore A. J. teamster; Warren.

Spore Benj. brakeman; Warren.

Spore H. retired; Warren.

Stanbro J. laborer; Warren.

Stansbrough Edwin, laborer; Sec. 33; P. O. Apple River.

Stanton J. E. constable and collector; Warren.

Sullivan D. laborer; Warren.

Surum M. C. shoemaker; Warren.

Switzer Walter, retired; Warren.

TALLMAN WM. laborer; Warren.

Taylor C. F. lumber merchant; Warren.

TEAR JOHN, Farmer and Stock Ra is er; Sec. 24; P. O. Warren; born in the Isle of Man, June 23, 1814; came to this Co. in 1851; Republican and Free Will Baptist; owns 425 acres of land; has held the office of Road Commissioner; married Betsey Buckman Dec. 24, 1838; she was born in Oneida Co., N. Y., Feb. 29, 1816; died Dec. 22, 1864; have nine children: Rosetta, born Oct. 16, 1839, Wallace, March 11, 1841 (he is in the regular service, 14th Reg't., stationed in Texas), Rosina, Jan. 21, 1343, Harmony, Jan. 20, 1845, Josephine, May 18, 1848, Matilda D., April 7, 1853, Henry C. and Harriett, March 5, 1856, Ada, Jan. 6, 1859.

Teft S. C, carpenter; Warren.

Tenyke E. gardener; Warren.

Terner B. baker; Warren.

Terry Michael, laborer; Warren.

Terry Pat. laborer; Warren.

Thomas David, blacksmith; Warren.

Thompson William, merchant; Warren.

Thornton T. D. shoemaker; Warren.

TOWNSEND GEORGE N. Retired; P. O. Warren; born in Vernon Co., New Jersey, Aug. 28, 1806; came to this Co. in 1827; Republican and Liberal; owns 800 acres of land, value, $32,000; has held the offices of Road Commissioner, Poor Master, School Director and Post Master; was Orderly Sergeant in the Winnebago War of 1827; married Mary Miner, of Schoharie Co., N. Y., Oct. 15, 1829; have 13 children: Samantha L., Amanda S., Samuel A., Geo. N., Annette, Joseph W., Jane C., Susan K., Olive A., Grazelle S., Hortense M., Hugh L., Emeline P.

TOWNSEND HALSTEAD S. Warren, Ill.; was born in Steuben Co., N. Y., April 11, 1814; came to Ill. in 1830; served in the Black Hawk War in 1832 under Gen. Dodge; was married in 1836 to Hannah Carver and settled permanently in the Town of Rush, where he bought a large tract of land and engaged in farming; ten children were born unto them, five girls and five boys, nine of whom are now living, and all married except the two youngest girls; their names are as follows: Robert K., Edward E., Samuel H., Winfield S. (died in 1869)

John M., Matilda R., Servilda, Cynthia A. Alice C. and Della; in politics he was formerly a Whig, but now, and for many years, one of the staunchest members and workers of the Republican party; he was the first Supervisor ever elected in the Town of Rush and was re-elected for nine years; in 1858 he was elected and served in the State Legislature; in 1869 he retired from his farm and moved to the Town or Village of Warren, where he now resides; in 1870 he was again elected to State Legislature.

TOTTEN ALBERT H. Furniture Dealer; Warren; born in Hamilton, Ontario, Canada, May 17, 1855; came to this Co. in 1856; Republican.

Tower M. carpenter; Warren.

Trague John, renter; Sec. 22; P.O. Warren.

Trague Josiah, farmer; P. O. Warren.

Tuttle A. M. physician; Warren.

Tuttle Lloyd, barber; Warren.

VAN DEUSEN RUFUS, salesman; Warren.

VAN DEUSEN JOHN, Farmer; P. O. Warren; born in Albany Co., N. Y., in 1823; came to this Co. in 1870; Independent and Liberal; married Margaret Jones in Feb., 1849; she was born in Albany Co., N. Y., Sept. 10, 1825; have four children: Robert (a medical student), Rufus P. (salesman), Rachel, and James H. (clerk).

Vandervert H. S. grain dealer; Warren.

Vandyke C. C. Sec. 33; P. O. Apple River.

Vandyke C. C., Jr., thresher; Warren.

Vandyke Perry, well-driller; Warren.

Vandyke Wm. retired; Warren.

Volglesang A. D. harness maker; Warren.

WALLACE JAS. Sec. 17; P. O. Apple River.

Ward E. T. painter; Warren.

Warren D. W.

WEAR ROBERT, Farmer; Sec. 34; P. O. Warren; born in England in 1810; came to this Co. in 1850; owns 170 acres of land; has held the office of Path Master; married Mary Lauton, of England, in 1841; have 9 children; Thos. Wear was in 7th Ia. V. C., Co. F; served 3 years and one month.

Wear Thos. Sec. 54; P. O. Warren.

Wear Wm. Sec. 34; P. O. Warren.

Weaver M. S. butcher.

Wells G. D. railroad man; Warren.

Wells W. C. artist.

West H. miner.

Weston R. renter; P. O. Warren.

Whaley D. laborer; Warren.

White Chas. Sec. 25; P. O. Apple River.

White Jas. farmer; Sec. 20; Warren.

White Joseph, Sec. 16; P. O. Apple River.

Whitham Jno. salesman; Warren.

Whitham Jno., Jr., salesman; Warren.

Whitham Wm. farmer.

WHITLOCK B. C. Retired Grain Dealer; Warren; born in Union Co., Ill., March 25, 1833; came to this Co. in 1866 and engaged in the grain trade, which business he has followed for 20 years; married Miss H. N. Poole, in Lafayette Co., Ind., in 1867; she was born in Clark Co., this State, in 1842; Mrs. Whitlock had two brothers in the army, William C. and Livien E. Poole; they served through the war with distinction, and were honorably discharged; her father, Dr. Sydney Poole, was born in Vermont in 1804; when he was 22 years of age he entered the Medical University at N. Y., from which he graduated; in a few years he came West and commenced the practice of medicine in Clark Co. in 1835, thus becoming the pioneer physician of that Co.; he was commissioned Col. during the war with Mexico; he died at his residence in Union Co. in 1861, respected and honored by all; Mr. Whitlock's father was born in Virginia in 1800; he came to Union Co., this State, in 1822, one of the first settlers in that Co., it being then a comparative wilderness, there being scarcely any inhabitants in the Co. at that time; Mr. Whitlock had a brother, James H. Whitlock, in the army; went in as Capt., was promoted to Major, and is at present a member of the State Legislature of Cal.; have four children: Laura M., born Dec. 9, 1868, Fannie J., Dec. 12, 1870, Maud, June 6, 1872, William Henry, June 27, 1875.

WILCOX G. H. & E. P. Merchants; Warren, Ill.; came to this Co. in 1872; were born in Chenango Co., N. Y., G. H. born June 7, 1840, E. P. born Nov. 4, 1846; Independent and Liberal; Wilcox Bros. are dealers in Dry Goods, Groceries, Notions, Boots and Shoes, Clothing and Gents' Furnishing Goods, Main St., opposite the railroad depot.

Wilkerson James, retired; Warren.

WILLIAMS BENJAMIN, Retired; Warren, Ill.; born in Saratoga Co., N. Y., May 7, 1804; came to this Co. in 1844; Republican and Free Will Baptist; has held the office of Road Commissioner and has been a member of the Town Board; Mr. Williams' parents were Quakers and he was raised in that belief; while a young man he experienced religion and joined the Free Will Baptist Church, and is a regular ordained minister of that denomination; organized two churches in this Co.; has always been a strong advocate of the temperance cause; an earnest abolitionist and is bitterly opposed to all secret societies; married So-

WARREN.

phronia Norris, Jan. 23, 1828; she died in June 1830; present wife was Soloma Hall; born in Conway, Mass., March 5, 1811; married Feb. 8, 1833; have five children living, two sons and three daughters.

Williams B., Jr., teamster; Warren.

Williams Benjamin, teamster; Warren.

Williams I. farmer; Sec. 19; P. O. Warren.

WILLIAMS SILAS L. Farmer; P. O. Warren; born in Scales Mound, Nov. 22, 1850; Republican and Liberal; married Florence F. Barron, Dec. 7, 1854; she was born in Milan, Cayuga Co., N. Y.; have one child, Elsie D., born Feb. 19, 1876.

Williamson R. Sec. 29; P. O. Apple River.

Wilson George W. Sec. 22; P. O. Warren.

Wilson James, Sec. 22; P. O. Warren.

Wilson John A. Sec. 22: P. O. Warren.

Wilson J. T. renter; Sec. 23; P. O. Warren.

Wilson Robt. farmer; P. O. Warren.

Wilson Wm. farmer; Sec. 22; P. O. Warren.

Woodworth J. C. hardware mercht.; Warren.

WOODWORTH LUTHER P. Farmer; Sec. 26; P. O. Warren; born in Bolton, Warren Co., N. Y., Oct., 16, 1812; Republican and Liberal; has held the office of Supervisor for 12 years, and Justice of the Peace for two years; married Marcia M. Babb, Dec. 13, 1832; she was born in Livingston Co., N. Y., May 19, 1816; have six children, Elmira, Martha, William, Benjamin, Eliza and Inez.

Woodworth W. H. farmer; P. O. Warren.

Wright Jesse, Justice of the Peace; Warren.

Wright W. F. drayman; Warren.

ZEIGLE L. T. grocer.

NORA TOWNSHIP.

BABCOCK LYMAN G. Farmer; Sec. 29; P. O. Nora; born in Putney, Windham Co., Vt., June 23, 1837; his parents moved to North Adams, Berkshire Co., Mass., when he was five years old; working in a cotton mill until the age of 17, when he went to Clintonville, Otsego Co., N. Y., where he took charge of carding room; here he was married to Julia J. Hosley, March 25, 1857; she was born in Binghampton, Broom Co., N. Y., Sept. 30, 1840; they moved to Cheshire, Berkshire Co., Mass., and after two years went to Chenango Co., N. Y., and six years later found them in New Hartford, Oneida Co., N. Y., where he took charge of cotton mills; came to Rush Tp., this Co., in 1869, and to this Tp. in 1876; John L. is their only child; Abigail Hosley, mother of Mrs. Babcock, who was born Dec. 25, 1818, resides with her daughter.

Ball Joseph, farmer; Sec. 9; P. O. Nora.

Bashan Wm. farmer; Sec. 16; P.O. Nora.

BAYNE JAMES, Jr., R. R. Ticket Agent; Nora; born in Norwich, Del., Jan. 3, 1849; he spent the early years of childhood in his native place, when he, with his parents, moved to Galena, Ill., and from there to Warren, in this Co.; here he worked five years for the Illinois Central R. R. Co.; he then came to Nora and has since had charge of this office; in Warren he was married to Josie L. Tuttle, in Dec., 1870; she was born, Jan. 29, 1854, at Ottawa, Ill.; Harry M. is their only child; Mrs. Bayne's mother and grandmother reside with them, making the unusual spectacle of four generations residing in one family.

Becox Charles, laborer; P. O. Howardsville.

Bishop L. S. farmer; P. O. Nora.

Blackman Charles, farmer; P. O. Nora.

BOND REV. DANIEL W. Minister; Sec. 19; P. O. Nora; born in Wayne Co., Ind., Nov. 28, 1835; in 1847 he came with his parents to this Tp., where he has since resided; he entered the ministry ten years ago, which calling he has since followed; owns 154 acres of land in this Tp.; he married Matilda Shaw; she was born April 8, 1842, in Nora, Jo Daviess Co., Ill.; John W., Silas W., George W., and Alvin S. are their children.

Bourne Samuel, blacksmith; Nora.

BOWER JOHN, Farmer; Sec. 21; P. O. Lena; born in Huntingdon Co., Pa., March 25, 1840; married Elizabeth Gunther, March 13, 1866, who was born in Allegheny Co., Pa., June 20, 1847; Mr. B. came to this Co. with his parents when he was but nine years old, first settling near Lena, Stephenson Co., Ill.; at this place he was married, and in Feb., 1870, he came to his present residence; Mrs. Bower came to Stephenson Co., Ill., when five years old; they are members of the German Baptist Church; the names of their children are: Mary J., Emma Nora, Aaron Edward, Ida Rose, and Clara Ann.

Bowman Peter, farmer; Sec. 17; P. O. Nora.

Bowman W. H. farmer; Sec. 16; P.O. Nora.

Breed A. J. farmer; Sec. 30; P.O. Greenvale.

Breed Chas. B. laborer; P. O. Warren.

Burr Eugene, Nora.

Burr Frank, Nora.

BURR MYRON H. Retired Farmer; Nora; born in Tompkins Co., N. Y., May 21, 1820; he left home at the age of 15 and went to Buffalo, where he learned the blacksmith's trade in a ship-yard; after two years he went to Cattaraugus Co., and from there to Chautauqua Co., working at his trade; he then went to Allegany Co., where he was married Oct. 8, 1843, to Mary E. Baldwin; she was born at Mt. Morris, Livingston Co., N. Y., May 10, 1823; in 1864 they came to Brady, Kalamazoo Co., Mich., where they lived five years, since which time they have resided in this town; Eugene and Frank are their children; Gustavus A. was born Dec. 19, 1844, and died Feb. 11, 1845; Congregationalist; Republican.

Burwell George, laborer; Nora.

Burwell J. mason; Nora.

Burwell James, laborer; Nora.

CAIN A. Nora.

Cain G. Nora.

CAIN WM. (Deceased) born in N. J. Feb. 10, 1816; married Ada Scheanck Jan. 6, 1839; she was born in N. J. Sept. 3, 1822; moved to Wis., where they lived four years, then came to Stephenson Co. in this state; lived there six years, and then went to Warren at the time the railroad was first put through; he started the first lumber yard, and also built the first hardware store in Warren; came in April, 1866, to the farm of 160 acres where his widow still resides; he died the following year; of their children, John, Amini D., George and Ada are living; Lucretia A., Emma M., William S. and Eva are numbered with the dead; John enlisted Nov., 1861, in 45th I. V. I. and served three years; Amini D. was born Oct. 2, 1847, in Lafayette Co., Wis., and married Eliza M. Helverin March 17, 1874.

Carpenter Chas. R. renter; Sec. 9; P.O. Nora.

CARPENTER JOHN L. Farmer; Sec. 19; P. O. Warren; born in Allegany Co., N. Y., May 23, 1841; in 1845 he came to this Co. with his parents; in the Spring of 1866 he went to Montana Territory, where he was engaged in various kinds of work; returned home in July, 1873, and went back to Montana in March, 1874; he came back to this Co. in the Fall of 1874; married Amelia Leonard Nov. 22, 1874; she was born in Jo Daviess Co., Ill., Jan. 3, 1851; Mr. C. moved on his present farm of 131 acres in the Spring of 1875; Republican.

CHAMPLIN JOHN H. Retired Farmer; Sec. 17; P. O. Nora; born in Livingston, N. Y., Aug. 11, 1813; when he was three years old his parents moved to New London, Co., N. Y.; here he taught school from the time he was eighteen years of age until he was twenty-two; came to Rockford, Ill., in 1835, and there married Jane R. Kellogg, May 12, 1839, who was born in New Woodford, N. Y., March 10, 1820; they moved on the north branch of the Kishwaukee, with one yoke of cattle, wagon, and one bed, which was used also as a table; went to Galena in 1841, where he was engaged in hauling wood for a livelihood; has resided on his present farm twenty years; Baptist; Republican; one child: Mrs. Alice E. Burns.

Colier John; Nora.

COON WILLIAM A. Minister of the Evangelical Association; P. O. Nora; born in Crawford Co., Ohio, Sept. 3, 1839; on April 12, 1857, his parents emigrated to this Co.; here he married Rachel J. Stock, Dec., 1861, who was born in Preble Co., Ohio, March 28, 1839; Mr. Coon enlisted on Jan. 24, 1864, in Co. F, 17th I. V. I., serving until Dec. 29, 1865; his regiment was in the battles at Allen Station, Boonville, California, Sedalia, Syracuse and Lexington; mustered out at Fort Leavenworth; Hattie C., Perry R., Berton W. and Frank W. are their children.

Cookson Silas, laborer; Nora.

Cooper R. J. painter; Nora.

Cowan John E. carpenter; Nora.

COX BRONSON, Farmer; Sec. 9; P. O. Nora; born in Wayne Co., Ind., July 7, 1848; at the age of thirteen he came to this Co. with his father, J. L. Cox, and settled with them in Rush Township; Feb. 25, 1875, he was married to Ruth Stock, who was born in Wayne Co., Ind., Nov. 23, 1849; Daniel and Sarah A. Stock, parents of Mrs. Cox, were old settlers in this county, coming here in 1853; they are now both dead, Mr. Stock dying at the age of sixty-five and Mrs. Stock sixty-one; in the Spring of 1876 Mr. Cox bought his farm of eighty acres in this township, and with his wife has since resided there; they have one child; Republican; neutral in church matters.

Crowell Hiram, laborer; Nora.

CROWELL MRS. JANE, Widow; P. O. Nora; Mrs. Crowell was born in Ontario Co., N. Y., Jan. 16, 1815; with her parents, moved to Allegany Co., N. Y., in 1821, and lived there until 1839, when she came to this township, her father, Asher Miner, having moved here in 1836; she taught school until 1841, when she married Sylvanus Crowell, who was born in Ontario Co., N. Y., Sept. 14, 1814; Mr. Crowell died Aug. 29, 1854; Mrs. Crowell adopted two daughters, Mrs. Jennie Luckner and Miss Viola Freeman, the latter now living with her.

Crowell Marvin, laborer; Nora.

CROWELL NELSON, Retired Farmer; P. O. Nora; born in Edenbush,

Herkimer Co., N. Y., July 13, 1811; when about six years old he moved to Allegany Co., N. Y., with his parents and resided there until Oct. 1836, when he came to this Co., and settled in Rush Tp.; at that time there was only one settler in Nora Tp.; Mr. Crowell was married, April 20, 1842, to Zilpah M. Buckley, who was born in Unadilla, Otsego Co., N. Y., Aug. 3, 1817; in Dec. 1837, Mr. Crowell returned to N. Y. and remained there until 1850, when he again came West, settling in this Tp. on the place now owned by William Pucket; Republican; Independent.

CUTLER IRVING L., M. D., Nora; was born in Lake Co., Ill., Jan. 29, 1850; the doctor's parents moved to Clinton, Worcester Co., Mass., when he was quite young, residing there about three years, then returned to Lake Co., Ill., but soon after permanently located in Cedar Lake, Lake Co., Ind., where they now reside; in 1870 the doctor took a trip to the West, and after visiting Denver and other points, settled in Kearney Junction, Neb.; subsequently was appointed ticket agent at Waverly and other places, by the C. B. & Q. R. R. and in the meantime studied medicine; returning to Chicago, he graduated at Rush Medical College, and has since been in the practice of his profession in Madison, Will and Jo Daviess counties; married Mary Alice Grant, Feb. 28, 1875; she was born in Jamaica, Vt., April 14, 1853.

DALEY JOHN, farmer; Sec. 6; P. O. Nora.

DAVIS OLIVER O. Retired Farmer; Nora; was born in New Gloucester, Me., Nov. 4, 1808; when nine years old he, with his parents, moved to Oxford Co., Me., there resided five years, after which they went to Milo, and then to Kennebec Co., Me., in 1841; here he married Sultana Smith, who was born in this Co.; they moved to Boone Co. in 1843, residing fourteen years, and emigrated in 1857 to Nora, where his wife died in 1868; married for his second wife Sarah A. McIntosh, who was born in Dundas, Canada, March 6, 1830.

Derr C. B., P.O. Nora.

Derr Delos, P. O. Nora.

Derr J. renter; Sec. 29; P. O. Nora.

Derr Reuben, P. O. Nora.

DIGGS ANTHONY, Farmer; Sec. Sec. 7; P. O. Nora; was born in Randolph Co., Ind., on Jan. 2, 1833; married Elvira C. Thomas on Jan. 5, 1854; she was born in Wayne Co., Ind., Sept. 4, 1834; they lived with parents until nearly three years after marriage, when they went to Dallas Co., Iowa, but the Co. there at that time was so devastated that he came to this Co., arriving in Nov., 1856; the following Spring he purchased 80 acres of land, and has since added another 80 to it; Anna J. is their only daughter; he has held the office of School Director, and was a member of the last Grand Jury of 1877; Republican; Independent.

DIGGS HENRY H. Farmer; Sec. 7; P. O. Warren; born in Randolph Co., Ind., July 11, 1830; commenced business for himself in the Fall of 1851, operating the first threshing machine ever run in Randolph Co.; the following Summer he farmed with his brother, and in Sept., 1852, bought a half interest in a saw mill; Oct. 23 of the same year he married Sarah Wright, who was born in Randolph Co., Ind., Nov. 25, 1829: he sold out and came to Rush Tp. in 1853, and bought 175 acres land; held that until 1864, when he sold it, and bought his present farm of 210 acres; has added much to the value of his farm by the improvements he has made; his wife died March 12, 1877; has three children living: Wm. L., Angelia C., and Iven I.; Effie Jane died March 19, '66.

Douglas Cameron, Sec. 33; P. O. Nora.

Dobler Sam. farmer; Sec. 7; P. O. Warren.

DOBLER SIMON H. Farmer; Sec. 6; P. O. Warren; born in Limestone, Lycoming Co., Pa., March 21, 1840; until the age of 24, he remained with his parents in his native Co.; Feb. 11, 1864, he took to himself as helpmeet Elvira A. Showers, who was born in Limestone, Pa., Oct. 14, 1843; went to Lafayette Co., Wis., in 1865 and lived on his father's farm till 1869, when he came to this Co. and bought his present farm of 155 acres; Mr. Dobler has served as School Director for seven years; Independent in politics; has six children: Sarah M., Joseph A., Mellie, Minnie Bell, Simon Peter, Cora.

Dobler T. H. farmer; Sec. 7; P. O. Warren.

Doidge Thos. renter; Sec. 21; P. O. Warren.

Douglass W. C. farmer; Sec. 33; P. O. Nora.

Drew Fenis, Nora.

Drew Theo. lumber dealer; Nora.

Durkee W. E. farmer; Sec. 32; P. O. Howardsville.

EIKERT JOHN F. boots and shoes; Nora.

EBY GEO. Farmer; Sec. 20; P.O. Nora; born in Franklin Co., Pa., March 31, 1831: married Susan Ferrenburg, who was born in Huntingdon Co., Pa., Oct. 8, 1833; in 1851 they came to this Co., first settling in this Tp., and 22 years ago settled on their present farm of 146 acres, on which they have made all the improvements; John F., born Sept. 10, 1854 (died Sept. 29, 1854); Nannie A., Oct. 3, 1855; Susannah, March 9, 1857; Joseph M., April 21, 1858; Lucy A., Nov. 20, 1859; Elvira, Sept. 25, 1861; Margaret, April 8, 1867; Lillie A., Feb. 7, 1869; George A.,

Jan. 26, 1871; Sarah C., Nov. 4, 1872; Enoch L., June 15, 1875, are their children.

FARLEY DAVID S. Shipper of Live Stock; Nora; born in Hastings Co., Canada, March 2, 1842; at the age of 21 he came to this Tp. and engaged in teaching school one year; in 1864 he went to Memphis, Tenn., but returned to Canada in the Fall of that year; after about one year's residence in his native country, he again came to Nora and married Eliza L. Taylor March 4, 1866, who was born in Norwich, Hampshire Co., Mass., Oct. 10, 1845; Mr. Farley was engaged in farming until the past four or five years, when he moved to this village, where he has bought grain and live stock; three children: Edith M., Edna B. and Ethel C.

Flynn C. D. tinsmith; Nora.

Foot C. C. farmer; Sec. 29; P. O. Nora.

FOSS LEONARD, Farmer; Sec. 9; P. O. Nora; born in Grafton Co., N. H., July 13, 1810; in 1829 he went to Boston, Mass., where he was engaged as a laborer for ten years, when he returned to his native county; a few years later he emigrated to Lafayette, Wis., and after ten years' residence he came to this Tp., buying his present farm of 80 acres; Nov. 20, 1850, he married Caroline Holmes, who was born in Campton, Grafton Co., N. H., Nov. 8, 1814: two children: Mary E. and Mrs. Sarah W. Holmes; Republican; Congregationalist.

FORESMAN JOHN T. Farmer; Sec. 22; P. O. Nora; born in Lycoming Co., Pa., July 7, 1847; went to Northumberland Co. in 1868, and remained eleven months, when he returned to his native county and lived until March 4, 1871, at which time he came to this Co. and worked by the month or year; he moved to Stephenson Co., but after a short residence there returned to this Co. and bought his present farm of 80 acres; married Katie Swartz Dec. 31, 1873; she was born in Centre Co., Pa., July 1, 1853; they have two children: Clayton B. and William W.; Methodist; Democrat.

Franklin Enos, Nora.

FRANKLIN FREEMAN, Retired Farmer; Nora; born in Easton, N. Y., Feb. 22, 1811; his parents moved to Delaware Co., N. Y., when he was one year old, residing there until he was sixteen, when they went to Allegany Co., N. Y.; here he married Sarah M. Baldwin April 10, 1839; she was born in Mt. Morris, Livingston Co., N. Y., Dec. 19, 1820; they came to this Co. in March, 1868, first settling in this Tp., buying a farm of 80 acres; two sons, Enos E. and James B.; the latter was born July 19, 1847, and married Clara A. Dobler Feb. 4, 1873, who was born in Stephenson Co., Ill., Feb. 21, 1856; one son, Clarence F.

Franklin J. B.

GESNER JOHN C. Farmer; Sec. 4; P. O. Nora; born in Hesse-Cassel, Germany, Nov. 2, 1825; remained with his parents until he was of age, after which he worked at linen weaving, a trade he had learned of his father; in 1848 he came to this country, first settling near Baltimore, Md., where he remained one year; he then went to what was then Claremont Co., near Pittsburg, Pa., and worked in the iron works and woolen factories four years; in 1852 he married Sarah Tippery and moved to this Co., first making a home in Rush Township, which home he sold after a fifteen years' residence, and purchased his present farm of 80 acres in this township.

HALL GEORGE, Resides on father's farm; Sec. 28; P. O. Nora; born in Canada, Feb. 16, 1852; came to this Co. when quite young with his parents, first settling on their present farm, where he has been a constant resident; married Nettie Bedford, Aug. 31, 1873, who was born in Madison, Co., N. Y., Feb. 11, 1855; she emigrated to Stockton Township, this Co., with her parents when seventeen years old; Lewis Edwin is their only child; Mr. Hall's father is now residing in Nevada Territory.

HARROWER ALONZO, Farmer; Sec. 9; P.O. Nora; born in Albany Co., N.Y., Sept. 8, 1825; he emigrated to Stephenson Co., Ill., in 1849, where he was married to Lavina Osterhout, on Oct. 25, 1855; she was born in Albany Co., N. Y., March 15, 1831; they moved to Nora Township, and on their present farm of forty acres, in 1864; Cora B. and Emma are the names of their two daughters; independent in religion; Republican.

Hay Andrew, renter; Sec. 20; P. O. Warren.

Hay Cameron, farm; Sec. 16; P. O. Warren.

Hay John, farmer; Sec. 20; P. O. Warren.

HOLLAND JAMES, Farmer; Sec. 21; P. O. Warren; born in Ireland, Jan. 6, 1833; he came to this country in 1840, first settling in Newport, R. I., where, in 1851, he married Julia Sullivan, who was born in Ireland; in 1853 they came to Stephenson Co., Ill., residing until 1867, when he came to this township, buying his present farm of 160 acres, on which they have made valuable improvements; Mr. H. commenced life as a ship-carpenter; he is now one of our best citizens, beloved and respected by all who know him.

Holland Jno. Sec. 4; P. O. Warren.

Holmes H. A. J.; P. O. Nora.

HOOD JAMES, Farmer; Sec. 4; P. O. Nora; was born in Doe Run, Chester Co., Pa., June 13, 1816; he emigrated to Iowa Co. (now Lafayette Co.), Wis., in May, 1839, and obtained there 160 acres of land;

Mr. Hood was one of the pioneers of the West, the Indians still roaming over their native prairies when he came here; was married June 30, 1854, to Margaret Stuce; she was born in Union Co., Pa., in Oct., 1817; they moved into this Co. Oct. 2, 1867; they now live in the house formerly known as the "One Mile House," on the stage route from Galena to Dixon; their only child is Annie A.; Independent in politics.

Hughs W. W. laborer; Nora.

HYNES JAMES H. Dealer in Agricultural Implements; Nora; born in Terrytown, N. Y., March 3, 1836; after his father's death he went with his mother to Hamilton, Ohio, where he remained one year; he then went to Elton, O., and learned the tinner's trade; he resided in Elton four years, and then moved back to Hamilton, where he engaged in the hardware business; he soon sold out his interest at this point, and went to Cincinnati, and tried the wholesale hardware business; this he left in 1865, coming to this Co.; his first venture here was on a farm, but after tilling the soil one year he concluded that selling agricultural implements was more lucrative than using them, and consequently moved into Nora and established a store in that line, and has carried it on continuously ever since; his wife was Anna K. Kline, who was born in Pa.

Johnson M. M. harness maker; Nora.

KEAST EDWARD, renter; P. O. Nora.

Keast Thos. renter; P. O. Nora.

KELSEY ANSON, Farmer; Sec. 16; P. O. Nora; born in Herkimer Co., N. Y., Jan. 5, 1827; left his native Co. for Schenectady, and then for New York City; from there to White Lake, Sullivan Co., returning again to New York; in 1842 he went to New Orleans, working for the government; we find him again in New York, where he shipped for coast surveying to Cal.; in 1849 he sailed for Panama, but returned to New York in a short time, shipping for Cal., and in 1854 returned to New York; emigrated to Wis.; came to this Co. from Wis., buying his present farm of 80 acres; married Hannah J. Stewart Nov. 18, 1856; she was born in Lockport, May 10, 1835.

Keely D. J. lumber dealer; Nora.

KEPNER BENJ. H. Farmer; Sec. 17; P. O. Nora; born in Juniata Co., Pa., July 21, 1817; married Sarah E. Bushey in this Co., May 13, 1841: she was born in Juniata Co., Pa., April 22, 1821; they resided in their native state until Nov. 4, 1848; then emigrated to this Tp., coming all the way in a wagon, and settled on their present farm, which now consists of 320 acres; a little log house 12 by 16 feet was about all the improvement on their place when they arrived, but now good buildings and fine improvements have taken its place, and are the results of honesty and industry; soon after their arrival in this place, they attended church one Sabbath through muddy roads, with two yokes of cattle attached to one wagon; now a German Baptist Church building is within a few rods of their house, to which they belong, and over which Mr. Kepner presides, as one of its speakers; Andrew L. (in Mo.), Erastus P., Aaron E. (in Mo.), Josiah B., Mrs. G. Wilson Myers, Mrs. S. Ellen Drew, Catharine A., Ida M., and Emma L. are their children.

Kepner Erastus P. son of B. H. Kepner.

Keplinger T. H. farmer; Sec. 20; P.O. Nora.

Keplinger M. farmer; Sec. 29; P. O. Nora.

KERLIN PETER J. Retired Farmer; Nora; born in Augusta, Northumberland Co., Pa., Sept. 5, 1793; married for his first wife Betsy Hull; she was born in N. J.; married for his second wife Mary M. Bighler; he lived in his native Co. till after his father's death, when he moved to Snyder Co., engaging in farming; after his sons left him, he sold out and spent a few years with friends; in 1871 he came to Nora, where he has since lived a retired life; when 74 years old, he bound grain in the harvest fields, keeping his station; few men of his years possess his vigor and youthful elasticity; he has followed hunting and fishing with avidity, and has still a keen relish for both; is still a sure marksman, without the aid of glasses.

Kitch Geo. P. O. Nora.

Kitch Robt. P. O. Nora.

Knotts A. H. renter; Sec. 4; P. O. Nora.

Knepley J. M. well driller; Nora.

LANE JOHN, farmer; Sec. 29; P. O. Warren.

LATHAM FRANKLIN A. Farmer; Sec. 33; P. O. Howardsville; born in Wadhams Grove, Jo Daviess Co., Ill., Jan. 10, 1844; married Elizabeth Shoesmith, Jan. 9, 1868; she was born in Kent, England, Sept. 4, 1846; when about one year old she, with her parents, came to this country, first settling in Stephenson Co., where she resided until married; Mr. Latham (with the exception of one year's residence in Stephenson Co.) has continuously resided in Wadhams Grove and Nora Township, in this Co.; he is the possessor of 80 acres of land; his father, Ezra Latham, was an old settler of this Co., coming here in 1838 from Vt.; he died a few years since, an honored and respected citizen; his wife is a resident of Lena, Stephenson Co., Ill.; Mr. F. Latham has two children: Lucy E. and Nancy L.

Lauver Edward, farmer; Sec. 28; P. O. Howardsville.

LAUVER JOHN, Farmer; Sec. 28; P. O. Howardsville; born in Juniata Co., Pa., March 28, 1824; on Aug. 3, 1848 he married Melissa Rhoads, who was born in Chester Co., Pa., Oct. 27, 1829; they started for Ill. the Oct. following their marriage, *via* the canal to Pittsburg, where they took passage on a steamer to Cincinnati, O., then they changed to the steamer "Colorado" for St. Louis, Mo.; when they reached Golconda, Pope Co., Ill., the steamer sank, and they remained in this place until the following April, when they went to St. Louis, and then to Stephenson Co., this state, living there fourteen years, after which they came to this Tp., and rented land three years, then bought his present farm of 80 acres; they have six daughters and one son; he has held the office of School Director; Baptist; Republican.

Lauver W. B. laborer; P. O. Nora.

LAWRENCE CHARLES, Proprietor of the Lawrence House; Nora; born in Springfield, Vt., Aug. 2, 1811; when very young, moved with his parents to Joy, Essex Co., Vt.; married Cornelia Way in 1833; had one child, Henry H.; married for second wife Sibyl H. Kennedy in 1838; came to this Co. in 1855; the Spring following his wife died; again married Lydia A. Atwood, April 27, 1857; she was born in Addison Co., Vt., Oct. 17, 1827; they resided on their farm eight years, and have kept their hotel ten years; two children: Perlie M. and Evangeline.

Leach Wm. B. wagon maker; Nora.

Leonard Isaiah, farmer; Sec. 16; P.O. Nora.

Lepper Harrison, farm; S. 32; P.O. Warren.

LEPPER WM. L. Traveling Agent; Nora; born in Trumbull Co., Ohio, July 4, 1831; married Perthana A. Ensign, Dec. 29, 1852, who was born in Trumbull Co., Ohio, Sept. 10, 1834; in 1856 they moved to what is now Brown Co., Kan., residing there two years; returning to Ohio, when, after one year, they went to Crawford Co., Pa., and after 15 months' residence, came to this Co., arriving in 1859; Sept. 4, 1861, he enlisted in Co. A, Fremont's Rangers Battery, and was wounded, near the headwaters of the Black River; after two years' service was discharged, at Houston, Mo.; their living children are: Erie W., and Ida E.; Seth H., born Jan. 20, 1857, was the first white child born in Brown Co., Kan., and died April 2, 1861.

Londergen Jas. farmer; Sec. 20; P.O. Warren.

LOVIN HENRY R. Meat Market; Nora; born in Wayne Co., Ind., Oct. 16, 1833; resided with his parents in Ind. 19 years, and learned the shoemaker's trade; came to this Co. in 1852, and was engaged successively in various kinds of work incident to settlements in new countries; married Lucia M. Cowan Jan. 1, 1857, who was born in Naples, Ontario Co., N. Y., Jan. 18, 1841; Mr. Lovin enlisted in the 142d I. V. I. and served one year, when he was honorably discharged; lived in Warren nine years and then came to this village; bought grain one year, when he entered upon his present business with a capital of $50; seven children living.

McCAFFERTY JAMES, laborer; Nora.

McNamara P. renter; P. O. Nora.

Mahan John, farmer; Sec. 5; P. O. Nora.

Mahaney M. farmer; Sec. 28; P. O. Warren.

Manley Daniel, laborer; Nora.

Marshall W. K. farmer; Sec. 9; P. O. Nora.

MESSICK GEORGE W. Merchant; Nora; born in Howard, Steuben Co., N. Y., March 24, 1846; resided in his native Co. until he was 20 years old, when he went to Arnoldsville to clerk, following that occupation two years; then removed to Marengo, McHenry Co., Ill., and from there went to DeKalb Center, DeKalb Co., where he clerked six months; afterwards traveled one year for a book agency; clerked six months in Polo; engaged in business in Warren two years; then bought a farm in Gratiot, Wis., but exchanged it for a stock of goods and moved to Nora, where he has since resided; married H. Zelida York, who was born in Brookfield, Madison Co., N. Y., July 8, 1835; she graduated at Oneida Conference Seminary at the age of 17; went to Dodgeville, Wis., two years later; taught in Brookfield Academy one year, two terms in Wis., two terms in Polo, Ill., and then came to this Co.; they have seven children.

Mill John P. farmer; Sec. 21; P. O. Warren.

MILLER CHARLES S. Farmer; Sec. 29; P. O. Nora; born in Centre Co., Pa., March 27, 1850; when 16 years of age he went to Hamilton Co., O., from there to Vane Co., and next to Stephenson Co., Ill., residing a few months in each of the counties named; then came to this Co., where he has since resided; married Prusilla Warner Nov. 24, 1870, who was born in Clarion Co., Pa., Dec. 12, 1846, and came to Boone Co., Ill., when she was nine years of age; ten years afterwards she moved to Stephenson Co.; they have three sons; Independent.

Miller Ellis, well driller; Nora.

Miner Bruce.

Miner S. K.

Moorehead Wm. laborer; Nora.

Morris C. E. farmer; Sec. 19; P. O. Nora.

Morris J. E. farmer; Sec. 18: P. O. Warren.

Morse G. C. renter; Sec. 4; P. O. Nora.

Moore W. K. farmer; Sec. 28; P. O. Nora.

MOYER JNO. Farmer; Sec. 33; P. O. Howardsville; born in Waterloo Co., Canada, July 4, 1858; emigrated to this country when he was but 17 years old, coming direct to Stephenson Co., where he married Maria C. Price; she was born in Centre Co., Pa.; she came to Stephenson Co., Ill., when but four years old, where she lived until coming to this Co. with her husband; they moved to Nora Tp. in Dec., 1876; the names of their children are: William H., Agnes and Robert A.

Murdick M. D. laborer; Nora.

Myers Enoch, farmer; Sec. 16; P. O. Nora.

MYERS ENOCH X. Farmer; Sec. 17; P. O. Nora; born in Juniata Co., Pa., Aug. 22, 1830; he, with his parents, moved to Mifflin Co., Pa., when he was five years old, and when twelve years old, to Huntingdon Co., Pa., where he married Nancy Garver Aug. 26, 1852; she was born in Huntingdon Co., Pa., July 29, 1835; in March, 1856, they came to this Co., first settling in this Tp.; now owns 250 acres land; Mrs. Myers died Jan. 21, ——; David R., Geo. W., Sarah K., Allen B., Ira E., Ida, Sherman B., Clarence and Laura are their children; married Harriet Garver Jan. 10, 1878; she was born Feb. 29, 1845, in Huntingdon Co., Pa.

Myers G. W., P. O. Nora.

MYERS RUDOLPH, Farmer; Sec. 16; P. O. Nora; born in Juniata Co., Pa., Feb. 28, 1833; married Harriet Musser Nov. 29, 1855; she was born in Juniata Co., Pa., Jan. 21, 1839; they came to this Co. April 11, 1856, first settling in this Tp., and moved on their present farm of 160 acres in March, 1868; are members of the German Baptist Church; have seven children living: Alfred, Clinton, Minnie M., Edward L., Cora E., Samuel W. and Maggie M.; Jennie W. was born Nov. 24, 1863, and died May 14, 1864.

Myers W. H. farmer; Sec. 21; P. O. Nora.

OTIS B. H. mechanic; Nora.

PARRIS WM. Farmer; Sec. 28; P.O. Lena; born in England Jan. 23, 1833; lived in his native country nine years, when, with his parents, he came to America, first settling in Susquehanna Co., Pa., where they resided five years; in 1847 they emigrated to Galena, Ill.; the following March they moved to Stephenson Co., where Mr. Parris married Louisa Shoesmith Feb. 24, 1857; she was born in England Feb. 17, 1836; fifteen years ago they moved to their present farm in this Tp., containing 210 acres, on which they have made the entire improvements; they have had six children: Robert J., John H., Lucy E., Frederick F., Wm. E. and Geo. E.; the latter was born Feb. 6, 1865, and died Sept. 16, 1866; Sept. 28, 1877, on his 23d birthday, Jas. S. Shoesmith, brother of Mrs. Parris, was killed by the kick of a horse.

Phelps A. O. farm; Sec. 30; P.O. Greenvale.

Phelps Max, farm; S. 30; P. O. Greenvale.

Phelps O. W. blacksmith; Greenvale.

Phelps W.W. farm; S. 30; P. O. Greenvale.

Pitcher J. mail carrier; Nora.

POMEROY WATSON Y. Was born March 16, 1813, in Otisco, Onondaga Co., N. Y. His parents were from Mass., and were among the earliest settlers of Onondaga Co. When the Erie Canal was building, his parents moved to Amsterdam and lived five years. Here his father died, in March, 1828. After the death of his father, he worked one year with a wagon maker, and then with mother; part of family moved back to Onondaga Co., where he worked a term of years on farm, and then entered academy in Village of Elbridge. One year later, with his brother-in-law, emigrated to Illinois, in Oct., 1835; at St. Joseph, Mich., he took steamer to cross the lake, but a furious gale shipwrecked nearly every craft, and they were obliged to go around the head of the lake the best way they could—part by stage and part on foot. The brother-in-law followed in a few days. They settled at Squaw Grove, DeKalb Co., near the present site of Hinkley. This was in 1836. Two years later they were found living eight miles south of Belvidere. Here Mr. Pomeroy married their first school teacher, Miss Ann Eliza Kellogg, Aug. 2, 1838. Their first child, Myron Eugene, was born Dec. 21, 1839. They moved to Galena in the Spring of 1840, and engaged in mining at "Fair Play" diggings. Here their second child, Eveline, was born, and died the same day, June 12, 1842. March 8, 1843, they buried their first born. They moved then to Galena, and manufactured small beer to take the place of strong drinks. Mr. Pomeroy was temperate, and thoroughly anti-slavery. Cyrus Watson was born July 31, 1844. In Fall of 1845, with A. B. Campbell, moved to what is now Nora, and engaged in farming. Here Mary Angeline was born, April 1, 1847, and Charles Henry, March 27, 1849. With a soldier's warrant Mr. P. located on southeast quarter of Sec. 8, on which he moved his house and now resides. April 14, 1851, Ella Jane was born; Myron Fremont, Sept. 6, 1856, now engaged in the house of Henry Sears & Co., Chicago; Charles Henry is a traveling agent for same house; Cyrus W. is traveling for Western Bank Note Engraving Co.; Horace Jay was born July 17, 1858; Hattie L. H., April 7, 1861; Cyrus enlisted July, 1862, in Co. K, 96th I. V. I., before he was 18; was wounded at Chicamauga and discharged at Chicago on account of the wound; Charles Henry enlisted before he was 17, in 17th I. V. C.,

Dec. 1, 1863, and was mustered out Dec. 18, 1865; Ella Jane died Nov. 8, 1856. Mr. P. moved to Iowa City and lived there two years to better educate his children. Oct. 29, 1868, Mary was married to Grandville C. Tucker; he lived south a while, teaching the freedmen, and returned home and died Aug. 2, 1876. Hattie, the only surviving daughter, died Nov. 17, 1877. Mr. P. has been a professing Christian since his 18th year.

PUCKET CYRUS J. Farmer; Sec. 7; P.O. Nora; born in Newport, Wayne Co., Ind., Dec. 26, 1840; he came to this farm with his father, Cyrus Puckett, in 1849; there being no railroads west of Chicago at this time, they came from Indiana to this Co. with teams, passing through Chicago, Elgin, Rockford and Freeport; on their way out the small-pox was caught by the family, and Mr. Puckett's eldest sister died with it soon after reaching their destination; married Lydia Franklin, Feb. 23, 1864; she was born in Angelica, Allegany Co., N.Y., March 15, 1840, and died Feb. 11, 1877, leaving three children: B. Frank, John W., and Willard; Wesleyan Methodist; Republican.

PUCKETT T. CLARKSON, Farmer; Sec. 8; P.O. Nora; born in North Carolina, Nov. 10, 1818; he moved to Randolph Co., Ind., with his parents, when very young; after attending school at Winchester Seminary, he taught school, and surveyed until May 10, 1852; when he married Emily E. Patchin; in 1853 he came to this Co., and in April of the same year he purchased the farm he now owns, and has since made many valuable improvements on it; the writer of this wishes to say upon his own responsibility, that Mr. Puckett's efforts to elevate a high standard in all that pertains to education, have been untiring and unceasing; the success of the Lecture Course, in Nora (a full account of which is given in another portion of this work), is largely due to the energy and devotion of Mr. Puckett, he being the president of the association.

PUCKETT WM. H. Farmer; Sec. 6; P. O. Nora; born in Wayne Co., Ind., June 22, 1838; came with his father, settling in this Co. in Dec., 1848; he remained at home until the breaking out of the Rebellion, when he enlisted in the 14th I. V. C., at Freeport; was mustered in as 2d Sergt., and promoted to 2d Lieut., Oct. 19, 1864, and received a 1st Lieut.'s commission, March 4, 1865; was engaged in the capture of Morgan, in Ohio, and fought in the battles of Cumberland Gap and Atlanta; was also on the Stoneman Raid, that ended in Stoneman's capture in Georgia; received an honorable discharge after three years' service; married Emerance Crowell Oct. 28, 1862; she was born in Belfast, Allegany Co., N. Y., June 6, 1843; Emeroy L., Nelson F., Harry C., are their children.

Puckett R. W. E. son of T. C. Puckett.

QUINN THOS. laborer; Nora.

RHODES ISAAC, farmer; Sec. 17; P. O. Nora.

Riddiough John, restaurant; Nora.

RICKER ALPHONSO E. Nora; born in Corinth, Penobscot Co., Maine, Jan. 7, 1837; came from Portland, Me., to Warren, Ill., in July, 1862, where he was engaged as clerk in dry goods store; came to Nora in Feb., 1867, engaging in the mercantile trade under firm name of Ricker & Stickney; sold out in 1870.

Roach D. farmer; Sec. 20; P. O. Warren.

Roach Jno. farmer; Sec. 20; P. O. Warren.

Roberts Jos. laborer; P. O. Nora.

ROCKEY RICHARD M. Druggist and Stationer; Nora; born in Clarion Co., Pa., April 29, 1841; remained with his parents, farming, until 18 years of age; then worked in the pineries during the Winter, and at the carpenter's trade during the Summer; enlisted in the 105th Pa. V. I., Co. C, Aug. 28, 1861, and remained with the regiment until June 16, 1862; came to Stephenson Co., Ill., in May, 1863, and for two years worked at the carpenter's trade and clerked in a store; Feb. 9, 1865, he enlisted in the 147th I. V. I., and was honorably discharged at Springfield Feb. 7, 1866; returning to Pa., he taught school one year, and then came back to Stephenson Co.; in the Spring of 1869 he drove a team through to Nebraska and Kansas, and pre-empted 160 acres of land in Osage Co., Kansas.; was married Dec. 15, 1870, to Almeda Dively, who was born Sept. 24, 1847; moved to this Co. in 1871; children are Margaret M., born Dec. 5, 1871; and A. Emily, Aug. 23, 1874; in the Fall of 1876 he was nominated by the Independent Greenbackers for Clerk of the Circuit Court, but was defeated.

Rockey Sam. B., P. O. Nora.

ROCKEY WM. F. Dry Goods and Groceries; Nora; born in Clinton Co., Pa., April 3, 1827; married Elizabeth Frasher in 1851; she was born in Clinton Co., Pa., March 28, 1820; in 1848 they immigrated to Ill., first settling in Stephenson Co., where he was engaged in milling; then moved to Cedarville and Rock Run, following the same business; he then took the Buckhorn tavern, in which he had a small store, but soon moved to McConnell's Grove, going into the mercantile trade; in 1871 he came to Nora, where he is one of the leading merchants; Samuel B. and Emma J. are their only children.

ROGERS FORDICE M. Farmer; Sec. 33; P. O. Howardsville; born in

F. M. Rogers

NORA TOWNSHIP

Turin, Lewis Co., N. Y., July 4, 1806; his father, in 1810, moved to Cape Vincent, Jefferson Co., N. Y., where Mr. Rogers, Jr., was married to Chloe Fiske Feb. 17, 1835; she was born in Boonville, Oneida Co., N. Y., Feb. 6, 1814; in 1841 they emigrated to Ill., with one span of horses, and one wagon, in which were packed a few necessary household goods, which comprised all their earthly possessions, first settling in this Tp. and on his present farm of 400 acres, building a little log house, which has since given way to a palatial dwelling; Mrs. Rogers died May 22, 1859, and Oct. 4, 1860, he married Emily Graves, who was born in Washington, Scioto Co., Ohio, June 18, 1817; at the first election after the Tp. organization, Mr. R. was elected its Supervisor; is the present Tp. Treasurer, which office he has held for 27 consecutive years; James H., Merick A., Ossian R. and Duane are the names of the children by first marriage; Wm. H. died at Lagrange, Tenn., while serving in the 92d I. V. I.

Roshong Wm. retired farmer; P.O. Nora.

Ryan P. foreman of railroad section; Nora.

SCHOCH WM. farmer; Sec. 32; P.O. Nora.

Shaw Charles, Sec. 18; P. O. Nora.

Shaw Henry, farmer; Sec. 19; P. O. Nora.

SHAW JOSEPH P. Farmer; Sec. 18; P.O. Nora; born in Angelica, Allegany Co., N. Y., April 6, 1828; at the age of 9 years he, with his parents, started on a raft at Olean Point, on the Allegheny River, and came to Pittsburg, and then down the Ohio River to Cincinnati, where they left the river and took a team and drove through to this Co.; he married Nancy A. Clay, May 4, 1854; she was born in Medina Co., Ohio, Nov. 18, 1836; Charles L., Lorin F., David C., Joseph P., and Enos W., are their children; Charles L., the eldest son, was married to Sarah Luther, Dec. 15, 1875; they have one child, Mabel P.; Mr. Shaw was one of the first settlers in this Tp.

SIMMONS ANDREW, Farmer; Sec. 30; P. O. Greenvale; born in Albany Co., N. Y., March 12, 1819; was married to Eliza Scofield, Jan. 8, 1840; she was born in Lysander, Onondaga Co., N. Y., Dec. 6, 1819; they remained in his native Co. until one year after marriage, when they moved to Baldwinsville, Onondaga Co., N. Y.; in 1850 he came to this Co. and settled in this Tp., which has since been his home; Andrew A. and Byron B. are his sons; Franklin D. is an adopted son; he has held the offices of Road Commissioner and School Director many terms; there were only ten or twelve families in the township when he came to it.

Simmons B. B. farmer; Sec. 30; P. O. Greenville.

Simmons Daniel, Nora.

Simmons B. F. Sec. 31; P.O. Howardsville.

Simmons Fred. B. Sec. 30; P. O. Greenville.

Simmons Irwin, Howardsville.

SIMMONS JACOB, Farmer; Sec. 31; P. O. Howardsville; born in Montgomery Co., N. Y., Aug. 25, 1816; when six years old his parents moved to Cayuga Co., N. Y.; here on Sept. 26, 1839, he married Mary Coppernoll, who was born in Montgomery Co., N. Y., Sept. 27, 1814; her parents moved to Oneida Co., N. Y., and then to Cayuga Co.; in 1845 they were emigrants to Ill., coming all the way by land; one span of horses and wagon, a few household goods, and a little money was their all, when they arrived in this Tp., Dec. 8, 1845; taking a claim of 200 acres of land in the above section; by perseverance they have acquired a competency, and have retired from active life, leaving their son, B.F. Simmons, in charge.

SIMMONS MICHAEL, Farmer and Manufacturer of Cigars; Sec. 30; P. O. Lena; born in Albany Co., N. Y., June 16, 1814; married Mary A. Manley, July 5, 1835; she was a native of Mass.; they came to this Co. June 29, 1844; from his birthplace in N. Y., he first settled in Rush Tp., then moved to this Tp. where he has 584 acres of land; he is an extensive raiser of tobacco, and manufactures cigars in Lena, Ill.

Smick Sam. farmer; Sec. 28; P. O. Nora.

Smith J. R. renter; P. O. Nora.

SNYDER LORENZO D. Farmer; Sec. 28; P. O. Nora; born in Jefferson Co., N. Y., Aug. 22, 1814; when 16 years old, he went to Onondaga Co., N. Y., and again, in 1834, to Laporte Co., Ind.; two years after his arrival in the above Co. he went to Ogle Co., Ill., where he lived four years; then he emigrated to Stephenson Co., Ill., and in 1867 he came to this Co. and to his present farm of 120 acres; married for first wife Catherine A. Bryant, May 18, 1836; she was born in Pa.; and again, on April 7, 1843, he married Amanda McAffee, who was born in Canada in 1852; married his present and third wife, Rachel Hull, Nov. 21, 1866; she was born in Janesville, Ohio, Feb. 14, 1825; by the first two marriages he had nine children; those living are: Henry, James, Jesse and Martha; those dead are: Ezra, Wm. W., Catherine A., Samuel, and Jessie; Wm. W. was killed in the battle at Buzzard's Roost, during the war of the Rebellion.

SPENCER OSCAR F. Dealer in Pumps and Wind Mills; Nora; born in Cayuga, N. Y., July 23, 1833; his parents moved to Jefferson Co., N. Y., when he was one year old, where he was married to Mary Daniels Sept. 10, 1854; she was born in Jefferson Co., N. Y., Sept. 10, 1834;

in 1865 they emigrated to this state, first settling in Christian Hollow, Stephenson Co., where they resided until Dec., 1869, when they moved to Nora; Mr. Spencer is a member of the Methodist Church and Superintendent of its Sabbath-school; J. Alden, Edson K., Evelyn O. and Alvin D. are their children.

Spencer Sam. retired farmer; Nora.

Sullivan Dan. laborer; Nora.

Sullivan Dennis, laborer; Nora.

Sullivan L. laborer; Nora.

Sullivan P. laborer; Nora.

Staplin W. H. farmer; Sec. 30; P. O. Howardsville.

STANCHFIELD GEO. B. Retired Farmer; Sec. 5; P. O. Nora; born in Wayne, Kennebec Co., Maine, Feb. 3, 1809: married Abigail Cookson in Oct., 1829; she was born in Cornish, Maine, April 28, 1804; after their marriage, they lived at Milo, Maine, until 1843, when they came to this state, making Boone Co. their first stopping place; after residing there about two years, they came to this Tp. and have since made it their home; Mr. Stanchfield was the founder of the Village of Nora; they have had seven children, all but two being now dead; Rud W. and James are the names of those now living; Geo. Henry, one of their sons, was captured during the Rebellion, and died while confined in Andersonville Prison.

Stanchfield J. M. carpenter; Nora.

Stanchfield B. W. carpenter; Nora.

STEVENS ALFRED, Stock Shipper; Nora; born in Ohio, Dec. 4, 1839; in 1841 he came to Stephenson Co. with his grandparents, and to this Co. soon after; and at this time he was quite young; he is one of our respected pioneer settlers and credited by his neighbors with always exerting his influence in furthering and advancing all undertakings for the improvement of the Tp.; his good name has won for him a place among the best stock dealers in the Co.; married Effie Haskell, Feb. 9, 1863; she was born in Nora Tp., this Co., May 21, 1846.

STICKNEY WALTER, Grain Dealer; Nora; born in Tyndinaga, near Belleville, Canada, March 22, 1840; until he was twenty-one years of age, he worked on his father's farm, going to school during the Winter months; after he attained his majority he studied nine months at Belleville Seminary, now Albert College, and then taught school two years; in Oct., 1863, he removed to Michigan, remaining there until the following Spring, when he went to Kansas City, Mo.; at this place he was engaged as one of the express messengers on a line belonging to Barlow Cotrel; this position he held until Dec., 1865, when he was engaged as a clerk in the Sutler's store of Pool & Lambert, at Fort Aubrey; he bought the stock of goods belonging to this firm in May, 1866, and continued the business at that point for two years, when he moved his store to Kiowa Springs; in 1868, he sold out his business, and came to this Co. in 1869; he was married Sept. 1, 1869, to Helen E. Cowan, who was born in this Co. in Jan., 1848; Mr. Stickney worked by the month for L. H. Clark, from 1872 till 1874; he then went into business with Mr. Farley, whom he soon after bought out; has two children, Irving E. and John H.; Methodist; Republican.

Stover Frank, laborer; Nora.

Stowell L. O. farmer; Sec. 4; P. O. Nora.

SWARTZ ELIAS M. Farmer and Raiser of thoroughbred Stock; Sec. 29; P. O. Nora; born in Centre Co., Pa., Jan. 28, 1838; at the age of 19 he came to De Kalb Co., Ill., only remaining three months, he continued his journey to Kaneville, Kane Co., Ill.; in 1859 he returned to De Kalb Co.; in 1860 he went to Stephenson Co., but returned to Kaneville, Kane Co., the same year; in July, 1861, he again went to Stephenson Co.; after a nine months' stay, he moved near Whitewater, Rock Co., Wis.; residing here only a short time, he returned to Stephenson Co., where, on Nov. 6, 1864, he was married to Susannah Rudy; she was born in Centre Co., Pa., Jan. 6, 1845; Mr. Swartz purchased his present "Evergreen Farm," consisting of 148 acres, in 1867; with his brother, under the firm name of E. M. and G. F. Swartz; they are engaged in raising thoroughbred stock, such as Shorthorned cattle, Berkshire and Poland China hogs; no man in the Co. takes a more lively interest in advancing the standard of stock raising; the pedigree of his herd of thoroughbreds show that they have been carefully selected from the best herds in the United States and Canada; all persons interested in raising the better grades of cattle, as well as those intending to purchase, will always receive a courteous welcome at "Evergreen Farm;" the proprietors have found their past experience so encouraging that they intend making this a permanent business.

Switzer W. H. renter; P. O. Howardsville.

TALBOT I. S. cooper; Nora.

Taylor Wm. postmaster; Nora.

Tirrenzo Anson, laborer; P.O. Howardsville.

THOMPSON CHRISTOPHER C. Farmer; Sec. 32; P. O. Howardsville; born in Plymouth Co., Mass., June 5, 1807; in the Spring of 1838 he emigrated to the West, first stopping for a few months at Winslow, Stephenson Co., Ill., but permanently settling in what is now Thompson

Township; this Tp. was given his name in honor of his public spirit of enterprise, and in assisting in making the Tp. what it is; immediately upon his arrival here he built the second saw mill in the Co., and in 1840 built the first large grist mill in the Co., which supplied Galena with nearly all its flour; he built the first frame school house in Rush Tp., and the first stone school house in Thompson Tp.; there were six families in his Tp. when he settled there; came to Nora Tp. in Oct., 1874; owns 931 acres land; married Almira Dunlap in 1842; she died in 1845; May 31, 1847, he married Mary A. Strong, who was born in Jefferson Co., O., June 14, 1821; two of their children, Whitfield J. and Tena, live with their parents; Winfield S., an adopted son, was killed in the army.

THOMPSON WOODMAN, Farmer; Sec. 29; P. O. Nora; born in the Tp. of Thompson, Jo Daviess Co., Ill., Jan. 13, 1851; he is the eldest son of C. C. Thompson, after whom his native Tp. was named, and who is one of the old settlers of this Co.; Woodman, Oct. 10, 1871, married Jenefor Eustice, who was born in Elizabeth Tp., Jo Daviess Co., Ill., Feb. 24, 1847; they came to this Tp. and to their farm of 20 acres about one year ago; they have two children, John C. and Raymond.

Thornton Thos. renter; Sec. 29; P.O. Warren.

Tilton B. F. town collector; Nora.

Tucker Ed. mechanic; Nora.

Tucker R. B. renter; Sec. 9; P. O. Nora.

Tucker W. J. painter; Nora.

Turner Forest, retired farmer; Nora.

WADDINGTON JOSEPH, Employe on Railroad; P. O. Nora; born in Yorkshire, Eng., Feb. 9, 1814; married July 8, 1838, Ellen Egg, who was born in Yorkshire, Eng., Dec. 21, 1816; they came to this country in 1849, first settling in Williamson Co., Ill., and residing there a little over two years; Chicago was their next stopping place, but after two years in that city they came to this Co. in 1854; for 23 years Mr. Waddington has been employed at Nora by the Illinois Central Railroad, and still holds his position; their children are: Sarah, George, Catharine, Will, John A., Martha and Mary (twins), John Ellen, Albert L. and Gilbert C.

WARNER GEO. P. Farmer; Sec. 8; P. O. Nora; born Jan. 17, 1832, in Strafford, Orange Co., Vt.; his father, Austin Warner, was born in Albany, N. Y., in 1801, and he moved to Montreal, Canada, with his parents, where he was married June 17, 1845; George came with his parents to this Co., settling first on Sec. 18, and afterwards moved to Sec. 32; here he resided ten years; he sold his farm and went into the lumber trade under the firm name of Drew & Warner; he sold out his interest in this after six years, and bought his present farm; married Phœbe Birdseye Sept. 28, 1859; she was born in Birmingham, Conn.

WARNER GOODRICH W. Farmer; Sec. 33; P. O. Nora; born May 30, 1824, in Strafford, Orange Co., Vt.; remained with his parents until 20 years of age, when his father gave himself and brother fifty dollars each and they came to Chicago, *via* the lakes, having five dollars left on their arrival; worked for $12 a month on a farm, during the Summer, near Aurora, Ill., and came to this Co. in the Fall of 1845, settling on Sec. 18, Nov. 6, 1847; he married Mary Davis, who was born in Wales, March 14, 1830; she came to this country when five years old, living in Ohio nine years, Keokuk, Iowa, one year, and since then, in this Co.; they have a farm of 137 acres, on which they moved July 1, 1860; their children are Mrs. Sarah L. Garver, Bessie B., Evert D., Mary E.; Republican; Congregationalist.

WASSON WALTER S. Manufacturer of Harness; Nora; born in Port Henry, Essex Co., N. Y., June 29, 1850; his father dying in 1854, he came with his mother to Lena, Stephenson Co., Ill., in 1855; married Alice J. Jones, Dec. 5, 1869; she was born in Lena, Dec. 13, 1850; in 1870 they moved to Harvard, McHenry Co., Ill., where he engaged in railroading; they came to Nora in April, 1875, where they have since resided; Mr. Wasson commenced his present vocation with but five cents in money, and by strict attention to business, has now a flourishing and lucrative trade; they have two children, Walter J. and Arthur L.

Way Manlove, blacksmith; Nora.

West John, farm; Sec. 19; P. O. Warren.

West Robert, farm; Sec. 19; P.O. Greenvale.

WILEY GEORGE W. Farmer; Sec. 21; P. O. Warren; born in Murray Co., Tenn., Dec. 1, 1809; his father moved to Jefferson Co., Mo., and in May, 1827, he emigrated to this Co., coming up the Mississippi on a boat as far as Fort Edwards (now Warsaw), walking from that place to Galena; he took part in the Black Hawk War; lived in this Co., and Wis., near Galena, until 1836, when he began to break and improve his present farm, now consisting of 335 acres of land in this Tp.; in 1838 he moved on the above land, and has continued living there since; married Mrs. Ann Durham, July 10, 1853; she was born in St. Louis Co., Mo., July 17, 1818; George E., Catherine, Perry and Anna B., are their children; Maria B., Keziah J., and Elizabeth Durham, were Mrs. Wiley's children by first marriage.

WILSON ROBERT M. Blacksmith; Nora; born in Tyrone, Ireland, Aug. 10, 1843; came to this country in 1847, with his parents, who settled first at Boston,

Mass., but soon after went to New York City; moved to Ogle Co., Ill., in 1853; at eighteen years of age he enlisted in the 34th Regt. I. V. I., Co. H, but re-enlisted in the regular army, Dec., 1862, joining Co. M., 4th U. S.; his discharge shows that he was engaged in the battles of Pittsburg Landing, Stone River, Snow Hill, Middleton, Franklin, Shelbyville, Chicamauga, Okolona, Miss., Dallas, Kenesaw Mountain, Noonday Creek, Lovejoy, Jonesboro, Rome, Ga., Nashville, Tenn., Selma, Ala., and at Columbus, Ga., April 15, 1865, the last battle of the Rebellion; Married Anna E. Dixon, April 7, 1870; she was born in Cambridge, Mass., Feb. 21, 1853, and came to this Co., in 1872; Mr. Wilson is a member of the Co. Board of Supervisors; they have three children: Joseph B., Florence A., and Robert M.; Independent; Congregationalist.

WIRE BENJAMIN F. Farmer; Sec. 29; P. O. Nora; born in Canada Jan. 21, 1839; in 1848 he, with his step-father, came to Dodge Co., Wis., and in 1852 moved to Ward's Grove, Jo Daviess Co., Ill.; here he was married to Mary A. Daws Nov. 10, 1857; she was born in England Dec. 23, 1838; the following year after marriage they moved to Stephenson Co., Ill., where they have resided until within the last year, when they came to this Tp.; their children are: Orpha V., Lydia A., Cora M., Æschylus A., Flora L. and Martha A.; Mr. Wire served one year in the 147th I. V. I.; Methodist; Republican.

YORK THOMAS, retired farmer; Nora.

YOUNG ANDREW J. Of the firm of Young & Waddington, dealers in Hardware; Nora; born in Herkimer Co., N.Y., May 27, 1849; in 1852 he, with his parents, emigrated to Stephenson Co., Ill.; some years after he was engaged in the butter trade in Lena, under the firm name of Newcome & Young; in 1870 he came to Nora, and in 1871 commenced the hardware trade in his present store; married Mary Waddington May 27, 1874; she was born in Williamson Co., Ill., March 11, 1851; have one child, Minnie.

APPLE RIVER TOWNSHIP.

ANDREWS JOHN, farmer; Sec.21; P.O. Apple River.

Armstrong Thomas, farmer; Sec. 27; P. O. Apple River.

ADAMS JOHN, Retired Farmer; Apple River; was born in Beaver Co., Pa., on the 12th of May, 1815; went from there to Wood Co., Ohio, in 1833; lived there until 1854; he then moved to Lafayette Co., Wis.; he remained there until 1867, when he moved to this Co., and it has since been his home; he was Supervisor a number of years in the Tp. which he lived in while in Wis.; is a member of the Presbyterian Church, and has been twice a delegate to the U. S. conference of that church; has been Elder since '45; married Mary Levitt in Wood Co., Ohio, on March 17, 1836; she was born in Yorkshire, England, Sept. 9, 1814; have had twelve children, five of whom are living; had one son, William T., in the army; he enlisted in Aug., 1862, in 96th Regt., I. V. I.; was discharged on account of sickness in 1863.

Appal Joseph, butcher; Apple River.

BAUMGARDNER JOHN, farmer; Sec. 34; P. O. Apple River.

BARRY JNO. Grain Dealer; Apple River; born in Co. Wexford, Ireland; aged 47; emigrated to U. S. in 1851; was 5 years railroad station-agent on the Watertown & Rome R. R., at Three-Mile Bay, Jefferson Co., N. Y.; came to Lafayette Co., Wis., in 1858, and engaged in farming; believes the Catholic to be the supernatural church; was a war democrat during the war of the rebellion, hence voted against peace resolutions in democratic convention held at Darlington, Wis., in 1861; has held offices of Village Clerk 4 years, Chairman of Supervisors 1 year; also School Dist. Treasurer 9 years, and has taught 9 winter terms at public school; moved to Jo Daviess Co., Ill., in 1873; engaged in the grain business, more or less, to the present time; has held the offices of Town Clerk 2 years, Assessor 1 year, and President of Village Trustees 1 year in Apple River, Ill.; married, in 1867, Miss Mary Catherine Kleeberger, aged 36 years, who was born in White Oak Springs (since Monticello), Territory (now State) of Wis.; the surviving children are: Mary H., born at Shullsburg, Wis., May 1, 1869, Elizabeth G., in Apple River, Ill., April 23, 1876.

Becker H. P. cooper; Apple River.

Beggin Terrence, farmer; P.O. Apple River.

Beggin Thomas, farmer; P. O. Apple River.

Bell William, laborer; Apple River.

Bennett William, farmer; P.O. Apple River.

BENSON B. B. Farmer; Sec. 27; P.O. Apple River; was born in Cortland Co., N. Y., in 1821; he came to this Co. in 1832; in 1849 he went to California; remained there until 1853, when he returned to this Co., and it has been his home since; has held the office of Assessor 1 year, and has held various other township and school offices; owns 180 acres of land; has been married twice; present wife was Mary Jane Kearns; they were married in this town on Dec. 26, 1874.

Benningham Thos. F. principal in High School; Apple River.

BERMINGHAM THADDEUS J. Lumber Dealer; Apple River; was born in Co. Clare, Ireland, on March 1, 1849; moved with his parents to Canada in 1859; lived there one year; thence to this Co. in 1860; entered the lumber business with Wm. Hoskins, in this place, in 1873; the business was established by Mr. Hoskins in 1855; Mr. Benningham is a graduate of the Galena High School; is one of the present Board of Town Trustees; was Principal of school in Elizabeth, in this Co., two years; also, Principal of High School in this place seven years; married Fannie Hoskins, July 30, 1873; she was born in this town Aug. 4, 1854; have one child: Willie, born in this town Dec. 10, 1875.

BERRYMAN WM. H. Farmer; Sec. 35; P. O. Apple River; owns 405 acres of land; was born in Lafayette, Wis., on Sept. 27, 1842; moved to this Co. with his parents in 1849; married Miss Gracie Pryor in Scales Mound, this Co., on March 13, 1863; she was born at Scales Mound on April 28, 1847; have had seven children, five of whom are living; Mr. Berryman is one of the present Directors of the School Board.

Bixby Beriah, retired; Apple River.

Blackson S. W.

Breen Daniel.

Bush Geo. A. laborer; Apple River.

Bush John A. blacksmith; Apple River.

Buche John, harness maker; Apple River.

Brunner M. M. blacksmith; Apple River.

CAMPBELL JAMES, laborer; Apple River.

Calvert William, carpenter; Apple River.

CASHMAN M. Dealer in Agricultural Implements; Apple River; was born in Ireland on May 15, 1839; came to this Co. in May, 1851; has been Deputy Sheriff twelve years, Constable fifteen years, Town Collector six years; was also Assessor a number of years, and has held various other offices; he has the reputation of being one of the most efficient officers in the Co.; he has always been a firm supporter of the Republican party; married Mary Jane White in Freeport, Stephenson Co., this state, on May 1, 1866; she was born in Ireland in 1849; have had four children, viz.: Mary Elizabeth, born May 26, 1867, Henry James, Feb. 27, 1870, John M., April 13, 1872, Francis E., July 3, 1876, died March 22, 1877; Mr. C. had one brother in the army (Henry Cashman); he enlisted in Co. E, 96th Regt., I. V. I., in 1862; was in many severe engagements; he was killed while making a charge on a rebel battery at the battle of Chicamauga, on Sept. 20, 1863; he was born in Ireland Aug. 7, 1843.

Chambers John W. Apple River.

CHRISTY D. W. Grain Dealer; Apple River; was born in Butler Co., Pa., Oct. 24, 1844; came from there to this state in 1855, and remained in it until 1862; he then went to Montana; remained there four years, at the end of which time he went to British Columbia, in which place he stayed one year; he then returned to Montana, this time remaining a little over a year; he came to this Co. in 1866; in 1873 he entered the grain business in this place, which business he has been engaged in since; married Rebecca Ingersoll, in Shullsburg, Wis., Nov. 19, 1866; she was born in Calhoun Co., this State, Jan. 1, 1831; they have four children, viz: Scovy Stewart, born Aug. 19, 1867; Mary Rebecca, April 19, 1869, Cora Belle, Feb. 6, 1871, Stella Maude, May 3, 1874; Mr. Christy is the present Town Treasurer in this place, which office he has held three terms.

Code Joseph L. wagon maker; Apple River.

Colvin Jas. farmer; S. 21; P.O. Apple River.

COLVIN WILLIAM, Farmer; Sec. 21; P. O. Apple River; was born in Washington Co., Pa., March 5, 1810; he was one of the 75 who came on the old Col. Bumford keel boat, in 1824, and planted a a little colony where Galena now stands; they were forty-one days making the trip from St. Louis; those persons were actually the first white settlers in this Co.; the country was then a most unpromising wilderness, mostly occupied by Indians; the first two years after their settlement they had neither law nor religion, and dishonesty was unknown among them; in 1826 they organized a church, elected a Justice of the Peace and Constable; it was then that rascality and trickery began, and have continued since; the first trial they had after they organized ended in a free fight, the Justice taking a hand in it; the only fee he ever received was a severe beating over the head with the jaw bone of a hog; at the breaking out of the Black Hawk War, Mr. Colvin entered General Dodge's command, and served until Black Hawk was finally driven across the Mississippi; he was engaged in many severe Indian fights; was in the battle of Bad Axe; in this battle the power of Black Hawk was completely broken; he fled, but was captured by the Winnebagoes; in a few days after was brought in and delivered to the whites; Mr. Colvin was married near Lawrenceburg, Indiana, in 1842; Mrs. Colvin was born in Boone Co., Kentucky, in 1821; she died in June, 1872; Mr. Colvin owns 191 acres of land; of the seventy-five pioneers who came up the Mississippi River on the old Col. Bumford keel boat in 1824, there are only four survivors, including Mr. Colvin.

Connarty Edward, farmer; Sec. 28; P. O. Apple River.

Copeland Gerrard, laborer; Apple River.

Corey Chas. H. physician; Apple River.

Craig Thomas, carpenter; Apple River.

Cunningham Hugh, farmer; Sec. 22; P. O. Apple River.

DE GRAFF HIRAM, Retired Farmer; Apple River; was born at Amsterdam, N. Y., on the 20th of April, 1817; he came to this Co. in 1835; at that time the Co. was rather thinly settled, the houses being about 25 miles apart; he was the first School Trustee elected in the Tp.; was elected Supervisor two years in succession (1865 and 1866,) and has held various other Tp. and School offices; during the early history of the Co. he took an active part in the organization of schools and churches; he is a member of the M. E. Church; has been Class Leader 29 years; Sabbath School Superintendent a number of years; Trustee 6 years; was also elected to the General Conference held at Joliet, Ill.; in politics he is Republican, being a firm supporter of that party since Fremont was nominated for President of the U. S.; he was one of the passengers on the ill-fated steamer Erie when she was destroyed by fire, he being one of the 35 saved out of the 200 on board; he has been married three times; first wife was Rachel Phelps, married 3d Oct. 1839; died 9th of April, 1849; second wife was Sarah Younce; married 23d Dec., 1849; died 7th of Dec., 1865; present wife was Sarah Crase; was married in Warren, this Co., 7th of June, 1866; she was born in Cornwall, England, on the 15th of Nov., 1828; came to this country in 1849; to this Co. 14 years ago; had one son killed in the army, Wm. Frederick; enlisted in the 96th Regt. I.V.I., in August, 1861; was wounded at Chicamauga; his father brought him home, and he had scarcely recovered before the brave fellow returned to his Regt. and was again wounded at Rocky Face Mountain, said wounds causing his death May 12, 1864; he was born in this town 3d of Feb., 1842.

DEMING ALBERT, Farmer; Sec. 21; P. O. Apple River; was born in this Co. on the 26th of April, 1841; has held various Tp. offices; owns 80 acres land; enlisted in Co. I, 25th Regt. Wis. V. I. in 1862; was Corporal; was in many severe engagements, and all through the Atlanta campaign; was honorably discharged in June, 1865; has been married twice; married present wife (maiden name Margaret Williams) in Warren, this Co., on the 16th of June, 1864; she was born in Ohio in 1849.

DIMMICK WM. OSCAR, Farmer; Sec. 22; P. O. Apple River; born in this town the 23d of Aug., 1852; owns 272 acres land; has held various School offices; married Miss Esther Stone, in Monticello, Wis., on the 20th of Oct., 1874; she was born in Monticello, on the 8th of Dec., 1854; have one child, Oscar Leroy, born in this place, the 17th of June, 1877. Lot L. Dimmick, father of W. O. Dimmick, was one of the pioneers of this Co., coming to Galena in 1825; was here during the Black Hawk War; was a member of the Presbyterian Church and lived a sincere, earnest Christian life; married Mary A. Mann, in Galena, the 10th of April, 1831; she was born in Cayuga Co., N. Y., the 20th of June, 1809; died the 3d of Feb., 1876; Mrs. D. was one of those early pioneer mothers in whom we all feel so justly proud; in 1820 she came West with her parents and settled near Kaskaskia, Randolph Co., Ill.; in the following year they moved to Waterloo, Monroe Co.; in 1829 she came to Galena, where she remained till her marriage, in 1831, when she came to the homestead now occupied by the family; she was one of the 36 inmates of the fort on what is now known as the Wiley farm, during the Black Hawk War; she was a consistent member of the Presbyterian Church for a period of 25 years, and was a teacher in the first Sabbath School organized in Galena; she had three sons in the War of the Rebellion, Daniel W., born in this town the 9th of Feb., 1840; enlisted in the 96th Regt. I. V. I., Co. E, as Corporal, in 1862; served until close of the war; Harry M., born the 23d of March, 1842; enlisted in Co. B, 45th Regt. I. V. I., in 1861; died at Corinth from typhoid pneumonia, contracted in the army, 19th of March, 1862; George W., born the 26th of March, 1844; enlisted in the 96th Regt. I. V. I., in 1862; was wounded and taken prisoner at the battle of Chicamauga, and died, after being exchanged, from disease contracted while in rebel prison, on the 15th of March, 1865.

DAUGHERTY DOMINICK, Farmer; Sec. 20; P. O. Apple River; was born in Ireland in 1812; came to this country in the year of 1842 and settled at Shullsburg, Wis., thus becoming one of the early settlers of that place; he came from there to this Co. a few years afterward; settled in this Tp. and it has since been his home; he owns 80 acres of land; married Ann McPike in Shullsburg, Wis., in 1858; they have three children.

Daugherty Terrence, farmer; Sec. 19; P. O. Apple River.

Down Edward B. retired; Apple River.

DOYLE WILLIAM, Farmer; Sec. 24; P. O. Apple River; was born in Lafayette Co., Wis., on the 17th of July, 1842; came to this Co. in 1865; owns the farm; married Miss A. Schank in Galena, this Co., March, 1870; she was born in Ohio in 1846; have two children, Frank and Mabel. His father, Andrew Doyle, was one of the first settlers in Monticello, Lafayette Co., Wis.

EADE GEORGE, butcher; Apple River.

EASLEY P. A. Telegraph Operator, I. C. R. R., Apple River; was born in Scott Co., Iowa, on the 21st of Jan., 1849; has been Town Clerk since 1875; and also is the present City Clerk; on the 10th of May, 1864, he enlisted in Co. B, 142d Regt. I. V. I.; served until the close of the war and was honorably discharged; he received the President's (Lincoln) thanks, and certificate of honorable service for gallant and meritorious conduct during the time he was engaged in the service of his country.

Eagan L. renter; Sec. 28; P.O. Apple River.

Ennor Martin C. miner; Apple River.

ENNOR W. D. Merchant; Apple River; was born in this Co. on the 10th of Jan., 1850; has been engaged in the mercantile business in this town (Apple River) two years; married Miss Elizabeth Atkinson in Winnebago Co., this state, on the 5th of July, 1874; she was born in Yorkshire, England, on the 12th of April, 1849, and came to this Co. with her parents at an early age; have two children, Jesse Clare, born the 10th of June, 1875, John Guy, 2d of April, 1877.

FENN JESSE, stone mason; Apple River.

Fenn T. farm; Sec. 22; P. O. Apple River.

FIELDING GEO. Farmer; P. O. Apple River; was born in Yorkshire, Eng., on the 20th of Sept., 1819; came from there to this Co. in 1842; owns 170 acres of land; has been a member of the Co. Board, and has held the office of assessor three years; married Harriet Levitt, in Lafayette Co., Wis., on the 25th day of April, 1849; she was born in Yorkshire, Eng., on the 10th of Nov., 1827; she came to this Co., in 1843.

Foley James.

Foley J. farmer; Sec. 31; P.O. Apple River.

Foley P. farmer; Sec. 31; P.O. Apple River.

Foley R. farmer; Sec. 31; P.O. Apple River.

FRANCOMB JAMES, Farmer; Sec. 33; P. O. Apple River; owns 120 acres land; was born in England, on the 16th of Aug., 1837; came from there to White Oak Springs, Lafayette Co., Wis., in 1858; lived there one year; then he went to New Diggings (same Co.); here he married Miss Agnes. Morton on the 22d of Aug., 1860; she was born in Yorkshire, Eng., on the 20th of March, 1842; they came to this Co. in 1864, and it has been their home since; have had eight children, the living are Emma, born 7th Oct., 1862, Anna Elizabeth, 8th of Feb., 1868, James Manly, 22d June, 1870, Agnes May, 12th Dec., 1872, Ella Eva, 14th Dec., 1874.

Freyboge Melchior, blksmith; Apple River.

Frost George, clerk; Apple River.

Frost George T. banker; Apple River.

FUNK EDGAR M. Railroad and Express Agent; Apple River; was born in Lafayette Co. April 7, 1849; he came to this Co. in 1862; has been railroad and express agent in this place seven years; is one of the present Board of Town Trustees; has held that office last three years; married Seraphina Maynard in this town, Aug. 20, 1873; she was born in Cuba, on May 27, 1853; have two children, Annita, born in this place on Oct. 5, 1875; Roy Alonzo, born in this town May 4. 1877. Mr. Funk's grandfather, Captain Funk, was one of the pioneers of this Co.; he settled here previous to the Black Hawk War; he served in that war as captain until its close; he also held various important offices in the early history of this Co.

GEDDIS R. farmer; P. O. Apple River.

Gellespie T. farmer; P. O. Apple River.

Goldsborrough Wm. renter; P. O. Apple River.

Grabham J. farm; Sec. 28; P. O. Apple River.

GRABHAM WILLIAM G. Farmer; Sec. 28; P. O. Apple River; was born in Durham, England, in May 13, 1843; came to this Co. with his parents in 1843; has been in California twice; married Athylinda Chapman in Galena, this Co., on Oct. 4, 1866; she was born in Shullsburg, Wis., on May 13, 1848; she died on April 18, 1873; have two children, Sarah Josephine, born on Feb. 27, 1869; Joseph E., Dec. 10, 1870; his father, Wm. Grabham, was born in England, in 1809; he married Miss Todd in Durham, England, in 1835; she was born in Cumberland Co., England, in 1810; they came to this Co. in 1853; had one son (John) in the army; he enlisted in Company E, 96th Regiment, I. V. I.; in Aug., 1862; served until the close of the war, and was honorably discharged; he was in most every battle the regiment was.

HALL R. L. druggist; Apple River.

Hamilton Thos. stock dealer; Apple River.

Hamson W. H. retired farmer; Apple River.

Haskins Wm. lumber dealer; Apple River.

Hastie T. F. retired; Apple River.

Henry Bevadill, laborer; Apple River.

Henry G. W., Sr., retired; Apple River.

Henry G. W., Jr., works for Joseph Vartz; Apple River.

Henson Richard, retired; Apple River.

Hill William, druggist; Apple River.

Hinkley Louis, laborer; Apple River.

Hodgson N. F. farm; Sec. 19; P. O. Apple River.

Horan Michael, farmer; P. O. Apple River.

HUME JOHN, Farmer; Sec. 33; P. O. Apple River; owns 140 acres of land; was born in Ireland in 1827; came to this country in 1852; and settled at new Diggings, in Lafayette Co., Wis.; remained there until 1857; he then came to this Co.; has held various town and school offices; married Miss Ellen J. White in this Co. in 1854; she was born in Ireland in 1830; they have six children living.

INGERSOLL S. S. retired; Apple River.

Irvine James M. merchant; Apple River.

IRVINE ROBERT, Grain Dealer; Apple River; was born in Ireland, 19th June, 1831; came to Wis. in 1842; lived in that state until 1854; he then went to California; remained there until 1859, when he returned; he came to this place (Apple River) and engaged in the grain business, which business he has successfully carried on ever since; married Miss Frances Ellen Maynard, in this place, in 1861; she was born in this town in 1841.

Irvine Robert, Sr., retired; Apple River.

Irvine Samuel, retired farmer; Apple River.

JACOBS JACOB, farmer; Sec. 23; P. O. Apple River.

James Isaac, retired farmer, Apple River.

KEARNS BERNARD, farmer; Sec. 34; P. O. Apple River.

Kearns Hugh, farmer; Sec. 34; P. O. Apple River.

Kearney John, laborer; Apple River.

Kindekens Joseph, pastor of St. Joseph's Church; Apple River.

King Andrew, laborer; Apple River.

KLEEBERGER GEO. L. H. Merchant; Apple River; was born in Germany, 30th Dec., 1830; came to this country in 1836; lived in N. Y. one year, then came to Monticello, Wis., in the year of '38, thus being one of the pioneers of that place; he came from there to this Co. in 1871, since which time he has been engaged in the mercantile business at this place; he married Harriet Funk in this Co. on the 28th Feb., 1843; she was born in Mo. on 14th Feb., 1823; her father (Capt. Benjamin Funk) settled near this place in the year of 1827, thus becoming one of the pioneers of the Northwest; he served as Captain during the Black Hawk War; he was born in Virginia in November, 1798; died on the 28th of Sept., 1851, respected and honored by the entire community in which he lived; Mr. Kleeberger had one son in the army; he enlisted in 1862; was honorably discharged.

Kramer Philip, laborer; Apple River.

LAMONT T. F. H. Hardware Merchant; Apple River; was born in Preston Co., Va., on 10th Nov., 1852; moved with his parents to Mo. in 1856, thence to this Co. in 1857; entered the hardware business at this place (Apple River) in the Fall of 1876; married Jennie C. Kevern, in Normal, this state (Ill.), in 1875; she was born in Council Hill, this Co., in 1857.

LAPPIN BERNARD, Farmer and Stock Raiser; Sec. 26; P. O. Apple River; owns 155 acres land; he was born in Ireland in 1817; came to this country in 1844, and settled at New Diggings, Wis.; lived there until 1850, when he came to this Co.; married Bridget Clark, in Ireland; they have nine children living.

Leamy Edward, laborer; Apple River.

Lemon Hans, laborer; Apple River.

LEMON PETER V. Farmer; Sec. 28; P. O. Apple River; was born in Canada on 14th Sept., 1805; came to this state in 1838; lived in Rock Island Co. one year; went from there to Mo.; lived in that state a number of years; came to this Co. in 1846, and it has since been his home; maiden name of wife was Nancy Scott; they were married in Shullsburg, Wis., in 1852; she was born in Ky. in the year 1811; Mr. Lemon owns 80 acres land.

Levitt Jos. T. harness maker; Apple River.

Levitt Robert, retired farmer; Apple River.

Levitt Robt. W. school teacher; Apple River.

LEVITT WILLIAM, Justice of the Peace; Apple River; was born in Yorkshire, England, in 1804; came from there to Ohio in 1831; lived there six years; was in Pa. one year; came to this Co. in 1838, and to this town in 1839; there were but few living here at that time, and there was not a house on either side for a number of miles; has been Justice of the Peace 15 years—nine years in this place; has also been assessor three years, and has held various other offices; married Cynthia Stone in Monticello, Wis., in 1852; she was born in Canada in 1814; she died in 1855; present wife was Ann Maynard (maiden name Ann Arthur); they were married in Monticello, Wis., in 1857; she was born in Cornwall, England, in 1812.

Geo. S. Wing

RUSH TP.

LICHTENBERGER CYRUS, Street and Highway Commissioner; Apple River; was born in Somerset Co., Pa., on 28th Jan., 1817; came to this Co. in 1827, and settled at East Forks (now Scales Mound), where he erected him a house and cultivated 10 acres land; this was then the greatest number of acres under cultivation in any one piece in what is now known as Jo Daviess Co. in 1827; he was engaged in the Winnebago War, in 1832; he served in the Black Hawk War; was elected Supervisor of this town in 1859; has been Commissioner 12 years, and has held various other offices for the last 20 years; in 1835 he discovered some of the best paying lead mines in the Co., the principal one being Vettegrand, better known as Blackleg Diggings; his father, Conrad Lichtenberger, was born in Pa., in 1789; he served in the war of 1812, and helped drive Black Hawk over the Mississippi in 1832–3; he died in this Co. on the 29th day of Oct., 1836; Cyrus Lichtenberger married Miss Hettie Harper, at Scales Mound, on 29th Dec., 1840; she was born in Ind. on 9th Feb., 1823; her father, J. Harper, came to this Co. in 1833, bringing his family with him; he was born in S. C. in 1797; he served under General Jackson in the war of 1812; he died in 1848.

Lichtenburger Eli L. superintendent lead mine; P. O. Apple River.

Lichtenburger Frank, clerk; Apple River.

Lichtenburger James, carp.; Apple River.

Lynch John, blacksmith; Apple River.

McAVIN JAMES, farmer; Sec. 31; P. O. Apple River.

McDONALD JOHN, Retired Farmer; Apple River; was born in Ohio on 10th Aug., 1807; moved from there to Va., in 1823; lived there until 1828; he then went to Mo., and remained there until 1831, when he removed to Greene Co., Wis., where he resided until 1834; he then came to this state; since then this Co. has been his home; he owns 323 acres land; has held various school offices, and in the early settlement of the Co. he took an active part in the organization of schools and churches; married Samantha Reed in Ohio, on 14th Aug., 1832; she was born in Vt., on 12th April, 1806; have had nine children: William, born 21st May, 1833, died 26th Oct., 1833; Laurilla (now Mrs. Phelps), 26th Oct., 1834; George, 16th May, 1836, died 30th Sept., 1856; Adaline, 6th May, 1838, died on 10th May, 1847; Mary, 24th Feb., 1840, deceased; William A., 25th Feb., 1842; he enlisted in Co. E, 96th I. V. I.; was honorably discharged; Amanda, 26th Oct., 1844, died on 29th of March, 1867; John L., 15th Oct., 1847; Marcus A., 7th Aug., 1850.

McDonald Marcus, miner; Apple River.

McFadden James, farmer; P.O. Apple River.

McFadden J. farm; S. 25; P. O. Apple River.

McFADDEN SAMUEL, Farmer; Sec. 34; P. O. Apple River; owns 100 acres of land; was born in Ireland in 1834; he came to this country when he was seventeen years old; lived in New York sixteen years; came to New Digging, Lafayette Co., Wis., in 1857; remained there until 1862, when he came to this Co.; it has been his home since; married Catherine Stevenson, in N. Y.; she was born at St. Johns, New Brunswick, in 1835; Mr. McFadden is one of the present Board of School Trustees; has also been School Director a number of years.

McFadden S., Jr., farmer; P.O. Apple River.

McHugh John, saloon; Apple River.

McQuade Jas. farmer; P. O. Apple River.

MANN JAMES H. Farmer; Sec. 23; P. O. Apple River; owns 160 acres of land; was born in this Co. March 26, 1846; went to Montana in 1867; lived there until Spring of 1873, when he returned and married Miss Clara Stone, in Monticello, Lafayette Co., Wis.; this, also, was the place of her birth; his father (Harvey Mann) was born in N. Y.; he came to this Co. in 1827; in 1832 he took part in the Black Hawk War, he and his family being driven from their home by the Indians.

Martin J., Sr., farm; S. 25; P.O. Apple River.

Martin J., Jr., farm; S.25; P.O. Apple River.

Mankey Alfred, blacksmith; Apple River.

Maynard H. J. D. dealer in agricultural implements; Apple River.

MAYNARD JOHN, Retired; Apple River; was born in Cornwall, Eng., Sept. 14, 1810; came to this Co. in 1841; remained two years; returned to England, where he remained ten months; went to Cuba; lived there nine years, when he again returned to England, remaining a period of two years; then to Jamaica; back to England for six months; back again to Cuba for one year; from there to this country by way of Havana, remaining only a short time; he crossed the ocean to Eng. in 1860; after crossing and re-crossing twice, he returned in 1863, making his home since then in this place; married Miss Elizabeth Drew, in Cornwall, Eng., in 1834; she was born in Cornwall, Eng., in 1817; have five children: Henry J. D., born in Cornwall, Eng., in Fall 1834, Malichi, in Cornwall, in 1837, Mary Eliza (now Mrs. Maynard), in Cuba, Sara Zina (now Mrs. S. J. Funk), in Cuba, Thomas Y., in Cornwall, in 1854.

Maynard M. merchant; Apple River.

Maynard Thos. H. dealer; P O. Apple River.

Maynard Thos. T. jeweler; Apple River.

Meade P. farm; Sec. 31; P. O. Apple River.

Moreley James, farmer; P. O. Apple River.

Murphy A. farmer; P. O. Apple River.

Murphy J. farmer; S. 31; P. O. Apple River.

Murphy Nicholas, merchant.

Murphy P. farm; Sec. 31; P.O. Apple River.

NEWTON FRANK, teamster; Apple River.

Nugent James, renter; Sec. 24; P. O. Apple River.

Nugent Michael, laborer; Apple River.

PAIGE E. D. farmer; Sec. 36; P. O. Apple River.

PAIGE GEORGE A. Farmer; Sec. 36; P. O. Apple River; owns 400 acres of land; was born in Windsor Co., Vt., on the 16th of Oct., 1819; came from that to this Co. in 1840; there were not over a dozen families located on farms in this Tp. at that time; he was instrumental in establishing the first post-office in this Tp. and was the first P. M. appointed, which position he filled a number of years; he has also been Deputy Co. Surveyor for 8 years, Justice of the Peace 9 years, School Treasurer 10 years; he took a prominent part in the organization of the Co. Grange at this place, and is an earnest supporter of the Greenback party; he married Louisa Towne, in Woodstock, Vt., on the 23d of July, 1841; she was born in Windsor Co., Vt., on the 30th of April, 1819; have had four children: Lucius, born 7th Sept., 1843, died 16th Oct., 1846; Edward G., 9th of Feb., 1847; Francis L., 16th Oct., 1849; Pluma C., 14th June, 1857.

PARKIN ROBERT, Carpenter and Joiner; Apple River; was born in Yorkshire, England, on the 4th of Nov., 1831; he came from there to this country in 1855 and settled in Lafayette Co., Wis.; he lived there two years; he then moved to this Co. and it has since been his home; he is one of the present Board of Trustees in this place; married Mary Heath, in this town, on the 15th of Dec., 1874; she was born in Canada on the 5th of May, 1849; have two children, Jane and Thomas; Mr. Parkin and family are members of the Episcopal Church.

PARKIN THOMAS R. Farmer; Sec. 24; P. O. Apple River; was born in Yorkshire, England, on the 11th of Jan., 1843; came to this country with his parents; they settled at New Diggings, Wis.; he lived there until 1857, when he came to this Co.; during the war of the Rebellion he enlisted in Co. B, 142d Regt., I. V. I.; served till the close of the war and was honorably discharged; owns 160 acres of land.

Parkin Wm. farmer; P. O. Apple River.

Parkinson, Thos. farm; P. O. Apple River.

Pearce Thomas, farmer; Sec. 35; P. O. Apple River.

PETERS THOMAS L. Farmer; Sec. 26; P. O. Apple River; was born in Mexico on the 24th of March, 1839; went from there to Cornwall, England with his parents when he was 7 years of age; lived there three years; they came to this Co. in 1849. Mr. T. L. Peters owns 160 acres of land; during the War of the Rebellion he enlisted in the 142d Regt., I. V. I.; served until the war was over and was honorably discharged; has been School Director a number of years; married Mary Ann Levitt, in Monticello, Lafayette Co., Wis., on the 9th of May, 1873; she was born in Monticello on the 25th of Nov., 1851; have two children: Benjamin Lane, born the 25th Nov., 1874, John Levitt, Aug., 1876.

Peters W. H. farmer; P.O. Apple River.

Phippin C. farm; Sec. 28; P.O. Apple River.

Phippin E. farmer; S. 28; P.O. Apple River.

PHIPPEN ORY, Farmer; Sec. 28; P.O. Apple River; was born in Allegany Co., N. Y., on the 3d of Aug. 1815; came to this Co. in 1838; married Elizabeth Benson, in Allegany Co., N. Y., in 1839; she was born in Cortland Co., N. Y., in 1815; had one son, Orlando, in the army; he enlisted in Co. E, 96th Regt., I.V. I., in 1862; he was honorably discharged at the close of the war; Mr. Phippen owns 160 acres of land.

Pierce Wm. T.

Power A. retired; Apple River.

Power Alvin, stone mason; Apple River.

Power N. farm; Sec. 30; P. O. Apple River.

Power Oscar, laborer; Apple River.

RADICAN MICHAEL, laborer; Apple River.

Renshaw C. M. carpenter; Apple River.

Rigster A. shoemaker; Apple River.

Rivenburg Wm. traveling salesman; Apple River.

Robbins G. F. restaurant; Apple River.

Robbins J. B. prop. Robbins House; Apple River.

ROBBINS MELZAR, (deceased) the subject of this sketch was born in the green mountains of Vermont, June 14, 1809; in 1831 he removed with his father's family to Chautauqua Co., N. Y.; in 1834 he married Aurelia Sprague, and engaged in farming, in which occupation he continued for several years; but hearing the glowing reports of the far West, and being favorably impressed with the many advantages claimed for the new country, he determined to brave all the hardships and privations that must necessarily be undergone by all the early settlers; he came to Illinois in the Spring of 1841, remaining until the Fall of the next year, when he returned to New York and brought his family west with him, thus becoming one of the pioneers of Northern Illinois; he located on a claim about one mile east of where now stands the Village of Apple River, and engaged in farming, in which business he remained for a number of years; he has reared a family of ten children, all of whom are living; he died at his residence in this village (Apple River) on the 11th day of April, 1876; many are they who will long cherish his memory for his unbounded generosity and large-heartedness; he was ever the poor man's friend, giving where-ever there was need, and many were the acts of kindness he has performed; he was a kind husband and indulgent father; the funeral services were held in the Presbyterian Church of this place, which was too small to contain the great number who followed the old citizen to his last resting place; such is the record left by him that we could fill a volume with recitals of his good deeds; but no words that we can employ would add any new lustre to the character he bore in the community where he lived so long.

Robbins W. H. restaurant; Apple River.

Robbins Welcome, miner; Apple River.

Roberts Chas. farm; S.22; P.O. Apple River.

Roberts J. farm; Sec. 26; P.O. Apple River.

Rowe J. farm; Sec. 26; P. O. Apple River.

ROWE JOSEPH H. Farmer; Sec. 26; P. O. Apple River; was born in Scales Mound, this Co., Jan. 11, 1847; owns 150 acres land; married Miss Cunningham in this place in 1873; she died in 1875; his father, Joseph Rowe, was born in Cornwall, England; came from there to this Co. in 1830, and settled near Galena; there were but few families in this Co. at that time; he died in this place in the 55th year of his age.

Rowe J. H. retired; Apple River.

Rule Wm. H. laborer; Apple River.

SCOTT THOMAS, Police Magistrate; Apple River; was born in Yorkshire, England, Oct. 31, 1824; came to this country in 1849, and settled in Lafayette Co., Wis.; he moved to this town (Apple River) in the year of 1873; Mr. Scott has held the office of Justice of the Peace two years, and was elected Police Magistrate in April, 1877; married Eliza Evans in Shullsburg, Wis., Sept. 26, 1851; she died March 6, 1873; had four children: John L., born July 21, 1852, Elizabeth, in Feb., 1854, died in May, 1855, Margaret A., Aug. 26, 1856, Thomas H., Aug. 16, 1859.

SIEBER JOHN, Cabinet Maker; Apple River; was born in Switzerland in Feb., 1831; came to this Co. in 1852, and settled in Galena; lived there until 1869; he then went to Kansas; remained there until year of 1872; then moved to this town and entered the furniture business, and has continued in since; married Catharine Krell, in Galena, in 1858; she was born in Pa. in the year 1843; have four children living.

SERVISS BEERI, Postmaster; Apple River; was born in this Co. Nov. 22, 1843; was appointed Postmaster in Aug. 1865, the duties of which office he has since faithfully discharged; on Aug. 5, 1862, he responded to his country's call and enlisted in Co. K, 96th Regt., I. V. I.; was in many severe battles, and through the Atlanta campaign; lost his right leg in the battle of Rocky Face Mountain; was honorably discharged in Nov. 1864, married Miss Huldah Bunker, in Stephenson Co., this state, on Sept. 29, 1872; she was born in N. Y., Oct. 3, 1851.

SHEEAN RICHARD, Farmer; Sec. 27; P. O. Apple River; owns 40 acres of land; was born in Ireland in 1830; came from there to N.Y. in '52; lived in that state two years; thence to this Co. in 1854; married Bridget Donald, in South Salem, N. Y.; she was born in Ireland.

SHEFFIELD D. A., M. D., Apple River; was born in New London Co., Conn., Aug. 29, 1836; when he was nine years of age his parents moved to Otsego Co., N. Y.; he remained there until 1856, when he came to Dixon, Ill., and commenced studying medicine in the office of N.W. Abbot, M. D.; at the breaking out of the late rebellion, he entered 96th Regt., I. V. I., as Assistant Surgeon; he served in that capacity until the Spring of 1863, when he resigned on account of ill health, and returned home; at this time his health was such that it unfitted him for the duties of his profession, in consequence of which he placed himself under medical treatment in Chicago, Ill., at the same time attending the Chicago Medical College, from which he graduated in 1867; his health now being restored, he came to Apple River, and has since practiced medicine here successfully; in Aug., 1869, he became editor of the Apple River *Index*; this paper was published by H. C. Gunn, and was republican in politics; in 1870 Dr. Sheffield's professional duties were such that he could no longer attend to its publication, and so resigned; he was married to Miss Mary N. Brookner, Dec. 1, 1859; she was born in Dixon, Aug. 3, 1839; have had nine children, three of whom are living: Mary Muriel, born Dec. 10, 1869, Catharine Elizabeth, Nov. 14, 1872, Helen Myran, July 25, 1877.

Sherridan William; P. O. Apple River.

Simmons Samuel, laborer; Apple River.

Sigafus Christopher, miner; Apple River.

Simmons G. P. confectionery; Apple River.

Simmons W. H. laborer; Apple River.

SMITH HENRY, Manufacturer and Dealer in Boots and Shoes; Apple River;

born in Derbyshire, England, May 15, 1832; came to this country in 1832; settled in Georgetown, Pa.; lived there five years; he then returned to England, remained there until 1852, when he came to Rochester, N. Y.; lived there until 1855, when he came to this place, which has since been his home, excepting in '60 and '61, when he was in Col.; commenced business here in 1863, and has been successfully engaged therein ever since; is at present one of the Board of Trustees; has been Town Collector three years, School Director six years; is a member of the M. E. Church, of which he is Steward and Trustee at present; married Miss Eliza Jane Heath in East Brighton, Monroe Co., N. Y., Nov. 19, 1854; she was born in Co. Sligo, Ireland, in 1823; have one child, William Henry, born in 1860; had one brother, John, in the army; he enlisted in 3d Mo. in the Fall of 1861; served until the close of the war, and was honorably discharged.

South Isaac, laborer; Apple River.

STAHL JOHN, Of the firm of Stahl Bros.; Proprietors of Meat Market, also Dealers in Choice Liquors, Wines and Brandies; Apple River; born in Germany in 1840; came to this Co. in 1854; July 27, 1862, he enlisted in the 96th I. V. I.; was in many severe battles: among them were Chicamauga, Nashville, Kenesaw Mountain and Atlanta; was wounded at Kenesaw, and was honorably discharged July 2, 1865; married Lena Rothmaer in Galena, this Co., in 1867; she was born in Germany in 1844.

Stahl Nicholas, butcher; Apple River.

Stinule Aug. saloon; Apple River.

Sullivan Jas. laborer; Apple River.

Sullivan Tim. section boss I. C. R. R.; Apple River.

Suggett Robt. G. laborer; Apple River.

Sutton Gaines, painter; Apple River.

Sutton M. B. wagon maker; Apple River.

Sutton Sylvester, carpenter; Apple River.

TIPPERT CHAS. shoemaker; Apple River.

Trevethan Benj. laborer; Apple River.

UNDERWOOD LLOYD, laborer; Apple River.

VARTY JOSEPH, Farmer and Stock Raiser; Sec. 22; P. O. Apple River; owns 288 acres land; born in Cumberland Co., England, Dec. 15, 1837; came to Lafayette Co., Wis., in 1857; remained there until the Fall of 1868; then came to this Co. and has remained in it since; has held office of School Director a number of years; married Marietta Adams in Lafayette Co., Wis., Oct. 1, 1867; she was born in Wood Co., Ohio, March 17, 1842; have had four children: John Lester, born July 19, 1868, died July 21, 1870; Joseph Allen, March 21, 1871; Lester Adams, Dec. 30, 1872; Mary Hannah, Nov. 14, 1874.

WATSON MARVIN, farmer; Sec. 20; P. O. Apple River.

WARNER SAMUEL, Farmer; Sec. 27; P. O. Apple River; was born in Mass. in 1810; he came to this Co. in 1829; there were only a few families in this Co. at that time; he entered the Black Hawk War at its commencement; he served in Gen. Dodge's command, in Capt. Clarke's Co., and was engaged in many sharp contests with the Indians; of the men now living in this Co. who served in Clarke's Co. and took an active part in Indian fighting, he and Wm. Colvin (whose biography we give in another place) are the only survivors; they served in the same Co., and fought in the same battles, and both are hale and hearty men at the present writing; Mr. Warner owns 180 acres land; he married Mary Ann, daughter of Jacob and Bethina Wood, who came to this Co. in 1829, in this town, July 3, 1834; she was born in Virginia, July 29, 1819; Mr. Warner had two sons in the army, Edgar and George P.; Edgar enlisted in Co. E, 96th Regt., I. V. I., as Color Bearer; in Aug., 1862, he was killed while his regiment were making a charge on the enemy at the battle of Chicamauga; George P. enlisted in 45th Regt., I. V. I.; he was killed at the battle of Shiloh.

White J. C. farm; Sec. 35; P.O. Apple River.

White W. L. farm; S. 35; P.O. Apple River.

White W., Sr., farm; S.34; P.O. Apple River.

White W., Jr., farm; S.34; P.O. Apple River.

WILLEY EDWARD D. Farmer; Sec. 23; P. O. Apple River; was born in Cornwall, Eng., Sept. 18, 1818; came from there to this Co. in 1842; owns 225 acres of land; married Mary Edwards, in Galena, Nov. 20, 1844; she was born in Cornwall, Eng., Nov. 5, 1822; have had nine children, viz.: Edward John, born Nov. 25, 1845, Margaret Jane (now Mrs. J. Rowe), Nov. 7, 1847, Mary Frances (now Mrs. C. S. Adams), Aug. 29, 1849, Hender Wesley, March 10, 1851, William Edward, Nov. 16, 1855, died Oct. 24, 1856, William E., Jan. 1, 1857, Edith A., July 16, 1859, Ada Luella, July 30, 1861, Clara Lincoln, Aug. 16, 1863.

Willey Hender W. Apple River.

Williams G. W. teamster; Apple River.

Williams Hugh, blacksmith; Apple River.

Williams J. farm; S. 34; P. O. Apple River.

WILLIAMS THOMAS, Farmer; Sec. 34; P. O. Apple River; was born in this Co. July 28, 1848; married Elizabeth Benson, in Franklin Co., Iowa, July 3, 1869; she was born in N. Y. in 1846; have four children living, viz.: Mary, born in

Iowa in 1870, Elmer, in 1872, Albert, in 1875, Edgar, in 1877; his father (Solomon Williams) was one of the early settlers of this Co., the county being comparatively a wilderness when he came here.

Winans S. Sec. 14; P. O. Apple River.

Wollam S. retired farmer; Apple River.

Woodward Geo. peddler; Apple River.

Woodward J. M. laborer; Apple River.

YUNGBLUTH ADAM, laborer; Apple River.

ZUCK EUGENE, blacksmith; Apple River.

SCALES MOUND TOWNSHIP.

ADAMS JAMES ADDISON, Contractor and Builder; Scales Mound; born in Wood Co., Ohio, April 11, 1845; came to this Co. in 1861; enlisted in Co. B, 45th Regt., I. V. I., in Aug., same year; participated in all their scouts and marches, and all the battles in which the Regt. was engaged, including Fort Donelson, Shiloh, Corinth, Jackson, Champion Hill and Vicksburg; was mustered out at Atlanta, Ga., Oct. 26, 1864; was married April 14, 1873, to Diana Allen; she was born in Canada in 1844; they had one child, Mary Augusta, born Feb. 22, 1874, died May 27, 1875; Mrs. A. died June 12, 1875; Mr. A. has followed the same business here for 12 years; attends the M. E. Church; Republican.

ALLAN JAMES, Sr., Scales Mound; born in Caithness, Scotland, in 1802; his father, John Allen, and mother (maiden name Janet Sanderson) were both natives of the same Co., also their forefathers; he superintended a large farm while renting one of his own; married Diana Williamson in 1825 — a noble woman; came to Canada in 1842; moved into the woods of Melbourne without a dollar; the children were then John, Euphemia, George, James, Janet, and Mary, aged, respectively, 16, 14, 11, 9, 7, and 5; their first child, William, born in 1827, died at the age of 5 years; another son, William, died on the Gulf of St. Lawrence, buried in Quebec; age, 18 months; Diana, Margaret and William were born in Canada in 1843, 1845 and 1847; he followed his sons here in 1868; Euphemia and Janet are married and living in Canada; Mary and Margaret died there in 1864; George, a business man of this place, was buried here in 1863; Diana, wife of J. A. Adams, of this place, died in 1875; hale, honest and contented, give this memorandum to their children; no enemies to punish, no debts to pay, only gratitude to God.

ALLAN JAMES, Merchant; Scales Mound; born in Caithness, Scotland, May 23, 1831; came with his father's family to Melbourne, Canada, in 1842; came here in 1855, poor, honest but healthy, qualities inherited from his parents, now living here, near 75 years old; married Elizabeth C. Phillips, April, 1871, who died in Feb., 1872, leaving a little girl named after her mother, Elizabeth Caroline; in Nov., 1874, married Isabella Phillips, who has a son William, the perfection of health and comeliness; in connection with his store, Mr. A. runs a grain house and farm; is Agent for the Express Co.; has worked at any thing honorable that presented itself; hopes if he dies poor, to die honorable.

Allan J. clerk and salesman; Scales Mound.

Allan Wm. works in brother's store; Scales Mound.

Allen Joseph, laborer; Sec. 15; P. O. White Oak Springs, Wis.

Allinson James, farmer; Sec. 19; P.O. Scales Mound.

ALLINSON JOSEPH, Farmer; Sec. 19; P. O. Scales Mound; born on this farm July 10, 1850; owns about 40 acres of land; married Isabel Brown Jan. 5, 1875; she was born at New Diggings, Wis., Aug. 27, 1852; they have one child, Martha E., born March 16, 1876; Mr. Allinson's father, Robert, came to this farm in 1849, where he remained until the time of his death, July 23, 1877, aged 73; left 196 acres of land; his widow is 67 years of age and resides on the home farm with Joseph, as also do her son and daughter, James and Hannah; Republican.

ALLINSON THOMAS R. Farmer; Sec. 20; P. O. Scales Mound; born in Shullsburg, Wis., Feb. 20, 1843; came to this Co. in 1849; owns 50 acres of land; married Ruth G. Robinson Aug. 21, 1869; she was born in Galena, March 11, 1844; they have four children living: Estella E., born April 7, 1870; Ezra C., Aug. 20, 1871, Florence A., Oct. 30, 1872, and Evaline, Feb. 11, 1877; lost one infant; Mr. A. is serving his second term as Collector; he met with a terrible accident in 1859; was on the horse power driving for a threshing machine, when his foot slipped, and, falling, his leg was caught in the wheel and cut entirely off between the ankle and knee; was entirely disabled for quite a while; is now able to get around pretty well with the aid of an artificial limb; they are members of the M. E. Church; Republican.

Annis John F. mail carrier from Scales Mound to Shullsburg, Wis.

Anschuetz Geo. E. farm; P. O. Scales Mound.

Arbour L. D. laborer; Scales Mound.

Atkinson Wm. renter; Sec. 28; P.O. Scales Mound.

BASTIAN GEORGE, Wagon maker; Sec. 35; P. O. Scales Mound; born in Galena, May 27, 1853; when 14 years of age he went to work in the Galena Woolen Mills; worked one year; afterward worked on one of the weekly papers of that place; learned wagon making with C. Bench, Galena; married Kate Webber, Feb. 1, 1877; she was born in Galena June 22, 1855; has been in business for himself since July, 1876; they are members of the German Catholic Church.

Belden Oregon, laborer; Scales Mound.

Bell J. farmer; Sec. 22; P.O. Scales Mound.

Bell J. with father; S. 22; P.O.Scales Mound.

BERRYMAN CHARLES, Farmer; Sec. 33; P. O. Scales Mound; born in Cornwall, Eng., in 1816; married Mary Roberts May 31, 1841; she was born in same Co. in 1822; they came to U. S. in 1842; settled near Hazel Green, Wis.; lived there until 1850, when they came to this farm; owns 330 acres land; have twelve children: William H., Mary G., Charles W., Caroline R., Elizabeth J., James, John, Stephen R., Sarah E., Martha J., Hester A. and Julia F.; attend the M. E. Church; Mr. B. has been class leader for 25 years; Republican.

BERRYMAN JAMES, Farmer; Sec. 34; P. O. Scales Mound; born in this town Oct. 17, 1850; lived here all his life except two winters spent in school at Galena; was married Nov. 25, 1873, to Maggie J. Annette; she was born in East Galena, March 5, 1853; was for three years previous to marriage engaged in teaching in East Galena; they have two children, Wilbur F. and Annie; owns 181 acres land; are members of the M. E. Church; Republican.

Berryman John, Sec. 32; P.O. Scales Mound.

Berryman S. R. Sec. 32; P.O. Scales Mound.

Bower John, laborer; Scales Mound.

Bowden Wm. farm; S. —; P.O.Scales Mound.

BOYLE PATRICK, Section Boss I. C. R. R; Scales Mound; born in County Tyrone, Ireland, in 1830; came to U. S. in 1846; lived in N. Y. till 1851, then came to Jo Daviess Co., Ill., where he has ever since been employed by the I. C. R. R., the last 18 years as section boss; owns 40 acres land; was married in 1852 to Alice Boyle; she was born in Co. Louth, Ireland, in 1837; they have nine children living: Lizzie, Ona, Con, May, Isabella, Alice, Patrick, Daly and John; lost one, Charles, died in Dec., 1876; are members of the Catholic Church.

Bray Jas. laborer; Sec. 20; P.O.Scales Mound.

Breed N. G. lab; Sec. 28; P.O.Scales Mound.

Briten John, laborer; Scales Mound.

Brown C. laborer; Sec.22; P.O.Scales Mound.

BURNS JAMES S. Agent for Magoon Estate; Sec. 22; P. O. Scales Mound; born in Ohio March 15, 1815; came to this Co. in 1849; owns 40 acres land in East Galena; married Rebecca Wright in 1852; she died April 5, 1860; they had two children: William M., born Jan. 11, 1854, and Zilpha M., April 5, 1859; Mr. B. was Assessor one year; they attend the M. E. Church; Democrat.

BUSHBY MOSES, Telegraph Operator, I. C. R. R.; Scales Mound; born in New Diggings, Wis., Dec. 27, 1845; lived on farm in Wis. till 1871, when he took charge of this office, where he has been ever since; married Mary E. Jackson Oct. 25, 1873; she was born in Hazel Green, Wis., Jan. 28, 1854; they have one child living, Floyd M., born Nov. 6, 1875; lost one, Mabel E., born July 19, 1874, died Jan. 4, 1875; attend the M. E. Church; Republican.

CANE JOHN, renter; Sec. 24; P.O. Scales Mound.

Canse Geo. farm; Sec. 34; P.O.Scales Mound.

Carey James, section boss, I. C. R. R.; Scales Mound.

CARR JAMES, Farmer; Sec. 31; P. O. Scales Mound; born in Ireland Oct. 26, 1846; came to this country in 1848; settled in N. Y. City; moved from there to New Diggings, Wis.; came to this Co. in 1859, and to this farm in 1867; owns 280 acres land; married Matilda Mullen April 23, 1867; she was born in New Diggings, Wis., Nov. 15, 1849; they have six children: Matilda A., born March 22, 1868; James R., July 29, 1869; Henry J., March 19, 1871; Harvey, Jan. 26, 1873; Wilbur, Dec. 13, 1874, and infant son, April 22, 1877; Mr. C. is Road Commissioner, also School Director; Democrat; they attend the M. E. Church.

CHAMBERS LEWIS K. Farmer; Sec. 30; P. O. Scales Mound; born in Richland Co., O., March 1, 1821; emigrated to Mo. in 1838; lived there four years, then came to this Co.; followed mining until 1847, then bought this farm, and has lived here ever since except two years (1850–51 was in California); crossed the plains in 63 days, which is said to be the quickest trip ever made with team; owns 240 acres land; married Mary Dickerson Oct. 2, 1851; she was born in Springfield, Ill., March 28, 1834; they have twelve children living: Mary F., John M., Susan A., Lewis E., Margaret E., James P., Nancy, Charles Wm., Aaron D., Jessie C., Robert S. and Milton O.; lost two, Sarah L. and Myron A., twin brother to Milton; Mr. C. is School Director, and has been for 15 years; was Road Master from the time the Tp. was organized until about six years ago; was intimately acquainted with both Grant and Washburne before they entered upon public life; the family attend the Methodist Church; Democrat.

CHAMBERS WM. H. Farmer; Sec. 30; P. O. Scales Mound; born in Allegheny Co., Pa., March 11, 1814; moved to Richland Co., Ohio, in 1816; from there to Missouri, in 1838; came to this Co. in 1841; only two brick houses in Galena; came to this farm in 1855; owns 368 acres land; married Mary Chambers in 1846; she was born in the same Co. in Pa.; have three children living: Martha A., Wm. H. and Jas. D.; lost one son, born March 4, 1847, died March 29, 1873; was Justice of the Peace eight years, and School Trustee and Chairman of the Board twelve years; Mrs. C. died Jan. 20, 1875, aged 65 years; Mr. C. has led the life of a pioneer in Ohio, Mo. and this Co.; the daughter is a member of the M. E. Church; the family attend same; Democrat.

Chambers Wm. H., Jr., Sec. 30; P. O. Scales Mound.

Chambers Wm. L. farmer; Sec. 30; P. O. Scales Mound.

Collins Ed. S. farmer; Sec. 20; P. O. Scales Mound.

COLLINS GEO. O. Farmer and Stock Raiser; P. O. Scales Mound; born in Lynn, Mass., May 8, 1812; married Miss Margaret M. Newhall, Nov. 21, 1839; she was born in Salem, Mass., April 22, 1815; came to Galena in 1843; remained there until 1867, when he moved on the farm where he now resides; owns 300 acres land; have three children living: Edward I., S. Theodate and Horatio N.; lost one daughter, Penelope, died Aug. 28, 1847; Edward I. was married Jan. 25, 1877, to Elizabeth Gratiot, of Gratiot, Wis.

Corrigan Chas. shoemaker; Scales Mound.

Coulson John, farmer; Sec. 19; P. O. Scales Mound.

COUCH CHAS. Proprietor Union Hotel; Scales Mound; born in Cornwall, England, Feb. 26, 1834; married Susan Kneebone May 20, 1854; she was born in same Co. in 1834; they came to this Co. in 1866; had six children; four living: Emma, Bessie, Ellen and John; buried two in England, Richard and Elizabeth; their mother died in Scales Mound Dec. 28, 1869; married again in 1871 to Mary Ann Sullivan; she was born in Va., Dec. 25, 1852; have four children: Mary Jane, Lillie, Frank and Annie M.; for ten years previous to leaving England, Mr. C. was driving omnibus from Truro to Plymouth; on arriving here, he first engaged in farming; followed it for three years; since 1869, has been in hotel business in this place; the family attend the M. E. Church; Bessie remained in England with friends until Aug., 1877, joining the family here after an absence of 11 years.

COUSIN JOHN, Farmer; Sec. 22; P. O. Scales Mound; born on this farm Oct. 8, 1850; owns 80 acres land; married Eliza H. Turner Jan. 31, 1871; she was born in N. J. April 29, 1853; have two children living: Mary J., born Feb. 21, 1873; and Wm. J., May 15, 1876; lost one, died in infancy; Mr. C. is serving his first term as School Director; his father came to this farm 30 years ago; died Jan. 28, 1868; mother makes her home here; she is 67 years of age; George Turner, Mrs. C.'s father also resides with them; her mother died May 11, 1875; Republican.

COX JOHN B. Proprietor Temperance Hotel, and Dealer in Chromos and Brackets; Scales Mound; born in Lincolnshire, England, Aug. 10, 1826; married Annie Greenfield April 27, 1850; she was born in Yorkshire, England, Feb. 29, 1831; they came to this Co. in 1853; owns property valued at $1,000; have ten children living: Walter W., Emma E., Annie M., Lizzie M., Jennie G., Minnie W., Eddie M. P., Charlie W., Bertie and Harvey; lost two, Willie and Clarence; Mr. C. was School Director six years; is now Street Commissioner; the family attend the M. E. Church; Republican.

Cox Walter, teacher; P. O. Scales Mound.

DRINK HENRY, laborer; Sec. 22; P.O. Scales Mound.

DE GRAFF JOHN N. Farmer; Sec. 25; P. O. Scales Mound; born in Montgomery Co., N. Y., in Dec., 1812; came to this Co. in 1836; built a cabin on this farm; afterwards built a house, and has lived here 41 years; owns 110 acres land; married Clarissa M. Phelps Oct. 3, 1839; she was born in Tolland Co., Conn., Dec. 2, 1815; have two children living: John H., now in Cal.; and Lizzie M., living in Scales Mound; lost five: William, Theodore, Charles, Natalia and Joel; Mr. De Graff has been Road and School Commissioner, Constable and Road Master for a number of years; when he came West, he crossed Lake Erie, by steamer, to Detroit; there they hired a wagon to haul their baggage; they came on foot from there to Chicago; there was not a house in Scales Mound when he came here; an old fort stood on Charles Mound; he crossed the plains in 1850 to Cal.; was there one year; returned by way of the Isthmus; is the oldest male settler in Scales Mound (living); has taken the Galena *Gazette* regularly since 1838.

Dunston Jno. retired miner; Scales Mound.

ENGLER HENRY, laborer; Scales Mound.

FARMILOE F. F. pastor M. E. Church; Scales Mound.

Ferguson Reuben, miner; Sec. 22; P.O.Scales Mound.

FOWLER H. M. Physician and Surgeon; born in Steuben Co., N. Y., Nov. 1, 1833; moved to Cass Co., Mich., in 1845; was among the first settlers in that Co.; lived on the banks of the Sister Lakes for 23 years; the Pottawattomie Indian boys were the only playmates he knew for many years; the nearest white neighbor was three miles off; worked in the harvest field for 37½ cts. per day; married Charity Arbour, of Livingston Co., N. Y., in 1856; moved to Galena, Ill., in 1863; studied medicine at Ann Arbor Medical College in 1864 and '65; then moved to Scales Mound, where he has been practicing medicine and surgery ever since; has buried three children; has two daughters living, Annie and Julia; is worth $3,300; is a member of the Methodist Church; Republican; is Postmaster here, a position he has held for nine years.

GARD JAMES, miner; Sec. 22; P. O. Scales Mound.

Glanvill John, P. O. Scales Mound.

GLANVILL SETH, Farmer; Sec. 24; P. O. Scales Mound; born in Cornwall, Eng., in 1814; married Elizabeth Vincent in 1839; she was born in same town in 1813; came to this Co. in 1846; lived here since except eight years he spent in California, the family remaining here; they have five children living: Elizabeth (born in Eng.), Jonathan, Thomas, Seth and John, born in Vedi Grand; also granddaughter, Henrietta, born same place; lost two, Elizabeth and Jonathan, buried in England; owns 248 acres land, this includes Charles' Mound, the highest point of land in the state; keeps on hand an average of 40 head of cattle, 20 of sheep, and 50 of hogs; attends the Methodist Church; Republican.

Glanville T. renter; S. 13; P.O.Scales Mound.

GRINDEY MARK J. Farmer; Sec. 36; P. O. Scales Mound; born in England Dec. 26, 1839; came to this Co. with his father, who, in 1840, settled on the farm they now live on; owns 310 acres land; married Margaret J. Phillips June 18, 1873; she was born in this Tp. June 16, 1851; they have two children: James F., born March 30, 1874, and John W., Aug. 27, 1877; James Grindey, father of Mark, was an early settler; lived on this farm over 30 years; now resides in Thompson Tp.; is 72 years old; Mr. Mark G. was Road Master one year; they attend the M. E Church.

Gundry Wm. renter; Sec. —; P. O. Scales Mound.

GUMMOW WM. Farmer; Sec. 24; P. O. Scales Mound; born in Cornwall, Eng., April 11, 1825; came to this Co. in 1855; owns 150 acres land; married Eliza Treseden in 1857; she was born in Cornwall, Eng., in 1829; they have no children; he was Assessor one year, Collector two years; was elected Commissioner of Highways last Spring; are members of the M. E. Church; Republican.

HANCOCK EDWARD, farmer; Sec. 23; P. O. Scales Mound.

Hancock Jos. laborer; Sec. 27; P. O. Scales Mound.

Hancock Wm. Sec. 15; P. O. White Oak Springs, Wis.

Hawkin A. G. station agent I. C. R. R.; Scales Mound.

Hedberg Benne, laborer; Sec. 16; P.O.White Oak Springs, Wis.

Helmsud Ernest, laborer; Scales Mound.

Herrington J. laborer; Scales Mound.

HICKS THOMAS, Farmer; Sec. 26; P. O. Scales Mound; born in Cornwall, Eng., July 15, 1818; came to this Co. in 1846; went same year to Lake Superior; worked in copper mines three years; in 1849 went to California *via* Cape Horn; stayed two years, then returned; stayed here two years; went to Australia; returned to this Co. in 1855; owns 160 acres land; married Phillipe White July 16, 1856; she was born in Cornwall, Eng., Aug. 29, 1835; they have five children living: Thomas H., Hester A., Phillipe J., Elizabeth A. and William W.; lost two: Martha L., died March 9, 1872, and Ida May, Oct. 6, 1874; family all members of the M. E. Church; Republican.

HOCH GEORGE, Grain and Lumber Dealer; Scales Mound; born in Baden, Germany, in 1833; came to this Co. in 1854; married Mary A. Hevberger in 1866; she was born in Sweden in 1840; have four children living: John, Georgie, Laura and Annie; lost one, Elizabeth, in 1873; Mr. H. is serving the fourth year as Town Clerk, third as School Director; is also President of Village Board of Trustees; handles annually about $5,000 grain, etc., and $4,000 lumber; enlisted in 3d Wis. V. I., first call, 1861; was in 17 battles; mustered out at Marietta, Ga., Aug., 1864.

Hocking John H. plasterer; Sec. 33; P. O. Scales Mound.

Hockin John, Scales Mound.

HOWE JOHN, Farmer; Sec. 23; P.O. Scales Mound; born in Cumberland Co., Eng., Sept. 5, 1818; married Alice Eadington in 1849; she was born in Northum-

John Moore

SCALES MOUND

Arneson Family Tree
Pics of Eliz Jane Jewell
& Wm Toy
M. Wendron
Nov 15 1835
Current tree
Lightcap-Davis
Priscilla Elizabeth Jewell

berland Co., Eng., April 28, 1820; came to U. S. in 1851, and to this farm same year; owns 111 acres of land here and 160 in Kansas; Mr. H. went to California in 1853; returned in 1855; in 1860 went to Pike's Peak; returned same year; was Collector four years, Assessor same, and School Trustee six years; they went to England in 1867 on a visit, remaining there one year; came back, went to their farm in Kansas; stayed one year and came back to the old farm, where they have been ever since; Republican.

INGRAM WM. miner; Vedi Grand; P. O. White Oak Springs, Wis.

JENSON IVER, laborer; Sec. 27; P. O. Scales Mound.

JEWELL ALFRED, Sr., Farmer; Sec. 34; P. O. Scales Mound; born in Cornwall, Eng., in 1833; came to this Co. in 1847; owns 145 acres of land; married Catherine Roberts in 1852; she was born in Eng. in 1837; have nine children living: Alfred, Katie, Lillie M., Frank, Eliza E., Parmelia, Henrietta, William and Arthur H.; three died in infancy; in 1850 Mr. J. went to California; stayed two years, came home, remained short time, then went to Australia; spent two years there; returned *via* Eng.; went to British Columbia in 1862; returned same year; has since resided here; family attend the M. E. Church; Republican.

Jewell A., Jr., Sec. 34; P. O. Scales Mound.

JEWELL EDWIN, Farmer; Sec. 29; P. O. Scales Mound; born in Cornwall, Eng., Jan. 25, 1830; came to this Co. in 1847; owns 370 acres of land; married Ann Reed in 1852; she was born in Devonshire, Eng., Aug. 9, 1834; they have nine children living: Frances, Edwin, William Alfred, Eliza E., Arthur, James H., Sarah J., John Franklin, and Alfred; lost two: Edwina and Albert; Mr. J. was Supervisor three years, Road Commissioner same, and School Director for fifteen years; he followed mining for two years after coming to this Co.; worked three years in the mines of California, and spent two years dealing in cattle in Australia; owns a mining interest in Cornwall, Eng.; attends the M. E. Church.

Jewell J. farmer; S. 22; P.O. Scales Mound.

JEWELL THOMAS, Farmer; Sec. 22; P. O. Scales Mound; born in Cornwall, Eng., April 14, 1815; married Elizabeth Rogers in 1835; she was born in Cornwall in 1810; came to this Co. in 1846; have seven children living: Thos. R., Elizabeth J., Mary, John, Grace, Priscilla and William; lost one son, died at sea, in 1846, and another in 1847; Mr. J. was Commissioner of Highways three years, Overseer, ten years, School Treasurer three years; is School Director now, a position he has held for twenty-four years; Mrs. J. died Oct. 22, 1853; afterward married Grace Jenkins in Aug., 1854; she was born in Cornwall, Eng., Aug. 23, 1813; owns 120 acres of land; belong to the M. E. Church; Republican.

KEMP JOHN, renter; Sec. 35; P. O. Scales Mound.

KISTLE JOSIAH, Farmer; P. O. Scales Mound; born in Cornwall, Eng., Jan. 1, 1817; came to this Co. in 1840; engaged in mining at Galena; stayed there ten years; came to this town in 1850, where he has resided ever since; owns 403 acres of land; married Phillipe E. Ford April 18, 1855; she was born in Eng., Nov. 19, 1833; have five children: Josiah C., born Feb. 15, 1856, John H., Dec. 18, 1857, Wm. T., Dec. 22, 1859, Estella S., Feb. 12, 1863, and Adella E., Oct. 20, 1871; Mr. K. has been Road Commissioner nine years, School Director thirteen years; followed mining ten years in Eng., often working 1800 feet under ground; worked four years in gold mines of California and six years in lead mines of Galena, where he once fell a distance of 85 feet and was crippled for life; attend the Methodist Church; Mrs. K. is a member of same.

Klenke Henry, shoemaker; Scales Mound.

KNEEBONE JOSIAH, Farmer; Sec. 25; P. O. Scales Mound; born in Cornwall, England, in 1834; came to this Co. in 1854; owns 207 acres of land; married Nannie B. Rowe April 16, 1861; she was born in England Jan. 26, 1840; they have five children living: Joseph T., born July 22, 1862; Phillippe J., Jan. 14, 1864; William H., June 16, 1869; John F., Jan. 7, 1872; and Elsie A., June 14, 1876; lost one: Amelia, died March 11, 1867; Mr. Kneebone was School Director eight years and Road Master one; they are members of the M. E. Church.

Knuckey Jas. T. druggist; Scales Mound.

KNUCKEY WM. Farmer; Sec. 34; P. O. Scales Mound; born in Cornwall, Eng., in 1826; came to this Co. in 1847; owns 250 acres of land; married Ellen Jewell in 1851; she was born in Cornwall; have eight children living: Sarah E., James, Francis, Mary, William, Alfred J., Eliza and Flora; lost two: William and Annie; family attend M. E. Church; Mr. and Mrs. K. are members.

Kreamer M. miner; S.22; P.O. Scales Mound.

Kyley Thos. laborer; Scales Mound.

LICHTENBURGER JAMES, carpenter; Scales Mound.

LYNE BENJAMIN, Farmer; Sec. 16; P.O. White Oak Springs, Wis.; born in Rutland, England, March 22, 1838; came to this Co. in 1844; owns 250 acres of land; married Eliza Rick in 1856; she was born in Leicester-

Buried in 1903 (Dec 7) Scales Mound (citizens) Cemetery
Eliz 1853 Oct 22 Grace Jewell 1904

shire, England, May 24, 1841; they have seven children living, Josie, Katie, John E., Benj. W., Martha F., Ella E., and Harry; lost two, Thomas W., died Feb. 24, 1876; and Louisa Florence, Aug. 29, 1876; Mr. L. was Commissioner of Highways for 3 years. Edward Lyne, his father, lives with him; is the oldest person in this Co. —93 years of age; came to this farm 33 years ago. In connection with farming, Mr. L. has been, for the last eight years, engaged in selling Agricultural Implements, making a specialty of the Marsh Harvester; sold more of them in this section than any other agent here; brought the first one here that was ever used in this vicinity; family attend the M. E. Church; Republican.

McDONALD JNO. L. carpenter; Scales Mound.

McBRIDE JAMES S. Proprietor of the Scales Mound Hotel; born in Oneida Co., N. Y., Jan. 19, 1812; was Railroad Contractor in that state for 24 years; from 1859 until breaking out of war, was building in Texas; came to this Co. in 1864; was married in 1835 to Helen Sloan; she died in 1849; afterward married Delia Cole; she died in 1858; third wife, Dorothy Moore, daughter of John Moore of this place; have six children living: James S., Minnie, Luella, John M., George and Richard; lost one son, Robert B., died Feb. 11, 1877; Mr. McB. was Assistant Superintendent of Rome and Watertown R. R. for six years; favorably known in railroad circles; kept this hotel for the last five years.

McKinnon Neil, farmer; Sec. 26; P. O. Scales Mound.

Martin H. farm; S. 26; P.O. Scales Mound.

Matson James, salesman farming implements; Scales Mound.

MATSON JAMES C. Teacher; Scales Mound; born in Thompson Tp., Jan. 28, 1849; married Lizzie M. DeGraff, Sept. 27, 1874; she was born in this Tp., Jan. 2, 1852; they have one son, John Franklin, born Nov. 4, 1875. Mr. Matson's father was a resident of Thompson from 1847 till April 8, 1875, when he died there; Mr. M. is dealing in agricultural implements during the Summer; also deals occasionally in blooded stock; the family attend the M. E. Church, of which Mrs. M. is a member.

Martin Joseph, retired farmer; Sec. 23; P. O. Scales Mound.

Martin Wm. H. with father; Sec. 26; P. O. Scales Mound.

Meeter John, blacksmith; Scales Mound.

MOORE JOHN, Retired Farmer; P. O. Scales Mound; born in Durham Co., England, May 29, 1809; came to this country in 1830; followed mining for eight years, two in Pottsville Pa., and six in Wheeling, Va.; married Mary, daughter of Samuel Bowman, an old Revolutionary soldier, in 1835; born in Pa., in 1806; they emigrated to Galena in 1838; was mining for 12 years; generally as Superintendent, his large experience being of great value; his services were sought by all the prominent companies at Galena, Dubuque, and throughout the entire mining district; he entered the mines in 1816, at the age of 7 years; quit the life in 1850; they have six children living; his wife died at this place April 13, 1863; married to Polly Harper, Nov. 8, 1863; she was born in Indiana, Nov. 14, 1816; came here in 1833; is the oldest settler in this town; Mr. Moore was Supervisor five times; Assessor and Collector two terms each; Justice of the Peace six times, holds the position now, also Notary Public which he has held two terms; Primitive Methodist; Democrat.

Moore Thomas, laborer; Scales Mound.

Moss T. miner; Sec. 22; P. O. Scales Mound.

MURLEY THOMAS, Tinsmith; Scales Mound; born in Penzance, Eng., Feb. 20, 1849; came to the United States in 1850; settled in Hazel Green, Wis.; lived there till 1872, since which time has been engaged in business here; married Annie M. Cox in 1873; she was born near Galena in 1855; have three children, Mattie, Mamie and infant; are members of the M. E. Church; Republican.

Murphy John, laborer; Scales Mound.

Murphy Patrick, laborer; Scales Mound.

Murphy Patrick, laborer; I. C. R. R.; Scales Mound

Murphy Wm. laborer; Scales Mound.

Musselman Henry, farmer; Sec. 34; P. O. Scales Mound.

NAPPER WM. Sec. 36; P. O. Scales Mound.

NAPPER STEPHENSON T. Farmer; P. O. Scales Mound; born in Yorkshire, Eng., March 13, 1815; came with his parents, two sisters and a brother to Knox Co., Ohio, in 1828; left there and came to Chicago in 1836; was there until 1838, when he came to this Co.; owns 720 acres of land in this Co. and 80 in Wis.; married Elfrida E. Toby; she was born in Fairfield, Me.; they have one child living, Stephenson T., born Aug. 13, 1869; lost one in infancy; in Ohio, was in the employ of Kenyon College from the age of 13 until 20; he was engaged in butchering in Galena, for 19 years, except two years spent in Cal.; he was Captain of men with 16 wagons from Galena, who crossed the plains in 1849; remained there two years; since 1857 he has been extensively engaged in farming and stock raising; has 25 horses, 200 head of cattle, 90 hogs, and 60 sheep, a fair average of the number he annually feeds; in coming West in 1836, he crossed the famous Black Swamps, the dread of all emigrants of that day, but having an excellent team he came through comparatively easy; has been Supervisor four terms; was one of the committee who, at Nashville, Tenn., in 1864, presented Gen. Grant with one of the finest swords he ever received; Mr. and Mrs. N. are members of the M. E. Church.

Neuschwanger C. farmer; Sec. 35; P. O. Scales Mound.

Neuschwanger Henry, with father; Sec. 35; P. O. Scales Mound.

Neuschwanger Henry, farmer; Sec. 35; P. O. Scales Mound.

Nichols J. laborer; Sec. 35; P.O. White Oak Springs, Wis.

O'NEIL JOHN, laborer; Sec. 29; P. O. Scales Mound.

PASCOE THOS. farmer; Sec. 21; P. O. Scales Mound.

Pascoe Thos. H. farmer; Sec. 21; P.O. White Oak Springs, Wis.

Perry John W. lives with father; Sec. 28; P. O. Scales Mound.

Perry Wm. farmer; Sec. 28; P. O. Scales Mound.

Perry William, farmer; Sec. 19; P. O. Scales Mound.

PHELPS WM. F. Farmer and Stock Raiser; Sec. 30; P. O. Scales Mound; born in Ohio, March 16, 1822; came to this state in 1837, and to this Co. in 1838; settled on this farm, where he has ever since resided; owns 192 acres of land; married Laurilla McDonald, Dec. 25, 1851; she was born in Mo. Oct. 26, 1834; they have seven children living: Lydia, born Nov. 27, 1854; Russell J., Nov. 7, 1860; Wm. Elmer, June 11, 1863; Arthur F., Aug. 25, 1866; M. Estella, April 14, 1869; A. Adelle, Aug. 17, 1875; and Eugene M., Oct. 10, 1877; Mr. P. was Commissioner of Highways for two years and School Director 15 years; settled on this farm six years before the land came in market; not a house between here and Wadhams Grove, except Chapman's Tavern; could stand in the doorway and shoot game or wolves almost any time; Warren, Apple River, and other towns of the present day were unknown; they are members of the M. E. Church; Republican.

PHILLIPS FRANCIS, Farmer; Sec. 27; P. O. Scales Mound; born in Cornwall, Eng., Jan. 9, 1805; came to America in 1842; settled in this Co. in 1845; owns 208 acres of land; married Elizabeth Piller in 1831; she was born in Cornwall in 1813; they have eight children: Ann, James H., Elizabeth, Richard, Francis, Margaret, William and Catherine; the family are all members of the M. E. Church; Republican.

Phillips W. farm; S. 14; P.O. Scales Mound.

Poyser J. farmer; S. 31; P.O. Scales Mound.

Pool H. miner; Sec. 22; P.O. Scales Mound.

Pooley Henry; Sec. 33; P. O. Scales Mound.

Pooley J. H.; Sec. 33; P. O. Scales Mound.

Pooley P. farm; S. 33; P. O. Scales Mound.

Pooley R. farm; S. 33; P. O. Scales Mound.

Pooley S. farm; S. 23; P. O. Scales Mound.

Pooley Wm. farm; S.33; P.O. Scales Mound.

REDFEARN GEORGE, miner; Sec. 22; P. O. Scales Mound.

Rittweger George, blacksmith; Sec. 35; P.O. Scales Mound.

Richards James, laborer; Sec. 26; P. O. Scales Mound.

Richards John, farmer; Sec. 16; P. O. White Oak Springs, Wis.

RICHARDS WM. H. Farmer; Sec. 33; P. O. Scales Mound; born in Cornwall, Eng., March 29, 1819; married in 1843 to Amelia Richards; she was born in same Co. July 14, 1819; came to this Co. in 1846; had a long and tedious journey; left Cornwall June 12; came in sail vessel to N. Y., steamer to Albany, canal boat to Buffalo, steamer to Chicago, thence in wagon to this place, reaching here Sept. 3; owns 85 acres of land; no children; are members of the M. E. Church; Republican.

Roberts George, farmer; Sec. 22; P.O. Scales Mound.

ROBERTS HENRY, Farmer; Sec. 27; P. O. Scales Mound; born in Cornwall, Eng., April 2, 1827; came to this Co. in 1851; owns 160 acres of land; married Ann Pryor in 1852; she was born in Cornwall in 1834; came to this Co. 40 years ago; have seven children living: Samuel H., Wm. A., Emma G., John E., Charles T., Joseph F. and Josiah F.; lost one, Mary A.; has been Justice of the Peace 16 years; Supervisor, Assessor, Collector and School Director for a number of years each; is now Trustee of Tp.; attends the M. E. Church; Democrat.

Roberts John, Sec. 22; P. O. Scales Mound.

Robson James R. farmer; Sec. 19; P. O. Scales Mound.

Robinson John, painter; Scales Mound.

ROBSON ROBERT, Farmer and Stock Raiser; Sec. 19; P. O. Scales Mound; born in Durham, Eng., Oct. 22, 1825; came to this country in 1846; spent the first three years in Burton, Hazel Green and Shullsburg, Wis.; in 1849 he crossed the plains to California with an ox team; was near six months making the trip; returned to the states and made another in 1852; came back in 1854;

bought this farm and has made it his home ever since; owns 330 acres of land; married Margaret Allinson in 1851; she was born in Schuylkill Co., Pa., April 24, 1833; have seven children living: James R., Wm. A., John F., Edith M., Thomas I., Christopher and Martha; lost five—four sons and one daughter; Mr. R. has been Supervisor 2 years, Assessor 12, Collector 7, Commissioner of Highways 2, and Justice of the Peace about 16 years; is a Republican.

Robson W. A. Sec. 19; P. O. Scales Mound.

Rogers James, Sec. 16; P. O. White Oak Springs, Wis.

ROGERS JOHN, Farmer; Sec. 16; P. O. White Oak Springs, Wis.; born in Cornwall, Eng., in 1821; came to this farm in 1849; owns 150 acres of land; married Betsey Perry, Oct. 19, 1845; she was born in Cornwall in 1817; they have six children: John (now in Colorado), James, Walter, Elizabeth, Richard and Tom; lost three, Mary, Mary Matilda, and one in infancy; Mr. R. was Overseer of Highways and School Director; the family attend the M. E. Church, of which Mr. and Mrs. R. are members; Republican.

Rogers Walter, Sec. 16; P. O. White Oak Springs, Wis.

Rowe Thomas, farmer; Sec. 27; P. O. Scales Mound.

Rummell Henry, farmer; Sec. 18; P. O. Scales Mound.

Rumell John, laborer; Sec. 26; P. O. Scales Mound.

SANFORD LaFRANK, laborer; Scales Mound.

Scott J. laborer; S. 35; P. O. Scales Mound.

Scott Thomas, laborer; Scales Mound.

SHERR JOHN, Farmer; Sec. 35; P. O. Scales Mound; born in Germany, Oct. 5, 1848; came to this Co. in 1860; owns 160 acres of land; married Mary A. Murphy Nov. 21, 1874; she was born in this Tp. May 6, 1854; they have two children: Annie, born Nov. 26, 1875, and John, Sept. 21, 1876; Mr. S. was Overseer of Highways one year; they are members of the German Catholic Church.

Sincock S. miner; Sec. 15; P. O. White Oak Springs, Wis.

Sincock Edward, miner; Sec. 15; P. O. White Oak Springs, Wis.

Sincock Thomas, farmer; Sec. 15; P. O. White Oak Springs, Wis.

Smart John F. with his father; Sec. 23; P. O. Scales Mound.

SMART NEWTON, Farmer; Sec. 23; P. O. Scales Mound; born in England in 1821; came to this country in 1848; settled in N. Y.; came to this Co. in 1855; owns 260 acres of land; married Jane Poyser in 1854; she was born in England in 1821; have five children: John F., Ellen, Mary J., Rosa N. and Fannie Ida; Mrs. Smart died in 1865; married again to Elizabeth Pooley; she was born in England in 1827; have one child by second marriage; Mr. S. was Overseer of Highways one year; family attend the M. E. Church; is a Republican.

Smart Wm. farm; S. 27; P.O. Scales Mound.

SPRY JOHN, Farmer; Sec. 36; P. O. Scales Mound; born in Cornwall, Eng., Jan. 8, 1819; came to this country in 1852; settled in Hazel Green, Wis.; remained there till 1867, when he moved on the farm where he now resides; owns 120 acres of land; married Mrs. Elizabeth M. Sherman (maiden name Wright), Jan. 24, 1265; she was born in England, Sept. 28, 1839; they have two children: John A., born Oct. 27, 1866, and Nathaniel W., Oct. 14, 1868; Mrs. Sherman, by first marriage, had two children: Benjamin F., born Aug. 1, 1859, and Mary E., Sept. 11, 1862; the family attend the Methodist Church; Republican.

Stephens Anton, saloon; Scales Mound.

TANGYE JOSEPH, Merchant; Scales Mound; born in Camborne, Cornwall, Eng.; came to the U. S. in 1854; worked in mines in Pa. about a year; moved to Shullsburg, Wis.; was mining twelve years; afterward kept store there till 1873, when he came here; been in same business here ever since; married to Elizabeth Osborn in 1858; she was born in Missouri in 1840; have two adopted children: Annie Tangye and Mary J. Rogers; are members of the M. E. Church; Republican.

Theas Fritz, miner; S.22, P.O. Scales Mound.

Tippet C. miner; Vedi Grand; P. O. White Oak Springs, Wis.

Trezona H. Sec. 35; P. O. Scales Mound.

TREZONA JOHN, Farmer; Sec. 35; P. O. Scales Mound; born in Cornwall, Eng., in 1818; married Maria Rowe in 1843; she was born in same Co. in 1824; came to this Co. in 1847; lived here till 1867, then moved to Shullsburg, Wis.; remained there until 1875; came back and settled on this farm; have eight children living: John T., Mary, Maria, Richard, Henry, Eliza J., Hester and William; four died in infancy; the family attend the M E. Church.

Treseder W. farmer; P. O. Scales Mound.

Turner E. J. lab.; S. 28; P.O. Scales Mound.

Turner Geo. Sec. 22; P. O. Scales Mound.

VIPOND JOSEPH, farmer; Sec. 28; P. O. Scales Mound.

WAUD E. P. laborer; Scales Mound.

WAUD ROBERT G. Saddle and Harness Maker, Dealer in Confectionery, Fruit, etc.; Scales Mound; born in Cohoes, N. Y., Sept. 24, 1816; came to Galena in 1837; married to present wife at Madison, Wis., Oct. 10, 1858; maiden name, Betsey L. Brumley; she was born in Hamilton, Madison Co., N. Y., in 1830; came to Wis. in 1854; Mr. W. is well known in Lafayette Co., Wis.; was Co. Treasurer six years in succession; would probably be in office yet, but has lost his hearing; have nine children living; attend the M. E. Church.

White John, farmer and stock dealer; Sec. 13; P. O. Scales Mound.

WHITE THOMAS J. Farmer; Sec. 24; lives with his father, John L. White, who was born in Cattaraugus Co., N. Y., Dec. 25, 1827; came West and settled in White Oak Springs, Wis., in 1846; in 1849 moved to the farm where he now resides; owns 247 acres of land; married in 1848 to Henrietta C. Phelps; she was born in Jasper, Steuben Co., N. Y., April 8, 1832; they have six children living: Thos. J., Cecil J., Delia H., Norman D., Orra L. and Ada; lost three: Charles, Aug. 17, 1859; May, July 18, 1862; and Paul, March 9, 1869; Mr. W. served two terms as School Director; deals extensively in horses; ships about forty head annually; also deals in hogs and cattle; the family attend the M. E. Church.

Wichler, Geo. shoemaker; Scales Mound.

WICHLER HENRY, Grocery and Saloon; Scales Mound; born in Germany Jan. 12, 1823; followed cabinet making for twelve years; married Christiana Schwartz, Feb. 21, 1853; she was born in Saxony, Feb. 21, 1830; came to this town May 14, 1856; have nine children: John Valentine, Anna, John, Adam, Henry, Christiana, Frederic, Elizabeth and Lorenzo; Lutheran; Democrat.

Wichler Valentine, works with his father, Grocery; Scales Mound.

Wilkins Egbert, laborer; Scales Mound.

Wilt Calvin, laborer; Sec. 28; P. O. Scales Mound.

WRIGHT JAS. Farmer; Sec. 29; P. O. Scales Mound; born in Fifeshire, Scotland, Sept. 8, 1827; came to this Co. in 1852; owns 291 acres land; married Eliza Grindey Jan. 30, 1860; she was born in Staffordshire, England, Sept. 16, 1838; they have eight children living: Thomas, Mark J., Robert, Eliza H., Margaret, Annie F., Chas. W. and Mary E.; lost one daughter, Ann; she died April 21, 1862, aged 1 year, 11 months and 27 days; Mr. W. enlisted in the 3d I. V. C. March 3, 1865; was mustered out Oct. 15, 1865; the family attend the M. E. Church; Mrs. W. is a member.

XANDER BERNT, blacksmith; Scales Mound.

YOUEL CHAS. Sec. 36; P. O. Scales Mound.

Youel J. farm; Sec. 36; P. O. Scales Mound.

ZENGRAF ADAM, laborer; Scales Mound.

ZIEGLER HENRY G. Wagon Maker; Scales Mound; born in Buffalo, N. Y., April 14, 1848; emigrated to this Co. in 1855; came on steamer from Pittsburg to Galena; his father died of cholera while *en route;* was buried a few miles north of St. Louis; at Galena he was apprenticed to Christian Koehler, Feb. 18, 1863, to learn his trade; worked with him till 1866; was married Feb. 10, 1871, to Mary Mueller; moved to Scales Mound, where he is now in business; has two children: Louis, born Nov. 14, 1872; and Annie, July 11, 1876; his mother, now 61 years of age, lives with him; his wife's parents reside at Sherrill's Mt., Dubuque Co., Iowa; he owns house and six lots, exclusive of his business.

GUILFORD TOWNSHIP.

ALTFELLECH MATTHIAS, farmer; Sec. 27; P. O. Avery.

AVERY ELIAS C. Farmer; Sec. 32; P. O. Avery; born in Tazewell Co., Ill., Sept. 20, 1823; came to this Co. with his father in 1828, who was one of the first settlers in this Co.; he can remember scenes and occurrences connected with the Black Hawk War, although not nine years old; his father was captain of a company of Light Horse; was too old to go into active service, but sent one or two of his sons, while he assisted in defending the home settlements; owns 90 acres land; married Mrs. Julia Wilson (maiden name Denio) in 1858; she was born in Buffalo, N. Y., March 1, 1834; they have six children living: Albert I., George G., Carrie, Mary A., Phœbe and Cyrus B.; lost three: John C., Emma I. and an infant; Mrs. Avery has one son by first marriage, William H. Wilson; Mr. A. crossed the plains to California in 1850; remained there till 1857; returned *via* Panama; attend the M. E. Church.

Avery Geo. S. farmer; Sec. 33; P. O. Avery.

BAKER JOSEPH, farmer; Sec. 22; P. O. Scales Mound.

BALBACK CONRAD, Farmer; Sec. 33; P. O. Avery; born in Hesse-Darmstadt, Germany, Jan. 1, 1831; came to this Co. in 1851; owns 214 acres land; married Elizabeth Menzemer Sept. 14, 1856; she was born in Baden, Germany, Sept. 30, 1839; they have seven children living: Henry, Caroline, Lizzie, Minnie, Louisa, Amelia and Josie; lost four: Louisa, died in 1859; Conrad, Aug. 6. 1872; Charles, Oct. 12, 1876, and Frederic, Oct. 21, 1876; Mr. B. was Commissioner of Highways three years, and School Director; family belong to Lutheran Church.

BALBACK GEO. Farmer; Sec. 33; P. O. Avery; born in Hesse-Darmstadt, Germany, Sept. 14, 1841; came to this Co. in 1853; settled on this farm; owns 130 acres land; was married Nov. 4, 1868, to Mary Riter; she was born in Germany in March, 1844; they have four children: John, Emma, Lizzie and Henry; Mr. B. was only 12 years old when he came here, and had his share of the hardships incident to the life of an early settler; he is Catholic; Mrs. B. is a Lutheran.

Bardel Chris. farmer; Sec. 34; P. O. Avery.

Bartell Francis, Sec. 18; P. O. Galena.

BARTELL HENRY, Farmer; Sec. 18; P. O. Galena; born in Cornwall, Eng., Nov. 1, 1817; came to this Co. in 1840, and to this farm in 1844; owns 200 acres land; married Mary A. Harvey in 1836; she was born in England in 1819; they have fourteen children: Elizabeth J., Mary, Sophia, Henry, John, Joseph, Caroline, Lavinia, William, Francis J., Thomas C., Benjamin A., Sarah A. and Jasper A.; Mr. B. was School Director and Overseer of Highways 14 years each; family belong to the M. E. Church.

Bartell John, Sec. 18; P. O. Galena.

Bartell Wm. Sec. 18; P. O. Galena.

BASTIAN HENRY, Farmer; Sec. 6; P. O. Council Hill Station; born in Cornwall, Eng., Jan. 5, 1825; came to this Co. in 1841; married Elizabeth Prisk Dec. 19, 1859; she was born in Cornwall, Oct. 22, 1836; they have six children living: Alfred H., Mary E., Carrie, Wilbur J., Laura J. and Ada S.; lost one, Sarah Jane, died Jan. 6, 1865; owns 93 acres land; Mr. B. has three brothers and three sisters all living in this Co., and a sister in Lafayette Co.; all came over in the "Cornwall" in 1841; were eight weeks making the voyage; Mr. B. is at present Town Treasurer, and was Collector three years.

BASTIAN JOHN, Farmer; Sec. 6; P. O. Council Hill Station; born in Cornwall, Eng., Sept. 9, 1809; was married in 1838 to Ann Holman; she was born in Cornwall in 1818; came to this Co. in 1841; came in the "Cornwall" with his father's family; owns 140 acres land; they have ten children living: John, Mary, Sampson, Thomas, Francis, Hester A., Elizabeth, William H., Annie M. and Orlando; lost one, Jane, died aged two years; has been School Director several terms, and Overseer of Highways one year; belong to the M. E. Church.

BAUS GEORGE, Farmer; Sec. 10; P.O. Scales Mound; born in Hesse, Germany, in 1815; came to this Co. in 1838; owns 120 acres land; married Miss Mary Wise in 1851; she was born in Baden, Germany, in 1825; they have two children: Mary, born in 1853, and John William, in April, 1859; the family attend the Lutheran Church.

BAUS JOHN, Farmer; Sec. 9; P. O. Scales Mound; born in Hesse, Germany, July 10, 1823; came to this Co. in 1838; lived in Galena till 1842, when he moved on this farm, where he has ever since resided; owns 200 acres land; is serving his fourth term as Assessor; was Collector two terms; was School Trustee one term; was School Director, with the exception of two or three years, since the Tp. organization; married Mary A. Haas in 1849; she was born in Germany Sept. 4, 1829; have six children: Catherine, Elizabeth, George C., Joseph H., Mary A. and Phœbe

C.; lost one son, John William, died March 11, 1870; are members M.E. Church.

Bear Henry, farm; Sec. 13; P.O. Houghton.

Bell B. laborer; Sec. 25; P.O. Scales Mound.

Bell Hiram, lab; Sec. 25; P.O. Scales Mound.

Bell Z. farmer; Sec. 26; P.O. Scales Mound.

Belden James, farmer; Sec. 32; P. O. Avery.

Belden M. farmer; Sec. 32; P.O. Avery.

Belden Napoleon, farm; Sec. 32; P.O. Avery.

Belden Thos. farmer; Sec. 32; P. O. Avery.

Bingham Geo. renter; Sec. 19; P.O. Galena.

Bousman Nicholas, Sr., farmer; Sec. 3; P.O. Scales Mound.

Bousman Nicholas, Jr., farmer; Sec. 2. P.O. Scales Mound.

BOUSEMANN PHILLIP, Farmer and Deputy Sheriff; Sec. 2; P. O. Scales Mound; born in Hesse-Darmstadt, Germany, July 8, 1817; came to this Co. in 1846; owns 259 acres land; has been Deputy Sheriff 11 years and Constable 16 years; married Julia Stoft in April, 1845; she was born in Germany Jan. 8, 1822; have five children living: Philip, aged 27; Nicholas, 24; William, 22; Henry, 18, and Julia, 14; the eldest daughter, Catherine, wife of Conrad Schneider, of Dodge Co., Neb., died there Aug. 4, 1874; the eldest son is in Story Co., Nev., engaged in mining; family belong to the Lutheran Church.

Bouseman Wm. Sec. 2; P.O. Scales Mound.

Brickner A. farm; Sec. 36; P. O. Houghton.

Bucher Felix, farmer; Sec. 31; P. O. Avery.

Bucher Jacob, farmer; Sec. 31; P.O. Avery.

Buck John, laborer; Sec. 33; P.O. Avery.

CABLE CHARLES, Farmer; Sec. 24; P. O. Houghton; born in Bavaria, Germany, in 1825; came to this Co. in 1849; owns 200 acres land; was School Director four years, and Overseer of Highways one year; married Eva Burn in 1850; she was born in Bavaria in 1823; they have five children living: Lena, Nettie, Charles, Katie and Eva; lost one, Mary, died in 1855; family belong to Presbyterian Church.

Callahan Hugh, farmer, Sec. 22; P. O. Scales Mound.

CALLAHAN JAS. Farmer; Sec. 29; P. O. Galena; born in Ireland in 1820; came to this Co. in 1848; owns 360 acres land; married Rosa Reynolds; she was born in Ireland; have one son, Edward; family belong to the Catholic Church.

Callahan Jno. farmer; Sec. 28; P. O. Galena.

Callahan T. farmer; Sec. 19; P. O. Galena.

Campbell Caleb, farmer; Sec. 24; P.O. Scales Mound.

Carrigan J. farmer; Sec. 31; P. O. Galena.

CARSON ROBT. Farmer; Sec. 23; P. O. Scales Mound; born in Ireland in 1814; came to the U. S. in 1838; lived in N. Y. till 1841, when he came to this Tp. and settled within three miles of where he now resides; owns 80 acres land; married Eliza Kelin in 1840; she was born in N. Y. City March 30, 1819; they have five children living: William J., Samuel, Robert and John (twins), and Rosamond; William and Samuel were in the army, the former in the 45th Ill., from the time of its organization till the close of the war; was in 17 battles; the latter was in the 96th, in the service one year.

Carson Sam'l, Sec. 23; P. O. Scales Mound.

Casper Geo. Sec. 1; P. O. Scales Mound.

Casper Jos. Sec. 1; P. O. Scales Mound.

Casper Julius, Sec. 1; P. O. Scales Mound.

CASPER THOS. Farmer; Sec. 1; P. O. Scales Mound; born in Switzerland in 1823; came to this Co. in 1841; owns 160 acres land; married Julia Frick in 1849; she was born in this Co. in 1827; had three children: Joseph, John and Julia; she died in March, 1854; married again, in 1855, to Maria Getz; she was born in Germany in 1835; they have seven children: George, Emma, Elizabeth, Thomas, Barbara, Henry and Peter; lost one, Christian, died March 23, 1871; Mr. C. is serving his second term as School Director; was Overseer of Highways four years; they are members of the Lutheran Church.

CLARK EDW. Farmer; Sec. 21; P.O. Galena; born in Ireland Feb. 1, 1845; came to N. Y. City when two years old, with his uncle, Jas. Clark; came to this Co. in 1857; enlisted in 1862, in Co. B, 90th I. V. I.; served until the close of the war; was in 20 general engagements; he and one other were the only men in his company that came through without a wound; was with Sherman from Chattanooga to Savannah, and thence to Washington; owns 120 acres land; married Sarah F. Sale in 1867; she was born on this farm Dec. 6, 1851: have four children: John E., Louis S., Philip H. and Geneva F.; Democrat.

Colin C. farm; Sec. 14; P. O. Scales Mound.

COLIN RENNY, Farmer; Sec. 14; P. O. Scales Mound; born in France Jan. 6, 1806; came over in 1830; traveled in different parts of the U. S. for ten years; went back to France; staid five years; returned in 1847, and settled on this farm; owns 342 acres land; married Mary A. Gabrois April 21, 1840; had three children: Edward J., Julius and Chas. H.; she died May 16, 1851; married again, Nov. 21, 1851, to Judith Ellsworth (maiden name Maloy); she was born in Ireland; has four children; three by first marriage; Mary, Alice and Annie; one by second, Josephine; has served two terms as Assessor and two as Collector; the family belong to the Catholic Church.

Combellick Thos. farm; Sec. 6; P. O. Council Hill Station.

Conlee Wm. laborer; Sec. 14; P. O. Scales Mound.

Corcoran D. farmer; Sec. 28; P. O. Avery.

DITTMER NICHOLAS, renter; Sec. 24; P. O. Scales Mound.

Durstein C. farmer; Sec. 21; P. O. Galena.

Durstein E. farm; S. 1; P. O. Scales Mound.

DURRSTEIN HENRY, Farmer; Sec. 16; P. O. Scales Mound; born in this Tp. April 6, 1842; owns 120 acres land; married Louisa K. Wilhelmi Sept. 6, 1870; she was born in Prussia in 1851; came to this Co. Sept. 20, 1869; they have two children living: Mary, born Sept. 20, 1872; Christian, Jan. 16, 1874; lost one, Lena, born Aug. 11, 1871, died Aug. 25, 1871; Mr. D. was Constable four years, and Overseer of Highways one year; his father, Michael Durrstein, came to this Co. in 1840; took up the land now owned by his son, and remained here until March 19, 1875, when he died, at the age of 75; his mother resides with him; is 73 years old; family attend the Presbyterian Church.

DUERR JNO. Farmer; Sec. 15; P. O. Scales Mound; born in Alsace, Germany, March 18, 1814; came to St. Louis in 1842, and to this Co. in 1843; married Lena Gerhardt June 30, 1860; she was born in Alsace May 14, 1824; she was first married to John Leux; he was killed in the mines near Galena in 1858; had two children: Lena and John; by second marriage have two: Philip and Frederick; owns 80 acres land; are members of the M. E. Church.

EDWARDS EMANUEL, farmer; Sec. 26; P. O. Scales Mound.

Ehredt M. farm; S. 27; P. O. Scales Mound.

Ehrler Frank, renter; Sec. 16; P. O. Galena.

Ehrler Jno. Sec. 17; P. O. Galena.

EHRLER MRS. MARY, Farming; Sec. 17; P. O. Galena; Widow of Michael Ehrler, who was killed July 4, 1877, by a pistol shot from the hands of John Hub, for which offense the said Hub is now serving a term in the penitentiary; Mr. Ehrler was married to Mary Basler April 29, 1849; she was born in Baden, Germany, May 18, 1825; came to this Co. in 1847; owns 360 acres land; has seven children living: Frank, Catherine, Michael, John, Willie, Mary and an infant; Mr. C. was Commissioner of Highways one term, Trustee one term, and School Director 13 years; belong to the Lutheran Church.

Ehrler Michael, Jr., Sec. 17; P. O. Galena.

Engle A. laborer; Sec. 18; P. O. Galena.

Engle Victor, farmer; Sec. 8; P. O. Galena.

Eversole C.C. blacksmith; S.22; P.O. Galena.

Eversoll Jno. renter; Sec. 22; P. O. Galena.

Evert G. farm; Sec. 1; P. O. Scales Mound.

FAHRIG WM. farmer; Sec. 33; P. O. Avery.

FAHRIG WM. Farmer; Sec. 34; P.O. Avery; born in Alton, Ill., July 3, 1845; came to this Co. in 1852; was driving team in Galena until 1868; then bought and moved on this farm; owns 90 acres land; married Emma Wencicker May 28, 1874; she was born in East Galena May 26, 1856; they have two children: William, born May 12, 1875; Josephine, July 12, 1877; are members of the M. E. Church, Galena.

Folan Mark, farmer; Sec. 20; P. O. Galena.

Foley John, Sec. 31; P. O. Galena.

Foley M. farmer; Sec. 31; P. O. Galena.

Ford Geo. laborer; Sec. 18; P. O. Galena.

Ford Richard, farmer; Sec. 18; P. O. Galena.

Ford Wm. farmer; Sec. 3; P.O. Scales Mound.

FORD WILLIAM N. Farmer; Sec. 5; P. O. Council Hill Station; born in Cornwall, Eng., June 20, 1831; came to this Co. in 1842; owns 360 acres land; married Elizabeth Cornbelick March 13, 1856; she was born in Cornwall June 9, 1837; they have six children living: Amos J., Cornelia A., Wallace M., Jesse W., Matthew and Samuel F.; lost three: Adaline J., Walter T. and one in infancy; Mr. Ford was Assessor three years, and is serving his third term as School Director; are members of the M. E. Church.

FRICK JOSEPH, Farmer; Sec. 15; P. O. Scales Mound; born in Selkirk Settlement, Red River of the North, in 1824; came to Galena with his father in 1826; was eight years old at the time of the Black Hawk War; has an indistinct recollection of the Indians, who were here at that time in great numbers; moved to this farm in 1833; owns 167 acres land; married Margaret Durrstein in 1854: she was born in Germany Dec. 15, 1833; they have six children: Elizabeth, Julia, Louisa, Mary, Emma and Joseph; family belong to Lutheran Church.

Fulton Peter.

GARBER HENRY, farmer; Sec. 20; P.O. Scales Mound.

GAUESHART VALENTINE, Farmer; Sec 4; P. O. Scales Mound; born in Baden, Germany, in 1835; came to this Co. in 1854; was married in 1860 to Elizabeth Heuberger; she was born in Switzerland in 1839; died in 1867; was married again to Margaret Sherr in 1871; she was born in Germany in 1851; have an adopted daughter, Kate Slyer; she was born in Cassville, Grant Co., Wis., May 20, 1870.

John W Taylor

GUILFORD TOWNSHIP

(DECEASED)

GEAR WM. T. Farmer; Sec. 9; P. O. Scales Mound; born in Cleveland, O., in 1816; came to this Co. with his father in 1826; settled on Fever River, near New Diggings, Wis.; moved to this farm in 1839; has followed farming and mining alternately ever since; owns 310 acres land; married Eliza Day Dec. 29, 1836; she was born in N. H. in 1818; they have nine children living: Charles E., James W., Hannah, John C., Sophronia A., Holland F., Sarah C., George L. and Eliza V.; lost one, Francis C.; Mr. G. was Register of Deeds in Wis. two years; is serving his ninth term as Supervisor of this Tp.; was School Trustee 16 years; family attend the M. E. Church.

Gesner John, Jr., Sec. 9; P. O. Scales Mound.

Gesner John, farmer; Sec. 9; P. O. Scales Mound.

Gill John, farmer; Sec.14; P.O.Scales Mound.

Glasgow J. G. farmer; Sec. 21; P. O. Galena.

Gleck Henry, farmer; Sec. 19; P. O. Galena.

Goodwin Wm. farmer; Sec. 26; P. O. Scales Mound.

GREEN CHARITY, Farming; Sec. 32; P. O. Galena; widow; maiden name was Springer; born in Dutchess Co., N. Y., March 5, 1800; was married to John Green, of Ontario Co., Aug. 23, 1824; he was born in Westchester Co. April 27, 1790; they came to this Co. in 1835; settled within two miles of here; have lived on this farm since 1846; owns 100 acres land; they have eight children: Noah, William H., James, Jeremiah, Jacob, Sarah, Maria and Barney; Mr. G. had four by a former marriage: Moses, Andrew, Amasa and John; lost one, George; Mr. G. died May 24, 1876.

Green J. O. farm; S. 27; P. O. Scales Mound.

GREEN JEREMIAH, Farmer; Sec. 32; P. O. Galena; in partnership with his brother, Barney, farming their mother's place; younger sons of Charity Green.

Gruber Valentine M. renter; Sec. 10; P. O. Scales Mound.

Gugler Gotleib, farmer; Sec. 7; P.O. Galena.

HAMMER BERNARD, farmer; Sec. 12; P. O. Scales Mound.

Hammer R. farm; S. 12; P.O. Scales Mound.

Harwick C. lab; Sec. 23; P.O. Scales Mound.

Harwick J. lab; Sec. 23; P.O. Scales Mound.

Harwick L. renter; S. 22; P.O.Scales Mound.

Harwick N., Sr., Sec.22; P.O. Scales Mound.

Harwick N.,Jr., laboror; P.O. Scales Mound.

Hathaway S.W.,Jr., farm; S. 17; P.O. Galena.

HATHAWAY SAMUEL W. Farmer; Sec. 18; P.O. Galena; born in Otsego Co., N. Y., Aug. 25, 1813; came to this state with his parents in 1818; settled in St. Clair Co.; his mother died here in 1822; his father moved to Sangamon Co. near where Springfield now stands, in 1822; died same year; in 1829 he came to the Galena Lead Mines; worked several years at any thing that offered, principally mining; was a private in Captain Allenwrath's company during the Black Hawk War; took up this claim in 1834; lived on it till 1847; when the land came into market, entered it at government price; owns 418 acres land; was Tp. Treasurer from time of Tp. organization up to March, 1877; was Town Clerk six years, Supervisor one term, and Justice of the Peace 16 years; married Sophronia J. Taylor, Oct. 18, 1845; she was born in Sangamon Co., Ill., Jan. 5, 1825; came to Galena in 1827, with her father, the first settler in Guilford Tp.; he built the first house, plowed the first furrow, and sowed the first wheat ever sown in Guilford; they have seven children: Mary J. Gear, of Clay Center, Kas.; Samuel W., Guilford Tp.; Sarah T., Eleazer J., Laura S., Abram L. and Margie L.; lost four children: Wm. H., died at the age of 22, and three died in infancy; the family attend the M. E. Church.

Hawkins George.

Hazelbacker John, farmer; Sec. 12; P. O. Scales Mound.

Hazelbacker John, Jr., farmer; Sec. 12; P.O. Scales Mound.

Heiser Geo. farmer; Sec. 28; P.O. Galena.

HENRY JAMES, Farmer; Sec. 34; P.O. Avery; born in Co. Antrim, Ireland, April 14, 1838; came with his parents to this Co. in 1842; enlisted in the 17th I.V.C. in 1864, at Dixon; went from there to Chicago, remained four days, and while there married Susan J. Isbell, Sept. 26; she was born in this Co. Dec. 15, 1841; he went immediately to his regiment at Rolla, Mo.; was with them in their scout and skirmishes until mustered out in July, 1865; they have six children: Ernest C., James W., David E., Robert F., Annie D. and Jennie B.; Mr. H. is Collector, School Director and Clerk of the Board.

Herr Christian, Sec. 13; P.O. Scales Mound.

Herr Henry, Sec. 13; P. O. Scales Mound.

Herr J. farmer; Sec. 13; P.O. Scales Mound.

Herr Thos. farm; Sec. 14; P.O. Scales Mound.

Heuberger Henry, Sec. 1; P.O. Scales Mound.

Heuberger Jacob, Sr., farmer; Sec. 1; P. O. Scales Mound.

Heuberger J., Jr., Sec.1; P.O. Scales Mound.

Heuberger R. farm; S.12; P.O. Scales Mound.

HEULMAN JOHN, Farmer; Sec. 18; P. O. Galena; born in Hanover, Germany, in 1824; came to this Co. in 1850; settled in West Galena; moved to this farm in 1857; owns 94 acres of land; married Mary A. Warborg in 1850; she was born in Hanover in 1826; they have five children living: Mary A. (now Mrs. Karle), Ann M., John M., Julia B. and Henry A.;

lost two: Henry and Elizabeth A.; are all members of the Catholic Church.

Hicks Jas. farm; Sec. 5; P.O. Scales Mound.

Hicks H., Jr., farm; S.5; P.O. Scales Mound.

Hocking G. farm; Sec. 35; P. O. Elizabeth.

Holland Geo. farmer; Sec. 34; P. O. Avery.

Holmes D.

Huffman G. farmer; Sec. 21; P. O. Galena.

ICHOLSE F. farmer; Sec. 28; P. O. Avery.

ISBELL ELLIOTT T. Farmer; Sec. 25; P. O. Houghton; born in Warren Co., Kentucky, Aug. 24, 1813; came to this Co. in 1832; was a member of Col. Dodge's Squadron from the beginning of the Black Hawk War till its close; followed mining exclusively till 1835; married Dorcas B. Steely, Nov. 11, 1835; she was born in Ky. in 1818; they had six children, five living; first wife died in 1849; married again in 1850 to Mrs. Annie Avery; maiden name, Cook; she had one child, Julia Cook; have eight children by second marriage, three boys and five girls. Mr. Isbell has been Supervisor, Town Treasurer, Trustee, School Director and Commissioner of Highways at various times since long before the Tp. organization.

Ivey Thos. farmer; Sec. 7; P. O. Galena.

JELLY HENSON, renter; Sec. 21; P. O. Galena.

Jelly J. S. farmer; Sec. 21; P. O. Galena.

JELLY WM. H. Farmer; Sec. 27; P. O. Galena; born in this township, Nov. 2, 1840; enlisted in the 15th I. V. I., in 1861; went with his Regt. to Mo.; was in the battles of Pea Ridge, Vicksburg, and five or six other general engagements; was with Sherman as far south as Resaca, Georgia; was sent north from there for muster out, his time (three years) having expired; owns 80 acres of land; married Mary Bartell, July 4, 1865; she was born in Guilford Tp., Dec. 11, 1843; they attend the M. E. Church; is a Republican.

KELLY EDWARD, Sec. 30; P. O. Galena.

Kelly Michael, farm; Sec. 30; P. O. Galena.

KELLER CHAS. Farmer; Sec. 16; P. O. Scales Mound; born in Baden, Germany, Sept. 17, 1834; came to this Co. in 1866; owns 120 acres of land; married Julia Keller in 1868; she was born in Galena, May 22, 1843; they have one child living: Herman, born Oct. 5, 1875; lost two: Albert and Edgar; Mr. K. was appointed School Director, Sept. 29, 1877, to fill vacancy; they have an adopted daughter, Elemeter Baker; are members of the Lutheran Church.

Kennedy D. labor; S. 5; P. O. Council Hill.

Kilmer H. T. laborer; Sec. 27; P. O. Galena.

Kline Jos. farmer; Sec. 33; P. O. Avery.

Kruser F. farmer; Sec. 28; P. O. Avery.

Kruser M. farmer; Sec. 28; P. O. Avery.

Kuntz C. farmer; Sec. 30; P. O. Galena.

LOGAN WM. H. farmer; Sec. 35; P. O. Avery.

Lindsey Robert, teacher; Sec. 29; P.O. Scales Mound.

McDONALD DANIEL, farmer; Sec. 29; P.O. Galena.

McDonald T. farmer; Sec. 26; P. O. Scales Mound.

McLane Thos. laborer; Sec. 31; P.O. Galena.

McMahon Jas. farmer; Sec. 29; P.O. Galena.

McPhillips B. farmer; Sec. 35; P.O. Avery.

Mahan L. farmer; Sec. 10; P.O. Galena.

Maloy D. farm; Sec. 26; P.O. Scales Mound.

MEFFLEY BARNHARD, Farmer; Sec. 36; P. O. Elizabeth; born in Wittenberg, Germany, in 1810; came to the U. S. in 1817; settled in Pa.; lived there as bound boy 12 years; came to this Co. in 1835; commenced work at once for old Capt. Gear, in mines near Buncombe; next year went to furnace at White Oak Springs, Wis.; worked there until 1847; then married Eve Weaver; she was born in Germany, in 1824; had nine children, three girls and six boys—Elizabeth, Harriet, John, Franklin, Jacob, Charles, James, Julia, and Barnhard; owns 120 acres of land.

Menzimer Chas. farm; Sec. 27; P.O. Galena.

Menzimer Fred. laborer; S. 33; P. O. Avery.

Metcalf D. H. painter; Sec. 17; P.O. Galena.

Metcalf F. P. laborer; Sec. 17; P. O. Galena.

Miller N. farm; Sec. 3; P. O. Scales Mound.

Miller V. renter; S. 4; P. O. Scales Mound.

Mineberg John, farmer; Sec. 2; P. O. Scales Mound.

MONNIER CHARLES A. Farmer; Sec. 36; P. O. Elizabeth; born in Switzerland, Dec. 22, 1806; came with his parents to the U. S. in 1822; settled in St. Louis Co., Mo.; he came to Hazel Green, Wis., in 1827; was engaged in mining at intervals there for seven or eight years; married Christine Rendisbacker in 1834; she was born in Switzerland, Feb. 20, 1811; they came to this farm in 1836; owns 256 acres of land; have seven children living: Emily, Elizabeth, Charles, Julia, Christine, Philip S., and Edward W.; lost three: Frederic, Frederic P., and David; the oldest son, Charles, enlisted in the 39th I. V. I., in 1864; was in the army of the Potomac; at Petersburg, etc.; was under fire for 25 consecutive days, and was present at the surrender of Gen. Lee; family attend the M. E. Church.

Monnier Edward W. farmer; Sec. 36; P. O. Elizabeth.

Monnier Philip S. farmer; Sec. 36; P. O. Elizabeth.

Montague Chas. farmer; Sec. 11; P.O. Scales Mound.

Mounder Michael, laborer; Sec. 2; P. O. Scales Mound.

Murray Ed. laborer; Sec. 32; P. O. Avery.

Musselman Christian, farmer; Sec. 13; P. O. Scales Mound.

MUMM GOTTFRIED, Farmer; Sec. 20; P. O. Galena; born in Prussia, Feb. 18, 1845; he was 14 years old when his father emigrated to this Co.; settled in Galena; was married, March 31, 1861, to Grace Gruber; she was born in Birne, Germany, in 1845; they have four children living: Mary, Grace, Lena, and Celia; lost one, Valentine, died March 5, 1875; Mr. Mumm's mother died in Prussia in 1847; his father, aged 62, is living with him.

NOLAN BARNEY, laborer; Sec. 31; P.O. Galena.

Nolan James, farmer; Sec. 31; P.O. Galena.

NADIG CHARLES, Farmer; Sec. 16; P. O. Galena; born in Germany in 1852; his father died there in 1853; he came to this Co. with his mother the same year; in 1854 she was married to Anton Pilz; she has six children; Peter, Leonard, Jacob, Caroline, and Mary; her eldest daughter, Katherine, died in 1854; she owns 120 acres of land; her father, Mr. Eisenhauer, was a soldier with the First Napoleon in all his campaigns; died in 1876, aged 96; they are members of the Lutheran Church.

PARTLOW M. laborer; Sec. 35; P. O. Avery.

Partlow W. H. laborer; Sec. 35; P.O. Avery.

Peters Francis.

Phillamallee Windle, farmer; Sec. 14; P. O. Scales Mound.

Phillamallee Wm. farmer; Sec. 14; P. O. Scales Mound.

Pilz Anton; farmer; Sec. 16; P. O. Galena.

Plaseh E. H. Apple River.

Pooley James, farmer; Sec. 4; P. O. Scales Mound.

Pooley John, Sr., farmer; Sec. 4; P.O. Scales Mound.

Pooley John, Jr., farmer; Sec. 4; P.O. Scales Mound.

Prisk Jas. miner; Sec. 6; P. O. Council Hill Station.

Promeuschenkel M. farmer; Sec. 12; P. O. Scales Mound.

QUINLEN JOHN.

RAWLINS L. P. farmer; Sec. 22; P. O. Scales Mound.

RAWLINS JAMES D. Farmer; Sec. 22; P. O. Scales Mound; born in Clark Co., Ky., Feb. 28, 1801; emigrated with his father to Mo.; lived there ten years; came to Galena Sept. 14, 1827; there were but few houses, two taverns and two or three groceries in the place; returned to Mo. and was married Oct. 5, 1828, to Lovisa Collier, of Howard Co.; she was born near Crab Orchard, Ky., May 2, 1803; her father was an old Indian fighter; he lived nine years in a fort, not daring to go out unless armed for defense; he returned in Nov., 1828, to this Co.; was here during the Black Hawk War; was not actively engaged fighting Indians, but was fully as much exposed, being engaged in hauling supplies from Galena to Dodgeville and Mineral Point, Wis., often within hearing of the guns of the combatants, not knowing at what moment he would fall into an ambush; has an inexhaustible fund of reminiscences of those early days; moved to this farm in 1834; owns 320 acres of land; have six children living: Mortimer C., residing in California, Lemon P., living on the farm here, Robert J., in U. S. Mint, California, Mary L., living in Iowa, Jas. S., in Custom House, Baltimore, Md., and Wm. D., Supt. Registry Dept., P. O. Chicago; Benjamin F. died in 1857, Jarrard O. in Dec., 1869, and John A. died in Washington, D. C., Sept. 6, 1869, an event that threw the whole nation into mourning, and was indeed a sad bereavement to to his aged parents, family and friends.

Rederick Isadore, renter; Sec. 10; P. O. Scales Mound.

Rederick N. A. farmer; Sec. 10; P. O. Scales Mound.

Retz G. farmer; Sec. 34; P. O. Avery.

Richter A. farmer; Sec. 21; P. O. Galena.

ROUSE SUSAN, Widow; farming; Sec. 4; P. O. Scales Mound; maiden name Nye; born in N. Y., April 10, 1805; emigrated to Ill. in 1817; settled in Carmi, on the Wabash River, thence to Peoria in 1820; was only one house in the place when they came there; was married to Thomas Ross, July 1, 1823; came to this Co., in 1827; Mr. Ross died Dec. 21, 1841; she was married to John Wilson, March 5, 1844; afterward married George Rouse Nov. 13, 1849; have five children by first marriage, Catherine M., John E., Isabella, Mary A. and Arabella; one by second marriage, Edmund Wilson; Mr. Rouse died May 10, 1865; she owns 160 acres of land; belongs to the M. E. Church.

SAAM CHRISTIAN, farmer; Sec. 11; P. O. Scales Mound.

Saam G. miner; Sec. 2; P.O. Scales Mound.

Saam Henry, farmer; Sec. 2; P. O. Scales Mound.

Saam J. farm; Sec. 2; P. O. Scales Mound.

Sale John A. laborer: Sec. 21; P. O. Galena.

Sale J. H. renter; Sec. 32; P. O. Avery.

Sale Thomas, P. O. Galena.

SCHMIDT JOSEPHINE, Widow, maiden name Fahrig; farming; S. 33; P. O. Avery; born in Alford, Prussia, in 1833; came to Alton, Ill., in 1844; moved to this Co. in 1851; was married same year to Adam Schmidt; he died June 15, 1869; had nine children, George, Henry and Cora are living; Adam, Charles, Conrad, Katie, John, and Mary died in childhood; her mother died Dec. 31, 1851; her father, Wm. Fahrig, makes her house his home most of the time; family belong to the German Methodist Church.

SHOENHARD VALENTINE, Farmer; Sec. 10; P. O. Scales Mound; born in Hesse-Darmstadt, Germany, Nov. 1, 1808; came to St. Louis in 1840; afterward to this Co. in 1843; married Mrs. Elizabeth M. Bell (maiden name, Young) in May, 1843; she was born in Germany in 1809; had five children by first husband: John, Jacob, Phillip, Katherine and Geo. P.; John is the only one now living; by second marriage: Ernest, born March 11, 1849; he was married to Elizabeth Baus, April 2, 1872; she was born in this Co; have three children: George C., Lilly and John V.; owns 160 acres; Mr. S., Sr., owns 360 acres; was Justice of the Peace, School Director and Overseer of Highways several years each; belong to the Catholic Church.

SCHUK JOHN, Farmer; Renter; Sec. 33; P. O. Avery; born in Germany, July 26, 1844; came to the U. S. with his father's family in 1852; stopped in Sandusky, Ohio, where his mother died of cholera; came the following year to Galena, where his father died in 1856; came to this farm in 1867; married Mary Fahrig, Feb. 17, 1870; she was born in Prussia, Aug. 12, 1841; they have two children: John W., born Dec. 1, 1870, and Mary, April 29, 1873; Mr. Schuk is a member of Steuben Lodge 321, I. O. O. F., of Galena; they belong to the M. E. Church.

Sheean J. farmer; Sec. 5; P. O. Council Hill Station.

Sheonhart E. farmer; Sec. 10; P. O. Scales Mound.

Sheridan J. farmer; Sec. 31; P. O. Galena.

SHULTZ JOHN, Deceased; born in Hesse-Cassel, Dec. 13, 1816; came to this Co. in 1847; settled in Guilford, and has lived within two miles of this farm ever since; lived 15 years where Henry Glick now resides; moved to this farm in 1870; owns 410 acres of land; was married in 1847 to Dorathea M. Schrump; she was born in Germany, Feb. 7, 1816; they have three children living: William, John A. and Sarah S.; Henry died in infancy; Mr. S. died Nov. 8, 1874, since which time the two sons have been farming the place; belong to the Evangelical Lutheran Church.

Shultz W. carp.; S. 12; P. O. Scales Mound.

Shutz Wm. farmer; Sec. 20; P. O. Galena.

Seferd F. farmer; Sec. 35; P. O. Houghton.

Seegle M. farmer; Sec.3; P.O. Scales Mound.

Sincock Wm. farmer; renter; Sec. 8; P. O. Council Hill Station.

SINCOCK WILLIAM C. Farmer; Sec. 6; P. O. Council Hill Station; born in this Tp. June 1, 1852; came to this farm in 1862; was married to Elizabeth Bastian, Dec. 10, 1874; she was born in Guilford, Dec. 8, 1854; they have two children: Casper W., born Nov. 22, 1875, and Francis, June 2, 1877; Mr. S.'s mother resides on the old homestead, consisting of 145 acres; she was born in Cornwall, Eng., in 1830; married William G. Sincock, Jan. 31, 1851, who died July 6, 1872; they had eight children: Wm. C., David, Annie, Thomas A., Sarah G. and Henry G. are living; John H. died at the age of 10 years and Thomas A. at 2 years; family attend the M. E. Church.

Sinclair Wm. S. teacher; P. O. Galena.

SINGER HENRY, Farmer; Sec. 9; P. O. Scales Mound; born in Bavaria, Germany, May 11, 1814; came to this Co. in 1840; settled on the farm where they now reside; owns 158 acres of land; married Margaret Saam in 1842; she was born in Bavaria in 1812; they have four children: Mary, Simon, Margaret and Theresa; lost two: Caroline and John; Mr. S. was School Director eight years and Overseer of Highways four years; Simon was married Jan. 25, 1870, to Ernestine E. Elbarth; they have three children: Bertha, Charles W. and Clara C.; Simon was in Co. D, 8th I. V. C.; enlisted in Oct., 1864; was in Shenandoah Valley; was in several skirmishes; mustered out at Benton Barracks, Mo., in July, 1865; are members of German Catholic Church.

Singer S. farmer; rents; Sec. 9; P. O. Scales Mound.

Smith Wm. farm; Sec. 30; P.O. Galena.

Stiefel J. farm; Sec. 23; P.O. Scales Mound.

Struble Chris. laborer; Sec. 20; P.O. Galena.

Studear Fred. laborer; Sec. 29; P.O. Avery.

Studear Otto, Sec. 29; P.O. Avery.

TACTHIO FREDERICK, Sec. 1; P. O. Scales Mound.

Tatchio Simon, Jr., S. 1; P.O. Scales Mound.

TATCHIO SIMON, Farmer; Sec. 1; P. O. Scales Mound; born in Selkirk Settlement, Red River of the North, in 1823; came to Galena in 1826; went to Gratiot Grove, Wis., where they remained till 1835, when they came to this Tp.; owns 140 acres land; was Commissioner of Highways three years, School Director two terms; remembers many incidents connected with the Black Hawk War; was in old Fort Gratiot most of the time; married Christiana Casper in 1847; she was born in Switzerland in 1820; they have five children: Simon, Péter, Frederick, Emma and Christiana; Mrs. T. died June 16, 1857; family are Presbyterians.

TAYLOR JOHN W. (Deceased). Died at his home in Clay Co., Kas., Nov. 29, 1877, aged 79 years. The fact that this good and noble man was one of the earliest settlers of Jo Daviess Co., and was for many years a leading citizen and a member of the Board of Supervisors, renders his biography one of peculiar interest to our readers. John W. Taylor was born in Luzerne Co., Pa., in June, 1798. In 1819, when 21 years old, he started West, going to W. Va., then to Ohio and Ind. In the Spring of 1824 he settled in Sangamon Co., Ill., where he became acquainted with Miss Temperance Stringfield, and married her in March, 1825. In 1827 he moved to Galena, settling first at Pilot Knob, but living afterwards in that part of the city now known as Oldtown. In 1829 he moved to Guilford, six miles from Galena, where he resided until 1870, when he removed to Kas. Mr. Taylor was the first Supervisor ever elected from the Town of Guilford, and was eight times re-elected, filling the office till he refused to hold it longer. His wife died April 10, 1849, after which he went to Cal., where he remained two years, returning to his home and family in Guilford in 1852. His sons, Henry H. and John R. Taylor, having settled in Kas., Mr. Taylor followed them there in 1870, where he remained till the time of his death. The remains were brought to this Co. for interment, accompanied by his son, Henry H. Taylor, and his daughter, Mrs. S. K. Troxell. The funeral, which was largely attended, took place from the residence of his son-in-law, Mr. S. W. Hathaway, in the Town of Guilford, on Wednesday, Dec. 5, Rev. James Baume, of Galena, preaching the funeral sermon. This is but a hasty sketch of the life of one of the noblest and best of the early pioneers of Jo Daviess Co. John W. Taylor was a good man in the very best sense of that term. He lost no opportunity to visit and minister to the comforts of the sick and afflicted, and to aid the destitute. Although he never attended a medical college, he was skilled in medicine and surgery, having read much on these subjects to the end that he might relieve the distress of his fellow beings at times when a physician could not be procured. In several cases he reduced the fracture of bones with such skill that the patients speedily recovered, some of whom are now living, with sound limbs. For all these deeds of kindness he invariably refused to receive the slightest recompense. Notwithstanding his well known liberality he amassed a fortune, and was enabled to leave each of his six children a good farm. He finished his work and it was well done. A comparatively young man remarked in our presence on the day that the remains arrived in Galena, "If I had done as much good as John W. Taylor has done, I think I should be willing to die." Mr. Taylor left three sons: Obadiah Taylor, of Guilford; John R. Taylor, formerly Co. Commissioner of Clay Co., Kas., now a resident of Fla., and Henry H. Taylor, formerly Co. Treasurer of Clay Co., Kas., and now president of a bank at Clay Centre. Also three daughters: Mrs. S. W. Hathaway, of Guilford; Mrs. S. K. Troxell, of Kas., and Mrs. C. Shaw, of Cal.

TAYLOR OBADIAH, Farmer; Sec. 17; P. O. Galena; born in this Co. Nov. 7, 1831; owns 218 acres of land; married Evaline Neville, April 1, 1858; she died June 23, 1867; he was married again April 15, 1868, to Eda M. Metcalf; she was born in East Galena March 23, 1841; they have five children: Sophronia E., Wilbur H., Orville E., Eda L. and Estelle May; also an adopted child, Elmer E., son of Thomas S. Taylor, deceased. Mr. T. is a son of the late John W. Taylor, (whose portrait appears in this work), who was the first to build a cabin in Guilford, and among the first settlers of the Co.; they are members of the M. E. Church.

Taylor Oscar, farmer; Sec. 29; P.O. Galena.

THACHER ALFRED, Farmer; Sec. 21; P.O. Galena; born on Cape Cod, Mass., Oct. 27, 1813; came to this Co. in 1829; followed mining for about three years near Galena; was with Capt. Stone, of Elizabeth, during the Black Hawk War until near its close, after which time he was with old Capt. Gear; moved on this farm in 1844; owns 80 acres land; married Elizabeth Liverton in 1837; she was born in Ohio in 1819; they have nine children living: Sarah T., Eleanor H., Esther H., Arminda J., Harriet, Lucy A., Emily E., Sophronia L. and Charles A.; lost three: Clarinda N., Henry P. and Elvira R.; family belong to M. E. Church.

TOBIN JOHN T. Farmer; Sec. 17; P. O. Galena; born on this farm May 7, 1845; his father came here in 1840, and bought this farm, where he resided until the time of his death, Oct. 4, 1864; he was born in Ireland in 1798; his mother was born in Ireland in 1812; she resides here with her son; he owns 170 acres of land; has one sister, Mary Ann, born July 10, 1847; she was married March 1, 1876, to John McKernan; live in Vinegar Hill Tp.; all members of the Catholic Church.

Trevarthen Frank, with his father; Sec. 6; P. O. Council Hill Station.

Trevarthen Thos. Sec. 6; P. O. Council Hill Station.

TREVARTHEN WM. Farmer; Sec. 6; P. O. Council Hill Station; born in Cornwall, England, Jan. 2, 1813; came to this Co. in 1842; came to this farm in 1850; owns 272 acres land; was married in 1837 to Jane Bastian; she was born in Cornwall in 1816; they have eight children living: Mary, John, Thomas, Philip J., Frank, Joseph, Lizzie and Wm. H.; Henry was drowned in the Platte River, near Fort Laramie, in 1864, while *en route* to Idaho; are members of the M. E. Church.

Trudgian C. farmer; Sec. 7; P. O. Galena.

TRUDGIAN MRS. MARY T. Farming; Sec. 7; P. O. Galena; born in Cornwall, England, May 23, 1825; Widow of Joseph Trudgian, who died June 3, 1857, aged 48 years; they were married in Cornwall, England, Dec. 25, 1845; came to this Co. in 1854: owns 160 acres land; she has five children living: Joseph Nicholas, Samuel, Thomas and Charles; Mr. T. had two by a former marriage: Eliza (now Mrs. Tressider, of Scales Mound), and William (who was in the army); he died in the hospital at Nashville, Tenn., in 1864; family belong to the M. E. Church.

Trudgian S. farmer; Sec. 7; P. O. Galena.

Trudgian T. farmer; Sec. 7; P. O. Galena.

Tyne M., Jr., farmer; Sec. 13; P. O. Scales Mound.

VARING FRANCIS, Farmer; Sec. 2; P. O. Scales Mound; born in Selkirk Settlement, Red River of the North; came to Galena in 1828; went from there to Schullsburg (Gratiot Grove), Wis., where they remained till 1843; came here and took up as a claim the farm he now lives on, and bought it when in market, in 1847; can remember many incidents connected with the Black Hawk War—Indian scares, etc.; married Sarah Derocher; she was born in Canada; they have ten children: Selina, Louisa, Joseph, Frank, Henry, Alice, Sarah, Willie, Clara and Louis; has held the offices of Assessor, Collector, Town Clerk and Justice of the Peace; belong to the Catholic Church.

WACHTER HENRY, Farmer; Sec. 20; P. O. Galena; born in Switzerland in 1824; came to this Co. in 1856; lived in Galena two years; married Mary A. Kiener in Feb. 1858; she was born in Lancaster Co., Pa., in 1840; they moved to this farm in 1871; owns 83 acres land; have ten children: Lavina, Caroline, Louisa, Julia, Annie, Mary, Lizzie, Willie, Christian and John; family belong to the Lutheran Church.

Weber Jacob, laborer; Sec. 19; P.O. Galena.

Weber John, farmer; Sec. 19; P. O. Galena.

Weber Mat. farmer; Sec. 21; P. O. Galena.

Wien A. farm; Sec. 25; P. O. Scales Mound.

Wein Frank, with his father; Sec. 25; P. O. Scales Mound.

Willard Francis, farmer; Sec. 13; P. O. Scales Mound.

Willard Henry, farmer; Sec. 13; P.O. Scales Mound.

Willson Edw. farmer; Sec. 4; P. O. Scales Mound.

Winter H. farm; Sec. 9; P.O. Scales Mound.

Wise Anton, farmer; Sec. 7; P. O. Galena.

Wise John, farmer; Sec. 7; P. O. Galena.

Wise Jos. farmer; Sec. 7; P. O. Galena.

ZIMMERMAN HENRY, renter; Sec. 9; P. O. Scales Mound.

Zawar Jos., Jr. farm; Sec. 12; P. O. Scales Mound.

ZAWAR MRS. MARY, Farming; Sec. 12; P. O. Scales Mound; born in Germany Feb. 24, 1807; Widow; maiden name was Baker; was married in 1836 to Joseph Zawar; he was born in Germany Dec. 27, 1803; died June 20, 1877, aged 73 years, 6 months and 7 days; she owns 230 acres land; has eight children living: Lizzie, Peter, Barbara, Mary, Lena, Caroline, Katie and Joseph; lost one, Maggie; she died in 1859; Joseph Zawar, Jr., was married May 24, 1877, to Emma Casper; she was born in this Co. May 22, 1857.

DUNLEITH TOWNSHIP.

ADELMAN ANDREW, employe I. C. R. R.; Dunleith.

ADAMS H. Watchman on D. & D. R. R. Bridge; Dunleith; born in N. H. March 2, 1825; resided in this Co. since 1851 except eight years spent in Dubuque, Ia.; married Artimesha Davis, from Ky., in 1854; has been employed by Bridge Co. six years.

Adkins A. carpenter; Dunleith.

Allenan Henry, night watch for I. C. R. R. Co.; Dunleith.

Allinson Wm. brakeman I.C.R.R.; Dunleith.

Alleway Patrick, railroad laborer; Dunleith.

Apfeld Chas. harness maker; Dunleith.

APFELD HUGO, Harness Maker; Dunleith; born in Prussia Feb. 14, 1841; came to this country in 1852; enlisted in Co. D, 27th Regt. Ia. V. I. Aug. 16, 1862; mustered out Aug. 8, 1865; was engaged in capture of Little Rock, Ark., and eight other severe engagements, under A. J. Smith, 16th Army Corps; married Caroline Boller, of Guttenburg, Ia., Sept. 16, 1866; have two children, Edward and Sophia; held office of City Treasurer 1872, Town Clerk two years.

ARMSTRONG ALEXANDER, Molder; Dunleith; born in Galena Feb. 15, 1846; came to Dunleith in 1856; married Margaret Shalfo, from Minn., in 1865; have one child, Charles; has been engaged with C. S. & S. Burt for the past ten years.

Armstrong Jno. day laborer; Dunleith.

Armstrong Wm. H. day laborer; Dunleith.

Ash Frank, day laborer; Dunleith.

Ashley Samuel, lumberman; Dunleith.

BAILEY BOUTON, railroad hand; Dunleith.

Bean Wm. laborer; Dunleith.

Beaty John, laborer; Dunleith.

Beck Gottleib, mechanical engineer in Burt's Factory; Dunleith.

Bergman M. H. carpenter; Dunleith.

Beyer A. laborer; Dunleith.

Bishop J. farmer; Sec. 20; P. O. Dunleith.

Black Geo. railroad hand; Dunleith.

Brady John, laborer; Dunleith.

Braustteter J. S. freight conductor; Dunleith.

Breason Peter, teamster; Dunleith.

Brula Anthony, charge of tunnel at Dunleith.

BUCKLEY JOHN, Baggage Agent Ia. Div. I. C. R. R.; Dunleith; born in Susquehanna Co., Pa., July 4, 1832; came to this Co. in May, 1855; has been in the employ of the I. C. R. R. 23 years; crossed the new bridge on the first train from Dunleith to Dubuque and took charge of the Baggage Department of the Iowa Division; married Catharine McMannus, of Galena, July 5, 1857; have ten children: James H., John B., Annie C., Daniel, William L., Charles J., Martin H., Bertha K., Henry L. and one not yet named; lost two; held office of Alderman two years, Mayor three years, member School Board for the past eight years.

Burhyte Chas. teamster; Dunleith.

Burhyte Jacob, miner; Dunleith.

Burns M. watchman on ferry boat; Dunleith.

BURT CHARLES S. Manufacturer of Shingle Machines and Agricultural Implements, Third St., Dunleith; born in Grant Co., Wis., in 1838; came to Dunleith in May, 1856; married Mariana Blanchard, of Concord, N. H., in Sept., 1861; have three children living: Angelo R., Frank A. and Claudine B.; lost one, Florence; held the office of Alderman several terms; holds the office of County Supervisor at this time.

BURT DANIEL R. Retired; P. O. Dunleith; born in Florida, Montgomery Co., N. Y., Feb. 29, 1804; moved to Canada West in April, 1826; moved to Mich. in 1830; married Miss Ashley, of Clermont, N. H., in 1831; located in Grant Co., Wis., in 1835, where he purchased 3,000 acres of land; in 1841 he was elected to the Territorial Legislature of Wis. and served four years; settled in Dunleith in 1856, since which time he has been extensively engaged in the manufacture of agricultural implements, smut machines, etc., together with his farming; two children, Charles S. and Roccy M.; wife died Sept. 19, 1864; married present wife, Mrs. Mary J. Enor, Jan. 16, 1866; his son, Charles S., and brother, Silas, carry on the manufactory.

BURT SILAS Manufacturer Shingle Machine and Farm Implements; Dunleith; born in Montgomery Co., N. Y.; came to Jo Daviess Co. in 1857; married Harriet Preston, of N. Y.; had two children, Charles S., Hattie M.; held office of Town Trustee 3 years, and School Director 5 years.

CALKINS HENRY G. conductor; Dunleith.

Campbell Augustus, physician; Dunleith.

CAVERLY H. P. Assistant Principal in High School; born in Strafford, N. H., May 10, 1839; married Lizzie M. Anderson, of Hanover, Ill., Nov. 21, 1861; had six children: May L., Allin B., Cora E., Clarence C.; two died in infancy; came to this Co. in 1861; held office of Town

Clerk, Hanover, 3 years; City Clerk, Dunlieth, this term; enlisted in Co. A, 15th Regt., I. V. I., Feb. 24, 1865; mustered out Sept. 16, 1865.

Chapman Ed., watchman on bridge; Dunleith.

CHAPMAN J. B. Painter; Dunleith; born in England, Oct. 14, 1826; emigrated to Ill., in 1848; settled in Jo Daviess Co. in 1856; married Betsey Winsor, from England, 1848; had thirteen children; three are dead.

Children A. G. machinist; Dunleith.

Children Edwin, manufacturer; Dunleith.

Chouteaw F. D. miner; Dunleith.

Clark Warren, laborer; Dunleith.

Clark Wm. J. fireman; Dunleith.

CLISE JOHN D. Postmaster and Hotel keeper; Dunleith; born in Virginia, 1833; came to Jo Daviess Co., 1836; settled in Dunleith in 1852; Married Amanda Williams, of Pike Co., Mo.; had three children: Josephine, Lucy and Cora; held the office of Postmaster 17 years; hotel keeper the past 8 years; held office of City Marshal 6 years and City Treasurer 2 years.

Cludry Edward, farmer; P. O. Dunleith.

Coyle F. farmer; Sec. 21; P. O. Dunleith.

Coyle John, laborer; Dunleith.

Coyle Thomas, ice dealer; Dunleith.

Cole Clinton, barber; Dunleith.

CONSALUS JOSEPH E. Freight Conductor I. C. R. R.; Dunleith; born in New York, Feb. 22, 1841; came to Nora, this Co., in 1856; to Galena in 1858; settled in Dunleith in 1867; married Lettie Beall, Galena, Dec. 5, 1866; had four children: Stella M., Wm. A., Celena B., and Joseph (deceased); enlisted in Co. A, 96th Regt. I. V. I., Aug., 1862; mustered out June, 1865; engaged in twenty-one hard-fought battles.

Conrad Chas. carpenter; Dunleith.

Creighton John, M.D.; Dunleith.

Crocket David, machinist; Dunleith.

Crocket Frank, laborer; Dunleith.

Cullen Edward, laborer; Dunleith.

Cullen Thomas, laborer; Dunleith.

Culton D. trackman, I. C. R. R.; Dunleith.

Culton D. J. fireman I. C. R. R.; Dunleith.

Curchill S. M. contractor; Dunleith.

DANES HENRY A. constable; Dunleith.

Dames Theophilus, Sr., street commissioner; Dunleith.

Dames T., Jr., molder; Dunleith.

Dangelmyer J. laborer, I.C. R. R.; Dunleith.

Donoghue Daniel, laborer; Dunleith.

Damuth John, carpenter; Dunleith.

Davis Samuel, laborer; Dunleith.

Dickman Chas. farmer; Sec. 21; P. O. Dunleith.

DISCH THEODORE, Mechanic; Dunleith; born in Germany, Sept. 9, 1849; came to this country in 1853; settled in Dunleith in 1856; married Elizabeth Pegel, in Dubuque, Iowa, in 1871; had two children, Emma and George; Emma died Oct. 16, 1873; have been in employ Dubuque Novelty Iron Works six years.

Disch Xavier, stone mason; Dunleith.

Ditmore J. track hand, I. C. R. R.; Dunleith.

Doggett J. M. insurance agent; Dunleith.

Dugan J. H. night watch I. C. R. R.; Dunleith.

Duncan Samuel, laborer; Dunleith.

EAGLEPOF THEO. farmer; Sec. 20; P. O. Dunleith.

Eberley P. farmer; Sec. 21; P. O. Dunleith.

Eckert Ernest, laborer; Dunleith.

Evans Sidney M. freight conductor I. C. R. R.; Dunleith.

FAIRFAX ALBERT, freight conductor I. C. R. R.; Dunleith.

Fairfax Andrew J. freight conductor I. C. R. R.; Dunleith.

Fairfax S. conductor I. C. R. R.; Dunleith.

Fargo G. H. express agent; Dunleith.

Farnam James, merchant; Dunleith.

Fogerty D. laborer; Dunleith.

Foltz Benj. B. laborer; Dunleith.

FOLTZ DAVID B. Farmer; Sec. 21; P. O. Dunleith; born in Onondaga Co., N. Y., Nov. 14, 1813; came to this Co. in 1868; married Mary Hoagh in Montgomery Co., N. Y., in 1835; had seven children: Frederick C., Albert, Richard D., Ransom B., Mary M., David B., Willie G., Richard (died with fever in the army, Sept. 18, 1861); Frederick D. was in the 3d Regt. W. V. I.; Ransom B. was in the 25th Regt. W. V. I.; David B. enlisted 44th Regt. W. V. I. Feb. 11, 1865; mustered out Aug. 28, 1865.

FOX CALVIN P. Foreman in Factory of C. S. & S. Burt & Co., Dunleith; born in New York Sept. 4, 1817; moved to Ill. in 1834; resided in Galena until 1843; settled in Dunleith in 1860; married Asenath Tyler in Pa.; had twelve children, five living; has held the position of foreman in this shop for ten years; Superintendent Public Schools three years.

Fox John, laborer; Dunleith.

FRENTRESS HENRY N. Farmer; Secs. 3, 32, 33, and 34; P. O. Dunleith; has charge of the Frentress Estate; was born on said estate Sept. 22, 1842; married to Mary J. Bidlock, Carroll Co., Ill., in 1868; had one child, Lois M.; he is the patentee of the Frentress Barbed Wire now being manufactured at Dunleith.

C. S. BURT.

DUNLEITH

FRENTRESS MRS. D. Farmer; Secs. 3, 32, 33 and 34; P. O. Dunleith; born in Vermont, Oct. 22, 1807; owns an estate of 1,100 acres of land; married to E. Frentress, Dec. 25, 1823; Mr. Frentress was born in North Carolina in 1800; they came to this Co. in 1827 and pre-empted portions of Sections 3, 32, 33 and 34; had thirteen children, six living; Mr. Frentress died in Dec., 1853; during the Black Hawk War he enlisted and went to guard Galena; he built the first house between Galena and Dunleith, and drove the first team from Galena to Dunleith.

Fustinger S. laborer; Dunleith.

GAINES CHAS. J. laborer; Dunleith.

Garnich James, gardener; Dunleith.

Gertenbach H. renter; S. 23; P. O. Dunleith.

Gibbs A. H. insurance agent; Dunleith.

Gillman Moses, laborer; Dunleith.

Glan Albert, fireman I. C. R. R.; Dunleith.

Gregoire Felix, farmer; P. O. Dunleith.

Groff John A. laborer; Dunleith.

Groff Lewis, saloon; Dunleith.

Groff Mich. laborer; Dunleith.

HALE PETER, retired; Dunleith.

Hall Ed. car cleaner I. C. R. R.; Dunleith.

Hall Ed. laborer I. C. R. R.; Dunleith.

Hall H. switchman I. C. R. R.; Dunleith.

Harney Harrison, laborer; Dunleith.

Harris Edward, laborer; Dunleith.

Hass Frank, blacksmith; Dunleith.

Haubt John, butcher; Dunleith.

Herold Henry B. carpenter; Dunleith.

Hill James, laborer; Dunleith

Hilliard J. farmer; Sec. 21; P. O. Dunleith.

Hilliard P. farmer; Sec. 21; P. O. Dunleith.

Holmes Henry, laborer; Dunleith.

Holmes Richard, drayman; Dunleith.

Honorback Jno, shoemaker; Dunleith.

Hutter August, laborer.

Hynes T. farmer; Sec. 21; P. O. Dunleith.

INGERSOLL DANIEL F. miner; Dunleith.

Ingersol Geo. freight conductor I. C. R. R; Dunleith.

Ingram Adam, saloon; Dunleith.

JEARDOE RICHARD, freight conductor I. C. R. R.; Dunleith.

Johnson Alvin, watchman on R. R. bridge; Dunleith.

Johnson Levi J. watchman on R. R. bridge; Dunleith.

Jones Sidney, laborer; Dunleith.

Jungbluth Philip, laborer; Dunleith.

KASS MATTHIAS, blacksmith; Dunleith.

Keane John, shoemaker; Dunleith.

KEEPINGS CHARLES, Brakeman on I. C. R. R.; Dunleith; born in Gloucestershire, England, April 2, 1836; came to this country in 1849; moved to Dubuque, Iowa, same year; settled in Dunleith in 1855; he was engaged with the Transfer Company nine years; spent 1861 and 1862 in mining in Idaho; was married to Miss Mary H. Whatmore in 1863; she died in 1874; was married to Miss Maria Burrows in 1874.

Kelly A. farmer; Sec. 21; P. O. Dunleith.

Kelly D. farmer; Sec. 21; P. O. Dunleith.

Kelly M. watchman I. C. R. R.; Dunleith.

Kennedy Thos. moulder; Dunleith,

Keonig John, saloon; Dunleith.

Kinslow James, laborer; Dunleith.

Kusse Jos. farmer; Sec. 21; P. O. Dunleith.

Kuch Jacob, laborer; Dunleith.

LAHEY WILLIAM, laborer; Dunleith.

LARKIN JAMES, Brakeman I. C. R. R.; Dunleith; born in Mass., Aug. 20, 1851; came to Galena in 1855; settled in Dunleith in 1865; married on Oct. 12, 1873, to Louise C. Rapp, of Dunleith; they had one child, Geo. T., born Dec. 30, 1874; been in employ I. C. R. R. 7 years.

Larkins Peter F. brakeman I. C. R. R.; Dunleith.

Laporte Lewis, Sr., Dunleith.

Laporte L., Jr., engineer on river; Dunleith.

Lavbly Wm. engineer I C. R. R. Dunleith.

Lacount Denis, laborer; Dunleith.

Lawler M., I. C. R. R. watchman; Dunleith.

Lenville Moses, laborer; Dunleith.

Lithuner Jas. clerk; Dunleith.

Letch Peter, wagon maker; Dunleith.

Lobstein Geo. carpenter; Dunleith.

Loeffler Chas. confectioner; Dunleith.

Ludwig Henry, clerk; Dunleith.

Lumley J. brakeman I. C. R. R; Dunleith.

Lutters Henry, laborer; Dunleith.

Lutters L. farmer; Sec. 27; P. O. Dunleith.

Lynch John, laborer; Dunleith.

Lynch Wm. employe I. C. R. R.; Dunleith.

McGEE JOHN, laborer; Dunleith.

McGuire Phil, section foreman I. C. R. R.; Dunleith.

MAGUIRE T. & J. Merchants; Dunleith, Ill.; members of firm are Thomas and John Maguire; they keep a general store and deal in all kinds of farmers' produce; commenced business in 1868; Joseph Leithner has been their faithful clerk for eight years; Thomas Maguire was born Aug. 22, 1839, in the Parish of Mullanghdun, Co. Fermanagh, Ireland, near Enniskillen; came to this country, and to this Co. in 1852; followed farming 5 years, taught school 11 years; graduated at Bryant & Stratton's College, Chicago, in 1866; held the office Town Clerk, Menominee Tp., 1 year, School Trustee 3 years, School Treasurer since 1863; served as Supervisor of Dunleith Tp. 6 years, and Mayor of Dunleith 3 years, in 1872-'73-'77; married, Nov. 4, 1868, to Miss Ellen J. Groff, of Dunleith, born Feb. 24, 1852, at Racine, Wis.; have four children: John E., born June 1, 1870; Thomas F., May 19, 1872; James O., March 23, 1874, and Henry C., Sept. 29, 1876. John Maguire was born Oct. 22, 1841, in Parish of Mullanghdun, Ireland; came to this country and to this Co. in 1850; pursued farming 15 years; spent the year 1863 in Pike's Peak, Col.; held the office of School Director 3 years, in Elizabeth Tp., School Trustee 3 years, in Dunleith, and Alderman in 1875-'76; is unmarried. Their parents' names are John Maguire and Elizabeth Cassidy, whose children are Mary, Thomas, John, Francis, James, Philip, and Henry, living, and Hugh, Margaret, Andrew, and Daniel, dead. In religion the brothers are Catholic; in politics, Democratic; they own 521 acres of land, besides their store, lots and other buildings in Dunleith; they are successful in business, and are closely identified with the interests of the city and county.

MacKnight Daniel, laborer; Dunleith.

McNulty, Edw. laborer; Dunleith.

Magbee Alex, saloon; Dunleith.

Mahoney Michael, farmer; Sec. 20; P. O. Dunleith.

Mahoney Timothy, laborer; Dunleith.

Maire Michael, laborer; Dunleith.

Martin Martinus, laborer; Dunleith.

Marshall Nicholas, blacksmith; Dunleith.

Maurer Albert, farm; Sec. 21; P.O.Dunleith.

Mayhew Mitchell, farmer; Sec. 21; P. O. Dunleith.

Medley Hiram, laborer; Dunleith.

Mechlet Jno. farm; Sec. 21; P. O. Dunleith.

Merry Chas. H. retired; Dunleith.

Mertess John, laborer; Dunleith.

Mertess Peter, clerk; Dunleith.

Meyer Chas. township clerk: Dunleith.

Michelle Antoine, laborer; Dunleith.

Miller J. M. farm; Sec. 34; P. O. Dunleith.

Milliner Geo. retired; Dunleith.

Moody A. H. hardware merchant; Dunleith.

Mortimer Frank, freight conductor I. C. R. R.; Dunleith

Moste Geo. carpenter; Dunleith.

MORGAN EDWARD, Engineer on Dubuque & Dunleith R. R. Bridge; Dunleith; born in Toronto, Can., Aug. 8, 1827; married to Harriet Welsh, Rochester, N. Y., 1859; employed on the Mississippi River until 1863; enlisted in Co. F, First Illinois Battery, in 1864; he took his present position Dec. 22, 1868.

Monton Nicholas P. clerk; Dunleith.

Muldowney Jas. stone mason; Dunleith.

Murray Jas., Sr., laborer; Dunleith.

Murray Jas., Jr., laborer; Dunleith.

Murray Thos. laborer; Dunleith.

Murray Wm. laborer; Dunleith.

Murphy John, teamster; Dunleith.

NELSON GEO. carpenter; Dunleith.

Newton Sherman, watchman; Dunleith.

Nugant Dennis, stonemason; Dunleith.

O'DONAGHUE DAN, laborer; Dunleith.

O'Neill Michael, lab. I. C. R. R.; Dunleith.

ODELL RICHARD E. Manufacturer shingle machines and agricultural implements; Dunleith; born in Conway, N. H., Dec. 24, 1817; came to Jo. Daviess Co. in 1855; married Mary E. Marshall, of Ross Co., Ohio, 1856; had four children: Lucie M., Carrie A., Arthur M., Elsie May; Elsie May died in 1868.

OLINGER JOHN, Merchant, Wis. ave.; Dunleith; born in Luxembourg, Prussia; emigrated to this country in 1853; settled in Jo Daviess Co. in 1854; has been in business since 1861; held the office of alderman one term, city treasurer one term; elected mayor three years.

Oster Henry, saloon keeper; Dunleith.

Oster John, farmer, Sec. 22; P. O. Dunleith.

PAUL EDWIN R., steamboat clerk; Dunleith.

Payton Decatur, miner; Dunleith.

Pierce D. O. carpenter; Dunleith.

Pierson Rob't F. lab. mach. shop; Dunleith.

Pinnel Peter, farmer; Sec. 22; P.O. Dunleith.

Platt Merrit, farmer; Sec. 20; P. O. Dunleith.

Platt Sterns, farmer; Sec. 28; P.O. Dunleith.

Powell W. W. engineer I. C. R.R.; Dunleith.

QUINN JOHN, laborer; Dunleith.

Quinn John, laborer; Dunleith.

Quinlan James, laborer; Dunleith.

Quinlan John, brakeman; Dunleith.

QUINLAN THOS. Freight Conductor Ia. Div. I. C. R. R.; P. O. Dunleith; born in Troy, N. Y., Dec. 4, 1849; came to Dunleith, 1856; stonecutter by trade; has been in employ of I. C. R. R. five years;

married Margaret Francis, Lena, Ill., May 1, 1871.

Quinlan Wm. laborer; Dunleith.

Quinlan Wm. E. brakeman I. C. R. R.; Dunleith.

QUIRK JOHN, Freight Conductor I. C. R. R., Ia. Div.; P. O. Dunleith; born in Ireland Feb. 1, 1835; came to this country June, 1850; came to Galena in 1852; settled in Dunleith 1855; married May 5, 1868, to Bridget Boyce, of Galena; had six children: Dennis, James W., John T., William F., and Lizzie, and one not named; three dead; has been in the employ of I. C. R. R. twenty-five years.

Quirk Philip, janitor High School; Dunleith.

RAPP GEO. butcher; Dunleith.

Reese Herbert, gardener; Sec. 21; P. O. Galena.

Rembold Fred. saloon keeper; Dunleith.

Rewell Geo. B. cigar maker; Dunleith.

Rewell John, cigar maker; Dunleith.

Rice Oliver, farmer; Sec. 20; P.O. Dunleith.

Richardson J. H. laborer; Dunleith.

Ropps Wm. fireman I. C. R. R.; Dunleith.

Rose Alonzo, merchant; Dunleith.

Roth Valentine, farmer; P. O. Dunleith.

Ryan John, laborer; Dunleith.

Ryan John S. engineer I. C. R. R.; Dunleith.

Ryan John S., trackman I. C. R. R.; Dunleith.

Ryan Thomas, laborer; Dunleith.

Ryder H. G. steamboat pilot; Dunleith.

SAUCE NICHOLAS, farmer; Sec. 15; P. O. Dunleith.

Schleuker Jno. M. lumber office; Dunleith.

Schroeder John, laborer; Dunleith.

Sixmith John, laborer; Dunleith.

Shower Henry, blacksmith; Dunleith.

Shumacher H. clerk lumber yard; Dunleith.

Slater James, carpenter; Dunleith.

Smith Andrew, retired; Dunleith.

Smith Daniel, farmer; P. O. Dunleith.

Smith E. brakeman I. C. R. R.; Dunleith.

SMITH GEORGE B. Master Mechanic, Car Dept., I. C. R. R.; Dunleith; born in Fairfield, Conn., April 11, 1814; came to Ill. in 1854; settled in Dunleith in 1855; married to Sarah Sherman, from Conn., July 2, 1835; had four children; Abbie J., Julius M., Mary F., and Ada S.; he built the first house on the Bluff in 1855; have been in the employ of the I. C. R. R. 22 years.

Smith H. farmer; Sec. 21; P. O. Dunleith.

Smith Peter, carpenter; Dunleith.

Standridge Jas. laborer; Dunleith.

STAUDENMYER JOHN, Merchant and Justice of the Peace; Dunleith; born in Germany May 2, 1826; came to Jo Daviess Co. in 1854; settled in Galena until 1856; moved to Dunleith May 20, 1856; married to Louisa Raisser, from Germany, in 1848; had six children, two dead; enlisted in the 2d Regt. Ill. Art. Co. A, Dec. 22, 1862; mustered out July 27, 1865; elected Alderman in 1866; elected Justice of the Peace in 1868; is a member of the Grand Army of the Republic.

STEVENSON ALBERT R. Proprietor Livery and Boarding Stable, opposite I. C. R. R. depot; Dunleith; born in Delaware Co., N. Y., Oct. 20, 1850; came to Dubuque, Iowa, in 1860; settled in Dunleith in 1875; married in 1870 to Miss Amelia C. McCormic, Grant Co., Wis.; had two children, Willard and Cora.

Stewart Marvin, yardmaster; Dunleith.

Stubenhaver Geo. laborer; Dunleith.

Stubenhaver John, cigar Dunleith.

Sutter Chris. hotel and livery; Dunleith.

Sutter Robert, liveryman; Dunleith.

SWITZER A. Dunleith; was born Feb. 16, 1821, near Hesse Cassel, in Germany, and came with his parents to the United States in 1832, landing at Baltimore Oct. 23, where the family remained one year, when they removed to Harrisburg, Penn., thence a year later to St. Louis; was here engaged in the Dry Goods business until 1842; was married Feb. 17, 1842, and the same year his store and entire personal property were destroyed by fire; he then went to Galena, where he arrived Nov. 13, and again started in business, continuing till 1854, when, with the proceeds of his successful business, he purchased a farm in Menominee Tp., whence he moved on account of the poor health of his wife; in 1860 he went to Dunleith and once more opened a general merchandise store; his wife died in 1872, aged 72 years, and in 1873 he was married again; was School Director in Galena one year; was the first Mayor of Dunleith, and has been re-elected many times since, besides filling many other offices both in Dunleith and Menominee; was very active in the enrollment of soldiers during the war, raising and disbursing bounties, etc., etc.; was instrumental in causing the government to make a new quota assignment, as the original was entirely disproportionate; has been identified with most of the interests of a public nature in Dunleith and Menominee, and has always exhibited a zeal in carrying out their details which has placed him in the front rank among the public spirited citizens of those places.

THAYER WM. conductor I. C. R. R.; Dunleith.

Thielen Anthony, saloon keeper; Dunleith.

Thill Chris. saloon keeper; Dunleith.

Thill Harry, with father; Sec. 27; P. O. Dunleith.

Thill N. farmer; Sec. 27; P.O. Dunleith.

Thompson G. H. eng. I. C. R. R.; Dunleith.

Tobin Michael, laborer; Dunleith.

Tulley J. engineer I. C. R. R.; Dunleith.

Tulley Pat. engineer I. C. R. R.; Dunleith.

Turner Chas. farm; Sec. 20; P. O. Dunleith.

Tyler A. H. farmer; Sec. 16; P. O. Dunleith.

VOGHT FRANK, farmer; Sec. 22; P. O. Dunleith.

WADDINGTON WILL, Freight Conductor I. C. R. R.; P. O. Dunleith; born in England, April 3, 1843; came to this country in 1850; came to this Co. in 1854; married Elsie Consolus, of Galena, in 1865; had five children: Bessie, Sarah H., Herbert A., Una M., Will H.; Bessie died; have been in the employ of the I. C. R. R. 16 years; his father is one of the oldest employes of the I. C. R. R. Co.

Waggoner J. farm; Sec. 21; P.O. Dunleith.

Walter J. farmer; Sec. 27; P.O. Dunleith.

Warden Benj. F. stonemason; Dunleith.

Webber Gotleib, machinist; Dunleith.

Webber Joseph, mechanic; Dunleith.

Webber Robert, laborer; Dunleith.

Weise Mathias, laborer; Dunleith.

Weuncher Wm. teamster; Dunleith.

Whatmore J. clerk I. C. R. R.; Dunleith.

Whalen John, laborer; Dunleith.

Whatmore James, R. R. clerk I. C. R. R.; Dunleith.

Wilson Augustus, laborer; Dunleith.

WILSON DAVID B. Freight Conductor I. C. R. R.; Dunleith; born in Potter's Mills, Centre Co., Pa., Nov. 7, 1836; came to Galena in 1846; settled in Dunleith in 1862; married to Margaret McKnight, of Galena, in 1866; had two children, Jessie May and Homer M.; enlisted in Co. K, 11th Regt. I. V. I., 1864; mustered out in 1865; have been in employ I. C. R. R. 17 years.

YOUNG CHAS. conductor; I. C. R. R.; Dunleith.

RUSH TOWNSHIP.

ARNOLD ADAM, farmer; Sec. 7; P. O. Warren.

Arnold E., farmer; Sec. 9; P. O. Warren.

Arnold F. farmer; Sec. 22; P. O. Greenvale.

Arnold H. farmer; Sec. 22; P. O. Greenvale.

Arnold J. farmer; Sec. 14; P. O. Greenvale.

Arnold L. farmer; Sec. 14; P. O. Warren.

Arnold S. farmer; Sec. 22; P. O. Greenvale.

Arnold Wm. A. farm; Sec. 15; P. O. Warren.

BACKUS J. C.

BACKUS E. M. Farmer; Sec. 34; P. O. Rush; owns 160 acres of land; was born in Erie Co., Penn., on the 20th Dec., 1837; moved from there to this Co. with his parents in the year of 1843; during the war of the Rebellion he enlisted in Co. F, 17th Regt. I. V. C.; served until March, '65, and was honorably discharged from the service; he has represented this Tp. in the County Board two terms, and at present holds the office of Justice of the Peace, and has held the office of Collector and Assessor of taxes; on the 15th of Feb., 1860, he married Miss L. S. Townsend at this place; she was born in Allegany Co., N. Y.; on 28th Aug., 1830; they have had eight children, viz.: Elfreda, born Dec. 1, '60, died Jan. 8, '63; Ruth, Aug. 2, '62; Charlie M., Aug. 30, '64, died Feb. 4, '72; Olive, Aug. 8, '67, died Feb. 16, '68; Lorretta G., April 23, '69; Lucia M., Nov. 18, '71; Wendell P., May 31, '74; Eugene Miner, Sept. 3, '76.

BACKUS J. G. Farmer; Sec. 34; P. O. Pitcherville; owns 142 acres of land; was born near Galena, in this Co., on Dec. 8, 1846; moved from there to this Tp. with his parents in the year of '49, and since then it has been his home; holds the office of constable at present; on the 8th of April, 1872, he married Lavina H. Renwick in this Tp. (Rush); she was born in this Tp. on the 3d of August, 1849; they have two children, viz: John R., born Feb. 27, 1873; Joseph F., Jan. 1, 1875.

BACKUS MRS. MARGARET, (maiden name Magaret Graham), Farming; Sec. 35; P. O. Pitcherville; owns 80 acres of land; she was born in Erie Co., Penn., on April 28, 1816; was married to Joseph Backus in that Co. on Sept 10, '35; he was born in Erie Co., Penn., on July 15, 1808; they moved to this Co. in the year of 1843, and settled near Galena, remaining there until 1849, when they came to this Tp.; Mr. Backus was a zealous member of the M. E. Church, in which church he was class leader and recording steward a number of years; he also held various Tp. and school offices in this place until the time of his death, which occurred at his residence, in this Tp., on June 15, 1877; they have six children, viz.: Wm. Nelson, born June, 1836; Ebenezer M., Dec. 20, 1837; Mary, April 8, 1839; James G., Dec. 8, 1846; Annie W., Feb. 5, 1854; Jay C., Nov. 5, 1855.

Baker W. physician; Sec. 20; P. O. Warren.

BALDWIN WESLEY, Farmer; Sec. 35; P. O. Greenvale; owns 163 acres of land; was born in Chenango Co., N. Y., on July 19, 1863; came to this Co. in 1856; married Miss Helen Coon, in this Tp., in 1861; she was born in Crawford Co., Ohio, in 1846; they have two children, viz.: Mary Melinda, born in the Town of Nora, this Co., in 1863; Nellie, in 1870.

BARRETT CHARLES, Farmer; Sec. 15; P. O. Warren; owns 60 acres of land; was born in Jefferson Co., N. Y., on April 25, 1836; went from there to Green Co., Wis., in 1854, in which place he was married to Almine Corsaw; she was born in Green Co., Wis., in Aug., 1839; she died in March, 1858; present wife was Julia C. Wolcott; they were married in Woodbine, this Co., on Jan. 22, 1864; she was born in this Co. Oct. 23, 1847; they have seven children, viz.: Mary E., born Nov. 25, 1864; Clara E., Feb. 26, 1866; Chas. Henry, Oct. 8, 1867; Laura E., Aug. 2, 1869; Bertha E., Sept. 2, 1871; Norman G., Sept. 18, 1873; Eliza, Jan. 11, 1876; during the War of the Rebellion Mr. Barrett enlisted in Co. A, 96 Regt. I. V. I; he was honorably discharged; his father, Nial Barrett, was a native of Vermont, in which place he married Ruth Coon; they moved from there to Berien Co., Michigan, in which place they have since resided.

Bates C. A. farmer; Sec. 23; P.O. Greenvale.

Bates J. H. farmer; Sec. 23; P.O. Greenvale.

BATTY ELIJAH H. Farmer; Sec. 28; P. O. Rush; owns 74 acres of land; was born at Council Hill, in this Co., on the 23d of Oct., 1853; married Miss Abbie Watts, at Hanover, in this Co., on the 25th of Jan., 1876; she was born in this Co. on the 20th of Dec., in the year 1858; they have one child, James Arthur, born in this Tp. on the 10th of July, 1877.

BATTY JOHN, Farmer; Sec. 28; P. O. Rush; owns 264 acres of land; was born at Council Hill, in this Co., June 10, 1843; married Miss Susan Spires, in this town, July 3, 1861; she was born in Iowa, she moved to this Co. with her parents when a child; they have two children: Frederick C., born April 6, 1871; Dewey, July 10, 1876.

Beacock George, farmer; Sec. 7; P. O. Apple River.

Bechtold Wm. farmer; Sec. 9; P. O. Apple River.

Bell Franklin, laborer; P. O. Apple River.

Burnett Jasper, retired; P. O. Warren.

Benson A. renter; Sec. 17; P.O. Apple River.

BENTON DATUS, Farmer; Sec. 28; P. O. Rush; owns 96 acres of land; was born in Green Co., N. Y., Aug. 21, 1808; Mr. Benton came to Chicago in 1832, remaining there only a few months; he then came to this Co., and remained in Galena a short time, thence to Dubuque, Iowa, in which place he erected the first cabin that was built in that place; in 1834 he returned to this Co., and with the exception of one Summer that he spent in Chicago, it has been his home since; he married Sophia Watts, at Elizabeth, in this Co., Nov. 30, 1842; she was born in Sussex Co., England, April 20, 1820; she came to Chicago in 1834, in which place she remained three years; she came to this Co. about the year of 1838; they had three sons in the army: William, who enlisted in Co. F, 17th I. V. C.—he served until the close of the war and was honorably discharged; Addison enlisted in the 96th Regt., and also served until the close of the war and was honorably discharged; Albert Eugene, enlisted in Co. K, 96th I. V. I. in 1862; he was killed in battle at Dallas, Georgia, fought May 30, 1864; his remains were buried in a soldier's grave where the Southern breezes sing a mournful dirge over the place of his rest, but he fell in a glorious work, a martyr to liberty's cause, and his short life was not spent in vain; he was not only a soldier of our country, but also a soldier of Christ ever trying to obey his Captain's commands.

Benjamin Geo. renter; Sec. 19; P. O. Rush.

BERRYMAN THOMAS G. Farmer; Sec. 19; P. O. Rush; owns 133 acres of land; was born in Cornwall, England, in 1840; came to this country with his parents in 1850; they settled in Lafayette Co., Wis.; married Mary H. Ivey in Lafayette Co., Wis., Nov. 22, 1860; they came to this Co. in 1871; they have six children: William G., born Aug. 4, 1863; Mildred, Feb. 20, 1865; May, Sept. 15, 1868; Louis, Dec. 5, 1870; Anna, March 9, 1874; John, April 26, 1876; Mr. Berryman is pastor of the M. E. Church in Nora Tp., this Co., also pastor of the M. E. Church in Thompson Tp.; he was ordained at Mendota, La Salle Co., this state, in 1873.

Binus Henry, farmer; Sec. 2; P. O. Warren.

Blackstone Everet, farmer; Sec. 9; P. O. Apple River.

Blackstone Franklin, farmer; Sec. 9; P. O. Warren.

BORTHWICK S. S. Farmer; Sec. 31; P. O. Rush; owns 110 acres of land; was born in Allegany Co., N. Y., Jan. 26, 1836; he came to this Co. with his parents in 1853; in 1862 he enlisted in Co. K, 96th I. V. I.; served until the close of the war and was honorably discharged; his father (George Borthwick) was born in N. Y.; he married Maria French, in that state, in 1832; she was also a native of N. Y.

Bonjour Henry, farmer; P. O. Apple River.

BONJOUR T. L. Farmer; Sec. 7; P. O. Apple River; was born in Switzerland Dec. 25, 1843; came to this country with his parents in 1852; he enlisted in Co. F., 96th Regt. I. V. I. on Aug. 14, 1862, was detailed to the 9th Ohio Battery, and afterward transferred to the 18th Ohio; was honorably discharged June 11, 1865; he was in many severe engagements, among them being the battles of Chicamauga, Lookout Mountain, Kenesaw, Nashville, Franklin, Jonesboro, and all through to Atlanta; he married Fannie J. Needham, in this township, on May 4, 1871; she was born in Lincolnshire, England, Jan. 14, 1852; they have four children: Elizabeth Ann, born March 7, 1872; William F., March 28, 1873; Thomas H., Dec. 7, 1874; Lydia Jane, July 2, 1876; Mr. Bonjour owns an improved farm of 160 acres of land.

Bowker Z. T., farmer, P. O. Warren.

Box James, farmer; Sec. 11; P. O. Warren.

BROWN JOHN D. Farmer; Sec. 6; P. O. Apple River; owns 520 acres of land; was born in Woodstock, Windsor Co., Vt., 1817; came to this Co. in 1839; located in this town in 1839; went from here to Cal. in 1852; returned in 1854; has held various offices since he has been in this Co., among them are the following: in 1847 being one of three commissioners elected to settle disputes between claimants on land, where there were two or more claims to the same lot of land, also, one of the trustees to attend land sales, that there should be no by-bidders on actual settlers land; among others that of Supervisor, Assessor, School Trustee, and Road Commissioner; the last office he has held for 21 consecutive years; has been married twice; first wife was Louisa M. Gillett, they were married in Stephenson Co., this state, 1846, she died in February, 1872; present wife was Emily McKenna; she was born in New Jersey, 1849, they were married in Stephenson Co., Oct., 1874.

Brown R. Henry, farmer; P. O. Apple River.

Burbridge Jackson, farmer; Sec. 10; P. O. Warren.

Burbridge Rolan, farmer; Sec. 2; P. O. Warren.

Burbridge Wm. renter; P. O. Warren.

Burch Thos. farmer; Sec. 3; P. O. Warren.

Burk James, Sr. farmer; P. O. Rush.

Burk James, Jr., laborer; Rush.

CALDWELL GEORGE, farmer; P. O. Warren.

Campbell Capt. renter, Sec. 34; P. O. Pitcherville.

CAMPBELL AMBROSE, Farmer; Sec. 34; P. O. Rush; was born in Allegany Co., N. Y., Feb. 18, 1818; owns 120 acres of land; he came to this Co. in 1849, remained in it until the Spring of 1850; he then went to California, remaining there until 1852, when he returned; he went to Kane Co., lived there a short time, and then went to Johnson Co., Iowa, and remained there several years; he returned to this Co. in 1868, and it has been his home since; he is at present one of the Town Central Committee; has been married twice; first wife was Calista E. Manley, they were married in New York, in October, 1837; she was born in Massachusetts, Feb. 22, 1819, died July 18, 1870; had seven children by this marriage; present wife was Mrs. S. B. Townsend (maiden name Matilda Ann Burnan); they were married in Warren, in this Co., April 27, 1871; she was born in Orange Co., N. Y., Oct. 14, 1829; she came to this state in 1839, was married to S. B. Townsend in 1842; he was murdered in Nevada, Iowa, in October, 1864; Mr. Campbell had two sons in the army (Charles and Miles E.); both were in many severe battles; they were honorably discharged at the close of the war; Republican.

Clay Chancey, farmer; Sec. 13; P. O. Nora.

Clancy Ed. farmer; P. O. Apple River.

Clancy John, renter; Sec. 5; P. O. Apple River.

CLANCY THOS. Farmer; Sec. 16; P. O. Warren; owns 290 acres of land; was born in Waterford Co., Ireland, in 1822; came to this Co. in 1851; married Margaret Hógan in Shullsburg, Wis., in 1854; she was born in Ireland in 1829: they have six children, viz.: Mary Ann (now Mrs. W. Tucker), Ellen (now Mrs. F. Fiddler), Thomas, John, Margaret, Catharine; Mr. Clancy settled in this township in the year 1856.

CLAY DAVID, Farmer; Sec. 24; P. O. Nora; owns 360 acres of land; was born in Centre Co., Pa., Oct. 10, 1813; he moved with his parents from that state to Ohio in 1820, in which state he married Sophina Matilda Snyder, Feb. 18, 1835; she was born in Lehigh Co., Pa., Oct. 22, 1817; they came to this state in 1840, and settled in Freeport, Stephenson Co., where they remained until the year 1850, when they came to this Co., and located on his present farm, where he has since remained; they have reared a family of twelve children, all of whom are in good circumstances.

CLAY GEORGE W. Farmer; Sec. 13; P. O. Nora; owns 120 acres of land; was born at Freeport, Stephenson Co., this state, Sept. 18, 1843; came to this Co. with his parents in the year 1850; he married Mary E. Laycock in the Town of Nora, this Co., Jan. 1, 1868.

Clay Levi, farmer; Sec. 24; P. O. Nora.

Clay Silas, farmer; Sec. 10; P. O. Nora.

Cornelius Allen, farm; Sec. 24; P.O. Warren.

Covington Bryant, renter; Sec. 21; P.O. Rush.

COX JEREMIAH L. Sec. 10; P. O. Warren; was born in Wayne Co., Ind., Jan. 30, 1823; came to this Co. in 1861; is one of the proprietors of the flour mill owned and run by J. L. Cox & Co.; this was erected by them on Clear Creek, Rush Tp., on southeast quarter of Sec. 4; it is a frame building, three stories high, and was completed at a cost of $10,000; Mr. Cox has represented this township in the County Board two terms, has also been Collector two years, and has held various other town and school offices; married Miss Delilah Garretson in Lafayette Co., Wis., Dec. 29, 1864; she was born in Highland Co., Ohio, Aug. 11, 1829; she is the author of several deservedly popular sketches, which do credit to her as a ripe scholar and racy writer; they have one child living, Robert L., born Nov. 27, 1865.

Cox Joseph, miller; Sec. 4; P. O. Warren.

Crawford A. Sec. 21; P. O. Apple River.

CRISSY BYRON, Farmer; Sec. 28; P. O. Rush; was born in Allegany Co., N. Y., in 1838; came to this Co. with his parents in the year 1840; he married Sarah E. Hamilton in Lafayette Co., Wis., March 4, 1858; she was born in Ohio in 1841; they have had six children, three of whom are living, viz.: Guy, born Nov. 17, 1859, Abel T., Oct. 22, 1865, Bella Ann, March 7, 1870; at the breaking out of the War of the Rebellion, Mr. Crissy enlisted in Co. B, 45th Regt. I. V. I.; was discharged on account of sickness in August, 1862, and returned home; his health being restored, he re-enlisted as veteran in Co. F, 17th Ill. Cav. in 1863; he was promoted First Sergeant April 17, 1875; he was in every battle that his company was in; this company traveled by rail, steamboat and marches, about 15,000 miles; it was in the engagement at Allen Station, Booneville, California, Sedalia, Syracuse and Lexington; those were a series of bloody disasters to the rebels; he was honorably discharged Dec. 18, 1865.

Crawford John, farmer; Sec. 21; P. O. Apple River.

DEAM ANDREW, Farmer; Sec. 28; P. O. Rush; owns 211 acres of land; was born in Germany in the year 1834; came to this country in 1840, and settled in Pennsylvania; he remained there until 1852, when he came to this Co. and settled in this township, which has been his home since; Mr. Deam is the Supervisor of this township at present writing, which office he has held for four years; he has also held various other offices; has been married three times; first wife was Miss E. L. Townsend; second wife was Amelia Bonjour; present wife was Annie J. Pucket; has five children living.

Dram John, farmer; Sec. 19; P. O. Rush.

Durr Wm. farmer; Sec. 23; P. O. Greenville.

ELSTON CHAS. retired; Apple River.

Elston Jacob, retired; Apple River.

Endress John, farmer; Sec. 28; P. O. Apple River.

Endress Joseph, farm; Sec. 28; P. O. Rush.

Eston Levi, retired; Apple River.

FARREN J. W. farmer; P. O. Warren.

Fielder Fred, renter; Sec. 21; P. O. Rush.

Fielder Martin, farm; Sec. 9; P. O. Warren.

FOSTER AMOS, Farmer; Sec. 29; P. O. Rush; owns 120 acres of land; was born in New Haven Co., Conn., May 17, 1806; he remained in that state until he was 21 years of age; he then went to N. Y., and lived there until the year of 1832 when he came to this state and settled in LaSalle Co., thus becoming one of the pioneers of that Co.; he lived there until 1855; he then removed to Crawford Co., Wis., in which Co. he remained until the year of 1866; he then came to this Co., and since then it has been his home; his first wife was Eliza Gaton; they were married at Earlville, LaSalle Co., in 1837; she was born in Conn., and died in LaSalle Co. in 1838; present wife Nancy Maynard; she was born in Genoa Co., N. Y., in 1820; Mr. Foster had two sons in the army, Amos B. and William; both served until the close of the war and were honorably discharged.

FOSTER CHARLES SIDNEY, Farmer; Sec. 31; P. O. Rush; was born in Oswego, N. Y., Nov. 14, 1836; in 1846 he moved with his parents to Wis., where he remained a number of years; at the breaking out of the late war he enlisted in Co. F, 3d Regt. W. V. C.; served until the war was over and was honorably discharged; he was in many severe engagements with the enemy; in the Fall of 1865 he married Annette Teeter, in Lafayette Co., Wis; she was born in Tompkins Co., N. Y., March 4, 1842; they have had four children: Charles Elmer, born Feb. 24, 1868; Harry, March 31, 1870; died Sept. 6, 1870; Helen, March 9, 1873; Emma Belle, Dec. 22, 1875.

Foster Wm. farmer; Sec. 29; P. O. Rush.

Fuller John, renter; P. O. Rush.

GARDINER WM. H. Farmer; Sec. 36; P.O. Howardsville, Stephenson Co.; owns 101 acres of land; was born in Albany Co., N. Y., Aug. 2, 1840, from which place he went to Wis., in the year 1866, thence to Iowa in 1869; from there to this

Co. in the same year; has held various local offices; married Cynthia A. Simmons in the Town of Nora, this Co., on the 4th of Dec., 1869; she was born in Onondaga Co., N. Y., on the 30th of June, 1840; they have three children: Gertie J., born Aug. 15, 1871; Alice M., Aug. 15, 1873; Berthie H., Jan. 4, 1875.

GOTICA EDWARD, Farmer; Sec. 7; P. O. Apple River; owns 80 acres of land; was born in Mo. on the 4th of Sept., 1832; he came to this Co. with his parents in 1835; married Alice White in Grant Co., Wis., on the 22d of Nov., 1854; she was born in Ireland June 2, 1836; came to this Co. with her parents when she was 11 years old; they have nine children living: John Edmund, born March 4, 1856; Margaret Emily, March 4, 1858; Mary Alice, June 10, 1860; Louis Constantine, Feb. 13, 1863; Louisa, April 23, 1866; Edward, July 27, 1868; Ellen, Oct. 4, 1870; Elizabeth Annie, Nov. 20, 1872; Julia, Nov. 4, 1874.

Grayham Edward, renter; Sec.—; P. O. Apple River.

Griffin Edward, farmer; P. O. Warren.

HAMILTON THOMAS, Farmer; Sec. 32; P. O. Rush; was born in Tompkins Co., N. Y., Sept. 20, 1815; he went from that state to Cincinnati, O., in the year 1834; he remained there until 1840; he then went to Rush Co., Ind., remaining there until 1852, when he came to this Co. where he has since remained; first wife was Melinda Willey; they were married in Rush Co., Ind., March 9, 1835; she was born in Hamilton Co., Ohio, in 1817; she died in this Co. on the 20th of March, 1854; present wife was Mrs. Rebecca Bowker (maiden name Rebecca Borthwick); they were married in this Tp. on the 10th of Oct., 1855; she was born in Albany Co., N. Y., in which place she married Mr. Bowker; they came to this Co. in 1837; Mr. Bowker died a few years afterward.

Harris Elisha, farm; Sec. 28; P. O. Rush.

HARRIS C. B. Farmer; Sec. 28; P. O. Rush; was born in this township Aug. 13, 1847; is Constable in this place at the present time; has held the office of Town Collector one term; has also held various other offices; during the late War of the Rebellion he enlisted in Co. R, 96th Regt. I. V. I., served until the close of the war, and was honorably discharged; May 25, 1869, he married Miss Annie Shultz in Lafayette Co., Wis.; she was born in Germany in 1850, and came to this Co. with her parents when she was a child; they have five children living, viz.: Cynthia M., George, Nelson, Frederick E., and Charles R.

Hatten John, laborer; Rush.

HIRST EDWARD, Farmer; Sec. 5; P. O. Apple River; owns 190 acres of land; was born in Yorkshire, England, Nov. 15, 1833; came to this country in 1855; married Mary Ann Brooks in New Jersey in 1856; she was born in Pennsylvania in 1838; they came to this Co. and settled in this township in 1866; they have two children living: Walter James, born in New Jersey, March 14, 1857; John, in this Co. Feb. 7, 1869.

Holcomb Albert, farmer; P. O. Warren.

Holcomb Alonzo, farm; S. 14; P.O. Warren.

Holcomb Reuben, farm; S. 16; P.O. Warren.

HOPKINS W. T. Farmer; Sec. 36; P. O. Pitcherville; owns 120 acres of land; was born in Whiteside Co., this state (Ill.), July 16, 1841; came to this Co. with his parents in 1847; during the War of the Rebellion he enlisted in Co. E, 4th Regt. I. V. I.; was in the battle of Shiloh; was honorably discharged; married Mary Helen Phelps in the Town of Stockton, this Co., Oct. 1, 1865; she was born in Chenango Co., N. Y., Dec. 13, 1842; they have three children: Alice H., born Feb. 26, 1867; Frances Emma, Dec. 22, 1872; Minerva, July 30, 1875.

Hughlett Samuel, laborer.

Hughs Timothy, laborer; Greenvale.

IVEY JOHN H. Farmer; Sec. 18; P. O. Apple River; owns 106 acres of land; was born in Cornwall, England, Oct. 13, 1846; he came to this country with his parents in 1848; his father (John Ivey) was born in England, in which place he was married to Mary Ann Mills; they came to this country in 1848 and settled in Wisconsin, in which state she died in 1876; Mr. John H. Ivey came to this Co. in 1874.

JONES OLIVER, farmer; Sec. 21; P. O. Greenvale.

Jones Nathan, farm; S. 24; P.O. Greenvale.

KANE J. R. laborer; Greenvale.

Kempthorn Thos. farm; S. 12; P.O. Warren.

KENNEY HENRY, Farmer; Sec. 17; P. O. Warren; owns 50 acres of land; was born in Pennsylvania April 6, 1841; came to this Co. with his parents in 1849; he married Mary E. Arnold in Winslow, Jan. 1, 1866; she was born in Ohio Dec. 9, 1844; they have four children, viz.: George C., born Oct. 8, 1867; Laura D., March 3, 1870; Viola, Oct. 2, 1871; Rebecca, Sept. 29, 1876.

Kenney Thos. farmer; Sec. 20; P. O. Rush.

KENNEY WASHINGTON, Farmer; Sec. 20; P. O. Rush; owns 80 acres of land; was born in Delaware Co., N. Y., Aug. 25, 1810; was married to Susan Arnold in Pennsylvania, in which state she was born Feb. 20, 1816; they came to this

RUSH.

Co. in 1851; they have had seven children, viz.: Emeline (now Mrs. D. Spencer), born Feb. 20, 1838; Hawley, Aug. 25, 1839, died in infancy; Catharine, Jan. 1, 1842, died in 1861; Darius W., Oct. 31, 1843, he enlisted in the 96th Regt. I. V. I., and was killed at the battle of Chicamauga; Levi, Nov. 25, 1845, died after he had reached his majority; Harvey and Harley, twins, March 3, 1850.

KING JAMES, Farmer; Sec. 25; P. O. Greenvale; owns 96 acres of land; was born in Poultney, Steuben Co., N. Y., on Dec. 30, 1827; moved with his parents to Allegany Co., N. Y., in 1829, in which place his parents still reside; he came to this Co. in 1863, and settled in this town, and it has been his home since; he is the present Town Clerk, which office he has held for eleven years; was married to Adelia E. Whitney in Belfast, Allegany Co., N. Y., on Nov. 25, 1855; she was born in Lee, Oneida Co., N. Y., on Nov. 12, 1836; they have had eight children, viz.: Carrie S., born Sept 1, 1856, died Sept 1, 1863; George H. M., April 6, 1858; Orville S., Feb. 28, 1861; Morris E., June 2, 1862; Nellie J., April 11, 1865, died Aug. 25, 1866; Robert W., Aug. 14, 1868; Edward E., Aug. 23, 1871, died Nov. 30, 1874; Winoa A, May 27, 1874.

KNISH WILLIAM, Farmer; Sec.21; P. O. Warren; owns 120 acres of land; was born in Germany in the year of 1816; came to this Co. in 1854, and settled in Galena, remaining there until 1863, when he moved to this town, and it has been his home since; Mr. Knish married Margaret Shultz in Germany, in which place she was born in 1822; they have five children living, viz.: Barbara E. (now Mrs. Wm. Shultz), born in 1853; Nicholas, in 1855; Frederick, in 1858; Minnie, in 1860; John, in 1862; during the War of the Rebellion Mr. Knish enlisted in Co. K, 96th Regt. I. V. I., in year of 1862; he served until the close of the war and was honorably discharged.

Kreitzer J. M. carpenter; Sec. 25; P.O. Greenvale.

Krink Jonces, renter.

LANDPHAIR HARLOW, Farmer; Sec. 32; P. O. Rush; owns 150 acres of land; was born in Madison Co., N. Y., on May 20, 1820; when he was fourteen years of age he moved with his parents to Ohio; he remained in that state until the year of 1838, when he came to this Co. and located in this Tp., which has since been his home; the maiden name of Mrs. Landphair was Jane A. Gates; they were married in Green Co., Wis., on July 19, 1862; she was born in Michigan on May 16, 1837; Mr. Landphair and family are members of the Evangelical Church; he had two brothers in the army (Hiram and Hoxie Landphair); Hiram enlisted in a Wisconsin Regt., and died in the service; Hoxie enlisted in the Ohio Zouaves; he also died in the service at Louisville, Ky.; Mrs. Landphair had three brothers in the army, viz.: (Noah, Leland and John Gates); all of them served until the close of the war and were honorably discharged.

Leman Theodore, farmer; P. O. Apple River.

Lehen T. farmer; Sec. 18; P. O. Apple River.

Lewis Jas. Sec. 33; P. O. Rush.

McCOWAN CHARLES, Farmer; Sec. 33; is Postmaster of Rush P. O.; owns 91 acres of land; was born in Scioto Co., Ohio, on Oct. 17, 1833; he remained in that state until the year 1855, when he came to this Co; Mr. McCown has held the office of Town Collector two terms, Assessor one term; during the War of the Rebellion he enlisted in Co. E, 17th Regt. I. V. C; he served until the close of the war and was honorably discharged; on the 16th of Sept., 1858, he married Miss Beulah A. Miner at Nora, in this Co.; she was born in this town on Sept. 9. 1840; they have had eight children, viz.: Lydia, Jan. 31, 1861; Hurlbut R., Sept. 5, 1862; Effie D., July 17, 1864; Justa L., Nov. 6, 1868; Mabel L., Nov. 10, 1871; Charles E., April 7, 1874; Arthur, June 23, 1876; lost one, Volney A., born June 11, 1859, died March 14, 1860.

McKee J. teamster; Millville; P. O. Warren.

McMahen John.

Marks J., Jr., farm; S. 26; P. O. Greenvale.

Metcalf G. farmer; Sec. 15; P. O. Greenvale.

Miller Peter, renter on J. D. Brown's farm; Sec. 8; P. O. Apple River.

MILLER R. R. Farmer; Sec. 31; P. O. Rush; owns 111 acres of land; was born in Colton Co., N. Y., on Aug. 9, 1828; moved to this state with his parents when he was a boy; has lived in Fulton Co. two years, McHenry Co. five years; the balance of the time he has resided in this Co.; he married Martha E. Russell in Lafayette Co., Wis., in 1858; she was born in this state (Ill.) in 1842; they have six children, viz.: Martha L., born in 1860; George R., July 19, 1862; Mary Jane, in 1864; Nancy R., in 1866; John S., in 1867; James D., in Nov., 1872.

MINER LUCINDA P. Farming; P. O. Rush; maiden name was Lucinda Post; owns 56 acres of land; she was born in Ontario Co., N. Y., in 1815; was married to Ransom H. Miner in Allegany Co., N. Y., in 1838; they came from there to this Co. in 1839, and located in this Tp.; Mr. Miner was a zealous member of the Baptist Church, and held various offices in this place up to the time of his death, which occurred at his residence in this place, March 7, 1855; they have had eight children: Beulah, now Mrs. McCowan, born Sept. 9, 1840; Luella V., May 9, 1842, died Aug. 14, 1842; Lydia N., now Mrs. J. Schofield, Nov. 20, 1843; Albert D., Dec. 7, 1847; John A., Nov. 24, 1850, died May 8, 1851; Mary, Dec. 14, 1845, died March 20, 1865; Gertie E., now Mrs. Jamison, Nov. 16, 1852; Jane, now Mrs. H. Hawes, Oct. 5, 1855.

Miner A. D. farmer; Sec. 33; P. O. Rush.

MURPHY JAMES H. County Surveyor; Sec. 25; P. O. Greenvale; was born in Lewis Co., N. Y., April 19, 1838, in which place he remained until 1858, when he came to this Co.; married Miss Phenie M. Simmons, in Town of Nora, this Co., July 16, 1867; she was born in Onondaga Co., N. Y., May 28, 1842; besides attending the duties of his office as County Surveyor, Mr. Murphy owns and manages a farm of 140 acres; also follows the profession of teaching, having taught 22 consecutive winter terms; he has also held the office of Township Treasurer seven years; was elected to his present office (County Surveyor) in the Fall of 1875.

NADIG JACOB, farmer; Sec. 22; P. O. Warren.

Needham James, farmer; Sec. 29; P.O. Rush.

Nicholsen John, farmer; Sec. 25; P. O. Greenvale.

ORMROD JAMES, Farmer; Sec. 17; P. O. Apple River; owns 136 acres of land; was born in England April 16, 1816; married Elizabeth Froggatt in Derbyshire, Eng., June 2, 1835; she was born in Eng., May 4, 1816; they came to this country in 1852 and settled in Rhode Island, in which state they remained until 1858, when they came to this Co.; they have had eleven children: Harriet, born June 4, 1838, died June 26, 1874; Sarah Ann, April 26, 1842, died May 14, 1848; Elizabeth, April 12, 1845; Ann, Oct. 12, 1846, died April 22, 1848; Eliza, July 24, 1849; James, Nov. 21, 1850; Mary, May 23, 1852; W. Permenter, May 9, 1854; Wm. Francis, Jan. 11, 1856, died April 12, 1856; Ellen May, May 24, 1857; George S., Feb. 19, 1859.

PALMER JOHN, farmer; Sec. 1; P. O Warren.

Parm Hartwell, lab.; Sec. 10; P. O. Warren.

Parm Hartwell, farmer; P. O. Warren.

PARKER F. J. Proprietor of Blacksmith Shop; Sec. 28; P. O. Rush; was born in Lancaster, Wis., in Jan., 1845; came to this Co. with his parents in the Fall of 1849; they remained here about three years, they then moved to Ogle Co., this state, thence to Wis., in which state they remained a number of years; they returned to this Co. in 1867, and it has been their home since; Mr. F. J. Parker's father (Joseph O. Parker) was born in Bennington Co., Vt., April 15, 1808; he married Maria Page in 1840; she was born in Jefferson Co., N. Y., June 19, 1812; they have five children living: Emma M., now Mrs. Parker, Harriet P., now Mrs. Weaver, Frank, Ellen M., and Melvin J.

Parker J. O. farmer; Sec. 28; P. O. Rush.

Parker Melvin, farmer; Sec. 28; P. O. Rush.

Phelps O. W. blacksmith; Sec. 36; P. O. Greenvale.

Posey Dennis, farmer; Sec. 29; P. O. Rush.

Posey Edward, farmer; Sec. 29; P. O. Rush.

Power Alvin, farmer; P. O. Warren.

Pryor Byron, laborer; P. O. Apple River.

PUCKETT NATHAN, Farmer; Sec. 2; P. O. Nora; he and his mother owns 140 acres of land; he was born in the Tp. of Nora, this Co., May 18, 1852; his father (Cyrus Puckett) was born in N. C. in 1806; came West and married Betty Thomas, in Wayne Co., Ind., July 24, 1828; she was born in S. C. in 1809; they came from Ind. to this state in 1848, and settled in Nora Tp., this Co., in which place they remained until 1869, when they moved to this Tp.; they had eleven children, eight of whom are now living; Mr. Cyrus Puckett died April 22, 1870, respected by all as an upright and honest man.

PULFREY CHARLES, Farmer; Sec. 31; P. O. Rush; was born in Winnebago Co., this state, Oct. 25, 1846; moved with his parents from there to the Tp. of Stockton in this Co. in 1858; during the War of the Rebellion he enlisted in Co. D, 153d Regt. I. V. I.; served until the war was over and was honorably discharged; married Gazelle Townsend in Galena, Jan. 14, 1875; she was born in this Tp. Dec. 13, 1850; they have two children, Burchard, born Nov. 22, 1875; Charlie, May 6, 1877.

RAWLINS O. P. farmer; Sec. 23; P. O. Greenvale.

Renwick Fred, farmer; P. O. Rush.

RENWICK JOHN G. Farmer; Sec. 32; P. O. Rush; owns 40 acres of land; was born in this Tp. Jan. 14, 1851; married Miss Mary Townsend in this Tp. August 25, 1872; she was born in this place Jan. 20, 1855; have two children: Laurilla Renwick, born July 14, 1873; Ortense Renwick, June 13, 1876.

Renwick R. D. farm; Sec. 21; P. O. Warren.

Reitzel James, farmer; P. O. Greenvale.

Richardson D. farm; Sec. 2; P. O. Warren.

Richardson Nathan.

Richardson Wm. farmer; P. O. Warren.

Rosenburg A. farmer; Sec. 34; P.O. Pitcherville.

SCHLADER M. farmer; Sec. 25; P. O. Greenvale.

Scofield Peter, farmer; Sec. 19; P. O. Rush.

Shea D. farmer; Sec. 6; P. O. Apple River.

SHEA JOHN, Farmer; Sec. 6; P. O. Apple River; owns 210 acres land; was born in Co. Cork, Ireland, in 1817; came to this country in 1840; married Margaret Murphy in N. Y. in '41; they came to this Co. in '44, and settled in Galena, in which place they remained about one year; they then moved to New Diggings, Wis.; they lived there 6 years; they then came to this Tp. and it has been their home since; they have eight children living: Dennis, Timothy, Ellen, Jeremiah, John, Catherine, Daniel and Johana.

Shipman Wm. renter; Sec. 34; P. O. Pitcherville.

Shipman W. renter; Sec. 36; P. O. Pitcherville.

Shultz Fred, farmer; Sec. 34; P. O. Greenvale.

Shultz George, farmer; P. O. Greenvale.

Shultz F. F. farmer; P. O. Greenvale.

Shultz H. S. farmer; P. O. Greenvale.

Shultz H. farmer; Sec. 27; P. O. Greenvale.

Shultz John, farmer; P. O. Greenvale.

Shultz N. farmer; Sec. 36; P. O. Greenvale.

Shultz Balzer, farmer; P. O. Greenvale.

Shultz Wm. farmer; P. O. Greenvale.

Shultz W. F. farmer; Sec. 20; P. O. Warren.

Simmons Delbert, farmer; Sec. 25; P. O. Greenvale.

SIMMONS H. A. Farmer; Sec. 36; P. O. Pitcherville; owns 82 acres of land; was born in New York Oct. 26, 1844; came to this Co. in 1852; has held various school offices; married Miss Mary J. Fuller in Onondaga Co., N. Y., Dec. 5, 1869; she was born in New York Aug. 11, 1850.

SIMMONS IRVIN, Farmer; Sec. 34; P. O. Howardsville; owns 80 acres of land; was born in Town of Nora, this Co., Dec. 18, 1846; married Miss Hattie Vanschaick at Howardsville, Stephenson Co., this state, Oct. 26, 1875; she was born in Jefferson Co., N. Y., April 2, 1855; they have one child, Mabel Gracie, born Nov. 4, 1876; Mr. Simmons' first wife was Hattie Howard; they were married in Sept., 1872; she was born in Stephenson Co., this state, she died in 1873; one child by this marriage, Hattie, born July 1, 1873.

Simpson Wm. farmer; Sec. 6; P. O. Apple River.

Simpson Thos. farmer; P. O. Apple River.

SIMPSON THOMAS, Sr., Farmer; Sec. 6; P. O. Apple River; owns 195 acres of land; was born in Ireland in 1787; he married Ellen Nesbitt in Ireland; she was born in 1803; they came to this county in 1838, thus becoming one of the pioneer families of Jo Daviess Co.; they came to this township in 1863; they have two children, viz.: Thomas, born in Galena Aug. 3, 1840; William, in Galena March 11, 1843; Mr. Simpson and family are members of the Presbyterian Church.

Smith Joseph, farmer; Sec. 10; P.O. Warren.

Smith Robt. farmer; Sec. 10; P. O. Warren.

Smith Simeon, renter; Sec. 19; P. O. Rush.

SPENCER AMZA LEWIS, Farmer; Sec. 32; P. O. Rush; was born in McCabe Co., Pa., Aug. 7, 1838; at the commencement of the War of the Rebellion he enlisted in Co. E, 15th Regt. I. V. I., April 18, 1861, being the first man from this Tp. to put his name on the muster-roll; he was mustered out in Dec., 1863; he re-enlisted as veteran in the same company and regiment, and served until the close of the war, and was honorably discharged; he was in many hard-fought battles, among them being the battle of Pittsburg Landing, siege of Vicksburg, Hatchie, and all through the Atlanta campaign; he was taken prisoner by the rebels after the fall of Atlanta, and consequently spent a few weeks at Andersonville Prison; he was wounded twice at Pittsburg Landing.

SPENCER J. H. Farmer; Sec. 31; P. O. Rush; owns 40 acres of land; was born in Lafayette Co., Wis., March 27, 1840; came to this Co. with his parents in 1842; he married Miss Abigail Hamilton in Winnebago Co., this state, March 8, 1866; she was born in Winnebago Co., Nov. 6, 1848; they have four children: Nettie A., born June 14, 1867; Mary Ettie, Nov. 17, 1869; Georgie Belle, April 26, 1871; Hiram Ernest, Nov. 26, 1873.

Spires F. M. farmer; Sec. 20; P. O. Rush.

STANTON ELIAS, Farmer; Sec. 24; P. O. Greenvale; owns 281 acres of land; was born in Jefferson Co., Ohio, Feb. 26, 1825; when he was 16 years of age he moved with his parents to Wayne Co., Ind., in which place his father (Benjamin Stanton) established the *Free Labor Advocate;* this was the first anti-slavery paper published in that state; Elias entered his father's printing office as Editor, which position he occupied until 1848; he then came to this Co. and located in this Tp., and it has been his home since; Mr. Stanton is the present P. M. at Greenvale, in this Tp.; he is the present Town School Trustee; he has represented this Tp. in Co. Board two terms; he has also held various other town and school offices; he married Matilda May in Greene Co., Ind., Feb. 4, 1847; she was born in Wayne Co., Ohio, Oct. 27, 1828; they had one son, Henry B., in the army; he served until the close of the war, and was honorably discharged.

Stanton H. B. farmer; Sec. 25; P. O. Greenvale.

Stanton Solan, farmer; P. O. New Westley.

Stephen P. farmer; Sec. 3; P. O. Warren.

STIDWORTHY WM. Farmer; Sec. 6; P. O. Apple River; owns 182 acres of land; was born in Devonshire, England, on the 29th of May, 1831; came to this country in 1846; he married Sophia E. Brooks, in New Jersey; she was born in Pa., Sept. 24, 1831; they came to this Co. in 1857; they have eight children: Mary Jane born July 8, 1854; Josephine, March 27, 1857; Sarah A., May 7, 1859; George H., Aug. 9, 1861; Lizzie, May 4, 1864; Daniel, Nov. 3, 1866; John, Nov. 10, 1867; Sophia A., Aug. 2, 1872; during the War of the Rebellion Mr. Stidworthy enlisted in Co. F, 96th Regt. I. V. I.; was transferred to Co. H, 21st Regt.; was honorably discharged Oct. 11, 1865.

Stock George, farmer; Sec. 24; P. O. Greenvale.

Sullivan C. renter; Sec. 20; P. O. Rush.

Swartz W. H. farmer; Sec. 12; P.O. Warren.

THOMAS WM. farmer; P. O. Warren.

THOMPSON CHARLES, Farmer; Sec. 30; P.O. Rush; was born in New Diggings, Wis., March 8, 1852; came to this Co. in 1858; has lived at Council Hill one year, and at Apple River seven years; has lived in this Tp. since 1876; married Annie McFadden in Apple River March 11, 1874; she was born in N. Y., Dec. 5, 1852; they have two children.

Thompson James, farmer; P. O. Warren.

Torrey S. retired farm; Sec. 32; P. O. Rush.

TOWNSEND G. N., Jr., Farmer; Sec. 34; P. O. Rush; was born in this town (Rush) May 23, 1837; at the breaking out of the War of the Rebellion he enlisted in Co. E, 15th Regt. I. V. I., May 24, 1861, in which Regt. he served until June, 1864, when he was honorably discharged; he then enlisted in the 4th Regt. U. S. V. V., in which Regt. he served until Nov. 28, 1866, when he was honorably discharged; he was in many severe engagements, among them were the battles of Wilson Creek, Pittsburg Landing, Corinth, Hatchie, Siege of Vicksburg, Fort Beauregard, and Champion Hills; he married Wilhelm Breckler, in Warren, this Co. March 28, 1867; she was born in this Co. June 17, 1843: they have three children living: Wilford D., born in this town June 16, 1869; Geo. N., in Glenelder, Mitchell Co., Kas., March 20, 1873; Elijah C., in this town, April 17, 1877; lost one child, Laura E., born Jan. 17, 1871, died March 25, 1871; Mrs. Townsend's father, Anthony G. Breckler, was born in France in Aug., 1794; he served under Napoleon 7 years and was in a number of bloody engagements, among them the battle of Waterloo; he afterward joined Selkirk in his Red River expedition; while on this expedition he met and married Elizabeth Rendisdacher; they came to this Co. in 1826, thus becoming one of the pioneer families of the Northwest; Mr. R. also took an active part in the Black Hawk War, in 1832; he died in this Co. July 14, 1876; his wife also died in this Co. in 1871.

TOWNSEND JOHN, Farmer and Stock Dealer; Sec. 26; P. O. Greenvale; was born in this town (Rush) May 2, 1848; owns 352 acres of land; married Miss Rosa Simmons in the Town of Nora, this Co., Jan. 1, 1871; she was born in this town; have three children: Bertha, born July 31, 1872; Albert, June 21, 1874; Nellie, Feb. 20, 1876,

TOWNSEND J. W. Farmer; Sec. 33; P. O. Rush; own 80 acres of land; was born in this Tp. Sept. 30, 1841; enlisted in Co. F, 17th Regt. I. V. C., as 1st Corporal; was promoted to 2d Duty Sergeant, and was honorably discharged in the Fall of 1864; on the 23d of Nov. 1862 he married Miss Hattie A. Lewis, at Warren, in this Co.; she was born in the State of N. Y., Oct. 10, 1841; they have five children: Lewis E., born Aug. 30, 1863; William N., July 16, 1866; George Chester, April 4, 1869; Joseph H., April 4, 1871; Frank Custer, Aug. 1, 1876; Mr. Townsend and family are members of the Evangelical Church.

Tucker J. farmer; Sec. 16; P. O. Warren.

TOWNSEND S. A. farmer; Sec. 33; P. O. Rush; owns 417 acres of land; was born in Allegany Co., N. Y., Oct. 16, 1834; moved to this Co. with his parents in the year of 1836, and married Miss Matilda Borthwick, in this Tp., March 15, 1855; she was born in Allegany Co., N. Y., Dec. 4, 1833; have had nine children: William F., born April 13, 1856; Eva C., Oct. 18, 1857; Mary L., Oct. 31, 1859; Bertha Jane, Nov. 17, 1861; James B., Jan. 20, 1863; Fannie G., Oct. 5, 1865; Nancy Lorena, April 20, 1869; Matilda, Jan. 23, 1873; S. A., Oct. 7, 1877; lost one child; Mittie Lavina, born Sept. 1, 1867, died April 26, 1869.

TUCKER J. M. Farmer; Sec. 16; P. O. Warren; owns 100 acres of land; was born in Adams Co., Ohio, Sept. 16, 1822; he came to this state with his parents when he was 16 years old; he came to this Co. in 1870; he married Mary E. Hancock at Wadham's Grove, in Stephenson Co., this state, Jan. 7, 1849; she was born in Sheffield Co., Pa., May 10, 1831; she came to Stephenson Co. with her parents in 1845; her father (J. M. Hancock) was born in Bedford Co., Pa.; he married Mercy Ogden; she was born in Pa.; they now reside in Nebraska; Mr. J. M. Tucker's father (Benjamin Tucker) was a native of Va.; he married Elizabeth Tucker; they came to Stephenson Co., this state, in 1836, thus becoming one of the pioneer families of that Co.

Tucker Martin, farmer; P. O. Warren.

Tucker Wesley, farmer; P. O. Warren.

Tucker Wm. farmer; P. O. Warren.

Typper T. C. farmer; Sec. 29; P. O. Rush.

VICK C. J. Farmer; Sec. 16; P. O. Warren; owns 210 acres of land; was born in England, Nov. 22, 1840; came to this Co. with his parents in 1844; married Hannah Redhern at Council Hill, in this Co., Oct. 11, 1868; she was born in this Co. June 5, 1842; they have two children: James Henry, born in this town (Rush) Feb. 19, 1870; Bertha Ella, Oct. 21, 1872; Mr. Vick has held several Tp. offices and school offices.

VICK MRS. JANE, Farming; Sec. 15; P. O. Warren; owns 212 acres of land; was born in England Jan. 10, 1808; her husband was Joseph Vick; they were married in England in 1831; he was born in England in 1813; they came to this Co. in 1842; Mr. Vick died in this town in 1866; they have had seven children, six of whom are living; two of them (Wm. A. and Joseph T.) served in Illinois Regiments and were honorably discharged.

VICK JOSEPH T. Farmer; Sec. 21; P. O. Warren; owns 160 acres of land; was born in England, March 2, 1842; came to this Co. with his parents in 1844; during the War of the Rebellion he enlisted in Co. H, 96th I. V. I.; was honorably discharged; married Mary M. Bates, in this town, Jan. 31, 1869; she was born in St. Lawrence Co., N. Y., Dec. 16, 1841, and came to this Co. with her parents in 1847; they have three children: Matilda Jane, born in Rush, Dec. 6, 1869; Effie May, March 14, 1873; William W., Aug. 7, 1877.

Vick O. J. farmer; Sec. 15; P. O. Warren.

Vick W. H. farmer; Sec. 15; P. O. Warren.

WALTERS JAMES, renter; Sec. 7; P. O. Apple River.

Warn Chas.

Washington George, farmer; Sec. 10; P. O. Warren.

Way Griffin, renter; Sec. 13; P. O. Nora.

Way Levi M. farm; Sec. 23; P.O. Greenvale.

WESTABY TOM, Farmer; Sec. 24; P. O. Greenvale; owns 94 acres of land; was born in Thompson Tp. in this Co., March 12, 1855; married Miss Martha Thomas, in Hazel Green, Wis., March 13, 1876; she was born in Hazel Green, Wis., Aug. 15, 1852; they have one child, James Albert, born Nov. 16, 1876; Mr. T. Westaby's father (George Westaby) came to this Co. at an early day, thus becoming one of the pioneers of this Co.

White Chas. renter; P. O. Apple River.

White George, laborer; P. O. Apple River.

White Oscar, renter, P. O. Apple River.

Wier John, farmer; Sec. 3; P. O. Warren.

Wilcot Wm.

WILLCOX JOHN E. Farmer; Sec. 30; P. O. Rush; owns 282 acres of land; was born in Somersetshire, England, Jan. 25, 1815; came from there to Pa. in 1851; lived in that state until 1856, when he came to this Co., July 11, 1864; he married Emily Shilliam in Hazel Green, Wis., she was born in Gloucestershire, England; in 1825.

Williams Alfred, farmer; Sec. 31; P.O. Rush.

Williams Chris. renter; S. 12; P. O. Warren.

WILLIAMS DAVID, Farmer; Sec. 30; P. O. Rush; was born in North Wales, Oct. 18, 1844; came to this country with his parents in 1855; they settled in Indiana, and remained there one year; then moved to Hazel Green, Wis., where they remained until 1866, when they came to this Co.; David's father, Wm. Williams, was born in Wales in 1817; he died Oct. 13, 1875; was married to Mary Williams in Wales, in 1840; she was born in Nov., 1822.

WILLIAMS G. W. Farmer; Sec. 31; P. O. Rush; was born in this Tp. Dec. 3, 1853; his father (Alfred Williams) was born in Canada in 1798; from there he went to Rockford, Ill., in 1838; he remained there until 1846, when he came to this Co.; he married Martha R. Marsh in the State of New York, March 10, 1827; she was born in Vermont, Nov. 3, 1808; they have seven children living, viz.: Angeline C. (now Mrs. T. Hatton), born Jan. 28, 1828; Maria (now Mrs. N. R. Miller), Nov. 9, 1833; Russell A., Sept. 10, 1837; he enlisted in Co. F, 12th Regt. I. V. I., and served until June, 1864; Providence, Jan. 25, 1840; Louisa, Oct. 7, 1846; Mary Ann, April 27, 1830; Mr. Williams and his son G. W. own 130 acres of land.

Williams John, farm; Sec. 32; P. O. Rush.

WILLIAMS R. A. Farmer; Sec. 31; P. O. Rush; owns 85 acres of land; was born in Canada, Sept. 10, 1837; moved from there to Rockford, Ill., with his parents in 1838, thence to this Co. with them in 1846; has held the offices of Town Collector, Commissioner of Highways, and has been School Director twelve years; at the breaking out of the War of the Rebellion he enlisted in Co. F, 12th Regt. I. V. I., and served until June 10, 1864, when he was honorably discharged; was in the battles of Fort Henry, Fort Donelson, both battles at Corinth, and all through the Atlanta campaign; was wounded at the battle of Fort Donelson; he married Miss Ellen Williams in the City of Galena, in this Co., Sept. 19, 1865; she was born in Wales, March 31, 1844; she came to this Co. with her parents when she was a child; they have six children, viz.: Eliza Ann, born July 5, 1866; William A., Feb. 7, 1868; Mary E., June 14, 1870; Fannie M., Sept. 14, 1872; Rosa E., March 16, 1874; Mabel Ruth, Aug. 21, 1876.

Williams R. H. farmer; P. O. Warren.

Williams Robert; farm; Sec. 9; P. O. Rush.

Williams Stephen, farmer; P.O. Warren.

Williams Wesley, farmer; P.O. Warren.

Willisen Samuel; farm; Sec. 32; P.O. Rush.

Willisen Sidney, carpenter; Rush.

Willisen Wm. renter; P.O. Rush.

Wilson Joseph, farmer; Sec. 25; P. O. Greenvale.

Wilson Henry, farmer; Sec. 25; P. O. Greenvale.

Wilson Wm. farmer; P. O. Warren.

Wilson Wm. farmer; P. O. Warren.

WING GEORGE S. Farmer; Sec. 16; P. O. Warren; owns 160 acres of land; was born in Bristol Co., Mass., Jan. 12, 1829, in which place he remained until 1856, when he came to this Co. and located on his present farm; Mr. Wing was elected Justice of the Peace in 1858, which office he has been the incumbent of since; he has also held the office of Town Clerk; in 1857 he was identified with the educational interests of the district wherein he resides, and took an active part in the organization of the district; on the 28th of Feb., 1859, he married Martha Woodruff, in Darlington, Wis.; she was born in Ashtabula Co., N. Y., Aug. 9, 1836; they have had eight children, viz.: Luther Porter, born Jan. 6, 1860; George Samuel, Sept. 27, 1862; Sarah Marcia, Jan. 1, 1863, died Oct. 8, 1863; Micah Edward, Feb. 6, 1865; Anna Sophia, Sept. 10, 1867; Mark Ellsworth, June 12, 1869; Philip Justis, in September, 1872, died June 25, 1873; Alvin Ephraim, Feb. 14, 1877; Mr. Wing's uncle (Abram Hathaway) was born in Mass. in 1787; he came to this state in 1816, and settled near Springfield, in which place he remained until 1827, when he came to this Co.; he has held various important offices in the early history of this Co., among them being that of County Commissioner, which office he held a number of years; he at present resides near Janesville, Wis.

WOLCOTT WM. A. Farmer; Sec. 14; P.O. Warren; owns 134 acres of land; was born in Lorain Co., Ohio, May 3, 1837; came to this Co. with his parents in 1839; he married Miss L. Godfrey in Woodbine, this Co., April 5, 1860; she was born in Genesee Co., N. Y., July 19, 1837; she came to this Co. in 1858; they have had four children, viz.: Charles Marion, born Aug. 17, 1863; Ira Augustus, June 18, 1869, died Sept. 5, 1871; Jesse Alden, Oct. 18, 1872; Lottie L., June 12, 1875; Mr. Wolcott has made three trips to California; his father (Henry A. Wolcott) was born in Lorain Co., Ohio, in 1807; he married Eliza Ann Williams in Lorain Co., Ohio; they came to this Co. in 1839, thus becoming one of the pioneer families of Jo Daviess Co.; Mr. H. A. Wolcott held various important offices in the early history of this Co; he died, honored and respected by all, May 21, 1858.

Wolfram Christopher, Sec. 3, P. O. Warren.

Wolfram John, farmer, P. O. Warren.

DERINDA TOWNSHIP.

ALBRITE FRANK, lives with his father; Sec. 25; P. O. Savanna.

Albrite Jno. farmer; Sec. 25; P. O. Savanna.

Anderson J. farmer; Sec. 36; P. O. Savanna.

Anderson Robt. lives with his father; Sec. 36; P. O. Savanna.

BARRETT WILBURN, farmer; Sec. 5; P. O. Elizabeth.

Baur Fred, farmer; Sec. 21; P. O. Derinda.

Baur Paul, farmer; Sec. 21; P. O. Savanna.

BELK ANDREW, Farmer; Sec. 16; P. O. Derinda Centre; born in South Carolina, in 1812; came to the State of Georgia in 1829; moved to the Indian Territory in 1830; to East Tennessee in 1831; moved to this state and to Galena in 1839; settled in Elizabeth Tp. same year; settled on his present farm in 1843; was married March 4, 1855, to Miss Clarissa Hackett; she was born in Will Co., Ill., in 1836; they have ten children, James B., Maggie E., Mary A., John D., George W., Millie E., Andrew J., Julia E., Olive A., Henry E.; he held the office of Constable seven years, School Director six years; has 262½ acres land in Sections 14 and 15.

Beck F. farm; S. 21; P. O. Derinda Centre.

Berch J. farmer; Sec. 30; P. O. Savanna.

Block J. farm; S. 12; P. O. Derinda Centre.

Bohn A. farmer; Sec. 14; P. O. Derinda.

Bowden Alfred, Sec. 14; P. O. Derinda.

Bowden Charles H. Sec. 14; P. O. Derinda.

Bowden H., Sr., farm; Sec. 14; Derinda Tp.

Bowden H., Jr., farm; Sec. 11; P. O. Derinda.

Brunner G. farmer; Sec. 2; P. O. Derinda.

CAMPBELL DAVID; Sec. 7; P. O. Hanover.

Campbell D. G. Sec. 18; P. O. Hanover.

Campbell J. farmer; Sec. 7; P. O. Hanover.

Campbell John, farm; S. 18; P. O. Hanover.

Campbell John, farm; S. 7; P. O. Hanover.

Campbell R. H. farm; S. 18; P. O. Hanover.

CAMPBELL WILLIAM, Farmer; Sec. 18; P. O. Hanover; he was born in 1830 in the British Possessions on the Red River, Headquarters Hudson Bay Fur Company; he came with his father and the family to this state and Galena in 1835; they moved to Hanover Tp. same year; they made a claim of his land and settled on it in 1838; it was purchased by his father, Robert Campbell, of government in 1844; he was married in 1859 to Miss Mary E. McDonald, from Elizabeth Tp.; her father, John McDonald, served through the Black Hawk War; they have six children: David H., Harriet A., Mary E., Louisa J., Cora E., William E.; he has 245 acres of land in Derinda Tp., and 120 acres in Hanover Tp.; he held the office of Justice of the Peace four years; School Director ten years; his father died Feb. 11, 1862, at the age of 71 years; his mother died Feb. 6, 1862 at the age of 67 years.

Curtis Geo. farmer; Sec. 11; P. O. Derinda.

DASHER HARMEN, laborer; Sec. 21; P. O. Derinda Centre.

Diehl Jacob, blacksmith; Derinda.

DITTMAR ALBERT, P. O. Derinda Centre; renter on his brother's farm; Secs. Nos. 9 and 10; he was born in Germany in 1847; he came to this country and Derinda Tp., in 1854; settled on his brother's farm in 1870; he was married in 1871, to Miss Annie M. Praeger, from Germany; they have had four children: George Walter, born April 1, 1872; J. Bettie, Dec. 19, 1873; M. Clara, Aug. 8, 1874; L. Herman, July 29, 1877; his wife died Dec. 24, 1877; he holds the office of Tp. Clerk at the present time; he held the office of Road Commissioner two years.

DITTMAR ERHARD, Farmer and Justice of the Peace; Sec. 10; P. O. Derinda Centre; born in Germany in 1838; came to this country and Michigan in 1854; came to this Co. in 1855; settled on his present farm in 1865; he was married in 1865 to Miss Eva B. Fehler, from Germany; they have five children: Annie M., born in 1867; Michael E., 1869; Emma M., 1871; Minnie B., 1873; Caroline M., 1875; he has 200 acres of land; Mr. D. enlisted in 1861, in Co. B, 45th Regt. I. V. I.; he was severely wounded in the battles of Donelson and Shiloh. He was in Sherman's campaign to the Atlantic; mustered out in July 1865; he has held the office of Justice of the Peace for five years; Tp. Assessor 3 years; School Director 3 years; Mr. and Mrs. Dittman have been among the most active members of the M. E. German Church since 1855.

DITTMAR GEORGE, Jr., Farmer; Sec. 13; P. O. Derinda; born in Germany, Dec. 6, 1836; came to this country and Co. with his parents in 1855; they settled on their present farm, Feb. 17, 1855; his father, George, Sr., who still lives with him, was born in Germany, Oct. 18, 1799; his mother was born in Germany June 24, 1810; she died March 12, 1864; George, Jr., was married Dec. 24, 1865, to Miss Charity Thain, from Derinda Tp.; they have had five children: John G., born April 11, 1867; Wm. A., Feb. 27, 1869;

Fredoline A., March 16, 1871; Rudolph O., June 20, 1873; George F., Oct. 18, 1875; his wife died April 22, 1877; he has 280 acres of land, Secs. 13 and 14; he has held office as School Director 9 years; Constable 4 years; Assessor 3 years.

Donahoe D. farmer; Sec. 12; P. O. Derinda.

Donigan J. Sec. 30; P. O. Hanover.

Donigan M. farmer; Sec. 30; P. O. Hanover.

Dupont A. farmer; Sec. 16; P. O. Derinda Centre.

EBERLY JOHN, Sec. 9; P. O. Derinda.

Eberley W., Sr., farm; S. 19; P. O. Derinda.

Eberly W., Jr., farm; Sec. 9; P. O. Derinda.

ELLINOR GEORGE, Farmer; Sec. 28; P. O. Savanna; born in Yorkshire, Eng., Dec. 10, 1810; he came to this country and Canada in 1831, to the States in 1840; started on his present farm in 1843; he was married in 1838 to Miss Mary G. Surmon from Dublin, Ireland; they had four children: Thomas, Sarah, Mary and John; Sarah died June, 1876; John enlisted in the 45th Regt. I. V. I, and died from disease contracted while in the army; Mary was married to Thomas Bradford, Marshalltown, Iowa; Thomas still lives with his father; Mr. Ellinor's wife is dead; he has 160 acres of land in Sec. 8; has held the office as School Director six years.

Ellinor Thos. Sec. 28; P. O. Savanna.

Endress A. farmer; Sec. 14; P. O. Derinda.

Espie Edward, laborer; Derinda.

FEHLER JOHN, Sr., farmer; Sec. 10; P. O. Derinda.

Fehler J., Jr., renter; Sec. 10; P. O. Derinda.

Fehler Michael, Sr., Sec. 10; P. O. Derinda.

Fehler M., Jr., farm; Sec. 33; P. O. Savanna.

Fraser H. laborer; Sec. 34; P. O. Savanna.

Frasher J. farmer; Sec. 34; P. O. Savanna.

Frey H. shoemaker; Sec. 33; P. O. Savanna.

Frymer Wm. laborer; Derinda.

GAMBLE DAN, Jr., Sec. 18; P. O. Hanover.

GAMBLE DANIEL, Farmer; Sec. 18; P. O. Hanover; born in Ireland, 1812; came to this country, and to the State of Delaware, 1832; moved to Philadelphia, Pa., 1833, then to this state and Hanover Tp., 1836; he made a claim of his land same year; he was engaged in blacksmithing in Hanover until 1838, when he settled on his farm; he made the purchase of the land of the government, 1844; he was married, in 1848, to Miss Eliza McCall, from Ireland; she was born, Jan. 10, 1828; they have nine children: James, born Feb. 15, 1849; Thos. July 18, 1850; Elizabeth, Sept. 9, 1853; Daniel, Jr., June 16, 1855; Jane Aug. 4, 1857; Samuel April 25, 1859; Martha A., Jan. 3, 1861; Wm. J., Dec. 9, 1866; Joseph U., Nov. 18, 1870; his neice, Agnes, lives with him; he has held the office of School Trustee 25 years, Assessor 1 year; he has 183 acres land in Derinda Tp. and 240 acres in Hanover Tp.

Gamble Jas. Sec. 18; P. O. Hanover.

Gamble Thos. Sec. 18; P. O. Hanover.

Gamer John, farmer; Sec. 23; P.O. Derinda.

GAYETTY L. WILLIAM, Farmer; Sec. 29; P. O. Hanover; born in Venango Co., Penn., June 18, 1834; he came to this state and Carroll Co. with his father in 1837; they moved to Galena in 1839; they came to Derinda Tp. in 1842; he left home to do for himself at the age of fourteen; through his industry and economy he accumulated money and bought his present farm, with gold, from the government in 1855; he was married in 1856 to Margaret Wagman from Bucks Co., Penn.; they had ten children, four are dead: Mary E., born Oct. 16, 1859; Harriet T., Jan. 14, 1861; Ida E., Aug. 12, 1862; Rebecca, Feb. 5, 1864; Lillie, April 8, 1869; Cora E., Sept. 22, 1875; his father died in 1840 in Carroll Co.; he has 160 acres land in Sec. 29; he enlisted in the 96th Regt. I. V. I., Co. A, in 1862; mustered out in 1863 on account of sickness; re-enlisted April, 1865; was mustered out Jan. 27, 1866; he has held the office of Assessor one year, Road Commissioner one year; Mr. G. has been very prominent in the interests of his district school and held the office of Director three years.

Gleason Michael, laborer; Derinda.

Gothard Isaac, farmer; Sec. 15; P.O. Derinda.

Gothard John, Sec. 15; P. O. Derinda Centre.

Gouse Marcus, Sec. 16; P. O. Derinda Centre.

Gouse Michael, farmer; Sec. 16; P. O. Derinda Centre.

Grabald John, laborer; P. O. Savanna.

Grass Fred, farmer; Sec. 16; P. O. Derinda Centre.

Groesinger Christian, farmer; Sec. 17; P. O. Derinda Centre.

Groesinger Christor A. farmer; Sec. 16; P.O. Derinda Centre.

Groesinger George, farmer; Sec. 5; P. O. Derinda Centre.

Groesinger Jacob, farmer; Sec. 22; P. O. Derinda Centre.

Groesinger John, farmer; Sec. 9; P. O. Derinda Centre.

HAAS GEORGE, farmer; Sec. 29; P. O. Savanna.

Haas John, farmer; Sec. 35; P. O. Derinda Centre.

Haas Wm. farmer; Sec. 24; P. O. Savanna.

Haas Wm. farmer; Sec. 24; P. O. Derinda.

James H. Murphy

COUNTY SURVEYOR,

GREEN VALE

Handel J. farmer; Sec. 33; P. O. Savanna.

Hardacre Jos. renter; Sec. 17; P. O. Derinda Centre.

Heer Andrew, farmer; Sec. 30; P.O.Derinda.

Heer George, farmer; Sec. 30; P.O. Derinda.

Heit Casper, farmer; Sec. 24; P.O. Derinda.

Helmick John, farmer; Sec. 15; P. O. Derinda Centre.

Henneberg Wm. farmer; Sec. 12; P. O. Derinda.

Hennesee Thos. laborer; P. O. Derinda.

Herald Dave, farmer; Sec. 19; P.O. Hanover.

Herron Albert, laborer; Sec. 28; P. O. Derinda Centre.

Herring C. farmer; Sec. 28; P. O. Savanna.

Herron Samuel, farmer; Sec. 5; P. O. Derinda Centre.

Hicks Jos. renter; Sec. 3; P. O. Elizabeth.

Hicks Wm. renter; Sec. 3; P. O. Elizabeth.

Hoffman H. farmer; Sec. 12; P. O. Derinda.

JESSE GODFRED, farmer; Sec. 1; P. O. Derinda.

Jesse Louis, Sec. 1; P. O. Derinda.

Jordan R. farmer; Sec. 34; P. O. Savanna.

KEARNEY HAMILTON, farmer; Sec. 19; P. O. Hanover.

KEARNEY JOHN A. Farmer; Sec. 19; P. O. Hanover; born in Ireland, March, 1837; came to this country and Carroll Co. 1855; came to this Co. in 1856; settled on his present farm in 1858; he was married, in 1868, to Miss Sarah R. McKinley, from Hanover Tp.; they have four children: Mary J., born Nov. 1, 1869; William E., Jan. 24, 1872; Howard L., May 11, 1874; Ruth J., Nov. 20, 1876; Mr. Kearney, in partnership with his brothers, Hamilton and Robert, owns 430 acres of land—230 acres in Derinda Tp. and 200 acres in Hanover Tp.; Mr. K. has held the office of Road Commissioner six years, School Director three years; his brothers came to this country at the same time that he did.

KEHL JOSEPH, Farmer; Sec. 15; P. O. Derinda Centre; born in Pa., 1836; came to this state and Galena in 1843; moved to Derinda Tp., 1844; settled on his present farm, 1866; married, in 1861, to Miss Barbara A. Knapp, from Germany; she was born, 1843; they have had eight children: Wm. G., Caroline F., Rosa C., Frank A., Catherine O., Hattie E., Emma D., and Oscar; Mr. K. has 188 acres of land; he has held the office of Township Collector 2 years, School Director 3 years, Commissioner of Highways 3 years.

Kehl Michael, Sec. 25; P. O. Derinda Centre.

Keller Michael, farm; S. 11; P. O. Derinda.

Kirkey J. farmer; Sec. 29; P. O. Savanna.

Knapp A. laborer; P. O. Derinda Centre.

Knapp Christian, farmer; Sec. 29; P. O. Derinda Centre.

LAUUER JOHN C.

Lauuer Wm.

Logan Jerry R. Sec. 3; P. O. Elizabeth.

LOGAN WILLIAM, Farmer: Sec. 3; P. O. Elizabeth; he was born in Jackson Co., Indiana, Dec. 2, 1815; he came to this state and New Boston, Mercer Co., in 1834; he moved to this Co. in 1835, and spent fourteen years in mining here and Wisconsin; he settled on his present farm in 1849; he was married in 1848 to Miss Elizabeth Claypool from Ohio; she was born April 25, 1822; they have had six children; Helen R., born Feb. 12, 1850; James P., Feb. 1, 1852; Jesse R., Oct. 1, 1854; Louisa H., April 26, 1857; Evans B., Dec. 16, 1859; Cora A., Aug. 1, 1864; he has 760 acres land located in Secs. 3, 4 and 10; 400 acres of his land he purchased of government in 1844; he has held the office of Supervisor for the past nine years, School Director eight years, School Trustee eighteen years; Mr. Logan is quite extensively engaged in stock raising; his cattle and horses all look fine.

McCALL THOMAS, farmer; Sec. 35; P. O. Savanna.

McEwen Adelbert, laborer; Derinda.

McGrath J. H. farmer; Sec. 8; P. O. Derinda Centre.

McGRATH ROBERT, Farmer, Merchant and Postmaster; Sec. 17; P. O. Derinda Centre; born in Penn. in 1831; came to this state and Galena May, 1836; settled in Derinda Tp. same year, and on his present farm in 1849; he was married, in 1857, to Miss Esther Weir from Penn.; they have had five children: Jane E., born April 23, 1858; Charles M., Feb. 15, 1863; Willmer W., Jan. 1870; Bennie R., May 17, 1873; Mary E., Jan. 31, 1868, died Oct. 8, 1868; Mr. McG. was elected constable when the Tp. was first organized in 1854, he held it four years; Township Constable one year, Postmaster since Jan. 27, 1873; he has 100 acres land in Secs. 9 and 11.

McGrath Sam'l, Sec. 9; P. O. Derinda Centre

McGrath T. D. Sec. 8; P. O. Derinda Centre.

McGrath Wm. farmer; Sec. 8; P. O. Derinda Centre.

McGrath W. A. Sec. 8; P. O. Derinda Centre.

McIntire J. Sec. 31; P. O. Derinda Centre.

Maas Jno. laborer; Derinda.

Madke Wm. farmer; Sec. 1; P. O. Derinda.

Mahood Wm. farm; S. 36; P. O. Savanna.

Miller J. G. farmer; Sec. 8; P. O. Derinda Centre.

Minges P. farmer; Sec. 33; P. O. Savanna.

Moffett Jas. farm; Secs. 25 and 26; P. O. Savanna.

Moffett John, Sec. 25; P. O. Savanna.

Moffett Thos. farmer; Sec. 7; P. O. Derinda Centre.

Mollison J. Sec. 17; P. O. Derinda Centre.

Morrison John, farmer; Sec. 17; P. O. Derinda Centre.

OLIVER RICHARD A. Farmer; Sec. 20; P.O. Hanover; he was born on the same farm he now occupies Jan. 15, 1843; he was married in 1863 to Miss F. J. Evans from East Galena Tp.; they have six children: Susie E., born Nov. 29, 1863; Florence G., Sept. 10, 1865; William T., Nov. 28, 1866; Katie H., May 24, 1871; Fannie J., Nov. 13, 1872; R. Leyle, Sept. 4, 1875; Mr. O. has 320 acres of land in Secs. 19, 20, and 22; he held the office of Tp. Clerk six years, Collector one year; Mr. Oliver's father, Thomas Oliver, was born in Yorkshire, England, in 1805; he served five years in the British army; he came to this country and Co. in 1833; he purchased the estate from government in 1844; he died in 1871.

Owens Thos. laborer; Derinda.

PAISLEY JOHN, laborer; Derinda.

Plush Valentine, farmer; Sec. 16: P. O. Derinda Centre.

Preiger L. renter; Sec. 10; P. O. Derinda Centre.

RADKEY JNO. farmer; Sec. 11; P. O. Derinda Centre.

Radkey M. laborer; Derinda.

Radkey Wm. laborer; Derinda.

Randecker Chris. farmer; Sec. 1; P. O. Derinda Centre.

Randecker J. C. farmer; Sec. 4; P.O. Derinda Centre.

Randecker J., Sr., farmer; Sec. 19; P. O. Hanover.

Randecker John, Jr., farmer; Sec. 19; P. O. Hanover.

Randecker Peter, farmer; Sec. 16; P. O. Derinda Centre.

Roberts Absalom, farmer; Sec. 3; P. O. Derinda Centre.

Robert Alfred, farmer; Sec. 4; P. O. Derinda Centre.

Rodgers John D. farmer; Sec. 30; P. O. Derinda Centre.

Rodgers Henry, laborer; Derinda.

SCHAIBLE GOTTLEIB, farmer; Sec. 20; P. O. Derinda Centre.

Schaible J. farmer; Sec. 6; P. O. Elizabeth.

Schaible Jno. farmer; Sec. 6; P.O. Hanover.

Schaerer Gottleib, farmer; Sec. 9; P. O. Derinda Centre.

Schueler Geo. farm; Sec. 13; P. O. Derinda.

SEYLER REV. THEODORE, Clergyman German Lutheran Church; Sec. 16; P. O. Derinda Centre; born in Bavaria, Germany, June 6, 1839; came to this country and Dubuque in 1854; he pursued his studies for the ministry in the Whatburg German Seminary, Clayton Co., Iowa, until 1859; he spent three years among the Indians as a missionary; he returned and finished his course in 1864; he commenced his ministry at Newbern, Jasper Co., Iowa, in 1865, where he remained three years; he spent three years and six months in Wis.; settled over his present parish in 1871; he was married in 1865 to Miss Mary Mance, from DesMoines, Ia.; they have had seven children; two died; names of living: Charlotte, Magdalena, Gotthold, Theodore, Jr., and Frederick; Mr. Seyler has two appointments besides the two regular; Rev. A. Myers assists him; the two churches in Derinda Tp., over which he is pastor, were organized as one in 1855, under the ministry of Rev. S. Fritschel; in 1849 there was a division made through the forms of holding worship; a part withdrew and built a church, in 1859, in Sec. 27; they now have a membership of 20 families; the church in Sec. 16 has a fine church built in 1872, with a membership of 28 families.

Shubert Fred. farmer; Sec. 24; P. O. Derinda Centre.

Skeem Wm., Jr., farmer; Sec. 2; P. O. Derinda Centre.

Speer Wm. farmer; Sec. 36; P. O. Savanna.

THEIN JOHN, farmer; Sec. 24; P. O. Derinda Centre.

Thein Lawrence, farm; S. 24; P.O. Derinda.

Thein Nichols, laborer; Derinda.

WETZEL S. farmer; Sec. 33; P. O. Savanna.

Wever John, farmer; Sec. 12; P. O. Derinda.

Williamson Adam, Sec. 34; P. O. Savanna.

WILLIAMSON DAVID, Farmer; Sec. 55; P. O. Savanna; born in Cavan Co., Ireland, in 1835; came to this Co. and Hanover Tp. in 1856; settled on his present farm in 1866; he was married in 1867 to Miss Letitia White, from Pleasant Valley Tp.; they have five children: John W., born April 8, 1869; James, Dec. 4, 1870; Elizabeth J., Aug. 20, 1872; Margaret B., July 5, 1874; Susan E., Feb. 16, 1876; he has 160 acres of land in Secs. 35 and 36 valued at $3,000.

Williamson David, laborer; Derinda.

Williamson Ritchie, farmer; Sec. 34; P. O. Savanna.

Williamson Robert, Sec. 34; P. O. Savanna.

Williamson Wm. Sec. 34; P. O. Savanna.

Wirbley Geo. laborer; Derinda.

Wouster Andrew, Sec. 16; P. O. Derinda Centre.

Wouster C. farmer; Sec. 27; P. O. Savanna.

Wouster Samuel, farmer; Sec. 16; P. O. Derinda Centre.

Wright Robert, farmer; Sec. 8; P. O. Derinda Centre.

ZINK BASSIE, farmer; Sec. 26; P. O. Derinda.

Zink B. farm; S. 23; P. O. Derinda Centre.

ELIZABETH TOWNSHIP.

ADAMS SAMUEL, miner; Elizabeth.

Adams Wm. J. laborer; Elizabeth.

Aiken A. farmer; Sec. 5; P. O. Galena.

ALLEN JOHN, Retired Farmer; Elizabeth; born in Derbyshire, Eng., March 25, 1811; came to Springfield, Ill., in 1840 and to this Co. in 1842; owns a farm on Sec. 7, Woodbine Township; married Miss Elizabeth A. Clark, in 1851; she was born in Jo Daviess Co. in 1830; they have nine children living: Sarah Ann, now Mrs. Gosnay, William, John, Charles, Alfonzo, Samuel Robert, Joseph Wilber; Mr. A. owns 330 acres of land; was one of the Co. in the Wishorn Diggings; he has now left his farm to be carried on by his sons and is now living in the retirement of his village home where he can enjoy the product of his energy and toil during the remainder of his declining years.

Armytage Benj. painter; Elizabeth.

Ashmore Bowman, printer; Elizabeth.

ASHMORE CHARLES, Farmer; Sec. 25; P. O. Elizabeth; born in Derbyshire, Eng., June 15, 1829; came with his mother to America in 1836; his father having come two years previous; has 186 acres of land; oldest settlers nearly all gone; very few here now that were in this section when they came; the Old Fort and a few cabins were all the marks of the settler's axe where now the village of Elizabeth is; John Flack built the first business shop and in that he sold whisky to the miners; his father bought the claim for the land where they now live, from Valentine Brazzel.

ASHMORE HENRY, Farmer; Sec. 25; P. O. Elizabeth; born in Jo Daviess Co. July 2, 1842; his father moved to the Co. from England in 1833; a great many Indians passed through the county after his family came, committing some depredations, marauding, and stealing from the white settlers; one day, while his father was mowing, a party of Indians came along; the one that seemed to be the chief rode up to Mr. A., and drawing out a long knife and brandishing it over his head, demanded a whetstone; Mr. A. being a stranger to their customs, hardly knew what was best to do, but not wishing to let them know that he felt any fear, gave him the whetstone; the Indian whet his knife, and then rode away, beckoning Mr. A. to follow, but he chose to remain and let Mr. Indian pass on; soon after a bee-tree was found a little way from the spot, and Mr. Ashmore always supposed the Indian wanted to show it to him. Henry Ashmore, the subject of this sketch, married Belle Claypool, Oct. 20, 1867; they have three children: Cora B., Jos. Sherman, and Nonie Elizabeth; Mr. A. has a farm of 160 acres of land.

AVERY WILLIAM, Retired; Sec. 5; P. O. Avery; born in Chenango Co., N. Y., Aug. 15, 1807; his father moved to Olean Point, Pa., by wagon; from there on a raft of pine lumber to Cincinnati; rented a piece of land near there, and raised a crop of corn; sold it in the Fall and started for the Wabash, but falling in company with Mr. Linsey, who told him of the transcendant beauties of the prairies of Illinois, he decided to abandon the trip to the woody banks of the Wabash, and, in company with his new friend, purchased a flatboat which had come from Pittsburg with iron, embarked upon it with their families, and floated down the Ohio to its mouth; there procured passage on a keelboat, which was officered by Spaniards and negroes, to St. Louis, Mo. The two families remained at St. Louis almost three years, with the exception of a six months' trip up to the Illinois River, but owing to disappointments by their employer, they were compelled to make their way back; they constructed a rude canoe,on each side of which they fastened a cottonwood log, to give the craft sufficient weight to withstand the surging waves of the Mississippi and rough Missouri; upon this the two families again embarked for St. Louis; to lessen the freight Mr. A., the subject of this sketch, was allowed to get into a canoe with some U. S. soldiers; soon a furious storm came up, and it was feared that the feeble barks would go down in the tempest's billows, and all be lost; but imagine the joy of the anxious mother and the little boy when they met again, safe, on the landing at St. Louis; they started late in the Fall for Peoria on a keel-boat; when about half way up the Illinois River, cold weather came on, and they found their boat fast in the ice, away from communication or civilization, but having sufficient provisions, they remained in their ice-bound vessel till navigation opened in Spring, and they sailed up to Peoria. Mr. A. came to Jo Daviess Co. in 1828, at the age of 21. He served as Captain of the U. S. troops during the Black Hawk War; he saw the council fires which glared on the wise and daring warriors go out, their arrows broken, their springs dried up, their cabins fall to ruins; the echoing whoop, the bloody grapple, the defying death song, all gave way to the onward march of civilization. Mr. A. was one of the very few settlers who beheld the remnant of Black Hawk's warriors take up their line of march toward the setting sun; after he had served his time, and peace spread her protecting wings over this part of the land, Mr. A. returned to Peoria and married Phœbe Reed, in March, 1834; she was born in Delaware Co., N. Y.; have five children: Col. Geo. S. Avery, at present Co. Clerk of Jo Daviess; Sarah M. Hallett, of Galena; Amos W., of Virginia City, Nev.; Cyrus R., of Virginia City, Nev., now at home taking care of his father; Alonzo M., M.D., of Iowa; Mr. A. is suffering at the present time with general paralysis, which has confined him to the house for many a year.

BAINBRIDGE JAS. miner; Elizabeth.

Barker Robt. farm; S. 22; P. O. Elizabeth.

Barnes J. farmer; Sec. 16; P.O. Elizabeth.

Barrett Herbert, merchant; Elizabeth.

Barrett Michael, retired; Elizabeth.

BARTON JAMES, Farmer; Sec. 28; P. O. Elizabeth; born in Co. Fermanagh, Ireland, in June, 1818; his father moved to this country and settled in Philadelphia in 1826; Mr. B. came to Galena and remained during the Summer of 1835; took a claim near where he now resides and had a cabin erected; returned to Philadelphia; the following year his father moved to this Co.; lived in the cabin upon the claim; in 1838 took a trip down the river; spent the Winter in New Orleans; worked two years for Wm. Goldthoy, near Galena, smelting; married Miss Elizabeth Tonkin in 1864; she was born in Jo Daviess Co.; have three children: George A., James W., Emma; owns 340 acres of land.

BARTON JEREMIAH, Farmer; Sec. 16; P.O. Elizabeth; born in the City of Philadelphia Jan. 27, 1828; came to Jo Daviess Co. in 1838; Mr. B. has 160 acres of good land and a fine residence, but the charms of the *fair* have never been sufficiently seductive, and he remains a single man; Mr. B. had a brother, John, wounded at the battle of Chicamauga and died from the wound, leaving a widow and five children; they have lived with him; the children are: Annie E., Samuel, Alice, Henry and William.

Bateman George, retired farmer; Elizabeth.

Bateman Jas. H. constable; Elizabeth.

Banwarth Charles, blacksmith; Elizabeth.

Bawden Richard, Sr., farm; P. O. Elizabeth.

BEEBE E. W. Physician and Surgeon; Elizabeth; born in Livingston Co., N. Y., Jan. 26, 1828; at the age of 24, having completed his course in medicine, he left his native state and commenced the practice of his profession in Michigan in 1852; during his residence there he returned to N. Y. and married Lucy Budrow, Jan. 2, 1860; came to Jo Daviess Co. in 1862; moved to Iowa in 1867; remained there nine years and returned to Jo Daviess Co.; they have four children living: Livingston, Edith, Gertrude, and Constance; Dr. Beebe is a gentleman of quick perceptive faculties and literary taste; is engaged in an extensive practice, takes a lively interest in the prosperity and progress of schools and churches, lending his influence to every enterprise calculated to encourage the young.

Bennett John, miner; P. O. Elizabeth.

Binns Abel, farmer; Sec. 3; P. O. Elizabeth.

Binns Mathew, Sec. 3; P. O. Elizabeth.

Black Daniel, farm; Sec. 29; P. O. Hanover.

Black Samuel, farm; S. 29; P. O. Hanover.

BLEYER JOSEPH, Farmer; Sec. 1; P. O. Elizabeth; born in Elcass, Germany, Feb. 13, 1836; came to America in 1866; lived in Rochester till the next Spring; went to Chicago, Bloomington and St. Louis; spent the next Winter in Louisiana; returned to St. Louis; went to Macon, Ga.; had ague; was advised to go north; returned to Burlington and St. Paul; returned south again and worked on Texas landing; came to this Co. in 1871; went south the third time to Natchez; came back by Port Byron; went to Fort Dodge, Iowa; then, returning to this Co., bought the farm of 40 acres where he now lives.

Blewett John, farmer; P. O. Elizabeth.

Blewett Thomas, farmer; P. O. Elizabeth.

Blower Ralph, laborer; Elizabeth.

Bowden George, miner; Elizabeth.

BOWDEN CHARLES, Farmer; Sec. 11; P. O. Elizabeth; born in Cornwall, England, May 16, 1829; came to this country by way of Quebec, direct to Jo Daviess Co.; married Miss Ellen Shimmin in 1851; she was born on the Isle of Man in 1837; came to America in 1845; Mr. B. has worked in the mines of Canada, Lake Superior mineral regions, and has traveled through nearly all the states and territories of the Union; visited California in the Summer of 1877; have ten children; Thomas P., now in Cal., John H., Eleanor A., Margaret J., Charles R., William C., George E., Joseph I., Clara A., Alice Mabel; owns 114 acres of land.

Bowden John.

Bowlesby James, stonemason; Elizabeth.

Boyle M. farmer; Sec. 8; P. O. Galena.

Bray Thomas B., Elizabeth.

Breed Nelson, Elizabeth.

BREED O. Farmer; P. O. Avery; born in Butternut, Otsego Co., N. Y.; came to Jo Daviess Co. May 12, 1835; started with a team, traveling through Canada, around Lake Michigan and crossed Rock River where now the beautiful City of Rockford is situated; at that time the only sign of a settlement was the cabin erected by Germanicus Kent, on the banks of Rock River; the cabin of James Flack, in Jo Daviess Co. was the next mark of a settler's axe on his route; disposed of his team and came on foot from Rockford to the mineral regions; Mr. B. followed mining for about seven years; now owns 240 acres of land, a part of which he pre-empted; married Mary A. Cook, July 23, 1844; she was born in Sheffield, England, Feb. 26, 1826, and came to Jo Daviess Co. with her parents at the age of six; they have had thirteen children: Lovisa, Melinda, Ann, Harriet Vesta, William, Nelson, Lucy, Mary, Lincoln H., Florence J., Olive and Ansel; Mr. B. is one of the Co.'s practical men; is extensively engaged in growing fine stock; has in his house one of those home comforts, an old fashioned fire place, almost a novelty now-a-days.

Breed Wm., Avery.

Bromley Albert, Sec. 12 P. O. Elizabeth.

BROMLEY RICHARD, Farmer; Sec. 12; P. O. Elizabeth; born in Montreal, Canada, April 11, 1823; his parents emigrated from the north of England. in 1815; he settled in this Co. in the Spring of 1844; came on the lakes to Chicago; from there on foot; would occasionally get a ride with teamsters; married Miss Harriet Williams; they had three children, Albert and Walter G. are living; lost the other child and his wife; married Mrs. Moyle; her maiden name was Miss Elizabeth Kemp; she was born in England, Co. Cornwall; came to this Co. in 1849; she had five children: Thomas Moyle, Elizabeth, Jane, Harriet and Mary; their home exhibits the evidence of a charitable and hospitable one as they now have two orphan girls for whom they care with all the fondness of a parent's relation.

Brown Samuel, Elizabeth.

Bryant Richard, farmer; P. O. Elizabeth.

BYERS GEORGE. Retired Farmer; Secs. 5 and 6; Derinda Tp.; resides in village of Elizabeth; born in Huntingdon Co., Pa., May 29, 1806; came to Jo Daviess in in 1838; followed mining in this and adjoining Cos. till 1852 when he went to the gold regions of California; returned in 1855; lived on his farm in Derinda till the close of the war; married the widow of Wm. Wayman May 20, 1856; her maiden name was Miss M. Price; born in Bucks Co., Pa., Jan. 16, 1811; came to this Co. in 1840; lost her husband in 1847; she has six children living: Thomas, Margaret G., Mrs. Ester Shipton; William, Mrs. Caroline Gable and Henry; have two grandchildren living with them: George Shipton and John Edwin Shipton.

CALVIN MICHAEL, farmer; P. O. Elizabeth.

Champlin Wm. laborer; Elizabeth.

Clark Felix, laborer; Elizabeth.

Clark Samuel, miner; Elizabeth.

CLEGG WILLIAM T., Agent; Elizabeth; born at Weston, Jo Daviess Co., April 16, 1856; his father came to the Co. in 1845; Mr. C. has resided in Jo Daviess since his birth except about six years, which he spent in the copper regions of Lake Superior; attended the High School in Galena; learned the trade of cigar maker; has a fine collection of specimens of copper, silver, crystals, English agates, Brazilian agates, etc., which show much care and taste in their selection.

Clegg Wm. miner; Elizabeth.

Cochrane Samuel, carpenter; Elizabeth.

Connor P. farmer; Sec. 6; P. O. Galena.

Cook Henry, farmer; P. O. Avery.

Cook Jas. farmer; P. O. Avery.

Cook John, Avery.

Cook Wm., Avery.

Corkery J. farmer; Sec. 2; P. O. Elizabeth.

Cornman G. miner; Sec. 10; P. O. Elizabeth.

CRUMMER JAMES, Farmer; Sec. 25; P. O. Elizabeth; born in the State of Delaware. July 24, 1824; his father and mother came from Ireland and settled on the Brandywine in 1818; Mr. C. came to Jo Daviess Co. with his mother in 1835, and his father came in 1834; first settlers in that section of county; has 240 acres of land; served as School Director for many years; married Miss Araminta Tart Oct. 7, 1847; has seven children living: B. F. Crummer, M.D., of Warren, Edwin M., Willis, Fremont, Lillis M., Schuyler Colfax and Joseph; lost his wife and one child, Horace; married Miss Sarah Wright July 1, 1865; she was born at Yellow Springs, Ohio; she went from Ohio to New York City, where she resided with an elder brother for eight years; lived in

Chicago for four years; came to Jo Daviess Co. in 1865.

Crummer Wm.

Cubbon T. farmer; Sec. 15; P. O. Elizabeth.

DANIEL WILLIAM, farmer; P. O. Elizabeth.

Davy W. J. miner; Elizabeth.

Doane Wm. stage driver; Elizabeth.

Draper William, retired; Elizabeth.

EADE JOSEPH, miner; Elizabeth.

Eade Samuel, miner; Elizabeth.

EADIE JOHN, Farmer; Sec. 33; P. O. Hanover; born in Renfrew, Scotland; came to America in 1842; remained a short time in Fulton Co., and came to mining district of this Co. same year; married Mary Statham Aug. 8, 1845; she was born in Derbyshire, Eng.; she came to America in 1828; remained at Albany, N. Y., till 1842, when she came to this Co.; Mr. E. was engaged in mining during the early times; spent eighteen months in California; visited Scotland in 1871: they have nine children: Benjamin, Elizabeth, Thomas, Hannah, John, Margaret A., Robert, Catharine S., Wm. Wallace; Mr. E. has a farm of 290 acres; fine residence and good stock buildings.

Eadie Thomas, Sec. 33; P. O. Hanover.

Etling George, saloon keeper; Elizabeth.

Eustice D. L. farmer; Elizabeth.

Eustice Jas. P. O. Elizabeth.

Eustice John G. P. O. Elizabeth.

EUSTICE RICHARD, Teamster; Sec. 22; P. O. Elizabeth; born in Cornwall, Eng., July 15, 1840; his parents came to America in 1841, when the subject of this sketch was quite young; they came direct to Jo Daviess Co.; Mr. E. has teamed from Hon. H. Green's smelting furnace, near Elizabeth for 16 years; married Miss Mary Tippett, Jan. 1, 1865; she was born in Weston, near where they now reside; Mr. E. has served for two terms as School Director, and five years as Commissioner of Highways; has five children: Edith A., William M., James E., Richard J., Charles R.

Eustice Richard W. retired; P. O. Elizabeth.

Eustice Samuel, P. O. Elizabeth.

EUSTICE THOS. W. Harness Shop; Elizabeth; born in Jo Daviess Co. Jan. 4, 1850; has lived in the Co. since, except three years spent in the copper regions of Lake Superior and Michigan; was there from 1872 to 1875; married Kitty Toben April 2, 1877; she was born in Galena July 14, 1849; they now reside in the village of Elizabeth, Jo Daviess Co., where Mr. Eustice is doing an extensive business in the line of harnesses, saddles, etc.

Eustice W. H. retired; P. O. Elizabeth.

FARRELL JAMES; laborer; Elizabeth.

Flemming Patrick, farmer; Sec. 29; P. O. Hanover.

Flemming Wm. P. O. Hanover.

FRASIER JAMES, Merchant; Elizabeth; born in Lanarkshire, Scotland, Sept. 24, 1822; came to America in 1842, landing at New York; went to Canada and lived there two years; came on to Apple River, in Jo Daviess Co. in 1844; during the gold excitement of 1850 went to that country across the plains; returned in 1852, and has since resided in Elizabeth; was employed as clerk in the store of Richard Brown for seven years; in partnership with Mr. D. Robinson—purchased Brown's stock; remained in the firm two years, and then purchased the store and stock from Mr. Barker, and has since been in business by himself—doing an extensive business; during an interval of two years that he was out of business visited New York; was in the city during the great riots; in 1845 married Miss Jane Pringle; she was born in Roxburyshire, Scotland, in 1826; she came to America in 1838; have ten children: Mrs. Sidney Marshall, John, Mrs. Margaret Crummer, James, Nettie, Fred, Frank, Wallace, Grant, Mable; Mr. F.'s father is still living in Canada, at the age of eighty-three.

Fraser Jas. A., P. O. Elizabeth.

Fraser John P. merchant; Elizabeth.

GALE WILLIAM, farmer; P. O. Elizabeth.

Gates Edmund, shoemaker; Elizabeth.

Gill W., Sr., farm; Sec. 22; P. O. Elizabeth.

Glessner H. retired; S. 24; P. O. Elizabeth.

Goble Jno. G. carpenter; Elizabeth.

GOARD JAMES H. Blacksmith; Elizabeth; born in Cornwall, Eng., Nov. 19, 1839; his father came to Galena with his family in 1841; Mr. G. has called Jo Daviess Co. his home ever since; served in the War of the Rebellion, 140th Regt. I. V. I., first corporal of Co. C; was in Memphis at the time of Gen. Forest's famous raid; married Margaret Z. Linsey; she was born in Jo Daviess Co.; they have six children: Cora A., Helen J., Fred, Maggie, Jenny and Harry; Mr. G. has an enviable reputation as a horse trainer and teacher; has two fine horses, and for him to command is for them to obey without halter-strap or bridle; has been in blacksmith business for fourteen years; is also the inventor of the Jim Goard Patent Harness Oil, which is known throughout the country as the best in the market.

GOLDSWORTHY THOMAS H. Merchant; Elizabeth; born in Cornwall, Eng., June 12, 1831; came to this Co. in 1845; remained in Penn. one year; went to California in Fall of 1855; lived there thirteen years; once during the time visited the Eastern States; returned to this Co. in 1868; married Miss Mary Eustice March 11, 1869; she was born in Wales April 6, 1844; they have three children living: Adella May, William A. and Thomas Eustice; lost two children: Nellie, died Feb. 16, 1870; Joseph Henry, June 5, 1877; his sickness was lingering disease of the spine; but a short time before he died there were some signs of improvement, and it was fondly hoped that he might recover; he was the delight of his friends young and old; his manly bearing and mature mind made him a companion of the old as well as the young; about a week previous to his death he told his father and mother that they must give him up, he could not live; he knew that the silver cord was almost loosened and the golden bowl was breaking at the fountain, but he was resigned, for he knew he had a *friend* in the great beyond who had said: "Suffer little children to come unto Me, and forbid them not, for of such is the kingdom of Heaven."

"Put away the little garments,
Harry needs them now no more;
Jesus watches safely o'er him
On that bright and happy shore."

Goldthorp Joseph; Elizabeth.

GOLDTHORP J. E. Farmer; Sec. 28; P. O. Elizabeth; born in Galena March 6, 1842; his parents moved to Elizabeth when he was two years of age; has been in Co. since except about two years at Rock River Seminary, Mt. Morris; married Miss Sarah E. Rankin Jan. 1, 1864, the day known as the cold New Year, a day to be remembered especially by some of our soldiers who were on duty that day; Mrs. G. was born on the American Bottoms opposite St. Louis April 20, 1842; they have two children: Elmer Elsworth, born Oct. 7, 1864; Clara W., Nov. 28, 1870.

GOLDTHORP T. R. Farmer; Sec. 27; P. O. Elizabeth; born in Jo Daviess Co.; married Miss Salina Angwin, March 10, 1868; Mr. G. and wife were reared and have always lived in this Co.; were born in Weston.

GOLDTHORP WM. Farmer; Sec. 22; P. O. Elizabeth; born in Yorkshire, England, April 5, 1812; came to America in 1829, settling at Philadelphia, Pa.; remained there three years; came to Jo Daviess Co. in 1832; went from Galena to Blue Mound, Wis., in 1833, mining there for 18 months; made his first $500 at that place; went to Lost Grove; remained there for one year in smelting business; then went on to Fever River, where he remained in the smelting business till 1844; moved to farm upon which he now resides; married Ellen Ellis Nov. 12, 1831, at Philadelphia; she was born in Yorkshire, Eng.; they have four children living: Elizabeth, Joseph E., Thos. R., and Araminta; has 1,380 acres of land; was Postmaster for 15 years at Weston; has been School Director for many years.

Gott Richard, laborer; Elizabeth.

Grady Patrick, farmer; Sec. 8; P. O. Galena.

Gray James.

Green Geo. carpenter; Elizabeth.

GREEN GEO. H. Retired; Elizabeth; born in Yorkshire, Eng., Nov. 23, 1832; came to America with his parents, landing at Galena in the Spring of 1841; the family resided about two years near the new diggings in Wis., then moved to Elizabeth Tp., Jo Daviess Co.; Mr. G. resided with his parents till 1853, after which, being 21 years of age, he commenced work with a firm in which his uncle, Henry Green, was a partner; remained in their employ for 10 years, then went to Washoe Valley, Nev.; engaged there on a ranch, where he remained for five years, becoming, at the expiration of one half the time, the superintendent of the work, a position which he sustained with dignity and honor; he was married July 4, 1854, to Mary T. Tredinnick; she was born in Cornwall, Eng.; they have had two children; lost a little girl, Martha Ann; Walter Henry, born March 30, 1868; Mr. G. has served as a member of the Board of Trustees for the Corporation of Elizabeth for three years; has been on School Board for five years; is a member of County Republican Central Committee; also of Town Committee; family attend M. E. Church; Mr. G. is at the present time living in the retirement of his home, enjoying the confidence and respect of all with whom he is associated.

GREEN HENRY, HON. Lead Smelter and Farmer; Sec. 23; P. O. Elizabeth; was born in the Village of Horbury, near Wakefield, in the West Riding of Yorkshire, Eng., on Feb. 13, 1819; his early life was passed as an operative in various branches of the woolen business, in which his father was a small manufacturer; in his twentieth year he left home and became superintendent of power-looms and "Jaquard Machinery," and designer and pattern-worker in a manufactory of ladies' dress goods at Shelf, near Halifax; in the Fall of 1841 he migrated to the United States, making his way directly to Galena, and entered the employment of the late Samuel Hughlett, Esq., with whom, two years later, he became associated in the lead smelting business, under the firm name of Tart, Greer & Co., and afterward Goldthorp, Greer & Co.; this business, after several changes in partnership, fell into Mr. Greer's hands, and is still carried on by him; he has also at the same time been engaged in mining, farming and store-keeping; he was married May 23, 1845, to Miss Sarah Roberts, of Horbury, who was born June 3, 1818; he brought with him to this country British free trade notions, but becoming satisfied that the true policy of a new country like this is a moderate, steady protection to manufacturing industries, he at once affiliated with the Whig party, and continued to act with it till its dissolution and the organization of the Republican party; his first Presidential vote was cast for Henry Clay; the confidence of his fellow-citizens has been expressed by repeated elections to the State Legislature; he has served six years in the House of Representatives, and four years in the Senate; for five years he participated in the county government as member of the Board of Supervisors, and from 1862 to 1865 was Chairman of the Board—the period in which the resources of the county were so freely used in support of the war; in early boyhood he united with the Methodists, and during most of his adult life has sustained some official relation to the church; he was lay delegate from Rock River Conference to the General Conference of the M. E. Church, which met in Baltimore in 1876; his early educational advantages or opportunities were very limited, the greater part of all acquisitions being made by study at home, with very little assistance; in his 33d year he thought he saw the long-sought opportunity for more extensive study and culture; he went to school, but after two years, when nearly ready to enter college, the demands of business called him home, and his projected collegiate course was abandoned forever; has 1,900 acres of land in Jo Daviess Co.; has a fine residence near Elizabeth; Mr. G. is known in the State of Illinois as one of its best financiers, and has a well-deserved reputation for high executive ability in any department of business, public or private; when he was chosen to fill the various offices of trust, he was not heralded by trumpets of fame or any desire on his part to be brought before the public, but for honest purposes and the good of his adopted country, allowed his name to be used; has decision and independence of character; is not afraid to express an opinion in advance of public sentiment; does not wait till public opinion is formed, and then step up to swell a majority.

Grundy John, farm; Sec. 20; P. O. Hanover.

HANCOCK JOSEPH, laborer; Elizabeth.

Hancock Stephen, laborer; Elizabeth.

Harkness John, Elizabeth.

HARKNESS JAMES, Farmer; Sec. 34; P. O. Elizabeth; born in Edinburgh, Scotland; came to America in 1843, settling in Fulton Co., Ill.; March 21, 1844, came to this Co.; first engaged in mining; bought a farm, and now has 300 acres of land; married Miss Hannah Statham Oct. 17, 1844; she was born near Manchester, Eng., March 18, 1827; her parents moved to America the following year; has seven children: Eliza, James, John, Peter, Benjamin, Mary, Hannah; Mr. H. is extensively engaged in growing stock.

Harkness James, Jr., S. 34; P. O. Elizabeth.

Harkness Peter, Elizabeth.

HASSIG LEOPOLD, Painter; Elizbeth; born at Baden on the Rhine, March 13, 1842; his parents moved to America when he was quite young; stopped at Buffalo a short time; from there to Chicago, where they resided six years, and in 1847 came to Galena; Mr. H. was in the Quartermaster's Department during the war; belongs to I. O. O. F. and A. F. and A. M. lodges; has traveled through Iowa, Montana, Nevada and California; married Miss Araminta Pilcher, Jan. 4, 1865; she was born in this Co. Jan. 31, 1843; has town property to the amount of $1,500; has six children: Raymond A., Jennie, Odell, Effie E., Franklin, and Mary A.

Harvey Joseph, miner; Elizabeth.

Hazelett C. farmer; Sec. 19; P. O. Hanover.

Hazelett D. farmer; Sec. 19; P. O. Hanover.

Hefty John, woolen factory; Elizabeth.

HOFFMAN JOHN, Grocer; Elizabeth; born in Zurich, Switzerland, Dec. 16; 1840; came to Jo Daviess Co., July, 1864; served in the Union army, 42d Regt. I. V. I. for one year; Mr. H. married Kunigunda Snyder who was born in Saxe-Coburg Gotha, Germany, Feb. 6, 1849; they were married April 23, 1868; have four children living: Maggie, born March 7, 1869; Annie, July 12, 1872; Edward, Oct. 27, 1874; John, July 4, 1876; lost one child, George F., born June 23, 1870, died Aug. 19, 1871. Mr. H. engaged in farming after returning from the war; traded his farm for town property in Elizabeth where he now resides; has a Billiard Hall and Grocery Store.

Holland E. farmer; Sec. 10; P. O. Elizabeth.

HOLLAND THOMAS, Retired Farmer; Sec. 9; P. O. Avery; born in Cheshire, England, Dec. 10, 1805; married Miss Mary Hamilton in Aug., 1830; came direct to this Co. from England in 1837; bought the claim of the land upon which he now resides from N. Morris; he is one of the pioneers of Jo Daviess Co.; has ten children living: Mrs. Ann Ransom, Mrs. Elizabeth Cook Ralph, of Page Co., Iowa, Thomas of Mossville, Edwin on Homestead, John of Kansas, George of this Co., Mrs. Mary Williams of Weston,

H. Green.

ELIZABETH TOWNSHIP

William of Nevada, Enoch of California; lost his wife in 1875; married Mrs. Spencer; one child; married Mrs. Shimmin; lost her and is now living in a neat cottage of which he is the sole monarch, at the age of 72.

Hoskings J. W., Jr., farmer; Sec. 12; P.O. Elizabeth.

HOSKING RICHARD, AND HOSKING JOHN, Farmers; Sec. 12; P. O. Elizabeth; John was born at Old Council Hill, this Co., April 7, 1850; parents came from England in 1834; resided at Hazel Green, Wis., Council Hill and Elizabeth; John went to California in 1871; lived there 18 months; returned and married Miss Mary Ransom in the Fall of 1875; she was born in Elizabeth Tp.; have one child, Lawrence Edgar. Richard was born in Elizabeth Tp. July 9, 1852; they hold an undivided interest in the homestead of 200 acres, and are engaged in farming and stock growing.

Howarth James, clerk; Elizabeth.

Howarth Thomas, painter; Elizabeth.

HOWARTH WILLIAM, Farmer; Sec. 16; P. O. Elizabeth; born in Yorkshire, England, Dec. 25, 1820; came to America in 1833, landing in Philadelphia; resided in Middletown, Pa., about 10 years; moved to Floyd Co., Ind.; was foreman in a saw mill preparing timber for boat and ship-building, and was part of the time watchman on a boat running to St. Louis, while he lived in Ind.; came to Jo Daviess Co. in the Summer of 1845; teamed from Galena to Chicago; has not been out of the Co. more than three weeks at a time for 32 years; married Miss Fannie Lawry Oct. 27, 1859; she was born on the Isle of Man, March 8, 1841; have ten children: Lewis P., Clara, Nettie, Dora, Bertha, Sarah, Hattie, Walter, Jane and William; has 100 acres of land; has served as Supervisor 5 years and as Assessor 4 years, and has always been one of this Co.'s substantial citizens.

HOWARTH W. T. Physician and Surgeon; P. O. Elizabeth; born in Jo Daviess Co. Aug. 30, 1850; commenced the study of medicine Oct. 12, 1870; attended the Chicago Medical College and graduated March 21, 1876; was known as an industrious and faithful student, and left the halls of the school with the confidence and respect of its Faculty; is now engaged in an extensive and lucrative practice in his native town, where he, by his frugality, temperance and industry has the esteem of all who know him.

Hutchinson John, farmer; P. O. Elizabeth.

IRWIN JAMES, farmer; Sec. 30; P. O. Hanover.

Isbell John K. miner; Elizabeth.

JENKINS EWD., laborer; Elizabeth.

JENKINS JAMES D. Retired Farmer; P. O. Elizabeth; born in Cornwall, England, Jan. 28, 1820; came to Jo Daviess Co. in 1837; in 1847 Mr. J. married Grace Rowe; they had five children: James H., now at Yankton, Dakota; the others, Edward R., and Frances M., reside in Jo Daviess Co.; Mr. J. lost his first wife in June, 1873; married Elizabeth Rogers Dec. 25, 1876; Mr. J. has spent most of his life in America in and near Jo Daviess Co.; was in the copper regions of Lake Superior eight months; during the years of 1837 and 1838, was at Mineral Point, Wis.; he is now out of business, and with his wife is living in retirement at Elizabeth, Jo Daviess Co., Ill.

Jenkins John, farmer; P. O. Elizabeth.

Johns Nathan, farmer; P. O. Elizabeth.

Johns Wm. L., laborer; Elizabeth.

Johnson W. S.

Jones William, lime burner; Elizabeth.

KAWL JOHN, farmer; Sec. 15; P. O. Elizabeth.

LAIGN JOHN, farmer; P. O. Elizabeth.

LAWTON J. J. Farmer; Sec. 20; P. O. Galena; born in Columbia Co., N. Y., near the City of Hudson, Feb. 13, 1837; came to Jo Daviess Co. with his father's family in 1848; married Miss Eliza J. Blake, July 8, 1858; she was born in Jo. Daviess Co.; her father was among the earliest settlers; have six children: John, Ann, Byron, Ada, Hannah, Alice; Mr. L. has a farm of 118 acres; is engaged in growing fine cattle, hogs and horses.

Levens Alex., Sec. 7; P. O. Galena.

Levens Edward, farm; Sec. 18; P.O. Galena.

Levens James, farm; Sec. 17; P. O. Galena.

LEVENS PATRICK, Retired Farmer; Sec. 7; P. O. Galena; born in County Louth, Ireland, May 15, 1805; married Miss Elizabeth McKeown June 9, 1831; she was born in County Down, Ireland, April 11, 1810; they came to America in 1833, landing at Philadelphia; remained there four years; came to Jo Daviess Co. in 1837; lived in Galena two years, then laid claim on land where he now resides; has 320 acres of land; has five children: Edward, James, Patrick, Alexander, Margaret; Mr. L. is among the oldest living settlers; visited his native country in 1875; traveled extensively along the eastern coast; attended the famous O'Connor celebration at Dublin in 1875; 10,000 Americans in attendance.

Levens Patrick, Jr., Sec. 7; P. O. Galena.

Lee John C. bridge contractor; Elizabeth.

LINGFORD ELECTA ANN, Mrs. Farm; S. 25; P. O. Elizabeth; born in Plattsburg, N. Y., Aug. 31, 1838; her maiden name was Electa Ann Holcomb; was quite young when her mother died; her father came to Jo Daviess Co., leaving her with friends in New York; her father married again, and she came on to live with them; married Mr. Robert Lingford Oct. 5, 1852; he was born in Nottingham, Eng., Feb. 23, 1818; came to America in 1849; settled with a colony at Rydott; has eight children: Eliza Viola, Florence A., Carrie E., Robert H., William A., Lawrence A., Wallace A., Thora May; has 80 acres of land.

Long John, harness maker; Elizabeth.

Long T. T.

Lowry Henry, retired; P. O. Elizabeth.

McCANNEY FRANK, farmer; Sec. 2; P. O. Elizabeth.

McCabe Jas. farmer; Sec. 6; P. O. Galena.

McCormick Michael, farmer; P. O. Galena.

McDermott Thos. miner; Elizabeth.

McDonald William, farm; P. O. Elizabeth.

McGough Edward, Sec. 4; P. O. Avery.

McGough Peter, farm; Sec. 4; P. O. Avery.

McGuire Henry, Sec. 1; P. O. Elizabeth.

McGuire John, Sr., farmer; Sec. 1; P. O. Elizabeth.

McGuire Philip, Sec. 1; P. O. Elizabeth.

McMath Wm. miner; Elizabeth.

McQuay John, laborer; Elizabeth.

McQuillian Patrick, farmer; Sec. 3; P. O. Elizabeth.

MANKEY THOS. W. Miner; Elizabeth; born April 11, 1812, at Devenport, Co., Devon, Eng., of Cornish parents; married Frances Hicks Jan. 25, 1840; she was born Oct. 25, 1819, near Chacewater, Parish of Kea, Co. Cornwall, Eng.; emigrated to the U. S. of America March 21, 1840; resided at Sharpsburg and Elizabethtown, near Pittsburg, Pa., two years; came to Galena, Jo Daviess Co., in April, 1842; Mr. M. has served the people in the capacity of Supervisor in the State of Wisconsin, where he lived for a while; he is now Street Commissioner Town of Elizabeth; they have four daughters living: Frances, Elizabeth, Annie Cly, and Susan Ellen; lost two, eldest daughters, Mary and Frances E.; the other daughters are married, leaving Mr. M. and his wife living alone at their home in Elizabeth.

Mason Michael, miner; Elizabeth.

MATTHEWS JOHN, Confectionery; P. O. Elizabeth; born in Town of Elizabeth Nov. 19, 1858; parents came to Jo Daviess Co. in 1857 from Cornwall, Eng.; Mr. Matthews is nineteen years of age; was left with two sisters early in life, having lost his father in 1863 and mother in 1868; has supported himself since he was twelve years old; is faithful and reliable, having worked three years in one place, nearly three and a half at another, one for another man, and lately has opened business in the confection line and is doing well.

Meter J. farmer; Sec. 1; P. O. Elizabeth.

Michael J. M. farmer; P. O. Elizabeth.

MILLER WM. ST. CLAIR, Miller; Elizabeth; born Feb. 17, 1837, in Greencastle, Franklin Co., Pa.; married Rebecca Miley Dec. 5, 1855; she was born in Bridgeport, Franklin Co., Pa.; Mr. Miller came to Ill. in 1856, settling in Carroll Co.; superintended the flouring mill of Holderman & Co. for nine years; was with Abram Polsgrove 4 years, and J. B. Shirk 2 years in the milling business; at the present time is foreman in the flour mill of Edward Mitchell; has no children except an adopted daughter, Hattie Victoria Jane Campbell; Mr. M's mother, a lady upward of 80, resides with him; she is very active in mind and body, often going to the neighbors and stores on errands.

Mounier C. farmer; Sec. 2; P. O. Elizabeth.

Moore Jas. farmer; Sec. 31; P. O. Hanover.

Moore Wm. farmer; Sec. 31; P.O. Hanover.

Morris A. farmer; Sec. 10; P. O. Elizabeth.

MORRIS NATHANIEL, Farmer; Sec. 10; P. O. Avery; born in Logan Co., Ky., Oct. 1, 1806; came to Jo Daviess Co. May 10, 1827, landing at what at that time was called "The Point," an Indian trading place of two or three cabins, afterward became the City of Galena; married Elizbeth Johnson July 4, 1829; she was born in Tenn., but reared in Randolph and Jackson Cos., Ill.; she came to Jo Daviess Co. with her parents in 1828; they were married in a cabin on the farm where they now reside; the dismal howl of the wild wolf in her lair, the screeching of panthers and the echoing whoop of the native savages, was the only music with which they were surrounded; they have seen the wigwams and huts give way to the palatial residences of advanced civilization; they passed through the dangers of the Black Hawk War and beheld the curling smoke of peace after the tiger strife was over; Mr. M. now owns 200 acres of land; they have had eleven children; Mrs. M. is now a lady of 65 years but is as active as a bright-eyed girl of 20, and during the past year has woven 550 yards of carpet upon her foot and hand loom, an article of furniture which she prizes higher than any other about her house.

Morris Nathaniel, Jr., farmer; Sec. 10; P. O. Elizabeth.

Morrison Alex.

MOSLEY RICHARD, Sr., Retired; Sec. 35; P. O. Elizabeth; born in Derbyshire, England, May 10, 1802; married Miss Mary White, in 1838; she was born in Derbyshire, England, Jan. 13, 1808; Mr. M. emigrated to Philadelphia, Pa., in 1830; his wife came in 1832; in 1833 came to Jo Daviess Co.; have one son: Richard Mosley, Jr., born Aug. 27, 1842, in this Co.; he married Miss Sarah L. Eastman Dec. 3, 1868; she was born in Delaware, Ohio, Nov. 27, 1847; came to Wis. with her parents in 1851; to Ill. in 1852; to Afton, Ia., in 1860, where they were married; their children are Wm. Ira, born Sept. 22, 1869; Cora E., June 24, 1871; Clara B., July 10, 1873; James R., May 29, 1875; Frank E., Aug. 22, 1877.

Mosley Richard, Jr., S. 35; P. O. Elizabeth.

Murphy Edward.

NEAL GEO. P. retired; Elizabeth.

NASH A. H. Jeweler; Elizabeth; born Nov. 4, 1853, at Yankee Hollow, Jo Daviess Co.; his father was among the first settlers of the Co., having come here in the Spring of 1845 from Chenango Co., N. Y.; Mr. N. is the youngest of a family of eight children; his father died when he was only a few months old, leaving the family in literally poor circumstances; he was obliged to work on the farm till he was 19 years old, having little opportunity of obtaining any thing more than a common school education; but having true courage and determination, Mr. N. went to Humboldt Co., Ia., where he spent two and a half years attending Humboldt College; taught school and learned the trade of watchmaker and jeweler; since then has spent most of his time in Jo Daviess Co., teaching school and working at his trade; is now located at Elizabeth, where he is doing a thriving business as jeweler.

Newkirk Cyrus, miner; Elizabeth.

Newkirk David, miner; Elizabeth.

Newkirk Reuben, miner; Elizabeth.

Noble James, miner; Elizabeth.

PAUL WILLIS, laborer; Elizabeth.

Powden John, butcher; Elizabeth.

Perry Wm. clerk; Elizabeth.

PILCHER PAYTON J. Carpenter and Joiner; P. O. Elizabeth; born near Fredericksburg, Va. May 15, 1808; his parents moved to Ky., near Lexington; the family came to Ill. in 1829, settling in Vandalia, Fayette Co.; remained there and in St. Clair Co. 8 years, and moved to Jo Daviess Co. in 1837; married Miss Anna B. Mitchell Nov. 8, 1832; she was born in Logan Co., Ky., Feb. 27, 1813; she came to Ill. in 1830, settling in St. Clair Co.; Mr. P. enlisted at Vandalia, in the Illinois Volunteers and served through the Black Hawk War; was mustered into service at the place where now the City of LaSalle is situated; only one log cabin at Dixon, only one at Rock River above there; was discharged at Dixon; he is the oldest living resident of the Village of Elizabeth; has five children: Sarah E., Wm. J., Araminta, Robert H., Amanda M.; Wm. J. is a deaf mute; was educated at the asylum; married a young lady in the same condition; have three bright, intelligent children: Sarah, James W. and Ettie, who understand two languages well; they converse freely with their father and mother in the language of the mute and can readily interpret into good Queen's English; Mr. P. owns a village residence and lots valued at $2,000; is a member of I.O.O.F.

Pilcher Wm. carpenter; Elizabeth.

Pogen Frank, potter; Elizabeth.

Potter Ed. renter; Sec. 20; P. O. Elizabeth.

Potter John, Elizabeth.

Price John, constable; Elizabeth.

Prisk Paul, retired; Elizabeth.

Prisk Wm. P. clerk; Elizabeth.

RANKIN GEO. W. Merchant; Elizabeth; born in this Co., Feb. 18, 1848; married Miss Margaret Etling, Nov. 15, 1871; she was born in Jo Daviess Co.; have two children: Carrie May Rankin, born Aug. 16, 1872; George Otto Rankin, April 27, 1874; in 1875 Mr. R. visited California, Montana and Nevada; has lately sold his farm and is now engaged in mercantile business in the Village of Elizabeth.

Ransom Jas. G. farmer; Sec. 10; P. O. Elizabeth.

Reid David.

Reed J. farmer; Sec. 1; P. O. Elizabeth.

Reed John, miner; Elizabeth.

Reed William.

Reese H. farmer; Sec. 12; P. O. Elizabeth.

Reese J. farmer; Sec. 12; P. O. Elizabeth.

Reynolds D. renter; Sec. 22; P.O. Elizabeth.

Reynolds Jno. E. wagon maker; Elizabeth.

RICHARDS JOSEPH, Farmer; Sec. 12; P. O. Elizabeth; born in Elizabeth, Aug. 21, 1854; never been away from his native village; born in a log cabin near his father's present residence; married Miss Parmelia Wishon March 6, 1873; she was born in Elizabeth Tp., near the famous Wishon Diggings, Sept 7, 1854; have two children: Martin Wishon Richards, born Jan. 11, 1874; Joseph E. Richards, May 14, 1876; Mr. R. has 163 acres of land, a fine house, and a well 228 feet deep, said to be the second in the Co. in point of depth.

RICHARDS THOMAS, Farmer; Sec. 24; P. O. Elizabeth; born in England Nov. 11, 1815; came to America in 1837; settled in Pottsville, Pa.; went from there to Big Sandy, 35 miles south of St. Louis; from there to Wisconsin, and then returned to Pa.; came to Jo Daviess Co. in 1850, and his home has been here ever since; married Peggy James at Bloomsburg, Pa., July 4, 1840; she was born Sept. 10, 1824, and came to America at the age of 6 years; they have six children living: John Henry, born Sept. 24, 1843; Thomas, June 27, 1849; Tobias, Aug. 21, 1852; Joseph, Aug. 21, 1854; Geo. W., June 29, 1859; Susan H., Jan. 27, 1866; have lost two children; Mr. Richards has been an extensive traveler during his life; he delights to talk of Pennsylvania as his home in America around which many pleasant memories linger.

Robinson Davis, merchant; Elizabeth.

Robinson J. Q. merchant; Elizabeth.

Roberts Henry, farmer; P. O. Elizabeth.

Roberts Walter, farmer; P. O. Elizabeth.

RODDEN JAMES, Farmer; Sec. 19; P. O. Galena; born in Galena in 1836; married Miss Eliza Bevard in May, 1858; had five children, three living: Eliza, George, Franklin; lost his wife and two children; married Miss Margaret E. Johnson March 10, 1871; she was born in Irish Hollow, in this Co.; they have had three children, two living, John and Matilda; lost one; Mr. R. has 160 acres of land.

Rodden John, Sec. 19; P. O. Galena.

RODDEN WM. Retired Farmer; Sec. 19; P. O. Galena; born in Holywood, Co. Down, Ireland, March 3, 1806; came to America in 1832, landing at Baltimore in August; lived in Philadelphia two years; came to Jo Daviess Co. in 1834; worked at bricklaying during Summer at Galena; located on the land where he now lives in Fall; only two cabins between there and Galena; advertised an estray on court house in Galena as being taken up by Wm. Rodden of Irish Hollow, hence the name of the ravine; married Margaret Flemming Aug. 31, 1832; she was born in Lisburn, Co. Down, Ireland; lost his wife in 1875; has three children: James, John, Eliza; sold wheat at 35c per bushel; has been back to Ireland since the War of the Rebellion in the U. S.; visited American Consul at Holywood, his native town; shook hands with him like any other American, without putting his hat under his arm or bending his knee, to the great astonishment of his acquaintances in the old country; has 480 acres of land; Protestant; Republican.

Rodman John, P. O. Elizabeth.

Rogers Joseph, P. O. Hanover.

Rogers T. B., P. O. Hanover.

ROGERS WM. Retired Farmer; Sec. 18; P. O. Hanover; born in Co. Monaghan, Ireland, Sept. 10, 1797; married Martha Todd Dec. 26, 1828; she was born in Co. Monaghan, Ireland, Aug. 20, 1809; they came to America in the Spring of 1837; lived in Pa. a short time, then came to Jo Daviess Co.; have been here since; have five children living: Michael, Joseph, Mary, William, Thomas B.; lost two girls and one son; four sons served in the Union army during the War of the Rebellion; William is at Omaha, Neb., the others at home; have two grandchildren living with them, William E. Mahood and Margaret M. Mahood; has 343 acres of land; obtained land upon which he resides from government; very few people living here now that were here when he came; Presbyterian; Republican.

ROTTMANN JOHN, Farmer; Sec. 11; P. O. Elizabeth; born in Bavaria, Germany, March 29, 1829; came to America in 1854; married Miss Regina Barbara Waldtman in Galena, Dec. 6, 1854; she was born in Bavaria, Germany; Mr. and Mrs. R. came to America in the same vessel while single, landing in New York, then went to Detroit, Mich. from there to Galena, and were married in the Fall; have 74 acres of land; have no children: they are educated and industrious people.

Rowley Chas. shoemaker; Elizabeth.

SAUCER GEORGE, Grocer; Elizabeth; born in Prince George Co., Md., Oct. 10, 1808; his parents moved to Kentucky, and from there to Ohio, where he lived about six years; in the year 1827, at the age of 19, he came to Jo Daviess Co.; Galena was called "The Point;" worked at the New Diggings two years; frequently run into The Point by reports that Indians were coming; in 1829 went on foot to Beardstown, on Illinois River; married Miss Ann E. Delany June 25, 1831; returned to Jo Daviess Co. about 1837; had three children: Eliza married Greenberry Powell Nov. 30, 1853, now living in Mo.; Nancy J. married J. M. Wier Jan. 1, 1857, died soon after her marriage; lost an infant son, William H.; lost his wife in 1876; has 136 acres of land besides his business property in town.

Schrader Ambrose, wagon maker; Elizabeth.

SCOTT ROBERT, Butcher and Shoemaker; P. O. Elizabeth; born in Fifeshire, Scotland, Oct. 22, 1831; married Catherine Smith, Aug. 1, 1851; she was born in Fifeshire, Scotland; the following year after their marriage they left their native land, arriving in Jo Daviess Co. in July, 1852; have four children living: Christina, Robert, Catherine and Mary: Mr. Scott established the first meat market and the first ice-house in the town of Elizabeth; is now engaged in conducting a meat market and shoe shop; also in superintending the work upon his farm;

has 80 acres in this Co., and 120 in Iowa; Mr. Scott is the champion of champions at the game of checkers; he now holds the first prize awarded him at a contest held in Galena, having carried off the palm where the states of Wis., Ia., and Ill., were represented by their best players; he is independent in politics; his family attend the M. E. Church, of which he has been an exemplary member for many years; Mr. Scott is known in this community as an affectionate husband, a kind, indulgent father and a good citizen; he is honest and upright in business, loyal to the government and generous toward his fellow men, always extending a helping hand to the needy and elevating the fallen to a higher and better manhood.

Shaw Charles, farmer; P. O. Elizabeth.

SHAW THOMAS B. Proprietor Union Hotel; Elizabeth; born in Jo Daviess Co., April 21, 1839; his parents came to this Co. from England at an early day; married Azildia Pogue June 8, 1862; she was born in Elizabeth Feb. 22, 1849; her father came to Jo Daviess Co. in 1830; he was a soldier in the Mexican War and died at Jalapa, Mexico, Dec. 8, 1847; Mr. Shaw has been in Nevada and Montana twice; went there first in the Spring of 1867; returned home in one year and went back to that country again in 1871 remaining three years; he is now the proprietor of the Union Hotel in the Town of Elizabeth; he is a genial, accommodating landlord and evidently knows how to "keep hotel;" they have four children: Eva, born March 26, 1863; Alma, Aug. 4, 1865; Reuben, May 22, 1867; Robert, Oct. 17, 1871; Mr. S. has in his possession an old English Bible, published in London, in 1772, which has been handed down from his forefathers with many other old books all of which are precious mementos and heirlooms in the family; an old family horse which his father always liked so well and cared for so kindly, died in Oct., 1876.

Sherard Geo. Sec. 30; P. O. Hanover.

Sherard Wm. farm; Sec. 30; P. O. Hanover.

Sincock Benj. laborer; Elizabeth.

SMITH E. R. U. S. Mail Carrier between Elizabeth and Galena and Justice of the Peace; born in Barre, Orleans Co., N. Y., Nov. 6, 1844; Mr. Smith went from N. Y. to St. Clair Co., Mich., in the Spring of 1861; from there to Sanilac Co., Mich., in 1863; came to Jo Daviess Co., settling in the Town of Elizabeth, Sept. 12, 1865; married the eldest daughter of John Weber, Sept. 12, 1872; has been engaged in carrying the mail from Elizabeth to Galena a great portion of the time, either as driver or contractor; Mr. Smith has been elected Town Clerk for two terms, 1876 and 1877; was elected Justice of the Peace in the Spring of 1877; his wife was born in the Town of Elizabeth and has been a resident of the Co. all her life; their home is surrounded by comforts that embellish life and make it happy.

Smith Edward, farmer; Sec. 6; P. O. Galena.

Smith George, miner; Elizabeth.

Smith Peter, laborer; Elizabeth.

Speer Wm. farmer and stock dealer; Sec. 8; P. O. Galena.

Staker J. J., Elizabeth.

Statham Jno. farm; Sec. 29; P. O. Hanover.

Strong John, miner; Elizabeth.

TART BENJ., retired; Elizabeth.

Tippert W. farmer; Sec. 21; P.O. Elizabeth.

Tippet Wm., Jr.

Tippet Wm., Sr.

Thomas John.

Tredinerick Richard, retired; Elizabeth.

TRESIDDER MRS. CATHERINE P. Farmer; Sec. 10; P. O. Elizabeth; born in Constantine, Eng., Sept. 23, 1825; her maiden name was Miss Rowling; married Mr. John Tresidder Feb. 16, 1854; came to America May, 1869, and settled in this Co.; have four children: Richard Rowling Tresidder, born Jan. 4, 1855; Mary Jane, Aug. 16, 1856, Elizabeth C. Morris, Feb. 9, 1859; Laura Annie, Jan. 21, 1863; Mrs. T. has 82 acres of land; lost her husband May 1, 1874; Mary Jane lives in Galena; she is an intelligent, industrious young lady and is interested in educational interests.

Trewartha Elisha, retired; Elizabeth.

Turner John, laborer; Elizabeth.

VIRTUE JAMES, Sr., farmer; Sec. 26; P. O. Elizabeth.

Virtue Samuel, farm; S. 26; P. O. Elizabeth.

Virtue Thos. farm; Sec. 30; P. O. Galena.

WADLEIGH JOEL, laborer; Elizabeth.

Wainwright Mark, laborer; Elizabeth.

WATTS JAMES, Farmer; Sec. 26; P. O. Elizabeth; born in Co. Monmouth, Eng., Dec. 25, 1827; came direct to Jo Daviess Co. in 1851; went to Wisconsin, lived there two years, and returned to this Co.; married Miss Lydia Jacobs, April 7, 1858, in Hazel Green, Wis.; she was born in Franklin Co., Ind.; came with her uncle, Wesley Jacobs, in whose family she was an adopted child, to Jo Daviess Co., in 1833; Mr. M. worked by the month many years for Hon. H. Green; now owns 164 acres of land, and is engaged in growing fine stock, especially hogs; have four children; William James, Mary Elizabeth, George Thomas and Charles Arthur.

Watts Philip, Elizabeth,

Watts Robert, farm; S. 22; P. O. Elizabeth.

WEIR JAMES M. Of the firm of Weir & Weir; Elizabeth; born in Mercer Co., Pa., July 21, 1832; came to this Co. in 1846; has been in business in Elizabeth twenty years; was married to Miss H. E. Marshall in 1860; she was born in Ill.; one child by this marriage, Winnie M.; wife died in June, 1867; married Miss M. R. Berry in March, 1870; she was born in Pa. April 28, 1846; three children: Annie M., James E. and Ira T.; has been P. M. at Elizabeth for seventeen years, Township Treasurer since 1864, Town Clerk three years; family members of Baptist Church; he is a member I. O. O. F.; visited Centennial *via* Niagara, N. Y., and Washington. A. H. Weir was born in Pa. July 3, 1836; married Miss M. J. Olney, of Mt. Carroll, in 1862; she died in 1863; was married again to Miss Maggie Huston in 1867; she was born in Champaign Co., Ohio; three children: Nellie, G. Russel and Sadie L. This firm is now extensively engaged in the hardware business, and will not be undersold; repairing and jobbing done to order.

Weir J. S. merchant; Elizabeth.

Westphal Julius, boot and shoe store; Elizabeth.

WENNER IRA H. Teacher; Elizabeth; born in Galena, Ill., Sept. 4, 1853; his father came to this Co. from Schuylkill Co., Pa.; his mother came from Syracuse, N. Y.; they were married in Jo Daviess Co.; Mr. W. was educated at the Normal School of Galena; has been engaged in teaching for seven years; married Miss Jennie Barns Nov. 25, 1875; she was born near Newark, N. J.; came to Jo Daviess Co. with her parents in 1855; have two children: Raymond E. and Leroy.

White Samuel, farmer; P. O. Elizabeth.

WHITE SAMUEL D. Farmer; Sec. 19; P. O. Galena; born in Irish Hollow, this Co., Dec. 20, 1840; Mr. W. served three years in Union army during the war, Co. D., 45th Regt. I. V. I.; was in the engagements of Fort Henry, Donelson, Shiloh, Corinth, Port Gibson, Ringwood, Champion Hill, Vicksburg, and many other hotly-contested battles; his regiment was the first to enter Vicksburg; was honorably discharged Nov. 20, 1864; married Miss Josephine Mongin Sept. 20, 1865; she was born in Rice Tp. July 19, 1849; have five children: Emily, Kittie J., Matilda, Nevada, Ida; lost a little son, Elsworth.

Wilcox Isaac, miner; Elizabeth.

Wilkinson John, laborer; Elizabeth.

WILKINSON ROBERT, Renter; Sec. 35; P. O. Elizabeth; born in Northumberland Co., Eng., June 8, 1824; married Miss Margaret Peart July 24, 1850; came to America same year; remained in N. Y. for two years, Pa. four years, and came to Jo Daviess Co. in Fall of 1856; engaged in mining twenty years; has been farming four years; have been members of M. E. Church twenty years; he has been a member of the I. O. O. F. for twelve years; have seven children: Elizabeth J., John W., Margaret A., William J., Mary H., Robert A., Sarah M.

Williams Geo. Elizabeth.

Williams Geo. W., Sr., farmer; Sec. 21; P. O. Elizabeth.

Williams Geo., Jr., farmer; Sec. 21; P. O. Elizabeth.

Williams G. W. farm; S. 21; P.O. Elizabeth.

Williams Henry, saloon keeper; Elizabeth.

WILLIAMS ISAAC, Farmer; Sec. 15; P. O. Elizabeth; born near the famous *Natural Bridge*, in Virginia, April 23, 1816; parents moved to East Tennessee, where he grew up to manhood; came to Jo Daviess Co. in 1850; married Miss Theresa Reynolds July 23, 1842; she was born in Tenn. and married there; they have seven children: William, Nancy J., James W., George, Thomas, John W., Isaac A.; have lost three children; Mr. W. has 160 acres of land and is engaged in growing cattle, sheep, hogs and horses.

Williams J. B. farm; S. 21; P. O. Elizabeth.

Williams Thos. Elizabeth.

Wilson Harvey G. miner; Elizabeth.

WILSON W. H. Farmer; P. O. Avery; born in Burlington, Iowa, July 8, 1852; came to Jo Daviess Co. when one year old and it has been his home since; married Angeline Lathlean, who was born at Council Hill, in Jo Daviess Co.; they have two children: Walter H., born Dec. 25, 1875; Winn, April 4, 1877; Mr. W. was thrown upon his own resources at an early age; was fond of social gatherings, and during his younger days played the fiddle for the dance many nights, and participated in the amusements of the gay and jolly, but now Mr. W. has changed his course of life and prefers to spend his leisure in some good cause; is now the superintendent of Col. Avery's farm and stock.

Winters Edward, miner; Elizabeth.

WISHON MARTIN, Retired; Elizabeth; born in Cumberland Co., Ky., Dec. 19, 1822; came to Jo Daviess Co. in the Spring of 1841; has since resided here; owns the land on which the famous Wishon Diggings were struck, from which more mineral has been raised than any diggings in the mining regions; owns 400 acres of land; has a fine residence in Elizabeth, surrounded by beautiful evergreens and shrubbery, which Shenstone might have envied; married Catherine Tenyck, July 20, 1850; she was born in Dutchess Co., N. Y., Sept. 27,

1831; they have five children living: Permelia, born Sept. 7, 1854; Nancy Jane, Sept. 25, 1858; Julia, Jan. 20, 1863; Cora B., March 16, 1867; Edith, Aug. 11, 1871; have lost five children; two of the daughters are now attending the Mount Carroll Seminary; Mr. W. is a genial, generous man, full of noble impulses; feels disposed to give his children all the chances for education and the accomplishments of music, drawing, etc., that wealth can purchase or fancy can suggest.

Woodward Eli, laborer; Elizabeth.

YOUNG CHARLES M. Farmer; Sec. 4; P. O. Avery; born in Mercer Co., Pa., June 24, 1836; came to this Co. in 1855; served three years and eight months in the Union army during the War of the Rebellion; enlisted at first call for 3 months' troops, in Co. I (Jo Daviess Guards), 12th Regt. I. V. I.; discharged at expiration of time; enlisted again under Maj. Avery, Oct. 1, 1861; was in many severe engagements, Little Rock, Camden, Hartville, Saline, charge of Chalk Bluff, etc.; during the advance on Camden was under fire of the enemy 26 days out of 30; was honorably discharged; married Miss Nancy E. Reed June 30, 1865; she was born in Washington Co., Pa.; have five children: John T, Chas. J., Charity M., Annie May, and Ida Clara.

YOUNG JOHN S. Farmer; Sec. 4; P. O. Avery; born in Mercer Co., Pa., July 22; 1838; came to this Co. in 1854; Mr. Young's mother still lives in Galena at the age of 72; he married Miss Amanda M. Keithly in 1859; she was born in Mo. and came to this Co. when she was quite young; have nine children: Horace H., born Aug. 25, 1860; Chas. L., Aug. 19, 1861; Ettie A. March 23, 1863; Elmer E., June 15, 1866; Minnie L., Nov. 30, 1867; Wilber R., Sept. 24, 1869; Lillie S., April 22, 1872; Bertie May, Sept. 25, 1873; Edna Beatrice, Nov. 12, 1877; Mr. Y. has taught school every Winter but one since 1858; served as School Director for many years; Assessor two years, Collector one year, and at present time is Supervisor of Elizabeth Tp.

HANOVER TOWNSHIP.

ANDERSON J. H. farmer; Sec. 35; P. O. Hanover.

Anderson J. farmer; Sec. 24; P. O. Hanover.

BABCOCK CHAS. carpenter; Hanover.

Bailey Chas. farm; Sec. 23; P. O. Hanover.

Bailey J. R. farmer; Sec. 13; P. O. Hanover.

Bailey W. S. laborer; Hanover.

Bain Robt. farmer; Sec. 33; P. O. Hanover.

Barrett P. farmer; Sec. 35; P. O. Hanover.

BEATY JOHN, Farmer; Sec. 4; P. O. Galena; born in Ind. Jan. 1, 1825; his parents emigrated to this Co. in an early day, and his father was the gentleman for whom Beaty's Hollow was named; was married to Miss Sarah J. Black in 1854; she was born in County Antrim, Ireland, Feb. 10, 1835; Mr. B. is known as a genial companion, of kind and generous impulses; his wife is no less remarkable for her generosity than for her faithfulness as a companion and a mother; they have two children, James and Mary E., who are the delight of their young friends and respected by all; Mr. B. owns 333 acres of land.

Belden Thos. laborer; Hanover;

Bennett H. V. farm; Sec. 28; P. O. Hanover.

Bennett M. farmer; Sec. 32; P. O. Hanover.

Bennett Wm. factory hand; Hanover.

Blake David, boarding house; Hanover.

Blake John, farmer; Sec. 2; P. O. Hanover.

Blake Joseph, factory hand; P. O. Hanover.

Brennan Jas. farm; Sec. 23; P. O. Hanover.

Browнter R. retired; Sec. 6; P. O. Hanover.

CALE J. M. Sec. 16; P.O. Hanover.

Cale P. farmer; Sec. 24; P. O. Hanover.

CARLEY WILLIAM W. Farmer; Sec. 28; P. O. Hanover; born in Petersborough, N. H., May 29, 1835; his father's name was Dexter D. Carley; he was drowned in the North Factory Pond at Petersborough; his mother's maiden name was Miss Nellie White; she died at Hanover, Ill., Jan., 1874, aged seventy-two years; Mr. C. came to Jo Daviess Co. in 1855; married Miss Mary J. James June 17, 1857; she was born in Syracuse, N. Y.; they have one son living, Fred Daney Carley, born April 9, 1858; lost one child, Clarence White Carley, died July 28, 1872.

Calvert John, laborer; Sec. 5; Hanover.

Cary Wm. R. laborer; Sec. 26; Hanover.

Chapman Ash, stone mason; Hanover.

Chapman Geo. laborer; Hanover.

Chapman J. R. Justice of the Peace; Hanover.

Chapman Joseph, stone mason; Hanover.

Chapman Thos. teamster; Hanover.

CHASE AUGUSTINE, Merchant; P. O. Hanover; born near Jamestown, N

Y., May 12, 1815; came to this Co. in 1840; married Miss Lavina Puddy of N. Y.; one child, Seth M. of Delhi, Iowa; lost first wife; married Miss Nancy M. Barnaby of Vt.; no children; she died, and he married Miss V. E. Fohs of this state; one child, Albert F. Chase; Mr. C. has been in the milling business fifteen years; has farmed some; merchandising twelve years; served as Collector four years, Assessor and School Director seven years; has been a prominent and influential member of the M. E. Church for thirty-five years; has served in the capacity of class leader most of the time.

Chase Edward, Sec. 1; P. O. Derinda.

Cheek Hamilton, farmer; Sec. 36; P. O. Hanover.

Chase Henry, farm; Sec. 25; P. O. Hanover.

Chase John, farmer; Sec. 11; P. O. Hanover.

Chase Wm. farmer; Sec. 2; P. O. Hanover.

CLARK GEORGE B. Prop. Hanover Hotel, Hanover; born at Westfield, Hamdon Co., Mass., Dec. 9, 1826; moved to West Springfield; was there four years; from there to the City of Springfield and remained fifteen years; came to Freeport in 1854; to Galena in 1856; married Miss Mariah C. Strickland in Sept., 1853; she was born in Palmer, Hamdon Co., Mass.; were married in Thompson, Conn.; have two children living, George A. and Clara E.; lost one child, Eva. Mr. C. served in the army during the war, 45th Regt. I. V. I.; was in the severe engagements of Vicksburg, Chattanooga, Kenesaw Mountain, Atlanta, Jackson, Nashville, and many others; was honorably discharged at close of war; returned and came to Hanover; purchased the hotel property, the business of which he has conducted since; on the 29th of Dec., 1877, Mrs. C. picked from the garden and had for dinner a dish of green lettuce which had grown spontaneously from the seed of the former Summer, something never before known; for the truth of this the writer of this sketch can bear witness, as it tasted as fresh as if served on a June morning.

Como Chas. A.

Cobim Thos. in factory; Hanover.

Cobim Wm. retired; P. O. Hanover.

COCHRAN ANDREW E. Farmer; S. 35; P. O. Hanover; born in Hancock Co., Ill., May 1, 1853; came to Hanover in 1856; married Miss Effie Farquher Feb. 25, 1875; she was born in Hanover, Jo Daviess Co.; they have one child, Bertie A. Cochrane, born Feb. 9, 1877; Mr. C. owns 265 acres of land.

Cooper Jacob, farm; Sec. 34; P. O. Hanover.

CRAIG NATHAN B. Merchant; P. O. Hanover; born in St. Charles Co., Mo., June 13, 1822; came with his parents to Galena in 1827; in the Spring of 1828 his father came to Hanover and took up the water power, and commenced at once the erection of a grist mill and a saw mill; the family came on in 1829; his mother was a granddaughter of the celebrated Daniel Boone, of Kentucky; her father was Nathan Boone, after whom the subject of this sketch was named; the family were here during the Black Hawk war; Mr. C.'s father served as Captain of Volunteers during the war, and was honorably discharged at its close; Mr. C. has his old muster rolls now in his possession; he also has in his possession an old family Bible, the property of his grandfather, Nathan Boone; the record of his mother's family is in it; Mr. C.'s first wife was Miss Nancy Chandler; they had six children, only one of whom is living, Mrs. Frances McLaughlin; married the widow Calamer, whose maiden name was Miss Margaret Pilcher; one child living, Olive M.; lost one; married Miss Elizabeth Milburn, born in Ind.; three children, viz.: Eva, Jessie, James E.; lost one; owns 527 acres of land.

Craig James, farmer; Sec. 20; P. O. Hanover.

Craig John, farmer; Sec. 20; P. O. Hanover.

CRUTTENDEN ZEBULON, Farmer; Sec. 12; P. O. Hanover; born in Ferrisburg, Vt., Jan. 24, 1824; came to Ill. in 1834; remained one winter near Dayton, Ohio; went to Fulton Co. in 1843; came to this Co. and settled on the farm where they now live in 1848; married Miss Margaret May in 1846; she was born in White Co., Ill., Jan. 19, 1825; her people were among the first settlers in Hanover; three children living: Henry, in California; Mrs. Clara Pilcher, and Matilda; owns 126 acres of land.

Cutler Suel, painter; Hanover.

Cundiff R. H. farm; Sec. 20; P. O. Hanover.

Cuniff Thos. J. farm; S. 15; P. O. Hanover.

DARAN LAWRENCE, farmer; Sec. 14; P. O. Hanover.

Daugherty Jno. farm; S. 25; P. O. Hanover.

Davidson Wm. farm; S. 22; P. O. Hanover.

Dawson G. H. blacksmith; Hanover.

DAWSON JOHN R. Farmer; Sec. 16; P. O. Hanover; born in Galena Nov. 22, 1838; lived in this Co. ever since; served in the army during the war from the first to the last; was the first to enlist in three months' service, in Spring of 1861; in Sept., 1861, enlisted in 45th Regt. I. V. I. for three years or during the war; was promoted from a private soldier to the rank of First Lieutenant; as a private he was known as a brave and willing soldier; as an officer, kind, generous and efficient; served four years and six months, only losing thirty days from duty; was in the severest engagements, as Vicksburg, Donelson, Shiloh, Kenesaw Mountain, Atlanta, Meridian, Champion Hill, Jackson, and

HANOVER

many other very severe fights and skirmishes; honorably discharged at close of war; married Miss Martha Miller Nov. 8, 1865; she was born in New York City Dec. 25, 1838; have two children: Mary R. Dawson and Elizabeth Dawson.

DAWSON ROBERT, Retired Farmer; Sec. 9; P. O. Hanover; born near Belfast, Ireland, Jan. 20, 1812; came to U. S. in 1832; lived in Philadelphia till 1834, when he came to Galena; married Miss Mary Robinson Oct. 13, 1836; she was born in Co. Fermanagh, Ireland, May 12, 1812; came to America with her parents in 1831; had ten sons, nine of whom are living: William, John R., George, James D., Eugene, Robert, Edward, Gibson, David, Benjamin; Joseph deceased; Mr. D.'s six eldest sons served in the Union army during the war; were on duty constantly, participating in the severest engagements from the first to the last; had their clothes shot, some slight wounds, but were all honorably discharged at close of war; Eugene contracted rheumatism, however, from which he has since lost a limb. The six served what would have been nineteen years for one man; Mr. D. has assisted his boys to a start in the world, and retains as a homestead 80 acres of land.

Dean Walter, retired farmer; Hanover.

Degear Able, fisherman; Hanover.

Dick John E. farm; Sec. 2; P. O. Hanover.

EDGERTON ASHER, Farmer; Sec. 11; P. O. Hanover; born in Coventry, Conn., Feb. 12, 1816; came to Illinois in 1831; to Quincy in 1832; came to this Co. in 1834; father came in 1836; went to Iowa in 1840; lived there four years; owned the land at one time upon which the City of Cedar Rapids has since been built; returned to Wisconsin and run a furnace one year; followed mining on Apple River two years; spent one year in the gold regions of California; owns 440 acres of land upon which he is now engaged in farming; married Miss Julia Deal in 1840; she was born in Ashland, Ohio; two children: James L., Mrs. Annie J. Griffith; lost a son in army, Washington Irving.

Edgerton Fred. farm; S. 13; P. O. Hanover.

Edgerton S. D. farm; S. 13; P. O. Hanover.

Edgerton Thos. E. farmer; Sec. 11; P. O. Hanover.

FABLINGER GEO. farmer; Sec. 3; P O. Hanover.

FABLINGER JOHN, Farmer; Sec. 14; P. O. Hanover; born near Cumberland, Md., Oct. 2, 1844; came to this Co. with his parents at the age of 4 years; mother died in 1861; father still lives in Co.; enlisted in 96th Regt. I. V. I. Aug. 8, 1862; served with his regiment till at the battle of Chicamauga was wounded through the upper part of left lung, fracturing shoulder bones; was there captured, and remained in the hands of the enemy about two weeks; there were so many to look after that his wounds were not properly dressed; was paroled and remained in hospital one year; never was able for active service again, and the disability will go with him to his grave; was honorably discharged at close of war, and is one of our country's defenders, disabled in the conflict, toward whom the government should ever extend the hand of charity; married Miss Jane Young in 1868; she was born in this Co. Jan. 22, 1845; her father, one of the earliest settlers, still lives with them, at the age of 81; have four children: Ellen May, John W., Mary J., Annie B.; lost one child; owns 80 acres land.

Fablinger Wm., Hanover.

Fisher John G. wagon maker; Hanover.

Flanigan M. farmer; Sec. 3; P. O. Hanover.

Frank H. farmer; Sec. 10; P. O. Hanover.

FRANCKE GUSTAV, Farmer; Sec. 10; P. O. Hanover; born in Rossla, Province of Prussia, June 26, 1826; came to the U.S. and settled in Milwaukee, Wis. in 1850; came to this Co. in 1852, and married Miss Christine Miller, same year; she was born in the same place March 31, 1833; she came to Milwaukee in 1849; has five children living: Herman H., A. Julius, Charles F., Wm. A. H., Wm.; owns 288 acres of land and is one of that industrious, intelligent class of whose adoption in this country the people may well feel proud.

FREEMAN MRS. JULIA, Farming; Sec. 30; P. O. Hanover; her maiden name was Miss Julia May; born in White Co., Ill., May 3, 1821; she came to this Co. with her parents in 1835; among the the first settlers; married Mr. John Freeman in 1843; he was born in Edensburg, Pa., in 1812; has four children living: A. Annie, Laura, John and May; owns 428 acres of land.

GALDEN JOHN, farmer; Sec. 8; P. O. Hanover.

Garrow P. farmer; Sec. 18; P. O. Hanover.

George John, laborer; Hanover.

George Lewis, plasterer; Hanover.

Gibbons W. farmer; Sec. 6; P. O. Hanover.

Gillett O. H. farmer; Sec. 27; P.O. Hanover.

Gillis J. farmer; Sec. 10; P. O. Hanover.

GREEN ANDREW, Farmer; Sec. 14; P. O Hanover; born Steuben Co., N. Y., June 24, 1819; came to this Co. in 1835; David Williams, one of the three men who captured Major Andre, the British Spy, was his great uncle; married Mrs. Grotton whose maiden name was Miss

Mary A. Collier, Oct. 15, 1861; she was born in Staffordshire, England, March 12, 1819; came to the U. S, in 1844; had ten children by her first marriage, only one of whom is now living, James B. Gretton: they now have two children, Marcus de Lafayette, and Louisa Montez; owns 200 acres of land.

Green L. farmer; Sec. 14; P. O. Hanover.

Green M. B. farmer; Sec. 6; P. O. Hanover.

HANNAH JAMES, farmer; Sec. 7; P.O. Hanover.

Hannah Wm. farmer; Sec. 7; P.O. Hanover.

Hammond C. M. farmer; Sec. 18; P. O. Hanover.

Hammond J. farm; Sec. 13; P. O. Hanover.

Hammond J. H. farmer and justice of the peace; Sec. 12; P.O. Hanover.

Hardy G. farmer; Sec. 28; P. O. Hanover.

HARPER MRS. JANE. Farming; Sec. 2; P. O. Hanover; her maiden name was Miss Jane McCall; born in Co. Monaghan, Ireland in 1840; came to the U. S. with her father when she was quite young; lived 12 years in the City of New York; came to this Co. in 1855; married Mr. M. Harper in 1857; he was born in same place in 1817; has three children living: Mary J., Elizabeth M., Ester; owns 400 acres of land.

Haslam J. Sec. 1; P. O. Hanover.

Haslom Moses, farm; Sec. 1; P. O. Hanover.

Hodgues E. retired; Sec. 6; P. O. Hanover.

Hull B. farmer; Sec. 12; P. O. Hanover.

Hunt Earnest, Hanover.

HUNT HIRAM B. Farmer and Engineer; Sec. 21; P. O. Hanover; born in Zenia, Ohio, April 19, 1822; in 1823 his father and two other families moved to what is now Galena—old town; first permanent settlers of Jo Daviess Co.; came up Mississippi on keel-boat "Col. Bumford;" no steamer had ascended the river so far. up as that; the steamboat, "Old Virginia," went up same Summer; came out to his farm in 1850; has been engineer on river boats for many years; married Abigail Comstock in 1843; have six children: Emma, Abbie, Arthur, Ernest, Kittie, and Irene E.; lost his wife in 1872; married Miss Amelia Vandorn; she was born in Ohio; Mr. Hunt crossed the plains in 1849, and remained in Cal. one year working gold mines; owns 565 acres of land; Republican; Rationalist.

HUNT JAMES S. Farmer and Engineer; Sec. 28; P. O. Hanover; born in Galena Oct. 9, 1824; first male child born of Anglo-Saxon parents in Jo Daviess Co.; commenced engineering on steamboats at the age of 19, and has been on the river nearly every Summer since; lived in Bellevue, Iowa, five years; married Sarah Armstrong in 1849; had five children: Edwin, William, Stella, Lewellen, and Lizzie; lost his wife in 1868; married Miss Mary Chapman in 1871; she was born in Lyons, Iowa, March 30, 1843; have four children: Charles, Frank, Eva, and Mary; Owns 120 acres of land.

HUNT ORSON A. Farmer and Stock Grower; Sec. 28; P. O. Hanover; born in Delaware Co., N. Y., Dec. 16, 1834; his father moved to Galena in 1840; they settled on Sand Prairie, where his father died in his 78th year; married Miss Emily Galpin in 1857; she was born in this Co. April 27, 1838; have six children living: Mrs. Cora Evans, wife of W. O. Evans, editor of Bellevue *Leader*, William T., Elmer S., Anna D., Florence A., and Fannie Fern; owns 750 acres of land.

HUNTINGTON A. C. Superintendent Hanover Woolen Factory; P. O. Hanover; born in Middlebury, Vt., Jan. 3, 1834; went to Wis. in 1861 and started the Appleton Woolen Mills; was trained to his business in Middlebury and Burlington; has been engaged in his business in many of the Eastern cities; has been in his present situation since 1872; married Miss Sarah E. Stearns in 1858; she was born in Middlebury, Vt., March 6, 1837; have two children, Carrie F., Sarah L.

Huntington H. H. merchant; Hanover.

HUNTINGTON JAMES P. Has charge of the Dyeing Department in Woolen Factory; P. O. Hanover; born in Middlebury, Vt., March 22, 1822; trained to his trade in his native city; came to Galena in 1854; in 1861 went to Fishkill, N. Y., where he followed his trade two years; came to Hanover in 1864; married Miss Charlotte E. Heath March 30, 1843; she was born in Molone, N. Y.; her parents moved to Middlebury, where they were married; they have one son, Howard H. Huntington, born May 24, 1844; his son has charge of his store in Hanover, where they are doing a lively business.

IRWIN ROBERT, Farmer; Sec. 4; P. O. Hanover; born in County Monaghan, Ireland, Aug. 1. 1819; came to New York in 1845; came to Jo Daviess Co. in 1848; returned and married Miss Helen Williamson in 1850; she was born in same Co. in Ireland Sept. 5, 1827; came to this Co. with her parents in 1840; parents died in this Co.; his father lives in Dubuque Co., Iowa, eighty-four years old; mother died here; they have seven children: Mrs. M. E. Kilpatrick, Thomas D., Ellen, Matilda, Robert, Rebecca, William D.; owns 343 acres of land.

JABE JEREMIAH, farmer; Sec. 20; P. O. Hanover.

Jabe S. farmer; Sec. 20; P. O. Hanover.

Jabe T. farmer; Sec. 20; P. O. Hanover.

Jameson S. farmer Sec. 20; P. O. Hanover.

Jeffers A. farmer; Sec. 9; P. O. Hanover.

JEFFERS GEORGE, Merchant; P. O. Hanover; born in this Co., Dec. 21, 1844; has lived here since except four years spent in the Union Army during the war; enlisted in Aug., 1862, in the 96th Regt. I. V.I.; served with his regiment one year, and was on detached duty in the quartermaster and commissary departments; he shared the toils and hardships of army life till the close of the Rebellion, when he was honorably discharged at Nashville; returned home about Jan. 1, 1876; married Miss Louie Rowan Jan. 14, 1867; she was born in New York City in 1845; came to Galena with her parents; removed to Chicago, where they were married; Mr. J. is now in business in Hanover, is Postmaster, and known as an efficient officer.

JEFFERS STEPHEN, Farmer; Sec. 15; P. O. Hanover; born in Broome Co., N. Y., Sept. 20, 1820; came to Whiteside Co. in 1836; resided there three years, and came to Jo Daviess in 1839; returned to Whiteside and married Miss Julia Maxwell Feb. 14, 1844; she was born in Delaware Co., N. Y., Feb. 22, 1819; they came from N. Y. in the same emigrant train, consisting of twelve wagons; were on the road twelve weeks; have four children living: George, Perry, Albert, Willard; lost two children, William and Ellen; only four houses in Hanover when he came to the place; Mr. J. enlisted in 96th Regt. I. V. I.; mustered in at Rockford Oct. 6, 1862; elected Quartermaster and served with the Regt. till commissioned Captain in Commissary Dept.; remained in army till close of war; was honorably discharged and returned to his home in this Co.; was in business for twelve or fourteen years; resigned his commission as P. M. when he enlisted; Supervisor ten years, Justice of Peace four years; has served as School Director, School Trustee, and Collector several years; owns 700 acres land.

Jeffers Willard, farm; S. 15; P. O. Hanover.

KEAMAGHAN ED. farmer; Hanover.

Keeler Henry, constable; Hanover.

Killough Thos. physician; Hanover.

KILPATRICK ANDREW, Retired Farmer; Sec. 4; P. O. Hanover; born in Co. Antrim, Ireland, Jan. 27, 1801; married Miss Elizabeth Stuart March 19, 1824; she was born in Co. Antrim; came to this country in 1825; lived ten years in City of Philadelphia; came to Galena May 11, 1835; came from St. Louis in the Warrior, a steamboat bearing marks of service in Black Hawk War; took a claim in Irish Hollow; sold, went back to Galena, settled on farm west of Galena; lost his wife Sept. 20, 1871; has five children: James, Andrew S., Eliza, Ellen and Robert; they own 300 acres of land; Mr. K. is now in his 77th year, hale and hearty, and during this Fall shoveled 6,000 bushels of corn.

Kilpatrick A. S. farm; S. 4; P. O. Hanover.

Kilpatrick Robt. farm; S. 4; P. O Hanover.

Kitty John, farmer; Sec. 24; P. O. Hanover.

Kirk James, laborer; Sec. 4; P. O. Hanover.

Klemper Henry, farm; S. 24; P. O. Hanover.

Klemper John, farm; S. 24; P. O. Hanover.

Klemper Jos. farmer; S. 24; P. O. Hanover.

Knapp Chas. farm; Sec. 21; P. O. Hanover.

Knapp Henry, farm; S. 15; P. O. Hanover.

LAMB JOHN, in factory; Hanover.

Lightner F. farmer; Sec. 8; P. O. Hanover.

Limage Anthony, carpenter; Hanover.

Limage Jos. teamster; Hanover.

LOVE JOSEPH G. Physician and Surgeon; Hanover; born in N. Y. City Jan. 9, 1840; educated in the public schools of the city; went to Detroit, Mich., there completed his education; took first course of medical lectures at Queen's College, Canada, in 1858; second in Buffalo Medical University in 1859 and 1860; graduated at the American Medical University of Pa. in 1861; enlisted in 40th Regt. N. Y. V. I.; served during war as Asst. Surgeon, rank of First Lieutenant; participated in all the engagements and endured the hardships of the Peninsula campaign; honorably discharged at close of war; practiced in Kankakee three years, in Richmond, Mich., two years; came to Hanover in 1868; married Miss Nellie M. Reynolds July 21, 1870; she was born in Elizabeth, this Co., May 12, 1851; have two children: Charles R. Love, John G. Love; the Doctor is a member of the Council and Royal Arch Masons.

McALLISTER DANIEL, Farmer; Sec. 12; P. O. Hanover; born in the north of Ireland June 18, 1822; married Miss Elizabeth Patton Feb. 8, 1844; she was born same place Oct. 3, 1823; emigrated to Philadelphia in June, 1844; worked in the city at the wheelwright business eleven years; came to Galena in 1855; in Spring of 1856 purchased the farm upon which they now reside; have five children: James H., Anthony, George, in California, Mrs. Annie Arnold, Mrs. Jane Burns; Mr. M. has served as Justice of the Peace; was commissioned by Gov. Palmer, Commissioner of Highways and School Director; owns 340 acres land.

McAllister J. H. farm; S. 13; P. O. Hanover.

McCabe Ed. farm; Sec. 16; P. O. Hanover.

McCALL THOS. Farmer; Sec. 5; P. O. Hanover; born in Co. Monaghan, Ireland, July 4, 1831; came to the U. S. in 1836; they settled in N. Y. City and lived there eight years; came to this Co. in 1844; married Miss Maria Coline in 1860; she was born in Ireland in 1840; have five children living: Elizabeth, William, Annie, George and Elsie; lost two children; Mr. M. owns 273 acres of land.

McCaun John, blacksmith; Hanover.

McCormack D. W. Sec. 7; P. O. Hanover.

McCormac D., Sr. farm; S. 7; P. O. Hanover.

McCormac D., Jr. farm; S. 7; P. O. Hanover.

McCormack Geo. Sec. 22; P. O. Hanover.

McCoy J. H. farmer; S. 22; P. O. Hanover.

McDermot Martin. laborer; Sec. 22; P. O. Hanover.

McDermot Thos. Hanover.

McKINLEY WM. Farmer; Sec. 25; P. O. Hanover; born in City of Philadelphia Nov. 4, 1830; came to this Co. with his parents in 1836; lived in Galena till 1848, when they moved on to farm; Mr. M. has circumnavigated the globe, went around the world; started in 1852 overland to California; from there to Sandwich Islands, Navigator Islands, New Zealand, Australia, Liverpool, and returned to his birthplace, N. Y. City; from there to Philadelphia, then home to Illinois, consuming a little more than three years on the trip: married Miss Ann Kearney in 1860; have eight children living: John M., Emma G., Wm. E., George L., Lillie J., Eva May, Ira J., Robert M.; works 280 acres of land; has been School Director 16 or 17 years; a member of A. F. & A. M.

McLaughlin Mike, shoemaker; Hanover.

MATHESON JAMES, Retired Farmer and Stock Dealer; Hanover; born in Sutherlandshire, Scotland, in June. 1800; came to British America, the Red River country, in 1821; came to Hanover in 1833; married Miss Margaret Southerland; had seven children, only one of whom is living, Mrs. Elizabeth Donelson; wife died in Hanover in 1846; married Margaret McGan, of Scottish birth; she died in 1871; Miss Maggie McKenzie, a granddaughter, lives with Mr. M.; he owns 400 acres of land.

Matheson John, farm; S. 15; P. O. Hanover.

May Alfred, laborer; Sec. 10; P. O. Hanover.

MAY BALAAM, Farmer; P. O. Hanover; born in White Co., Ill., Sept. 15, 1827; came to this Co. in 1835; father died in 1875; his mother, Mrs. Amanda May, born in 1805, still lives on the homestead where they settled in 1835; Mr. M. learned the blacksmith trade in Hanover; has worked at the business over eighteen years in this Co.; married Miss Eliza J. Nesbitt in 1852; she was born in Co. Monaghan, Irelnad, in 1830; have six children: Alfred W., Mary E., George W., Wm. H., Charles R., Clara Belle; lost three children; has been School Director fourteen years.

May Jas. farmer; Sec. 12; P. O. Hanover.

MILLER JOHN, Retired Farmer; Sec. 12; P. O. Hanover; born in Co. Monaghan, Ireland, Dec. 14, 1801; came to U. S. in 1823; settled in City of New York; lived there fifteen years, being a part of the time in Brooklyn and Jersey City; worked in carpet and hat factories, and was engaged in a publishing office; married Miss Eliza Gray Aug. 13, 1828; she was born in same place in 1805; were schoolmates in old country; came to this Co. May 1, 1838; bought claim from his brother; among the earliest settlers; eight children living: Mrs. Mary Jane Campbell, Joseph, Robert J., John Q., Mrs. Martha Dawson, Dr. George, of Savanna, Phœbe E., William N.; the original homestead contained 441 acres.

Miller John Q. farm; S. 18; P. O. Hanover.

Miller N. Hanover.

Miller R. J. farmer; Sec. 12; P. O. Hanover.

Miller Samuel, laborer; Hanover.

Miller Wm. G. farm; S. 22; P. O. Hanover.

Miller Wm. N. Sec. 12; P. O. Hanover.

Milligan Ed. farmer; S. 20; P. O. Hanover.

Milligan Jas. E. carpenter; Hanover.

Montgomery E. renter; S. 29; P. O. Hanover.

Montgomery Wm. farmer; Sec. 29; P. O. Hanover.

Moore Thos. clerk; Hanover.

Moorhead Albert, farm; S. 6; P. O. Hanover.

Moorehead T. A. farm; S. 6; P. O. Hanover.

Moorhead Thos. painter; Hanover.

Morris Levi, teamster; Hanover.

Murphy Mike, lab; Sec. 9; P. O. Hanover.

NESBITT CHAS. farmer; Sec. 10; P. O. Hanover.

Nesbitt Josiah, farm; S. 10; P. O. Hanover.

Nesbitt Jas. farmer; Sec. 10; P. O. Hanover.

OTTEN HENRY, Hanover.

PEARCE MOSES, farmer; Sec. 2; P. O. Hanover.

Pearce R. M. farm; Sec. 2; P.O. Elizabeth.

Phillips J. L. carpenter; Hanover.

PILCHER REV. LEWIS A. Sec. 2; P. O. Hanover; born near Lexington, Ky., March 16, 1824; son of Jane and Nancy Pilcher; they were born in Va., respectively June 2, 1783, and May 5, 1787; father died in 1857; his mother had fourteen children; she is now 91 years old; has eighty grandchildren; sixty-five great grandchildren and four great-great grandchildren; Mr. P. is a Baptist Minister, and has preached the Gospel for many years; married Miss L. Beer in 1847; she was born in Ill., Oct. 23, 1825; had three children, one of whom is now living, Mary A., wife of David P. Kuhns, a carpenter and joiner; he was born in Guernsey Co., Ohio, Aug. 10, 1852; came to this Co. in 1864; they have one child, Leroy D. L. Kuhns, born Dec. 2, 1877; has 49 acres of land; Mr. P.'s wife died Dec. 22, 1852, since which time he has kept his family together by aid of his mother.

Pratt Samuel, Hanover.

RAVENSCRAFT THOS., Hanover.

REYNOLDS ABRAM, Proprietor Carriage and Wagon shop, Hanover; born in Rome, Oneida Co., N. Y., July 21, 1821; lived in St. Lawrence Co. 8 years, Chautauqua Co. 10 years, La Fayette Co., Ind., 2 years; came to this Co. in 1841; resided here until the California gold excitement in 1850, when he crossed the plains with ox teams; was four months on the route; were harrassed by Indians who stole their horses and other property; after losing horses walked 1,000 miles in order to get provisions to send back to the train; was compelled to depend on shooting game sufficient to supply them while footing it ahead of the teams; was there 2 years; Mr. R. entered the land on which the Village of Elizabeth stands; was there at the land sale in 1847; the sale was at Dixon; Mr. P. J. Pilcher is the only man there now that lived there at that time; Mr. R. learned the trade of blacksmith in his native town and has followed it for 42 years; married Miss Ellen Marshall in 1848; she was born in New Hampshire in 1827; came to Rock Island in 1836 and to Elizabeth in 1843; have four children living: Mrs. Mary Moore, Mrs. Augusta, wife of Dr. Killough, Carrie and Hattie.

Reynolds Jno. B. wheel-wright; Hanover.

ROBINSON ARCHIBALD, Farmer; Sec. 8; P. O. Hanover; resides in the village; born in Co. Donegal, Ireland, in 1807; came to the U. S. in 1826; settled in Philadelphia; remained there till 1834, when he came to this Co.; his sister Catherine, born in 1802, and another sister who died in 1839, came with him; his sisters Eve and Ann lived at home in this Co. till 1849, then moved to Galena; were there 15 years; removed to St. Louis and were there 8 years; have lived in Hanover since; Catherine married James Robinson who died Dec. 24, 1871, since which she has lived with her brother; Mr. R. is one of the pioneers in this Co.; there are only two persons in Hanover Tp. now who lived here when he came; owns 80 acres of land.

ROBINSON CHAS. T. Farmer; Sec. 34; P. O. Hanover; born in Carroll Co., Ill., Feb. 10, 1845; his grandfather, John Armstrong, came to this Co. from N. Carolina, about 1827; Mr. R. moved into this Co. in 1870; married Miss Abbie Hunt in 1868; she was born in Galena May 17, 1847; have five children: Arthur, Ella, Mylus C., Lillie, Ada; owns 160 acres of land; Mr. R. served the last year of the war in the 15th Regt. I. V. I., was honorably discharged at the close of the war.

Robinson G. farmer; Sec. 5; P. O. Hanover.

Robinson H. G., Hanover.

Robinson James, Hanover.

Robinson John, Hanover.

Robinson J. H. Hanover.

Rogers Michael, Hanover.

SANDERSON WM. Sec. 25; P. O. Hanover.

Smith Rev. J. D. Pastor U. P. Church; Hanover.

Smith John, Sec. 2; P. O. Hanover.

SPEER CHARLES, Farmer and Stock Dealer; Sec. 4; P. O. Hanover; born in Elizabeth Tp., this Co., Feb. 18, 1842; married Miss Nancy Campbell March 21, 1866; she was born in Galena Feb. 18, 1844; have six children living: Isaac, William J., James W., Mary E., Joseph A., Henry; owns 419 acres land; at the present time Mr. S. is Supervisor of Hanover; takes a lively interest in the agricultural affairs of the Co.; a faithful officer and worthy citizen.

SPEER JOHN, Farmer and Stock Dealer; Sec. 5; P. O. Hanover; born in County Monaghan, Ireland, July 20, 1828; came to Philadelphia with his parents at the age of five years; his father came to this Co. in 1834, and the family followed in 1835; remained in Galena three years, where Mr. S. was sent to a select school a part of the time; no public schools; moved on farm in 1838; being the oldest son, his father being in delicate health, much of the business management devolved upon him and his mother; as he grew older found his education deficient; applied himself nights and so schooled himself as to fit him well for the business duties of life; in 1857 engaged to pay $21,000 for 945 acres of land in addition to the home farm; by the untiring industry of the family, farming, running threshing machines, etc., paid the debt, to the astonishment of some of their neighbors; the father died in 1862; mother still living at the age of 80 years; married Miss Mary Moore Oct. 20, 1857; she was born in Hanover: they have six children living: Josiah, Mary H., Elizabeth J., John M., Agnes I., Margaret T.; owns 361 acres land.

Speer J. R. farmer; Sec. 8; P. O. Hanover.

STEELE CYRUS, Farmer; Sec. 4; P. O. Hanover; born in Peterborough, N. H., May 21, 1829; came to Hancock Co.,

Ill., in 1853; lived there three years and came to this Co. in 1856; married Mrs. Cochran, whose maiden name was Miss Susan Gates, in May, 1856; she was born in N. Y. Dec. 14, 1816; she had five children: Mrs. Nancy J. James, Charles A. Cochran, Andrew E., Anna E.; Mr. S. has one son, George Edwin Steele; has an adopted daughter, Eda Steele; owns 250 acres land.

Stewart James, Hanover.

Stryker William, Hanover.

Sullivan Florence, Sec. 23; P. O. Hanover.

Sullivan Jerry, Sec. 23; P. O. Hanover.

Swift D. Hanover.

TIPP HENRY, farmer; Sec. 24; P. O. Hanover.

UPSON H. U. in factory; P. O. Hanover.

WAUSEY WM. Sec. 15; P. O. Hanover.

WATTS JAMES B. Farmer; Sec. 19; P. O. Hanover; born in Sussex Co., Eng., Aug. 13, 1817; went to Manchester in 1832; from there to London in 1833; lived in that city till he sailed for America; came to Chicago in 1834; clerk in court house two years; came to Galena in 1836; clerk for Amerys two years; moved to Elizabeth, and in a miner's cabin set up the first store in that village in 1838; started carding mill there in 1845; purchased grist mill in 1855, and introduced carding business and saw mill in connection with same power; remained there till 1867; moved to his present home in 1868; married Miss Abigail Hunt in 1842; she was born in Ulster Co., N. Y., July 28, 1825; four children: Eugenia A., Amelia C., Mrs. Ella A. Miner, Mrs. Abbie L. Batty; owns 296 acres land; is a member of I. O. O. F.

Wells John, harness maker; Hanover.

WHITE A. B. Clerk; Hanover; born in Hanover Oct. 4, 1848; was educated at the University of Notre Dame, Ind.; married Miss Martha S. Reynolds in 1874; she was born in Jo Daviess Co.; have one child, Ella R. White, born Nov. 16, 1875; Mr. W. is a member of the Masonic Lodge, and has been "honored with supreme command" as Master.

White Charles, supt. of pulp mill, Hanover.

WHITE JAMES W. General Manager Hanover Manufacturing Company; P. O. Hanover; born in Amherst, N. H., July 2, 1818; parents moved to Lowell, Mass., 1831; lived there till 1837, when they came to Savanna, Ill.; Mr. W. carried on merchandising in Savanna from 1839; extended his business to Elizabeth, 1841, and moved to the latter place in 1843; married Miss Almira Jenks in the Spring of 1843; she was born in Beverly, Va.; came to Savanna with her parents in 1838; she died in 1852; had three children, two of whom are living, Albert B. and Ella M.; lost one daughter, Anna; married Miss Harriet E. Fowler in 1853; she was born in this Co.; have four children: Mrs. Florence Howard, of Mass., Ralph W. Frank F., Wm. J.; in 1845 came to Hanover and purchased the water power and nine acres of real estate belonging thereto; commenced the improvement of the power, built dam, erected flour mill and saw mill; in 1845 the walls of the flour mill gave way, and in 1857 the present large and substantial stone building took the place of the former structure; continued the flouring business till 1864, when the present company was organized, and commenced the manufacture of woolen goods, using the stone building for a factory and erected a new one for flouring near by; Mr. W. is also the general manager of Hanover Paper Pulp Co.'s Mills, situated four miles below Hanover; owns 400 acres of land; Mr. W. and his kindred are known as unassuming, honest, and industrious people, having the confidence and respect of all who known them.

WHITE JOHN KELSO, Retired Farmer; P. O. Hanover; born in Peterborough, N. H., July 22, 1819; married Miss Mary H. Swan, Dec. 19, 1844, in their native town; she was born in Peterborough April 26, 1823; they came to Hanover, Jo Daviess Co., in 1855; Mr. W. has been engaged in farming till 1874, since which they have been living in the retirement of their village home; they have one child living, Mrs. Mary A. Dawson; lost one daughter, Mrs. Agnes J. Lightner, whose four children are now living with their grandparents: Claud O., Oma W., Charles A., Ray Albert.

WHITE JONATHAN, Jr., Miller; Hanover; born in Lowell, Mass., Dec. 25, 1833; his father, whose name the subject of this sketch bears, moved to Amherst from Peterborough in 1812; engaged in the manufacturing business till 1830, when he removed to Lowell, where he could have the aid of water power in carrying on his business; in Lowell he was many years a member of the Common Council, but declined other municipal offices; moved to Hanover in 1850, where he engaged in various pursuits, and was Postmaster of the village till he resigned in his 80th year; J. W., Jr., served in the army during the War of the Rebellion; in 1862, six months, in the enrolled militia of Mo.; returned to this Co. and joined the 45th I. V. I. at Vicksburg; was with Sherman on his "March to the Sea"; was honorably discharged at the close of the war; married Miss Ellen H. Treganoun in 1855; have four children living:

Jennie H., Harriet B., Caroline S., and Charles; lost first wife Jan., 1872; married Awilda J. Lightner Aug. 25, 1874; she was born in Mercer Co., Pa., in 1844.

Wilcox F. farmer; Sec. 27; P. O. Hanover.

Wiley Henry, Sec. 10; P. O. Hanover.

Wiley J. H. farmer; Sec. 10; P. O. Hanover.

Wiley Wm. Sec. 10; P. O. Hanover.

WILSON JAMES, Clerk; Hanover; born in Canada near Niagara Falls Aug. 2, 1836; his father owned a part of the ground upon which the battle of Lundy's Lane was fought; moved to Niagara in 1837; came to this Co. in 1859; his parents came in 1862; father died April 14, 1866; mother died Aug. 5, 1870; Mr. W. married Miss Isabella Warner in 1859; two children living: Jenet M. and Nellie I.: lost one child, James M., in 1870; his wife died in 1871; was married to Miss Sarah Kaye of England; one child, Mary S.; lost his wife in 1873; his present wife was Miss Elizabeth L. Dick, whom he married Sept. 4, 1876; she was born in Beaty's Hollow, this Co., Sept. 3, 1843.

Wilson R. R. merchant; Hanover.

WOLCOTT HENRY O. Farmer; Sec. 24; P. O. Hanover; born in Ohio May 31, 1838; started in 1859 in a company with ox teams for Pike's Peak; went as far as Kan., traversed that state, and in Oct. with six others went 200 miles west on a buffalo hunt; returned to this Co. in Dec.; in 1867 with another party started overland for Montana; was detained fourteen days at Ft. Reno; Gen. Smith of Galena came up with a train of 120 government wagons bound for Ft. Phil Kearney; went to Ft. Smith; arrived at Helena Aug. 15; worked in the mines till following July, when he returned to this Co., where he has since resided; married Miss Helen R. Carpenter Dec. 2, 1863; she was born in N. Y. Oct. 2, 1845; they have four children living: Etta F., Cyrus H., Lois O., Robt. R.; lost one child, John H., Jan. 15, 1876; owns 200 acres of land.

YOUNG HENRY, butcher; Hanover.

YOUNG JONATHAN, Farmer; Sec. 3; Bellevue, Ia.; born in Manchester, N. H., Jan. 3, 1825; married Miss Margaret Ann Moore in Aug., 1846; she was born in same city Feb. 12, 1829; removed to Dubuque Co., Iowa, in 1858; to Delaware Co. in 1859; lived in Londonderry nineteen years before coming West; came to this Co. in 1861; owns 140 acres of land; deals extensively in stock; they have four children living: Israel H., Lucy E., Addie A., David H.

Young Z. H. teacher; Hanover.

WOODBINE TOWNSHIP.

ADAMS CHARLES, farmer; Sec. 13; P. O. Woodbine.

ARMITAGE JOSEPH, Carpenter and Farmer; Sec. 19; P. O. Elizabeth; born in Yorkshire, Eng., Sept. 4, 1838; came to America in 1843; came to Jo Daviess Co. in 1843; has lived at Galena most of the time; has made five trips to the gold regions of the mountains; married Miss Catherine Ann Bray May 7, 1862; she was born in Cornwall, Eng., in 1840; they have five children: Frank S., Mary Grace, Sarah B., Nettie, and an infant not named; Mrs. A. is a sister of T. B. Bray, a prominent citizen of Elizabeth; he was born in June, 1835, at Cornwall, Eng.; he came to th's Co. in 1843; married Miss Lucretia Robinson, a daughter of Davis Robinson, Esq., in 1857; they have three children: Harry Clyde, John Albert and Charles H.

ARTMAN JOSEPH J. Farmer; Sec. 34; P. O. Elizabeth; born in Prussia Nov. 15, 1847; came to this country with his parents in 1851 *via* New Orleans; on the route up the river his mother was taken with the cholera and died, and was buried at Memphis; he and his father came to this Co. and settled on his present farm, formerly owned by his uncle; his father, who now resides with him, was born in Prussia April 16, 1814; he married Miss Josephine Benworth in Nov., 1869; she was born in Switzerland; have four children: Charles A., Annie R., Henry J. and Andrew; owns 336 acres land.

Artman Joseph, farmer; Sec. 30; P. O. Elizabeth.

Atchinson M. W. farmer; Sec. 35; P. O. Derinda.

BAINBRIDGE GEO. farmer; Sec. 19; P. O. Elizabeth.

Barret Geo. farmer; Sec. 29; P. O. Elizabeth.

Bastian Leonard, farmer; Sec. 14; P. O. Woodbine.

Batmann George, retired farmer; Sec. 19; P. O. Elizabeth.

Batman James, constable; Elizabeth.

Baumgarten Frank, farmer; Sec. 16; P. O. Elizabeth.

Bauworth Fred. farm; S. 30; P. O. Elizabeth.

Bauworth Geo. farm; S. 31; P. O. Elizabeth.

Bauworth Jno. farm; S. 31; P. O. Elizabeth.

Bauworth Wm. farm; S. 31; P. O. Elizabeth.

Bawden Francis, farmer; Sec. 36; P. O. Elizabeth.

Bawden Jas. farm; Sec. 24; P. O. Elizabeth.

BAWDEN JAMES H. Farmer; Sec. 36; P. O. Derinda; born in Fayette Co., Wis., Nov. 24, 1842; went to California in 1862; returned and enlisted in 7th I. V. C. at old Council Hill; was at Nashville, East Port, Iuka, Okalona, Custumbia and Decatur; was honorably discharged at Nashville at the close of the war; married Miss Eliza J. White March 11, 1869; she was born near Galena, in Beaty's Hollow; lost her parents when she was quite young; have four children living: James H., William N., Francis W., Annie E.; lost one child, Eva Lena; owns 125 acres land.

Becker John, farmer; Sec. 1; P. O. Elizabeth.

Blake Jesse, farmer; Sec. 19; P. O. Elizabeth.

BOARDWAY PETER, Farmer; Sec. 29; P. O. Elizabeth; born in Canada, of French descent, July 13, 1806; was employed by the American Fur Company, and came to Mackinaw in 1827; went to Green Bay; under the protection of the U. S. troops they went to Fort Winnebago; the Indian chief Red Bird offered the pipe of peace to the commander of the troops, who refused it in scorn, knocking it from his hand; the chief in anger arose and said he had killed many whites and escaped; he was a brave and a chief, and to shield his tribe he would suffer the penalty; he was sentenced to be hanged, but starved himself in prison before the day of execution. Soon after he settled in this Co. he enlisted in the volunteer army and served during the Black Hawk War; he was sent on an expedition to rescue the Hall girls, who had been captured by the Indians; he received an honorable discharge and returned to his home; he was married in 1836; he has three children living: Margaret, Charles and Louisa; his first wife died; he afterwards married the widow Walcott, whose maiden name was Eliza A. Williams; she was born Nov. 3, 1817, in N. Y.; she married Mr. Walcott in Ohio in 1833; came to this state in 1836; he has eight children living: William A., Henry O., Mary H., Sarah, Nancy, Julia C., Ellen, Olive; Mr. Boardway owns 200 acres land.

Boman Chas. laborer; Sec. 20; P.O. Elizabeth.

Bower John, farmer; Sec. 6; P. O. Elizabeth.

Bowden Benjamin, farmer; Sec. 24; P. O. Elizabeth.

BOWDEN ISAAC, Farmer; Sec. 23; P. O. Elizabeth; born in Luzerne Co., Pa., Jan. 1, 1811; his father was in the revolution under the command of Gen. Washington; was wounded at Brandywine and carried English lead to his grave; went to N. J. at the age of 19; lived there eight years and went to Ohio, where he resided till 1854, when he came to this Co.; married Miss Rachel Watson in N. J.; she was born there; have eight children living: Hiram, Neoma, John, Benjamin, Mary, Robert, Isaac, Elizabeth; lost one son, who died in the army, of measles; John and Hiram also served in army.

Bowden I. farmer; Sec. 24; P. O. Elizabeth.

Bough P. farmer; Sec. 23; P. O. Woodbine.

Bogle C. farmer; Sec. 24; P. O. Woodbine.

Bray Jas. farmer; Sec. 36; P. O. Derinda.

BRAY JOHN, Farmer; Sec. 36; P. O. Derinda; born in Cornwall, Eng., Jan. 15, 1826; came to America in 1842; remained a while at Mineral Point and Dodgeville, Wis.; came to Jo Daviess Co. in 1844; returned to England in 1847, having spent most of the time in America in the Lake Superior Copper Regions; married Miss Elizabeth Bellman, while visiting England, in 1848; she was born in Cornwall, Eng., Aug. 15, 1825; returned to Jo Daviess Co.; has made four trips to copper mining regions of Lake Superior; after his second trip bought a farm on Rush Creek; lived in Dubuque, Iowa, six months; Mr. B. has been engaged in mining many years—St. Louis, Ottawa, Dubuque, Lake Superior and in Johnson Co.; has seven children: Mary J., John, Elizabeth, James, Maria D., Richard, Caroline; Mr. B. has 147 acres of land, and is now engaged in farming and growing stock.

Bray John, Jr., farm; Sec. 35; P. O. Derinda.

Burnes Hugh, miner; Sec. 19; P.O. Elizabeth.

CARPENTER CYRUS, Farmer; Sec. 17; P. O. Elizabeth; born in Orange Co., Vt., Nov. 17, 1822; moved to Lawrence, N. Y., 1836; married Miss Lois E. St. John Nov. 28, 1844; she was born in Rutland Co., Vt.; her parents moved to Bangor, N. Y., when she was quite young; then to Lawrence; they came to Ogle Co., Ill., 1848; came to this Co. in 1850; they have two children: Mrs. Helen R. Walcott, Mrs. Frances H. Brady; Mr. B. is a graduate of Evanston University; he is a member of the Mich. M. E. Conference; Mrs. Carpenter's youngest sister, Lydia E., after the death of her parents, came West with them and made her home with them until she married Mr. Aden Richardson, of Jackson Co., Ia.; a nephew, Frank St. John, lives with them; Mr. C. owns 190 acres of land.

CLAYWELL SHEDRACH, Farmer; Sec. 22; P. O. Elizabeth; born in Cumberland Co., Ky., April 9, 1816; came to Sangamon Co., Ill., with his father in 1825; mother died in Tenn.; in 1831 returned to Ky.; went from there to St. Louis, to Springfield, to Chicago, in 1833; was there at treaty with Indians; worked for Claybourne four months; for Epperson

G. V. Townsend

WARREN.

two months; carried mail from Chicago to Blue Island; found a woman supposed to be killed by wolves; had been to the garrison in Chicago to beg food for her children; carried mail, in 1834, for Mr. Dixon, from Chicago to Dixon, weekly; laid the first claim in Franklin Grove; in 1835 carried mail for Winters from Dixon to what was called Dad Jo's Grove; came to this Co. in 1835; carried first mail from Galena to Freeport, blazing his track with a hatchet to Burr Oak Grove; worked for Winters till 1840; another driver on the line came into the hotel one cold, stormy night, with his horses, having left his hack and passengers, consisting of an emigrant family—a man, his wife, and three children—in a snow drift; they were left to pass the night in the bitter cold; no ray of hope to cheer, but snow drifting over the bleak and houseless prairie; the wind whistling around them, every sound of which seemed like a death knell or wailing requiem; Mr. C. could not lie down "to pleasant dreams" that night, till he went to the barn, harnessed his four horses, proceeded alone through the merciless storm, found them, hitched his wheel horses to the end of the tongue and drew them from their snow-bound prison; the spirit of humanity was exhibited, the perishing were rescued and taken from what would have been certain death, to a comfortable tavern, where gleamed and glowed a hospitable fire that snapped and crackled as it sent its cheerful sparks heavenward through the chimney of an old-fashioned fire-place; the joy of that father's heart and the rapture of that mother's soul can only be imagined; words fail to express it; Mr. C. married Miss Martha J. Winters, a niece of John D. Winters, in whose employ he was, Dec. 15, 1840; she was born in Fayette Co., Pa., Feb. 8, 1819; she came to Ill. with her uncle, who had been to Washington, and called to visit her father at his home in Pa.; was married and remained here 30 years before she returned to her native home; Mr. C. had been called "Shed" so much by men along the line, that they went by the name of Mr. and Mrs. "Shed" for years, many of their friends not knowing what their right name was; have three children living: George E., Mrs. Cynthia J. Shepler, and Joanna; owns 422 acres of land.

Cox E. farmer; Sec. 8; P. O. Elizabeth.

Cox Geo. farmer; Sec. 8; P. O. Elizabeth.

Crawford J. farm; Sec. 15; P. O. Woodbine.

Crawford W. J. farm; S. 15; P. O. Woodbine.

Crawford W. S. farm; S. 15; P. O. Woodbine.

DETMER E. farmer; Sec. 5; P. O. Elizabeth.

Dobkins M. V. farmer; Sec. 17; P. O. Elizabeth.

ERTMER JOSEPH, farmer; Sec. 33; P. O. Elizabeth.

EVANS JOHN, Farmer; Sec. 11; P. O. Woodbine; born in Wales, March 13, 1821; came to this country in 1845, landing at Quebec; came to Racine, Wis., from there to Iowa Co., and then to Galena; worked in New Diggings as a miner; married in Galena, Miss Catherine Hughs, April 18, 1851; she was born in Wales in 1830; came to America with her parents when quite young; has been School Director 5 years; commissioned as Justice of the Peace by Gov. J. L. Beveridge in 1874; also by Gov. Cullom in 1877; owns 165 acres of land; has eight children living: Mary E., Elizabeth, Hannah, Flora Bell, Owen, Margaret, John, Ebenezer; lost one son Sept. 7, 1854.

Evans Rev. John E. farmer; Sec. 2; P. O. Elizabeth.

FARRELL JOHN, Jr., farmer; Sec. 17; P. O. Elizabeth.

FARRALL JOHN, Retired Farmer; Sec. 8; P. O. Elizabeth; born in Co. Longford, Ireland, in 1811; came to America in 1832; remained in New York and New Jersey 3 years, coming to Galena in 1835; married Miss Elizabeth Dwyer in the Spring of 1834; she was born in Co. Wexford, Ireland, in 1812; she came to America in 1832; remained in Galena 2 years; mined for some time; bought a claim and obtained a deed when the land came into market; sold out and returned to Galena, remaining there six years for the purpose of school privileges for his family; then came out to Apple River and bought the place on which he now resides; has four children living: James, Thomas, William H. and John; Mr. F. has 296 acres of land and is now living in the retirement of his home, enjoying, during his declining years, the products of his honest toil; his word is his bond and he enjoys the confidence and respect of all who know him.

Farrell Thomas, Elizabeth.

GABLE BENJ. farmer; Sec. 25; P. O. Elizabeth.

Garthart J. farm; Sec. 23; P. O. Woodbine.

Gates R. B. farmer; Sec. 16; P.O. Woodbine.

GATES MRS. PASSINGFAIR, Farm; Sec. 16; P. O. Elizabeth; her maiden name was Miss Shore; born in Cumberland Co., Ky., Oct. 28, 1806; came to Ill. in 1827; married Mr. Edmond Gates May 1, 1828; he was born in North Carolina May 15, 1805; came to Jo Daviess Co. in 1834; settled first on a claim where she now lives; moved on to another claim on Apple River which was afterward taken into the mineral reserve, and they sold out and returned to the first claim; lost her husband Sept. 26, 1875; has four children living: Robert B. married Miss Barker;

they have three children living: Ira E., Edith M. and Lewis C.; Mrs. Emeline E. Wilkinson, Mary Ann E., and John F. who is in Kansas; has 120 acres of land.

GOLDHAGEN IGNATZ, Farmer; Sec. 21; P. O. Elizabeth; born in Prussia, Germany, April 3, 1839; came to America in 1854, remaining in Chicago during the Winter; in the Spring of 1855 came to Jo Daviess Co.; married Elizabeth Pohl; she was born in Hanover, Germany; they have three children living: Mary Josephine, Annie and Elizabeth; lost one, Catherine; Mr. G. owns a farm of 60 acres upon which he now lives engaged in grain and stock business.

Gosing John, farm; Sec. 18; P.O. Elizabeth.

Goult Matthew, stock buyer; Sec. 27; P. O. Elizabeth.

Green Joseph, lab; Sec. 22; P.O. Woodbine.

Grosinger C. farmer; Sec. 34; P. O. Derinda.

Grosinger J. farmer; Sec. 34; P. O. Derinda.

Gundry J. farmer; Sec. 17; P. O. Elizabeth.

HAIG JOHN, farmer; Sec. 20; P. O. Elizabeth.

Haig Peter, farmer; Sec. 20; P.O. Elizabeth.

Hardacre, Ed. renter; S. 25; P. O. Derinda.

Harms H. farmer; Sec. 16; P. O. Woodbine.

Harms Klous, Woodbine.

HEIDENREICH JOHN, Farmer; Sec. 14; P. O. Woodbine; born in Rottenburg, Germany, June, 18, 1830; came to Pa. in 1848; lived there about two years, and married Miss Margaret Barager in 1850; she was born in Briar Creek, Pa.; they moved to Ogle Co. in 1865, and soon after to this Co. and settled in Woodbine; have ten children living: Lavina, William, John, Alexandria, Charles, George E., Philip, Jacob, Annie C., Margaret; owns 100 acres of land; William, the eldest son, since he grew to manhood has been in Whiteside Co. about one year; went to Nebraska in 1873; returned and has been engaged in farming and running a threshing machine for several years, and by his untiring industry and energy, coupled with commendable economy, has, from small beginnings, become able to purchase the Woodbine Store, of which he is sole proprietor; he is doing a thriving business in Dry Goods, Groceries, Boots and shoes; he proposes by honest dealing to furnish every thing in his line as cheap as the cheapest; he has lately been appointed Postmaster of the Woodbine Post-office, which he keeps in his store.

Heidenrich Wm. farmer; P. O. Woodbine.

Hermann Fred. farmer; Sec. 15; P.O. Woodbine.

Herring James, farm; S. 34; P. O. Derinda.

Hess George, farmer; P. O. Elizabeth.

Hewit John, farmer; S. 28; P. O. Elizabeth.

Hicks Nathaniel, farmer; Sec. 28; P. O. Woodbine.

Hilderbrand Chas. farmer; Sec. 13; P. O. Woodbine.

HILDEBRANDT WILLIAM E. Farmer; Sec. 1; P. O. Elizabeth; born in Zehlendorf, between Berlin and Pottsdam, Germany, Aug. 18, 1834; came to Jo Daviess Co. by way of New Orleans, in Spring of 1857; married Miss Anna M. Schuchardt April 17, 1861; she was born in Germany, and came to America with her parents when quite young; Mr. H. served in the army during the war; enlisted at Dixon in the 96th Regt. I. V. I.; when the time of that regiment expired he was transferred to the 21st Regt. I. V. I.; was at Camp Butler and Nashville; went down the river to Texas, and was honorably discharged at the close of the war; has been School Director for four years, an office which he now fills; has 120 acres of land.

Hitt Leslie, farmer; P. O. Elizabeth.

Hitt Nelson, farmer; S. 19; P. O. Elizabeth.

HITT MRS. REBECCA K. Farming; Sec. 30; P. O. Elizabeth; born in Jefferson Co., Ky.; her maiden name was Miss Brown; married Mr. Thaddeus Hitt in Rushville, Ill., July 29, 1831; he was born in Virginia, Nov. 19, 1793; he served in the war of 1812; her grandfather, Fields, was wounded at the battle of Tippecanoe; they were in the Apple River Fort during that Summer; she is one of the few survivors; her grandson, Thaddeus Hunter, lives with her; he was born in Ogle Co., Ill; Mrs. H. retains her memory remarkably well, and related some interesting history, which will appear in the body of this work.

Hitt Samuel, farmer; S. 32; P. O. Elizabeth.

Hoffman Geo. farmer; S. 5; P. O. Woodbine.

Holcomb Geo. teacher; S. 26; P.O. Elizabeth.

Holcomb Ira B. farm; S. 26; P.O. Elizabeth.

HOLCOMB NEWELL, Farmer; Sec. 26; P. O. Elizabeth; born on an island in Lake Champlain, Grand Island Co., Vt., Aug. 15, 1819; his father moved to Plattsburg, N. Y.; lived there and in St. Lawrence Co., N. Y., till the subject of this sketch was 19 years of age; came to Ill. in 1838; lived at Springfield first Winter; then to Galena; worked at coopering at Gillett's mill and Thompson's mill; then went to Jule's prairie and bought a farm; married Miss Louisa Kellogg July 9, 1845; she was born in Chautauqua Co., N. Y.; have two children living: Maria L. and George W.; lost his wife; married Nancy A. Crissy May 12, 1850; have five children living: Bertha J., Marietta, Ira B., Henrietta, William H.; lost his second wife, both having died of consumption; married Miss Sarah A. Montgomery July 4, 1871; she was born in Galena Jan. 8, 1845; her father came to this Co. from St.

Louis; have three children living: Jennie M., Edward M., Mabel A.; Mr. H. has 268 acres of land; is extensively engaged in growing cattle, hogs and horses.

HORSCH SAMUEL, Farmer; Sec. 12; P. O. Elizabeth; born in Bavaria, Germany, Feb. 12, 1818; came to America in 1851, by way of New York, to Jo Daviess Co.; married Miss Catharine Horsch in May, 1851; she came over in the same ship that her husband came in, but were not married till they came to this Co.; have 120 acres of land; have nine children living: David, William, Mary, Louisa, August, Annie M., Samuel, Elias H. and Frederick; lived near Galena; from there went to Scales Mound, and have now lived sixteen years at their present residence.

Hubbard Thos. farm; S. 18; P.O. Elizabeth.

Hughes Ewd. farm; S. 10; P. O. Elizabeth.

HUGHES HUGH R. Farmer; Sec. 10; P. O. Elizabeth; born in Wales Feb. 17, 1831; came to America with his parents in 1841; lived in Pittsburg three months, and moved to Wisconsin, where they resided till 1847, when they came to Jo Daviess Co.; married Miss Ellen Caldwell in Sept., 1857; she was born in Jo Daviess Co. April 2, 1839; her parents came from Ky. to Ill. at an early day, and settled in Jo Daviess Co. in 1837; were among the earliest settlers of the Co.; have nine children living: Edward F., William J., George T., Frances M., Joseph L., Cora E., John Sherman, Ella and Martha; have 140 acres of land.

Hughes Owen, farm; S. 11; P. O. Elizabeth.

Hughes Rich. farm; S. 10; P. O. Elizabeth.

Hurst August, farm; S. 12; P. O. Elizabeth.

Huth John, farmer; Sec. 23; P.O. Woodbine.

Hutton John B., P. O. Elizabeth.

Hutton William, P. O. Elizabeth.

ISABELL TAMP, miner; Sec. 19; P. O. Elizabeth.

JOHNS HUGH, Elizabeth.

Jones John F. Sec. 1; P. O. Elizabeth.

Jones John L. blacksmith; Sec. 1; P. O. Elizabeth.

Jones John W. Sec. 1; P. O. Elizabeth.

KOLB JOHN B. farmer; Sec. 32; P. O. Woodbine.

Krell G. farmer; Sec. 22; P. O. Woodbine.

Krell Wm. P. O. Derinda.

LANG ADAM M. farmer; Sec. 23; P. O. Elizabeth.

Lang Thos. farmer; P. O. Woodbine.

Lewis T. farmer; Sec. 3; P. O. Elizabeth.

Lewis Wm. farmer; Sec. 3; P. O. Woodbine.

Lewis Wm. W. farm; Sec. 3; P. O. Elizabeth.

Libert A. farmer; Sec. 5; P. O. Elizabeth.

Loyd A. laborer; Sec. 2; P. O. Elizabeth.

Loyd Thos. farmer; Sec. 2; P. O. Elizabeth.

Lynch James, farmer; Sec. 26; P. O. Woodbine.

Lynch John, farm; Sec. 26; P. O. Woodbine.

Lynch John A. farm; Sec. 26; P. O. Woodbine.

Lynch O. farmer; Sec. 24; P. O. Woodbine.

Lyons H. farmer; Sec. 23; P. O. Elizabeth.

McCOY JOHN G. Farmer; Sec. 27; P. O. Elizabeth; born in Yorkshire, Eng., Oct. 4, 1830; came to America with his parents at the age of four, landing in Jo Daviess Co. in 1834; his father was one of the pioneer settlers on head of Small Pox Creek; his father died at the age of ninety-six, and is next to the eldest person buried in the cemetery at Elizabeth; remained with his parents till 1852, when he went to California; remained there seven years and returned to call for his aged mother; she died in 1864; married Miss Sarah Ashmore in 1860; she was born near Elizabeth, this Co., Aug. 31, 1838; they have four children living: Lorenzo, Bowman, Alice and Charles; lost three children, one girl and two boys; served in army during war; was at Nashville, Knoxville, etc.; was detailed as ward master in hospital at Knoxville; honorably discharged at Springfield, Ill., at close of the war; has been School Director for many years, a position which he now holds; has 83 acres of land.

McGregory R. farm; S. 6; P. O. Elizabeth.

McGuire F. farmer; Sec. 26; P. O. Elizabeth.

McGuire T. farmer; Sec. 7; P. O. Elizabeth.

McKENZIE DONALD, Farmer; Sec. 27; P. O. Elizabeth; born in Glasgow, Scotland, June 18, 1819; came to America in 1835; lived in Maryland about seven years; went to St. Louis, Mo.; remained two years; came to this Co. in 1844, and has since resided here; married Miss Catherine Williams in 1849; she was born in Wales; no children; lost his first wife; married the widow of James Madge in 1858; her maiden name was Miss Sarah Atchison; they have three children living: John, Mary G. and Wm. L.; lost one child, Sarah C., in 1877; Mr. M. crossed the plains in 1850 to California; returned in 1852; has been engaged in farming and mining; his boys discovered lead in a ravine on his farm after a wash that bids fair to prove valuable; has served as Supervisor seven years; served three years and withdrew; was out three years and was called to the position again and is now serving the fourth year; has been School Director three years.

Mathews R. farm; Sec. 19; P. O. Elizabeth.

Medough G. lab; Sec. 35; P. O. Elizabeth.

Miffly F. farmer; Sec. 36; P. O. Elizabeth.

Miller John T., P. O. Elizabeth.

Miller Royal, P. O. Woodbine.

Mitchell Edward, Jr., Sec. 18; P. O. Elizabeth.

MITCHELL EDWARD, Owner of Elizabeth Mills; P. O. Elizabeth; born in Cornwall, Eng., May 2, 1821; came direct to this Co., arriving at Galena on June 6, 1842; married Miss Amelia Sincox in Aug., 1843; she was born in Cornwall, Eng., in 1822; she also came to America in 1842; in Fall of 1845 Mr. M. went to the Lake Superior copper regions and returned the next Summer; went across the plains to the gold region of California in 1852; was there eight years; came back to Jo Daviess Co. in 1860, and has since resided here; he has been for seven years and is now the sole proprietor of a large and flourishing grist mill on Apple River near the Village of Elizabeth; his son Edward is now running the mill; they have ten children: Mary Annie, born Nov. 18, 1844; Samuel, March 29, 1847; Edward, Sept. 2, 1848; Richard, Feb. 12, 1850; Emma J., Oct. 2, 1851; Wilber B., April 25, 1860; Lorenzo, Oct. 2, 1861; Evalena G., Jan. 26, 1863; Wallace E., July 31, 1864, Alfred W., May 26, 1866.

Mitchell S. farmer; Sec. 4; P. O. Elizabeth.

Musselman C. farm; S. 24; P. O. Woodbine.

Myers J. farmer; Sec. 21; P. O. Elizabeth.

Myers Lee, farmer; Sec. 21; P. O. Elizabeth.

NOBLE JAMES, laborer; Sec. 19; P. O. Elizabeth.

Noble Wm. laborer; S. 19; P. O. Elizabeth.

OLD JOHN, Farmer; Sec. 9; P. O. Elizabeth; born in Cornwall, England, Feb. 6, 1841; came to Elizabeth, this Co., in 1845; was in the Lake Superior copper mines 2½ years; went to Cal. in 1863; returned in 1866; in 1873 purchased the farm of 156 acres upon which he now lives, in the seclusion of his bachelor home, where he is "Monarch of all he surveys;" the order and neatness of his house should be a reproach to some of the women of the land; of this I speak with confidence, having enjoyed the hospitality of his table; he is no less remarkable for his sociability than for his generosity; is a member of the A. F. and A. Masons.

PHILLIPS JAMES, Farmer; Sec. 21; P. O. Elizabeth; born in Cornwall, Eng., Oct. 13, 1838; came to America in June, 1842, with his parents; settled in Grant Co., Wis.; then moved to Scales Mound about 1845; he went to California in 1862; remained there three years, returned to Jo Daviess Co., moved on the farm where he now resides; has 340 acres of land; married Miss Emily H. Grindey Feb. 22, 1868; she was born in Staffordshire, Eng., Oct. 22, 1842; she came to America in 1845; have two children: Isabella H., born Jan. 1, 1867; Samuel J., May 31, 1871; has been School Director four years; is engaged in farming and growing stock.

Pierce Franklin, farmer; Sec. 33; P. O. Elizabeth.

POTTER MARTIN C. Farmer; Sec. 21; P. O. Elizabeth; born in Bedford Co., Pa., Jan. 19, 1844; came to Jo Daviess Co. in Fall of 1865; married Miss Jane R. Rogers Sept. 13, 1866; she was born in Cornwall, Eng., July 21, 1842; came to America in June, 1846; Mr. P. enlisted in the army at Harrisburg, Pa., Feb. 3, 1862, in 101st Regt. Pa. V. I.; was in the severe engagements of the siege of Yorktown, Williamsburg, seven days' battle before Richmond, Kingston, Whitehall, Fair Oaks and Goldsboro; was wounded in the head at Fair Oaks May 31, 1862; served till expiration of three years, and then reenlisted, and was taken prisoner at Plymouth, on the Roanoke, in N. C.; was in Andersonville Prison six months, and at Florence, N. C., five months — eleven months' imprisonment, the serious effects of which he feels to this day; visited his native Co. in Pa. in 1867; has five children: Elmer W., Eliza J., Delilah A., Lillie and James W.; has 131 acres of land; Mr. P. and wife are members of the M. E. Church; he belongs to the I. O. O. F.

Powell Milton, lab; Sec. 35; P. O. Derinda.

PRISK MRS. GRACE, Farming; Sec. 25; P. O. Derinda; her maiden name was Miss Grace Williams; she was born in Cornwall, Eng., Dec. 25, 1815; she married Mr. Samuel Prisk about 1832; he was born in Cornwall, Eng., in 1814; came to America in 1844, and settled near Council Hill, in Jo Daviess Co.; has eight children living: Samuel, Grace, Mrs. Sarah Tucker, Honora, Joseph, in California, Elizabeth H., Mary, Mrs. Susan A. Hardacre; lost her husband July 31, 1861; has 216 acres of land; Miss Mary Prisk and her sister, Elizabeth H., are engaged in teaching, a business for which they have prepared themselves well by their untiring industry and unflagging zeal in the cause of education.

Prisk Samuel W. farm; S. 36; P. O. Derinda.

RANKIN ARTHUR V. Sec. 34; P. O. Elizabeth.

Rankin James, Sr., farmer; Sec. 26; P. O. Elizabeth.

Rankin James, Jr., farmer; Sec. 34; P. O. Elizabeth.

Rankin James J. farm; S. 34; P.O. Elizabeth.

Rankin John W. farm; S. 35; P.O. Elizabeth.

Reber Jas. farmer; Sec. 10; P. O. Woodbine.

Reber Samuel, farm; S. 11; P. O. Woodbine.

Redington Frank, laborer; Sec. 36; P. O. Elizabeth.

Reed S. R. teacher; Sec. 6; P. O. Elizabeth.

RETZ GEORGE, Retired Farmer; Sec. 33; P. O. Elizabeth; born in Wurtemburg, Germany, on St. John's Day, June 24, 1809; married Miss Sophia Brenner in 1843; she was born in Wurtemburg, Germany, in 1813, came to America in 1858, settling at Galena; went to Jefferson, Wis., for some time, and returned to Jo Daviess Co., and have since lived here; have three children living: Godleip, Jacob and Christianna; the boys own 144 acres of land in this Co.; they are an industrious family, having an intelligent idea of popular education and the general progress of the country.

Reynolds John T. farmer; Sec. 28; P. O Elizabeth.

REYNOLDS SARAH S. Farm; Sec. 28; P. O. Elizabeth; maiden name was Miss Sarah S. Cliff; she was born in Cornwall, England, May 27, 1831; came direct to this Co. with her parents in 1844; resided at Elizabeth and Weston, Jo Daviess Co.; married Mr. Thomas Reynolds Nov. 24, 1853; he was born in Cornwall, England, June 14, 1813, and came to America in 1842; in 1850 Mr. R. went to the gold fields of California; returned to his home on Rush Creek, and died in 1875, leaving his wife and seven children to mourn the loss of an estimable husband and affectionate father; the children are: John T., Sarah A., George W., Wm. W., Samuel B., James W., Lemuel H.; lost two children; they have 215 acres of land.

REYNOLDS WM. LAW, Farmer; Sec. 14; P. O. Woodbine; born in Hertfordshire, England, Nov. 23, 1829; came to America in 1851; remained one year in Vermont and two years in Rochester, N. Y.; came to Jo Daviess Co. in 1856; married Miss Mary Green June 7, 1857; she was born in Yorkshire, England, Oct. 15, 1836; came to Wisconsin with her parents in 1842; Mr. R. served in the army during the war; was mustered into the 124th Regt. I. V. I. at Dixon; was at Camp Butler, Vicksburg; was at the siege of Spanish Fort, a severe engagement, lasting 13 days and nights; went to Montgomery, and returned to Vicksburg where he was honorably discharged at the close of the war; have three children: Martha, Anne E., George W., and Jessie Green; has 110 acres of land.

Richards John, Sec. 30; P. O. Elizabeth.

Roberts Paul farm; Sec. 9; P. O. Elizabeth.

Roberts Jas. farmer; Sec. 8; P. O. Elizabeth.

ROBERTS WM. Retired Farmer; Sec. 8; P.O. Elizabeth; born in Cornwall, England, March 15, 1810; married Miss Mary Sparzo in March, 1832; she was born in Cornwall, England, April 1, 1810; came to Jo Daviess Co. in 1855; went to Lake Superior copper regions soon after arriving in this Co., remained there about nine months; came back and has been here since; has 218½ acres of land and lives in the enjoyment of a pleasant home in which to pass his declining years; has eight children living: William, Henry, John, James, Mary Jane, Paul, Elizabeth and Grace.

Roberts Wm., Jr., farmer; Sec. 9; P. O. Elizabeth.

Rogers Geo. farmer; Sec. 14; P. O. Woodbine.

ROGERS JAMES, Farmer; Sec. 14; P. O. Woodbine; born in Cornwall, Eng., in 1820; married Miss Eliza Roberts in Jan., 1842; she was born in Cornwall, Eng., Feb. 4, 1819; they came direct to Jo Daviess Co. in 1846, settling at Scales Mound; Mr. R. has always taken an active interest in the advancement of the M. E. Church; was one of four men who instituted and set on foot the erection of Scales Mound M. E. Church in 1851; was a miner in the old country, and has been engaged in the same business here till some years since; turned his attention to farming, in which he is now engaged; owns 271 acres land; took an active part in the organization of Jewl's Prairie M. E. Church, of which they are prominent members; have four children living: Mrs. Jane Potter, Walter, George and John J. C.; lost two children, buried at Veto Grand Burying Ground, afterwards removed to Scales Mound.

SASS JOHN, farmer; Sec. 7; P. O. Elizabeth.

Sass Leonard, farm; Sec. 7; P. O. Elizabeth.

Schrack Frank, farm; Sec. 33; P.O. Elizabeth.

Schrack Lewis, farm; Sec. 29; P.O. Elizabeth.

Schrack Mickel, Sr., farmer; Sec. 33; P. O. Elizabeth.

Schrack Mickel, Jr., farmer; Sec. 33; P. O. Elizabeth.

Schugert John, farmer; Sec. 11; P. O. Woodbine.

Scisler Jno. farmer; Sec. 14; P. O. Elizabeth.

SHORE SOLOMON, Farmer; Sec. 15; P. O. Woodbine; owns 132 acres land; born in Cumberland Co., Ky., Dec. 6, 1810, six miles from Burksville, on Marrowbone; came to Morgan Co., Ill., Nov. 23, 1827; moved to Galena July 1, 1836; followed mining and driving stage; spent three years around Madison, Fort Winnebago, and Mineral Point, Wis.; came back to Jewl's Prairie, Jo Daviess Co., and improved a claim, following mining principally till 1843; was elected Constable in what was then McDonald's Precinct June 28, 1844; the County Court also appointed him School Trustee; married Miss Elizabeth Simpson in March, 1845; she was born in Jamestown Jan. 12, 1826; Mr. S. was again elected Constable in 1847, and in 1851 the County Court made him Judge of Elections in Elizabeth; was elected Justice of the Peace in 1853, commissioned by Gov. Mattison; was again elected Justice and commissioned by Gov. Palmer April 27, 1869; was elected Supervisor and served on Board for the year 1872, and in 1873 was again elected Justice and commissioned by Gov. Jno. L. Beveridge April 25, 1873; Mr. S. has always been known as one of the substantial citizens of Jo Daviess Co., and he has seen the pioneer cabins give way to the onward march of improvement; has nine children living: Margaret Ann, John F., Susanna E., Samuel S., David M., Nancy E., Charles W., Catherine P. and George H.

SIMPSON SAMUEL, Farmer; Sec. 18; P. O. Elizabeth; born in Washington Co., Tenn., near the Virginia line, which ran through the field in which the house stood where he was born, July 23, 1798; his parents moved to Pulaski Co., Ky., carrying the subject of this sketch across the mountains on a pack saddle; remained there till 1830, when they came to Ill., locating in Adams Co.; remained there and in Warren Co. till 1842, when they came to Jo Daviess Co.; Mr. S. and his father built the first boat for the Cumberland River Coal Mines; married Miss Susanna Fry in 1822; she was born on Cumberland River in Ky. April 14, 1806; have eleven children living: Edward C., Margaret Ann, Elizabeth, Mary Jane, Laverina, Amanda, Matilda, Emma, William L., Susanna V. and Samuel S.; has fifty-six grandchildren and three great-grandchildren; two grandchildren at home with the old folks, James E. and Annie.

Simpson Samuel, Jr., farmer; Sec. 18; P O. Elizabeth.

Snodgrass Soloman, farmer; Sec. 35; P. O. Derinda.

Stafford John, farm; Sec. 8; P. O. Elizabeth.

Stiffins Frederick; farmer; Sec. 26; P. O. Elizabeth.

Sudenburg Peter, farmer; Sec. 29; P. O. Elizabeth.

THOMAS EDWARD, farmer; Sec. 9; P. O. Elizabeth.

THOMAS DAVID, (Deceased) born in Bryntrefeiler, Llandwrog, Carnarvonshire, North Wales, Sept. 2, 1821; he came to America in 1845, settling in Galena, then removed to Blackleg, Wis., from there to his last residence in Woodbine, Ill., in the year 1849; married Miss Elizabeth Evans, daughter of Hugh Evans and Jane (Roberts) Evans, March 21, 1849; they have three children living: Hugh D., born Jan. 4, 1854; Henry E., Dec. 13, 1855; Mary Ann, Nov. 14, 1858; have lost two children: Thomas, born Feb. 26, 1852, and Mark, March 1, 1860; Hugh D. Thomas was educated at the Normal School in Galena; has been engaged in teaching, but has now abandoned it and turned his attention to the farm; has 200 acres land.

Thomas H. D. farm; Sec. 9; P. O. Elizabeth.

THOMAS MARK, Jr. Farmer; Sec. 9; P. O. Elizabeth; born in Cornwall, England, and came to this country with his parents in infancy; his father, Mark Thomas, Sr., was born in Cornwall, England, in 1810; his mother's maiden name was Miss Mary Harris, born in Cornwall, England, in 1809; emigrated to America in 1839; resided in Pa. till 1856, when they came to this Co.; Mr. T., Jr., has held the office of Town Clerk 3 or 4 years; Assessor 2 years; Collector 2 years; School Trustee of the Tp. 3 years, and at the present time is serving the second term as School Trustee; is a member of A. F. & A. Masons; owns 80 acres land.

Thomas M., Sr., farm; S. 9; P.O. Elizabeth.

Thompson W. farm; Sec. 9; P. O. Elizabeth.

Toms Wm. farmer; Sec. 29; P. O. Elizabeth.

Toms W., Jr., farm; Sec. 29; P.O. Elizabeth.

Thrane Jos. farmer; Sec. 22; P.O. Elizabeth.

VIRTUE ROBERT, farmer; Sec. 6; P. O Elizabeth.

Vogole W. Sec. 32; P. O. Elizabeth.

WAUD ANDREW, farmer; Sec. 32; P. O. Woodbine.

Waud Joseph; P. O. Woodbine.

Waud Philip, Sec. 16; P. O. Woodbine.

Weir Geo. W. Sec. 29; P. O. Elizabeth.

Weir Jas. Sec. 29; P. O. Elizabeth.

WEIR THOMPSON, Farmer; Sec. 29; P. O. Elizabeth; born in Westmoreland Co., Pa., Dec. 10. 1803; removed to Mercer Co., where he married Miss Sarah Mossman Oct. 31, 1831; she was born in Mercer Co., Pa., July 8, 1808; came to Jo Daviess Co. in May, 1846; lived in various parts of this section of the county till 1848, when he bought 120 acres of land, upon which his house now stands; has 161 acres land; has nine children living: Jas. M., John Steele, A. H., Francis A., Mrs. Caroline Wilson, Mrs. Maria Barrett, Mrs. Sarah Ann McDonald, Mrs. Austic Fablinger and George T., who is still at home; Mr. W. has served the town as Supervisor for many years, and at the present time is the Treasurer of the Tp.; he is now in his 75th year, and is actively engaged in superintending his farm.

Wilcox A. farmer; Sec. 18; P. O. Elizabeth.

Wilcox J. L. farm; Sec. 18; P. O. Elizabeth.

Wilcox S. farmer; Sec. 18; P. O. Elizabeth.

Wilcox W. farmer; Sec. 18; P. O. Elizabeth.

Wixson John, Sr., farmer; Sec. 14; P. O. Woodbine.

Wixson John, Jr., farmer; Sec. 14; P. O. Woodbine.

STOCKTON TOWNSHIP

ARNOLD D. farmer; S. 7; P. O. Winters.

Arnold J. renter; Sec. 8; P. O. Winters.

Arnold S. farmer; Sec. 18; P. O. Winters.

BACHELDOR R. farmer: Sec. 22; P. O. Winters.

Bacheldor Wm. B. renter; Sec. 23; P. O. Stockton.

Baker A. H. laborer, Morseville; P. O. Plum River.

Baker Robert, blacksmith, Morseville; P. O. Plum River.

Ball J. G. farmer; Sec. 21; P. O. Winters.

Bartch J. F. farmer; Sec. 28; P. O. Winters.

Bates H. U. farmer; Sec. 4; P. O. Winters.

Beam W. C. farmer; Sec. 34; P. O. Yankee Hollow.

Bearson Jake, blacksmith; Sec. 30; P. O. Derinda.

BEDFORD C. E. Farmer; Sec. 12; P. O. Pitcherville; born in Canada, near Kingston, in 1818; has lived in Madison Co., N. Y., and seven years in Lake Co. O.; at the age of 16 commenced to sail on the lake, and followed that sixteen seasons; has lived in this Co. seventeen years; has a farm of 209 acres, valued at $18,500; was married to Caroline Stebnan, who was born in Mass. in 1822; has seven children: Ella M., Emma, Charles E., Florence, Susan, Frankie, Augusta.

Benton Ira, farm; S. 11; P. O. Pitcherville.

Benton John, laborer, Morseville; P. O. Plum River.

Benton L. D. farm; S. 11; P. O. Pitcherville.

BENTON IRA T. Farmer; Sec. 10; P. O. Stockton; was born in Stockton Tp., Oct. 25, 1851, and remained until 1868; his parents dying, he went to Wis. and lived with his aunt; after his return, worked by the month until 21 years old, when he came into possession of the farm he now lives on; went to Cal. and remained about one year; was married Feb. 24, 1876, to Elnora Manley, who was born in this Tp. in 1855; one child, named Bessie; Independent in politics; was elected Tax Collector in 1877.

Billings Wm. farmer; Sec. 13; P. O. Plum River.

BIXBY GEORGE A. Hotel Landlord, Morseville; P. O. Plum River; was born in Springfield, Windsor Co., Vt., July 2, 1835; at the age of 4 years he removed with his father to Canada, near Dundas, where they lived one year, and then moved to Battle Creek, Mich.; lived there nine years, and then came to this Tp., where they arrived Nov. 22, 1849; lived with his parents until Dec. 25, 1857, when he was married to Diadama Clark, of Jo Daviess Co., who was born June 11, 1835; Mr. Bixby has been engaged extensively in farming and as a stock buyer, and was so engaged until the Fall of 1877, when he bought the hotel at Morseville, and has since been engaged in that capacity; has four children: Frank, Noble, Hetty and Juventus.

Blair James, farm; S. 25; P. O. Plum River.

Bonjour F. renter; Sec. 5; P. O. Rush.

Bough Ed. farmer; Sec. 32; P. O. Derinda.

Boyle James, farm hand; Sec. 18; P. O. Elizabeth.

Boyle John, farm; Sec. 18; P. O. Elizabeth.

Boyle Pat. farmer; Sec. 18; P. O. Elizabeth.

Breed B. farmer; Sec. 2; P. O. Pitcherville.

BREED C. A. Farmer; Sec. 3; P. O. Pitcherville; born in Otsego Co., N. Y., in 1830, and lived there until 25 years of age, when he came to this Co., and has lived here ever since; was married in 1849 to Catherine Smith, who was born in Otsego Co., N. Y.; they have five children: Hil, Charlie, Mary Alice, Aleric and Amos Worth; owns 102 acres of land, valued at $4,000; Greenback in politics.

Breed Eugene, Sec. 2; P. O. Pitcherville.

Breed Jehial, Sec. 3; P. O. Pitcherville.

Brower A. renter; Sec. 2; P. O. Pitcherville.

Burkhardt Jos. farm hand; Sec. 2; P. O. Pitcherville.

Burns Wm. farm hand; P. O. Winters.

Burton T. farmer; Sec. 17; P. O. Winters.

Byrnne A. B. farmer; Sec. 13; P. O. Plum River.

Byrnne E. E. farmer; Sec 3; P. O. Pitcherville.

Byrnne J. farmer; Sec. 10; P. O. Stockton.

CANNON CHAS. butcher; Morseville; Plum River.

Carpenter M. F. farmer; Sec. 11; P. O. Pitcherville.

Chown R. teamster; Morseville; P. O. Plum River.

Clay B. renter; Sec. 27; P. O. Winters.

Claypool B. R. farmer; Sec. 6; P. O. Rush.

CLAY JOHN, Farmer; Sec. 27; P. O. Winters; born in Southold, Upper Canada, in 1824; remained there until 27 years of age, engaged in farming; then came to Michigan and bought a farm, but only staid 8 months and then came to Winnebago Co. this state; was there two years, and then went to Boone Co. where he remained three years; came to Jo Daviess Co. in 1856, and settled on the farm he now owns; has 180 acres of land; was married to Jane H. Clark, Aug. 11, 1849; she was born in Canada, Feb. 8, 1828; has eight children: Louisa, Henry B., Ada A., Samuel E., Willard W., William L., Chas. Minnielaus, and James Lovell; has been School Director for several terms; farming has always been his occupation; Republican.

Clay U. F. farmer; Sec. 33; P. O. Winters.

Coppernoll E. C. renter; Sec. 11; P.O. Pitcherville.

Cox Jas. farmer; Sec. 8; P. O. Winters.

Crackenberger P. farm; Sec. 12; P. O. Pitcherville.

Creighton Geo. Sec. 20; P. O. Winters.

Creighton O. farmer; Sec. 20; P. O. Winters.

Crummer H. farmer; Sec. 19; P. O. Winters.

Crummer T. farmer; Sec. 19; P. O. Winters.

Crummer W. T. farm; S. 19; P. O. Winters.

DEEDS JOHN, renter; Sec. 24; P. O. Plum River.

Dow G. L. farmer; Sec. 34; P. O. Yankee Hollow.

Doyle Owen, farmer; Sec. 23; P. O. Plum River.

Doyle Peter, Jr., farm; S. 26; P. O. Winters.

EADE S. T. merchant; Pitcherville.

Ebert Mike, blacksmith; Sec. 18; P. O. Winters.

Edwards A. B. farm hand; Yankee Hollow.

Ehrler A. farmer; Sec. 4; P. O. Rush.

Ehrler C. farmer; Sec. 4; P. O. Rush.

Ertnur J. farm; Sec. 13; P. O. Pitcherville.

FARRELL W. H. harness maker; Morseville; P. O. Plum River.

Flinn D. J. farmer; Sec. 31; P. O. Derinda.

Foster A. farmer; Sec. 12; P.O. Pitcherville.

Foster W. Y. farmer; Sec. 23; P. O. Winters.

GAGE Z. farmer; Sec. 29; P. O. Derinda.

Gates E. W. farmer; Sec. 24; P. O. Plum River.

GATES ISAAC, Physician; Sec. 24; P. O. Plum River; born in Otsego Co., N. Y., Feb. 13, 1815; lived there two years, when he removed with his parents to the Western Reserve, Ohio, and lived there until 1842; lived with his mother and brother-in-law, until 18 years old, when he began the study of medicine with Dr. Cox, his brother-in-law; studied, read and practiced with him some four or five years; practiced in Ohio on his own account some time, and then came to Aurora, Ill., where he lived and practiced until 1850; then started to California with a company of 22 men, but only got as far as St. Joseph, Mo., when he turned back and came to this Co.; bought property here; sold his Aurora property, and has since lived here, practicing medicine and farming; was married Sept. 6, 1838 to Aurinda Millett; she was born in Ohio, Aug. 16, 1816; have had thirteen children, ten of whom are living: Wm. E., Edward W., Solomon D., Chilleon Oreatas, Harmony Logusta, Abigail J., Emily Annette, Florence Lovina, Eliza Rosalia, Helen Aurinda; Republican.

Gates S. D. billiard hall; Morseville; P. O Plum River.

Gibbs J. shoemaker; Morseville; P. O. Plum River.

Grace J. farmer; Sec. 30; P. O. Derinda.

Grace John, farmer; Sec 30; P. O. Derinda.

Grace T. farmer; Sec. 26; P. O. Winters.

Gray Orange, retired farmer; Sec. 13; P. O. Plum River.

Graghagan J. renter; Sec. 16; P. O. Winters.

Greenman P. farm; Sec. 31; P. O. Derinda.

GRIER D. C. Physician; Morseville; P. O. Plum River; was born June 18, 1828, in Washington Co., Pa.; attended the Jefferson Literary College four years, and studied medicine under Dr. Murray, of Cannonsbury, Pa., three years; in 1847 and 1848 attended the Jefferson Medical College, and commenced practicing in 1848; practiced about five years in Penn.; in 1856 moved to Loran, Stephenson Co., where he practiced about twelve years; came to Morseville in 1867, where he has since resided, practicing medicine; in 1852 married Eliza Jane Chambers, who died three years afterwards; one child, Martha Araminta; Aug. 5, 1856, married Rhoda M. McCune, who was born March 27, 1838, at McConnellsville, Pa.; she came West in April before her marriage; in 1867 she commenced the millinery business in Morseville in company with Mrs. Bixby, it being the first establishment of the kind in this vicinity; sold to Mrs. Bixby in about three months, and in about one and one half years bought the shop, and has since conducted the business; they have three children: Ida, Elmer and James.

Groesbeck Peter, laborer; Sec. 25; P. O. Plum River.

Grosscup C. W. farm; Sec. 2; P. O. Pitcherville.

Gunsolby Ed. farmer; Sec. 13; P. O. Plum River.

HAIGHT ED. renter; Sec. 2; P. O. Pitcherville.

Haight F. renter; Sec. 10; P. O. Stockton.

Haight J. J. farmer; Sec. 2; P. O. Pitcherville.

Hall D. renter; Sec. 13; P. O. Plum River.

Alex. Burnett

WARREN.

HAMMOND MERWIN K. Farmer; Sec. 14; P. O. Stockton; was born in Summit Co., Ohio, in 1830; lived there until ten years of age, and then moved to Knox Co., Ill., and remained there seven years; then came to Galena, where he remained one Winter, the following Spring moved to Sand Prairie, near Hanover; in 1852 went to California and went into the mines; remained there until Nov., 1857, when he started home via the Isthmus and New York, arriving here in Dec.; was married July 7, 1858, to Samantha Fowler, who was born in Hanover, Jan. 14, 1836; they then came to this place, and have made it their home since; bought 80 acres of land at first, but now has 320 acres in the homestead, 84 acres of timber, and 200 acres of Mississippi island land; Mr. Hammond makes a specialty of dairying, milks from thirty to forty cows, and has the finest barn in the Tp.; they have eight children: Willis F., Charles A., Alice E., Anna S., Frank M., Royal K., Fred and Nellie; was Supervisor three years; independent in politics.

Harrison Robert, farmer; Sec. 13; P. O. Plum River.

Hartsough Ben. Sec. 6; P. O. Rush.

Hartsough Dan. Sec. 6; P. O. Rush.

HARTSOUGH PETER, Farmer; Sec. 6; P. O. Rush; was born in Tompkins Co., N. Y., in 1813, and came to this Co. in 1845; was married in 1845 to Mary Arnold, who was born in Newfield, Tompkins Co., N. Y.; have six children: Cornelia, Lafayette, Benjamin, Daniel, Franklin, Sarah; owns 210 acres of land, valued at $6,300; has always been a farmer, and is a straight Democrat.

HASTINGS HENRY F. Merchant, Morseville; P. O. Plum River; was born in LaFayette Co., Wis., in 1842; came to Ward's Grove when a child, and when about 5 years old was brought into Stockton Tp.; in 1862 enlisted in Co. H, 96th Regt. I. V. I. and remained three years; in the Spring of 1866 went into business here as one of the firm of Hastings & Tyrrell; in 1873 bought out Mr. Tyrrell's interest, and has since conducted the business alone; was married in Spring of 1870 to Abbie C. Tyrrell, who was born in Wis. Nov. 23, 1849; one child, Viola M.; Republican.

Hatch A. S. renter; Sec. 20; P. O. Winters.

Hawes Enoch, farm; S. 12; P.O. Pitcherville.

Henderson A. renter; Sec. 24; P. O. Plum River.

Hewit M. farmer; Sec. 31; P. O. Derinda.

Hickman Jos. farm; Sec. 18; P. O. Winters.

HOFFMAN CHARLES, Farmer; Sec. 5; P. O. Rush; was born in Prussia May 7, 1815, and came to America in Aug., 1836; landed in N. Y,; staid in Pa. about one month; then went to Ohio, and then to Indiana, where he remained two years; removed to Jo Daviess Co., landing in Galena in July, 1838; worked five years for one man three miles north of Galena; worked eighteen months in the lead mines; in 1846 came to Stockton Tp. and took a claim on his present location; went to Cal. in 1850, and returned in 1854; was married in 1857 to Elizabeth Brickler, who was born in Shullsburg, Wis., in 1828; has one child, Linnie L.; owns 170 acres of land; Republican.

Hogan Pat. farmer; Sec. 19.

HOLLAND THOMAS, JR., Wagon Maker, Morseville; P. O. Plum River; born in Galena March 7, 1840; when quite young moved on a farm near Elizabeth, and lived there until 1862, when he joined Co. I, 96th Regt. I. V. I.; remained with regiment about 1½ years, then went with the pioneers, and the next year was transferred to the engineer corps; was detailed for topographical duty, and remained in that capacity until the close of the war; after his return worked at carpentering and wagon making; married Rachel Guard in 1871; have one child, Cora; run a wagon shop in Elizabeth, and came to Morseville in 1869, where he has since been engaged in business; Republican.

Howell John, renter; Sec. 38; P. O. Winters.

Hoy Pat. farmer; Sec. 18; P. O. Elizabeth.

Hughes P. renter; S. 24; P. O. Plum River.

INMAN ED. farmer; Sec. 12; P. O. Plum River.

JOHNSON A. M. Sec. 18; P. O. Winters.

Johnson H. H. farm; Sec. 28; P. O. Winters.

Johnson M. F. farmer; Sec. 35; P. O. Plum River.

Johnson S. H. farmer; Sec. 25; P. O. Plum River.

Johnson Wm. storekeeper; Sec. 18; P. O. Winters.

Johnston Stephen, farmer; Sec. 25; P. O. Plum River.

Justus F. E. renter; Sec. 10; P. O. Stockton.

JUSTUS GEORGE, Farmer; Sec. 10; P. O. Stockton; was born in Geauga Co., Ohio, April 14, 1822, and lived there until 1856; worked in a tanyard until about 20 years old, when he learned the shoemaking trade, and worked at that until he came to this state; was married April 11, 1847, to Huldah M. Byrum, who was born in Ohio July 3, 1830; came to this town in Jan., 1857, and lived on Sec. 3 the first Summer; has held the office of School Treasurer sixteen years, and has been Justice of Peace seventeen years; has been Postmaster at Stockton about three years; Republican until about four years ago, when he endorsed the Independent movement: has four children living: Charles T., Florence S., Frank E., Delia C.; lost one child.

KELLER G. farmer; Sec. 35; P. O. Plum River.

Kemper A. merchant, Morseville; P. O. Plum River.

Kenney David, farmer; Sec. 5; P. O. Rush.

Kentrey James, laborer; Morseville; P. O. Plum River.

Krell Lewis, farmer; Sec. 29; P. O. Derinda.

Krucht Jacob, farmer; Sec. 15; P. O. Winters.

LACOCK WM. teamster; Morseville; P. O. Plum River.

Lawrence A. farmer; Sec. 26; P. O. Plum River.

Lawrence Frank, farmer; Sec. 26; P. O. Plum River.

Lawrence S. farmer; Sec. 26; P. O. Plum River.

Lawhorn W. L. farmer and stock dealer; Sec. 20; P. O. Winters.

Lebanon A. farmer; Sec. 26; P. O. Plum River.

Lyon R. M. farmer; Sec. 36; P. O. Plum River.

Lyon Wm. retired; Sec. 36; P. O. Plum River.

MANLEY J. N. farmer; Sec. 3; P. O. Stockton.

Manley Kingsley, farmer; Sec. 10; P. O. Stockton.

Mapes M. F. farmer; P. O. Winters.

Mapes W. E. farmer; Sec. 11; P. O. Stockton

Marks Jos. farmer; Sec. 1; P. O. Pitcherville.

Marshmun W. farmer; P. O. Winters.

Miller Geo. farmer; Sec. 27; P. O. Winters.

Millet Emery, miner; Morseville; P. O. Plum River.

Millet H. laborer; Morseville; P. O. Plum River.

Momenteller A. Sec. 15; P. O. Winters.

Momenteller J. farm; Sec. 15; P. O. Winters.

Monon John, mail carrier; Morseville; P. O. Plum River.

Morse Amos, tinner; Morseville; P. O. Plum River.

Morse Chas. farmer; Sec. 25; P. O. Plum River.

Morse Ed. cheese factory; Morseville; P. O. Plum River.

Morse H. farmer; Sec. 25; P. O. Plum River.

Mosley Wm. renter; Sec. 16; P. O. Winters.

Murdick Robt. farm; Sec. 16; P. O. Winters.

Murray John, Sec. 16; P. O. Winters.

Murray M. Sec. 16; P. O. Winters.

Murray Thos. farmer; Sec. 16; P. O. Winters.

NASH N. S. machinist; Morseville; P. O. Plum River.

NASH WM. S. Glove Maker; Morseville; P. O. Plum River; born July 31, 1844, in Oswego Co., N. Y.; came to Jo Daviess Co. when about one year old, his parents settling in Pleasant Valley Tp.; lived with them until Aug. 15, 1862, when he enlisted in the 96th I. V. I., Co. F; served three years, and was in the battles of Chicamauga, Lookout Mountain, Missionary Ridge, the Atlanta campaign, Franklin and Nashville; was severely wounded in the shoulder and in the chin; after the close of the war came home to Pleasant Valley; was married Oct. 9, 1866, to Rachel Vanderlinder, who was born in Steuben Co., N. Y.; in 1868 they went to Union Co., Ia., and lived there six years; while there was engaged in farming, real estate business, and reading law; returned to Ill. in the Fall of 1874, and in Oct., 1877, came to Morseville; since his return to this state has acted as auctioneer, been engaged in farming, glove making, and the practice of law; have five children: Ida B., Francis A., Katie L., Willie R. and Jennie; Republican.

NELSON SYLVESTER, Justice of Peace; Morseville; P. O. Plum River; was born in Rutland Co., Vt., March 27, 1817, and lived there until 1839; brought up on a farm, but worked most of the time at mason work; went to Mich. in 1839, and was there and in Pa. about 18 months, and then returned to Vt.; was married in 1841 to Maria L. Gibbs, who was born in Rutland Co., Vt., May 14, 1820; in 1844 moved to Rock Co., Wis., and lived there until 1855, when they came to this Co.; was elected Justice of Peace in 1857, and served until 1864; in 1862, after prospecting a long time, struck the first paying mineral that was taken in this vicinity; moved to Mo. in 1868, and remained there four years, working in the mines and at his trade; went to Texas in 1872, where he worked at plastering two years, and then returned to this place, where he has since remained, working at his trade, etc.; was elected as Justice of Peace in 1877; is agent for Insurance Co.; was Township Treasurer four years; has four children living: Elwin O., Hiram W., George W., Hattie A.; Democrat.

Olmstead O. H. teamster; Morseville; P. O. Plum River.

PARKER ALANSON, Farmer; Sec. 34; P. O. Yankee Hollow; was born in Chittenden Co., Vt., in 1805; this was his home until 1834, when he went to Mass. and remained about six months working to get money to come West; then went to Ohio, and walked from Geauga Co., Ohio, to Kendall Co., Ill., and back; the following Spring started with his wife to Detroit, where he procured a conveyance for her to Chicago, he, himself walking through to Kendall Co., which he reached in the Spring of 1835; during his walk he often walked 40 miles per day, and one day made 60; was married March 22, 1835, to Sophia Johnson; she was born in Windham Co., Vt., in 1815; remained in Kendall Co. until 1838, when he came to this township with his brother, and they together made a claim about two miles long and one and a half miles wide; in the Fall they went for their families, returning in the Spring of 1839, being the first permanent settlers in the south part of the Tp.; has lived on the same farm ever since, and now owns 700 acres of land which he has made from the land, never having borrowed a dollar of money to buy land with; has four children living: Leonora, Frank, Harriet, Adeline; five sons dead; George died in the army; Republican.

Parker Chas. blacksmith; Sec. 18; P.O. Winters.

PARKER CHESTER, Farmer; Sec. 28; P. O. Winters; was born in 1809 in Vt., and lived there until 1844, living on a farm all of the time; in 1845 he came to this Co. and Tp. and settled on the farm he now owns where he has since resided; Mr. Parker's two brothers came here before him, and made the claim for his farm; the three men with two others had a desperate fight with fifteen men who attempted to jump their claims; axes and other weapons were used and several men severely injured; was married in 1848 to Alma Humphrey who was born in Vt. in 1812; have three children: Jonas, Warren and Charles; Republican.

Parker W. farmer; Sec. 27; P. O. Winters.

Parker J. farmer; Sec. 28; P. O. Winters.

Parks S. farmer; Sec. 6; P.O. Rush.

Patterson Ed. farmer; Sec. 13; P. O. Pitcherville.

Perry H. A. farmer; Sec. 22; P. O. Winters.

Phelps J. S. farmer; Sec. 1; P. O. Pitcherville.

Phelps Reed, farmer; Sec. 1; P. O. Pitcherville.

Plankerton H. farmer; Sec. 2; P. O. Pitcherville.

Polker A. farmer; Sec. 32; P. O. Derinda.

Polker C. farmer; Sec. 29; P. O. Derinda.

Polker H. farmer; Sec. 30; P. O. Derinda.

Polker L. farm; Sec. 35; P. O. Plum River.

Pulfrey H. farmer; Sec. 27; P. O. Winters.

Pulfrey J. E. farmer; Sec. 22; P.O. Winters

PULFREY JOHN, Farmer; Sec. 22; P. O. Winters; was born in England in 1804, and came to this country in 1845, and landed in New York; while in England was a farm laborer; came to Winnebago Co. where he lived 14 years, and then came to this Tp. in 1859, and has since been engaged in farming here; was married in 1832 to Ann Weston who was born in England; has had twelve children: Henry, William, Jane, Weston and Annie came to this country with their father; two of his sons were in the army; Republican in politics, and a Methodist; owns 100 acres of land.

Pulfrey W. farmer; Sec. 22; P. O. Winters.

Pulfrey Weston, farmer; Sec. 11; P. O. Stockton.

REED RICHARD S. Miner; Morseville; P. O. Plum River; born in Cornwall, England, June 5, 1832; came to this country in 1833, his parents settling first at Pottsville, Pa.; from there to Virginia, where they lived 5 or 6 years; then back to Pa., and then to Cuyahoga Co., Ohio, where they lived about 9 years; they then came to Wis.; was 4 years in the Lake Superior mines; in Oct., 1863 enlisted in Co. C, 21st Regt. W. V. I., and served until Sept. 1865; was in every fight on the Atlanta campaign, and was under fire 40 days in succession; after his return from the army went to Wis., and remained there until 1867 when he came to the Village of Morseville; has been engaged in mining ever since; was in the Utah mines about 18 months; was married in March, 1868 to Mrs. Jane Rayen, who was born in Ohio in 1839; Mrs. Reed was first married in Jan., 1858, and her husband was killed at the battle of Kenesaw Mountain, in 1864; had two children, Flora and Elliott; Mr. Reed has three children: William F., Louis F., Rosa May; Republican.

Reynolds D. R. farmer; Sec. 17; P. O. Winters.

RINDESBACHER FRED, Farmer; Sec. 9; P. O. Winters; born in the Selkirk Settlement, on the Red River of the North, in 1822; his parents came down the river in Mackinaw boats, and landed at the old portage on Fever River, in Nov., 1826; they passed the Winter at Gratiot's furnace, and in the Spring moved to Wisconsin, where they remained three years, when they went to St. Louis, Mo.; staid there until 1838, and then came to this Co.; afterwards was in Wis. one year, and five years near Galena; in 1845 came to this Tp. and located his present claim, it being on the mineral reserve; in 1850 went to California, and remained until 1855; while there mined one year, and the balance of the time was engaged in teaming and staging; was married in 1857 to Elvira Claypool, who was born in Woodbine Tp. in 1839; has four children: P. M., Frederic C., William C., Frank S.; owns 770 acres of land, and has a fine house, good stables, cattle sheds, and one of the best stock farms in Jo Daviess Co.; Republican.

ROBERTS JOHN, Sr., Farmer; Sec. 8; P. O. Rush; was born in England in 1821, and came to this country in 1848; worked in N. Y. and Pa. two years, and then came to Council Hill; worked there six years, and then moved to his present location, in 1850, where he has since followed farming; owns 300 acres of land valued at $10,000; married Elizabeth Roberts in 1845; she was born in England; have six children: John, Jane, Annie, Mary, William, Joseph; John and Jane were born in England; Republican.

Roberts John, Jr., farmer; Sec. 7; P.O. Rush.

Roberts Thos. farmer; Sec. 8; P. O. Winters.

SCHLEGEL D. renter; Sec. 8; P. O. Winters.

Scrantz Peter, renter; Sec. 12; P. O. Pitcherville.

Schwendle F. farmer; Sec. 12; P. O. Plum River.

Seavey Rufus, Sr., farmer; Sec. 16; P. O. Winters.

Seavey R., Jr., farmer; Sec. 16; P. O. Winters.

Sellers E. laborer; P. O. Plum River.

Seegar Conrad, farm hand; Sec. 1; P. O. Pitcherville.

SHARP JEREMIAH N. Physician; Morseville—P. O. Plum River; born in Warren Co., Mo., May 2, 1835; until five years old lived in that Co. with his parents, and then removed to Dubuque Co., Ia.; he lived there until about the age of 18, when he went West on a surveying trip in government service; afterwards returned to Dubuque Co., and commenced the study of medicine under Dr. John Warmoth; remained there, studying and practicing about four years, when he closed up his business and went to the Rocky Mountains in 1859, going into the mines; was in the mines nearly four years, when he came back to the States and resumed his medical studies, going to Ann Arbor, Mich., and graduated at Keokuk, Iowa, in June, 1863; then went to St. Louis, passed examination, and was commissioned into the 32d Mo. V. I. as First Assistant Surgeon; he remained in the army until 1866, being engaged most of the time in the U. S. military hospitals; he then engaged in mercantile business, but this proving disastrous, he sold out and came to Hanover, in this Co., and commenced the practice of his profession; in Oct., 1869, he bought out Dr. Crouse, of this place, and has since practiced here; was married, May 2, 1865, to Miss Mary Adams, who was born in Grand Rapids, Mich., Oct. 27, 1839; Mrs. Sharp was in the military hospitals under commission from Mrs. Livermore, of the Sanitary Commission, and spent nearly four years at Chicago, St. Louis, Vicksburg, and Memphis; have one daughter 12 years old, Carrie B.; Methodists; Republican.

Sheridan J. farmer; Sec. 28; P. O. Winters.

Sheridan Pat, farmer; Sec. 28; P. O. Winters.

Sheridan Peter; farmer; Sec. 28; P. O. Winters.

Shannon R. M. farm; Sec. 3; P. O. Pitcherville.

Shertz I. farmer; Sec. 2; P. O. Pitcherville.

Shook F. miner; Morseville; P. O. Plum River.

Shugrue M. renter; Sec. 18; P. O. Elizabeth.

Skeine J. farmer; Sec. 28; P. O. Winters.

Skeine R. farm; Sec. 24; P. O. Plum River.

Smith R. S. retired; Morseville; P. O. Plum River.

Smith T. M. farmer; Sec. 31; P. O. Derinda.

Smith W. R. farmer; Sec. 31; P. O. Derinda.

Spitler Dan, farmer; Sec. 7; P. O. Winters.

St. John Fred, miner; Sec. 25; P. O. Plum River.

Straight W. farmer; Sec. 8; P. O. Winters.

STARKEY WM. H. Farmer; Sec. 13; P. O. Plum River; was born Nov. 5, 1826, in Geauga Co., Ohio; lived in that state nearly all of the time until 1852; while there worked at carpentering and painting, commencing to learn the trades when about eighteen years of age; when twenty years old went to Washington Co., Ohio, and worked one year at cabinet making, and taught school two winters; then went to Geauga Co., where he worked one season, then moving to Conn.; there he worked at painting and carriage painting, and traveled nearly over the whole State of Conn. peddling; came here in 1852, and has since worked at his trade, teaching school and farming; was married in 1855 to Diancy Gray, who died one year after her marriage; Nov. 12, 1858, was married to Ada C. Baker, who was born in Prince Edward Island Nov. 8, 1840; they have six children: Charles B., Cora H., William F., Lottie L., Nellie A., Louis H.; Democrat.

Stayner J. farmer; Sec. 14; P. O. Stockton.

Stayner S. farmer; Sec. 14; P. O. Stockton.

Stayner W. farmer; Sec. 15; P. O. Stockton.

Strickland R. postmaster; Morseville; P. O. Plum River.

Stoker T. M. farm hand; P. O. Plum River

TEETER FRANK, farmer; Sec. 6; P. O. Rush.

Teeter Jerome, farmer; Sec. 6; P. O. Rush.

Terpening W. W. farmer; Sec. 28; P. O. Winters.

Tucker Frank, clerk; Morseville; P. O. Plum River.

Tucker H. A. farmer; Sec. 1; P. O. Pitcherville.

Tucker N. W. farm; Sec. 23; P. O. Stockton.

Tucker W. C. farmer; Sec. 1; P. O. Pitcherville.

TYRRELL FRANCIS, Farmer; Sec. 24; P. O. Plum River; was born in Hillsboro Co., N. H., March 12, 1832; when four years old moved with his parents to Mass., where he lived five years; in 1841 came to this Co., settling in Ward's Grove Tp.; at the age of fifteen commenced to work out by the month, and continued to do so until Aug., 1856, when he went to Mitchell Co., Iowa; remained there two years, and then returned to this Co.; was married in 1859 to Chloe C. Bixby, who was born in Windsor Co., Vt., in June, 1840; after returning from Iowa bought a half interest in a general store in Morseville, where he lived five years; not being satisfied with the profits of this, he sold out and bought the farm he now lives on in June, 1870; farm contains 206 acres; has three children: Francis M., George M. and Herman D.; Democrat.

Tyrrell H. B. newspaper correspondent; Morseville; P. O. Plum River.

Tyrrell. J. F. teamster; Morseville; P. O. Plum River.

TYRRELL MILES, Druggist; Morseville; P. O. Plum River; was born June 12, 1820, in Hillsboro Co., N. H.; lived there until about fifteen years old, and then went to Winchendon, Mass., and worked in a cotton factory; remained there until 1838, when he came here, arriving Nov. 2, 1838; settled in Ward's Grove and had his home there, being a part of the time in the pineries and lead mines of Wisconsin; in 1850 went to California and returned in 1851; the next year commenced business here, and has since been continuously in business here; Mr. Tyrrell is one of the oldest settlers in this county, there being but few people here when he came; he is the oldest business man here; held the post office here for some time, when Plum River office was first established; was married in 1875 to Mrs. Clair; Democrat.

VAN DELINDER LUTHER, farmer; Sec. 9; P. O. Winters.

VAN DELINDER DANIEL W. Glove Maker; Morseville; P. O. Plum River; was born in Pleasant Valley Aug. 21, 1852, and lived there with his parents until April, 1875, and was engaged in farming all of the time, except two winters, when he taught school; in 1875 went to Lincoln, Neb., but only remained two months, and then returned to his home in this Co.; since that time he has spent his summers farming in Bureau Co., and his winters in teaching in this Co.; his home was with his parents until they moved to Kansas in December, 1877, since when he has lived in Morseville, working at glove making.

Vipond I. K. wagon maker, Morseville; P. O. Plum River.

WARNE CHAS. renter; Sec. 6; P. O. Rush.

Warne S.. retired, Morseville; Plum River.

Warne W. H. farmer; Sec. 29; P. O. Winters.

Waters Robert, renter; Sec. 23; P. O. Plum River.

Westaby Stephen, farmer; Sec. 21; P. O. Pitcherville.

Westfall A. farmer; Sec. 7; P. O. Winters.

Westfall James, farm; S. 19; P. O. Winters.

Westfall John, farmer; S. 19; P. O. Winters.

Wheelock A. J. renter; Sec. 24; P. O. Plum River.

Wheelock Oscar, farmer; Sec. 14; P. O. Plum River.

Wiegant Carl, farmer; S. 17; P. O. Winters.

Wilson Jake, farmer; Sec. 16; P. O. Winters.

Wilson J. D. farm; S. 24; P. O. Plum River.

Wilson Jesse, farmer; Sec. 24; P. O. Winters.

Winter Henry, blacksmith; Pitcherville.

WINTER & JOHNSON, Merchants; Sec. 19; P. O. Winters; William Johnson was born in Jackson Co., Ill., in 1814, and lived there until 1830, when he came to this Co., and has lived here ever since; has lived near Galena, in Millville, and in Derinda Tp., and was engaged in various occupations: milling, keeping restaurant, etc.; has had mail contracts for sixteen years; in 1871 came to this Tp. and entered into his present business; now has a contract for a mail route from Winters to Mt. Carroll; was married in 1833 to Sarah Ann Johnson, who was born in Jackson Co., Ill., in 1818; has seven children living: Elvira Jane, Jasper Newton, Henry Harrison, Minerva Samantha, Amanda, Louisa, Adolphus Manley. Henry Winter was born in Prussia in June 22, 1841, and came to America in 1848, settling in South Hadley Falls, Mass; removed to Northampton, Leeds; thence to Ware Village; thence to Whately; thence to Holyoke; thence to Rockville, Conn., and in company with his father, to Illinois, and settled on a quarter section of Government land in Woodland Township, in the County of Carroll. In August, 1861, he enlisted as bugler in Co. A, 45th I.V. I., in the War of the Rebellion; aware of his abilities, however, to serve his country better as a marksman, he soon after shouldered a musket and stepped into the ranks; participated in the battles of Fort Donelson, Medon, and Woodland Plantation as a private in the ranks, but after having been severely wounded by a gunshot in the head at Fort Donelson, was unable to bear the fatigue attendant upon field duty, and to modify the same he was transferred to the drum corps, where he served as drummer in the battles of Thompson's Hill, Iron Bridge, Raymond, Jackson, Champion Hills, Siege of Vicksburg, Columbus, and the Siege of Washington; he was taken prisoner at Champion Hills, and paroled; his term of three years' service expired on Aug. 31, 1864, while on a scouting expedition in search of guerillas in the mountains of Pennsylvania; on returning from this expedition, he was honorably discharged at Harrisburg, on the 5th day of Sept., 1864, and returned to the old homestead in Illinois; on Sept. 20, 1864, he married Minerva Samantha Johnson, daughter of Wm. Johnson, one of the early settlers of the West, better known as "Bushy" Bill; Mr. Winter suffered continuously from the effects of the wound received at Fort Donelson; was compelled to quit his favorite occupation of farming, and very reluctantly entered the mercantile arena, in opening a general store at Derinda; soon after his marriage, during a five years' residence here, he served as Postmaster of Derinda, and also as Justice of the Peace; in 1869 he removed to Morseville and opened a jewelry and notion store, but this enterprise proved unsuccessful, and in the Fall of 1870 he entered into a partnership with his father-in-law in a general store in the Town of Stockton, where they carry on a lively business, with a stock of $8,000, consisting of almost every thing required by the farmer; in 1874 a post-office was established, to satisfy the demands of the many people visiting the store; this office was christened by the Hon. H. C. Burkhard, and called Winters, and Mr. Winter appointed Postmaster.

Wright C. P. farm; S. 26; P. O. Plum River.

Wurster A. farmer; Sec. 29; P. O. Winters.

COUNCIL HILL TOWNSHIP.

ABLY HENRY, shoemaker; Council Hill Station.

Armer Joseph, miner; Sec. 22; P. O. Buncombe, Wis.

Arnett Jas. F. miner; Council Hill.

Arthur A. farm; Sec. 25; P. O. Council Hill.

Arthur W. H. farm; S.25; P. O. Council Hill.

Atkinson D. farm; S. 20; P. O. Council Hill.

Atkinson Geo. H. Sec. 20; P. O. Council Hill.

Atkinson Reuben, Sec.20; P.O. Council Hill.

BELL WM. farmer; Sec. 25; P. O. Council Hill.

Bennett J. farm; S. 23; P. O. Council Hill.

BETHEL JOHN, (Deceased) Farmer; Sec. 30; P. O. Council Hill; born in Nelson Co., Va., June 6, 1816; came to this Co. in 1833; settled near New Diggings, Wis.; lived there 9 years; was married to Eliza Dougan in May, 1842; she was born in Dublin, Ireland, in 1818; came here with her father in 1833, who settled on this farm; they had six children: John, now in N. Y. City; Mary J. and William, now living; Thomas, drowned in 1858; Harriet A. and John, died when young; Emily Alston, a sister of Mrs. B., is living with her; Mr. B. died Aug. 27, 1876; they own 502 acres of land.

Bethel W. farm; Sec. 30; P. O. Council Hill.

Birkbeck Samuel, farmer; Sec. 27; P. O. Council Hill.

Birkbeck Samuel A.; Sec. 27; P. O. Council Hill.

Birkbeck T. farm; S. 27; P. O. Council Hill.

Branton H. farm and hotel; Council Hill.

Branton Thos. farm and hotel; Council Hill.

Brinskill Simon, farmer; Sec. 20; P. O. Council Hill.

Buck Jas. nurseryman; Council Hill Station.

Buzza S. renter; Sec. 24; P. O. Council Hill.

CARPENTER HENRY, miner; Sec. 23; P. O. Council Hill.

Carpenter John, laborer; Sec. 19; P. O. Council Hill.

Cross Philip, miner; Sec .22; P. O. Galena.

Cross Wm. miner; Sec. 22; P. O. Galena.

DAILEY PATRICK, farmer; Sec. 35; P. O. Council Hill Station.

Davenport George W. renter; Sec. 20; P. O. White Oak Springs.

Davies Jacob, carpenter and builder; Council Hill Station.

Davies Jno. carp. & build; Council Hill Sta.

Day James, farmer; Sec. 22; P. O. Galena.

Dougherty Michael, miner; Sec. 36; P. O. Council Hill Station.

EVA HENRY, miner; Sec. 26; P. O. Council Hill.

Eva Wm., Sr., miner; Sec. 26; P. O. Council Hill.

Eva Wm., Jr., miner; Sec. 26; P. O. Council Hill.

Ewing Benj. blacksmith; Council Hill.

Ewing John, lab; Sec. 25; P. O. Council Hill.

GOODBOURNE HENRY, farmer; Sec. 22; P. O. Council Hill.

Gould A. T. miner; Council Hill Station.

Green Henry, nurseryman; Council Hill Sta.

Green Jesse, nurseryman; Council Hill Sta.

Gundry Henry, farmer; Sec. 29; P. O. Council Hill Station.

HANEY JOSEPH, clerk; Council Hill.

HARRIS THOMAS, Farmer; Sec. 25; P. O. Council Hill; born in Cornwall, Eng., in 1817; came to this Co. in 1837; owns 125 acres of land; was married in 1844 to Margaret Chalder; she died same year; married again in 1846 to Ann Edwards; had three children; Thomas H. and Elizabeth J. are living; Mrs. H. died in 1849; he went to California in 1850, staid three years, returned, and in 1854 married Jane Arthur; she was born in Cornwall May 10, 1810; Mr. H. went to Idaho in 1864; was gone 17 months; they are members of the M. E. Church.

Harris Thomas H. farmer; Sec. 23; P. O. Council Hill.

HARVEY WILLIAM, Merchant; Council Hill; born in Cornwall, Eng., April 5, 1818; came to this Co. in 1842; followed mining until 1853; commenced mercantile business in this place, where he has been ever since; is also Postmaster, a position he has held about twelve years; was married in 1850 to Caroline Ne Collins; she was born in Cornwall, Eng., in 1823; they have four children living: Christopher, Joseph J., James H. and William; lost three girls: Caroline, Mary E. and Mary Jane; has been Town Clerk twelve years; is a local preacher in the M. E. Church, of which his family are members.

Haskins Wm. lab; S. 32; P. O. Scales Mound.

Hayden Patrick, watchman I. C. R. R.; Council Hill Station.

Hayden Thos. Sec. 22; P. O. Galena.

Hazer Joseph, farmer; Sec. 34; P. O. Galena.

Hazer Nicholas, farmer; S. 34; P. O. Galena.

HICKMAN WM. Teacher; Council Hill; born in Buffalo, N. Y., Nov. 24, 1854; came to this Co. in 1873; attended the German-English Normal School in Galena; graduated in 1877; has been teaching ever since; was married Dec. 25, 1876, to Lydia Wenz; she was born in Dubuque, Iowa, Oct. 16, 1855; graduated in same school, at Galena, in 1875; is now employed teaching in the same school here; are members of the M. E. Church.

Hocking Jas. miner; Council Hill Station.

Hogan Rich'd, lab; S. 30; P.O. Council Hill.

JAMES RICHARD T. farmer; Sec. 31; P. O. Council Hill Station.

KANE JAMES, section boss I. C. R. R.; Council Hill Station.

KEELING GEO. F. Engineer I. C. R. R.; born in Middletown, Conn., Oct. 10, 1843; enlisted Oct. 22, 1861, in Co. F, 24th Mass. V. I.; was mustered out at Richmond, Va., Jan. 20, 1866; was in 34 general engagements; came to Ill. in 1866; was run over by an engine on I. C. R. R., and disabled for 18 months; came to this place in 1870, and has run stationary engine ever since; was married Dec. 26, 1871, to Marietta Williams; she was born in this place in 1853; have three children: Charles W., George W. and Gertrude; attend the M. E. Church,

LAIRD JOHN, farmer; Sec. 19; P. O. Council Hill.

LAIRD HUGH S. Farmer; Sec. 19; P. O. Council Hill; born in Co. Down, Ireland, in 1807; came to the U. S. in 1832; was married in Philadelphia, in 1837, to Ellen Campbell; she was born in Co. Antrim, Ireland, in 1817; they came to this Co. in 1843; owns 355 acres of land; they have five children: James, now in Kansas, William, Sarah, John and David; lost four, three died in infancy, and Hugh died April 10, 1872; Mr. L. was Supervisor seven years, and Trustee and School Director since 1852; family attend the M. E. Church.

LETHLEAN WM. Farmer; Sec. 31; P. O. Council Hill Sta.; born in Cornwall, Eng., Nov. 25, 1839; came to this Co. with his parents in 1841; went to Montana in 1864, staid three years, returned, and was married Nov. 5, 1868, to Mary Trevarthen; she was born in Cornwall May 20, 1836; they have five children: William H. T., Mary E., Emma H., Benjamin F. and Thomas J.; are members of the M. E. Church.

Loughorn James, miner; Council Hill.

Lukley Chas. W. farmer; Sec. 26; P. O. Council Hill.

Lukley James F. farmer; Sec. 27.

Lukley John T. farmer; Sec. 27; P. O. Council Hill.

Lupton John, farmer; Sec. 30; P. O. Council Hill Station.

Lupton Joseph, S. 30; P. O. Council Hill Sta.

Lupton Wm. farmer; Sec. 30; P. O. Council Hill Station.

Lupton Wm., Jr., S. 31; P.O. Council Hill Sta.

Lyne Edward, farmer; Sec. 17; P. O. White Oak Springs, Wis.

Lyne Wm. farmer; Sec. 17; P. O. White Oak Springs, Wis.

McALLISTER GEO. miner; Council Hill.

McAllister Jno. C. miner; Council Hill.

NEWSOM JOHN A. Farmer; Sec. 34; P. O. Mill Brig; born in Yorkshire, England, May 19, 1825; came to Wabash Co., Ill., in 1842, and to this Co. in 1847; owns the undivided half of 170 acres of land; was married in 1851, to Elizabeth Evans; she was born in Chesshire, England, in 1832; they have five children living: William, Clara, Elizabeth, Maud and Martha; lost one—Sarah Lois, died in 1853; Jas. Diehl, an orphan boy, is also living with them; are members of the M. E. Church.

NEWSOM KENRICK A. Farmer; Sec. 34; P. O. Mill Brig; born in Yorkshire, Eng., June 8, 1827; came to Edwards Co., Ill., in 1841, and to this Co. in 1847; owns the undivided half of 170 acres of land; was married Oct. 2, 1850, to Martha Wilde; she was born in Pa. July 2, 1833; they have five children living: Mary, John, Richard, Carrie and Martha; lost three: Sarah, James and an infant; are members of the M. E. Church.

OATEY WILLIAM, Farmer; Sec. 32; P. O. Council Hill Station; born in Cornwall, England, July 17, 1817; was married to Mrs. Jane Rodda, maiden name Thomas, in 1840; she was born in Devonshire, April 10, 1817; owns 160 acres of land; they have two children, Alice (now Mrs. Jeffries), born Nov. 20, 1849, and Samuel, Feb. 26, 1857; Mr. O. went to California, in 1851; returned in 1854; bought this farm and has resided here ever since; Mrs. O.'s first husband was killed while mining in Cornwall in 1838; her son, John Rodda, was killed at Chicamauga, Tenn., Sept. 20, 1863; are members of the M. E. Church.

Oxman Wm. miner; Sec. 24; P. O. Council Hill.

PARKINS JOHN B. Station Agent and Telegraph Operator, I. C. R. R., Council Hill; born in Hamilton, Ontario, Oct. 18, 1836; was married in Detroit, Mich., in 1859, to Thomisina Cragg; she was born in England Oct. 9, 1837; came to this Co. in 1865; have four children: Mary E., Ella R., Charles, G. W., and John B.; they belong to the M. E. Church.

PASSMORE WM., Blacksmith and Carriage Maker; Council Hill; born in Devonshire, Eng., Nov. 5, 1822; came to this Co. in 1846; owns 7½ acres of land; married Elizabeth Hughes in 1849; she was born in Wales; she died same year; was married again in 1850 to Sarah Hughes; they have seven children living: Mary A., Catherine, George F., Lizzie Ella, William Y., and Sarah O.; lost three —died when young; he was Supervisor 11 years, Town Clerk for a number of years; is Coroner of the Co., and Postmaster at Council Hill Station, a position held by him for the last 15 years; was Justice of the Peace 16 years.

Perkins James, miner; S. 15; P. O. Galena.

Penalma Alex. farmer; Sec. 25; P. O. Council Hill.

Penalma John, farmer; Sec. 25; P. O. Council Hill.

Phipps Harry, laborer; Council Hill Station.

Pinking John, laborer; Council Hill Station.

Polkinghorne John, farmer; Sec. 35; P. O. Council Hill Station.

Puckey Walter, farmer; Sec. 25; P.O. Council Hill.

RAW JOSEPH, farmer; Sec. 26; P. O. Council Hill.

Raw Peter, farmer; Sec. 25; P. O. Council Hill.

Raw Simon, farmer; Sec. 36; P. O. Council Hill.

REDFEARN GEORGE, Retired; resides in Council Hill Village; born in Durham, England, in 1808; was married in 1829, to Ann Seward; she was born in the same Co. in 1806; came to the U. S. in a sail vessel in 1830; stopped in Pa. until 1834; thence to Michigan where he lived five years; came to this Co. in 1839; has resided in this Tp. ever since; followed mining until 1841, when he went to farming; acquired land to the amount of over 600 acres which is now divided among his children; has eight: Mary A., Margaret, Thomas, John, George, Adeline, Hannah, and William; Mrs. R. died Sept. 11, 1874; Mr. R. was Commissioner of Highways 18 years, and has held a number of minor offices for a number of years each.

Redfearn Geo., Jr., farmer; Sec. 19; P. O. Council Hill.

Redfearn John, farmer; Sec. 24; P. O. Council Hill.

REDFEARN THOMAS, Farmer; Sec. 24; P. O. Council Hill; born in Michigan, Aug. 23, 1835; came to this Co. in 1839; was married March 7, 1869, to Sarah Jane Robinson; she was born in Benton, Wis., April 26, 1850; they have four children: Chas. W., Eddie C., Thomas H., and an infant daughter; owns 310 acres of land; Mr. R. enlisted Sept. 19, 1861, in the 45th Regt. I. V. I.; was in 13 engagements, and mustered out in Sept., 1864; family attend the M. E. Church.

Richards Ed. miner; Sec. 25; P. O. Council Hill.

Richley Thos. miner; Council Hill Station.

RICK EDWARD, Farmer; Sec. 17; P. O. White Oak Springs, Wis.; born in England, Jan. 9, 1801; married Martha Rear, April 6, 1849; she was born in Leicestershire, Eng., June 10, 1807; she was

T. C. Puckett

NORA TP.

the mother of ten children, six living; Mrs. R. died Aug. 9, 1865; Mr. R. married again Dec. 5, 1868, to Louise Lyne; she was born at Mackinaw Island, Feb. 27, 1850; has two children; Mr. R. bought this farm when he first came here in 1850; the family attend the M. E. Church.

Roberts Simon E. farmer; Sec. 23; P. O. Council Hill.

SCANDLYN T. farmer; Sec. 25; P. O. Council Hill.

Schader Edward, shoemaker; Council Hill.

Scott Owen, laborer; Sec. 25; P. O. Council Hill.

Sincock John, farmer; Sec. 24; P. O. Council Hill.

Sincock Joseph, Council Hill.

Smart John, farmer; Sec. 19; P. O. Council Hill.

Smart Rowland, Sec. 19; P. O. Council Hill

Southcot Wm. farmer; Sec. 25; P. O. Council Hill.

Spencer Simeon, farmer; Sec. 20; P. O. Council Hill Station.

STACY WILLIAM, Farmer; Sec. 22; P. O. Galena; born in Buncombe, Wis., Oct. 17, 1846; has been living in this Co. since 1858; is now superintending farm for James M. Day, Esq.

Steel Wm. farmer; S. 26; P. O. Council Hill.

Swift George, farmer; Sec. 29; P. O. Council Hill Station.

TAYLOR JAMES, laborer; Council Hill Station.

Temperly Thos. farmer; Sec. 22; P. O. Council Hill.

Temperly Vickers, farmer; Sec. 14; P. O. Council Hill.

Temperly Wm. farmer; Sec. 32; P. O. Council Hill.

Thomas Thomas, miner; Sec. 32; P. O. Council Hill Station.

Thompson Geo. laborer; Council Hill Sta.

Thompson Joseph, miner; Council Hill.

Thompson Peter, miner; Council Hill.

TODD GEORGE, Miner; Sec. 22; P. O. Galena; born in White Haven, Eng., Sept. 6, 1807; came to the U. S. over fifty years ago; settled in Pa.; was married to Isabella Gray in 1832; she was born in Durham Co., Eng., Oct. 2, 1815; they came to this Co. in 1834; have four children living: John, Ellen, Margaret and George H.; lost two: Thomas died in Virginia City, Nev., Dec. 20, 1863, and Elizabeth Ann (Mrs. Spensley) at Mineral Point, Wis., in 1873; Mr. and Mrs. T. are members of the Grant Hill Primitive Methodist Church.

Todd Geo. H. miner; Sec. 22; P. O. Galena.

Todd John, farmer; Sec. 22; P. O. Galena.

Travis Wm. farm; S. 20; P.O. Council Hill.

Trefz Theodore, blacksmith; Council Hill.

Tuttle Ben W. farmer; Sec. 34; P. O. Galena.

WEBSTER JOHN, farmer; Sec. 32; P. O. Scales Mound.

Webster Thos. Sec. 32; P. O. Scales Mound.

Welsh John, renter; S. 35; P.O. Council Hill.

Wilcox Thos. P. O. Council Hill.

Williams Edward, farmer; Sec. 32; P. O. Council Hill Station.

Williams Jas. S. 32; P. O. Council Hill Sta

Wills John, farm; S. 25; P. O. Council Hill.

Wilt Calvin B. laborer; Sec. 20; P. O. Council Hill Station.

YELLAND ALBERT, farmer; Sec. 36; P. O. Council Hill Station.

Yelland Wm. H. farmer; Sec. 26; P. O. Council Hill Station.

THOMPSON TOWNSHIP.

ALTZ JOHN G. renter; Sec. 30; P. O. Houghton.

Appel Valentine, farmer; Sec. 8; P. O. Scales Mound.

Armstrong William, farmer; Sec. 27; P. O. Houghton.

Atkinson Wm. K. farm hand; Sec. 10; P. O. Apple River.

Auglin Pheanas, farmer; Sec. 31; P. O. Elizabeth.

BAHR HENRY, farmer; Sec. 18; P. O. Scales Mound.

BARNINGHAM JAMES, Farmer; Sec. 10; P. O. Apple River; born in North Riding of Yorkshire, Eng., July 22, 1818; came to this state in 1839; lived five years in St. Clair Co., moved to Galena, thence to Council Hill; came to his present home in 1855; owns 320 acres, valued at $9,600; is an American Reformer in politics, a Methodist in religion, and radically opposed to all secret and oath-bound societies; was married at Council Hill in August, 1851, to Miss Catherine Reisbeck, also a native of Yorkshire; they had seven children; oldest six are living, viz.: Sarah J., Marr, Margaret, Elizabeth Ann, Hannah and Mary Helen; youngest died in infancy; he is also raising and educating an orphan from the New York Juvenile Asylum, John Wesley Gregory, of whom Mr. B. seems very fond, and says he is a very intelligent youth of 20 years, truthful, and of remarkably good morals.

Bastin John, farm; S. 14; P. O. Apple River.

Bastin Thos. farm; S. 14; P. O. Apple River.

Bauer Martin, farmer; Sec. 7; P. O. Scales Mound.

Bell Geo., farmer; Sec. 16; P. O. Houghton.

Bell Richard, farmer; Sec. 6; P. O. Scales Mound.

Bell Wm. farmer; Sec. 16; P. O. Houghton.

Berryman Richard, farmer; Sec. 23; P. O. Houghton.

Boell John, farm; S. 18; P. O. Scales Mound.

Boldt John, farmer; Sec. 30; P. O. Houghton.

Bonhoff Fritz, farmer; Sec. 8; P. O. Scales Mound.

Bottner John, farm; S. 29; P. O. Houghton.

Brukner Philip, farm; S. 27; P.O. Houghton.

CAHIL JAMES, farmer; Sec. 27; P. O. Apple River.

Chapman Wm. farm; S. 23; P. O. Houghton.

Chrisburk Simon, farmer; Sec. 30; P. O. Houghton.

DARNILL MRS. MARY JANE, Widow; Sec. 25; P. O. Rush; owns 330 acres, valued at $6,600; she was born in Rush Tp. April 3, 1845; was married March 20, 1862, to Wm. Westaby, a native of Lincolnshire, Eng.; he was killed Jan. 14, 1870, while rolling a log at Thompson's mills; on Jan. 18, 1871, she married Richard Darnill, a native of England; he died Sept. 29, 1874; she has six children: Joseph Henry, Nellie May, and Charles James Westaby; Richard Wm., Peter Gideon, and Frederick Edmond Darnill; she is independent in religion.

Davich Constantine, farmer; Sec. 13; P. O. Apple River.

Dittmar Casper, farm; S. 20; P. O. Houghton.

Dittmar J. G. farm; S. 20; P. O. Houghton.

Dittmar John, merchant; Sec. 30; P. O Houghton.

Durish Geo. farmer and stone mason; Sec. 18; P. O. Houghton.

DURRSTEIN GUSTAV, Farmer; Sec. 6; P. O. Scales Mound; born in this Co. in 1847; owns 209 acres of land, valued at $5,250; Democrat; Mennonite; married, March 31, 1872, Miss Rosy Elizabeth Beeler, born in Guilford Tp. in 1852; has two children, viz.: Annie Katie, born Aug. 22, 1874, and George Christian, on Good Friday, March 30, 1877; his mother, a native of Saxe Coburg, a very intelligent, respectable and healthy lady, aged 74 years, lives with him; his father died Feb. 5, 1877.

Durrstein John, farmer; Sec. 5; P. O. Scales Mound.

DURRSTEIN LOUIS, Farmer; Sec. 6; P. O. Scales Mound; born in Guilford Tp., this Co., March 31, 1845; owns 24 acres, valued at $7,200; Democrat; Mennonite; married, Feb. 28, 1870, Miss Ursulina Beeler, born in Guilford Tp. Dec. 30, 1849; they had three children, viz.: William, born May 4, 1871 (died Sept. 25, 1872), Louisa, Nov. 14, 1873, and William Henry, Feb. 23, 1877.

EAUSTICE JOHN R. Sec. 24; P. O. Houghton.

Estorf Wm. farmer; Sec. 16; P. O. Houghton.

Evans David H. farmer; Sec. 35; P. O. Elizabeth.

EVANS HENRY H. Farmer; Sec. 35; P. O. Elizabeth; born in Carnarvonshire, Wales, Feb. 2, 1837; came to this Co. in 1845; married, June 8, 1861, Miss Sarah, daughter of Andrew Jackson Gordon, of Pike Co., Mo., where she was born May 24, 1841; her parents moved to this state when she was a child; they had nine children, seven are living: David T.; Sarah J., Florence A., Elizabeth A., Margaret, William H., and Alice; two daughters—Cora and Hannah—died in infancy; he owns 244 acres, valued at $4,800; Republican; independent in religion; has held the office of School Director.

FUNK REV. JOHN E. Pastor of the German Presbyterian Church, Schapville, P. O. Houghton; born in Hesse Cassel, Aug. 13, 1848; came to Wis. in 1853; made his preparatory studies at Hazel Green; was six years a student at the German Presbyterian Theological Seminary, Dubuque; received a call from the German Presbyterian Church of Frank Hill, Minn., while a student, accepted and officiated there two years; received and accepted a call from Nazareth Church, Gasconade Co., Mo., of which he was pastor 19 months, and in 1875 responded to a call from the pastor of which he is now pastor; was married near Dubuque, Oct. 7, 1872, to Miss Sophia C., daughter of Henry Kortemeyer of that place; she was born in Lippe Detmold, Germany, April 16, 1852; has three children: Lydia, born Jan. 17, 1874; Henry D., Nov. 5, 1875; and Jno. G., Sept. 19, 1877; Republican, and is highly spoken of as a zealous minister and exemplary man.

GALLAGHER D. J. farmer; Sec. 16; P. O. Houghton.

GALLAGHER PATRICK, Farmer; Sec. 13; P. O. Apple River; born in Tully, Roscommon Co., Ireland; was married there in Oct., 1850, to Miss Nancy, daughter of Michael and Eliza Glancey; came to this Co. in 1852; lived in Galena 18 years; moved to his farm in 1870; owns 240 acres, valued at $6,000; is a Democrat and a Catholic; their children are: James, born in Ireland, Thomas, John, Christopher, Mary Jane, Ann Eliza, William and Peter, born in this Co.; he buried two children that died in infancy.

GALLAHER JAMES A. Farmer; Sec. 16; P. O. Houghton; was born in Frederick Co., Md., August 15, 1811; was married in Baltimore, Jan. 8, 1833, to Miss Mary C. Schwatka, who was born in that city March 30, 1814; her parents were natives of Prussia; he came to this Co. and settled in Galena in 1837, when it had only one brick building; carried on the business of carpenter and builder, filling various public offices; first was elected Constable, and when the village became a city was elected Marshal; was Deputy Sheriff in 1846–'7; served two years as Harbor and Lumber Master; in 1849 he started for California, but was taken sick at Panama; he remained six years on the Isthmus working as ship carpenter repairing Chagres River boats, etc.; in 1855 he returned to his family at Galena and was again elected City Marshal; served 3 years; in 1869 he moved to his farm; has served one term as Tp. Supervisor; is now School Trustee and Justice of the Peace; has nine daughters and one son: Charlotte A., Annie E., Mary C., Sarah M., Rebecca P., Helena C., Daniel J., Emeline E., Mary M., and Louisa S.; owns 160 acres, valued at $4,000; Democrat; Catholic.

Gilbert Thomas, farmer; Sec. 9; P. O. Apple River.

Gilbert Wm. farmer; Sec. 9; P. O. Apple River.

Gorman Michael, farmer; Sec. 1; P. O. Apple River.

Grebeur Valentine, farmer; Sec. 28; P. O. Houghton.

Greiburg S. farm; S. 30; P. O. Houghton.

Grindy James, farmer; Sec. 10; P. O. Apple River.

Grindy Mat. farm; Sec. 4; P.O. Apple River.

Grube C. A. farm; Sec. 30; P. O. Houghton.

GRUBE GEORGE, Blacksmith; Schapville, Sec. 9; P. O. Houghton; born in Hesse Cassel, Germany, in 1849; came to the United States in 1857; lived in Hazel Green, Wis., 15 years; came to this Co. in 1870; Nov. 15, 1871, he married Miss Lena, daughter of Charles A. Cable; she was born in Galena in 1853; has four children: Henrietta, born Oct. 2, 1872; Emma S., April 17, 1874; Eveline, Jan. 17, 1876, and Matilda C., Nov. 10, 1877; owns 33 acres, residence and shop, valued at $2,500; Republican, and Elder in the German Presbyterian Church.

Gunn Hugh, Sr., farmer; Sec. 10; P. O. Apple River.

Gunn Hugh, Jr., Sec. 10; P. O. Apple River.

Gunn John, Sec. 10; P. O. Apple River.

HAMAN FRED, farmer; Sec. 24; P. O. Houghton.

Hartwig H. farm; Sec. 29; P. O. Houghton.

HAYES PATRICK, Farmer; Sec. 1; P. O. Apple River; born in County of Wexford, Ireland, in 1816; came to this county in 1845; married Miss Ellen White in 1849; went to California in 1851; worked in the gold mines three years; was fairly successful there; returned in 1854; lives on his Mount Sumner farm of 400 acres, valued at $14,000, where he was many years Postmaster of Mount Sumner P. O. (now discontinued); Mr. Hays is a well preserved, young-looking man, of most pleasant, genial, and hospitable disposition; seems to enjoy the comforts of a well-spread table, and true domestic felicity, being surrounded by his nine fine sons, five amiable and finely deported daughters, and their good, lady-like mother; his children are aged in the order named: William, Margaret, Richard, George, Kate, Robert, Ellen, John, Patrick, Moses, Alice, Mary, Joseph, and Edwin; the latter is in his second year; they are all single, Catholic, and Democratic.

Hayes Richard, farmer; Sec. 1; P. O. Apple River.

Hayes Wm. farmer; Sec. 1; P. O. Apple River.

Hess John.

Hilt Ferdinand H. renter; Sec. 5; P. O. Scales Mound.

Hodgins G. farm; Sec. 28; P. O. Houghton.

Hodgin M. D. farm; S. 17; P. O. Houghton.

Hoppe T. farm; Sec. 30; P. O. Houghton.

Horsh Wm. wagon maker; Sec. 30; P. O. Houghton.

Humphrey J. B. farmer; Sec. 15; P. O. Apple River.

Humphrey J. W. farmer; Sec. 15; P. O. Apple River.

Hynes Andrew.

JAGGER JAMES, farmer; Sec. 2; P. O. Apple River.

Jagger Wm. farmer; Sec. 2; P. O. Apple River.

Jelly Matthias, farm hand and miner; Sec. 30; P. O. Houghton.

KEAYES JAS. framer· Sec. 23; P. O. Houghton.

Keenan Francis, farmer; Sec. 7; P. O. Scales Mound.

Keenan Michael, Sr., farmer; Sec. 7; P. O. Scales Mound.

Keenan Michael, Jr., farmer; Sec. 7; P. O. Scales Mound.

Kent J. farmer; Sec. 28; P. O. Houghton.

KETTERER ANTON, Boot and Shoe Maker, Schapville; P. O. Houghton; born in Baden, Germany, May 3, 1850; came to the United States in 1868; lived in Wisconsin 6 years; came to this Co. in 1874, and married Miss Sophia, daughter of Charles A. Grube, in April, 1875; she was born in Germany in Aug. 1857; they had two children that died in infancy; he owns a nice, new residence, a good workshop, and two village lots valued at $1,600; is a Catholic and Greenbacker.

Kingsley S. P. miner; S. 24; P.O. Houghton.

Kreeger Andrew, farmer; Sec. 9; P. O. Scales Mound.

Kyle Jas. farmer; Sec. 27; P. O. Houghton.

LAUR GEORGE farmer, Sec. 20; P. O. Houghton.

Laird Wm. farmer; Sec. 3; P. O. Apple River.

Lappin B. farm; Sec. 22; P. O. Houghton.

Lapien F. farmer; Sec. 32; P. O. Houghton.

Lappin M. farmer; Sec. 22; P. O. Houghton.

LEAVITT JEREMIAH, Farmer; Sec. 28; P. O. Houghton; born in New Hampshire in 1835; came to this Co. in 1856; owns 100 acres valued at $3,500; in 1860 he married Miss Julia, daughter of the late Michael and Margaret Lynch of this Tp.; she was born in 1837, in Co. Cork, Ireland; they have five children living: George A., Frank, Abigail, William S., and an infant son, not named; before he began farming he was by trade a house carpenter; on Oct. 10, 1864, he enlisted in the 1st Regt. I. V. Lt. A., Co. I; went to Nashville and Eastport, Miss.; lay in Division Hospital at the latter place about three weeks; went thence to Evansville, Ind., and was discharged at Louisville, June 5, 1865; has been four years a Justice of the Peace; several years Town Clerk; was School Trustee and is Secretary of the Thompson and Guilford Mutual Fire and Lightning Insurance Company; Greenbacks; Independent in Religion.

Livingston Alfred J., school teacher; Sec. 5; P. O. Scales Mound.

Livingston J. Sec.5; P. O. Scales Mound.

Livingston W. H. school teacher; Sec. 5; P. O. Scales Mound.

LIVINGSTON WM. Farmer; Sec. 5; P. O. Scales Mound; born in Ennisharron, Monaghan, Ireland, in 1815; came to this Co. in 1851; lived about two years at Council Hill; moved to his present home in 1854; owns 270 acres of land, valued at $10,800; was married in Ireland in 1844, to Miss Jane McKnight, native of Monaghan; has five children: Eliza A., born Nov. 21, 1846; Margaret, July 4, 1848; Alfred J., Oct. 21, 1852; Wm. H., March 21, 1855; and Mary Ella, April 26, 1858; Eliza A. is married to Wm. W. Claypole, of Franklin Co., Iowa, and Margaret is the wife of Henry Thuirer of Washington Co., Kansas; Mr. L. has been President and Treasurer of the Board of Road Commissioners for 15 years; several years School Director, and one term Tax Collector; Republican; Methodist.

McDONALD JAS. farmer; Sec. 4; P. O. Apple River.

McDonald Pat. Sec. 4; P. O. Apple River.

McDonald Peter, Sec. 4; P. O. Apple River.

McGee J. farm; Sec. 27; P. O. Houghton.

McKILLIPS WM. P. Farmer; Sec. 34; P. O. Elizabeth; born in Bath Co. in 1831; came to this Co. when four years old; was married in 1856 to Miss Amanda L. Miller of this Co.; she died Nov. 21, 1871; has seven children: Wm. A., Matilda, George, Henry, Edward, Ella A., and Frank, aged respectively, 21, 19, 17, 15, 13, 11 and 9 years; he owns 160 acres valued at $4,000; he followed the smelting of ore for 16 years; Republican; independent in Religion but a believer in Christianity.

McManus T. farm; Sec. 26; P. O. Houghton.

McQUILLAN FRANCIS, Farmer; Sec. 2; P. O. Apple River; born in Co.

Fermanagh, Ireland, March 16, 1825; came to this Co. in 1847; bought property and lived in Galena 22 years; moved to his present residence in 1869; owns 240 acres valued at $6,000, and property in Galena worth $2,000; was married to Miss Mary Ann Deery, native of Fermanagh, May 6, 1856; has nine children: George P., Mary C., John F., Wm. J., James H., Sarah A., Peter, John and Eliza, all living with parents; Mr. McQuillan is School Director, and has filled the office for six years; is a Democrat and a Catholic.

McQuillan Geo. P. Sec. 2; P. O. Houghton.

Mann B. F. farm; Sec. 17; P. O. Houghton.

Mann J. A. carpenter; S.— P. O. Houghton.

Marks J. farmer; Sec. 17; P. O. Houghton.

Matson Frank, farmer; Sec. 5; P. O. Scales Mound.

Miller John, Sr., farmer; Sec. 21; P. O. Houghton.

Miller John, Jr., farmer; Sec. 21; P. O. Houghton.

Millhouse J. farm; Sec. 30; P. O. Houghton.

MUSSELMAN MICHAEL, Farmer; Sec. 6; P. O. Scales Mound; born in Bavaria, July 25, 1829; landed in New York City, May 1, 1846; lived two years in Lancaster Co., Pa.; came to this Co. in 1848; owns 190 acres, valued at $5,000; was married on Oct. 16, 1853, to Miss Elizabeth, daughter of the late John and Louisa Durstein, of this town; has nine children living: John, Louisa, Christian, Gustav, Elias E., David, Michael, Benjamin and William; his wife died June 9, 1875; he has been nine years School Director, one term Trustee and twelve years Road Commissioner; Democrat; Mennonite.

O'NEIL JOHN, farmer; Sec. 11; P. O. Apple River.

O'Neil J. C. school teacher; Sec. 11; P. O. Apple River.

O'Neil Joseph, farmer; Sec. 11; P.O. Apple River.

Osborne Page, farmer; Sec. 15; P. O. Scales Mound.

Otto —— renter; S. 18; P. O. Scales Mound.

Owens Thomas, renter; Sec. 33; P. O. Elizabeth.

PARKIN PHILIP, Farmer and Postmaster; Sec. 29; P. O. Houghton; was born in the Parish of Camborn, Co. of Cornwall, England, Oct. 20, 1817; came to this Co. in 1840; married in April 1845, Mrs. Margaret Lee, a native of Ky.; they have no children; own 123 acres, valued at $3,690; was elected Commissioner of Highways when the Tp. was organized; filled the office 8 years; has been overseer of Highways; is one of the Board of Supervisors; has filled the office six years; is Postmaster, Justice of the Peace (an office he has held 15 years), and President of the Thompson and Guilford Mutual Fire and Lightning Insurance Company; he donated one acre, the site of Mill Creek school house, Dis. 3, Sec. 29; Republican in politics; Independent in Religion.

Polkow Wm., Sr., farmer; Sec. 31; P. O. Houghton.

Polkow Wm., Jr., farmer; Sec. 31; P. O. Houghton.

Potter L. miller; Sec. 24; P. O. Houghton.

RACE GEORGE.

ROMMEL MRS. ANNIE, Widow; Sec. 6; P. O. Scales Mound; she was born in the Canton of St. Gallen, Switzerland, July 11, 1831; came to this Co. in 1845; lived in Galena about ten years; married Henry Rommel (native of Prussia), in Jan., 1850; husband died in 1869; she has ten children living: Annie K., Henry, John, Charles, Elizabeth, Fannie, Emma L., William, Valentine and Mary; Annie K., and Henry are married; the family are Lutheran; sons are Republican.

Rommel John, Sec. 6; P. O. Scales Mound.

Redamer Casper.

Redamer Jacob.

Remer Lewis.

Roberts W. farmer; Sec. 36; P.O. Elizabeth.

Rogers E. farmer; Sec. 33; P. O. Houghton.

Rowe John, farmer; Sec. 8; P. O. Scales Mound.

Russel John, farmer; Sec. 1; P. O. Apple River.

SAMPSON A. R. farmer; Sec. 27; P. O. Houghton.

Sampson Ichabod, farmer; Sec. 34; P. O. Houghton.

Schap A. carpenter; S. 30; P. O. Houghton.

Schnieder Joseph, Sec. 8; Scales Mound.

Schoenhardt Jacob farmer; Sec. 18; P. O. Houghton.

Shirdan Richard.

Shoemaker J. farm; S. 30; P. O. Houghton.

Sincox Edward, farmer; Sec. 14; P. O. Apple River.

Sincox John, Sec. 14; P. O. Apple River.

Sincox Wm. farmer; Sec. 14; P. O. Apple River.

Smith Andrew, renter; Sec. 4; P. O. Scales Mound.

SMITH JOHN W. Farmer; Sec. 8; P. O. Scales Mound; born in this Tp. in 1844; enlisted in 1862 in the 96th Regt. I. V. I., Co. E; drilled two weeks at Rockford; went to the front; fought at Chicamauga, Lookout Mountain, Mission Ridge, Kingston and Kenesaw Mountain; had many skirmishes to Atlanta; marched thence, under Gen. Thomas, to Franklin, and Nashville where he was last engaged in battle; was mustered out there in June, 1865; was paid off at Chicago; on Aug. 24, 1867, married Miss Evaline Willard; born in Guilford Tp. in 1846; buried four children; has one living, Emily Marion, born Oct. 14, 1868; he owns 40 acres, valued at $1,000; Republican; Methodist.

Soule Elijah farm; Sec. 26; P.O. Houghton.

Soule G. H. carpenter; S. 24; P.O. Houghton.

Stadale Gotleib, Sr., farmer; Sec. 30; P. O. Houghton.

Stadale Gotleib, Jr., farmer; Sec. 30; P. O. Hanover.

Stadale W. farm; Sec. 20; P. O. Houghton.

Steiner Henry, farm hand; Sec. 22; P.O. Apple River.

Steiner Michael, farmer; Sec. 22; P. O. Apple River.

Stephens Christian, farmer; Sec. 16; P. O. Scales Mound.

Stephens John, farmer; Sec. 8; P. O. Scales Mound.

Stephens Valentine, farmer; Sec. 17; P. O. Scales Mound.

Stich Matthias, Sr., farmer; Sec. 30; P. O. Houghton.

Stich Matthias, Jr., farmer; Sec. 30; P. O. Houghton.

Stich Wm. Sec. 30; P. O. Houghton.

Strauss J. H. farm: Sec. 19; P.O. Houghton.

Sweeney Edward, farmer; Sec. 1; P. O. Apple River.

Sweeney T. renter; Sec. 23; P. O. Houghton.

TIPPERT C. H. farmer; Sec. 20; P. O. Houghton.

THOMAS THOMAS H. Farmer; Sec. 36; P. O. Elizabeth; born in Carmarthenshire, Wales; came to this Co. in 1850; had been married in Wales to Miss Elizbeth Jones, who died in that country; he had one son and a daughter whom he brought with him to the United States; the son, John, died in hospital at Nashville, Tenn., in 1864; his daughter Ann is the wife of Henry Hartman of Black Oak, Colorado; he was married on Feb. 21, 1868, to Mrs. Fanny, widow of Daniel Williams; is a native of Anglesey; was first married in Wales, and with her late husband and two children came to this Co. in 1846; he died here March 5, 1865, leaving ten children: Hugh, born Sept. 3, 1842; Ellen, March 31, 1845; Wm., Feb. 17, 1847; John, July 18, 1849; Elizabeth, June 9, 1851; Richard, July 17, 1853; Robert, May 1, 1855; Daniel Dec. 17, 1857; David, Feb. 29, 1860, and Mary Ann, March 31, 1863; Mrs. T. owns 204, and Mr. T. 40 acres, all valued at $4,000; she is a Methodist, he is Independent in Religion and politics.

Totzel Jno. renter; Sec. 21; P. O. Houghton

Tregoning John, farmer and miner; Sec. 34; P. O. Houghton.

UHREN WM. farmer; Sec. 3; P. O. Apple River.

VAUGHAN EDWIN, Farmer; Sec. 36; P. O. Rush; was born in this Co. Feb. 28, 1853; his father was a native of Cardiganshire, Wales; died here April 12, 1872; his mother in May, 1874; they are buried in Thompson Cemetery; his brother James served in the 96th Regt. I. V. I., Co. A, and was killed at Rocky Face skirmish, May 9, 1864, aged 18 years; he owns 200 acres, valued at $5,000; is single; a successful hunter, fond of the chase, and is a terror to the wolves and other vermin that prowl among the hills and woodlands and often prey upon the sheep and poultry of the farmers of Thompson; Republican; Independent in Religion.

Vaughn Richard, farmer; Sec. 36; P. O. Elizabeth.

Vaughn Wm. farm; S. 36; P. O. Elizabeth.

WAGNER CHRISTIAN.

Weich H. farmer; Sec. 28; P. O. Houghton.

WENNER JOHN, Farmer; Sec. 9; P. O. Scales Mound; born in Lebanon Co., Pa., Jan. 31, 1819; came West in 1839; worked at the carpenter trade in St. Louis; moved to Galena in 1841; worked at his trade, mined and farmed there 14 years; came to his present farm in 1855; owns west of Galena 73 acres, and 560 acres in this Tp., all valued at $20,500; was married at Galena Oct. 8, 1852, to Miss H. E. True, a native of Syracuse, N. Y.; has four children: Ira H., aged 24; Alice M., 19; E. E., 16, and Helen D., 2 years; was nominated in 1850 by the Whigs for Representative and repeatedly asked to accept nomination for the office of Sheriff; has filled the offices of Tp. Treasurer 18 years, Supervisor 2 years, is now School Director; in 1847 was appointed Tp. bidder at government land sales for the Tp. of West Galena.

Westaby C. farm; Sec. 25; P. O. Houghton.

WESTABY GEORGE, Farmer; Sec. 23; P. O. Houghton; son of Thomas and Mary Westaby, of Barron, Lincolnshire, Eng., where he was born Nov. 19, 1822; was married April 12, 1850, to Miss Ann, daughter of Wm. and Maria Wilson, of Alton Le Moor, Lincolnshire, and emigrated to this Co. same year; she was born Oct. 22, 1822; they have four children: Stephen, born June 12, 1852; Tom, March 12, 1855; Wilson, July 17, 1857, and George Rice, March 29, 1863; they lost by death two daughters and one son; they are raising a grand-nephew of Mrs. Westaby,

Thomas Wilson, born in Eng. Aug. 28, 1864, whom she brought to this country on her return from a visit to her native home and relations; Mr. W. owns 584 acres valued at $11,680; is Road Commissioner; has been Overseer of Highways; School Director four terms; Assessor and Collector several years; Republican in politics; Independent in Religion; donated site (one acre), for the Salem M. E. Church, and was a member of the Building Committee.

Westaby S. farm; Sec. 25; P. O. Houghton.

Westaby W. farm; Sec. 25; P. O. Houghton.

White John C. renter; Sec. 12; P. O. Apple River.

White J. H. farmer; Sec. 14; P. O. Apple River.

White Wm. farmer; Sec. 11; P. O. Apple River.

Whitham W. farm; S. 28; P. O. Houghton.

Wigler Fred. farm hand; Sec. 6; P.O. Scales Mound.

Williams J. farmer; Sec. 34; P. O. Elizabeth.

Williams J. E. farm; S. 35; P. O. Elizabeth.

Williams J. F. farm; S. 33; P. O. Elizabeth.

Williams Robert, with brother; Sec. 25; P. O. Rush.

WILLIAMS WILLIAM, Sec. 25; P. O. Rush; was born in this Co., Feb. 17, 1847; he rents 320 acres from Mrs. Mary J. Darnill; enlisted in the 96th Regt. I. V. I., Co. F, on Oct. 8, 1864; participated in the last battle of Nashville, and was honorably discharged at Springfield, on the 30th day of Oct., A. D., 1865; was married Dec. 4, 1872, to Miss Annie M., daughter of John and Ann Hutchinson of Elizabeth. Tp.; has three children: Fred Russel, born Nov. 4, 1873; Cora E., April 27, 1875, and Jesse, Jan. 3, 1877; Republican in politics and Independent in Religion.

Williams Z. farm; S. 34; P. O. Elizabeth.

Wilson T. farm; Sec. 27; P. O. Houghton.

Winter Conrad, Sr., Sec. 29; P.O. Houghton.

Winter Conrad, Jr., farmer; Sec. 20; P. O. Hougton.

Winter H. farm; Sec. 29; P. O. Houghton.

Winter J. farm; Sec. 30; P. O. Houghton.

Winter M. farm; Sec. 18; P. O. Houghton.

Wise J. farmer; Sec. 19; P. O. Houghton.

ZICK FREDERICK farmer; Sec. 20; P. O. Houghton.

BERREMAN TOWNSHIP.

ASHER CONRAD, farmer; Sec. 21; P. O. Loran.

Aurand Benj. farmer; Sec. 28; P. O. Loran.

BARNAKING FREDERICK, farmer; Sec. 9; P. O. Loran.

Beals John, laborer; Loran.

Bechler Calvin, farmer; Sec. 5; P. O. Willow.

Bishop Peter, merchant; S. 5; P. O. Willow.

Bowman Josiah, laborer; Willow.

Brininger Benj. farmer; Sec. 5; P. O. Willow.

Brininger Henry, farm; S. 5; P. O. Willow.

BRININGER JOHN, Farmer; Sec. 5; P. O. Willow; born in Ohio July 31, 1843; came West in an early day with his parents; served in army in the 39th I. V. I., and remained until the close of the war; was in front of Richmond and Petersburg; was honorably discharged at Norfolk, Va.; married Catherine Oberheim March 6, 1864; she was born in Centre Co., Pa., Oct. 24, 1847, and came to this Co. when a child; have three children living: Lewis T., Manie E., Ervie M.; three dead: John E., Orin S., George A.; owns 40 acres of land, house and lot, valued at $2,000.

BRUSHOUS JACKSON, Farmer; Sec. 17; P. O. Loran, Stephenson Co.; was born in Pa. Sept. 24, 1827; his father died in 1831, but his mother married again, and in 1844 the family moved to this Co.; married Mary A. Bishop in 1853; she died May 28, 1874; married Mrs. Brumgard Aug. 15, 1875; her maiden name was Catherine Brean; she was born in Clinton Co., Pa., April 11, 1844; she married Mr. Brumgard, by which marriage she had three children living: Newton, Harrison, Valentine; lost one, Ida Jane; Mr. Brushous has ten children living by his first marriage: George, Peter, Josiah, Mary Catherine, Parmelia, Barbara E., Julia A., Emma F., Wallace, Jackson; lost one, William; one child by second marriage, Sylvester; owns 280 acres of land.

Bucher Adam, farmer; Sec. 30; P. O. Pleasant Valley.

BUCHER JOHN, Farmer; Sec. 31; P. O. Pleasant Valley; born in Nederweingen, Switzerland, March 8, 1812; married Esther Huber in 1836; came to the U. S. in 1854; she was born in Dulsdorf, Switzerland, March 1, 1814; they came direct to this Co.; have four children living: Jacob S. Bucher, Mrs. Dorothea

White, Mrs. Anna Kaufman, and John J. Bucher; Jacob S. Bucher was born Jan. 18, 1837, in Switzerland; married Elesta McIntyre Aug. 30, 1860; she died in 1875; served in Union army during the war, in the 45th I. V. I.; was in battles of Fort Donelson, Shiloh, Corinth, Jackson, siege of Vicksburg, and Champion Hill; was honorably discharged after serving three years and three months.

Bucher Johannes, farmer; Sec. 13; P. O. Pleasant Valley.

CALHOUN NOAH W. Farmer; Sec. 5; P. O. Willow; was born in Bedford Co., Pa., April 18, 1838; when quite young his parents moved to Maryland, where they lived until 1857; then came to Ogle Co., Ill.; lived there one year, and in Stephenson Co. three years; in 1861 came into Jo Daviess Co.; enlisted in 57th Regt. I. V. I., and served until the close of the war; joined Sherman's army at Savannah, and came up through the Carolinas to Washington, and was honorably discharged at Chicago; married Julia A. Parkinson Jan. 10, 1861; she was born in this Co. March 11, 1843; have seven children living: Roberta, Crissie, Manly J., Russell W., John S., Hattie, Josephine; owns 213 acres of land; was Assessor two years, Supervisor two years, School Director three years, and Highway Commissioner.

Church Martin, lab; Sec. 7; P. O. Willow.

Chambers M. R. teacher; P. O. Willow.

Clay Daniel, farmer; Sec. 9; P. O. Willow.

Claywell Geo. E. farmer; S. 28; P. O. Loran.

CLAY JEREMIAH, Farmer; Sec. 5; P. O. Willow; was born in Summit Co., Ohio, Feb. 22, 1830; his mother with her family came to this Co. in 1849, and this has been his home since that time; Sept. 20, 1855, married Martha Stahly, who was born in Summit Co., Ohio, Nov. 12, 1837; have eight children living: Mary C., Lovina J., William H., Mollie A., Samuel F., Charles S., Fannie A., Elliott R.; was a member of the 153d I. V. I., and was honorably discharged at Springfield at the close of the war; Mrs. Clay's mother (Mrs. Catherine Stahly) lives with them; she was born in Wurtemberg, Germany, April 16, 1806, and came to America in 1831; owns 198 acres of land; was Postmaster two years and School Director six years; member of M. E. Church and A. F. and A. M.

Clevidence Daniel, farmer; S. 9; P. O. Loran.

Cormony Henry, farmer; Sec. 31; P. O. Pleasant Valley.

Cullens Geo. E. farmer, Sec. 32; P. O. Loran.

CULLENS JAMES, Farmer; Sec. 33; P. O. Loran, Stephenson Co.; born in Pa. Dec. 8, 1817; came to Stark Co., Ohio, and married Miss Esther Zerbe Oct. 2, 1842; she was born in Stark Co., Ohio, April 25, 1825; came to this Co. in 1856; was Commissioner of Highways six years, Justice of Peace four years (commissioned by Gov. John M. Palmer); was School Director for many years; have ten children living: Wm. H., George E., Sarah C., Margaret A., Julius F. J., Esther A., James Wesley, Josephine, Emma A. and Ward H.; lost five; owns 280 acres of land; his mother, Mrs. Mary Cullens, resides with them; she was born in Huntingdon Co., Pa., in 1795.

Cullens Wm H. farmer; Sec. 32; P. O. Loran.

DARR JOHN C. Farmer; Sec. 19; P. O. Pleasant Valley; born in Westmoreland Co., Pa., Jan. 24, 1835; came to this Co. in 1856; was married May 13, 1860, to Ann Harkness, who was born in Canada June 27, 1837; one child living, Oscar E.; have lost five children; Sept., 1862, enlisted in 96th I. V. I., and served until the close of the war; was at Atlanta, Buzzard Roost Gap, Resaca, Dallas, Kenesaw Mountain, Peach Tree Creek, Lovejoy Station, Franklin, Nashville; served as Sergeant and Corporal, and was honorably discharged at Nashville; owns 200 acres of land.

Davis John, farmer; P. O. Willow.

DAWSON JOHN, Farmer; Sec. 5; P. O. Willow; born in Lincolnshire, Eng., Aug. 7, 1831; came to U. S. in 1842; suffered shipwreck on the voyage off the banks of Newfoundland; all survived but one; lived in Freeport two years, and returned to England; came to America again in 1845; married Miss Phœbe J. Baker May 5, 1868; she was born in Canada Aug. 22, 1850; came to the U. S. with her parents in 1860; have three children: Julia Ann, Henrietta A., Jennie Maud; lost one child, Franklin Eugene; Mr. D. owns 60 acres of land.

Ditsworth Samuel, farm; S. 28; P. O. Loran.

Ditsworth Wm. farmer; P. O. Loran.

Dixon Alvin, farmer; Sec. 28; P. O. Loran.

FLICKINGER JACOB, farmer; Sec. 21; P. O. Loran.

Fickes John, farmer; Sec. 19; P. O. Willow.

Fike David, laborer; Sec. 5; P. O. Willow.

Fox Anthony, farmer; Sec. 33; P. O. Loran.

Fox Wm. farmer; Sec. 29; P. O. Loran.

Frederick A. S. P. lab.; P.O. Pleasant Valley.

GARKE AUGUSTUS, farmer; Sec. 16; P. O. Loran.

Garke Wm. farmer; Sec. 16; P. O. Loran.

GATES SAMUEL B. Farmer; Sec. 6; P. O. Willow; born in Wayne Co., N. Y., June 4, 1822, on shore of Lake Ontario; his father emigrated to this Co. in 1837; were first permanent residents in

C. C. Thompson

NORA TOWNSHIP

Berreman Tp.; his mother, whose maiden name was Phoebe G. Crane, born in New Hampshire April 21, 1797, still lives with him; she was the only woman in this section for eighteen months after they came to the country; she is the only one of nineteen brothers and sisters now living; his father died Aug. 18, 1847; he was born in N. Y. Oct. 26, 1779; married Miss Mary E. Mahoney Sept. 15, 1851; she was born in Indiana Nov. 8, 1827; have six children living: William W., now in Washington Territory, Mrs. Clara Davis, John W., Alice A., Rosilla M., Thomas M.; a little nephew lives with them, Ellis A. Evans; have lost four children; Mr. G. served in 57th Regt. I. V. I.; joined Sherman's command at Savannah, Ga.; passed in review with the army at Washington; was honorably discharged in 1865; owns 320 acres of land.

Glassner Nicholas, farm; S. 8; P. O. Willow.

GRAY GEORGE W. Farmer and Stock Dealer; Sec. 29; P. O. Loran, Stephenson Co.; born in Owen Co., Ind., March 19, 1844; served in Union army during War of the Rebellion, in 97th Regt. Ind. V. I.; participated in battles of Vicksburg, Jackson, Missionary Ridge, Dalton, Resaca, Atlanta, Savannah, Bentonville, N. C., and a number of others; was honorably discharged at Indianapolis at close of the war; went to Pittsburg, Pa., in 1866; came to Jo Daviess Co. in 1868; married Cordelia Mitchell Oct. 14, 1875; she was born in Stephenson Co. July 1, 1854; have one child, Bessie Irena, born Oct. 7, 1876; works 200 acres of land.

HARMON DAVID, farmer; Sec. 31; P. O. Pleasant Valley.

Hoy Henry C. farmer; Sec. 9; P. O. Willow.

KELTNER HENRY, Farmer and Stock Dealer; Sec. 21; P. O. Loran, Stephenson Co., Ill.; was born at Dayton, O., Dec. 25, 1817; in 1834 his father moved to Elkhart Co., Ind., where they lived 18 years; married Welthy A. Cook in 1847; she died in 1850; had two children, one of whom, Julia A. Benner, is living; married Catherine Eisenbise March 13, 1851; she was born in Miami Co., O., Sept. 8, 1833; came to Ill. to Carroll Co. in 1853, and to Jo Daviess Co. in 1872; have nine children living: Peter R., who has been a teacher six years; John H., Henry, William, Cora E., James A., Lewis E., Effa M. and Malinda; lost four children; owns 177 acres land.

Klump C. A. farmer; Sec. 19; P. O. Willow.

KLUMP JACOB B. Farmer and Justice of the Peace; Sec. 5; P. O. Willow; born in Wurtemburg, Germany, Dec. 24, 1834; came to the U. S. with two sisters in 1853, to Lake Co. and to Elgin; to this Co. in 1854; went to Galena; declared his intention to become a citizen; traveled in Iowa and Minnesota; returned in 1860; went to Peoria to see sisters; there enlisted in 39th I. V. I.; served 4½ years during rebellion; never was off duty; had close calls from bullets; passed through his clothes; drew some blood; was in the severest engagements—16 battles—Winchester, Black Water, Morris Island, Petersburg, charge and capture of Ft. Gregg, and others equally severe; pursuit and capture of Gen. Lee; while at home on veteran furlough married Miss Jane Parkinson Feb. 29, 1864; she was born near where they now live; was the first white child born in Ward's Grove precinct; have six children living: Sophie E., Herman R., Julia M., William F., Mary and Rubie; lost two children, Helen and Joseph; Mr. K. was honorably discharged from army at Springfield Dec. 16, 1865; has been commissioned by three governors of Illinois as Justice of the Peace, John M. Palmer, John L. Beveridge and Shelly M. Cullom; owns 323 acres land.

Kock Henry, farmer; Sec. 17; P. O. Loran.

Koehler Frederick, farmer; Sec. 32; P. O. Pleasant Valley.

LEAY AUGUST.

Lopshire Wm. H. farm; Sec. 5; P.O. Willow.

Lyde N. Allen, carpenter; Sec. 8; P. O. Willow.

McGINNIS ENOCH, Farmer; Sec. 19; P. O. Loran, Stephenson Co.; born near Indianapolis, Ind., June 23, 1828; father emigrated to McLean Co., Ill., in 1841; came to this Co. in 1842; lived eight years in Stephenson Co.; went to Wis. in 1859; remained there till 1867; moved to this Co.; married Beulah Buckley in 1850; she was born in Lycoming Co., Pa., Sept. 20, 1828; have ten children living: James B., John F., Samuel A., Thomas D., Mary J., Ida A., Joseph S., Clunson B., George A. and Orpha E.; lost two children: William F. and Sarah E.; owns 320 acres of land; Commissioner of Highways three years.

McGINNIS FRANCIS, Farmer; Sec. 21; P. O. Loran, Stephenson Co.; was born near Pittsburg, Pa., March 8, 1801; at the age of 15 moved to Ky., and remained there six years; married Jane Coffar in 1822; she died June 9, 1849; they had twelve children, five of whom are living: Enoch, Mary, Sarah, Margaret, Nancy; emigrated to Ind. when it was a new country, and remained till 1841, when he moved to McLean Co., Ill., and in 1842 came to this Co.; two of his sons, James and Joseph, died in the army; James was the owner of the famous Wisconsin eagle; he was color-bearer in the regiment to which it was attached, and cared for it until he died at Jacksonville, Tenn., in 1862; had they both lived, James intended to present this eagle to his father, but it became the common property of the Regt. after his death, and at the close of the war was presented to the Governor of Wisconsin; the bird was taken to the Centennial, and while there attracted a great deal of attention; Mr. McGinnis married Eleanor Bartlow Oct. 10, 1851; she died Oct. 17, 1870; owns 61 acres of land; member of church of Brethren of the Abrahamic Faith.

McGinness James, farm; S. 19; P. O. Loran.

McPEEK ROBERT, Farmer; Sec. 19; P. O. Pleasant Valley; born in Guernsey Co., Ohio, March 18, 1831; came direct to this Co. from Ohio in 1856; married Nancy Aduddell in Oct., 1854; she was born in Ohio Dec. 11, 1829; have nine children living: Sarah M., Mary I., Amanda J., Benjamin A., Perry O., Orpha A., Margaret A., James G., Josephine B.; lost one child, Nancy; owns 195 acres of land; has been School Director four years; they have been active and influential members of the M. E. Church twenty-four years.

MACHAMER THOMAS J. Farmer; Sec. 4; P. O. Willow; born in Union Co., Pa., March 28, 1839; parents emigrated to this Co. in 1845, when the subject of this sketch was quite young; served in the Union army in the 45th Regt. I. V. I.; enlisted Sept. 14, 1861; was in battles of Fort Henry and Donelson; was wounded at Shiloh; honorably discharged on account of wounds received July 17, 1862; married Mary E. Solt Sept. 24, 1864; she was born in this Co. March 10, 1848; have four children: Daniel Lafayette, John Wilbert, Russel C. and Lottie B.; owns 40 acres of land.

Mader Wm. H. S. 30; P. O. Pleasant Valley.

MITCHELL MARTIN M. Farmer; Sec. 33; P. O. Loran, Stephenson Co.; born in Vermillion Co., Ind., April 21, 1827; his father emigrated to Stephenson Co., Ill., in 1842; married Thirza Herrington April 18, 1853; she was born in Upper Canada July 14, 1830; came to Carroll, Ill., in 1839; have five children living: Mrs. Cordelia A. May, Anna M., teacher; Almeda A., Phœbe R. and Stephen M.; owns 433 acres of land; was School Director fifteen years; lost three children: Wm. H., Isaac A., and an infant not named.

Mowry Wm. laborer; P. O. Loran.

Mowery Wm. farmer; Sec. 16; P. O. Loran.

Muper Henry, farmer; Sec. 29; P. O. Loran.

NEFF HENRY, farmer; Sec. 4; P. O. Willow.

NOBLE ARTHUR, Farmer and Stock Raiser; Sec. 29; P. O. Loran, Stephenson Co., Ill.; born in Co. Tyrone, Ireland, in 1825; came to this country in 1850, and settled at Pittsburg, Pa., where he lived ten years; was married March 8, 1860, to Jane Conn, who was born in Co. Down, near Belfast, Ireland, in 1843, and came to America with her parents when 5 years old; came to Jo Daviess Co. in 1867; seven children: Alice E., Margaret W., William J., Mary A., Joseph R., Sarah J., Emma R.; owns 310 acres of land; is School Director of the Union School District.

OBLEY CHRISTIAN, Farmer; P. O. Loran, Stevenson Co., born in Germany, and came to U. S. when young; settled in Westmoreland Co., Pa.; married there Miss Catherine Darr, in 1844; she was also born in Germany, and came to this country when a child; came to Galena in 1854; Mr. O. served in the army, in 96th Regt. I. V. I.; participated in all the severe engagements through which his regiment passed; was honorably discharged at close of war; have eight children; Catherine married Mr. Wm. H. Mader; both born in this Co.; they have one child, Leonora.

PARKINSON MRS. CHRISTINE, Farming; Sec. 8; P. O. Willow; her maiden name was Miss C. Hoy; she was born in Centre Co., Pa., Aug. 31, 1812; married Mr. James Parkinson in 1832; he was born in Centre Co., Pa., April 29, 1806; they emigrated to this Co. in the Spring of 1839; second family in this section; Mr. P.'s brother, Isaac W., who is now P. M. at Willow, came with them; they were educated and enterprising men, and were valuable to the society in a new and sparsely settled country; James was the first Justice of the Peace in this precinct, and served as first Supervisor of Berreman Tp.; eight children living: Jane (now the wife of J. B. Klump, Eng.), Mrs. Julia A. Calhoun, Isaac W., Mrs. Fannie Lopshire, Cressie E., Geo. W., Silas D., Josiah B., now at Rock River Seminary; lost three sons in army: John died of disease; William killed at Pittsburg Landing; James died of disease; lost one daughter, Rebecca.

PARKINSON GEO. W. Farmer; Sec. 5; P. O. Willow; born in this Co. May 8, 1850; married Miss Julia A. Wise Dec. 7, 1873; she was born in Ward's Grove, Dec. 7, 1852; Mr. P. is the Leader of the Willow Helicon Band; he is teacher of instrumental and vocal music; owns 41 acres of land; they have one child; W. Bliss Parkinson.

PARKINSON ISAAC W. Farmer; Sec. 5; P. O. Willow; born in Berreman, this Co., Jan. 23, 1845; has since resided here; served in the Union Army, as Sergeant Co. B, 142d Regt. I. V. I.; served his time in that Regt. and enlisted in the 39th Regt. I. V. I.; joined this Regt. the next day after Lee's surrender at Appomatox; was honorably discharged Dec., 1865; married Miss Maggie C. McLenahen, Sept. 16, 1866; she was born in Mifflin Co., Pa., Nov. 2, 1848; came to Freeport with her parents in 1850; have five children living: Minnie A., Warden W., Fannie B., James W., Benjamin F.; Mr. P. is now serving as Supervisor for the second term, a position he is worthy and well qualified to fill; has been Assessor one term; owns 135 acres of land.

Parkinson Isaac W., Sr., postmaster; Willow.

Parkinson J. B., Willow.

Parkinson N. farmer; Sec. 6; P. O. Willow.

PARKINSON SILAS D. Farmer; Sec. 8; P. O. Willow; born Aug. 27, 1852; in this Co.; married Miss Florence A. Chambers in Sept., 1877; she was born in Winona, Minn., June 4, 1859; Mr. P. owns 140 acres of land.

RAY G. W. farmer; Sec. 19; P. O. Loran.

Reiss John M. farmer; P. O. Loran.

Renner David, farmer; Sec. 31; P. O. Pleasant Valley.

RINEBARGER JOSIAH, Farmer; Sec. 18; P. O. Loran, Stephenson Co.; born in Dolphin Co., Pa., Oct. 14, 1829; his father emigrated to Ohio in early times; was principally reared in Wayne Co., Ohio; came to this Co. in 1854; married Elizabeth Mader Nov. 12, 1857; she was born in Union Co., Pa., Sept. 7, 1829; came here with her parents when quite young; they were early settlers; have four children living: Susan J., Eveline R., Mary E., and Carrie Bell; Dolly Ray, niece of Mrs. R., also resides with them; own 220 acres of land; Mr. R. was School Director 3 and Commissioner of Highways 9 years.

Robinson Chas. farmer and Tp. collector; Sec. 7; P. O. Willow.

Rumsey G. W., Sr., farmer; Sec. 32; P. O. Loran.

Rumsey G. W., Jr., farmer; Sec. 32; P. O. Loran.

Rumsey S. farmer; Sec. 33; P. O. Loran.

SCHLAFER GEO. Farmer; Sec. 5; P. O. Willow.

Schmeck G. W. farm; Sec. 6; P. O. Willow.

SCHMECK LEVI F. Farmer; Sec. 5; P. O. Willow; born in Mountour Co., Pa., July 26, 1834; came to this Co. in 1854; served in the Union Army, 3d Regt. Mo. V. C., as Commissary Sergeant; was under fire of the enemy most of the time from Balls Bluff to Little Rock; was honorably discharged Dec. 31, 1864; married Miss Rebecca A. Ruble, 1866; she died in 1867; married Miss Julia A. Lyle, Jan. 20, 1869; she was born in Jefferson Co., Pa., Sept. 4, 1845; came to this Co. in 1863; has two children: Susan M. and Luella; Mr. S. has been Collector one term, and School Director three years; belongs to the M. E. Church.

Shaffer P. farmer; Sec. 16; P. O. Loran.

Sharron H. laborer; Sec. 31; P. O. Loran.

Solt D. farmer; Sec. 5; P. O. Willow.

SOLT ISRAEL, Merchant; P. O. Willow; born in Clinton Co., Pa., April 7, 1840; came to this Co. in 1848; served in the army during the Rebellion in the 34th Regt. I. V. I.; was promoted to 1st Lieutenant Co. I; was in the severe engagements of Shiloh, Stone River, Murfreesboro and Chattanooga; re-enlisted in 1864; returned home on veteran furlough and married Miss Kate Bishop in Feb., 1864; she was born in Centre Co., Pa., Dec. 7, 1842; have three children: Cora E., Theophilus A., and Hettie; Mr. S. was wounded at Jonesboro, Ga., Sept. 1, 1864, through the left thigh; was honorably discharged at the close of the war; has been engaged in merchandising 5 years at his present stand where he is doing a thriving business.

Spurgeon Joseph, farm; S. 19; P. O. Loran.

Staley Frederick, farm; S. 4; P. O. Willow.

TAYLOR JOHN, Jr., laborer; Sec. 9; P. O. Loran.

Taylor John, Sr., farmer; S. 9; P. O. Loran.

Tiffany C. J. farmer; Sec. 6; P. O. Willow.

TIFFANY DELZON, Farmer; Sec. 6; P. O. Plum River; born in Wayne Co., Pa., Feb. 24, 1820; lived in N. Y. two years; came to this Co. in 1839; settled on farm where he now resides; among first settlers; married Miss Betsy Lyon Dec. 31, 1847; she was born in Wayne Co., N. Y., June 7, 1825; have eight children living: Albinus, Columbus J., Mary E., Charles H., Palmer, Douglas, Orlena, Reuben; have lost three children; lost his wife June 28, 1871; has been Supervisor five years; owns 476 acres of land; he and his son, C. J., both members of A. F. and A. M.

Treuckenmeller G. L. farmer; Sec. 28; P. O. Loran.

WAGNER LAFAYETTE, Farmer and Teacher; Sec. 32; P. O. Mt. Carroll; was born in Stark Co., Ohio, Jan. 15, 1828; when quite young his father moved to Wayne Co.; in 1850 he left home and crossed the plains to California, and was in the gold mines ten years, then returned to Ohio, and in 1860 came to this Co.; Aug. 26, 1877, married Mrs. Keyser, whose maiden name was Nancy McGinnis; she had six children by her first marriage, four of whom are living: Mary J., William E., Elizabeth R., Rosanna. Mr. Wagner has taught school for 20 years; has been Supervisor and Justice of Peace; owns 207 acres of land.

WILLIAMS Z. TAYLOR, Farmer and Teacher; Sec. 29; P. O. Loran, Stephenson Co.; was born in this Co. Sept. 4, 1848, and has made his home here ever since; traveled through Iowa and Central Illinois; attended Mt. Hope school, Pleasant Valley, and Union school, Mt. Carroll; married Lucinda Mader April 14, 1870; she was born in this Co. May 5, 1852; one son, Wilber; owns 120 acres of land; he is now engaged in teaching the Union school in Berreman Tp.

WISE MRS. ESTHER, Farming; Sec. 4; P. O. Willow; maiden name was Esther Wolfley; she was born in Union Co., Pa., Dec. 15, 1822, and moved with her parents to Centre Co.; was married Dec. 8, 1845, to Frederic Wise, who was born in Germany, near the French line, Feb. 14, 1820; came to the U. S. in 1823, and in 1849 to Jo Daviess Co.; Mr. Wise died March 2, 1873; has seven children living: George, Henry, Mrs. Julia A. Parkinson, Mrs. Mary C. Calhoun, William, Randolph D., Jacob; William and Jacob are at the Rock River Seminary; owns 265 acres of land.

Wise George, farmer; Sec. 4; P. O. Willow.

WISE HENRY, Carpenter and Joiner; P. O. Willow; born in Ward's Grove, this Co., April 25, 1850; went to Neb. in 1871; was there three years; came back to this Co.; served an apprenticeship at his trade in Stephenson Co.; married Miss Mary J. Troxell Nov. 9, 1875; she was born in Pleasant Valley, this Co., Nov. 9, 1856; they have one child, Orus M., born Sept. 11, 1876; Mr. W. has lately erected a mill, in which he has a steam engine for grinding feed, and is already doing a good business.

Womer John, blacksmith; Willow.

YEOMANS JOHN, laborer; Willow.

Yeomans Wm. laborer; Willow.

PLEASANT VALLEY TOWNSHIP.

ADAMS ROBERT, laborer; Sec. 9; P. O. Pleasant Valley.

Allbright Henry, farmer; Sec. 18; P. O. Pleasant Valley.

Atchinson T. C. farm; Sec. 4; P. O. Derinda.

BERNAN JOHN, farmer; Sec. 10; P. O. Yankee Hollow.

Bradford Wm. farmer; Sec. 32; P. O. Polsgrove.

Rryant —, farmer; Sec. 36; P. O. Pleasant Valley.

Buckley John, farmer; Sec. 10; P. O. Pleasant Valley.

Buckley J. R. farmer; Sec. 10; P. O. Pleasant Valley.

Buckley Wm. farmer; Sec. 8; P. O. Derinda.

CAHILL JAMES, farmer; Sec. 4; P. O. Yankee Hollow.

Cahill Patrick, farmer; Sec. 4; P. O. Yankee Hollow.

Calend Ed. farm; Sec. 2; P. O. Plum River.

CAMPBELL DAVID, Farmer; Sec. 1; P. O. Plum River; born in Allegany Co., N. Y., July 12, 1834; came to this Co. in 1846; settled near Elizabeth; was married to Mary Miller, Sept. 30, 1859; she born in Cortland Co., N. Y., Nov. 27, 1832; two children living: Almira and Daniel De Forrest; lost seven: George H., Charles, Clarinda, Mary A., Henry Harry and Hattie; owns 189 acres of land; was Overseer of Highways two years.

Carroll Con, farmer; Sec. 18; P. O. Pleasant Valley.

Carroll Daniel, farmer; Sec. 10; P. O. Pleasant Valley.

Carroll Denis, farmer; Sec. 7; P. O. Derinda.

Carroll John, farmer; Sec. 7; P. O. Derinda.

Carroll John, Jr., farmer; Sec. 18; P. O. Derinda.

Carroll Jeremiah, Sr., farmer; Sec. 18; P. O. Derinda.

Carroll Jeremiah, Jr., farmer; Sec. 7; P. O. Derinda.

Carroll Robt. farmer; Sec. 18; P. O. Pleasant Valley.

Carroll Tim. farmer; Sec. 7; P. O. Derinda.

Carroll Wm. farmer; Sec. 7; P. O. Derinda.

Cashman Michael, farmer; Sec. 10; P. O. Pleasant Valley.

Clark Jacob, P. O. Pleasant Valley.

Cormany A. C. farmer; Sec. 36; P. O. Pleasant Valley.

Cormany George, farmer; Sec. 36; P. O. Pleasant Valley.

Cormany John, farmer; Sec. 36; P. O. Pleasant Valley.

Crowley Cornelius, farmer; Sec. 10; P. O. Pleasant Valley.

Crowley Dennis, farmer; Sec. 11; P. O. Yankee Hollow.

CROWLEY JEREMIAH D. Teacher; Sec. 2; P. O. Derinda; born in Boston, Mass., April 25, 1850; accompanied his father to this Co. the same year; has resided here ever since; was married Oct. 17, 1876, to Anna Shay; she was born in this Tp., Nov. 30, 1850; they have one daughter, Maud Ella, born July 23, 1877; Mr. C. is serving his first term as Supervisor; family are members of the Catholic Church.

Crummer John, farmer; Sec. 29; P. O. Pleasant Valley.

DARR DANIEL F. Assistant Postmaster; Pleasant Valley; born in Pa., Feb. 8, 1843; enlisted May, 1861, in the 8th Pa. Reserve; was in nine general engagements and numerous skirmishes; was mustered out in June, 1864; came to this Co. in 1872, to settle up his brother Henry's affairs, who died here in that year.

Davis Aaron, farmer; Sec. 15; P. O. Pleasant Valley.

Davis Cyrus, farmer; Sec. 15; P. O. Pleasant Valley.

Dawes Henry, farmer; Sec. 1; P. O. Plum River.

Davis James, farmer; Sec. 15; P. O. Pleasant Valley.

Davis John, farmer; Sec. 15; P. O. Pleasant Valley.

Davis Robert, farmer; Sec. 15; P. O. Pleasant Valley.

Davis Wm. J. Sec. 15; P. O. Pleasant Valley.

DEEDS DELILAH (Widow, maiden name Williams), Stock Farm; Sec. 27; P. O. Pleasant Valley; born in Tenn. Sept. 24, 1812; came to this Co. in 1833; her father was one of the settlers on Plum River; owns 1,264 acres of land; was married Sept. 29, 1840, to Thomas Deeds; he was born in Ky., Feb. 20, 1813; came to this Co. in 1833; served several terms as Supervisor; School Director a number of years, and Postmaster 20 years; died June 27, 1874; Mrs. Deeds is a member of the Church of God.

Diviny Wm. laborer; Sec. 13; P. O. Plum River.

Donahoe Cornelius, Sec. 15; P. O. Pleasant Valley.

Donahoe Dennis, farm; S. 7; P. O. Derinda.

Dunahue Daniel J. farmer; Sec. 7; P. O. Derinda.

Dunigan M. farmer; Sec. 7; P. O. Derinda.

EATON AMOS, farmer; Sec. 9; P. O. Yankee Hollow.

Eaton Daniel, farmer; Sec. 3; P. O. Yankee Hollow.

Eberly G. farmer; Sec. 32; P. O. Polsgrove.

Eberly M. farmer; Sec. 32; P. O. Polsgrove.

EDWARD GEORGE, Farmer; Sec. 9; P. O. Yankee Hollow; born in Monmouthshire, Eng., Dec. 8, 1826; came to this Co. in 1856; owns 432 acres of land; was married in 1860 to Emily Buss; she was born in Sussex Co., Eng., June 16, 1839; came to the U. S. in 1850; settled in Lena; they have no children of their own; a relative, Carrie Buss, makes her home with them, and has since she was a little child; she was born in Sussex, Eng., Sept. 29, 1854; came here in 1868.

Edwards Richard, farm; Sec. 3; P. O. Yankee Hollow.

Elfline George, farm laborer; Sec [illegible] P. O. Pleasant Valley.

Eutress John, farmer; Sec. 19; P. O. Pleasant Valley.

Eutress Michael, farm; Sec. 19; P. O. Pleasant Valley.

FARRISEE ROBERT, farmer; Sec. 9; P. O. Derinda.

Farisee Wm. farmer; Sec. 9; P. O. Derinda.

Finn Tim. farmer; Sec. 12; P. O. Plum River.

FITZSIMMONS ABRAM M. Farmer; Sec. 13; P. O. Pleasant Valley; born in Allegany Co., N. Y., March 17, 1836; came to this Co. in 1846; was married July 5, 1859, to Frances Sortore; she was born in same Co., May 22, 1842; they have six children living: Homer G., John F., Florence R., Charles M., George W. and James L.; lost two: Mary, died March 24, 1861, and one infant; Mr. F.'s father came here in 1846; the country was a wild prairie, a portion of which has since grown up with timber.

Fitzsimmons H. farm; Sec. 11; P. O. Pleasant Valley.

Fitzsimmons John, farmer; Sec. 22; P. O. Pleasant Valley.

Flack James, farmer; Sec. 4; P. O. Derinda.

FORBES GEORGE H. Merchant and Stock Dealer; Sec. 27; P. O. Pleasant Valley; born in Wooster, Ohio, Aug. 8, 1839; came to this Co. in 1859; enlisted Sept. 21, 1861, in the 3d Mo. Cavalry; was with them in all their marches, battles, etc.; was discharged Nov. 14, 1864, expiration term of service; was married March 10, 1867, to Helen W. Welden; she was born in Oswego Co., N. Y., Jan. 27, 1849; have four children: Maude C., born Nov. 20, 1867; Claude, May 16, 1872; Mark, Oct. 31, 1874, and Oliver, March 29, 1877; owns 250 acres of land; has served three years as Justice of the Peace, and four years as School Director.

Forbes J. H. farmer; Sec. 27; P. O. Pleasant Valley.

Forbes Roxwell, farmer; Sec. 29; P.O. Pleasant Valley.

Foust Andrew, farmer; Sec. 20; P. O. Pleasant Valley.

Foust Jacob, Sr., farm; Sec. 20; P. O. Pleasant Valley.

Foust Jacob, Jr., farmer; Sec. 20; P.O. Pleasant Valley.

Frederick Henry, farmer; Sec. 36; P. O. Pleasant Valley.

GARNER JOHN, farmer; Sec. 30; P. O. Pleasant Valley.

Gill Jerome, farmer; Sec. 23; P. O. Pleasant Valley.

Goodmiller Frank, farmer; Sec. 21; P. O. Pleasant Valley.

Goodmiller Lewis, farmer; Sec. 21; P. O. Pleasant Valley.

GOODMILLER MICHAEL, Farmer; Sec. 20; P. O. Pleasant Valley; born in Germany, Sept. 29, 1813; came to this country in 1839; was married in 1842 to Dorothea Keck, of Iowa; she was born in Germany, June 13, 1819; they moved to Galena in 1843, and to this farm in 1844, then a wild prairie; built his cabin and cleared up a farm; owns 560 acres, of which 400 are under cultivation; their children are: John, Margaret, Lewis, Michael, Caroline and Sarah; the oldest son, John, was a member of the 45th Ill.; served three years; Mr. G. has served four terms as School Director; belongs to the Lutheran Church.

Goodmiller Michael, Jr., farmer; Sec. 20; P. O. Pleasant Valley.

Green Wm. farmer; Sec. 23; P. O. Pleasant Valley.

Guild Benj. farmer; Sec. 3; P. O. Yankee Hollow.

Guild S. A. farmer; P. O. Pleasant Valley.

Gump George, farm; Sec. 36; P. O. Pleasant Valley.

HALL JAS. farmer; Sec. 21; P. O. Pleasant Valley.

Harpster John, renter; Sec. 2; P. O. Plum River.

Hazlebecher Adam, Sec. 20; P. O. Pleasant Valley.

Herrington J. B. S. 27; P.O. Pleasant Valley.

Hilliard Byran, farm; Sec. 8; P. O. Yankee Hollow.

Hilliard L. H. farmer; Sec. 4; P. O. Yankee Hollow.

Hillmer Henry, farmer; Sec. 2; P. O. Plum River.

Hoffman Adam, farm; Sec. 30; P. O. Pleasant Valley.

Horton George, farmer; Sec. 3; P. O. Yankee Hollow.

HOUSE RANSOM, Farmer; Sec. 2; P. O. Yankee Hollow. Born in Berkshire Co., Mass., July 14, 1804; was married in 1826, to Laura Williams; she was born in Chenango Co., N. Y., March 26, 1806; they came to this Co. in 1845, settled on this farm (then wild prairie), where they have ever since lived; owns 5 acres of land; they have five children living: Bradford, Albert E., Harriet (now Mrs. Eaton), Freeman H., and Leroy S.; lost seven: William, Walter, Seth W., Edwin, Anna M., and Mary J.; their granddaughter, Lillie R. Harrington, is also living with them.

Humphrey A. farm; S. 1; P. O. Plum River.

KEHOE ED. farmer; Sec. 16; P. O. Pleasant Valley.

Keller A. farmer; Sec. 19; P. O. Derinda.

Keller Bartol, farmer; Sec. 19; P. O. Derinda.

Kennedy D. farmer; Sec. 8; P. O. Derinda.

KENNEDY JAMES, Farmer; S. 12; P. O. Plum River; born in Ireland in 1810; was married to Alice Callahan in 1840; came to the U. S. in 1853; lived in N. Y. three years; moved from there to Stephenson Co., where they remained until 1865, then came to this Co.; owns 80 acres of land; they have three children living: John, James, and Mary; lost three: William, John, and Bridget; the oldest son, John, was a member of the 65th I. V. I.; mustered out in 1865; family all Catholics.

Kennedy J., Jr., Sec. 12; P. O. Plum River.

Kolb C. farm; Sec. 1; P. O. Plum River.

KUHNS DAVID, Farmer; Sec. 17; P. O. Pleasant Valley; born in Guernsey Co., O., May 6, 1819; was married in 1844, to Margaret A. Conden; she was born in Philadelphia April 17, 1823; came to this Co. in 1864; owns 120 acres of land; have eleven children living: Milley A., Mary J., Joseph, David P., Arabella, William L., Samuel C., Melissa M., Newel E., Hattie I., and George W.; lost two: Elizabeth and Margaret; Milley A. (Mrs. Barton) also lives here; she has five children: four girls and one boy; belong to the M. E. Church.

Kuhns W. L. farmer; Sec. 17; P. O. Pleasant Valley.

LAUGHRIN B. farmer; Sec. 29; P. O. Pleasant Valley.

Laughrin John, farmer; Sec. 15; P. O. Pleasant Valley.

Looney Patrick, Pleasant Valley.

Lytle Wm, laborer; Sec. 14; P. O. Pleasant Valley.

MALONE CON, farmer; Sec. 5; P. O. Derinda.

Malone Henry, P. O. Pleasant Valley.

Malone John M. laborer; Sec. 11; P. O. Yankee Hollow.

Malone William R. laborer; Sec. 10; P. O. Pleasant Valley.

Marlow Isaac, farmer; Sec. 16; P. O. Pleasant Valley.

Marlow Thomas, laborer; Sec. 16; P. O. Pleasant Valley.

Miller A. farmer; Sec. 2; P. O. Plum River.

Mitchell A. S. farmer; Sec. 16; P. O. Pleasant Valley.

Morarity Pat. farmer; Sec. 6; P. O. Derinda.

Morehead Jas. farmer; Sec. 21; P. O. Pleasant Valley.

Morehead Robt. renter; Sec. 23; P. O. Pleasant Valley.

MYERS DARIUS, Farmer; Sec. 9; P. O. Pleasant Valley; born in Oswego Co., N. Y., Dec. 18, 1816; came to this Co. in 1845; owns 160 acres of land; was married in 1852 to Melissa Appleby; she was born in Wayne Co., N. Y., March 20, 1836; they have ten children living: Epaminondas, Rebecca, Louisa, Marietha E., Lydia B., Darius E., Judah, Nebuchadnezzar and George (Twins) and Flora; lost two, Euclid died Jan. 15, 1860, and Jane Nov. 3, 1867; Mr. Myers served as Supervisor one year, Commissioner of Highways 3, and School Director several years; Religious belief Seventh Day Adventist.

Myers Epaminondas, teacher; Sec. 9; P. O. Pleasant Valley.

NASH AMASA, plasterer; Sec. 3; P. O. Yankee Hollow.

ORR GEO. renter; Sec. 27; P. O. Pleasant Valley.

PERRY JAMES, H. farmer; Sec. 1; P. O. Plum River.

PICKARD ALBERT, Farmer; Sec. 2; P. O. Plum River; born in Onondaga Co., N. Y., Aug. 27, 1833; came to Stephenson Co. when 4 years old; enlisted in Aug., 1861, in the 37th Regt. I. V. I.; was in the service till June 1, 1862, when he was discharged for disability; came to this Co. in Jan., 1863; was married Sept. 22, 1863, to Adaline Manzer; she was born in Hancock Co., Ill., Sept. 12, 1843; they have three children living: Roy W., born July 9, 1864; Anna M., Nov. 25, 1866, and Lucina J., April 25, 1875; lost one, Cora A., born June 24, 1869, died Oct. 20, 1876; owns 50 acres of land; was Overseer of Highways 3 years.

Pulley Adam, farmer; Sec. 20; P. O. Pleasant Valley.

Pulley Jos. farmer; Sec. 20; P. O. Pleasant Valley.

PULLEY WILLIAM, Farmer; Sec. 20; P. O. Pleasant Valley; born in Guernsey Co., Ohio, Jan. 20, 1820; was married in 1841 to Mary Kuhns; she was born in same Co., Aug. 15, 1812; owns 158 acres of land; have seven children living: Joseph S., Adam, Eliza, Mary C., Elizabeth A., Susie A. and Sarah J.; Samuel died in 1842, and William died of Small Pox, March, 1863, while South with his Regt., the 45th I. V. I.; Mr. Pulley came to this farm in 1860; served three terms as School Director.

RANDECKER MARTIN, farmer; Sec. 19; P. O. Pleasant Valley.

Rawlings J. C. farmer; Sec. 33; P. O. Pleasant Valley.

Reed Geo. farm; Sec. 1; P. O. Plum River.

Reed James, farmer; Sec. 17; P. O. Pleasant Valley.

Reed Lee, teacher; Sec. 17; P. O. Pleasant Valley.

REED JAMES, Farmer; Sec. 17; P. O. Pleasant Valley; born in Crawford Co., Pa., in Dec., 1815; was married June, 12, 1849, to Julia A. Weir; she was born in Mercer Co., Pa., Feb. 10, 1828; they came to this Co. in 1850; moved to Wis. in 1852; remained there till 1865, when they returned, and in 1867 bought the farm where they now reside; owns 211 acres; have six children: William, Cora E., Campbell, Lee J., John B. and Amos R.; Mr. R. was Tp. Trustee one term; belong to the U. P. Church.

ROBINSON HARVEY, Farmer; Sec. 14; P. O. Pleasant Valley; born in Delaware Co., N. Y., Oct. 16, 1836; emigrated to Ogle Co., Ill., in 1848, and to this Co. in 1868; owns 80 acres of land; was married Jan. 1, 1856, to Sarah Davis; she was born in Randolph Co., Ill., Oct. 11, 1833; they have five children living: Martha J., (now Mrs. McGinnis) Mary E., John P., Amos and Amanda; lost two, Henry and an infant; Mr. Robinson is serving his first term as School Director; is a Republican. Robert Davis and wife the father and mother of Mrs. Robinson are residents of this Tp., are both very near 80 years of age, have been married 56 years; he was a soldier during the entire Campaign against Black Hawk.

ROCK GEORGE M., Farmer; Sec. 13; P. O. Pleasant Valley; born in Lafayette Co., Wis., April 4, 1844; came to this Co. in 1850, with his mother, his father having died in 1846; owns 80 acres of land; was married Dec. 22, 1869, to Almira C. Frederick; she was born Dec. 1, 1851; they have three children living: Oscar O., Marion W., and Orin H.; one died in infancy; Mr. R. enlisted in the 45th I. I. V., in 1861; was with the regiment in all their marches, etc.; was in thirteen general engagements; mustered out in 1865: is now serving his first term as Town Collector; family attend the Church of God.

RUBLE GEORGE, Farmer; Sec. 13; P. O. Willow; born in Mifflin Co., Penn., Dec. 15, 1844; enlisted in June, 1863, in the 26th Pa.; served three months; came to this Co. in 1865; was married Dec. 15, 1871, to Clarinda Fulton; she was born

April 17, 1853, in the house they now occupy, her father being among the first settlers in this valley; they have one child living, Charles Wilbur, born March 8, 1875; lost one, Olla V., born Aug. 17, 1871, died Aug. 19, 1875; they are members of the M. E. Church.

RUBLE JACOB, Farmer; Sec. 12; P. O. Willow; born in Mifflin Co., Pa., Dec. 17, 1838; came to this Co. in 1866; owns 42 acres of land; was married in 1865 to Elizabeth Williams; she was born in Centre Co., Pa., Oct. 24, 1841; they have three children, Mary A., Regina E., and Margaret E.; Mr. R. enlisted Aug. 1, 1861, in the 1st Pa. V. C.; was in about twenty general engagements, and numerous skirmishes; was discharged Sept. 9, 1864; is serving his first term as School Director; they are members of the M. E. Church.

RUBLE JOHN, Farmer; Sec. 12; P. O. Willow; born in Mifflin Co., Pa., Jan. 14, 1801; came to this Co. in 1842; settled on this farm (then wild prairie, not yet in market); owns 225 acres; was married in 1825, to Julia A. Parkinson; she was born in Centre Co., Pa., in 1805, died in 1854; have five children living, Elizabeth J. (Lutz) resides in Ohio, Christiana, Susan, Rachel, and John; lost seven, James, Louis, William, Jacob, Rebecca, Becka A., and Julia A.; family attend the M. E. Church.

RUBLE JOHN C., Farmer; Sec. 13; P. O. Willow; born in Mifflin Co., Pa., Dec. 17, 1842; enlisted April 18, 1861, in the 1st Pa. V. C.; was with the regiment in twenty general engagements; was wounded at the battle of Malvern Hill; was a prisoner three months; discharged in June, 1865; came to this Co. in 1866; was married Nov. 28, 1867, to Susan Ruble; she was born in this Tp. Dec. 16, 1845; they have one daughter, Julia A., born July 16, 1868; Mr. R. is serving his second year as Road Commissioner, first as Justice of the Peace, and has served four years as School Director; Mrs. R. is a member of the M. E. Church.

Ruble J. W. farm; S. 12; P. O. Plum River.

Russell O. renter; S. 3; P. O. Plum River.

SAGE J. B. farmer; Sec. 23; P. O. Pleasant Valley.

Shay Michael, farmer; Sec. 8; P. O. Derinda

Smith J. R. minister; Sec. 16; P. O. Pleasant Valley.

Smith William S. farmer; Sec. 16; P. O. Pleasant Valley.

Sughroe Martin, farmer; Sec. 24; P. O. Pleasant Valley.

Sughroe Timothy, farmer; Sec. 4; P. O. Yankee Hollow.

Sunimy Chris. farmer; Sec. 23; P. O. Pleasant Valley.

Sunimy Samuel, farmer; Sec. 23; P.O. Pleasant Valley.

STRICKEL EDWARD, Farmer; Sec. 14; P. O. Pleasant Valley; born in Norfolk Co., England, Feb. 20, 1833; came to the U. S. in 1853; resided in New York until 1856, when he came to this Tp., where he has ever since resided; owns 198 acres of land; was married in 1852, to Mrs. Ruth Foster (maiden name, Price); she was born in Greenbriar Co., Va., Feb. 4, 1818; she has two children by first marriage, Rachel V. (now Mrs. Hilliard), and Hannah M.; they are all members of the Church of God, Pleasant Valley.

THOMAS ELI D. Farmer; Sec. 22; P. O. Pleasant Valley; born in Warren Co., Ky., Aug. 16, 1817; his father moved to Dubois Co., Ind., in 1819; from there to Vermillion Co., same state, in 1829, where he died in 1831; Mr. T. went to Coles Co., Ill., in 1837; was married Dec. 31, 1840, to Sarah Gaston; she was born in Meigs Co., Ohio, Nov. 16, 1820; they have seven children living: John W., Louisa A., George W., Lucretia G., Stephen M., Sarah E. and Eli A.; Joseph M. enlisted in the 45th I. V. I. in 1861; was in the battles of Ft. Donnelson, Pittsburg Landing and several other actions; died of small pox at Lagrange, Tenn., Feb. 13, 1863; Mr. T. was Commissioner of Highway four years; Assessor one year, and School Director ten years; owns between 400 and 500 acres of land.

Thomas Geo. farm; Sec. 29; P. O. Pleasant Valley.

Thompson James, farmer; Sec. 32; P. O. Pleasant Valley.

Thompson Thos., Sr., farmer; Sec. 33; P. O. Pleasant Valley.

Thompson Thos., Jr., renter; Sec. 33; P. O. Pleasant Valley.

Tolbet Jas. farmer; Sec. 32; P. O. Pleasant Valley.

Trainor Peter, laborer; Sec. 26; P. O. Pleasant Valley.

Troxell E. B. farmer; P. O. Plum River.

TROXELL JACOB, Farmer; Sec. 12; P. O. Plum River; born in White Deer Co., Pa., Aug. 14, 1830; came to this Co. in 1842; owns 280 acres of land; was married Feb. 7, 1856, to Mary E. May; she was born in Hancock Co., Ky., Dec. 23, 1833: have eight children: Mary J., Sarah A., Henry T., Webster D., Emma M., Sylvester G., William J. and Fannie G.; Mr. T. was Road Commissioner one year, and School Director six years; family attend the Church of God, Pleasant Valley; Mrs. T. is a member of the same.

TROXELL JACOB, (Deceased) born in Union Co., Pa., in 1794; was married Oct. 23, 1819, to Sarah Grimm; she was born in Berks Co., Pa., Feb. 14, 1798; came to this Co. in 1842, and to this farm in 1844; owns 280 acres of land; have eight children living: Elizabeth Pratt,

G B Stinchfield

NORA.

Henry, Mary Mackay, Jacob, Leah Fitzsimmons, Edward B., William and Sarah J.; lost two: Lucy, died in Pennsylvania, and John, died in Elizabeth, in 1845; Mr. T. was a soldier of 1812, and for a long time Captain of Melitia in Pa.; he died in 1852; Edward B. is in charge of the farm; he was Supervisor 7 years, Commissioner of Highways 3 years, Collector 2 years, and Township Trustee 16 years.

Troxell Wm. farmer; Sec. 12; P. O. Plum River.

VANDERHEYDEN EDWARD, farmer; Sec. 4; P. O. Winters.

Vanderheyden John, farmer; Sec. 9; P. O. Pleasant Valley.

WALTER ADAM, farmer; Sec. 31; P. O. Pleasant Valley.

Walter John, farmer; Sec. 31; P. O. Pleasant Valley.

WEIBLE MARTIN, Farmer; Sec. 20; P. O. Pleasant Valley; born in Germany, Jan. 15, 1837; came to this Co. in 1846; owns 180 acres of land; was married March 8, 1861, to Catherine Hauk; she was born in Germany, Feb. 22, 1842; they have three children living: Maggie, Anna M. and August; lost two: John, died Oct. 18, 1867, and Joseph, April 11, 1872; attend the Lutheran Church, of which Mrs. W. is a member.

WELDEN SHERMAN W. Farmer; Sec. 13; P. O. Pleasant Valley; born in Oswego Co., N. Y., July 17, 1820; was married April 18, 1848, to Charlotte Weed; she was born in same Co., Dec. 2, 1825; moved to Elgin, Ill., in 1853, and to this Co. in 1866; owns 175 acres of land; they have ten children living: Helen O., Frances A., Ella C., Amelia M., Allen J., Lucy M., Clara E., Edwin S., Cora E. and Minnie L.; Flora R. died Sept. 10, 1876, aged 18; Mr. W. has been School Director eight years.

White John, farmer; Sec. 30; P. O. Pleasant Valley.

Williams Preston, farmer; Sec. 22; P. O. Pleasant Valley.

Williams T. Sec. 22; P. O. Pleasant Valley.

Williams Watkins, farmer; Sec. 22; P. O. Pleasant Valley.

WINTERS GEORGE, Farmer; Sec. 31; P. O. Pleasant Valley; born in Prussia, July 24, 1827; came to this Co. in 1843; settled in Derinda; lived there till 1852, when he went to California; returned in 1854; was married July 5, 1857, to Theresa Haines, of Kansas; she was born in Hesse-Darmstadt, in 1838; bought this farm in 1857; was then a wild prairie; owns 375 acres of land; they have two children living: George W. and Sebastian; lost two: John and Louis; Mr. Winters was Town Clerk 2 years, Assessor 1 year, Supervisor 4 years, Justice of the Peace 16 years, and School Director 10 years; are members of the Lutheran Church.

ZELLERS LEE, renter; Sec. 27; P. O. Pleasant Valley.

Zink Jos. farmer; Sec. 29; P. O. Pleasant Valley.

Zink John, farmer; Sec. 29; P. O. Pleasant Valley.

WARD'S GROVE TOWNSHIP.

ANMAN JACOB, farmer; Sec. 28; P. O. Kent.

Appleby Leonard, farmer; Sec. 18; P. O. Plum River.

AURAND ALFRED, Farmer; Sec. 32; P. O. Kent, Stephenson Co.; born in Stephenson Co. Jan. 8, 1849; came to this Co. in 1866; married Mary T. Hodge, Nov. 30, 1871; she was born in Oxford, Wis., Aug. 20, 1853; have two children: Lillian M. and Harvey M.; owns 120 acres of land; Mrs. A.'s mother, Mrs. Margaret Hodge, whose maiden name was Moore, lives with them; she was born in Luzerne Co., Pa., Nov. 13, 1808; married Samuel Hodge, Esq., June 30, 1829; emigrated to Wis. in 1850; came to this Co. in 1861.

BEDFORD EDWARD, farmer; Sec. 4; P. O. Howardsville.

Biehl Joseph, farm; S. P. O. Howardsville.

Biehl M. farmer; Sec. 9; P.O. Howardsville.

Blair Wm. farm; S. 28; P. O. Plum River.

Borsdorf Augustus, farmer; Sec. 7; P. O. Pitcherville.

Bush A. farmer; Sec. 17; P. O. Plum River.

CLAY ALFRED, farmer; Sec. 32; P. O. Willow.

CRAFT WM. Farmer; Sec. 28; P. O. Kent, Stephenson Co.; born in Manc, Germany, July 15, 1829; came to the U. S. in 1854; married Elizabeth McCausland in Sept., 1851; she was born in Bath Co., Ky., Nov. 3, 1828; her father emigrated to Ill. in 1845; have five children living: Henry, Mrs. Georgianna Boguereif, Frank, Mary A., and Sarah; owns 150 acres of land; Mrs. C's mother, Jane McCausland (maiden name Price), was born in Lawrence Co.,

Ky., Sept. 8, 1808; she married Andrew McCausland, Esq.; he was born in Bath Co., Va., Feb. 20, 1807, died Sept. 5, 1877; her mother resides with them.

Cookson Abraham, farmer; Sec. 4; P. O. Howardsville.

Coombes Thos., Jr., Howardsville.

DICK ROBERT, Farmer; Sec. 31; P. O. Plum River; born in Co. Antrim, Ireland, May 24, 1843; parents moved to Co. Down when the subject of this sketch was quite young, and lived near Belfast till 1856 when they emigrated to America, coming direct to this Co.; married Mary E. Wilson Feb. 6, 1868; she was born in Hanover, this Co., Feb. 4, 1851; her father came to this Co. from Vermont in an early day, and married in this state; her mother was born in Southern Ill.; they have three children: Rachel Jane, Cora Ellen and Olive Veretta; owns 200 acres of land.

ERLEWINE DAVID, farmer; Sec. 30; P. O. Plum River.

FINKINBINDER D. farmer; Sec. 16; P. O. Kent.

Finkinbinder Emanuel, farmer; Sec. 17; P. O. Kent.

Finkinbinder John, farm; S. 17; P. O. Kent.

Finkinbinder Wm. farm; S. 16; P. O. Kent.

Fracher L. farmer; Sec. 33; P. O. Kent.

Furbeck Jacob, farmer; Sec. 5; P. O. Howardsville.

GATES E. W. farmer; Sec. 29; P.O. Plum River.

GRAVES HOMER, Farmer; Sec. 5; P. O. Howardsville; born in Sciota Co., Ohio, March 31, 1811; came to this Co. in the Spring of 1835; took up the claim upon which he now resides; he returned to his native home in the Fall, and in the year 1837 again came here, coming the entire distance on horseback; he started the 20th of March, arriving the 12th of April; was married Nov. 23, 1842, to Almira Maccomber, who was born in Worcester Co., N. Y., Feb. 23, 1822; his home was made desolate on July 23, 1865, by the death of his wife, and again on the 8th of Dec., 1869, by the death of his daughter Mary; has nine children living: Horace, Julia L., Homer J., Cyrus E., Emily, Charles, Annie E., John Q., George W.; Republican; Independent in religion.

GRAVES WILLIAM, Farmer; Sec. 8; P. O. Howardsville; born April 23, 1815, in Sciota Co., Ohio; at the age of twenty-two he came to this state, stopping first in Stephenson Co.; in 1838 he came to this Co.; he commenced life as a farm laborer, working by the month, and secured a piece of land in Sec. 8; as soon as getting $50 ahead he would go to Dixon and get forty acres more land until he acquired the beautiful home upon which he now resides; he was married Feb. 11, 1858, to Mary Dillon, who was born in Canada, Oct. 24, 1832; they have had four children: William B., George L., living; Charles H., Consider, dead; Republican; Independent in religion.

Groesbeck Dow, Farmer; Sec. 8: P. O. Plum River.

HASTINGS GEO. F. farmer; Sec. 16; P. O. Plum River.

Heidenreich Carl, farmer; Sec. 4; P. O. Howardsville.

Heleman John, farmer; Sec. 7; P. O. Plum River.

Hopkins H. E. farmer; Sec. 18; P. O. Plum River.

JOHNSON ALLEN, farmer; Sec. 31; P. O. Plum River.

KEESTER JNO. F. farmer; Sec. 16; P. O. Kent.

LACOCK ELISHA, farmer; Sec. 29; P. O. Plum River.

Lawfer Freeman, renter; Sec. 29; P. O. O. Plum River.

LAWFER JOSEPH, Farmer; Sec. 29; P. O. Plum River; was born in Monroe Co., Pa., Sept. 15, 1816; married Elizabeth Frantz April 28, 1839; she was born in Monroe Co., Pa., May 15, 1818; came to Stephenson Co. in 1856, and Jo Daviess Co. in 1857; they have seven children living: William, Mrs. Mary A. Tyrrell, Freeman, Mrs. Julia A. Shearer, Mrs. Lucinda Shearer, Lucy, wife of Wallace Gates, and Elizabeth; lost three children: James, Geo. H and Josiah; owns 207 acres of land; Lucy, their daughter, lives with them; has two children: Delma and Edith.

Lockington A. farmer; Sec. 28; P. O. Kent.

MACHAMER GEO. farmer; Sec. 33; P. O. Kent.

Metz J. farmer; Sec. 28; P. O. Kent.

MITCHELL ISAAC G. Carpenter; Sec. 29; P. O. Plum River; was born in Washington Co., Pa., Feb. 15, 1816; married Lydia Stillians Nov. 12, 1835; came to this Co. in 1849; two children living: Ellen Anna Maria and Joseph W. Blair; lost three children; has been Town Clerk fifteen years; is Justice of the Peace, and has been a successful teacher forty years: served in the 8th Regt. I. V. I., Co. K; was at battles of Stoneman, Muddy Branch, Fairfax Court House, and other important engagements; one son was killed at battle of Champion Hills, Miss., May 16, 1863; Mrs. Mitchell was born in Wilmington, Del., Dec. 14, 1819.

Mitchell J. W. B. Sec. 29; P. O. Plum River.

MOORE JOSEPH, Farmer; Sec. 19; P. O. Plum River; born Dec. 26, 1822, in Sciota Co., Ohio; at the age of fourteen he in company with his mother and elder brothers (his father being dead) left their native state to seek a home in the West; they first stopped in Stevenson Co., this state, remaining here but a short time; they in March, 1838, moved to this Co., settling on Sec. 5; in 1847 he moved on his present farm, where he has resided ever since; Mr. Moore started in life as a farm laborer, working three years at ten dollars per month, and by industry, economy and strict attention to business he stands to-day the acknowledged king farmer of Jo Daviess Co., owning 1,527 acres of land in one body, upon which graze 400 head of cattle; July 19, 1860, he married Calista Byron; she was born Nov. 22, 1832, in Tompkins Co., N. Y.; they have four children: Mittie M., Philip, Mary E., Florence; Republican; Independent in religion.

NUSS JOSEPH, farmer; Sec. 21; P. O. Kent.

PEMBERTON JOSEPH, farmer; Sec. 30; P. O. Plum River.

Pemberton Winfield, P. O. Plum River.

Phelps Harvey, farmer; Sec. 8; P. O. Lena.

Pierce Jacob, farmer; Sec. 29; P. O. Plum River.

REBER JACOB, Farmer; Sec. 21; P. O. Kent; born in Centre Co., Pa., Jan. 27, 1808; was married to Miss Sarah Kern Dec. 5, 1830; she was born in Centre Co., Pa., and died May 11, 1848; he has six children living by this marriage: Eliza, Mary, John, Jacob, Catherine, and Wm. G.; in 1850 married Mrs. Frese, whose maiden name was Reninger; she was born in Union Co., Pa., in 1824; she had two sons by her first marriage, both of whom she lost in the army; they have six children living: Frank H., Jackson, Samuel, Ira, Adaline, Adaline; lost one child, Douglas; Mr. R. owns 418 acres of land; he was among the earliest settlers of this Co., and is one of its most respected and honored citizens.

REBER WM. G. Farmer; Sec. 33; P. O. Kent, Stephenson Co.; was born in Ward's Grove Tp., July 24, 1841; enlisted in 92d I. V. I., Sept. 4, 1862, and served during the war; went with Sherman to Martelle, Ga., and returned to Indianapolis; was troubled with sore eyes while in the army; honorably discharged at Chicago in 1865; married Miss Mary A. Fisher, Feb. 24, 1867; she was born in Lancaster Co., Pa., June 30, 1843, and came to Ill. in 1855; three children living: Louemma, John O., Winnie M.; three dead; owns 300 acres of land.

Reiland Nicholas, farmer; Sec. 4; P. O. Howardsville.

ROGERS MRS. CYNTHIA, Farming; Sec. 8; P. O. Howardsville; her maiden name was Miss Perkins; was born in Oneida Co., N. Y.; her parents emigrated to Ohio when she was eight years old; then to Schuyler Co., Ill.; returned to Ohio, and from there back to Vermillion Co., Ill.; came to this Co. in 1847; was married to Mr. Abner W. Rogers in 1848; he was born in Lyme, N. Y., and died in 1869; one son living, Walter N. Rogers, born June 18, 1855, in this Co.; he married Miss Ada Weelock, Dec. 25, 1876; they have one child, John W.; Mrs. R. owns 647 acres of land, and her son, Walter N., 200 acres.

Rogers Walter; Sec. 8; P. O. Howardsville.

Roths John, farm; Sec. 7; P. O. Pitcherville.

SCHLOTMAM, CHAS. farmer; Sec. 16; P. O. Howardsville.

TUCKER ALFRED, shoemaker; Plum River.

TYRRELL ARTHUR (Deceased); born Sept. 29, 1815, in Hancock, Hillsborough Co., N. H.; in the year 1835 he came to this state, first stopping in Kane Co., and in Oct., 1836, he came to this Co., and settled in Ward's Grove Tp. upon a claim; he remained here and improved his claim until the year 1849, when he started for California by the overland route; it was late in the season when they started, and they encountered many hardships, most of their stock perishing from hunger on the way; on this trip he contracted the chronic diarrhœa from which he never fully recovered; returned to Jo Daviess Co. in 1853, and died June 13, 1872; was married to Louisa J. Partridge Jan. 8, 1846, who was born June 7, 1831; he left his widow and eight children in good circumstances: Omar A., Franklin S., Cassius N., Abby P., Charlotta E., Miles M., Dudley B., Mary A., living, and Eliza A., Julia A., dead; Democrat; Independent in religion.

Tyrrell Franklin, farmer; Sec. 17; P. O. Plum River.

Tyrrell Jas. L. farmer; Sec. 19; P. O. Plum River.

Tyrrell Omar A. farmer; Sec. 28; P. O. Plum River.

TYRRELL SAMUEL, Farmer; Sec. 19; P. O. Plum River; born Aug. 18, 1810, in Hancock, Hillsborough Co., N. H.; he remained at home working on a farm until the Spring of 1830, when he went to Lowell, Mass., and worked in the cotton mills there until the year 1837; in Nov. of this year he came to Jo Daviess Co., this state, settled on a claim in this Tp., in Sec. 20; was married Sept. 9, 1855, to Mrs. Lucy Tyrrell; her maiden name was Lucy Ellis, she having been previously married to Alden Tyrrell, a cousin; she was born Nov. 7, 1813, in Springfield, Windsor Co., Vt., in 1839; he was elected Justice of the Peace, which office he has held almost continuously, and is now serving his ninth term of four years each; in 1846 he was elected Treasurer of the School Board, which office he has held ever since; he is now Chairman of the Board of Supervisors, to which office he was elected in 1856, and has served his Co. in this capacity ever since; Mr. Tyrrell was one of the earliest settlers of this Co., and has acquired and held the confidence of his neighbors since coming here; he is a strict temperance man, not having touched spirituous liquors since he was 16 years old; no children; Independent in religion.

WALDO LYMAN, farmer; Sec. 18; P. O. Plum River.

Waldo S. E. farm; S. 7; P. O. Plum River.

WARD BERNARD, Farmer; Sec. 17; P. O. Plum River; born Nov. 8, 1808, in Underhill, Chittenden Co., Vt.; left his native state when 19 years of age; coming to Ohio, he spent the Winter there, and in the Spring of 1828 came to Galena, in this Co.; he remained around the mining districts for some time, and in May, 1836, came to this Tp., settling on Sec. 17, where he has remained ever since; the subject of this sketch was the first settler in this Tp., the Tp. deriving its name from him; he erected the first log cabin, in which he taught the first school in the Tp, which was taught gratuitously; has served as Justice, also as Town Clerk; Mr. Ward has always taken an active part in the advancement of all that pertains to education, and is regarded as an honest and honorable man; never married; Spiritualist; Republican.

Workheiser Armandus, farmer; Sec. 9; P. O. Kent.

White Wm. farmer; Sec. 16; P. O. Lena.

Wolffe Wm. renter; Sec. 31; P. O. Willow.

YEAGER PETER, farmer; Sec. 30 P.; O. Lena.

VINEGAR HILL TOWNSHIP.

ALLEN JAMES, miner, Sec. 25; P. O. Galena.

Allison J. farm; S. 22; P. O. Excelsior Mills.

Allison L. farm; S. 22; P. O. Excelsior Mills.

Allison J. farm; S. 22; P. O. Excelsior Mills.

Augfang M. gardener; Sec. 35; P. O. Galena.

BACKER CONRAD, farmer; S. 26; P. O. Galena.

Backer Jacob, farmer; Sec. 26; P. O. Galena.

Bedford F. farm laborer; S. 33; P. O. Galena.

Bell Wm. miller; Sec. 28; P. O. Mill Brigg.

Bennett G. merchant; Sec. 20; P. O. Galena.

Beggin Barnard, miner; S. 20; P. O. Galena.

Beggin John, miner; Sec. 20; P. O. Galena.

Biggins M. miner; Sec. 20; P. O. Galena.

Boher John, Sr., miner, S. 29; P. O. Galena.

Boher John, Jr., miner; S. 29; P. O. Galena.

Boher Thos., Sr., miner; S. 29; P. O. Galena.

Boher Thos., Jr., miner; S. 29; P. O. Galena.

Bolton J. merchant; Sec. 20; P. O. Galena.

Bussau G. farmer; Sec. 34; P. O. Galena.

Bussau H. farmer; Sec. 34; P. O. Galena.

Butter Jer. miner; Sec. 28; P. O. Galena.

CAIN CHARLES, miner; Sec. 21; P. O. Galena.

Champion H. miner; Sec. 21; P. O. Galena.

Champion J. miner; Sec. 21; P. O. Galena.

Conners B. H. farmer; Sec. 26; P. O. Galena.

Conners John, farmer; Sec. 26; P. O. Galena.

Conners Michael, teamster; Excelsior Mills.

DALLYN JOHN, farmer; Sec. 36, P. O. Galena.

Dawson John, miner; Sec. 21; P. O. Galena.

Day James, miner; Sec. 21; P. O. Galena.

Day John, miner; Sec. 21; P. O. Galena.

Day John, miner; Sec. 21; P. O. Galena.

Day Patrick, miner; Sec. 21; P. O. Galena.

Day Thomas, farmer; Sec. 20; P. O. Galena.

Dolsing J. E. farm; Sec. 27; P. O. Excelsior Mills.

Doyle James, miner; Sec. 28; P. O. Galena.

Doyle Michael, miner; Sec. 28; P. O. Galena.

Doyle Moses, miner; Sec. 28; P. O. Galena.

Doxey Jacob, farmer; Sec. 24; P. O. Galena.

Doxey Thos. farmer; Sec. 24; P. O. Galena.

Doxey Wm. H. farm; Sec. 24; P. O. Galena.

Duggan James, miner; Sec. 21; P. O. Galena.

Duggan John, miner; Sec. 21; P. O. Galena.

EDWARDS SAMUEL, miner; Sec. 21; P. O. Galena.

FEEHAN MARTIN, farmer; Sec. 25; P. O. Galena.

Flynn David, miner; Sec. 29; P. O. Galena.
Flynn J., Sr., miner; Sec. 29; P. O. Galena.
Flynn J., Jr., miner; Sec. 29; P. O. Galena.
Funk George, farmer; Sec. 26; P. O. Galena.

FURLONG JOHN E. Retired Farmer; Vinegar Hill; born 16th of Nov., 1837; was married to Catherine C. Murray in 1864; have six children: Ann C., Lawrence, Wm. P., James E., Mary and Agnes E.; the Tp. was named by his father, John Furlong, in 1827; married Ann Carroll Oct. 28, 1828; married by the Rev. Father Bading; William F., his brother, was the first child born in Vinegar Hill; was born Aug. 30, 1829; Mr. F. is the present Supervisor, and owns 360 acres of land in Vinegar Hill.

GAUSS J. F. farmer; Sec. 33; P. O. Galena.
Gauss Philip, farmer; Sec. 33; P. O. Galena.
Gavin Joseph, miner; Sec. 28; P. O. Galena.
Gavin Simon, miner; Sec. 28; P. O. Galena.
Glasson Benj. miner; Sec. 21; P. O. Galena.
Glasson James, miner; Sec. 21; P. O. Galena.
Glasson John, miner; Sec. 20; P. O. Galena.
Goodburn J. miner; Sec. 21; P. O. Galena.
Graham Geo. farmer; Sec. 36; P. O. Galena.
Gray John W. miner; Sec. 16; P. O. Galena.

HINCHY ANDREW, miner; Sec. 28; P. O. Galena.
Hocking J. miner; Sec. 21; P. O. Galena.
Hocking Jos. miner; Sec. 21; P. O. Galena.

HOCKING THOMAS, Miner; Sec. 21; P. O. Galena; born in Co. Cornwall, England, July 29, 1847; came to this country and to this Co. in 1849; has been engaged in mining for eighteen years; owns 1½ acres of land valued at $300; married Sarah Walton, April 28, 1869; she was born in Durham Co., England, Feb. 15, 1849; they have four children: Sarah Jane, Thomas H., Alice and William, and one dead; Mr. and Mrs. Hocking are members of the M. E. Church.

Horan J., Sr., miner; Sec. 29; P. O. Galena.
Horan M. J. miner; Sec. 29; P. O. Galena.
Hull Thomas, miner; Sec. 21; P. O. Galena.

JACKSON JOHN, Sr., farmer; Sec. 24; P. O. Galena.
Jackson J. P., Jr., farmer; Sec. 24; P. O. Galena.

KELLY CON. miner; Sec. 21; P. O. Galena.
Kennedy M. farmer; Sec. 21; P. O. Galena.
Kennedy T. farmer; Sec. 21; P. O. Galena.
Kennedy T. farmer; Sec. 21; P. O. Galena.
King H., Sr., farmer; Sec. 36; P. O. Galena.
King H., Jr., farm; Sec. 36; P. O. Galena.

LANE HENRY, farmer; Sec. 33; P. O. Galena.
Lane Thos. farmer; Sec. 33; P. O. Galena.
Liddle Foster, miner; Sec. 21; P. O. Galena.
Liddle J. E. miner; Sec. 21; P. O. Galena.
Lifker B. farmer; Sec. 22; P. O. Excelsior Mills.
Lindsey T. farmer; Sec. 22; P. O. Excelsior Mills.
Lulwing H. farmer; Sec. 22; P. O. Galena.

McCARTY PATRICK, miner; Sec. 25; P. O. Galena.
McClaren, miner; Sec. 21; P. O. Galena.
McCormick M. farm; Sec. 26; P. O. Galena.
McGuire H. farmer; Sec. 24; P. O. Galena.
McGuire M. teacher; Sec. 29; P. O. Galena.
McGuire T. miner; Sec. 29; P. O. Galena.
McKernan D. miner; Sec. 21; P. O. Galena.
McKernan J. miner; Sec. 21; P. O. Galena.
McKernan J., Sr., miner; S. 20; P.O. Galena.
McKernan J., Jr., miner; S. 20; P.O. Galena.
McKernan W. miner; Sec. 29; P. O. Galena.
McManus A. farmer; Sec. 36; P. O. Galena.
McManus M. farmer; Sec. 26; P. O. Galena.
McManus P. farmer; Sec. 26; P. O. Galena.
McManus W. farmer; Sec. 26; P. O. Galena.
Madden P. farmer; Sec. 36; P. O. Galena.
Mahoney D. farmer; Sec. 23; P. O. Galena.
Mahoney J. farmer; Sec. 23; P. O. Galena.
Manly M. miner; Sec. 25; P. O. Galena.
Manly P. farmer; Sec. 25; P. O. Galena.
Mann Daniel, farmer; Sec. 25; P. O. Galena.

MANN HARVEY, Whose portrait appears in this work, was born in Aurelius, Cayuga Co., N. Y., Oct. 21., 1805. From tradition he is a descendant of one of four German brothers that emigrated to America on the "Mayflower." His grandfather came from the State of Vermont, when he was 84 years old, to Aurelius, Cayuga Co., N. Y., where he died and was buried. His father, Frederick Mann, died at the age of 67, and was buried in Waterloo, Monroe Co., Ills. The subject of this sketch came to the State of Illinois in April, 1830, and lived one year on a farm two miles south of Port Deposit (now Chester). He also lived six years in Waterloo, Monroe Co., Ills., engaged mostly in farming. In June, 1827, he came to Fever River (now Galena River), and followed mining until the Fall of 1828, when he came to Galena, and contracted for grading the streets and building a wharf by the "Big Spring," near where the iron bridge now is. In the Fall of 1829 he also took a contract to build a Government warehouse, for the storage of lead. In 1830 he commenced making a farm on Government land, in Vinegar Hill Tp. In 1835 he was engaged in smelting, and in 1836 built a saw mill on the "Sinsinawa River." He is now engaged in farming. Has served two terms as Co. Commissioner, one term as Chairman of Board of Supervisors, and two terms as a Magistrate in Vinegar Hill Tp. He married Catharine Sidner, Feb. 14, 1837, in what is now Menominee Tp., in this Co. She was born June 4th, 1824, in Pike Co., Missouri. They had thirteen children: Lydia Anna, born Aug. 24, 1840; Adelia Margaret, Dec. 26, 1842; Frederick, Jan. 28, 1845, died April 18, 1845; James Harvey, March 26, 1846; William Henry, March 30, 1848; Susan Violet, April 2, 1850; Joseph, Aug. 22, 1852, died Nov. 20, 1872; Daniel, Nov. 28, 1854; Mary Lucy, Feb. 14, 1856; Alvina Jane, March 1, 1858; Thomas Ezekiel, May 5, 1860; Charles, April 10, 1862, and George Eugene, Aug. 17, 1864.

Murphy A. farmer; Sec. 26; P. O. Excelsior Mills.

Murphy D. miner; Sec. 20; P. O. Galena.

Murphy P., Sr., miner; S. 20; P. O. Galena.

Murphy P., Jr., miner; S. 20; P. O. Galena.

Mylan John, miner; Sec. 21; P. O. Galena.

NOBLE THOMAS, farmer; Sec. 21; P. O. Galena.

O'ROURKE DANIEL, farmer; Sec. 28; P. O. Galena.

O'Rourke T. farmer; Sec. 28; P. O. Galena.

O'Roure Wm. farmer; Sec. 28; P. O. Galena.

PEIRT JACOB, miner; Sec. 21; P. O. Galena.

Poling J. D. farmer; Sec. 24; P. O. Galena.

QUIRK FRANK, farmer; Sec. 35; P. O. Galena.

READY DENNIS, miner; Sec. 28; P. O. Galena.

Ready M. miner; Sec. 28; P. O. Galena.

Rewarth John, miner; S. 21; P. O. Galena.

Richards John, miner; S. 20; P. O. Galena.

Roberts John, farmer; S. 14; P. O. Galena.

Roop George, miner; S. 20; P. O. Galena.

Ryan James, miner; Sec. 29; P. O. Galena.

Ryan Patrick, miner; S. 25; P. O. Galena.

Ryan Thomas, miner; S. 29; P. O. Galena.

SCHERKEY FRANK, miner; Sec. 26; P. O. Galena.

Scherky Fred. miller; Excelsior Mills.

SCOTT JAMES W. Farmer; Sec. 32; P. O. Galena; born in Jo Daviess Co., Ill., March 10, 1842; he has been engaged in farming over eighteen years; Republican, and a member of the M. E. Church.

Scott Thomas, farmer; Sec. 32; P.O. Galena.

Seward R. miner; Sec. 29; P. O. Galena.

Shaber Louis, farmer; Sec. 33; P. O. Galena.

Shortell W. miner; Sec. 25; P. O. Galena.

Sidner Fred. farmer; Sec. 26; P. O. Galena.

Skehan R. miner; Sec. 26; P. O. Galena.

Snair Henry, Sr., farm; S. 24; P. O. Galena.

Snair Henry, Jr., farm; S. 24; P. O. Galena.

Speeker C. farmer; Sec. 26; P. O. Galena.

Spensley Mason, smelter; Sec. 27; P. O. Excelsior Mills.

Spensley Richard, smelter; Sec. 27; P. O. Excelsior Mills.

Spilane Daniel, Sr., miner; Sec. 29; P. O. Galena.

Spilane Daniel, Jr., miner; Sec. 29; P. O. Galena.

Spilane T. miner; Sec. 29; P. O. Galena.

Springer L. laborer; Sec. 13; P. O. Galena.

Stockle Henry, farmer; Sec. 27; P. O. Excelsior Mills.

Stockle John, farm; Sec. 27; P. O. Excelsior Mills.

Stoots Leonard, farm; Sec. 23; P. O. Galena.

TEMPE CLEMENT, farmer; Sec. 34; P. O. Excelsior Mills.

Thompson John, farmer; Sec. 36; P. O. Galena.

Thompson Joseph, farmer; Sec. 36; P. O. Galena.

Thompson S. farmer; Sec. 36; P. O. Galena.

Trevarion John, miner; Sec. 20; P.O. Galena.

Turnbull Louis, farmer; Sec. 34; P. O. Excelsior Mills.

WALCH JAMES, farmer; Sec. 36; P. O. Galena.

Walch John, miner; Sec. 36; P. O. Galena.

Walch John, Sr., farmer; Sec. 36; P. O. Galena.

Walch John, Jr., farm; Sec. 36; P.O. Galena.

Walker Thos. miner; Sec. 21; P. O. Galena.

Walton James, miner; Sec. 21; P. O. Galena.

Walton J. miner; Sec. 21; P. O. Galena.

Walton Wm., Jr., miner; Sec. 20; P. O. Galena.

Waters John, miner; Sec. 20; P. O. Galena.

Wenner Chas. farmer; Sec. 33; P. O. Galena.

Wermouth N. miner; Sec. 21; P. O. Galena.

Wevan F. farmer; Sec. 33; P. O. Galena.

Wilkinson Hugh, miner; Sec. 28; P. O. Mill Brigg.

Williams J. farmer; Sec. 14; P. O. Hazel Green, Wis.

Williams Paul, farmer; Sec. 14; P. O. Hazel Green, Wis.

Wilmarth P. M. farm; Sec. 33; P. O. Galena.

Wilmarth W. farmer; Sec. 33; P. O. Galena.

Wylan Wm. farmer; Sec. 21; P. O. Galena.

YOURT GEORGE, Sr., miner; Sec. 20; P. O. Galena.

Yourt Geo., Jr., miner; Sec. 20; P. O. Galena.

Yourt Peter, miner; Sec. 20; P. O. Galena.

RICE TOWNSHIP.

ARNOTT GEORGE.

BAKER HOWARD, miner; P. O. Galena.

Baker Jacob, renter; P. O. Galena.

Bouatal Peter, retired farmer; P. O. Galena.

Boutch Francis, farmer; P. O. Galena.

Boutch John, farmer; P. O. Galena.

Brooks T. farmer and miner; P. O. Galena.

Brein Rudolph, farmer and fisherman; P. O. Galena.

Brink Rudolph, farmer; P. O. Galena.

Burns Morris, farmer; P. O. Galena.

Burns Thos. farmer; P. O. Galena.

CALVERT RICHARD, laborer; P. O. Hanover.

Campbell David, farm; Sec. 2; P. O. Galena.

Campbell Jas. farmer; Sec. 2; P. O. Galena.

Creighton John, Sr., farmer; Sec. 23; P. O. Galena.

Collins M. farmer; Sec. 25; P. O. Galena.

DATER ANTON, farmer; P. O. Galena.

Dater Bernard, farmer; P. O. Galena.

DICK ROBERT K. Farmer; Sec. 25; P. O. Galena; owns 400 acres of land; was born in Co. Antrim, Ireland, in Oct., 1810; came to this country in 1829, and settled in Pa., in which state he remained eight years; during his stay in that state he was married to Miss Margaret Marshall, Feb. 9, 1836; she was born in Ireland Dec. 23, 1808; they came to this Co. in 1837; Mr. Dick has held various town and school offices during his residence in this Tp; they have had seven children; the living are: Ann Jane, now Mrs. James Speers, born Aug. 10, 1838; John E., May 20, 1844; Elizabeth L., Nov. 3, 1845, she is now Mrs. J. Wilson; Robert K., Dec. 25, 1846; William H., Aug. 17, 1849.

Dick Wm. H. farm; Sec. 25; P. O. Hanover.

Donavan Daniel, farmer; P. O. Galena.

ENTWHISTLE ROSS, farmer; Sec. 24; P. O. Galena.

FANNAN JAMES, farmer; P. O. Galena.

Feist Bernard, miner; P. O. Galena.

Fidler Edward, miner; P. O. Galena.

Freil Charles, renter; P. O. Galena.

Freil Frank, renter; P. O. Galena.

Funston Adam, farmer; P. O. Galena.

Funston David, farm; Sec. 15; P. O. Galena.

Funston George C. farmer; P. O. Galena.

Funston John, farm; Sec. 14; P. O. Galena.

Funston William S.

GAMMON JAMES, farmer; P. O. Galena.

GINN JAMES, Farmer; Sec. 12; P. O. Galena; owns 350 acres of land; was born in Philadelphia, Pa., Dec. 29, 1830; moved to this Co. with his parents in 1834; on the 2d of Feb., 1859, he married Miss Jane Funston, in Town of Rice; she was born in Ireland Nov. 1, 1839; Mr. Ginn was elected Supervisor of this Tp. last Spring (1877) and is the present incumbent of that office; he has held the office of Sheriff of Jo Daviess Co. two years; was also Deputy Sheriff two years; in 1861 he enlisted in Co. H, 3d Mo. V. I.; served as a Sergeant; was honorably discharged at St. Louis, Mo., Nov. 2, 1864; he has been in many severe engagements, among them being the battles of Vicksburg, Atlanta, and a series of battles around each one of those places; his father (Johnson Ginn) came to this Co. in 1834, thus becoming one of the pioneers of the Northwest, resides in Galena.

Golden H. farmer; Sec. 26; P.O. Hanover.

Gray David, farmer; Sec. 35; P. O. Hanover.

Gray James, farmer; Sec. 35; P. O. Hanover.

Gray Wm. J. farmer; Sec. 9; P. O. Galena.

Guebsmith P. farmer; P. O. Galena.

HECKELSMILLER PHILIP, farmer; P. O. Galena.

Heckelsmiller Peter, renter; P. O. Galena.

Heffern V. farmer: Sec. 22; P. O. Galena.

Hemes Max. farmer; P. O. Galena.

Henry Robert, farmer; Sec. 10; P.O. Galena

Hines John, farmer; P. O. Galena.

Hughs Ellis, retired; Galena.

Hysel G. W. miner; Galena.

Hysel Wm. A. teamster; Galena.

JENNINGS ANDREW, renter; P. O. Galena.

Jerome Ambrose, laborer; Galena.

Johnston John C. farm; Sec. 2; P.O. Galena.

KAMPHOUSE WM. miner; Galena.

Katen Patrick, farmer; P. O. Galena.

Kipp Bernard, farmer; P. O. Galena.

Kipp Henry, farmer; Sec. 4; P.O. Galena.

LAMPA BERNARD, farmer; P. O. Galena.

Lucy Dennis, laborer; Galena.

Lucy Jerry, miner; Galena.

Lucy Michael, laborer; Galena.

Lyden Martin, farmer; Sec. 26; P. O. Galena.

McAFEE WM. laborer; Galena.

McAllister A. farmer and school teacher; Sec. 35; P. O. Hanover.

McCormack D. farm; Sec. 13; P. O. Galena.

McCormack John, farmer; P. O. Galena.

McCormack Patrick, retired; Galena.

Miller John, laborer; Galena.

Morris James, renter; P. O. Galena.

Mougin A. farmer; Sec. 15; P. O. Galena.

PERSHANG NICHOLAS, farmer: Sec. 27; P. O. Galena.

QUIGLEY JNO. farmer; P. O. Hanover.

Quinlin John, laborer; Galena.

ROBINSON ADAM, farmer; Sec. 2; P. O. Galena.

Robinson David, farm; Sec. 2; P. O. Galena.

Ross R. M. farmer; Sec. 35; P. O. Hanover.

SANDERS FRANCIS, miner; Galena.

Sanders Joseph, renter; P. O. Galena.

Sanderson David, renter; P. O. Galena.

Sanderson James, renter; P. O. Galena.

Sanderson John, school teacher; Galena.

Sanderson Saml. farmer; P. O. Galena.

Sanderson Stewart, renter; P. O. Galena.

Sharp A. farmer; Sec. 16; P. O. Galena.

Sherrill John, renter; P. O. Galena.

Sherrill Lafayette, laborer; Galena.

Shubert August, farmer; P. O. Galena.

Shuleyr G. farmer; Sec. 9; P. O. Galena.

Shuleyr Wm., miner; Galena.

Sincox John, miner; Galena.

Spratt Geo. W. miner; Galena.

Spratt John, farmer; Sec. 5; P. O. Galena.

Steele R. farmer; Sec. 35; P. O. Hanover.

Steele John A. laborer; Hanover.

Steele John J. school teacher; Hanover.

VIRTUE DAVID A. farmer; Sec. 11; P. O. Galena.

VIRTUE DAVID, Farmer; Sec. 12; P. O. Galena; owns 100 acres of land; was born in County Donegal, Ireland, in the year of 1805; came to this Co. in 1845, and located in this Tp., and it has been his home since; in looking among the Tp. Records we find that he has held most every office known in the catalogue of Tp. and School offices, among them being that of Justice of the Peace, which office he has held twelve years, Town Treasurer twenty-four consecutive years; he is the present incumbent of the offices of Justice of the Peace and Town Collector; he has been twice married; first wife was Catherine Read; she was born in Ireland in 1804; they were married in 1828; she died in 1829; present wife was Margaret Roe; they were married in Ireland; they have had five children, viz.: William Roe, born Nov. 10, 1830; Eliza Jane (now Mrs. J. Gray), Nov. 16, 1834; Robert, Nov. 28, 1837; he enlisted in Co. A, 96th Regt. I. V. I.; was in many hard-fought battles, among them being the battles of Nashville and Franklin; he died on Dec. 6, 1865; Ellen, in 1842; James, April 20, 1845, died in infancy.

Virtue J. S. farmer; Sec. 12; P. O. Galena.

Virtue John, farmer; Sec. 12; P. O. Galena.

VIRTUE WILLIAM I. Farmer; Sec. 13; P. O. Galena; owns 200 acres of land; was born in Galena, in this Co., on Sept. 25, 1841; in 1861, when the dark clouds of war overshadowed our land and armed hands threatened the dissolution of the union of our fathers, he answered his country's call and enlisted in Co. A, 96th Regt. I. V. I., in which Regt. he served three years; he was honorably discharged; was in every engagement with the enemy that his Regt. was; he was promoted Corporal in 1863; was married to Miss Martha Campbell in this town (Rice) on March 7, 1867; she was born in Galena in 1842; they have six children: viz.: Adam Howard, Feb. 14, 1868; Mary Jane, April 14, 1870; Margaret Eliza, Nov. 11, 1871; Anna G., July 11, 1873; David Samuel, Jan. 9, 1876; Sarah Rebecca, Nov. 12, 1877.

VIRTUE WILLIAM ROE, Farmer; Sec. 12; P. O. Galena; owns 140 acres of land; was born in Ireland Nov. 10, 1830; came to this Co. with his parents in 1845; in politics he has always been Republican, casting first vote for Winfield Scott; is the present School Trustee, which office he has held for the last sixteen years; he married Miss Jane Virtue in this town on May 3, 1860; she was born in Galena on Oct. 12, 1839; they have had two children: M. Emma, born Aug. 15,

James Hood

NORA.

1861; Addie Lavina, March 7, 1864, died March 17, 1874.

Few the starry Summers,
That o'er her path had flown,
Ere the angels called her
To the far unknown.

Smiles of gleaming brightness,
Wreathed that fair young face;
Till its placid whiteness
Told of death's embrace.

Mrs. Virtue's father (Adam Virtue) was born in Ireland in 1809; he embraced religion in 1832, when he identified himself with the M. E. Church, of which he remained a faithful member; he came to this Co. in 1836, thus becoming one of the pioneers of Jo Daviess Co.; he worked earnestly for the establishment of schools and churches in the community in which he lived; his wife was Margaret Boyd; they were married in Ireland; he died in this Co. on Sept. 12; 1863.

WATSON JOSEPH, farmer; P. O. Galena.

White Hugh, farmer; P. O. Galena.

White Matthew, farmer; P. O. Galena.

Wise John, miner.

Wollweaver H. farmer; Sec. 4; P. O. Galena.

Wollweaver John, laborer; Galena.

Wright Adam, Galena.

YOUNG HUGH, farmer; Sec. 25; P. O. Hanover.

MENOMINEE TOWNSHIP.

ARTS HENRY, Farmer; Sec. 21; P. O. Excelsior Mills; has 100 acres; born May 6, 1842, on same farm on which he now lives; married May 1, 1862, to Miss Augusta C. Gotiea; had six children: Julia A., Mary A., Louisa S., Catharine J., Gusta M., Rose C.; held office of Constable 6 years; held office of Assessor and Collector of Menominee Tp. for 6 years, which he now holds.

BAKER PETER, laborer; P. O. Excelsior Mills.

Bony P. farm; Sec. 23; P. O. Excelsior Mills.

Bower J. F. farmer; Sec. 31; P. O. Galena.

Bower N. laborer; Sec. 31; P. O. Galena.

Brumer Henry, farmer; Sec. 23; P. O. Excelsior Mills.

Brumer Hannen, farmer; Secs. 23 and 26.

Brumer John, laborer; P. O. Excelsior Mills.

Brummer Gorb, farmer; Sec. 24; P. O. Excelsior Mills.

Brew P. S. farmer; Sec. 6; P. O. Galena.

BUDDEN GERARD H. Farmer; Sec. 30; P. O. Excelsior Mills; 140 acres; born in Kingdom Hanover, Prussia, Jan. 6, 1818; came to this country and Ohio in 1842; came to this Co. in 1843; settled on his present farm in 1846; married in 1846 to Miss Mary Hobbman, of Galena; had six children: Clemens, John H., Bernard, Harmon, Jacob and Catharine.

Bur Dominick, laborer; Galena.

CORDING CHRISTEL F. & CORDING JOHN F. Farmers; Sec. 5; P. O. Galena; C. F. Cording was born in Germany May 16, 1853; John F. Cording was born in Germany Sept. 2, 1855; they came to this country and Co. in 1869; they purchased the farm in partnership in 1875; they have 152 acres of land, valued at $6,000; their parents are still living in Germany; the brothers are not married.

Coyn Wm. farmer; Sec. 17; P. O. Galena.

DEAGON MICHAEL, farmer; Sec. 24; P. O. Excelsior Mills.

Doonen John, farmer; Sec. 6; P. O. Galena.

Doulavey Thos. laborer; Galena.

Dunne Thos. farmer; Sec. 16; P. O. Galena.

FAIRWEATHER HENRY, laborer; Sec. 32; P. O. Galena.

Fairweather J. lab; Sec. 32; P. O. Galena.

FENLEY MRS. EMILY, Farmer; Sec. 17; P. O. Excelsior Mills; born in Kentucky May 1, 1814; came to Missouri in 1821, to Wis. 1835; settled on present farm in 1837; married to Mr. Joseph Fenley Feb. 26, 1831; had ten children: Mary J., Eliza, Caroline, Sarah E., Drusilla, Emily, John H. Mordicai, Squire, Joseph J.; Mr. Fenley died July 6, 1876; John H. and Mordicai enlisted in 96th Wis. V.I.; John H. died in the army Aug. 31, 1863; Mordicai died in the army Nov. 11, 1864.

Fleege B., Sr., laborer; P. O. Excelsior Mills.

Fleege B., Jr., farmer; Sec. 30; P. O. Excelsior Mills.

Fleege Harman, farmer; Sec. 20; P. O. Excelsior Mills.

Fleege Henry, laborer; P. O. Excelsior Mills.

Fleege Henry, farmer; Sec. 16; P. O. Excelsior Mills.

FLEIGE JOHN BERNARD, Farmer; Sec. 20; P. O. Excelsior Mills;

owns 174 acres land; born in Galena Tp., July 21, 1848; settled on his present farm in 1850; married to Miss Mary Bruening of Grant Co., Wis., in 1872; had three children: Clemens A., Mary L., Theresa.

Fleege Jos. laborer; P. O. Excelsior Mills.

Foht Bernhard, farmer; Sec. 7; P. O. Excelsior Mills.

Foht F. farm; Sec. 7; P. O. Excelsior Mills.

Foht J. farm; Sec. 7; P. O. Excelsior Mills.

GANNON JOHN, farmer; Sec. 17; P. O. Galena.

GAFFNEY JOHN A. Farmer; Sec. 5; P. O. Galena; has 160 acres land; born in Ireland Jan. 6, 1843; came to this country and Co. in 1849 and settled on his present farm; married to Miss Sarah E. McGinnis, Feb. 8, 1863; who was born in this Tp.; names of children now living: John M., Andrew T., Esther E., William B., one not named just born; held office of School Director 12 years; held office Supervisor past 3 years.

Gray Curtis, miller; Sec. 28; P. O. Excelsior Mills.

Gray Jno. J. school teacher; P. O. Excelsior Mills.

GRAY JOHN R. Miller, Farmer, Postmaster; Excelsior Mills, Menominee Tp; Sec. 28; born in Cornwall Co., England, June 11, 1820; came to this country and Penn. in 1841; came to Shullsburg, Wis., in 1842; spent 1850 in California; returned to Wis. in 1851, where he followed mining and engineering until 1860; he settled in his mill and on his present farm same year; married Isabella Brodwell in Oct. 1848; had seven children: John J., Curtis B., Agnes A., Henrietta, Isabella, Lincoln H., Cobden G.; Henrietta dead; he has held the office of Postmaster 12 years; Justice of Peace 4 years; he has 200 acres of land.

Greenwald C. farm; Sec. 12; P. O. Dunleith.

Greenwald F. farm; Sec. 12; P. O. Dunleith.

Greenwald J. farm; Sec. 12; P. O. Dunleith.

Greenwald T. farm; Sec. 2; P. O. Dunleith.

HARGRAFEN B., Sr., farmer; Sec. 20; P. O. Excelsior Mills.

Hargrafen B., Jr., farmer; Sec. 20; P. O. Excelsior Mills.

Hargrafen B. A. farmer; Sec. 20; P. O. Excelsior Mills.

Hanfelt Henry, farmer; Secs. 25 and 30; P. O. Excelsior Mills.

Hanfelt Harmen, laborer on Sec. 30; P. O. Excelsior Mills.

Hanfelt Jno., Sr., carpenter; Sec. 30; P. O. Excelsior Mills.

Hanfelt Jno., Jr., farmer; Sec. 30; P. O. Excelsior Mills.

Heitcamp C. farmer; Sec. 29; P. O. Excelsior Mills.

Heitcamp Henry, farmer; Sec. 29; P. O. Excelsior Mills.

Hendricks H. renter; Sec. 35; P. O. Dunleith.

Hesing Jno. farmer; P. O. Excelsior Mills.

HESLING MRS. MARGARET, Farm on Estate; Sec. 18; P. O. Excelsior Mills; born in Prussia in 1815; came to this country in 1844; settled on their farm same year; she married Henry Snyder in 1846; he died in 1850; she married Henry Hesling in 1851; she had four children: Mary A. and John Henry by Mr. Snyder, and William J. and Annie C. by Mr. Hesling; her son John H. works the estate, 60 acres; Wm. J. works his own farm of 117 acres; Sec. 25.

Hesling Wm., Sr., farmer; Sec. 19; P. O. Excelsior Mills.

Hesling Wm. J. farmer; Sec. 25; P. O. Excelsior Mills.

Hilpy Jos., Sr., farm; Sec. 8; P. O. Galena.

Hilpy Jos., Jr., farm; P. O. Excelsior Mills.

Hilly Dan. farmer; Sec. 8; P. O. Excelsoir Mills.

Horan Jas., Sr., farm; Sec. 33; P. O. Galena.

Horan Jas., Jr., farmer; Sec. 33; P. O. Excelsior Mills.

HORAN MARTIN, Farmer; Secs. 19 and 25; P. O. Excelsior Mills; born in Ireland in 1813; came to this country and Detroit in 1834; settled on his present farm in 1835; married Catharine Dunlavey of Ireland in 1848; had eleven children: Mary A., Michael, Bridget E., Thomas J., Bernard P., Mark P., Martin F., Katie S., James O., Margaret T., Julia A.; Mr. Horan has 240 acres land; he is the oldest settler now living in Menominee Tp.

Horan Thos. laborer; Sec. 19; P. O. Excelsior Mills.

How Geo. farm; Sec. 23; P. O. Fair Play, Wis.

Hughes Geo. farmer; Sec. 8; P. O. Excelsior Mills.

Hughes Pat. farmer; Sec. 8; P. O. Galena.

IMHOLD HENRY, farmer; Sec. 28; P. O. Excelsior Mills.

JOHNSON LOUIS, carpenter; Sec. 27; P. O. Excelsior Mills.

KIEFFER NICHOLAS, Farmer; Secs. 25 and 26; P. O. Excelsior Mills; born in Luxembourg, Nov. 11, 1846; came to this country and Co. in 1869; settled on this farm in 1871; married Mary Brummer April 18, 1871; she was born in Menominee Tp., Dec. 8, 1848; had three children: John, Francis, Harmon; he owns 160 acres land.

Kimler Fred, farmer; Sec. 16; P. O. Galena.

Klieth Chas. farmer; Sec. 21; P. O. Galena.

Knall Harmon, farmer; Sec. 30; P. O. Excelsior Mills.

Knoll Harmon, Jr., laborer; Sec. 30; P. O. Excelsior Mills.

Knoll Wm. farmer; Sec. 30; P. O. Excelsior Mills.

Kopel Bernard, farmer; Sec. 29; P. O Excelsior Mills.

Kuhl A. farmer; Sec. 21; P. O. Menominee.

KUHL HENRY, Retired; P. O. Excelsior Mills; born in Kingdom Hanover, Prussia, March 26, 1816; came to this country and St. Louis in 1840; settled in this Co. in 1841; entered 80 acres land in Sec. 21 in 1847; married Miss Mary Welp from Prussia, April 6, 1842; she was born on Dec. 7, 1814; they had six children: Mary, born June 4, 1843; John, Jan. 1, 1845; Bernard, May 8, 1847; Anton, Aug. 17, 1849; William, Oct. 2, 1852; Christine, May 18, 1857; Anton lives with his parents and works his farm, 324 acres; Sec. 21.

Kuhl Jno. farmer; Sec. 19; P. O. Excelsior Mills.

LIST ADAM, Sr., farmer; Sec. 8; P. O. Excelsior Mills.

List Adam, Jr., farmer; Sec. 8; P. O. Excelsior Mills.

List Jacob, farmer; Sec. 8; P. O. Excelsior Mills.

List J. farm; Sec. 7; P. O. Excelsior Mills.

Long Gregory, renter farmer; Sec. 29; P. O. Excelsior Mills.

Long S. farmer; Sec. 25; P. O. Excelsior Mills.

MADDEN JNO. farmer; Sec. 33; P. O. Excelsior Mills.

MANEMAN BERNARD H. Farmer, Blacksmith and Wagon Maker; Sec. 20; P. O. Excelsior Mills; born in Prussia, Sept. 29, 1844; came to this country and this Tp., March 1, 1846; married to Miss Mary Ann Muller, Grant Co., Wis., June 25, 1867; had six children, one dead; held office as School Treasurer 2 years; Tp. Clerk 10 years; his father Clemens Maneman, born in Prussia, Oct. 30, 1813; lives with him and does the wood work; his brother John Maneman is partner in the business, and also, held office Tp. Constable 2 years.

Maneman C. farmer; Sec. 20; P. O. Excelsior Mills.

Maneman Jno. farmer; Sec. 20; P. O. Excelsior Mills.

Mann Wm. farmer; Sec. 8; P. O. Galena.

Mitten Jno. farmer; Sec. 2; P. O. Dunleith.

Mulroy Pat. farmer; Sec. 18; P. O. Galena.

Murphy Jno. laborer; P. O. Galena.

NEIGHOONER GARET, farmer; Sec. 19; P. O. Excelsior Mills.

OPRIM MICHAEL, farmer; Sec. 18; P. O. Galena.

Oprim John, laborer; Galena.

PEALER CONRAD H. carpenter; Excelsior Mills.

Plear Nicholas, farmer; Sec. 25; P. O. Excelsior Mills.

Power James, laborer; Galena.

Power John, laborer; Galena.

Power Wm. farmer; Sec. 32; P. O. Galena.

READMOND THOS. farmer; Sec. 6; P. O. Excelsior Mills.

Readmond Wm. farmer; Sec. 6; P. O. Excelsior Mills.

Rhondius P. farm; Sec. 35; P. O. Dunleith.

Richard F. laborer; P. O. Excelsior Mills.

Rickey Bernard, farmer; Sec. 23; P. O. Excelsior Mills.

Roach Wm., Sr., farm; Sec. 7; P. O. Galena.

Roach Wm., Jr., farm; Sec. 7; P. O. Galena.

Rogers Michael, laborer; Galena;

Rolling H. laborer; P. O. Excelsior Mills.

Rollins Henry, farmer; Sec. 30; P. O. Excelsior Mills.

Roney Wm. farmer; Sec. 32; P. O. Galena.

Ryan Philip, farmer; Sec. 32; P. O. Galena.

Ryan Thos. laborer; P. O. Galena.

SCHMIDT C. HENRY, farmer; Sec. 11, P. O. Galena.

Schoussie A. carp; P. O. Excelsior Mills.

Schoussie G. laborer; P. O. Excelsior Mills.

Sheean Dave, farmer; Sec. 5; P. O. Galena.

Sherman J. farmer; Sec. 23; P. O. Dunleith

Shutting H. farmer; Sec. 36; P. O. Galena.

Smerback L. farmer; Sec. 1; P. O. Galena.

Snider Henry, farmer; Sec. 18; P. O. Excelsior Mills.

Soat B. farm; Sec. 29; P. O. Excelsior Mills.

TALLEN MORRIS, laborer; P. O. Galena.

Tarbalt Jno. renter; Sec. 1; P. O. Excelsior Mills.

Tranell Bernard, farmer; Sec. 24; P. O. Excelsior Mills.

Tranell G. H. laborer; P. O. Excelsior Mills.

Tranell H. farmer; Sec. 31; P. O. Excelsior Mills.

Tranell H. H. laborer; P. O. Excelsior Mills.

Tranell Henry, Jr., laborer; Sec. 24; P. O. Excelsior Mills.

Tranell H., Sr., farmer; Sec. 30; P. O. Excelsior Mills.

Tranell John, farmer; Sec. 24; P. O. Excelsior Mills.

Timerman Math. farmer; Secs. 25 and 26; P. O. Excelsior Mills.

Timerman Pat. farmer; Sec. 36; P. O. Excelsior Mills.

VANDERVEAL H. farmer; Sec. 31; P. O. Galena.

Vanderveal A. laborer; P. O. Galena.

VERHOEF REV. W. C. Clergyman Menominee Parish; Sec. 30; P. O. Excelsior Mills; born in Holland in 1828; came to this country and Wis. in 1855; settled in this Co. in 1864 and was settled over this Parish same year; he has officiated 13 years; his Parish numbers about eighty families Irish and German; he assisted in organizing a new Church and in erecting their new and beautiful edifice, which is 96 by 44; it was commenced in 1875 and finished in 1876.

Vesterbeck Albert, carpenter.

Vogal A. farmer; Sec. 16; P. O. Galena.

Vogel Henry, farmer; Sec. 16; P. O. Galena.

WALIN LAWRENCE, laborer; Sec. 7; P. O. Galena.

Walin M. laborer; Sec. 7; P. O. Galena.

Walin Pat. farmer; Sec. 7; P. O. Galena.

Wederhold Chas. farmer; Sec. 31; P. O. Excelsior Mills.

Weders H. farmer; Sec. 9; P. O. Galena.

Welter Mark, farmer; Secs. 25 and 26; P. O. Excelsior Mills.

WEST JOSEPH, Farmer; Sec. 28; P. O. Excelsior Mills; born in Kingdom Hanover, Prussia, Jan. 31, 1844; came to this country and Lyons, Iowa, in 1860; moved to Grant Co., Wis., in 1863; settled on his present farm in 1866; married to Miss Christine Fleege in 1866; she was born in Menominee Tp. in 1848; had five children: Philo M., Clemens A., Mary J., Frances M., Joseph Leo; he has 185 acres land.

White Pat. farmer; Sec. 19; P. O. Dunleith.

WHITE WILLIAM, Farmer and Miner; Secs. 19 and 25; P. O. Dunleith; born in Ireland, Wexford Co., in 1808; came to this country and Vinegar Hill Tp. in 1846; settled on his present farm in 1847; he has 119 acres land; married to Miss Margaret Furlong in 1837; she was born in Ireland in 1812; had eight children; Moses E., Ellen, Alice, Esther, John H., Richard, Patrick H., William W.; Patrick H. lives with his father and mother and carries on the farm.

Wilking Jno. farmer; Sec. 21; P. O. Excelsior Mills.

Williams Garrett, farmer; Sec. 29; P. O. Excelsior Mills.

WUBBEN BERNARD H. Merchant and Justice of Peace; Sec. 21; P. O. Excelsior Mills; born in Prussia, Nov. 9, 1834; came to this country and Ohio in 1850; enlisted in 15th Kentucky Regt. in 1861; promoted to sergeant in 1862, mustered out in 1865; settled in this Co. in 1865; married to Elizabeth Hargrafen, Menominee Tp., in 1867; had five children: Henry, Mary, Anna, Bernard, Theresa; held office of Justice of Peace 10 years.

WUBBEN JOHN G. Farmer; Sec. 19; P. O. Excelsior Mills; born in Amt. Friern, Prussia, Jan. 7, 1837; came to this country and Cincinnati, Ohio, in 1854; came to this Co. in 1855; settled on his present farm April, 1864; he owns 141 acres land; married to Mary T. Fleege Feb. 3, 1863; she was born Sept. 18, 1840 in Amt. Friern (Hanover) Prussia; had five children: Regina H., Mary A., Clemens A., Annie C., Annie Louisa; held office of School Director 6 years.

PHYSICAL GEOGRAPHY.

(Taken from Illinois Geological Reports.)

This large and important county is situated in the extreme northwest corner of the state. It is bounded on the north by the State of Wisconsin; on the east by Stephenson County, in the State of Illinois; on the south by Carroll County; and on the west by the Mississippi River. From north to south it extends twenty-one miles; from east to west, along the south line, twenty miles, and along the north line, thirty-six miles.

PHYSICAL FEATURES AND CONFIGURATION.

These are more diversified and interesting than are to be met with in any other county in this part of our state. The whole county is a part of the side of an extensive water shed, with a slope to the southwest. The county is excellently well watered. All the streams flow in nearly the same direction; from the northeast to the southwest. The principal of these streams, commencing at the eastern part of the county, and going westward, are: Plum River, Camp Creek, Rush Creek, Apple River, Small Pox Creek, Galena or Fever River, Sinsinawa River, Little Menominee and Big Menominee Rivers. Apple River and Fever River are considerable streams; the latter, in high stages of water in the Mississippi River, will float the largest steamers from that river to the City of Galena. Most of the others afford abundant mill sites for light mills and manufactories. At Hanover, on Apple River, there is quite a heavy power used, for the purpose of driving the machinery in an extensive woolen mill. Along the southwest part of the county there is some alluvial bottom land, made up of deep, black Mississippi mud bottoms and sand prairies; but these are not extensive. Some of the smaller streams have narrow and fertile alluvial bottoms. These are walled in in most cases with bluff ranges, more or less precipitous and rocky. The trend of the bluff line along the Mississippi River winds and bends with the general course of that stream. These bluffs are high, and gently rounded along the northwestern part of the county, but assume a more picturesque and castellated appearance as they enter Carroll County on the south.

It is almost impossible to give a correct description of the surface of Jo Daviess County, without a minute reference to almost every township in it. In general terms, there are all varieties of surface found in the northern part of the state. Level prairie, rolling and undulating prairie and oak openings, uneven, hilly, rocky, and bluffy timbered and farm land tracts, may all be found in almost any portion of the county. The eastern and northeastern townships are generally prairie; soil rich, warm and deep; some of its regular level Illinois prarie land; some of it, towards the centre and south of the county, undulating, uneven, partly covered with scattering and scrubby timber. The southern tier of townships is uneven, sometimes hilly, sometimes rocky, with some prairie in Berreman, Pleasant Valley and Hanover. The western and northwestern townships are generally timbered, hilly, rocky, and even bluffy. The central townships are generally uneven and partly timbered.

The prairies of Jo Daviess County are not excelled in fertility by any upland prairie in the state. The soil of the rough, uneven and hilly land, when cleared of its timber and underbrush, and laid open to the genial influences of good cultivation, is quick and fertile, being composed of a clayey, somewhat marly base. Numerous farms, some of them quite large, open in the rough lands in every part of the county, attest the truth of this statement, and amply repay their owners for the labor of putting them under cultivation. Some of these reddish clayey soils might not look fertile to the husbandman used to the blacker prairie soils, but the large yield of cereal grains and grasses would soon convince him that their producing powers were almost equal to the vegetable molds and humas-charged soils of the leveler portions of the state. Indian corn, of course, is not so heavy a staple crop here as in other portions of the state farther south; still, good crops are raised with reasonable certainty.

Stock raising is also an important element of wealth in the county. The range is good, and sheltered situations for the Winter are abundant. The citizens of the county, many of them, are largely engaged in this very remunerative business.

The agricultural resources, stock raising capabilities, and mineral wealth hidden away in the underlying rocks, are all leading elements of wealth in this county.

The county has an abundant supply of timber, for its own consumption, for many years to come. The oak family is largely represented among its trees; basswood, hickory, walnut, and, in short, all the trees, wild fruits and shrubs, catalogued for this part of the state, may be found in the bottom timber, barrens and groves.

Fruit growing and vine raising may both be carried on successfully. The hills about Galena, and in many other portions of the county, produce the hardy fruits and grapes in great abundance. The business has not been gone into extensively, but there is no reason why wine making might not be made to pay in favored localities. On the Galena hills I have seen grape vines purple with thick hanging clusters, while apple trees near by bent beneath their ripened fruit. The garden fruits attain also to great perfection.

A prominent feature in the landscape of portions of the county, is a number of natural mounds, rising to a considerable height above the general surface.

Pilot Knob is the most conspicuous of these. It is about three miles south of the City of Galena, and about two miles from the Mississippi River. It is a conspicuous landmark to tourists and river men, passing up and down that stream. Towering above the surrounding high bluffs, it reaches an altitude of 429 feet above ordinary water mark in Fever River, according to barometrical measurements, made by Whitney.

There is a chain of some half dozen of these mounds, running northeast of Pilot Knob four or five miles, among them Waddell's and Jackson's Mounds, well-known local elevations. Around the City of Galena there are several mound-like elevations and ridges, the most conspicuous of which terminates in a group of castellated rocks, near the residence of Mr. Hallett. These rocks overlook the city, and crooked valley of Fever River, for some distance.

Charles' Mound, near the north line of the county, is supposed to be the highest point of land in the state. Its ridge-like, rocky backbone is 295 feet above the Illinois Central Railroad track, at Scales' Mound station; 951 feet above low water in the Mississippi River, at Cairo; and 1226 feet above low tide in the Gulf of Mexico. These are the figures given by Whitney.

Scales' Mound, about a mile south of the last, is a well-known locality. Around this latter, and within a radius of two or three miles, there are several other similar but smaller mounds.

East and southeast are Woods' Mounds, in the south part of Apple River Township; Bean's Mound, near Apple River; Powers' Mound, in the northwest corner of Rush Township; Paige's Mound, near the south line of Courtland Township; Simmons' Mound, near the northeast corner of the Township of Stockton; Benton's and Rice's Mounds, a little north and west of the latter; one or two mounds or mound-like elevations east of Elizabeth, whose names I did not ascertain; an elevated, mound-like plateau of several miles in extent, commencing about two miles north of the Village of Elizabeth; and several other such plateaus in various parts of the county.

The geological structure of these mounds gives them the appearance of gentle sloping hills, for a part of the distance up their sides, crowned by abrupt, fancifully weathered, castellated rocks, of a reddish-brown or whitish-yellow appearance. Some of these views, from a distance, have a great resemblance to old mural walls and baronial towers, and vividy recall to memory the wild architectural structures of the middle ages.

These same Niagara Rocks outcrop in long mural escarpments along the Mississippi and Apple River Bluffs, and along many of the smaller streams in those portions of the county where this geological formation is heavily developed. The ledges and exposures, and some of the abrupt outliers of the Galena rocks, also present the same picturesque, wild appearance. Some of them present scenes almost as attractive as any in Jackson County, about the Devil's Backbone and the Mississippi Bake Oven.

It will thus be seen that the topography and physical features of this county are well marked, and attractive in the extreme.

SURFACE GEOLOGY.

Alluvium.—The small water courses of the county have the usual narrow alluvial bottoms. In some places these spread out wide enough for small farms. Pleasant Valley, along the north branch of Plum River, extends from Morseville to the Carroll County line, a distance of some ten miles; it is from a quarter of a mile to almost a mile in width, and contains some of the very best farming lands in the county. These narrow alluvial bottoms are composed of a rich, brown, marly soil, made up in great part from the wash and detritus from the hills on either side. In but few places can there be noticed the black silt or mud or washed sand of river alluvium. The valleys are all ancient valleys of erosion, floored or built up by recent detritus from the hills, not transported to great distances, nor greatly mixed, and belonging to very recent Quaternary deposits.

The Mississippi River bottom, in the upper part of its course along this county, is very narrow—in fact that stream almost washes the rocky base of the bluffs for many miles. There is, however, a chain of sloughs opposite Galena, and along the mouths of Fever River and Small Pox Creek, where there is a low alluvial bottom, timber grown, and made up of Mississippi mud and sand. This is the flood plain or flood bed of the stream, over which the annual overflows of high water extend. Farther down the river this bottom spreads out to several miles in extent. In the western part of the Township of Hanover, bottom timber land, alluvial grass land, and table land high and dry, and susceptible of cultivation, exhibit all the characteristics of ordinary Mississippi alluvial bottoms.

Loess and Modified Drift.—The regular marly loess of the Mississippi bluffs, such as is found opposite Fulton City, at Warsaw, and at other localities further down, is not a marked feature along the western limits of Jo Daviess County. Its bluffs are mostly composed of massive rocky formations. The bald bluffs, composed of whitish, partially stratified sands and clays, were not observed; but there are mound-like elevations, and masses of brown, marly, sandy clays along, among, and overcapping some of these chains of bluffs, which undoubtedly owe their origin to the same agencies which deposited the loess of the bluffs, lower down the stream. These brown deposits are loess marls and clays, slightly modified by local conditions. Within the limits of the City of Galena, and at other points in Fever River Valley, and forty or fifty feet above ordinary water level of Fever River, there are heavy outcrops of a well marked, distinctly stratified clayey deposit, which shows every characteristic of the most marked and well defined loess of the lower Mississippi bluffs. Thin seams of reddish clayey marls alternate regularly with thin seams of a whitish, tough, unctuous-feeling clay. The seams are from one to four inches thick; the stratification is complete; the lithological character seems to be identical; the thickness is from ten to eighteen feet; and the extent into the hills indefinite, but probably limited. In the marly seams I found great quantities of a fluviatile shell, in a fair state of preservation. These shells are quite small, running from the size of a wheat grain to that of a large barley corn. I have several times, within a few years, noticed the same shell, or a closely allied species, strewn thick over the silt and mud after the floods of the Mississippi had subsided, and the flood bed had become overgrown with a dense growth of grass. Beneath the shadow of the grass the damp ground looked as if it had been thickly sown with large wheat kernels. Subsequent overflows no doubt imbedded these, and where antiseptic properties mingled with the silt, they will no doubt be preserved, and present an appearance exactly identical with those picked out of the outcrop near the Illinois Central Railroad depot in Galena. It will thus be seen, I think, that the evidences of the desposition of loess deposits in this county are incontestible.

In the Fever River Valley, within the City of Galena, a mile or two above the city, and at several places between the city and its confluence with the Mississippi River, there are well defined river terraces of modified or river drift. These are about twenty feet above ordinary water mark in that stream. Similar traces were observed by Professor Worthen at the mouth, and up the valley of the Small Pox Creek; and a broad, distinctly marked river terrace may be observed in the lower part of the Mississippi bottom, extending down into Carroll County.

Drift Proper.—The productive lead field has been written down as "a driftless region;" and to some extent this is true of that part of it within Jo Daviess County. But in attempting to account for this supposed absence of the drift in the lead region, eminent geologists have fallen into a controversy, or difference of opinion.

Whitney contends that when the lead region was uplifted from the Silurian seas, no subsequent submergence ever took place; and that all the changes which have since taken place on its surface have been produced by agencies, such as we now see producing dynamical results upon dry land. When the broadly extended drift forces—whether broad creeping and grinding glaciers, or broad water currents, or ice-bergs and water acting together—moved the drift on its southwest course, according to this theory, the lead region rose as an island in the midst of the moving forces, and the drift stream was divided—thrown to the east and west—and united again after passing the obstruction. Such being the case, the lead basin, supposed then to have been elevated above the surrounding country, escaped the action of the drift forces. During all this time, more peaceful geological causes are supposed to have been at work over the uplifted island, whose action has produced all the geological changes supposed to have taken place. Atmospheric and chemical agencies disintegrated the hard Silurian rocks. The surface rocks changed slowly into the clays now overlying the bed rocks, except so far as rains and winds may have transported these clays and subjected them to a mixing process. This being true, the superficial deposits of the driftless lead region are substantially *in situ*, at the very places where they were formed by the decay of the parent rock.

Percival believed that the high water shed, extending from the mouth of the Wisconsin eastward, rose as a reef in the drift epoch waters, and turned the drift to the west, through Iowa, and to the east, round the lead region. This reef may have permitted a sheet of shallow water to flow over it, and submerge the lead basin. In this way the action of the drift forces would be greatly modified.

My own observations upon the drift phenomena in this county have not been altogether satisfactory. In the first place, I do not think it a driftless region. In addition to the drift pebbles and copper nuggets referred to by Professor Worthen, as having been found at the California lead diggings, I have observed numbers of large boulders lying over the prairie land in the eastern and southeastern portions of the county; and I am credibly informed that, on the high upland some three miles north of Galena, many boulders of a sort of buhrstone, whose parent outcrop is far north in Wisconsin, are strewn over the ground. Many of the clay deposits covering the very lead veins themselves, do not differ materially from the buff and yellow clays treated, and recognized every where else in the northwest, as true drift clays. The river terraces and stratified loess deposits, above spoken of; the lithological character of the clays just referred to; the few "nigger heads" and lost rocks found in several places in the county, show unmistakably, I think, that the drift forces, especially towards the close of the drift epoch, had much to do in cutting down, carrying away, and arranging the great rocky formations which once existed, but which have now disappeared over large portions of the county. Over more than half its area, perhaps, the whole thickness of the Niagara limestone and the Cincinnati shales have disappeared, except the mounds left standing as sentries, at long intervals; and the very galena bed rocks below where they used to stand have had their surfaces denuded, to a considerable extent, in the operation. To one standing upon one of these mounds, and looking over the valley-like expanses between them, with the eye of a geologist, the conviction that he is standing upon the old Silurian level of the country grows into a certainty. Eroding and denuding influences have removed from three hundred to three hundred and fifty feet of Magnesian limestone and shales. It is impossible to suppose that simple atmospheric or chemical causes, acting no matter how long, could produce such gigantic results. Many submergencies and upheavals may have taken place; the dynamical powers of heavy bodies of water and water currents, and other drift forces, must have acted long and powerfully in bringing them about.

While these things all appear to be true, it can not be denied that the superficial deposits covering the bed rocks are, in part, derived from their disintegration, by rains, frosts and other atmospheric and chemical agencies. I have examined many clay banks through the lead mine region which bore unmistakable evidences of this. Those peculiar red clays, characteristic of the lead region, if dug into, show, first, the clays and hard pan, without rocks of any description, but, as the deposits are penetrated, rocks begin to appear in detached pieces, becoming more abundant at a greater depth, until the regular strata of the bed rocks are reached. Now, these pieces are unworn by atmospheric influences; they lie in horizontal beds, parallel to the strata below, and are evidently the harder portions of the mass, which resisted the influences that changed a rock bed into a clay bed. Nearly all the float mineral, or clay bed mineral now found, is, also, nothing but the ore which has settled down from the decayed rocks, in which it was once held in veins, and mineral-bearing lodes.

This is also true of the clays covering some of the Niagara and Cincinnati outcrops or bed rocks, for they partake largely of the underlying rocks, from which they have probably been derived. I think a chemical analysis of these clays would show a great similarity or exact identity with the rocks under them.

Professor Whitney's theory of atmospheric agencies, and no submergence of the lead basin since its upheaval from the Silurian ocean, explains well these unmixed clays, *in situ* apparently, at the very places where formed; but it does not explain the great erosion and denudation which has taken place through the productive part of the lead basin, and is utterly inconsistent with the terraces, loess and drift phenomena plainly manifest in almost every part of this county. If we knew exactly what the drift forces were, and how they acted, we would probably have no difficulty in seeing what influences modified their force in the lead basin. That such a modification did take place in some way, there can be no doubt.

The blue plastic clays, which lie near the bottom of the drift in other parts of the state, are sparingly developed here, so far as I have been able to observe. The boulder drift and coarse gravel drift, which lie near the top of the true drift, except the few loose boulders already noticed, are, also, substantially wanting in this region. The yellowish brown clays, red clays, and hard-pan are developed here to a considerable extent; but the average depth of the superficial deposits covering the rocks in Jo Daviess County is a good deal less than in portions of the state farther east and south. The great denudation which took place here seems to have been followed by transporting agencies, which bore away a large portion of the materials thus disengaged to other regions.

The phenomena here observed are probably best explained by supposing two epochs, when causes somewhat different in their results were at work. The first was the epoch of erosion and denudation, accompanied by vast transporting agencies of some kind, probably flowing water or modified drift forces. During this epoch the Niagara limestone was worn down, and the Cincinnati shales suffered disintegration, and most of the detritus thus formed was removed. The second epoch was one in which the waters or modified drift forces had partially or wholly subsided; chemical and atmospheric agencies worked upon the comparatively naked rocks, and the lead basin clays settled down in the places where the underlying rocks had decayed. Such a condition of things would, I think, explain all the phenomena observed in the lead region of this county. How far it might apply to other portions of the northwest lead region, I am unable to state.

The Niagara Limestone.—All the mounds, mound-like ridges, and plateaus mentioned in speaking of the topography of the county, are capped by massive irregularly-bedded dolomitic Niagara limestone, ranging in thickness from about fifty to one hundred and seventy-five feet. Tapestried with lichens and mosses, of a dull brown or red color, with castellated and fantastic forms, these rocks at once attract the attention of the most careless observer. In addition to the mounds, they cover other portions of the county in the south and southwest; and their ledges and exposures all round the edges, along the bluffs, and where the streams have cut deep channels into their midst, show the same massive, ragged and picturesque appearance observable on the mounds; except that they resemble more, long, irregularly shaped reddish-brown mural escarpments or walls, carpeted with soft green mosses and feathery ferns.

The probable extent of the county covered by this formation, is a little less than one third. There are many places throughout this extent where the eroding streams have cut down through the Niagara, into the Cincinnati shales, and even reached the Galena limestone below both.

Such is the superficial area covered by this rock, stated approximately. Its lithological character has been so often written that it seems superfluous to speak of it here. The rock is generally massive, irregularly bedded; tough, of a yellowish color on fresh fracture, but weathering to a reddish-brown. It is full of chert bands; and some of the Niagara hills are macadamized with a thick floor of finely broken, dendrite-speckled flints, which remain from the decay of the strata formerly enclosing them. These flint hills, or flint covered hills, are characteristic of the Niagara limestone formation. The maximum thickness of the Niagara limestone in this county can not be accurately stated. The denudation which has taken place on its top, and the difficulty of ascertaining the bottom, make it almost impossible to measure its thickness correctly. Its heaviest outcrop is probably along Small Pox Creek, where it reaches a thickness of over two hundred feet. As developed in this county it is exceedingly homogenous in character—the varieties observed at Racine, LeClare and Cardova, being wanting. In chemical analysis, lithological character, and general appearance, it is very similar to the Galena limestone. If a difference can be detected, it is less sandy and crystalline, and tougher than the latter formation. Its type or characteristic fossils are also different.

These are chiefly *Pentamerus oblongus; Favosites favosa; Halysites cateularia; Astrocerium venustum,* and one or two species of *Stromapotora* formed corals. The *Pentamerus* are the traditional "petrified hickory nuts," so often spoken of by the miners and well-diggers. Huge blocks of the stone, in places, are sticking full of them. On the silex sown hills, bushels of rough weather-stained specimens of the *Favosites* can be collected. These old Niagara seas swarmed with the coral builders; and many of the Niagara beds of rock were little else than coral reefs.

The Cincinnati Group.—The green and blue shales and limestones of the Cincinnati group underlie the Niagara limestone wherever the latter is developed in the county. There are not many natural outcrops of these shales, and they never stand out in ledges or rocky exposures, unless where quarries are opened into the covered rocks. Even where quarries are opened into this formation and then abandoned for a few years, the rapid disintegration soon covers up the rocks with a gently sloping talus.

The parts of the county underlaid by this formation can be told at a glance. All around the mounds and mound-like elevations; all around the outer boundary lines of the Niagara formation, up either side of all the valleys of erosion which have cut through it, the gentle slopes extending from the general level of the country up to the base of the bold Niagara exposures, are underlaid by rocks and shales of the Cincinnati group. These slopes may be represented by a narrow band two or three hundred yards, more or less, in width, encompassing all the Niagara fields and outliers in the county, and running up either side of all the valleys that are cut through it. When this is said, the superficial area underlaid by the Cincinnati group is as well indicated as it could be by many pages of description. One or two localities, however, deserve a passing notice.

At the northern terminus of Terrapin Ridge, near Elizabeth, the milky looking clays and shales are washed and furrowed out by the rains, exposing many fine specimens of the hemispherical-shaped coral *Chætetes petropolitanus*. I have found dozens of good specimens of this coral in the clay-washed road at this locality.

East of Scales Mound the track of the Illinois Central Railroad is laid for several miles almost upon the top of the Galena limestone. Several rather heavy cuts in that locality show good exposures of the overlying Cincinnati shales. These beds contain in certain layers a very great abundance of minute fossils, principally a small *Nucula*.

The general character of this group in Jo Daviess and Carroll Counties is almost identical. The upper layers are thin-bedded argillaceous and silicious shales, of a light buff or creamy color. Where thick-bedded enough to quarry, the stones have a kiln-dried, dusty appearance. Lower down, the shales become blue or greenish in color, sometimes separated by thin bands of green, marly clay; still lower, some massive strata of a deep ultra-marine blue color may be found, exceedingly hard, and giving out a clear ringing sound when struck with a steel hammer; below these there is found in some localities a black carbonaceous shale, so highly charged with carbon as to burn with a bright flame as though impregnated with oil, and the bottom of the deposit is made up of thinner strata of alternating yellow, blue and green shales and clays. Wherever the rain cuts through the soil into these shales, or the little streams wash them, the wet clays have a greasy look, and the trickling waters a creamy and greenish color. There are no gradual beds of passage into the overlying Niagara or the underlying Galena limestones; but the formation preserves well its distinctive characteristics.. The beginnings of its foundation stones and its cap rocks are always easily recognized.

The thickness of the deposit can not be accurately stated. A true section, as developed in the Mississippi River bluffs, from Bluffville, in Carroll County, to the mouth of Fever River, would run from eighty to one hundred and twenty feet. In the interior of this county it nowhere, perhaps, reaches to one hundred feet, and in some places it is only from forty to sixty feet.

The deposit is full of well preserved fossils. The *Orthoceratite* beds in Dubuque County, Iowa, have long been famous for the number of well preserved *Orthoceratites* with which they are crowded.

The *Chætetes petropolitanus* is a characteristic fossil, and is found in great abundance at Elizabeth, and in the washes and ravines at other places.

Fragments of a branching coral, and the small bud-like heads of an *encrinite*, are generally found in the same localities. In a few places I observed immense numbers of the fragments of *Isotelus gigas;* also several species of *Orthis*, among them *Orthis lynx*; associated with *Ambonychia radiata*, *Strophomena alternata*, fragments of two or three species of *Orthocera*, and one or two of the new fossils described in the Third Volume of the Illinois Geological Reports, *Strophomena unicostata* and *Tentaculites sterlingensis*, were also observed.

The Galena Limestone.—This is the great bed-rock of the county. From Dunleith to about the mouth of Small Pox Creek it forms the rocky bluffs on the Mississippi River. All the northwestern, northern and northeastern part of the county, except a few of the mounds heretofore named, is underlaid by it. The eastern part of the county, extending a short distance south of Morseville, is also underlaid by the same rock. All the larger streams in the county, including Sinsinawa, Fever and Apple Rivers, Rush, Small Pox and Plum Creeks, with their principal tributaries, flow along the surface or cut into this formation. It immediately underlies the surface deposits of something like two thirds of the county.

The maximum thickness of the Galena rocks in this county is not known. It is probably not far from three hundred and fifty feet. At Elizabeth, shafts are sunk one hundred and fifty feet deep, and what is known as the flint strata among miners was not reached. At the places of these shafts the Galena had been considerably denuded. The flinty strata generally is characteristic of the middle of the formation. It may be, however, that the estimate from this basis is too great. No outcrop observed was over about two hundred feet thick.

Its lithological and stratigraphical character is too well known, and has been too often given in these reports, to require an extended notice here, as all into whose hands this report will be likely to fall will probably have access to those descriptions. The rock is a thick-bedded, sub-crystalline, compact, cream or chrome colored dolomitic or magnesian limestone. It weathers out into forms almost as fantastic and picturesque as the Niagara above it. Along the streams its weathered out ledges present the same castellated and mural appearances; and some of its outliers rise into towers and chimneyed shapes of the most striking outlines.

Fossils are not so numerous in the Galena limestone of this county as in that of Carroll, Stephenson, or Winnebago. At Morseville, among the stones and debris thrown out from the lead diggings, I obtained several fine specimens of *Bellerophon*, the only fossil there observed. *Illaenus crassicauda* and *I. taurus* have both been found at Galena; a large species of *Cypricardites* is also frequently found, especially in the quarries in Carroll County. *Murchisonia bellicinta* and *Receptaculites Oweni*, two of the most characteristic Galena fossils, are found less frequently here than in any other portion of the formation in neighboring counties. A section of the largest *Orthocera* ever discovered in the lead region, perhaps, was found in the Galena limestone at Morseville, some two years ago, by some of the miners. It was eighteen or twenty inches long; a siphuncle nearly three inches in diameter projected about four inches at one end; the septa, somewhat loose, looked somewhat like a ribbed human body with a projecting neck. Of course those who saw it supposed that a petrified human trunk and neck had been discovered.

Trenton Limestone.—This limestone is only met with in two localities in the county. At Dunleith, and a little above it, there is a low outcrop along the banks of the Mississippi River. It is here a light bluish-gray rock, regularly and rather thinly bedded, with shaly partings, showing many of its characteristic fossils. These layers are near the top of the formation and have some of the characteristics of the superincumbent Galena. They, in fact, begin to partake of the nature of beds of passage into that rock.

Other exposures of this limestone may be seen along the north branch of Fever River, commencing about three miles northeast of Galena, and continuing until the Wisconsin line is reached. The outcrop attains a thickness of about twenty-six feet at its heaviest exposure, at Tuttle's mill.

This is the lowest formation any where outcropping in the county, or that can be regarded as belonging to a section of Jo Daviess County rocks. We are now prepared to give that section, naming the approximate average thickness of the formations:

SECTION OF JO DAVIESS COUNTY ROCKS.

Quarternary Deposits. Alluvium, loess, river terraces, clays, sands and hard-pan	20 to 75 feet.
Niagara Limestone. Heavy-bedded reddish-brown dolomitic limestone, weathering into cliffs and castellated exposures, similar in lithological character and appearance to the Galena limestone	40 to 200 "
Cincinnati Group. Green and blue and buff-colored shales; thin-bedded gray limestone, and hard, thick-bedded glassy rock	42 to 80 "
Galena Limestone. Heavy-bedded, cream-yellow dolomitic limestone, the lead rock of the Northwest; somewhat granular, and crystalline, and showing beds of passage into Trenton below	100 to 275 "
Blue Limestone. Thin-bedded gray limestone and shales and glass rock of miners	10 to 26 "

ECONOMICAL GEOLOGY.

Building Stone.—There is the greatest abundance of good building stone in this county, so distributed as to make it of easy access to all its citizens. All the formations are quarried. In Pleasant Valley a number of good quarries are opened in the Cincinnati group of rocks. These quarries are in the brows of the hills, on either side. The stone obtained is sufficiently thick-bedded and compact to make a good building stone. It has a dry, dusty, kiln-dried appearance. Several farm houses are built of this material in the valley. So far it seems to answer well for farm uses, without exhibiting a tendency to disintegrate. The best of it would, I think, be unsafe for massive and long-enduring masonry, but for light masonry it seems to answer well.

The blue limestone outcrops, along the north branch of Fever River, afford some good building stone. This is a light-gray limestone, rather thin-bedded, and of enduring properties. The outcrop at Dunleith also splits into a conveniently handled stone, and is used extensively for economical purposes.

The massive ledges, exposures, and natural outcrops of the Niagara and Galena limestone along nearly all the streams, in the brows of all the bluffs and hills, and in all those parts of the county where these heavy deposits are the bed rocks, furnish an inexhaustible supply of a coarse, enduring, valuable stone, suitable for all sorts of heavy masonry, such as bridge piers and abutments, foundations, cellar walls, and even public buildings, and private residences. They require considerable dressing for these latter purposes, but when dressed into good shape, their rich, warm, brown and cream colors, and the fact that they season into almost the hardness of a granite, and have an enduring, solid, substantial appearance, makes them prominent among the materials of economical value in the county.

Lime.—The abundance of timber and the abundance of good magnesian limestone, afford all the facilities for manufacturing large quantities of good, coarse, strong lime.

Clays and Sand.—The clays associated with the Cincinnati shales are sufficiently pure to furnish a potters' clay, good for the manufacture of common crockery ware. At Elizabeth I noticed several outcrops of this potters' clay in some of the streets and lots of the village. Four or five miles south of Elizabeth, on the Mount Carroll and Galena road, the Jenkins' pottery is located. This establishment has been in operation for quite a number of years, and has built up quite a remunerative business. The clay is obtained near by. It is not altogether pure and free from foreign substances; but these difficulties seem to be mostly overcome by the processes through which it is put in manufacturing. The result is, a ware largely used in this part of the state, as the Jenkins' pottery wagons are well known in all the neighboring towns, villages, and cities.

Common yellow and red clays, for ordinary brick, exist everywhere in the greatest abundance. Sand, suitable for building purposes, is not so universally distributed, neither is it so scarce as to be a matter of serious inconvenience.

The Associate Minerals.—Associated with the galena, and deserving a passing notice before that important mineral deposit is referred to, are several other mineral substances well known in the lead region. The most important of these is the sulphuret of zinc, blende, or "black jack" of the miners. This is a useful ore of zinc, but is quite difficult to reduce. The carbonate of zinc, smithsonite or "dry bone" of the miners, is considered a more valuable mineral. Iron pyrites also occur in connection with these minerals, in considerable abundance. At the celebrated Marsdens' lead, all these associate minerals may be seen associated with each other and with the galena, with the Galena limestone, and with spar and other substances. This mine has offorded the best cabinet specimens of these minerals in combination to be found any where in the lead regions. Brown hematite, and several other mineral substances, occur in occasional small quantities, but they are not of interest, in an economical point of view. None of these associate minerals have become articles of commerce, except, perhaps, the carbonate of zinc; and it is doubtful if even that exists in sufficient quantities to make it an article of value in the economical resources of this county.

Galena or Lead Ore.—The great mineral interest of the county, as every one knows, is lead. Indeed, it is second to mineral interest in the state, except that of coal. The leading ore of this metal has given its name to the great and important rocky formation in which it is chiefly found in this part of the country, to an important city in the midst of its heaviest deposits, and to the township in which that city is located.

The scope of this county report does not embrace a very extended essay upon the mining or metallurgy of lead, or a topographical survey or description of the crevices, leads, lodes and diggings, nor a scientific discussion of the modes of occurrence and phenomena observed in its workings. It is rather the province of this report to present the geological formations of the county, and some general remarks upon the extent of its mineral and other resources. The "Lead Region" has been closely examined and ably written upon by Professor J. D. Whitney, for the three States of Illinois, Wisconsin and Iowa. It will be unnecessary to repeat here what he has presented so well in the first volume of the Reports of the Illinois Geological Survey. That volume will be as accessible to the common reader as this, and to that volume we refer the reader for surveys and descriptions of the crevices and leads, and a detailed account of the different diggings, their positions, peculiarities of form, extent of working, amount of ore produced, and facts collected in regard to them. A brief *resume* of some of the facts and history of lead and the lead region may not however be out of place.

Galena, or the sulphuret of lead, called in the common speech of the lead region "mineral," when pure, is composed of 86.55 pure lead and 13.45 sulphur. It crystallizes in the form of the cube and its secondaries, has a perfect and easily obtained cleavage, and a bright, silvery, metallic luster on fresh fracture. The lead ore obtained in this county is nearly pure galena. It sometimes contains faint traces of silver.

From 1827 the mines rapidly grew in importance and multiplied in numbers. From 1840 to 1850 the greatest degree of prosperity was reached in the mines, about midway between those years being the very acme of mining prosperity. Galena became the mining metropolis of the Northwest. Thousands of rough miners swarmed through her streets. All sorts of moving vehicles were seen in her thoroughfares, and every language was spoken, every costume worn. The miner generally spent all he made, was poor, and held his own remarkably well. And that reckless spirit, bred of all uncertain pursuits, was abundantly manifested among the miners who assembled in the lead region. Card playing and whisky drinking, quarrelling, and that rough desperate life developed among adventurers of all classes gathered about Galena, was characteristic of those of all other mines. But in the midst of it all, the City of Galena grew to unexampled prosperity and wealth, and for hundreds of miles round was the centre of commerce and trade for the whole country. Treasures came up out of the ground, flowed into the city, and there remained and built it up. The discovery of the California gold mines swept from the lead mines all that floating part of its population ready for a new excitement, and also much that was of a more permanent nature. The lead mining interest rapidly decreased in importance, until the financial troubles of 1857 drove many back to mining as a matter of necessity. At the present time considerable attention is paid to mining, and it is probably a fact that mining labor generally is better and more uniformly paid now than at any period in the history of the mines. With all the vast amounts of mineral found, it is also a fact that but a very small proportion of the ground has been proved.

We can not arrive at even an approximately accurate amount of the mineral mined in Jo Daviess County. According to Mr. Whitney, the amount of lead received at Chicago and St. Louis, as per records of the Chamber of Commerce and Board of Trade, from 1853 to 1859, including both years, was about 181,000,000 pounds. This was from all sources. Of this amount, he thinks about one sixth was derived from the mines in Illinois, almost exclusively in this county. This would give about 30,000,000 for this county for that period, which period was the least prosperous time for mining known to exist for many years. From the detailed descriptions given of particular leads and ranges, by the same gentleman, in the first volume of the geological report of Illinois, we find that he gives the produce of certain enumerated mines up to that time at about 64,000,-000 pounds. The Apple River diggings are supposed to have produced from one half to one million of pounds. The Elizabeth group of mines are stated, by Henry Green, Esq., an old miner and smelter, to have produced from 60,000,000 to 75,000,000 pounds. Mr. Green is probably below the amount actually produced. The Vinegar Hill diggings, being a group of about forty lodes or mines, are supposed to have produced 100,000,000 pounds. This statement is made upon the authority of Mr. Houghton's pamphlet upon the Marsden lead. From the same authority we learn that the maximum production of the Jo Daviess County mines, in 1846, was 56,000,000 pounds. The Council Hill mines are supposed, by D. Wilmot Scott, Esq., to have produced 19,000,000 pounds. The Morseville mines are stated to have produced from one quarter to one half million pounds. Captain Beebe stated a few years ago that five furnaces were in operation in the county, smelting annually 8,750,000 pounds of pure lead, some of which was obtained outside of the county. The Marsden lead is said to have produced 3,000,000 pounds of mineral..

From these figures—and they are imperfect enough—it can be seen that the mineral interest of this county in the past has been a matter of great magnitude. Together with Shullsburg, Mineral Point and Dubuque, this Northwestern lead basin has been, and yet is, one of the greatest mining localities in the world.

The superficial area of the country underlaid by productive lead deposits, so far as known at the present time, is limited, embracing but a small fraction of the area of the Galena limestone. The lodes or ranges are principally located in groups. The diggings, mines or workings are in patches; but seem to have many features in common. The most southern productive mines in the county are on the great east and west range of mineral passing through, and just north of Elizabeth. This mineral range commences at the mouth of Yellow Creek, a few miles southeast of Freeport, in Stephenson County, where an old shaft exists, which used to be heavily worked a good many years ago. The next group of mines on this range to the west is at Morseville, in the southern part of Jo Daviess County. Here lead has been mined more or less for many years.

The next heavy mines westward, on this same mineral range, is the group at Elizabeth and Weston. About 2,500 acres here are prospected over and mined in. It is an irregularly shaped tract of land, about six miles long from east to west. The Village of Elizabeth is located upon its southern edge, a little east of its centre.

The Elizabeth mines were discovered at a very early day, and worked to some extent. In 1846 more than 800 miners are stated to have been engaged in mining about Elizabeth and Weston. At this time one ninth of all the mineral raised in the lead region is supposed to have been obtained here.

Leaving the Elizabeth lead fields, the next heavy mines are found a few miles west, on the east and west slopes of the bluff range, bordering the Mississippi River. These are the New California mines, discovered accidentally only a few years ago, by a fisherman, who resided in a wild glen on the Mississippi River. At this point the rocky bluffs rise abruptly. The ranges are found by drifting into them a little above water level, going in where a crevice is noticed rising vertically through the rocks. The mineral found is heavy mineral, existing in large cubes or cogs in some instances. It resembles the large bodies of mineral found in the Marsden lead. On the east slope of the bluff range, where the hills fall away gradually to the level of the interior, several lodes are struck by sinking shafts down to the ranges. The following ranges have been struck in these mines, and perhaps a few others, the names of which I did not learn: Wise Range, McKenda & Graham, Davis & Brownell, Bernard & Co., Lester, Sanders & Hony, Felt & Clymo, Wakefield & Co., Marble & Young, Dye & Co., Samuel Taylor. Other valuable ranges will doubtless be discovered, when all the crevices are examined.

Five or six miles north of the New California diggings, the celebrated Marsden lead may be found.

This range is celebrated not only for the amount, but for the variety and beauty of its mineral deposits. Large cubes and diamond-shaped masses of lead ore have been found here, perfectly coated with a beautiful covering of iron pyrites. Galena, black-jack, spar, and iron pyrites, are found in wonderful combinations, furnishing the finest cabinet specimens found any where in the lead region.

The Marsden lead, the New California diggings, the Ambruster & Co. lode, recently discovered, and most of the mineral found along the western limits of the lead field in this county, have certain resemblances, both in the character of the lead ore and its associated minerals, not observed in the mines in the eastern part of the county.

The next important group of ranges to be noticed, is within and immediately around the City of Galena.

These ranges and diggings are situated within a circle of about three miles in diameter, of which the City of Galena would be the centre. They are principally on the west half of section 21, the northwest quarter of section 16, the west half of section 9, the northwest quarter of section 28, east fractional section 8—all in township 28, range 1 east, 4th P. M.; and on the east half of section 12, the east half of section 23, the south half of section 13, the north half of section 26, and the east part of section 27—all in township 28, range 1 west, 4th P. M.

The Vinegar Hill diggings are about five miles north and a little east of Galena.

These are located principally on the fractional sections 14, 15 and 16, on fractional sections 20 and 29, on sections 21, 22 and 23—all in township 29, range 1 east, 4th P. M.; and on the east part of sections 24 and 25, township 29, range 1 west, 4th P. M. On the west part of the last section named, on the northeast corner of section 35, and on the north half of section 23, in the township and range last aforesaid, there are also groups of diggings not enumerated in the foregoing ranges. The Vinegar Hill mines are among the heaviest in the lead region, if we consider the amount of mineral they have furnished, but they are not now worked to a very great extent.

About three miles east and a little south of Vinegar Hill Diggings, the Council Hill ranges are located. The heaviest ones are situated on the north half of section 25, and the south half of section 24, township 29, range 1 east. They are known as the North Diggings, and cover a tract of about forty-seven acres, on which are over one hundred veins running northeast and southwest. The principal, medium, and smaller shafts, number nearly one thousand. The South Diggings, on the south of the Hill, are of small importance. The east half of section 36, township 29, range 1 east, and the west half of section 31, and the south half of section 30, township 29, range 2 east, have upon them diggings, the most important of which is the Rocky Point and Bolt's Lots.

Price.—The following table shows the price of mineral per thousand pounds, for the last sixteen years, as delivered by the miner to the purchaser, at the mouth of the shaft. The ore was always paid for in gold, until the greenback era drove gold out of circulation:

Year	Price	Year	Price
1853	$37	1861	$28
1854	38	1862	40
1855	32	1863	55
1856	35	1864	75
1857	34	1865	65
1858	29	1866	60
1859	30	1867	60
1860	32	1868	55

Modes of Occurrence.—The crevices, veins and caverns in which the lead ore is found, are all, perhaps, cracks of shrinkage, into which the lead subsequently became deposited. The most common and widely disseminated form in which lead ore occurs, is known among miners as "float mineral." In many places the beds of red ferruginous and orchery clay have scattered through them galena in considerable quantities. It is generally found in small, irregularly-shaped pieces; sometimes in small grains, and sometimes in good sized crystals and chunks. Although widespread in its occurrence, no heavy bodies of mineral are found as float mineral. This form of mineral deposit results from the decomposition of the overlying Galena limestone, and in many cases it has settled down almost in the exact spot where the rock containing it once existed.

The mineral in the rocks occurs in what is known as "gash veins," and takes the forms of cog, dice, chunk, sheet, float, or fibrous mineral, as modified by circumstances. The predominant forms of deposit are the vertical crevices, and their modifications into the flat sheet and flat sheet openings. A crevice is a perpendicular or nearly perpendicular opening in the rocks, of varying width and depth. When filled with galena, the deposit is called "sheet mineral." The sheet varies in thickness, from a mere seam the thickness of a knife blade, up to three inches or more in thickness. The vertical crevices have a certain well-marked parallelism to each other, and an approximate north and south and east and west direction. The east and west are, by far, the most fully developed, and contain, by far, the largest deposits of mineral. These crevices are known by the various names of "leads," "lodes," "cracks," "veins," "ranges," and "diggings." The predominant form of mining in this county is that of the working of the vertical crevices. These are, by far, the most productive, and are characteristic of the upper and middle of the Galena limestone. The modifications of the vertical crevice are the crevice opening, pocket opening, chimney opening, and cave opening. They are all produced by the same causes. The crevice opening is an expansion of the crevice to the width of several feet in some instances; the cavity is often filled with red ocher and ferruginous clays, intermixed with loose stones and heavy masses of galena. The pocket openings are a succession of irregularly-shaped small openings in the crevices; the chimney opening is a rather large expansion of the crevice, extending upwards to a point resembling a chimney; and the cave opening is a large crevice opening, widening out into cave-like proportions, floored often with stratified clays. In these openings the galena is found lying over the bottom, mixed with the materials with which they are filled, crystallized in blocks or cubes over the walls, and hanging pendant from the roof. Some of the masses of mineral weigh thousands of pounds, and it is said one mass was found in the mines of Captain Harris weighing half a million of pounds, and worth thirty-five thousand dollars.

These various openings are caused by the decay or disintegration of the rock on the sides of the crevices, owing to chemical agencies working round the mineral deposits. If the dirt remains where it was formed, the mineral and nodular masses of the rock will be found imbedded in it; sometimes the dirt has been removed and the lead alone remains. Sometimes these openings extend to the surface clays; sometimes they are covered by a cap rock. They often extend into the flint strata, characteristic of the middle and lower portions of the Galena limestone. There are often several crevices, or sets of these various openings, one over the other; often three, sometimes as many as five; but one opening or set of openings is usually larger than the others, and contains the heaviest bodies of mineral.

The flat sheets or flat sheet openings are similar to the vertical, both as to themselves and their modifications, except that they lie flat in the rocks, parallel to their stratification, instead of standing upright. The saddle-shaped openings and pitching openings are but the transition openings from the vertical to the flat. These flat openings are characteristic of the lower parts of the Galena limestone and of the underlying blue and buff limestone, and are not found extensively developed in Jo Daviess County. The "green" or "calico" rock, below the flint beds; the "brown rock" and the "glass rock" are characteristic of the lower Galena limestone, their beds of passage into the blue, and the blue itself. In these occur the pipe clay openings; and in the buff limestone the "lower pipe clay opening" is found. These are flat openings, filled with shaly limestone and a peculiar clay, from which they take their name. These lower flat openings are also peculiar in having more of the associate mineral deposits, such as tiff, blende, the ores of zinc, etc., than the upper vertical openings.

In this connection, I do not intend to say much as to the origin of the lead ore in the Northwest, nor to speak of the various theories as to the origin and deposition of mineral peposits in general. The question as to the origin of our lead is unsettled, perhaps. J. D. Whitney, the best living authority on the Galena lead basin, believes the galena and its associate minerals were deposited in the aqueous or humid way in the crevices of the rocks, and that the veins were filled from above downwards. This theory supposes that the metals were held in solution in the waters of the primal ocean, in the form of sulphates, and were deposited in crystalline forms in the shape of the sulphurets. The decomposition of organic vegetable or animal matter throws off a sulphuretted hydrogen gas, which, acting upon solutions containing sulphates, is supposed to cause a reduction and precipitation of the metals in the form of sulphurets. The decay of sea plants and the abundance of organic life in the Trenton Period are thought to have been sufficient to produce the great precipitation of lead ore found in these rocks. The writer argues his theory with ability, and it may now be considered as the one generally received. I hazard the suggestion, however, that electrical action may have had much to do with the precipitation, crystallization and arrangement of these minerals.

Early and Recent Mining Processes.—The primitive mining processes in the Galena lead basin were of a very simple character. Two men selected the spot where they wished to try their fortunes. They were generally guided by certain signs in making the selection, such as depressions in the ground, unusual luxuriance in the growth of vegetation, color of the clay, or ravines supposed to indicate crevices in the rocks below. A shaft was sunk through the clay, and cribbed by building up timber, until the rock was struck. A rude windlass, bucket and rope, a few shovels, picks, and pieces of tallow candle constituted all the tools needed, to which was sometimes added a few blasting tools. If a crevice was struck, it was followed down, and drifts were driven from it in various directions. The man at the top laboriously hoisted with his windlass the material necessary to be removed. The digging was abandoned when worked down to the water, or a pump is put on, driven by horse power. The mineral is brought to the bottom of the shaft or rude car, running on wooden rails. Instead of sinking a shaft, an inclined plane or drift is run into the hill, in case the outcrops of the rock show lead crevices. If a heavy body of mineral is found at any considerable depth, a whim is put on. This is a large wooden wheel or barrel, revolving at some height above the ground, propelled by horse power, and containing coils of a strong rope, to which are attached rude cars or tubs, so arranged, in many instances, that one goes down as the other comes up. With the whim and the horse-power pump, a range can be worked considerably below the water level.

The first attempts at smelting were also quite rude. The Indian squaws melted the ore by roasting it in a rude stone furnace, in which they were able to melt out but a small portion of the lead. The log furnace succeeded this when the white men began to work in the mines. A "reverberatory furnace," in which the ore was melted in an oven, where the blaze passed over and through the charge, was next tried, and was a great improvement in smelting processes.

But they have all been superseded of late years by the Scotch Hearth or Blast Furnace, now universally used throughout the lead region. The following detailed description of the Scotch Hearth is taken from an article in *Harper's Magazine*, and is understood to be the production of a lady of Galena, whose name I do not know:

"The hearth consists of a box of cast iron, two feet square, one foot high, open at top, with the sides and bottom two inches thick. To the top of the front edge is affixed a sloping shelf or hearth called the work stone, used for spreading the materials of the 'charge' upon, as occasionally becomes necessary during smelting, and also for the excess of molten lead to flow down. For the latter purpose a groove one half an inch deep and an inch wide, runs diagonally across the work stone. A ledge, one inch in thickness and height, surrounds the work stone on all sides except that towards the sole of the furnace. The hearth slopes from behind forward, and immediately below the front edge of it is placed the receptable or 'melting pot.' An inch from the bottom, in the posterior side of the box, is a hole two inches in diameter, through which the current or 'blast' of air is blown from the bellows.

The furnace is built under an immense chimney thirty to thirty-five feet high, and ten feet wide at its base. Behind the base of the chimney is the bellows, which is propelled by a water-wheel, the tuyere, or point of the bellows, entering at the hole in the back of the box. The fuel, which consists of light wood, coke, and charcoal, is thrown in against the tuyere and kindled, and the ore is placed upon the fuel to the top of the box. The blast of air in the rear keeps the fire burning, as the reservoir or box is filled with molten lead, the excess flows down the grooved hearth into the 'melting pot,' under which a gentle fire is kept, and the lead is ladled from it into the molds as is convenient. Before adding a new 'charge' the blast is turned off, the 'charge' already in is turned forward upon the work stone, more fuel is cast in, and the 'charge,' is thrown back with the addition of fresh ore upon the wood. The combustion of the sulphur in the ore produces a large amount of heat required for smelting. The furnace is thus kept in operation sixteen hours out of the twenty-four.

The ore is of different degrees of purity, but the purest galena does not yield on an average over sixty-eight per cent of lead from the first process of smelting. The gray slag is very valuable, though the lead procured from it is harder than that of the first smelting. There is left about 75,000 of gray slag from each 1,000,000 pounds of ore. The slag furnace is erected under the same roof with the Scotch Hearth, and has a chimney of its own a few feet from that of the hearth, and the 'blast' is secured from the same water power by an additional blast pipe driven by the same wheel. It consists of a much larger reservoir, built of limestone, cemented and lined with clay, with a cast iron door in front, heavily barred with iron. It will burn out so as to require repairs in about three months. Open at the top, the slag and fuel are thrown in promiscuously. Under the iron door is an escape for the lead and 'black slag.' In front of this escape and below it is the 'slag pot.' It is an oblong iron basin about a foot in depth, with one third of its length partitioned off to receive the lead, which sinks as it escapes, while the slag, being lighter, flows in a flame-colored stream forward, and falls into a reservoir that is partly filled with water, which cools the slag as it is plunged therein. As the reservoir fills, a workman shovels the scoriæ into a hand-barrow and wheels it off. The scoriæ is black slag, and worthless; the lead having now been entirely extracted. The smelter now and then throws a shovel full of gray slag into the furnace, which casts up beautiful parti-colored flames, while the strong sulphurous odor, the red-hot stream of slag, with the vapor arising from the tub wherein the hissing slag is plunged, the sooty smelters, and the hot air of the furnace room, suggest a thought of the infernal regions. Outside, the wealth of 'pigs,' not in the least porcine, gives one a sort of covetous desire that, if indulged in, we are taught, leads directly to said regions. The Scotch Hearth requires less fuel than any other furnace. It 'blows out' in from six to twelve hours, while the Drummond Furnace was kept in operation night and day."

After examining the process of smelting, I concluded the above description could hardly be improved on, and hence give it a place in this report.

LEAD AND LEAD MINING.

The immense deposits of lead ore, or "mineral," as it is called, in the mining region, have long been known and have extensively worked for nearly sixty years, and are far from being exhausted yet. The old leads known to the early settlers were "worked out" and abandoned, long ago but the hills of Jo Daviess County undoubtedly contain enormous deposits yet undiscovered. The ore is principally of the species termed "galena," or sulphuret of lead. This mineral is usually found in crevices or leads, running either north and south, or east and west. Sometimes, but not often, the mineral lies close to the surface, as was the case in the famous "Buck Lead," and the "Marsden Mine," but generally the prospector must dig or sink a shaft from six to thirty feet if the lead is on level ground. At the "New California Diggings" about nine miles south of Galena, the miners "drift" into the bluff horizontally. Experienced miners say that in the Spring when the grass first begins to start, they can determine the location of "crevices" from the fact that the grass starts more luxuriantly over them, but they can not tell whether mineral exists below until they "prove" them by digging.

Lead ore, in the form of galena, is usually found crystallized. The primary form is the cube, sometimes truncated but never in any other than that form, or its modifications, and the cubes broken, break into smaller cubes. The carbonate of lead occurs occasionally, mingled with the sulphuret, but in irregular lumps or masses, never crystallized. It is nearly or quite as rich and smelts easily. Mineral is taken from the "wash-dirt" in which it is embedded, in masses from one or two, to hundreds of pounds weight. In the crystalline form these "junks" look like masses of cubic crystal partially fused together and suddenly cooled. These cubes are of all sizes, from minute specks to several inches square, and weighing from a single grain to 80 or 100 pounds. Native or pure lead has never been found except in a single locality, in Vinegar Hill Township, but pure sulphur occasionally occurs. "Wash-dirt" is a yellowish, clayey substance in which the mineral is embedded, and is full of small pieces of mineral. It is *washed* to separate these from the sulphurous earth, and generally the product of the "wash-dirt" will pay expenses of mining. Zinc ore, or "blende" occurs in this region in immense quantities. It is called "black jack" by the miners and in former times was considered worthless, being used for the streets and roads. "Black-jack" appears generally to underlie lead deposits. This was the case in the Marsden Mine, now extensively worked for zinc. At the New California Diggings, there are apparently inexhaustable deposits of blende under the mineral.

Sulphuret of iron, or pyrites occurs in great abundance in connection with both lead and zinc. The crystals of mineral are often covered with a coating of crystallized pyrites, as if the mass had been dipped in a liquid solution and suffered to remain until coated. Capt. D. S. Harris, in his extensive and valuable cabinet has some exceedingly rare and beautiful specimens of pyrites that look as if they might be small branches and twigs changed, in the mysterious and wonderful alchemy of nature, into this beautiful but useless mineral. These are of various sizes, from the size of a large knitting needle to an inch in diameter. In this cabinet are also some most beautiful specimens of crystallized galena taken from the Marsden mine and other localities.

In some localities, particularly in the "New California diggings" in Rice Township, there is overlying the heavy deposits of mineral a stratum of very fine white clay. The miners call it "pipe clay." It is plastic when first taken out, but hardens when exposed to the atmosphere.

The lead ore of Northwestern Illinois and Southwestern Wisconsin is very rich, yielding under modern appliances 90 per cent pure lead, and the combustion of the sulphur it contains is made to aid the smelting process.

But in the ruder log and ash furnaces of early times, the yield averaged probably from 60 to 70 per cent.

Prior to the arrival of the white miners in 1821–'2, mining in this region was done exclusively by the Indians, although traces of early operations by Dubuque's men were discovered. The natives, however, only skimmed the surface. The work was done by the old men and squaws, the braves considering it beneath their dignity to "raise" mineral. It occurred, therefore, that all the rich leads discovered and worked at least until 1824, were these Indian diggings struck anew and effectually worked by the whites. Wherever the miners could find a place where the Indians had worked, they were almost certain of valuable "discoveries."

The windlass and bucket and other methods employed by the miners were unknown to the Indians who operated before them. They sunk no shafts, and did they not understand the use of gunpowder. When the mineral was near the surface, as in the "Buck lead," and they could raise it easily, they did so. Some times they "drifted" into the sides of the bluffs for some distance, and when they reached the "cap-rock," which overlies mineral, surrounds or encloses it, they kindled fires on it, and when the rock was thoroughly heated, they threw water upon it. This was the Indian method of blasting. Their tools were buck-horns, with which they removed the rock partially crumbled by the action of fire and water. Early settlers have found these horns in old Indian "drifts." In later years they used hoes, shovels and crow-bars, obtained from traders to whom they sold lead.

After the old Indian leads were exhausted, new and enormous deposits were found by the enterprise and energy of the miners, and the amount of mineral "raised" in this region is simply fabulous. Sometimes it was necessary to sink shafts through twenty or thirty feet of rock before arriving at the openings or "leads" containing the mineral, but when "struck" it was found in large quantities. At the Sanders' lead, a mile and a quarter from Galena, it is said that three men dug and raised 56,000 pounds of mineral in one day, valued at $21 per thousand at that time. This lead was an east and west opening, in a cave, long since "worked out," but one to one and one half millions pounds of mineral were taken from it.

The following extract is from the *Spirit of the Press*, edited by H. H. Houghton, Esq., of October 9, 1871:

Valuable mines of lead ore are being wrought within the city, and within the compass of six miles the number that has been discovered is very large. They are all comparatively shallow diggings. Some of them have been worked out, as is generally supposed, and others are still yielding large returns for labor.

The proportion of land that has been "prospected" on, is insignificant compared with what has never been molested by a miner. The reader will find below the names by which a number of these lodes are designated. They are written from memory, and are very far from comprising a full list, nor can we form an estimate of the quantity of mineral they have yielded.

Harris Leads, Tomlin & Burrichter, Tomlin, Buck, Doe, Kringle, Gaffner, Hog Range, Graves, Comstock & Rosemeyer, Wallou & Quick, Sanders & Co., Muldore. Bolton, Stephen Marsden, Allenrath, Eagan, Frysinger, Crumbacker, Evans & Adams, A.C. Davis, Armbruster & Co., Ottawa Diggings, Drum, Rare & Co., Benninger & Co., P. Smith & Co., Hostetter & Co., Duer & Co., Allendorf & Co., Tom Evans, Brittan & Wilkins. Cady Range, Robert's Range, Wm. Richards, Wilcox & Co., J. E. Comstock.

The above are within a short distance of the City of Galena, and a great many more not enumerated.

VINEGAR HILL DIGGINGS.

These mines are located some three or four miles northeast of Galena. The following are some of the ranges or mines that have been discovered there, to-wit:

Bailey, Gear, Meighan, H. Mann, Indian, Feehan, Blood, Campbell & Reppy, Furlong & Feehan, Talbott, Kennedy, Rogers, Hogan, Trover, Liddle, Sidener, Smelt, Foley,

Cooney & Ryan, Wylram, Gray, Leekly, Beadle, Briggs, Manly, Myers, Bruno, Cottle O'Meara, K. Orwick, Whim Ranges, Hawkins, Hart, Dugan, Hoskin, Shattruk, 15 Strike, H. H. Gear, Cox, Richards.

These mines extend some two miles in length, and it is estimated that they have yielded one hundred millions of pounds of mineral.

At this date (1878) there are some mining operations near Galena, but these are trifling in comparison with former years. The West diggings, 2½ miles west of the city, the Pilot Knob diggings, recently discovered, and a lead on what is called the old Buck Hill, near the old Buck lead, are among the principal in the immediate vicinity of Galena. At Elizabeth, Vinegar Hill, Apple River, mining is still carried on to some extent. The best diggings now, however, are what are called the "New California," or Sand Prairie Diggings, about 9 miles south of Galena, in Rice Township, first discovered by —— Lafayette about 1852. These are on the east bank of the Mississippi. At that point the high bluffs approach very near the river, leaving in many places only a narrow roadway between the cliffs and the water. Here also some years ago the work of grading for the Illinois Central Railroad, which it was then proposed should reach Galena by that route, under the old charter, was commenced. Here the miners drift horizontally into the bluffs for thousands of feet, following the crevices or leads, taking out the mineral and wash dirt as they proceed. In the tunnel so made, sometimes so small that the miner must almost creep, and at others expanding into caverns several feet wide and ten to thirty feet high, a wooden railway is laid, and the mineral and debris are brought to daylight in tubs, or miniature cars pushed by the men. Some of these tunnels are hardly ten feet above low water, and in very high water would be likely to be flooded. There are several good mines or leads now being worked in that locality, but the most extensive here, and in fact in all Jo Daviess County, is that of J. H. Burrichter, Esq., and Capt. D. S. Harris, on the Kamphous estate, on the south side of a little creek that pierces the bluffs at this point. This is said to be one of the largest deposits of mineral ever discovered in the mining region. It was discovered in January, 1875, and up to January, 1878, over 3,000,000 pounds of mineral had been taken out, and there appears to be an almost inexhaustible quantity still remaining.

The author visited this mine January 29, 1878, accompanied by Mr. John Dowling, of Galena, and it may not be uninteresting to the future reader if here is recorded a brief

DESCRIPTION OF A LEAD MINE.

At the foot of the bluff stands the engine-house, a rude shanty, in one end of which we found one of the owners, Capt. Harris, who personally superintends the operations, and who received us very cordially. The engine is kept constantly in operation, to keep the mine free from water, as the workmen are below the level of the river. Nye's vacuum pump is used for this purpose, which, although it raises less water than some others, is less liable to get out of repair, and is, therefore, the "best and most economical," Capt. Harris thinks, "for miners' use." A short distance from the engine-house is a door, not unlike the door of a root-house, in the side of the bluff. This is the entrance to the tunnel. Above, on a little bench, and perhaps forty or fifty feet higher than the engine-house is another small building containing a windlass, worked by horse power. Here is the mouth of a shaft, sunk to the bottom of the mine, seventy or eighty feet or more, and here all the mineral. wash-dirt and debris are raised. The wash-dirt is dumped on the side of the bluff, where a huge heap of yellow dirt is accumulated. This is washed, and "from it," says Captain Harris, "we get mineral enough to pay expenses of mining." At the side of the building built over the mouth of the shaft, lie three or four hundred thousand pounds of mineral ready for smelting.

Borrowing rubber coats from the engineers, and each furnished with a miner's lamp, we are now ready to descend into the mine, with Captain Harris for our guide and instructor. Entering the door above mentioned, we find ourselves in a tunnel, perhaps thirty inches in width and about four feet high. In the middle, in an open wooden aqueduct, runs quite a little stream of water, raised by the pump from the galleries below. Stooping low and stepping on each side of the aqueduct, we slowly make our way perhaps a hundred feet; here the tunnel enlarges and we are able to stand erect, and a short distance further we arrive at the perpendicular shaft. Here, on a rudely constructed, but strong, ladder, we descend, one by one, about twenty-five feet, and find ourselves in a gallery stretching away several thousand feet into the heart of the bluff. At the bottom is laid the little wooden railway before described, by means of which the miners transport the mineral, etc., to the shaft. In some places, for some distance this gallery is so narrow and low that it is only with difficulty that the inexperienced visitor can make his way; at other parts it expands and we are able to walk erect. This tunnel or gallery is simply the fissure or vein from which the mineral has been removed. At the sides are pockets or side leads, from which have been taken large quantities of mineral. In several instances, the gallery opens into natural caves of considerable size. "Some of them," says our guide, "were open, and others full of mineral when we reached them." Ever and anon we find ourselves walking on the narrow track over a black abyss or chasm from which the mineral has been removed. In one of the caves the cap-rock has been shored up with timbers. Slowly we grope our way along by the dim light of our lamps—above us, beneath us, all around us, the yellow clay the miners like to see, glistening with mineral. Ever and anon we must stop and stand close to the walls to permit the passage of the "miners' trains." After traversing several hundred feet, we descend by a ladder sixteen or eighteen feet, to still another and larger gallery below. We are nearly a hundred feet below the surface, and 1,000 or 1,500 feet from the entrance. We are in the midst of one of Nature's mysterious laboratories, where for ages she has been accumulating lead for the use of man. Her processes are beyond his knowledge. He can only witness the results. Who shall say that these processes are not still in active operation, and that in these hills, in this strange yellow earth, crystallization of mineral is still going on? It can not be that all this mineral wealth stored away was created in a moment, and if it be the result of slow processes and these have stopped, what stopped them?

Following this lower gallery for some distance we arrive at a cave of respectable dimensions. Clambering up its sides on a ladder and creeping around a jutting point, on steps cut in the clay, we suddenly come upon the miners at work, picking the lumps of mineral from the yellow, sulphurous earth, in which, and perhaps from which, it has been formed. These lumps are of all sizes, from the little crystals that can only be obtained by washing the dirt, to large masses of aggregated cubic crystals weighing hundreds of pounds. The miners are working by the light of tallow candles. The air is tolerably pure, for a little distance away, a hole has been bored from the surface to admit fresh air. The miner's pick strikes a mass of mineral and in a moment he throws out a lump weighing, perhaps, 150 pounds. We break off a piece as a souvenir of our visit. We have seen the mineral in its native bed, we have seen it removed by the sturdy miner, and now we start on our toilsome journey to the world of sunlight above. Returning to the upper, or rather the first mineral gallery, our guide informs us that this stretches away for about 2,000 feet beyond us and terminates in a large cave, the bottom of which is covered with water, and which has not yet been explored. Here Capt. Harris picked from the wall of the gallery a bit of the "pipe clay" that overlies the heaviest deposits. It is white, plastic, cuts like a piece of old cheese, and doubtless may be valuable for pottery. Why it should be spread over the chemical laboratory below, is a problem for the scientists to solve. "In this mine," said Capt. Harris, "we have found pure sulphur, both in powder as it is sold in the shops, and in crystallized form." But we must not tarry here to speculate upon the mysterious and wonderful processes of nature, the results of which only we have witnessed, and we soon find ourselves again in the sunlight of heaven.

From seven to twenty men are employed in this mine. Ten are now at work raising about 25,000 pounds of mineral per week. Beneath the lead, we are informed by Capt. Harris, are immense deposits of sulphuret of zinc, blende, or "black jack," as it is called by the miners, and in the future, when the lead is exhausted, this may be profitably mined.

Thanking our kind host for his attentions, we returned to Galena.

Miners seldom smelt the ore they raise. Mining and smelting are separate and distinct occupations. The miner sells his mineral to the smelter, and this custom prevails at the present day. Mineral is sold by the 1,000 pounds and at this time is worth $18. This is considered low and miners are holding for better prices.

SMELTING.

The Indian furnaces for smelting were simple affairs. They were constructed of stones and sand on the side of a hill or bluff, so built that the lead could run off on the smooth inclined plane of earth below. In this manner, rude as it was, they succeeded in obtaining a larger percentage of lead than the whites obtained in their log furnaces at the first smelting, it is said, because the latter applied too much heat at first. These old Indian furnaces were rich "finds" for the early miners. The ashes were rich in lead, and the banks of earth over which the molten metal flowed from the furnaces were full of pure lead. The heat cracked the earth in innumerable places, and these "cracks" were full of metal.

The first furnaces employed by the early smelters were the "log furnaces," and the ashes, etc., from that, were re-smelted in what they called an "ash furnace." These furnaces went out of use when the "blast" and "cupola" furnaces were introduced. The first or primitive log furnaces were simply heaps of logs properly piled on the hill side, the largest logs on the down-hill side. On these logs was piled the mineral and this covered with smaller wood, a hole was excavated on the lower side which received the lead as it run down from the burning pile. Later, these furnaces were constructed of stone and mud. The following description is given by Harvey Mann, one of the early smelters:

Selecting a proper spot near the foot of a hill sloping down at an angle of about forty-five degrees, a wall about two feet thick was built along the line of the hill, ten feet long and about eight feet high. At each end a wall of same thickness was built *up the hill;* another of same thickness was built in the centre, dividing the furnace into two compartments or pits, each four feet wide, and from the surface of the ground at the top to eight feet deep at the bottom. These "pits" were paved with flat stones on the bottom, and at the sides were placed stones about six inches high to keep the logs from resting on the sloping floor down which the lead ran. Through the head wall, at the bottom was made a hole in the centre of each pit. These holes, or "eyes," served the double purpose of giving draft for the fire and for the escape of the melted lead which ran down the inclined plane through these, and by channels was conducted into a basin excavated in the earth below, and from which it was dipped with iron ladles into the moulds and converted into "pigs" or bars weighing seventy-five or eighty pounds each. Smelters usually had at least two of these furnaces, so as to charge one while the other was burning and cooling off.

To charge a furnace, oak logs were sawed into lengths of four feet, the largest were rolled down to the bottom and smaller ones succeeded until there was a floor of logs, raised about six inches from the stone floor from the bottom of the enclosure to the top. Then smaller wood stood on end around three sides of the pit, and about 2,500 pounds of mineral packed in on the logs in each, the largest pieces at the bottom; wood was then piled on the top of the mineral, and the furnace was ready to fire. In burning, fresh wood was constantly piled on the top and the fire kept up until the logs were burned out underneath, and then allowed to die out. When the furnace was sufficiently cool the pits were cleared out; the largest pieces of mineral remaining, taken out to be added to the next "charge," and the ashes thrown into a pile to be washed and re-smelted in an ash furnace. A log furnace of this description costs about $25. A "charge" usually burned out in sixteen to twenty-four hours, depending on the size of logs used.

The ash furnace was a different and more expensive affair. Selecting a proper spot at the foot of a hill, a sort of box, with bottom and sides of stone (not unlike a mason's mortar-bed in form) was made. This was generally about six feet long and three feet wide. On one side was an eye, on the level with the floor, but filled with clay, and on the other side another, higher up. Over this was built a structure of masonry, and extending far enough below or *from* the hill for the fire, which was fed through an arch in front, something like the arches of a brick kiln. From the other end of this structure was a long flue, three feet wide, floored and covered with stone, something like a chimney built on the ground up the sloping side of the hill, fifteen or twenty feet, with a flue three feet wide and about one foot high. Here, then, we have a huge fire box, with the "lead box" in the up hill side, w th a chimney from it lying on the ground at an angle of about forty-five degrees. The fire kindled, the ashes, after being washed, are thrown in at the top of the chimney, smelted by the heat and draft from the fire passing over them, the lead runs down into the box prepared for it below, which is kept hot by the fire which passes over into the chimney. Here the liquid lead accumulates, the "slag" or dross, which floats on top running out of the upper hole in the "box." When the lead gets high enough to run out of the same "eye," the clay is knocked out of the lower "eye" on the other side, and the pure lead is drawn off and cast into "pigs." The "eye" is then plugged again, and the process is repeated. The "slag" was for a long time considered worthless, but when the cupola or blast furnace was introduced, it was smelted, yielding, in some cases, fifty per cent pure lead.

The introduction of the "cupola" furnace, and improvements invented by N. A. Drummond, in 1837, and called the "Drummond Furnace," and the "blast furnace," entirely superseded the rude log and ash furnaces above described. The "cupola" or chimney of the furnace of that name was from thirty to forty feet high, with a flue about eighteen inches in diameter, and was so constructed as to cause the blaze and heat from the fire to pass over the mineral, and it was necessary to keep it in operation constantly, day and night. The "blast furnace" was so called because a strong and constant current of air was sent into the fire from a bellows, driven by water or other power. The blast furnace "blows out" in from six to twelve hours. The blast furnace requires more labor and less fuel than the "cupola." Ordinary furnaces smelted from sixty to one hundred and fifty pigs of lead, of seventy pounds each, per day. At some of them two hundred pigs per day were manufactured in the palmy days of the mining interest.

In 1846-'7-'8, there were at least twenty-four smelting furnaces within Jo Daviess County in active operation. The mines reached the maximum of production about 1846, during which year about 25,000 tons of lead were manufactured. The importation of lead into the United States in the year ending June, 1859, amounted to about 64,000,000 of pounds. This shows that the importation of lead into the United States that year much exceeded the whole production of this county in 1846.

At this date (1878), there are only five furnaces in regular operation in this county, and these are not run to their full capacity. These are as follows: T. B. Hughlett, Galena, who is the largest smelter; M. Spencely, Vinegar Hill; Richard Bowden, Council Hill; Henry Green, Elizabeth; T. G. Stevens, Rice. There is also a small furnace at Warren. Mr. Hughlett, smelted during 1877, about 1,500,000 pounds of lead, and the total production in the county last year, he estimates at 3,300,000 pounds, or a little over 1,600 tons, against 25,000 in 1846.

In February and March, 1877, mineral was worth $35 per 1,000 pounds, and lead was sold at $6 per 100 pounds. In April following, mineral went up to $38 per 1,000, and lead to $6.25 per 100. In February 1878, mineral was worth only $18 per 1,000, and lead was dull at $3.50 per 100.

It is thought by some, because the product of the lead mines has decreased, that the mineral has become exhausted, but this is not a correct conclusion. It will undoubtedly be found that the proper development of these mineral deposits has only just commenced. Capital and labor, directed by science and observation, and rightly applied to deep mining, will produce more wonderful results than any yet attained. The Burrichter & Harris mine, which has been described in the preceding pages, may be cited in corroboration of this statement. It is probable that many old leads now abandoned, will be found to yield abundantly under the skillful application of labor and capital.

The lead mines of Cumberland, Durham, and York, in England, are said to resemble these in this country in their general features, and from these are raised more than one half the entire lead products of Great Britain.

The production of these English mines is more than double that of all the lead mines of the United States, and this result has been brought about by deep mining. An English miner stated to Mr. Houghton a few years ago, that his father, who was also a miner, well remembered the time when it was believed in England that their lead mines were nearly worked out. Capitalists then took hold of the matter, invested prudently but boldly, sunk deep shafts, and made discoveries astonishing for their richness, and which are apparently inexhaustible.

The same process should be inaugurated here. That it would be successful in a high degree there is no doubt. The old mines will be taken up by and by, drained of their water, sunk to the depth of English mines, if necessary, and be worked as successfully.

ZINC AND ZINC MINING.

The mineral wealth of the territory embraced within the limits of Jo Daviess County is not developed as it must be in the future. The application of capital and labor in deep mining for lead will probably utilize immense deposits of lead now only supposed to exist. But the treasures hidden in these hills are not confined to lead. Zinc ore has been found more or less intermingled with galena in nearly all the lead diggings, and in some instances, at least, it is known that the mineral has rested upon inexhaustible deposits of zinc in the forms of sulphuret (blende, or black-jack), and carbonate of zinc (calamine, Smithsonite, or dry-bone). The sulphuret, or blende, underlies the lead in the Burrichter & Harris mine, and undoubtedly under all the Sand Prairie leads. The carbonate of zinc which frequently occurs in lead mines, is called "dry-bone," by the miners, probably from its fancied resemblance to old bones in color and appearance.

In March, 1854, the celebrated Marsden mine, was discovered by Stephen Marsden, about four miles south of Galena. The spring on the farm at the foot of the hill, in a ravine, had become choked up and for some distance around, it was boggy; the water was unfit for use, and the place was unhealthy. Mr. Marsden determined to drain it. In digging the drain he found "float" mineral, and when he reached the spring he struck a large mass, indicating a lead. For twelve hours the water ran off through the drain, perfectly black. He then followed the lead about 20 feet into the hill and discovered a cave 20 or 30 feet in diameter from which the water had been drained, and which accounted for its color. This cave contained a large amount of mineral blende and pyrites, the cogs, or cubes of lead and formations of blende being coated in some instances to the thickness of half an inch with beautiful crystallized sulphuret of iron. From this another vein led to an immense deposit in circular form, in some places fifty yards wide, and from the inner edge of this circle it was found that the mineral "fell off," on an angle of about 45 degrees. From the cave to the "pitch" is a distance of about 75 yards. This mine has yielded probably 8,000,000 pounds of mineral, and was worked from that until 1868. Large quantities of blende had been raised and thrown away as worthless, but about this time it was found to be valuable. Mr. Marsden sold the first "black-jack" from this mine for $12 per ton. Since that time he worked it for blende principally, taking out immense quantities and shipping it to La Salle.

In January, 1877, Mr. Marsden sold the mine to the Illinois Zinc Company of Peru, for $20,000, by whom it is now extensively worked under the skillful superintendence of Mr. August Pein.

About $15,000 worth of machinery has been put in operation including an air-compressing machine for operating the drills. The miners have reached a depth of about 90 feet, and are still working downward on the inclined plane of about 45 degrees. The ore here is mixed with lead which must be separated from it before smelting, but the farther down they go the less lead is found. The ore is worth $16 per ton, and is shipped by railroad to the company's factory, in Peru, Ill., to be smelted. It yields about 45 per cent pure zinc. Eighty men are constantly employed producing about 120 tons of ore per week. Galena, black-jack, pyrites, spar, etc., are found in wonderful combinations in this mine. Immense quantities of sulphuret of iron are raised and thrown away, as the blende was until within ten years. It is more than probable that this now worthless mineral will be utilized in the coming future and become valuable. The finest cabinet specimens of mineral, black-jack, pyrites and spar, and other strange and beautiful combinations, ever found in this country have been obtained from the Marsden mine.

Other zinc mines will undoubtedly be worked in this county in the not far distant future, and wonderful discoveries of mineral wealth in this region are yet to be made. For a more extended and scientific account of the mineral treasures of Jo Daviess County, see the chapter on Physical Geography and Geology, which will be found very interesting.

ANCIENT MOUNDS.

The history of Jo Daviess County would be incomplete without some mention of a subject which properly, perhaps, should have been mentioned first, and would have been, but for the fact that the first occupants of this region have left no records from which their history can be written, and there are no traces of their existence except the mysterious mounds they built containing the bones and some of their singular implements of war and household utensils to mark the spot where they once lived a numerous semi-savage people—the Mound Builders.

The high bluffs on both banks of the Mississippi, from its head waters to the low lands of Louisiana, are thickly dotted with these remarkable mounds, which are also found along many other water courses of the West. These mounds have largely attracted the attention of antiquarians, who have proposed many theories of their origin, plausible enough, perhaps, but which thus far are only vague speculations, for there is no voice from these wonderful old sepulchres, the only traces now of the pre-historic age, except to tell that they were built by the race that occupied this country and became extinct many centuries ago.

On the top of the high bluffs that skirt the west bank of the Mississippi, about two and a half miles from Galena, are a number of these silent monuments of a pre-historic age. The spot is one of surpassing beauty. Standing there, the tourist has a view of a portion of three states—Illinois, Iowa and Wisconsin. A hundred feet below him, at the foot of the perpendicular cliffs, the trains of the Illinois Central Railroad thunder around the curve; the Portage is in full view, and the "Father of Waters," with its numerous bayous and islands stretches a grand panorama for miles above and below him. Here, probably thousands of years ago, a race of men now extinct, and unknown even in the traditions of the Indians who inhabited this region for centuries before the discovery of America by Columbus, built these strangely wonderful and enigmatical mounds. At this point these mounds are circular and conical in form. The largest one is at least forty feet in diameter at the base, and at least fifteen feet high now, after it has been beaten by the storms of many centuries. On its top stands the large stump of an oak tree that was cut down about fifty years ago, and its annular rings indicate a growth of at least 200 years. Whatever may have been the character of these mounds in other localities, these could not have been the dwelling places of their builders.

The mounds on the bluff have nearly all been opened within the last two or three years by Louis A. Rowley, Esq., Mr. W. M. Snyder and Mr. John Dowling, assisted by Sidney Hunkins and Dr. W. S. Crawford. These gentlemen have taken much interest in these pre-historic structures, and have very carefully investigated them. In all that have been opened the excavators have found in the centre a pit that was evidently dug about two and a half feet below the original surface of the ground, about six feet long and four feet wide, in the form of a paralellogram. The bottom and sides of this pit are of hard clay. The bones found in this pit indicate a race of gigantic stature, buried in a sitting posture around the sides of the pit, with legs extending towards the centre. In some cases the position of the bones indicate that they were placed back to back in the centre with their feet extending toward the walls of the pit. Over these bones are found layers of anhydrous earth of dark color, hard from pressure, but easily crumbles into fine powder. Above this is a strata of hard-baked clay or cement, on the top of which is found a layer of ashes mingled with burnt shells and bones, indicating that after the bodies were barely covered with dry earth, a layer of the clayey cement was spread over the earth and a fire kindled upon it perhaps in the performance of some rite—perhaps to harden the cement, or both. This done, a huge mound of earth was with infinite toil heaped above the pit thus filled and finished, and what is remarkable, the most of it was evidently brought from a distance, as it is unlike the surrounding soil, and there is no evidence of excavations in the vicinity.

It will be seen that thus hermetically sealed from air and moisture, the bones became indestructible and will be preserved until the world ends or they are exposed to the action of the elements. Removing the superincumbent earth, penetrating the shell of baked clay and carefully removing the earth beneath, Mr. Rowley and his associates invariably found several skeletons at the bottom of the pit before described, and in most cases, but not all, mingled with the bones, or lying beside them, were found various implements of stone. Axes, arrow and spear-heads made of a species of flint not found in this region; a singular and finely finished pear-shaped implement of stone, flat, four or five inches long and sharp at the edges, probably used for skinning animals; large pearls perforated to be strung; very finely wrought copper chisels and wedges; great numbers of the large teeth of some carnivorous animal supposed to be the bear, in some instances with a piece of the jaw attached and carved, and each pierced with holes like the pearls; ornaments made of copper mingled with silver, indicating that the metal came from the Superior region; copper implements somewhat resembling a bodkin, about the size and length of a lead pencil, pointed at one end and chisel-shaped at the other. Lastly, and most important as indicating some civilization and knowledge of arts, a piece of pottery, about twelve inches in height, urn-shaped, round on the bottom and ornamented. This was made of clay, but when broken the fracture shows in the centre a substance like pounded lead or silver and ground flint.

The skulls found are packed with earth. Some of them testify that the original owners were killed, as they are pierced with holes made with some blunt, sometimes sharp, instrument. Generally they have low, receding foreheads, are long from front to back, narrow across the top and indicate a preponderance of back brain; a patient, plodding people with some little intelligence, and a brain formation unlike the modern Indian.

It must be admitted that these mounds were built and the race who built them had vanished from the face of the earth long before the Indians occupied the land, but the date must probably forever baffle human ingenuity to discover. There seems but little doubt that these are as old as the pyramids and indicate that in the days of "Cheops and Cephenes" the American continent, at least this part of it, was densely populated by a semi-civilized people, perhaps more civilized than these pre-historic relics indicate. At best, however, the origin of these mounds can be only a matter of speculation. Only the "Ancient of Days" can unravel the mystery.

In this connection it is to be stated that in several localities in this county, miners have found at a depth of 100 to 150 feet below the surface, the bones of animals now extinct. These have been found in Elizabeth, and have been pronounced by eminent savans to be the bones of the cave bear, and an animal of the buffalo or bovine species. The position of these bones says Hon. Henry Green, indicate that they were either carried into the caves, which in ages past abounded in this region, by the action of water, or that the animals fell into deep crevices and remained there, sometimes being washed into the caves. It is a problem whether since that period this entire region has been submerged beneath the waters of an ocean which deposited the superincumbent clay, filled the almost bottomless chasms, broke into and filled up many of the caves, covering the bones where they are now found. Some geologists do not coincide with this view, but it is the opinion of many intelligent men that since the mysterious mounds were built, this entire region has been for ages submerged, and was the bed of an ocean for ages before it was again thrown up to become the dwelling place of a great and prosperous people. However this may be, close observers, says Mr. Green, can not fail to recognize the action of water in connection with these fossil bones.

This index was prepared by Genealogy Committee of The Winnetka Public Library of Winnetka, Illinois and graciously provided for this reprint.

Index of Names

BAUER
Anton, 626
Henry, 377
Joseph, 391
Martin, 790